The Last C

Two thousand years ago there lived a man who sold some valuable information for a fee of thirty silver coins. His name was Judas Iscariot, and he is no longer with us. The coins, however, still exist – and still hold an elusive power over all who claim them …

The Paper Grail

A strange man (named Howard) on a strange quest (for a Paper Grail) in a strange land (California) … A lot of fuss for a folded scrap of paper. But considering all the odd people searching for the Grail, it must be something special. Something magical …

All the Bells on Earth

Walt Stebbins runs a small catalogue business out of his garage, and he has no notion of a demonic presence in his town until a package is mistakenly delivered to him. The contents are not the inexpensive Chinese toys and novelties he deals in. The nasty-looking pickled bluebird of happiness piques Walt's interest, and he keeps it when he rewraps the box and passes it on to the addressee: the one person in the world Walt loathes, his former friend Robert Argyle. But Walt's keeping back the bluebird of happiness is the best thing that could have happened to Argyle – and the worst thing that could happen to Walt. What price is happiness? If you have to ask …

Also by James P. Blaylock

The Elfin Series
The Elfin Ship
The Disappearing Dwarf
The Stone Giant

Langdon St Ives
Homunculus*
Lord Kelvin's Machine*

Other Novels
The Digging Leviathan
Land of Dreams
The Last Coin
The Paper Grail
The Magic Spectacles
Night Relics
All The Bells on Earth
Winter Tides
The Rainy Season
Knights of the Cornerstone

Collections
Thirteen Phantasms
In for a Penny
Metamorphosis

* Not available as SF Gateway eBooks

James P. Blaylock
SF GATEWAY OMNIBUS

THE LAST COIN
THE PAPER GRAIL
ALL THE BELLS ON EARTH

GOLLANCZ
LONDON

First published in Great Britain in 2013 by
Gollancz
An imprint of the Orion Publishing Group
Orion House 5 Upper Saint Martin's Lane
London, WC2H 9EA

An Hachette UK Company

A CIP catalogue record for this book
is available from the British Library

ISBN 978 0 575 11755 6

1 3 5 7 9 10 8 6 4 2

Typeset by Jouve (UK), Milton Keynes

Printed and bound by CPI Group (UK) Ltd, Croydon, CR0 4YY

The Orion Publishing Group's policy is to use papers
that are natural, renewable and recyclable products and
made from wood grown in sustainable forests. The logging
and manufacturing processes are expected to conform to
the environmental regulations of the country of origin.

www.orionbooks.co.uk
www.gollancz.co.uk

CONTENTS

ENTER THE SF GATEWAY . . .

Towards the end of 2011, in conjunction with the celebration of fifty years of coherent, continuous science fiction and fantasy publishing, Gollancz launched the SF Gateway.

Over a decade after launching the landmark SF Masterworks series, we realised that the realities of commercial publishing are such that even the Masterworks could only ever scratch the surface of an author's career. Vast troves of classic SF & Fantasy were almost certainly destined never again to see print. Until very recently, this meant that anyone interested in reading any of those books would have been confined to scouring second-hand bookshops. The advent of digital publishing changed that paradigm for ever.

Embracing the future even as we honour the past, Gollancz launched the SF Gateway with a view to utilising the technology that now exists to make available, for the first time, the entire backlists of an incredibly wide range of classic and modern SF and fantasy authors. Our plan, at its simplest, was – and still is! – to use this technology to build on the success of the SF and Fantasy Masterworks series and to go even further.

The SF Gateway was designed to be the new home of classic Science Fiction & Fantasy – the most comprehensive electronic library of classic SFF titles ever assembled. The programme has been extremely well received and we've been very happy with the results. So happy, in fact, that we've decided to complete the circle and return a selection of our titles to print, in these omnibus editions.

We hope you enjoy this selection. And we hope that you'll want to explore more of the classic SF and fantasy we have available. These are wonderful books you're holding in your hand, but you'll find much, much more ... through the SF Gateway.

www.sfgateway.com

INTRODUCTION

from The Encyclopedia of Science Fiction

James P. Blaylock (1950–) is a US author, born and based in California, whose first published sf was 'Red Planet' for *Unearth* #3 in 1977, and whose 'The Ape-Box Affair' (1978) may be the first consciously Steampunk tale; his first books were two fantasies in his Elfin series, *The Elfin Ship* (1982) and *The Disappearing Dwarf* (1983). The series, which includes the later and more assured *The Stone Giant* (1989), is remarkable for its geniality and quirkiness, and the general likability of most of the characters, even the unreliable ones. Though dwarfs and elves are featured, it is difficult to imagine a fantasy series less like J. R. R. Tolkien's in tone, if for no other reason than its constant subversion of any underlying premise that travel to perilous regions lies at the heart of fantasy.

A similar tone could be heard in Blaylock's next two books, which more closely resemble sf: *The Digging Leviathan* (1984) and *Homunculus* (1986), the latter being the winner of the Philip K. Dick Award for best paperback original (coincidentally appropriate, since Blaylock had been a friend of Philip K. Dick during Dick's last years). It was by now clear that Blaylock's talent was strong, but sufficiently weird and literary as to be unlikely to attract a mass-market readership. His earlier books in particular feature grotesques and eccentrics, whose fantastical relationship to the world is viewed with whimsical but sometimes wearying affection. The protagonists of later books continue to have crotchets and obsessions, but live in increasingly mutable worlds whose deep strangeness, as it were, transcends both their own eccentricities and their attempts – sometimes earnestly scientific – to make sense of things. The things of the world (there are many) in Blaylock's books tend to fall into odd patterns rather than linear plots, though the later works have a stronger narrative drive. *The Digging Leviathan*, the first volume set in what may be called the Digging Leviathan world, takes place in a modern Los Angeles, beneath which stretches a giant underground sea (it may be the first Los Angeles novel to feature one, though it is certainly not the last), which some Los Angeles inhabitants hope to traverse in order, somehow, to reach the center of the Hollow Earth. An interior world indeed serves as the primary venue for *Zeuglodon* (2012), where the entire inner reality may be the invention of a man asleep, who may be a Secret Master, or who may not.

Homunculus, a kind of thematic prequel to *The Digging Leviathan*, and which also does service as the first volume of the Langdon St Ives sequence, is set in a Dickensian nineteenth-century London, and is likewise imbued with the spirit of scientific or alchemical inquiry, along with space vehicles, zombies and the possibility of Immortality gained through an application of essence of carp. *Lord Kelvin's Machine* (1992), a direct sequel, carries on in the same vein; both have been assembled as *The Adventures of Langdon St Ives* (2008). The sequence, which variously and lovingly explores Steampunk's initial and continuing nostalgia for scientific method, continues with a novella, *The Ebb Tide* (2009), plus *The Affair of the Chalk Cliffs* (2011), which is longer, and *The Aylesford Skull* (2013), a full-length tale in which St Ives's resemblance to Sherlock Holmes is perhaps more marked.

These spirited concoctions are reminiscent of the more-benign work of Blaylock's good friend Tim Powers; indeed, Blaylock's *Homunculus* and Powers's slightly earlier *The Anubis Gates* (1983) – both set in an Alternate History quasi-animate London in which Urban Fantasy motifs are driven by magically efficacious steam-driven technologies in language also evocative of various pulp sf conventions – are generally crediting with central roles in fathering Steampunk. Blaylock and Powers, in fact, share not only a steampunk vision and venue, but also certain characters, and their work as a whole could almost be regarded as comprising a kind of metaseries. The best-known character shared by the two is the fictional nineteenth-century poet William Ashbless, originally a joint pseudonym for poetry published while at college, later a character in various fictions, and the 'author' of more than one pamphlet. Like many of his Postmodernist generation of writers, including Powers and another of his friends, K. W. Jeter, Blaylock has never been interested in maintaining generic purity, mixing tropes from Fantasy, Horror, sf, magic realism, adventure fiction and mainstream literature with great aplomb, as if it were the most natural thing in the world.

Blaylock's later singletons, beginning with *Land of Dreams* (1987), increasingly settle into a supernatural fiction default, but with sophisticated glosses from other patterns of the fantastic in literature, and increasingly convey a sense of some deep sadness magically averted, for the nonce. *Land of Dreams* is set in the same fantastic northern-Californian coastal setting as Blaylock's excellent short story *Paper Dragons*, which won a World Fantasy Award, and is drenched with love for the venue. *The Last Coin* (1988) and *The Paper Grail* (1991) (for both see below) expand upon this model. More recent novels, like *Night Relics* (1994) and *All the Bells of Earth* (1995) (see below), continue to explore supernatural fiction concerns; some of them are clearly imbued with autobiographical intensity, and increasingly address what could be called – not at all frivolously – the Matter of California. In these novels, which may be his best, he has travelled very far from sf; he has become a mature, sagacious, complexly competent author, whose travels into California have not ceased.

The Last Coin (1988), the first novel reprinted here, is perhaps the most exuberant of the later works, featuring an ex-travelling salesman who turns out to be the Wandering Jew, and is anxious that the 30 pieces of silver used to betray Christ should be kept from the hands of a Mr Pennyman, who will use them for apocalyptic purposes. *The Paper Grail* (1991), which comes next, is, unusually for Blaylock, a quest tale, set as usual in northern California, and featuring the curator of a small museum caught into a search for the eponymous relic, which has manifested in the form of a Hokusai image rendered into origami. The technology is Steampunk, the aesthetic pre-Raphaelite. The last novel here is *All the Bells of Earth* (1995), which reverses the flow of *The Paper Grail*: instead of a protagonist on quest, it features a protagonist to whom all too many mysterious artifacts are delivered: which somehow seems ill-intended, and proves so. In the end the chaos created by the Devil himself subsides, and California is still there. It is the good California that remains, the California we want never to end. Blaylock is its scribe.

For a more detailed version of the above, see James P. Blaylock's author entry in *The Encyclopedia of Science Fiction*: http://sf-encyclopedia.com/entry/blaylock_james_p

Some terms above are capitalised when they would not normally be so rendered; this indicates that the terms represent discrete entries in *The Encyclopedia of Science Fiction*.

THE LAST COIN

For Viki

And this time,

For my friend Lew Shiner,
Pen Pal and Surfing Buddy

And for the lovely Edie
and her mint brownies, raccoon houses, and coffee –

From the four of us

'—*Nay, if you come to that, Sir, have not the wisest of men in all ages, not excepting Solomon himself,—have they not had their Hobby-Horses;—their running horses, their coins and their cockle-shells, their drums and their trumpets, their fiddles, their pallets, their maggots and their butterflies?—and so long as a man rides his Hobby-Horse peaceably and quietly along the King's highway, and neither compels you or me to get up behind him,—pray, Sir, what have either you or I to do with it?*'

LAURENCE STERNE,
TRISTRAM SHANDY

BOOK I

The Second Joke

*'There is no duty we so much underrate as the duty of being happy ...
A happy man or woman is a better thing to find than a five-pound
note.'*

ROBERT LOUIS STEVENSON,
'AN APOLOGY FOR IDLERS'

PROLOGUE

He sat in the back seat of a sherrut, a whirling dervish taxi, slamming down the road out of the Jerusalem Highlands toward the Ben-Gurion Airport in Tel Aviv. The driver was a lunatic, and Pennyman bounced and rocked on the back seat of the old Mercedes-Benz as it wheeled around curves and plunged over dips. In his pocket was a leather bag of silver coins, uncomfortably hot. The day was declining behind them, and the buildings of old Jerusalem were sun-washed and pale. Ahead, the high-rises of Tel Aviv threw shadows out over the flat Mediterranean landscape. Pennyman could barely recognize it. It had been years.

He'd been through the airport once before, when it was the Lod Airport. Before that, uncounted years earlier, he'd sailed from Haifa to Cyprus on a fishing boat, carrying another of the coins — only the third he'd ever possessed. The crew had sensed that he was fleeing from something, and when a storm had blown up in the night and nearly capsized them, the ship's cook, a Jordanian with wide, holy eyes, had called him a Jonah, and Pennyman had come close to being pitched into the sea. They had taken the coin from him when it had begun to crackle with St Elmo's fire in the static-charged air. They'd flung *it* over the side instead, and then watched silently when a vast shadow rose from the dark sea and swallowed up the glowing coin as it tumbled into the depths.

The years had shuffled his memory, dealing away bits and pieces of it. Time diminished a man; there was no denying it – even a man who possessed certain methods. Now the coins in his pocket made him feel almost young again, although it was a feeling that was tainted and corrupted, like the youthful flush of a well-nourished vampire.

He looked back out the window. There appeared to be no sign of pursuit. In well under an hour he'd be in the airport, and then on a Pan American jet to Paris and New York. He would angle across to Vancouver on the way to Los Angeles in order to pay a visit to his old coin-collecting friend, Pfennig. Pfennig might have heard about the murder of Aureus by then, of course, and might have fled. He might as easily have decided to sell. Perhaps Pfennig was the sort who would come cheap, or at least who could be convinced that it was better to come cheap than dead. The world was filled with fools, it seemed, who thought they'd been called upon to be Caretakers. He himself had been called upon to be something; but it was he, and no one else, who would determine what that something was.

He'd left the old man named Aureus dead in Jerusalem, and with any luck the man's corpse would lie in his locked shop for days before it was found. The shades were pulled and a sign hung in the window. He was gone, it said – on holiday. No one on earth expected the store to reopen for another week. The blind beggars in the man's employ would know that something was wrong. They sensed something, no doubt about it, behind their strangely Asiatic, sightless eyes. But they were almost certainly mad. One had followed Pennyman for half a block, and then had cocked his head, as if listening, when Pennyman had climbed into the taxi and driven off. Pennyman had made the mistake of rattling his bag full of stolen silver out the window at the man, just as a lark. At the sound of it, coins had flown out of the beggar's cup like popcorn out of hot oil, and the man had thrown open his mouth and howled so high and shrill that his howling was silent, and the rising lamentation of baying dogs had followed the taxi out of the city to the highway. None of the beggars would have keys to the shop, though. Old Aureus wouldn't have trusted them with a bag of shekels much less with the coins. His corpse would have ample time to ripen.

Pennyman patted his coat pocket. His papers, as the saying went, were in order. It was too bad he had to fly out of Tel Aviv. Security at Ben-Gurion was tight and mean, and there was nothing of the bazaar atmosphere of Athens or Beirut airport. That would keep the beggars out, though, which was just as well. Tackling the metal detector would be interesting. He'd send the coins around it with the papers of requisition from the British Museum. Carrying out old Hebrew coins would have been tricky, but these thirty silver coins – of which Pennyman possessed twenty-five – had their origins farther east, much farther east, and so weren't of local historical significance. He wouldn't be accused of trying to smuggle out relics from the Holy Land.

The coins were old when the Cities of the Plain had burned, and they had been scattered in the years since, to be collected, all of them together, only once in the last thousands of years. The man who had held all of them briefly in his grasp had cast the coins into the dirt and hanged himself in remorse for the ruination his greed had fashioned.

But he hadn't been allowed to die. The thirty silver coins, all together, had assured his immortality, and he had wandered the earth since, for over two thousand years, seeking to redeem himself by assuring that the coins were kept forever scattered. Old Aureus, trusted as a secret Caretaker, had sought to betray him, and had sought out more and more of the coins, hoarding them. Aureus had failed, though, in the end. Jules Pennyman didn't intend to fail.

Some few of the coins had been used by temple priests twenty centuries ago to buy the potter's field where wandering strangers would be buried –

the first one of whom was interred with two of the coins pressing his eyelids shut. And so it was thought by the priest who had buried the man that even if twenty-eight of the coins were gathered again in a distant time, at least these two would be lost forever. But in the end he betrayed his own secret, for his own meddling with the coins had tainted him.

When the grave in the potter's field was robbed, though, the coins were gone, and it was said that the weight of the coins had driven them through the dead man's head and that they'd burnt through the winding sheet and into the earth beneath it and that one day, ages hence, they would complete their travel through the earth and appear on the other side of the world to set into spinning motion the prophecy of revelation.

The twenty-eight unburied coins had been carried off singly, and now and then two or three together. Most had been squandered, sometimes sold as curiosities. In the right hands, though, they were something more than curiosities. Benjamin Aureus, finally, had buried fourteen of them in the sand beneath the floor of his shop, and it was said that early on autumn mornings, an hour or two before sunrise, the air over the shop seemed to be agitated by flitting spirits, like an illustration of the opening of Pandora's box.

Jules Pennyman had long suspected that Aureus possessed some of the coins, but he hadn't half-expected what he'd found. Powerful as Aureus was, he couldn't have hoped to keep the coins silent. The coins had a way of finding Caretakers, and of searching out weaknesses in them. In the absence of weaknesses, the coins would create some. Aureus at first had been nothing more than a Caretaker himself, a disciple of the Wandering Jew whose penance for the sin of betrayal was the two-thousand-year task of keeping the coins apart. But Aureus had fallen to greed and to the corruption that came inevitably from the process of accumulating the coins. And now he was dead.

Jules Pennyman wasn't anyone's disciple. He was a stone in the desert – linked to nothing at all, a self-contained, self-satisfied entity. And unlike Aureus, he was alive, and he possessed nearly, but not quite, twice the number of coins. His power would be incalculable. Unlike Judas Iscariot, he wasn't a man given over to remorse …

At the thought of Judas Iscariot he pulled a flask full of Pepto-Bismol out of his coat and drank off half the contents. He had more in his luggage.

The taxi banged over a pothole as the driver felt around on the floor, coming up with a bottle of sweet Carmel wine. Pennyman leaned forward to complain, but the man shrugged and tilted it back, then spat the wine through the open window, cursing and throwing the bag and then the bottle out after it, muttering about vinegar. He turned and glared at Pennyman, as if the wine's turning was his fault. And in a way it was.

Just then it began to rain, great muddy drops that fouled the windshield. Pennyman peered up out the rear window at a nearly cloudless sky. Overhead, as if following them, was a single black cloud, and out over the desert a thousand little wind devils seemed to be whirling up, dancing in a riot of dust and dry twigs. They raced along beside the car for a way, the twigs and debris swirling into vaguely human shapes, like spirits again, peering in at the window. A dead bird plummeted from the sky, thumping onto the hood of the taxi, and then another followed, slamming against the windshield. The rain of birds lasted half a minute, and then the sky cleared abruptly and the wind devils died away. Pennyman waited. He had expected something, but he hadn't known what.

There was a lead box waiting at the airport, in his suitcase in a locker. He ought to have brought it along. The leather bag wasn't enough to *contain* the coins. Even the weather, suddenly, was sensitive to them, as if it knew that they'd fallen into – what? – not evil hands. Evil wasn't the word for it. Evil was a word used by the ignorant to explain powers and forces they feared. Jules Pennyman feared nothing at all, short of being stopped when he was so close to winning through.

The rearview mirror spontaneously cracked to bits just then, showering the front seat with tiny fragments. The driver glanced sideways at Pennyman. He had a look of frightened incomprehension on his face now. The taxi swerved toward the shoulder, then back again, and then started to slow down. Pennyman had seen that look before. He pulled out his wallet, withdrew a wad of shekels, and waved it at the man. The taxi drove on. In ten minutes they'd be in Tel Aviv.

It was true that Pennyman didn't yet have all of the coins. There were still two in the earth, and the one that had been thrown into the sea. Pfennig, it seemed certain, possessed another one – or rather the coin possessed him. And then there was the coin in California. That one was veiled by mystery. He would have them all, though, in the very end; for the more he possessed, the more certain he became of the whereabouts of the rest, as if the coins sought each other out.

'Skirt the city,' Pennyman said, not wanting to get caught in the downtown press of people. The road had flattened, and the air was sticky and warm. The muddy rain had given out, but the sky over the Mediterranean was black with approaching clouds.

Something was happening to the weather. The pressure was dropping and the atmosphere seemed to be bending and warping – tensing like a coiled spring. When the taxi lurched to a halt amid honking traffic and Pennyman stepped out onto the curb, the ground shook, just a little, just enough to make the hurrying masses of people put down their luggage and stop, waiting.

Pennyman paid the taxi driver and strode toward the airport doors – casually, nodding at an old woman with a dog, and pausing for one precious moment to hold back the milling crowd so that she could drag her bags and her dog in through the door. He didn't want to seem to be in a hurry to get to the locker, to be a man possessed, although in truth there wasn't a man in the world at that moment more thoroughly possessed than he was.

He peered up at what he could see of the sky and grimaced as lightning arced across it. An immediate blast of thunder rattled the windows, followed by a wash of wind-driven rain. The air suddenly was full of the smell of ozone and sulphur, and the ground shook again, as if it were waking up.

ONE

'I was told that he was in his heart, a good fellow, and an enemy to no one but himself.'

ROBERT LOUIS STEVENSON,

PRINCE OTTO

Andrew Vanbergen used a pruning ladder to get to the attic window – the sort with flared legs and a single pole for support. The pole clacked against the copper rain gutter and then hung uselessly, the top rung of the ladder seesawing back and forth across it. He looked over his shoulder at the silent midnight street and wiggled the ladder, worried that it might slide down along the gutter and pitch him into the branches of the camphor tree that grew along the side of the house. But there was nothing he could do about it now; it was the only ladder he had.

He could hear Aunt Naomi snoring through the open window. The whole street could hear it. That's what would give him away – not any noise he'd make, not the scraping of the ladder against the gutter, but the sudden stopping of the snoring if she woke up and saw him there outside the window, peering in. Neighbors would lurch awake in their beds, wondering. Had they heard something? It would be like in an earthquake, when you're not aware of the rumbling and the groaning and creaking until it stops.

An hour ago he had lain in bed beside his sleeping wife in their second-story bedroom, listening to Aunt Naomi snoring through the floor. It drove him nearly crazy, the snoring and the mewling of her cats. He couldn't sleep because of it. He had pitched and tossed and plumped up his pillow, watching the slow luminous hands on the clock edge toward morning. He swore that if he saw the coming of twelve o'clock, he'd act. Midnight had come and gone.

He had lain there knowing that the old woman would sleep the night through, like a baby. She'd awaken in the morning, about five, proud of herself for rising early but complaining about it anyway. She couldn't sleep: her poor nerves, her 'sciatica,' her sinuses, her this, her that. She'd demand tea with milk in it. Her bed would be covered with cats, and the air in the room would reek of mentholated vapor rub and litter boxes and old clothes. Taken altogether it would smell like – what? Words couldn't express it. They *wouldn't* express it; they'd mutiny first and become babble.

It was the hottest April he could remember. Even at nearly one in the morning it was seventy-seven degrees and not a whisper of wind. The ocean sighed through the pier pilings half a block away, just over the rooftops. Now and then the light of headlamps would swing around the curve from Sunset Beach, and a car full of sleepy night owls would go gunning up the Pacific Coast Highway toward Belmont Shore and Long Beach. They were too far off to see him though, hidden as the house was down the little dead-end street that it shared with half a dozen other houses. Lights shone in one; the others were dark.

Andrew climbed the ladder slowly, his faced blacked out with ash from the disused fireplace. He wore a black shirt and slacks and black burlap shoes with crepe soles. A long fiberglass pole with a loop on the end lay tilted against the ladder. On the shingled gable in front of him was an empty flour sack and a bit of rope with a loop already tied in one end. Lying there awake in bed an hour earlier, hot and tired and unable to sleep through the mewling and the snoring, he'd committed himself to the idea of tackling the cat problem that very night. Sleeplessness was maddening. There was nothing else on earth like it when it came to sheer, teeth-grinding irritation.

The idea now was to snatch up a cat, hoist it into the flour sack, and tie the sack off with a slipknot, then go in after another cat. One of them stared at him through the open attic window. It seemed to find his sudden appearance boring and tiresome. He smiled at it and touched two fingers to his forehead, as if tipping his hat. Civility in all things, he muttered, peering in at the window, past the cat. Thank God there wasn't a window screen to remove.

He listened – to the snoring, to the sounds of distant, muted traffic, to the faint music coming from a tavern somewhere down the Pacific Coast Highway, probably the Glide 'er Inn. It drifted past him on the warm night, reminding him of the world, stealing away his nerve, his resolve. The moon was just rising over the rooftops. He'd have to hurry.

'Nice kitty,' he whispered, making smacking noises at the cat. They liked that, or seemed to. He'd decided that he wouldn't throw the cats into the salt marsh after all. A half hour ago, when he was crazy with being kept awake, it had seemed like the only prudent course. Now that he was up and about, though, and had put things in perspective, he realized that he had nothing against cats, not really, as long as they lived somewhere else. He couldn't bear even to take them to the pound. He knew that. Cruelty wasn't in him.

He hadn't, in fact, entirely worked out what he *would* do with them. Give them away in front of the supermarket, perhaps. He could claim that they'd belonged to a celebrity – the grandmother of a movie star, maybe; that would fetch it. People would clamor for them. Or else he could give them to the neighborhood children and offer them a dollar-fifty reward for every cat they took away and didn't come back with, and another dollar apiece if the kids hadn't ratted on him by the end of the month. That would be dangerous, though; children were a mysterious, unpredictable race – almost as bad as cats. Pulling a smelt out of his shirt pocket, he dangled it in front of the open flour sack. The cat inside the window wrinkled up its nose.

He smiled at it and nodded, winking good-naturedly. 'Good kitty-pup. Here's a fishy.'

The cat turned away and licked itself. He edged up a rung on the ladder and laid the fish on a shingle, but the cat didn't care about it; it might as well have been an old shoe. Andrew's shadow bent away across the shingles, long and angular in the moonlight, looking almost like a caricature of Don Quixote. He turned his head to catch his profile, liking that better, and thinking that as he got older he looked just a little bit more like Basil Rathbone every year, if only he could stay thin enough. He squinted just a little, as if something had been revealed to him, something that was hidden to the rest of mortal men. But the shadow, of course, didn't reveal the knowing squint, and his nose needed more hook to it, and the cat on the sill sat as ever, seeming to know far more than he did about hidden things.

He reached for the pole, jumping it up through his right hand until he could tilt it in through the open window. The pole wasn't any good for close work. The cat in the window would have to wait. He peered into the darkened room, waiting for his eyes to adjust, listening to the snoring. It was frightful. There was nothing else like it on earth: snorts and groans and noises that reminded him of an octopus.

He had been tempted at first, when he was seething, to poke the pole against her ear and shout into the other end. But such a thing would finish her. She'd been ill for ten years – or so she'd let on – and an invalid for most of them. A voice shouting into her ear at midnight through a fifteen-foot pole would simply kill her. The autopsy would reveal that she'd turned into a human pudding. They'd jail him for it. His shouting would awaken the house. They'd haul him down from the ladder and gape into his ash-smeared face. Why had he shouted at Aunt Naomi through a tube? She owned cats? She'd been snoring, had she? And he'd – what? – got himself up in jewel-thief clothes and crept up a pruning ladder to the attic window, hoping to undo her by shouting down a fiberglass tube?

Moonlight slanted past him through the tree branches, suddenly illuminating the room. There was another cat, curled up on the bed. He would never get the noose over its head. There was another, atop the bureau. It stood there staring into the moonlight, its eyes glowing red. The room was full of cats. It stank like a kennel, the room did, the floorboards gritty with spilled kitty litter. An acre of ocean winds blowing through two-dozen open windows wouldn't scour out the reek. He grimaced and played out line, waving the loop across the top of the bed toward the dresser. The cat stood there defiantly, staring him down. He felt almost ashamed. He'd have to be quick – jerk it off the dresser without slamming the pole down onto the bed and awakening Aunt Naomi, if that were possible. A *little* noise wouldn't hurt; her snoring would mask it.

He had practiced in the backyard when the family was gone. His friend Beams Pickett had helped him, playing the part of a surprised cat. Then they'd pieced up a false cat out of a pillow, a jar, and a gunnysack and snatched it off tree limbs and out of bushes and off fences until Andrew had it refined down to one swift thrust and yank. The trick now was to balance the pole atop the windowsill in order to take up some of the weight. Another arm would help, of course, if only to hold open the sack. He'd asked Pickett to come along, but Pickett wouldn't. He was an 'idea man' he had said, not a man of action.

Andrew let the pole rest on the sill for a moment, watching the strangely unmoving cat out of one eye, the cat inside the window out of the other eye. He picked up the flour sack, shoving the hem of the open end into his mouth and letting it dangle there against the shingles. He was ready. Aunt Naomi snorted and rolled over. He froze, his heart pounding, a chill running through him despite the heat. Moments passed. He worked the pole forward, wondering at the foolish cat that stood there as still as ever. It was a sitting duck. He giggled, suppressing laughter. What would Darwin say? It served the beast right to be snatched away like this. Natural selection is what it was. He'd get the cats, then pluck up the corners of Aunt Naomi's bed sheet and tie them off, too. It would be a simple thing to lock her into the trunk of the Metropolitan and fling her, still trussed up in the sheet, into the marsh in Gum Grove Park.

It was easy to believe, when you looked at the wash of stars in the heavens, that something was happening in the night sky and in the darkened city stretched along the coast. The whole random shape of things – the people roundabout, their seemingly petty business, the day-to-day machinations of governments and empires – all of it spun slowly, like the stars, into patterns invisible to the man on the street, but, especially late at night, clear as bottle glass to him. Or at least they all would become so. Clearing the house of cats would be the first step toward clearing his mind of murk, toward ordering the mess that his life seemed sometimes to be spiraling into. He and Pickett had set up Pickett's telescope in the unplastered attic cubbyhole adjacent to Aunt Naomi's bedroom, but the smell of the cats had pretty much kept them out of it – a pity, really. There was something – a cosmic order, maybe – in the starry heavens that relaxed him, that made things all right after all. He couldn't get enough of them and stayed up late sometimes just to get a midnight glimpse of the sky after the lights of the city had dimmed.

All this talk of unusual weather and earthquakes on the news over the past weeks was unsettling, although it seemed to be evidence of something; it seemed to bear out his suspicions that something was afoot. The business of the Jordan River flowing backward out of the Dead Sea was the corker. It sounded overmuch like an Old Testament miracle, although as far as the newspapers knew, there hadn't been any Moses orchestrating the phenomenon. It would no doubt have excited less comment if it weren't for the dying birds and the rain of mud. The newspapers in their euphemistic way spoke of solar disturbances and tidal deviations, but that was pretty obvious hogwash. Andrew wondered whether anyone knew for sure, whether there were some few chosen people out there who understood, who nodded at such occurrences and winked at each other.

The city of Seal Beach was full of oddballs these days, too: men from secret societies, palm readers, psychics of indeterminate powers. There had been a convention of mystics in South Long Beach just last week. Even Beams Pickett had taken up with one, a woman who didn't at all have the appearance of a spiritualist, but who had announced that Andrew's house was full of 'emanations.' He hated that kind of talk.

He shook his head. He'd been daydreaming, so to speak. His mind had wandered, and that wasn't good. That was his problem all along. Rose, his wife, had told him so on more than one occasion. He grinned in at the cat on the dresser, trying to mesmerize it. 'Keep still,' he whispered, slowly dangling the noose in over its head. He held his breath, stopped dead for a slice of a moment, then jerked on the line and yanked back on the pole at the same instant. The line went taut and pulled the cat off the dresser. The pole whumped down across the sill, overbalanced, and whammed onto the bed just as the weirdly heavy cat hit the floorboards with a crash that made it sound as if the thing had smashed into fragments. The cat inside the window howled into his ear and leaped out onto the roof. The half-dozen cats left inside ran mad, leaping and yowling and hissing. He jerked at his pole, but the noose was caught on something – the edge of the bed, probably.

A light blinked on, and there was Aunt Naomi, her hair papered into tight little curls, her face twisted into something resembling a fish. She clutched the bedclothes to her chest and screamed, then snatched up the lamp beside her bed and pitched it toward the window. The room winked into darkness, and the flying lamp banged against the wall a foot from his head.

The pole wrenched loose just then with a suddenness that propelled him backward. He dropped it and grappled for the rain gutter as the ladder slid sideways toward the camphor tree in a rush that tore his hands loose. He smashed in among the branches, hollering, hooking his left leg around the drainpipe and ripping it away, crashing up against a limb and holding on, his legs dangling fourteen feet above the ground. Hauling himself onto the limb, trembling, he listened to doors slamming and people shouting below. Aunt

Naomi shrieked. Cats scoured across the rooftops, alerting the neighborhood. Dogs howled.

His pole and ladder lay on the ground. His flour sack had entangled itself in the foliage. He could climb back up onto the roof if he had to, scramble over to the other side, shinny down a drainpipe into the backyard. They'd know by now that he wasn't in bed, of course, but he'd claim to have gone out after the marauder. He'd claim to have chased him off, to have hit him, perhaps, with a rock. The prowler wouldn't come fooling around *there* any more, not after that. Aunt Naomi couldn't have known who it was that had menaced her. The moment of light wouldn't have given her eyes enough time to adjust. She wouldn't cut him out of her will. She would thank him for the part he'd played. She'd ...

A light shone up into the tree. People gathered on the lawn below: his wife, Mrs Gummidge, Pennyman. All of them were there. And the neighbor, too – old what's his name, Ken-or-Ed, as his wife called him. My God he was fat without a shirt on – out half-naked, minding everybody's business but his own. He was almost a cephalopod in the silver moonlight. His bald head shone with sweat.

There was a silence below. Then, hesitantly, Rose's voice: 'Is that you, Andrew? Why are you in the tree, dear?'

'There's been some sort of funny business. I'm surprised you didn't hear it. I couldn't sleep, because of the heat, so I came downstairs and out onto the porch ...'

'You did what?' His wife shouted up to him, cupping a hand to her ear. 'Come down. We can't hear you. Why have you got the ladder out?'

'I don't!' he shouted. 'A prowler ...' but then Aunt Naomi's head thrust out through the open window, her eyes screwed down to the size of dimes. She gasped and pointed at him, signaling to those below on the lawn.

'I'll go to her,' said Mrs Gummidge, starting into the house.

Andrew had always hated that phrase – 'go to her.' It drove him nearly crazy, and now particularly. Mrs Gummidge had a stock of such phrases. She was always 'reaching out' and 'taking ill' and 'lending a hand' and 'proving useful.' He watched the top of her head disappear under the porch gable. At least she paid her rent on time – thanks to Aunt Naomi's money. But Aunt Naomi held the money over her head, too, just like she did with the rest of them, and Andrew knew that Mrs Gummidge loathed the idea of it; it ate her up. She was sly, though, and didn't let on. The wife couldn't see it. Rose was convinced that Mrs Gummidge was a saint – bringing cups of tea up to the attic at all hours, playing Scrabble in the afternoon as long as Aunt Naomi let her win.

'Of course she lets her win,' Andrew had said. 'She feels sorry for the woman.'

Rose hadn't thought so. She said it was generosity on Aunt Naomi's part that explained it – natural charity. But it wasn't. Andrew was certain it was something loathsome. It would almost be worth it to have Aunt Naomi gone, and her money with her. They'd get by somehow. If they could just hold on a couple of weeks, until tourists began to flock through, until he could get the cafe into shape and open up for dinners. They'd see their way clear then.

He shivered. It had gotten suddenly colder. An onshore wind had blown up, ruffling the leaves on the tree, cutting through his cotton shirt. At forty-two he wasn't the hand at climbing trees that he'd been at ten. There was no way he was going onto the roof of the house. He was trapped there. He'd stick it, though, at least until Pennyman left – Pennyman and Ken-or-Ed. The man's head was a disgrace. He looked like a bearded pumpkin.

There he was, down on the grass, peering at the looped end of the rope attached to the pole. Tied into it was the head and shoulders of the plaster statue of a cat, its red glass eyes glowing in the moonlight. Andrew Vanbergen had risked his life and reputation to snatch a painted plaster cat off a dresser at one in the morning. He shrugged. Such was fate. The gods got a laugh out of it anyway. Pickett would see the humor in it. So would Uncle Arthur. Ken-or-Ed pitched the cat head into the bushes and leaned the pole against a branch of the camphor tree, shaking his head again as if the whole business were beyond him, as if it beat all.

Murmuring voices wafted up toward Andrew from the lawn. 'Are you coming down, dear?' his wife asked suddenly, shading her eyes and peering up into the branches.

He waited for a moment, then said, 'No, not for a bit. I'm going to wait. This man might return. He could be lurking in the neighborhood right now. Wait! What's that! Off toward the highway!'

Ken-or-Ed loped away, looking around wildly, alert for prowlers. Pennyman watched as if unconvinced, then muttered something and strode off into the house. When he found nothing at all to confront, Ken-or-Ed slouched back up the street and onto the lawn. He explained loudly to Andrew's wife just what it was a prowler was likely to have done under the circumstances. He had done some police work when he was younger, he said, and it paid off in situations like this. Andrew rolled his eyes and listened from up in the tree, shivering again in the breeze off the ocean. He could just see the top of his wife's head.

'I'm certain it does,' Rose said diplomatically, and then she excused herself and said 'Don't be long' to Andrew, up into the branches of the tree. 'And don't tackle him alone! Just shout. There's enough of us here to help you, so forget any stupid heroics.' Andrew loved her for that. She saw through him as if he were a sheet of glass. He knew that. She hadn't swallowed any of it, but here she was letting him off.

She deserved better than him. He made up his mind to turn over a leaf. He'd start tomorrow. Maybe he'd paint the garage. It needed it, certainly. Thinking about it depressed him. He'd do something, though. He watched as Rose followed along in Pennyman's wake, shutting the front door after her. Finding himself alone on the lawn, Ken-or-Ed went home, squinting back up toward the tree as if he only half-believed there was anyone in it. Aunt Naomi's window slammed shut just then, and Andrew sat by himself in the filtered moonlight, sheltered by the canopy of leaves, listening to the lonely chirping of night birds and the quiet splash of seawaves.

Andrew's family had come from Iowa, all of them Dutch with remarkable last names. There'd been dozens of them: aunts and uncles and cousins and far-flung this and thats who had never been entirely explained.

Rose's family was the same way, but Dutch with Scottish mixed in. They'd grown up in Alton, he and Rose, and had married out of love. There'd been farms and corn and shiftings west, to Colorado and California. The family had scattered. Like old home movies, elements of it had been grand, but you had to have been there. There were bits and pieces of it, though – largely uninteresting even to those who *had* been there – that *meant* something. Andrew was pretty sure of it. Beams Pickett would be positive. They kept swimming into focus through the murky waters of passing time, refusing to be submerged and swept away into the gray sea of lost memories. That's the way things went: the crumbling of empires, the front-page news, the blather yodeling out of the television; all of that was nothing, a blind, a red herring.

It was the *trifles* that signified: the cut of a man's beard, the too-convenient discovery of forgotten money in a disused wallet, the overheard conversation between two fishermen early in the fog-shrouded morning as one of them hauls out of the ocean a crab trap with an ink-stained note in it. There was a secret order to things.

In Iowa, in 1910, almost forty years before she was born, Rose's family had lived on a farm. There were a dozen of them in all, including the vast grandmother, who was so wide that her voluminous skirts wedged tight in doorways. There were aunts and uncles, too – Rose's Aunt Naomi, for one. Uncle Arthur lived nearby. He wasn't exactly an uncle, but was an old and trusted friend, and now he lived some two miles down Seal Beach Boulevard at the Leisure World retirement community.

Family legend told how, one autumn morning, back on the farm, there had been a furious clatter on the back porch. It was as if a portable earthquake were rattling the windows. It was hot and muggy outside, and somehow the banging and shaking didn't surprise anyone, not even the children. Jars toppled off the pantry shelf and broke; the porch railing groaned; the house shuddered as if some fearful Providence waited impatiently outside, tapping its foot and frowning, checking its pocket watch.

The grandmother, clutching a fireplace poker, cast the door open. A half-score of children peered past her skirts.

There on the stoop had stood a pig, broad as a buggy, with a silver spoon in its mouth. It waited, watching the family gaping there, until the grandmother, very calmly and solemnly, took the spoon from between its teeth. The pig turned and ran away on idiotic legs, lumbering around the side of the chicken coop, out of their lives. The thin spoon was dented on the edge from the pig's teeth, and there was an almost rubbed-off profile on the concave surface of it. If you held it in moonlight, and tilted it just so, it seemed to be the bearded face of a pharaoh, perhaps, or an Old Testament king with a stiffened beard and an unlikely hat. There was a moon on the other side, or maybe a curled up fish, or both, one inside the other; it was too dim and rubbed to tell.

It created a stir in Alton for a week. Conversations sprang up around it, as if one of the grandmother's ten children had been born with the same article between *its* teeth. By week's end, though, the business of the spoon dwindled until nobody, in the family or out of it, cared any more. But Rose's grandmother polished and kept it, and it fell out, years later, that the spoon was given to Naomi, who met her husband because of it – or so the story went – and that the husband had considered it some sort of talisman. The spoon disappeared when he died – or was murdered, as some thought. Rose had heard that years later his young widow had had his corpse exhumed and cut open, and the spoon was found in his stomach and recovered.

Even more years later – almost seventy-five years after the arrival of the pig at the family farm in Iowa – Andrew and his wife had moved from Eagle Rock to Seal Beach, and bought, at least partly with Aunt Naomi's money, a thirteen-room craftsman bungalow with the idea of renovating it and opening up an inn and a restaurant. They would rent out rooms, by the day, week, or month. They'd take in boarders and feed them breakfast. There would be a cafe with a price-fixed menu and a bar, open on weekends. Aunt Naomi would live upstairs.

Her spoon came west with her and sat now in a mahogany china hutch, along with a collection of old Delft pottery and the last cracked pieces of a porcelain chocolate set.

There was something about the spoon. Andrew couldn't define it. It was vaguely loathsome, like an enormous snail, maybe, or the wrong sort of toad, with an almost visible trail behind it leading through a dusty old Iowa graveyard and into antiquity. Maybe it was the idea of the thing's having been cut out of the stomach of a dead man. It all signified, somehow.

It meant something, but what it meant he wasn't sure. Rose was indifferent to it. It was just another bit of family history – probably lies. She hadn't yet been born, after all, when the fabled pig had arrived on the back porch. It sounded suspiciously like one of Uncle Arthur's tales, Andrew had to admit. It sounded *just* like one of Uncle Arthur's tales – which made it all the more curious.

They'd moved into the bungalow and rolled up their sleeves, uncrating boxes for weeks. They painted. They crept around in the cool cellar replacing galvanized pipes. They ran electrical conduit to replace the old single line and insulator wiring that rats had chewed into rubble. Andrew converted one of the rooms into a library, with a couch and easy chairs and footstools and a painting of a clipper ship on the wall. He hauled out his aquaria with an eye toward setting up half a dozen.

Rose objected to Andrew's aquaria. There wouldn't be time for them. There never had been. They had been a mess half the time – a brown muddle of half-eaten waterweeds and declining fish. Andrew insisted, though. He would set up *one*, he said, to house a Surinam toad. It was the only aquatic creature he wanted anymore, and she could hardly object to his caring for it. A Surinam toad reminded him of Aunt Naomi, poor thing. Outside her aquarium-like room she'd dry up and wither. Without the family gathered round to conceal her, Aunt Naomi was a sort of unlikely horror, and couldn't be expected to survive without their charity. His wife scowled at the comparison, but she understood Aunt Naomi's plight well enough. Unlike Andrew, though, she rarely said anything ill about anyone, especially about Aunt Naomi, whose money they were almost completely dependent on.

Andrew shook his head sadly over the plight of the toad, which, in fact, he'd already bought from the aquarium shop that used to belong to poor old Moneywort, before he'd been murdered. The toad lived at that moment on the back porch, in a five-gallon bucket lidded with a copy of *Life* magazine. Andrew wouldn't treat the creature shabbily. He *was* his brother's keeper, after a fashion. His soul wouldn't be worth a drilled-out penny if he abandoned the toad now. In the end he had set up the aquarium on the service porch just behind the kitchen and beside their bedroom.

He and Rose slept in a downstairs room during the first two months they lived in the bungalow. One night late, a week after the setting up of the aquarium, there'd been a fearful clatter on the porch – a scuffling and sloshing and a banging of aquarium lids, and then the odd, Lovecraftian sound of something slurping across the floor of the kitchen. Rose had awakened in a sweat. It was a burglar; she was certain of it. The noise was unnatural – the noise of a fiend. Andrew had picked up a shoe, but he was thinking of the pig, making its racket seventy-five years ago on the back porch of an Iowa farm. He dropped the shoe, certain that he wouldn't need it. In his nightshirt he peeked out through the half-open door. There was the escaped toad, scurrying across the linoleum floor toward the front of the house, toward the living room, chirping as it ran. He confronted it on the threshold of the kitchen, scooping it up and dropping it back into its aquarium, then weighting the lid with a brick before going back to bed.

It wasn't until dawn that it occurred to him that the toad must have had a destination. In the living room, against the far wall, sat the china cabinet in which lay the pig spoon. It seemed unlikely at first, then possible, then wildly likely that the toad had been bound for that china cabinet, that it, too, was caught up in the adventure of the spoon. Andrew lay for an hour thinking about it, and then, without waking his wife, he tiptoed out onto the service porch, scooped the toad out of the tank, and set it onto the floor. It sat there, pretending to be dead.

Of course it *would* with him looking on and all. He'd missed his chance – bungled it. It might have been very different: the toad, thinking itself undiscovered, making away across the floor toward the hutch, wrestling it open somehow, plucking out the spoon, going out the mail slot with the spoon gripped in one of its webbed paws. Andrew might have followed it – to the sea, to a den beneath the old pier, into the back door of one of the derelict carnival rides at the Pike. It would have demonstrated, at the very least, a symphony of mysterious activity. At best – and not at all farfetched – it hinted at the sort of veiled, underlying order that bespoke the very existence of God.

But the toad had sat mute. After long minutes had passed, Andrew plucked it up and returned it once again to its aquarium, where it sank innocently to the bottom and pretended to sleep. He hadn't proved anything, but he was left with the uncanny suspicion that one foggy morning there would come a rattle at the door handle and a scuffling on the front porch. He would rise, wondering, and throw open the door. On the porch, giving him the glad eye, would be the pig, come round for the spoon. The toad would appear, yawning and stretching, and the two of them, the toad and the pig, would take the spoon and go.

Andrew sat at the kitchen table, surrounded by open boxes of breakfast cereal. He scowled into his coffee. It had gone stale. He would mail-order another two pounds that very morning. Coffee shouldn't sit in the refrigerator for more than two weeks. *One* week was plenty. The precious aromas were lost, somehow. He'd read about it. He'd compiled a notebook full of coffee literature and was toying with the idea of ordering a brass roasting oven from Diedrich. Rose wasn't keen on it.

She held her coffee mug in her hand, satisfied, not understanding his passion for brewing perfect coffee. She didn't see that it *had* to be done just so, or it was barely worth doing at all – they might as well boil up jimsonweed. A cup of coffee was a cup of coffee to her. Well, that was overstating it. She lacked some sort of vital instinct for it, though. 'What I don't get,' she said, peering at him over the top of the mug, 'is why you smeared ashes all over your face.'

'I tell you I really *was* after 'possums,' he said, putting down the coffee and gesturing. 'Do you know what 'possums would do to the wiring in the roof if they got up there and built a nest? We might as well burn the place to the ground ourselves. They're nocturnal. You know that. I went out after them, that's all. Traps don't work. They're too smart for traps.'

'Did you *try* traps?' She looked at him skeptically. He rolled his eyes, as if to suggest that he didn't see the necessity of *trying* anything, when a man could round up a ladder and noose and just lasso the creatures. 'One got in through the window, you say? In among the cats?'

'That's right.' He nodded broadly. That was it exactly. In among the cats. He'd seen it leap in, and knew there was going to be trouble. Anyone who understood 'possums could have seen it. It wouldn't do for the beast to awaken Aunt Naomi. *She'd* think it was an enormous rat that had gotten in. So he had gone after it with the noose affair he and Pickett had put together. The beast had run across the dresser, and he'd looped the noose over the head of the statue by mistake. If Aunt Naomi's bedroom hadn't been so full of trash, he'd have gotten the 'possum instead of the statue. But as it was, the thing went back out through the window – made a rush at him and nearly toppled him onto the ground. Rose had heard the racket, hadn't she? Fat lot of thanks he'd gotten for the effort, too.

'What was all that rigamarole about a prowler on the roof, and then him running down toward the boulevard?'

He blinked at her, stared into his empty coffee cup, and then blinked at her again. 'Health Department,' he said. 'With neighbors looking on, I had to pretend it was something other than 'possums. They'd report us, and the Health Department would close us down in a shot. I don't half-trust Ken-or-Ed. Did you *see* him parading around out there? And then there's Pennyman. Do you think he'd stick it here for another moment if he thought there were 'possums around? He'd be packed and gone, and there goes two hundred a month, like clockwork. It's the psychology of a 'possum that you've got to understand. A common criminal leaves when he knows you're onto him. A 'possum doesn't care. He moves in wholesale, meaning to stay, and Pennyman moves out. There goes the two hundred, like I said, in a shot. And then the cry goes round that there's 'possums positively haunting the place, and we don't get a nickel's worth of customers this summer. There's your inn for you ... 'Possums could have the place; they've nearly got it already.' He shook his head darkly, as if he was surprised that he had to explain such a thing.

'Have another cup of coffee?' his wife asked, looking at him sideways and picking up the Chemex beaker. 'What's wrong with the electric drip pot?'

He shook his head at the proffered coffee. 'Temperature's not right. Too hot. Over 180 degrees the water releases all the bitter oils. Wrecks your stomach. And it shouldn't sit and stew on the hot coil, either. All that does is make the coffee taste like turpentine.'

'Wash your face a bit,' she said. 'There's still ashes all over it. And later on this morning you might look in on poor Aunt Naomi. Explain things to her. I wouldn't half-wonder at her packing up and leaving.'

'You wouldn't half-wonder at her making *me* pack for her, and then drive her down to the train station in order for her to sit around for three hours before relenting and coming home again.'

'Just look in on her. Mrs Gummidge is with her now, but *she* shouldn't have to do all the smoothing over. Not when it was you chasing ...'

''Possums. I was chasing 'possums.' He turned away and walked toward the door. 'I'm going out to the restaurant and inventory supplies. Have you seen my copy of *Grossman's Guide*? I can't make another move without it.'

'There's work that needs to be done worse than that.'

'Later. I promise I'll do it this afternoon. Draw me up a list. Either the restaurant will open or it won't. I don't think you're as keen on it opening as I am.'

'I think we need a chef, and I don't think we can afford one.'

'That's just it. *I'm* the chef, Pickett has volunteered as *maître d'* until we get onto our feet. But unless I get things squared away out there, we don't have a chance. I'll need more money, by the way. I'm over budget now.'

'Talk to Aunt Naomi.'

'Maybe *you* should, what with this 'possum business and all.' He bent across and kissed her on the cheek, trying to look cheerful and matter-of-fact and swearing to himself that he *would* set in to paint the garage that afternoon. For certain he would, just as soon as he finished the business of shaping up the bar. Talk to Aunt Naomi – the idea of it appalled him.

'Square it with her this afternoon,' Rose said. 'She doesn't bite. Explain yourself a little bit, and she'll see reason. And don't carry on about 'possums, for heaven's sake. She thinks you're insane. You know that, don't you? Remember when you told her about how many baby 'possums could sit in a teaspoon, and then tried to say that that's how 'possum mothers carried their babies around? In a spoon? Don't talk that way, not in front of Aunt Naomi. You can talk nuts like that all afternoon with Pickett, but for goodness sake, leave it alone in front of people who don't understand it.'

He nodded, as if he thought Rose had given him good advice. But she gave him a look, seeing through him again, so he winked at her and went out, trying to seem jolly. She was right, of course. He'd have to confront the old woman after lunch. He'd bring her chocolates and flowers and explain about the mythical 'possum – not terrify her with it, of course, or say anything nuts. He'd just tell her about how it was big as a dog and had threatened her cats and about how the beasts burrow under bedsheets and build nests. If he spread himself a little bit, there'd be no telling what he might convince her of.

Jules Pennyman crouched outside the kitchen door, dabbing at his shoes with a rag. The shoes were already polished – they were new, in fact – and so didn't, maybe, need much dabbing. But he dabbed at them anyway, with the same methodical squint and tilt of the head with which he regarded himself in the mirror each morning when he trimmed his mustache and beard. His feet hurt, actually, as if his shoes were two sizes too small. There was damn-all he could do about it though, except hide the pain and wait for it to get worse.

He wore a Vandyke beard, razor-cut to a point that could have impaled a potato. His silver hair was brushed back cleanly – the sort of hair that wouldn't allow itself to become tousled unless the situation absolutely called for it. He might have been a barber, talcumed and rose-oiled and with a mustache that curled at the ends. What he was, though, no one was certain. He was 'retired' and had been in the import-export business. He wore white suits. He collected silver coins. He was a product, he said, of the 'old school.' He had appeared at the doorstep some weeks back, having returned from travel in the east, and looking for a place, he said, where he could 'watch the sea.' And he had the habit of paying his rent on time – even early. This last virtue alone was enough to recommend him, at least to Rose.

He was well read, too. Andrew had liked that at first, and had made a show of consulting him when it came to setting up the library. They had two dozen old stackable bookcases, which, along with the furniture, the clipper ship, a pole lamp and an old Chinese rug made for a tolerably comfortable room. Andrew picked through his own books, finding copies to fill the shelves. The idea of transient tourists thumbing through anything good, though – perhaps slipping volumes down their pants and into their purses – made him cautious. He took Pickett's advice and plied Aunt Naomi with chocolate truffles and latex cat toys, and the following day he and Pickett made a serious trip to Bertram Smith's Acres of Books and, spending Aunt Naomi's money, brought out enough crates to half-bury the old pickup truck.

But the shelves still weren't quite filled up. Rose suggested knickknacks, but Andrew stood firm against them. Pennyman, in a show of kindness, lent them two hundred or so volumes from his own considerable library. His books looked right – old dark spines, dusty, comfortable – but most of them had to do with faintly unsavory subjects or were written in foreign languages, mostly German. Andrew secretly doubted that Pennyman knew the languages. He was just being ostentatious. 'Pennyman is a phony,' Andrew had said to Pickett, showing him an old German volume inked up with what appeared to be alchemical symbols. Pickett shook his head and studied the drawings, then asked to borrow the book. There were other books – on Masonic history, on the Illuminati, on gypsies and Mormons and suppressed Protestant ritual.

Andrew saw a clear link between Pennyman's obsessive self-barbering and his interest in secret knowledge. There was something slimy about it. Rose didn't see it at all. She didn't say so, but he feared that after she would talk with Pennyman she would size Andrew up – study his old shirts, his burlap shoes torn out in the toe, his hair rumpled west in the morning and east in the afternoon. Andrew couldn't stand Mr Pennyman. He couldn't, in fact, call him *Mr* Pennyman. The name was idiotic.

Pennyman adjusted his collar, dusted off his hands, and stepped into the kitchen. He bowed just a little to Rose – something which had struck her from the first as being 'European' and gallant. 'Trouble with opossums, then? I didn't mean to listen, but I couldn't help hearing just a bit of your conversation.'

Rose hesitated a moment, smiled weakly, and admitted that there was, apparently, trouble with 'possums. Nothing that should concern Mr Pennyman, though. Andrew had taken steps. It was poor Aunt Naomi that they were worried about. A 'possum in her room could be the last straw. She had such delicate health.

Pennyman nodded his head. 'I might stop in and see her this morning, in fact. She was understandably upset last night. She quite likely still doesn't fathom all the clamor.' He paused and picked up Andrew's empty coffee cup, peering at the trout painted on the front of it. He set it down, frowning. 'I'm not sure, now that I think of it, *that I* entirely understand all the ruckus. Andrew, though, has it all sorted out, I'm certain. He's a stout lad, Rosannah, a stout lad. You won't find another like him.' He nodded at her pleasantly. 'May I call you Rose, do you think? I feel as if we've gotten rather closer in the last month. All this formality wears me out. I'm a simple man, really, with simple ways. That's why I admire your husband. He's so – what? Simple, I suppose.' He gestured at the tabletop, at the half-dozen boxes of breakfast cereal: Captain Crunch, Kix, Grapenuts, Wheat Chex.

'Rose will be just fine. That's what everyone calls me.' She blushed faintly and stood up to pour Pennyman a cup of coffee. He watched her, smiling. He seemed to admire the way she moved – sure, quick, never a wasted gesture. She worked almost like a machine – washing the stove front and wiping down cabinet doors even as she poured coffee. He nodded for no reason at all, except to communicate his admiration.

'Aah,' he said, sipping the coffee. 'Wonderful.' He sloshed it around inside his mouth, making noise, as if he were tasting wine. 'Quite a lot of fancy coffee-brewing apparatus, eh? What is that affair there with the tube and valve?'

'It's a milk steamer. He's got three of them, actually. Lord knows why.'

Pennyman grinned and shook his head slowly. 'Rather like a child with toys, I suppose.' He held up a hand as if he anticipated a response. 'I don't mean anything by it. I appreciate that sort of thing, in fact. I'm a fan of – what is it? – eccentricity, I suppose. It's ... charming in its way. That creamer there – the elongated toad with the open mouth, sitting on the stump; that's it, the one wearing trousers and a cocked hat. I bet that's something Andrew brought home. Am I right? I knew it. This place has his mark on it. Positively.'

He grinned again and nodded wisely while he looked around, as if he were appreciating the labored artwork of a six-year-old. 'He has so much *fun* when he's at it. I envy that. I've always been a little too serious, I think. Too ... well, grown up.' And he said this last bit in a theatrically deep voice, as if to indicate that he saw very clearly through his own shortcomings, and that his seeing through them made them all right after all. He drank his coffee and regarded Rose with the eye of an artist.

'You're French,' he said, squinting.

'On my mother's side. Originally, anyway. They were – what do you callums? – Huguenots. Always sounds like Hottentots to me. They were filtered through Holland for a few years, though, before transplanting to Iowa.'

'You can see it in your cheekbones. Very finely chiseled. My own ancestors were French. We've a certain amount in common, it seems.'

Rose smiled at him and pushed a wisp of dark hair out of her eyes, tucking it back in under the scarf that she wore tied across the top of her head. 'I've got to get these dishes washed, I'm afraid.'

'Of course,' he said. 'Of course. *Devil* of a lot to this business of opening up an inn, isn't there? I shouldn't wonder that you were ready half the time to throw it all over. Looks like six months' work to me, and here you are struggling to be ready for the public in June. Andrew will fetch it all together, though. He's quite a character, quite a character. I don't mean to muscle in, but if this were *my* inn, I'd throw another coat of paint on the west wall outside. The sun and the ocean will alligator that paint off quick.'

'Andrew mentioned something of that sort. It's on his list.'

'His list! Of course; he's a man of lists. I should have guessed it. Pity you can't get a real workman in to do it, though. I have faith in this little venture of yours, Rose. I've loaned my books to Andrew; I could loan you the price of a housepainter.' He held up a hand again to cut off any objections. 'I wouldn't suggest it except that we Huguenots have to rally round. Don't give me a yes or no. Just remember that the offer stands. I like this place. The ocean air suits me. I shouldn't wonder that I'll spend a few years here, God granting me the time. I rather feel as if I have a right to offer.'

'Thank you, Mr Pennyman. Andrew has it on his list, though, as I said, and he's promised to get at the list this afternoon.'

'*Jules*, Rose. No more Mr Pennyman. No backsliding now.'

'Jules, then.'

Pennyman touched his forehead and smiled. Then, as if suddenly remembering something, he asked, 'Tell me, does Naomi collect coins? She has the look of a person who might – a sort of – what is it?' Rose shrugged and shook her head. 'Not at all then? Perhaps when she was a girl, or a young woman? You haven't heard her talk about such a thing – a particularly valuable coin, perhaps?' Rose said she hadn't, wondering at Pennyman's curiosity. Under the right circumstances, she might rather like him for it. He seemed to make such an effort to *talk* to people. The world needed more of that, when it was genuine. She wondered whether with him it *was* genuine, or whether he was simply playacting. She watched him stride out, brisk and humming, his shoulders square. In a moment the front door slammed and he walked away down the sidewalk toward Ocean Boulevard, just as he did every morning, tapping along with a stick topped with an ivory sea serpent that curled back around onto itself.

TWO

'—Mr Shandy, my father, Sir, would see nothing in the light in which others placed it;—he placed things in his own light;—he would weigh nothing in common scales.'

LAURENCE STERNE,
TRISTRAM SHANDY

Andrew stood in what had become the bar. He very carefully poured cold coffee into a cup. Beams Pickett watched him. 'So I fill it once,' said Andrew, 'like this.' He finished, set the coffee down, and picked up the cup. 'And I drink half of it, like this.' He drank half of it, then set the cup down. 'Now I fill it up again, and, once again, drink it.' He poured the coffee down his throat, finishing it off entirely, then set the cup down once more, with a flourish, like a stage magician. 'So this cup has been entirely full of coffee twice. Is that right?'

Pickett squinted at him for a moment before nodding.

'And now it's empty, right?'

'That's right. Empty.'

'And yet,' said Andrew, smiling, 'though the cup has been full two whole times, I only drank a cup and a half of coffee, and the cup is *empty*.' He turned it upside down to illustrate. A single dark drop plunked down onto the countertop.

'I think I see,' said Pickett, calculating. He touched the first two fingers of his left hand with the index finger of his right, as if working the problem through thoroughly. 'My advice to you is to drop it entirely. There's no profit in it at all. I swear it. Einstein was in ahead of you anyway.'

'Einstein? He worked with cups of coffee, too?'

'No, cups of tea I think it was. And it didn't have anything to do with drinking the tea, either, like yours does. His had something to do with rivers – oxbows, I think. He figured them out.'

'Did he? Einstein? From reading tea leaves?'

Pickett shrugged. 'That's what I've read.'

Andrew rather liked that. Science was a satisfactory business all the way around. One of Rose's cousins had spent years whirling frog brains in a centrifuge, with the vague hope, apparently, of working the experiments into something telling. The papers he'd written were full of the most amazing illustrations. One man whirls frog brains, the other measures coffee in a cup, and one day – what? A man walks on the moon. Another steps into a black hole and disappears. Who could say what might come of it all, for good or ill? That was the wonder of it. 'It's rather like infinity at first, isn't it, this vanishing coffee business? Like the notion of endless space. When I was a boy I always imagined that there was a chain-link fence out there somewhere, like on the edge of a schoolyard, where things just ended.'

'Couldn't you see through it? Chain-link, after all ...'

'I can't remember. Coffee?' He held the rest of the cold coffee out toward Pickett and slid a clean cup down toward him. Pickett shook his head. 'I love mathematical mysteries,' said Andrew, 'especially when you bring them down to earth, to where they apply to cups of coffee and that sort of thing. Not an unprofitable consideration for a restaurant man.'

Pickett nodded, but looked puzzled. 'You know, I don't think it *was* filled twice; I think ...'

'Of course,' said Andrew. 'Of course. I figured that out myself – last night. It's a matter of language, isn't it? What do we mean when we use the word "filled"? Do we refer to the empty cup having been filled up twice, or do we mean that it's merely been topped off? It's rather like the word "window." Look that one up in your *Webster's New International*. No one on earth can tell you whether "window" refers to the solid business that keeps the wind from blowing in or to the hole in the wall, the hiatus itself. You can close the window and you can climb through it and you can wash it and you can break it. Imagine being able to climb through something solid enough to break.

'It's an astonishing business, language, and I'll tell you that it seemed a lot more astonishing last night after a couple of glasses of scotch. I thought at first that I'd fallen onto the secret of the bottomless cup of coffee, except that it seemed to work against me. I could see straightaway that I couldn't profit from it. Just the opposite. I pour two cups and the customer only gets a cup and a half out of them. I lose a half a cup for every two I pour. Imagine the loss over the years. What is it? Say two hundred cups a day, two days a week, and half a cup each disappearing due to mathematics – that's fifty cups a day gone, multiplied by … Will we close this place down on holidays?'

'And Mondays, maybe. Everything closes down on Mondays.'

'Yes,' said Andrew. 'We weren't going to be open on Mondays anyway. Now I've lost count. Fifty times what?' Andrew shook his head and shrugged. 'Anyway, I wanted to show it to you. I've written up a brief explanation and mailed it off to the "Mr Wizard" program, just as a sort of joke. Kids love this sort of thing. Don't tell Rose, though. She'd think I was wasting time.'

'I won't. Don't worry about that.' Pickett sat on his stool and stared out toward the street, as Andrew sipped at the cold coffee and studied his copy of *Grossman's Guide*. 'How are people going to find you here, tucked away like this off the highway?'

Andrew looked up from his work. He was drawing up a list of bar implements – three lists, actually: the necessary, the desirable, and the questionable. He'd rulered the page into three columns and headed each with an N, D, or Q. Neatness was impossible in broad matters, so he made up for it in small ways when he could. The first list covered an entire column and spilled over onto the back of the page; the Q list had only one item on it – flex straws, which it seemed to him were children's items. He didn't intend to cater to children, not from the bar anyway.

'Reputation,' he said.

'You need to do some footwork. Xeroxed flyers aren't enough. The best menu in the world isn't enough.'

'I rather thought we might slip something into the *Herald*, with you on the staff part time and all.' Andrew picked up a comical napkin and studied the grinning, pipe-smoking dog on the front of it. 'Do you know anyone in advertising?'

Pickett nodded. 'There's Pringle, but he's a wash-out. He hates me for the gag letter I printed with his name on it. He'd boasted about being one of the founders of the Pringle Society, but that turned out to be a lie. They wouldn't even let him in. Anyway, I ribbed him about it and now we can't stand each other. He'd ruin any ad we ran. I could trust Mary Clark, though. She's sharp. Has an eye for design. Speaks French, too.'

'A pity no one else in Seal Beach does. We'd better run it in English, I think.'

'Of course, of course,' Pickett said, gesturing. 'But it should have a Continental air to it. This isn't going to be a hamburger joint. I'll draw something up. Leave it to me. Have you worked out a menu yet?'

'No. I'm still experimenting. Never having worked in the restaurant business is a handicap. I can see that. But I can turn it to advantage, I think. The customer is bound to find something here to surprise him. The Weetabix, for example. Show me another restaurant that serves them. They don't. All they've got are those variety pack cereals – the same everywhere. That's the truth of it. A man in the business sees nothing but the business; he's hidebound, blown by the winds of the obvious. A man from outside, though, he'll take his chance on the peculiar, because he doesn't know it's peculiar. Success out of naivete. That's my motto. Speaking of the Weetabix, when are you driving up to Vancouver?'

'Day after tomorrow. Are you *sure* they're contraband? I can't fathom the idea of contraband breakfast cereal. Can't you just order them from some local distributor?'

'Not a chance of it. And as I was saying, there's not a restaurant in the continental United States that serves them, not that I've heard of. All the best restaurants in England and Canada wouldn't open up without a supply. Used to be you could get something called Ruskets. These Ruskets weren't identical to Weetabix, of course, but they were close – flat little biscuits of wheat flakes. Some people broke them up before pouring on the milk and sugar; other people dropped them into the bowl whole, then cut them apart with a spoon. I had a friend who crushed them with his hands first. What's the use of that, I asked him. Might as well eat anything – Wheaties, bran flakes; it wouldn't make a lick of difference. That's the point here, the strategy. Give the customer something out of the ordinary. Make it wholesome, but don't make it like the competition makes it or you're good as dead.'

'But all the way to Canada in the pickup truck?'

'Don't use the truck. They'd probably just confiscate the crates of Weetabix at the border – spot them in a second. They'd wonder what in the world a man is doing smuggling Weetabix in an old pickup truck when he's supposed to be in Vancouver at a convention for writers of columns for the lovelorn. The truck doesn't run worth a damn anyway. Fill the trunk of your car. That'll be enough. We'll make another run somehow in a few months.' He paused for a moment and thought. 'I'll pay for gas.'

Pickett nodded, as if he trusted Andrew's weird native genius for this type of thing, for seeing things roundaboutly and inside out and upside down. It was too easy to doubt him, and if there was anything that Beams Pickett distrusted, it was anything that was too easy. Simplicity almost always wore a clever disguise. If he was caught with the Weetabix at the border, he could claim ignorance. 'Contraband? Breakfast cereal?' What would they do to him, shoot him?

'When does the first lovelorn column appear, anyway?' Andrew asked.

'Friday after next. I'm still putting it together. It'll run daily in the *Herald*, but if it's good enough, I don't see why I can't syndicate it sooner or later. Georgia's helping me with it.'

'Lots of letters? How does anyone know to write?'

'I'm making them up, actually, addresses and all. Georgia's answering them. She's too bluff, though. Too unkind for my tastes. Her advice to everyone is to dry up. I submitted a letter by a woman in Southgate whose husband had lost interest. "Lose weight, get a face lift, and tell him to go to hell," that was Georgia's response. *My* advice was to buy diaphanous nighties and packets of bath herbs. That's going to be my standard response, I think.'

'Bath herbs?'

Pickett nodded. 'You can order them through women's magazines – little bags of dried apples and rose hips and lavender. You mix them into the tub water along with bath oils and then climb in, winking at your mate, you know, provocatively. Turns them into sexual dynamos, apparently.'

'And all this stuff floats on the bathwater? God help us. Isn't there an easier method?'

'It's the rage,' said Pickett. 'The word from the public is that they want whatever's the rage. That's one reason I'm going up to Vancouver. The convention up there is the cutting edge of the lovelorn business.'

'That's where we part company,' said Andrew. 'The science of breakfast cereals runs counter to that, and I mean to prove it. To hell with the rage. To hell with the cutting edge. If it were my column I'd advise celibacy. Either that, or go wild in the other direction. Advise them to heap the bed with suggestive fruit – peaches, bananas, split figs, that sort of thing. Call it the Freudian approach, just to give it legitimacy. And use *Dr* Pickett as a byline.' Andrew studied his list again, then went after it with his eraser. 'I've got ice picks, ice tongs, ice scoops, ice shavers, ice buckets, ice molds, and ice dyes. What have I left out?'

Pickett shook his head. 'What kinds of molds?'

'Mermaids, toads, comical hats, and high-heeled shoes. I'm purposely staying away from gag items. No eyeballs, bugs, or naked women.'

'Wise,' said Pickett, nodding. 'No trash.' He looked over the list. 'What's a muddler?'

'I don't know, entirely. I looked it up but there was nothing in the dictionary after muddleheaded. It has something to do with stirring things up, I think.'

'Couldn't just use a spoon, then?'

'Go down to the Potholder if you want spoons. Here we use muddlers. At least I think we do. I've got to call down to Walt's to find out what they are.'

Pickett stepped across to the street window and rubbed off a little circle of glass wax so that he could peer out better. 'I've been having a look at Penny-man's books. At several of them.'

Andrew nodded. 'Anything telling?'

'I think he bears watching.'

'In what way? Has an eye for the silver, does he? Waiting to rob us blind and go out through the window?'

'Hardly. I don't think he needs to rob anyone. I've got a hunch that your Uncle Arthur would know something about him – though he'd never let on. It's more than just his name.'

'Names, names, names. Remember what you said about old Moneywort. If anyone was less likely than Moneywort to be involved in that sort of thing, I can't think who it might be. Poor devil, crippled by some wasting disease. What was wrong with him, anyway?'

Pickett frowned. 'I'm not sure, exactly. Age, maybe. A bone disease. He couldn't get up from his chair there in the end.'

'And then cut to bits in his shop by a dope-addled thief! My God that was grisly.' Andrew shuddered, remembering the account in the newspaper. 'I'll say this, though, if Moneywort was up to some sort of peculiar shenanigans, that wouldn't be the way he'd die. You know that. It would be something exotic. Something out of Fu Manchu.'

'That's exactly what it *wouldn't* be. Not necessarily. That's where you've got to get 'round them. Sometimes it's the slightest clues that give them away, rather than anything broad. You won't see them driving up and down in limousines. Have you gotten a glimpse of Pennyman's walking stick?'

'Of course I have.'

Pickett squinted at him, nodding slowly. 'Remember Moneywort's hat – the one that was all over fishing lures?'

'Vaguely.'

'Well *I* remember it. There were things hanging from that hat that no sane man would try to entice a fish with. Most of them were smokescreens, if you follow me. But there was one that signified – a sea serpent, curling around on itself and swallowing its own tail. What did he hope to catch with that? A blind cave fish? That wasn't any lure, and you can quote me on it. And the devil who sliced him up wasn't some down-and-out dope addict looking for a twenty. Do you know that the murderer died before coming to trial?'

Andrew looked up at Pickett, widening his eyes. 'Did he?'

'For a fact. Poisoned. Fed the liver of a blowfish, scrambled up in his eggs. Pitched over nose-first into his plate. I got it out of the police report.'

'Just like – what was his name? The man with the eyeglasses. Or with the name that sounded like eyeglasses – impossible name. Must have been a fake. Remember? Sea captain. Died in Long Beach back in '65. *You* told me about it. Didn't they find blowfish poison in his whisky glass?'

Pickett shrugged, but it was the shrug of a man who saw things very clearly. 'That was one of the explanations that turned up later. Hastings made an issue of it, but the man was dead and buried, and ninety-odd years old to boot. Nobody cared what killed him. He could have been carried away by a pterodactyl and it wouldn't have interrupted anyone's lunch. There goes Pennyman,' Pickett said, watching through the window again. 'Where in the devil does he go every morning? Why haven't we followed him?'

Andrew shook his head. 'Haven't time. Rose is all over me with her list. It's long enough to paper the hallway with. She doesn't understand the fine points of setting up a bar – of setting up the whole damned restaurant, for heaven's sake. She has doubts about my chefing. She doesn't say so straight out, but I can sense it. I'll be damned if I'll back down now. There's got to be something around this place that I can do right. Rose got the upstairs coming along, though. I'll give her that.'

'Well,' said Pickett, sitting back down, 'for my money, your fellow with the walking stick there amounts to more than we can guess. I bet *he* could tell you a little bit about poisoning a man with the guts of a fish, except that you couldn't get anyplace close to the subject in a conversation with him. You'd suddenly find some damned half-eaten thing in your sandwich and him grinning at you across the table. That's the last thing you'd see this side of heaven.

'Look at this.' Pickett reached into his pants pocket and pulled out a newspaper clipping – a photograph. He glanced around the room before opening it up. In the clipping was a picture of a man on a hospital bed – apparently dead. Three other men stood by the bedside: a doctor; a trim, no-nonsense looking man in a suit; and a man who looked for all the world like Jules Pennyman. It was a fuzzy shot, though, and the third man, really, could have been anyone.

'Who is it?' asked Andrew.

'Pennyman,' said Pickett, plonking out the answer without hesitation.

'Does it say so?'

'No, it doesn't say so. It refers to an "unidentified third party." But look closer.'

Andrew squinted at the picture. The Pennyman figure held something in his open palm – two coins, it seemed, as if he were handing them over or had just had them handed to him or as if he were getting ready to do something else with them, like lay them on the dead man's eyes. 'Good God,' Andrew said, mystified. 'Is he going to put coins on the corpse's eyes? I didn't think they did that anymore.'

'That depends upon who "they" are, doesn't it?'

Andrew looked at him. 'They?' he asked.

'The ubiquitous "they,"' said Pickett. 'Who do *you* suppose we mean by using the term?'

Andrew shook his head again. 'I don't know. It's just idiom, I guess. Just a convenience. Like "it," you know. Like "*it*," won't rain this afternoon.' Nothing more to it than that. If you try to put a face on it you go mad, don't you? That's schizophrenia.'

'Not if it's *true* it isn't. Not if it actually *has* a face. And in this case I'm afraid it has. Any number of them, known in fact as "Caretakers."'

'Pardon me,' said Andrew, smiling. 'Who are? I lost you, I'm afraid.'

'*They* are. That's what I'm trying to tell you. This reference to "they" isn't idiom, not in any local sense. It comes down out of antiquity, and it has specific application – deadly specific.' Pickett let his voice fall, casting another glance at the door to the kitchen. 'You've read of legends of the Wandering Jews?'

'Was there more than one of them? I thought it was singular.'

'There might have been a heap of them, over the years. Throughout Europe. The peasantry used to leave crossed harrows in fallow fields for them to sleep under. It was a magical totem of some sort, meant to protect them. Animals brought them food. There was a central character, though, a magician, an immortal. The rest of them were disciples, who extended their lives by secret means. I'm piecing it together bit by bit, and it involves fish and coins and who knows what sorts of talismans and symbols. What I'm telling you is that this is not fable. This is the real McCoy, and like it or not, I think we've been pitched into the middle of it.'

'So you're telling me that there's – what? – a whole company of "them"? What do they want with you?'

Pickett shrugged. 'I don't know enough about it, mind you. And any ignorance here is deadly dangerous. But it could be that they control everything. All of it. You, me, the gatepost, the spin of the planet for all I know.'

Andrew snapped his fingers. He had it suddenly. He'd read about it in a novel. 'Like in Balzac! What was it? – *The Thirteen*. Was that "them"?'

Pickett looked tired. He shook his head. 'What Balzac knew about it you could put in your hat. Some few of them might have been assembled in Paris, of course. Or anywhere at all. Here, even.'

'*Here*, at the inn?'

'That's what I mean. One of them's here already, not at the inn *necessarily*. Here in Seal Beach.'

'So Pennyman, you're telling me ...'

'I'm not *telling* you anything. Some of it I know; some of it's speculation. Go easy with the man, though, or you'll find yourself looking at the wrong end of a blowfish.'

Andrew wondered which end was the *right* end of a blowfish. He poked idly at the newspaper clipping, still lying in front of him. 'Who's the dead man, then?'

38

'Jack Ruby,' said Pickett.

Andrew suddenly seemed to go cold. He looked again at the picture. It *could*, certainly, be Pennyman. But coins on a dead man's eyes ... The idea was too morbid. And it didn't amount to anything either. What did it mean? 'Why coins on his eyes?' Andrew asked, folding the clipping in half and handing it back to Pickett. Somehow, he'd seen enough of it. It hinted at things he really didn't want to learn more about.

'*I* didn't say anything about coins on his eyes; you did. I don't believe it's that at all. It's payment, is what I think. Somebody's dead, and somebody else has killed him. The coins are payment for services rendered. Payment for a long series of betrayals.'

'Comes cheap, doesn't he?' said Andrew, referring to Pennyman, or whoever it was.

'We haven't seen the coins, have we?'

'Why did They do it?'

'I don't think They did. I think *one* of Them did, working at cross purposes to the others. There's something in those coins ...'

Andrew tried to study *Grossman's Guide* again; all of a sudden *Grossman's* talk about appropriate gins and bitters had begun to sound wholesome and comfortable. When it got around to particulars, this talk about conspiracies gave him the willies. Something was pending. He'd felt it last night when he was in the tree. He wasn't sure he was ready for it. Pickett and his mysteries! The truth of it was that if you didn't go looking for them you'd never see them. Let well enough alone; that was what Rose would advise. And it would be good advice, too. 'Why do you suppose he recommends stainless steel fruit knives?'

'Who? Pennyman?'

'No, Grossman. What's wrong with a carbon steel knife? It holds an edge better.'

'Turns the fruit dark. Stainless steel doesn't. It's chemistry is what it is. I can't explain it better than that. A *glass* knife is what I'd advise. That's what they use somewhere.'

'*They?*' asked Andrew, picturing Pennyman stepping out of the fog with a glass knife in one hand and a frightful looking fish in the other.

'No, not *Them*. I forget where. Hotel in Singapore, I think.'

Andrew nodded, relieved. 'How about one of those Ginzu knives? I saw them on television. Apparently you can beat them with hammers if you want to.'

Pickett gave him a puzzled look. 'Why do you want to do that?'

'I don't have any idea,' said Andrew, shaking his head. 'Just on general principles, I should think. I'll stick to *Grossman* here, though. Distrust anything modern, that's my motto. Stainless steel fruit knives it is – three of them.'

His list looked pretty healthy, all in all, but it would cost him a fortune to buy the whole lot of it. He couldn't bear the idea of a half-equipped bar, though. He was an all-or-nothing man at heart. 'The Balzac book,' he said to Pickett, 'have you read it?'

'Years ago.'

'What was the old man's name? Ferragus. That was it. Remember? "A whole drama lay in the droop of the withered eyelids." Fancy such a thing as "withered eyelids." I love the notion of all that sort of thing – of the Thirteen, the *Devorants*.'

'You'll love it a lot less when they come in through the door.'

'So you think this is Them, then?'

'No,' said Pickett. 'This is not the same crowd. That was the wrong Them. This isn't the Thirteen nor ever has been. This isn't a fiction. Mr Pennyman is who it is, and I'm telling you that you'd better be careful of him.'

'But is there thirteen of Them, of our Them?'

'How on earth do *I* know? There might be ten; there might be a dozen.'

'A baker's dozen, for my money. That's what we'll call the inn.'

'What, The Baker's Dozen?'

'Sounds foody enough, doesn't it? And with all this Thirteen business, it seems to fit. It'll be our joke.'

'Sounds cheap to me. Like a chain restaurant, a coffee shop.'

'Then we'll call it The Thirteen. Just like that. And it'll work, too. That's our address, isn't it? Number 13 Edith Circle. Destiny shoves its oar in again. That's just the sort of thing that appeals to me – the mysterious double meaning. To the common man it's merely an address; to the man who squints into the fog, though, it signifies. You like that notion, too. Admit it. The number is full of portent.'

Pickett shrugged. 'It has a ring,' he said. 'But …'

'But nothing,' said Andrew. 'It has an inevitability, is what it has.' He looked up at Pickett suddenly and then stepped across to peer through the half-open door that led down the hallway to the kitchen. Apparently satisfied, he said in a whisper, 'Speaking of poisons and conspiracies, what's the name of your man at Rodent Control? The guy you interviewed for the newspaper?'

'Biff Chateau.'

'That's the one. Fancy my having forgotten a name like that. What's he got in the way of poisons?'

'Mostly anticoagulants.'

'Work quick, do they? Feed a 'possum a dose of one of them and – what? – he's dead in an hour?'

Pickett shook his head. 'I don't think so. Most of them are cumulative. Rat nibbles a little bit on Monday, Snacks on it on Tuesday, still feels in top form on Thursday. A week later, though, he's under the weather. Then, as I understand it, all his blood turns to vapor or something and just leaks out through every available pore. Grisly sort of thing, but effective.'

'Do they ever murder a dog by mistake?'

'In fact, yes. It's rare, though. A dog has to eat a heap of the stuff. They could kill an elephant with it, I suppose, if they took the time to do it right.'

Andrew nodded and stroked his chin. 'Can this man Chateau get me a dead 'possum?'

'More than one, I should think. They're always turning up dead in someone's backyard and being taken for enormous rats. They probably have a half dozen in the dumpster right now.'

'I only need one,' said Andrew. He stepped across to the window and looked out, as if he were suddenly in a hurry. The street was in shadow, since the sun was behind the house, but the rooftops blazed with sunlight, and Pacific Coast Highway, a block away, was thronged with barefoot beach-goers, taking advantage of the hot spring weather. Andrew peered back down the hallway, listening.

A vacuum cleaner rumbled somewhere on the second floor. Rose was working away. God bless her, thought Andrew, as he and Pickett slipped out through the back door and headed toward Andrew's Metropolitan, parked at the curb. Knowing that Rose was at work wrestling the bungalow into submission was like knowing there was coffee brewing in the morning. It gave a man hope. It made things solid.

There were days when it seemed to him that the walls and the floor and the chairs he sat on were becoming transparent, were about to wink out of existence like snuffed candle flames, leaving only a smoky shadow lingering in the air. But then there was Rose, looming into view with a dust rag or a hammer or a pair of hedge clippers, and the chairs and walls and floors precipitated out of the air again and smiled at him. He'd be a jellyfish without her, a ghost. He knew that and reminded himself of it daily.

So what if she was short-sighted when it came to beer scrapers or imported breakfast cereals or just the right bottle of gin or scotch? She had *him*, didn't she? He had a genius for those sorts of things. She didn't have to bother with them.

The Metropolitan grumbled away toward the highway, blowing out a plume of dark exhaust. If he was lucky, Rose wouldn't have heard them go, and he could slip back in later, undetected. Pickett would want to stop at Leisure World and look in on old Uncle Arthur, but there wouldn't be any time for that. This was business. He'd have to settle the score with Aunt Naomi that afternoon, or there'd be trouble.

Good old Aunt Naomi. In the light of day – when she wasn't snoring, when her cats were out stalking across the rooftops – it was easy to take the long view. The idea of Rose pulling things together made it even easier. Sometimes. In truth, sometimes it just made it easier to feel guilty. He sighed, unable to keep it all straight. Well, *he'd* look to the delicate work. It was the best he could do. No one could ask more of him than that. What had his father said on the subject? If it was easy, his father had been fond of saying, they would have gotten somebody else to do it. Or something like that. It seemed to apply here, in some nebulous way that didn't bear scrupulous study. He realized suddenly that Pickett was talking – asking him something.

'What? Sorry.'

'I said, what do you want with poison?'

Andrew stayed up late that night reading in the library. Mrs Gummidge and Aunt Naomi played Scrabble upstairs until nearly eleven; then they went to bed. Rose had been asleep for hours. Pennyman had turned in at ten. By midnight the house was quiet and dark; only the pole lamp in the library burned. Andrew felt like a conspirator, but in fact he wasn't conspiring with anyone. This was *his* plot, from end to end. He hadn't even discussed it with Pickett, although his friend had agreed to come round early in the morning, pretending to be on his way to the pier to fish. At 6AM, Andrew thought, smiling, the tale would be told.

He waited for the stroke of midnight, just for the romance of it. Then, feeling as if his chest were empty, he tiptoed up the attic stairs carrying the dead 'possum in a bag. It was starting to ripen, having been found yesterday in Garden Grove, already dead and torn up by something – cats, probably. That would be a stroke of luck if he played his cards right. It was dark on the stairs, but he couldn't use even a flashlight. Being discovered now would mean ... He couldn't say. They'd take him away. Men in lab coats would ask him deceptive questions. They'd whirl his brain in a centrifuge and come to conclusions.

He let himself into the little, gabled cubbyhole, so that he could climb out the window onto the roof. The ladder had been a wash-out the night before; he wouldn't chance it again. He could see the shadow of Pickett's telescope in front of the casement. Slowly, carefully, he hauled it aside, eased open the window, and stepped out. Thank goodness there wasn't much of a slope. He pulled the bag out after him, left it lying on the roof, and edged down the asphalt shingles toward where the pole lay tilted against the house, hidden by the foliage of the camphor tree. There it was.

He pulled it up through the leaves, scraping it over a limb, and then set it on the roof with the noose in front of him. The moon wouldn't be up for an hour yet; last night he had learned that much, anyway. The 'possum cooperated admirably. Dead 'possums tell no tales, he thought, grinning. He tightened the noose around its neck, and, towing the pole behind him, crept toward Aunt Naomi's window.

It was closed. Of course it would be. She wouldn't want any more marauders. Last night had been enough to put the fear into her. Andrew slipped a hand into his back pocket and pulled out a long-bladed spatula, then shoved it through the gap between the two halves of the ill-fitting casement windows. It was the work of an instant to flip up the latch. In the hot, still night there wouldn't even be a breeze to disturb the sleeping Aunt Naomi.

If there was trouble, if she awoke again, he could just let the 'possum lie and drop the pole back down into the tree. He'd go across the roof and climb down onto the carport, and from there onto the top of his pickup truck. The library window was wide open, and there was a pile of bricks outside it. He'd be reading in his chair inside of two minutes, and all they'd find on the roof would be a dead 'possum. He had thought it through that afternoon – studied it from the street. It was as if Providence had come round to set it up: the bricks, the 'possum, the pole already lying beneath the tree; all of it had been handed to him with a ribbon tied around it. But if his luck held, he wouldn't need to use the escape route. It would be a neater job all the way around if he could plant the 'possum in Aunt Naomi's bedroom and let her find it in the morning.

Nothing stirred inside. Aunt Naomi snored grotesquely; the cats slept through it. He slid the pole in through the window, barely breathing. Dropping the 'possum onto her bed would lead to spectacular results, except that she'd probably wake up on the instant and shriek. Near the door – that would be good enough – as if the beast were trying to escape, but hadn't made it. He positioned the pole just so, paused to breathe, then played out the line. Immediately it went slack; the 'possum whumped to the floor, and Andrew hauled the pole out into the night.

He pulled the casement shut and slid along on his rear end toward the tree, dropping the pole down through the leaves so that it rested on the same branch that it had been tilting against all day. Crouching, listening, he counted to sixty. The snoring continued, uninterrupted. She hadn't even stirred.

He crept back to the casement, pulled out his spatula again, and pushed the latch back into place, neat as you please. In a moment he was back in at the window, shifting Pickett's telescope, shoving the 'possum bag in behind the foil-backed insulation stapled into the unplastered studs. He tiptoed back down the narrow stairs, washed his hands in the kitchen sink, and opened a beer to celebrate. It was 12:13 by the clock, and he'd already accomplished a night's work.

Far too full of anxious energy and anticipation to sleep, he lay down on the couch with the idea of reading a book, and in a half hour got up to pour himself another glass of beer. He read some more, half-heartedly, his mind wandering away from the book, until he found himself studying in his mind the complexities of coffee mugs. That led him on to silverware and to copper pots and pans and enormous colanders suitable for draining twenty pounds of fetuccini. He dreamed about extravagant chefs' hats, about his wearing one, standing in front of an impossibly grand espresso machine that was a sort of orchestrated tangle of tubes and valves, reaching away to the ceiling.

A pounding on the front door awakened him. There was a simultaneous screaming, coming from somewhere – from overhead, from the attic. Andrew stumbled out into the living room, rubbing his face. He felt like a rumpled, dehydrated hobo. Wrapped in her bathrobe, Rose pushed past him, bound for the front door. She threw it open. There was Pickett, holding a fishing pole and tackle box and wearing a hat. He started to speak, to play out the role he and Andrew had written for him the previous afternoon, but Rose dashed away toward the stairs, shouting at Andrew to follow along.

Upstairs, Mrs Gummidge stood with her hand across her mouth, outside the open door of Aunt Naomi's room. Somehow the 'possum had deteriorated sadly in the early morning hours. In the closeness of the room, it outstank the cats, which had, apparently, been at the corpse just a little bit – investigating it, but finally giving up and leaving it alone. It was perfect. Andrew bit his lip and winked at Pickett.

Aunt Naomi sat in bed, her hair curled as it had been the night before. She breathed like a tea kettle. 'How,' she demanded in a hollow, lamenting voice, 'did that creature get into my room?'

Andrew cleared Mrs Gummidge out of the way. 'Bring me the scoop shovel,' he said, taking command. 'Out of the garage. The broad, aluminum scoop.'

'I'll get it,' said Pickett, hurrying away down the stairs.

Andrew examined the dead 'possum. 'Cats have done for it.' He nodded at Aunt Naomi, who stared at him as if he were talking like an ape. 'The cats,' he said, louder. 'They've worried the beast to death. Look at him, he's all over scratches. Like the Chinese – the death of a thousand cuts. Very nasty business.' He shook his head. Pickett came stomping up the stairs, carrying the short-handled shovel. 'What do you think of this?' asked Andrew stoutly.

Pickett stared at him, then said, 'Looks like – what? – the cats got him, I guess.' He bent over to have a closer look, then screwed up his face and backed away. 'He's rather had it, hasn't he?'

Andrew nodded. 'Does he look like the fellow we saw on the back fence two days ago? Same size, I'd say.'

Pickett nodded. 'I'm certain it is.' He looked up at Rose, who seemed to be staring at him particularly hard. 'Couldn't *swear* to it, of course, not absolutely. Wouldn't want to sign an affidavit. If he were in a police line-up, you know ...' He let the subject drop and pretended to examine the creature again, shaking his head at the very idea of it.

Rose sat down on the bed beside Aunt Naomi and patted the coverlet over the old woman's leg. 'Can't you get it out of here?' she asked Andrew, nodding toward the door.

'At once. Back away there, Mrs Gummidge. One dead 'possum coming down the stairs. Call Rodent Control, will you? There's a man there named Biff Chateau who has done some work for me in the past. This is right in his line. Thank God for the cats, eh? This place would be hell on earth without them. There wouldn't be a room in the house safe from monsters like this. He stinks to high heaven, doesn't he?'

There were more footfalls on the stairs, and Mr Pennyman hove into view. Imposter, thought Andrew. He's taken the time to massage his scalp before coming up. There might have been any kind of trouble at all up here – thieves, cavemen, Martians – *he* wouldn't have been worth a curse. It occurred to Andrew that he could trip right then, and pitch the spoiled 'possum into Pennyman's face. No one would claim it wasn't a flat-out accident. But he wouldn't. This was art, this 'possum business. It demanded subtlety. There wasn't any room for farce.

'Excuse me, Mr Pennyman,' Andrew said, shoving past the man on the landing. 'There's been a 'possum fooling about in Naomi's bedroom. Half-terrorized her before the cats got to it. God bless the cats, like I was saying. Lord love a cat. Nothing like them.' He angled away down the stairs, holding the scoop shovel out in front of him, Pickett following. 'A cat by any other name ...' he said over his shoulder. 'Sacred in Borneo, I understand.' He continued to chatter long after Pennyman could no longer hear him. If he stopped, he'd pitch over laughing. He'd convulse. They'd have to call in a doctor to sedate him. The whole successful business would be spoiled like an old fish.

There was Mrs Gummidge, looming out of the kitchen. She'd gotten nothing but a recording over the phone at Rodent Control. Of course she would have. He'd known it when he'd sent her off, but *she* hadn't thought of it. What Mrs Gummidge didn't think of would fill a book. It wasn't even six in the morning yet. She'd left a message, and Chateau would discover it later. He'd send a man out in a van later in the day, full of stories about renegade 'possums, about the land being overrun with them.

Andrew was vindicated. That was the long and the short of it. He held the truth on a scoop shovel. They'd been suspicious of his 'possum, had they? Now here one was, giving them all the glad eye. Or the glazed eye. Andrew very nearly laughed out loud. He had taken up the reins and steered the morning out of chaos, right under the nose of Pennyman. He would look in on Aunt Naomi later that morning, after she'd had a chance to compose herself, to haul the god-awful curl papers out of her hair. He would ask her for a small sum, for the restaurant. Five hundred dollars would ... Well, it wouldn't go far. A thousand, though, would buy him the bar implements on his list, with money left over to buy single malt whiskies. His importer listed forty-two, at an average of thirteen dollars a bottle. That was five hundred and what, altogether? Something. He wasn't any good at sums.

He paused to smile at Mrs Gummidge on his way out the door, thanking her for making the useless phone call. She grinned back at him and nodded. Pickett stood silently, holding his hat. His mustache desperately needed trimming.

'I'll just go to Naomi,' said Mrs Gummidge. 'I'll bring round her tea.'

Andrew winked at her. 'You do that, Mrs Gummidge. I'd suggest chamomile, for its soothing properties. Avoid anything containing caffeine. I'd fetch it up myself, but this fellow here ought to be dumped into a trash can and lidded, before the whole house moves out on account of him. Then I'm going fishing. You've met Mr Pickett, I believe.'

Mrs Gummidge nodded, still smiling, her teeth set.

'Yes, of course you have,' said Andrew. 'Any number of times. Goodbye, then. If Rodent Control calls back, tell them the beast is in a trash can behind the garage. Normally it's the animal shelter that handles this sort of thing, but I particularly wanted Rodent Control to be in on it. They're equipped to test for plague fleas.'

Mrs Gummidge blinked. Andrew nodded to her and went out through the door, dumping the 'possum in an empty trash can and shoving the lid on, then leaning the shovel against the clapboard wall of the garage. Pickett followed along into the cool darkness inside, waiting in the doorway until Andrew turned on the lights. 'She's the grinningest woman I've ever seen,' Pickett said, putting his hat back on. 'I'd guess she was a waxwork statue if I didn't know any better. Or an automaton. You can't trust a face like that. Impossible to read.'

Andrew nodded, messing with a little bag full of white granules on the workbench. On the side of it, in black felt pen, was scrawled something impossible – a chemical name. 'She has a vocabulary of about thirty stock phrases, most of them involving tea and Scrabble and changing poor Naomi's bed linen. All of it sounds programmed. For my money she's got some dark motive beneath it all.'

Pickett watched him untie and then tie the plastic bag. He looked uncomfortable. 'Which one is that again? Chloro-what?'

'Chlorophacinone,' Andrew said. 'No, I haven't mixed it up yet. You use wet cornmeal – press it into cakes.' He put the bag down on the bench, as if he suddenly found it distasteful. 'I'd thought of setting the cakes around as if I were poisoning 'possums. Rose would have to take the whole business more seriously then.'

'I dare say she would,' Pickett said. 'What if you *do* poison something – a 'possum, say? What if by accident you poison a *cat*, for God's sake? You'd never get out of the soup.'

Andrew stared at the powder in the bag. 'I'd hate myself if I poisoned anything at all. It was just going to be a blind, a ruse. Only because the cat-stealing trick went bad. I'm certain Rose saw through it. So I've got to press on, somehow, and make her doubt herself. Make her see that I'm serious about this 'possum business.'

'*Are* you serious about this 'possum business? My advice is to let it drop. Cut bait and get out. It's a shame there *isn't* a 'possum around the neighborhood. That would settle things.'

Andrew sighed. 'There is, actually. I think there's one living under the house. That's where I got the idea in the first place.'

'Well there you are! Point him out to Rose. There's your evidence, right where you want him.'

'I can't let on that there's *really* one living under the house. She'd want him out of there.'

Pickett stared hard at Andrew, as if trying to make sense of nonsense. 'So you're telling me that despite the poison and the dead 'possum in Naomi's room and your fears about having been caught up on the roof in the middle of the night, what you really want to do is *protect* the 'possum living under the house?'

Andrew shrugged and then nodded weakly. 'They're such great-looking little guys, with that nose and all.'

'I can't do anything for you then,' said Pickett. 'You've made a mess of your priorities.'

'I can't stand talk about "priorities." They tire me out.' Andrew picked up the sack full of poison. It seemed suddenly to contain a coiled snake or a nest of spiders. 'I ought to pitch it into the trash, right now, while I'm thinking straight. Don't tell Chateau, though, will you? I don't want him to know that I tossed it out after begging five pounds of it off him to assassinate non-existent rats.'

Pickett shook his head. 'Toss it out. That's what I'd do. I'm afraid of poisons, especially with Pennyman around. There's no telling what you'll find in your beer.'

Andrew nodded. 'Done,' he said, and he stepped out into the daylight, dropping the bag into another trash can and hauling the can across the backyard, away from the garage so that Rodent Control wouldn't find it while looking for the 'possum.

'I left my pole and tackle box in the living room,' said Pickett, remembering suddenly.

'Go after them then. I'll get my stuff together. I'd better not go back in – not just now.' Somehow the idea of coming face-to-face with Rose filled him with terror. He'd wait until the dust settled.

Just as Pickett turned to go, the house door slammed shut, and there was Mrs Gummidge, carrying a dripping coffee filter full of steaming grounds. She grinned at them. 'Can't put these down the disposal,' she said. 'They'll clog the septic tank.'

'We haven't got a septic tank,' Andrew said, grinning back. 'Nothing but sewers for us.'

She stepped across and lifted the lid from the trash can that Andrew had just moved. She set the lid down and looked in suspiciously, then dropped the grounds in. 'No 'possums in that one,' she said cheerfully, bending over to pick up the lid. She banged it back down onto the trash can and hurried away toward the house, muttering about 'poor Naomi' and 'given such a fright,' her voice trailing away into nothing.

The door slammed again, and Pickett stood watching the empty porch, lost in thought. His eyes had that vacant, dangerous look that meant he was 'onto something,' that he was beginning to see things clearly at last. He was lost in plots, assembling and disassembling them, thinking of blowfish and assassins and lights in the sky, thinking of Moneywort and Pennyman, thinking of Uncle Arthur steering across foggy midnight oilfields in his red, electronic car, bumping over ruts, watching, perhaps, for the telltale glow of a suddenly uncovered lantern that would reveal to him in the instant of illumination the secret tiltings of world banks, the moment-to-moment machinations of governments. He turned around stiffly and set out after his fishing pole.

THREE

'See the rings pursue each other;
All below grows black as night …'

ROBERT LOUIS STEVENSON,
'LOOKING GLASS RIVER'

Whatever was happening had the feeling of nightfall about it, the feeling that twenty centuries of battles and betrayals, of civilizations and the shifting of continents, were crashing to a stony close. Something was coming full circle – slouching in on a wind out of the east. It was hot and thin – a desert wind with the smell of sagebrush and riverbeds on it, yanking off roof shingles in the night and scattering sycamore leaves and blowing spindrift off the back of the cold north swell as it hammered through pier pilings and surged up onto an almost deserted spring beach.

The wind tore fruitlessly at the newspaper in the hands of Jules Pennyman, who sat at a redwood table in the shade of the old pier and drank black coffee from a Styrofoam cup. He knew as he sat there, idly sipping his coffee and watching the sea across the top of his newspaper, that something had loosened in the world; something had awakened, and was plodding toward him, or with him, across the aimless miles. He smiled and stroked his beard, then flicked a bit of thread from the knee of his white trousers. He could hear the deep, hoarse breathing of it on the wind, like an out-of-tune, bedlam orchestra. There was just the suggestion of the first trumpet behind it all, and there would follow in the days to come a rain of hail and fire and blood, maybe literally. He rather hoped so.

Pennyman's coffee was terrible – probably brewed early that morning and then burnt up on a hot plate. Andrew Vanbergen made a good cup of coffee. You had to give him that much. It didn't matter much to Pennyman anymore, though; coffee was coffee. He drank it because he had to fill his stomach; that much was still required of him. He would have liked to see the world rid of its curious little habits. If it were up to him – and it soon might be – he'd have the beaches swept clean of sand and its seashells ground into powder and mixed into cement. He'd pave everything, is what he'd do. The pattern of mussels and barnacles and starfish on the pier pilings offended him, almost as much as the sunlight did. The shouted laughter of an unseen fisherman up on the pier rasped across the back of his brain like the serrated edge of a scaling knife.

He'd gotten back just four weeks past from his trip to the Middle East. His coins were tucked away, waiting against the day that he'd possess them all. There was still only one of the remaining five that puzzled him, and he suspected that somehow, somewhere in antiquity, something had been done to it to render it unrecognizable. He'd find it, though. Someone knew what it was and where it was, and it was only a matter of time before, one by one, he'd wring the information out of them.

He wasn't the only one who sensed that something was in the wind. There'd been a rash of odd stories in the newspaper over the past months – and not in the tabloids, either, but in big-city papers. A goat had climbed into a truck owned by a shadowy delivery service and had knocked the hand-brake loose and steered the truck down a hill and into a tree, jumping out the open window a moment before the truck had caught fire and burned, along with its contents. Two pigs a month back had terrorized a doughnut shop, making away across a parking lot with half a dozen glazed doughnuts and rooting through a drive-in dairy until the startled clerk had given them milk to drink. When they were rounded up at last they seemed to be playing a complicated game on the asphalt of the parking lot, snuffling the doughnuts up and down with their noses. And then there were reports in Huntington Beach of a hippopotamus that had appeared through the mist of a foggy morning and then disappeared just as thoroughly and quickly. Thirty whales had beached themselves in Mexico.

It had all been very funny to the journalists, but it wasn't funny to Pennyman; it reminded him a little too much of the demoniacs and the Gadarene swine. It was as if an unseen hand were stirring nature out of her long lethargy, as if there were counterplots and divine conspiracies that he didn't entirely see or understand. There was nothing he liked less than something he didn't understand.

Someone would rise up to take the places of Moneywort and Aureus. And when Pennyman had his way with Pfennig, there would be a person in the world unwittingly ready to take his place, too, if any of the coins found him. The trick was recognizing them when they appeared; and they *would* appear – one of them possessing the untraceable coin. It had been thousands of years that they'd worked as one, all the Caretakers, and all the time there was someone's shadow cast across their enterprises. There were surreptitious visits, disappearing coins, coins reappearing in the possession of apes or in the pouches of opossums after being lost for decades – all of it a sort of shadow symphony, orchestrated by – whom?

Pennyman knew the secret identity of the man who conducted the orchestra; he knew who the overseer *really* was. And he knew that the man sought to ransom himself by keeping the coins apart. It was a two-thousand-years-old good deed. The man's *assumed* identity was a mystery to him, though. One couldn't simply look up 'Iscariot, Judas' in the Seal Beach phone directory and come up with an address. It might be the mayor, or a television repairman, or, even more likely, the hobo that slept right now against the wall of the concrete rest room beneath the pier. He might call himself anything at all. There were certain tests that betrayed the identity of one of the Caretakers, but their master wasn't susceptible to tests, not unless you caught him out – in the moonlight. Well, he would show his hand soon enough, whoever he was. Pennyman would force it. He'd been forcing it for close onto two hundred years now – hoarding and hiding the coins, giving up one here to gain two there, committing any sort of atrocity, buying and selling kings and presidents and piling up the silver coins one on top of another. And now the pot was almost full. Almost.

Things were falling into disorder – a condition that suited Pennyman just fine. He sometimes, more often lately, preferred white noise to music on the radio. He sought out the hoarse, chaotic cry of nighttime terror and closed his ears to the insipid laughter of human beings pretending to be jolly. He found his flask in his coat pocket and drained off the rest of the chalky, pink antacid in it. The skin of his scalp felt as if it were crawling, and for a moment it seemed as if he were breathing dust. He could almost feel his pulse creeping along like a tired, rusted engine. With a shaking hand he fumbled after a glass vial in the pocket of his trousers. He squinted at the little dribble of elixir in the bottom of it, and he shook his head, as if dissatisfied. Then, grimacing, he drank it off, capped it and put it away.

He poured the rest of his coffee onto the ground and nodded his head at a man who approached along the sand. He felt the elixir from the vial seeping along his arteries, bracing him. The man coming toward him was a bore, all full of drivel about flying saucers. He'd insisted Pennyman come to a literary society thereabouts, and he wouldn't take no for an answer. It was always possible, of course, that the man knew more than he let on – that he was a Caretaker, that he had the coin. Maybe it was in his pocket right now. Maybe he possessed it and didn't know what it was. Was he the one? Pennyman gestured toward a chair and half stood up, as if in greeting. He rummaged in his pocket for a silver quarter, and winked as the man sat down, a wide, stupid grin on his face. 'Take a look at this,' said Pennyman, flipping the coin end over end. The coin seemed to vanish, and then, as if by a miracle, Pennyman, looking vastly surprised, hauled it out of the man's ear.

Halfway down the pier, affixed to an old, rusted swivel that used to be painted a jaunty red and white, stood a telescope that you could aim out to sea on a clear day in order to catch a glimpse of Catalina Island. Or you could point it north, toward Los Angeles Harbor or south toward the oilfields of Huntington Beach. A tall old man with brush-cut hair dropped a dime into the slot and cranked it around toward the beach, slowly turning the focus. Parked beside the telescope was a red car, a little electric car like a golf cart, that was about twenty percent interior space and eighty percent fins, as if it were an old Cadillac shrunk down by an urban witch doctor. It was driven by a twelve-volt battery that plugged into a wall socket for a recharge, and you could drive it on the pier if you were old enough or if your legs were no good.

Arthur Eastman squinted through the lens. He could read nothing in the face of the man he watched, except that the man was waiting for something, or someone. There was desperation in the wind, the slow creak of a century turning fitfully to a close, the quiet whisper of the shuffling of the last pages of a book. Uncle Arthur didn't like it a bit. The next week would tell. He swung the telescope around and scanned the sea. There was nothing.

The telescope shut off, and Arthur stepped down off the little plinth that the thing stood on. He might as well stroll down the pier and see what people were catching. The air would do him good. He caught sight, just then, of

Naomi's nephew, Andrew Vanbergen, fishing by the bait house along with young Pickett, both of them laughing out loud. Apparently they hadn't seen him yet. It was best, perhaps, to leave them alone. Pickett would ask too many questions. The pot was boiling, and there were too many cooks as it was. He didn't need Pickett to come staggering toward the broth with a salt-shaker. He was a good man – both of them were – and their time would come. But right now wasn't their time. He would let them fish.

Climbing into his car, he noticed that Jules Pennyman had struck up a conversation with one of Andrew's idiot friends. Pennyman was desperate – but then desperate men were as often as not dangerous men. He was plying the man with coin tricks. Uncle Arthur sat and thought for a minute, then looked out once again at the open sea before motoring silently away up the pier and down onto Main Street.

The doctor visited Aunt Naomi that afternoon. 'She's had a fright,' he said under his breath when Andrew poked his head into the room. The doctor stepped out onto the landing and half-shut the door behind him. Andrew shook his head sadly, hiding a bag full of chocolates behind his back. The doctor paused to take his glasses off, then wiped them slowly and carefully with a shred of tissue before putting them back on, squinting, taking them off again, and wiping some more, turning the activity into a sort of drama. Andrew stared at him, controlling himself.

'Bed rest; that's what I'd advise. And a certain amount of quiet, too.' The doctor was a fraud. Andrew could see that in an instant. There was a look in the man's eyes that advertised it, that seemed to say: 'I know nothing at all about anything, and so I look very grave instead.' He was perfect for Aunt Naomi, who wanted a doctor that knew nothing. A decent doctor would merely tell her to get out of bed, to quit whining, to pitch out the cats and air the room for a week.

The doctor had almost no chin, as if he were inbred or had evolved in a single generation from the fishes. And his hair had fallen out in two symmetrical clumps, so that he was bald as a vulture above his forehead and on the very crown of his head, and combed the little strip of wispy hair in between so that half of it fell forward and half of it backward, making him look as if he were wearing a rare sort of foreign hat.

He made housecalls, though, for an exorbitant sum that Aunt Naomi gladly paid. Andrew was happy enough about that, for it would be he, if anyone, who would otherwise have to cart her across town to the doctor's office. Doctor Garibaldi, he called himself. He wore a black suit and tie in the sweltering heat. 'She needs exercise, you know,' he said, peering sideways at Andrew as if he were revealing a secret that he ought not to reveal.

Andrew nodded. 'Bed rest and exercise,' he said. 'How about chocolate?'

The doctor shook his head violently. 'I wouldn't. Too rich for her.'

'Liquor?'

'No more than a glass of dry white wine with a meal.'

'What exactly is wrong with her,' asked Andrew, 'besides her being an invalid?'

'Well,' said the doctor, 'it's a complicated business for a layman. The veins and arteries, you understand, are like little subways, let's say, for the blood to – what is it? – traverse, perhaps.' He gestured with both hands, driving one through the other like a car through a tunnel. 'Do you follow me?' he asked. Andrew smiled and nodded. 'When we're young, they have a certain elasticity to them, not unlike rubber tubing.'

Andrew widened his eyes, as if struck by the extent of the doctor's knowledge of anatomy. 'I begin to see,' he said. 'Elasticity?'

'Yes indeed. The pressures, you know. The heart is like a pump ...'

'There's biblical precedent for all of this, I believe – all of this elasticity. In Exodus, if I'm not mistaken.'

The doctor looked at him sharply and shook his head, as if he didn't quite follow.

'Moses,' said Andrew, 'was out in the scrub – how did that go? He was looking for something. I don't remember what it was; the fatted calf, I think. We can look it up if we have to. It says, if I recall the substance of the text, that he tied his ass to a tree and walked half a mile.'

The doctor stared at him. Andrew smiled. It wasn't worth laughing out loud over, maybe, but it was worth more than six seconds of staring. Nothing came of it, though, except more staring. He thinks I'm insane, Andrew thought. That sort of thing happened to him a lot. It was like the baby 'possums in the teaspoon business. The world wasn't built with a sense of humor. It took itself too seriously. He'd once laughingly informed a gas station mechanic that there was something wrong with the 'Johnson rods' in the Metropolitan. The man had wiped his greasy hands on his pants and given him a look that matched exactly the look that the doctor was giving him now. 'Ain't no such thing,' the man had said, and shook his head over it, as if of all the living idiots he'd seen in his life, none had amounted to half as much as Andrew amounted to.

The doctor opened his bag, looked inside quickly, and stepped toward the stairs. 'And no coffee, either. Especially no coffee. The acid could ruin her stomach lining. And the caffeine! – well, leave it at this: She simply shouldn't get worked up. At all. It's the worst thing. I've prescribed Valium. It's tranquility that she needs, poor soul. I gather there was some sort of disturbance this morning – an animal or something in her room.'

'That's right,' said Andrew, feeling ashamed of himself now. 'A 'possum, actually. Cats tore it to shreds in the night. I've read that they're on the march, in their way – migrating south. There's talk of a coming ice age, according to *Scientific American*. Do you read it?'

'Yes … That is, when I can. I'm a busy man, what with house calls and all. Are you talking about cats?' He wiped his glasses again, peered at Andrew, and backed away down the stairs. 'I'll come round again in a week. Keep these creatures out of her room, cats or no cats.'

Andrew followed him down, thinking that if he himself were a bald man he'd have something tattooed on the crown of his head – on the very top, so that almost no one could see it unless he bent over. He thought briefly of writing something on Dr Garibaldi's head with a felt-tipped pen, but it would quite likely be impossible unless the doctor were asleep or dead. And if he were dead there wouldn't be much point to it, beyond exciting a certain amount of wonder and suspicion among coroners and immediate family. Something completely unfathomable would be best. If you were going to do a job, he thought, watching Dr Garibaldi step out into the living room from the stairs, then you do a job. You'd have to write something on a man's head that had no sane explanation. Nonsense syllables might do the trick. And if they rhymed, then it would be all the better, since it would seem as if they signified something. He could imagine Beams Pickett innocently noticing such a thing written onto the top of the doctor's head. His eyes would expand like pond ripples until he fell face-first into the bushes.

The doctor went out through the front door and onto the porch. Andrew shook his hand, which, it occurred to him, felt rather like a mushroom, as if pressing it too hard would release a little cloud of spores. He dropped it abruptly. 'About animals in the room, Doctor Garibaldi – the cats, that is. All the hair and noise and cat boxes and half-eaten food. That can't be healthful. It would be hard for me to see them go, of course, but perhaps they should. We're fond of them, my wife and I, but we could sacrifice ourselves just a bit if it would improve Naomi's health.'

The doctor grimaced. 'If it were a matter of asthma or allergies I'd concur,' he said. 'But this is general debility, so to speak. The cats are a boost to her lagging spirits.' He paused, then winked broadly at Andrew. He bent forward and whispered, 'She'll outlive us both if she's kept away from rich foods, liquor, and tobacco.' And then he turned and hurried away like a fat little animal, a marmot or a raccoon, toward his car.

Andrew stepped into the house, and popped back up the stairs whistling, still carrying his chocolates. He tapped twice on the door before shoving it open a crack and looking in. There sat Aunt Naomi, propped against pillows. She looked tired – but who wouldn't, lying around all day in a room full of cats? In fact, when he looked more closely, it wasn't so much tired as put-upon that she looked – by circumstance, by doctors, by 'possums, by the world in general.

Aunt Naomi was inscrutable; that was her problem, or one of them any-way. Either that or she was merely empty-headed. In truth, Andrew hadn't ever been able to figure her out – not entirely. He had always had mixed thoughts about inscrutable people, about eastern mystics or people claiming to be geniuses or certain sorts of knowing, pipe-smoking men whom he'd meet in bookstores or aquarium shops. Their knowledge could never be clearly defined, and although when he was younger he had assumed that he simply hadn't the brains to fathom that knowledge, when he'd gotten older he began to develop suspicions.

Aunt Naomi's suffering was the same sort of thing. It was this, it was that, it was the other: twinges, pains, general listlessness. Iron capsules accom-plished nothing. Orthopedic pillows brought on headaches. An army of doctors had come and gone over the long course of her life, and those that had gone the quickest had been the ones to suggest that her maladies were 'psychosomatic.' Uncle Arthur had recommended something called a 'Bed Massage,' which he had peddled, in his day, door to door. It was an electronic contrivance that hummed and rippled the stuffing in the mattress. Somehow it had gone haywire, though, after Andrew had hooked it up, and had, through some kink in the laws of physics, caused the leg on the nightstand to collapse and then couldn't be turned off until, hearing an ominous hammer-ing on the floorboards and Aunt Naomi shouting, Andrew had dashed up the stairs and jerked the plug out of the wall socket.

Andrew preferred maladies that were more sharply defined. If he were a doctor he wouldn't have lasted ten minutes with Aunt Naomi. One time when discussing the death of Naomi's husband after only two years of mar-riage, Andrew had said to Rose, 'Who wouldn't have died?' thinking to be funny. It hadn't been funny, though, and Rose had given him a look.

There were secrets in Aunt Naomi's past, skeletons in the closet. The cir-cumstances of her husband's death was one of them. Mrs Gummidge was familiar with them. The women had been fast friends in school, if such a thing were possible. There had been a falling out. The two had been in love with the same man – Miles Lepton, but it had been Aunt Naomi who had married him. He'd been fascinated with the story of the pig spoon and had actually come to possess it, or so Rose had heard. Mrs Gummidge – who hadn't, of course, been Mrs Gummidge at the time – toad felt jilted and swore to do them ill, but Lepton had died, and old wounds slowly began to heal. But it was years afterward that the reconciliation between the two women occurred. Mrs Gummidge had come west, down on her luck, and Aunt Naomi had condescended, charitably, to take her in. That gave Andrew a pain. It was *his* house, after all. It had been *him* who had taken Mrs Gum-midge in, and yet Aunt Naomi had become a sort of saint because of it.

He regarded Aunt Naomi with a smile. 'How are you feeling?' he asked, sitting softly on the end of the bed. She opened one eye and looked at him as if he were some creature in a zoo and had wandered inadvertently into the wrong cage. 'Piece of chocolate?'

'I can't tolerate chocolate,' she said, sighing, 'You can't imagine what it does to me.'

'Really?' Andrew shook his head, trying to imagine it, but failing. 'I've brought truffles. All natural. I'd be wary of preservatives. I read an article about chemical preservatives in chocolates – a list of poisons half a mile long.'

Naomi lay silent for a moment, then opened her eyes and looked at the bag of chocolates. A warm afternoon breeze billowed the window curtains. 'Could you adjust an old lady's pillows?' she asked suddenly.

'Of course, of course,' Andrew stood up and, as Aunt Naomi bent forward, he plumped up the half-dozen pillows, arranging them into a little box canyon. She leaned back and immediately pitched forward again, as if he'd hidden a cactus among them.

'My back,' she cried, screwing up her face. 'Mound them, Andrew. I can't stand that sort of thing.'

'Of course!' he said, not knowing, exactly, what it was her back couldn't stand. There was no satisfying her, no dealing with her unfathomable maladies. 'Here now. There it is. Slide back just about an inch. How's that now?'

She settled into the pillows, as if into a too-hot bath, hunching her shoulders and souring her face. Then she shook her head, tolerably dissatisfied. She didn't invite him to rearrange them again, though. She'd given up on him, the look on her face seemed to say. 'What do you mean, natural?'

'Cream,' he said, 'and cocoa and butter. That's it, except for flavoring. And not chemical flavoring, either – walnut extract, liqueurs, berries. All very healthful. Dr Garibaldi particularly recommended them.'

She gave him a look. Andrew smiled, thinking that by the time Dr Garibaldi left the house next week he *would* have recommended them. Aunt Naomi would see to it. She plucked out a cocoa-covered piece and nibbled it. Then, without a word, she nodded toward the nightstand as if commanding him to set the bag down, to leave it.

'I've rather brought these as a peace offering,' Andrew said, shrugging just a little. 'The incident with the 'possum – I blame myself for that. If it hadn't been for your cats ...'

She said nothing. She might have been dead, except that she was still chewing on the chocolate.

'I've set traps all around the house – a sort of Maginot Line. I think I can guarantee that there won't be any more of the creatures in at the window.' There was a silence, during which Aunt Naomi finished chewing, then sucked the chocolate from her fingers. Andrew smiled down at her. 'Would you like a telephone in your room?' he asked.

Her eyes shot open. 'What on earth for?' She looked at him as if he'd uttered an obscenity. 'A telephone would drive me mad, ringing all day long. That's what you want, isn't it? I've seen through you from the start, and I told Rose so when she introduced you. A telephone.'

'I meant your own phone, of course. Not an extension. Your own number. You could ring up your friends, the drugstore. You could call downstairs. We could put a phone in Mrs Gummidge's room. It would be better than a bell on a rope.'

'I have no friends.'

'Well,' said Andrew, stopping the compulsion to merely shrug and nod. 'There's Mrs Gummidge.'

'Mrs Gummidge,' said Aunt Naomi flatly – as if that was all she had to say on the subject of Mrs Gummidge. She squinted into space, looking, perhaps, at some little piece of distant history, when she and Mrs Gummidge had been young together.

'What *do* you want, then?' asked Andrew patiently. 'A television?'

She waved the suggestion aside.

'New glasses?'

She pretended to sleep.

'A subscription to a book-of-the-month club?'

Nothing would satisfy her but that Andrew would leave her alone and send Mrs Gummidge up. He would, said Andrew. Straightaway. It was rest she needed. He paused, trying to think up some way to ask her for the thousand dollars for the restaurant. A lie would do, and nothing less. He could hear a flock of wild parrots, out ravaging the neighborhood carob trees, probably. They'd been hanging around lately, about thirty of them, big Amazon parrots, up from Mexico. 'I do have one little surprise besides the chocolate,' he said, smiling.

She waited, breathing deeply, fanning herself with a little Japanese fold-out fan from the nightstand.

'I've found a chef for the restaurant. I think you'll approve. I had you in mind, in fact, when I talked to the man. He studied in Paris, under Girot. He ran a pastry kitchen in Pasadena. In fact, he made these truffles. That's partly why I brought them up, to give you an inkling of the sort of man we'll have in the kitchen.'

She opened one eye, almost imperceptibly, like a toad regarding an unsuspecting fly. She had, somewhere along the line, developed a reputation as a gourmet, although Andrew was fairly sure that she couldn't tell milk-fed veal from dairy cow. He'd found that she liked a drink well enough, but again, maybe just out of perversity, he'd concluded that it didn't much matter how you defined 'drink'. Mrs Gummidge, he was fairly sure, had the same tastes, and kept Aunt Naomi well enough satisfied. Rose would have been too temperate. Dr Garibaldi's advice would have struck home with Rose.

The news of the hiring of the French chef seemed to revive Aunt Naomi just a little. She nodded at Andrew in almost a 'good man' sort of way. 'And you say you've actually hired this man? When?'

'Yesterday,' Andrew lied. There was no such man, although there might be someday soon. It was only half a lie. 'He's given notice, but he has to stick it out for two more weeks at the pastry shop. The honor of the French, you know. Then he'll be here. I'm hustling to get the restaurant in order. They're installing the equipment that you helped buy, in fact. But it's still an expensive thing – hiring chefs, buying this and that, stocking the shelves. These foreign chefs want fresh materials. It's not just a matter of hauling a truckload of canned goods back from the market. I've got three different suppliers on the hook – two of them importers. Pickett is drawing up a menu. We'd be grateful to you – Aunt – if you'd give it a look-over when we've got it roughed out.'

'I should be glad to,' she said. 'It wouldn't be excessive to say that I've had some experience along those lines.'

'I'm certain you have.' Andrew sighed. 'I'm afraid the menu won't be – what? – as *nice*, maybe, as you're accustomed to.' He cleared his throat. 'As I said, the expenses of a hired chef and all ...'

She squinted at him. 'How much do you want?'

'No, no. That isn't it at all. Dr Garibaldi tells me that you've got a delicate constitution. That's all. Under the circumstances a foreign chef isn't a luxury, is it? That's what I said to Rose.'

'How much do you want?'

Andrew shook his head, half-sadly, and, hating himself, patted her on the shoulder. 'Well,' he said, 'not to put too fine a point on it, there's wages for the man in advance for a month and the price of copper mixing bowls and pots and pans. He won't have anything less. And he insists on an espresso maker. You won't argue with that, I'd bet. Would you like a cup now, in fact?'

'Have you already bought it? The espresso maker? I thought you were asking for money for it. Now it's suddenly in use.'

'No, no, no.' Andrew laughed and slapped his knee theatrically. 'I've got a small one – one cup at a time. And a milk steamer. For the restaurant we would need something sizeable. I was just thinking that a big cup might go right along with another of these chocolates. Since you press me, though, let's call it ... two thousand. At month's end I should have a good bit of it back. Rose says we're almost ready for boarders – by the end of the week, she thinks. I've drawn up a placard, and there's a man coming round to hang it out front, facing the boulevard.' All the talk about getting the money back was perfunctory. Aunt Naomi had never asked for it back, which made Andrew feel guilty, and so he was doubly scrupulous about offering to give it back, even if that were impossible.

Aunt Naomi nodded tiredly and mechanically, and gestured Andrew out of the room.

'I'll just brew up that coffee,' he said, and went away whistling, down the two flights of stairs to the kitchen. He loved meddling with coffee machinery – grinders, steamers, even thermometers if he were doing the job right. He poured beans into the hand grinder on the wall, cranked the setting to super fine, and smashed out nearly a half-cup of powdered coffee, which he heaped into the coffee trap in the stove-top espresso maker. In minutes, thick, black liquid, dark as sewer sludge but smelling wonderful, was bubbling up out of the depths of the pot, and his milk steamer hissed through the pressure-release hole. He steamed a third of a mug of milk, topped it off with coffee, and then, before dumping in two teaspoons of sugar, he poured the leftover coffee across the copper bottom of a pan in the sink, tilting it this way and that to cover the entire pan bottom. In twenty minutes the copper would shine like a new penny.

Aunt Naomi handed him a check when he set the mug down next to the chocolates. He could tell that she'd been shoving the truffles down while he'd been out. The checkbook had vanished. She kept it hidden. With it she kept a little spiral binder listing all the money she'd doled out over the months. She had let him catch a glimpse of that more than once, to remind him, possibly, that he wasn't getting away with anything.

He steeled himself, then bent over and kissed her on the cheek. In two minutes he was out the door, striding up the alley toward the bank. Two thousand – it was double what he'd hoped for. He might have asked for three. But if he had, and she'd laughed in his face, then the whole business of the chocolates and the French chef would have come to nothing. And besides, if she'd written a bigger check, the bank might easily have kept it for a week to clear it. They weren't entirely satisfied with the quality of Andrew's banking. They weren't anxious to speculate in questionable new businesses. Bankers were men of little imagination; that was the truth of it. The further truth was that the two thousand would go some distance toward paying the bills. They seemed to pile up so quickly these days. It wouldn't be long, quite likely, before certain of their creditors would get nasty. But then their desperation might be enough to make Aunt Naomi advance them a bit more. Her will was drawn, after all. It would all belong to Rose when Naomi died. Surely it didn't matter to the old woman whether she gave it to them now or waited until the end.

So the two thousand would have to do for the moment. If he were lucky, Rose would never hear about it until, on some future, grim day, Naomi would haul out her binder and show Rose what sort of spendthrift husband she was married to. By that time though, Rose couldn't possibly remember what had happened to any single piece of that money. True, she'd be flabbergasted at the size of the debt they'd run up. But such was life. It would be spilled milk by then. There would be no inn without it, and certainly there'd be no restaurant – no real restaurant, anyway. Speculation was in his blood. There wasn't a winner in the world that didn't bet, and timidity wouldn't buy copper pots. He'd have to work on the French chef business, though. Faking up a beard and mustache for Pickett wouldn't answer. He'd heard of a chef's school in Bellflower, and it would be the work of a moment to ring them up and inquire about the availability of graduates. He could hire one for a week to satisfy Naomi and Rose, then toss him out and do the cooking himself.

It was early evening when Andrew drove along the Coast Highway, listening to an odd rattle in the engine of the Metropolitan. He was entirely ignorant of mechanics, happily so. He didn't have time in his life to meddle with it. There were better things to do, any number of them. In fact, he'd been doing some of them that very afternoon. He'd paid a visit to Polsky and Sons liquor importers and distributors on Beach Boulevard in Westminster, and come away with two cases of scotch, four dozen pint glasses, and most of the items on the list he'd made up out of *Grossman*. The trunk and back seat were full of stuff, and he still had the bulk of Aunt Naomi's money in his wallet. He whistled tunelessly and looked out the window.

The warm weather seemed to be passing. The sky was gray out over the Pacific, and the wind had fallen off. Twilight cast long shadows across the weedy marshland ruins of boatyards and clapboard bungalows. He drove past heaps of rusted anchors and piles of painted buoys and what looked like an old concrete bridge, collapsed now and sunk into the shallows of the Bolsa Chica Salt Marsh. The Seed Beach Naval Weapons Station loomed off to the right, a broad expanse of what looked like pastureland and farmland, with here and there in the dim distances a weapons bunker sitting toad-like and ominous between grassy hillocks. There were broad wooden doors in the ends of some of the hillocks, with grass and canteloupe vines growing right in around the jambs. What lay under the grass and vines was a mystery.

He slowed the car, bumping off onto the shoulder. A knot of people stood around in front of the roadside stand that sold strawberries and corn and tomatoes in the spring and summer, and pumpkins in the fall, all of it grown on government property, which wore the fruits and vegetables as a clever disguise. Hinged sheets of plywood had been dropped across the front of the stand to close it up for the night, so the people – a couple of families with children from the look of it – weren't buying anything. They were clearly up to something else. Another carload pulled in directly behind Andrew, and what seemed to be a half-dozen children piled out and went shouting away past his car, a large woman in a wraparound garment climbing ponderously out after them and yelling them into submission.

Andrew followed just for the adventure of it – something that Beams Pickett would approve of. There was a sign posted, advertising, of all things, a treasure hunt. It referred to a companion ad in the *Seal Beach Herald*, Pickett's newspaper. The newspaper advertisement no doubt explained the carloads of curious people. Treasures were to be buried, the sign said, no end of them, and the public could come dig for them, on the night of Sunday the 24th, by moonlight. Penlights were allowed, nothing bigger than that, though, and the public could keep what it found. There was a diamond ring, it said, in a hermetically sealed glass box, and a glass paperweight in a wooden box, and tickets for two dinners at Sam's Seafood, which weren't, Andrew assumed, in any sort of box at all. There were five hundred children's toys, and a real treasure chest full of quartz crystals and fluorite and bags of rhinestones and glass beads. No maps would be provided. The public would furnish their own spades.

Andrew recalled such a thing from the past. What was it? – almost thirty-five years ago. It had been a fairly common practice in central Orange County, when vast tracts of houses were routing out orange groves and bean fields, and driving up the price of land so that small farmers couldn't afford to keep it. For a time it had been the fashion for farmers to let the populace spade up their acreage for them. They'd bury rolls of pennies and such, and let suburban hordes do a week's worth of work in a night. It had always seemed an unlikely practice to Andrew, although he approved of the notion because of the mystery and romance associated with digging for spurious treasures in a weedy pasture by moonlight. It appealed to his sense of – what? He couldn't quite define it.

He drove away mulling it over. It made a certain amount of sense two score years ago, when hundreds of farmers owned little tracts of land up and down the roads leading south toward the beaches – just a couple of acres or so – and sold roadside produce to wring out a living. But that was all gone years since, and now what farmland was left was owned by vast real estate companies that, in some indefinable way, let out bits of land for farming in order to gain some sort of nebulous tax profits. Nobody 'spaded up' the land anymore.

Still, that didn't mean that there was some sort of secret motive in this moonlight-spading business, did it? He'd have to watch that sort of jumping-to-conclusions. It was too easy to raise people's eyebrows. He suspected, somewhere inside him, that Rose 'put up with him' sometimes. In the best possible way, she was conventional. There wasn't any more to it than that. She was conventional; he wasn't. His antics made her tired. He knew that, and he wished it weren't so. But they seemed to inhabit different worlds sometimes, different universes. Hers was neatly mapped out. The streets that seemed to run north and south *did* run north and south, seven days a week, and if a farmer planted pumpkins it was simply because Halloween was drawing near and he could sell them at a profit. Andrew's world was cut with streets that angled and twisted. Fogs rolled through at inopportune moments, seeming to hide the shifting landscape. Slouching farmers planted pumpkins so that the crawling vines would cover hillocks beneath which lay unguessed weapons, cleverly hidden from the eyes of satellites sweeping past overhead, themselves veiled by distance.

And although he was certain that he understood her world easily enough, saw through it clearly, he was equally certain that she had little notion of his. She understood him to be simply frivolous, cockeyed for no apparent reason at all. His enthusiasms were a mystery to her, a closed book. At worst he was stark, staring mad, which didn't, he thought as he drove along, particularly bother him. What was far worse was that she thought him childish, with his coffee makers and his books and his paperweights, his preoccupation with beer glasses and breakfast cereal and his odd car, which, she'd once said when she was angry, no grown man had any business driving. But he was deadly serious about it all. Those sorts of things were the threads which knitted up his world. Pulled out one by one and examined, maybe they were foolish and frivolous things, but if you pulled them all out and pitched them into the dumpster, then what was left? Nothing that was worth bothering with. A lot of airy trash fit for the junkman. That was the truth of it, and Rose didn't quite understand it. She pretended to when he tried to explain it, but in her eyes and in her voice there was something that made him feel as if he were six years old, showing his mother his favorite toy. It made him mad just to think about it.

He drove along feeling half-sorry for himself, neglecting to turn his headlights on. He couldn't tell Rose about Pickett's Caretaker nonsense. It would be evidence of something. Lord knows what would have happened if she were to discover that he'd shamelessly talked two thousand dollars out of Aunt Naomi that afternoon, when what he was supposed to be doing was generally smoothing things over. Now he'd promised a French chef and spent a quarter of the money on exotic liquor, and Beams Pickett was on his way to Vancouver to load up the trunk of his Chevrolet with cartons of Weetabix, charging gas to the company credit card, which Rose had insisted he not use unless it were an absolute emergency. He hadn't *wanted* to give Pickett the credit card, but his wallet had been empty. Now it was full, only a few hours later. That's how life went. It was unpredictable. Just when you thought that the way was clear, that the script was written, wham! there was some new confusion, flying in at the window, overturning chairs.

A horn blared and a car swerved out of the lane in front of him. He'd drifted across the line, into oncoming traffic. He jerked the car back into his own lane, his heart hammering. Rose paid attention when she drove. He didn't, it was true. He couldn't argue with her when she pointed it out. The only human being on earth, she said, who drove worse than he was Uncle Arthur, who was ninety-two.

And she had her doubts about his seeing so much of Beams Pickett. Pickett had developed the reputation of believing in plots and threats, and Rose understood, although she never said it, that Andrew had been contaminated. Pickett believed in the theory that what was obvious was probably lies; the truth lay hidden, and you got at it by ignoring what passed as common sense.

Andrew's mind wandered again as he drove along. He thought about their eventful morning, about the 'possum trick and Pickett's suspicions about Mrs Gummidge. What was true about Pickett was that he was skeptical of skeptics. He had almost hit one that very morning in a cafe near the pier, after the two of them had dumped the 'possum and went fishing. They had had some luck with bonita, keeping at it until after nine in the morning. Then they'd left the fish in a gunnysack in the back of the Metropolitan and gone in for breakfast at the Potholder. A man named Johnson sat at the counter, sopping up egg yolks with a slab of white toast. They knew him from the bookstore, where they'd attended meetings of a literary society for a time.

Johnson saw through everything. There was nothing that would surprise him. He had 'no regrets', he had insisted at the literary society in a hearty, chest-slapping tone, and he'd drained his beer glass at a gulp and smacked his lips. There at the counter at the Potholder he had sat poking at egg yolks and shoving down half a slice of bread without bothering to chew it more than twice. Pickett couldn't stand him, and Andrew could see, as soon as they had walked in through the door, that Pickett was going to go for him straightaway, although what Andrew wanted to do was to nod and sit at the opposite end of the cafe, so as to avoid starting Johnson up. Pickett, braced by four hours of sea air, had wanted to start him up very badly.

Johnson had been reading – old issues of science fiction magazines. He'd come upon an essay that made a hash of Pickett's flying saucer enthusiasm – knocked the pins out from under it, Johnson had said, grinning. He'd nodded at Andrew and motioned down the length of the empty counter. Andrew didn't like sitting at counters. He felt too conspicuous there. But Pickett sat down at once and fingered the menu, grinning at Johnson, who droned along about unidentified flying objects.

'The telling thing,' Johnson had said, wiping his face with a napkin, 'is that when these things appear, they're always described in the fashion of the day. Do you get me?'

'No,' said Pickett.

'I mean to say that a hundred years ago they were a common enough business, weren't they? But they looked like hay wagons, then, with wings and propellers and paddle wheels. I was reading an account of a man in Sioux City, Iowa, who claimed to have seen an airship – this was in 1896, mind you – that was shaped like an Indian canoe with an inflated gasbag above it. It dropped a grappling hook, he said, that caught in the slack of his trousers and dragged him across a cow field.' Johnson grinned and laughed to himself, humping up and down with the force of it. He looked sharply at the remaining egg on his plate, as if seeing it for the first time, and then hacked it to bits with the corner of a piece of toast.

'A *cow* field!'

'I'm still not certain,' said Pickett, 'what you mean to say. It's an amusing story, but ...'

'Isn't it?' said Johnson, interrupting. 'Concentrate, now. It's not difficult to grasp. Really it isn't.'

Pickett sat stony-faced.

'You see,' said Johnson, waving his toast, 'that's how it went in 1896. In 1925 it was the same business, only no canoes by then, no airbags, no propellers. They were those inflated-looking rockets that you see in the pulps. After that it was saucers, and now there's cylindrical ships made of polished metal that go very, very fast. What next? That's the point. It's all fakery, imagination, humbugging. If it weren't, there'd be some consistency to it. That was the crux of this essay, anyway.'

'Who wrote it?' asked Pickett, sitting very still and stirring his coffee.

'Asimov. He's hard to argue with. Rock solid logic, from my point of view. Shreds the whole UFO business at a single swipe. What do you think?' He leaned past Pickett to put the question to Andrew.

'Absolutely,' said Andrew. 'It's a dead issue I should think.'

Pickett gaped at Andrew, then turned back to Johnson, heating up. Andrew could see it. Pickett was about to burst. It always happened that way with Johnson. That was why they'd given up the literary society. Pickett would be fired up to have a go at him, and then the conversation would drive him mad, and Johnson would go off grinning, having won.

'Of *course* they keep showing up in different craft,' Pickett said. Their breakfasts arrived and Andrew started to eat, but Pickett ignored his. 'That's the beauty of it. They don't *want* to give themselves away, for God's sake. It's a matter of disguise, is what it is. I wouldn't be half-surprised if the aliens who dragged your man across the cow pasture are the same crowd who appeared in the flying egg six years ago over San Francisco. Why not? If they've got the technology to sail in from the stars, then certainly they've got the technology to design any sorts of ships they please. Look at Detroit, for heaven's sake. They can build a truck on Monday and a convertible on Tuesday, just like that. And what's more …'

But Pickett hadn't gotten a chance to finish, for Johnson was suddenly ignoring him, talking to the waitress and paying his bill. He laid a quarter on the counter by way of a tip and then scratched the end of his nose. 'Do you know what it was in the airship?' he asked, grinning at Pickett and Andrew.

Pickett blinked at him. 'What? What airship?'

'In Iowa – the cow field ship. Pigs. That's what the man said. It was pigs. And they stole his money – a rare coin. That's what he said. I swear it. He was robbed by pigs. Of course, the whole story went to bits, didn't it? It's simple enough. You don't need Sherlock Holmes to piece together the truth. The way I figure it he'd had a run-in with pigs. They were probably out on the road and knocked him into a ditch. That explains how his trousers came to be ruined. And he'd lost money of some sort, probably a silver piece or something, which he shouldn't have had anyway because his wife needed it for groceries. He was on his way to spend it on a bottle, probably. Well, he couldn't just up and admit it, could he? I mean *pigs*, after all. He'd look like a fool. So he made up the story, lock, stock, and barrel: alien pigs, hooks, draggings across cow fields, rare coins. He's a hero, isn't he, and not a fool at all, no longer a poor sod manhandled by pigs.' Johnson stopped and squinted at them, nodding his head knowingly. 'He lost a pocketful of change in ditch water, that's what I think, and soiled his pants. So he explained it away with the wildest lie he could invent, knowing that the public would go for it. They always do – the wilder the better. But mark me, gentlemen, you can bet that his wife didn't much believe him. Am I right? Yes I am. Right as rain. There isn't a wife alive that isn't ten times as shrewd as the public. What do you think, Andrew?'

Andrew gawked at him, not at all knowing what to make of all this talk about pigs and rare coins. But there was no fathoming Johnson. There was nothing to fathom. Johnson wasn't deep enough. You could see the bottom just by looking into his eyes. 'I think,' said Andrew, 'that if you laid the public out end to end they wouldn't reach from here to Glendale.'

'You're a scholar!' shouted Johnson, standing up. 'You, too, son,' he said to Pickett, and he grabbed Pickett's hand and shook it before Pickett had a chance to snatch it away. 'Got to go,' he said. 'I've got to see a man about a horse. Do you know what I mean? Spaceships – very interesting business all the way around. We'll take this up again.'

Pickett started to speak, to get in the last word, to finish what he'd started. 'Anyway, as I was saying, convertibles on Tuesday …'

'Yes,' Johnson said, setting out. 'That's right. Convertibles. Maybe the aliens will be driving convertibles next. Pigs in sunglasses.' And with that he giggled and strolled away, letting the glass door slam shut behind him and waving back over his shoulder.

Pickett had left his cold eggs on the counter, Johnson having ruined his appetite. They paid and left, forgetting entirely about the car and the fish and walking the two blocks back to the inn. Andrew tried to bring the subject around to the successful 'possum episode, but his enthusiasm was lost on Pickett, who insisted that he was going to have Johnson killed, that he'd ridicule him in the *Herald*, that before he was done he'd do half a dozen things to ruin the man, to make his life a living hell. That very afternoon, while driving north, he'd compose lovelorn letters in order to publish them in the *Herald* under Johnson's name. 'What did you make of the pencil line down the center of his face?' Pickett asked suddenly. 'Evidence of insanity, I'd call it.'

Andrew shrugged. 'Just more of his nonsense. It was best not to ask. He *wanted* you to ask, obviously. He'd probably have had some idiotic explanation prepared, some gag line and we'd be the butt of the joke.'

Pickett nodded. 'He must have forgotten it, though, if he'd put it there on purpose. Did you see him smear it up with the napkin?'

'He was too fired up about his cow pasture story. You shouldn't work him up so. It doesn't do you any good.'

'I'll sell him to the apes,' said Pickett, climbing into his Chevrolet. 'See you.' He started the car up with a roar and drove away toward the Coast Highway, carrying Andrew's credit card, bound for Vancouver. He'd be gone nearly a week.

It had been the middle of the afternoon when Andrew discovered that he'd left the Metropolitan parked at the pier. He'd jogged back down and opened the trunk. There lay the fish, stiff as papier-mâché ornaments. He had emptied the gunnysack into the dirt of the alley behind Señor Corky's restaurant, and was immediately surrounded by half a dozen cats. He waved goodbye, driving away south to visit Polsky and Sons and feeling generous.

Now here he was, parking the car at the curb, home at last after a hellishly long day. He hadn't gotten around to painting the garage, as he'd intended to, but there'd be time enough tomorrow to tackle it. Haste was never any good. The street was dark, and Aunt Naomi's window was shut against night creatures. Andrew locked up the car. It wouldn't do to start hauling stuff in. He'd wait until Rose went out or went to bed. He'd tell her he'd been to Bellflower to interview student chefs, which wasn't entirely a lie. He'd called the chefs' school, after all, and had gotten the name of a likely graduate, a young Frenchman who had grown up in Long Beach but still had a trace of an accent.

Fog blew in billows now, in between the houses and over rooftops. It would be a good night for some cat sabotage, but he'd probably worked the 'possum angle hard enough already. In fact, he'd been pressing his luck all day long. Maybe he'd go to bed early. That would make Rose happy. It would be evidence that there were traces of sanity left in him. He stepped up onto the front porch, humming, tolerably satisfied with things. Then he jumped in spite of himself to see Pennyman sitting in a rattan chair, smoking his pipe. He looked far too polished and stiff, like a waxwork dummy or a preserved corpse, and it seemed to Andrew as if he had the smell of fish about him, as if he'd been swilling cod liver oil. Pennyman pulled his pipe out of his mouth and pointed at an empty chair. 'Sit down,' he said.

FOUR

'Similarly, a stone with little discs upon it is good to bring in such coins; and if a man found a large stone with a number of small ones under it, like a sow among her litter, he was sure that to offer a coin upon it would bring him the one pig.'

SIR JAMES G. FRAZER,
THE GOLDEN BOUGH

Andrew stared at the figure of Pennyman smoking on the darkened porch. Suddenly he was filled with Pickett's fears, with visions of blowfish and secret societies. The glowing ash in the bowl of Pennyman's pipe burned like a hovering eye in the evening gloom. Andrew opened the door and reached into the house, flipping on the porch light. 'I'm home!' he shouted, not wanting to seem to be any later than he was.

Rose answered from somewhere within. 'Oh,' she said.

Andrew turned and shrugged at Pennyman. 'Sitting in the dark, are you?'

'Yes, indeed,' came the reply. 'I find it strangely relaxing, darkness. It's like the womb. Or the tomb. Funny business, language. Full of that sort of coincidence. Makes you wonder, doesn't it?'

'Of course it does.' Andrew sat down across from him, where he could see Rose through the window, angling back and forth across the kitchen. It was a comforting sight, but it made him feel vaguely guilty, and he wondered suddenly where he'd put his painting paraphernalia. He'd have a go at the garage in the morning, before the day heated up. It wouldn't take him long.

The day's newspaper lay in a heap beside Pennyman's chair. A crumpled piece lay in the shadows, half atop the pile, as if Pennyman had read something in it that he didn't at all like, and had wadded it up in a rage. There was an odd quality to it that caught Andrew's eye. He bent forward to have a better look and discovered that it wasn't a crumple at all, but was an inflated origami fish, with spiny little fins, folded up out of the comic section of the *Herald*. The sight of it was unnerving, although Andrew couldn't entirely say why.

Fog wisped across the lawn, obscuring the curb trees. A soft ocean wind blew, scraping tree limbs across the eaves of the porch, sighing through the bushes and unclipped grass, swirling the fog. The pale mists were a perfect accompaniment, somehow, to Pennyman's white suit and reeking pipe. He cast Andrew a mysterious sideways glance and said, 'I've spent some time in the Orient.' Then he nodded at the origami fish by way of explanation. 'Delicate things, aren't they? Like flower petals. The fog will half-dissolve it in the night – like the fleeting years, like life itself.' He sighed and waved his hand tiredly, gesturing, perhaps, at life.

Andrew nodded. He couldn't stand Pennyman. The man acted as if he were on a stage. 'I never did get the knack of folding up paper,' Andrew said. 'Couldn't even fold a paper hat.' Pennyman stared at him, as if he expected something more, something philosophic, as if the reference to paper hats couldn't, alone, have been the point of Andrew's utterance. Andrew's hand shook on his knee. He grinned widely. 'My sister could, though. She could fold up ... well, anything.'

With a flourish of his wrist, Pennyman opened up his hand. A quarter lay in his open palm. He widened his eyes at Andrew, as if to say, 'Watch this,' and he tumbled the coin over onto the back of his hand with one smooth movement of his thumb, flip-flopping it back and forth across his knuckles. Then he rolled it around into his palm again, caught it between his thumb and forefinger, and snapped his fingers so that the coin vanished up the sleeve of his coat.

Andrew was at a loss. It was a neat trick, to be sure, but he couldn't at all guess what Pennyman meant by it. He grinned, though, and produced a coin of his own, a nickel, which he balanced on end on the tip of his finger. It seemed to him that their encounter on the front porch was shaping up into a sort of contest, a test of cleverness or harmony or reason – as if they were competing students in some rare breed of martial arts school, learning to tread on rice paper without making any noise or balance on one leg like a swamp bird.

Pennyman nodded at the upended nickel, then smiled in appreciation when Andrew drew back his forearm, allowing the nickel to roll down his tilted finger onto the edge of his palm and then down his arm and off his elbow into the air, where he snatched it up. He bowed just a little. All in all it beat Pennyman's knuckle-rolling. And the open-sleeve trick was amateurish. Anyone could do that.

Pennyman said nothing. He flourished his quarter again, and, looking very grave, seemed to shove it into his ear. Then with a look of sudden surprise he hauled it out of his mouth, rattled it in his cupped hands, opened them, and seemed mystified to find no quarter at all.

That was cheap, thought Andrew, wondering what other coin tricks he remembered. Somewhere, in a shoebox tied with twine, he had a nickel with a nail welded to it. You'd pound the nail into the floor, then laugh and point at people who tried to pick it up. He made a mental note to remember it and play it on Pennyman later, when he suspected nothing. It would do him no good at the moment, though. He was at a loss for another trick. He could wedge quarters into his eyes, or dimes into his nose and ears, but the effect would be lost on Pennyman. It would be lost on anyone, for that matter – which was something in itself. There was always some profit merely in confounding people. Pennyman would at least wonder what Andrew meant by it. There was a certain indignity involved in shoving dimes into one's nostrils, though.

His hesitation made Pennyman tired, it seemed, and he couldn't wait any longer for Andrew to fire a shot. He produced a penny from his shirt pocket, held it up in front of Andrew's face, canted his head at it, and dropped it neatly into the bowl of his pipe, nearly covering the glowing coal. Andrew waited, wondering what in the world the man had in mind. Pennyman winked, and just as he did the penny caught fire – flared up just for an instant, then died, then seemed to be consumed into the tobacco. The penny had disappeared. Pennyman removed his pipe and bowed, acknowledging himself the winner.

Andrew, being gallant, shook his hand regretfully, secretly seething at being taken in by the burning penny trick. Obviously it was a cheap gag bought for fifty cents in a joke shop – a penny pressed out of dry, copper-colored tobacco. That's why he'd had it in his coat pocket instead of his pants pocket – so that it wouldn't be crushed. Pennyman probably had a whole handful of such pennies that he hauled out and burned in his pipe to impress strangers and influence competitors in the world of import and export. He'd probably bought them in the Orient when he'd tired of learning to fold paper.

'You're a good sport,' said Pennyman, slapping his knee and settling back into the chair. 'You're – what? – playful. I like that in a man. You don't find it often. Everyone's so damned *serious*.' And he growled this last word out in order to make fun of it, then tamped his pipe and relit it, blowing an enormous billow of smoke toward the porch roof. 'You've traveled, haven't you?'

'Well,' said Andrew, fuming, 'not extensively. To the midwest. Or rather *from* the midwest. I spent some time in Canada, too. Rose and I manage to get away to San Francisco sometimes. We love San Francisco.'

Pennyman nodded. 'I have contacts in Chinatown. I've spent some time there myself. You haven't been off the continent, though?'

'Not besides Canada ...' Andrew began. Then he stopped, catching himself in a stupidity and inwardly blanching. 'No. I'd like to, of course, but, with the inn and all ...'

'How true.' Pennyman sighed. 'You have a European air about you, actually. That's why I asked. It's the casual cut of your trousers, perhaps. Reminds one of the Provinces – vineyards, cobbled streets, bent old men in backyard gardens. Or, no, this is it – of the Mediterranean. Greek fishermen.' He paused and shook his head sadly, as if remembering. Then, in an inflated tone, he said, ' "I grow old ... I grow old ... I shall wear the bottoms of my trousers rolled." ' He squinted at Andrew silently, assessing him. Andrew considered poking him in the eye. Pennyman sat back with the air of a successful man, a man who has expressed himself tolerably well. 'And your hair – that tousled look. Do you do that on purpose? I mean, is it contrived? It's so ... so ... well, *you*. Do you follow me?'

'Not entirely. No. I just don't comb it, that's all. Waste of time, combing hair.' He meant this last bit to sting, but even as he said it it sounded like a petty insult. Whatever game they were playing on the porch, Andrew was losing, and he knew it.

'I mean to say that few men would have, well, the *guts* that it takes to wear their hair like that. That's all. I admire the hell out of that. Blast the world! What does it know?' He shook his head again and stared at the floorboards of the porch, and his look seemed to say that he'd found out this truth too late in life, that his manicured nails and sculpted beard were nothing but vanity, nothing but a childish fear of letting himself go.

Andrew saw through the whole despicable charade. There was nothing in Pennyman's chatter, though, that would justify Andrew's hitting him – bonking him on the conk. Or even of outright insulting him. Pennyman suddenly cheered up, as if he'd just then remembered where he'd left a twenty-dollar bill that he'd thought he'd lost, or as if he'd forgotten his name and it had just come to him in a flash. He produced a quarter again. 'One more,' he said, waving it in the air. 'Wait. Let's be sporting about this. I'll bet you a dollar that you can't pull this one off, and as a handicap, I'll let you watch the trick first. If you want to have a go at it, then we'll both ante up a dollar. If you think you can't hack it, we're quits. What do you say?'

'Go,' said Andrew, who, with fourteen hundred of Aunt Naomi's dollars in his wallet, could afford to lose one. And he was clever enough at coin tricks. He'd take Pennyman's money and walk away singing.

Pinning the quarter flatwise between both forefingers, Pennyman pressed the edge of it dead center on his forehead, right at his hairline, and then, with his fingers acting like axles, he rolled the quarter down over his nose, across his lips and down his chin. That was it – a manual dexterity trick. Pennyman half stood up and dropped the quarter into his trouser pocket.

'You're on,' said Andrew, fishing out a dollar.

Pennyman pulled a bill out of his shirt pocket, waved it, then thrust it back in, as if to imply that he was certain it would stay there, and that in a moment Andrew's would keep it company. 'Have one of mine,' he said, producing yet another quarter from his coat pocket and handing it to Andrew, who pinned it at once between his fingers, jammed it against his forehead, and rolled it down his face slowly. Just like that, right off the end of his chin. He could have driven it down into the collar of his shirt if he'd wanted to, and he gave Pennyman a look that seemed to say so. Pennyman frowned and shrugged, then handed across his dollar. 'It's not many people can do that,' he said. 'You've got a steady hand, sir; a steady hand.'

'Look,' said Andrew suddenly, staring at Pennyman's quarter, which he still held, 'it's silver. Don't lose it.'

'Is it?' asked Pennyman, acting astonished. 'Well I'll be damned …' He held it out so that the dim porch light glinted off the curve of George Washington's head. 'Would you look at that? How much is it worth, do you suppose, a dollar?'

'I'd suppose,' said Andrew, shrugging. 'Something like that.'

Pennyman widened his eyes in mock astonishment. 'Imagine,' he said. 'A whole dollar.' He put the coin away, sat back, and smiled, as if the smile were meant to suggest that it was Andrew's turn to dream up the next bit of front porch sport.

Andrew caught sight of the newspaper just then. Partly visible beneath the origami fish was the ad about the treasure hunt. He picked it up and read it, swearing that he wouldn't say another word to Pennyman until Pennyman said something to him – something civil. He could find nothing in the ad that explained the real purpose of the hunt. It was some sort of promotional gimmick, apparently. A charity of some sort, based locally, had leased the farmland for a night. Ah, there it was – the fine print. It would cost five dollars for adults, three for children. How many cars, full of people, would drive up, spades thrusting out of tied-down trunks, only to discover that they had to *pay* to dig for treasure, that they could dump all the five dollars and the three dollars in a box and have their own treasure without dirtying their hands? But it would be too late for them. They'd have to pay, or their children, intent upon digging gold in the moonlight, would wail the tops off their parents' cars.

It seemed the money was going to a good cause, though, although what that cause was the ad in no way made clear. It had slightly liberal political overtones – world hunger, world peace, world sanity – all too nebulous to define clearly.

'What do you make of that?' asked Pennyman suddenly, startling Andrew into dropping the paper.

'What? I mean, I don't know. Looks like fun, I suppose, digging treasures and all. Just the sort of thing I'd have liked as a child.'

'I knew it when I saw it. I said to myself, *here's* something that Andrew Vanbergen would appreciate. It would appeal to ...' He stopped and smiled. 'I bet you read Stevenson, don't you?'

Andrew nodded, wondering what would follow.

'I knew it. *Treasure Island*. I read it when I was thirteen. I was attracted to his essays, too, as a boy. Nothing brilliant in them. I can see that now. But they shined when I was a lad. All that adventurous optimism and moody reflection. Playing at soldiers with wooden swords – that's what his writing always reminded me of. Yes indeed. All style though. Not much substance. Great for children. To hell with substance, in fact. Let's ban it. Let's all read boys' books again and go off pirating, eh?' He nodded his head vigorously, then broke into a snatch of piratical talk, saying 'aargh,' afterward, which, if Rose hadn't shouted just then from the kitchen, might have cost Pennyman his life. Seething and grinning past his teeth, Andrew nodded at him and walked away into the house muttering, leaving him there.

He obligingly flipped off the front porch light so that Pennyman could do all the wombing and tombing he wanted. The man had figured out, somehow, that Andrew was keen on going to the treasure hunt. How he'd figured it was impossible to say, but he'd purposefully been making sport of him, that was sure. All that talk of adventure and tousled hair. The idiot. Nothing brilliant! No matter that most of it happened to be true and that Pennyman was full of lies and falseness. That's why Pennyman despised it. That's why he despised Andrew, for that matter. The truth always appeared despicable to the eyes of someone inherently false. Well to hell with him! The man wouldn't frighten him away from the treasure hunt. Andrew would be there and would take Pickett along. He'd talk Rose into going, by God. They'd bring a midnight lunch, a bottle of wine. Cheese. Smoked oysters. Sardines. Baskets of strawberries.

'What?' asked Rose. 'Run this plate up to Aunt Naomi, will you? Mrs Gummidge has gone out.'

'Yes. Nothing. I was just talking out loud.'

'Sounded like you said something about oysters. Remember when we had that picnic on the bluffs in Mendocino and ate smoked oysters and chocolate?'

'Yes,' said Andrew, smiling. 'You liked that. You were happy then.'

'I'm happy now,' she said, then stopped, looking at him as if puzzled. 'What's that on your face?'

'What? On my face?'

'Look in the mirror.'

He peered into the mirror over the kitchen sink. There, running down his forehead and nose and chin, dividing his face evenly in half, was a line of graphite or charcoal dust or something. In an instant it was clear to him – the quarter trick. Pennyman had hoaxed him, had played him for a fool. Pennyman had rubbed the serrated edge of the quarter across a pencil lead, perhaps, then tricked Andrew into rolling it down his face. Andrew would kill the man, he'd … Suddenly he remembered Johnson, smearing through an identical line with a torn napkin at the Potholder. He slumped, wondering what it meant, nearly putting his hand into Aunt Naomi's chicken.

'What on earth is wrong?' asked Rose, pulling out a chair.

Andrew waved her away. 'It's nothing,' he said. 'I was shaken to see it, that's all. I've apparently interviewed a man at the chefs' school in Bellflower while all the time I've looked like a fool. Heaven knows what they made of it.'

'*I* don't know quite what to make of it, actually.'

'It's nothing. An experiment, that's all. I was reading psychology. Certain sorts of madmen have faces which are utterly symmetrical. Sane people don't. There's subtle differences – one eye squints, maybe, or one cheek angles toward the chin just a hair steeper than the other. But madmen … cut their face in half – or rather a photograph, say – and flop the halves over and … Well. It's fascinating, really.'

Rose nodded while he talked, as if she were sympathetic to the notion of cutting photographs of madmen's faces in half, or whatever it was that Andrew was suggesting be done, and as if she saw very clearly why Andrew, after having come to understand the peculiar facial characteristics of lunatics, had drawn a line down the middle of his own face and gone out on the town. 'Naomi's food is getting cold,' she said, patting him on the arm.

Andrew started to wipe his face clean with the dish towel, but Rose snatched it away and handed him a paper towel, tucking the dish towel through the handle on the refrigerator door. 'I just took it out of the drawer,' she said. 'I wish you'd get into the habit of using paper towels instead. It just makes more work using tea towels all the time.'

'I will,' said Andrew. 'I lost my head.' He rubbed away with the paper towel, smearing the line. To hell with it; he had to take a shower anyway. He felt as if he'd been wearing the same clothes for a week. *Damn* Pennyman. Andrew would work the nailed-nickel trick on him tomorrow – in public. He'd laugh out loud and point; then he'd twist Pennyman's nose for him and send him packing. They'd do without his stinking two hundred dollars. He gave up and dropped the wadded paper towel onto the countertop, then went back out into the living room, carrying the plate for Aunt Naomi. Inconspicuously, he peered out onto the porch. Pennyman was gone.

*

The door to Aunt Naomi's bedroom was ajar, although the room was dim. Assuming she was awake, Andrew pushed the door farther open with his shoulder and stuck his head in. 'Dinner,' he said cheerfully. The bed was empty. Naomi sat in a chair, staring through the little gable window that looked out toward the ocean. There was the muffled boom of waves breaking, punctuated by the footfalls of someone walking on the sidewalk below, but nothing could be seen through the open window except hovering gray mist. A cat rubbed against Andrew's leg, pretending to be friendly.

'Chicken a la Rose,' said Andrew, setting the tray down. 'And rice, too, and – something. Looks like eggplant, maybe, in little squares.' He smiled at the back of Aunt Naomi's head, wondering if the woman was alive or had died in her chair. He caught himself inadvertently petting the cat, so he gave it a hard look and stood up. 'See anything out there?'

'Too much fog,' said Aunt Naomi, not turning around. 'I love to watch the ocean. I wish there were a widow's walk on the roof. I'd spend all my time out of doors, watching.'

'For what?' Andrew asked. 'Your ship coming in?'

'It went down years ago, I'm afraid. But there's no telling what might be out there waiting. Have you read this business in the newspaper about the whale trying to swim up the Sacramento River? What do they call him – some foolish name. If they understood it they'd laugh out of the other side of their mouth. I wonder where they think he's going.'

'I don't know,' said Andrew, trying to think of something funny to say – some ridiculous destination for the off-course whale. If it *was* off course. Aunt Naomi didn't seem to think so. He wasn't much in a joking mood, though. Somehow the presence of the old lady, staring out into the fog and talking about things lurking in the sea, took the edge off his sense of humor. It occurred to him that in a moment she'd turn around to confront him, her face a grinning skull, like something out of a late-night horror movie.

She swiveled round suddenly, regarding him strangely, then gasped and half stood up, as if *he* were the grinning skull. He reached down and flipped on the bedside lamp, but the sight of his illuminated face made her recoil even more, and for a moment he was certain that she was going to topple backward out the window.

'Who's done that to you?' she asked.

Andrew was at a loss. He touched his cheek and shrugged. 'Pardon me?' he said. He'd humor her. That's what he'd do. It was instantly clear to him. She'd gone round the bend. She was seeing things. She looked straight at him and saw – what? – her long-dead husband, perhaps, or Saint Augustine, or her old grammar school principal. He couldn't deal with this sort of thing at all. He shouldn't have to. She was Rose's aunt, after all. He'd get Rose up here. *She'd* know what to do. She was a marvel in this sort of situation. She'd say it

was the 'possum business, though, that had driven Aunt Naomi crazy. If it
was ever discovered that he …

'The line on your face,' she said. 'Who did that to you?'

The line, thought Andrew. Of course. She hadn't run mad. 'No one *did* it
to me,' he said. 'I was reading a book about schizophrenics. Strangely frightening business, really, about symmetrical faces, and …'

'*Books.* You weren't reading books. Someone did that to you and you don't
have the foggiest notion why. You're like a child. Tell me. Who was it? It's
smeared, isn't it? It must be smeared.'

Andrew was seething again. Who was she to call him a child? She was
driven half-wild by his having a line drawn down his nose, and she was calling *him* a child. But she'd given him two thousand dollars just that morning,
hadn't she? He thought hard about the money in his wallet, about the trunk
full of liquor, about the chances of wrestling another thousand or so out of
her in a few days, after he'd introduced her to the French chef from Long
Beach. It was best not to take offense. Old people as often as not didn't mean
any offense to be taken. And she was right, wasn't she? 'Mr Pennyman,' he
said. 'Yes, it's smeared. I'm just going in now to wash it off.'

'Pennyman!'

'That's right. A little gag of his. A quarter rubbed in pencil dust. Very
funny. Kid's trick, actually. We were horsing around on the porch.'

'Yes. A silver quarter.'

Andrew stared at her, washed by an entirely new wave of emotion; nearly
drowned in it. 'How did you know that?'

She waved the question away. 'I knew it. Stay away from him. Everything
he says to you is significant. There's no such thing as a casual conversation
with a man like Pennyman. I know who he is now. Take my word, and steer
clear of him. And here,' she said, dipping her napkin into the water glass
beside her bed, 'see if you can wipe that off.'

Andrew grinned and took the napkin. Humor her, he thought. Don't say
anything. He rubbed at the line, then looked at the smudged napkin. Peering
into the mirror over the dresser, he wiped some more until the mark was
gone. He handed the napkin to Aunt Naomi, thanked her, and turned to
leave.

'Wait,' she said, peering at him closely. 'Do me a grand favor, will you?'

'Anything,' he said.

'Fetch that old silver spoon from the china cupboard. The one Rose calls
the pig spoon.'

Puzzled, Andrew hopped away down the stairs and was back in a moment
carrying the spoon.

'I want to give this to you,' Naomi said.

'To Rose?' asked Andrew.

'No, to you. Despite our differences, I'm pretty sure you're a man of honor. Listen closely. This spoon is yours now. It's been mine for a long time, but I'm quit of it now. It belongs to you. Do you want it?'

Andrew blinked at her. In truth, he didn't much want the spoon. It had a curious history and was a moderately interesting relic, but it couldn't be *worth* anything. It was simply a dust collector. He tilted it into the light and stared at the delicate scoring on the concave surface. It seemed to be pulled down into the handle, so that the markings were proportionate at the top of the spoon and then stretched away below. It was thin enough so that he could have bent it in half between his thumb and forefinger. The silver of it was warm, almost hot, but that came from his holding it in his hand, he supposed. It *was* an interesting piece. He'd always been fascinated by it. It felt almost like some sort of magic wand in his hand. Suddenly he didn't want to give it up. He wanted to keep it. And almost as suddenly he felt vastly tired. Of course he did. He'd been up half the night and then awakened at dawn. His back was stiff, too. A hot shower *would* be nice. It would pick him right up. 'I'd love to have it,' he said. 'I'll just put it back into the hutch.'

'God bless you,' said Aunt Naomi, smiling one of her very rare smiles. It was genuine, too. Andrew felt a sudden liking for her, and he wondered at the tinge of sadness that flavored her smile. That came from age, he guessed. There was always some sadness flavoring your smiles when you stood in the shadow of the gravestone. It was regret, is what it was, for the passing of time. She had fond memories of that spoon. It was all she had left of her husband – aside from his money, of course. It was the last link to the Iowa farm. She lowered her voice suddenly and said, 'But I wouldn't put it back into the hutch if I were you. I'd find a safer place. It's really far more valuable than you suppose – very old, actually. In a sense, it will make its value known to you. You'll see. Put it somewhere safe for now.'

Andrew smiled back at her. She'd gone mystical on him, obviously. 'I'll keep it safe as a lamb,' he said. And then, hearing Rose calling from downstairs, he tipped a non-existent hat to Aunt Naomi and stepped out onto the landing, tucking the spoon into his pocket, muddled with mysteries. Halfway down, it occurred to him that Naomi might easily have overheard his conversation with Pennyman, down on the porch. Both of them had exclaimed over the silver quarter. Of course she had. She wasn't filled with arcane knowledge after all; she just wanted to *seem* so.

Rose stood in the living room holding the telephone. It was a long distance call – from Vancouver. Puzzled, Andrew took the phone, half-expecting, impossibly, to hear Pickett's voice on the other end.

But it wasn't Pickett. It was a man who claimed to be named August Pfennig – a dealer in coins and books and curiosities, calling from his shop on the waterfront. He asked whether Andrew was of the Iowa Vanbergens and whether he wasn't related by marriage to the Iowa Zwollenveters, and when Andrew said that he was, Pfennig sighed, as if happy at last. The man's name was vaguely familiar to Andrew, as if he'd run across it in a magazine article, perhaps, and remembered it because of its curious sound. He thought hard while the man rambled on, but he couldn't fit the name with a face.

Pfennig's voice was slow and careful, as if he were half-old and half-calculating. There was a false joviality to it, too, that Andrew recognized at once to be the empty, pretended interest of a salesman. He couldn't stand salesmen, especially salesmen who muttered about mutual friends, since that was always a lie right on the face of it. It was interesting, though, that one had called all the way from Canada. At least it wouldn't be insurance that the man was peddling. Maybe it was light bulbs. Andrew had got a rash of calls about light bulbs – a charity of some sort selling them for fifteen dollars a bulb, guaranteed to outlast everything, still to be glowing after you were dead and living with the worms.

The man wasn't selling light bulbs. He was buying – not selling anything at all. He dealt in estate jewelry and libraries. Andrew had been a hard man to 'track down.' Since the death of his brother-in-law, said Pfennig, he'd rather lost track of what went on in Southern California, and he said this in such a way that it sounded as if Andrew ought to know who this brother-in-law was.

'Well,' said Pfennig, carrying on, 'I do like to renew old acquaintances. Things seem to go to bits these days, don't they? The years sail past so.'

Andrew admitted that they did, thinking that somehow the conversation was at an end, that Pfennig, whoever he was, had called all the way from Vancouver to chat. Perhaps he was one of Rose's old school friends, a casual acquaintance from Orange City. He covered the mouthpiece and whispered the name to Rose, who stood waiting, curious. Rose shrugged and shook her head. Andrew shrugged back. The man's voice trailed off into nothing.

'Pardon me?' asked Andrew politely. 'I'm afraid I missed that last part. Bad connection.'

There was heavy breathing on the other end, like someone hyperventilating. 'I'm not well,' the man said suddenly. 'I'm ... ill. Bedridden. If you could speak up ...'

Irritated, Andrew spoke directly into the mouthpiece, talking roundly, 'I said, "*What?*"'

There was more breathing, and for a moment Andrew thought the conversation had gone entirely to bits, but then the man Pfennig continued. 'I was led to believe,' he said, 'that you were a collector, and I hoped that we could trade this for that, in the spirit of collecting, of course. I'm not in this for the money.'

Andrew nodded. Here it was. He wasn't in it for the money, wasn't he? He was in it for sport. He was calling from Vancouver for the jolly spirit of collecting. Pfennig droned on, asking about family Bibles, hymnals, Dutch translations, perhaps, of old prayer books. He worked his way into cookbooks and volumes of medical arcana and books describing home remedies. Andrew didn't have any of them. He had a falling-apart copy of *The Whitehouse Cookbook*, but Pfennig wasn't interested in it. 'Not in my line,' he said, and then went on to arts and crafts pottery and hammered copper.

'I've got a Roseville vase,' said Andrew helpfully. 'Fuchsia pattern – green and pink. Fairly rare, actually. But I don't want to sell it.'

'Too bad,' said Pfennig, clucking his tongue. 'My brother-in-law led me to believe you might put me in the way of some rare coins. What do you have along those lines?'

Andrew paused, thinking. He had the remnants of an old childhood penny collection and a half-dozen oval dimes flattened on a railroad track, but beyond that ...' Are you sure it's me?' he asked. 'Maybe ... My wife's *cousin* collects coins. He's always regretting that he can't put his hands on a curly quarter. Too expensive by half. It would cost him the value of the rest of his collection.'

'This is an *old* coin, that I'm talking about,' said Pfennig, and he went on to describe the thing – the hawk-nosed face on the one side, a curious rune on the other. A silver coin, but not as worn as you'd guess, given the thing's great age. They didn't have much silver of this quality any more, not very much at all.

'I'm really very sorry,' said Andrew. 'Someone's mistaken. I'm just not much of a coin man, actually. I'm afraid that I don't go in much for the kind of collecting ...'

'You're telling me you don't own this coin, then?'

'That's correct, Mr ...'

'*Have* you owned it? Sold it, maybe?'

'No, really I ...'

'Think about it. I'm prepared to offer a substantial sum. More than the man you're dealing with now. On no account let him have it. I'll be in touch.'

'I don't have any coin!' Andrew began. 'What *man?*' But Pfennig hung up. In a moment there was a dial tone.

'Who was it?' asked Rose.

Andrew shrugged. 'I don't know. Man from Vancouver buying and selling things.'

'You shouldn't let them waste your time like that. Tell them very firmly that you won't talk to them and then hang up. You're too polite for your own good, letting people like that waste your time away.'

'What do you mean "people like that"? What kind of person was he? He was an old acquaintance of some sort. How did I know? "People like that"! I go in for politeness. That's my way. Cheap as dirt, politeness.'

Rose shook her head and disappeared into the kitchen, not seeming to want to argue about how cheap politeness was. Andrew took a step toward the kitchen, thinking to press the issue. What, he would ask, did Rose have against politeness? And how on earth, not having listened in to the conversation, did she know that … But thinking about the conversation with Pfennig muddled things up. What *was* it all about? A wrong number, likely. Or rather a case of mistaken identity. Surely no one would have recommended Andrew as a collector of rare coins.

'Food's getting cold,' Rose said from the kitchen. She looked tired, Andrew thought as he stabbed away at his chicken. This business of opening an inn was wearing her out. She'd run an ad in the *Herald* already, and she was working doubly hard just in case it paid off early. It was premature, certainly, but she was right when she said that it might take time to draw customers. 'Anything come from the ad?' Andrew asked, deciding to let the politeness issue drop.

Rose nodded. 'One man. A nut from the look of him. Reminded me of Moses. He came around this afternoon and had a chat with Mr Pennyman on the porch. I thought he was a friend of Mr Pennyman, but it turned out he wanted a "semi-permanent" room. Those were his words. I don't know exactly what he meant.'

'Did you tell him two hundred a month?'

'No, never got around to it. And if I *had* gotten around to it, I wouldn't have told him any such thing. He had a beard. You should have seen it. He looked like Gabby Hayes and he was wearing a robe.'

'A bathrobe?'

'No, a sort of Oriental robe, I guess. He said he was a member of a "society." I don't remember which. He was fascinated by the place, or so he said – particularly in your books. He said the house had "a feel" to it. You should have seen his hat.'

'My books? You let him handle my books? What hat?'

'It was a sort of what-do-you-call-it hat, like an old-fashioned clown's cap – a sort of cone with a round brim and coming to a rounded point on top.'

Andrew nodded, still not liking the part about the books, but happy now that Rose hadn't rented him the room. That was just what they needed, a zealot of some weird stripe. Probably an Atlantean. Why were such people drawn to Southern California, to the coast, to the inn? 'So you pitched him out?'

'No, *I* didn't. Mr Pennyman rather discouraged him, I think.'

'Pennyman again! And there goes two hundred a month. What filthy business does Pennyman …'

'His business isn't filthy at all. *You* wouldn't have rented a room to this man. Oh, wait. Yes you would have. Out of politeness, I suppose.'

Andrew fumed. 'What *I* would have done isn't … Pennyman can keep out of our business. We don't need his filthy money and we don't need the stench of rosewater and fish oil all over the place.'

Rose stood up and began clearing away the plates, saying nothing. After a long minute of silence, she asked, 'Why are you so against Mr Pennyman? Is it that he keeps his hair cut and combed?'

Andrew's own hair was a mess. He'd admit that. It needed cutting badly and had taken on the appearance of a sort of wind-blown bush. He was above it, though. He had calculated once how many hours he'd spent in front of the mirror, arranging his hair, thinking, perhaps, that if he got it just so he'd be able to see someone else in there, the *real* Andrew Vanbergen, self-assured, rock-steady, able to walk on avenues of cobwebs without leaving an imprint. But his hair hadn't ever cooperated. Little curls of it would spring out on the end of a straight shock while the rest of it would stay put, giving his head the appearance of a broken cartoon clock with a ruined spring nodding from the top. The hours he'd wasted dabbling at it added up to about a year and a quarter. Well, no more.

Rose clinked dishes in the sink. 'You don't have to be afraid of people just because they're different,' she said, 'just because you don't understand them. Sometimes you seem to despise everything you don't understand.'

'*Me?*' said Andrew. 'It was *you* who wouldn't rent the room to this poor bearded man just because he wore a hat. Who cares about his hat? *I* wouldn't have given a damn about his hat. I'd have envied the man his hat. God bless a hat.'

Mrs Gummidge wandered through just then, small and gray and bent and humming to herself as she stopped to root in the junk drawer. 'I'll just be a sec,' she said apologetically. 'Don't pay a bit of attention to me.'

'Fine,' Andrew said agreeably. 'What was I saying …?'

'Don't we have a little plastic case of tiny screwdrivers?' said Mrs Gummidge, fluttering her eyelids at Andrew.

'We?' Andrew widened his eyes, as if the phrasing of the question had thrown him for a loop.

'In the back,' said Rose.

'Ah.' Mrs Gummidge inclined her head at Andrew, almost sympathetically, seeming to say that she knew just how tough things were for him, and didn't take offense. 'I'm just repairing that lock on the bathroom door that you haven't got around to yet, Mr Vanbergen. I *like* a little job like that.'

He let it pass, smashing down the urge to hurl a chicken bone at her. When she left, insisting that she was sorry for the 'intrusion,' he said to Rose, 'We? *Our* screwdrivers? What damned lock? What business does she have with locks on the bathroom doors?'

Rose looked at him blank-faced. 'Settle down,' she said. 'Who cares? Don't be petty. She didn't mean anything by it.'

They both fell silent. Andrew hated to be told to settle down. But you almost *had* to do it when you were told to, because if you didn't it was further evidence that you should have. You wanted to run wild, to scream and break things, but you couldn't. You had to see reason. He tried to force himself to see reason, realizing that because of Mrs Gummidge he had utterly lost track of the conversation he'd been having with Rose. In the silence he could hear the toad chirruping on the back porch, talking, maybe, to one of the cats.

'And I'm *not* afraid of Pennyman,' he said, lowering his voice. 'But I can spot slime easy enough. I'm going to pitch him out; that's what. He's cost us two hundred a month, and that rather negates the two hundred he's paying us, doesn't it? We pitch him out and we're dead even.'

Rose washed the dishes, hosing off bubbles and stacking the clean dishes on the sink. 'Add it up again,' she said simply.

'Add nothing. This isn't mathematics, it's – what? – morality. That's what it is. Hanging about with something diabolic. Pretty soon all sorts of rottenness starts to seem normal to you. Let a man like Pennyman get a toehold and all of a sudden he's running the place. He acts like he does already. Chasing this bearded man off! Talk about offensive beards.'

'Done with your plate?'

'What?' asked Andrew. 'Oh, yes. I guess so. What did this man want with my books?'

'He didn't want *anything* with your books. He simply peered at them for a moment. In the library. And anyway, it was Mr Pennyman's books he liked, not yours at all. The foreign ones on the middle shelves. He pulled one out and started to thumb through it, and Mr Pennyman rather discouraged it. I can't say just how. He simply made it clear that the man was taking liberties of a sort. The two of them didn't like each other a bit. I could see that right away. The man said that he'd decided he didn't need a room after all, but I think he was just mad about the books. He went out looking haughty anyway. But then he stopped for a moment on the front porch to chat some more with Mr Pennyman, who was really quite nice about it all.'

'Nice!' said Andrew. 'How does he get off being nice? What does *nice* have to do with anything?'

'You wouldn't know, perhaps, but I rather like it. Cheap as dirt, niceness.'

Andrew kept silent. She had him there.

'Anyway, the man hung around on the porch talking to Mr Pennyman about coin tricks. It was easy as that. I don't believe he was ever serious. He just wanted to poke around, like people looking through houses for sale. Nosiness is what it was.'

'Well,' said Andrew 'why in the world did Pennyman loan us the books in the first place if he didn't want the public meddling with them? They're nothing but trash anyway. And coin tricks, you say?'

'That's right. I wouldn't know about his books. I've got a few things to do yet. Can you find time to bring down Aunt Naomi's plate?'

'Yes, I can find time.' Andrew shrugged out of the kitchen, feeling like a wreck. Somehow the evening had gone to smash. The pain in his back was murdering him. It must be his sciatic nerve … That's how the day had gone: He had come home rich and jubilant and then, through no fault at all of his own, had run into no end of treachery from Pennyman and Mrs Gummidge. Well, he'd do something about it. A man's home, after all, was supposed to be his castle. He'd throw the knaves into the moat. His conversation with Pfennig still bothered him. Half of him wanted to think that the whole thing was a case of mistaken identity; the other half of him muttered that he ought to know the name, that no mistake had been made.

He pushed into the bedroom, thinking to change into looser clothes and to idle away a few minutes before having to confront Aunt Naomi again. Heaven knew what she'd be up to – sitting in a trance again, probably, watching the foggy night through the open window.

His books – his good books – lined two walls. There was Burroughs and H. G. Wells. There was Wodehouse and Dickens. None of the volumes were worth much. He was a book-owner rather than a collector. He was a hoarder. That was the truth of the matter. He thought about it as he sat on the edge of the bed, leaning back against his elbows. His books added something to his existence – a sort of atmosphere. No, it was more than that. They were a barrier of sorts. They were like a concrete foundation on a house; they kept the structure of his life up out of the dirt. They kept the termites out of the sill and kept the whole place from shaking to bits when the earth quaked. Looking at them was satisfactory, even when he was in a foul mood. Pennyman! There was one insect that had crept in, disguised, to gnaw on the floor joists. He was a bug, and no mistaking it, even if Rose didn't see it.

Of course Andrew couldn't just throw him out. It was too much money, after all. Rose would hand him the hedge trimmers and the vaccuum and tell him to fix the place up himself. She'd quit, and then there'd be no inn, no nothing. He pictured himself happy, ten years older, maybe, a little bit stouter, sitting at a corner table in the restaurant, a cheery fire in the grate, a pint glass of Bass Ale in his hand, things upstairs being seen to, the chef going about his business in the kitchen, the money rolling in. It was a pleasant enough dream, all in all – a comfortable dream. And it was true that it wouldn't come to pass if he was all the time throwing the guests out.

He sighed, tugging on his slippers. Squinting at the bookshelves, he stood up and cocked his head sideways, reading titles. There was a book gone, missing. He was certain of it. He looked closer, studying the titles, remembering how the books had been arranged. There were two books gone … three. He'd been robbed.

FIVE

'Now therefore, I think that, without the risk of any further serious objection occurring to you, I may state what I believe to be the truth – that beauty has been appointed by the Deity to be one of the elements by which the human soul is continually sustained ...'

JOHN RUSKIN,
LECTURES ON ARCHITECTURE AND PAINTING

'What the hell?' he muttered, thinking at first that he must recently have been looking at the missing books and then forgotten to put them back. Or maybe he hadn't unboxed them yet. Maybe they were in the garage. They weren't, though, and he knew it. It was impossible; they were gone. That was the long and short of it. Someone had taken them, and it was fairly clear who that someone was. Angry, he plucked up a pen from the dresser and looked about for a bit of paper. Finding nothing, he wrenched his handkerchief out of his pocket, and, stretching it tight across the top of the dresser, he wrote down titles on it: *I Go Pogo* was gone, and it had been signed, too, to Morton Jon-wolly from Walt Kelly. There were two Don Blandings gone – *Hula Moons* and *Vagabond's House* – both signed, although the signatures were almost worthless. What else? Not much of value. An unsigned copy of Wither-spoon's *Liverpool Jarge* and a copy of Gerhardi's *Pending Heaven*. That was it, at least from a hasty glance. It had been a weirdly selective thief – either a lunatic or someone who had taken the time to study things out.

Andrew shoved the pen into his pocket. There was the spoon, still in there. He plucked it out, looked around for some place to put it, and when nothing better suggested itself he slid it onto a bookshelf, in behind Charles Dickens.

'Rose!' he shouted, striding toward the door. Thievery in the house – that was the last straw. 'Rose!'

Rose stepped out of the den, a swatch of fabric in her hand. 'What's wrong?' she asked. 'What's happened?'

'Thievery, that's what. My books, stolen.'

'*All* of them?'

'No, just selected volumes. He knew what he was after. It was your man in the hat. It had to be. I thought you said he only fingered the books in the library.'

'Well he did,' said Rose. 'At least while I was there. He might have sneaked in, I guess, while I assumed he was on the porch with Mr Pennyman.'

'I dare say he did. Let *me* interview these people from now on, will you? We'll be robbed blind at this rate.'

Rose turned back toward the den. 'Gladly,' she said. 'Interview anyone you please.'

'And I *will*, too,' shouted Andrew, thinking immediately that the retort sounded weak and foolish. He wasn't sure *he* knew what he meant by it. By golly he wouldn't be robbed though, not in his own house. And by a fat man in an Oriental robe, too, and wearing a clown hat. What was the world coming to? Was it rotting away under his nose? He slammed upstairs and into Aunt Naomi's room, ready to give hell to the cats if they asked for it. But they'd gone out the window, apparently, and Aunt Naomi was asleep in the chair. He picked up her half-empty plate and went back out, muttering his way down the stairs.

He laid the plate on the kitchen counter and stepped outside into the backyard where he opened the lid to the trash can, thinking that he'd been hasty to throw out the bag of poison, though he had no clear idea why at that moment he wanted to keep it – who or what he wanted to poison. The thief, certainly, was long gone by now.

He realized suddenly that he was striding around aimlessly, as if frantic to keep the world from collapsing on his head but not knowing what to prop up first. He had to do *something*, though. He was apparently living in a world full of rats, and they were growing more bold by the day. The trash can was empty. The poison was gone. Surprised, he checked the other can. The 'possum was gone, too. Rat control must have come around for the 'possum, found the pitched-out poison and taken it, too. Well to hell with them.

He slumped back inside. It was just nine o'clock, and all in all the most hellish night he'd spent in months. Rose would be going up to bed within the half hour, and wouldn't speak to him first. She was miffed. But by golly, her inviting criminals in to have a go at his books – that was no damn good. He walked into the library and sat down, realizing at once that he couldn't sit. He needed a walk, that's what. A walk in the fog. He loved the smell of fog on concrete with the smell of the ocean just beyond. It was like an elixir.

He started for the front door, realizing as he reached for the doorknob that he couldn't just walk out. Rose would think he'd left in anger and there'd be no way later to insist that he'd just gone out to clear his head. He turned around and poked into the den, where she sat sewing up a slipcase for the cushion on the library window seat.

'Thought I'd step out for a bit,' Andrew said, grinning at her.

'That would be nice.'

'Just for a walk. I've got to think this out.'

'What a good idea.'

'That damned robed man ...'

Rose shook her head and frowned. Then she held up the business she was sewing and turned it right-side-out, inspecting the seam at the corner. She didn't say anything more.

After a moment Andrew ducked away and out the front door, into the misty evening. He felt more doomful than ever. It seemed as if there were forces that conspired against him. He remembered suddenly Aunt Naomi's two thousand dollars, and it seemed that perhaps some few things had gone right that day after all.

But then, as if all the ghastly business this evening had seen its opportunity and leaped in to pollute things utterly, the money in his wallet was suddenly loathsome to him. What did it mean but that he was dependent on old Aunt Naomi? Here was Rose, sewing away in the den, *doing* something, for goodness sake. And what was he? – a man who lounged around and hoodwinked money out of an old cockeyed woman whom he pretended to despise but didn't. *He* was the despicable one. He was mean and base; there were no two ways about it. Rose had seen through him at last. He would be a lucky man if she ever spoke to him again. She hadn't stolen his books either. She put up with them, in fact. They cluttered up every room in the house. Rose didn't say a word about them. She dusted them. She shelved them happily when he left them lying around. It wasn't *her* fault if men from secret societies sneaked in and pinched them.

And what about this 'society' business? What about the funny hat and the robe? There was a good deal too much of that sort of thing in the wind recently: Pickett with his talk about blowfish; Pennyman lounging about in the dark with the air of a man possessed of secret knowledge; Aunt Naomi with her spoon and her sudden fear of silver quarters; and now this Atlantean, or whatever he was, snatching books. He seemed to know what he was after, too, as if he'd been in the house before, perhaps, and had snooped things out.

The fog hovered heavy and wet. There wasn't a breath of a sea breeze. He walked down the alley, past the back of Señor Corky's, and then left on Main Street, past Walt's and the Potholder and a half-dozen darkened stores and out onto the old pier, scuffing along. What did it mean? Was Pickett right? Was something going on? Something secret and vast? Did a scattering of ancient men control the turnings of the world, and if so, what were they doing in Seal Beach? The idea struck him suddenly as being very funny. He nearly laughed out loud; only the night was so dark and foggy and silent that laughter wouldn't have worked. It would have made things horrible.

But the thought of it – a few old men like master puppeteers, working the rest of them, making them caper and dance and bow and scrape, as if humanity were a sort of enormous farce and in the sad position of never being able to see the joke because they *were* the joke. Somehow it seemed reasonable enough, especially on such a night as this.

Well, so be it. What did he care? *Someone* had to run the show. It might as well be these wandering Caretakers. Andrew couldn't begin to run an inn. It was a damned good thing that the business of running the world hadn't been left to *him*. Rose might make a go of it. All in all, though, it made little difference who was pulling the strings, as long as they left him alone, as long as they didn't yank the wrong string and bring the whole thing down in a heap. But they weren't entirely letting him alone, were they?

He found himself at the end of the pier, by Len's Bait House, staring off into the mist. He could just see the gray Pacific below, the ground swell humping through oily and smooth, almost the same color as the fog. The scarred iron railing, beaded with mist, lay cold beneath his hands and the air smelled of fish. Along the side of the bait house, water drip-dripped into a vast sink where fishermen, on more hospitable evenings, cleaned their catch.

All at once the shifting ocean seemed to him to symbolize all the mysteries in the universe. He recalled reading, as a boy, an account of the netting of a marine coelacanth by fishermen off the coast of eastern Africa. There had been a drawing of a black fish with an odd arrangement of fins and great scales the size of thumbnails and a mouthful of teeth. Science had been surprised. Such a fish was extinct. It had been relegated to the job of being a fossil. Now here was one in a net, which meant that there were more in the depths of the ocean, swimming through the dark waters among – what? Who could say?

The surprising thing was that anyone had been surprised. The fishermen, certainly, weren't surprised. They'd spent their lives on the ocean, bobbing along in small boats, peering over the side into seas of sargasso weed, tangled in the topmost branches of kelp forests, watching the sun sink and the night drift in and the green-tinged moon rising out of the water like a transmarine Venus and hearing the quiet splash of restless things disturbing the surface of the dark waters and then disappearing again into the depths.

They must have wondered a thousand times at the shadows that shifted beneath the evening swell, beneath their puny tacked-together boat. Nothing that came from the sea would really have surprised them. Something in them would have nodded and said, 'At last. Here it is. It's come.' That's how Andrew felt – as if nothing at all would surprise him: aliens landing in saucers, pigs bringing around a spoon early in the morning, the discovery that the Wandering Jew was at work tinkering with the earth as if it were a clockwork mechanism. He had read in a book of myths the story of a wizard who had gone out fishing on the Mediterranean Sea, trolling with a magical coin. The wizard had caught an enormous fish – the Leviathan itself – and just as the beast had swallowed the coin, a great, shadowy counterpoint fish had descended out of the shadows of the heavens and swallowed the moon. Coins, coins, coins. And now this telephone call from the man Pfennig. It was maddening, but it would put itself right in time. Everything put itself right in time. Either that or it didn't.

Andrew shivered. He'd forgotten to put on his jacket. He was wearing his bedroom slippers and it felt to him suddenly as if the loose, slip-on shoes were full of fog, as if he were tramping down the pier wearing a pair of ghostly fishbowls. Rose would have gone up to bed by now. She'd be asleep. He dreaded having to wake her up to set things straight. He wouldn't let the night slip by without it, though. There'd be no weighty silence at breakfast.

He turned around to set a course for home, nearly pitching over onto his face at the sight of Pennyman, holding his stick in one hand and with his reeking pipe in his mouth, not fifteen feet distant, all alone on the pier. He wore his white coat and he bent over the railing as if to catch a glimpse of the sea. It looked to Andrew as if he held a spool of fishing line and was dangling it over the side, thinking to hook a flounder, perhaps, and then pull it in with his hands. Lamplight shone off whatever it was that was tied onto the end of the line – a fishing lure, maybe a bass spoon; it was too dim and foggy for Andrew to see it clearly. There sounded the plunk of it hitting the water and it seemed that at that instant the pier shook, as if a monumental wave had broken across the pilings. It was coincidence, of course, as if the universe were playing along with Pennyman, abetting him in his posing and pretense.

Andrew decided that he wouldn't even ask about Pennyman's fishing. He would ignore Pennyman and all of his affairs. He was one down every time he showed an interest in the man. Without looking up, Pennyman said, 'Out for a stroll, are you?' and he tugged a couple of times on his line.

'That's right.' Andrew's heart flailed like a machine stamping out nails. He set out at once toward Main Street. He could see the comfortable glow of streetlamps disappearing down toward the highway, and the headlights of a car that motored toward the mouth of the pier then swung off down the alley.

'Looking for something?' asked Pennyman as Andrew strode past.

'No, just walking. Getting a little air.'

'Something *in* the air tonight, isn't there?'

'Fog,' said Andrew, nodding and clumping away, wishing he weren't abroad in his bedroom slippers. He thought suddenly of what the fog must have done to his hair, but he chased the thought off, noticing that it hadn't, somehow, ruined *Pennyman's* hair, and wondering why that was. There *was* something in the air tonight; just as Pennyman had said. And it wasn't just fog and darkness, either. It had been drifting in for a week or more, and it would no doubt keep on drifting in until its features coalesced out of the gray and it made itself known.

The moon peeked through the parting mist just as Andrew stepped off the pier and out onto the sand, as if it were having a quick glance at what sort of man it was who was out fishing after mysteries. A wave broke softly along the shore, glowing with an eerie phosphorescence in the light of the moon, which looked uncommonly pale and distant and lonesome up there, winking and bobbing in the briefly starry heavens like the reflection of a dream. Then, in the slip of an instant, the fog billowed through again, swallowing the moon utterly. Andrew set out for home, scuffing along the deserted beach. He could just see the dim figure of Pennyman slouched over the railing at the end of the pier. In the now moonless night the waves no longer glowed, but out in the water, beneath the rolling swell, there gleamed a whitish light, as if a company of water goblins were gathering mussels from the pier pilings by the guttering light of an undersea candle, or as if some glowing, deep-water monster had drifted up out of a submarine grotto, attracted by Pennyman's lure.

The house was dark – everyone asleep. Pennyman, of course, was out fooling away the night on the pier, up to whatever it was he was up to. As Andrew stood outside, leaning against the curb tree looking at the house, he wondered exactly what it was he'd say to Rose. He decided to have a drink first – a glass of beer, maybe. He still was on the edge of feeling foul. The walk hadn't entirely done the trick. His books were gone; Pennyman had made a fool of him; and worst, he'd made a fool of himself, whining at Rose about nonsense.

He half-wished he smoked a pipe; it would be just the thing – outdoors on a night like this. It would be a comfort. But he numbered smoking among the vices he'd been spared, and he put the thought aside. There was a rustling off in the bushes – no doubt one of Naomi's cats, out fouling the flowerbeds. Damn them. He'd have to hit Farm Supply for some of those anti-cat stakes. If he couldn't bring himself to trap the creatures, then the least he could do was make it clear to them who ran the show – put them in their place.

But it wasn't a cat. It appeared just then, a 'possum, sniffing along behind its foolish pointy nose. It was a big one, out marauding. It wandered along to the crawlspace under the house, where it hooked its paw behind the wood-framed screen that covered the space and tore the screen loose, frame and all, ducking away into the darkness. Andrew went across and examined the frame and screen. It had never been fixed properly to the house, just tilted in, sort of holding itself up – as barriers went, it was apparently no match for a determined 'possum.

In the soft dirt around the space were a dozen of the creature's footprints, plain as day. Maybe Pickett was right; maybe he *would* show them to Rose. That would cement things. All suspicion would be swept away. He tilted the little door back into its hiatus and then stood up, debating with himself. He was a fan of 'possums. He liked the idea that there were wild creatures out and about in the neighborhood, living in the urban sprawl of Southern California as if the coastal chaparral and grasslands hadn't been swept away a hundred years earlier.

He remembered the first time he'd seen the flock of wild parrots fly past overhead. It had been in the autumn, some years back. There was something mystical about the green, raucous flock of tropical birds cutting across the gray skies above Long Beach, winging down to roost in the broken-out windows of an abandoned building. Parrots and 'possums – they were a sort of weird counterpoint to the deadening, soulless technology of the modern age.

He grinned. It *must* be late, for him to start dredging up shopworn philosophies over a 'possum living under the house. Having made up his mind, he bent down again and dusted away the thing's footprints. He wouldn't tell Rose after all. She might have taken him seriously about what sorts of monsters 'possums were, and demand that he trap them, get them out of there. And they were sort of an ace in the hole anyway. When push came to shove, and it was generally assumed that he was a madman, he could lead them all to the crawlspace and point. The nest of 'possums would be vindication.

Vindication, though, wasn't worth much to him at the moment. In fact, thinking about it made it all come flooding back in again, all of the day's lost battles. He went inside and into the kitchen to pour that drink. Drink, fortunately, was not one of the vices he'd foresworn. He jerked open the kitchen cupboard door and surveyed the glasses, wavering between the temptation of beer out of pilsner glasses and wine out of cut-glass stemware. Both had their advantages. The right glass was almost as important as the right drink.

It would be a glass of wine, he decided, instead of beer. Beer had a deadening effect on him; wine seemed to settle him down. It filled him almost at once with a sense of proportion. It was a balancing effect, a keel-evener. Except that if he drank too much of it he overbalanced and sank.

The wine glasses were wedged in behind non-descript, dimestore quality tumblers, and when he edged the tumblers out of the way with his hand, one toppled off into the sink, shattering into fragments. He stopped dead, not even breathing, waiting for the rustling to begin. Mrs Gummidge would scurry in, chattering like a gibbon ape, lunging after the broom and dustpan, saying, 'You just leave *that* little mess to me, Mr Vanbergen. *I'll* see to it. Dropped a glass did you? Well, care killed the cat, as they say,' and uttering this lunacy she'd shoulder him out of the way and turn the whole business into a production, further ruining the evening.

She didn't awaken, though. There was no rustling, no whispering, no sudden illumination. He'd have to clean the glass up himself.

He pulled out a paper sack and started fingering the larger pieces very daintily out of the sink, shoving the tip of his thumb almost immediately into a glass sliver. He blushed with heat, feeling the sliver half-buried there and not wanting to look at it. In a moment he held his thumb to the light. There it was. If he hadn't kept his fingernails chewed short, he might have plucked it out. As it was he had to go for the tweezers. Taking care not to brush his thumb against anything, he knocked the bathroom door open with his knee. Then, holding the tweezers in his left hand, he worried the piece of glass out, a drop of blood bubbling slowly out in its wake. He squeezed his thumb against the possibility of blood poisoning, and, cursing, dropped the glass sliver into the trash, put away the tweezers, and walked back into the kitchen. He wouldn't touch another piece of glass. There was nothing more treacherous than broken glass. He seemed to have gotten all the sizeable fragments anyway. He turned on the water, washing the last few chips down into the garbage disposer. Then he flipped it on. Immediately there was a terrible grinding and howling. He hadn't gotten all the big pieces after all. The disposer ground to a sudden stop, locked tight against a wedge of glass.

He stood in silence, listening to the laboring of the engine, thinking vaguely that he'd let it go until it overheated and burned itself out. That would show it. He'd catch hell for it, though, and it would mean having a man in to fix it, and the man would no doubt steal a half dozen of his books on the way out. So he reached up and flipped off the switch. He'd get a pipe wrench, is what he'd do, and beat the living daylights out of the garbage disposer. That was the only sane course. Except that it would awaken the house. That wouldn't do at all. Mrs Gummidge would appear and, wiggling something, would have the disposer running again. Had he tried to grind up a glass? Had he this? Had he that? Didn't it seem as if the trash bag under the sink? …

Shaking, he opened the cupboard door to confront the glasses once again. There were the tumblers standing like so many smug little swaggering fools. There was nothing at all to recommend them, not even age. They were a sort of olive green, splashed with gold glitter – a half-wit's idea of elegance. He and Rose had gotten them as a wedding gift – from a blind man, it would seem. Andrew had always detested them. There'd been eight of them, and in the long years since only one of them had broken – the one he'd dumped into the sink. At that rate, losing one, say, every fifteen years, there would still be a set of them, four at least, when he was dead. The idea of it appalled him. And that was if he lived to be ninety. He'd die broken and gibbering, and in the cupboard, barely showing the use they'd had, these foul tumblers would wait, knowing that, barring major earthquakes, they'd see another sixty years out easily enough. He couldn't stand it.

He *wouldn't* stand it. He hauled two of them down – it would be madness to do for all seven of them at once – and he carried them out the back door. In the garage he found a gunnysack and an old paint-stained T-shirt. He wrapped the glasses in the rag, put the rag into the gunnysack, and, after laying it on the sidewalk just off the back porch, he wrestled a melon-sized chunk of smooth granite out of the flower bed, ascended the porch, and dropped the rock onto the glasses. There was the satisfying thunk of something smashing; not the tinkle of flying fragments, but the deadening smash of the glasses having gone flat. He felt as if he were striking a blow, literally, for – what? – art, maybe. Sensibility. General principles. He retrieved the rock and carried it up the stairs for another go, dropping it just as the porch light blinked on.

The rock thumped down again, rolling off onto the grass. Rose stood in the open door, looking puzzled. Andrew grinned at her, feeling like the prince of fools. He started to speak, but managed only to croak and shrug. He searched desperately for a plausible lie. Fish in the sack, perhaps. He'd gone fishing and caught two bonita and he wanted to kill them and clean them. No use letting that sort of job go until morning. Best get them into the freezer tonight. It wouldn't wash, though, him killing them with a rock as big as his head.

'What are you doing?' asked Rose, utterly humorless.

'Nothing,' said Andrew. 'That is to say, I'm messing with an idea I've had about glass – about building odds and ends out of shattered glass and melted lead. I got the idea down on the pier tonight. There was a burner for sale at the bait house, for melting lead into fishing weights. Why not cast it into shapes, I thought, mold it around scatterings of colored glass? Paperweights, bookends, doorstops – all that sort of thing.' He smiled at her and stepped off the porch, fetching up the stone again, very purposefully, and setting it back into the flowerbed.

'Pickett called,' said Rose. 'He wanted to tell you about a pair of apes that escaped into San Francisco. A psychic, apparently, had a vision of them eating ravioli in a North Beach restaurant.'

'He called to tell me that? What was the point of it?'

'I'm not sure. I thought at first it was a joke – apes and psychics and ravioli and all that – only there didn't seem to be any punch line. Maybe I've told it wrong. He seemed to be fascinated by it all and assumed you would be, too. Anyway, I'm going back to bed. I heard the noise and I didn't know what it was.' She looked over the porch railing at the gunnysack. Then she yawned, shoved either hand up the opposite sleeve of her bathrobe, and walked away into the darkened house without saying anything else.

Andrew heard a cupboard door open in the kitchen, and then, a moment later, shut again. He looked down at the gunnysack. It was a sad, foolish object, lying there on the fog-damp sidewalk. Rose would know what he'd been up to, and her knowing would foil any future efforts at smashing up the glasses. If he broke one by accident now it would seem as if he'd gone mad and done it on purpose. He was as transparent as a sandwich bag. He'd have to use Aunt Naomi's money now to buy the sinker molder at Len's. Then he'd have to fake up some way to build something out of lead and broken glass, as he'd said. What it would be he hadn't any earthly idea, but he *had* to do it. If he didn't do it, he was doomed. He couldn't be caught in a lie. He had to turn the lie inside out, to meddle with reality until things were put right. Just like he'd done with the 'possum. He could do that again with the broken glass. If there was method to his madness, then it couldn't be madness after all, could it?

As he dumped the gunnysack onto the bench in the garage he wondered if that's how Pickett's Caretakers worked. If they effected vast upheavals of economies or governments or whatever they did by setting into motion, say, a trifling little calculated lie, or a wink tipped in just the right direction – some little bit of gravel, which, bouncing down a broadening hillside, would knock loose rocks and boulders, one of which, out of nowhere, would whack on the head some poor banker in a three-piece suit as he stood contemplating interest rates. Maybe he'd drop dead on the spot, and when alerted associates began to suspect that the stone out of nowhere signified something, there would begin a surreptitious movement of money in and out of vaults and through the electronic links of computer networks until the public got wind of it and undertook a fear-induced run on the bank. Just like that, an empire would sink in the dust, ruined entrepreneurs would leap out of windows, third-world governments would topple, and no one ever suspecting that the first jolly pebbles were kicked loose by a pottering old man in baggy trousers, pruning rose bushes with one hand and manipulating the lever-action works of the universe with the other.

Two weeks earlier, Uncle Arthur had bought twenty-two Exer-Genies from a door-to-door salesman. In the Leisure World retirement community door-to-door salesmen were frowned on. There was a wall around the place to keep them out. One had got in, though, past the guards, with a trunk full of these Exer-Genies, which a person would recline on in the interest of being folded up over and over again at the waist, fearfully fast, until he was healthy again. Uncle Arthur had bought the lot of them. He had become 'the West Coast rep,' as the salesman had said. And now the devices were stacked in the plywood cabinet screwed to the wall of the carport.

He'd done it on the afternoon of a full moon. Rose had pointed that out. Uncle Arthur was an old man. Rose couldn't remember a time when Uncle Arthur *hadn't* been an old man. It had always been common knowledge in the family that his age seemed to affect him most when the moon was full. When there was no moon, or just a sliver of it, he seemed chipper and spry and canny. It was a strange business. Andrew couldn't puzzle it out, except that it seemed to imply that the derivation of the word 'lunatic' was a product of something more than mere superstition. That's how it went sometimes; there was often some little grain of truth behind the wildest folktales.

Uncle Arthur shouldn't live alone, Rose had said in reference to his moon-madness and to his buying the Exer-Genies. The family had shaken its head – the poor old man, swindled again. Last time it was a case of rechargeable batteries and a device to do the recharging, which had burst into flames after having been left plugged in all night and had nearly burned the house down.

Pickett knew better than the family. Senility, he said, didn't enter in. One didn't second-guess Uncle Arthur – not even Pickett, who suspected he knew who Uncle Arthur *really* was – *what* he was – although he said he couldn't tell anyone yet, not even Andrew. Why the twenty-two Exer-Genies had to have been bought, Pickett couldn't say. Where they were bound was an utter mystery. They might very well sit in their plywood cupboard until doomsday, what did it matter to you and me? They'd sit there because they *had* to sit there, because when it came to Uncle Arthur's dealings, said Pickett, *nothing* he did or said was random and without purpose. Everything was calculated. That's what Pickett had said about the Exer-Genies and about Uncle Arthur's late night sojourns in his red, electronic car. Don't question the Exer-Genies, that had been Pickett's advice, at least that had been his advice until the arrival of Pennyman. Then Pickett had begun to question everything.

There were simpler answers, of course. There nearly always were, but Pickett didn't see any value in them. Uncle Arthur had been a prodigious traveling salesman in his day – going door to door, town to town, state to state, and, years past, continent to continent, wandering the earth like a tinker, peddling his wares. There was nothing he hadn't sold, to hear Aunt Naomi tell it, no front stoop he hadn't stood on, no bell he hadn't rung. He had accumulated the careers of ten standard-issue salesmen stacked one on top of the other, and there was scarcely a corner of the globe, no matter how far-flung, that he hadn't memories of.

Such instincts die hard, Andrew thought, wandering through the quiet house, carrying a glass of beer. The wine that had been in the refrigerator was gone – Mrs Gummidge again, no doubt. It was after midnight, and he couldn't sleep. Squaring it with Rose had become impossible, what with their confrontation on the back porch. He sat down in the library, staring up at the books. He would read something to take his mind off things. It should be something substantial, nothing unsettling. Dickens would do – some funny Dickens. Or *The Wind in the Willows*. That was the ticket. It was clover-strewn meadows that he needed, running down into babbling rivers. It was talk of firesides and Christmas and glasses of ale, of picnics and boating and jolly companions. Things were out of balance, and if he didn't have a glass of wine to put them right, then a book would have to do.

He opened the book at random – he'd read it often enough so that beginnings and endings meant nothing any more – and found himself dabbling through 'The Piper at the Gates of Dawn.' Ratty and Mole were off to find the baby otter, lost down the river. Dawn was near. The world was turning toward the morning. There was faint music on the breeze, which stirred through the rushes. Something was pending – something … For a moment Andrew thought he knew what it was, that something. He *did* know, but he couldn't at all put it into words. It wasn't something you knew in your mind; you felt it with your spine, maybe, and with your stomach. And it wasn't the obscure machinations of men like Pennyman that you felt, either; it was something else, something that such men were ignorant of, or that they hated – that they didn't have or want any part of, that they wanted to ruin. For that moment at least, Andrew knew that he himself wanted a part of it very badly, whatever it was. He closed the book and sat there. The late hour lent itself nicely to that sort of thing – to things of the spirit, so to speak. When the day dawned with its garages needing to be painted and its men in mystical hats coming around after rooms for rent, the feeling would be gone, dissipated, hovering just out of sight. But he would stumble upon it again when he wasn't at all expecting it – the promise of heaven on the soft wind, 'the place of my song-dream,' as Rat put it.

Andrew glanced up, surprised to see a light on in the kitchen. He'd turned it off an hour earlier. It must be late, one or two in the morning. There was the scraping of a chair being pushed back and of a spoon clanking against the side of a bowl. He stood up and tiptoed along. It might easily be Pennyman. Andrew had had enough of Pennyman for one day.

But it wasn't. It was Aunt Naomi in a bathrobe. Andrew stood gaping for a moment, startled by the idea of Aunt Naomi out and about. She so rarely left her room that he'd begun to think of her as another fixture there, and he'd have been no more surprised to see her nightstand or her coatrack dressed in night clothes and wandering through the kitchen. She was after a bowl of cereal. There were a half-dozen boxes on the table and she sat looking at them, unable, perhaps, to decide. The sight of them reminded Andrew that he was ravenous. It seemed to him that he hadn't eaten in months. Cereal would be just the thing.

'Hello,' he said, smiling in at her.

She looked up sharply, surprised, it seemed, to be caught in the act of eating breakfast cereal at such an hour.

'Having a bowl of something?'

She nodded. 'In fact I am.'

'Mind if I join you then?'

'Not at all,' she said, nodding toward the chair opposite. She seemed almost friendly, as if the act of eating breakfast cereal was naturally cheering.

'I'm a Cheerios man myself,' said Andrew, digging a bowl out of the cupboard. 'Most people pour the milk on first, then sprinkle on the sugar. I do it the other way around, to wash the sugar to the bottom. Then you can scrape it up later, when you're spooning out the milk. It's wonderful that way.' It occurred to him as he said this that it was just the sort of thing that Rose had warned him against – the sort of nutty talk that a woman like Aunt Naomi wouldn't understand.

She nodded her head, though, as if she *did* understand, and she picked up the box of Wheat Chex and dumped out a third of a bowlful. 'The trick,' she said, 'is not to fill the bowl. You want a taste of each of them. It's a matter of temperance, really. You don't want to give into the urge to stuff yourself with the first sort you pick up.'

This advice sounded rock-solid to Andrew, who'd always felt more or less the same way. He was happily surprised to discover that Aunt Naomi possessed some cereal lore. 'What about flakes? I've always said that the problem with bran flakes is that they didn't hold up. Immediately soggy.'

She nodded again. 'You put in too much milk,' she said, 'and drown them. Use less, then dig for the milk with your spoon. Leave half the flakes high and dry. They've gotten round that with Wheaties, I've noticed. They hold up longer. And with sugar-sweetened cereals, too. It's the sugar glaze that keeps the milk out. Until it melts off, of course. I've never had much faith in them, though. I've felt that it was gimmickry from the outset.'

Andrew shrugged, not wanting to contradict her. In fact, he was partial to both Trix and Sugar Pops. But he was still half-afraid of setting her off, despite the growing evidence of her sanity. His coming in on the side of sugar-sweetened cereal might cause unlooked-for trouble. 'Do you remember Ruskets?' he asked.

'Those little biscuits of pressed-together flakes?'

'Indeed I do.' She paused and squinted at him. 'Were you a crusher or a non-crusher?'

'A non-crusher. Absolutely. The only way to do it was to lean them against the sides of the bowl, so that half of them were out of the milk, like you were saying before, then skive off sections with a spoon so that you got a little bit of the dry flakes with the rest. There was always a heap of soggy flakes in the bottom, of course, but that couldn't be helped. Have you, by any chance, come across Weetabix?'

'Not in years,' she said, remembering. 'I ate them in London, when I was feeling better. I used to travel a good bit, alas. That's the problem with being bedridden. The world isn't your oyster any longer.'

'Well,' said Andrew, 'it happens that I've got a line on some Weetabix. For the cafe. My friend Pickett is driving them down from Canada. I think I can keep you supplied, actually.'

'I'd like that. A person has so few surprises nowadays, so few little comforts.'

'It must be rotten,' said Andrew. 'I don't at all mean to be nosey, Aunt, and you can tell me to mind my own business, but I've never entirely understood what it was that ailed you. It must be something fairly grim, to keep you holed up like that.'

She shook her head, staring out toward the kitchen door. 'It's merely a cross,' she said euphemistically, 'that I've had to bear.'

'I see,' said Andrew, who actually saw nothing at all. He decided not to press the issue, though, just in case there was nothing, really, to see, or in case it was some sort of vaguely indefinable female trouble that he didn't want to hear about anyway. 'How did the chocolates agree with you?'

'They were quite moderately nice, thank you. You say your new chef made them?'

Andrew blinked at her. Lies seemed to have a way of perpetuating themselves. He was stricken with the urge to haul out his wallet and give Aunt Naomi the leftover fourteen hundred dollars and to admit everything. He gasped instead and grinned and nodded, and just then Rose walked in, squinting in the light, and saved him. 'Well!' he said, standing up. It was awfully good to see Rose all of a sudden, and not only because her arrival clipped off the French chef discussion. It was a chance to make amends. 'Bowl of cereal?'

She looked at the table, winked pleasantly at Aunt Naomi, and said, 'Yes, I believe so. That looks awfully good.'

Andrew scrambled around after another bowl and spoon. Anticipating her, he picked up the box of Grapenuts and inclined his head at it. She smiled and nodded, yawning and putting her hand over her mouth. 'Aunt Naomi and I have just been discussing the mysteries of breakfast cereals,' said Andrew.

'She's something of an authority.'

They ate in silence for a moment, and there was no sound but the scraping of bowls. A cat wandered in just then, looking around. Andrew bent down to pet it. He laid his cereal bowl on the linoleum floor. The cereal was gone, but it was still half full of sweetened milk. The cat sniffed it and then set in to lap it up, pausing now and then to look around, as if wondering why it was he hadn't made this a regular practice long ago.

'I'm finished,' said Aunt Naomi, standing up and leaning on her cane. She looked dangerously thin, with sharp cheekbones and an aristocratic face that made it clear she was once frighteningly handsome. Andrew was struck with her resemblance to Rose. Both of them were tall and patrician, as if they'd come from some royal family in the mountains of Bohemia. But whereas Naomi was polished and prim, Rose was slightly disheveled and earthy. Taken together like this, they made Andrew feel just a little bit like a bumpkin.

'This has been delightful,' Aunt Naomi continued. 'Perhaps we'll meet again like this. I'm feeling very much better this evening. Better than I've felt in thirty years. It's as if I've had a fever for years and it's finally broken. Good night, Rosannah, Andrew.' And with that she hobbled away, shaking her head at Rose's offer to help her up the stairs. Rose let her go.

'Time for bed, don't you think?' she asked, smiling at Andrew. 'You've had a tiring day.'

Andrew shrugged. That was the truth. 'So have you,' he said.

'That's why I've been sleeping. You've been wearing yourself out, wrestling with things. Quit thinking so much. Sleep more. Why don't you go fishing more often? Do you remember when we used to get up in the morning and be out on the pier at dawn? Why don't we do that any more?'

'Not tomorrow, you don't mean. Not at dawn?'

'No, not tomorrow. But sometime.'

'Of course,' said Andrew. 'I didn't think you liked that sort of thing anymore.'

'Quit thinking, then, as I said. It's not doing you any good. You're full of anticipation – worrying about things that haven't happened yet and probably won't. You're half wornout just getting ready to dodge phantoms. You don't have to dodge me. You know that, don't you?'

'Sure,' Andrew mumbled, unable to say anything more. He *did* know it, too. What he didn't know was why he so often failed to remember it.

'You're probably right.' He stood up and cleared away the dishes, running water into them and stacking them in the sink. 'Look,' he said, 'paper towels. I'm being good.' And he yanked two towels off the roll, dried his hands, and threw them into the trash. Rose shook her head, giving him a mock-serious look.

He was frightfully tired all of a sudden. It had been a long day. With Rose following, he wandered into the library to turn out the reading lamp. On an impulse, he read her a bit out of his book, and she took the book from him and read a little more to herself. Then she shelved the book and switched off the lamp, and the two of them went up to bed.

BOOK II

Reason Not The Need

'Oh, reason not the need! Our basest beggars
Are in the poorest thing superfluous.'

WILLIAM SHAKESPEARE,
THE TRAGEDY OF KING LEAR

SIX

'Let James rejoice with the Haddock, who brought the piece of money to the Lord and Peter.'

CHRISTOPHER SMART,
'JUBILATE AGNO'

All in all, the changes in Vancouver appealed to him – the ruination of Gastown especially. Every second shop was littered with tourist goods, with ceramic dolls and souvenir plates, with idiot wood carvings of non-existent totem poles and with pot metal ferry boats – the china-hutch dreams of travelers who preferred a homogenized, cleaned-up waterfront to what had been the dark and gritty reality of the place. Jules Pennyman was indifferent to the place itself, except that in general he preferred a sterilized world with the wrinkles ironed out of it. The deadening, prefabricated emptiness of the new tourist-appealing waterfront was just the sort of thing he approved of. It had become a place almost without spirit, a shallow place of surfaces and mirrors. Although some of the old shops were left – a few bookstores and bars – they'd be modernized and sanitized in time, too, and the sooner the better.

His meeting with August Pfennig had been interesting. Pennyman hadn't wasted words; he'd finished his dealings with Pfennig and slipped away, the whole business reminiscent of his meeting with Aureus in Jerusalem. He had driven south, boarded a ferry, and now had stopped at Vashon Island with about an hour to spare before the outward-bound ferry departed for Seattle. His flight left Seattle/Tacoma in four hours.

Fifty yards away, at the base of a hill, sat his rented limousine, its driver polishing the dust from the fenders with a rag. Pennyman sat on his unfolded handkerchief atop a step stool outside the rusty, white-painted metal shed that passed for a gas station. There were two pumps anchored in dirty asphalt, and beyond the asphalt was forest and more forest, with here and there a house hidden in the trees. It was too idyllic – all the greenery and outdoorsy atmosphere of the place, but its lonesome silence was attractive, empty and cold as it was and devoid of human illusion. Away behind him stretched Puget Sound, the gray and shifting home of pilot whales and porpoise and octopi. There was too much life beneath the surface of the sea to satisfy Pennyman. He could barely stand thinking about it.

The Cascades, snowcapped and stretching away south toward Oregon, were what the common man would call majestic and sublime. Pennyman didn't believe in such things; he despised the tendency of stupid people to want to turn dirt and rock into something more than it was. His shoes were murdering his feet, and he'd run out of Pepto-Bismol on the ferry. His throat was full of acid. This morning his hair seemed to have gotten back some of its life. It had begun to fall out in clumps, just before he'd paid his visit to Adams and then traded the carp for another bottle of the elixir. It hadn't seemed to have the same restorative effect on his feet, though. And of course it wouldn't have. He didn't dare remove his shoes, although it felt as if there were a rock in each, jammed in against his toes. It was as if his shoes were three sizes too small now and shoved onto the wrong feet. He thought he knew why.

He looked at his watch. It wouldn't do to miss his plane. There was no use exciting suspicions among the members of his new-found family in California – Rose especially. He rather liked the look of her, and there was a certain satisfaction in using her to torment her idiot husband. Alone, Andrew was too easy a mark; there was more sport in bringing the whole family down together.

Someone was coming from up the road. It was the gas station attendant and the boy. The boy had been the only witness to the sinking of a rowboat and the drowning of an old man, whom Pennyman knew to be a bearded Caretaker named Simon Denarius. Pfennig had told him that much before they'd parted company.

There had been a trifling little article in yesterday's *Tribune*. Pennyman would have missed it, except that Pfennig had circled it in red ink, and left the newspaper laid open on the countertop in his shop. There was damn-all Pennyman could do about it now, of course, except to make certain. A fish had been caught, according to the article, fouled in a drag net in Puget Sound. It had been enormous – the few eyewitnesses had agreed to that. It might have been a whale, they supposed, except that it was impossibly large and was coruscated with undersea life, as if it wore a thousand years of coral polyps and hydra and sea fans and blue-green algae – a deep-ocean coat of many colors.

They had towed it to Vashon Island and cut it open, only to find another fish in its vast stomach, and then another fish in *its* stomach and yet another and another, like a set of dwindling, Peruvian gourd dolls. Out of the stomach of that last fish – so the newspaper article read – they'd taken an old silver coin. Early the next morning the coin was bought for an unlikely sum by an old man with a vast beard like an Old Testament prophet, who'd come in out of the fog on the Seattle ferry. Directly afterward he'd rented a rowboat and gone fishing. That was the end of Simon Denarius.

The boy who finally stood goggling in front of Pennyman had a baseball cap cocked around sideways and pulled down over one ear. His jeans were torn out at the knees, and there were dirty, candy-stained smears around his leering mouth and down his chin. He chewed moodily on something – his tongue, maybe, or a half-dozen sticks of gum wadded together. Dull wasn't the word for his eyes; vacant was better. Probably inbred, Pennyman thought, repelled by the boy, who might have been eight. Pennyman shivered inadvertently and a wash of acid churned up into his throat. Children in general were intolerable, but a filthy, gum-chewing urchin like this was an argument for something. A hundred and fifty years ago he might have been crippled and set to begging, but in the modern world he was merely useless, a bit of filth. Pennyman smiled at him. 'So you saw the big fish, did you?'

'I ain't saying nothing.'

'You're not?'

'I ain't saying I ain't, but I ain't saying I am, neither.'

The gas station attendant grinned stupidly. 'That's it, Jimmy,' he said, nodding and blinking his eyes. 'What'd I tell you?'

The boy looked up at Pennyman, screwing his eyes half-shut, and spit between his teeth at the ground, the result landing on his own foot. 'How much will you pay me? If you don't pay, I ain't telling you nothing.'

'Pay is it!' laughed Pennyman, pretending to be vastly amused. 'This is a surprise.'

'It ain't no damn surprise,' said the gas station man, running a greasy hand through his hair. 'This is business. The boy got a living to earn, ain't that right, Jimmy?'

'Yep,' said Jimmy, and he chewed his gum and squinted. 'Maybe I see the old man go out, maybe I was asleep, maybe you can kiss my ass.'

'How much do you want?' said Pennyman flatly. He'd had enough of both of them.

'Soak him, Jimmy!' said the attendant, and he slapped Pennyman on the shoulder as he said it, as if Pennyman would especially appreciate it.

Pennyman recoiled in horror, in sudden revulsion, as if he were a slug curling away from a droplet of lye or as if he'd discovered a rat's nest in a clothes closet. He flailed at the sleeve of his white coat, which was smeared with dirty oil from the man's hand.

The attendant grinned at him. 'Sorry, pop,' he said, wiping his hands on his pants as if to make amends. 'Jumpy bastard, ain't you?'

'Talk first,' croaked Pennyman, pulling forty dollars out of his wallet.

Jimmy stared at it with faint loathing on his little-boy face. 'That ain't shit,' he said.

Pennyman started to speak, but stopped himself. His chauffeur lounged against the newly polished fender, talking to two men in overalls, one of whom waved happily back up toward the gas station and shouted something that sounded like, 'Ream 'im, Gus!' The gas station man smiled wider. 'That's me,' he said, nodding. 'Gus.' He held a tire iron in his right hand and slapped it against his left.

'What do you got in your shoe?' asked Jimmy, blowing an enormous bubble that popped across his nose and chin. He plucked the gum out of his mouth, rolled it in his dirty hands, then, using it as stickum, tugged the glued-on gum off his face.

'In my shoe?' asked Pennyman, suddenly horrified.

Gus said, 'He means give him all you got. And if you got any in your shoe, cough it up. We ain't a-going to talk to the whole world. First it was the newspaper, then yesterday a guy name of "Fence post" or something who come all the way up from L. A. in a beat-up Chevy. Burnt oil like a fry pan. He give Jimmy fifty bucks, and here's a cheap-ass slick like you waving two twenties. This ain't the Salvation Army, Holmes. Empty it out.'

'That's right,' Jimmy said. 'This ain't the Army.'

Pennyman sighed, trying to contain himself. He couldn't afford to be beaten with a tire iron. He couldn't afford to miss his plane. He couldn't afford to think that the limousine driver would do a damn thing to help him. In fact, all he could be sure of was that the two men talking to the driver were doing something more than passing the time of day. He angled his open wallet at Gus and Jimmy and pulled out all the visible money inside – almost three hundred dollars altogether.

Gus yanked it out of his hand, then snatched up the wallet itself, pulling out bank cards and papers and dropping them onto the asphalt. Pennyman let them lie there. If it had been within his power, he would have killed both of them then and there. They found a folded hundred dollar bill hidden under a flap, and Gus said, 'Look-a here,' and nodded down at Jimmy, who in one swift movement kicked Pennyman in the knee, then dodged in around behind Gus, who cocked his head on the side and gave Pennyman a don't-you-try-nothing stare.

Pennyman shook with rage, biting his tongue until it bled, thinking that he'd be back for a visit. Soon. When he was immune, when all the coins were his and he could do as he pleased. He forced a grin, trying to look as if he'd come up against better men in his life and laughed at them, too. 'You've got it all,' he said. 'Now what about the old man and the coin? What about the coin?'

'He was nuts,' said Jimmy. 'Sewed that coin up in the belly of one of them fish, rented a boat down at the dock from Bill Nayler, and rowed out onto the Sound, trolling with a big old marlin rig and using the fish for bait. Set out there for half an hour burnin' crap in a bowl. I heard him singin' to himself. Then this thing come up out o' the ocean and ate him up, boat too, like in Pinochio. I got that movie on video. Same fish, I suppose.'

'You think the boy's *lyin'* to you,' said Gus flatly, making it a statement rather than a question. 'Goddamn rich bastard driving down here in a stinking limo. Ain't you a ungrateful ...'

But Pennyman had turned to go, walking stiffly across the weedy asphalt toward the limousine. In fact, he didn't disbelieve it at all. It was just the sort of thing he expected – and half-feared. He wasn't sure what it meant. He anticipated a tap on the shoulder at any moment, Gus's hand spinning him around, a greasy shove on the back. He wouldn't travel again without carrying a gun. But there was nothing except wild laughter and the blubbering rip of a tremendous raspberry – probably the high-spirited work of Jimmy. Then a credit card zinged past his ear. There was the sound of small feet running. He stiffened up, ready for a blow, just as a hand shoved him on the back. It was the push of a small hand – Jimmy's hand, no doubt.

Pennyman stumbled forward, caught himself, and strode on. He wouldn't turn around. They wanted him to turn around. He bent into the limousine and ordered the driver to back out and go. He settled into the seat, and then, thinking for the first time about the man from L. A. with fifty dollars to spend, he bent forward to loosen his shoelaces. That was when he felt Jimmy's wad of gum stuck onto the back of his coat, stretching away from where it had glued itself to the upholstery.

The sunlit fog was white instead of gray – as if Andrew were sitting in a house among the clouds. It seemed to be thickening, though, as the morning wore on, and there wasn't a bit of a breeze. Everything was wet – sidewalks, tree trunks, roof shingles, the windshield of the Metropolitan. Andrew sat in his car, idly working the wipers and watching the street.

There had been dead sea gulls all over the lawn and sidewalk that morning. Andrew had kicked one, not seeing it in the fog. Then he'd kicked another, and when he had bent over to have a closer look, there was yet another, lying in the gutter. They were everywhere, fallen as if shot. Alone in the fog, he had collected sixteen of the creatures up and down the street, dropping them into a cardboard box and then lugging the box down the alley, pitching it into a dumpster. The whole business struck him as bizarre, and he wondered if there'd been a leak of some sort of poison gas in the night, maybe a screw-up at the Naval Weapons Station.

The news on the car radio had been odd too – reports of flooding back up the San Gabriel River, as if there'd been a monstrously high tide. Only there hadn't been. It was almost as if the river had flowed backward all of a sudden, and brackish tidal water had spilled out into backyards and overflowed storm drains. Andrew wondered at it all: the odd phosphorescence in the ocean last night, the storm surf, the rain of birds, the river. It all had a biblical ring to it, as if something were 'coming to pass.' The morning was peaceful now, though, and wearing on. He glanced at his watch.

It was past ten. He'd slept late – later than he'd slept in almost fifteen years. He sipped at a mug of coffee that had gone half-cold in the morning air. There was no sense in painting the garage, not in weather like this. It wasn't at all a day for work; it was a day for thinking and reading and generally recovering from the previous day, which had been arguably the longest he could remember.

He was happy and satisfied sitting in his car, though. He had run the heater for a few minutes, taking the chance of being discovered, and now he was warm and almost sleepy. There was something in the smell of the interior of the car, something familiar and enclosing, which, when combined with the fog and the coffee and the sea air drifting through the narrow window gap, seemed altogether to conjure up a sort of feeling; he couldn't quite describe it. It was as if he were aloft in a balloon, very comfortable and with a glass of something nice to drink and watching the crazy-quilt earth slip past below.

The fog seemed to weigh everything down gently, like a gray overcoat thrown across the shoulders of a huddled world. Water dripped from the curb tree onto the top of the car, slow enough so that until the next one came each drip seemed sure to be the last, and from somewhere, layered between the muffled noise of distant traffic and the occasional lonesome cries of wheeling gulls, came the slow rumble of waves collapsing along the shore not half a block away.

It would be a good morning for walking on the beach. The heavy surf of the past night would have tossed up seashells and polished stones, and what with the fog and cool weather, tourists wouldn't yet have picked them over. Andrew finished his coffee and set the cup on the floor of the car. He had intended to wait for Pennyman, if for no other reason than to have some-thing to report to Pickett when he returned from Vancouver with the Weetabix. Pennyman hadn't come out, though, and it had begun to seem suspiciously like Andrew had missed him. Such were the risks of sleeping late.

He hunched out onto the street, shut the car door as silently as he could, and locked it. The fog was so thick that he wouldn't be seen from the house, either by Rose or by Pennyman, and although he would have liked to wear his hat, he couldn't risk going in after it. He thrust his hands into his pockets and walked southwest toward the beach, angling down a narrow alley past where he'd given the bonita to the cats and wondering all of a sudden if they hadn't been Aunt Naomi's cats. That would be just like fate, wouldn't it? Here he'd been working hard to rid the house of the fiends, unsuccessfully, and then very graciously feeding them whole fish in the alley. They'd think he was a lunatic. Everyone sooner or later would think he was a lunatic – the cats, Aunt Naomi, Rose, Pennyman – everyone except Beams Pickett, who wasn't the sort of pot who called the kettle black. It was funny, actually, his having given the cats a treat. Even death row prisoners were given a top-notch meal before they were led away, or so the stories had it.

And the cats seemed to like him for it. Over the past couple of days it seemed as if they'd been hanging about him. One had even wandered into his bedroom early in the morning. Andrew had drowsed awake to see the beast standing there, looking as if it wanted to tell him something or as if it were standing watch while he slept.

At the edge of the beach he took his shoes and socks off, stuffed the socks down into the shoes, tied the laces together, and hung the shoes around his neck. Then he rolled his pantslegs up to his knees. The sand was damp and cold and it scrunched under his feet. He couldn't see the ocean, but he could hear it. Momentarily he was entirely adrift on the open beach, with nothing in the gray morning but a little circular patch of sand surrounding him, and not a sound of human manufacture to be heard. He was utterly alone, and the idea of it suddenly terrified him. He was struck with the notion that *They* were out there: Pickett's bogeymen, contriving the fog itself, perhaps, with a machine bolted to the underside of the pier.

Just then a man loomed up out of the mists, extraordinarily fat and with a glittery sort of helmet on and a shirt with moons and stars on it. An alien, Andrew thought, and he very nearly leaped back to hide himself in the mist, but the man's thrift-store trousers and down-at-heel shoes made it clear that he hadn't flown in from the stars, and he seemed easily as surprised to see Andrew as Andrew was to see him. He was obviously a local eccentric – like the bearded man yesterday at the inn – some sort of mystic. He nodded and passed on mumbling, walking toward the pier. Immediately someone else appeared, and behind him another three or four, all of them dressed like maharajas and carrying little tambourines like you'd win at a penny carnival. Andrew hurried past, careful not to make eye contact with any of them.

In his haste he kicked an enormous seashell and it rolled away down the sloping sand toward where the edge of a wave licked the pebbly shore. He chased after it and picked it up – a black murex the size of his hand, which had been wrenched up out of deep water by storm surf. Near the water's edge the sand was littered with seashells and jellyfish and tangles of kelp and pickleweed and eelgrass. There were moonsnails and owl limpets and brittle stars and leathery, purple nudibranchs and sea lemons and pipe fish. It was as if half of the denizens of the sea had stolen ashore in the night and decided to stay. Enormous codfish with bulbous eyes lay tangled in the weeds. Half-buried in the sand, the cold tide swirling around its whip-like tail, was a bat ray bigger than the hood of Andrew's Metropolitan. Andrew wished he had a sack with him. There was enough wonderful flotsam on the beach to fill a sea chest with.

He could see, farther up, a man in a tweed coat and with an uncanny sort of Prince Valiant haircut poking at something with a bit of driftwood. Andrew pulled his collar up and headed that way. The beach, clearly, was as full of eccentrics as it was full of odd sea life. Maybe he'd find his Atlantean there, reading one of his stolen books. Maybe he'd find the remnants of Atlantis itself, tossed up onto the beach along with pop bottles and fishing line and cast-off shoes. It was impossible that it was all coincidence, all of these oddballs sifting through things and the rain of birds, all of the talk of backward-flowing rivers. The strange people on the beach were looking for something, perhaps, or else, just like Andrew, they suspected that there was something to look for but didn't entirely know what it was and had come out to browse around on the chance that it would make itself known.

All in all, despite his haircut this fellow seemed safer than the maharajas or the man in the glittery helmet – less likely to run mad or to strike up a conversation with a ghost. And the thing he poked at appeared to be a body. Andrew strolled up and nodded a greeting. It wasn't a body, not a human body anyway. It was an impossible squid, eighteen or twenty feet long, half-buried under the sand and with its doleful, sightless eyes staring at nothing. It smelled awful, too, and not as if it had rotted there on the beach. It smelled burnt, somehow, like a smouldering electrical outlet or like badly scorched meat in a hot steel pan.

'Big, eh?' said the man, smiling at Andrew and gesturing with his pipe at the squid.

Although he already knew what it was, Andrew said, 'What is it, a squid?' in order to give the man a chance to show off. But as soon as the words were out, Andrew noticed the line drawn down the center of the man's face, and his heart jumped like a spooked rabbit. He forced his own face to relax and glanced quickly around just in case Pennyman was somewhere nearby, watching them through the fog.

'That's just what it is,' the man said, and he looked up at Andrew and shifted his pipe. 'Genus *Loligo*. The French call them *poulps*.'

Andrew nodded, breathing through his mouth very slowly in an effort to calm down. There was no sign of Pennyman, who was probably farther up the beach now, playing the quarter trick on the rajas. 'The French do?'

'That's a fact. The Spanish eat them in sandwiches. The Italians fry them in olive oil or stuff them with herbs and cheese. The Japanese eat them raw on little moulded rectangles of rice. And in the South Seas the natives make a sort of jelly out of the eyeballs, which they eat on toast.'

'You don't happen to be a chef, do you?' asked Andrew, thinking for a moment to solve the current Aunt Naomi problem. The man could certainly pass for a Frenchman, with his hair and all. But he wasn't a chef. He shook his head. Andrew squinted at his face, which was honest enough, but was pale and almost transparent, as if the man got out into the sun about once a year, early in the morning. There was no mistaking it; down his face was drawn the same line that Johnson and Andrew had been afflicted with.

'Something wrong?'

'No,' said Andrew. '*That* is, your face … Seems to be something smeared on it. Pipe ash, perhaps. Sorry to stare.'

The man produced a handkerchief and scoured away, the line rubbing off easily in the foggy air. Andrew inadvertently touched his own forehead. 'Haven't seen a man out and about this morning, have you? A man in a white suit, beard? Carries a cane?'

'Yes, indeed. I saw just such a man. Had a nice long talk with him, too. He was an amateur stage magician; showed me some of the most amazing coin tricks, and card tricks, too.'

Andrew nodded. 'Had you roll a quarter down your face, didn't he?'

'By golly,' said the man, 'how did you know?'

'He's always up to that sort of thing. Out walking, was he?'

'He was fascinated by the squid. Said he'd been an ichthyologist from Scripps, down south. Interested in the glandular functions of carp, he said. If you live long enough you'll meet people who specialize in any damn thing; do you know what I mean? Apparently squids were a sort of sideline with him, carp glands being his heart's desire. Look here.'

Andrew looked. The squid had been sliced open lengthwise, the cut so clean and straight that Andrew had taken it simply for a natural flap of skin. What the slice meant, though, Andrew was at a loss to say. Had Pennyman been out on the beach dissecting sea creatures? Grimacing just a little, Andrew pulled the skin back to expose an enormous cuttlebone and organ cavity. The inside of the beast was burned black, as if someone had kindled a fire in it. Andrew stood up and stepped back, turning toward the ocean and gasping in a lungful of sea air.

'Damndest thing, isn't it? Stinks like anything,' said the man, staring into the bowl of his pipe. 'Your friend seemed to expect it though, the burned organs. Put his nose nearly in 'em, as if they were cut flowers. He had a pair of gloves to put on and a sort of apron. Didn't want his white trousers soiled, I guess. Do you know what he did?'

Andrew shook his head, half-expecting to hear that Pennyman had made a sandwich out of the squid's heart and eaten it.

'He rummaged around in there and came up with a silver coin tangled in a bit of fishing line. He nipped it free with a nail clippers, and then he washed it in ocean water, dried it on his apron, put it in his pocket, and walked away. Just like that. He had me going, too, for a moment. I didn't know what to think, until I remembered the magician business. It was a gag, is what it was, and I was taken right in. There was a stage magician in Las Vegas who did that – with a gold ring and a loaf of bread out of the oven. He'd get a ring from someone in the audience, you see, very valuable, and make it disappear, and then ten minutes later he'd holler at a random waiter to bring over a hot bun, and ...'

But Andrew wasn't listening any longer. The story of the ring and the bun didn't signify. The story of the coin in the squid did – somehow. Had Pennyman been fishing for squid last night from the end of the pier? It certainly seemed so. He'd caught one, at least – and a big one, too. It must have broken his line, of course, and he'd come out that morning looking for it – which was odd, unless he was certain that the lure, whatever it was, would kill it and that the heavy surf would wash it ashore. That scenario worked, given what Andrew knew. What it *meant*, though, was hidden from him as he trudged back up the beach, idly rubbing sand off the murex shell.

He stood looking out over the ocean. The fog had thinned suddenly, and he could see the glassy green humps of smaller waves breaking inside on the sandy, suddenly shallow seabottom. Pennyman seemed to be fishing for more than just the idle squid. Andrew and Pickett and maybe Rose, too, were schooling around his lure. One day soon, if they didn't look sharp, he'd give it a bit of a jerk and they'd jump for it. He'd reel them in, just like that, and stuff them into an old gunnysack.

Well, Andrew would be ready for him. Pennyman foolishly underestimated him and Pickett. That was his error. It was high time that Andrew struck back – subtly, of course. It was enough at first merely to make Pennyman wonder, merely to make him peer over his shoulder a little more often and be a little less carefree and smug. Andrew nodded at the ocean and squinted into the fog, thinking that for Rose's own protection he'd keep this whole unsettling business away from her. Let Rose think anything about Pennyman that she'd like to think. When the time was right, Andrew would unmask him; he'd splash mud onto Pennyman's trousers; he'd muss up his hair; he'd clip the point off the bottom of his beard; he'd play the nailed nickel trick on him; he'd ...

'Hey!' shouted Andrew, leaping and waving his hand in the air. 'What!' He pitched the giant murex onto the wet sand and shook his right hand. A drop of blood oozed out from the soft skin between his fingers. He'd been pinched, and it hurt like hell. He rubbed it and bent over the shell. A hermit crab leaned out, enormous and hairy and menacing him with a single pincer. Its eyes stood on stalks, like the eyes of a moon creature, and it seemed to be looking at him from about sixty different directions at once. It hiked up its seashell and walked away into the ocean. For a moment Andrew could see it beneath the clear water – a dark shadow making for the open sea, going home to a pleasant, weedy grotto, where it had an easy chair, maybe, set up in the shade of a sea fan.

The sun broke through the mists just then, in shafts of piercing white light, and Andrew saw that he wasn't fifty yards from the pier. The beach was dotted with people now, sitting in folding chairs and setting up umbrellas. Suddenly there were children laughing and running. A trio of smart-aleck-looking surfers ran past, sliding their surfboards into the morning swell and leaping onto them in one smooth motion, letting a glassy little wavelet slap across the nose of their boards and full into their faces.

On an impulse, Andrew waded out into the shallows, thinking that the saltwater might brace him. It had been years since he'd swum in the ocean. He remembered how good it had been just to get wet. The water was stingingly cold, though, and when a wave washed through, splashing across his rolled-up pants, he turned around and fled, his feet already numb. Youth, thought Andrew, shaking his head. Go figure it. He waved two fingers back over his shoulder at the departing hermit crab to show it that there were no hard feelings. He understood well enough. A man's home … after all. He'd said as much himself, just last night. It was time to reach out of the shadows and give Pennyman a pinch. He grinned. There were a thousand ways to do it.

SEVEN

'… but when the truffle pigs were driven into the forests of Fontainbleau a great fat sow escaped into a stand of birch, from which it emerged with a spoon in its teeth and a beggar at its heels, escaping withal from master and beggar both, and never seen again in the region.'

LOUIS VINTEUIL,
AHASUER: LE JUIF-ERRANT
C. K. DEXTER HAVEN, TRANS.

The trick was to befuddle them. That's what would strike terror into their shabby hearts. You could send a man an anonymous letter that would paralyze him without his half-understanding it. Tom Sawyer had been a genius at it after all, but he hadn't known why. Andrew sat in the bar, doodling on a scrap of paper. It wasn't enough to write 'You'll die at midnight' or 'Beware the singing corpse' or something like that. Theatrical notes weren't worth a penny when it came to literate men like Pennyman. Nor was it worth anything to be straightforward, like 'Quit meddling in our affairs' or 'Cross me once more and you'll suffer for it.' That sort of thing was childish. There could be no hint of the Marquis of Queensberry about it.

The message had to be cryptic, almost nonsensical. There could be no sane explanation for it on earth. 'Give me back my sister's chewing gum' wouldn't be bad, but it might be misconceived to be humorous, which wouldn't at all do. Andrew scratched his head. It had to be something short, and it had to seem to be complete, although it couldn't *really* be, not in any recognizable sense. He had the envelope addressed and stamped. He'd purposely misspelled 'Pennyman,' making it 'Pengleman' instead, just to frost the cake, to raise Pennyman's eyebrows before he'd even torn the letter open. And Andrew had perfumed the envelope, too, and picked out a stamp from the post office's fish collection – a Japanese koi, appropriately enough. Pennyman would be steamrollered by it.

He was struck suddenly with inspiration, and grinning, he bent over the paper, shifting the pencil to his left hand in order to make a general mess of the note. 'MOKE DAT YIGARETTE,' he wrote, in a laborious, back-slanted hand, all the letters cockeyed and barely resembling each other. It was perfect. It meant nothing at all, but it seemed to imply something – smoke, perhaps, maybe poison smoke, maybe what? Ziggurats, mystical pyramids – certainly nothing that Pennyman could be sure of.

Andrew had debated cutting letters out of a magazine and gluing them on, but that was cheap, certainly, and would deflate the whole thing accordingly. He traced over the letters, darkening them, and dotted the *i* with a happy face. That would kill him. Andrew nearly laughed out loud. What would Pennyman make of it? Nothing. There was nothing on earth that he *could* make of it, and therein lay the beauty of it.

It would purely and simply flatten him out, like drinking undiluted grain alcohol by mistake. He'd think it was written by a foreigner at first, but then it would seem less and less likely to him that a foreigner would choose to utter such a phrase at all, and less likely yet that he would so weirdly misspell it. After the first few moments of numbed confusion that would surely follow Pennyman's opening it up and reading it, then rereading it and turning it over, a fog of genuine bewilderment would rise in his mind. There would follow a moment of fear and wild alarm. Here, he would say to himself, is something I don't at all understand. And the idea of it would paralyze him.

Pickett would be proud of Andrew, although Pickett would be shy of sending it. In truth Pickett had a little too much fear of these Caretakers, whoever they were, and would balk at the idea of taking them on. He was the man to *study* them. It was up to Andrew to step out of the shadows and confront them. He misfolded the letter, crammed it into its tiny envelope, and sealed it with Scotch tape. All in all it was an impressive package. He decided to drive to the Naples post office to mail it, just to throw Pennyman off the scent. And on the way back he'd stop by the telephone company and order up a phone for Pennyman's room and an extension for the attic observatory.

Andrew would graciously offer to pay the charges, except for long-distance calls, of course. Pennyman needn't know about the extension.

He considered for a moment whether he ought to push things just a little bit: not a bloody horse's head in Pennyman's bed or anything like that – but a lizard in his shoe, perhaps, or some fairly horrible substance like honey or cornstarch or sulphur dissolved in his hair oil, or maybe a gag from the joke shop – rubber excrement, say, – on the toe of his shoe. Andrew started to write out a list, a battle plan, but then he thought better of it and tore the list apart, stuffing it into his coat pocket. He'd keep no records. And for the moment at least he'd abandon the idea of those sorts of gags. They were the sort of thing that would give a man away, and they weren't half the ploy that the note was. The note was a corker.

It was just two in the afternoon. The fog had burned off entirely, but there was still just the hint of moisture in the air. He'd break out the paint and brushes in an hour, when it was drier. How long could it take to get a good section of wall painted? A couple of hours? He'd have a really solid go at it later, after he'd mailed the letter and hit the phone company.

Writing the note had cheered him considerably. He was finally *doing* something, for heaven's sake, and was no longer just the passive observer idling away his time in a chair and getting his toe trod on by people with destinations. He went out the door whistling, driving slowly past the house on his way toward the boulevard in order to assess this business of painting it, and calculating as he drove just how much a man like him might accomplish once he rolled up his sleeves and pitched in.

He hadn't driven for more than eight minutes – up the Coast Highway and across the bridge onto Second Street – when he saw Pennyman tapping along the sidewalk. He looked poorly, somehow, as if he were showing his age. In fact, with the afternoon sunlight shining on him he looked almost like a walking mummy, and his hair was slick with oil, as if it had taken half a gallon or so to make it cooperate. The sight of him in that state almost made Andrew whistle a tune.

He stepped on the brake and started to turn off onto one of the little streets leading up to the Marine Stadium, but then he swerved back onto Second Street again and angled in toward the curb. It wouldn't do to lose Pennyman. There were a thousand streets for him to disappear into. It was better to park the car and follow on foot. He locked the doors and jumped out, fed dimes and nickels to the parking meter, and loped along up the sidewalk in order to catch up. Pennyman was walking briskly and determinedly.

Andrew waited for a break in the traffic, keeping well away down the block and lingering now and then in the storefront shadows so as to appear leisurely. Pennyman rounded a corner and disappeared, heading toward the isthmus and Alamitos Beach, and Andrew jogged across the street in pursuit, slowing down as he came to the corner and half-expecting Pennyman to be waiting there for him, just out of sight. He found himself in front of Moneywort's Tropical Fish, run now by Moneywort's nephew, a man referred to only as 'Adams' who'd worked there for years, making Moneywort's life miserable while Moneywort was still alive. He was a nasty sort altogether, and the place had declined and lost much of its magic since Moneywort's death.

Andrew put his hands in his pockets and slouched along. He'd have a quick look around the corner, and if Pennyman were there, anticipating him, he'd pretend that he was simply heading for Moneywort's, to buy feeder goldfish for the Surinam toad – which wouldn't, in fact, be a bad idea. The toad would be happy with some goldfish, and there was something cheerful and solid about the notion of a happy toad. He'd buy dried shrimps for Aunt Naomi's cats, too, just to cement the impression that he was a friend to cats. Well ... He admitted it to himself. He seemed almost to *be* a friend to cats. It was a half dozen of them all at once in the attic that gave him the pip.

Here was the corner. He stepped past it, down off the curb and heading across toward the Texaco station, where he would conspicuously get a drink of water at the fountain. He'd wait until he was almost there to glance down the street, and make it look as if there was nothing anxious about him, as if the last thing in the world he was doing was following someone. But he couldn't wait. Halfway across the street he turned his head to the side and pretended to scratch his neck. The long block stretching away toward Naples Lane was empty; there wasn't a soul on it except for a woman in hair curlers who was watering her lawn.

Andrew continued straight on across, cutting over to the gas station drinking fountain, which was clogged with chewing gum. He turned away in disgust after having pretended to drink. Either Pennyman had slipped into one of the houses farther along the block or else he'd gone into Moneywort's, through the back door. Of course he had.

Andrew would have to make up his mind quickly. He couldn't appear to be hanging about. The die was cast. He pushed into the tropical fish shop, reaching up immediately to shush the bell that would jingle to announce his arrival, and prepared to be pleasantly surprised to see Pennyman there. But there was no sign of Pennyman. The outer room of the shop was empty.

Feeling like a private investigator out of a forties movie, he eased the door shut behind him and let go of the bell. There was silence except for the hum of aquaria. The shop was almost dim, lit only by a couple of incandescent lamps near the counter and by countless twenty-five-watt bulbs in aquarium reflectors, the light of which was darkened, somehow, by the shadowy water in the tanks, and cast a shifting, murky glow over the dank concrete floor.

There was the sound of bubbling airstones and the pleasantly musty smell of waterweeds and wet sand and fish.

The shop comprised a half-dozen small rooms with corridors leading back and forth. Pennyman could be in any one of them, waiting for him. Andrew cocked his head and listened. There was the faint sound of murmuring in the back of the shop, and then the sound of low, unpleasant laughter.

He tiptoed past the counter and in among the aquaria, watched by a thousand hovering fish that blinked out of grottoes built of waterfall rock and weighted driftwood and kelp-like stands of elodea and foxtail and Amazon swordplant. The murmuring grew louder and then fell away. There sounded a brief clattering and splashing and then silence again. Andrew peered past a narrow doorway into another room of aquaria. Beyond that was a broad storeroom with a door that fronted the alley down which Pennyman must have come. *If* he were in the shop at all. He mightn't be, of course. Andrew slid into a shadow, peered back over his shoulder, and then crouched down onto his knees, peeking around the jamb. There was Pennyman all right, just as he'd guessed, but alone in the storeroom. He stood with his back to Andrew.

One wall of the storeroom was simply an enormous aquarium – easily a thousand gallons, probably more like two thousand. It stretched from halfway up the wall to the ceiling, encased in hammered steel along the perimeter and braced every four feet or so. It must have opened into the attic, so that it would seem from the floor of the attic to be a sort of rectangular pool. A dozen stupendous carp, scaly and golden in the glow of hidden, overhead bulbs, clustered in the corner of the tank. The water was agitated and water plants were torn loose and floating.

Suddenly a broad net plunged into the water of the aquarium, and directly after that a head appeared along with the hand and arm holding the net. It was the head of Adams, Moneywort's worthless nephew, who was trying to dip out a fish. He was shirtless and wore a skin-diving mask and snorkel, and his dark hair swirled in the moving water as he looked out through the thick glass at Pennyman, who gestured impatiently toward the tank. The man swung the net ponderously at a big carp that had strayed away from the crowd huddling on the bottom. The net crept along through the water, though, and the carp easily eluded it, but made the mistake of fleeing into a back corner. The net wavered in toward it, and the carp nosed frantically against either wall of the tank, befuddled by having too many options. It burst away in a wild rush, swirling up sediment from the bottom, straight into the net, which Adams hauled up and out of the water.

There were noises in the attic: drippings and splashings, a curse and the sound of compressed air being blown into a plastic bag. Then Adams appeared on the little tilted stair-ladder that angled into the attic crawlspace, struggling to carry a long, lidded Styrofoam box. Pennyman stepped across to grab the end of it, and Andrew pulled back out of sight. It wouldn't do to be seen crouching in the doorway. Then he stood up slowly and straightened his coat, expecting the two men to wander out toward the front of the shop now, and find him. Just then the bell over the front door began to jangle.

Andrew hunched over to peer into a tank full of marine tropicals. Reflected in the glass of the tank he could see two doors – the door to the storeroom and a kitty-corner door leading out to the corridor that connected to another room full of aquaria and also led out to the rest of the shop. He pretended to study the fish in the tank in front of him. Adams appeared and disappeared past the second doorway, going out to see who it was that had come in. He hadn't seen Andrew. Then there was the sound of the back door shutting; that would be Pennyman, going out the same way he'd come in.

Andrew thought hard and fast. Pennyman was gone – or so it seemed – and that was good. Should he follow? It would be easy enough to slip out the same door. Adams wouldn't see him that way – wouldn't wonder how Andrew had got in without dinging the front door bell. But somehow Andrew didn't want to leave, or rather, he didn't much want to follow Pennyman any longer. There was something mortally dangerous about the man and in the power he seemed to have over people. Today especially. In the watery light of the storeroom he had looked like Mr Death, like the personification of evil and decay. Andrew would wait for Pickett. Pickett was due home soon enough. Why press it?

But where was Pennyman going with the carp? Certainly not back to the inn. Andrew wouldn't stand for that, for Pennyman setting up aquaria. Was he going to eat it? Bring it to Rose as a gift? It was probably a taste he'd acquired in the Orient. Heaven knew what kinds of tastes he *hadn't* acquired in the Orient. Adams slipped past the door again and into the storeroom.

The sudden appearance of Adams had been startling, but in a moment Andrew realized he was safe; he still hadn't been seen. There would be no chance of sliding out the back door, though. He waited. There was nothing to panic about. He was a customer now, and nothing else. He still wanted those feeder fish and the shrimps for the cats. In a bit, when he was sure it was a good idea, he'd step quietly back out to the front of the shop and tug on the bell a couple of times, pretending that he had just that moment come in.

He focused on the fish gliding around in the aquarium before him: fat clown fish lazying back and forth through the poisonous tentacles of blue anemones. Somehow it seemed to signify to Andrew; it seemed as if it ought to be a metaphor or something, and he thought idly about how the most disconnected things developed secret connections when you saw them in the right sort of light – moonlight, maybe, or the suffused light of an aquarium. He wondered what it might mean – the clown fish and the anemones – and he listened to the momentary silence and then to Adams in the back room whispering, 'Mr Pennyman?' Adams waited, as if he were listening, too, and then he said it again, like a conspirator, very low and urgently. Mr Pennyman, of course, didn't answer.

There was a hand on Andrew's shoulder suddenly, and Andrew nearly shrieked. He couldn't, though: There was a hand over his mouth, too. He stiffened, wondering whether to slam his assailant in the rib cage with his elbow or to pretend to be a surprised customer – which he was, really. The hand on his shoulder had a ring on it that Andrew recognized – a round signet sort of ring that looked like an old doubloon, or some other vaguely familiar old coin.

He turned his head slowly, and the hand released his shoulder. There was Uncle Arthur, standing behind him, the hand with the ring on it just touching his lips. The old man shook his head and took his other hand away from Andrew's mouth. Andrew relaxed. He'd been holding his breath, and he let it out now in a long whoosh. He started to speak, but Uncle Arthur cut him off with a gesture, then shook his head again and jerked his thumb back over his shoulder toward the front door. Andrew nodded and set out alone, muffling the bell again and squinting at the bright sunlight when he opened the door.

It wasn't until he was outside and walking back up Second Street toward his car that he began to wonder why in the world Uncle Arthur was messing around in Moneywort's shop. He and Moneywort had been friends, but now Moneywort was dead, and Arthur had little interest in tropical fish – no real reason for visiting the shop. Andrew would have plenty of mysteries to lay at Pickett's feet, although he wouldn't, alas, have any shrimps to lay at the feet of the cats.

So what was Uncle Arthur doing there? That's what Andrew wondered as he motored away up Second Street toward the post office. Coincidence wouldn't answer. Over the past week Andrew had come to disbelieve in coincidence. There were only two answers that were any good: Uncle Arthur had come 'round to Moneywort's shop for the same reason Pennyman had – to buy an enormous carp – or else Arthur himself had been *following* Pennyman, a development that wouldn't much surprise Pickett.

Pennyman had got home before him. He was going in through the front door when Andrew pulled in along the curb. And he wasn't carrying the Styrofoam box, either. Andrew sat in the Metropolitan again, thinking. It was nearly four o'clock, and once again Andrew had managed to do nothing at all that day but avoid Rose. He'd gone out after seashells that morning but had collected mysteries instead, each of which was pretty enough, in its way.

But one wanted the mysteries to add up somehow. What Andrew had was a jumble of them, like shells rattling in a bag, and he had the growing suspicion that one day soon he'd reach into the bag to draw one out and he'd be pinched by it. He had to get them sorted, to see which of them contained hidden crabs, which of them stank of dead things, which of them he could hear the distant murmur of the ocean in. He turned on the car radio and then turned it off again. There was no excuse on earth for wasting the rest of the day. He reminded himself of what had happened yesterday, a day that had started out so promising and then declined into despair. The 2AM Cheerios powwow around the kitchen table had fetched it all back together just a bit, had saved him. Now here he was idling away his time, losing the little tract of ground he'd got back with Rose and Naomi.

It was time to haul out the paint. He had painter's coveralls in the garage. It wouldn't take him six minutes to pull them on and get started. He had the sudden urge to announce his intentions to Rose, but he squashed it. Let her stumble upon him at work. He'd be whistling away, paintbrush in hand, cap pulled down over his eyes. He'd hang his paint scraper in the loop in the coveralls and shove a rag into his back pocket, next to his putty knife. People would drive by on the street, and, mistaking him for a professional painter, they'd stop and ask him for an estimate, appreciating his work, happy that these old houses were being sparkled up. He was working late in the afternoon, wasn't he? Well, he'd say, nightfall was the only clock *he* paid any attention to – nightfall and sunrise, the two great motivators of mankind. He was a philosopher-painter. Which one of the Greeks had talked about that sort of thing? Plato, maybe.

He picked up his coffee cup, which had lain there on the floor of the car since that morning. There was a little dribble of coffee in it, dried on the inside in a sticky line. He wished suddenly that the cup were full, but he couldn't risk going in to brew up a fresh one. He couldn't risk going after a beer, either. He'd have to paint dry, which was a pity, really, painting being such a boring job. Having something to drink – whatever it might be – was an end in itself, a pastime. Hose water would have to do. He sat up abruptly, realizing that another ten minutes had passed. He'd been daydreaming again.

In a fit of determination he climbed out of the car, closed the door softly, and stepped around into the backyard, hurrying into the garage. There on the bench was the sack full of smashed glass. The sight of it depressed him hugely, and he picked it up and flung it into the trash can in the corner. To hell with melting lead. He hadn't the time to waste on it. There was no use trying to fiddle away old mistakes anyway; Rose wouldn't be fooled. Not for a moment. All he would accomplish would be to look like an utter moron, and he couldn't afford that sort of thing any more. He yanked on the coveralls, pried open his paint, and hurriedly stirred it with a piece of stick. In minutes he stood alongside the house, spreading out a canvas dropcloth. To hell with painting the garage, too. The house was bigger game.

He began to dust off the house with a horsehair brush, intending to clean

a good-sized area before starting to paint. It was nothing, this painting business. He studied the edge of his paintbrush. It was a good one, a Purdy four
inch – sharp and clean. He dipped it into the paint, slipped the back edge of
it across the metal can rim, and cut in a two-foot section of one of the clap-
boards, catching a drip and smoothing it out nicely. He stepped back and
looked at it happily. It seemed to him to be evidence of something – that he
wasn't entirely a worthless crud, perhaps. He dipped the brush again and
then stopped and listened. There were voices murmuring, one of them angry.

He laid the paintbrush across the mouth of the can and rubbed his hands
on the rag. It sounded like Rose; the angry voice did. He wouldn't have that.
He would put a quick stop to it. There was no one in the house who had the
right to argue with her, except maybe himself. If it was Pennyman giving her
trouble … A hot flush of anger surged through him and he stepped around
toward the front door, nearly breaking into a run, his fists clenched. Then
there came another voice; it *was* Pennyman, but he wasn't arguing with Rose.
The woman's voice belonged to Mrs Gummidge, and both voices were coming through the open window of Mrs Gummidge's ground-floor bedroom.
She was the only one of them who occupied a room down below – a sort of
maid's quarters with its own bath and kitchenette. The window was open just
a fraction.

Andrew braked and then skipped backward two steps, spinning around
and lunging after the paintbrush and paint. He fetched them, then tiptoed
back around until he stood just beside the open window, and then very
quietly and haphazardly he began to paint the siding. He hadn't brought the
horsehair brush, and there wasn't time to waste going back after it, so he
splashed the paint on over ten years worth of grime. He barely breathed, listening to the rising and falling of voices.

'I should think I'd get more than that,' said Mrs Gummidge tearfully.

There was a pause, then Pennyman's voice: 'I haven't got more. You can
appreciate that. It's a tiresome, slow process, wringing it out like that and
distilling it down and decanting it and aging it. It isn't done in a day. And the
fish themselves are fearsomely rare. When Adams killed them all out of stupidity, with his cheap thermostats, it was six months before the damage could
be put right. If it hadn't been for the quick trip up to San Francisco … Well …
Thank heavens for Han Koi's man up in Chinatown. It's only in the last
month that Adams has got it all going again, and that means a month or two
more before there's a surplus.'

'A surplus! I'm not asking for a surplus. I'm asking for a very little bit. A bit
of yours is what I'm asking for. You can spare it. You'd think it was narcotics.'

'And it works that very way,' said Pennyman in a soft and fatherly voice.
'You don't need any more than I've given you. I *do*, though. Certainly you can
see that. Don't cut any capers now. We're days away from it. You know that. *I*

can't sacrifice a drop. If my powers aren't honed and strong, then we're done for; we might as well not have bothered.'

There was silence for a moment as Andrew continued to slap paint on the wooden siding, paying no attention to the finer points of his work. He idly painted upwards and sideways and crossways, his head cocked, waiting for the conversation to continue. He could hear Mrs Gummidge crying almost silently – stifling it, as if she didn't want to be overheard by anyone chancing to pass by in the hallway. Andrew smiled. They had no earthly suspicion that the enemy stood right outside their window, got up in coveralls and a hat. He was killing two birds with one stone; that was the truth of it.

The conversation started up again. There was the sound of glass clinking against glass and of Pennyman muttering something about cups of tea. Andrew couldn't make it out.

'Just a little at a time,' Mrs Gummidge said.

'Why don't you give that up? This has nothing to do with personal vendettas. We're above that.'

'I don't believe we are,' she said after a moment. 'What about the books? Aren't we above that, too?'

'Damn the books. What books?'

'Don't think I don't see anything. Don't think it's not me that does a bit of dusting and vacuuming around this house.' Her voice rose. In a moment she'd be hysterical.

'Shh!' Pennyman hushed her up, cutting her off before she had revealed anything at all.

Andrew was baffled. The whole conversation was baffling. Now there was another baffling silence during which he heard the back door shut. That could only be Rose, coming outside. She'd see that the garage door was open and she'd go in to have a look. Then she'd find the lid to the paint can and his jacket hanging over the bench vise, and she'd come around to the front to see if her wondering eyes had deceived her.

There was a grunt of loathing, as if Mrs Gummidge had swallowed a toad, and then an ungodly sort of fishy smell wafted out through the window, so putrid and overpowering that Andrew reeled back, turning his face away. There was Rose, standing on the sidewalk. He might have predicted it. He *had* predicted it. He smiled at her and waved his paintbrush. At least he hadn't been crushing water glasses or experimenting with cups full of cold coffee.

He moved away from the window before he said anything, hauling his paint can back around to where his dropcloth lay and setting it down. 'Thought I'd take advantage of the sunlight and get in a bit of painting.'

Rose nodded – not happily, it seemed to him. He stepped back and looked at the house. There were two short strips of clapboard painted very neatly on the corner where he'd started in. Then there was a sort of mess of fresh paint near Mrs Gummidge's window. It looked something like a psychological test. He waved his brush at it, as if in explanation, thinking hard for something to say. He'd been caught out again. But at least he'd been caught by Rose and not by Pennyman. It would have gone hard on him if Pennyman had discovered him listening at the window. And of course he *would* discover it, too, as soon as he saw the weirdly painted patch of siding. Pennyman wasn't an idiot.

'I'm amazed,' said Rose, seeming suddenly to be happy with Andrew's antics, as if she'd taken the long view and come to the conclusion that *any* work was good work, any painting good painting. 'What's the point of being so wild with it, though?'

'Bad grain in the wood. The redwood seems to be delaminating there. Probably a matter of too much afternoon sun. When that sort of thing happens you have to scrub it on, to get it in under the grain lines where the wood is coming apart. It acts as a sort of adhesive. Looks bizarre now, I'll admit, but once the whole thing is painted ...'

Rose nodded. 'Why don't you stick to one side at a time. That way if you don't get it all done, it won't look quite so peculiar.'

'Absolutely,' said Andrew. 'I got carried away, I guess. I saw what the problem would be with the wood and all and decided to have a go at it. I couldn't resist. You know how I am when it comes to tackling little problems like that.'

Rose nodded. 'Shouldn't you clean it first? All that dirt ...'

'Bonding agent,' said Andrew, hating himself. 'It'll look good freshened up, won't it?'

'*I'll* be pretty happy with it,' said Rose. 'But why don't you clean up? You don't have much of the afternoon left anyway.'

Andrew picked up his paint can and moved across toward the open window again, talking loudly to alert Mrs Gummidge and Pennyman, if they were still in the room, that he was out on the lawn. His spying was pretty much at an end. If he were smart, he'd haul out a floodlight and an extension cord and try to get the mess of paint smoothed out and cleaned up before he quit for the evening. Rose would admire his sticking to it, and Pennyman wouldn't wander out in the morning and find anything suspicious.

'Bring my dinner out on a plate, will you?'

'If you want,' said Rose, heading back up the sidewalk toward the garage. 'Don't wear yourself out, though.'

That was just like Rose, worrying about him. He dipped his brush into the paint, straightened up, and looked square into the face of Pennyman, which was regarding him out the window, grinning slyly. 'Good evening,' rasped Andrew, startled.

Pennyman nodded, giggling just a little bit, then laughing harder, then bursting into such a paroxysm of laughter that for a moment Andrew thought he'd choke. And for as long as Pennyman laughed, Andrew couldn't step a foot nearer the house, and he began to hope very fervently that Pennyman *would* choke, that the laughter would simply explode him like an overfilled balloon.

EIGHT

'Our affections and beliefs are wiser than we; the best that is in us is better than we can understand ...'

ROBERT LOUIS STEVENSON,
VIRGINIBUS PUERISQUE

It was late – after midnight. Pennyman hadn't come in all day. Andrew was sure of it. He would give the old man another hour, maybe catch an hour of sleep himself, if he could. It was high time he had a look inside Pennyman's room, and this was as good a night as any. He punched buttons on his little battery-operated kitchen timer, setting it for sixty minutes. In order to muffle it, he shoved it under the pillow on the couch. Then he lay down and fell asleep almost at once.

He woke up from a dream involving pigs, wondering where he was, wondering at the ringing buzz in his ear, and he groped for the alarm clock. Then he remembered. He sat up groggily, rubbing his eyes. He could barely keep them wedged open. His back was nearly murdering him, and he was stiff in the joints. He suddenly wanted very much to go back to sleep, to lie on the couch forever. But he couldn't. He had a mission. When he stood up, though, he almost tumbled forward onto his face. An hour's worth of sleep had just made him more beat; his mind was a sandy pudding. Then he thought about the pending adventure, and the thought woke him up. He stretched, tucked in his shirt, and stepped out into the livingroom.

The tennis ball he'd set against the front door still sat there. Pennyman hadn't come in. He was gone for the night – something fairly common lately. Mrs Gummidge had mentioned having spoken to him before dinner. She had said that Pennyman had spent most of the day in his room and then had gone out to a relative's house in Glendale, where he would doubtless spend the night. But neither Andrew nor Rose had seen Pennyman that morning, and Andrew suspected that he'd gone off early and hadn't returned, that Mrs Gummidge had lied. Pennyman was using Mrs Gummidge for an alibi, it seemed. From Andrew's point of view, a man who needed an alibi was usually guilty as a gibbon ape.

Andrew didn't much trust Mrs Gummidge, not since he'd overheard them at the window. He was certain that they were up to something together, that they'd joined forces since coming to live at the inn. In one way it relieved him just a little. Mrs Gummidge, after all … One would have thought that Pennyman could find more capable allies. Perhaps his liaison with Mrs Gummidge was evidence that Pennyman was mostly show, mostly facade. He was the sort, certainly, who *seemed* to be. That was something Andrew could sniff out pretty accurately. Andrew had a good nose for falseness.

He looked around for something else – something that would make a clatter. The fireplace tools would do. He left them hanging precariously in their wrought iron holder and tilted the whole business against the door. If Pennyman came in now, the whole house would know it. Andrew would have some explaining to do, but it would be better than Pennyman sneaking in and catching Andrew rummaging in his room.

He creaked up the stairs, listening to the snores echoing down the stairwell from Aunt Naomi's room in the attic, listening for sounds of restlessness from the bedroom where Rose, by now, had been asleep for three hours. He couldn't help grinning. There was excitement in skulking around a dark house after midnight, doing battle with the forces of evil – or the forces of something.

One of Aunt Naomi's cats strolled down from above and stood blinking at him on the stairs. Then it jumped past him and ran down the stairs to the ground-floor landing, where it sat on its haunches and stared out toward the front door. Another cat appeared above, coming along down to rub against Andrew's leg. It sat down outside Pennyman's door and meowed softly. The cat below meowed as if in response. Andrew had the uncanny feeling that the cats were up to something – that they were signaling each other. He was certain somehow that they were on his side, though – that once again they were watching over him.

He suddenly felt surefooted and keen. The thrill of it all had scoured the sleep from his head. He could picture the interior of Pennyman's bedroom – the chair, the bureau, the bookcases, the single bed tucked into an alcove in the wall and with a curtain hung across in front of it. He'd found and bought the furniture himself. Rose had sewed the bedchamber curtain, and Andrew had installed it on a wooden rod across the front of the bed alcove. There wasn't a square inch of the room that he wasn't familiar with. He really didn't need the penlight in his pocket; he could feel his way from stem to stern in the dark.

Suddenly and without a tickle of warning, he sneezed. He squelched it with his hand, sort of moomphing it into his palm. He pinched his nose to stop an inevitable second sneeze as he froze there on the darkened stairs, listening again, his heart slamming. No one stirred. The snores continued unabated from overhead, and in the still, enclosed air of the stairwell hung just a hint of the smell of cats. It was comforting, somehow, and hadn't the power anymore to disgust him or set him into a rage.

He still didn't like the idea of a house full of them, though. His resolve to deal with them had weakened a bit, but he still had a score to settle there. He had to be the master of his own house. One thing at a time, though; that was how it had to be. Pennyman first, the cats afterward. He wouldn't make the mistake of overreaching himself. He tiptoed past the cat, bending over to pet it and feeling guilty again for plotting against it. He paused outside Pennyman's door, listening for one last time. Then he steeled himself, shoved the door open slowly, and stepped into the dark interior of the room.

There was the smell of books and rosewater and bay rum. An octagonal, hinged mirror sitting atop the bureau caught a glint of moonlight through the window. Arranged atop the bureau were carefully laid out toiletries: tortoiseshell combs and brushes, a mustache scissors, bottles of hair tonic and skin lotion, an emery board and another mirror – for admiring the back of his head, apparently. It was an unimpressive lot of credentials, but it was all Pennyman had to recommend himself. Mess his hair up and he was a sorry-looking scarecrow.

Andrew abruptly considered tumbling the lot of it out the window. He could watch Pennyman's pride crack to bits on the stones of the pathway below. Walk with the proud, he thought, and you shall be scornful. That was true enough. If there was one thing that Pennyman surely was, it was scornful. Andrew was – what? – scornful of it. He grinned again. That's what tripped him up every time – his pride in being humble. It beat all. There was no way to lick it.

He found himself contemplating a hairbrush, idly thinking about philosophy. He shook his head, clearing it again. There was no time for that. At any moment the fireplace tools might clatter down on the hardwood floor and Andrew's mission would come to a bad end. What if Rose, waking up and stepping into the hallway, caught him sneaking out of Pennyman's room? What if she got downstairs before him and found the fireplace tools strewn across the floor? Who would appear to be the fool, the lunatic? He or Pennyman? He knew the answer to that. He also knew that Rose wasn't the sort to lie in bed and shake when there were strange noises in the house. She was every bit as likely to pull on her bathrobe and have a look. He wondered suddenly what he was doing there at all, meddling in Pennyman's room.

The business of the fish tonic – that was central. Come to think of it, that was the other odor, mingling with the hair tonic and the bay rum and the general old-house smell. And there was something more, too – the faint smell of something sweet and chemical. What was it? – perfume, perhaps. A woman's perfume.

His eyes were adjusted to the dark, but the faint moonlight wasn't quite enough illumination to do the trick. He pulled out the penlight and switched it on, shining it first at this, then at that. There was a plethora of drawers in the room – five in the bureau, two in the desk, six in the built-in cupboard below the bed. He wished he could look through them all, but it would be folly. What if Rose awakened and went downstairs out of kindness to him, to wake him up on the couch and urge him to come up to bed? He'd have to hurry.

There it was, as if it had been left for him. On the little mahogany table next to the head of the bed alcove sat a half-filled bottle, open and with a glass vial lying beside it. It was odd that Pennyman would leave it open, and even odder that he'd leave it out like that, unless he were so conceited and sure of himself that he couldn't imagine anyone slipping in like this. Andrew pulled his silver flask out of his coat pocket, twisted open the cap, tilted the fish elixir bottle over it, and drained off a quarter inch or so – no more than a half ounce, just enough to have a bit of laboratory work done on it.

He set the bottle down, recapped his flask, and put it away. He was torn between hauling open drawers and getting the hell out. What might he find there? Anything at all; that was the answer. It was odds-on that there was something incriminating in Pennyman's goods – some telling affidavit, some revealing letter, a photograph, a recipe for brewing up poisons out of blow-fish. It was tempting, but far too dangerous. He'd be back – when it was safer and he had more time. He'd bring Pickett along and do the job right; one of them to rifle Pennyman's goods and the other to keep watch.

He shined the penlight once more around the room, but the tiny beam wasn't enough to reveal anything telling. One bit of real information; that's all he asked for. The elixir was well and good, but what could it reveal? That it had been extracted from a carp? He already knew that much, or at least suspected it.

He turned to the curtain across the bed, reached up and grabbed it below its wooden rings, and slid it open in a rush.

Mrs Gummidge lay there, asleep.

Andrew shouted, hoarse and silent as if in a dream. He jammed his fist partly into his mouth and reeled back into the desk, paralyzed with heart-hammering fear and flinging his penlight away onto the floor. It blinked out when it hit, and he scrabbled after it, down onto his hands and knees. It had rolled under the chair. He flailed for it, looking back over his shoulder, certain now that Mrs Gummidge was dead. He couldn't bear to have his back turned to her.

He twisted around and stood up, abandoning the flashlight and stepping toward the door in long, silent strides, squinting at Mrs Gummidge and breathing through clenched teeth. He paused there for a moment. If she was dead he'd have to take action … Steeling himself, he squinted at her, lying there in the shadow of the alcove, stiff and awful like an old-woman doll. She was breathing, though. And she stirred just a little.

It struck him suddenly that it wasn't Mrs Gummidge at all, but was Pennyman in a Mrs Gummidge mask, and the thought propelled his hand toward the doorknob like a shot out of a sling. But that was madness, and he told himself so as he whipped the door back, stepped out into the hallway, and threw himself past the waiting cat and nearly head-first down the stairs. Straight into the kitchen he went and out into the bar. He poured a shaky drink out of the scotch bottle, and then for reasons he couldn't define he slipped out through the street door into the night air, striding around and into the backyard and then into the garage, where he set the scotch onto the bench and then held onto the bench himself, breathing like an engine.

He stood just so for minutes, not daring to turn on the light. All the old night fears of his childhood had rushed back in upon him. Mrs Gummidge's curl-encircled face had been horrible. She'd nearly gorgonized him. He shuddered and drained his glass, listening in anticipation for the sounds of pursuit. He could picture Mrs Gummidge coming out through the back door like a wraith, like Lady Macbeth, drifting toward him through the night air with bloody hands and a loathsome automaton grin on her face. He shuddered again, cursing himself for not having hidden a bottle of scotch somewhere in the garage. Minutes passed and his breathing leveled out. It was cold. The concrete floor felt frozen through his socks. There was no sound of pursuit – no lights blinking on or back doors whispering shut. What he wanted more than anything, suddenly, was to go to bed. Rose's company, even if she was asleep, was worth a fortune to him.

The next day, Andrew was sitting in the overstuffed chair in the library when Pennyman came home. Andrew was happy to see him. It was late in the afternoon, and the mail had dropped through the slot just a half hour earlier. The note was there.

Luckily, it had been beaten up in transit, no doubt having been routed through the downtown station, and seemingly used as a coffee cup coaster for a day or two and then trodden on before delivery. It had become a happy mess of wrinkles and dirty Scotch tape, of unidentifiable stains and childish, semi-literate lettering.

Andrew had avoided Mrs Gummidge most of the day, but she'd gone about her business as if she'd no idea that Andrew had come across her sleeping in Pennyman's bed. In fact, she seemed weirdly high-spirited, winking at him once in an appallingly suggestive way. Andrew could hardly accuse her of being in the room, but in the cold light of day he'd begun to generate theories to explain things. It seemed fairly likely that, if nothing else, Pennyman and Mrs Gummidge were tolerably familiar with each other, that they'd been carrying on in secret. There was nothing he could do about his suspicions except dwell on them, and he had been engaged in doing just that when in had come Pennyman, through the door, almost on the heels of the mailman.

Pennyman was carrying his coat, folded over his arm. He looked particularly proud of himself; he had almost a youthful, damn-all appearance to him, as if he'd just finished off a half-bottle of wine and the world was a rosy place. The sight of him in such a state would normally have made Andrew seethe, but given the circumstances, the arrival of the anonymous letter and all … Andrew looked up and winked and said that Pennyman looked surprisingly well today, in such a tone as implied that on most days Pennyman looked uncommonly miserable and tired. Then Andrew began to whistle the tootling little melody from 'Steamboat Willie,' and pretended to read his book while actually watching Pennyman sort through the mail and willing him to open the note then and there and not carry it away to his room.

Pennyman picked it up and peered at it. Then he thrust it away at arm's length and cocked his head, wondering at it with what seemed like vague loathing, as if he'd supposed at first it were a twig and then discovered that actually it was a cleverly camouflaged insect. He looked up at Andrew, but Andrew was reading harmlessly, swept up in his book and with a pencil in his hand. Pennyman produced a pocketknife and slit the envelope open, holding it suspiciously now between his thumb and forefinger. He peered inside, removed the folded message, and flattened it out. Andrew looked out over the top of his book, watching Pennyman's eyes sweep back and forth across the note. He read it and then read it again, uncomprehending. He blinked at it, reading it once more, his lips moving this time as if he were concentrating furiously, thinking it to be in code, perhaps, and trying to unscramble it, to make sense out of nonsense.

'Something wrong?' Andrew asked innocently, sitting up straighter in his chair as if ready to come to Pennyman's assistance.

'What?' said Pennyman. 'No.'

'Not bad news, I hope?'

'Not at all. It's nothing at all.'

Andrew shrugged, implying that it was none of his business unless Pennyman wanted to make it so. 'You seemed to go pale there for a moment. Not feeling under the weather are you? Sit down for a moment.'

Pennyman's face seemed to stiffen into something resembling the face of a skull, and he looked at Andrew with such a rictus of suppressed fury that a wave of cold fear washed down along Andrew's spine, and for a moment he wished to heaven he hadn't sent the note at all. Then the moment passed and Pennyman relaxed just a little, gaining control of himself. 'I'm feeling very fit, thank you. I have no desire to sit down. The contents of this letter, I believe, are none of your concern.' And with that he gave the missive one last glance and refolded it – neatly this time – and slid it back into the envelope. Then he looked up suddenly at Andrew again, his expression having changed once more. He seemed to be studying the episode, seeing it and Andrew both, perhaps, in a new light.

Andrew stretched his face into a look of indifferent resignation, shrugged, and said, 'Sorry. None of my business. You're right. Didn't mean to butt in. You seemed almost helpless there for a moment, though, and … Well …' He waved the whole incident away, trying to give the impression that he would forget about it, that he had already forgotten about it, that *he*, certainly, wouldn't be the cause of Pennyman's further embarrassment. 'By the way, the phone company came around today and installed a phone in your room. I thought it was high time. It's on the house – all but long-distance calls, of course.'

Pennyman was forced to thank him, although the effort of it was apparently painful. Then he turned toward the stairs, whacking his stick a couple of times against the carpet as if to recall the spirit of determination that he'd first come in with. He strolled away, humming now, brushing at his sleeve.

He stopped at the first step, looking downward. Then he bent just a little, leaning on his stick. Andrew watched, biting his lip, suppressing laughter. Pennyman stooped to pick up the nickel that seemed to lie there on the bottom tread.

It wouldn't come up. It was stuck. He flicked at it with his finger, then whacked at it with his stick. Andrew leaned forward in his chair, ready with a comment. 'Coin trouble?' he would say, raising one eyebrow as if mystified at Pennyman's antics. That would do the trick. It would imply things. The day belonged to Andrew, and no doubt about it – the nailed nickel trick coming on top of the anonymous letter. Pennyman was a living ruin: one moment a thing of clockwork dignity tricked up out of hair oil and an ostentatious cane, the next moment a slouched old humbugging fake, scrabbling after joke nickels on the stairs.

Pennyman stood up suddenly, not turning around. He gazed up the stairwell, straight ahead of him, thinking about something. Andrew couldn't force himself to talk to the man's back. He wouldn't be able to speak if Pennyman didn't look at him. Ah, well … Silence, perhaps, would say more under the circumstances. He watched Pennyman climb the stairs, humming again. Andrew didn't like the humming. There was something in the humming that wasn't good, as if Pennyman were humming him out of existence. Andrew popped up and stepped into the kitchen, pulling a little claw hammer out of the drawer and then heading out toward the stairs to pry out the nickel. It was a pity, really, to have driven the thing into the stair tread, although the runner would hide the hole easily enough. He worked out the nickel, shoved it into his pocket, and then pushed at the rug a little to press the hole shut. There it was, disappeared, and no one the wiser.

The cafe, finally, was almost put right. It seemed to Andrew as if there were merit in the mere bulk of kitchen apparatus – all the stuff that Aunt Naomi had sprung for six weeks back and was only now being delivered and installed. He sat at the bar polishing years of dust from old salt and pepper shakers and taking notes in his spiral binder as three men in blue jeans and shrunken T-shirts hooked up a Wolf stove. It was enormous – six broad burners, a griddle the size of a playing field, and two ovens, each of which could accommodate a Thanksgiving turkey. Alongside it was a vast warming oven, and next to that was a cupboard with a cutting board top. Andrew had designed the cutting board himself, and was moderately proud of it. It was as big as would fit comfortably into the relatively small cooking area, and it had stainless steel bowls mortised in, so that a chef could sweep chopped odds and ends off into the bowls, pluck the bowls out, and dump the odds and ends into pans on the stove.

He was itching to mess with it all, to make it work. It was impossible that the equipment could produce anything in the food line that wasn't first-rate. A friend of Pickett's had built the cabinetry and the bar – had done all the woodwork, in fact, under Andrew's supervision, and it all looked just right. Andrew had bought the half-dozen draw-leaf tables for ninety dollars apiece from an importer of English antiques, and had searched out three dozen oak chairs at thrift shops in downtown Long Beach. He'd paid out ten or fifteen dollars for each of them, and so he had no *sets* of chairs to speak of, just a random lot of them that Pickett's friend had worked over, regluing joints and replacing missing spindles and shimming up short legs.

Andrew admired the general mess of old furniture and had decided to continue the theme. He'd bought up random silverware and cups and saucers and odd bits of china and porcelain and napkin rings. He'd found no end of old tablecloths of mid-fifties vintage, with deep pastel flowers and rectilinear designs. And he had collected pairs of salt and pepper shakers: comical ducks and head-bobbing dogs and painted clowns riding on happy-go-lucky pigs.

Every table would be a mish-mash of shapes and colors, would remind you of a carnival, of a kaleidoscope, of a wooden box full of marbles, of the kitchen and pantry in Mr Badger's house. It would be a comfortable place, with a cheerful fire in the winter and the casement windows thrown open in the summer. There wouldn't be two forks the same, or two wine glasses either, and serious, frowning businessmen, talking about updating supplies and finalizing documents and impacting infrastructures, would suddenly find themselves salting their potatoes out of the end of an elephant's nose. He saw it as an experiment in the principles of Ruskin and Morris. It wouldn't just be the food that sent them out satisfied; it would be something else, too, something that they couldn't quite define. Satisfied and mystified at once, that's what they'd be – and better off for it, too.

He had sprung for the espresso maker just that morning. The old Andrew would have frittered away the bulk of Aunt Naomi's money on odds and ends, and then looked about frantically for a means to buy the espresso maker. But he'd turned over a leaf on the night of the Cheerios meeting. He was working hard now at developing a strain of practicality in himself, at becoming the-man-who-got-things-done. The house painting was evidence of it. For the past couple of days, since the victory of the letter and the nailed nickel, he'd let Pennyman go pretty much about his business; he had acted as if what Pennyman was up to was no concern of his. He'd been tempted to listen in on one of Pennyman's phone calls, but he hadn't done it. Pennyman would suspect that very thing. Andrew would wait for Pickett's return, and then the two of them would hold a council of war. After that, who could say?

He'd been fiddling with a promotional notion, too – the idea of sewing up a couple of enormous chef's hats, one for himself and one for Pickett. There was no reason at all that they couldn't be inflated, say, with helium, like clouds hovering over their heads as they manipulated whisks and spatulas in the kitchen. A photo in the *Herald* would do nicely. It would advertise that here was no ordinary cafe, operated by ordinary chefs.

Ordinariness was cheap; everyone owned it by the bucketful. Here at the cafe was something you didn't quite expect, such a picture would reveal. What? – something pleasant, certainly, something compelling and utterly removed from the tedious humdrum of the workaday world. He'd get Rose to sew the hats up. She'd see the value in them. They were a practical matter, really, an advertisement. The tops, of course, might have to be cut out of thin, beach ball vinyl and the seams glued shut. It would be nothing for Rose – two hours' work. Andrew sketched a hat in his binder, then flipped the page and sketched another one, bigger. He drew a comical picture of Pickett with a caricature mustache and a fabulous inflated hat perched on his head, like a double-dip mound of vanilla ice cream balanced on the wrong end of a cone. There was no point simply in a *big* chef's hat. It had to be enormous – the sort of thing to make the public's eyes shoot open; a tall order in these odd latter days, when men in helmets and wizard shirts searched for mysteries on the foggy seashore.

Thank goodness the workmen were leaving. Andrew hated to have strangers mucking around in his cafe; they violated it, somehow, with their cussing and loud laughter and hooting out the doorway at women a block away on the highway. When their truck finally rumbled off, Andrew set in with a rag and a spray bottle of cleaner, swabbing down stainless steel and generally neatening things up. It was then that Ken-or-Ed walked in. Another man followed him, carrying a clipboard.

'Ken,' said Andrew, standing up.

'Ed, actually. Look here. I'll get straight to the point ...' At that juncture, though, the man with the clipboard snorted, and Ed looked at him, losing the point entirely. On the bar was a salt and pepper shaker set – two tiny ceramic tornadoes, interlocking and hanging on a ceramic fence rail. They each had winking eyes and flipper-like arms and hands, one arm of each entwined around the other one's shoulder. Of the two free arms and hands, one held a sheaf of wheat, the other a sign that read, 'I been to Kansas.' Andrew had been trying to wangle the jammed corks out of them.

The man with the clipboard winked broadly at Ed and fumbled at his shirtpocket, pulling a ball-point pen out of an inky pen holder. He jotted something down.

Andrew squinted at them both, wondering what in the devil they wanted. This didn't seem to be a social call. 'What's the point, again?'

His neighbor crossed his arms, looking uncomfortable. 'I was saying that some of us have just learned about the cafeteria you're starting up here, and ...'

'Cafeteria?'

'That's right. You can hardly deny it, can you?' He swept his hand around in a broad gesture, taking in the newly installed equipment. 'This inn idea wasn't quite as bad – was it? It wouldn't have ruined the neighborhood. But a cafeteria is ...'

'Cafeteria?' said Andrew. 'Do you mean like Clifton's or something – hot turkey sandwiches and meat loaf and roast beef with gravy? Mashed potatoes? People in a line serving themselves with enormous spoons?' Andrew looked at him incredulously, as if he couldn't quite imagine that the cafeteria subject had been broached. The second man wandered away, taking notes.

Ed gestured the whole business into oblivion. 'I don't care about mashed potatoes. Will you listen to me? By God, we won't have it. That's what I'm saying. Mashed potatoes or no mashed potatoes. We don't want this neighborhood turned into a fast-food restaurant! It's illegal. This is Jack Dilton from the planning commission. He's a personal friend of mine.'

'I can easily imagine that he is,' said Andrew. 'Even the least of us needs a friend. I have a variance, actually. This was all settled long ago. You're a little late. And who set you off, anyway? Just the other night you were running around in the streets half-naked. It was an insult to my wife and to Mrs Gummidge. Put on some clothes next time.' Jack Dilton stepped back across, sensing trouble. Andrew nodded to him and smiled politely. 'Glad to meet you, Mr Dilman.'

'Dilton,' the man said. 'I'd like to see a copy of the variance if I might.'

'You can't,' said Andrew. 'You can't stay here another moment. Do you have a warrant of some sort? No, you don't. You can't have a warrant, because they don't entrust warrants to petty officials from the planning commission. What you've come around here for I can't imagine, but I have a tendency to think that it has something to do either with thievery or malicious mischief. Someone has been systematically stealing valuable books from my library and letting 'possums loose in the attic bedrooms at night. What *were* you doing on the street that night, Ken?'

'My name is Ed. Ed Fitzpatrick. *Mr* Fitzpatrick. *You're* crazy. I'm going to have this place shut down. There isn't any parking and the neighborhood isn't zoned commercial.'

Andrew's face stretched with astonishment. He reached out suddenly and pumped his neighbor's hand, then let it drop just as suddenly. 'You aren't *the* Eddie Fitzpatrick? – who played for the Dodgers one season? Old *Slider* Fitzpatrick?'

Just then the door to the house kitchen swung open and Rose peered in, holding a glass of lemonade. 'Didn't mean to interrupt,' she said.

Andrew stepped across to take the lemonade. He waved back at his neighbor. 'Rose, this is Eddie *Fitzpatrick*, of the Dodgers, remember him? Relieved Wally Moon that one night at the Coliseum. Walked eight batters in an inning. *You* remember. It was on the night that the hot dog vendor tumbled down the stairs and broke his leg. Who'd have thought? And right across the street, To ...' He grinned at Jack Dilton. 'Baseball fan, Mr Dilman?'

Rose gave Andrew a hard look, a drop-this-nonsense look, and started to say something to the neighbor. Ken-or-Ed interrupted her though, his face having gone red. 'Your husband is an idiot,' he said, glaring past her at Andrew. 'And what's more, he's a filthy Peeping Tom. That's what I think. That's why he was up in that damned tree the other night, peering into windows. By God, my wife heard a noise last night, too, and ...'

Andrew had hauled off his jacket by then and tossed it onto the bar, accidentally knocking off one of the tornadoes, which cracked to bits on the hardwood floor. Doubly enraged by the broken saltshaker, Andrew pushed Ken-or-Ed's shoulder, spinning him half-around. 'I don't care *who* you are,' he shouted, waving a fist. 'Call me an idiot! Call me a Peeping Tom! I'll ...'

Ken-or-Ed hunkered over, both hands in front of his face in the style of a turn-of-the-century boxer. 'Try me,' he said. 'C'mon!'

'Try nothing!' Rose shouted, stepping in between them. 'Get out of my house, you and your friend both.'

'That's right ...' said Andrew, endeavoring to move Rose out of the way. This was a man's work. He'd bloody the fool's nose. One good blow ...

'You shut up, too. You're both fools. Now get out. Andrew, sit down, for God's sake, before you turn yourself into the idiot he says you are. There's the door, Mr Fitzpatrick.'

Dilton had already retreated toward it, and was busily measuring it with a pocket tape measure. Suddenly Mr Pennyman was standing behind him, having materialized, it seemed, out of the afternoon air. Dilton hopped back into the room, prodded by the tip of Pennyman's cane and turning around to protest. The idea of Pennyman showing up at all further infuriated Andrew, who was mad now in such a variety of directions that he couldn't speak.

'What seems to be the trouble?' asked Pennyman slowly, uttering the syllables in a voice that sounded as if it had come out of a machine. Instantly a quiet descended on the room, and Ken-or-Ed blinked at him, seeming to wonder why his simple presence was enough to strike them all silent.

Pennyman leaned on his stick and smiled. 'You're from the planning commission,' he said to Dilton.

'That's right. This entire business is illegal, if I'm not mistaken. The doorway isn't broad enough, there's no ceiling sprinklers – not even a smoke alarm. It's a shame.'

'Save your catalogue, sir. I represent these fine people, and I can assure you that everything that goes on here is legal and aboveboard. I believe they attained a variance some months back and have a moderately good relationship with the Coastline Steering Committee and the Chamber of Commerce.'

Andrew started to protest. Pennyman *represent* them! He wouldn't be represented by Pennyman on a bet. 'We can ...' he started, but Rose stepped meaningfully on his foot, and he shut up.

Dilton stared at Pennyman and Ken-or-Ed stared at Dilton. 'Let's go,' Dilton said, sliding his pen back into his pocket.

'This is pointless.'

'We'll be back!' shouted Ken-or-Ed over his shoulder, but the threat didn't amount to much, and Andrew yelled 'Hah!' just to show him. It made him feel almost happy to see that the fat man's shirt had come untucked in the melee, and what was left of his hair had been jacked up into a sort of wonderful hedge.

'Tuck in your shirt!' Andrew shouted out the door, but Rose dragged him away. He was giddy with victory for a moment, but then there was Pennyman, smiling benevolently.

'I'll see what I can do,' he said to Rose.

Andrew plucked up his coat and put it on. 'Don't bother,' he said. 'There's nothing to be done.'

Rose cast Andrew another look. 'Thank you,' she said to Pennyman.

Andrew started to speak again, but Pennyman had very gallantly kissed Rose's hand and was tapping toward the door, and the sight of the hand-kissing froze Andrew's words before they'd had a chance to be uttered. Speaking was no good at all here. The more he spoke, the worse it got. Andrew would have simply slammed Pennyman in the back of the head then and there, except that there was something in him that wouldn't allow for the striking of an old man. Or else there was something in him that made him afraid to. He pushed this last thought out of his mind and bent over to sweep up the fragments of the broken tornado. And just before Pennyman disappeared, Andrew heard him mutter the words 'upset' and then 'he'll calm down.' Then he was gone, giving Andrew no chance at all to murder him.

Andrew stood staring at the backs of his hands on the bar. Then, calmly and deliberately, he picked up the unbroken tornado and threw it hard at the wall. It exploded in a spray of black pepper, the 'I been to Kansas' sign snapping off entire and spinning away across the bar like a top. Rose gaped at him. Without looking up, he slammed his fist down sideways onto the little, hollow ceramic sign, crushing it. He could feel it slice into the side of his palm, and he was glad for it. It would show Rose something; that was for sure. *What* it would show her he couldn't say; not enough, maybe. To complete the picture, he smashed his closed fist into one of the wooden panels fronting the bar, with far more force than he'd intended. He winced in spite of himself, and blood from the cut sprayed back onto his pants. Rose walked silently through the door, back the way she'd come. Andrew watched her go, the wild energy emptying from him. He pressed his left hand over the bleeding cut and flexed his fingers, wondering if he'd broken one of them. He half-hoped he had. He deserved to. But then he'd have to live with the day-to-day reminder of it for the next six weeks, and that he didn't deserve. That would be too much.

He seemed to go limp all of a sudden. All his rage had leaked away like water out of a cracked jar. He wanted suddenly to chase after Rose, to explain himself. It was easy enough. It was Pennyman, is what it was – kissing her hand. He couldn't have that. It wasn't gallant, it was … a perversion. Pennyman was laughing at both of them. Andrew could stand the laughter; he was big enough to shoulder it; but he couldn't have the slimy old fake making up to Rose that way. He nearly punched his hand into the bar again, but he didn't have enough jazz. He was drained, empty. He slumped into a chair and stared out through the street door, thinking of nothing.

At dinner that night Rose didn't say a thing about the trouble in the afternoon. She was cheerful, in fact, and had opened a bottle of Spanish champagne, which Andrew was happy enough to see. He kept wanting to bring the subject up, conversationally, as if by chance, in order to get around to explaining himself. He knew, though, that he oughtn't to be *explaining* anything. He ought to be apologizing. There was a vast difference. It was easy enough for him to do the one; the other was tough.

And here was Rose, pouring him a third glass of champagne. Pennyman was out; Mrs Gummidge was upstairs, eating with Aunt Naomi. It was just the two of them. That sort of rage – that cold sort of smashing and breaking – was something entirely foreign to Rose. She didn't engage in it. She couldn't be made to understand it, any more than a tropical native could be made to understand ice … But there he went again, thinking of explanations.

If she just weren't so damned pleasant, with the champagne and all. She very clearly had 'forgotten all about it,' so as to make it easier on him. And she *meant* it, too. There was nothing deceitful in it. She was simply good, in about a hundred ways, thank God, and her goodness made Andrew feel worse.

Then it occurred to him abruptly that she was taking Pennyman's advice, and letting him 'calm down.' That wasn't so good after all. Thinking of Pennyman made Andrew go cold. The champagne wasn't worth anything all of a sudden. The pleasant sense of proportion it had given him evaporated and he felt only a dull headache.

Things changed so fast. The days seemed to bolt past while he hurried blindly toward a destination that no one on earth could define for him. He never seemed to get there either. More than half his life was gone, and he seemed no closer to any of his nebulous goals than he'd ever been. He'd been closer, in fact, when he was eighteen and was full of dreams and spirit. What had Aunt Naomi said? The world wasn't your oyster any more. Well, that would take some getting used to.

He could remember when, not so very long ago, he'd been as even-tempered as the next man, more so even. Laugh-a-minute Andrew; that's what he'd been. Now the tiniest thing would set him off. The bad, out-of-temper mornings came around more often than the mornings full of cheerful whistling. Would it get worse? Would Rose tolerate him? Why in the hell *couldn't* he have just a little bit of Pennyman's gallantry and self-assuredness?

The champagne was gone. He couldn't suggest opening another; that would be going too far. It would be a disaster to end the day in a drunken stupor, desperately pretending that he wasn't. He smiled at Rose, marveling at how pretty she looked. She hadn't ever needed make-up, although she looked smashing when she had it on. When she was half-disheveled, at the end of a long, tiresome day like this one, she looked prettiest. *Capable* was what she looked, and just a little bit tough, as if there was nothing that she might do that would surprise you. How in the world had he ended up with a woman like her? Why didn't she just pitch him out? He felt the wild urge to ask her, but he stepped on it. There was no use pushing his luck.

Maybe things hadn't gone so badly for him after all. When you looked around, why there was a comfortable house full of books and the smell of the sea, and there was Rose being good to him, and a business to dabble in that let him do just what he wanted – even if doing it made him feel guilty. It occurred to him for the first time – as if the champagne, or something, had whispered it very clearly into his ear – that he'd be more satisfied, perhaps, if he thought less about his regrets and more about – what? – his many blessings, maybe.

He must be drunk. He was getting maudlin. In a moment he'd start singing, counting them one by one. He pushed himself away from the table in tolerably better spirits, though. There was nothing for it but to keep going, to put one foot in front of the other. Steady-on – that was what was demanded of him. And besides, Pennyman would get his one of these days soon. Andrew would have to bring it off in such a way that it was Pennyman, and not himself, who was made to seem mean and small, especially to Rose.

'I'm going out to work on the cafe,' Andrew said, kissing Rose on the cheek. 'It's pretty nearly ready.'

Rose nodded. 'I'll just clean up. Why *did* that man come around this afternoon? He turned out to be far more horrible than I'd have guessed.'

Andrew shook his head, grateful that the subject, finally, had been brought up. 'I don't know what set him off. He must have known all along what we were doing here. Now he's taken it into his head to start trouble. He's a lunatic. That's all I can think of. He can't touch us, though. Don't worry about it, for heaven's sake. I'll take care of it. I'll call Uncle Arthur tomorrow. He's connected; maybe he can help.'

'I'd be relieved if you did. Don't go brawling with the neighbors, though. Promise me that. You know how you are. You'll hurt someone and then there'll be trouble. That seems to be what he wants, you know. To start something.'

Andrew nodded. That certainly seemed so. 'I wouldn't have hurt him much,' he said. 'Just a little poke in the nose.' He was moderately proud of the idea. Once he got hold of a man, he didn't let him go until he'd wrung him out.

'And what was that nonsense about a baseball game? I don't believe I've ever been to one.'

'That was good, wasn't it?' Andrew grinned, recalling how easy it had been to make Ken-or-Ed or whatever his name was both furious and mystified at the same time. That took a certain technique. 'Sent him straight through the roof, didn't it?'

'But was it a *good* idea to send him straight through the roof?'

Andrew shrugged. 'It did the trick. I'm glad you stopped me, though. I *might* have hurt the man after all. I'm a pretty dangerous character, aren't I?'

'That's why you need me around. Admit it.'

'I admit it. Happily.' He kissed her again and went out whistling. He'd have another go at the menu. It was due at the printer's day after tomorrow. Pickett would be home late tomorrow night, and could give him a hand. Then, as a gesture, he'd run it past Aunt Naomi the following morning. Who could tell? – she might have something smart to say about it after all. He glanced back at Rose as he shut the door behind him. She winked at him very jolly and then gave him a mock-serious look, a no-nonsense look, a behave-yourself look, as if she were keeping him in line. And it made him feel almost whole again.

NINE

'Hey diddle diddle, the cat and the fiddle, the pig and the coin in the spoon ...'

ARCHAIC RHYME

Andrew decided to risk a phone call or two. Pickett would be dead set against messing around like that. He would want to use the attic phone to listen in, simply in hopes of discovering something telling. Making prank calls on it would accomplish nothing, Pickett would say. But Andrew couldn't hang around halfway up the stairs all day, waiting for Pennyman's telephone to ring. He was a busy man, what with the painting and all.

He was getting the hang of it – this painting business. What sickened him was the idea of having to scrape all the old, flaked paint off the eaves. With the money left from Aunt Naomi, he could hire someone to clean the house up, to do the preparatory work; then he could wade in and paint it. But after his boasting and all to Rose, he would look like a fool hiring someone. It would be an admission of incompetence and laziness, among a number of other things – including the fact that he somehow had a large chunk of money in his pocket.

But that damned old paint seemed to chip off right under his nose. The slightest vagaries of weather set it off. He had been brushing away late that very afternoon when the most astonishing wind had blown up, seemingly from under the house. Hot and dry, it had come rushing out through the crawlspace, carrying almost chalk-fine dust on it and the dried exoskeletons and spindle legs of dead beetles. There had been a moaning, too, as if some-one with an awful hangover were waking up beneath the house. The wind had come curling up around him, billowing out his shirt, dirtying his hair, and, weirdly, the old, dried paint on the clapboards had begun to alligator off in a little hailstorm of yellow chips, the loosened paint snapping, the clap-boards groaning. A half-dozen nails had half-pried out with a single desperate skreek. Then the wind fell, the chipping paint lay still in the grass, and the moaning stopped.

Andrew had gotten a hammer out of the garage and beaten the nails back in, all the time wondering what on earth had gone on. The moaning, certainly, would simply have been wind blowing through the cracks around the crawlspace – either that, or it might have been the 'possum, yowling at the wind like a dog yowling at sirens. It was still under there, the 'possum was, coming and going at night. But where did the wind come from? Through the crawlspace on the far side of the house? It was sheltered over there. Andrew had gone back to scraping, half-expecting another blast of wind, which you *would* expect, if it were a natural wind. But there had been nothing.

If the phenomenon had occurred three weeks back, he'd have shrugged. He'd have forgotten it by dinnertime. But now, with things astir on the south coast … Maybe this wind was one of the 'emanations' that Pickett's friend Georgia had carried on about. She was full of talk of positive ions. In fact she had said that the air around the house was saturated with them, and that Andrew ought to get some sort of machine, he couldn't remember quite what – an orgone box? An ionic bomb? She had said that the house was at the eye of a mystical *foehn* wind. As he understood it, the whole thing was a matter of electrical charges cast off by spirit forces – ghosts bumping into each other, like raindrops in clouds. It had struck him as funny. Ghosts lead the damndest lives.

But now this wind … And even if there were some sort of mystical business going on, what did it mean? Perhaps Pennyman was behind it. They were going at it blow for blow, he and Andrew were. Pennyman still reeled from the effects of the note and the nailed nickel. The old man had come back at Andrew there in the cafe, mumbling to Rose just loud enough to be overheard. And now, to leap ahead in the war, maybe he had manufactured this scaling paint business, although heaven knows how he'd done it. It seemed to argue that it was Andrew's turn. The telephone would do nicely.

Andrew decided not to go about it in any slipshod manner. It was just possible that he was involved in something more grand than he had suspected. If so, then subtlety was vital. What was called for was tomfoolery with a delicate touch.

He mixed up a pitcher of lemonade in the kitchen, then sneaked up the stairs to make sure Pennyman's door was shut. He would have to place the call from his bedroom phone, and his bedroom was just down the hall from Pennyman's room. He couldn't afford to be seen going past in the hall or hustling up and down the stairs. He couldn't call any attention at all to himself, not if he wanted to accomplish anything.

After the call, there was the chance that Pennyman would phone out, that he had accomplices, that he was part of a more nebulous conspiracy and that he would want to keep them informed. In that case, Andrew would have to listen in. He'd have to slip up the stairs into the attic to where the extension was. Clearly, if Pennyman spotted him going up, Andrew would have to pretend to be paying a visit to Aunt Naomi, and forget about listening in. Coming back down afterward, of course, would be riskiest. He could still claim to have been up visiting Naomi, but Pennyman would be certain he hadn't been. And if Pennyman tumbled to the gag phone call, or to the existence of the attic extension, then he'd be certain about the origins of the note, too, and would be on his guard. Andrew's entire battle plan would be exposed. He tiptoed along, holding his breath, listening hard. The coast was clear; the door was closed.

He got the best effect by talking through a Melitta coffee filter – a black plastic cone with a paper filter still lined with wet grounds. The effect was astonishing, like a voice out of an orbiting satellite. He slipped into his bedroom, and eased the door shut. Then, holding the coffee filter against the telephone mouthpiece like an upended bullhorn, he shoved his face into the cone and dialed Pennyman's number. He heard the phone ring across the hall an instant before he heard the manufactured ring inside the telephone. 'Mr Pennyman?' he asked, suppressing a giggle.

'Yes,' Pennyman answered, immediately suspicious.

'Mr Jules Pennyman?'

'Yes, what do you want?'

'I have a message for you. From a friend in the east.' Andrew snickered, immediately sniffing and clearing his throat, as if it hadn't been a snicker at all. He pinched himself hard on the leg.

There was a silence, then Pennyman saying, 'You do, do you?'

Very slowly and ponderously, enunciating as if he were talking to a half-wit or a foreigner, Andrew said, 'He wants you to know that the key to the dilemma is a chew of tobacco. Tow-bak-ko. A chaw of ... *terbackky*. His advice is Redman brand. This is generally unknown.'

There was another silence, a long one, which Andrew had to break by hanging up. He buried his face in his jacket, laughing like a fool. Pennyman was right down the hall. If he heard Andrew laughing like that, heading up to the attic, it would be curtains for the whole campaign. Andrew pinched himself again, trying to make it hurt, then ditched the coffee filter under the bed and went out swiftly and silently, up the stairs, sliding past Pennyman's room. The door was still shut.

He waited in the attic for a full minute. Timing was the key here. He couldn't afford to pluck up the receiver while Pennyman was dialing. Pennyman would hear the empty silence of the off-the-hook extension. If he were talking, though, to a line already open ... Andrew's hand hovered over the phone until, on the count of sixty, he eased the receiver out of the cradle. There was the sound of Pennyman's voice, already in conversation.

'Yes, that's correct.'

'When?'

'On the agreed-upon night.'

'Look, I'm not sure that the kind of money you're offering is worth the trouble that ...'

The voice trailed off, interrupted, if that were possible, by an enormous silence – the silence of Pennyman listening, judging, and coming to conclusions. The owner of the voice on the other end had somehow understood the silence, had felt its weight pressing against his own words, his own whining.

Andrew listened hard. A moment of revelation was at hand. What did it mean, 'the trouble'? The silence lengthened. Then Pennyman's voice again: 'On the agreed-upon night.'

'Yes. Of course. I just ...'

Andrew wheezed into the phone just as the man paused.

'I just ...'

Andrew made a noise like a bird, a sort of canary twitter involving his tongue and upper lip, only an instant of it.

'Pardon me?' asked the voice, half-apologetically.

'What?' said Pennyman. 'I didn't ...'

Andrew hung up – desperately carefully – and then slid out and down the stairs just as fast as he could manage. He heard Pennyman murmuring behind his door as he stepped past, and he was in the kitchen in seconds, lifting the receiver to the downstairs phone and dialing Pennyman's number again. It was busy, so he re-dialed – once, twice, three times, and then it rang. Pennyman picked up the receiver and listened for a moment before saying, 'Hello?'

Andrew switched the faucet in the sink over to spray and turned both taps onto full, then, without saying a word, shoved the receiver down into the sink, aiming it at the cataract. He counted to ten slowly before pulling it out, biting his jacket sleeve, and mumbling through a mouthful of cloth, 'Redman brand. Everyone agrees upon the night.' Then he hung up, tense, wondering if he'd gone too far.

He started whistling very loud and stomping around in order to give the impression that he was hard at work. He poured a tall ice-filled glass of lemonade, then stamped away up the stairs, still whistling, but softer now, more subtly. He rapped on Pennyman's door, and the old man opened it almost at once, as if he'd been standing right there.

'Glass of lemonade?' asked Andrew. 'Made in the shade by an old maid with a spade.' He winked. 'Just now brewed it up in the kitchen. I've been outside painting.' He looked past Pennyman, into the room. Only a slip of it was visible through the crack between Pennyman and the jamb. On the floor, weirdly, was one of Aunt Naomi's cat boxes, or rather, one of her cats' cat boxes, well used, and with a little slotted metal scooper shoved into the sand.

Upon opening the door, Pennyman regarded him evenly, then glanced at the glass with a look of profound contempt. He started to speak, but Andrew's face betrayed his puzzlement over the cat box, and suddenly Pennyman's countenance changed. He pushed the door open a little wider, as if he had nothing to hide, and gestured back into the room with his free hand. 'Looks odd, doesn't it?' he said. Andrew shook his head, trying to grin. 'I thought I'd do my part. These little domestic chores ... Rose is too busy for them, and heaven knows, what with the painting and all ...'

'Of course,' said Andrew. 'And Naomi, certainly, still isn't up to it entirely. By golly. We appreciate it; I can assure you.'

Pennyman took the lemonade now, smiling widely. Andrew was one up on him, and he knew it. Scowling wouldn't accomplish a thing for him. He stood for a moment, as if unsure what to do next, like a child who had been caught at something and had managed to lie his way out of it but was still edgy about the lie.

Andrew raised his eyebrows, thinking to follow up his little victory. 'Something gone wrong?'

'No,' said Pennyman, recovering. 'Why?' His tone of voice seemed a challenge to Andrew to make something of the cat box.

'Nothing. This is really first-rate of you. Humbling sort of job, mucking out cat boxes – calls for something more than lemonade, really. And this is out of a can, I'm afraid, but not at all bad.' The conversation had come to an impasse. Pennyman was clearly anxious to close the door.

'It will do just fine,' he said. 'I'm really rather busy.'

'Yes,' said Andrew. 'I can see that. Well, there's more in the kitchen. I've mixed up a jumbo can. It's in the fridge.'

Pennyman stared at him. He was gaining ground. 'In the *fridge*,' he said flatly. Then he smiled an ingratiating smile, started to close the door, but evidently thought better of it. 'I'd like to recommend a book to you, by the way.'

'Ah,' said Andrew. 'Which one.'

'Anthropological text, actually. I know that's not your meat, as they say, but you'd find it ... informative. Wonderful book, actually. All about a race of early men in South America who dismembered their dead, afraid that they'd walk again otherwise. Sawed them into pieces. Very nasty business, don't you think?'

Andrew gaped at him. 'Yes. Now that you point it out. I mean to say – sawed them up?'

'Into fragments. Then generally mixed up the pieces of a half-dozen corpses and buried them like a salad. If the corpse still managed to rise from the dead it wouldn't have any idea who to haunt – wouldn't know whether to go after the cousin of its arm or the landlady of its right ear.'

'Fascinating,' said Andrew. 'I'll look forward to it. But right now I've got to get on with the cafe, actually. Been at it steady. I just took a break to bring you up a glass. I mean to say that I've got to get back to the painting. Horrible job.'

He turned around and fled back down the stairs, cursing himself. Why had he thought it necessary to face Pennyman down? His momentary advantage over the man had gone up in smoke, and he had quite likely given himself away, to boot. If he had just let it go after the phone in the sink gag! Maybe headed back upstairs in another half hour to make a third call – a breather call – and then another a half hour later. By dinnertime Pennyman would have been jumpy as a flea. Now Andrew had gone and spoiled the effect. And the old maid with a spade business had been far too hearty. He would have to train his face and his voice not to give him away. But the cat box … What in the world? Pennyman was going to lengths to ingratiate himself with Rose and Naomi, but for what reason? Just to be in a better position to do Andrew down? He picked up the lemonade pitcher, looked around guiltily, and drank off a third of its contents before wiping the rim and putting it into the refrigerator.

Andrew looked again at his pocket watch: almost one o'clock in the morning. Pickett was late. He had called from somewhere outside Bakersfield and had been driving for sixteen hours, all the way from Portland. He had sounded very mysterious, as if he'd learned something; he wouldn't say what – not over the phone. That was at ten. Anyone could have made it from Bakersfield to Seal Beach in three hours, even in Pickett's rattling old Chevy.

Andrew peered through the window at the deepening fog. Headlights loomed through the mists on the highway, appearing and disappearing like the glowing eyes of deep-water fish. It was eerily silent, as if the fog muffled all noise. He could just hear the drip, drip, drip of moisture plunking down into the saturated dirt of the windowbox from an overhanging branch.

The menus were finished. At first, until they got their sea legs under them, they'd offer a price-fixed menu – only two choices for the main course. There'd be a different theme, so to speak, every Friday and Saturday night, and breakfast served Saturday and Sunday mornings. But that wouldn't start for a week or two. Andrew had ordered handbills with the idea of giving them out to early-morning, weekend pier fishermen.

On Saturday, when they opened, Andrew would lead off with Cajun food, which was in vogue – something that was irritating, since Andrew had fancied it for years. He couldn't much stand the idea of liking things that were fashionable. People would assume that he liked them *because* they were fashionable, when in fact it was most often true that the opposite was the case. Cajun food though … He'd make a gumbo that would wake them up. With Rose and Mrs Gummidge waiting tables, Andrew cooking, and Pickett generally *maître d*'ing and helping out here and there, they'd do tolerably well. He'd have to give Mrs Gummidge clear orders not to speak, though. He couldn't have her start yammering in front of the guests; that would be the end of their patronage.

Andrew's mind wandered, sorting through his list of current troubles. It seemed that there was always something leering in at the window, some ruinous little piper demanding to be paid. Rose still had no idea that he'd loaned Pickett the credit card merely to stock up on Weetabix. It would do her no good at all to know. She couldn't fathom it, and for very good reasons, too. Yesterday evening, after his making up with Rose, Andrew had popped down to the supermarket to search out sesame oil and oyster sauce in anticipation of Chinese night, and there in the import foods aisle he'd run into a shelf of Weetabix. His information had been wrong. They weren't contraband at all. They were a dollar and a half a box. With a dozen biscuits in a box, and two in a serving at ninety cents per serving, that was a profit margin of two or three hundred percent, not subtracting for overhead. Andrew sighed. He had sent Pickett after the Weetabix in good faith, anyway. He couldn't be expected to know *everything*.

Pickett wouldn't have charged more than sixty or eighty dollars in gas. Andrew would have to keep the thing silent and nab the credit card bill before Rose got to it. He couldn't afford to forget – as he'd forgotten about the coffee filter under the bed. She had found it later in the evening while searching for a bedroom slipper. After trying in vain to dream up a lie, Andrew had said simply, 'You wouldn't believe it if I told you,' and she had nodded in agreement, not asking him to try. It depressed him, though, her having to protect him with her silence and her continually taking the long view. The house painting had made up for some of it. And when this whole thing was over, he would quit staying up late every night. That would help. She rarely said anything about it, but he was certain she felt his absence, so to speak, and he was happy she did.

Tonight, though, he had business to attend to. Rose was long ago in bed, and it would be a simple thing tonight to unload the cases of Weetabix like he'd done the whiskey, stow them away, and later on pretend that they'd come from some standard issue distributor in Los Angeles.

But where was Pickett? He'd been on edge when he'd called, had mumbled something about a newspaper clipping from the Vancouver *Tribune*, about a murder, about a curious book he'd bought in a Gastown bookstore. Andrew had pressed him for details but Pickett had clammed up.

Headlights swung round the corner and there sounded briefly the churning rumble of the Chevrolet. Then the lights blinked out and the motor coughed quietly and cut off. Andrew stepped out onto the side porch just as the pale bulk of Pickett's car coasted out of the mists and slanted in toward the curb. The door opened and Pickett hunched out from behind the wheel, carrying his leather briefcase. He grabbed Andrew's elbow and hurried him back in after shutting the car door softly behind them but leaving the window down. He stood inside the cafe, watching the street.

Andrew started to speak but Pickett shushed him, still holding onto his arm. His grip tightened as another pair of headlights appeared, and a taxi, navigating through the fog, stopped at the curb opposite. The door opened and out stepped Pennyman, smoking on his pipe. He handed the driver a bill, then counted change out of his open palm before tapping across the street with his stick, up onto the lawn. They heard the front door swing open and then shut, and then Pennyman's tread sounded for a moment on the stairs.

Andrew stepped across to the bar and with a shaking hand poured Pickett a glass of bourbon, neat. Pickett looked as if he needed it. His suit was rumpled and moist, and his hair had been blown silly by the wind on the open road. His shirttail was hauled out in back, and he made a gesture at tucking it back in, but accomplished nothing.

'He spotted me out near Leisure World,' Pickett said, wrinkling up his face. 'I saw him through a gap in the fog just as I was pulling off onto the boulevard. That beard of his is a dead giveaway.' Pickett stared into his glass, then rapped against the bar with his fist. 'What does he want? That's the trick. We don't know what he wants.'

Andrew nodded as if giving Pickett's question serious thought. He determined to play the fool. It would be better all the way around to cool Pickett down. He was fatigued from the trip, and so all the more likely to make a mistake. There was no room for mistakes now. 'Maybe he doesn't *want* anything. It's not much of a coincidence, is it? Nothing odd about Pennyman's being out and about this late. Night before last he didn't come home at all. Tonight he could have been anywhere. Mrs Gummidge tells me he's got a relative of some sort in Glendale. That would be about right. If he came home down the Long Beach and the San Diego freeways, then he'd have every reason on earth to be passing Leisure World. You don't put enough faith in simple coincidence.'

'He didn't come home at all night before last?'

'That's right. He's a grown-up. He can stay out all night.'

'Mrs Gummidge has been telling you this, about relatives in Glendale?'

'That's exactly what she's been telling me.'

Pickett looked steadily at him, then brushed his hair back out of his face. 'And you believe her?' He asked the question in a flat sort of tone, as if he'd been wondering whether it might have come down to this at last.

Andrew thought for a moment and then said, 'No. I don't suppose I do. But it's possible just the same. We don't want to overreach ourselves, do we?

We don't want to get jumpy now. Our big advantage is that he thinks we're largely ignorant.'

'Maybe,' said Pickett. 'Look at this.' He handed Andrew the newspaper clipping that he'd mentioned over the phone – the grisly account of a murder, of a man sawed in half lengthwise, so cleanly that the precision of it utterly baffled the authorities. He'd been frozen first. That was the consensus, although a coroner had speculated that a laser scalpel might have done the trick. He'd been found – both halves of him had – holding a silver quarter in either hand, for reasons no one could fathom. Had he been murdered in the midst of making change? It hardly seemed likely.

Andrew was almost giddy with dread as he skimmed through the article, wondering why on earth Pickett had brought it along and knowing why at the same time. It was ghastly, to be sure, and was the sort of utterly unlikely incident that would give the gears in Pickett's head a good cranking. But beyond that, beyond all notion of reason and of reasons, was a muddle of instinct and gut fear – nothing but more unwoven threads from a tapestry they only suspected the existence of.

'The name,' said Pickett. 'Look at the man's name.' Andrew staggered against the bar. It was August Pfennig who'd been sawed in half August Pfennig – dead. That made it certain, didn't it? It made *something* certain anyway. But there was no way on earth that Pickett could know that Andrew knew the name. When had Andrew gotten the phone call, after all? Pickett was in Vancouver himself at the time. 'This Pfennig – who do *you* think he is?' asked Andrew, giving his friend a sharp look.

'He was Moneywort's cousin,' said Pickett flatly. 'We met him that night in Belmont Shore, at Moneywort's shop. You remember. No, strike that. *I* met him. You weren't there that night, were you?' Andrew shook his head and said nothing. Pickett continued: 'He had a tricolored koi that he'd paid a fortune for. I thought at the time that it was pretty weird, all of them fascinated with a big carp …' He stopped and looked edgewise at Andrew. 'Who in the devil did *you* think he was, for goodness sake? You knew the name. How many August Pfennigs can there be?'

Andrew told him about the phone call, about the coin business. Pickett listened, his eyes narrowing. He slammed his fist into his open palm and waved Andrew to silence, then paced back and forth across the floor.

'It doesn't matter. All of this proves a theory of mine. I called the authorities in my official capacity as a member of the press. I asked them straight out whether the murder was connected with the recent death of Pfennig's cousin – Leyman Moneywort. The officer on the phone professed ignorance of any such cousin and insisted that I come around to talk. Then he covered up the mouthpiece and mumbled for a moment before another detective got on and said he knew all about Moneywort, and that the murders were unrelated. A string of bad luck for the Pfennig-Moneywort family, that's all. He accused me of sensationalizing the case – as if it needed such a thing.'

Andrew nodded. 'And this didn't satisfy you?'

'Satisfy me! Heavens yes it satisfied me. What could the denial be but confirmation of a *connection*. Pfennig isn't two days dead, and here's the police professing the certainty that the two murders are unrelated. That was a carefully calculated tale; you can take it from me.'

Andrew shrugged. 'Let's haul those Weetabix in before the fog through the open window turns the boxes to mush.'

Pickett shook his head. 'Wait a bit. Let your man upstairs fall asleep first.' He put his finger to his lips to silence Andrew, then crept across toward the door that led to the kitchen. He snatched it open and stepped back, as if he were certain that Pennyman would be crouched there, perhaps with a glass tumbler pressed to his ear and a look of surprise on his bearded face. No one was there. Somewhere overhead a clock tolled – once, twice. 'Two o'clock,' said Pickett, and then pushed the door shut and turned once more to face his friend.

'Let me tell you about my little bit of detective work. I found a telephone book is what I did. And do you know what? There was a listing for August Pfennig Books and Arcana in Gastown. The man was dead – horribly murdered – but the shop was open for business as usual. That's where I bought this.' Pickett snapped open his briefcase and produced an old book. The cover was ochre-colored morocco, brittle and torn with age. Pickett set it onto the top of the bar and then nodded at it, as if to say, 'Look at *that*.'

There was gilt writing on the cover, but it was so faded and dim that Andrew opened the book to the title page. *Le Cochon Seul* it said, translated by the Marquise de Cambremer. Andrew looked up at Pickett. 'No author?'

'I think it's all old legends. Probably a pocketful of authors, like the Bible. I imagine that this marchioness had nothing at all to do with the writing of the thing.'

'Sounds rather like a cheese, doesn't it?'

'A cheese?' asked Pickett, mystified.

'This woman's name.'

'That's Camembert, the cheese is. This has nothing to do with cheeses. And it's not her name we care about anyway. It's the book itself, for heaven's sake.'

'It's Greek to me,' said Andrew, grinning.

'Well hold onto your hat, then. The title means "The One Pig," or something very much like that. I can't quite figure it as a title, but look at the frontispiece. That's what struck me. The clerk was studying it when I came in.'

Andrew did. There, badly drawn in sepia-colored ink, were back and front drawings of a serrated-edged coin with the likeness of a man on one side and of a moon-enclosed fish on the other. It was a crenelated-looking fish, like a sea serpent, perhaps, like the Leviathan, and it was swallowing its own tail.

Pickett looked moderately pleased with himself and started to talk again. Andrew stared at the picture, disbelieving in its existence. His chest felt hollow all of a sudden, and he found that he was breathing in little gasping breaths. He started to speak, to interrupt, but then he didn't. He decided to let Pickett go on. Pickett had been driving for nineteen hours, waiting for the chance to confound Andrew with this book, with whatever bit of coin lore the French text revealed. Andrew wouldn't upstage him yet.

'Well, the fact that it was an illustration of a coin struck me straight off,' said Pickett, warming to his story. 'But what fetched me up short was that I'd seen such a thing before. You'll never guess where.'

Andrew shrugged. All he was sure of was that Pickett hadn't ever seen Aunt Naomi's spoon, or rather *his* spoon. He was suddenly short of breath again.

'On Moneywort's hat. Remember me telling you about his fishing lures? Well, this is the fish, swallowing its tail. It's a common enough symbol in mythology, of course, serpents swallowing their tails. But it struck me like a ball bat that the likeness of this very fish should have been hanging from Moneywort's hat. Think about it: Moneywort's dead, murdered. And so is Pfennig. And the book is in Pfennig's shop. And here's the clerk with a hell of an unhealthy interest in it. Look at the picture – the multiple dorsal fin and the too-big head and the way there's a crescent moon laid in behind it, half-hidden. There isn't a shadow of a doubt – a miniature copy of it had been hanging on Moneywort's hat. I saw it there. Ho, I said to myself. Here's an unlikely coincidence. And the more I thought about it the unliklier it seemed.

'So just for the dickens of it I asked for the proprietor, for Pfennig – you know, just to feel the clerk out. Pfennig was gone – out of the country, said the man. Which was a lie, of course. Pfennig was lying in a bag on a slab at the morgue. The clerk couldn't have been ignorant of it. I mentioned that I'd been a friend of Moneywort's, but the clerk shrugged. I asked to buy the book, which, like I said, the clerk had been messing with when I came in through the door. He was nervous about it – tried to put me off. He said he couldn't sell it at any price. It was just a "curiosity," he said. Nothing valuable. Nothing I'd want, really. I told him that in fact I wanted it very badly, and then he said that it was sold already. That he was holding it for a man who was a friend of Pfennig. I told him *I* was a friend of Pfennig and then told him to name his price. That's just what I said: "Name your price, sir!" I said, and snapped your credit card down onto the counter when I said it. The long and the short of it is that he named it. These days a credit card is as good as cash.' Pickett winked broadly, as if to underscore the story of his victory.

'I don't doubt it,' said Andrew, sinking into a chair. Rose was going to kill him. He debated asking Pickett how much the clerk had soaked him for, but he didn't. It was too late at night. He'd never get to sleep if he knew. He'd have to watch for the bill to come in the mail, just as he'd planned, and pay it off entirely, then destroy the record. 'So what about this clerk?'

'He knew about Pfennig; you bet he did. You could see it in his eyes – raw terror. I thought he'd bolt before he got the book into a bag; and he nearly did. He sold me the thing, stuffed all the cash from the register into his pocket, and was out the door and locking it before I'd walked halfway down the block to my car. I've thought it over all the way down from Vancouver, and what I think is that we have a book that we shouldn't have, and *that's* why I didn't at all like the idea of running into Pennyman out by Leisure World. And now you tell me he was out of the house for nearly thirty-six hours on the day Pfennig was murdered. He was in Vancouver himself; that's what I think. And what's more, I think he was the "friend" who wanted the book.'

Andrew was suddenly overwhelmingly tired. His head spun with the bits and pieces of the mystery. He thought about the squid on the beach, sliced lengthwise, and Pennyman rummaging in its guts to retrieve a silver coin. He thought about the spoon lodged behind the books in his room, about the face on the front of it and the moon and fish on the convex curve of the bottom. He thought about Aunt Naomi giving it to him, almost making a production out of it, a ritual. He thought of Pfennig, sawed in two. Then a new thought chilled him – the thought of the credit card. 'They've got my name,' he said flatly.

Pickett shrugged. 'Forget about names,' he said. 'They're living in your house, for God's sake. They don't need your name.' He poured himself another glass of bourbon, and sat down, looking desperately fatigued.

Pickett was right, of course. Andrew opened the book again, to the frontispiece, just to make sure. 'There's something else living in the house,' he said flatly. 'Wait half a minute.'

And with that he walked out tiredly, slumping through the kitchen and up the stairs to fetch the pig spoon.

He knew that the penlight belonged to Andrew Vanbergen, but he didn't know what it was doing under the bedroom chair. Someone had been in his room while he had been traveling. He smiled, regarding himself in the mirror. He tipped his head. There was a clinic in Paris that performed hair transplants in such a way that one didn't emerge with a head that looked like a palm grove. And there was a shaman, a Professor M'gulu, in Zambia who could restore hair outright. The African's process, though, involved the application of loathsome substances to one's scalp and the chanting of mystical phrases. Jules Pennyman rather preferred a more clinical approach. He didn't function at all well in earthy, ritualistic settings. That was the enemy's territory, for the most part. Pennyman preferred the antiseptic cleanliness of stainless steel and vinyl and Formica scrubbed down with chemical sterilizers.

While the coins worked well enough prolonging life, they weren't at all kind to hair. There was a subtle, gradual decay and debilitation that they generated, even after one had got around the initial wasting away, the aches and pains and brittle bones. Pennyman had been plagued with random baldness for the last fifty years. The elixir manufactured by Moneywort and his cronies had done its work, and as long as he had it, he felt tip-top. Not even a cold. But he was beginning to suspect that there was a limit even to the elixir's effects; it was as if slowly but surely he'd become immune to the elixir's effects – as if it were an opiate – and now even with increased doses … That would be the effect of the coins again. But there was nothing he could do about it. There was always a price.

He could see in the mirror that his hair was thinning, unnaturally, in patches. He brushed it back carefully, checking the effect in the hand mirror. He'd have to have something done to his ears, too. There were certain body parts that kept growing, regardless of age, and their growing was enhanced by Moneywort's potion. Ears were the worst of them, because you couldn't cover them up. He despised the idea of surgery. One was so vulnerable when lying on a surgeon's table. But he couldn't abide looking comical either, and oversize ears were nothing if not comical.

There were aspects of the problem that he wouldn't have minded when he was young – those bodily members which, unlike ears, *could* be covered up. It had got to the point at which he could command a ducal salary on the club circuit, but he'd lost his taste for that sort of thing long years ago. Debauchery had worn thin after a while, and he had abandoned it as he had abandoned everything else. Even when he was young, he'd never understood the nature of the urgings that the common man referred to as love. They were nothing but fear – a matter of clinging to each other, just as a blind man, finding himself on the edge of an unfamiliar street, might cling to a tree or a lamp-post simply to keep his bearings as he listened to the traffic whiz by. Pennyman had no such fears. The unknown held no secrets from him, and he was no stranger to darkness.

He liked to think of the human heart as a clockwork mechanism, a thing of gears and crystals. He'd seen one at a laboratory in Munich, during the war. It had been removed from its host and maintained artificially in a sterile glass box, a complication of rubber tubes and circulating fluids. There was nothing sentimental about it; it was merely a mechanical device, more ghastly, perhaps, than a man-made contrivance because of its awful fleshiness, because it was more authentically alive.

If his plans failed, he'd go to the Paris clinic and have his ears attended to. If his plans *didn't* fail, then it wouldn't much matter.

What he couldn't quite fathom was the faint smell of perfume on his blanket. He knew whose perfume it was, but what had she been doing lying atop his bed? They'd never had any such relationship. The idea of it appalled him. The idea of physical contact of any sort appalled him, and that sort doubly so. What in the world had she been up to? Some sort of odd fantasizing? If so, then she'd come unhinged, and he'd be better off if she disappeared off the end of the pier on the next foggy night. His mind wrangled with the mystery. Why on top of the bedclothes and not under them? Clearly it hadn't simply been a matter of her sleeping in his bed. And why Andrew Vanbergen's penlight? Had she taken it from him? Andrew carried it clipped into his shirt pocket on occasion; it would be a simple enough thing to steal. But why would she bother?

There was the possibility, of course, that she hadn't been in his room at all – that it had been Andrew all along, and that he'd soaked a tissue in her perfume and rubbed it onto the blankets. But again, why? Why not slip in and out again? Why leave telltale signs? Simply out of lunacy? That would almost seem the answer, especially when Andrew Vanbergen was involved. He was raving mad; that was the truth of it. There was no other explanation, certainly, for the note that had come in the mail. The idiot's face had been an open book. And the contents of the note, too – senseless, decayed jabber. There was no question about its being Andrew's work. The man was a case study in several of the more novel forms of insanity. And he was a pest. Sooner or later it would be necessary to reach out and crush him, too, now that Pennyman had ascertained that Andrew wasn't a Caretaker.

Why leave the penlight, though? And why the stolen elixir? Pennyman hadn't hidden that half well enough. He'd been sloppy. On an impulse he put away his brush and mirror and bent down by the bed, hauling open one of the drawers below it. Behind folded sweaters lay a package wrapped loosely in brown butcher paper. Next to it was a leather bag, a lidded Plexiglas cube, and a lead-lined silver and pewter box designed by Archibald Knox and made by Liberty and Company in 1904, during a time when Pennyman had fancied the trappings of wealth and pretended an interest in art. He had come to see through that, finally. It was as transparent as the rest, art was, and not worth his time. His energy had been focused over the years onto a tinier and tinier target, and he had shed his trivial, youthful enthusiasms for art and liquor and tobacco and the rest of the 'productions of time.' Let heaven be in love with them. He was in love with – nothing. Maybe love was the wrong word.

The boxes in the drawer hadn't been touched. He took the silver box out anyway. He'd have to find a safer place. *Someone* had been skulking in his room when he was out – at night, to judge from the penlight. Surely a nitwit like Andrew Vanbergen would have no interest in the coins. But Pennyman had traveled too many miles, dealt with too many powerful men, to take any chances now, especially with a man as irrational as Vanbergen.

And there was the matter of the last four coins. He'd see the emergence of two of them soon enough. And the third, he knew, he would have to fish for. The fish would come to him, though. He had discovered that accumulated coins drew the scattered coins; and the more he had accumulated, the stronger had been their attraction. He possessed twenty-six of them, and the few missing coins were even now tumbling and burrowing and swimming toward him through the earth and sea. And when they arrived, he wouldn't need to drink carp elixir in order to drag out a few more years of life. As had happened when Judas Iscariot had been tempted to suicide out of remorse; immortality had been thrust upon him as a curse. Well, it wouldn't be a curse to Pennyman.

Pfennig knew that too – what it was the coins granted. All his kind did. And they pretended not to be attracted to the idea of it. They hoarded their coin or two and assumed the role of Caretaker. But it was all affectation. Pennyman was certain of it. Old Aureus had accumulated more of the coins than had been good for him, and their attraction had begun to work on him, to debilitate him. He was tainted with them. The possession of any single one of them would have turned a common man into an invalid. Fourteen of them had brought Aureus enough power so that he'd been a formidable enemy, with his obedient beggars and his calling up of spirits. Pfennig and Money-wort had been nothing. Caretakers! If their business was to keep the coins dispersed, then they were a sorry lot, weren't they? And one by one they were a dead lot.

But the fourth coin – where was it? It clearly had been altered some time in the past, and then lost. Pfennig had been on the track of it. It was there somewhere. He was tolerably sure, though, that neither Andrew nor Rose *knew* it was there. He would have sensed it long ago if they had. The coin *had* been altered – that was the truth of it – and cleverly, too.

A vague doubt flickered across the back of his mind – just the ghost of one. What if Andrew Vanbergen and his idiot friend weren't the fools that he took them for? What if their tomfoolery was monumental cleverness? What if they knew *exactly* what they were doing, but were operating at depths that he couldn't fathom, on wavelengths that he couldn't detect? Andrew wasn't a Caretaker; their meeting on the front porch had told Pennyman that much. When Pennyman had confronted Pfennig for the first time on his way home from Jerusalem, his silver test quarter had been torn from his hand and had slammed Pfennig in the forehead. Pennyman hadn't had to bother with the pretense of coin tricks. If Pfennig had been smart, he would have left the country then and there. But he hadn't been smart. Was Andrew Vanbergen smart? Had he managed to hide the altered coin more cleverly?

Then there was the old lady – Aunt Naomi. Pennyman would look in on her that very afternoon. She'd be a tougher case. Interesting her in idiotic coin tricks would be more difficult than it had been with Andrew or with any of the rest of them. Naomi wouldn't be in the mood for light-hearted parlor tricks. He'd have to flatter her – bring her a bit of a present, perhaps. If she had one of the coins on her person, he'd … No he wouldn't. He couldn't; not with the alleged 'treasure hunt' just a couple of days off. Anyway, he had promised to leave her to Mrs Gummidge. He'd have to be patient.

Pennyman slid the drawer shut and carried the silver box back over to the dresser, where he examined himself in the mirror again. He stepped back, admiring the sharp thrust of his bearded chin. He would put the coins in a safe-deposit box. That would do nicely until the day of Andrew's treasure hunt. He'd better have them out by then or else there'd be an astonishing whirlwind of silver in the bank when the two earth-bound coins neared the surface. He didn't know whether there'd be enough attraction to yank out silver fillings or tear silver rings off fingers, but it was possible, especially if the last of the coins *was* in the vicinity. Then all thirty of them would be in close enough proximity so that their power might provoke anything at all. And he, possessing the coins, would wield that power.

Smiling, feeling better just thinking about it, he examined his teeth in the mirror, then opened the lid of the box. He heard a high-pitched keening, the sound of manufactured wind swirling the dust outside, and he heard the snapping of old paint buckling off the clapboards of the house and the strain of old nails yanking loose. Would the coins simply dismantle the house, turn it to rubble? Bring it down on the head of that idiot Vanbergen who painted stupidly below? He was half-tempted to see. But that, of course, would needlessly complicate things, just for a few moment's pleasure. And it might mean his own death, too. He shut the box lid, picked up his walking stick, and went out, startled despite his half expecting it when a dead sparrow plummeted out of the sky onto the lawn. He regarded it for a second with a smile and then went on.

Out on the pier, two days after Pickett's return, Andrew pushed a hook through a piece of frozen anchovy, then cut a chunk of shrimp with his slimy fishing knife and baited a second hook with it. On the third hook he hung an orange-brown remnant of mussel, then tipped the baited hooks over the iron railing and let them whiz down into the gray ocean. It was just sunrise, and he and Pickett had the pier pretty much to themselves. 'Have another Mounds bar?' he asked, raising his eyebrows at his friend.

Pickett shook his head. 'Another cup of coffee, actually. I slept till three in the afternoon yesterday. I must have been beat.'

'And no wonder,' said Andrew. 'There's nothing easy about battling the forces of evil. It takes it out of you in spades. I slept late myself.'

'We've got to go back in. Soon, I'd say.'

Andrew nodded. He felt the same way about it. He hadn't learned half enough in Pennyman's room. There were answers there somewhere, but they wouldn't reveal themselves to timid men. He and Pickett would have to wade in. 'What's wrong with today? Mrs Gummidge said something about going out. Rose is driving Aunt Naomi over to Leisure World later on. Pennyman's bound to be out most of the day doing whatever it is he does. Let's slide in as soon as he leaves.'

Pickett nodded, staring over the railing at the sea. Andrew reeled in his line. The anchovy was gone – nibbled off by perch. He broke off a piece of Mounds bar and pressed the sticky coconut and chocolate around the hook, dropping it back into the water and letting line reel out until the lead weight whumped onto the bottom. He gave Pickett a studied look and said, 'But *why* was she in his room? Why was she sneaking around when they're in league together?'

'Maybe she *wasn't* sneaking around. If they're in league together then maybe she can come and go as she likes. Maybe he doesn't care if she's in his room.'

'I don't buy that. They're not equal partners, that's for sure. He's the general. She's not even a lieutenant, if you ask me. She's a private with aspirations. There's no way he'd be happy to know she was in the room.'

'Then she was after the elixir,' said Pickett. 'Just like you were. She heard you sneeze on the stair and hid behind the curtain, just like in a movie. When you yanked the curtain back, she pretended to be asleep. And you're right about his not wanting her to be there. If she weren't worried about being discovered, then she'd confront you with *your* being there. She couldn't do that, though, because *neither* of you was supposed to be there, lucky for you.'

They fished in silence for a moment. Then Pickett tossed the dregs of his coffee onto the pier and said, 'It's clear, of course, what happened to Pfennig.'

'Is it?' asked Andrew.

'As a bell. He was sawed in half because there was something in him that had to be fetched out.'

'Like the squid on the beach,' said Andrew.

'Almost exactly like the squid on the beach. I don't suppose Pfennig had swallowed the coin, though. I think it had been surgically implanted.'

'Why on earth …' began Andrew, but Pickett interrupted him impatiently.

'To keep it out of someone's hands – out of Pennyman's hands, to be precise. All the evidence points to it. The newspaper clipping of Jack Ruby dead. The phone call from Pfennig. Pennyman slouching around town trying out the quarter trick on every eccentric he runs into. He sawed Pfennig in half is what he did, and retrieved a monumentally important coin.'

'Rose's cousin has a coin collection,' said Andrew. 'Some of them can be valuable as hell. He needs a curly quarter, apparently, but you can't get one for love nor money – or at least not for love. He'd need half a million to buy a good one, I understand.'

'This is not that kind of coin. You know that as well as I do. Nobody beats that sort of coin into a spoon. It wouldn't make sense. They'd beat a coin into a spoon to alter it, to disguise it. Pennyman isn't a coin collector in *that* sense. Offer him a curly quarter and he won't react; take my word for it. How about all that nonsense in Puget Sound about the fish with the coin in its belly? That was no curly quarter either.' Pickett shook his head, remembering his hurried trip down from Vancouver. 'The man at the gas station there said I needed new rings. They'll always try to take you for something. He made fun of my name, too. Damned rustics.'

'What is it then?'

'What? The coin? I don't know. I think ... I'm not sure. But I'd bet my bottom dollar that it's ancient as hell. Coins, originally, were magical totems. You know that, of course.'

'Of course,' said Andrew. 'Common knowledge, isn't it? Were they?'

'For a fact. Moon disks is what they were. Playing cards are the same sort of thing, distilled down from the tarot deck, which itself was a distillation of an even more ancient deck. I wouldn't at all wonder if the most commonplace coins were tainted with some little bit of magic which has strayed down out of antiquity. This spoon of yours, take my word for it, was fashioned out of a coin that's incredibly old. Older than either one of us would guess. The same with carp.'

'What?' asked Andrew, puzzled. The mention of carp reminded him that he was fishing, and he reeled up his line to find a starfish eating the candy. He plucked it off and threw it back.

'Carp. You've seen pictures of two carp curled around each other like a yin and yang. That's part and parcel the same as the fish or the serpent swallowing its own tail. Like on top of Pennyman's stick and Moneywort's hat. And guess what – they were carved into a wooden sign over Pfennig's door in Gastown. Now you might think I'm nuts, but I'll tell you that all this magical talk isn't just symbolic: carp curled around into circles, like moon disks, like coins, like the buttons on your shirt, like bus tokens and the pattern of seeds in a flower and the cycle of the seasons and the planets going round and round in the sky. Read Jung. It's all the same thing. We're awash in magical totems. Surrounded by little portholes looking out into infinity, at glimpses of immortality, if you bring it down to earth. The most trivial flotsam and jetsam scattered on the beach and cluttering shelves of junk stores *means* something, if you look at it from the right angle, through the right sort of spectacles.'

'But *what* does it mean?' asked Andrew, reeling in his line again. He had no real patience. That was his problem when it came to fishing. The Mounds bar hadn't accomplished anything. The mussel was gone and the shrimp was half-eaten. He hacked another anchovy into bits, baited all three hooks with it, and swept the head and tail off into the ocean as chum.' I have these nagging doubts,' he said as he released the catch on the reel. 'Let's say it's all true, all this business you've been talking about. Let's say my shirt buttons *mean* something besides just being buttons. So what? I mean, what about the man who's ignorant of it? What about the man who doesn't see – how does it go? – "infinity in a grain of sand"? He just buttons up his shirt and heads down to the cafe for a hamburger. *You* look at a hamburger and think about circles and then about moon disks and about curled serpents and about planets swinging through space. This other man looks at a hamburger and sees ground beef. Do you know what I mean? If you were both struck dead coming out of the cafe, you'd go to your grave with a head full of puzzles; he'd go to his with a full stomach. So what does it all *mean – really*?'

'I haven't any idea on earth,' said Pickett. 'But I mean to find out.'

TEN

'*After having referred to a report that Paracelsus was not dead, but was seated alive, asleep or napping, in his sepulchre at Strasburg preserved from death by some of his specifics, Labavius declares that he would sooner believe in the old man, the Jew, Ahasverus, wandering over the world, called by some Buttadaeus, and otherwise, again, by others ...*'

S. BARING-GOULD, M. A.,
CURIOUS MYTHS OF THE MIDDLE AGES

The Metropolitan putted along up Seal Beach Boulevard toward Rossmoor Leisure World. Andrew and Pickett still smelled of fish, because of cutting up anchovies, but Uncle Arthur wouldn't much care. There was no way at all to anticipate how he'd react to anything, given that he was ninety-two years old, maybe older – probably older – and that he grinned and winked and looked vastly surprised at what seemed to be randomly chosen moments. So the fishy smell and the tarry, scale-smeared jeans wouldn't matter a bit. Their wearing ape masks or space helmets wouldn't have mattered. Uncle Arthur would be every bit as likely to leap in startled surprise at the sight of them in a coat and tie, fresh from the barber.

They turned in past the enormous, skeletal, revolving globe that marked the Leisure World gate and were grilled by an octogenarian guard, who rang up Uncle Arthur's townhouse on a wall-hung telephone and then entered into a baffling conversation. He put his hand over the mouthpiece, turned to Andrew, and said, 'He wants to know if you're the man with the sheep.'

'Indeed we are,' said Andrew.

The guard peered uncertainly into the back seat, suspicious, perhaps, that there weren't any sheep riding along.

'In the trunk,' said Andrew. 'Stuffed toys, for the grand-niece. Christmas.' He winked at the guard, who nodded, as if he understood Christmas despite its being eight months away, and then he muttered into the phone again before hanging up. Suddenly cordial, he waved them through and watched as they headed west, toward the townhouses and apartments that skirted the oilfields. The air was heavy with the smell of oil-saturated earth mingling with the salt air in the onshore ocean breeze.

'Stinks, doesn't it?' said Pickett, rolling up his window.

'I love it,' said Andrew. 'It's a gift, is what it is – our ability to smell the world as well as see it and hear it.'

'I say it stinks. What was that nonsense about sheep? We haven't got any sheep.'

'Always agree with everyone. That's my motto. If they were expecting sheep, and we say we've got them in the trunk, then it's suddenly *us* they were expecting. *Ipso facto*, as the logician would say.'

Pickett nodded. It made sense. 'Isn't that Uncle Arthur over there in the rose bushes?'

Andrew angled in toward the curb, parked the Metropolitan in a visitor's space, and set the brake. 'Ho!' he shouted, thinking to make themselves known. It wouldn't do to slip up on Uncle Arthur unawares. The old man turned and gave them a baffled look, as if he were expecting the men with the sheep, and this wasn't them. Then, squinting and shading his eyes with his hand, he seemed to recognize them, and he waved and motioned them over.

'Help me get this fellow out of here,' he said.

Pickett peered past him, a look of intense interest on his face.

'What fellow?'

'Turtle. Big one. There he is. See him there? His shell is almost the color of the stucco. Here, help me haul him out. Fellow wants to hibernate some more, I guess, and tried to disappear under the ivy.'

There it was – the light brown shell of a desert tortoise. Its feet were drawn in and its little pointy tail bent sideways, as if the creature meant to weather a storm. Pickett bent in and pulled it out, grunting in surprise at the weight of it. It was as big around as a hubcap. 'Where do you want him?' asked Pickett.

Uncle Arthur started away toward the garages. 'In the car,' he said. Pickett gave Andrew a look, and Andrew shrugged as both of them followed along.

The red electronic car sat in its stall like something landed from the stars. Andrew had always admired it, with its immense fins and tiny cab. It was what cars were meant to look like in an alternate universe. A cut-down cardboard box lay on the floor, wedged up against the steering bar. Pickett fitted the turtle into the too-small box, in among lettuce leaves, which it had to sit on.

'Won't steal your car, will he?' asked Andrew, grinning.

Uncle Arthur looked at him blankly. 'Coffee?' he asked.

'Yes indeed,' said Pickett. 'I'll take a cup.'

Uncle Arthur regarded Andrew again, seeming to see him for the first time. 'Aren't you the nephew?' he asked.

'That's right. Rose's husband. Naomi's nephew-in-law.'

'That's just what you are. Of course. And you must be Spigot.'

'Pickett, sir. Beams Pickett. We met some months back, I think. On the pier.'

'Ah.' Uncle Arthur stared as if in disbelief at Pickett's face.

'I remember the mustache.' He grimaced. 'You were bent over cleaning a halibut, I recall, almost upside down. It looked as if your mouth were in your forehead for a moment, and that you had an inconceivable head of hair underneath it. Then I saw my mistake. It was a mustache after all. Fancy a mustache. Grotesque notion. Do you know that in my day they patented a device for burning off beards and mustaches?'

Pickett blinked, his hand going inadvertently to his face. 'Did they?'

'A mechanical device. Reduced them to ash. Touted as the end to razors. It was a miracle of the future.'

'I don't doubt it,' said Pickett.

Uncle Arthur gazed at him, as if he suddenly supposed that Pickett *did* doubt it. 'I sold them. Door to door. It wasn't like vacuum cleaners. There was no live demonstration. Just a patented dummy. Head was stuffed with hair. You'd pull out a beard's worth through holes poked in his chin, apply the machine to it, and immolate the beard. Made a terrible stink. That was what got in the way of sales. Set the dummy on fire once.'

'Huh,' said Pickett sympathetically, stepping into the living room of Uncle Arthur's townhouse. It smelled like a barn. Arthur turned to Andrew, winked broadly, and jerked his thumb in Pickett's direction. Andrew was mystified. He had no idea on earth whether the old man was playacting or was cockeyed with age. There was an atmosphere of shrewdness behind his eyes, of tired knowledge that gave the lie to the senility business. Andrew had faith in his own ability to read another man's eyes. And Uncle Arthur's talk wasn't so very odd, either. It often seemed so because of the old man's leaping from one bit of conversation to another; as if as soon as you broached a subject he would play the coming exchange through in his mind in an instant, and then leap ahead to some distant point, or some tangentially related subject. And there hadn't been anything the least bit off-key about Uncle Arthur when he'd appeared at Moneywort's shop. He hadn't been engaged then in loony pursuits; on the contrary. It was his baffling activities, more than anything else, that made people wonder about him.

'Excuse me for having forgotten,' said Pickett, 'but I'm confused about *your* name.'

'Arthur,' said Uncle Arthur, looking as if Pickett were insane.

'Arthur …?'

'Eastman.'

'Ah, of course. Eastman. Somehow I had it mixed up with another name. What was it Andrew? It was you who told me, wasn't it? When we were chatting about the old days, back in Iowa. I can't quite get it Lique-something. That can't have been it.'

'Laquedem,' said Uncle Arthur. 'That was a good long time ago. I've anglicized it just a little.'

There was a scuffling back toward the hallway. Both Andrew and Pickett turned around, and there was another tortoise, bigger than the first, wandering out of the bedroom. Someone had painted a landscape scene onto its shell. Behind it was yet another, nosing along the light green carpet, thinking, perhaps, that the carpet ought to be edible, and that if he nosed around long enough he would find a patch that was.

Uncle Arthur stepped away toward the kitchen, and so Pickett, as if seeing his chance, slipped off down the hall. Following along, Andrew found himself in Uncle Arthur's almost-empty bedroom. In it was an ancient pine table, tilted on wobbly legs, and an old straight-back chair that must have been almost inhumanly uncomfortable. In the center of the room lay a bed – an oversize cot. It might easily have been the room of a hermit. A third turtle peeked out at them from under the bed. There were two bits of ornament in the room: a short length of hempen rope hanging on the wall, so old and so fragile-seeming that it might have crumbled to bits at the slamming of a door. It was looped around and tied into a noose. And then over the bed, strung by more rope, were two old, earthy ploughshares, crossed and hanging from the ceiling.

Pickett glanced around nervously, seeming to Andrew to be looking for something telling. 'This is a crime,' he whispered to Andrew, who shrugged.

'He likes it this way,' said Andrew. 'He used to sleep on a gunnysack filled with coconut fiber, but Aunt Naomi made him switch to the cot. It was his only concession to comfort, as if he's trying to expiate some monstrous guilt or sin. Part of his nuttiness if you ask me.'

'I don't buy that,' Pickett said. 'I don't hold with nuttiness. There's always something more behind it.'

The turtle came creeping out just then, angling toward Pickett's shoe. Andrew leaned down to pet it, just as Uncle Arthur shuffled in bearing a coffee cup.

'They're everywhere,' said the old man, gesturing tiredly. 'Don't mind them. They won't hurt you. Did either of you know that squids, of all creatures except pigs, have the highest degree of innate intelligence?'

Pickett shook his head, accepting the cup of coffee – cold coffee, it turned out. The three of them went back out into the hallway.

'Ice?' asked Uncle Arthur.

'I don't think so,' said Pickett. 'Too early in the morning for ice. Pigs, you say?'

'No, squids. They've put them in lidded jars, science has, and the squids figure out within moments how to unscrew the lids. Give the jar to a child and watch him work at it.'

'Maybe if the child had suckers on his fingers ...' said Andrew, reaching down to pet the painted tortoise, which had lumbered out into the living room proper.

Pickett shook his head in quick little jerks at Andrew, meaning for him to keep his mouth shut, to leave off with his jokes. 'What fascinates me are pigs,' Pickett said, sipping the thin, chicory-flavored coffee. It tasted like ant poison.

Lying on an end table next to Andrew's chair was a Xeroxed catalogue. 'Gators of Miami,' it read across the top. On each page was a list of available, mail-order animals: hippos, giraffes, caiman, antelope, even elephants and wildebeests. You could pick them up COD at the air freight depot at Los Angeles airport. All you needed was a truck. Amused, Andrew thumbed through it idly until he came to a section on barnyard animals. Someone had filled in half a dozen of the blanks, as if to put in an order to outfit a farm.

'Nothing like a pig,' said Arthur.

Pickett slapped his knee. 'That's my feeling entirely,' he said. 'I understand you can house-train them, like dogs and cats. There was a fellow over in Buena Park who taught one to count. He had a sow that would stamp on the ground, counting out numbers, and then grunt when she'd calculated a sum. It was amazing.'

'Makes you think about the glories of the universe, doesn't it?' asked Andrew, clicking his tongue at the painted tortoise, which had lodged under the coffee table and was attempting to paddle itself free.

Uncle Arthur nodded sagely. 'I've always been a friend to pigs,' he said.

Conversation waned. Pickett seemed to be grappling with some means of opening the old man up, but the talk kept going awry.

'Ordering animals, are you?' asked Andrew, waving the catalogue.

Arthur shrugged. 'After a fashion. Years ago I set up for a time as a wildlife biologist. Took quite an interest in the migratory habits of certain animals, especially of swine – of feral pigs. Most people have no notion what happens to farm animals that escape the confines of the barnyard. They exercise certain – functions, perhaps. There's more of them out there than you'd guess, living their own lives, out from under the yoke.' Uncle Arthur paused, gazing at Andrew shrewdly. Then he said, 'Quite a race, pigs. Let one of them out of a barnyard and there's no telling where he'll go. Rather like letting loose a balloon with a message inside, if you follow me. Liable to end up in the most puzzling lands, largely because of air currents, of course. Feral pigs are the same sort of phenomenon, except that they're indifferent to air currents. It's another sort of – what? – force, let's say, that drives a liberated pig. I've written a monograph on the subject, in fact. But that was fifty-odd years ago.'

Pickett nodded sagely and winked at Andrew. 'Quite a history in pigs, isn't there?'

'A deep one, sir.'

'By golly, Andrew,' said Pickett abruptly, as if he had just then remembered something. 'Wasn't it a pig that brought the spoon around to Naomi's farm? Tall tale, I suppose?'

'No, the gospel truth or so I've been told. You haven't heard that story, have you, Uncle?'

The old man shrugged. 'It's true enough. Old silver spoon. Very curious. I wouldn't touch it with a dung fork. And neither should you boys. Don't, for God's sake, eat from it. Leave it alone. Pig didn't want it, did he?'

Pickett shook his head.

'Does anyone want it?' asked Uncle Arthur.

'What?' asked Andrew, thinking that the old man was speaking generally. '*Want* it? I don't suppose so.'

'Only Jules Pennyman,' said Pickett, and he looked at Andrew in such a way as to imply that he'd purposely ripped the lid off the conversation.

'Pennyman, is it? And has he got it?' Uncle Arthur yawned suddenly, as if he were beginning to find the conversation trivial and tiring.

Andrew shook his head. 'Not at all. He …'

'Then keep it that way.' The old man took out a pocketknife and began very slowly to pare his fingernails. He looked up suddenly at the open front door. 'Damnation!' he cried, standing up. 'Another one's got out.'

Sure enough, there was the painted turtle, having heaved itself free of the coffee table, gone out through the door, and making away across the lawn. The third turtle teetered on the threshold, inches from freedom.

'I'll fetch him,' cried Pickett, springing up.

'Put him in the car,' Uncle Arthur said. 'On top of the other one. I'm taking them out. For air.'

In minutes three of the tortoises lay in a heap in the box, and the fourth sat on the passenger seat. Pickett sorted the boxed tortoises out so that the biggest was on the bottom. Together they made a little pyramid of turtles, like an icon to a pagan god.

'Quite a load,' said Pickett. 'Where are they going again?'

Uncle Arthur buttoned his tweed coat, then hauled out his pocket handkerchief and dusted off the car fender. 'Out and about. Bit of a constitutional and all. Naomi tells me you boys are coming along to the treasure hunt.' He climbed into the cab, putting on a pair of thin leather gloves with the fingertips cut out of them.

Pickett looked baffled. 'Treasure hunt ...?' he started to say, but Andrew interrupted.

'That's a fact. I'd forgotten all about it.' He wondered wildly how in the world Aunt Naomi knew about their going on the treasure hunt. It must have been the overheard conversation on the front porch again. But why had she thought it necessary to inform Uncle Arthur?

'Do an old man a moderate favor, will you, boys?'

'Absolutely,' said Pickett.

'Carry your pig spoon along to the treasure hunt. I'd like to have a look at it. I haven't seen it in heaven knows how long. It would bring back memories, to tell you the truth.'

'Sure. Of course. If you'd like to see it,' said Andrew. 'I can bring it around tomorrow – later today, if you want. There's no need to wait on something like that.'

'No, no.' He shook his hand at Andrew, almost wildly, and his face seemed to pale. 'I don't want it. Keep it tight between now and the treasure hunt. It's on the night of the hunt that I'll want you to fetch it along. We might have need of it. And not a word of this to Pennyman or anyone else. You two can't leave town for a couple of days, can you? Take it with you?'

'Impossible. The cafe is opening tomorrow night. And we've got to get the chef's hats ready. We're being filmed by KNEX – a little promotional gag I've cooked up. Why?'

'Nothing. Keep it tight, though. Don't trust Pennyman.'

'Not very damned likely,' Andrew said. 'What do you know about him?'

'That he's no damned good. He and I have had our differences. But don't tell him I said that. Don't mention me at all. He doesn't know that we've had any differences. Don't mention turtles or pigs or anything at all. Mum's the word.' Uncle Arthur winked in the manner of a secret conspirator and started up the humming little electric engine. There was a click, and the car navigated back out of the parking stall and weaved away down the drive. Halfway to the street, as if heeding an impulse to take a shortcut, the car shot off across the lawn, bumped over the corner of a brick flowerbed border, and banged down the curb. The car wobbled on its miniature tires, then hummed away out of sight, heading southeast.

'Let's go!' shouted Pickett, and immediately he was off and running toward the Metropolitan. Andrew followed, swept up by Pickett's urgency, and the two of them flung the car doors open and slid in, Andrew firing up the engine and the car leaping into the empty street in a cloud of black exhaust.

'Turn left at the corner, along the wall,' Pickett said. 'We've got to follow him. Out for a constitutional! Turtles, for God's sake!'

Andrew banked around the corner. There was Uncle Arthur, disappearing three hundred yards down, behind a bank of parking garages. 'There's no exit gate down here,' Andrew said, shifting down into second gear as he approached the little alley that ran along the garages. 'He's not going out.'

'Just follow him.' Pickett gripped the metal dashboard, his face hovering inches from the windshield. 'Don't lose him. This is vital.'

Andrew peered sidewise at his friend's livid face. 'No problem,' he said. 'I won't lose him.'

But just then they lost him. The alley behind the garages swung around in a slow arc, dead-ending against a fire hydrant which sat at the edge of a sward of grass and flowerbeds. Uncle Arthur didn't care about grass and flowerbeds; he'd shunted between the fire hydrant and a cinderblock wall and was tearing across the lawn, straight through a shower of lawn sprinklers, the tires of the electronic car leaving little curvy ruts.

'Back out, for the love of ... Go around!' Pickett was wild with the chase.

Andrew threw the Metropolitan into reverse and slammed away backward down the alley, weaving with the speed of it, almost out of control. He rammed the palm of his hand down onto the horn, honking his way out onto the street again as a carful of gray-haired women jerked to a stop to let him in. The Metropolitan roared off, making a false turn into a cul-de-sac, squealing to a stop, and backing out of it, too. A horn honked in the street, but Andrew didn't bother to look back. He was fired with his driving, and he tore away, shouting with laughter, punching Pickett in the shoulder. 'Relax!' he hollered. 'We'll catch him!'

Lousy driver, was he? If only Rose could see him now, catapulting around the grounds of Leisure World, chasing a tiny automobile carrying God's own mob of turtles and driven by an impossibly strange old man. How many people could say they'd done that? He realized all of a sudden that Uncle

Arthur had disappeared, and he throttled down as they approached a corner, swinging out toward the right gutter. What did the racing man say about turns? Go in slow; come out fast – something like that. He set his teeth and jammed down on the accelerator, sliding around, tires squealing. Maybe it was best that Rose *couldn't* see him.

'There he is again!' cried Pickett, grabbing his forehead.

'Hold on!' cried Andrew, and he bounced the left side of the car up over the curb, the right side rolling up a little concrete wheelchair ramp. They started off across the lawn as Andrew surveyed the rearview mirror for signs of pursuit. The idea of a earful of ancient Leisure World police tearing along behind appealed massively. Rose would have to bail him out of a makeshift prison on the grounds. Maybe she would bring him the clothes of a washer-woman as a disguise. She'd find him manacled to a shuffleboard pole. He laughed out loud. Stay out of the sprinklers, he told himself, angling away toward the street again. If the Metropolitan bogged down …

'Slow up, for God's sake!' shouted Pickett. A garage wall loomed ahead. Andrew hauled on the wheel, skidding past the edge of it, the tires skiving out a strip of wet sod. A woman carrying a golf club across the lawn ran for an open door, shouting. Andrew hooted and jammed his foot down onto the accelerator, spinning the wheels and then abruptly heading for the street again. They'd saved a hundred yards taking the lawn. He'd learned some-thing from watching Uncle Arthur. The old man had guts; you had to give him that.

And there Uncle Arthur was, driving on the street again, down toward the shopping center. He was going out the south exit. They were traveling too quick now; in a moment they'd be upon him, and it would be evident that they were following. Andrew spun the steering wheel and they rocketed in behind a collection of dumpsters, where he braked to a stop. 'Give him a second,' Andrew said, breathing hard.

'Don't give him more than that,' said Pickett. 'We've got to get out of here. If anyone calls the gate and reports us, the guards will shoot us on sight. They carry weapons, damn it. These old men can't be expected to take the long view when it comes to ripping up lawns.'

'Well it was you who were so hot to trail him. I was just …' Andrew sud-denly put the car in reverse, backed around, and then headed out onto the street, looking back over his shoulder. He'd seen an official-looking car creeping along slow across the mouth of the alley some hundred yards dis-tant. 'They're after us!' he said, feeling a flush of excitement again.

'Out the gate!' cried Pickett, swiveling around to look out the rear window. 'Quick, before they spot us and radio ahead.'

Andrew hesitated. He was tempted to make a U-turn and confront the prowling search car – speed past it honking his horn, lean out of the window and gesture insanely with both hands, lead it on a wild chase through the twisting streets, clipping off fire hydrants, crunching down mailboxes, scattering pigeons on the lawns, straightaway through the fence and onto the oilfields, dragging fifty feet of chain-link with him. Motive? he'd say when they booked him. And then he'd laugh.

He grinned at Pickett as they set out – approaching the gate. There was a car in front of them, slowing down to cross the little, bent steel fingers that thrust out of the road. A single guard lounged in the gatehouse. Andrew could hear the phone ringing as the car in front of them sped off. On a wild impulse, he tromped on the clutch and shoved the Metropolitan into first gear, gunning the engine and rolling down his window.

'Don't,' whispered Pickett.

Andrew nodded with an air of utter confidence. 'I'll handle this.'

The guard, holding the phone now, hunched down suddenly and peered out through the window at them, astonished. He hollered into the receiver. 'Yes!' he shouted. 'It's them!' and he let the phone drop and lunged toward the door.

'Go!' shouted Pickett desperately.

There was a click and a bang, and a long wooden gate began to sweep down across the road. Andrew regarded it coolly. Pickett slammed Andrew's shoulder and shouted. 'For the love of God!' The guard fumbled in his coat – for what? A gun, a badge, a can of Mace? Andrew laughed out loud and started to speak, but then his foot was kicked off the clutch and Pickett's shoe was suddenly jammed atop his own on the accelerator. The Metropolitan shot forward, under the half-shut gate, careening toward a concrete planter, the steering wheel twisting to the left.

Andrew jerked around and grappled with the wheel, shouting incoherently and pulling it too far to the right, the car skewing around in a fishtailing slide. 'Get your damned foot … !' Andrew shouted, pulling the wheel back again. All in an instant, Pickett sailed against the door. Off balance now, he pressed down all the harder on the accelerator and on Andrew's shoe as Andrew slammed his left foot down onto the clutch. The engine screamed, a cloud of exhaust shot out, and Andrew let up on the clutch, anticipating the sound of smashing engine steel. He heaved again at Pickett's foot.

'Oh!' Pickett yelled. 'Damn!' and they skidded past the tail end of a parked car, spinning around into the parking lot of the Leisure Market. A shopping cart flew. Andrew pulled his foot, freed at last, off the accelerator, jammed on the brake, and then, his hands shaking on the steering wheel, he drove slowly and deliberately across the parking lot, out the exit onto Westminster Boulevard and up the street until he turned into the parking lot of the Haynes Steam Plant, pulling in among a clutch of cars and cutting the engine.

He sat for a moment in silence and then said, 'They won't find us here.' He breathed heavily to counteract the slamming of his heart. Then he got out of the car and went around to the back to examine the hubcap that had scraped the curb. It was mashed in all the way around, as if someone had beaten it with a hammer. 'Aw hell,' said Andrew. It wasn't just anywhere that you could get a hubcap for a Metropolitan. The front bumper was dented too, where he'd hit the shopping cart. The chase had taken its toll.

Pickett still sat in silence when Andrew climbed back in. 'Sorry about the foot on the accelerator,' he said. 'But what in the world did you want to tell the guard? I told you they were licensed to carry weapons.'

'I had the wild urge to quote poetry to him,' Andrew admitted, grinning suddenly and recapturing some little bit of the outlandish feeling that had surged through him when he had confronted the guard.

'Poetry!'

'Vachel Lindsay, actually.' Andrew let out a whoosh of breath, calming down now. '"Boomlay, Boomlay, Boomlay, Boom!"' he quoted, slamming his fist against the dashboard. '"Banging on the table with the handle of a broom!" What do you think? Would it have done the trick?'

'Of course,' said Pickett. 'Of course it would have. That's just what it would have done.' He twisted around and looked past the cars, back toward the street. 'He wasn't in the shopping center.'

'Who? The guard?'

'No. Your uncle. His car wasn't parked in the shopping center. He's gone on. Where in the world? We lost him because we were screwing around.'

Andrew frowned. 'Say it – *I* was screwing around. Let's go. They're not going to chase us. The guards don't have any jurisdiction off the grounds, and they aren't going to call the police over something like this. The city police don't send out squad cars over a chewed-up lawn. I didn't mean to do that – to cause any damage. I got carried away.'

Pickett kept silent.

'Let's head down to rat control and talk to Chateau – see what he's found out about the fish elixir.'

'Good enough,' said Pickett, sighing. 'But where the devil was the old man taking those turtles, and why? How are we going to find out? This is vital. I'm sure of it.'

Andrew shrugged as they turned off into traffic, driving up Westminster Boulevard toward Studebaker Road, intending to make a U-turn, then head back again east, along the edge of the oilfields. *Vital* – Andrew couldn't fathom it. What was vital were about a dozen things: painting another swatch of house, getting the kitchen together, being *responsible* for a change. And here he was out hoodwinking around, as if he were eighteen. What he *wasn't* responsible for was the godamned fate of the world, for the machinations of

Pickett's bogeymen. Damn all this business about coins and magic. What had come of it but a dented hubcap?

And damn the pig spoon, too. He hadn't wanted it anyway. Not really. He was half-ready to *give* it to Pennyman, just to have done with it. Except that Pennyman was a foul slug, and Andrew wouldn't give him a nickel, unless it was attached to a nail driven into the floor. He grinned despite himself. Well, he and Pickett could stop around to talk to Chateau, who would, of course, know nothing about the elixir, which was probably just fancy cod liver oil. Then they'd hotfoot it home. They could be there by eleven if they hurried. Andrew would make an issue of their returning, as if they were just then wrapping up a really solid morning of fishing. It wasn't *lying*, actually, to carry on like that; it was something like self-preservation. It would be the last time, too. For a couple of days he would be wrapped up utterly in the business of the cafe and the chef's hats, which Rose, in her infinite wisdom, had agreed to assemble. She was giving him a chance to prove himself in his own oddball way. He knew that. It was a matter of trust on her part. He couldn't betray her.

He banged his hand against the steering wheel. He'd very nearly disgraced himself that morning. For what? Well, he would turn over that leaf now; he'd be good, worthy of her …

'Speed up,' said Pickett.

'What?'

'I said pick it up a little bit. This is a 45-mile-per-hour zone. What are you doing, about 20?'

'Yeah, sorry.' He *had* been doing about 20, and drifting toward the shoulder on the right. He set his teeth and sped up, making the turn at the light and reversing direction in the suddenly gloomy morning.

A fog had hovered in, and the sunlight brightened and waned with each blowing drift. Dark oil derricks stood alien and lonesome in the mist, and the insect heads of oil pumps rose and fell like iron grasshoppers scattered randomly across two hundred acres of dirt wasteland. There was a tang of oil seeping into the trapped air of the Metropolitan even with the windows rolled up. The fields were deserted, empty of people and of structures, except for a couple of rusted shacks way off in the murk. Andrew slowed the car despite his determination. The rush of energy he'd gotten during the chase had entirely drained out of him.

'There! Wait!' shouted Pickett suddenly. 'Pull over!'

Mechanically, Andrew twisted the wheel and bumped up a driveway into the dirt of the oilfield, the car behind them rushing past with a blaring horn.

'Around behind that shed,' Pickett ordered, rolling his window down and shoving his head out.

The car slowed and stopped. Andrew cut the motor, listening to the foggy silence and to the creak, creak, creak of the pumps.

'What?'

'Off to the north. That way,' he said, pointing. 'Isn't that his car? Of course it is.'

Andrew squinted. The windshield was fogging up. Pickett was right. There was the rear end of Uncle Arthur's car, half-hidden behind a pile of wooden pallets. 'Do you see him?'

'No,' said Pickett. 'Yes. There he is, off by the fence, by the oleander bushes. He's up to something. Let's go.'

Before Andrew could protest, Pickett was out the door and running at a crouch toward a distant oil pump. Uncle Arthur was a hundred yards away, busy with something involving the turtles. Andrew could see the cardboard box lying on the ground ten feet beyond where the old man was bent over. Pulling the keys out of the ignition, Andrew followed Pickett, feeling like a fool. They'd be caught, is what they'd be, and arrested for trespassing. And when the police got a look at the Metropolitan, the two of them would be identified as the thugs that had terrorized Leisure World.

He hunched in behind Pickett, who was jammed up against a rusting chain-link fence and partly hidden by the machinery of the oil pump. 'He's got the turtles,' said Pickett. 'What's on the other side of the fence?'

'Naval Weapons Station,' said Andrew.

'What in the devil is he doing? Let's get closer. We can't mess up here.' With that Pickett scuttled away toward the mountain of pallets, and Andrew followed again, looking back over his shoulder toward his car. There was still no one in sight. The traffic on the highway zoomed along, dim through the fog. He should have driven farther onto the fields, where the Metropolitan couldn't be seen from the road. That's what would give them away. Maybe they'd be lucky, though. Maybe the police, if they drove past, would suppose it belonged to workmen.

They peered around the edge of the pallet heap, deadly silent. They could just hear Uncle Arthur humming or singing to himself. Either that or he was talking to the turtles. He bent over and picked one up, then crouched into the oleanders, disappearing. There was a rustling of brush, and then he stooped back out and reached into the box, where the last of the turtles waited. He seemed to be setting them free, shoving them in among the bushes, maybe under the fence. It was obvious: He was directing his squadron of turtles, running them out into the fields of the weapons station. This was the last one.

There was something odd about the turtle; it seemed to be wearing a gaudy sort of belt. 'What in the world …?' Andrew muttered. Then suddenly he saw what it was – a belt all right, made of Navajo silver in the form of great, strung-together squash blossoms. Uncle Arthur pushed his way into the oleanders again.

'It's the treasure hunt,' Andrew whispered into Pickett's ear. Pickett turned to give him a look. Andrew put his finger to his lips and jerked his head back toward the car, tiptoeing along the pallets. They'd have to make a rush for the road, get out before they were seen. But it was too late. Uncle Arthur had got rid of the last turtle and was stepping along toward his machine, oblivious to their presence. If they ran for it now he'd see them for sure. Pickett, clearly realizing it, crouched as low as he could and jerked on Andrew's jacket, pulling him down, too. Both of them edged around clockwise, keeping just out of sight. They heard the tiny slam of the door and the click and whir of the engine. Quickly they hunched around counter-clockwise now, as Uncle Arthur drove away forward. They stayed hidden, watching the old man make a wide U-turn around an oil derrick and head back toward them, beeping his horn as he swept past on the far side of the pile, humming away east, bumping across ruts, bound, apparently, for home.

'Damn it,' said Pickett out loud, standing up and thrusting his hands into his coat pockets. 'He was honking at *us*. He knew we were here. We haven't fooled him for a moment.'

'He couldn't have known. The Metropolitan is lost in the fog, and he sure as hell didn't *see* us. He was honking at the turtles, I think.'

Pickett peered at him as the two of them set out toward the highway. 'What do you know about this? It doesn't seem to surprise you? – him covering turtles with silver and scattering them in the fog? What about this treasure hunt? He's hunting treasure with turtles?'

They drove back toward Seal Beach Boulevard and the freeway as Andrew told Pickett about the mysterious treasure hunt. Pickett, true to form, didn't seem to find it half so innocent as Andrew had. Andrew told him about how such treasure hunts were carried out in the old days, implying that this wasn't any sort of precedent, any sort of real mystery. But Pickett swept his suggestions away with a belittling wave of his hand.

'It's the *key*, is what it is,' said Pickett. 'And the old man wants the pig spoon there. Why? Why the turtles? Why in heaven is he trafficking in farm animals? That's what I want to know. What's all this pig business? *The One Pig* – strange title for a book, isn't it? It wouldn't signify much, though, except for the rest of this. I've got some work to do in the library. Care to run into L. A.?'

'Not me,' said Andrew. 'I'm shot for the rest of the day. For the week. Are you still *maître d*'ing?'

'Of course I am,' said Pickett. 'I'll be there with bells on.'

'Well, look – don't take all this so damned seriously. It's probably a lot of silly nonsense and none of our business. It looks awfully wild and important at two o'clock in the morning, but in the light of day it's exposed as foolishness – a couple of old men cutting senile capers. Am I right?'

Pickett gave him a withering look. 'A man has been sawed in half in

Vancouver. Another man has been swallowed by a fish in Puget Sound. There's a herd of decorated turtles scouring across the pumpkin fields of the Naval Weapons Station. There's … Wait a minute. Where did you put the spoon, anyway?'

'In behind my books,' said Andrew.

'I'd do better than that if I were you. You rooted through Pennyman's bedroom; we better suppose that he's going to root through yours. Get it out of there. Bury it under the house.'

'I hate getting under the house. There's spiders under the house.'

'Put it out in the cafe then. He doesn't go out there much, does he?'

'No,' said Andrew. 'He's afraid to run into me, I guess. He's a coward when you get right down to it, and doesn't want a confrontation. I'll put it somewhere safe. Leave it to me.'

Pickett nodded, gazing out the window, lost already in the idea of killing the day in the library, of stumbling onto The Answer. They drove off into Garden Grove, bumping up into the parking lot of Rodent Control, where two brown-shirted employees mashed cornmeal and rat poison in an enormous wooden tub. Andrew slipped into a parking space and cut the engine. Pickett twisted the mirror around and peered into it, smoothing away at his hair and mustache. 'Damn it,' he said, unable to subdue his fog-frizzled cowlick. Andrew grinned at him, and Pickett frowned and got out.

Pickett pretended to be very businesslike when they pushed in through the glass door, nodding at the receptionist, who at once smiled broadly and raised her eyebrows as if of all the people she hoped would walk in that day, it was Pickett she hoped to see most of all. He reddened and looked at Andrew, who grinned at him. Then he croaked just a bit, as if he had something in his throat. 'Georgia busy?' he asked.

'She's in the euphemism.'

'Ah,' said Pickett.

Just then there were footfalls on the carpet behind them, and Pickett's girlfriend appeared. Andrew wondered whether, in her Oriental shirt and black, Chinatown slip-on shoes, she didn't look more like a mystic than a secretary.

'Andrew,' Pickett said, gesturing too widely, 'you've met Georgia?'

'About a half-dozen times, actually.'

'Of course,' said Pickett. 'Of course.'

'Hi, Beamsy,' she said, winking at Andrew.

'Beamsy?' Andrew whispered, and Pickett grinned crookedly at him.

She was slight and pretty, with crinkly eyes and a nice mouth and half-unruly curly hair. All in all she radiated a sort of go-to-hell attitude – necessary, maybe, for a psychic in a world full of doubters. Andrew said to her, 'Would you and Beamsy like to be left alone for a bit?'

She blushed, and Pickett stuttered for a moment, then bent down suddenly to peer at a display of stuffed rats in a case along with various examples of their enormities: a gnawed wire, a chewed bit of avocado encased in Lucite, the stuffing out of a chair. 'Very informative,' he said weakly. 'Imagine what a rat could do in your attic.'

'Almost inconceivable, isn't it?' said Andrew, smiling at Georgia, who stepped toward the counter as if to explain the curiosities in the case. Andrew motioned toward a nearby door that stood half-ajar. 'Is Mr Chateau in his office?'

'Yes,' she said. 'I don't think he's up to anything. There was a gentleman in there ten minutes ago, but he's gone out.'

'I'll just pop in, then, and leave you two to hash over the rat display.'

Pickett looked half-betrayed and half-relieved, and as Andrew pushed through the door and out of the room, the two launched into earnest conversation that Andrew made no effort to overhear.

'What ho?' said Andrew cheerfully to the man who sat holding his head at the cluttered desk.

'What!' he half-shouted, sweeping an illustrated book on insects off onto the floor in a gesture of startled bewilderment. His face had on it the look of someone who half-expected to see something ghastly coming in through the door. 'Mr Vanbergen! Why ... It's you, is it?' He grinned oddly. He had a jolly round sort of a face, almost cherubic, but it was tainted now as if with the memory of a recent fright, and he peered past Andrew, toward the parking lot visible through a far window. He seemed to relax suddenly. The wall behind him was covered with tray upon tray of beetles – thousands of them, some enormous, some microscopic, and all, except for their size, identical to the untrained eye. Andrew had always thought that a man would be worn down by the perpetual stare of countless beetle eyes, and here, perhaps, was evidence to support it.

'Feeling well?' asked Andrew. 'Sorry to have burst in.'

'Yes. No. I'm ... I dozed off for a moment. I ... I think it's a matter of biorhythms. I'm in a downswing. Feeling poorly, to tell you the truth.' He waved his hand in a little explanatory squiggle.

'Sorry about that. I won't waste your time. I'm in a hurry myself. What did you come up with on the fish elixir?'

The man grinned again weakly. 'Oh, yes. The ... what did you call it? Elixir? It's nothing for you to worry about, actually.'

'Excuse me?' said Andrew, blinking at him. 'I wasn't actually *worried* about it; I was wondering what on earth it was.'

'Of course, of course. I'm terribly sorry about it.'

'Sorry?'

'It broke. In the sink. Slippery stuff, I'm afraid. Cracked to bits on the porcelain and went down the drain. Nothing but cracked glass. All of it gone. And the water was running, too. That was the pity of it. Washed all the goop off the fragments even. There wasn't enough left over to have a look at. I was disappointed, of course. It appeared to be fascinating stuff, although not entirely in my line.' He bent over to pick up the insect book, avoiding Andrew's gaze.

'It's *all* gone?'

'I'm afraid so.' He coughed into his hand. 'Swept the glass into the trash can. Jaycox hauled it away this morning at six.'

Andrew opened his mouth to speak, then stopped and stared at the man. He took a step closer to the desk, bent over, and stared harder. He knew he was revealing too much curiosity, too much wonder. He was giving himself away entirely, but he didn't care. Down the center of Biff Chateau's forehead was drawn the telltale line, charcoal gray, wavering where the silver quarter had crossed onto the bridge of his nose, and smudged where he'd been leaning against his arm when Andrew had come in.

ELEVEN

'The Egyptians have observed in the eyes of a Cat, the encrease of the Moonlight, for with the Moone, they shine more fully at the full, and more dimly in the change and wain …'

EDWARD TOPSELL,
HISTORIE OF FOURE-FOOTED BEASTS

'Bought off!' shouted Pickett as they bumped out of the parking lot and turned toward the freeway.

'I don't think so,' Andrew said. 'He was terrified. I've never seen the like. He thought I was Pennyman coming in through the door like that – coming back to deal with him further. You should have seen the look on his face. Stark terror. I think he put up a fight before he gave in. He's an honest man, Chateau is, and he wouldn't have given the elixir up easily. Maybe Pennyman threatened him with the same sort of business he'd pulled on Pfennig.' Andrew shivered with a sudden chill, thinking about it.

Pickett nodded. 'Well, now we know what we're up against, don't we? We've been pretty casual about all of this so far. Pennyman's probably already found the spoon. He probably hunted it out this morning while we were hightailing it around Leisure World. *He* hasn't been lounging around. Clearly, he followed you yesterday morning when you hauled the elixir down here. He's a careful man. We know that. You say you heard him refusing Mrs Gummidge – wouldn't give her a drop of it even though she begged. The whole business becomes plain: It was out in his room that night because Mrs Gummidge had been setting in to steal it. You sneezed out in the hallway and she hid, just like I said. You only took half an ounce, but then, maybe, she took a bit more. And here comes Pennyman to find his store of it depleted while he's out of town sawing Pfennig in half. Maybe there's only an ounce gone – not much, we say. But who knows? What if it were drugs of some sort – an ounce of cocaine, an ounce of heroin? There'd be murder in his eyes, wouldn't there? So what does he do? He looks around a bit and finds your penlight; simple as that. One, two, three. And he follows you down the freeway next morning, and figures he's struck pay dirt when you stop in to talk to Chateau. He waits for you to leave, and then he goes in and has a little talk with Chateau himself. Do you know what Pennyman told Georgia?'

'No,' groaned Andrew.

'He said that there were two very persistent rats that he wanted to exterminate. He finds their "droppings," he said. Shooting was too good for them – that's what he said. He was going to trap them, cut them up into a stew, and feed them to the cats in the house – one spoonful at a time. That was this morning. Not half an hour ago. He thinks it's funny.'

'I'm afraid he ...'

'And what's more,' interrupted Pickett, 'there can't be any doubt at all that he was tailing me the other night when I got in from Vancouver. No doubt at all. Am I right? Admit it. No more talk about coincidences. I don't believe in them.'

'You're right, so help me. I've said this before and I'll say it again. We've got to act.' Andrew stared out the window at the empty fields trailing past, fields across which trooped Uncle Arthur's league of silver-bearing turtles. 'What I can't quite fathom,' he continued, squinting at Pickett, 'is what in the hell is going on.'

Pickett checked his watch. They banked down the off-ramp and turned up onto the boulevard, heading home. 'I'll come around later,' said Pickett. 'I've *got* to spend a couple of hours in the library. Maybe I'll find out. Wait for me, though. If he catches you snooping through his room alone ...'

'He won't,' Andrew said. 'He won't *catch* me at all. I'm too many for him. I know how to handle his sort. You should have seen his face when he got the note in the mail – utter bewilderment. He was a rudderless boat.' Andrew was cheered for a moment by the memory, but it didn't last. He gritted his teeth with determination. Pennyman! The son of a bitch. Andrew would take steps, immediately.

'He's got to be kept that way then – off-balance. Especially until we've got a handle on this.'

'Leave it to me,' said Andrew.

Pickett slammed his fist into his open palm. 'What we've got to know is *why* he's going around town threatening people. And don't lose that spoon, for God's sake. Get on it as soon as we're home. I'll go up with you.'

'No, don't. Rose and all. We've got to make it look as if we've been out fishing all morning. We can't burst in full of mysteries and plans. Did you shove your tackle box into the gunnysack?'

Pickett nodded as Andrew pulled into the curb. 'Haven't got much done on the painting end, eh? What's that mess of paint by the window there?'

Andrew cut the engine. 'That's the result of espionage. How about the tackle box?'

'Yes. It's in the gunnysack, along with my fishing jacket and my thermos.'

'Great,' said Andrew, climbing out of the car and going around to the trunk. In a slightly too-loud voice, just for the sake of an open window, he said, 'Not bad for a morning's work, eh?' And he held the weighted gunnysack up with both hands, winking at Pickett.

His friend took it from him. 'Heavy!' he said. 'Must be – what? – twenty pounds if it's an ounce.'

'Whoppers,' said Andrew. He felt guilty suddenly, but faintly proud of himself for not actually lying. And no one was listening anyway, probably. Or watching. He slammed the trunk and watched Pickett deposit the sack in his car, climb in, and finally drive away after an elaborate amount of warming up the engine and racing the motor. Then, steeling himself, he walked into the backyard whistling, as if he'd spent a satisfactory morning.

Rose was in the kitchen, washing dishes, and Aunt Naomi sat at the table sipping coffee, looking oddly well. 'You smell like fish,' Naomi said, wrinkling her nose.

Andrew smiled cheerfully. 'One of the hazards of the sport. What's this? Trix? Aunt! Trix? You? You're after the prize! What is it?' He picked up the box and studied the back. 'A glow-in-the-dark squid! Have you got it out of there yet?' He tilted the box, angling the little colored balls of cereal so as to see to the bottom, and nearly spilling them onto the table top. 'Here it is!' He hauled out a little cream-colored, glitter-sprinkled squid, three-inches long and made out of rubbery plastic. Grinning at Naomi and then at Rose, he said, 'You two should have been quicker. It's mine now. My advice is that you empty the whole box into a bowl next time. Then root out the prize, and pour the cereal back into the box. You don't really even have to wash the bowl afterward – just dust it out.' He pocketed the squid.

Rose whacked him on the shoulder with the dish towel. 'I'm glad you made a morning of it,' she said, hanging the towel up and dusting the sink with scouring powder. 'It's what you need. The prize in the Trix is your reward for getting up early. Catch any fish?'

Andrew nodded weakly. 'You should have seen the starfish I caught on a Mounds bar.' He clicked his tongue, as if to imply that the sea had been full of creatures that morning, that there was nothing he hadn't hauled in. 'Pickett just tossed a full gunnysack into his trunk – must have weighed twenty pounds.'

He was a pitiful case – sneaking around. It was shameful, and he knew it. If he'd been up to something important, really important, if he were sure of it, then why in the hell didn't he just up and *tell* her? Because he wanted to protect her? Partly. Because it all looked very much like nonsense? Yep. Because he wanted desperately to play the hero, to make it clear in the end that he'd had the entire business in hand all along, and that, like Uncle Arthur, his seeming madness had deadly serious method in it? That was it. He'd like to be a hero, wouldn't he? – casting down the villain Pennyman. It was pride and vanity. He saw through himself too damned clearly, and sometimes, when he was in a mood, he half-hated himself for it. Why couldn't he let himself rest? Why was he possessed day to day with the knowledge that he just wasn't good enough? Sometimes it made him want to throw up. He kissed Rose on the cheek and hurried up the stairs and into the bedroom before he was forced into any more lies.

The spoon was still there behind the books. It was faintly warm when he picked it up, and his palm seemed to retract at its touch, to draw back into itself like the antenna of a snail, repulsed by the feel of it. And it seemed monstrously heavy. The weight of it made him sag. He was suddenly tired. He'd been up early. All this Pennyman business was draining him. It was Pennyman, God damn him, that possessed Andrew with all these doubts about himself. That was the man's nefarious strength. That was how he worked. Andrew's back ached awfully, and there was nothing in the world that he wanted to do more than lie down and sleep.

He fought it though. Sleep was too easy. There was a job to be done. There was the matter of his shredded self-respect. He pocketed the spoon and headed back downstairs slowly, hanging onto the rail, saying nothing to Rose or Naomi as he ducked out into the cafe. He looked around, wondering, then picked up a pint glass, chose a half-dozen random spoons from the silverware box, and dropped them in, sliding the pig spoon in among them. It was a perfect disguise. He put the glass up on the wooden shelf that ran around half the room, ending against the stones of the fireplace. Sitting among books and knickknacks, the glass full of spoons looked innocent – just another decoration – and well above eye level so as not to catch anyone's casual attention. Feeling considerably lighter, but still fighting the compulsion to sleep, he headed out for the garage to fetch the paintbrush pickling in thinner. It was time to roll up his sleeves.

*

Pennyman's room was almost exactly as it had been two nights earlier. The man was psychotically neat. The only change was that the room smelled differently – only the old-house smell now; the window was shut against the ocean breeze, and there was no telltale hint of fish elixir or perfume.

The rest of the house was quiet. Rose had gone out with Aunt Naomi – the old woman's first outing in nearly a year. Dr Garibaldi had come around that morning and been sent away after exclaiming that Naomi's recovery had been almost miraculous. He'd never seen anything like it. But then he'd never seen anything like the disease, either, which he still referred to euphemistically as 'general debilitation,' and so his surprise, perhaps, didn't signify as heavily as it might have. He'd found just a hint of internal bleeding, and that bothered him, but until Naomi could come in for tests … Naomi, at the moment, wasn't interested in tests.

Pennyman was out, too. Mrs Gummidge was out. Andrew and Pickett had fastened the chain locks on the doors. If someone tried the front, the two would hear the rattling and close things up, then head out through the back door and into the garage, leaving that door unlocked, and pretending – if the locked-door business were commented upon – that they had no notion that the front door had been locked at all. No one would guess that they'd been up rifling Pennyman's things – except Pennyman, of course. He was the type to glue hairs to drawer fronts with saliva, then check later to see if the bond had been broken.

Who cared though? Pennyman knew that they were on to him; and they knew he was on to them. So what were the odds? Andrew was tempted to make the break-in obvious. Maybe he should slip in two or three times a day all week long, just to confound Pennyman, who would have to begin to think that all the breaking in and subtle ransacking was without purpose – which it very likely was, since neither Andrew nor Pickett had the foggiest notion what it was they were after.

Andrew patted his pocket. In it was the rubber squid out of the cereal box. He pulled it out and regarded it, grinning at the look of morose wisdom on its face. It was bound for one of Pennyman's socks. Pickett wouldn't approve at all. He took this whole business deadly seriously. What he didn't grasp was that Pennyman apparently did, too, and therein lay the beauty of the squid-in-the-sock notion. Pennyman wouldn't be able to fathom it, any more than he'd fathomed the letter in the mail. And Andrew was fairly sure that the letter business had been over Pickett's head too. 'What did you write?' Pickett had asked, puzzled. Then he repeated Andrew's phrase several times to himself, as if trying it out on his tongue. 'I don't get it,' he said finally. 'Why cigarettes? Wasn't there a song like that – "Smoke, smoke, smoke that cigarette"? How did that go?' He had hummed a bit, remembering, convinced that there was a message hidden in the lyrics; there must have been. He'd never caught on. That sort of thing was entirely a matter of instinct, not brains; you couldn't think through it and come up with anything but nonsense. That's why it worked so wonderfully on men like Pennyman. Andrew knew it was best not to tell Pickett about the squid until later. He nearly laughed out loud, thinking of Pennyman slipping the sock on, unawares, and then starting in horror. Was it a tremendous insect? A severed toe? He'd shake the thing out onto the floor, standing back out of the way. His face would go blank, and he'd curse …

'You take the bureau,' said Pickett suddenly from across the room. 'Wake up. Let's get this done and leave, for heaven's sake.'

Andrew blinked at his friend. 'Of course.'

Pickett bent down in front of the bed alcove and carefully slid open a drawer. 'Easy does it, now. Let's not give him the slightest clue.'

'Call me Slippery Sam,' said Andrew, sliding open dresser drawers until he found the socks. There they were, all of them folded flat, arranged in neat little heaps from light to dark. Andrew slipped the squid into a cream-colored sock, halfway down the first pile, then very carefully felt around the edges of the drawer and between the socks. There was nothing. The drawer beneath it was filled with underwear – most of it silk. Andrew was disgusted with the idea of searching through it, but he did. Beneath the shorts and T-shirts was a monumental elastic supporter, strung with mesh plastic to better keep its shape and bringing to mind the exoskeleton of a cephalopod or a particularly loathsome amphibian. It was obviously custom-built. Andrew whistled under his breath and held it up.

'Put that back!' hissed Pickett.

'What on earth …!' Andrew began. 'Certainly no human being …!' He was struck suddenly silent with the idea of retrieving the squid and of dropping it into the elastic garment like a bucket down a well. He could stretch the waistband across the frame of the casement and fire the squid through Ken-or-Ed's living room window. He eased the sock drawer open again in order to fetch out the squid, wondering if he was allowing things to go haywire. Shooting the squid out of the supporter would pretty clearly break the cardinal rule demanding artistic subtlety. Somehow. It was best not to determine exactly how. He would compromise, and merely leave the squid in the supporter. Pickett had agreed that Pennyman be kept off balance, hadn't he? Andrew glanced at Pickett, whose back was turned, and then shoved the doctored supporter back in among its neighbors, smoothing the whole mess out and sliding the drawer closed.

In the middle drawer he found nothing but shirts – a tiresome lot of them, starched, buttoned, and folded. It occurred to him that, in the interests of excess, he could with very little risk dredge up about a hundred rubber creatures and load up every blessed piece of Pennyman's clothing …

He found nothing in the fourth drawer but ties and handkerchiefs and a pair of suspenders in a plastic case. The top drawer was the inevitable junk drawer – very neat, though, and three-quarters empty. There was a can of spare change, a couple of pocketknives, and several road maps – one of downtown Vancouver. Andrew held it up for Pickett to see and then put it back. Next to the maps lay a vinyl checkbook – the broad sort of double book that a businessman would carry.

Here was pay dirt. Each of the checks had been torn off of an attached stub, and each stub had written onto it a neat record of whom the check had been paid to. It was Pennyman's fetish with neatness again – everything orderly and labeled. Andrew wondered how many times a day Pennyman washed his hands. The information on the stubs meant almost nothing to him – just random names and dates. He and Pickett could run the lot of them down, of course, but it would take weeks, and what good would it do them in the end? They'd discover, no doubt, who it was that cleaned Pennyman's shirts and where he had his hair cut, but they hadn't time for that sort of wasted effort.

On a sudden hunch, Andrew counted back on his fingers, calculating the date on which he'd tracked Pennyman to Moneywort's shop. Sure enough, there'd been a check paid out – to a man with an Asian name, on The Toledo. Andrew couldn't quite make out the spelling of the name, beyond the fact that it was short and started with a *K*. It was substantial, too – nearly a thousand dollars. That would be for the elixir. Pennyman had walked away in that direction carrying a live carp in a bag, and had appeared at home two hours later carrying a vial of the elixir. It stood to reason. Andrew pulled the pen off the checkbook and wrote the information on the palm of his hand, just as a precaution against forgetting it, then idly flipped to the next check stub. It had been written out to Edward Fitzpatrick.

Ken-or-Ed. Right across the street. Andrew was flabbergasted. What did it mean? Pennyman had paid the man off. All that business about the planning commission – that was all a charade, a hoax. Pennyman had set it up. It had cost him two hundred dollars. Jack Dilton! He was probably some drunk they'd found slumped on the counter down at Wimpy's.

For a moment Andrew was tempted to fly into a rage, to turn Pennyman's room upside down, the lying, stinking … Kissing Rose's hand! The whole incident rushed back in upon him, and it took an effort of will not to rip the checkbook in half. He counted to ten, very slowly. He heard Pickett whistle just as he was telling himself to put the checkbook back. He could *use* the information. If he tore it up, Pennyman would know all. Andrew would have played his hand, and a damned poor one at that.

'Look at this,' Pickett said. Andrew slid the checkbook back into the drawer, closed it, and stepped across to help Pickett, who kneeled in front of the lower, right-hand drawer beneath the bed. In it, spread open, was a leather bag of silver dimes – thousands of them. 'What in the world ...'

'All silver?' asked Andrew.

Pickett slid his hand through them, letting them run through his fingers as if he were an adventurer in a pirate's cavern. He nodded.

'Looks like.'

'Do you think he just *keeps* them? I keep pennies, for heaven's sake. They're not evidence of anything.'

'You're not going around town sawing people in half, either. Lord knows what they're for, though. They don't do us any good, do they?'

Andrew shook his head. 'What's that wrapped in paper there? Looks like books, doesn't it?'

Pickett hauled it out – an almost-square parcel wrapped in butcher paper and with the ends folded and taped like the ends of a Christmas present. 'Tape is pretty new,' Pickett said, worrying up a corner of it. 'It hasn't stuck tight yet. Should we chance it?'

'Of *course* we'll chance it. Let's steal them and replace them with *Reader's Digest* condensed.'

'None of that,' said Pickett. The tape pulled back without ripping a bit of the paper. It would stick down again well enough. Andrew bent in over Pickett's shoulder, watching his friend unfold the package carefully. The sight of the top volume staggered him: *Hula Moons*, by Don Blanding, the poet – one of the five books that had been stolen from Andrew's bedroom. It hadn't been the Atlantean after all. It had been Pennyman all along.

'The son of a bitch ...' Andrew said. They were all there: the Walt Kelly, the Gerhardi, *Liverpool Jorge* – all five of them. Andrew plucked the pile out of Pickett's hands.

'Hey, watch it!' his friend said. 'Don't mess them up.'

'What do you mean "mess them up"? They're my books. I'm taking them back, right now. Pennyman's a common thief! I had him pegged for a world-class criminal, and he stoops to stealing another man's books!'

'We've got to put them back.'

'*Got* to? We've got to do nothing but expose him. I'll show these to Rose, wrapped up just like this. Evidence is what I call it, and so will she. She'll know they're my books. We'll give Pennyman the bum's rush. Him and his processed hair.'

Pickett shook his head meaningfully. 'I believe Pennyman to be one of the most powerful and dangerous men in the world. Don't even think about tackling him this way.'

'If he were such a man, then why *steal* books? These aren't *rare*, for God's sake. He could find copies just by driving around town. He could buy copies at Acres of Books. That's where I got most of these. Aside from the Pogo, there aren't ten bucks worth of books here. The most powerful man in the world doesn't *need to* steal books.'

'Don't try to reason it out,' said Pickett. 'There's presidents and priests cutting the most amazing capers right now. Depend on it. They arrested that judge up in Bellflower just last week for going out naked except for a hat. He didn't *need* to go out naked, did he? God almighty, man, he sure as hell didn't need the *hat.* I drove a thousand miles to buy contraband breakfast cereal for you. What would Rose say if she knew it? Forget any of this business about what people need. Also, if you tell Rose that Pennyman stole these books from you, wrapped them in paper, and then hid them in his drawer, she's going to wonder, isn't she? She knows you've got it in for him.'

'I'll show her the checkbook.'

Pickett squinted. 'What checkbook?'

'Pennyman's checkbook,' said Andrew, tossing his head toward the dresser. 'There's evidence that he paid off the fat man across the street. Sent him over to cause trouble. Rose witnessed the whole thing.'

'Maybe,' said Pickett, looking doubtful. 'What will you tell her when she asks you what you were doing going through Pennyman's things?'

'I don't know.'

'In fact, what if she *does* believe it and wants to take action, to confront him? He's a dangerous man, like I said. We don't want to start him up over some damned petty thing like this.'

'Petty!'

'Yes,' said Pickett. 'Petty. Compared to what he did to Pfennig, this is petty as hell. A couple of books ... Even you say they aren't *worth* anything much. Wait and watch, that's my advice. Don't involve Rose. Trust me. She doesn't want to be involved.' He took the books away from Andrew again and folded them up laboriously, rubbing a finger across the tape to heat the glue and slipping the package back into the drawer. 'One more box. Looks like opaque Plexiglas sealed with a neoprene gasket. Maybe some sort of waterproof ... Let's have a look.'

Andrew was silent, fuming about the books. He'd get them back; that was for sure. And he'd confront Pennyman with them, too. He'd make him sweat before he was through, he'd ... 'Damn it!' cried Andrew, reeling back. 'What the ... Close it up!'

A putrid, decaying stench filled the room. Andrew gagged and staggered toward the windows, throwing them open and leaning against the screens, sucking in air. He heard Pickett scrabbling around behind him. Gasping a lungful he turned and stepped back to where his friend wrestled with the box, trying desperately to shut the lid clean and tight enough so that the spring latch would compress the top of the box down into the neoprene. Pickett half-threw the box at Andrew, leaped up, and raced out, starting to retch, barely pausing at the door. Steeling himself, Andrew fitted the lid carefully, set the corner of the box against his knee and leaned into it, snapping the latch into place. Then he put it back into the drawer before jumping away toward the window again.

There was a heavy onshore breeze, thank heaven, angling in up the alley, straight through the window. In minutes it would have flushed out most of the reek. Andrew knew that he wasn't in any risk of being sick anymore. But that first whiff ... Pickett had barely made it.

Again, why? Why a box full of decayed – what? Andrew had seen just a bit of it, and it made no sense at all. What he thought he'd seen was a scrap of the snout and eye of a dead 'possum – a severed head, probably. But that couldn't be, could it? It was too bizarre to believe. And there was more than that in the box – unbelievable filth. There leaped into his mind the memory of Pennyman and the cat box. It was incredible, preposterous. There could be only one explanation – it was a joke. A sick joke. Pennyman had anticipated them, and he'd had a sealed box built *just so that they'd find it*. He had probably laughed himself sick over it. Rodent Control hadn't gotten the 'possum out of the trash can at all. Pennyman had. Andrew could imagine him cutting it up, just like the squid on the beach, just like Pfennig, and then going upstairs to strain the sand in the cat box. The man was a living horror.

Andrew shut the windows, took a look around to see that nothing was out of place, and went out. The idea of setting more traps of his own hardly appealed to him. He'd lost his appetite for that sort of gag.

'I can't imagine why,' Mr Pennyman said, sitting on the stool in the kitchen. Rose worked at the sink. It was evening. Andrew was out in the cafe chopping vegetables.

'Was anything gone? Stolen?' The information clearly bothered Rose. This wasn't good – someone sneaking into Mr Pennyman's room. News of it would do nothing but ruin their chances of making a go of the inn.

'No, nothing stolen. Not that I could discover. I haven't much, really, that's worth anything. What is there to steal in an old man's room? Not even a pocket watch. It's the idea of it though – having one's sanctum sanctorum, as they say, invaded by garden-variety thieves. Thank God I was out. They probably came in through the window – rather like the crowd Andrew chased off the other night. I'm half-surprised that Andrew didn't hear them. He was probably busy with his cafe, clanking glasses and such. You wouldn't think a sleepy neighborhood like this was such a hotbed of garret thieves, would you?'

Rose shook her head, saying nothing for a moment, but looking as if she were collecting her thoughts. Finally she said, 'Should we call the police?'

Now it was Pennyman's turn to pause. He shrugged and gave his head a little noncommittal jerk. 'I suppose not. No need to drag the police in, is there? Nothing stolen after all. There's always the chance that suspicion is cast in the wrong direction when the police meddle in these sorts of affairs. They can be inventive. And then there's your troublesome neighbor across the street. If he came around yammering about Andrew's having been up in the tree ...'

'Well,' said Rose, 'I'll take your advice here. I'd rather this got no further, actually. If Andrew could be spared ...'

'Say no more.' Pennyman held his hand up. 'This is a stressful business, opening an inn. Andrew's eccentricities can be explained. Even justified. How is he feeling, better?'

Rose looked at him. 'I don't know how you mean, but to finish my sentence, if Andrew could be spared knowing about the break-in, I'd appreciate it. It would only work him up.'

'Of course, of course. I knew just what you meant. After the business with the planning commission the other day ... I'm not a practicing psychologist, Rose, but Andrew seemed to me to be rather dangerously close to the edge there. Far be it from me to butt in, though. That's his affair – and yours, of course. I'm afraid he's already conceived a dislike for me. I rather wish he hadn't. I admire him, men like him ...'

'I'm sure you exaggerate. He's determined, is what he is, and I wish sometimes that he weren't. I wish he'd put on his bedroom slippers and relax. But he can't. He's always got to be up to something, meddling around with half-finished projects, trying to make sense of things that maybe can't be made sense of. I'm pretty sure, though, knowing him like I do, that if he got rid of all his demons, what was left afterward wouldn't be worth as much as it should be. I rather like him the way he is, and I can tell you that you don't have to worry about him. I'll tell him half the truth. I'll tell him that you were afraid that someone had been in your room, but that nothing had been stolen and so it must have been Mrs Gummidge straightening up. It might have been, I suppose?'

Pennyman nodded and widened his eyes. 'We'll suppose so, won't we? She was out, though, wasn't she? I admire the hell out of your loyalty, do you know that? If I were a younger man, and you weren't attached ... Well ... You'd have to be curt with me.' He smiled and winked. 'Hold onto that husband of yours. He can use a bit of your energy and strength.' Pennyman strolled away, out of the kitchen, out the front door. Rose stood without moving, staring through the kitchen table.

Out in the cafe kitchen Andrew chopped vegetables on his cutting board. Every now and then he stopped and looked around him, satisfied. Tomorrow night would tell the tale. There were two reservations so far, but he expected more. The cable station was coming around to do a piece of filler on the chef-hat gimmick. He was damned lucky that they had called around to suggest it. It beat a simple photograph in the *Herald*.

Everything would have to roll out smooth and easy. Timing was the key in the cooking business – that and advance preparation. He hated cutting up onions. Somehow he always lost track of what he was doing and ended up with his face six inches away from the damned things, crying all over them. How many had he chopped? – eight? That ought to do it. There was no use making ten gallons of gumbo to feed a dozen people. He wouldn't be cheap with it, though.

He raked a heap of chopped bell peppers into one of the cutting board bowls, then dumped peppercorns into a mortise and ground them to dust. He'd already mashed garlic and cut up a picnic ham and three pounds of sausages. He'd peeled the shells off a mountain of shrimp, but had left the heads attached for style, and he had a flotilla of crab legs soaking in fresh water in order to leach out some of the salt.

When Pickett knocked on the street door at eleven, Andrew was three-fourths done. Aunt Naomi's cats had been in and out all night, looking around, winking at the shrimps, generally making themselves at home. At first Andrew had half a mind to throw them out, but he didn't. He had to admit that he'd developed a kind of regard for them, solitary creatures that they were. He wouldn't half-mind being a cat; they seemed so well informed. He was vaguely puzzled by his having come to like them. He could remember having been wild to pitch them out not two weeks past, and now here he was, feeding them the odd shrimp. It was what he'd felt on the stairs when he'd first gone into Pennyman's room – the strange notion that the cats were looking out for him, that they were players in the same game, on the same team. He wouldn't be surprised to find that Uncle Arthur fraternized with cats.

'Sit down,' said Pickett, looking as if he were wild with discoveries. 'They had to throw me out at ten. I would have spent the night there if I could have. This is monumental. I've been talking to Robb, the reference librarian. Do you remember him?' Andrew drained the oil off the sausages and ham fat he'd been simmering, pouring the fat through a heap of cheesecloth into a measuring cup. 'Slow up,' he said. 'You're about to explode. *I've* been taking it slow and easy – machine-like, that's my way tonight. Everything done just so. Measure twice, cut once; that's my motto. Rob who?'

'Randall Robb. At the literary society. He threatened Johnson that one night over Johnson's misquoting a phrase from Leviticus.'

'Steely-eyed fellow with bushy eyebrows? Fierce?'

'That's the man! He's been running me all over the basement of the library. You wouldn't believe the stuff he's got stored down there: secret society stuff, apocryphal Masonic texts, suppressed Illuminatus tracts, hollow-Earth literature. It's astonishing. And just between the two of us, the authorities think that the recent library fire wasn't just a case of simple pyromania. There's stuff in that basement collection that someone wanted destroyed.'

'Whoa,' said Andrew. 'I thought this man Robb worked up in one of the branch libraries. Up in Glendale.'

'Eagle Rock. That was years ago. They transferred him uptown. A branch library wasn't big enough to hold him. He's one of the old-school librarians – wild hair, spectacles, arcane knowledge. They get that way. Nickel-and-dime information isn't worth anything to them. They run into an odd bit here, an unlikely coincidence there, and suddenly they're following a trail of hints and clues and allegations back into the murky depths of *real* history – the stuff that's glossed over and rearranged; the stuff they don't want us to know.'

'They again?'

'That's right. Depend on it. But listen. He knows Pennyman. Tell me this, where did Pennyman say he came from? Back east, wasn't it? Just blew into town like Billy Bones, right? Looking for a berth where he could watch the sea? Well it was lies. Robb knew him from the library. He'd been hanging around for six months, looking to find something but too sly to reveal what it was. He said he represented the British Museum in some sideline way. His research had to do with coins, though, and with biblical arcana. That much was sure. You and I know which coins he was after. But why? We ask ourselves that, don't we?'

Andrew nodded and turned the flame on under his cast iron kettle, arranging a big whisk and a long-handled spoon on the range top next to it. 'Just this afternoon,' he said. 'But there's the "what" element, too. I've seen a picture of this coin, and I seem to own one that's been beaten into a spoon and carried around Iowa in the mouth of a pig, but I don't have the earthliest idea what that means.'

'Well hang on to your hat. Robb's looked over my Vancouver book. The coin is definitely one of the thirty.' Pickett uttered this last phrase slow and meaningfully.

'Ah,' said Andrew, noting that the oil in his kettle was starting to smoke, and distracted by the process of gumbo-making.

'Thirty pieces of silver.'

'Ah. Thirty of them. Here goes nothing.' He poured three cups of flour into the smoking oil and began flailing at it with the whisk, knocking out lumps. Flames shot around the blackened sides of the kettle, scorching the hairs on his arm. 'Pot holder!' he shouted.

'*Thirty* pieces of silver,' said Pickett again, looking at him fixedly.

'All right,' Andrew shouted, grabbing the whisk with his left hand and waving his right hand out away from the pot to cool it. 'I'll pay. Just give me the damned pot holder, will you, and then turn down the flame here. God almighty this is hot!'

Pickett blinked at him, then got up to fetch the pot holder, which Andrew had carelessly left lying out of reach on the counter.

Andrew transferred the whisk to his right hand and slipped his left into the pot holder. Pickett turned the flame down by half and peered hesitantly into the pot. 'What the hell?' he said.

'Black roux. Or at least it will be. Touchy process. Watch, you can almost see it turn color. If you quit whisking for a moment, it's burnt like a cinder. Nothing to do then but pitch it out. Back away there.' With that he picked up the bowl full of heaped vegetables and poured them into the bubbling oil and flour. A great reek of steam poured up out of the kettle, and Andrew dragged it off the flame, still whisking. The worst was past. The whole business was a success. He whisked away until the mixture quit bubbling.

'Looks like the devil, doesn't it?' said Pickett. 'What do you do with it? You're not still thinking of trying to poison the cats, are you?'

'I was *never* going to poison the damned cats! You eat it,' said Andrew. 'After you've mixed it into three or four gallons of broth and tossed in all this meat and shrimp and such and a little cayenne.'

'All that oil? What is this, oil soup?'

'It's God's reward for our meager virtues,' said Andrew, rinsing off the whisk. He shut down the stove and closed the cookbook that had been lying on the counter.

Pickett, looking cross, picked the book up and took a look at the cover, on which was a picture of a startlingly fat man with a pudding face, grinning out across an appalling lot of sausages and crustaceans. 'You're cooking out of this man's book?'

'Look at him,' Andrew said. 'The man knows how to eat. He's eaten more than the rest of us put together. What that man hasn't eaten you could put in your hat. What cookbook would you suggest, the *Hindu Diet Book*?'

Pickett shook his head. 'Oil soup with shrimp heads. *Burnt* oil soup with shrimp heads.' He sat down pettishly, took out his pocketknife, and pretended to scrape his fingernails, saying nothing.

'Well, where were we?' asked Andrew, smiling pleasantly. Tomorrow's cooking would be a piece of cake. The yeoman's work was done, and at barely eleven o'clock, too. Rose would be proud of him. She was upstairs gluing up the chef's hats. She had protested mildly about the dimensions of the hats, about them being sewn up out of an expanse of rubberized nylon roughly the size of a bedsheet. Andrew had prevailed though, explaining to her his theory of the virtue of excess. In the morning Andrew would run down for a canister of helium. The camera crew from KNEX was due at four o'clock in the afternoon, an hour before the doors would open. It was a miracle, them calling and offering to do the story. They'd heard of the cafe, they said. They wanted to do a human interest story – local citizens make good, that sort of thing. The chef's hats were a natural, just the sort of comic slant the public would like. Things were certainly falling together.

Andrew became aware suddenly that Pickett was in a state. He'd been almost crazy with the idea of the coins, and Andrew had lost interest because of cooking up the roux. It was time to get back on track. 'Oh, yes. That's right. That was it. Thirty pieces of silver. Just like out of the Testaments. Judas Iscariot and all.'

'Not *just like*,' said Pickett, folding up his knife. 'The *same damned coins*! That's what I'm telling you. I've suspected it for days, but what I've found in L. A. cinches it.'

Andrew whistled. 'They must be worth a heap. How can anyone tell though? It would be just like any religious relic. Sell a man an old sea gull bone and tell him it's what's left of St Peter's ring finger.'

'Nope. Not this time. There were always only thirty of these coins.'

'What do you mean, "always"?'

'I mean as far back as anyone can discover. I mean thirty *magical* coins minted in antiquity.'

'If you plant them, will they grow?' Andrew was giddy with the success of his gumbo, with the satisfaction of something going right. He grinned at Pickett, thinking to cheer him up.

'If you collect them all together,' said Pickett evenly and deadly serious, 'you can … Lord knows what you can do. But the point is that Pennyman's been after these coins, and it looks as if he's got them.'

'What do you mean, "looks as if"? He certainly hasn't got them all, and won't, either.'

'It's a damned long story, let me tell you. I haven't been sitting idle. But listen. All of a sudden ten million things fit. That's what struck me – even little things. Have you ever thought about the business of kicking over the money changers' tables in the temple? I mean really *thought* about it?'

'Because He didn't go for money-changing in the temple.'

'Half that story,' said Pickett, 'has never been told. The coins were being gathered. That's what I think. Right there, by the priests. A conspiracy so massive and far-reaching that it set the course of modern history. It was the collected coins that brought about the inevitable betrayal – the fall, if you want to put it that way, of heaven on earth. They're a physical incarnation of evil, and they've been purposefully scattered these two thousand years since, and …'

'And now Pennyman's got them together again. The two coins in the photo of him and the dead Jack Ruby …'

'Betrayal upon betrayal, evil stacked on top of evil.'

'But he hasn't got *all* of them, because we've got …'

Pickett sprang at him, waving his hands and shaking his head. 'Don't say it. Wink twice when you want to refer to it. Where is he, anyway?'

'Out, as usual. Or he was an hour ago.'

'Is it hidden?'

Andrew nodded. 'Brilliantly. But what is he going to do, anyway, when he gathers all the coins?'

'Save that,' said Pickett. 'I don't know. I don't want to find out, though. There's more to it. I haven't scratched the surface here. Look what Robb turned up. It's part of a dozen legends in the farthest-flung reaches of Europe and the Middle East. Latch on to something, though. It's going to throw you.'

Pickett held up a Xerox and read: '"When the moon is old, he is very, very old, but when the moon is young he turns young again." And now this: "… and he can only rest beneath two crossed harrows or *ploughshares*."' Pickett put the Xerox down and sat silently.

'Who says?' asked Andrew.

'One Chrystostum Dudulaeus Westphalus. Seventeenth century.'

'*Westphalus?*'

'Assumed name. And the name doesn't matter anyway. The legend is everywhere, dating back to at least the second century. This man Westphalus just wrote it down. And here, listen to this from something called *Curious Myths of the Middle Ages*: "We hear of the Wandering Jew again at the royal palace in Bohemia, in 1505, where he is assisting the prince to find certain coins which had been secreted by the great-grandfather of the prince, sixty years before. The coins were found in a leathern bag, beneath a boundary stone cut into the shape of a sow and her litter. On the advice of the Jew, the coins were dispersed, all but one, which the ill-fated prince hid beneath his tongue and later paid to a stranger for the murder and betrayal of the king, his own father. The prince's tongue clove then to the roof of his mouth, and during the course of his two-year reign, which ended when he hanged himself, he was known as Walter the Mute.'

'Pigs again,' said Andrew.

'Pigs is right. Here's another; this one translated from the French. It's an account – get this – of the legendary *Isaac Laquedem*. What do you think about that? The name is corrupted from the Hebrew and means Isaac the Old or Isaac of the East. He was believed to be the Wandering Jew, and had a sort of Francis of Assisi affinity to *farm animals*, for God's sake, especially pigs. Listen: "When the truffle pigs were driven into the forests of Fontainebleau, a great fat sow escaped into a stand of birch, from which it emerged with a spoon in its teeth and a beggar at its heels, escaping withal from master and beggar both, and never seen again in the region. Six years later, its master identified it as one of a trio of swine driven along the roadway outside Chateau Landon by a man in monk's robes, who was identified by a passing peasant as Isaac Laquedem, the Wandering Jew, who had been alive at the time of the Passion of Christ."'

'So who is he?'

'Wait, one more. Here's the *Britannica*, tenth edition: "As Cain was a prototype of Judas, so was Judas of such doomed wanderers as Malchus in Italy and Ahasuerus in Germany, who along with a score of similar wanderers, were known variously as the Legion of the Coins or the Legion of Iscariot." '

'Iscariot? A sort of general then, of a band of wanderers? And you're telling me that they've been hightailing it across the western hemisphere keeping an eye on these thirty coins?'

'That's the long and the short of it. But they've failed, largely, in recent years, and what's gone around, as they say, is coming around.'

Andrew sat for a moment, considering all this. Then he asked, 'Who is Uncle Arthur?'

Pickett shrugged. 'You know what I know, almost. It's all there, isn't it: the name, the murky past, the pigs, the farm animals, the phases of the moon, even the crossed ploughshares. For my money, every last dime of it, Uncle Arthur is Judas Iscariot.'

Andrew stood for a moment in unbelieving silence, then said, 'But living in Seal Beach? In Leisure World? Driving an electronic car?'

'Why not?'

Now it was Andrew's turn to shrug. Why not indeed? 'And you think he's hustling to – what? – keep Pennyman from collecting the coins?'

'That's just what I think – to keep *anyone* from collecting the coins. Did you know that Pennyman was recently in the Middle East – at a time that corresponds exactly with all the mystical stuff, the rain of dead birds and the Jordan River flowing backward? What does that tell you about the impossible tide last week? About the sea gulls all over the street? Remember what Georgia said about the psychic disturbance in the area?'

'Are they still here, do you think? They weren't in his room. We'd have found them.'

'Yeah, we would have. He wouldn't keep them here, not now that he thinks we're onto him. Where is it, by the way?' Pickett winked twice.

Andrew winked back. 'That'll be my little secret, won't it? It's safe. So tell me, what about Pfennig? What about Moneywort?'

'Caretakers, just as I'd suspected. In league with Uncle Arthur. Aunt Naomi, too, the way I figure it. She inherited the you-know-what from her late husband. You know the story. She's lucky, though. She's still alive.'

'Because she's given the damned thing to me!'

Pickett shrugged. Then he started, as if he'd had a chill, and he slapped his hand on his knee. 'I just thought of something,' he said. 'Johnson was right – that morning down at the Potholder. It *was* pigs – back in Iowa, involved in the cow-pasture business. Of course it was pigs. And they took the man's coin! Wouldn't that cook you? I can't stand the creep anyway. It was a lucky guess on his part, an eyes-shut home run. Anyway, what I've pieced together is that Pennyman traced all the Caretakers down and stole the coins from them, ruthlessly. It was just like I said with Pfennig. Robb found mention of two of the coins in the Apocrypha. They were never recovered after Iscariot hung himself unsuccessfully; they were buried by a remorseful priest in the potter's field that's mentioned in the Testaments. Without any doubt, a third coin is in the belly of that fish up in the Sound. How it got there I can't begin to say. And do you know what? For my money that fish isn't in the Sound at all anymore. He's off the south coast, or on his way.

'The balance of the coins, we have to imagine, were scattered, and have been turning up far and wide and doing their mischief ever since. It was the coins that bestowed immortality on Judas Iscariot. That's their effect. When he tried to hang himself, he couldn't, and he set himself to a quite possibly endless lifetime of penance. He's had a mission for two thousand years.'

'But he seems so happy, so cheerful, driving over lawns and all. You don't suppose that piece of rope on his wall ...'

'Of course I do. And why shouldn't he be happy? He's turned back around, hasn't he? He wakes up every morning with a purpose. He's been a moderate success at orchestrating a vast and intricate plan – up until now. Then his officers start to die, to be murdered, and here comes Pennyman, pocketing a coin here, two coins there ...'

'It must have taken him ages. How old can he be? How old can *any* of these Caretakers be? I get the immortality part as far as Uncle Arthur is concerned, but why the rest of them?'

'I'm not sure, but I suppose that possessing even a couple of the coins might have such an effect. And then there's the fish elixir, isn't there? I've got a few leads to run down there, including your Asian man on The Toledo.'

Andrew groaned. 'I wish I could help. But with the cafe and all ...' He swept his hand in a wide arc, gesturing at the stove. 'And if I slipped out again, Rose would kill me. She'd pack my bag and leave it on the porch. I'm going to have to leave the fate of the world to you.'

'On the contrary,' said Pickett seriously. 'As I see it, the world rests on the shoulders of the last of the Caretakers.'

'The last of the Caretakers?'

'Keep it well hid.'

'Oh,' said Andrew. 'Yes. No wonder I've felt worn out. Call me Atlas.' But he said this last without much humor. It wasn't very funny to him.

Pickett stared at his friend's face. 'Step over here by the window for half a mo. Let's check the street.'

Half-dazed, Andrew followed his friend. The two of them stood in the light of a gibbous moon, which had risen above the ocean. The fog had dispersed, and moonlight shone through the window glass, casting an ivory glow over the rubbed oak of the table tops. Pickett stared at his friend's forehead, but Andrew was lost in thought. 'If we had a silver quarter and a bit of powdered ash … But it would mean your death if Pennyman saw the results.'

'He's already played that trick,' said Andrew.

'When he did, he had the wrong man.'

'What was he looking for?'

'Stigmata, of a sort. There's mention of it in the *Britannica* and in the Vancouver book, both. Sympathetic markings that the silver and the ash would cause to materialize. The markings would fade eventually, but for a time they'd be indelible.' Pickett produced another Xerox from his bundle, and read from it. ' "Such a mark was indeed supposed to be on the Wandering Jew's forehead. Xemola says it was a red cross concealed by a black bandage, on which account the Inquisition vainly tried to find him." That's the *Britannica*. Here's from *The One Pig*, Robb's translation of it. He's written it out for me. "The mark of Iscariot can be drawn from the forehead of his followers by the use of silver and palm ash …" '

'His followers,' said Andrew, idly rubbing his forehead. 'I'd never have pegged myself as a follower of anybody, and certainly not of Judas Iscariot.'

'He's not the same man now as he was in the Testaments. And it's not *you* who does the pegging anyway. You're one of the chosen few. For the moment, you're the *last* of the chosen few. Many are called,' Pickett said ponderously, 'but few are chosen.' He shoved his Xeroxes and notes into his coat, reached for the doorknob, and said, 'There's a full moon on the night of the treasure hunt.'

'Is there?'

'That's right. It'll be a dangerous business. We can't depend on Uncle Arthur then, not if all this phase-of-the-moon stuff is accurate. He'll be feeble, doddering. Maybe outright loony. It'll be up to us.'

'Up to us,' Andrew muttered as Pickett went out through the door, into the night. Andrew stood at the window, looking out at nothing, only vaguely seeing Pickett's car whoosh away toward the highway. He turned and looked in at the kitchen, which was a mess of splattered roux and the remnants of chopped vegetables. Somehow the mundane notion of cleaning a kitchen, when set against the mystical knowledge that Pickett had revealed, made Andrew dizzy. He decanted the roux into lidded plastic tubs and shoved them into the refrigerator, working in a sort of haze. His back ached. He was tired out, and tomorrow would be worse. He would clean the kitchen in the morning. It was sleep he needed now. His eyes were drawn to the pint glass full of spoons. It seemed to glow and jiggle in the gloomy twilight of the cafe.

'The last of the Caretakers,' he breathed. 'Maybe the single most important man in the world ...'

The idea flitted around in his head like a sparrow, never really alighting anywhere long enough for him to grasp it, to study it, to draw some satisfaction from it. He went out and climbed wearily up the stairs, wishing he could tell Rose, but knowing he couldn't.

BOOK III

The One Pig

'... One pig to rule them all, One pig to bind them,
One pig to bring them all and on the pier-end find them
In Seal Beach, on the Coast.'

WILLIAM ASHBLESS,
MYTHS OF THE PACIFIC COAST

TWELVE

'I am a man more sinned against than sinning.'

WILLIAM SHAKESPEARE,
THE TRAGEDY OF KING LEAR

The telephone rang at five in the morning. Andrew groped for it, nearly pushing it off the nightstand. It was Pickett, whispering. He sounded desperate. There was trouble. He was in the basement of a Chinese restaurant, the Bamboo Paradise, down on Broadway, near Cherry.

'What?' said Andrew, half-groggy. 'Speak up. What time is it?'

It sounded as if the phone banged against something on the other end, as if it had been dropped maybe. Then it was hung up; there was a click and a dial tone. Andrew swung around and sat on the edge of the bed, trying to think. It was barely daylight.

'Who was that?' Rose asked.

'No one. Pickett.'

She turned over and plumped up her pillow. 'What for? More escaped zoo animals eating ravioli?'

Andrew forced a laugh in order to humor her. But this clearly wasn't any laughing matter. The ax had fallen. The enemy was finally moving against them. Andrew wondered if it was the squid in the supporter that had set them off, if that had been the last straw. He stood up, picked his pants up off the floor, and pulled them on, squinting around the room for yesterday's shirt.

'You're not thinking of going out,' said Rose, waking up now. 'Where?'

Andrew acted hearty, as if he'd had a little outing planned all along. 'Fishing. There's a warm current in. Fish'll be biting like crazy. *You* were the one who advised it, after all, and now I'm just taking the advice. It's simple as that. I'll be back early.'

'But we're opening today. *You're* opening today.'

'No sweat,' said Andrew, tying his shoelaces. 'I got it all squared away last night. It's in the fridge. There's a couple of veggies to chop for the salad and the dressing to whip up, but that'll save for this afternoon. You might send Mrs Gummidge in to tidy up the kitchen, though.'

Rose pushed herself up onto her elbows. 'Mrs Gummidge isn't a maid. She's a paying guest. The kitchen is a mess and you're going out fishing?'

'Only for a bit. I'll be back in no time, like I said. I've got to meet Pickett down at the Potholder before word leaks out that I'm coming. There won't be a fish left this side of the Belmont Pier if I stop to scrub the kitchen down first. News travels fast in the ocean. Mr Sardine tells Mr Perch, Mr Perch tells Mr Flounder, Mr Flounder tells Mr Mackerel. Pretty soon it's a fish exodus. You know how it is. They live in fear of me and Pickett.' He laughed, kissed her on the cheek, and went out before she had a chance to complain. He'd have to throw his fishing rod and tackle box into the Metropolitan, just to keep things straight. And this time he'd stop in at the fish market on the way home and buy a couple of cod or something to flesh out the gunnysack.

He was halfway down the stairs before he hesitated, turned, and crept back up, holding his breath. He tiptoed down the hallway to where the door of Pennyman's room stood slightly ajar. The door didn't creak; Andrew knew that. He pushed on the top panel, evenly and lightly. It swung open an inch, two inches. It was dark inside. Andrew was certain he could hear heavy breathing. A ghastly smell lingered in the air of the room, and Andrew wrinkled up his face at it, recognizing it. Could it still be the stink from Pickett's opening the box in the drawer? Surely by now it would have faded …

Pennyman himself must have been at the box. Strange, thought Andrew, his eyes adjusting. There was Pennyman, asleep on the bed, the curtain open enough to reveal his face. Satisfied, Andrew left the door where it was and backed away down the hall.

Just then the phone rang again. Andrew gasped and staggered, hurrying toward the bedroom, hoping to God it was Pickett, talking sense this time. There was another half-ring and then silence followed by someone murmuring. He stopped to listen outside the bedroom door. Rose wasn't talking to anyone; she was asleep again. It hadn't been their phone at all. He loped to the stairs and then down them three at a time, as noislessly as he could, out through the kitchen door, ducking through the garage, grabbing his rod and tackle box, and sliding into the Metropolitan, shoving his rod in through the open window. He threw the car into gear and cranked the ignition, leaning on the gas smoothly as the engine caught and the car leaped forward. It had been Pennyman's phone, and Pennyman had answered it.

In five minutes he was out on the Coast Highway, driving northwest, into Long Beach, wishing he'd brought – what? A gun? A ball bat? He had his pocketknife, a multi-bladed little toad-sticker. He could picture himself pulling the knife out, menacing thugs. How was that sort of thing done, exactly? Pickett was in trouble; there could be no doubt about that now. What was the restaurant called? The Bamboo something.

There was a fog bank out over the ocean. Andrew could see little trailing wisps of it stealing ashore as he sailed up Ocean Boulevard, the traffic lights still blinking yellow. Almost no one was out and about except him, which was moderately pleasing. He was a man with a mission. Maybe with a deadly mission. He recalled last night's conversation with Pickett. He *should* have told Rose, informed her, very placidly but squinting with secret knowledge, that he'd become the most important man in the world, that the mystical weight of the millennia had fallen on his meager shoulders. By God, he was bent, but not broken. She would have sighed and shaken her head. Who'd have thought? Then when the phone rang at five o'clock in the morning it wouldn't surprise her, although she'd react to the element of danger in it. 'Do you have to go?' she'd say. 'Stay with me another five minutes.'

'It's duty,' he'd tell her, his jaw set, his eyes focused on eternity. 'They've called.' And out he'd go, brushing back his hair, to face the bastards down.

There was an old green panel truck parked on Cherry, just around the corner, off Broadway. 'Han Koi' it said on the side of it, and beneath the words was painted a stylized goldfish. Two Asian men, Chinese probably, stood beside it, eating doughnuts out of a Winchell's box. That had to be it, although what exactly *it* was Andrew didn't know. There was the restaurant, the Bamboo Paradise. Lights burned inside. Andrew drove on past, up Cherry, swinging around onto Appleton. He cut the motor and coasted to the curb.

The neighborhood was neat and fresh – old bungalows and Mediterranean-style flat-roofed houses sitting atop banked front yards with clipped lawns. The sycamores along the curbs were just starting to leaf out. A dog barked a few doors down and then abruptly shut up, as if he were sorry for it. Andrew sat and thought for a moment, realizing that he had no idea on earth what he was doing there. He hadn't been built for this kind of work, this saving-the-world business. Or had he? It seemed vaguely like fate to him, like destiny – his having ended up with the spoon – his being the last of the Caretakers. He wondered abruptly if that made him one of Them. It pretty clearly did. Maybe this *was* what he was built for. Maybe on this foggy morning the curtain had opened on the final act, and he was stepping out onto the stage to play out his destiny and the destiny of the world. He regarded himself momentarily in the rearview mirror in order to see whether he looked the part. His hair stuck up like flowerettes on a broccoli stalk. He worked for a moment winnowing them out with his fingers and smoothing them down but gave it up. They'd have to take him as he came.

He sat for a moment and thought. Pickett had been in danger – clear enough. But what sort of danger? How could Andrew go wading in? They'd both be up to their necks in it if he weren't careful. He had an edge, though. He'd been smart enough to check Pennyman's room. He'd heard the phone ring. If the old man had already been out, then Andrew could assume he was here, at the Bamboo Paradise. But Pennyman hadn't been out; he'd been home in bed, sleeping like a baby, at least until his phone had rung. Andrew had got the jump on him. What was Pennyman doing now? Styling his hair?

Fetching out the blowfish? The laser scalpel? Until Pennyman arrived, Andrew could assume fairly safely that there was no one here who knew him, who would recognize him. But when Pennyman showed up …

Han Koi. That was the name on the check stub in Pennyman's book – the man on The Toledo! The carp truck fit. The way Andrew figured it, Pickett had gone meddling around down there late last night, trying to make sense of that corner of the puzzle. He'd run afoul of them, and now, for some unknown reason, they'd brought him around to this Chinese restaurant. There flashed through Andrew's mind the picture of Pickett lying on a Formica table, held down by hired men, and Pennyman setting in to saw him in half. And it wasn't a far-fetched notion at all.

He slid out of the car, feeling helpless. Then, in a fit of inspiration, he tugged one of his shoelaces out and tossed it back into the car. He yanked half his shirt out and went around to the trunk after his fishing jacket, which was coffee-stained and smeared with ten years worth of tar and fish scales. He mussed up his hair, although it didn't need it, and then kneeled in the muddy gutter, soiling his pants and smearing the wet dirt with his hands, wiping them off on his jacket. Three doors down, on a front lawn, was a thrown-away bag with an empty bottle in it – just the thing. Andrew retrieved it. He looked good – a custom-built hobo, the tongue protruding from his laceless shoe. No one would imagine who he really was, *what* he was – Andrew Vanbergen, restaurateur, Caretaker, last of the Legion of the Coin, a sort of twentieth-century Odin going out disguised into the foggy morning.

He made sure both sides of the car were unlocked, and he left the key in the ignition. It was risky, but it was a good neighborhood and there might easily be no time to be fumbling after keys. This might be a matter of running for it. He slumped away down the sidewalk, around onto Cherry, heading downhill toward Broadway. Overhead there sounded the raucous cackle of wild parrots, dozens of them, jerking along toward the south, toward wherever they went.

Andrew forced himself not to look up. He had to affect the indifference of a wino just having waked up on someone's stoop. But he was happy to hear the parrots anyway, strangely so, as if he suspected without knowing why that, like Aunt Naomi's cats and like Uncle Arthur's turtles, the parrots were allies, were looking out for him, were part of an ordered plan.

That was nonsense, though. He'd have to pay attention. This was no time for flights of fancy. The doughnut eaters were slouched against the side of the truck, sipping coffee now and talking. Andrew shuffled along silent as death in his crepe-soled shoes. If they looked up and saw him, he'd weave past and head south on Broadway, entirely unremarkable. If they didn't he'd …

Quick and quiet he angled across into the cramped parking lot behind the restaurant, forcing himself to walk slowly, straining to watch the two men out of the corner of his eye. They paid no attention to him. One of them laughed aloud and said something in Chinese. The other one laughed, too, and said something back. One more step, two … and they were gone, lost to sight behind the edge of the building. Andrew quickened his pace, ducking in past an open, foul-smelling dumpster, half full of garbage. He shoved the bag and bottle into the inside pocket of his coat.

There wasn't any time to wait. At any moment a taxi might pull up to the curb and spill Pennyman out; then he was lost, or at least the whole business would become frighteningly more complicated. A line of windows showed just above the pavement of the parking lot, dusty and covered with hardware cloth fixed with screws and strips of wood. They'd be basement windows. Pickett had claimed to be in a basement. The windows were large enough for a man the size of Pickett to squeeze through.

Andrew made up his mind. This was no time for debate. He pulled his knife out of his pocket, prying out the screwdriver and kneeling in front of one of the windows.

But he was in clear view of the street. Anyone cruising past would see him and suppose him a burglar. They'd sound the alarm and he'd be given away. He stood up and bent along toward a heap of cardboard cartons, pulling two big ones over to where he had been working, careful not to scrape them on the asphalt. Then he went back for two more, piling them up so as to hide him entirely when he crouched behind them. He went to work again.

There was no use trying to alert Pickett. Not yet anyway. What could Pickett do to help? Andrew would take it on faith that Pickett was inside. If he weren't, then Andrew would go in through the window anyway to have a look around. Either way, unscrewing the hardware cloth was a good idea. The screws turned easily in the weathered wood, but were too loose to back out. Andrew pried on them, shoving a big splinter of wood from a packing crate in under the blade to get some leverage. He peered around the boxes at the street. The seconds slipped by. The screws one by one popped out onto the pavement, and he brushed them away with his free hand. Finally two of the wood strips fell away and the corner of the hardware cloth was loose. He realized he was sweating in the cold, foggy air, but he was working silent and sure, surprising himself, thinking about Rose, thinking that if he tackled painting the house with this much attention and persistence …

He yanked on the corner of the steel screen, gouging his palm against one of the jagged edges. The still-attached wood strips cracked, popping loose past the screws. He tugged again and tore the screen away entirely, pitching the hardware cloth into the weeds beyond the parking lot and then leaping up and sweeping the litter of screws and wood fragments away with his foot before hustling in behind the dumpster again to lie low.

The smell was god-awful – old rotted fish and coffee grounds and cigarette butts. He crouched there, catching his breath, half-waiting for the sound of the doughnut eaters coming to investigate the noise. There was nothing. He counted to ten, giving them time. Still nothing. He peered beneath the dumpster, past its little wheels. The parking lot was empty and silent. Back to the window he went, folding the screwdriver back into the pocketknife and drawing out the long blade.

Clearly, he was born to be a burglar. This was going as neatly as had the dead 'possum job. The transom window had a spring latch at the top. That was it. Over the years the building had slumped, the windows had worked their way out of square, and there was no end of gaps where gaps weren't intended to be. He slid his blade in, pressed the half-rounded point against the angled side of the spring-set metal triangle that formed the moveable half of the catch, and pushed it in, simultaneously pushing on the window.

He nearly tumbled against the wall as the window fell open, and at once there was the smell of garlic and fish and the sound of distant voices. The basement was almost dark. Clearly, Pickett wasn't in there. He'd have heard and seen Andrew breaking in. He'd be at the window, pulling himself through. There was nothing for it but to go in – head first, on his back.

It was easy. Inside, above the window, was a concrete ledge – the top of the foundation most likely. Andrew grabbed onto it, scrabbling for a hold on the rough wooden mudsill running along the top of it, and held on as he slid through and dropped to the floor, landing in a crouch and waiting again – this time for the talk to stop, for the hue and cry. There was nothing – just more hushed voices, a laugh, the sound of glasses clinking.

What if Pickett weren't there? What if, thought Andrew suddenly, he hadn't even been in trouble? What if he'd only been zealous, thinking that Andrew was equally so and wouldn't mind being awakened by a five o'clock phone call? What if he'd simply been cut off? Those were grim thoughts. It would mean that Andrew had broken into an innocent Chinese restaurant, that when frightened cooks took him apart with meat cleavers, there'd be nothing to do but grin and bear it.

That couldn't be the case though, not with the truck parked out at the curb. What had Pickett said about not believing in coincidence? Andrew crept forward. Despite the deepening fog, there was plenty of light outside, now that his eyes adjusted, to illuminate the basement. It was smaller than it appeared to be from the street, only a half basement, really, with almost a quarter of it taken up by a single restroom. Boxes of canned goods and crates of vegetables were stacked everywhere. A bare, unlit incandescent bulb hung from the ceiling by its cord. The scrape of table and chair legs sounded from above.

Andrew crept across the concrete floor and up the stairs, pausing with each step to listen. All he wanted was a peek. If Pickett weren't there, out in the restaurant itself, then Andrew would go back out through the window, weaving bum-like up the road, waving a groggy hello at everyone he saw. But if he were confronted now, on the stairs …

He'd act drunk, pretend to have broken into the basement in order to sleep. He wished to God that he had liquor on his breath instead of tooth-paste, but he was glad he hadn't stopped to shave that morning. He paused long enough to pull the bag out of his coat pocket and unscrew the lid on the bottle. There were a few drops left inside. 'Night Train,' the label on the bottle read. He dribbled them onto his coat, surprising himself at the sudden, winy reek. He put the bottle away. It was a good prop.

Feet shuffled past above. There was clanking in the kitchen – off to the right he supposed, although he couldn't see the door. He crept up the last six treads on his hands and knees, ready to drop down and feign sleep. He was shaking wildly, as if he had a chill, and he knew if he were caught he'd never be able to convince anyone of anything. They'd have him. At best he'd find himself downtown, in a cell.

He could just see over the top tread, through the table legs. Three Chinese men in aprons, one of them a head taller than the other two and with oddly wavy hair, scurried around, setting tables, wheeling carts full of water glasses and plates. They were garden variety waiters, clearly, putting things right. An old man, very old, white-haired and thin and with a goldfish earring in one ear, sat a table sipping tea. There was no Beams Pickett. It looked suspiciously as if there was no Beams Pickett in the entire building. Pickett was probably sitting at the counter at the Potholder eating steak and eggs. By God if he was … What if Pickett *had* simply been cut off, and had called home again and talked to Rose, asking after Andrew …?

Andrew would kill him – and to hell with saving the world. He backed away down the stairs, half-sliding. He had to get out of there. Suddenly he couldn't breathe. He was hyperventilating. He felt faint. If he tumbled back down the stairs … He sat down hard, fighting vertigo, shoving his head between his knees and forcing himself to breathe regularly. He would just take a second – it was better than passing out.

There was a shifting noise, like someone moving – below him. He listened sharp. It was impossible, unless someone had come in through the window after him, in which case he was trapped, fore and aft. He started down again, looking sharp, and there was the shifting and scraping, followed by a sigh. It was coming from the bathroom, which had, weirdly, a bolt on the outside of the door. The bolt was pushed in. Someone was locked in the bathroom. Andrew grinned. He knew who it was. This would be good – dangerous, but good.

He glanced backward up the stairs, turned the knob at the same time that he slipped the bolt, and swung the door open, dropping down into a sort of

James Bond crouch, as if he were ready to tear to pieces whoever was on the other side. It was Pickett, wild-eyed, backed against the sink, expecting Lord knows what – Pennyman, no doubt, carrying some loathsome instrument of death and torture.

Pickett sagged like a stuffed doll, steadying himself against the sink. He opened his mouth to speak, but Andrew shook his head, gesturing, looking again up the stairs, and then nodded him out of the restroom, shutting the door and throwing the bolt. He pointed toward the rear of the basement and winked, then set out with Pickett at his heels. He helped his friend through first, and then Pickett half-dragged him out onto the asphalt of the parking lot. Andrew reached back in and pulled the window shut just as the basement light clicked on. Both of them sprang for the dumpster.

The seconds ticked by. They could just see someone moving around within, shifting crates, juggling vegetables. There was an airy little snatch of song, and then the light shut out again and all was silent. Andrew nudged Pickett in the ribs and grinned at him. His friend looked awful – rumpled and baggy-eyed – but he clearly hadn't been beaten. They were saving him for Pennyman, no doubt. There'd be time to discuss it in the car.

Andrew felt very satisfied with himself, and nearly laughed out loud. Quickly, he formulated a new plan, whispering it to Pickett, warning him about the thugs on the street, about the manifold dangers. Andrew would slouch out, bum-wise, toward the sidewalk, and if the doughnut eaters were gone, he'd give Pickett the high sign and Pickett would follow, the two of them beating it up to the Metropolitan and away. It was easy as that. He'd get Pickett out of there yet, and Pennyman could go hang.

Steeling himself, Andrew started out, peering past the edge of the dumpster and shoving his foot forward just as a yellow cab whipped around the corner onto Cherry and bumped to a stop at the curb. The rear door swung open and Pennyman himself hunched out, shoving his arm back in through the window to pay the driver.

Andrew ducked back, whispering 'Pennyman!' and hauling Pickett down onto the asphalt, the two of them huddled and listening. A car door slammed and the taxi motored away. They'd wait for Pennyman to go in, and then they'd run for it. To hell with anyone at the curb. Once Pennyman unbolted the bathroom door and found that the prey had disappeared, there'd be half a dozen men at the curb.

But Pennyman didn't go inside. He walked straight in their direction, whistling 'Zip-a-Dee-Doo-Dah,' as if he were in tip-top shape and the morning was a good one.

Andrew and Pickett crouched amid the rubble of broken crates and cardboard boxes, watching beneath the dumpster as Pennyman's white bucks strode along toward them, the tip of his walking stick tapping along beside.

There was no time to pull a carton over their heads; no time for elaborate plans. Andrew gave Pickett a look that he hoped suggested toughing it out. Between the two of them they could throttle Pennyman despite his canes and blowfish. If he carried a gun though ...

Pennyman stopped when he got to the dumpster, close enough to it that he must have been gripping the edge, with his face nearly in the garbage. There was no way on earth that he could see Pickett and Andrew unless he walked around to the other side. What was he looking for? Some sort of vile fish guts to grind into poison? He stood just so. Andrew and Pickett held their breath. The morning was deadly silent.

No, not quite silent. There was a deep, almost hoarse irregular breathing and sniffing. Garbage shifted in the dumpster, as if Pennyman were stirring it with a stick, and the reek issuing from the rotted fish and vegetables and table leavings redoubled. Andrew nearly gagged, covering his mouth with his hand, still watching Pennyman's feet. The old man groaned, sliding the toe of one shoe up along the back of his calf, as if caressing it. He stood suddenly on tiptoe, bending farther over into the dumpster, and uttered a low, moaning wail, breathing like an engine, quicker and quicker, the toes of his shoes twitching on the asphalt.

Andrew was dumbstruck, and Pickett, given the look on his face, was nearly blind with disgust – not at the ghastly odor of decay and rot that had settled around them, but at Pennyman's insane passion, which, from the look of his twitching feet and the sound of his dwindling, throat-rasping wheeze, was almost spent.

Andrew suddenly stood up, slamming his open hand into the steel side of the dumpster, which thrummed like a bass drum. His vision had narrowed down into a tight little focus, as if he were looking down a tube. He couldn't speak. But playing through his head like a looped tape was the loathsome knowledge that this monster, ecstatic now with rot and filth and decay, had kissed Rose's hand, had been gallant, had been ...

He lashed out with his right fist, pulling himself up and across the rim of the dumpster, taking Pennyman utterly by surprise. The old man reeled back, safe by inches, his mouth working. He raised his stick and swung it at nothing, as if he were half-blind. Andrew leaped around toward him, picking up an empty bottle and hurling it wildly, past Pennyman's shoulder. It smashed straight through the basement window where he'd torn off the screen. Glass shattered, crates toppled. Pennyman shouted, and there was the sound of running feet punctuated by a weird raucous chattering, coming, it seemed, from the sky.

Pickett slammed into Andrew's side, deflecting him away from Pennyman, who stood with his stick upraised, watching him rush in. 'C'mon!' Pickett screamed, pulling at Andrew. 'Leave him! Let's go!'

Andrew reeled after him, but turned back after half a step. Give up! Not now he wouldn't give up. He would finish Pennyman off and damn the consequences he'd beat Pennyman with his own cane, by God! He'd …

The two doughnut eaters rounded the corner of the building just then, one of them carrying a little wooden baseball bat, and both of them springing straight toward Andrew. Pickett waded in behind them, smashing one of them with a packing crate, the spindly wood cracking to splinters against the man's head. He stumbled, mostly out of surprise, but he was up again in an instant.

The air was a tumult of sounds: Pennyman's cursing, Andrew's shouted threats, feet running on pavement, the airborne shriek of suddenly-appearing parrots. Andrew turned to meet the two new attackers just as Pickett threw himself onto the back of the one who had stumbled. But two more men – two of the white-aproned waiters from the restaurant – burst out through the back door just then, and although Andrew landed one good punch on his man's shoulder, half-spinning him around, the two reinforcements slammed Andrew against the stucco wall, pinioning his arms. Pickett lay on the parking lot, the man with the ball bat having shaken him off and standing over him now, the club poised in the air.

'Stop!' commanded Pennyman, and the man with the bat lowered it, snatching Pickett to his feet. Pennyman smiled, raising his left hand to his mouth and nibbling on his finger. 'I'll attend to that,' he said. 'Hold them.'

Andrew was aware that he was breathing hard, but he felt calm, considering what he faced. He vowed not to lose control over himself the way he had that afternoon with Ken-or-Ed. Pennyman fed off that sort of chaos. 'Your hair is mussed,' Andrew said matter-of-factly and squinting with disapproval. 'I'd let you borrow my comb, but I don't …'

The tip of the cane whistled through the air, stopping a half inch from Andrew's nose. Pennyman grinned when Andrew flinched and gasped. He paused to take out a pocket comb, which he pulled through his hair with a trembling hand. Andrew wouldn't be put off. He was fired up and thinking. The morning was wearing on. Traffic had picked up. There was every reason in the world to waste time, to spend a few more minutes in the parking lot in order to attract the attention of neighbors or passing cars.

'Why those five books?' Andrew asked.

Pennyman looked sharp at him. 'What?'

'The five books you stole. Why those five? They aren't worth anything, not really. I don't get it. Those are the five *I* might have stolen.'

Pennyman made no effort to act surprised, to pretend. He shrugged. 'It doesn't matter.'

Pennyman liked to talk. He fancied himself a philosopher.

Andrew knew that – all the wombing and tombing business had taught him as much. 'I can't figure it out, especially the Pogo.'

Pennyman widened his eyes, as if to tell him to go on, that he would hear him out.

'A month ago,' said Andrew, 'I'd have said that any friend of Pogo was a friend of mine. Anyone who reads Walt Kelly *has* to have the right inclinations. Nitwits and pretenders wouldn't understand it. I'd have taken you for the sort who nods over – who? – Sartre? Maybe Mann. Someone polished and full of ... shit, I guess. But not Pogo. What does that mean, I ask myself. And it seems to mean that, well, you're something in the way of a lost soul. There's something in you yearning to be ... might I say, good? Something that isn't at all fond of ... of ... collecting cat waste, let's say, or drooling over rotted garbage in a dumpster.' Andrew beamed at him curiously, but with the moony-eyed, meaningful smile of a self-help psychologist, a benevolent, compassionate look, guaranteed to drive Pennyman insane. He tensed, readying himself to duck the inevitable blow of the walking stick. But there was none. Pennyman stared at him, breathing shallowly. A heavy pall of embarrassment had descended.

'Are you through?'

Andrew shrugged, glancing sideways across the parking lot. The street was empty. Talking was useless.

'Take them in.' Pennyman's mouth was set, frozen in an expressionless line. 'Into the kitchen,' he said, with such a ghastly intonation as to make it sound as if the kitchen weren't a kitchen at all, but were a medieval chamber of horrors.

Andrew screamed, simultaneously ducking away, carrying his captor with him. Taking Andrew's lead, Pickett screamed, too, and Pennyman, caught by surprise, stepped backward, thinking that Andrew was lunging at him, and swung the stick wildly, thudding it off the back of the man that held Andrew's arm. Andrew stamped his foot behind him, still shouting and screaming, trying to smash the man's toe and swinging around so as to keep the man between himself and the cane.

It was worthless. The man sprinted forward, driving Andrew into the wall of the restaurant. It was over, and all Andrew had managed was to drive Pennyman into a fury. He could hear the parrots circling above, and he stumbled as he was pushed toward the door.

Then, without warning, the parking lot was chaotic with parrots, flapping and reeling and shrieking. There was a cloud of them, a green, clamoring, raucous cloud of heavy parrots, dropping in like dog-fighters and slamming around and around them, tearing at faces with pronged beaks and claws, screeching and gouging. Pennyman threw his hands over his head after taking a wild cut at them with his cane. One of the waiters ran for the street, pursued by three or four parrots that tore at his ears like demons.

Pennyman hunkered lower, trying to keep the birds away from his neck, trying to curl up into a ball but terrified lest his white trousers touch the dirty asphalt of the parking lot. One of the parrots, a great, red-headed Amazon with an almost three-foot wingspan, clung to Pennyman's back and burrowed into the collar of his coat as the old man let go of his head with one hand and flailed away at the bird uselessly, trying first to bat it away, then to get a grip on it.

The parrots took no interest at all in Andrew and Pickett. It was as if the cavalry had arrived in the nick of time. For the long space of half a minute Andrew watched amazed, wafering himself against the wall of the restaurant, as he was jerked back and forth by the doughnut thug, who still gripped his left arm but was weaving and dancing and waving his free arm to keep off the parrots. Seeing his chance, Andrew hit his man in the stomach with his elbow, twisting away at the same time and kicking him in the knee.

Two parrots sailed in as if to help him, one of them clutching at the man's cheek with its talons and biting his nose, wrenching it back and forth as if to tear it off. Howling, he grabbed the bird but couldn't pull the parrot off without losing the end of his nose into the bargain, and so reeled away shrieking for help, blood spattering his shirtfront. Andrew ran for it, up Cherry, toward the Metropolitan, thanking heaven that the parrots were on his side, and that one hadn't latched onto *his* nose by mistake. Pickett pounded along after him as the men back in the parking lot were slowly backed up against the wall, fighting just to keep the birds away from their eyes.

None of the parrots followed Andrew and Pickett, and as they topped the hill and sprinted across a lawn, angling toward where the car was parked, they looked back to see Pennyman lurching through the door into the rear of the restaurant, his pants tattered, his hair wild. He tore at his coat, which still sagged under the weight of the determined parrot.

Andrew fired the engine and sped away, Pickett pulling himself into the weaving car and slamming the door on the run, the Metropolitan barreling through two stop signs and sliding around the corner onto Wisconsin Street, bound for home. It was when they'd got to Ximeno that the flock of parrots passed squacking overhead again, heading out over the ocean. Mystified, Andrew and Pickett watched them through the windshield until they disappeared beyond the rooftops.

It was early yet, too early to go home. Heaven knows there was enough to do at home, but there was no way on earth that Andrew could claim to have done any serious fishing yet, and, at least for the moment, there was no way they could simply walk in and confess. Not yet anyway. They talked about it as they sat in a booth at the Potholder, eating breakfast.

What profit would there be in generally revealing things? Rose would become involved; that was bad. It would be expected that they'd call the police, now that kidnapping had entered the list of villainies. But what, the authorities would want to know, had Pickett been doing breaking into a house on The Toledo?

That's what he'd done, it turned out, just as Andrew had suspected. Pickett had driven off late last night with Andrew's Toledo address in his pocket, and just for sport he'd parked in Naples and walked to the right. It fronted the water and backed up onto an alley. There'd been an unlocked door, as if it were an invitation. Pickett had sneaked in, crept downstairs and into a basement, knowing he was an idiot for doing it, but fired up with his successes at the library. The basement was a laboratory, full of books and what seemed almost to be alchemical apparatus. A great carp lay flayed upon a table, laid open with a scalpel, but with its heart still beating, weirdly, as if Pickett had just that moment interrupted some half-finished experiment.

Which, of course, he had. They'd stepped out of the shadows and cut off his retreat, almost as if they'd been waiting for him. He'd sat tied to a chair for hours, waiting almost until dawn, unable to sleep. The man wielding the scalpel – an old Chinese who looked like Fu Manchu with goldfish earrings – had been friendly, although not out of compassion, but out of the certainty, it seemed, that Pickett was a dead man and so posed no threat and could be talked to with impunity.

Three hundred years old; that had been the man's age, or so he said. Pickett believed him. Why not? He looked it, certainly, in some vague and undefinable way – as if he'd seen at least three hundred years worth of tumult and mystery and wonder. He excised a little gland from the carp, a gland from which, he said, he generated the elixir that Pennyman guarded so jealously. It was a longevity serum, a way to circumvent the ruinous effects of possessing the coins. 'Mr Pennyman needs the elixir very badly,' the old man had said, shaking his head as if it made him sad. 'Very badly. He came to me in a sedan chair, a mummy, unable to walk, barely able to swallow. And now ...' He shrugged, as if Pickett could see for himself. 'He is a good customer. A very good customer.'

Grinning, Han Koi had offered Pickett an ounce of the elixir, mixed in orange juice, thinking, maybe, that it was funny to offer a man something in the way of immortality one moment, knowing that the man's life would be snatched away the next.

One thing that Pickett became sure of before they hauled him away to the Bamboo Paradise was that Pennyman was merely a customer of Han Koi, an old and treasured customer, but not a partner. Pennyman paid well for the elixir – as the check stub testified – well enough so that Han Koi was happy to do Pennyman the favor of holding on to the snooping Pickett for a few hours, until dawn, until Pennyman had finished his sleep and would want to ask a few delicate questions.

Pickett sipped his coffee and shook his head, remembering. It had been a long night. They had driven him to the restaurant and led him inside, untied – very sure of themselves. They'd dead-bolted the street door and pocketed the key, going into the kitchen to brew tea. Pickett had lunged for the pay phone, dialing Andrew's number, barely able to get a sentence out before they were onto him. They locked him in the bathroom then, and there he'd sat, thinking that the first person he'd see when the door opened would be Pennyman. But there was Andrew ...

'It was a pretty spectacular escape, wasn't it?'

Pickett nodded.

'And how about the parrots? If it hadn't been for the parrots ...'

Pickett drew a finger across his throat, illustrating what would have become of them if it hadn't been for the parrots.

They ate in silence, both of them nervously watching the door. 'What do we do about Pennyman?' asked Andrew.

'Nothing,' said Pickett.

'Nothing? We let him get away with this? How about that garbage business. You don't think that he was ...'

'I think that explains the filth in the drawer, doesn't it? Some men clip out pornographic pictures, some ...'

'Good God,' gasped Andrew. 'He's twice the monster I had him pegged for. I can't allow him to stay in the house. He *won't*, I bet. For my money we won't see him again. He'll send for his things.'

'Nope,' said Pickett. 'He'll be back looking sleek and happy and full of flattery. And you'll have to let him stay. The treasure hunt is two days away. The pot is on the burner, and we've got to let it boil. This isn't something that can be stopped; it's something that will *come to pass*, like it or not. And for your sake and Rose's sake and the sake of the inn, we better let it play itself out with as little mess as possible. If Pennyman tries to brass it out, we'll outbrass him, that's all.'

Saying nothing, Andrew sopped up the last of his egg yolks with a piece of toast. Maybe what Pickett said was true. The sails were furled, the ship slanting through the growing swell. There was nothing to do but ride out the storm. Someone, Andrew was sure, was at the tiller – maybe it was Uncle Arthur, maybe an unseen hand. This was no time to start throwing over ballast, to try to shift course.

After breakfast they drove to the fish market on Ocean Boulevard, watching through the rear window for a tail. Then, with two rock cod and a sheepshead in the gunnysack, they drove to Naples, where Pickett's car was parked. Pickett drove off. He intended to be at the cafe later that afternoon, to do his part. It promised to be a curious evening.

When Andrew got home it was barely nine o'clock. He walked through the back door carrying his fish. He looked like hell, still wearing his jacket, although he'd tucked his shirt in and replaced his shoelace. Rose gave him a look.

'Catch anything much?'

'Didn't do too bad.'

'Out on the pier?'

'Off the end.' He held up the gunnysack.

'Cold out there?'

'Not bad,' said Andrew, beginning to wonder. Rose was distant, clearly not chipper. He grinned to cheer her up.

'I wouldn't think that old jacket would be worth much. The wind must cut right through it.'

Andrew nodded. 'It *was* cold out there. But when you're fishing ...'

'KNEX called early this morning and changed the time.'

'What? To when?'

'This evening, while you're cooking.'

Andrew grimaced. 'That's no good. I can't actually *wear* one of these hats, not while I'm cooking. My idea was to get them in and out of here. Clear the decks, you know, before we opened up.'

Rose shrugged.

'You should have told them I was out, that you couldn't change it. You should have told me first.'

'In fact,' said Rose, wiping the countertop with a rag, 'I did more than that. I went out onto the pier looking for you, about seven.'

'Damn,' Andrew lied. 'That's when we were down at the Potholder, eating breakfast.'

'No you weren't,' said Rose. 'I looked for you there, too. The waitress said she knew the two of you and that you hadn't been in yet. When I couldn't find you anywhere I figured there was nothing to do but call them back and okay the time change. It seems to me that if this inn or the cafe made the least bit of difference to you ...'

'Of course it does!' It looked as if she were going to cry, just out of tired desperation, sick of his sneaking around, his weird behavior. Andrew stepped toward her, thinking to take her by the shoulders, to give her a bit of a hug. Maybe he *would* explain things to her. Maybe she should know. But she wrinkled her nose and stepped aside.

'What in the world ...'

'What?' said Andrew. 'Nothing. Alcohol from the kelp worms we use as bait. They pickle them.' He spread his arms in a gesture of assurance, a gesture that revealed the bag and bottle in his inside pocket. The sight of it horrified him. Why hadn't he …? He pulled it out, gesturing more wildly now, almost frantic at what this must look like. He was innocent. He was *more* than innocent. He …

The bottle slid out of the bag onto the linoleum floor, smashing to bits. Fragments of green glass slid away. The label, with a nebula of shards glued to it, spun 'round and 'round like a dervish until it slowed to a stop at the door to the living room, where Aunt Naomi stood in surprise, looking on. The old lady turned and hurried away, leaving the two of them alone.

THIRTEEN

'Let Tola bless with the Toad, which is the good creature of God, tho his virtue is in secret, and his mention is not made.'

CHRISTOPHER SMART,
'JUBILATE AGNO'

Andrew was horrified. He was empty. This had knocked the stuffing out of him. He couldn't bring himself to grope for another lie; the kelp worm business had been bad enough. Rose very deliberately opened the cupboard in the little pantry where they kept the broom and dustpan.

'Let me do that,' said Andrew.

'No.'

'This isn't what it looks like.'

'It looks like broken glass.'

'What I mean is …'

Rose stopped dead still and gave him a level gaze, her jaw set. 'For God's sake *don't* start up about making paperweights out of old bottles or something. Don't say anything at all about it. Don't carry on. Let it alone. Go out and clean up the kitchen in the cafe. I don't want to know what you've been up to this morning. I can't imagine what it could be. I don't *want* to imagine what it could be. Get out of here and let me clean this up. I've got to take Aunt Naomi in to see Dr Garibaldi in a half hour, so please stay out of my way; that would help me more than you could guess.'

Andrew nodded. 'Yes. Sorry,' he said, stepping toward the door to the cafe. 'I'll be ready to go tonight. Don't worry. I've got it under control.' Rose was silent, sweeping glass from under the kitchen chairs. 'I'd be happy to take Aunt Naomi over …'

Rose interrupted him with a meaningful look, and he scurried away, into the sanctuary of his cafe.

He managed to keep up a cheerful front all day, as if there were nothing wrong, as if he took what Rose had said to him at face value and that the morning's blunders had been scoured away. It was lousy for that to have happened right on top of his foiling Pennyman, though. Apparently he wasn't meant to revel in glory.

But he knew that the cheerful front was a lie. He couldn't get around that even for an instant. He was filled with the hollow fear that the bottle incident had caused damage that couldn't be repaired by winking and grinning and apologizing. It was a final sort of blow. And whose fault was it? His own. He'd masterminded Pickett's escape, but he couldn't, it seemed, keep himself out of trouble at home. He couldn't get through the most mundane chores around the house without everything going to bits and him looking like a jabbering clown.

Of course, part of it was Pennyman's fault. It was important to keep that in mind. It was Pennyman who was driving the wedge.

And it was Pennyman who rolled in at noon, dapper and smiling and without the look of a man who'd been torn to bits by parrots. Andrew was struggling with a rented helium canister. It would have been worlds cheaper to haul the chef's hats down to the gas and chemical company to have them filled, but that would require a truck with an enclosed bed to transport the full hats home in, and he didn't want to rent one. Also, if one of the hats leaked, then he'd have to run it home again for repairs and then back down for more helium, and the day wasn't long enough for that.

He was just levering the canister out of the trunk of the Metropolitan when Pennyman's cab pulled in. Andrew could feel his blood race. Would there be a confrontation? Pennyman wouldn't give him any slack at all next time. He'd strike first and talk afterward. Andrew would have to be ready for him.

But how, without starting Armageddon right there on the sidewalk? It would make a strange setting for the Last Battle.

Pennyman waved at him, very cheerfully. 'Bringing in the sheaves, are you?' he called. 'Give you a hand?'

'No thanks,' Andrew croaked. He cleared his throat, determined once again to outgrin him. 'Just one sheaf, actually, and I've got a dolly here. Nothing to it, really.' The canister cooperated nicely, thunking down onto the little metal dolly and settling there. Andrew strapped it down. It wouldn't do to have it fall and the valve be knocked off. He heaved it up over the curb and across the parkway, making away toward the rear. He ignored Pennyman entirely, although he could see out of the corner of his eye that the old man stood there watching, as if Andrew might need him after all.

What he wanted, probably, was a chance to bandy words. Andrew had best not give him that chance, not with Rose home again. It was tempting, but dangerous. Andrew might easily lose control and reveal that he possessed the spoon, and that the spoon was the coin, and then he'd be a dead man. He couldn't take a chance on it. Uncle Arthur had advised getting out of town. Lying low was the best alternative – starting now.

Andrew would have liked to mention the parrots, though, just to see how Pennyman reacted. It would be nice to imply that Andrew hadn't at all been surprised to see them, that he half-expected them, or perhaps that he himself had timed their arrival for just that crucial moment, that his shouting and screaming had summoned them. Pennyman would respect him then; that much was certain. He would think that Andrew wasn't blundering along blind; he was part of an Organization, an officer in the War of the Coin, that each step he took was toward a fully anticipated destination.

But what did Andrew care for Pennyman's respect? That had been his problem all along – wanting to be liked or respected by people he loathed. What he ought to do was simply tweak Pennyman's nose, right there and then, on the sidewalk. But Rose was home now, along with Aunt Naomi, who was still bleeding internally. Dr Garibaldi couldn't grasp the ailment. It was worsening, too. Her blood was thin. He'd prescribed megadoses of vitamin K and an avocado diet. That was a tough break.

Andrew found himself feeling bad for the old bird as he clunked up the steps into the cafe, hauling the canister. Just when she'd gotten the invalidism licked, this new ailment set in. On an impulse, he filled a bowl with Weetabix, sprinkled sugar on them, poured milk into a pitcher, and headed upstairs. He knocked on Aunt Naomi's door and went in. The sight of the Weetabix seemed to cheer her.

She'd been watching out the window again, staring at the lonesome ocean. She looked at him wistfully and said, 'Don't worry, it'll be all right.' At first he thought she was talking about her own troubles, but she wasn't. She was talking about Rose and him. 'She'll see things straight soon,' Naomi said, spooning up the Weetabix. 'Just do what you have to do.'

Andrew went back downstairs feeling a little bit cheered, and he stopped to pet the cats on the bottom landing. He chatted for a moment with the toad on the service porch on his way back to the cafe, asking after its health, but the thing just floated there with its fingers outspread, doing nothing. Andrew realized abruptly that he half-expected it to respond. This, he told himself, is insanity. But then he remembered the parrots, and he shrugged.

Turning toward the cafe door, he noticed that Rose had taken the brick off the top of the toad's aquarium and was using it to block the back door open. He stopped again and considered it. If *he* had done that, Rose would have pointed out his mistake. She still wasn't enthusiastic about the creature, and wasn't fond of the idea of it slipping out of the tank and making away through the house. And here she was, giving it just such a chance. Well, he'd be big about it, and not point out the contradiction in her behavior, not remind her of the lecture she'd given him. And if she neglected to put it back, and the toad got out … Andrew shrugged. It would give him a certain edge, wouldn't it …?

He felt suddenly like a jerk. He was working hard at feeling sorry for himself is what he was doing. If he could *invent* misdeeds for Rose, then it would seem to even things out. What he was thinking of doing was using this petty brick business against her, in order to gain back some lost ground. Only it wouldn't gain *anything* back, and he knew it; it would only make him contemptible.

He had caught himself – nipped his self-pity in the bud. He hadn't let himself make the stupid error of picking a fight over nothing, just to cast blame. His spirits lifted. He saw Rose heading across the backyard, toward the open door, carrying the library rug, which she'd been beating in the yard. He stood smiling at her. He would say something about the brick, is what he'd do, something lighthearted, that showed that he was aware of the possible trouble connected to removing it from the top of the toad's aquarium, but that he had too much faith in Rose to remind her to replace it.

But then just as abruptly as his spirits had lifted, they fell again. He was puffed up with pride, and he knew it. He marveled at the shifting of virtues and emotions. You couldn't keep them straight. One was always edging the other one aside or swamping it entirely. You had to juggle them continually, and when you thought you had them all balanced and spinning just so, down they came, in a tumble, and you were reminded all over again that you were the biggest fool of all when you put on airs. Well, sometimes that was a healthy reminder – because it was true, you were. And it was when you congratulated yourself most loudly that you were in the most trouble; that's when the fall was greatest.

Andrew laughed for the first time that day. There was a certain humor in the irony of it, in the up and down tangle of guilt and remorse and desire and joy that drove people along as if they were sitting in motor cars built by madmen, trying to steer but finding that the wheel kept coming loose in their hands and that the tires were out of round. And yet somehow, in the face of it all, he was sure that he would get to where he wanted to go – wherever that was – despite the fog and the joke car and the crooked and roundabout route.

He resolved again not to tell Rose the Pennyman business. He was big enough to shoulder it. He knew that he would have liked to abdicate some little bit of his responsibility to her in order to lighten the burden on himself, just like he'd left the mess in the cafe kitchen, half-hoping that Rose or

Mrs Gummidge or elves or cats or someone would clean it up for him. This was his chance to turn that around, his chance to come through.

When the battle was won or lost, when his tour of duty in the Legion of the Coins was through, Rose could be made to understand what had gone on. All would be revealed. He needed patience, that and a clear head, because he could feel it in his bones that there would be trouble tonight.

This had come down to a personal battle between him and Pennyman – an almost petty contest of wills that had begun that night on the front porch and had become a quite possibly deadly affair. Pennyman would act, and soon, too. That's why he had come home starched and pressed and cheerful today. Inside he was a festering mass of hatred; outside he wore the mask. But he would rip it off that evening. You could bet on it.

Trouble came early. It was six o'clock and KNEX hadn't shown up. Andrew's frantic calls to the station were useless. The crew was out in the field. They couldn't be called back. Canceling the piece was out of the question; if it was going to be done at all, then tonight was the night. There was static clicking and a dial tone. Subsequent calls turned up nothing but a busy signal, until finally, after a half-dozen tries, it seemed as if Andrew had got a connection again, except that on the other end there was nothing but silence and then a distant chattering voice sounding like a humanoid insect. Andrew was gripped with the suspicion that the phone trouble was manufactured, and he thought he heard muffled laughter just before the connection was cut.

Too many people were showing up at the cafe. It began to seem as if he wouldn't have enough gumbo, and if he were going to make more then he'd have to hustle. Even with help the process would kill a couple of hours. He felt like sitting in a chair. He wanted a pint of beer, but the keg wasn't working worth a damn. It was pouring out a steady stream of foam, leaving a quarter inch of beer in the bottom of the glass. Pickett had gone to work on it and failed, so now Rose was having a go. But Andrew would have to call her away to chop onions and bell peppers.

And just an hour earlier it had seemed as if everything was set. The fire was lit, and a pile of split eucalyptus logs sat on the side of the hearth, ready. Each table was arranged just so, with a tiny bouquet of blue sweetpeas arranged around a pink carnation; Rose had done that. There were ceramic salt and pepper shakers on each table along with a cut-glass sugar bowl and a pair of candlesticks and the flowers. The whole effect, with the print tablecloths and oak chairs and mismatched silver and china was so homey that he had suddenly wished *he* was eating there, carefree and waited upon. Then it had struck him that the idea of it meant that he had succeeded, that the cafe was going to work. Rose seemed to think so, too.

Pickett had come dressed in a black jacket and a bow tie and with his shoes polished. His very appearance made it clear that he was putting aside his demons and devils for the evening and was rallying 'round. He took Mrs Gummidge in hand, the two of them agreeing on the folding and place-ment of napkins, on the topping off of water glasses. Mrs Gummidge would pour conventional coffee; Pickett would brew more exotic coffees in the espresso maker and tend bar. Rose would bus tables and wash dishes, helped out generally by Mrs Gummidge when Pickett could spare her. Aunt Naomi would tally and distribute the checks and would keep the cats out.

The cats insisted on coming in – hiding behind counters, under tables. Andrew had chased them out again and again, losing the patience he'd developed for them over the past few days. They wouldn't be persuaded, though. They *would* come in, like it or not, and Andrew finally threw in the towel, warning Aunt Naomi to keep them at bay, and to be ready in an instant to pitch them out if a customer complained. He had been certain, by four in the afternoon, that everything would work as smoothly and accurately as a seven-day clock. With only two tables reserved, they couldn't fail. They would come close to outnumbering their guests.

By five everything had been ready and there hovered in the air an atmos-phere of anticipation. Pickett had polished glasses that were already clean, holding them up in the evening sunlight gleaming through the casements and buffing out traces of fingerprints and waterstains. Mrs Gummidge had brewed Aunt Naomi a cup of tea out in the house kitchen. She insisted that tea was a natural curative, and that Aunt Naomi drink half a dozen sugared cups a day, which the old lady did, perhaps to humor her. There had been a generally cheerful bustle as the minutes ticked away toward six o'clock.

Andrew, finished for the moment in the kitchen, had stepped out to sur-vey the bar – the pint glasses, the bottles, the little refrigerator case full of beer and white wine, the debris he'd picked up from Polsky and Sons. Their liquor couldn't be argued with. Most of it would be wasted in a mixed drink, though. They'd discourage mixed drinks. They weren't Pickett's forte any-way. Andrew had felt like a general, surveying the field before a battle, satisfied with the troops ranked just so about the hillsides, with the cannon and camouflage and with the satisfying smell of victory already in the air.

Then the first party arrived, dressed in suits and furs and looking very cheerful. Pickett had just seated them near the fireplace when the second party came in through the door, a very old couple and a very young couple – the young couple evidently the grandchildren. The old man was nearly deaf, and seemed to think he'd been mistreated. Pickett seated them three times, before, with a gesture of contempt, the old man was satisfied and asked immediately for dry toast. Pickett explained graciously about the set menu, about the unavailability of dry toast, and the old man had to be humored by the rest of the party. He picked up the saltshaker, a blue ceramic doggy with inflated cheeks. He stared at it as if in disbelief and then put it down, hiding it behind the flowers. That's where the cat trouble will come from, thought Andrew, looking out through the kitchen door.

Then there was another party, without reservations: four women from Leisure World. They revealed that they were on the staff of the *Leisure World Recliner*, and did the restaurant column. Behind them, to Andrew's indignant surprise, was Ken-or-Ed, looking very cheerful and accompanied by his wife. He caught sight of Andrew in the kitchen and swarmed in toward him, waving his hand and apologizing and leaving his wizened wife standing by the street door, wearing, of all things, a mumu intended for a woman six times her size.

Andrew gritted his teeth. This stank. Something was rotten in Seal Beach. Here was Ken-or-Ed, being big about it all. Andrew could hardly accuse him of being a hireling of Jules Pennyman, not with Rose and Aunt Naomi there, not without seeming to be a lunatic in front of the contingent from the Leisure World newspaper.

Andrew rousted himself. He would have to work like a fiend. He couldn't afford to drink beer. Rose had done something to the keg, and now it was flowing moderately well. There was a cat on the counter staring into the gumbo and another wandering out into the cafe, looking for a lap to leap into. Andrew hissed at the passing Mrs Gummidge to see to the cats, but she hurried off to 'lay tables' as she put it, and was looking for silverware,

KNEX finally strode in almost at seven o'clock – two of them altogether, with video equipment and looking tired and out of sorts, as if it had been a long day. God almighty, Andrew thought, watching the sudden turmoil in the cafe. Pickett ushered the crew into the back corner, then went around to the tables explaining things. The old man was skeptical. He squinted at the video camera and said, throwing down his napkin, that he didn't want a salad, that he couldn't stand 'roughage.' He wanted soup. Pickett grinned at him. The soup would be right up, he said, and explained again about the camera crew, who waved equipment around and talked too loud, joking between themselves. The old man asked where his toast was, and the young lady at the table patiently explained that there wasn't any toast.

Andrew hid in the kitchen. He hadn't even inflated the hats yet. He had no idea whether they'd inflate at all. His brilliant notion of publicizing the restaurant by wearing floating chef's hats was turning out to be a nitwit idea, and he felt suddenly defensive about it. He heard the old man, talking too loud out of general deafness, say, 'I've been told that there *isn't* any toast!'

Mrs Gummidge came through the kitchen smiling just then, looking around. She had a vacant, bemused expression, as if she only half-remembered why she was there at all. She found a spoon on the counter, rinsed it off, dried it, and went back out, humming. Another batch of guests had arrived. The place was filling up. They needed salads, they needed silverware, they needed this and that and the other. Andrew was tired. His back ached and his elbow joints hurt. He had to have aspirin. He felt as if he'd aged ten years in the last two days.

Suddenly there was a shout from the cafe. Andrew knew the voice. He would have guessed it would come from the dry toast man, but it hadn't. It was Ken-or-Ed, cutting up rough. 'You're God damned right!' he shouted, evidently at Pickett. 'In my *salad!*'

A woman shrieked. Leaving his cast iron kettle on the fire, Andrew stepped across to the door and looked out. There was Mrs Ken-or-Ed, standing up, her hands thrown across her chest, a look of surprised horror on her face. Her water glass was tipped over, her chair thrown back. The rest of the patrons were obviously restless, peering under their tables and lifting napkins. The cats! Andrew thought, suddenly seething.

But it wasn't the cats. 'It was a beetle!' shouted Ken-or-Ed. 'A big damned beetle! In my damned salad!'

'Must've been an olive,' Pickett said.

'I saw it, too,' said Mrs Ken-or-Ed.

Pickett brassed it out. 'Seems to have disappeared, doesn't it?' He turned around and looked at Andrew in the doorway. Pickett's face was white. Out of nowhere came a man from KNEX, waving a video camera, grinning. He was a tall Asian, Chinese probably. He looked familiar as hell.

'Come, come,' said Andrew, strolling out among the tables. 'I put that salad together myself, piece by piece. I can assure you that there was nothing at all in it that shouldn't have been. I'd have seen anything out of the ordinary, wouldn't I? It's not one of your tossed-together salads. It's a bit of salad nouvelle. The arrangement, you see, is at least as important as the flavor. Texture is as important to the eye as it is to the palate. The byword in salad-building is … Ah, here's our man's toast!'

Rose had appeared, carrying two slices of quartered, dry toast. The old man was suddenly full of goodwill, as if at last he'd found someone in the restaurant who wasn't certifiable.

'And something's knocked over my water glass!' cried Mrs Ken-or-Ed. 'I don't know what it was. Something was on the table.'

Andrew smiled at her and then, grinning almost wildly, he patted Ken-or-Ed on the back. The man jerked away, looking as if he would kick the table down. Andrew righted the water glass. 'Did the bug kick it over?' he asked. Then to Pickett he said, 'A fresh glass for Mrs Fitzpatrick.'

Meanwhile the camera whirred away, filming the whole thing. Andrew turned to confront the cameraman, grinning into the lens. 'I'll sue you blind,' he whispered, winking at the man. The Fitzpatricks snatched up their coats and stormed toward the door, slamming out, Mrs Ken-or-Ed giving Andrew a look that resembled the face of someone who'd drunk turpentine. Suddenly Andrew knew who the cameraman was. He'd seen him just that morning, at work at the Bamboo Paradise.

So that was it. A beetle! 'Sorry folks,' Andrew said. 'I'm afraid that the couple who left weren't feeling up to snuff. That was Eddie Fitzpatrick, who used to play for the Dodgers. He was hit by a line drive in his last season. In a coma for a year and a half. Maybe you've read about it. Never been the same. They live across the street, and we invited them 'round tonight to eat on the house. They haven't been out for nearly fifteen years, because he's developed a fear of insects. I thought we'd have a go at breaking him of it. But I guess ...'

Rose angled in toward him, smiling very nicely. 'The kitchen, perhaps ...' Andrew waved at the troubled guests, hurrying back toward the kitchen where his kettle sat red hot on the stove. He collared Pickett on the way.

'Shit!' Andrew said, looking at the smoking kettle, 'It's *hot* enough anyway,' and with that he dumped in two cups of oil and two cups of flour, whisking away at the mixture. Rose went out carrying the first bowls of gumbo. 'Pour everyone a drink on the house!' Andrew said to her. Then to Pickett he said, 'Do you recognize the guy with the camera? The Chinese man?'

Pickett shook his head.

'He was one of your hosts this morning.'

'Get the hell out of here!' said Pickett, incredulous.

'Honor bright. Hand me the damned pot holder.'

'Well listen to this. There *was* a beetle in that idiot's salad.'

'Couldn't have been.'

'Big as a damned mouse. Must have been some sort of imported variety.'

'Then the bastard put it there himself. It sure as hell wasn't in there when I put the salad together. Where would something like that come from?'

'My bet is ...'

'Of course,' said Andrew, anticipating him. 'From Chateau, from Rodent Control. It was one of those prize bugs of his. Pennyman must have walked out with it, the dirty ... It had to have been him. And KNEX, too. I should have known when they called out of the blue like that ...'

'Wait,' said Pickett. 'That's not the half of it. Do you know what kicked over the water glass?'

'*She* did, I suppose. Or else her stinking husband ...'

'Uh uh. Neither. It was your *toad*. That damned pancake toad from your back porch.'

Andrew handed the whisk to Pickett and ran out to look in the aquarium. The toad was gone. The tank was empty. The thin reflector lid lay on the linoleum, and a trail of water led away toward the cafe door. Andrew hustled back into the cafe kitchen, where Pickett scoured away at the kettle with the whisk.

'Where the hell did he go?' asked Andrew, taking over.

'In among the logs by the fireplace. He's in there now, eating the beetle. He came out of nowhere – snatched the bug off the table and ran for it. Thank God she didn't see *him*. She'd have to be hospitalized.'

'We'll give him a medal,' said Andrew. 'It's the Toad Hall of Fame for him now.' How convenient, he thought. Fancy Rose having left the brick off his lid today, of all days. And then the toad … Talk about timing.

Aunt Naomi stuck her head in through the door. 'Mr Pennyman's here,' she said.

Andrew rolled his eyes. 'Holy mother of …'

'Take my word for it, ' said Pickett. 'He's just here to watch. He'll be puzzled that your man across the street is gone.'

The man with the camera loomed in the open door, filming Andrew just as a great splop of napalm-hot grease slid off the whisk and into the open flame, igniting in a wash of leaping fire. Andrew plucked up a dish towel and slapped away at it, dropping his whisk. Hunks of burning grease splattered across the back of the stove.

'Baking soda!' shouted Pickett, looking around wildly as the camera zoomed in.

Andrew flailed away with the towel. 'What!' he shouted. 'Out in the other kitchen. In the house!'

And right then Rose pushed in past the cameraman, shaking a can of beer, her thumb over the popped top. She slid her thumb aside and cascaded beer foam onto the islands of burning grease, then stoppered the can, shook it, and sprayed it on again. The fire smothered itself out under the foam.

'Turn the fire out first thing,' she said to Andrew, who was just then twisting the knob under the burned-up gumbo. The kitchen was filled with smoke. Rose turned on the fan in the flared hood and a swoosh of smoke was sucked up and out. Then she closed the open door in the face of the man with the camera in order to keep the smoke out of the cafe itself. 'I've got Mrs Gummidge serving sorbets. That should kill some time. There's enough gumbo for almost everyone, although I had to tell the camera crew that there wasn't.'

Andrew waved his whisk, furious at the burned muck in the kettle. 'I'll tell them more than that …'

'Where are the hats?' Rose asked, cutting him off.

'What? Out back. With the helium.'

'Let's get that over with then. Get them out of here.'

'That's a damned good idea,' said Andrew. 'See to it, will you?' He nodded at Pickett. 'There's a flap in back with a clip to seal it off. Fill it there. The tank's simple. Just a valve. Don't overfill it though. We don't want a balloon; we want a sort of floating cloud effect. Tell them that I'm busy as hell in here, and that they'll have to get in and get out just as soon as you're ready.'

'Right,' said Pickett.

Andrew nodded cheerfully at Rose. 'This will be good,' he said. Secretly, though, he knew that it wouldn't be good. His chef's hat plan was spoiled. No matter how good the idea had been at the outset, this new Pennyman twist wrecked it. KNEX would find some way of making a hash of it. Pennyman would see to that.

But Andrew couldn't let on to Rose, could he? She had put hours into the hats, into his damned, cockeyed hats. He *had* to tough it out – to be entirely surprised when the whole hat plan went to bits. He couldn't reveal that there was a Pennyman plot afoot. He couldn't reveal anything. He had to pretend to be an entirely innocent victim. 'So – what?' he said to Rose. 'No more gumbo?' He was relieved about that. Making another pot of gumbo was the last thing he wanted to do. He put the kettle into the sink and turned the water on.

'Not now,' said Rose as Pickett went out the door.

The other member of the KNEX crew, a man dressed like a lumberjack and with a beard, looked in just then and growled something about its getting late.

Rose shut the door in his face. 'Mr Pennyman is the last of the guests, I think, for the evening.'

'Pennyman,' said Andrew in a hollow voice. 'Let's serve him dead rats just for the hell of it.'

Rose ignored him. 'He's sitting with the ladies from Leisure World. They're really very sweet. They loved the salad and place settings and the fireplace. One of them apologized on behalf of Mr Fitzpatrick. She said it was terrible about his being so long in a coma.'

Andrew smiled at her. Then the thought that Pennyman might actually fancy a plate of dead rats wiped the smile from his face. He pushed the door open and leaned out, to give things a look. The place had settled out now that the Fitzpatricks were gone. There was Pennyman, dressed all in white, sucking up to the four old ladies, gesturing expansively, talking about China. He tipped a non-existent hat at Andrew and smiled a jolly greeting. Andrew shut the door and took a deep breath.

'Are you all right?' asked Rose.

'Tip-top. Still recovering from the fire. The beer foam trick was neat.'

Rose nodded. 'Yes, well, portion out the gumbo then. We shouldn't need but five more.'

'Piece of cake,' said Andrew. He opened a cupboard, hauled out two cans of beef broth, opened them, and poured them into the finished gumbo. What else did he have – a big can of crab meat, a bottle of oysters ... He'd flesh the pot out a little. To hell with making more. Rose went out into the cafe just as Pickett was coming in – or trying to.

He wore one of the hats, about three-fourths inflated. The whole cafe watched in disbelief. The old toast man had half stood up, gesturing with his spoon. The hat wanted desperately to float off, but Pickett had strapped it around his neck. He forced it through the doorway into the kitchen, plumping it sideways as if it were an enormous pillow.

'Put the apron on him,' said the KNEX lumberjack. 'This is good. This is theater, is what it is. Here, give him this big whisk. Dip it into the pot there, Mr Pickett. That's it. What the *hell* is that thing there? A shrimp? That's a *shrimp*? Good God. That's right. Hang it from the whisk there. You getting this?'

The cameraman grunted, the camera whirring away.

'*Do* something with it,' said the lumberjack.

'What?' asked Pickett.

'Bite its head off.'

'Are you picking up voices, too?' asked Andrew. 'Because if you are ...'

'To hell with the voices. We'll dub this later. Who the hell are you?'

'I'm the owner ...'

'Stand back, then. That's right, wave that thing around. Get a close up of that goddamn shrimp, Jack. Then back off and pan the whole kitchen. Get the hat. Hey! I got it. Let loose of the strap, Spickett. Let's float the hat out into the cafe. "Runaway Hat," we'll call it. That's it.'

And before Andrew could intervene, the lumberjack leaned in and unsnapped Pickett's hat, which floated toward the ceiling. The man batted it toward the door, then tried to yank it through. It caught on the corner of a hinge, though, and hung itself up, at which the man jerked on it, pulling loose a seam. The hat deflated in a whoosh, sinking to the floor like a bottled genie that had granted its wishes and gone home.

'Shit,' said the lumberjack. 'Sorry. Someone fetch the other one.'

Andrew gritted his teeth. '*Forget* the other one. That's plenty. You've got enough, I should think.'

'Edited down, though ...'

They were interrupted by the clatter of a plate hitting the floor out in the cafe. The cameraman flipped around, his eyes round with anticipation. What would it be, wondered Andrew: Cats? Ken-or-Ed having come back with an automatic rifle? The toad terrorizing the Leisure World women?

It was Mr Pennyman, having a fit. He sat perfectly rigid in his chair. His bread plate lay broken on the tiles of the hearth. His face was all moony, and he was breathing quick and shallow, as if he were hyperventilating. Andrew had seen that look on his face before. Little gasping noises came out of his throat, throttling together second by second into a sort of high-pitched keening. His hair – perfectly neat when he'd sat down – seemed to dishevel itself in a little storm of dandruff flakes, and his shoes thumped against the floor, each thump causing a spasm of pain to lance across his face, only to reveal a mask of even more intense pleasure.

The street door opened and Ken-or-Ed surged in, followed by Jack Dilton.

'I'm the health inspector!' Dilton said aloud. Then he saw Pennyman carrying on and he lapsed into a grimace of startled surprise. He turned helplessly to Ken-or-Ed.

There was a sickening smell in the air – the odor of long-decayed fish, of bacteria, of sewer sludge. On the end of the bar, not two feet from Andrew's elbow, lay the pint glass of spoons that Andrew had put away on the shelf. Half the spoons were gone. It didn't take three seconds to figure things out. Mrs Gummidge had found the pig spoon, and had given it, very innocently, to Mr Pennyman, who had shoved it into his gumbo.

'For God's sake don't eat with it.' That's what Uncle Arthur had said.

Mr Pennyman was almost helpless, his strange urges uncontrollable. Pickett and Andrew launched themselves toward his table at the same time, Andrew arriving first, but when Andrew snatched up the fouled gumbo and tried to haul it away, Pennyman groped after it, mewling, and pitched out of his chair onto the floor, snatching out the spoon in one last heaving effort, just as Andrew shouted, 'He's got it!' in order to warn Pickett to stand by.

Pretending to go to Pennyman's aid, Andrew tried to wrench the spoon away as the old man's face shuddered and shook inches from his own, livid and vibrating.

But Pennyman was recovering. His helpless grin was turning into a calculated smile. Andrew pinched him under the armpit, hard, leaning into it, twisting his hand as if to tear out a piece of flesh, pinching him for the sake of the whole human race. 'There now, Mr Pennyman!' he said through his teeth. 'You'll be fine. Did you forget to take your medicine?'

'Poor man!' cried one of the Leisure World ladies, saddened at the very thought of Mr Pennyman's having neglected his medicine.

'Brain lesion,' said Andrew, just as Pennyman hooted in pain and released the spoon, half-throwing it toward the fire. Quick as a flash, one of Aunt Naomi's cats scooped it up and was gone – out the door, into the night.

'I'll just have a look at that soup!' Jack Dilton said to Pickett, who headed toward the door in the wake of the cat.

'Jesus! What …!' Ken-or-Ed began dancing and twisting, and Jack Dilton, giving him a wondering look, instantly did the same. The doorway was suddenly full of cats, an ambush of them, shredding pants legs, honing their claws on the legs of the two men who danced there, cursing and stomping. 'Get 'em off! Hell!' Dilton yelled, and then pushed Ken-or-Ed so hard on the shoulder that he reeled, bending over to slam at the cats.

Pickett pushed through them with the soup, setting out to dump it in the alley. Aunt Naomi hobbled across, shouting 'Shut the door! You're letting in every cat in the neighborhood. This is a restaurant, not a kennel!'

The man with the camera slouched in, filming the whole thing. Rose collared him, smearing a fingerful of peanut butter over the lens of the camera as if by accident.

'Hey!' he said, as she led him outside, pushing Ken-or-Ed and Jack Dilton in front of them both. Aunt Naomi shut the door. The cats had gone. The spoon was gone. The fouled gumbo was gone. Pennyman, his face clenched like a skeletal fist, apologized very graciously to the Leisure World ladies. He was beaten and was acting the gentleman.

'I'll just go lie down,' he forced himself to say. Andrew could see in Pennyman's eyes the most obscene sort of pure hatred he'd ever witnessed. The sight of Pennyman's face struck him cold. He wanted to wink, to say something that would put the old man away, but he couldn't. He nodded and pulled off a weak sort of smile. Pennyman went out, followed by Mrs Gummidge, whose head shook as if she were palsied. Rose came back in just then, followed by Pickett.

Andrew walked into the kitchen, rummaged in the cupboard until he came up with the kitchen bottle, and poured two inches of scotch into the bottom of a tumbler. He filled the tumbler with water and drank it down, steadying himself against the counter. Then, breathing evenly, he went back out into the hushed cafe and announced that they'd all be able to use a round on the house. He pulled down bottles of sauterne and port and sherry, and nodded at Pickett. 'Where's the spoon?' Andrew asked.

Pickett shrugged. 'Trust the cats,' he said, and set out to take orders.

'Where's Fitzpatrick?' Andrew asked Rose, as she pulled down glasses.

'I chased him off. Told him I'd call the police. He didn't want that. You were right. The man's stark. The other one, Dilton, wanted to fight him, right there on the street, and said something about his hundred dollars. They're out there right now, for all I know, beating each other up. I don't pretend to understand it.' Andrew grinned, half-thinking to go out and watch. But things were too hot for that.

Aunt Naomi, appearing to be utterly unruffled, went over to talk to the four ladies. In a moment they were shaking their heads and clucking their tongues and exchanging reminiscences about medical troubles that they'd known. Aunt Naomi moved away, toward the old couple and the young couple.

'What was that *god-awful* smell?' the old man demanded. The couple at the adjacent table, the ones who had arrived first, nodded and leaned in.

Andrew heard Aunt Naomi say, 'That's rather delicate, isn't it?' and he stepped up, clearing his throat, to save her the embarrassment.

'Sorry, folks,' he said. 'This has been a rough night. Poor Mr Pennyman. When he's taken with this sort of fit, he suffers total muscle relaxation. I'm afraid he's ...' And he bent over and whispered into the ears of the young man and the gentleman at the next table. Each of them whispered into the ears of their wives, and the young lady whispered to her grandmother, who said, 'Oh, the *poor* man; *what* an embarrassment!' and then whispered the grim truth into the ear of the old man, who sat stock still and with a look of puzzled dissatisfaction on his face.

His mouth fell. 'He *what*! Soiled his ... The filthy ...'

'He couldn't help it, for goodness sake. It was uncontrollable.'

'A hanged man does that,' the old man announced out loud.

'I dare say he does,' muttered Andrew, moving off but happy enough that the old man had said it. The rest of the restaurant knew now. Or at least they thought they knew.

Rose collared him as he slipped toward the kitchen. 'What on earth did you tell them about poor Mr Pennyman?' she asked.

'Well,' said Andrew. 'I told them the only thing I could think of – that he'd had a fit and lost control of his bodily functions. What else would explain it? It's no crime. The man is old.'

Rose looked at him steadily. 'What was wrong with the gumbo? What did you do to doctor it up, to stretch it?'

'Not a thing!' said Andrew, looking hurt. 'Take a look in the pot.'

Rose did. In fact there wasn't anything wrong with it. It was fine. 'Well,' Rose admitted. 'Don't get a swelled head, but the woman from the *Recliner* said she'd never eaten better than this or felt so at home in a restaurant.'

'Did she?'

'Yes, and the couple across the way said the same. Your gumbo was a hit, apparently.'

Andrew wiggled his eyebrows at her. Then the street door opened and into the cafe came the cameraman and the lumberjack, having put away their equipment. Andrew's face clouded and he headed out of the kitchen, but Rose grabbed his arm. 'I've asked them to drink a beer. Let's not aggravate things. I told them that we were very anxious that their program, if they aired it, would reflect well on the restaurant and hinted that if it didn't we'd take action. But I don't want to put too fine a point on it. I don't want to make them mad.'

'Ah,' said Andrew, thinking hard. 'Settle them down, is it? A beer, a friendly chat. Sure. You're right. They can take a stab at the gumbo, too. What the hell. There's some left. It's in their blood, I guess, waving cameras like that.' He smiled at the two of them and gestured toward a table.

A half hour later the cafe was almost empty. Aside from Andrew and Rose and Pickett, only the two from KNEX were left. Aunt Naomi had gone up to her room, but had to have Rose's help climbing the stairs. Andrew considered every word he said to the two from the cable station. He was breezy, unconcerned, nonchalant. He supposed that they were mystified by the night's proceedings. They certainly couldn't have imagined that they'd be witness to such a wild display.

When they left, the cafe was six beers down, but the two seemed congenial enough. It was just possible that they'd changed sides, that they'd been good men who had been caught up in Pennyman's web without half-knowing how they'd gotten there, and had, over the course of the evening, been wooed away from the enemy by the cafe and the gumbo and the beer and the cheerful talk. Andrew almost felt friendly toward them.

Five seconds after they were out the door, the shouting began. Andrew, Pickett, and Rose headed for the street. 'Trouble!' Andrew shouted, thinking that the two of them had – what? – been jumped? Maybe Ken-or-Ed had come back again, out of his head finally. But no, there the two were, arguing on the parkway. Yelling. The Chinese man was nearly out of his mind. Some damned thing had gotten at the camera, had torn all the tape out. Something with claws.

'It was the stinking cats!' shouted the lumberjack, suddenly sober and enraged.

But it hadn't been the cats; Andrew was sure of it. An almost electric thrill of joy and mystery shot through him, and he felt suddenly like a man with friends, like a shaman who could call up the wind and the birds and send them on missions, who could make oak trees dance in the forest. The frame over the crawlspace had been pushed aside. Andrew squinted at it surreptitiously, hardly believing that it could be true, but knowing it nonetheless. It was the 'possum that had dealt with the film, that had scuttled Pennyman's last ship. There it was, under the house. Andrew could just barely see it in the soft glow of the streetlight, looking out at him with goggly eyes. It ducked back into the shadows.

There was a monumental amount of tape on the street, ragged and dirty and trailed nearly to the beach and back. A car or two had run over it. Andrew wouldn't have guessed there'd be half so much tape in a video camera. Every last inch of it, apparently, had been hauled out and shredded, chewed and trampled on, heaped into the gutter, tangled in the bushes.

'Hell,' said the cameraman, standing very still. And it seemed to Andrew as if he was worried, as if he had someone to answer to. Five minutes later they were gone, the wadded-up tape nearly filling one of the trash cans in the backyard.

Within a half hour, Pickett was gone, too, and Rose had shuffled wearily upstairs to bed. Thank God, thought Andrew, they wouldn't be open tomorrow night. Just cleaning up would kill half the day. So what? He whistled merrily despite his aching joints. Pennyman had come in smug and gone out a wreck. Ken-or-Ed was a broken man. The cafe would get a bang-up review in the *Recliner*, not to mention the *Herald*, Pickett's newspaper. Pickett had written his review three days ago; Andrew had helped him.

He went outside for the last time that night, wearing the second chef's hat, which he'd inflated dangerously full, and carrying with him a saucer of milk. Clicking his tongue outside the crawlspace to alert the 'possum, he lay the milk just within the shadow, and then strolled around to the front of the house.

A light burned in the Fitzpatricks' living room, but as Andrew drew up across the street, the light blinked out, as if they'd seen him, and wanted, perhaps, to hide behind the drapes and watch. He stood on the sidewalk, his hat billowing around his head, lit by the streetlamp and valleyed with shadowed folds, like a cumulus cloud blowing in the sea wind. After a moment he turned and headed back around, satisfied that they wouldn't know what to make of him, that the sight of him wearing the floating hat and standing dead still on the midnight sidewalk was a vision from outside their ken. They wouldn't be able to fathom it.

He slipped back into the house, tolerably satisfied, and climbed the stairs to bed.

FOURTEEN

'Since we have explored the maze so long without result, it follows, for poor human reason, that we cannot have to explore much longer; close by must be the centre, with a champagne luncheon and a piece of ornamental water.'

ROBERT LOUIS STEVENSON,
'CRABBED AGE AND YOUTH'

The spoon was in his pants pocket next morning when he awakened early, well before dawn. It fell out and bounced on his foot when he picked the pants up. Who had put it there? The cats? Why not, Andrew thought, tiptoeing around the bedroom. The cats were probably downstairs right now, playing gin rummy with parrots and 'possums and toads, plotting against the Soviets.

Rose still slept, and the house was dark and quiet. Hustling downstairs, Andrew went out onto the service porch, took the brick and the lid off the toad tank, and buried the spoon in the gravel at the bottom, laying a lump of petrified wood over it.

The toad floated as ever, innocently, as if he hadn't just last night thwarted a lunatic and hid out among eucalyptus logs until Andrew had found him and put him back. Toads, thought Andrew, were an inscrutable lot. Andrew wished there was some sort of toad treat he could give it, but nothing came to mind. The toad drifted down to the bottom of the tank and sat on the petrified wood, giving Andrew the slack-faced, deadpan look of a serious martial arts assassin, as if anyone who dared retrieve the spoon would have to deal with him first, and would regret it.

Satisfied, Andrew went off to work, and an hour later was washing dishes moodily in the cafe kitchen. The casements were open, and he could smell the Santa Anas blowing again, the warm desert and sagebrush odor mingling with the smell of popping soap bubbles. The cafe itself was cleared and swept clean and the tables arranged despite their having to sit idle until next Friday night. On the counter next to him lay a cheap walkie-talkie, silent, but with the volume turned all the way up.

It might be today that the crisis would come. The treasure hunt was that night. The moon would be full, the tale told. The dawn light radiating now above the eastern rooftops was a bloody slash, dwindling into a gray and violet sky, and the air was heavy with the sighing wind. There had been a pair of jolting little earthquakes some time after two in the morning, and then a third two hours later, a deep, rolling quake that had brought him up sharp out of a dreamless sleep. Rose had got out of bed and wandered through the house when the first of the quakes struck, convinced that she'd heard something fall downstairs. She had slept through the third, though, and that's when Andrew had climbed wearily out of bed, thinking to get a jump on cleaning the cafe.

He had never before been so filled with premonition, with the absolute certainty that everything in the world was connected, that like Pickett's circles and serpents, everything whirled in a vast, complex pattern – the wind, the rhythmic crashing of ocean waves, the wheeling gulls and the distant cries of parrots, the earth-muted grumbling of subterranean cataclysms – all of it was linked, and all together it was the embodiment of something bigger, something unseen, something pending.

If Andrew were called, he would go. No trickery with fishing poles, no gunnysacks full of junk. Come tomorrow, Rose would understand. She might think he was crazy, but she'd understand. It was his destiny that was blowing on the Santa Anas, sailing along on the backs of newspapers and tumbleweeds and dust and dead leaves.

He'd been to the window a half dozen times, watching the sky pale and wondering at the cool, silent morning. There was fire in the foothills, out in the San Gabriels, and the northwest horizon was sooty-black despite the rising sun. He felt weirdly enervated, as if he were light and weak, built out of Styrofoam or woven out of the ashy smoke blowing up out of the hills. With luck, he'd have got through the dishes and drained the sink before the call came. That way, when Rose looked in and found him gone, at least she'd see that he hadn't been idle, that he hadn't left a mess again for Mrs Gummidge.

He was just polishing the last glass when the walkie-talkie erupted into static. Andrew pushed the talk button and said, 'Yo.'

'He's come out.' It was Pickett's voice.

Andrew threw down the dish towel. 'Is there a cab?'

'Around on your side. You can see it through the window. Don't bother to look, though. Go out the back and around through the garden gate. I'm down on the seat. Don't make for the car until I honk. He'll have left. Then run like hell so we can catch him. He was carrying the bag of dimes.'

'Dimes?'

'The bag of silver dimes that was in his drawer. He's got them.'

Andrew switched off the machine, shoved it into his coat pocket, and rummaged in the pantry for a bite of something to take along. Then, leaving the light on so that Pennyman wouldn't see it blink off abruptly, he slipped out through the back door, leaped across Mrs Gummidge's weedy garden, and pushed the gate open, peering past the corner of the house at the departing taxicab. Immediately a horn honked, and there was Pickett, sitting up and gunning the engine of the Chevrolet. Andrew was off at a dead run, climbing in through the thrown-open door as Pickett sped off.

They followed him down to the Pacific Coast Highway and around onto Seal Beach Boulevard. There was little traffic, so they stayed almost two hundred yards back. Andrew tore open the top of a variety pack box of Corn Pops, shaking out a handful and eating them one at a time, cracking them like nuts with his teeth.

'What else do you have?' asked Pickett.

Andrew patted his coat. 'Let's see. Frosted Flakes and Honey Smacks.'

They crossed Westminster, Pickett driving with his left hand and shaking Honey Smacks into his mouth with his right. 'Bet you ten cents I know where he's going.'

'Of course that's where he's going. But what's he up to? Is he going to dig?' Pickett shrugged.

'Maybe we better head into Leisure World – roust Uncle Arthur. Maybe he ought to know that the game's afoot.'

'Let's not,' said Pickett. 'Let's just follow along. If we sidetrack now we might miss the whole business. Besides, after the other day they might be watching for us at the gate. We can't afford trouble. Not now.'

Andrew nodded, dropping his empty carton into the sea of trash and books and jackets on the floor. The cab pulled in just then at the Leisure Market. Pickett slid past, angling up a driveway farther on and cutting the engine in front of Mrs Chapman's Doughnuts. 'Duck,' he said.

Both of them hunkered down, and Andrew watched above the seat as Pennyman tapped his way across the lot and onto the dirt shoulder of the street, down toward the oilfields. He disappeared from sight beyond the edge of a cinderblock wall. Andrew and Pickett were out, scrambling toward the wall and peering over. Pennyman picked his way along the road, dust blown up by the wind swirling around his feet.

'Half a sec,' said Andrew, heading in after a doughnut.

'Two glazeys,' Pickett said at his back. 'And leave the coffee. This might take some running.'

In minutes Andrew was back, trying to fit the edge of one of Mrs Chapman's puffy, angel food doughnuts into his mouth. 'I got a break on a half dozen,' he said, holding out the open bag.

Pickett plucked one out. 'He's heading for the oilfield across from the steam plant, where Arthur let the turtles loose. There's no use following him yet; he'd spot us in an instant. When he goes through the oleanders, though ...'

'Right,' said Andrew, looking again over the fence. Pennyman was a good way down now, cutting across and into the field.

'There he goes,' said Pickett. 'Give him to the count of ten. Now!' The two loped across the road and down, ducking around into the field and behind an oil derrick fence, then across and behind the mountain of pallets from where they'd watched Uncle Arthur launch the turtles.

Pennyman peered through the foliage into the oleanders, then bent over, ducked in, and disappeared.

Pickett thumped Andrew on the shoulder. 'There he goes. Give him a moment. Let's go!'

They were off and running again, as quietly as they could, certain that Pennyman couldn't see them but anxious not to be heard. The wind would cover most of the noise. The oleander was dense and deep, maybe fifteen feet broad, and from three yards away it looked impenetrable. Just inside the perimeter of leafy branches, though, someone had hacked out a tunnel, and you could shove in past the outer branches and get around to the back, in against the chain-link. The oleander grew right through the links, so that over the years the old barbwire-strung fence had disappeared into the bush.

'There it is,' whispered Andrew. He could see where the fence had been cut and then hooked back together along one side with baling wire so that it was sort of hinged, the cut panel held up by oleander branches. The baling wire was clean and free of rust, very likely wound through the cut links within the last couple of months. On beyond the fence were the fields of the Naval Weapons Station, half of them up in tomatoes now, the other half fallow, waiting for autumn pumpkins. Bundled tomato stakes were the only cover in the open fields, so there was no question of their following; they'd be seen for sure. And besides, they could see Pennyman clearly, stepping through the clods of the harrowed pumpkin field. Some distance away to the west rose a cloud of dirt where a tractor cut the earth, and off to the east sat the green humps of sod-covered weapons bunkers.

Andrew could hear flies buzzing and the drone of a distant, unseen airplane. 'God, it's lonesome out here,' he whispered, polishing off a second doughnut.

Pickett was silent.

'What's he doing, do you figure?' Andrew bit into his third Mrs Chapman's and knew at once that he didn't want it. But he ate it anyway, wondering why he had such a passion for doughnuts, why he couldn't leave them alone.

'Watch,' said Pickett.

Andrew watched, and it became clear at once what Pennyman was doing. He was sowing the field with silver dimes – handfuls of them, which he threw out in a glittering spray. Then he moved on, twenty feet farther, scattering dimes in a wide, purposeful circle that would lead him back around to the oleanders.

'What on earth …?' Andrew muttered.

'Same as the belted turtles,' Pickett said. 'To attract the two coins.'

And it was just then that Pennyman found one of the turtles. They saw him bend over to pick it up, and then drop it abruptly when the thing urinated almost heroically on his pantslegs and shoes. They could hear the curse in the still air. Then he bent over again, and meddled with the creature, removing the silver belt before sowing another handful of dimes, peering closely at the ground now, alert for more turtles.

They were home by seven-thirty, after a half-dozen cups of coffee at the Potholder. The Santa Anas had kicked up, and the air was full of the rustling of tree limbs and the random banging and pounding and howling of the wind-blown seacoast. Andrew went up to visit Aunt Naomi, carrying another bowl of Weetabix and the fixings just in case. Predictably, she was sitting in front of the window again, watching the ocean over the several rooftops. Two of her cats sat with her.

Surf stormed through the pier, the wave crests licking the bottom of it and blown to foamy white by the offshore wind. The long, booming waves began to break some two hundred yards out, quartering hard in a tumble of churning ocean, re-forming quick and steep and slamming down in the shallows with a crack that must have been audible for miles. City lifeguards had cordoned off the entrance to the pier, which shuddered under the pounding surf, and every now and then a monstrous wave humped up along the horizon, drove in, and smashed straight through the pier railing, surging around the bait house and pouring off again in spindrift sheets of lacy white. The beach was almost inundated, and the tide was still rising.

Aunt Naomi's radio murmured. The early morning earthquakes had centered in the Hollywood Hills, and there'd been damage at the zoo. Griffith Park was alive with escaped beasts – apes and peccaries that had gone to ground, some few of them escaping over the hills and into the backstreets of Chinatown. Clouds of bats had swarmed out of the canyons from previously unknown caverns and rifts, and the dry bed of the Los Angeles River had cracked like the shell of a walnut, releasing torrents of subterranean water through a dozen fissures.

'Sounds almost like the first trumpet, doesn't it?' Andrew said, fixing up the bowl of Weetabix.

Aunt Naomi nodded. 'I didn't think I'd live to see it.' She petted one of the cats, who was looking hard at the cereal.

'Coming along to the treasure hunt tonight?'

She shook her head. 'I'm too tired.'

'Maybe Dr Garibaldi ...'

'Dr Garibaldi is off the case,' she said with a dismissing wave of her hand. 'It's cancer, I suppose, all this bleeding, and he's too much the fool to see it.'

Andrew didn't know what to say. Somehow he had come to like Aunt Naomi and her cats, once he'd understood what made her tick, or rather what had got in the way of her ticking. She'd become a sort of kindred spirit, what with her Weetabix enthusiasm and the joy she took in a cup of coffee. It had turned out, when he paid attention, that she wasn't a fool after all; she no doubt understood very well what he was doing with the money she advanced him – approved of it even.

Last night, before the cafe doors opened, she had talked seriously about drinking glasses, about the differences in beer drunk out of pilsners and pint glasses and mugs, pointing out the easy to overlook virtues of paper cups. He had risked telling her about his war with the tumblers in the kitchen cupboard, and she had offered to do her part. She had been full of philosophy, and saw very clearly that all the cheerful little details of day-to-day existence, all the wonderful trifles, were, as she put it, knick-knacks of the human spirit. Andrew was almost teary-eyed now thinking about it.

'Well,' he said, 'Pickett and I are going to be there, at the treasure hunt. I expect it's going to be an adventure.'

'Probably more of an adventure than you'll want,' said Aunt Naomi.

There was a silence. Then the radio began to chatter about a collision at sea, about a fishing boat heading in toward San Pedro, trying to beat the rising swell and colliding off the tip of Catalina Island with a vast, barnacle-encrusted whale ...

Andrew puzzled over it. 'Something in the wind,' he said.

'And in the ocean.' She was silent for a moment. 'Why don't you spend some time with Rose today? It's Sunday. Take a walk. Here.' She hauled her purse out from under the night stand and fished around in it. 'Have dinner somewhere nice.' She handed him four twenties and squeezed his hand, not bothering to write anything down in her book.

Darkness came early. There was hardly any dusk. The full moon rocked above the troubled ocean, throwing a silver sheen across the plowed dirt of the pumpkin field, where two or three hundred people milled about, eating late-night picnic lunches and talking in hushed voices. The apocalyptic weather had somehow leached away the carnival atmosphere that Andrew would have expected. It was almost as if the mass of people, sitting on tailgates and at suitcase tables, felt the coiled tension in the air. The occasional ringing voice of a child sounded as out of place as it would have in church, and almost made the night vibrate.

Someone had brought along oil drums full of cut-up construction lumber, which had been doused with gasoline and lit, so that here and there around the parking area little imprisoned bonfires burned, throwing shadows onto the dirt. Somehow the effect was weird, almost cataclysmic, rather than warm or cheering.

When they pulled up in the Metropolitan, Andrew felt almost as if the people ought to applaud him, as if they ought to know who he was. But they wouldn't believe it even if they were told, and they were anxious only to dig, to find the hermetically sealed ring or the seafood dinner tickets. They'd brought spades and collapsible army shovels and clamming forks. Children carried trowels. Andrew had brought the spoon, and Pickett was empty-handed.

They spotted Pennyman straight off, walking alone fifty yards distant. And there, parked at the head of the line of cars, was his taxi, the driver waiting inside, reading a paper. Pennyman walked with a limp, as if he had something in his shoe. Andrew bet that it was some sort of detecting device, contrary to rules, but that even if Uncle Arthur's charity knew about it nothing would be done. For the principal players, the rules would be abdicated that night. Rules were perfunctory now.

Two tables with folding chairs had been set up between the bonfires, and a half-dozen ladies of Leisure World vintage sat around them, taking five-dollar bills, issuing tickets, handing out little maps, ready to keep track of unearthed treasures on lists drawn up on college-ruled paper. Andrew recognized the woman from the *Recliner*, but he was too nervous to make small talk. So after he and Pickett had paid their money, they hurried across toward the dirt trail that led into the field from the road, where a little rising cloud of dust swirled up from the wheels of the red electronic car, which bumped along toward them, swerving from side to side, carrying the oldest man on earth. It was Uncle Arthur finally, and Andrew was glad to see him.

His relief waned, though, when the old man pushed the door open and stumbled out. He was tousled and rumpled, and he looked so ancient that he might have passed for an unwrapped mummy in a glass case. Andrew and Pickett stopped short. The very sight of him cut off Andrew's hearty wave. Pickett stepped up and shook his hand delicately, unable to hide his fascination with Uncle Arthur's forehead, which was marked quite clearly with a cross-shaped slash of pink. If Pickett and Andrew didn't know what they knew, they might have taken it for a scar.

The murmuring night was shattered suddenly by a voice behind them that said, 'You!'

Andrew spun around, and there was Mr Pennyman, looking past them at Uncle Arthur's forehead.

For a moment the old man's rheumy eyes cleared and he peered straight at Pennyman. 'Me,' said Arthur simply.

Pennyman laughed out loud, and Andrew wanted to hit him, to pop him one on the snoot. But they'd been through that, and there was no time for it tonight. Up close, Andrew could see that Pennyman wore an ostentatious belt of silver dollars in a triple row and linked with silver chain mail. He didn't have his stick, but rested instead against a silver-shod spade. He didn't in any way acknowledge Andrew's or Pickett's presence, but seemed satisfied simply with knowing at last who his real adversary was. He turned around and hobbled off toward the assembled crowd that pressed in anticipation against the ribboned starting rope.

'We've got the spoon in the car,' Andrew whispered when Pennyman was out of earshot.

Uncle Arthur cupped a trembling hand to his ear and said, 'Eh?'

'I say we've got the spoon!'

'God damn the moon!' the old man rasped, but the effort of it seemed to shake him. He stepped back, almost stumbled, and closed his eyes for a moment.

Then he blinked at them, as if he were just waking up, and gave Andrew a squint-eyed look. 'I was up in Alberta once,' he said, nodding.

Andrew swallowed hard, his mind racing to make sense of the Alberta business. It didn't compute, somehow. Maybe Uncle Arthur hadn't come to the point yet ...

But it seemed he had. He stood blinking at them, swaying in the wind. 'Little bit of railroad work,' he said.

'Ah,' said Andrew. 'About the *spoon* ...'

There was an explosion just then – a blast of yellow fire that lit up the whole western horizon, as if the entire city of Long Beach had detonated.

'Oil fire!' cried Pickett. 'Looks like Signal Hill!'

Another explosion rocked the night, and a tongue of bright blue flame shot away and licked the sky. The air was suddenly full of the shriek of sirens and the hot wind blew out of the east.

The masses of people stood staring. If one had run, all would have followed. But in the full minute that they stood immobile, unbelieving, it became clear that there was nothing to do, no place to run. The fire didn't pose a threat; it was several miles away. They'd paid their five dollars ... The woman from the *Recliner* rallied them, snatching down the rope, letting them out into the field, shouting about rolls of coins, diamond rings, toys. 'Hurray!' someone shouted, and all of a sudden there was cheering and running, as if it had been fireworks igniting in the west, and not oil storage tanks.

Uncle Arthur squinted at Andrew suddenly and said, 'Are you the son?'

'God help us,' muttered Pickett.

'I'm the nephew,' said Andrew. 'Do you remember me?'

'Of course,' said the old man. 'Sure. The bearded man, with the sheep. Did you cut it off?'

'Cut what off? I don't wear a beard.'

'We had a device,' he said, thinking hard, 'that would burn your beard straight off. Roast your head like a potato if you didn't look sharp. I sold them door to door. At least I think I did. Wish I had one now.' He gave Pickett a particularly hard look. 'Did I tell you I was in Alberta? Why don't you shave off that damned silly mustache?' he said. 'Looks like a damned caterpiller.'

'Get the spoon,' said Pickett, smiling and nodding at Uncle Arthur. He jerked his hand at Andrew, as if to propel him toward the car. 'Sit down, sir! Take a load off.'

'Ach.' Uncle Arthur waved him away in disgust, and then slumped back down onto the seat of his car. Lord knows how he'd driven that far, but his part in the War of the Coins was over, at least for the evening.

'The damned moon!' said Pickett as Andrew hurried back toward him, the spoon in his pocket. 'This *would* have to happen tonight.'

'Maybe we better do something for him. Call someone.' Andrew looked sadly at the old man, whose head slumped against his chest now. He appeared to be sound asleep, breathing laboriously.

'He's two thousand years old,' said Pickett, heading out toward the fields. 'He won't die until it's time, and if it's time, then heaven help all of us. All the doctors in the world wouldn't be worth the quarter it took to call them.'

*

232

For an hour they had no luck. Andrew carried the spoon in his back pocket, and somehow he didn't like it at all. He'd always felt it was vaguely repellent, but now it felt as if his back pocket housed a throbbing, poisonous lizard. It was warm, too, and not simply because it was pressed against him. For ten minutes it had got hotter and hotter, and he had taken it out and wrapped it in his handkerchief. But then it cooled again, only to heat up and cool twice more during their stumbling search of the fields.

All around them people dug happily in the moonlit earth. There were shouts and cries. A boy ran past howling with joy, carrying a little plastic treasure chest filled with rhinestones. Another waved a tangled handful of chandelier crystals. A thin woman in a too-short dress unearthed a fist-sized hunk of amethyst, and then cursed under her breath and flung it down again, and then a little girl who couldn't have been above four picked it up and tilted it into the moonlight, oohing and ahing at the watery purple glow. A little over a half hour into the hunt there was a shriek from near the perimeter of the field. The diamond ring was found. Half the treasure hunters left grumbling.

There were silver dimes aplenty, scattered here and there. And they found a turtle, Andrew and Pickett did, beltless, and wandering purposefully toward the oilfield fence. They let it go. One o'clock came and went. Pennyman was still at it; they could see him methodically shoving the silver tip of his spade into the earth at calculated points.

Then the spoon started to heat up again. That's when Andrew figured it out. It was like a child's hot and cold game – literally. He would stake his fortune on it. They quit wandering then, and followed the spoon, pretending for Pennyman's benefit, though, that they weren't up to anything at all. When they passed the old man at a distance of some ten yards, the tip of his silver shovel jerked into the air and the shovel spun end over end, torn from his hands, skiving down into the dirt six feet away so that the whole blade was buried.

'Let's go!' whispered Pickett urgently, and Andrew pretended not to have seen the shovel's weird behavior. When they looked back, Pennyman spaded furiously in a cloud of rising dust, throwing big clods back out of the way.

'Did the *spoon* make it do that?' asked Andrew.

'We have to think so,' said Pickett. 'Either that, or he's found one of the coins. But even so we have to go on. We can't wrestle him for it. Not yet. Not with the spoon in your pocket. He'll end up with all of them that way. Is it still hot, or is it cooling off?'

'Heating up even more,' Andrew said. 'Whew!'

'There!' cried Pickett under his breath.

Down among the clods shown a glint of reflected silver moonlight. They bent over to look. The spoon began to vibrate in Andrew's pocket, and he was possessed with the intense desire to drag it out of there, to throw it as far and as hard as he could. It seemed to weigh a ton, as if it would push his feet right down into the dug-up earth and anchor him there forever.

It was a turtle that Pickett had seen. It was half-buried, as if he'd dug in to hibernate the rest of the spring away. On his back was the landscape painting, half-flaked off, and girding it around was the belt of Navajo silver.

'Watch it,' Andrew said as Pickett bent over to pick it up. 'Remember what happened to Pennyman this morning.' The thought of Pennyman reminded Andrew that the old man might well be watching, and so he stepped in behind his friend in order to shield him. It wouldn't do to have Pennyman figure them out. Andrew could see that he still dug away, though less furiously now, as if he were tiring.

'Holy smoke,' muttered Pickett. 'Will you look at this.'

On the turtle's underside, clinging as if magnetically to the silver belt, was a ball of fused dimes, big as an orange. Pickett jerked it off and turned it over in his hand, tilting it into the moonlight. 'There's one,' he said, tracing the outline of the edge of a larger coin that thrust up through the dimes. 'No, both of them. They're sandwiched together, back to back. We've got them both.'

Andrew slammed his hand against his pocket, where the spoon jerked and danced. He was certain that if he didn't hold it down it would tear the pocket right off. Both of them set out, pretending still to be searching. Pennyman was hard at it, poking randomly with his silver spade, having given up on the hole he'd been digging. Andrew was sure that at any moment he would figure out what had happened with the spade business and be onto them. He would certainly think it monumentally suspicious when they left the field and went home. Almost everyone had by now, but Pennyman would assume that Pickett and Andrew would stay until they were successful or else had been defeated. Their leaving now would point to their success.

The bonfires were out. Only a big propane lantern burned on the table where the woman from the *Recliner* sat reading a book. She waved cheerfully to Andrew, pointing toward her list and widening her eyes, as if wondering whether he hadn't found something nice. He waved back, trying hard to look calm and maybe just slightly disappointed, but nearly shaking with anxiety. If Pennyman hadn't seen them talking with Uncle Arthur, if he hadn't seen the cross on the old man's forehead, there would still be the chance that he thought they were simply there to dig for rhinestones and nickels, and were going home because they were tired, like the rest of the people.

He would know, though. Andrew was sure of it. 'Put the ball of dimes in the trunk,' he said to Pickett as the two of them hurried toward the Metropolitan. 'I'll take the spoon up front with us.'

'Right,' said Pickett. 'Keep them apart. Let's take it easy driving out of here. If Pennyman catches on and heads for the taxi, then step on it.' They eased the trunk lid shut, then climbed in and backed out.

Andrew forced himself to drive slowly, bumping over ruts. 'What the hell's he doing?'

'I think … Yeah. He's found it. The turtle. We should have taken the damned belt! Why the hell didn't we take the belt? He's onto us. He tossed his shovel away. Here he comes. Step on it.'

Andrew stepped on it, shifting back down into second and swerving toward the edge of the road where it was smoother going.

'Don't get stuck in the field!' warned Pickett, as they slewed into a rut.

'You know me,' said Andrew, grinning at him and jerking the car back out, 'The Terror of Leisure World.'

The Metropolitan slammed along like a camel over the desert. The lights of the highway shone ahead, a couple of lonesome cars full of people thinking they had somewhere important to go. The moon was enormous and yellow, as if it reflected the fires that burned in the north and west. Signal Hill was almost entirely ablaze, a leaping ribbon of wind-driven flame. Dust swirled and flew as gusts buffeted the car.

'What a night,' muttered Pickett.

'Just about what you'd expect,' said Andrew. 'Are they after us?'

'No. Yes. There's his headlights.'

The Metropolitan banged down onto the highway, screeching left on Studebaker Road. 'It's too open out here,' said Andrew. 'There's no place to hide, nowhere to lose him.'

'Just go like hell. I'll watch for cops.'

Andrew drove toward home. If it came to a fight, he wanted it to be on familiar ground, near allies – Rose and Aunt Naomi. And somehow the beach drew him, the pier, the crashing waves. He was jacked up with adrenaline. He felt sharp and canny. Things along the roadside seemed almost to glow. He could hear the ocean, too, as if in a giant seashell, rushing and sighing, the sound of the collapsing ages.

They rocketed down the highway, angling back onto the Pacific Coast Highway toward the San Gabriel River. 'Look!' Andrew shouted.

'What, what?' Pickett's head ratcheted around, staring, expecting Lord knew what.

It was a pig that Andrew saw. A monumental pig, big as a pygmy hippopotamus, coming up out of the bed of the river and bound for Orange County. It rollicked along on its too-tiny hooves, its eyes set on an unseen destination, glancing for an instant at the Metropolitan as they sailed past. Andrew slowed down, both of them craning their necks, and for no reason he could easily define, Andrew waved over the top of the car at it and then blinked his headlights. They banked around into town, past residential streets.

'He's going our way!' shouted Andrew, elated but not knowing why.

'Yeah,' said Pickett. 'That's a good sign. I can't see Pennyman. We lost him, I guess. We got out of there in time.'

They slid around the corner onto Main Street, then down the alley and around beside the house. There was a light on in the kitchen. Aunt Naomi, no doubt, or Rose, waiting up for them, having a bite of something.

It was Mrs Gummidge. Andrew was dumbstruck. On the kitchen counter lay a plastic bag full of white powder. On the stove was the tea kettle, singing away, and on the counter lay Aunt Naomi's mug and a box of Earl Grey tea.

'Oh!' she cried, throwing a towel over the plastic bag. But Andrew had recognized it. She hadn't been quick enough. It was the anti-coagulant rat poison that he'd stupidly thought to fool Rose with a week ago. Mrs Gummidge had plucked it out of the trash can. The rest of the story was clear as well water – Pennyman's talk of 'personal vendettas,' Mrs Gummidge's insistence that Aunt Naomi consume cup after cup of tea, the mysterious internal bleeding …

'Assassin!' cried Andrew, throwing aside the towel and upending the bag into the sink. He turned on both faucets, flushing the powder down the drain, damning himself for ever having been fool enough to …

'Don't!' Pickett cried, waving the ball of dimes. 'It's evidence! Don't pour it out!'

'Ow!' shouted Andrew, slapping at his back pocket. Smoke curled up from it, and there was the sharp smell of burning cloth.

'The spoon!' yelled Pickett, and Andrew flailed away at it with his hand, hauling out the smoking, handkerchief-wrapped spoon and dropping it immediately onto the floor, where it bounced free of the cloth and began to revolve, faster and faster, like a compass needle gone mad.

Mrs Gummidge burst from her chair. She slammed past Andrew, who tried to push in front of her to cut her off, and she grabbed at the spinning spoon, understanding what it was now and hungry to possess it. Andrew kicked it away, toward the back door and the toad aquarium, then turned to chase it. 'Get her out of here!' he yelled at Pickett.

Mrs Gummidge backed away toward the living room, as if she were giving up, but then whirled around and jerked open the knife drawer, coming up with a carving knife. Without a word she slashed at Pickett, who yowled and tumbled backward out of the way. Astonished, Andrew abandoned his pursuit of the spoon and grabbed a ceramic pitcher off the counter, cocking his arm to throw it at her. She ducked out through the open door, cursing, with Andrew at her heels, carrying the pitcher, thinking to stop her and her murderous rage before she could do any damage with the knife.

The living room door flew open and there stood Pennyman, alone, with a pistol in his hand. His face was deadly white, and his hand shook dangerously. The corners of his mouth trembled, spasming downward in random jerks, and his head was twisted around stiffly, his chin thrust forward, as if he were being pressed on the back of the head by some unseen force. 'I'll take that,' he said to Pickett.

FIFTEEN

'Patience, children, just a minute –
See the spreading circles die;
The stream and all in it
Will clear by-and-by.'

ROBERT LOUIS STEVENSON,
'LOOKING GLASS RIVER'

Before Pickett could move, could drop the ball of dimes or throw it, or cosh Pennyman in the head with it, the old man stepped forward, pressed the gun to his forehead, and clicked back the hammer.

There was the sound of a slamming door, and feet on the hallway upstairs. It was Rose, without a doubt, getting up to see what was going on.

Stay upstairs, Andrew thought, half-closing his eyes. Stay the hell upstairs. Don't come down.

Cats peeked out from behind chairs, slinking around corners and blinking out of doorways. There was a scrabbling beneath them, under the house. What was it? – 'possums? The wind buffeted the casements and moaned through the mail slot.

'Now the other one,' Pennyman said. He turned the pistol on Andrew, who shrank away in horror. 'Quick, or I'll shoot you in the stomach.' The old man stank like a demon, his breath rasping out through darkened, mossy teeth. His eyes glowed with loathing and desire and corruption. There were footfalls on the stairs.

'It's on the kitchen floor,' Mrs Gummidge hissed. 'He dropped it.'

Pennyman waved them toward the kitchen with his pistol, then abruptly shoved it into his pocket, leaving his hand on it. Rose confronted them from across the room, tugging her bathrobe around herself.

'Well,' she said, smiling sleepily. 'Back from the hunt?'

'That's right,' said Andrew. 'Wonderful time. Plenty of treasures. I'll just be up in a moment.'

Rose nodded. 'I won't join you, if you don't mind,' she said. 'I'm not dressed for socializing.'

'Of course,' said Pennyman, controlling himself with a visible effort. Rose didn't seem to sense any trouble. She nodded and climbed back up the stairs. Andrew deflated. He didn't care what happened, not really, not if Rose could be kept out of it.

Waving the pistol again, Pennyman herded them into the kitchen. 'Where?' he said.

Mrs Gummidge hesitated, betrayal in her eyes. Quick as a lizard, Pennyman slapped her on the cheek with the back of his gun hand, knocking her into the kitchen cabinet. She mewled with pain, cowering there.

Andrew started forward, but Pennyman spun toward him, covering him with the pistol. 'Stinking coward,' said Andrew, cursing himself for his helplessness. 'It's on the damn floor. Under the aquarium. Take it.'

All of them pushed toward the back door. The spoon wasn't there. Andrew glanced at the lid of the aquarium, thinking that maybe the toad … But no, the toad floated as ever, hovering, watching them, the brick securing the lid.

'Where?' Pennyman grunted, threatening Mrs Gummidge again.

'It was there!' wailed Mrs Gummidge, her eyes full of hatred. 'I swear it was. Five minutes ago. I tried to get it for you. I tried …'

'Shut up!' shouted Pennyman. 'Witch! You murdered your lover to get your hands on that coin. You'd betray me in a moment. I'll have it out of you though, before the dawn. See if I don't. Out the door.'

They cut across the backyard in a herd, through the gate and around into the alley, heading up toward Main Street. Andrew strode along, keen and alert but having no idea in the world what to do with all his keenness. Run? What would that avail him? Should he jump on Pennyman and then be shot and left in the alley? Or worse, bring about Pickett's death? He wished he could communicate with his friend, make some sort of sign, but Pickett looked pale and tired and watched the ground as they stumbled along.

Pennyman walked on his heels, painfully. Halfway there, back behind Señor Corky's, he hobbled to a stop. With his free hand the old man rummaged in his pants pocket, hauling out a clasp knife. Watching them all the while and covering them with the pistol, he thumbed one of the blades out of the knife, shoved it through the leather on the side of his shoe, and slit the shoe open, his face sagging with relief. He sawed across the top of the shoe, excising the toe, tearing his sock out entirely when the knife blade caught in it.

Andrew nearly gagged. He hadn't expected what he saw inside Pennyman's cut-away shoes, in the dirt and trash of the alley. There were no toes visible, no real flesh. Instead there was the cleft, scaly black callous ridge of a cloven hoof, obscene in the moonlight. Pennyman worked the knife into his other shoe, cutting chunks away.

His face twitched and shuddered, and his hair stood out in patches from his head, his scalp flaky and mottled. He licked his lips with a tongue that was almost snake-like. Mrs Gummidge watched him, fascinated, unbelieving, frightened. She had the look of someone both repulsed and attracted by evil, the eyes of a half-repentant torturer, whose special sickness was a groveling, hand-washing contrition.

Andrew backed away from her and the pistol swung toward him. He stopped dead. Pennyman stood up, smiling now. He threw the pocketknife into the weeds, reached into his coat, and hauled out his silver, jingling, lead-lined box. Steam seemed to seep from under the lid, smelling sulphurous and hellish. The bulge of the two dime-encased coins danced in his pants pocket, and he licked his lips again, wondering, maybe, if he could afford to pull the fused coins out, break off the covering of dimes, and add the two to his collection. He put his face into the reek and breathed deeply. His features stiffened and his gun hand jerked and spasmed as if he wanted to throw the gun away, to tear open the box right there and scoop out the tainted silver and let it run through his fingers.

The temptation tore at his features, but he put the box away again, unable, perhaps, to accomplish the juggling act without putting down the gun. He wanted two more coins. That's all. Two more coins before the sun rose again over the tired earth.

They were off once more, out onto the deserted asphalt of Main Street. He waved them toward the pier. The surf cracked and boomed, shaking the pilings. The pier lamps still burned, dim and watery in the light that shone from the now enormous moon hanging over the city like a gas lamp, threatening to blow out on the instant. Wind sheered across the face of the waves, blowing sand, scouring the beach where the tide had fallen. A wash of shooting stars fell into the sea.

Andrew watched for his chance as they ducked under the rope that the lifeguards had used to cordon off the pier. He didn't have any idea when it would come or what form it would take. He knew without doubt that he'd leap into the ocean gladly if, say, Rose were there and had fallen in and needed saving. He would step in front of a bullet to save Pickett. But would he do the same to save the faceless world? To stop Pennyman? Would the desperate time come when he would say damn the gun, and just wade in? Or would he leave it to Mrs Gummidge? She certainly seemed posed for it. She half-hovered when she walked, watching Pennyman out of the corner of her eye, knowing that he carried with him a malignant treasure that it had taken a lifetime to amass, and that in one calculated move she could ...

But no, Pennyman was no longer entirely human. He was a thing born of the coins, a thing of evil, and he understood the Mrs Gummidges of the world far too well. He knew how far to trust them. He prompted the three of them along, down the pier, past the concrete restrooms, the fish cleaning sinks, the lifeguard tower, the snack stands, toward Len's Bait House, which stood dark and wind-lashed on the pier's end.

The ocean was a vast, oily plain lined with the humps of waves driving in toward shore. An ivory ribbon of moonlight ran out across it like a dwindling highway, illuminating the depths with a weird, silver-green glow. In the west the oil fire burned on Signal Hill, low and intense now, casting an aura over north Long Beach. All of them stood in the wind finally, in front of the bait house, waiting for Pennyman to make his demands, to reveal his plan. Do what he might, Andrew couldn't help him with the spoon. He had no idea at all what had happened to it. The cats, perhaps, had made away with it, just as the pigs had done in Johnson's entertaining tale. The spoon was out of Andrew's hands now, and good riddance. Still, he would do his part …

Menacing them with the revolver, Pennyman took out the silver box of coins and laid it on the shuddering pier. Andrew hung on to the iron railing, watching the flying spindrift, anticipating the wave that would wash them all to their death in the sea. A vast black shadow passed across the ribbon of moonlight on the ocean just then, as if a single cloud had blown in on the night wind. But the sky was clear, and lit with a thousand stars. There was something in the water – *under* it – not in the sky at all.

Andrew watched the sea. There it was again. He could see the dark hump of it behind incoming swells, edging along over the sandy bottom – a whale, surely, summoned by the coins, and on hand, perhaps, to do the bidding of the man the coins possessed. The radiant sea was full of fishes despite the Leviathan, the waiting monster. Andrew could see them: schooling bonita and mackerel and jack smelt; plate-sized perch swarming around the pilings; hidey-hole fish, sculpin and rock cod, blennies and eels, nosing up toward the surface. The sandy bottom was alive with shellfish and creeping things, with sea slugs and hermit crabs and lobsters and moon snails. It was as if he were watching them in a dream. But it wasn't a dream. Pickett saw them, too. And Pennyman, surely he was aware of the thing in the sea. Of course he was; it was what he was there for. The creature contained within it the last of the thirty coins.

The pier shuddered just then, as if a wave had slammed through it. It rocked on its pilings, creaking and groaning, threatening to tear apart, to twist itself in half and pitch into the ocean. Andrew held on, flung sideways as it moved again. There was the sound of splitting wood and concrete, and one of the pilings shivered into bits, slamming down into the water.

Pennyman cracked the fused dimes like an egg on the old worn slats of the pier, cupping his hands over the two coins, trapping them as they fell out together, the dimes rolling away in a dozen directions. He tipped back the hinged lid of the box, and the two coins popped in among their brothers like tiddly winks and drew the silver lid down after them with a bang as the pier heaved again in counterpoint to the slamming of the box lid. Pennyman stumbled and caught himself. He smiled and looked out over the sea.

He was scarcely human. His white suit was ragged and soiled with dirt from the treasure hunt and from kneeling in the alley. His ripped-apart shoes only half-hid what his feet had become, and his face, as if in keeping with the rest of him, had warped into a goat-like parody of a human face. His tongue lolled above his pointed beard as if there wasn't room for it in his mouth. In the west the moon was setting over the sea, and its reflected light made Pennyman's eyes seem opaque yellow, like disks.

'I'll begin with you,' he said suddenly to Pickett. 'You seem to be the detective, the clever man. Let's see how smart you are when smart is at a premium. Tell me where the coin is, or I'll blow you to kingdom come.' He aimed the pistol. Andrew tensed, ready to jump.

'It's here,' said a voice behind Andrew, and he turned in disbelief to see Rose standing in the cast-open door of Len's Bait House.

Pennyman turned the gun on her, a flicker of surprise and the hint of a smile appearing and disappearing on his face, replaced in turn with a look of grimacing idiocy.

'Look!' Andrew shouted, pointing away down the pier, where a tiny car bumped up off Main Street humming along toward them. It stopped, and someone got out to take down the rope. It was Uncle Arthur.

The pistol cracked. Too late, Andrew threw himself wildly at Pennyman, caring nothing about saving the world, but wanting only to turn the pistol on him, to … His hand and arm smashed into something that felt like a wall of cold, wet clay, and then he slammed into it bodily, rolling down onto the deck of the pier and against the bottom railing. He was up in an instant, puzzled, but throwing himself without thinking at Pennyman again, who stood holding the smoking pistol. Pickett reeled away, grasping his shoulder, and when Andrew leaped the second time, Pennyman was leveling the pistol at Rose, who flung herself back against Aunt Naomi, the two of them disappearing into the bait house.

Again Andrew smashed into the clammy, rubbery, invisible wall and found himself on his back. He looked wildly behind him, only to see Uncle Arthur buzzing toward them at full throttle, agonizingly slowly. Pennyman turned and fired at the oncoming car, and the windscreen spiderwebbed with cracks as the car swerved, caromed off the railing, and came on again.

Mrs Gummidge sprang out of the shadows just then, with a shriek that stood Andrew's hair on end. He'd almost forgotten her, so intent was he on foiling Pennyman. She flew at Pennyman's back when he shot at the car, and maybe because his guard was down, there was no barrier to stop her as Andrew had been stopped.

The shriek gave her away, though, and the old man turned as he fired, sweeping his arm around savagely, roaring through his wide-open mouth, his eyes lit with hatred and with the joy of knocking her down. She slammed back against the pier railing, which caught her in the small of her back, and in an instant Pennyman's hand was at her throat, smashing up into her chin with adrenaline-charged strength, cutting off her scream as her head snapped back with an audible breaking of bone, and she flew backward over the railing, falling headlong into the sea, all of it done in a moment.

Aunt Naomi pushed through the bait house door, swinging her cane at Pennyman's head as he turned back toward them, howling pointlessly, as if he knew that the killing of Mrs Gummidge called for some expression of emotion – laughing or yipping or hooting – but was no longer human enough to puzzle out what sort. His eyes flew open and he snarled into Aunt Naomi's face.

Andrew saw her cane shudder to a slow stop a foot from the old man, as if Pennyman were walled-in again by magic, protected by the accumulated coins. He snatched the tip of the cane out of the air, and before Andrew could react, could clamber up and leap, Pennyman jerked Aunt Naomi toward him, grabbing her wrist and twisting her around, pointing the pistol at her head.

Everyone stood as if frozen. The electronic car stopped fifteen feet away. Andrew was stymied. Heroics would accomplish nothing at all. He couldn't get near Pennyman, not while Pennyman held the coins, not while he threatened Aunt Naomi. The pier shuddered, nearly throwing the lot of them onto their faces. The ocean had grown weirdly calm, and the shuddering now could have nothing to do with storm surf. There *was* no surf; it had fallen strangely flat, as if it were waiting. Pennyman laughed again hoarsely, like fingernails on a chalkboard.

'Take it,' Rose said, holding out the spoon.

'Yes,' said Pickett. Blood seeped through the fabric of his jacket in a growing patch. 'He still doesn't have them all. There's one in the fish. He can't get that one. The fish doesn't care about his gun.'

Pennyman nodded sagely, as if in response to the conclusions of an intelligent four-year-old. 'Put it in my pocket,' he said to Rose.

'Don't go near him!' Andrew shouted.

Pennyman shrugged, tipped the gun up, and shot through Aunt Naomi's hair. Rose screamed at the crack of the pistol, staggering against the doorway. Aunt Naomi flinched and bent forward, unhurt. Pennyman laughed. 'I want it now,' he said.

Rose stepped forward to give it to him. He couldn't take it, though, not with one hand on Aunt Naomi and the other on the pistol. She would have to put it into his pocket, as he'd said. Andrew waited, poised, ready to leap. If

Rose wasn't repelled by invisible walls, then he wouldn't be either. He'd knock the old man down, kick him to bits. If he touched Rose …

But Pennyman jerked Aunt Naomi around, covering Andrew with the pistol, waving it back and forth between him and Rose. In an instant the spoon was in his pocket, and when Rose grabbed Aunt Naomi's shoulders and pulled the old lady away from him, Pennyman let her go.

His eyes were rolled half up into his head, so that crescents of bloodshot white shone under each iris. His teeth chattered and his breath came in gasps. He seemed to be twisted from within, as if he'd swallowed a handful of ten-penny nails, and his hand shook as he clutched at his silver box, laying it on the pier and pulling it open. Twenty-eight silver coins lay within, glowing an almost sickly green in the lamplight. There was a ghastly, rotten smell on the wind, as if Pennyman were a ripe cheese or was riddled with dead, gangrenous flesh. The pier shuddered again, the creature in the sea, perhaps, growing impatient.

The spoon wouldn't fit in the box. It was too long. The lid closed against the handle. The surface of Pennyman's face moved as if it were a swarm of insects, betraying a dozen emotions in a moment, and he sniffled and drooled over the box, kneeling on it finally to warp the lid down around the spoon handle. There was the snap of the lid catching, and Pennyman stood up, holding it, backing toward the very corner of the pier, staggering as the pilings shook, his mouth working, but nothing but babble croaking out of his throat.

He climbed onto the railing. The great fish lolled on the surface of the sea – an immensely long undulating whale, looking like something out of an illustration of a Paleozoic ocean.

It came to Andrew abruptly that the great fish was Pennyman's destiny. Pickett was wrong. Pennyman didn't need the pistol any longer. He was merely going to leap into the gaping mouth of the fish, into the belly of the fish where lay the last of the coins. Pennyman was a modern-day Jonah. But he was a corrupted Jonah. And when the fish spit him up finally onto a Southern California beach, it wouldn't be the grace of God that brought him forth. Nor would Pennyman any longer be a man. He would be something else entirely.

There sounded the beeping of a tinny little electric horn, and Andrew threw himself out of the way as Uncle Arthur's red car surged past. It angled arrow-straight toward where Pennyman was perched on the corner of the pier railing, squatting like a wind-bedraggled sea bird, clutching the box, the pistol, and – in the crook of his elbow – the iron lamppost. He stood up boldly, flinging the pistol into the sea just as Uncle Arthur's car smashed feebly into the post. Andrew lunged forward, grabbing futilely for Pennyman's foot, over the tiny hood of the stalled car.

Pennyman swung around the iron pipe of the lamppost, waving the box of coins in his free hand, a wild, damn-all look in his eyes, intoxicated with coin-magic. He flailed at the railing, at the post, scrabbling to steady himself, waiting for the moment to deliver himself into the mouth of the fish.

The pier shuddered again, a vast, heaving, concrete-snapping quake that threw Andrew backward and into the railing. He grabbed for a hand hold, his legs slewing around and through, between the parallel rails. His head banged hard against an iron post as he latched onto the wooden curb along the very edge of the pier and hung on, nearly sobbing with the effort of stopping his fall and looking down at the roiling water, seeing Pickett out of the corner of his eye, hunkering along toward him as the pier tossed and groaned.

Andrew shook his head, and pain lanced across the back of his skull where he'd hit the post. He sagged with the weight of fatigue and defeat and pain. He hadn't slept for two days. What could anyone expect of him? He was powerless to help himself, let alone the world. He could do nothing but hang on, and steel himself for the sliding rush, the smash of cold ocean water.

Blood from his lacerated scalp dribbled down past his shirt collar, and somehow the wild rush of the world around him paled and he focused on that little tickling dribble. It would be simplest just to hold on and wait, to be acted upon instead of acting.

Pickett hadn't made it to him. He couldn't help. He hugged the railing ten feet farther down, his left arm bloody. Rose huddled with Aunt Naomi against the wall of the bait house, and Andrew could hear Rose shouting at him, hollering unnecessarily for them both to hang on.

Then Aunt Naomi lurched forward across the pier toward Andrew. She shouted something, but he couldn't make it out. She stopped, nearly pitching forward, then steadied herself for a moment and flung her cane. It bounced, clacked down, and skittered toward Andrew, and he let go of the precious rail to grab it, shaking his head hard, letting the shot of pain wake him up – call him back to the world.

Andrew twisted his face into the wind as the pier heaved again. He hauled himself to his feet, the cane in his right hand. He could see Uncle Arthur slumped behind the wheel of his car, the electric motor still humming. Pennyman balanced on the top railing for a long, gasping moment. A hundred sea birds swarmed around him, snatching at his clothing, pecking at his eyes. He batted at them, slamming away with the box. There was one last shuddering quake, and Pennyman was thrown backward, off balance, clutching the coins to his chest as the entire corner of the pier – deck, lamp post, sink, railing, and all – began to crack loose from the rest of the pier with a groaning of twisting metal and a snapping of wood and bolts.

Andrew lunged, shouting, and swung the cane like a baseball bat, with both hands, slamming the hooked end across Pennyman's knuckles. There was a shriek and a clang – the sound of Pennyman screaming and of his coin box banging against the cold iron of the lamppost that fell now as if in slow motion into the sea.

Andrew whipped the cane back to hit him again, just as the badly latched box sprang open and the coins sailed out in an arc, into the ocean, across the pier. For an instant Pennyman had a look of horrified, uncomprehending defeat in his eyes, and then he went down end over end, scrabbling after the flying coins like a man in a cartoon as the corner of the pier collapsed piecemeal into the sea. Andrew dived back toward the railing to save himself, throwing away Aunt Naomi's cane, tearing out the knees of his trousers on the rough deck of the pier and hugging the splintered wooden curb.

He held on and watched Pennyman fall, watched his cloven hooves shiver and metamorphose into the feet of an old, old man, his magic gone, the coins no longer his. Pennyman turned his face to the sky, betraying the yellow, sunken-eyed features of a mummy, of a man long dead but half-preserved by potions. And then he splashed into the sea like a something built of sticks and twine.

The red electronic car geysered in after him, carrying Uncle Arthur inside its little cab. And just as Andrew thought of letting loose, of sliding in after it all, of trying to drag poor Uncle Arthur out of there, the dark bulk of the whale gave one last heaving lash and it opened its mouth like the door of Aladdin's cave, swallowing them up, Pennyman and Arthur both, and the car into the bargain.

The great fish humped around and slipped away, into the shadowed depths, and was gone.

The surface of the sea boiled with fish, but almost immediately it was still, and the dawn light illuminated the depths enough for Andrew to see that the fish were diving toward the bottom, darting after the coins that shimmered and disappeared into deep water.

The sky suddenly, was full of birds – sea gulls and pelicans, parrots and crows and curlews – dropping down and pecking at the scattered coins on the pier, flying off with the coins in their beaks. Andrew heaved himself through the twisted railing, rolling over onto his back on the deck of the ruined pier. Something gouged him in the shoulder blade. He sat up and looked. It was the spoon.

He picked it up, and on an impulse, cocked his arm to throw it into the sea, into the newly rolling swell and the ribbon of sunlight that had just then blazed up across the blue-green water. Let the fish have it, he thought. Let them swim it away to some other continent, out of his life entirely. But then he stopped himself.

The light of the rising sun shone on the back of something running toward them down the center of the pier, running with an odd, short-legged, rolling gait. It was The One Pig, and no mistaking it, its hour come 'round at last. It trotted indifferently past a company of sleepy fishermen just arriving with the dawn, and followed the course of the Uncle Arthur's lost car, straight through the hovering birds, past Aunt Naomi and Rose, past the open-mouthed Pickett, trotting to within a foot of where Andrew sat holding the spoon in his outstretched hand.

Neat as clockwork the pig plucked it up, turned immediately around, and trotted off again. Andrew watched it grow smaller and smaller and smaller, disappearing up Main Street, bound for heaven alone knew where.

EPILOGUE

Beams Pickett felt a little like Tom Sawyer, as if his wound were a badge, a trophy. He'd only been winged. He liked the sound of the word – 'winged.' It seemed to conjure up the notion of it having been very close, his ducking away and foiling the concentrated efforts of a world-class murderer.

Georgia had announced that the inn was almost clean of mystical emanations. There was a residue, maybe in the dust under the house, like the lingering smell of aromatic cedar in a sweater just out of the chest. Ocean winds would sweep it away.

The little car he rode in jolted as it went off the curb, straight out into traffic, weaving crazily around a stalled truck and under the nose of a startled pedestrian. Pickett held on, one hand on the dashboard and another on the edge of the cardboard carton wedged behind his seat an Exer Genie. Apparently they were marvelous things for toning stomach muscles. Heaven knew he could use some of that. The thirty-five bucks had been well spent. Georgia had him on a new regime – diets, stylish clothes, twenty-dollar haircuts. She was going to civilize him, bring him up to date. Rose had been threatening the same ever since Andrew had made a clean sweep of things and admitted to the credit card outrage. She seemed to be softening, though. Georgia, on the other hand, had taken Pickett on as a sort of challenge.

'New battery, then?'

Uncle Arthur nodded, looping the car around an insanely wide turn and onto Main. 'Corroded all to hell. Bumper all strung with kelp. They patented a machine for processing kelp. Did you know that? I sold them off the coast of Maine.'

'No, did they? Where were you these three days, anyway?'

'Out. Constitutional and all. Holiday. Ever been to Scottsdale?'

Pickett shook his head. 'No, is that where you've been? Arizona? We thought you were drowned.'

'Not me.'

'You weren't in Scottsdale?'

'I wasn't drowned. What happened to your mustache?'

'My girlfriend made me shave it off.'

'She's a good woman. Keen eye.'

'So you were in Scottsdale?'

'Once. Hell of a place. I sold rain gutters. Losing proposition in Scottsdale, you'd think. A man would go broke.' Uncle Arthur grinned at Pickett and widened his eyes, possibly to imply that he hadn't gone broke.

Pickett was satisfied. *He* knew where Uncle Arthur had been. You could smell it in the upholstery. That the car still ran after being dumped in the ocean and swallowed by a fish was a testament to something – although whether to something mechanical or something spiritual he couldn't quite figure. Maybe both.

Pickett had tried to make it clear to Rose and Andrew. He himself had anticipated Arthur's return. Pickett had driven out to Leisure World on a hunch that morning. He had knocked on Arthur's door, and when it opened, there the old man had stood, in reading glasses and a suitcoat. He had got Pickett's name wrong and then taken him out to the garage and sold him the Exer-Genie. Just like that. Now they were on their way to the Potholder, together.

Pickett grinned and slapped his knee. The real corker was that Andrew and Rose still thought the old man was dead. In almost exactly a minute and a half – less, even, if Uncle Arthur ran another red light – Pickett and he would lurch up to the door of the Potholder, maybe take out a parking meter or slam into the curb, maybe park on the sidewalk. Andrew and Rose, sitting at the window table, would doubletake, spill their coffee. Andrew would choke and stagger out of his chair, toppling it over. They would rush outside, wild with wonder and joy, appearing to be lunatics, and Uncle Arthur, very calmly and deliberately, as if there were nothing else in the world to interest them, would talk about selling rain gutters in the desert, the red electronic car smelling of whales and kelp and the sea, like a tiny, deep-water submarine, a tangle of waterweeds still trailing from the smashed front bumper.

They couldn't fish off the pier because of what the storm supposedly had done to it. It was cordoned off again, and from where they sat they could see the sparks of a cutting torch where three men worked on a scaffold above the ocean. Rose and Andrew, of course, knew that it hadn't been the storm at all, that it had been a giant fish that had knocked the end of the pier to bits, but there was no profit in saying so. The less said the better.

So they fished off the rock jetty just to the south, Andrew and Rose did, drinking coffee out of a thermos. The fish weren't biting so far, but it didn't matter to either one of them. The sunrise had been worth getting up for. And fishing there together like that, with all the turmoil and villainy behind them, was like a holiday. In a little under an hour they were meeting Pickett at the Potholder for bacon and eggs. There was summer in the air, and the morning was warm and fine.

'So it was you,' said Andrew. 'You were onto the whole business all along.'

Rose shrugged, flipping her plastic lure twenty yards out into the water.

She reeled it in slowly. 'It belonged to me, too, just as it belonged to Aunt Naomi when her husband died, or when Mrs Gummidge murdered him, I guess. *That's* something I didn't know. I should have though.' She sat silently, thinking. 'Poor Uncle Arthur,' she said at last.

'I wish, well ...' He let the thought go and pressed on to more cheerful subjects. 'So you were feeding the 'possum under the house, weren't you? Admit it. And the brick on the toad tank – you left that off on purpose. I'm astonished. I wouldn't have thought it. Not for a minute. I bet you're a closet Weetabix eater, too. Sometimes ... Sometimes I don't figure you very well. Sometimes I wish ...' His cheerful train of thought had sidetracked again.

'Sometimes you should quit figuring. The house looks great, by the way – the paint that is. Did I tell you that?'

'Yeah,' said Andrew. 'You did. But you can tell me a couple more times if you want. God I hate painting.'

'Want some help?'

Andrew started to say no. Then he caught himself. Actually he wanted help very badly. 'Sure,' he said. 'Mounds bar?' He held one out to her.

Rose looked skeptical. 'A Mounds bar? This early in the morning? Where did you get that?'

'I keep a few in the tackle box, actually. There's nothing like them when you're fishing.'

She slid one of the pair of candy bars out of the wrapper and ate it. A crab sidled out from under the rocks and looked at her. She tossed it a hunk of coconut and chocolate and called him Mr Crab.

Andrew grinned at her. The crab scuttled out of sight, carrying the treat. Rose folded up the fishing knife and dropped it into the tackle box. There was only a half hour to go before they were due at the Potholder. She reeled in her line and began to dismantle her pole. 'We'd better get,' she said.

Andrew nodded. 'One more cast.' He was using an old spinning reel with fourteen-pound line and a one-ounce pyramid sinker. 'Watch this,' he said, and he baited the bottom hook with a hunk of Mounds bar and cast it way out into the water in a long, low arc. He waited for the telltale thunk when it settled on the bottom. Rose, cheerfully skeptical, watched Andrew take the slack out of the line.

Then, almost at once, as if the universe were playing along, the line jerked, then jerked again, and Andrew set the drag down just a bit, winked at Rose, and leaning back against the heavily bent pole, began to reel in his fish.

THE PAPER GRAIL

To
Viki

and this time,
to
Tom and Venta Streff
Here's to friendship, food, philosophy, and the future

and to the memory of
Roy Squires

The author would like to thank some people for their help and their friendship:

Dorothea Kenny, Merrilee Heifetz, Randal Robb, Kirk Schumacher, and Tim McNamara, the Secret King of the North Coast. And especially Lew Shiner, the no-holds-barred story doctor. And Tim Powers, from whose tin shed full of plots, images, and ideas I've always stolen ruthlessly.

… that harmony is now broken, and broken the world round: fragments, indeed, of what existed still exist, and hours of what is past still return; but month by month the darkness gains upon the day …

JOHN RUSKIN

… to draw out the soul of things with the syllogism is as impossible as to draw out Leviathan with a hook.

G. K. CHESTERTON

His body is perfectly spherical,
He weareth a runcible hat.

EDWARD LEAR

1

The skywriting in his dream wasn't a word or phrase; it was five white clouds drifting in a blue sky. There was no airplane gusting out smoke, only the five clouds very gradually appearing, exactly positioned, like a constellation growing visible in evening twilight. This time there was the heavy, rhythmic sound of the ocean in the distance, and Howard confused it with the sound of the seasons turning like a mill wheel. He knew in the dream that it was autumn. The pattern of the cloudy skywriting was always the same, and always suggested the same thing, but the seasons kept changing, following the course of the waking year.

In the dream, Howard walked into the mill, which was built of stone, and he stood before the fire in the hearth. A cold wind off the ocean blew at his back. There was no heat in the fire at all, and so he stirred the coals with a stick that he found in his hand, only half surprised that leafy green tendrils sprouted from the stick and twined up his arm in the few moments that he held it.

The fire popped and leaped, throwing embers onto the hearthstones. He knew he was dreaming, and he knew that in a moment he would kneel on the hearth and burn his knee on a hot ember, and that he would feel the pain of the burn even though it was a dream and the fire was cold. And then he would touch the clear fluid that seeped from the burn and taste it, only vaguely surprised that it had the piny smell and flavor of tree sap. There would be a message in the five clouds now, spelling out his fate, but when he walked back outside to read it, the mill wouldn't be a mill any longer. It would be a stone house on a cliffside with the ocean pounding on rocks below and the sky above dark with impending rain.

He woke up this time to the sound of waves breaking along the Point Reyes coastline. It was just dawn. He had slept that night in the back of his camper, parked at Stinson Beach, having driven the few miles from the campground at Mount Tamalpais yesterday morning. Already the dream was fading from his mind. As always, he couldn't remember why it had seemed so vastly important to him, but it had left him with the ghostly suggestions of urgency and dread, and with the peculiar certainty that the five white clouds hadn't been real clouds at all, but had been painted by some unseen hand on the sky above his dream.

*

After driving north out of Point Reyes, Howard stopped at Inverness for breakfast and then used up the rest of his half-frozen anchovies fishing in a big tide pool north of town, throwing chunks of bait at wheeling sea gulls and thinking about his job as assistant curator at a small and dusty museum in southern California. He had come north to pick up a single piece of art-work – what he understood to be a nineteenth-century Japanese woodcut sketch, perhaps by Hoku-sai.

He remembered the sketch as having been faded, with heavy crease lines where some idiot had folded it up, trying to construct, or reconstruct, an ori-gami object. That had been nearly fifteen years ago, when he had spent a rainy weekend at the cliffside house built by Michael Graham, the old man who owned the sketch. Graham had kept it in a curious sort of box, hidden behind the stones of the fireplace, even though there had been prints on the wall, in plain view, that were more valuable.

Howard's cousin Sylvia had been there, too. She had guessed that the rice paper sketch had actually been folded into any number of shapes, and had wondered if a person could refold it, using the creases as a sort of road map. Every now and then, and especially lately, after his dreams about the mill wheel and the fireplace, it occurred to Howard that the road map metaphor fit better than either he or Sylvia had guessed.

Hanging from the rearview mirror in Howard's truck was an origami flower, a lily that had yellowed to the color of old ivory. It was dusty and torn, but too delicate by now to clean up or reshape. Young and romantic, he had given Sylvia a lily on the night they decided against making love, and she had given him the paper flower the following morning, folded up out of paper pressed from linen and leaves.

They were just twenty years old then, and the fact of their being cousins meant that they had very nearly grown up together. It also meant that when their feelings for each other began to grow romantic, there was something that made such feelings troublesome, if not impossible. In her junior year at college Sylvia told him she had decided to move north to Fort Bragg, where her parents lived, and against his own desires he had let her go without arguing.

A month ago he had found the paper lily in a box full of old college mem-orabilia, and had hung it in the cab of his truck. It turned out to be a sort of catalyst, suggesting Sylvia to him, stirring in him the desire to travel up the coast after all these years and pay her a visit. He told himself now that when he arrived in Fort Bragg today or tomorrow he would take it down before she saw it and misread his intentions – or, perhaps, read them correctly. Who could say what either of them would feel these many years later? Nothing had changed, really.

He thought about this as he fished in the pool above Inverness. Either there weren't any fish in the pool or else he was a lousy fisherman. A pelican landed on a nearby outcropping of rock and watched him with a dreadful eye. Howard said hello to it, and the bird clacked its beak open and shut, then cocked its head and fixed its eye on the remaining anchovies. One by one Howard fed them to the pelican, finally showing it the empty carton. The pelican stood there, anyway, watching him past its ridiculous beak, until Howard reeled in his line and picked his way across the rocks toward where his truck was parked on the roadside. Then the bird flew north, following the coast, disappearing behind grassy bluffs and then reappearing out over the ocean, skimming along a foot above the swell, while Howard followed in the pickup, driving at erratic speeds in order to keep the bird in sight and trying to remember whether signifying seabirds were good omens or bad.

He wasn't due in Fort Bragg until tomorrow, but there was no reason at all that he couldn't drive the few hours north today, maybe stop at Graham's house this very afternoon and get business out of the way, after which he could head on up to his Uncle Roy's house and get on with his vacation. He wondered idly whether Sylvia still lived there or had gotten a place of her own, and whether she still saw anything of the man she had very nearly married. What had he called himself then? An animal name of some sort – skunk, maybe, or weasel. Stoat, that was it. Howard had got the news roundaboutly, through his mother, and had insisted to himself that he was happy for Sylvia, that there were no hard feelings. How could there be, after all these years? He was a good deal happier, though, when he heard that Sylvia hadn't married, after all. So much for taking the long view.

On Highway One, above Point Arena and Elk, the road was cut into the cliff face, barely wide enough for two cars to edge past each other. He slowed down, hugging the side of the highway, occasionally looking for the pelican, holding out hope even though he hadn't seen it for two hours. Tangled berry vines snaked down almost onto the asphalt, massed around the bleached pickets of rickety hillside fences. Above him the hills were dry and brown except for stands of cypress and Monterey pine and eucalyptus. Below him were hundreds of feet of rock-strewn, almost vertical cliffs that disappeared into the fog that was drifting ashore now. Here and there, when the road skirted the cliff, he could see the gray Pacific churning below on cathedral-sized rocks.

Occasional mailboxes appeared along the ocean side of the road, marking the driveways to isolated houses on the bluffs. Uneasily Howard started watching for Graham's house, matching landmarks along the highway with the little symbols on the pencil-sketched map on his dashboard. He remembered the house fairly clearly from his stay there years ago, and even more clearly from his dreams, where, because of some trick of dream architecture, Graham's house and the old stone mill were in some subtle way the same thing.

He drove straight past it, not seeing the fence-post mailbox or the weedy gravel drive until it was too late. Immediately the highway twisted around and began climbing, making it impossible to turn around. Somehow, missing the driveway didn't bother him. It was almost a relief, and he realized that the house filled him with an indeterminate sense of foreboding, like heavy weather pending on a muggy and silent afternoon.

He slowed the truck, though, and turned off the highway, up Albion Ridge Road, stopping at a little grocery store with a pair of rusty old gas pumps out front. Far below the ridge, the Albion River wound down out of the coast range. The north coast was in the middle of a long drought, and the river was a muddy trickle. On the bank sat a campground, nearly empty, with a dirt road running through it, leading beneath the bridge and down to a deserted beach that was strewn with driftwood and kelp. It looked like a good place to go shelling, especially this time of the year, when the first of the big north swells dragged the ocean bottom and threw seashells and long-sunken flotsam onto the rocky beaches.

He thought about spending the night at the campground. Maybe it was too late to stop and see old Graham that afternoon, anyway. The old man might easily be doubtful about strangers in pickup trucks appearing out of the fog so late in the day. Howard would call back down to the house in order to make an appointment – for tomorrow noon, say. He felt grimy and salty, and his clothes smelled like fish bait. Tomorrow morning he could find a laundromat in Mendocino, and then backtrack the ten miles to Graham's house. The plan sounded fine to him, very rational, except that he knew he was simply avoiding things, and was beginning to feel as if the north coast, like the two poles of a magnet, was conspiring to attract and repel him about equally.

The gas station was actually a sort of country store, covered in rough-cut redwood planks and with a few chain-sawed burl sculptures out front that had turned gray in the weather. Old macramé and bead curtains covered the windows, which were dusty and strung with cobwebs and dead flies. The junk food in the rack on the counter was a little disappointing – carob brownies and sticky-looking granola bars in plastic wrap, all of it sweetened with fruit juice instead of sugar. It was guaranteed to be organic, put together by a local concern called Sunberry Farms. It certainly *looked* organic, especially the carob, which might as easily have been dirt.

There wasn't a Twinkie in sight, so he grabbed a pack of gum and one of the brownies and laid them on the counter. Gas was nearly a dollar and a half a gallon, and his old Chevy Cheyenne drank it like champagne. The attendant stood out by the truck, talking to a man carrying a tackle box, who set the box down and held his hands apart, obviously telling a fish story. Nobody was in any hurry up here, which satisfied Howard entirely. It seemed to be the first time in months, maybe years, that he wanted to be exactly where he was, drunk on the weather and the solitude and the sound of the sea.

He found a wire rack of postcards and window decals, and he sorted through them, pulling out a half dozen decals that advertised north coast sights – the Skunk Train, Shipwreck Aquarium, the Winchester Mystery House, Noyo Harbor. It didn't matter to him that he hadn't been to most of these places. What he wanted was to glue decals all over his truck and camper shell windows. He had a couple dozen of them already, from places in Arizona and Nevada and New Mexico. Soon he'd be out of room, and would have to start layering the decals, perhaps covering just the inessential edges and corners at first, and then ultimately losing one after another of them altogether. Once he had gotten started on it a couple of months ago, it had become a sort of compulsion, and he had come to believe in the virtues of excess, almost as if someday he would reach a sort of mystical decal threshold, and something would happen.

Normally he avoided any decal that didn't advertise a place. He didn't want slogans or political statements or any indication that he meant anything consistent. Obvious meaning would subvert the entire effort, and he'd have to scrape the whole mess off with a razor blade. Up until now he never bought too many at one time. The thing shouldn't be rushed. There was something about the air up here, though, that overrode that instinct, and he found that within moments he was holding a whole sheaf of the things. He picked out one last decal of a comical pelican, which he bought as a souvenir of the bird he'd shared his anchovies with. If there was any meaning in that, no one except him would be able to guess it out.

He wandered up the center aisle of the little store, toward a display of fishing tackle and rental poles on the back wall. Thumbtacked to a piece of corkboard beneath the carded fishing tackle was a faded and dog-eared bumper sticker advertising a local roadside attraction. It had holes in the corners so that it could be wired to your bumper while you weren't looking. In small letters it read, 'Honk if you've seen,' and then below, in larger letters, 'The Museum of Modern Mysteries.' Alongside was a sketchy illustration of ghosts flitting through a redwood grove with a shadowy automobile running along below, the front end of the thing lost in the foggy night. Howard unpinned it, instantly losing interest in his hand full of decals.

There was the scraping of shoe soles at the door, and Howard turned to find the attendant sliding in behind the counter. The man looked doubtfully at the brownie, pushing it with his finger. 'This yours?' he asked, as if he couldn't quite believe it.

Howard nodded, suddenly regretting it. The thing cost nearly a dollar, the price of two decals. 'Is this bumper sticker for sale?' Howard held it up for the man to see.

'Oh, that,' the man said, sitting down on a stool. 'That's a couple years old. It ain't no good. Place went broke.'

Howard wondered for a moment whether his question had been answered and then decided that it hadn't been. 'Don't want to sell it, do you?' He tried not to sound too anxious. The man was right, from his point of view, and was clearly having a hard time putting a price on a scrap of old faded paper.

'Used to have a decal, too.' He leaned heavily on the first syllable of the word and nodded at the wire rack.

'Don't have one now, do you?'

'Nope,' the man said. 'Place went bust.'

Howard widened his eyes, as if in surprise that such a place as a spirit museum could go bust. 'People don't much believe in ghosts anymore,' he said, trying to make it sound noncommittal, as if he were ready to believe in whatever the attendant believed, and blame the rest of the world for believing something else and causing trouble.

'People don't know from ghosts.' The man switched on a portable television behind the counter. A game show appeared on the screen – a family of six wearing funny hats and jitterbugging furiously in front of a washer and dryer hung with enormous price tags.

The sound of the television ruined the atmosphere, and Howard was suddenly desperate to leave. He set his credit card down on the counter along with the decals and made one last try at the bumper sticker. 'I'd be glad to buy the sticker,' he said.

'Won't do you no good.' The man stared hard at his credit card, as if Howard had handed him something inexplicable – a ham sandwich or a photograph of the Eiffel Tower. He read the name several times, looking at Howard's face, and then checked the number against a little book of bad-risk numbers shoved in alongside the cash register. 'Barton,' he said. 'You ain't any relation …' He looked closely at Howard's face again and then smiled broadly. 'Sure you are!'

'He's my uncle,' Howard said. 'On my father's side.' It was no good to lie. Now he would have to pay triple for the bumper sticker. Howard's Uncle Roy had founded and owned the Museum of Modern Mysteries and then had gone broke with it. Howard had never even been there, although he had always loved the idea of it. And now, these years later, here was a long-lost bumper sticker advertising the place. Clearly he had to buy it as a memento. The man knew that now. He sat there as if thinking about it, about soaking Howard for the rectangle of sun-faded paper.

'Roy Barton,' he said, shaking his head. 'That old son of a gun. Hell, *take* the damned thing. You going up to his place now?'

'That's right,' Howard said, surprised. 'I'm up here on business, mostly.'

'Roy Barton's, or your own?'

'My own, actually. I haven't seen Roy for a few years. I don't know what kind of business he's in now.'

The man gave him a curious look, as if Uncle Roy were in some sort of business that didn't bear discussion. Then he said, 'Roy Barton's pretty much in business with the world. Nobody'd be surprised if your business and his business didn't cross paths down the line. He used to call himself an "entrepreneur of the spirit." And by God he ain't far wrong. He'll liven up your day.'

'I hope so,' Howard said. 'I could use it.'

'Give him a howdy from me, then, will you? Tell him Cal says hello. He used to come in here pretty regular when he was working the ghost angle up to the museum. He had a lot of idle time. It wasn't but a half mile up the road. Building's still there, sitting empty. Ever been up there?'

'Never was,' Howard said. 'Always wanted to, but I put it off. Then he went under and it was too late.'

'Too damned bad, too. He's a character, Roy Barton is. He *seen* some things out in the woods ...' The man laughed, shaking his head, remembering something out of the past, some sort of Roy Barton high jinks. 'Hell, I believe him, too. I'll be damned if I don't.' He turned around to a glass-fronted drink cooler, opened it up, and pulled out a six-pack of Coors. 'Take this along for him, will you? Tell him Cal Dalton says hello and why don't he stop in.' He handed Howard his credit card along with the beer, and Howard signed for the gas and decals. Cal shook his hand. 'Look for it on the right, three or four bends up. You can pass it easy if you aren't looking out.'

Howard thanked him and left. Fog had settled into the campground below, making it look inhospitable and cold. Somehow the man's carrying on like that had lifted Howard's spirits, making him feel less like an outsider. The idea of having a look at the abandoned spirit museum appealed to him. There was a couple of hours of daylight left.

He had heard all about the museum from his mother, who had done her best to make the whole cockeyed thing sound reasonable. His mother was fiercely loyal to Uncle Roy, who had looked after them, in his way, in the years following Howard's father's death. Howard had picked up bits and pieces of family gossip lately about the museum's sad decline and about how Uncle Roy had borrowed himself into lifelong debt to make a go of it. The rotten thing about it was that his poor uncle had believed in it, in the ghosts. Despite the gimmicky bumper stickers and decals, he had been convinced that he had seen a carload of spirits appearing out of the north coast dawn and gunning away up the highway, dressed in out-of-date clothes and driving a Studebaker.

Why a Studebaker? That's what had torn it, had wrecked the museum, just as surely as if the Studebaker had driven through the wall. It was a car that lacked credibility. The ghosts might as well have been pedaling unicycles and wearing fright wigs. If only it had been some sort of generic Ford or Chevy, people might have bought the idea.

For Uncle Roy, though, the ghost museum had been a scientific study in the paranormal. He didn't care what sort of car the ghosts drove. He didn't require a ghost to follow fashion. The public ridiculed a Studebaker, largely because it had a front end that you couldn't tell from the rear; it was a sort of mechanical push-me pull-you. But if such a vehicle was good enough for the ghosts, then to hell with the public; it was good enough for Uncle Roy, too. That's what made it about ten times as sad when the museum closed down – Uncle Roy's sincerity.

Realizing that he wasn't very hungry, Howard opened the glove compartment in order to put the brownie away. A glass paperweight lay inside, dense with flower canes and ribbons that looked like Christmas candy. He meant it to be a gift for Sylvia, who had always loved pretty things. It had cost him a couple hundred dollars, though, and it might seem like an ostentatious gift. He would have to be subtle with it.

A half mile north of Albion there was a turnout on the land side of the highway. Howard slowed the truck and bumped off onto the shoulder, which widened out behind a line of trees into a gravel parking lot that had been invisible from the road to the south. Sitting at the far edge of the lot, overhung by fir and eucalyptus, was a long bunkhouse-like building, empty and boarded up. There was a fence of split pickets running along in front, with three or four cow skulls impaled on random pickets. A painted, weathered sign over the front porch read, 'Museum of Modern Mysteries.'

He cut the engine and sat on the edge of the lot, just able to hear the muted crash of breakers through the rolled-up windows. So this was it. He had known it was out here somewhere, sitting lonesome and empty along the highway. Somehow he had expected more, although exactly what he had expected he couldn't say. He was tempted at first to climb out and have a look, but the windows were shuttered, and the longer he sat there, the sadder the place seemed to be. Some other time, maybe. He was planning on spending a couple of weeks; he could always get Uncle Roy to drive him back out and show him around, if his uncle was up to it and still had a key.

Howard thought about the Hoku-sai sketch, hanging on the wall of Graham's house, back down the road. It was time to have a look at it. To hell with laundromats and appointments. He had waited long enough. It was almost two years ago that he had written a letter suggesting that Graham give the sketch to the museum in Santa Ana on what was called permanent loan. Graham could write it off on his taxes. Howard would use it as the focus of a new wing of oriental artwork.

Two years ago that had sounded enterprising – something new. But for nearly a year after he sent the letter he hadn't heard anything in return, and

had almost forgotten about the sketch. Then, unexpectedly, he had got a letter back, agreeing to the permanent loan business. Graham wouldn't ship the
piece, though; Howard would have to come after it. He had done nothing
about it for most of a year. Then a month ago something shifted in him – the
dreams, the accidental rediscovery of the origami lily – and he began to feel
like a man whose spirit was beginning to recover from a long dry spell.

He came up with the idea of going up north, of taking a slow, zigzag route,
driving back roads out of obscure beaches and primitive campgrounds. It
would be nothing less than a matter of sorting out his life. He would visit
Uncle Roy and Aunt Edith in Fort Bragg, get to know Sylvia again. He would
take a month to do it, just like in the old days. Mrs Gleason, his boss, hadn't
liked the idea of month-long vacations, but Howard showed her Graham's
letter, and that had done the trick. He had kept his thumb over the date.

Fog settled around the pickup truck as he sat on the roadside now, and
water dripped onto the roof of the cab from an overhanging tree limb. The
sea wind gusted around the doors, and Howard started the truck in order to
fire up the heater. Once the engine was idling, his sitting there seemed pointless, so he rolled up to the edge of the asphalt and peered downhill into the
gloom. A pair of headlights swung around the curve of highway below, the
car itself still invisible in the fog. It was impossible to tell how far away it was,
so Howard waited it out, letting it have the highway to itself.

Howard recognized the characteristic cheese-grater roar of a Volkswagen
engine before the microbus actually materialized out of the wall of fog. It was
moving slowly, even for a Volkswagen, like a deep-water fish prowling
through submarine canyons. One moment it was a ghost, obscured by mist;
the next it was solid. Howard thought suddenly about his uncle's Studebaker,
full of top-hatted spirits, and on impulse he shifted the transmission into
reverse, as if he would escape it by hurtling backward into the forest.

As it drew near, it appeared at first to be covered with sticks and leaves, like
something that had driven up out of the deep woods. But it wasn't leaves; it
was stuff from the ocean that had been glued onto the body of the bus in
layers, so that only the front windows were clear. Dried kelp and sea fans,
starfish and barnacles, clumped mussels and fish skeletons and seashells
covered the bus in layers so that it looked like a tide pool on wheels. It was
impossible to be sure it was a car any longer, except that it ran on tires and
had a windshield. Even the rumbling engine might have been a cobbled-
together mechanism of tube worms and starfish gears and pumping seawater.
It growled uphill, lit within by the strange green glow of the instrument
panel. The driver's face was a shadow.

Howard shifted back out of reverse, realizing that his mouth was open in
disbelief. He watched the bus disappear into the fog around the curve of the
hillside, noticing that a big patch of stuff had evidently fallen off the outside

of the engine compartment – too much heat, probably. The effect was suddenly one of shabbiness, something like a ghost story ruined by missing paragraphs.

Still, something about the bus, about seeing it, reminded him of his uncle's museum and of Michael Graham's stone house, with its passages and turrets. The very atmosphere of the north coast was compulsive – the overgrown countryside and the perpetual mist, the strange appeal of a wire rack full of gaudy decals. It struck him that there was something right and natural about the deep-sea bus, as if it stood to reason. He laughed uneasily, reminding himself that eccentrics were common on the coast. They must issue cards, like a Mensa ID. After another week of solitude and fog he would be ready to apply for one himself.

No wonder Uncle Roy had been possessed with notions of ghosts. The foggy air seemed to be thick with them. For the first time since he'd left home a week ago he wanted company – even old Graham's company. He rolled out onto the highway, heading south again. He would make it to the stone house with an hour's worth of daylight to spare.

2

The limousine crept along through the San Francisco traffic, down Grant Street, through Chinatown toward North Beach. It was July, and the streets were full of tourists, the heavy stream of cars barely moving in either direction and people cutting warily back and forth between bumpers. Why the fool of a driver had missed his offramp and tied them up in crosstown traffic, Heloise Lamey couldn't fathom. Stupidity, maybe. Some sort of smart-aleck malice – wasting the time of a poor old woman out alone, at the mercy of the world.

She said nothing, though. It was already spilled milk. She could rant and rave and it wouldn't get them to their destination one moment sooner. And the hired driver wouldn't care anyway. She could buy the limousine service and have the man fired and he wouldn't care. Her insisting on justice would simply provoke abuse. Despite his snappy uniform, he was sullen and dull and false-looking. She could see it in his eyes. She could take the measure of a man in an instant. In her sixty-eight years on earth she had learned to do that with a facility that she was proud of. It was the key to her success as a businesswoman.

People weren't what they used to be. The tradespeople didn't keep to their stations. Duty was a thing of the past. Everywhere she went people were full of abuse. There was trouble of some sort from almost everyone she ran into. She seemed to remember a time in the distant past when that wasn't so, when people and life were simple and direct. When that had changed, she couldn't at all say.

Before the war she had almost married a sailor. She remembered how handsome he had looked in his uniform on the day he shipped out. On the night before, they had danced to Benny Goodman. Now his bones were on the bottom of the ocean somewhere, and that's what life had to offer you ultimately – death and disappointment. The world hadn't changed in that respect. People had, though. Now there was nothing but grasping, people clawing their way through life at your expense. A person had no choice but to get in ahead of them. There was no middle ground. She stayed home as much as she could, but even there she was forced to carry on a war with a lot of backwoods hicks who didn't know progress when they saw it, or destiny, either.

Her mouth set and her eyes narrowed, she sat in the center of the backseat and stared straight ahead out the front window, trying not to see the awful gaggle of people swarming on the sidewalks and in the gutters. She believed that there was a certain dignity in her face, which was long and thin and with a prominent chin and the eyes of a monarch – the sort who saw straight through her subjects and their pitiful little games. There was nothing weak in her face, nothing watery. It was the sort of face that wasn't easily forgotten. She peered at herself in the window reflection now, refastening a strand of hair that had come loose.

Her attention was broken by the high-pitched shouting of an old Chinese news vendor, arguing, probably, over a nickel. At the curb the rear door of a van swung open and a man stepped out carrying a flayed goat over one bloody shoulder and a string of plucked ducks over the other. Life, like so much scurrying vermin, went on around her. She thought for the sixth time how necessary it had been to hire a limousine. Then she realized they were stopped again, and she checked her watch. 'I'm *very* late,' she said to the driver, who said nothing in return.

The traffic cleared just then, as if it, at least, were paying attention to her. The car moved forward slowly, making nearly a half a block's worth of headway before stopping again. The lights of a tow truck whirled in front of them now, blocking oncoming traffic while the tow truck driver walked around an illegally parked Mercedes-Benz, looking in the windows. He pulled a clutch of flat plastic slats out of his coat and slipped one in along the edge of the front door of the parked car in order to jimmy it open, a policeman directing the cars around it, holding the limousine at bay with an upturned hand.

Skeptically Mrs Lamey watched them work. Nothing was safe from them. Even the police would steal your car. 'Honk the horn,' Mrs Lamey said to the driver.

'At the cop?' He turned and looked at her.

'Just *honk the horn,* young man. I've been patient with you up until now, but this takes it too far. Honk the horn.'

The driver squinted into her face. 'You gotta be kidding,' he said.

'I never *kid,* if I take your meaning. I assure you I'm very serious. Honk your horn. I've hired this car, and I demand it.'

'Why don't you climb up here and honk it yourself, lady? Then *you* can talk to the cop.' He turned forward again, ignoring her. Opening the glove box, he found a pack of gum, pulling out two sticks and shoving them into his mouth, settling into his seat contentedly to wait out the tow truck, even if it took all afternoon.

Mrs Lamey leaned forward, unable to believe it. She had expected grief of some nature, but this sort of outright impudence from a driver ... 'I *insist.* Honk the horn or I'll have your job.'

'You can have the fuckin' job, lady, and the horn, too. Calm the hell down. Where you going, anyway? Just up to North Beach. It's easier to *walk* from here. If I was you, that's what I'd do. I'd get out and walk. You'd have been there twenty minutes ago.'

'Your advice is worthless to me, young man. Here, look, they've gotten out of the way. Pull around these cars, for heaven's sake.' She waved a limp-wristed hand toward the street.

He shrugged and edged the limousine past the tow truck, which had straightened out now and was towing the Mercedes out into traffic. They stopped and started a half dozen times down the last two blocks to Portsmouth Square, slowing in the press of cars swinging up onto Broadway and Columbus. Small gangs of youths lounged on the sidewalk along the square, shouting and smoking cigarettes.

Mrs Lamey carefully kept her eyes straight ahead. There was nothing here that she wanted to see. She felt vulnerable, even inside the limousine, but with a little bit of work she could ignore the world outside utterly. As they turned up Columbus, though, she saw three young men with weirdly miscut hair bend toward the limousine and make obscene gestures with both hands, all three of them laughing and hooting. Mrs Lamey concentrated hard on the windshield, on the car ahead of them, on the tip of her nose, blocking out their existence, eradicating the whole brief scene.

'That's rich, ain't it?' the driver said, chuckling in the front seat. 'What it is, is the limo. Happens all the time. Can't go nowhere without people flipping you off. You know what I mean? It's a social statement is what I think.' He shook his head, clearly pleased, able to take the long view. 'You got to admire it, though.' He looked at her wide-eyed in the rearview mirror, as if inviting her to admire it as much as he did, to talk a little bit of philosophy.

Mrs Lamey was silent. There was nothing on earth she had to admire. Where she came from limousine drivers spoke when spoken to. They weren't street-corner sociologists. He shook his head after a half minute of her refusing to speak, and they drove in silence up Columbus to Vallejo.

She directed him up an alley between graffiti-scrawled brick façades. Midway down, the alley opened onto a courtyard. 'Stop here,' she said suddenly.

'Here?' He turned and looked at her incredulously, having expected, perhaps, some more reasonable destination.

'That's right. Here. In the alley. I won't be needing your services any longer. I'm getting out here. *Can* you fathom that?'

He shrugged. 'Suits me.' He got out and went round to her door, opening it and gesturing gallantly at the littered asphalt.

'I won't be giving you a tip of any sort,' she said to him, staring at his chin with a look of determination. 'I don't know what you're accustomed to, but I'll tell you right now that I had thought at first to give you two dollars. You can ruminate on that for the rest of the afternoon. I'm moderately certain that I would have gotten quicker, more courteous service from a taxicab. One expects a certain amount of gracious behavior from a driver, a certain level of professionalism and expertise.'

She took two steps to distance herself from him, then turned around to face him squarely. With an air of someone having the last word, she showed him the two crisp one-dollar bills that might have been his. She tucked them away finally and irretrievably into her pocket, turning away into the courtyard without a backward glance.

She hadn't gone three steps, though, when a horn honked. Without thinking she looked back at the alley, where the limousine accelerated slowly past the mouth of the courtyard. The driver was bent across the front seat, waving out the open passenger window. He shouted a parting obscenity which somehow involved eating. Mrs Lamey closed her ears to it just a second too late, continuing across the courtyard and resolutely listening to nothing now but the *tap, tap, tap* of her shoes on concrete, blocking out the whole filthy world round about her.

There was a breezeway at the corner of the courtyard, opening onto another small, winding alley that ran steeply uphill. At the top she crossed a small parking lot and went in through the side door of a white concrete building with red letters on the side proclaiming itself to be the 'Whole Life Mission.' Below that, in italic lettering, was the legend 'The Church of the Profiting Christian.'

Inside the church the air was heavy, still, and musty. The building was bigger than it appeared to be from the street, and Mrs Lamey walked through the nave, past rows of empty pews built of wood-grain Formica. She peered into the empty sacristy and then into an adjacent chair-lined room, also empty of people, and containing a glass-fronted, water-filled tub. Heavy-looking television cameras and big reflecting lights hung from the ceiling and stood in the corners. She went on, pausing to knock on an office door and listen at the cloudy glass window. A sign on the door read, 'Reverend White, Ministry Office.' There was nothing but silence inside. Reverend White, apparently, was somewhere on the second floor.

She climbed a stairs and with a key from her purse let herself into a kitchen. Beyond it was a corridor with rooms leading off to either side. There was the smell of carbolic acid and alcohol in the air now, and the floors were tiled in white linoleum. A chrome pole on wheels stood in the corridor, hung with an IV bottle and with plastic tubing and clamps. Through one open door she glimpsed a gurney and a surgical table. A thrill of fear and anticipation surged through-her, and she was struck with the notion that in the air of that room her destiny hung like a rain cloud.

She knocked twice on the window of the next door down, then pushed the button on an adjacent intercom.

'Who is it?' asked a man's voice.

'Heloise.'

The door opened an inch and a man peered out, as if to ascertain whether it was really Mrs Lamey standing in the hallway or somebody playing a trick. Satisfied, he smiled broadly and waved her in. He wore a white coat over a red shirt and black trousers. His patent-leather shoes matched his shirt. 'Heloise!' he said, as if he'd been waiting for this moment for weeks. 'I half expected you wouldn't come.'

'Well, I'm here, Reverend,' she said sarcastically. 'Let's get this over with.'

'It would be better to call me "doctor." I'm a minister downstairs, a doctor upstairs.'

'An abortionist, maybe. "Doctor" is a weighty word.'

He shrugged. 'I don't perform abortions anymore, actually. I was an abortionist when it was illegal and more profitable. Now I perform elective surgery – reconstructive surgery, mostly.'

Mrs Lamey made a face, imagining what he meant despite herself.

He grinned at her for a moment and then put on a serious, bedside, medical-man face. 'It's a fact,' he said. 'People come to me from all over the city. Up from Los Angeles, too. Men and women both. In fact, half a block up the street, at a bar called the Cat's Meow, there's a dancer who owes her entire career to me. You'd be surprised what people will pay to see. Enormous breasts are a dime a dozen in North Beach. People are tired of that sort of thing. But there's a certain fascination for – what can I call it? Alien results, let's say. For anatomy that's … physiologically wrong.' He watched for her response, but she stood stony-faced. He couldn't phase her. He shrugged. 'Anyway, even that's going by the boards. They're turning the Cat's Meow into a dinner theatre, and my client is out of a job. Your case is comparatively simple, though, isn't it? You've got too low an opinion of my talents, Heloise, which is a mystery to me.'

'A mystery? A back-alley surgery like this. Performing whatever sorts of ghastly operations fifteen years after your license was revoked. And my opinion is a mystery to you?'

'Oh, no, not that. I don't have any problem with that at all. What mystifies me is why you seem to want my help and yet insist on insulting me.' He lit a cigar and sat down, leaning back in his swivel chair, shifting the cigar from side to side in his mouth.

Mrs Lamey brushed the heavy smoke away from her face. 'Because I pay you not to ask questions,' she said. 'And I'd rather not hear about your loathsome work, thank you. How long will this take?'

He shrugged. 'Moderately simple surgery. No exterior cutting at all. One just hauls the plumbing out through—'

'Save the filthy talk, Mr White. How long will this take – until I'm home again?'

'A week in bed, under observation. You'll need a nurse, someone trained. Then four or five weeks before a full recovery. There's the threat of infection, of course. This is a moderately risky surgery, you know. I can't fathom why you'd elect to have it unnecessarily at this … late age.' He smiled at her.

'Business,' she said. 'That will have to suffice.'

He nodded. 'You undertake the strangest sort of business, Heloise, don't you? I have faith in you, though. Our business efforts always seem to end satisfactorily. And, of course, I make it a point not to pry into my patients' affairs.'

'Don't, then. There's the matter that we discussed over the telephone, too. Can we take care of that right now, do you think, before we carry out this surgery?'

'That requires a different coat,' he said, standing up and gesturing toward the door. They went out, back through the kitchen and down the stairs into the church. He unlocked the door to the ministry office, letting Mrs Lamey through first and then locking the door behind them.

The office was large and ornately decorated, with oil paintings on the walls and an oriental carpet on the parquet floor. A six-panel Japanese screen covered half of one wall, and on a low, gaudily carved table in the center of the room sat a glass-encased collection of Franklin Mint coins. The Reverend White stepped straight across to the wall opposite the door where he lifted and took down a Norman Rockwell painting. 'This is an original,' he said, nodding at it and squinting. 'Cost me plenty.'

'I'm sure it did.'

'I love Rockwell, though, don't you? He captures a sort of spirit, a sort of ...' He lost track of the thought as he turned the dial of a wall safe that had been hidden behind the painting. The safe door swung open, and he carefully removed a velvet-wrapped bundle, laying it gently on the edge of the rug. He untied a ribbon at either end and unrolled the bundle, revealing two long, pale bones, streaked with brown and black. The bones themselves, looking porous and dry, seemed to have crumbled partly away at both ends.

'And these are what we discussed?' she asked, looking at the bones doubtfully.

'Yes, they are. They come with papers detailing their history over thousands of years, and not a particularly complicated history, either. I got these at a bargain-basement price, I can tell you. I've dealt in relics for years, and I know the man I bought these from personally. Here's his affidavit.' He held out a signed paper, insisting that the bones were from the forearms of Joseph of Arimathea, the first of the so-called Fisher Kings, according to some of the Grail legends. The bundle included the two radii, recovered from beneath a church in Lithuania.

Mrs Lamey looked the document over. It was signed by four different people, the signatures unreadable and full of flourishes as if the document were intended to be framed and hung on the wall alongside spurious doctoral diplomas. 'This is certainly worthless,' she said. 'But then what isn't? I have moderately sure methods of proving their authenticity. And I'm entirely certain that you wouldn't defraud me, Reverend. You wouldn't sell me a couple of old monkey arms, not at a hundred thousand dollars.' She paused and looked hard at him, waiting for his response.

'No,' he said, as if surprised that she'd suggest such a thing. 'Of course not. You have my word on it as well as this affidavit of authenticity.'

She smiled at him and stood up, moving toward the door. 'Keep the affidavit of authenticity,' she said. 'Line the birdcage with it. Leave the bones in the safe for now. We'll settle my account after my recovery. Any news of the Ruskin skeleton? I want him, too. All of him.'

'No news at all. I've got feelers out, though. If it's available, we'll get it. You've got my solemn oath on that. My man in England has confirmed that the bones aren't in Coniston.'

'I don't give a tinker's damn what your man in England confirms. If the bones aren't in Coniston, then they've got to be somewhere else. John Ruskin, for heaven's sake. It's not like the man was unknown. Don't they keep track of the corpses of great thinkers and writers? I can't believe they'd be so careless as to misplace such a thing.'

The Reverend White shrugged. 'It appears as if the bones were taken ages ago. Maybe he was never interred at all. My man can recover his flowered shroud, though, if that will be of any use to you. There was a claim made once that vines grew out of the shroud when it was sprinkled with holy water. If my man can recover it …'

'Tell your man to recover his wits.'

'I've got him pursuing the matter. As I said, you've got my solemn oath …'

She interrupted him. 'Your solemn oath. That's very good. There's no chance, is there, that the gentleman we spoke of has the skeleton? He might have had access to it, you know.'

'In fact, I do know. I make it my business to know. Someone would have heard of such a thing. This gentleman you refer to is a noted lunatic, isn't he?'

'He's very subtle. A deceptive man. It's hard to say what he is.'

'Well, he isn't the owner of the Ruskin skeleton. I'll make further inquiries, though, if you're serious about this.'

'I've never been more serious, I assure you. And I would be very disappointed if you had dealt with him instead of with me. Don't play games with me.'

'I'm impervious to games, I assure you.'

'Then let's get on with the afternoon's business, shall we?'

'Happily,' he said. 'That'll require a different coat, though.' He put the bones back into the wall safe, rehung the painting, and led the way back up the stairs to where, in the surgery, a gowned nurse was already laying out instruments.

Howard turned down the gravel drive, which dipped steeply into the darkness of the woods. It must have been nearly impossible to navigate right after a heavy rain. As it was, the truck wheels spun a little in the gravel and the pickup wallowed from side to side, in and out of deep ruts. He crept along, taking it slow through the ghostly, overgrown cypress trees, which ended abruptly on the meadow's edge, fifty yards or so from the cliff.

There was the house itself, half cloaked in fog, the whole thing a beautiful driftwood gray, the color of the ocean, with moss growing between the stones and with the meadow wild around it. Howard was amazed at how clearly he remembered it – how much it was like the house in his dreams. It was uncanny – troublesomely so. It was fifteen years ago that he had last driven down this gravel driveway, and yet it seemed to him that he could recall even the shapes of individual stones in the walls of the house and the weathered ends of exposed roof rafters.

He had been climbing the stairs in his dreams, the old mill having turned into Graham's stone house. The stairs hung to the outside wall of the turret, wrapping around to a landing and second-floor doorway. The steps were built of irregular, chunked concrete, sledgehammered out of a sidewalk and reinforced underneath with lengths of angle iron from an old bed frame torched into pieces. There was an iron pipe handrail along the wall where the steps were mortised into the stones of the turret, but the other three edges of each step hung in the air, and now it made him dizzy just to look at them.

In his dream he had climbed slowly, looking hard at the wide lines of cleanly troweled mortar between the stones. He had seemed to be looking for something, but he didn't know what. Abruptly he realized that odds and ends of things had been shoved very carefully into the wet mortar: cheap, colored-glass perfume bottles laid sideways, tiny iron toys, a faded ceramic Humpty Dumpty wearing a polka-dot shirt and a green tie with a stickpin and with a broad, leering, know-it-all grin.

One moment he had been halfway up; the next he was at the top of the stairs, facing the weathered door; his heart hammering in his chest. He had turned and gone back down, taking the irregular steps two at a time, thinking that something had come out of the door and was watching him, had noticed him for the first time. He had gone straight out onto the bluffs, where the driveway ended in weeds, and had nearly stumbled headlong into an old truck from which two workmen were off-loading straw-stuffed crates of the ceramic Humpty Dumptys.

It was a ridiculous dream, that part of it was. He could see that clearly in the daylight. At night, though, at two in the morning … Darkness tended to multiply the significance of dreams. Dream mathematics acquired its own logic after dark. And night was falling quickly now. In twenty minutes there wouldn't be much daylight left.

Howard watched the house for a moment longer, waiting for the door to open, for someone to peer out. Anyone in the house would have heard him rattle up. Berry vines grew so dense as to nearly cover the west-facing downstairs windows, and had been hacked away to let in sunlight. Split shingles lay in a pile on the meadow, alongside a telephone pole that had been sawed into foot-and-a-half lengths. There were piles of sand and gravel with sun-shredded plastic tarps staked over them, and an old cement mixer hooked up to a rusty gasoline generator on wheels. Heaps of size-sorted stone lay stacked along the wild edge of the vines, most of the stones covered up by new growth. Beyond the open door of a long, low, lean-to barn in among the cypress and eucalyptus trees, a chain-saw mill sat in the middle of a mountain of wood chips.

The place seemed empty, deserted. He climbed out of the truck, taking his keys with him. There was a heavy odor of cedar and moldering vegetation and fog, and the thick silence was cut only by the low sound of a foghorn moaning somewhere to the north. He walked around the house toward the cliffs, stopping next to a prefabricated tin shed, probably bought out of a catalogue from Sears and Roebuck. The house appeared to be dark.

The fog cleared momentarily, and there was enough daylight left to see the black rocks nearly a hundred feet below the cliffs. Waves broke across them, surging up the cliffside and then washing back down. On one of the rocks, partly submerged and crumpled up, sat an old car like a piece of statuary on a plinth. It had obviously gone off the cliff. What was it? Something peculiar; he couldn't tell at first if he was looking at the front end of the car or the back end. A Studebaker? The ocean rushed out to feed an incoming wave, exposing the car entirely. It *was* a Studebaker – an old one, from some year in the early fifties. What a coincidence; it might have been the ghost car itself.

Howard chuckled to himself. He loved the whole idea of ghosts driving around in oddball cars, getting into trouble, maybe robbing a liquor store or setting fire to someone's shoes. Then he thought about the empty spirit museum and Uncle Roy's sad bankruptcy, the loss of his house and his having to rent it back from one of his creditors who had come to own it as a piece of collateral. What with all that and the fall of night, the subject of ghosts wasn't very funny at all.

The ocean raced in again, parting around the smashed front end of the Studebaker, water streaming off the fenders. The car hadn't rusted much, either, from what Howard could see of it. It must have gone over pretty recently.

Straight behind him, uphill, was the garage end of the barn. It looked as if someone hadn't set the brake, and the car had rolled across the grass and off the cliff edge. It would have continued to roll for a long ways, down the steepening slope, which was strewn with scree and loose boulders. There was a gnarled old piece of scrub half torn out of the cliff face some twenty feet above the beach, and hooked to it was the car's rear bumper, which had no doubt slowed the car's descent and explained why it wasn't an utter ruin now.

A pelican appeared from around the headland, angling along the back of a swell, into Howard's line of sight. It pulled up when it neared the beach, and perched on the front of the car like a hood ornament. Howard stepped back away from the cliff edge, suddenly dizzy, the sound of the waves becoming disturbingly rhythmic, like the sound of the mill wheel in his dream.

He wondered what he should do. Stay? That seemed presumptuous to him – to hang around the foggy meadow when no one was home. He would feel like a sneak. And it was very possibly pointless, too. Graham might easily be gone for the night. Howard would drive into Mendocino and find a hotel room, after all. In the morning he would wash his clothes, then call Fort Bragg to announce his arrival to Uncle Roy, explaining that he happened to be in the area a couple of days earlier than he had thought, and … It was weak, but it had the advantage of taking Sylvia by surprise and therefore not scaring her off. Howard could easily check into a local hotel if things weren't looking up at his uncle's house.

He was still watching the ocean when he heard footsteps behind him. He turned around, expecting to see Graham, after all. A stranger stood there, though, smiling slightly. Surprised, but not wanting to seem to be up to something, Howard stuck out his hand, salesman-like, and the man immediately shook it very heartily, one big shake before dropping it.

'Mr Jimmers,' the man said, introducing himself. He didn't look happy as he waited for Howard to explain what he was doing there, prowling around the premises. But then he didn't really look like trouble, either. His face was broad and fleshy, like a comical drawing of a gentleman toad, and he had a mess of salt-and-pepper hair. He wore a comfortable-looking wool sweater, a pair of old dungarees, and down-at-heel bedroom slippers, as if he had just been reading by the fire. He was short and squarely built, although not really fat, and might have been sixty or sixty-five.

'Howard Barton,' Howard said. Then there was a silence. 'I'm looking for Mr Graham, actually. I'm from the museum, down south.'

'About the Orientalia?'

'That's right.' Howard was happy at that. The man knew about him. He was expected. 'Roy Barton is my uncle, up in Fort Bragg.' There wasn't much chance that Mr Jimmers would know his uncle, perhaps, but it made Howard sound a little less dubious, his having an uncle in Fort Bragg.

'You don't say! Roy Barton of the spirit museum? The ghostly automobile Barton?'

Howard nodded. Apparently there was no escaping his uncle's reputation.

The look on Mr Jimmers' face suggested that he found the whole business suspicious. He turned his head, fixing Howard with one eye and looking him up and down, as if taking his measure. 'Haven't gone into the shed, have you?' Mr Jimmers drummed his knuckles against the wall of the red and white metal shed. The car must have come very close to taking it out when it went over the cliff. In fact, there was a big crease in the side of the thing, about bumper height. It had a pair of cockeyed sliding doors, half rusted by the weather and secured by a ridiculously big lock. The idea of Howard's having 'gone into' it was foolish, although a burglar with a can opener could have done it in an instant.

'Not me,' Howard said. 'Is Mr Graham at home?'

Mr Jimmers was pretty clearly off his rocker, an eccentric rustic. But despite that, Howard instantly wondered what was in the shed that he wasn't supposed to have meddled with. It sat dangerously close to the crumbling edge of the bluffs, resting up on wooden skids in the weeds. Surely they wouldn't store anything but garden tools in such a run-down shed.

A flurry of raindrops plinked down onto the metal roof, the sound reverberating hollowly inside, and for a moment it sounded as if voices could be heard within – the voices of surprised ghosts, maybe, arguing with each other. It must have been a trick of the echoing raindrops. Abruptly Mr Jimmers squinted at Howard again, as if vaguely surprised and seeing him in a new light. Then, shading his face against the rain, which had already ceased to fall, he turned around on the path and trotted off toward the house, gesturing for Howard to follow.

When they got around to the front, Howard discovered that the truck door on the passenger side was ajar. He pulled the door open and saw that the glove box was open, too, and nearly empty. His paperweight was gone along with almost everything else: a box of fuses and odds and ends of spare change, nuts and bolts, an air gauge, pencils, an unopened package of Mr Zog's surfboard wax, and ten years' worth of useless kipple – most of it completely worthless to whoever stole it. He'd very nearly been cleaned out, although none of it was valuable except the paperweight. They'd left him the brownie and the decals – most of them, anyway; the pelican was gone.

Mr Jimmers held the arched door of the house open, and Howard slammed out of the truck and hurried up the curving walk toward the porch. 'Shoes not allowed,' said Mr Jimmers. Howard took his off and left them by the door, sitting neatly alongside three other pairs.

'Someone stole everything in the glove compartment,' Howard said, 'including a glass paperweight that cost me nearly two hundred dollars. Can you believe that?' It occurred to him for the first time that Mr Jimmers himself was suspect, but he took another look at the man and gave the notion up.

Mr Jimmers wasn't paying attention, though, but was looking out at the evening sky. 'I thought you'd brought rain with you for a moment,' he said, sighing afterward and giving Howard one of his shrewd, sideways glances. 'My advice is to keep your car doors locked. They'll rob you blind – like crows. They've got a fearful appetite for any kind of junk, especially little things. Steal the buttons off your coat if you let them. They go through the local parks carrying paper sacks, picking up all manner of stuff – bottle caps, bits of colored glass, anything they find on the ground. They'll steal your kitchen utensils right off the table, too.'

'Who?' asked Howard.

'The whole damned crowd of them,' Jimmers said, polishing his glasses on his vest. 'They stay away from me, though. I'm a mean outfit, and they know it. "Give Mr Jimmers the road" – that's what they say when they see me coming. "No quarter," that's my motto. It's a good one, too. I recommend it to you. You're from down south, aren't you?'

'That's right,' Howard said, wondering what in the hell the man was talking about and whom he didn't want to give any quarter to. 'Who is it again?'

'Gluers is what they're called. They work a couple of communes back in the woods, up above the fog line. They put out the Sunberry products, natural foods. Very healthful. Always building, too. They built half of this house.' He gestured at the stone walls and the open beamed ceiling. 'They were …

fond of Graham, you might say. Very nearly worshipped him. Looked after him like he was royalty. You won't see much of them, though. They don't come into town much. But leave your car door unlocked and see if they don't rob you blind. They've got a crow's eyesight for any damned kind of bauble and nut.'

'Thanks for the warning,' Howard said.

'Well ...' Mr Jimmers shook his head darkly. 'You've got a lot to learn, my boy. You people from down south ... It's not like that up here. My advice to you is to learn it quick, too, because there's those up here that will give you less quarter than I will. Gluers aren't the worst of them, either. Far from it. You might find friends among them before you're through, depending on who you *really* are. Take me, now. I've got a wooden keg, down in the shop. I toss in any old thing – the odd screw and washer, bent nails, the broken-off heads of tin toys. First Sunday of every other month, starting in January, I leave it out on the meadow. Next morning it's empty. They respect me for that. I'm hard, but I treat them right if they let me.'

Howard nodded. 'I think I see,' he said, although he didn't, really. The heads of tin toys? It wasn't like *what* up here?

Mr Jimmers put a fatherly hand on his shoulder. 'You'll see a lot more before you're done. You can take my affidavit on that. You can put everything you know into your hat, and still have room for the rabbit. And don't for a moment think you can swindle me, either. Did I tell you I was an astronomer? I believe there to be a flat constellation – two-dimensional – made up of five stars in the shape of a chalice. Nobody's made out the shape of it because it's tilted exactly perpendicular to the rotation of the earth. The dog star, Sirius, is at the base, and points the true direction of the celestial mill wheel. There's a cosmic wind, though, that's about to blow it around edgewise, and when it does ...' He shook his head. 'Do you believe me?'

'Of course,' Howard said, thinking to himself that the man was pretty clearly a fourteen-carat loony. Mention of the celestial mill wheel might have thrown Howard pretty hard, except that it was too mixed up with nonsense. That's what was in the shed, probably, the two-dimensional constellation. Mr Jimmers didn't seem dangerous, though. 'Is that your observatory? Out in the shed?' Howard smiled, thinking to humor the man, but realizing too late that what he had said might be taken for an insult.

'What do you know about the shed?' Mr Jimmers asked, suddenly wary. 'Did you go into it?'

'No,' Howard said. 'I don't know anything. Not a thing. I just got here.' The conversation had gone off down a foggy tangent. He decided to take a stab at changing it. 'So where is Mr Graham?' he asked again.

'Dead,' Mr Jimmers replied.

3

'Dead?'

Mr Jimmers nodded seriously and sadly, but still with an air of suspicion, as if to suggest that Howard, maybe, knew more about the business than he was admitting. 'He went over the cliff just a couple of weeks ago. That's his car down on the rocks. A man can't survive such a fall as that. Body was never found. It's my notion that he was thrown clear of the wreckage. Longshore currents probably swept him down south by now. You'd have done better to stay home and waited for *him*.'

Dazed, Howard followed Mr Jimmers into an ill-lit sort of living room. 'You don't have such a thing as a drink around the house, do you?' Howard asked. This was no time for being polite. His stomach was curiously hollow. His plans had been thrown for a loop, and he was somehow certain that his entire life had altered course on the instant.

Mr Jimmers looked a little puzzled about the mention of a drink, as if he couldn't quite see the point in it, but he nodded after a moment and stepped along, disappearing into yet another room. Howard heard the satisfying clink of glass against glass. At least that sounded right to him – almost the only familiar sound he could remember having heard in a week.

The house was cold, with a stone floor and roughly plastered stone walls. Candles guttered in little hollows, making the room look like a shrine, but not lighting it up enough to do any real good. The fireplace was built of stone, too, and clinker brick, and all of it, the whole room, was stony cold, despite the hearty-looking fire. Howard stepped up closer to it, wondering if he could remember which of the stones disguised the cavity where the sketch had been hidden fifteen years past. Nothing was visible, though, no cracked joint or missing mortar.

His feet were nearly frozen, and he held them in front of the fire, wiggling his toes. He would have liked to keep his shoes on or else go out to the truck now for a second pair of socks. It was dark and foggy outside, though, and the truck was invisible through the murk, and there were odd thieves lurking in the woods.

He thought again about the paperweight stolen from the glove box – a two-hundred-dollar lesson. And now Graham was dead, too …

He patted his coat pocket, where he had Graham's letter. Thank God he hadn't left it in the cab of the truck. He half wanted to show it to Mr Jimmers straight off, before the probate courts, or whoever it was, hauled Graham's possessions away and the sketch was forever lost. But then who the hell *was*

Mr Jimmers, anyway? The man was tolerably comfortable there. Or at least he went around with the air of someone who had made himself at home. And then there was the strange business of the shed ... Suddenly Howard wanted very much to get a glimpse inside it – just a little peek.

But that was childish, wasn't it? If he were caught fooling around in either the shed or the fireplace, it might botch up the whole business of the Hoku-sai sketch, which had already gotten pretty shaky. He noticed right then that the walls were full of paintings and photographs and no end of wall hangings of one sort or another. In the dim light it was impossible to make any of them out clearly. Howard stepped over to have a look at a few of them.

Most of what hung on the walls wasn't of any note – reproductions of hunting scenes and of women with flowing hair and dressed in clothes that couldn't have been worn seriously during any historical era. There were some grisly-looking African masks and some wooden puppets and a wall-hung china cabinet crammed full of depression glass. Where in the world was Mr Jimmers? Or more to the point, where was the drink?

He wandered into the next room, taking the direction that Jimmers had taken. This second room was brighter, having an honest-to-goodness electrical lamp burning in it. He wondered what the point of the candles was. Maybe Mr Jimmers was the atmospheric type. He remembered this room all at once – the oriental carpets, the confusion of oak furniture, the wooden chandelier.

There on the wall were three badly framed, collodion photographs, antiques, hanging in a vertical row. He remembered those suddenly, from a class in Pre-Raphaelite photography that he had taken in graduate school. The photos had been taken by John Ruskin – when? 1855? 1860? They were very old, anyway, and, if they were authentic, might be worth a fortune to the right collector. He peered at them, unbelieving. He knew what they were now, although he hadn't known when he saw them years ago – three of Ruskin's Tintern Abbey photographs.

Ten years ago Howard had eyes for nothing but the work of the Pre-Raphaelite Brotherhood, and he had struggled through Ruskin's *The Seven Lamps of Architecture* and his rambling lectures on the Pre-Raphaelites. He was fascinated at least partly by his knowledge that Michael Graham himself was the great-grandson of James Graham, the Pre-Raphaelite photographer. But there had been more to his study than that. John Ruskin had been a curiously enigmatic figure – a sexually impotent genius surrounded by a cabal of artistic zealots who were strangely loyal to him and to his fierce esthetic desire to embody nature in art.

Anyway, it made sense that Michael Graham possessed these photographs. He had probably been willed them. Fancy them having hung on the wall all these years, gathering dust. The house was a treasure trove of collectible stuff.

He was suddenly aware that Mr Jimmers was regarding him from the doorway. He held a glass in one hand and a wine bottle in the other. Howard would rather it was a beer bottle, but right now that didn't seem to matter half as much to him as did the letter in his pocket. 'I was wondering about the Japanese sketch,' Howard said, getting straight down to business. Mr Jimmers knew why he had come; he might as well say what he meant.

'So was I,' Mr Jimmers said. 'What do you know about it?'

'Nothing. Not beyond Mr Graham's having offered it to the museum.' He pulled the letter out of his coat and held it up.

'And you've come up after it, have you? After all this time? What compelled you? Was it greed, or something else? I've always been a student of compulsion, and I see something in your eyes that intrigues me.'

Howard gave him a look that wasn't meant to be intriguing. What was this? Suddenly he was being interrogated. Suspicions were being aired.

'This thievery nonsense,' Mr Jimmers continued, 'this imaginary glass bauble gone from your pickup truck – that could easily be a clever ruse, couldn't it? An effort to throw suspicion elsewhere, to make it look as if you, too, were the victim of these thieves.' He nodded shrewdly and then nodded again in the general direction of the wall. 'It's been stolen, hasn't it?'

'What? My truck?' Howard took a panicked step toward the door before realizing that Mr Jimmers wasn't talking about the truck or the paperweight. He meant the sketch. 'Stolen? When? I've been a week on the road …' Howard found himself speaking in a tone of denial, explaining himself, laying out an alibi.

'A week? Driving up from L. A.? A day would have done it. Eleven hours, say. What if, my mysterious stranger, you've been skulking around up here for days?' Mr Jimmers raised his eyebrows theatrically. 'I'm thinking that you might be the one to shed some light on the business of the missing sketch, and perhaps on poor Graham's murder, too.'

'Murder!' Howard almost shouted.

For the space of twenty seconds Jimmers stared at him, letting the idea soak in. Then suddenly he laughed out loud, bending a little at the waist and slapping his knee. Apparently he had only been fooling, playing a little game with the bumpkin from down south. He was suddenly cheerful. He ran his hand through his hair, frazzling it, and then strode toward Howard, holding out the glass, his face stretched into a toad-like grin.

'Cheer up,' he said. 'You can't trust anyone nowadays, can you? They'll rob you from east to west if they get a chance. "Beard them in their den," that's the byword around here. And if you can't, then beard them somewhere else.' He winked like a conspirator and pulled at the strap of his suspender, letting it snap against his chest. 'Come along upstairs,' he said, taking the bottle and glass with him. 'I've got something to show you.'

Howard wondered if he'd ever get a chance at the wine. He was vastly relieved, though. The sketch must be all right, after all. Mr Jimmers had hidden it upstairs, fearing thieves. The man was a crank, a joker, but he was wily. There was no use getting mad at him or trying to second-guess him. But how about this business about old Graham? *Had* he been murdered? And if he had, why? Who would bother to murder a ninety-year-old?

He followed along up the stairs, winding around past a second-story landing and then onto a third, where there was a stained-glass window looking out into the darkness. The window depicted what might be a wall built of salmon-shaped stones, or else a dry river littered with flopping fish. In front of it lay a broken Humpty Dumpty, and racing down out of the wooded hills beyond were two strangely shaped automobiles, pieced together with delicate ribbons of copper foil and jeweled with bits of faceted glass.

That's where I got the Humpty Dumptys from, Howard thought, relieved just a little bit. He had no doubt seen the window years ago and had carried the Humpty Dumpty around with him since, hiding back in the shadows of his mind. He reminded himself that there was almost always some reasonable, day-today explanation for even the weirdest aspects of one's dreams. The notion satisfied him for about fifteen seconds, and then it occurred to him that this window might just as easily be another mystery and not any sort of explanation at all.

He hadn't any time to study it out, though, because Mr Jimmers opened a door into the attic right then, and leaned in to switch on the light. He stepped back to let Howard into a broad room with exposed rafters and roof sheathing and the undersides of shingles. Two big leaded windows were boxed into the roof, serving as skylights, and there were two more windows in the wall that looked out on the ocean. There was a seven-inch telescope on wheels in the corner and star charts on the wall around it. An oak desk and a couple of comfortable-looking Morris chairs with low footstools sat in the center of the room. Books lined the walls, stacked up sideways and endways and ready to tumble off the edges of shelves. The room was heavy with the smell of pipe tobacco.

'Keep the bottle,' Mr Jimmers said.

'Sorry?' asked Howard, turning around.

Mr Jimmers still stood outside in the hall. He had set the wine bottle and the glass on the floor just inside the room. He waved, wiggling his fingers by his ear, and then shut the door. Howard heard the click of the lock being thrown before he'd taken half a step forward. A tiny panel opened in the door, and Mr Jimmers peered back in. Howard could just see his nose and eyes. 'Ham sandwich suit you?' Mr Jimmers asked.

Howard didn't answer. He stood there mystified and furious.

'Think of this as a credentials check,' Mr Jimmers said. 'Imagine that you've just made a border crossing into eastern Europe and you're being detained while the authorities have a look at your papers. Is everything in order, they wonder, or do we beat him with rubber hoses?'

Laughing, Mr Jimmers shut the panel, and there was the sound of his footsteps descending the stairs. Then there was silence. Howard waited for him, expecting the door to open again at any moment. Certainly this was another joke. Mr Jimmers had a sense of humor that had been honed in outer space.

When the panel opened again, though, ten minutes later, Mr Jimmers clearly wasn't in any mood to let Howard out. He shoved a ham sandwich through the hole, and then a bag of Fritos and a too-ripe banana. Then he poked the corner of a quilt through, and Howard gratefully enough hauled the whole thing into the room, like a magician pulling an immense scarf through the mouth of a tiny bottle. 'Watch the heater,' Mr Jimmers said. 'Might blow a fuse if you're not careful.' Then the panel slid shut and he was gone.

Apparently Howard was being kidnapped. He *had* been kidnapped. That part was over and done. What should he do? Threaten? Scream? Bang against the door with a tin cup? He didn't have a tin cup. And anyway, the entire adventure was so monumentally crazy that he almost certainly didn't see the whole picture yet. Mr Jimmers was up to something subtle. Surely in a few minutes …

He waited, but Mr Jimmers didn't return. The man was gone. Howard *was* kidnapped, shut up in an attic in an old stone house perched on a lonely cliff. Abruptly he was stricken with fear. It washed over him like a sea wave, and he walked across to the door and pounded on it. 'Hey!' he shouted. 'What the hell!' His voice was loud and foreign-sounding, and he immediately fell silent, not liking the noise. He listened, but could hear nothing except the pounding of the waves out on the reefs. He strode back and forth, furious with Jimmers, clenching and unclenching his fists at the utter irrational helplessness of things and wishing in his heart that he was home again, sitting in his own living room with his stereo going. He wondered why on earth he had left; what had possessed him?

He tried shouting again, but it was no good, and after a half hour passed and Mr Jimmers hadn't reappeared, Howard resigned himself to his fate. There was no dignity, anyway, in screaming and flailing and demanding things. His best bet was to play the role of someone utterly confident but getting a little tired of it all. Surely Jimmers wouldn't keep him prisoner long. There was no point to it. But then what point had there been to anything lately? He was starting to feel a little like Alice, lost in a north coast wonderland.

He stood up suddenly and tried the two doors in the east wall. One was a half-full closet; the other was a bathroom with a toilet and a sink. He turned the water on and off. There were soap and a drinking glass on the sink and an electric space heater on the floor, which he pulled out and plugged into the only wall socket he could find. To hell with blowing a fuse; it was better than freezing to death.

The attic was well equipped, anyway. A man could pass many a pleasant month there, what with Mr Jimmers pushing food through the door panel and all. Howard walked hurriedly to the windows, pulling one open. Foggy air blew in, smelling of wet rocks and the ocean. It would be easy enough to slide out through the window, except that it was a hundred and fifty feet to the rocks below. The back edge of the house was a mere continuation of the rocky cliff. In a pinch he could cut the quilt apart, using his teeth, maybe, and fashion a rope ladder. He would contrive to steal a spoon and would sharpen it on the stone walls, devising a weapon. Of course if he were only fed sandwiches, he would never get hold of a spoon ...

He laughed out loud, shutting the window and then wrapping himself in the quilt. This was too bizarre to be believed. He shuffled across to the door. Thank heaven for small comforts, he thought, picking up the wine bottle and examining the label. Almost instantly his spirits plummeted again. 'Wild Blackberry Wine,' it stated proudly, 'Sunberry Farms.' Below that was a Norman Rockwell-like drawing of a woman in a patchwork gown picking blackberries from vines that grew out of the engine compartment of a Studebaker turned into a sort of garden. Roses sprouted from the backseat and daisies grew out of the roof. The fenders were spiked with the suggestive tips of asparagus, thrusting from the tires. A peach tree shoved up out of the trunk, its branches heavy with fruit. Below the drawing was the legend 'Natural and Healthful.'

'Curiouser and curiouser,' Howard said out loud. Then, steeling himself, he tilted the bottle back and tasted the wine. He grimaced and put it back down by the door again, his mouth filled with the sour taste of weeds and unripe berries. Clearly this was another of Jimmers' little gags. This wasn't wine at all; it was some sort of fluid used for polishing pan bottoms.

He went into the bathroom to fill his glass with water. Then he sat down on one of the Morris chairs to think things through. Even then he half believed that the door would swing open and Jimmers would let him out.. His plans had disintegrated at a startling rate, only to be replaced by oddly disconcerting patterns and implications and dreamlike suggestions, and he felt a little like a fish swimming in a dark river and just getting its first startled glimpse of the slowly encircling net. He thought up explanations for Mr Jimmers' behavior, abruptly remembering the oceanic Volkswagen bus and how weirdly compulsive it had seemed. Along with everything else – the stained-glass window, the wine label, the ubiquitous Studebaker, the glove-compartment theft – it argued that the north coast was its own universe, hidden by weather and isolation and mist, and working according to its own set of natural laws. Thinking about it was unsettling.

Years back there had been a lot of serious cult activity along the coast – severed heads perched on guardrail posts, disappeared hitchhikers, blood rituals on deserted beaches. He wondered uneasily what had happened to all of that, whether the cultists had gotten day jobs and were working at the pulp mills now, or whether they were still out there, lurking in the deep woods.

And who *had* stolen the stuff out of his truck? What had Jimmers called them? Gluers? What the hell was that? And when you came right down to it, who was Mr Jimmers? Maybe the high priest of some fungal religion. No, Howard thought. That was unlikely. He was clearly too settled in here, with his books and telescope and all. He had lived here for years, and old Graham wouldn't have put up with any oddball shenanigans from his boarders.

Howard couldn't remember having gone into the attic when he stayed in the house fifteen years ago. Maybe Mr Jimmers had been living here even then, holed up, searching the skies for his unlikely constellation. There had been other boarders at the time, besides him and Sylvia. He remembered an herbalist, very proud of his profession, and the Bay Area artist who drew underground comics – the man Stoat, whom Sylvia had nearly married years later.

Howard hadn't liked the man even then, before Sylvia had anything to do with him, or at least Howard told himself so. He was artsy and theatrical in the worst way. He had worn a single black glove back then and had called himself by a different alias. What the hell was it? Something idiotic. Morc, that was it. Morc of Fomoria. Black Hand Comics. The adventures of the Kings of the Night. He was a Norwegian, tall and blond and handsome – Aryan to a fault.

Besides him and the herbalist, there had been a crowd of standard-issue coastal hippies who worked for Graham as day laborers, coming and going out of the hills and along Highway One. Hadn't one of them driven a car that was glued over with something? Howard searched his memory. Clock parts. That was it – gears and springs and lenses. All manner of dismantled clocks and watches. The hood ornament was a brass sundial.

Thinking of his stay there reminded him of Sylvia – her face mostly. Howard had been timid back then, a tendency that was often mistaken for standoffishness. He wasn't so timid anymore, and couldn't afford to be if his stay in the north coast was going to amount to anything at all. His hanging around Sylvia certainly hadn't amounted to anything, although both of them had agreed on the night he brought her the lily that all was for the best. You didn't carry on with your cousin. Or did you? There wasn't any law against it, strictly speaking.

He realized abruptly that the passing years hadn't settled anything at all, hadn't made anything clear to him. He wondered idly whether she was as pretty now as she had been then, and whether she was still as full of momentary passions. She had been able to find almost anything and anybody interesting and worthwhile – one of those people who were so essentially good and honest that they thought everyone else was, too. Howard always expected to hear that she had bought real estate in a Florida swamp.

Stoat himself had been a sort of Florida swamp, Howard thought. Sylvia was like her father when it came to being gullible. Uncle Roy had been a moderately successful salesman when he was younger because he always believed so completely in whatever he was trying to sell, no matter its flaws. People and things were allowed to have flaws.

Perhaps that's why Howard had always found it so easy to be around Sylvia. She gave him the same break she gave everyone else. Also, she had always made plain things nice, somehow. She was a knockout in thrift-store clothes. He would have flown coast-to-coast to eat the plainest sort of casserole if she had made it. There would have been a flowered tablecloth on the table, and cut flowers, and there wouldn't have been any trace of self-consciousness in any of it, or in her cook-with-honey, mother-nature ways that made the simplest chores seem like a sort of dance. He wasn't the only one who saw her like that, either, and that had bothered him. He had always wished that she was his secret, but she wouldn't submit to being anybody's secret.

Howard sighed. He let his mind spin, feeling a little guilty about dredging up old jealousies and passions. All that was water under the bridge, wasn't it, no matter what he ran into on the north coast? Or who. He got up abruptly and walked across to where the wall plaster was discolored or smudged. It wasn't just a smudge; it was something set into the plaster, its color showing through.

He rubbed at it, curious, and the thin coat of plaster covering it chipped off. Underneath was a small, convex bit of metal, painted red. He hesitated for a moment and then decided that prisoners were allowed, even expected, to chip away at the walls of their cell. Following tradition, he dug around the metal with his pocket knife, discovering it, strangely, to be the fender of a toy car. There were other objects, too, under the curve of the fender, as if the collection were meant to be a tiny shrine.

He cleaned the plaster away carefully, like an archeologist at a dig, exposing first a carven Japanese god. Howard recognized it. It was Dai-Koku, the god of luck, carrying the tools that he used to dig out the treasures of the earth. There was a steel dog, too, out of a Monopoly game, and a clay marble and a little stoppered perfume bottle, stained purple by the sun and containing what looked like a sprig of dried violets.

Hastily he considered what he knew about Michael Graham – not very much, obviously. Plastering these odd miniatures into the wall couldn't have been his work, though, not unless Howard had misjudged him wildly. Graham hadn't been frivolous in any way at all. He worked from sunup to sundown, ate plain food, read his Bible, went to sleep. Howard had seen him fish once, off the rocks in the cove, but that seemed to have been the only lighthearted sort of activity he allowed himself. There was no way on earth that he would have been so full of momentary fun as to plaster toys up in a wall.

And if they hadn't been so near the surface, they would have remained hidden forever, until the house fell down. They weren't meant as decoration; they were meant as something else entirely.

Howard ran his hand across the wall below them, suspicious that there might be more buried there. There was a suggestive bump, and immediately he chiseled away at it, scraping the plaster off in a little dusty cloud. Underneath, still half hidden, were the red-glazed soles of Humpty Dumpty's shoes.

4

There was something about lilies that was attractive to Heloise Lamey – their heavy, fleshy flowers, perhaps, or the way the flower stalks thrust up through the earth, reminding her of a certain kind of lush scene in a D. H. Lawrence novel, although she would never admit this to anyone. They were easily susceptible to mutation, too, and color alteration. Their odor, when they had any, was most often intense and repulsive, as if they were dense with the stuff of decay, of excretion and death.

Her front-yard garden was laid out in orderly rows. It wasn't the sort of garden she would have chosen to lay out if she were gardening for the mere enjoyment of it. She did almost nothing, though, for the mere enjoyment of it. She had come over the years to lead a life of purpose, void of mere entertainment.

Across the street, nailed to the roof of a house, sat a plywood Humpty Dumpty the size of a man. It was still and inanimate in the windless morning – a small blessing. Onshore breezes would stir it up in the afternoon, and it would undertake its eternal waving, along with all the other wind-driven gewgaws in her neighbor's front lawn. Movement for the sake of movement, that's what it was. His wooden gizmos had no object that she could fathom, other than simply to drive her mad. They were utterly frivolous. She would contrive to deal with them, though, and with him, sooner or later.

For the moment she concentrated her energies on her garden, which was a geometric copy, row for row, of the vegetable garden planted somewhere by her half brother, Michael Graham, a man with an authentic green thumb. Lord knew where his garden lay. She hadn't actually seen it, just as she hadn't ever seen his garden at the cliff house. But she had understood the design of that garden, too. She had felt it in her joints, as a person with arthritis feels pending rain. She had never felt it so clearly, though, as she had since her recent trip to San Francisco.

She had planted eight rows of flowers, all hybrid tubers and bulbs. There was still more to plant. On her porch sat a half dozen pots of dye, all of it mixed up out of things of the earth – berries and roots, autumn leaves and iron filings and blood. Two sea hares nosed around in a bucket of clear ocean water. She had hauled them out of a tidal pool a half hour ago. Carefully she picked one of them up, holding it by the head over a clean glass bowl, and began to squeeze it, gingerly at first and then harder when it wouldn't give up its ink. A rush of viscous, vivid-purple fluid gushed out into the bowl. She let it drip for a moment, then tossed the creature into a clean ceramic jar. She picked up the second sea hare and milked it of its ink, too, pitching it into the jar along with the first.

Then, very carefully, she unstoppered a jar of hydrochloric acid, sizzling the liquid in over the writhing bodies of the two sea hares. Within moments they were still, their soft flesh disintegrating in the shallow pool of acid. She had no idea at all what would come of cooking the two creatures down, but the acid was already turning an interesting color of greenish brown. Traces of the purple ink trailed out of the things, deepening the color nicely.

Nearby lay the two forearm bones she had brought back from San Francisco. When she told the Reverend White, very truthfully, that she was going to turn them into a dowsing rod, he had shrugged. He hadn't understood it, but he knew her too well to doubt her. The bones were connected now at the elbow end, lashed together with strips of animal hide and ivy vine. He had supplied some of the animal hide, too – the more interesting fragments – although necessarily in strips too small to do any real tying up. She had contrived to weave them into the lashings, though, along with the rest. The result wasn't pretty, and for a week it had smelled worse than almost anything she could think of, but the awful smell had faded as the object dried out.

Picking up the V-shaped dowser, she limped into a clear spot in the garden, focusing her concentration on the earth, on dirt and humus and worms and percolating rainwater. She closed her eyes and pictured the symphony of movement in the soil – roots unfurling, creeping downward; billions of grains of earth shifting, settling, giving way; rock decomposing; leaves and dead roots rotting; seeds opening and pushing toward the surface; ants and moles and gophers and earthworms creeping along in the darkness; the entire surface of the dry world stirring, crawling, heaving with motion just as steadily and surely as the surface of the sea.

The tip of the dowser bent downward, drawn toward the soil, twisting in her hands so that she could barely hold on to it. 'Cabbages,' she said out loud. It was as if she had seen them herself, like slide film played against the back of her eyelids. He had put out cabbages. She opened her eyes and swayed there, nearly losing her balance and blinded by the bright sunlight. With an effort she managed to clear her mind, bringing herself back around to her own garden. She marked the spot with a piece of stick, and then using the dowser again, she traced out the row, some twelve feet of it, wondering what to plant there, what sort of maleficent vegetation might wither his cabbages.

She worked by instinct. Someday soon she would know where his garden was hidden, where *he* was hidden, and she would have a look at her handiwork. It struck her as funny that she was engaged in a vegetable war, probably the first in the history of the world. It was a war she must ultimately win. He was old and feeble and dying, and his power was dying with him.

She fetched a trowel from the porch and began to dig holes in the dirt, humming now and laying a tuber in the bottom of each. A sea breeze ruffled her hair, and she scowled, looking without wanting to at the thing on the roof across the street. Its plywood arm caught a gust and slowly straightened out in a long, sardonic salute, jerking upright in order to repeat the gesture, probably over and over for the rest of the afternoon. She hummed louder, drowning out the world, pausing to pour sea hare ink over each tuber in turn and then filling in the holes with dirt.

Howard woke up stiff. Sleeping on the Morris chair had required a certain degree of exhaustion, and it had taken him half the night to attain it. He had slept hard in the early hours of the morning, though, and now he felt disheveled and drooly and wrinkled, and his neck was kinked and stiff.

Abruptly he knew what had awakened him – his name had been called. A key rattled in the lock, the door swung open, and there stood Mr Jimmers and, for God's sake, Sylvia. Howard pulled himself up and hurriedly wiped his face and ran his hands through his hair. He unwrapped himself from the quilt and stood up, the pain in his spine nearly arching him over backward. 'Sylvia!' he said, trying to sound cheerful and robust but actually just croaking. He tried to clear his throat. Like a proud father, Mr Jimmers stood beaming at Sylvia, the look on his face seeming to assure Howard that although he had waited a long time for this moment, the wait must clearly have been worth it.

He was right. Sylvia seemed not to have aged. Her skin had the same pale cast to it, almost a translucence, and her hair was full and dark and an absolute sculptured mess. She wore red lipstick, too, which was gaudy, but right at the moment she seemed custom-built for gaudy, even though it wasn't what Howard remembered or expected. And her eyes were larger than he remembered them, too. She reminded him of a woman out of a Rossetti painting, modernized with twentieth-century makeup and natural, handmade-looking clothes. She would have looked terrific even in a flour sack or a mu-mu. Almost laughing at him, she said, 'You look awful.'

'Do I?' he managed to say. He was flattered, somehow, that she would say such a thing to him, willing to joke around when they hadn't seen each other or even spoken in years. He tried to think of a way to quit looking awful, but there wasn't any.

'Utterly awful. It's my fault that you had to sleep in a chair all night, too. Mr Jimmers couldn't get through to me until this morning, because I was out late. He said that he had a man locked into the attic who might be a thief and murderer but claimed to be my cousin. We didn't expect you until the end of the week, actually.'

'I got impatient. Solitude wears you out after a while.'

'And you've had years of it, haven't you? No wonder you look like you do.' She smiled at him, clearly assuming that his sense of humor had held up. She might easily have seen him last week, It was as if there were nothing about him that she had forgotten, which either was a good thing or wasn't. Howard wasn't awake enough to tell yet, but he remembered that this was another reason he had never gotten rid of his memories of her.

He dropped the quilt and managed a smile. He was a fairly ridiculous sight. The whole adventure in the attic was funny as hell if you looked at it right, through the Sylvia spectacles, so to speak. He realized that he was staring at her, and he looked away, bending over suddenly to pick up the quilt from the chair. He folded it carefully.

'And I'm awfully sorry about all this,' Mr Jimmers said to Howard. 'There's been dirty work recently, though, what with Mr Graham going off the cliff and all. Things along the north coast are ... unsettled, you might say, and your sudden appearance, I'm afraid, was fraught with suspicion. I hope you forgive me.'

'Sure,' said Howard. 'Not at all. Of course I do.' Forgiving him was easy all of a sudden. He was a friend of Sylvia's, after all. Howard wondered exactly how he was a friend of Sylvia's, and whether he could use that friendship to pry the sketch out of Jimmers. This was no time for that sort of selfish thinking, though. He would tackle Mr Jimmers some other time. He'd had enough of the man for the moment.

Mr Jimmers hurried across the room just then and pulled the plug on the space heater, looking skeptically at the frayed cord. He threw open one of the windows. 'Close in here,' he said, wrinkling up his face. Then he caught sight of the chiseled wall, blinked at it in surprise, started to say something, and fell silent. He picked up Howard's pocket knife, which still lay open on the desk. 'Burrowing out through the wall?' he asked, gesturing at the hacked plaster. Sylvia looked at it, seeming mildly surprised. 'This man is a curious man,' Mr Jimmers said to Sylvia. 'You must always be a tiny bit vigilant around a man who suspects that things are hidden in the walls.' He closed the knife and handed it across carefully.

Sylvia peered more closely at the plaster now. 'Things *are* hidden in the walls,' she said to Mr Jimmers.

'I wonder if this man didn't put them there himself,' Jimmers said.

'I ... Of course I didn't. How would I have done that?' Howard found himself fumbling again. Mr Jimmers couldn't seem to stop pummeling him with nonsense.

Jimmers shrugged, as if he would believe Howard mainly out of politeness. 'Well,' he said. 'I'm nearly certain that you *would* have put them there, if you'd been given half a chance. Don't you think so, Sylvia?'

'Of course he would have. So would I. I think right now, though, that I have to get back to the shop. Some of us have to work. Where are you going?' she asked Howard.

'Why ... I thought I'd drive up to Uncle Roy's,' he said. 'Up to your place. You're still there, I guess.'

She nodded.

He felt a little like he was inviting himself, despite his having sent the letter telling them that he was coming – which is to say, the letter inviting himself.

'It isn't any sort of palace,' she said.

'I don't need a palace, really. I'm not the palace type.'

'You never were,' she said, and she stepped across and kissed him on the cheek in a sisterly way. 'Father is a little down on his luck right now. He's not what you'd call solvent. I think you two will hit it off, though.'

Howard couldn't remember a time when Uncle Roy *wasn't* down on his luck. He was a *businessman* – something that he would tell you proudly, making the word sound less generic than it really was. But as a businessman he was a spectacular failure. He had done moderately well as a salesman when he was younger, then managed to force a living out of the pet store trade for a few years. But then he had sold the business and borrowed heavily to open the spirit museum, which had cooked his goose financially.

'I want to help out,' Howard said. 'I haven't done anything for the last two years but squirrel money away.'

'Father isn't fond of charity,' Sylvia said flatly. 'I wouldn't bring it up to him.'

'I didn't mean that. I meant that I don't want to mooch off him or anything.'

Mr Jimmers appeared to be uncomfortable listening to the two of them talk. He edged toward the door, as if to hurry things along. It was checkout time for Howard.

Sylvia beamed her smile at him again and fingered the quartz crystal that hung around her neck on a copper chain. 'Duty calls,' she said, turning to leave. 'Can you find the house all right?'

'Sure,' Howard said. 'No problem. I've got the address.' Suddenly he wanted nothing more than to be out of there – out of the attic and out of the house. He wanted elbowroom and space to think, to rearrange what he knew about the world. He realized that his shirt was half untucked, so he shoved it back in, excusing himself and heading for the door of the bathroom. Mr Jimmers went out, following Sylvia, and when Howard appeared downstairs a few moments later, Mr Jimmers asked him if he wanted breakfast. 'My hospitality hasn't been worth much so far,' he said, looking abruptly downcast. 'I'm a scientist, in my way, an inventor, and I'm afraid that I overlook the niceties sometimes. I live rough, you see, with no one to care for but myself ...'

This was a new Mr Jimmers. Howard hadn't thought of that. It must be terribly lonely, living out on the deserted bluffs like this. And now with Graham dead, maybe murdered, Mr Jimmers was alone and pretty clearly frightened of strangers, and rightfully so.

'I'm afraid that all I've got are these cans of chop suey,' Mr Jimmers said, hauling one of them out of the cupboard. 'You can scramble them up with eggs. It's not bad, actually, on toast. Pity we don't have any toast. The sandwiches last night were the end of the bread. I've got salt, though. I don't eat breakfast myself. It runs my metabolism ragged, breakfast does. I take a cup of Postum, actually, with hot water out of the tap in order to flush the system.'

'Thanks,' said Howard, trying to sound sincere. 'I've got to get up to Fort Bragg, though. I'm not a breakfast man, either.'

Jimmers put the chop suey away. 'Cup of Postum, then?'

Howard held up a restraining hand. 'System's fine. I'll just run, I think. The ham sandwich last night was tip-top, though.'

'You're too kind,' said Jimmers, ushering him through the room with the fireplace and out toward the front door, where Howard fetched his shoes back. Having sat outside through the foggy night, they felt damp and sticky to the touch. The truck heater would dry them. 'Goodbye, then,' said Mr Jimmers, starting to close the door as soon as Howard stepped out onto the front stoop. 'Nice of you to drop by.'

The sky was clear and blue and the air was cold. Out over the ocean the fog lay like a gray blanket, but it was a long way off. The day would be a warm one, and Howard was almost cheerful, anticipating breakfast in Fort Bragg. He went around to the camper door, thinking to throw his jacket into the back. On the window, dead center, was the pelican decal. These were *gluers*, all right, just like Jimmers had said. They'd stolen the damned decal and then stuck it onto the first window they'd come to. Oh, well, Howard thought. That's pretty much where he would have put it, anyway. They'd saved him the work.

After a moment he drove away north, mulling over the last twenty-four hours. Mr Jimmers had told him nothing. *Had* the sketch been stolen? Or had Mr Jimmers put it somewhere for safekeeping? Is that what he had in the mysterious tin shed? Howard hoped not. The thing wouldn't be worth hanging in an incinerator after a week outdoors in a misty climate like this. You might as well throw it in the ocean. Howard would have to deal with Mr Jimmers again soon. He would get Uncle Roy to help him. Maybe he could fake up some sort of story about the museum paying a commission so as to be able to slip poor old Uncle Roy a couple of hundred dollars. He'd have to be canny about it, though.

He thought momentarily about being trapped in the attic last night, how he had been scared half witless and then had been furious with Jimmers. It still wasn't funny. Not really. But it wasn't a matter for the police, either. There was too much that he didn't understand, too much mystery hovering on the fog. Maybe he was done with it; maybe not. He would ask Sylvia, appeal to her inherent honesty. Sylvia wasn't the cipher that Jimmers was.

Sylvia. Things had started off unevenly there. It seemed to him suddenly that he had made an off-key, Blinky the Clown impression on Sylvia. On an impulse he sucked his stomach in a little and sat up straighter, regarding himself in the mirror. He wasn't hopeless, anyway. His face was still pretty lean. Some people developed moon faces when they gained weight, but he had never had that problem. He had a rapid-fire metabolism that let him eat anything at all without regret, and he took that to be a sign of good health. At times, when he really overdid it, he developed a moderate spare tire, which, unless it got out of hand, was easy to hide. At least the north coast beaches didn't lend themselves to sunbathing. He could keep his shirt on and his stomach pulled in.

Maybe he would start jogging again, too. And no more junk food, either – no doughnuts or Twinkies. It would be a new regime, the Sunberry Farms approach, starting after breakfast, which he'd eat in Fort Bragg and which would consist of a hell of a stack of pancakes. An hour a day chopping wood for Uncle Roy wouldn't hurt him any, either. He would earn his keep is what he would do. He rolled down the window and inhaled hugely. The air was full of the ocean and the musty smell of autumn vegetation. He was surprised at how good he felt, despite having been tortured in an attic. It was a brand-new day.

Maybe he'd be better off if the Hoku-sai *were* gone. It would almost sever his connection with the museum. Over the past week the sketch had become a sort of carrot on a stick. Its having disappeared would free him, wouldn't it? If he managed to get hold of it, he'd have to haul it back down south, out of duty, and actually put together the display of Japanese artwork that he'd been mouthing off about. He had worked hard at selling the idea to Mrs Gleason, although now he didn't know quite why. The museum seemed a long, long way off. If he walked back into it today, it would seem utterly alien to him. Before long he would forget where the paper clips were kept and how the coffee-maker worked. Maybe he had come north to stay, and he was just now realizing it.

He flicked sand out of the corner of his eye, which looked almost unnaturally blue because of the reflection of the sky in the rearview mirror. His hair was cooperating, too. It was a little long, but what the hell. He would have to shave, though. His beard, when he tried to grow one years ago, had looked like something bought cheap at a swap meet. It was getting gray, too – a constant blow to the vanity, and a reminder that the years were flying past, that he was older now. The thought sobered him just a little, and suddenly he was cold from the sea wind blowing in through the open window.

He passed the first turnoff into Mendocino and looked back into town, and there was Sylvia standing next to a yellow Toyota parked at the gas station. In an instant he lost sight of her. That's where her store was, on Main Street in Mendocino. He had heard all about her opening it up, running it on a shoestring, half her stuff selling on consignment. On impulse he turned back down Lansing Street, driving toward Main.

The gas station was empty now, which was just as well. He didn't really want her to see him and think he was skulking around, spying on her. He was just curious about her shop, about what her life had become during the years that he hadn't known her. He drove slowly down Main, surprised at the number of cars on the street. It was as if Mendocino had become a sort of shoppers' amusement park. There was the yellow Toyota, parked along the curb. He slowed, wondering which store was hers. Too many of them qualified as 'boutiques.'

Suddenly there she was, standing on the sidewalk in front of an ice cream store. She saw him and widened her eyes, starting to wave, actually looking happy and surprised to see him. Howard grinned, made a waving gesture of his own, and then looked away stupidly, pretending he was just passing through. He would have stopped, to explain to her that he was curious to see what she was up to, to thank her for having come to rescue him from the clutches of Mr Jimmers. But he couldn't. Standing next to her, shaking his head and gesturing, was a tall, blond man, nicely dressed, fit-looking. He didn't wear a single black glove anymore, but Howard knew who he was.

'Shit,' Howard said out loud, mad at himself for having been so utterly incapable of dealing with things. Intending to circle back toward the highway, he turned right down Albion and nearly drove straight into an oncoming car. The driver honked, shouting incoherently out the window. Shaking, Howard pulled to the shoulder, staring in disbelief at the roof of the house across the street. Fixed to the shingles, gazing placidly down at him, was a tremendous wooden egg man with a by-now familiar face. After a moment the thing waved at him. Howard drove slowly away, looking back at it once in the rearview mirror just to make sure he hadn't imagined it.

His hands shook on the steering wheel, and not entirely from the near accident. He had never before felt so cut adrift, so entirely out of his element and broken off from everything he was familiar with. He had fallen among pod people. Yesterday he had whistled a tune while he fed that pelican his fish bait and then innocently followed it up the coast. He possessed dependable road maps drawn up by the Triple A. And in his pocket, folded like a passport, was a signed letter from Michael Graham. The headlights on his truck were new and so was the battery. He had the receipt from the Pep Boys to prove it.

So what the hell had happened? He had apparently turned up the highway to Loonyville by mistake, because he was watching the pelican instead of the road map. His worries and his troubles hadn't vanished into the landscape, after all; they had merely taken new faces, and for a few idle days they had been harder to see because of the shifting shadows of north coast vegetation. He watched the cars whiz past on the highway, thinking that with a flick of his hand he could trip the right-turn blinker instead of the left and simply go home.

Opening the nearly empty glove compartment, he pulled out the Sunberry brownie, unwrapped it, and bit the corner off, unprepared for the dirt-and-ground-weeds taste of the thing. There was nothing at all in the flavor that suggested food. Even the pelican wouldn't eat such a brownie. He bundled it back up in plastic wrap and dropped it onto the floorboards. This was it – the last insult he would take. He had half a mind to drive back into town and throw the brownie at Stoat, take him straight out of the contest.

He had a pretty good picture all of a sudden of the way things had fallen out in Mendocino. A week ago Michael Graham had heard Howard's engine start up, way down in Orange County. 'Let's move,' he had said to Jimmers. 'Break out the Humpty Dumptys.' He had tottered to his feet, leaning heavily on his cane, and as one last arcane joke, he had made his way out to the garage, climbed into the old Studebaker, released the hand brake, and rolled straight off the cliff into the sea. Like the faithful subject he was, Jimmers had waited Howard out, watching through the window, giggling over the idea of giving the high sign to the gluer boys and then locking Howard into the attic, feeding him on old bananas and on wine fermented out of root mulch by the selfsame lunatics who had robbed him, finally staging the rescue by Sylvia at precisely the moment that Howard, slumped into his attic chair, had begun to drool and snore. But that hadn't been the end of it. Howard had driven off happily enough despite it all, and what had Jimmers done? He had called Stoat, probably on a car phone. 'Here he comes,' Jimmers had said. 'Comb your hair, for God's sake, and get out there onto the sidewalk.'

There was something deep going on. Howard could see that much even if he couldn't yet make out the shape of it. He watched the smoke billowing like overweight ghosts out of the Georgia-Pacific mills on the edge of Fort Bragg and realized that he was hungry. Maybe that's the trouble, he said to himself. He would attempt the patented pancake cure.

Right then, flapping its big, fateful wings, a pelican flew overhead, perpendicular to the highway, and Howard immediately turned down Harbor Drive, in order to follow it, admitting out loud that he was a born sucker.

He pulled into the parking lot of a restaurant called the Cap'n England, stopping alongside an old stake-bed truck and climbing out, noticing with a start that a waxwork dummy with a staved-in head sat on the truck bed, leaning tiredly against a half dozen cinder blocks. 'Me, too,' its face seemed to be saying to him as it looked sadly out at Howard from between the slats, its hair clotted with fake blood and one of its eyeballs dangling from tendrils of stretched putty. Howard gaped at it for a moment, surprised to discover that he wasn't at all surprised. Of course, he said to himself. It was the sort of thing you came to expect after a day on the coast. Locking the door of his truck, he went inside to eat.

5

Uncle Roy's house lay at the end of Barnett Street, backing up against a fir grove that seemed to run on forever, up into the hills. It was a tumbledown Victorian that needed paint. Pieces of its gingerbread trim had cracked and fallen apart over the years, and here and there bits of it were broken off or hanging by rusted nails. Someone had started to patch the place up, sanding and repairing the wooden fretwork, but the work was sketchily done, a long time ago by the look of it, and the rickety two-by-four scaffolding nailed to the west side of the house where some-one had once been scraping eaves had turned gray in the weather. The yard was brown and overgrown, with old yellowed newspapers, still in their rubber bands, lying discarded in the weeds.

Howard shut the motor off and sat there. He was still full of pancakes and bacon, and he had managed that morning to wash and dry a load of clothes. All his errands were finished. He had arrived at his destination, ready to knock on Uncle Roy's door and introduce himself – the long-lost nephew from down south. He felt relieved at last. He was among family again, and as run-down as the house was, there was something comfortable in the very notion that it was a shelter from the crazy hailstorm that had been pounding him since yesterday afternoon.

He eyed the house a moment longer, slowly changing his mind about it. It didn't just look run-down, he decided – it looked haunted. Uncle Roy could have opened *it* up as a spirit museum and no one would have scoffed. Ragged lace curtains blew out of an open upstairs window, and on the front porch a willow rocker tilted slowly backward, then slowly forward. Somewhere, around in back maybe, a door slammed shut in the wind. The neighborhood was quiet otherwise – empty of people.

Howard climbed out of the truck, leaving his suitcase for the moment, and stepped up the front walk to the wooden porch, where the paint in front of the door had long since been trodden away. He knocked hard. There was no use being timid about it. The door creaked open slowly on its own; there was no one there. Inside lay a dark room of heavy, shadowy furniture. Beyond the entryway stood a turned newel post at the bottom of a stairs. There was a brass lamp fixed to the top of the post – the head of a dog with illuminated glass eyes.

Howard waited, wondering who had opened the door. No one appeared. He knocked again on the casing. Maybe the door hadn't been latched, and he'd knocked it open himself. It hadn't felt like that, though; the door was too heavy. Beside him, the rocking chair creaked in the breeze. 'Hello,' he said, although not too loud. There was something hushed and still about the place, as if it were abandoned. It wasn't a place for shouting.

The first notes of somber organ music drifted down from upstairs somewhere, and there was a sudden banshee wail, distant and tormented like the sound of something muffled in a locked closet. A faint patch of gauzy brightness lit the stairs, and for a moment someone seemed to be standing there, halfway up. It was a woman in a lacy dress or shroud, her hands held out in supplication, her eyes wide with a sort of horrified passion.

Howard found himself backpedaling into the yard. His heart chugged like an engine. The door of the house slammed shut, and laughter echoed out of an upstairs window – the deep and throaty stage laughter common to ghosts with a sardonic sense of humor. Heavy chains rattled and the laughter turned to a tormented moaning. Then there was the amplified scratch of a needle scraping across a phonograph record, followed by a curse. 'Damn it!' a voice said.

A head appeared through the lace curtains of the window just then. It was Uncle Roy, with a face like a melon. Howard hadn't remembered him as being fat. 'Nephew!' he shouted, then knocked the top of his head on the window frame. '*Damn* it!' he said again. 'Don't stand in the yard. Come in!'

He disappeared, and Howard climbed the porch stairs again, happy and puzzled. Clearly Uncle Roy had been expecting him. Home at last, he said to himself, and nearly laughed out loud. Again the door opened, but it was his uncle this time, rubbing his head. He pumped Howard's hand, dragging him into the house and turning on a light, cheering the place up considerably.

'What did you think of it?' Uncle Roy asked.

'Very impressive,' Howard said. 'The woman on the stairs did the trick. Knocked me right back onto the lawn.'

'Cheesecloth. You drape a few single layers of it across the stairs and then play a bit of film across it from a projector. You don't get much of an image, but then you don't want much of an image, do you?'

'Not for a ghost, no. That one was about right.'

'It's the *effect* that's paramount here. You either have it or you don't – effect or nothing. I've learned that from studying business. I've got rubber bats, too, on pulleys, and a skeleton from the university in Sonoma. And look at this.' Howard followed him into the kitchen. Uncle Roy climbed onto a step stool and pulled open a high cupboard, hauling down a jar. 'Eyeballs,' he said. 'Honest-to-God eyeballs in alcohol.'

'Really?' Howard looked at the bizarre things. They were eyeballs, all right, of various sizes, clearly not all taken from the same sorts of creatures. 'What are you going to do with them?'

'Game of marbles between corpses. I've got a couple of waxwork dummies on their hands and knees. They're obvious corpses – hair all grown out and stringy, skin like a burn victim, ragged old suits of clothes ...'

'Really?' Howard said. 'I think I met one of them this morning.'

His uncle nodded at him, apparently not finding the idea crazy in any way. 'The trick is to have them shooting eyeballs into a ring drawn in blood. Very nice effect again. Repellent, too. Makes the public veer off, I can tell you, when they see the eyeballs. They'll pay you for it, though, and come back again and pay you some more. There's nothing the public won't pay for if you trick it out in the right kind of hat.' He put the jar back into the cupboard and shut the door.

Howard reconsidered the notion of the spirit museum as a 'study in the paranormal.' He had been led to believe that his uncle was serious about the ghost business, that the museum had failed because he refused to ham it up with waxwork corpses and projected dead women. He had stuck by the Studebaker because it was true and right. Now here was Uncle Roy, loaded with tomfoolery and with a jar full of eyeballs in the cupboard.

'My boy,' Uncle Roy said, turning to him suddenly and grabbing his hand again. Howard felt like the prodigal son, guilty for having stayed away so long. 'How is your poor mother?'

'Very well, actually. She's feeling absolutely fine. Happy, I think.'

Uncle Roy shook his head, as if Howard had said she was living in the street – on a grate, maybe, with her possessions in a bag. 'I'm certain she never recovered from your father's death. None of us did. He was my brother, after all. He had his faults, but …' He looked at Howard suddenly, as if reading his face. 'In a way it was lucky you were so young. I don't mean it's easy growing up without a father, but sometimes it's harder on an older child, one who's come to know his father. I tried in my way to make up for it, at least until we moved up here. Can you ever do enough, though?'

Howard nodded, surprised at his uncle talking like this. Uncle Roy was obviously sincere, and Howard was moved by it. He hadn't expected this. 'I know you did,' he said. It was true, too. It was Uncle Roy that had taken him to ball games and driven him to the beach and told him jokes and winked at him covertly on serious occasions. Now he sensed that his uncle doubted all that. He had clearly been worrying, maybe for years, that he ought to have done more for Howard. On impulse, Howard put his arms around his uncle's shoulders and hugged him, and after an awkward moment Uncle Roy hugged him back, wiping at his eyes afterward and sighing heavily. 'Time passes,' he said.

'That's the truth.' Howard sat down in a stuffed chair. 'You don't look much different, though.'

'I'm a fat man now,' Uncle Roy said. 'I used to be fit. There was a time when I could work like a pig in the sun, all day long, and then get up the next morning and start in again. You remember those days.'

Howard nodded.

'About your mother, though? How is she? Her letters sound melancholy sometimes – between the lines, if you follow me.'

'No, really,' Howard said. 'She's doing well – working at the library, actually, putting together stock for the new bookmobile.' Uncle Roy put his hand on Howard's arm, to console him, perhaps. Conversation fell flat. 'Sorry just to stop past early like this,' Howard said, changing the subject after a moment's silence. 'I didn't mean to surprise anybody, but—'

'Not at all. We got your letter and all. This is no surprise. Sylvia called up this morning and said she'd found you in Jimmers' attic, tied into a chair. That damned Jimmers … It gave me plenty of time to set up the woman on the stairs, though. How long can you stay?'

Howard shrugged. 'My plans aren't definite yet. I don't want to put you out …'

Uncle Roy waved the idea into oblivion.

'Do you know this Mr Jimmers?' Howard asked, anxious to get on to new subjects. 'I'm not sure I understand him. Tied into a chair, did she say?'

'Jimmers is a case. Completely sideways, if you know what I mean. He'll be coming when the rest of the world is going. Did he tell you about his tin shed?'

'A little,' Howard said uncertainly.

'What did you think of the door opening all by itself?' Uncle Roy broke into another grin.

Howard tried to fathom it, to recall one of Jimmers' doors opening all by itself. Did he mean the door of the shed?

'Sorry ...' he started to say. Then he caught on – he meant the front door of Uncle Roy's house, just five minutes ago. 'I give. How did you do it?'

Uncle Roy opened the refrigerator door and bent over to haul something out – a pickle bottle full of severed fingers, maybe. 'Mechanics. Leave it at that. What did you study in school?'

'Art history, mostly. Some literature.'

'Both worthless. Can't earn a living with them. Don't know anything about magnetism, do you? "The country that controls magnetism controls the earth." Who said that?'

Howard shook his head again. 'I don't know.'

'Diet Smith. I thought you read literature. Sandwich?'

'No, actually. Thanks, anyway, but I just ate breakfast.'

'Not down at the Jersey Deli?'

'No, someplace down at the harbor. Captain somebody.'

'That would be the Cap'n England. Owner's a pal of mine. Not a bad breakfast. Skip the Jersey Deli, though. It's last year's grease. I got a spoiled egg in there once that nearly killed me. Location's bad, too. They'll be out of business inside the year, just like the last nine jackasses that opened up there. Anyone can see it. Location is paramount.' Uncle Roy slathered mayonnaise on two slices of white bread and heaped on six or eight layers of packaged cold cuts. 'Pickle?' he asked, unscrewing the lid from a jar full of kosher dills.

Somehow the eyeballs were too fresh in Howard's mind. 'No thanks. You go to town, though. Do it justice.'

'It's early for lunch, but my life doesn't run according to schedule, if you know what I mean. No liquor before four, though. Can't have your vices wear you down. They've got to be harnessed, controlled. "Every excess carries within it the seed of its own decay." Sigmund Freud said that, when he was sober. The rest of what he said was dope talking. Have you read psychology?'

'Not much, I'm afraid.'

'Good man.' He walked back out into the living room and sat down heavily in a chair, sighing deeply, as if he'd been at it since dawn and was only now getting a rest. His jacket, which years ago might have fit him, was too tight now – a shabby tweed coat bunched tight under his arms and with the buttons in opposite hemispheres. He wore baggy cotton trousers with it and a pair of scuffed penny loafers that actually had pennies wedged in under the leather bands. He worked at his sandwich in silence.

'Hey,' Howard said, suddenly remembering. 'I ran into another friend of yours down in Albion. Wait a sec.' He went out the door, hurrying to the truck. Uncle Roy's talk of being sober had reminded him of the beer, which he had iced up down at the laundromat. He pulled the six-pack out of the cooler, locked the camper door, and went back in. 'It's a gift from Cal, at the Albion grocery. He said to tell you to stop in sometime.'

'That old horse thief,' Uncle Roy said, jiggling with laughter. 'He used to tell the damned stupidest jokes.' After a moment's thinking he said, 'What do they get when they cross an ape and a mink?'

Howard shook his head.

'A hell of a coat, but the sleeves are too long.' Uncle Roy laughed twice, slapping his knee hard. Then he cut it off, nearly choking on his sandwich. 'Beer?' he asked, yanking a Coors out of the six-pack. He pulled the pop top and took a long swallow.

'No thanks,' Howard said. 'I'm full of coffee and pancakes.'

'Normally I don't drink before four, like I said. But I don't look a gift horse in the mouth, either. There's bad luck in that.'

Howard acknowledged that there was. His uncle finished the first beer, bent the can in half with his hands, then stomped it flat on the rug and opened a second can.

'It *has* been a while,' he said finally, smoothing his hair down, although it was already straight and smooth and combed flat across the crown of his head, where the hair was thin. Getting fat had given his face a jolly and genial man-in-the-moon look, which was perfect for him.

Howard nodded. 'Nearly fifteen years.'

'That long? No! Really? I always wondered about you and Sylvia. Did something happen there? Is that what's kept you away?'

'No, nothing, really.' He blushed despite himself. He was talking to Sylvia's father, after all, and his own uncle to boot. It didn't matter what he told himself about Sylvia, the truth had a way of making itself known. 'You know how that is,' he said. 'Four or five hundred miles might as well be a million. You write, you quit writing. There's no excuse for it really, and no reason, either.' He gestured uneasily.

Uncle Roy and Aunt Edith had come to live in Los Angeles after Howard's father died. Howard and Sylvia had been toddlers then, and for the next eighteen years had been down-the-street neighbors. Then his uncle and aunt had moved north to Fort Bragg, where life was less expensive and where, his uncle had been fond of saying, a man could carve his niche. Uncle Roy had done that, in his way, although it was a strangely shaped niche.

'What about all of you?' Howard asked. 'How's Aunt Edie?'

'She's well.' Uncle Roy jerked his thumb toward the door. 'She's downtown, doing the grocery shopping. Damn crust,' he said, dangling the edge of his sandwich over his plate. He pulled the two strips of crust apart and liberated a bit of lunch meat still glued to the mayonnaise, then stepped across to the front door, opened it, and threw the remains out onto the lawn. 'Squirrels,' he said. 'They love a crust.'

Almost at once the door opened again and Aunt Edith stood there, look-ing in uncertainly past a cardboard carton full of groceries. 'Was that you throwing something out onto the lawn?' she asked.

Uncle Roy winked at Howard. 'The boy did it,' he said, jamming the crushed beer can under his chair cushion and nodding at the half-drunk beer, then winking at Howard. Howard caught on and picked it up just as Aunt Edith pulled the door shut, looking bright-eyed at him. Surreptitiously Uncle Roy shoved the six-pack across the floor with his foot so that it sat next to Howard's chair, and at the same time he took the carton out of his wife's arms so that she could rush at Howard and hug him. 'Look at you!' she said, thrusting Howard away and standing back in order to do just that. He set the beer down.

'You're a long, tall drink of water, aren't you? How tall?'

'Six three,' Howard said.

'I can remember when you were like this.' She held her hand out, waist-high, and shook her head. 'You should put on a little weight, though. You were always thin.'

'If you ate my cooking you'd be thin, too,' Howard said.

Uncle Roy went into the kitchen and laid the box of groceries down on a Formica table. Then, dutifully, he set about putting things away.

'There's more in the car,' she said to him, giving Howard another quick hug. 'We're letting Howard cook, Roy. Maybe he can thin us both down.'

'Let me get the stuff in the car,' Howard said, wanting to help. He went out into the front yard again, past where the crusts lay in the weeds now, and found the family station wagon in the driveway. There were two more car-tons of groceries in the back, and he set one of them awkwardly on top of the other.

He noticed several books of food stamps slid down along the side of the carton, next to a loaf of bread. So that's how it is, he thought sadly. He was doubly determined to help out somehow, to solicit Uncle Roy's help in get-ting the sketch away from Mr Jimmers. He would broach the subject that very afternoon. He picked up the boxes, balanced them with one arm, and slammed the cargo door of the wagon, then carried the boxes into the house. Aunt Edith was just then hurrying out the back door, carrying a sandwich on a plate. Howard was certain that she had shut the door quickly, as if in order to hide something.

Uncle Roy put away the lunch meat and bread and mayonnaise, mopped up the counter with a tea towel, and hung the towel back up from a peg on the wall. 'I like to help out in the kitchen,' he said. 'Some men don't like that kind of work, but I don't mind. Any work is good work, that's the byword around here. We'll get help in when things click for me.' He began uncrating more groceries, half pulling out the loaf of bread and then dropping it back down into the box. 'What's that?' he asked suddenly, peering out the window.

Howard looked out, expecting to see something going on with Aunt Edith. She was gone, though, perhaps out of sight around the side of the house. There was nothing out the window but fir trees, the forest floor overgrown with berries and lemonleaf and poison oak. The pointed leaves of wild iris grew in clumps along the edge of the trees beside a little path that ran out into the woods. For a moment Howard thought he could see his aunt's red jacket moving along the path, some distance through the trees. He couldn't be sure, though.

When he turned back around, Uncle Roy was putting away the bread. The leftover food stamps were gone from the box. One of them, in fact, protruded from where it had been shoved into his uncle's coat pocket. Howard glanced away, turning on the water in the sink as if he wanted to wash his hands, and out of the corner of his eye he saw Uncle Roy push it down farther into the pocket and then hurriedly shove the balance of the stamps into a kitchen drawer and shut it. 'Just dry them on the dish towel.'

Howard nodded, pulling the towel from its peg. They talked for a time, Howard telling him about his trip north, omitting any mention of the past twenty-four hours. There was no use sounding like a paranoid nut. Uncle Roy listened, nodding his head. He took the towel and began swabbing down cupboards and mopping up spots from the floor. Then, abruptly, he shot a glance out toward the front window, as if he'd just then seen something wonderful or puzzling out there. Howard followed his gaze, not able to help himself even though he suspected he was being hoodwinked again. Uncle Roy headed into the living room, gesturing at Howard, indicating that Howard should follow him along to the door. When he opened it, though, nobody was there. There hadn't been any knock; Howard was certain of it.

'Must have been the wind,' Uncle Roy said, and at that moment, as if to prove him right, there was the sound of a door slamming – the same that Howard had heard when he first arrived.

'Toolshed door.' Uncle Roy stepped outside and down the front-porch steps, continuing around past the side of the house, past the abandoned scaffolding. Tilted against the back side of the garage was a lean-to shed with a plywood door, which wobbled open in the sea wind. It hung there for a moment, as if deciding something, and then banged shut. 'Damned latch,'

Uncle Roy said, shoving the hasp shut and driving a pointed stick down through it to keep it tight. 'This is my current project.' He waved at an immense pile of old weathered lumber, full of nails, as if it had all been pried off the side of dilapidated houses. 'Barn lumber. There's a fortune to be made in it if a man's got any gumption. Gumption's the thing, you see, out here. This is like the frontier.'

'What do you do with it?' Howard asked.

'Clean it up. Sell it. Yuppies buy it for twice the price of new lumber in order to make new houses look old. It's all fakery, of course. The only people they fool are each other. Still, it's good wood. They did a study – concluded that hundred-year-old redwood planks, pulled off a house roof, hadn't lost more than two percent tensile strength.'

'Really?' Howard reached down and pulled up the end of one of the boards. A grisly-looking spider darted out, scampering away into the weeds as the board slammed down again. 'Beats bulldozing the stuff, doesn't it?'

'That's it,' said Uncle Roy. 'Conservation is what it is. Recycling. Pull out the nails, trim the ends, stack it up, and wait for the trucks to roll in. I'm just now getting started on it. My back's been acting up, though, and I've had to take it easy.'

Howard looked at the old dry Bermuda grass, curling up through the heaped wood. Clearly no one had touched it for months, perhaps years. 'Maybe I can help you with it. I can pull nails and trim ends easy enough. I'd like to do that.'

Uncle Roy hesitated, thinking it through, as if he had talked too much and gotten in too deep. 'We'll buy another six-pack and draw up plans,' he said, winking. 'Tonight. After four.'

A telephone rang. 'Roy!' came a shout from the kitchen.

'That's Edith. Come on.' He hurried past the garage, up onto the back stoop, and into the service porch. There was an old washer and dryer there, vintage twenty years ago, and one of those fold-up doweled-together wooden clotheslines with underwear hanging on it. A door led into the kitchen, where Aunt Edith was just then hanging up the phone.

'What?' said Uncle Roy. 'Who was it?'

'Syl.'

'Why did you shout? Did she want to talk to me?'

'No. She might have, though. I wanted you to be ready at hand.'

'What did she want? Is she all right?'

'Heavens, yes, she's all right. Why shouldn't she be all right?'

'Then why on earth did she call? We were just discussing the issue of the barn lumber. Howard's got an idea for selling it down south. That's where the housing market is. We were just starting in on it.'

'Dressed like that? Howard's just arrived. Don't make him work until he's had a chance to sit down for a moment. That wood's been lying there since who knows when. Let it be until after lunch, anyway. Give the boy a breather. Sylvia's coming for lunch. She's upset about something, I think.'

Aunt Edith went on about Sylvia, for a few minutes, about the store and her making things to sell in it. They were dependent on the tourist trade in Mendocino. It was easy for a shop to founder and sink. You got around it by diversifying. Tourists loved a trinket, and they were certain that the north coast was a haven of creativity. They didn't want a shirt that they could buy in a mall down south. They wanted whales and wool and driftwood and natural foods.

'That's her now,' Uncle Roy said. There was the sound of an engine cutting off out on the street.

Edith nodded. 'She called from right down at the Safeway. She's picked up some salmon for dinner tonight, in honor of Howard being here. I told her—'

'Good,' said Uncle Roy, interrupting her. 'It's time we had something high-toned for dinner. I'll cook it up myself. A little dill weed, a little white wine. Have we got any wine?'

'No,' Edith said.

'We'll remedy that. Always cook with the wine you intend to drink,' he told Howard seriously.

The front door opened and Sylvia walked in. She might easily have been crying. Howard was suddenly furious, ready to murder someone – Stoat, the dirty pig. He forced a smile, thinking that it would be a disaster to fly off the handle now, even in Sylvia's defense.

'What the hell's wrong?' Uncle Roy asked, seeing the same thing in her face.

'I don't think they're going to renew my lease. I'm going to have to move the shop, probably back off Main Street.'

'The sons of bitches!' Uncle Roy slammed his fist on the kitchen table.

'Roy!' Aunt Edith said, glancing at Howard, pretty clearly embarrassed for him.

'They're talking about redevelopment along Main,' Sylvia said.

'What the hell is that, "redevelopment"?' Uncle Roy looked disgusted. 'Of all the damned things ...' he said.

'That's when they tear down whatever's interesting and put up something shabby and new,' Howard put in. 'They're always up to that down in my neighborhood.'

'Is this certain?' Uncle Roy squinted at her. The look on his face suggested that he read an entire plot into the notion. 'Who told you, the old lady?'

'No, Stoat. This morning. I saw you drive past,' she said to Howard. 'I'm kind of glad you didn't stop, though. I wasn't in any mood to talk.'

So Stoat, somehow, had become – what? Her landlord? A landlord's agent? Guiltily he found that he was wildly relieved. Happy even. This explained the sidewalk conversation. Stoat was a backwoods Simon Legree, twisting his blond mustache.

Uncle Roy paced up and down, dark looks crossing his face. 'They're moving,' he said.

'Oh, Roy.' Aunt Edith started putting together sandwiches on the counter.

Howard wondered what his uncle meant – who was moving? What did the word mean, exactly?

Roy stopped. Looking hard at Howard, he asked, apropos of nothing at all and in the cryptic manner of Mr Jimmers, 'Are you a man who likes to fish?'

6

Uncle Roy brooded while Sylvia and Edith ate their sandwiches. Looking nervous, as if he had nothing to do with his hands, he got up finally and opened the refrigerator door, staring in at Tupperware containers full of left-overs. He hauled out an open tin can, holding it up and widening his eyes at Howard. 'Peach?'

Howard shook his head. 'Still full from breakfast.'

'Anyone else?' Sylvia and Edith shook their heads. 'Don't mind if I do?' No one minded. Uncle Roy poured milk into the peaches, fishing a clean fork out of the drawer. He waved for Howard to follow him and took the can out into the living room and sat back down in his chair, sipping milky peach syrup out of the open can. Howard could hear Sylvia and Aunt Edith talking between themselves, having cranked the conversation up once the men were out of the room.

'Slippery little devil,' Uncle Roy said, biting into a peach, eating it off the end of the fork. Howard waited for the subject of the unrenewed lease to surface again, but it didn't, and he became aware that Uncle Roy was studiously avoiding it. After a couple of minutes Sylvia left, heading back down to Mendocino. Uncle Roy assured her that nothing would happen, that he would work things through. 'Don't worry,' he said to her, but it was unconvincing.

Then Aunt Edith came in, wiping her eyes with a handkerchief and immediately climbing the stairs. Howard sat there uncomfortably. His uncle had sunk into his chair. He sat now with his head pulled down into the flesh of his neck and chin, as if he had turned into a sort of human pudding. There was more in his face than sorrow or worry. He was thinking hard about something, making plans. He started to speak, but was interrupted almost at once by the sound of footfalls on the front porch and then a heavy knock.

Uncle Roy shook his head, meaning for Howard to stay in his chair.

After a moment a woman's voice spoke from outside, very loud, as if she were shouting through a bullhorn. At first Howard thought it was Sylvia come back, apparently in some sort of rage. 'I know you're in there!' the woman shouted, and then banged on the door again. It was an old woman's voice, though, loud and thin like the voice of the Witch of the East.

'Ssh!' Uncle Roy put a finger to his lips. The house was silent for a moment. There was no movement from upstairs.

'Open this door!' came the voice from the porch, followed by a rapping on the window. 'Your car is apparent! Don't pretend! You'll find yourself living under the bridge!'

Howard sat very still. He heard the sound of something scraping on the porch – the rocker being hauled aside – and then someone's face, just a slice of it, appeared in the window beyond the one-inch gap between the curtains. 'I can see the back of your head, Roy Barton!'

'That's not me!' shouted Uncle Roy. 'I have my *lawyer* in here! He's a bull dog when he's riled up! He's come up from San Francisco, and he means business. With a *capital B*!'

The woman laughed, high and shrill. 'Send him out!' she shouted, banging on the window again. Howard saw that Aunt Edith had descended the stairs now, carrying her purse.

'Put that damned thing away!' Uncle Roy hissed. Then to Howard he said, 'Never let them see the color of money. Drives them wild – like the scent of blood to a shark. They won't rest till they've torn your belly out.' He nodded toward the porch. 'It's the landlady.'

Howard nodded. 'Wait here,' he said, getting up and heading for the door.

Uncle Roy grabbed his pant leg. 'Just let her rant,' he said. 'She'll tire out and go away. We've got to hold her off until after Halloween. I'm going to make a killing on the haunted house, and then we can pay her.'

'I see,' Howard said, although actually he didn't see anything at all. What haunted house? He found that he didn't have any faith in the notion of his uncle's making a killing, in haunted houses or otherwise. 'Let me deal with her. I've handled her sort before.'

'She's a bugbear …'

'Let me at her.'

'Go to town, then,' Uncle Roy said, letting go of Howard and sitting up a little straighter. 'It's all right,' he said to Aunt Edith, who still hesitated on the stairs. 'Howard's got a line on this woman. He's just been telling me about it. He'll settle her hash.'

Howard smiled and nodded at his aunt, mouthing the words 'No problem' and opening the front door.

On the porch stood a tall thin woman in a red dress. She had the face of a pickle with an aquiline nose, and she glared at him from behind a pair of glasses with swept-back frames dotted with rhinestones. Immediately she tried to push him aside, to rush into the house. Howard forced her back out, weaving across in front of her and pulling the door shut as if he would happily crush her sideways if she didn't move quickly. She folded her arms, seeming to swell up there on the ruined porch.

'If you're a lawyer,' she said, looking him up and down, 'I'm a Chinese magistrate.'

'Mr Barton is willing to make a partial payment,' he said in a low voice. 'I've advised him not to let the issue go to court.'

'Wise,' she said, eyeing him steadily. 'A partial payment against what?'

Howard hesitated. He wasn't sure what. Uncle Roy had said that this woman was the landlady, but what did that mean? Did this have something to do with Sylvia's store, or with the house? It didn't matter to him, really. 'What do you recollect the total to be?'

'*Recollect!* There's a payment of four hundred-odd dollars a month against a principal of forty-two thousand at twelve percent amortized over thirty years. The house is mine, my smarty-pants lawyer, unless he empties his pockets, which he can't do, because they're full of moths!'

'Calm down,' Howard said gently, laying a hand on her arm. 'Try to relax.'

She whirled away, as if his hand were a snake. He smiled benignly, trying to put just the hint of puzzlement into his eyes, as if he were confused and sorry that she'd gotten so carried away. 'Breathe regularly,' he advised her, using a soft, clinical psychologist's voice – the sort of voice designed to drive sane people truly mad.

He pulled the rocker back over from where she'd shoved it aside, adjusting its position carefully, wondering what the hell to say to her. He gestured at the rocker then, as if she might be anxious to sit down, to take a load off, and he widened his eyes like a happy dentist coercing a child into the tilting chair. Uncle Roy, he could see, was watching through the gap in the curtains now. The curtains moved, parting another couple of inches. His uncle grinned out at him and wiggled his hand in a sort of coy wave, and then whirled his finger around his ear, making the pinwheel sign.

The woman took another step backward, nearly to the edge of the porch. It was clear that she wouldn't go anywhere near the chair and wouldn't settle down, either. Howard's theatrical patience had worked her into a fury. Her eyebrows were arched and her forehead furrowed, as if she had eaten a slug.

Then abruptly she caught herself, her face instantly composing. It seemed to have taken an effort, though. 'I sent Mr Barton a notice that I'd no longer accept late payments. I meant what I wrote in that letter. It's incontestable. The law is the law.'

'Surely two or three more weeks ...' Howard said, calculating when Halloween was.

'In two weeks Mr Barton will be living out of the back of his automobile,' she said, interrupting him. 'I pity his poor wife, but she's brought this upon herself, marrying the likes of him.'

The front door squeaked fully open just then, and a rubber bat as big as a pigeon dropped down into the doorway, flapping on the end of a black thread. His uncle stood hidden inside somewhere, probably manipulating a pulley. Howard could hear him stifling his laughter in the palm of his hand. The woman made a rush for the open door again, but Howard was there before her, pulling it shut, trapping the bat outdoors. It dangled in front of the closed door, its nose thumping against a panel like a rubber knocker.

She cast Howard a faint grin and shook her head tiredly, as if the rubber bat trick had very nicely illustrated exactly what sort of man Roy Barton was. Which of course it did, to Howard's way of thinking. 'My client is willing to offer you ten cents on the dollar,' he said. 'Right now. Instantly.' He pulled his checkbook out of his jacket pocket, took out a pen, and opened the book, as if ready to sign it.

'Tell Mr Barton he can park his car behind the Texaco station at the comer, in back along with the other wrecks. He can utilize the gas station rest room that way.' She turned around and stepped off the porch, heading for the curb. The sound of chains and recorded laughter echoed out of the upstairs window, very slow and throaty this time, as if played at a too-slow speed. Howard saw the back of her neck flush pink, but she didn't turn around.

He caught up with her on the street as she was climbing into her car. Keeping his back to the house, he talked through the open passenger window. She started the car right up, as if she meant to drive off. 'Four hundred even?' he asked.

She gave him an assessing squint, her eyes traveling to his checkbook, as if a little disappointed to see it. 'Four hundred forty-two. It's already three weeks late. There's another payment due within eight days. Precisely. Or I'll take action.'

'Here then.' He tore off the check and handed it through the window. She hesitated for a moment, but finally she took it, as if she couldn't stand not to.

'You're a very small boy,' she said. 'And it's a very big and badly designed dike that you're trying to stopper up.' She blinked rapidly, but her voice was slow and studied now, like the voice of an aged and nearly psychotic schoolmarm delivering a standard lecture on behavior for the ten thousandth time. She suddenly changed her tone, though, looking him in the eyes. For a moment it looked to Howard as if she had gone into trance, and then she gave him a sideways look and asked, 'Who are you, really?' She seemed to be seeing him clearly for the first time, and for a moment he was overwhelmed with confusion, as if he had just been caught stealing something.

Howard fought for something to say. She obviously hadn't swallowed the lawyer gag. 'Just a friend from down south,' he said. 'He's in pretty tight straits right now, but he'll pull out of it. He's got a couple of irons in the fire.'

She gazed at him, smiling faintly, as if he had said that Uncle Roy was really a Persian prince, just about to inherit the kingdom.

'The water you're swimming in is deeper and darker than you can imagine,' she said. 'And you won't be able to find the bottom when you tire out, which you will, very shortly. I don't know who you are, but if you've come out here to challenge me, you've made a fatal error. I'll see that old fraud on the street. See if I won't. He won't stand in my way, and neither will you.' She gave him a pitying look then, as if what she was telling him was purely for his own good. 'Mark me, he'll bleed you dry, too, if you let him. Go back home. Don't throw good money after bad. There's nothing for you here. You don't understand anything.'

She pulled away from the curb just then, and Howard had to step back quick to avoid being clipped. He ditched the checkbook in his coat, and after pulling his bags out of the truck, headed back into the house, wondering at her strange speech. It hadn't sounded as if she were merely talking about finances.

'What came of it?' asked Uncle Roy. 'Did she react to the props?'

'Infuriated her.'

'Good, good. So much the better. Will she hold off until the end of the month?'

'Yes, but I had to threaten her,' Howard said. 'I guess the lawyer scam worked on her.' Howard didn't like to lie to his uncle, except that Uncle Roy would feel good about the ruse, and that was worth something and would explain why the old woman had gone off without any money. 'These landlord types want the check,' Howard said. 'They don't want to foreclose. They can't afford it. They're in the business of being paid, not of renovating houses. I guaranteed her the money come November. It was as simple as that.'

'And we'll get it, too. This haunted house business can't fail. You've seen what I've got going here – the corpses, the ghost woman, the bats.'

Howard nodded. 'The eyeballs,' he said, finishing the list. He realized that his hands were shaking. The meeting outside had worked him over pretty thoroughly. Now he had involved himself in a lie, and in the end it would probably be impossible to hide it from Uncle Roy, who, regardless of what sort of deadbeat he was, wouldn't put up with Howard paying his bills for him. Sylvia hadn't made that part up.

'Who is this woman?' Howard asked.

'One Heloise Lamey. She owns half the coast. Part of a consortium of some sort. This man Stoat is part of it. They're an octopus – a finger in every damned sort of pie.'

'So she's Sylvia's landlady, too, down at the shop?'

'One and the same. Stoat wasn't a bad sort, years ago. Money is the root, though. Don't ever let anyone tell you different. Money is the stinking root.'

'What's their problem?'

'They're millionaires, aren't they? Rough crowd, millionaires. All this talk of redevelopment … There's oil in it for them, too – offshore. They'd pave the ocean if there was money in it. Take your man Stoat. He's drunk my beer, dated my daughter. He was always a little slick, of course. But I don't hold that against a man. That's all appearances, and we know what those are worth. But then he fell in with the old woman and made a couple of bucks. That frosted it. He turned into a damned chameleon, changed the color of his scales. Started to live for his bank account.'

Howard found the anti-Stoat talk very pleasant, and he wished that he knew more about the man so as to be able to run him down even more expansively. His mouth was dry, though   probably a nervous reaction from his bout with the landlady. 'I'm going to grab a glass of water,' he said, leaving his uncle in the living room. Aunt Edith had gone back upstairs. He circled around into the kitchen, working things over in his mind. He had been there about an hour and a half and already the complications were descending on him. He might have expected it. Nobody told him it would be easy. There were never any guarantees. He drank a glass of water at the sink, staring out the window at the woods, lost in puzzled thought. The sound of a voice made him jump.

'That's not a friendly place, those woods.' It was Uncle Roy, who had slipped into the kitchen. He nodded at the window, at the forest beyond. His face was serious, almost fearful. 'There's bears in them. Can you believe that? Mountain lions, too. Those woods are stalked by carnivores.'

'Really?' Howard said. 'Right out there?'

'Can't tell by looking, can you? Trees are too dense. The creatures might be watching us right this moment, hiding in the shadows. They don't take well to civilization. It ruins them. They develop a taste for garbage over the years. They'll tear a man's head clean off, too, and eat his entrails.'

'Not often, I hope.'

'Doesn't have to happen to a man more than once, does it?' Uncle Roy smiled at him, having deliberately misunderstood. 'Nope, those are inhospitable trees – nothing but poison oak in there. The poison vapors get into the lungs, finally. Throat closes up tight. Death by constriction, the medical men call it.' He shook his head darkly, not relishing the idea of a man's throat closing up. 'Cultists, too. All varieties of them, but not half as bad as the dope farmers.'

'I hear they're a dangerous crowd,' Howard said. 'I can understand it, I guess, price of dope and all. Must be profitable.'

'Oh, there's money in it. Yes indeed. Money's paramount in a backwater like this. Guns, dogs, trip cords, Claymore mines, razor wire, spike pits, bear traps – you name it; the dope farmers have the lot of it, the whole megillah. I wouldn't go into those woods on a bet.'

Howard shook his head, as if he wouldn't either, for the moment anyway. Aunt Edith had gone into them quick enough, though, and carrying a sandwich, too.

'Then there's the logging roads. They'll run you right down, loggers will. They'd take a man like you for an environmentalist. Nothing they hate worse. They'll shoot you on sight. The only crowd that won't shoot you are the cultists. They want you alive.'

Uncle Roy seemed to have gone crazy, rattling off his catalogue of forest horrors. He peered into the refrigerator again, pushing things around, trying to find something that appealed to him. 'Coke?' he asked.

'Thanks. Shall we ask Aunt Edith?'

'For permission? Or whether she wants one, too?' He looked angry all of a sudden, as if the question had set him off. 'She's retired, actually. Taking a nap. You won't see her until it's time to cook dinner.' His face softened a little then. 'She's worried about Sylvia, to tell you the truth. What she wants is more faith. Things iron themselves out. She's got the usual motherly instincts, though, and they run her ragged. Survival is paramount in a business like Sylvia's. If she survives the winter …' He shrugged and then grinned abruptly, as if having thought of something more cheerful. 'Edith is ticked off about the rubber bat, actually. She wasn't keen on my putting on the laugh record, either. She takes the old woman too seriously.'

Howard couldn't think of anything to say about taking the old woman seriously that wouldn't irritate his uncle, so he changed the subject entirely, trying to force Uncle Roy to slip up and be a little bit candid for a change. 'Tell me,' he said. 'What are they, these gluers I keep hearing about? Mr Jimmers mentioned them to me. They seem to have stolen a bunch of junk out of my glove compartment. Are they some kind of cult?'

'Nobody knows, really. Almost nobody. Live back in among the trees. Anarchists to the last man jack of them. Won't wear matching socks to save their mortal souls. Won't cut their hair. Spend their days gluing stuff up, layer on top of layer, usually on their cars. Coral reef syndrome; that's what I call it. Kids all ride skateboards – break into churches and schools. Won't work. Some people think it's primitivism, the decline of man. They distill a hell of a bottle of whiskey, though, just between the two of us.'

'I can tell you that their wine isn't worth anything at all. I tried some last night. I was forced to drink water instead.'

'That bad?' Uncle Roy grimaced, as if finding it hard to imagine. 'They don't drink the stuff themselves, that's why. They don't know a lick about wine, except that all these natural-sounding fruit wines are big with the tourists, especially the teetotalers. They bring home a bottle of herb wine and offer it to company as a joke. It's like taking the cure. The gluer elders can drink whiskey, though. They smoke the malt over fires like the Scots do, only they don't use peat; they use green redwood skived out of root balls with an adze.'

'Root balls?'

'That's right. Got to be done that way. Hand me down a couple of those glasses.'

Howard reached into the cupboard over his head, pulling out two green tumblers. Behind them, sitting in the back corner of the cupboard, was a collection of salt and pepper shakers – ten or twelve pairs. Sitting among them, smug and leering, was a porcelain Humpty Dumpty. Howard was stricken speechless. Here, too, he thought.

'Do you know what the oldest living thing in the world is?' asked his uncle.

Howard shook his head, unable to guess.

'A root ball from a stand of redwoods. They've got redwood trees out there that are two thousand years old if they're a day. Where do they come from? you might ask. Not from seeds, mostly – from root balls. One tree puts down roots and then one day another tree comes up from the roots of that first one. Then along comes another, and all of these new ones putting down new roots. First tree grows old and dies, finally – falls over. Maybe it's a thousand years old, maybe two. And this goes on for twenty thousand years through God's own generations of trees, all of them growing and adding roots to this root ball. *It* doesn't die, though. Fires don't touch it. Bugs can't get at it. How old is it? How big is it? You tell *me*. Nobody can guess. Bigger than the pyramids, older than the woolly mammoth.'

He squinted at the unopened Coca-Cola cans. 'Anyway, that's what they use to smoke the whiskey. Older the root material, the better the spirits. That's paramount. You're a literary man. Have you read Morris' essay on age?'

It seemed to Howard as if he must have, but he couldn't calculate it right now. The coincidence of the Humpty Dumpty still played in his mind. He reached into the cupboard again and pulled it out, waving it at his uncle. 'What *is* this, anyway?' Howard asked. 'I seem to be running into a lot of them lately.'

His uncle eyeballed him, as if he were trying to fathom the question, or, perhaps, as if he were considering how much he could safely say on the subject. 'That's Humpty Dumpty,' he said. 'One of Edith's dust collectors. Nothing you need to worry about.'

'Right. It's just that they seem to *mean* something, don't they? Maybe it's the look on his face. He's such a know-it-all.'

'Mean something? I'm not sure … They've got a fascinating history, I suppose. They're an incredibly ancient business involving fertility and reproduction. Sort of a metaphoric root ball, aren't they? Nobody knows how long they've been around. That lad is one of your vegetation kings; that's my notion. Early incarnation of the thing. Your friends the gluers are fond of him. They revere a fat man. Consider themselves to be the king's men, if you know what I mean.'

'I'm not sure I do,' Howard said, putting the little porcelain egg back into the cupboard. 'Who's the king, then?'

Uncle Roy hesitated for a moment before speaking. 'Maybe you're putting too fine a point on it,' he said. 'Safer to think of it as a myth. It's easy in this climate to get swept up in the wind and rain and forest, to start thinking in terms of weather. Things up here can be supernaturally green, and would be, except for the drought. People drift north talking about "getting back to the land." But they don't know what that means. Not really. That's what I was telling you a moment ago – that business about the woods. They're a dangerous place. Do you follow me?'

Howard shook his head. He didn't follow anything except that his half-innocent question about the Humpty Dumpty had sailed the conversation straight into the realm of the mystical. What was wrong with people up here? Everyone was a puzzle waiting to be solved. First Mr Jimmers and then the landlady. Now Uncle Roy. And what the hell *was* Aunt Edith doing out in the woods with a sandwich on a plate?

'Look here,' Uncle Roy said, suddenly animated. 'It's nearly four o'clock. Forget the Cokes. Let's make a little run down to Sammy's. I usually drop in about this time. We've got a couple of hours to kill before dinner. We can work out the elements of the barn lumber scheme.'

What scheme? Howard wondered, following his uncle out the door. Now suddenly there was a scheme, although nobody on earth could lay out the particulars of it. In his mind, Uncle Roy was probably certain that Howard had given serious thought to the barn lumber angle. He hoped the haunted house plans were less imaginary.

'We'll take your truck,' Uncle Roy said, climbing heavily into the passenger side and looking down furtively into his jacket pocket.

Howard went around opposite and fired up the engine, driving down Oak Street toward the highway, swinging south finally, and then back up Cypress. 'Across the street there,' Uncle Roy said. 'By the warehouse.'

The tavern was long and almost windowless, sided in dark redwood with the name 'Sammy's' painted on it. Its roof was a shambles of different-colored composition shingles in layers – strips and pieces having broken or blown off over the years. A neon cocktail glass stood atop a rusted steel post outside, lit dimly despite it being daylight. Only a couple of cars were parked in the gravel lot when they pulled in, including what might have been an old Chevy from around 1965. Only you couldn't quite tell now, because it was utterly covered in layers of cheap religious icons – Day of the Dead skulls and bleeding Christs and robed Virgin Marys made out of painted plastic and plaster of Paris.

'Gluers,' Uncle Roy whispered.

7

'Trouble?' Howard asked, and almost at once he felt a little foolish, a little childish. He realized then that he was full of a vague, bulk-rate uneasiness. There was a shadow lying across the landscape, and he suspected that it had some sort of fearful shape and that he was on the verge of making it out. Here was another piece of that shadow, he had thought, seeing the car parked beneath the neon sign.

Uncle Roy shook his head. 'No,' he said. 'You can relax about that. You won't be running into any trouble from them. I'd guess just the opposite. Follow my lead, though. There might be profit in this. You do the knocking, I'll do the talking.'

Howard followed him into the bar, suddenly unable to see in the darkness. There were illuminated beer signs on the walls and a light over a pool table in one corner, but it was dim and cool and smelled like spilled beer. He stood for a moment just inside the door in order to let his eyes adjust. Uncle Roy moved off, negotiating the furniture easily – from long practice, probably. In a moment Howard made out the bulk of shadowy tables and chairs and the long bar against the wall.

The place was almost empty aside from a couple of hunched men drinking beer at the bar and talking to each other about basketball. One of them turned and gave Uncle Roy the high sign, saying, 'What's new?'

'Easy livin',' Roy said, and the man laughed, going back to his beer and basketball. In the back corner, a man who must have been a gluer sat talking to another man in a shirt and tie and with the face of a grocery store manager. This second man stood up as Uncle Roy angled toward the table. He picked up a carton of bottles and took it with him as he moved away, heading toward the bar and nodding to Uncle Roy.

315

The gluer looked like an old hippie – the brother of the Patchwork Girl from Oz. His clothes resembled a quilt sewn by a drunkard, and he had a mess of graying hair that hung halfway down his back. Howard stood for a moment, wondering whether to join his uncle or order something from the bar. The gluer didn't look like a happy man, though; he looked like a zealot, like the Holy Man of the Moab, maybe. And so going after a drink struck Howard as a better idea. He wouldn't meddle in his uncle's affairs any more than he had to – for the moment, anyway. He stepped across and asked the bartender to draw two draft beers.

When the man turned around to pull the tap, Howard slipped one of the bottles out of the cardboard carton and glanced at it. It was unlabeled, but the amber-colored liquid inside, and its seeming to have come in with the patchwork man, convinced him that the bottle held the fabled Sunberry Farms whiskey that his uncle had talked about. No doubt about it.

'What's that to you?' the bartender asked suddenly, surprising him.

'What?' asked Howard. 'Nothing. Just curious. Wondering what it was. Can I order a glass of this?' Sheepishly he slid the bottle back into the case.

'I don't know what you're talking about,' the bartender said. 'Why do you want a glass of it if you don't know what it is? This belongs to that man over there.' He nodded toward the corner. 'It's urine samples that he's running up to the lab. Terrible outbreak of hepatitis around here. Some new San Francisco strain. You know how that goes – disease capital of the world. Health department's hired these poor bastards to collect samples.'

'By the quart?' Howard asked.

The man shrugged. 'Who the hell are you, anyway? Do you want something to drink, or are you just here to ask questions?' He picked up the box and set it on the floor behind the counter. Then he stood up and looked Howard straight in the face, not smiling at all.

'Roy Barton's my uncle. I'm visiting from down south.'

'Barton family, eh? So you're here with Roy. That's all right, then. Where you from, L. A.?' He relaxed, smiling again and turning around to pull a bottle of Scotch off the shelf. He poured a couple of ounces into each of a pair of Old-fashioned glasses, talking all along about the last time he was down in L. A., about the smog and the dirt and the freeway killings as if he wanted to bury Howard's interest in the gluer whiskey beneath a dump truck full of words. He put the bottle away. 'Tomatin, this is called. Not a bad whiskey. You aren't going to find it just anywhere.'

Howard took a polite sip, turning around to have a look at what his uncle was up to. The gluer was just then handing him a couple of bills – tens, it appeared – and Uncle Roy handed over a few folded food stamps. The whiskey was raw and fiery, and Howard nearly choked on it. He took the other three glasses from the bar, croaking out his thanks, and headed for a table near a half-dead potted palm, wondering whether he would have to pay for the Scotch. He didn't want the damned stuff. Maybe the potted palm wanted it. Clearly the bartender had poured it in order to take Howard's mind off the gluer bottles.

Uncle Roy was walking back across toward him. He tipped Howard a huge wink, as if he'd just done a pretty bit of business. Howard wondered what the going rate for food stamps was – sixty cents on the dollar? The gluer walked out of the bar, without his case of whiskey. Howard heard gravel scrunch outside as the car crept out of the parking lot.

'What's this?' asked Uncle Roy, nodding at the Scotch glass.

'Scotch. On the house, I think.'

His uncle nodded. 'You tried to order some of the Sunberry malt, didn't you, and he talked you into this? What did he tell you was in the case?'

'Urine samples.'

Uncle Roy chuckled. 'This Sunberry whiskey isn't exactly aboveboard, if you follow me. They don't serve it down at the Hungry Tiger. Sammy took you for a cop. He knows you aren't a local. You must have thrown him, walking up to the bar like that and hauling one of the bottles out.'

'I didn't mean to. It was all that talk about root balls, I guess. The whole idea's pretty astonishing.'

Uncle Roy nodded. 'Anyway, I figure to have the haunted house open by next week,' he said, as if they'd been talking about the haunted house scheme all along. 'That'll give me seven days to run kids through before the thirty-first. Once we pass Halloween the thing'll be a dead bust. Everyone's gearing up for Christmas by then. I've been toying with the idea of doing a sort of Santa's village, too, with reindeer and all – maybe hire a little carnival to dress it up with. I make a hell of a Santa Claus.'

'Quite a bit of work, isn't it?' Howard asked. 'Converting a haunted house to a Santa's workshop, or whatever it is, in just a couple of months?'

'It's just a matter of imagination, of picturing the details. "God dwells in the details." Mies Van Der Rohe said that. I wrote it down on my hand with a ballpoint pen once. That's the way to remember a thing – write it on your hand. Or else write it in mirror writing on your forehead.'

Howard suddenly became aware of a framed photograph on the wall near the table. At first he couldn't make it out, because it was full of unfamiliar shapes. He peered more closely at it. It was a picture of the Watts Towers, built by Sabatino Rodia starting around 1920 in south-central Los Angeles. Rodia had spent years building the towers out of old, found materials – rebar and pipe, China plates and seashells and trinkets and pieces of colored glass – until he had put together a cluster of tall spires in junkman-Gothic style. The truth struck Howard forcibly, like a stone in the back of the head.

'Rodia was a gluer!' he said to Uncle Roy.

His uncle nodded, as if it were common knowledge. 'He was touched by the instinct,' he said. 'And do you know what else?' He looked furtively around, as if he were about to reveal a secret. 'Under each of the feet of those towers, there's a pair of 1938 Buicks with reinforced roofs and frames. Welded steel I-beams. Banks of steel-belted truck tires on quadruple axles. Eight-speed gearboxes. All of it underground, where you can't see it.'

Howard looked again at the photograph. 'What do you mean "under" them?'

'They're built on top of automobiles – the towers are. Engines are ready to go. Tanks topped off. One of these nights, when the weather's right and the wind's blowing out of the east and the constellations are set just so in the sky ...'

Uncle Roy sat back and widened his eyes, waving his right hand with a sort of flourish that reminded Howard of Mr Jimmers talking about his two-dimensional constellation, which was just about as unlikely as this. The two must belong to some sort of fabulists' club.

'So why are they built on top of cars?' asked Howard. 'They're going to drive off or something? This fleet of Buicks? Where to? Up the coast?'

Suddenly laughing, Uncle Roy tilted forward and slapped Howard on the shoulder. 'That's rich, isn't it? Up the coast highway in the night! You've got a hell of an imagination for a nephew. Here, let me buy you another beer.' And with that he stood up and walked off toward the bar, leaving Howard to wonder what sort of an imagination nephews usually had – nothing that could touch the imagination of an uncle, apparently. How much weight *could* a bunch of old Buicks stand? Even reinforced ... He looked more closely at the photo. They were immense. What – a hundred feet tall? He couldn't make out the base of the towers, which were buttressed with arched steel – tons of it – rising out of a fenced backyard. His uncle returned with two fresh, full glasses.

The door opened just then, flooding the floor with sunlight. Stoat walked in. One of the men at the bar stood up hurriedly and went out through the back, not even looking around. The other man at the bar nodded over his beer, keeping to himself. Stoat squinted for a moment in the dim light before heading across to the table. 'Mr Barton,' he said, cheerfully enough.

How on earth can he know who I am? Howard wondered, and then realized that it was Uncle Roy that Stoat was talking to. The man's hair was perfect, as if it had been shaped with a laser scalpel, and he looked both well off and comfortable in his clothes. Howard didn't trust his looks – too chiseled, too careful, with no hint of eccentricity and no humor in his face at all even though he was smiling. He had changed over the years, lost the affectations that he had sported back in his underground-comics days, which was the way with all affectations. You either lost them or came to believe in them, and Stoat was obviously too clever for that. Success and his own cleverness had worked him over, perhaps.

Howard could see that his uncle was sweating. He looked nervous and he smiled self-consciously. His left eye twitched just a little as he took a long pull on the new glass of beer, drinking half of it off at a single swallow.

'Mr Barton,' the man said again.

'Are you addressing me, my good fellow?' Uncle Roy asked. Howard tensed, knowing that here was another piece of the mystery, about to be unveiled. His uncle was pretending, and Howard wondered what he would have said if Howard hadn't been there. Abruptly Uncle Roy looked surprised, as if he'd just then recognized Stoat. 'Well,' he said, gesturing toward an empty chair. 'My good friend Stoat. What brings you into a dump like this? Must be woefully important business.'

'That it is,' said Stoat, looking at Howard as if he wondered whether he could discuss such business in front of a stranger.

'This is my nephew,' Uncle Roy said. 'Howard Barton. He's an assistant director at the Getty Museum. Expert in oriental artifacts. He's up here for a little breather, a little constitutional, if you know what I mean. He was a special forces agent in Southeast Asia, highly connected.'

'I think we've met,' Stoat said. 'Southeast Asia? I thought you'd managed to avoid that part of the world. Now you're with the Getty? That must run you in and out of elevated circles.'

Howard nodded again. 'That's right. I'm doing a little troubleshooting.'

'Troubleshooting? Up here in the woods?'

'Vacation, really.'

'Well,' said Stoat, 'this is the country for that. Nothing but peace and quiet.'

'I've gone into the barn lumber business since I talked to you last,' Uncle Roy said to Stoat. 'With any luck I'll be able to cut a deal with the Getty. They're going to build a new wing, out of my lumber, I hope. It's a hell of a project, but they're loaded. Swimming in green. There's a bunch of old houses coming down up Eureka way, part of a downtown bypass. I've got *bracero* labor up there right now, prying the places apart. Howard's acting as my liaison down south. This kind of deal is delicate.'

Howard kept silent. His uncle had pretty clearly leaped in with his wild tale in order to keep Howard from talking. Howard had explained his trip in his letter. It had been no sort of secret – up until now, anyway.

Stoat was sucking on a eucalyptus drop, and he shifted it back and forth in his mouth when he talked. It was his only mannerism that was less than magazine-photo quality. 'The world is full of delicate deals,' he said. 'I talked to Sylvia today. I guess you know that by now.'

Uncle Roy stared at him, not trusting himself to speak, perhaps. Howard had plenty to say, but he forced himself not to say it now. There was too much room for error, for making things worse.

'What I mean to say is that I'm afraid she's overreacted to what I told her. I didn't mean to be making threats. To be truthful, I don't like the idea of redevelopment along Main any more than she does. As an artist I appreciate the beauty of that little town. I want to see it preserved. I'm not the only member of the consortium, though, and I was only passing on to her what was in the wind. I don't want her to be taken by surprise. I'm going to do what I can to head things off.' He hesitated, letting this sink in. Then he said, 'Heloise Lamey and I don't always see eye-to-eye on these issues.'

'Heloise Lamey doesn't see eye-to-eye with anyone,' Uncle Roy said. His face didn't betray what he was thinking, though, and what he said sounded like a flat statement rather than an acceptance of what Stoat was telling him.

Stoat sat back in his chair. 'A certain amount hangs in the balance,' he said. 'Nothing's certain.'

'True enough,' Uncle Roy said, not giving an inch.

'You know she's wild for that ... object we discussed.'

'I remember the object in question. It's disappeared, apparently. Gone from the face of the earth.'

'I almost wish it were,' Stoat said. 'You don't have to come cheap, you know. You can take her straight to the cleaners. And she doesn't care about the old man, either.'

'The cleaners couldn't help her,' Uncle Roy said. 'Too much dirt. Too many years of wallowing with pigs.'

Stoat sighed deeply, as if he took this last statement to be a personal insult, but would swallow it in order to maintain the delicate balance of things. He produced a pen, though, and wrote a number on the bottom of a bar napkin, five or six figures – not enough for a phone number, but plenty if it had to do with dollars and cents. Howard caught only a glimpse of it before Uncle Roy tucked it into his coat pocket.

'Another round of drinks here,' Stoat said to the bartender as he stood up. He widened his eyes at Uncle Roy. 'Think about it,' he said. Then he nodded to Howard, walked across and laid a five-dollar bill on the bar, and walked out.

Uncle Roy sat still for a moment, as if waiting for Stoat's return. A car started up outside, though, following the labored, metallic whine of a bad starter. Uncle Roy relaxed then, all in a heap, producing a handkerchief and mopping his brow. The atmosphere in the bar seemed to ease just then, and Howard could smell the wind off the sea, tainted with candy-drop eucalyptus.

'Put that in the tip glass, Sammy,' Uncle Roy said, waving at the bill on the bar. 'Let's go,' he said to Howard. 'I won't drink on that bastard's money. Go ahead – I'll meet you in the truck.'

Without asking about it, Howard went outside, squinting in the late-afternoon sunlight. He sat in the truck for a moment warming up the engine before his uncle came out, carrying a paper sack. Uncle Roy winked at him after he hauled himself in and waved the paper bag. There was a bottle of Sunberry Farms whiskey in it. 'No need to tell Edith about any of this,' he said.

'Not a word,' Howard said. 'I'm not sure what went on myself.'

Uncle Roy gave him a sideways look. 'There's nothing to tell, really. Damn all creditors,' he said. 'There's nothing worse than a landlord. Bunch of vultures. Money's not enough for them, they want your soul, too. Give me a psychotic with a loaded gun anytime.'

'Anything to do with that sketch I'm after?' Howard asked, working on a hunch.

Clearly his uncle didn't want to discuss it. Let the matter slide, his face seemed to say. And the sketch wasn't Howard's in any real way, despite Graham's letter. Although if he, or rather the museum, wasn't going to get it, someone owed him an explanation – some story he could take back south with him.

'Don't worry about Stoat,' Uncle Roy said, as if that answered Howard's question. 'I've already forgotten him. He draws pictures of copulating machines. What can you say about a man like that? Steer clear of him. That's the advice I gave Sylvia, and I'm going to give the same advice to you. I'll show him a thing or two if he comes meddling around us again.'

Uncle Roy went on in a more determined voice. 'Look, I won't pretend here. You've come up north at a ... tenuous time. Things are shaky. The ground's rumbling. Pressure's dropping. Do you follow me?'

'Yeah,' Howard said. 'The haunted house and all. The landlady. I'm willing to help, though.'

'I know you are. God bless you. But it's not just that. There's some of this business that you ought to steer clear of. This man today ... this Stoat – he's a dangerous character. And you come up here on vacation and run straight into him.'

'And Sylvia was crazy for this guy.'

'After a fashion. She's fond of a handsome face and she trusts damned near anybody until they give her reason not to. He's not her sort, though. And if she knew he was hounding me ...!' Uncle Roy shook his head at the thought of what Sylvia might do.

'Well, look,' Howard said, pulling in at the curb in front of the house. 'I've got a sort of proposition for you. A business deal. It wouldn't mean much money, I'm afraid, only a couple hundred. And I wouldn't ask you at all if I thought it might be wasting your time. It seemed like a sure thing to me yesterday, but after visiting with Mr Jimmers last night, I'm not so sure anymore.'

'Sure about what? I'm happy to help. I don't need any commission, though – not from my nephew.'

'Of course, of course. It's the museum, though, that's offering the commission. They've sent the money up with me – part of an expense account. It's this bit of artwork that I'm supposed to obtain – I don't know how much I told you about it in my letter. It's a piece owned by Michael Graham, a sketch for a Japanese woodblock print. But now Graham's dead, and I can't get anything sensible out of Jimmers. I'm a foreigner up here, and what I need is a local – someone these people trust. You, actually, if you'd tackle it. I've pretty much come to the conclusion that I can't accomplish it alone. I hate to foist this off on you, what with the haunted house and all …'

His uncle was as pale as one of the Studebaker ghosts. Abruptly he held up the paper bag and pulled the cork out of the bottle with his teeth. He offered the bag to Howard, who immediately looked into the side mirror, a little bit uneasy with the idea of opening the whiskey in the car.

'No thanks.'

'That's the stuff,' his uncle said, after swallowing a mouthful. 'That's the feathers on the bird.' He replaced the cork with a shaking hand. 'My advice to you is to forget this – what did you call it?'

'It's a sketch by an old Japanese artist. Hoku-sai, I think. Graham had it hidden. Jimmers claims that it's gone now, but I can't make out whether Jimmers has made off with it or if the piece has been stolen. I don't mean to accuse him, of course.'

'Well, you know how it is up here. Lots of mysteries. Jimmers is one of the biggest of them. It'll probably surface in one of the oriental antique shops down in San Francisco, and Jimmers will be in groceries for a couple of months. I'll level with you. This is nothing you want to be involved in. If the thing's gone, it's gone. I'm certain that if Jimmers still had it, he'd ante up. Think of it as spilt milk.'

'Maybe,' Howard said. 'I've got to try to recover it, I guess. I've got to have something to tell them back at the museum. I'll need advice, though, from someone who knows the territory. But I won't take it for nothing, so this commission business still stands. If you won't help, I'll have to go elsewhere, which I don't want to do.'

'I'm telling you that I can't do you a shred of good. You're pumping money down a rat hole.'

'Fair enough. I've been warned.'

'Of course if push comes to shove,' Uncle Roy said cryptically, 'then I'm your man. You won't be working alone.'

Howard nodded, grateful for the promise but wondering how to apply it. He pulled in at the curb in front of the house and the two of them got out.

Howard decided not to press it any further, not to mention the 'object' that Stoat had referred to back at the bar. Easy does it, he told himself.

'Follow me,' Uncle Roy said, heading toward the back, past the scaffolding again. He stopped at the lean-to shed, pulling the splinter of wood out of the hasp, then stepped inside. There was a trouble light hooked up, hanging from the ceiling, a heavy orange extension cord leading away beneath the house. Uncle Roy turned the light on, pulled open a drawer, hauled out an inch-thick stack of sandpaper, and shoved the bottle in under it.

'Edith's not much on hard liquor,' he said. 'I've got a house bottle, too, but I'm pretty sure she keeps a weather eye on it. She's a fierce one when she's got a measuring stick in her hand. Doesn't mind a couple of bottles of beer gone, but a bottle of whiskey had better last a man six months; either that or he's a rummy. Better to humor her than to argue the case, though. That's paramount in a marriage. Argue for fun, if you want to, but not for profit.'

Together they strolled toward the back door, Uncle Roy telling Howard about his plans for the haunted house, calculating ticket prices and overhead and then going on to the barn lumber issue, and from there into talk about video game arcades and the profit to be made hauling chicken manure, carrying the conversation farther and farther away from landlords and rice paper sketches and the manifold mysteries that rode on the evening sea wind.

8

Howard found himself that evening in Sylvia's yellow Toyota, riding down the coast highway toward Mendocino and Sylvia's shop. Dinner had been a little rough. Uncle Roy talked so seriously and optimistically about the haunted house that he might have been soliciting investments in it. It was set up in an abandoned icehouse down on the harbor, behind the Cap'n England. His friend Bennet was 'working on it night and day.' It wasn't clear to Howard whether 'Bennet' was the man's first name or last name. Uncle Roy was the business end of the thing and the creative genius behind it. The man Bennet could use a hammer and nails and had been willing to work 'on spec.' Uncle Roy promised to haul Howard down there tomorrow, first thing in the morning, and show him a thing or two.

Uncle Roy's cheerful and convincing notions about the haunted house did nothing to enliven things, though. Aunt Edith had a look about her that suggested she found the haunted house tiresome, or worse – that she saw it as another looming financial disaster. Howard knew that they were in such straits that the loss of a couple of hundred dollars qualified as a financial disaster.

Sylvia said little. The subject of haunted houses seemed to embarrass her slightly, as if she had her opinion but couldn't state it without causing trouble between her parents. Howard smiled and nodded, uttering pleasant statements in a sort of oil-on-the-waters way. It had been a strain, though, and when he had suggested, after dinner, that he and Sylvia go out for a drink, she had accepted without hesitation.

Now Howard tried to make small talk while driving into Mendocino, but she seemed depressed and was untalkative. 'This haunted house business might just work,' he said. 'Those are popular things down south. Kids line up for blocks.'

Sylvia glanced into the mirror and shrugged. 'Maybe,' she said. 'Mr Bennet's sunk most of the materials into it. They're mostly salvage. If it fails, there won't be too much loss, financially speaking.'

'Right. That's what I was thinking. Uncle Roy's got some nice props, anyway – the eyeballs and ghost woman and all.'

Sylvia looked at him as if she thought he was kidding. 'It isn't money, though, that's bothering Mom. Not mainly. I think she can't stand to see him make a fool out of himself. She believes in him like crazy, and so every time he jumps on a new idea she suffers for it. She's seen him fail, and she doesn't want it to happen again, for his sake.'

'I talked to the old landlady today, what's-her-name.'

'That would be Mrs Lamey. She can be awful. Sometimes I think that it isn't just money she's after.'

'He gave her a thrill with the rubber bat.'

Sylvia smiled just a little bit, as if there were something about Uncle Roy's eccentricities that pleased her, after all. Then the troubled look came into her face again. 'If I lose the store,' she said, 'we lose the house.'

'That's too bad. The store floats the house?'

'In the spring and summer, when the coast is full of tourists, but the rest of the year it's a matter of squeaking by. Dad gets a Social Security check, but you know what that's worth these days. Anyway, I'm squeaking now. I operate these private New Age parties on the side, selling catalogue stuff, and that helps. That's what I was doing last night. That's why Jimmers couldn't find me. Mother and Father were out playing pinochle. Anyway, Father has the capacity to sort of fritter money away when we get a little ahead. Before the haunted house it was an aquarium down at the harbor. He got hold of a lot of heavy window glass and had the idea of gluing up aquariums and piping water in out of the ocean. He even applied for a grant to study marine life. He was going to sell fish and chips on the side.'

'It didn't work?'

'No.' She shook her head.

'He means well.'

'Of course he means well. And he's optimistic, too. He's always on the verge of making a killing. The spirit museum was going to make a killing, and it bled him nearly dry. It's almost a blessing that he doesn't have any real money to invest anymore.'

'He's got a certain innate genius, though. I'm sure of it. If he'd only find out how to put it to use.'

'Before we all go broke.'

'As I understand it, he believed pretty strongly in the museum.'

Sylvia looked hard at him. 'Why shouldn't he have?'

Howard shrugged. 'Sounds a little implausible, that's all. He was in competition with all those other roadside attractions, where gravity abdicates and water runs uphill and all. Hard to imagine tourists stopping at any of them, unless maybe their kids force them at gunpoint. What sorts of gimmicks did he have?'

'Gimmicks? None, if I understand what you mean. It wasn't fakery. He had a historical interest in the paranormal. He was sure there was something out there, along that stretch of highway. He was picking mushrooms early one morning, and … He's an amateur mycologist, did you know that? He used to be very well thought of, actually.'

'No,' said Howard, 'I didn't know. Anyway, he was out picking mushrooms …'

'And he saw a car full of ghosts drive past in the early-morning fog. They were apparently in Michael Graham's car.' Sylvia looked straight ahead, down the highway.

'I heard about that. He wrote a letter to my mother. How did he know they were ghosts?'

'He said they just evaporated there, while he was watching. The car was sort of drifting up the highway, and there were three men in it, wearing out-of-date hats. The car was slowing down as it passed him, and the three inside just … the car disappeared in the fog. It was Father that drove it back down to Graham's after it rolled to a stop against the guardrail. There wasn't anyone in it and not a soul around.'

'These ghosts were car thieves?'

She shrugged. 'I guess they were.'

'And so on the basis of this he invested twenty-odd thousand dollars?'

'That's just what he did.'

'You know, maybe he opened the place too close to town. If it was out in the middle of nowhere, people would stop in hoping to buy a snack or just to stretch their legs. But there's no use stopping when there's restaurants and motels five miles down the highway. They'd breeze right past him. He's big on location. I wonder why he didn't see that.'

Sylvia didn't say anything for a moment. Howard realized that what he was saying wasn't new to her. She and her mother had agonized over all this for years. His dredging it up now wasn't helping to cheer her up.

'You still don't understand it,' she said. 'Dad believed in these ghosts, and he thought that there was something out there that accounted for them. That explains the location problem. Why on earth would he have set up the museum anyplace else?'

'Sure,' said Howard. 'I wasn't thinking. I guess it's just that I wish he would have made a go of it. I'd like to go out there sometime. See what it's all about. Building's still there, I see. I passed it on the way in yesterday afternoon.'

'Yes, it's still there. Mrs Lamey owns it. It's pretty worthless, though. The roof leaks and there's termites in the walls. It's too small for a restaurant, and there's a moratorium against new building out there, so no one can do any-thing with it. There was talk of it being opened up as a gift shop, to sell redwood products, I think – lamps and carvings and all. Nothing's come of that, though.'

They pulled off the highway into Mendocino. There was the hint of mist in the air, and a fuzzy red-tinted ring around the full moon. A scattering of cars was parked along the sidewalk, but almost no lights shined in any of the shops except at the Mendocino Hotel, where the bar was fairly quiet.

'Can I have a look at the boutique?' Howard asked.

Sylvia nodded, fumbling in her purse for her keys. They clomped down the boardwalk and opened up the darkened shop. It was neat and sparse, a sort of study in minimalism, with blond fir paneling and a pine floor and what seemed to Howard to be almost no clothing at all on the wooden racks. It looked very high-toned, being empty like that, but there couldn't be much money in it. He fingered a roughly woven wool scarf, taking a peek at the price tag that dangled from it. Eighty-nine dollars, it read.

'Sell this stuff?'

'In the summer. Local folks can't quite afford most of it.' Sylvia slipped behind the counter and began to fiddle with papers while Howard looked around.

There was a pile of wooden bowls turned out of burls, a couple of rugs, a few pieces of art glass, and two Plexiglas trays full of folksy jewelry. All of it was expensive, backwoods designer stuff. There didn't seem to be a lot of anything but space. At one side of the counter were half a dozen books on origami art as well as patterned paper, cut into big sheets and slipped into plastic bags along with step-by-step folding instructions. Alongside lay an origami bird standing next to an origami egg, the egg so finely folded and faceted that there seemed to be almost no hard edges.

Hanging overhead were a half dozen more folded creatures, most of them fish. They were startlingly intricate – thousands of tiny folds in what must have been enormous sheets of paper to begin with. 'Still folding paper?' Howard asked.

'Yeah,' Sylvia said. She seemed distant, angry perhaps at what she had conceived Howard's attitude to be, or upset about the lease business and about the tense dinner.

Howard wondered if this was the time to bring up having found the paper lily, but he decided against it.

'It's therapy of a sort.'

'Ah,' said Howard. 'Therapy.' Somehow the notion of therapy spoiled things just a little. Sylvia opened the cash drawer and banged a roll of pennies hard against the edge, breaking the roll in half. Howard noticed that the several bills in the drawer were folded up, too, into bow-ties and stockings and elfin-like shoes. He reached across, picked out a bow-tie dollar, and widened his eyes at her.

She shrugged. 'Lots of time to kill, I guess.'

On the other side of the counter lay a couple of Chinese baskets full of crystals – mostly quartz and amethyst – as well as big copper medallions and bracelets and small vials of herb potions and oils. Alongside were racks of books full of New Age advice on the mystical properties of rocks and about reincarnation and out-of-body travel. There was some Rosicrucian flapdoodle on a throwaway pamphlet and a calendar of local events starring self-made mystics and seers and advice-givers of nearly every stripe.

Howard put the folded dollar back into the drawer and picked up the Rosicrucian ad. On it was a drawing of Benjamin Franklin seeming to be impersonating Mr Potatohead. The legend below read, 'Why was this man great?' Howard grinned, thinking up a couple of possible answers.

'You don't have to stand and sneer at it,' Sylvia said suddenly.

'I wasn't sneering, was I? I didn't mean to sneer. Look at Benjamin Franklin here, though.' He held the paper up so that she could see it. 'What's wrong with this man's face?' he said in what he hoped was a sufficiently serious and compelling voice, and then puffed out his cheeks and crossed his eyes. He started to laugh, but Sylvia's frown deepened, and so he controlled himself with an effort.

'Really,' he said, gesturing at the crystals and books. 'It's very … modern, isn't it? Very up-to-date. I like all of this sort of New Age stuff. It's so easily replaceable, like a paper diaper. This year your piece of quartz crystal cures arthritis or summons up the spirit Zog; next year it's a mantelpiece ornament, and you can't sleep until you own a three-thousand-dollar Asian dog. What was it last year, Cuisinarts and biofeedback? Or was that the seventies? I thought the Rosicrucians went out with *Fate* magazine.' He caught himself then. He had started out thinking to be funny, but now he was being something else. Uncle Roy would advise against the truth, or at least his version of the truth. There was no profit in it. It would make things worse.

'You see through things so clearly,' Sylvia said.

He shrugged, deflating a little but stung by her getting ironic with him. 'Well,' he said. 'I guess I wasn't taking the long view. People can't afford a hundred bucks for a hand-knit pair of gloves, but they can fork out twenty easily enough for a copper bracelet that lets them talk to the dead.' He tried to look cheerful, full of play.

Sylvia looked steadily back at him, though, and he realized that he had messed up, perhaps fatally. Sylvia didn't seem to have any sense of humor about this sort of thing. Like her father, she had probably developed a rock-steady belief in her products. She was too honest to do anything else. Howard reminded himself that he hadn't known her for fifteen long years. She might have come to believe in anything. Back when they were younger she had accused him once of despising whatever he couldn't understand, and there had been some truth in that. He hadn't forgotten it, but maybe he hadn't changed much, either. Life was safe and restful that way. You didn't have to tire yourself out developing new interests, and you could feel virtuous about being narrow-minded, too.

'I don't care about turning a profit. Not like you mean it,' Sylvia said. 'I'd like to make things a little easier on Mom and Dad, though.'

'Sure.' Howard felt a little ashamed of himself now that she had put it like that. 'I didn't mean ...'

'And besides, you seem to think this is all a fake. Everything's a fake to you. I was thinking you might have outgrown that sort of cynicism by now. And what's worse, how do you know what *I* think? How do you know what I believe and don't believe? Don't go around insulting people before you know what they're all about.' She paused for a moment and then looked him straight in the face, glaring just a little bit. 'In fact,' she said, 'there's evidence that I've lived past lives – lots of them. If you'd open your mind, instead of closing it down like a trap, you might find out a few things about yourself that would interest you.'

'What sorts of lives?' Howard was suddenly defensive again. He couldn't help himself. Maybe it was because she'd let him spend the night locked in Jimmers' attic while she hustled crystals to New Age loonies. He knew what she would say, too, about these past lives – that she was some sort of princess, Egyptian, probably, maybe Babylonian, or a serving girl who had caught the eye of the prince. There must have been a raftload of them back then, all waiting to die a few times in order to have a shot at being modern girls.

'I was a servant in the court of Ramses III, if you're really interested. Once, about a year ago, I underwent trance therapy and drew hieroglyphic figures in the sand with a stick. They had meaning, too. They weren't just scribbles. My therapist translated them. I had never seen any such things before, either. So you explain it, Mr Skeptic; nobody else can.' She still stared straight at him, waiting for him to scoff.

He widened his eyes at her. 'Do you mean like bird-headed men and ankhs and people doing that bent-handed Egyptian dance? I always loved that stuff. I had an elementary school teacher whose name, I swear it, was Rosetta Stone.'

'Seen enough?' she asked, heading toward the door.

'I guess. Look, I'm sorry. I was just being funny.'

'You're a riot. You don't believe in anything and so you make fun of people who do. Are you frightened of something, or what?'

'I don't know. I haven't thought about it that way.'

'Well, think about it. You don't half understand what's going on up here, do you? Maybe you ought to go back down to L. A. and leave us alone. Get lost on the freeways or something.'

Howard followed her out of the store, into the moonlight. His mind whirled. He'd been stupidly facetious, even though he could have predicted it would cause trouble. If he were utterly confident that he *did* understand some central mystery, then maybe he could put up with that sort of behavior from himself. But truthfully he had come to think, over the last couple of years, that he understood almost nothing. And the last two days had pretty much made him certain of it.

'I'm sorry,' he said. 'Actually I'm a little nervous. I *don't* know what's going on, just like you said. Everybody's telling me that, and I think it's getting to me. I don't know anything about anybody's past lives, and I'll admit it. I promise I won't make fun of it anymore. Let's get something to drink, like we set out to do. A bottle of wine.'

'I'm pretty busy,' she said, clearly still miffed about his attitude.

'What busy? What's there to do?'

They stood on the boardwalk near the duck pond. The full moon shone on the weedy water. It might have been romantic under other circumstances, but at the moment it was just cold and windy and uncomfortable. It occurred to Howard that he and Sylvia had gotten remarkably familiar with each other in the last two hours. The fifteen years had simply disappeared, like Uncle Roy's ghosts. Somehow, though, it had gone just as quickly sour. And it was Howard's fault, mostly. He tried to think of why it was partly Sylvia's fault, but he couldn't come up with anything good except for the reincarnation nonsense.

'I'm sorry I got smart,' he said.

She nodded. 'I think you say that too often.'

'Say what?'

'That you're sorry. Quit saying it. Just do something about it.'

'Right. Bottle of wine?'

Without saying anything more she headed up the street. He followed along, catching up to her at the corner, where she turned, angling across toward the Albatross Cafe. The bar upstairs was nearly empty, only a couple of people playing darts and eating popcorn. Geriatric-sounding New Age jazz played softly over hidden speakers. After being careful to consult her, Howard ordered a bottle of white wine and two glasses, and they sat in silence for a time.

'Mr Jimmers tells me you were robbed yesterday,' she said finally.

Howard nodded, then went on to tell her about the adventure at the turn-out on the highway, about the gluer microbus and the stolen paperweight. The news didn't seem to surprise her. 'Did you tell Father about it, about the paperweight?'

'Nope. Subject never came up.'

'I'll see if he can get it back for you,' she said. 'It might be sold by now, or traded away. There's a fairly hot black market operating up here. Lots of bartering and contraband. Father's had a hand in it. He's got connections that might have seen it. You might check out the antique stores downtown, too, or right here in Mendocino.'

'Good idea,' Howard said. 'I wouldn't mind buying it back.' He paused, thinking hard. Seconds passed while he stared into his glass. Finally he spoke, taking his chance on the wine and on Sylvia's inherently romantic nature. 'Actually I was bringing it up as a gift for you.' He gazed into his glass as the moments slipped past, hoping that the silence was underscoring his meaning. When he looked up in order to meet her eyes, she wasn't there; she was standing at the popcorn machine, holding the empty bowl from the table.

'I can't stand not to eat popcorn when it's around,' she said, returning with a full bowl.

'Me neither.' He snatched up a big handful and munched on it, trying to think of how to rephrase the statement about the paperweight. He topped off their wineglasses, noticing that the level in the bottle had gone down quickly. That wasn't a bad thing, except that if he were depending on the wine to loosen the evening up, a single bottle might not do it. And yet if he ordered a second, she might think he was up to something, or else drank like a fish along with the rest of his vices and bad attitudes.

'Anyway, this paperweight was a Mount Washington weight. I'm not sure how old, but nineteenth century for sure.'

She nodded at him and said, 'I almost feel like an appetizer. What do you think?'

'Sure,' he said, putting the lid on the urge to make a silly joke out of her statement. 'I mean, I'm pretty full of salmon. Something light, maybe. You choose it.'

'Be back in a sec.' She stood up and moved away, studying a menu that lay on the bar and then talking to the bartender for a moment. Howard could hear her laugh, but she was speaking too low for him to make out any of the conversation. Clearly they knew each other well. He felt like a tourist as he pretended to watch the dart game. Now he would have to bring up the paperweight a third time. That was almost impossible.

'Want anything to drink?' Sylvia asked from the bar.

'A beer,' he said. 'Anything local, thanks.' He turned back to the dart game. He might as well leave the rest of the wine to Sylvia.

She sat back down, smiling and with his beer and a glass. 'The bartender's a friend of mine,' she said. 'His name is Jean Paul. He's a martial arts expert and owns – what do they call it? – a dojo up in Fort Bragg. He has to moonlight here four days a week in order to keep the dojo open. Martial arts is a spiritual thing with him, a way of life.'

Howard decided to say nothing. He couldn't tolerate Jean Paul. Clearly it was a fake name. The subject of Jean Paul would just get him into trouble. The man had probably been a ninja assassin during the Ming dynasty. Wasn't a dojo some sort of aquarium fish? Martial arts stank on ice. It was another New Age phenomenon pretending to have lived exotic past lives.

'Say,' he said. 'I ran into Stoat down at a tavern in town.'

She was silent on the subject of Stoat.

'What's he up to these days along artistic lines? Does he still paint, or is he mostly a financier?'

'He paints pictures of complicated-looking microcircuitry, with bits yanked out of it. It looks sort of ... physiological. Fleshy, I guess you'd say, but it's cold and empty and nasty. Very nasty. To my eye it's just dead on the canvas. He's heavily into cybernetics.'

'You two aren't ...'

'Aren't what?'

'Seeing each other.'

'I saw him this afternoon. You drove past, remember.'

He nodded. 'Of course. I just ...' Howard let the subject die. Somehow the jovial bartender had made him jealous, and the jealousy had reminded him of Stoat. He had caught himself, though. There was no percentage in taking that line. 'So anyway, this paperweight ...' Howard started to say.

'Oh, yes,' Sylvia said, interrupting. 'You were worried about getting it back.'

'Well, no. Not exactly. You see, I remembered back when you used to have a couple. Remember that French one that you had – the St Louis weight with the little running devil in it?'

She nodded, but the conversation was interrupted by the arrival of the food – two plates, a tray full of potato skins, and a wire rack full of condiments and a couple of spoons. Sylvia studied her wineglass, her eyes distant, her mind troubled again. The paperweight subject had evaporated.

On the theory that desperate times called for desperate measures, Howard picked up the two spoons and wedged one into each eye so that the handles thrust away on either side of his head like dragonfly wings. He stared in her general direction, his face screwed up to keep the spoons from falling out. He swore to himself that he wouldn't relinquish the spoons, no matter what, until she did something – hit him, walked out, asked to use a spoon, anything.

She let him sit for a long minute, until he began to think about the other people in the bar and the spectacle he was making of himself. He started to wish he could see something past the edges of the spoons. What if she had left – gone to the popcorn machine or the rest room? What if she slipped out and drove home? Finally she laughed, though, as if she couldn't help herself, and shoved the end of a potato skin into his mouth when he tried to say something.

'Cheer the hell up,' he said, swallowing the thing.

'*You* cheer up. Better yet, don't talk. You keep getting into trouble when you talk.'

'I won't. I promise. I mean I will. Anyway, this paperweight …' He wanted more than ever for her to know that he had brought it as a gift.

She pursed her lips and nodded. 'I'll see what I can do. I can see that it's really bothering you. Like I said, if it's still around, maybe Father can get it back. You'll just have to be patient about it. It's really got you worked up, hasn't it? That's probably why you're on edge, why you're so catty about things.'

It was hopeless. Giving her the paperweight now, even if he had it, wouldn't work. He had made too big an issue of it. He decided to cut his losses and drink his beer. He poured the rest of the bottle of wine into her glass.

'I'm warning you right now,' she said, 'that if I drink that, you're going to have to drive home.'

'Fine. I'm sober as a judge. It's still early, though.'

She checked her watch. 'Just nine o'clock.' She drank her wine meditatively for a moment. Then she said, 'You know, for a minute there I thought you were going to tell me that you'd brought the paperweight up to give it to me.'

His eyes shot open. 'That's what I did,' he said. 'That's what I've been trying to tell you.'

She laughed. 'That's okay,' she said. 'You don't have to say that now. I know what the thing means to you. You were like that when you were a kid, too. Remember?'

'I guess I was.' He wondered what she meant, what she was up to. 'Like what?'

'Remember you had that one marble, the one with the red and blue swirls? That favorite one? What did you call it? "Martian Winter." Remember that? You were sure cornball sometimes.'

'I …' He shrugged. He *had* actually made up names for his marbles, but how on earth had she remembered them?

'You went absolutely stark when it disappeared. Remember? You cried for about a week.'

'Me? I never cried about that.' He'd been about eight at the time. He could still remember it clearly. It was one of those disasters that loom monumental in the mind of a child. He certainly hadn't cried about it, though – not in public, anyway.

'Did you ever figure out what happened to it?'

He shook his head. 'Lost it under the couch or something.'

Now she shook her head. 'Nope. I stole it. I gave it to Jimmy Hooper.' She smirked at him, finishing off her wine.

'I knew you did.'

'You *liar!* You never knew anything about it.'

'And I never drew bird men in the dirt, either, and had my trance therapist scope them out.'

'Neither did I. I was lying about that. I knew it would about kill you. I really didn't steal your marble, either.'

'I knew you didn't,' he said. 'And I really did bring that paperweight up here to give it to you.'

'You're sweet,' she said, still not believing him. 'I know what let's do, let's go out to the museum.'

'Now? In the dark?' Suddenly he regretted letting her finish the bottle of wine by herself.

'I've got a flashlight in the car. Don't forget that I'm pretty familiar with the place. I grew up there, nearly.'

'Would tomorrow be better? Tomorrow afternoon – I'm supposed to work on the haunted house tomorrow with Uncle Roy, but not all day.'

'You're scared,' she said. 'Just like when you lost the marble. Tell me your pet name for it again. I've forgotten. I want to hear you say it just once, just for the sake of old times.'

He sat like a stone idol, smashing his mouth shut, and then made the motion of turning a key in front of his lips, locking them tight.

'Remember when you set marbles all over the floor and said they were the "ice planetoids," and then you went to the bathroom and I brought Trixie into the house and played "deadly comet"? I think that's when the Martian one disappeared, don't you? It went down the heater vent in the floor.'

'No. Forget the marble. We were talking about going down to the museum. I can't believe you're serious about that.' He found himself hoping that she was, though. He could picture them hand in hand in the moonlit museum, waiting for the arrival of the ghost car. It was something they might have done in high school.

'Why not?' she said. 'What are you afraid of, ghosts?'

'What the heck,' he said. 'Not me.' Not for the first time, it struck him that Sylvia looked astonishing in her sweater. It gave him a new appreciation for the overpriced clothes in her shop. 'Let's go,' he said. 'I'll drive.'

9

Thank God for the moonlight, Howard said to himself as they wound their way down the highway, south through Little River. The road was empty save for one set of headlights a half mile behind them. Howard was ready to pull off the road and let the car pass rather than drive with its lights shining into his rearview mirror, but it stayed well back – always one or two bends behind them, pacing them evenly.

Without the moonlight it would have been utterly dark. As it was, there were patches of silvery light, illuminating here and there a bit of road or beach cut by the shadows of rocks and trees. The wind and the darkness had sobered Howard up quickly, but Sylvia leaned against his shoulder with her eyes closed, softly humming. The wine had relaxed her and she had managed to forget the day's troubles. Howard wished that it had been something else that had relaxed her – him, specifically. But he hadn't been able to.

This was home to her, this wild stretch of twisting ocean highway. He was in strange territory, though, and it made him nervous. No, that didn't entirely explain it – even as kids she had twice his sense of adventure, half his sense of fear. He watched for the headlights behind them. There they were, right on track. He couldn't see the car, even with the moonlight. 'Slow down,' she said, sitting up straight in the seat. 'Here it comes.'

He turned off the highway, past the picket fence with its cow skulls and across the weedy gravel parking lot where he pulled up against a wooden berm and shut the engine off, leaving the keys in the ignition. The windows in the building were tightly covered with plywood shutters, and even in the darkness, maybe especially so, the place had a long-disused look about it that somehow made him skeptical about going in.

Sylvia climbed right out, though, pulling a parka out of the backseat along with a flashlight. Howard reached for his corduroy coat, wishing he had brought something warmer. The ocean wind rushed straight up at them from across the road, and he could hear the crash of breakers, unnaturally loud in the silent night. They scrunched across the gravel toward the rear of the building, back into the shadows of the forest. The smell of eucalyptus leaves was heavy in the air along with the smell of the sea.

Sylvia shifted a little pile of granite rocks beneath an electrical circuit-breaker box, carefully lifting the grapefruit-sized rocks, as if wary of bugs, and shining her light in among them. 'There's a key here somewhere,' she said. Beyond, at the end of the building, was a padlocked door.

On an impulse he stepped back around into the parking lot and waited. Nothing. There wasn't a car in sight. He thought without meaning to of the gluer microbus on the highway and of the Chevy in the parking lot at Sammy's. Where was the car that had been following them? It should have gone past while they were fishing out their coats, but it hadn't. It had vanished.

There were driveways off the highway, of course, dirt roads leading down to houses on the bluffs or else up into the hills, up to the land of the cultists and dope gardeners. That would explain it. The car had turned off. It was as simple as that. It wasn't the fabled ghost car making a run down the coast. Graham's Studebaker was smashed to scrap on the rocks, anyway. Even ghosts wouldn't care to drive a wreck like that.

Cutting off the urge to whistle, Howard walked hurriedly around back, to where Sylvia ought to have been searching for the key. She was gone.

'Syl!' he whispered, suddenly terrified. There was no answer. He looked around wildly for a rock, a stick, anything. He hunched down and scuttled across to the pile of rocks she'd been messing with, picking one up and hefting it. Then he stood still, listening, and very slowly edged toward the building to get his back to a wall. He gripped the rock. There was nothing – no sound at all.

Until the door swung open and Sylvia stepped out onto the little wooden stoop, shining her flashlight into his face. He shouted – something between a scream and a groan – and threw the rock straight at the ground, as if he wanted to pulverize a lizard.

'What on earth is wrong with you?' she asked in a normally pitched voice. It sounded insanely loud. 'What were you going to do with that rock?'

He stood blinking at her, his heart pounding against his ribs. 'I thought you were gone,' he gasped out. 'I thought there was some sort of trouble.' He whispered this last bit, knowing that there was no reason to and that it made him seem twice as terrified.

'Aren't you gallant?' she said, laughing. 'Coming to my rescue like that. There's nothing out here.' Then she was silent, listening, as if to let the night provide its own evidence. There was nothing but the low rumble of breakers from across the road and the sound of the wind sighing in the trees.

The stillness didn't make Howard feel any better. That was just the trouble, wasn't it? – that there was nothing at all out there. He would have been more comfortable surrounded by the familiar noises of a southern California suburb.

He picked up the rock and tossed it back into the pile, calming down enough to be embarrassed at having thrown it like that. Sylvia went back into the darkened museum, playing the flashlight around on the walls. Howard followed, expecting – what? – ghosts, maybe, the Studebaker crowd in their top hats playing chess.

The place was dusty and deserted. It looked as if even in its heyday it had never amounted to much. He had expected some kind of fun house – with a mysterious cellar, maybe, and with different rooms and passages – but there was only the one big room and what looked to be a tiny office and bathroom off to the side.

Because of the darkness, nothing was particularly visible. Faint moonlight shone through the open door, but there was almost no light at all through the shuttered windows. Only the little beam of Sylvia's flashlight illuminated the room. She shined it across low tables built of redwood planks, like picnic tables. They were covered with dust, but nothing else.

'He used to sell literature on the supernatural,' she said. 'All kinds of stuff, some of it serious, some of it completely nuts. It was all over two of these tables. I used to keep it straight, which wasn't hard, since there were hardly any customers to mess it up. There was a wonderful model of the Studebaker, too, with the ghosts sitting in it. Mr Bennet built that. It had a table to itself. I kept it dusted. Father's got it somewhere, in a closet at home or something.

'Wait,' she said, 'there's a picture.' On the wall was an enlarged photograph, out of focus, of a Studebaker on the highway. In it sat a trio of half-evaporated men. One of them was looking out the window at the camera, his face indistinct.

'Uncle Roy took this?' Howard asked. 'I thought he was out picking mushrooms when it drove past.'

'He was out photographing them, actually. It was pure luck. There he was with the camera in his hands. Impressive, isn't it?'

Truthfully it looked to Howard like a bunch of dressed-up guys in a car, driving through the fog. 'It's weird, all right,' he said, not wanting to cross her. 'I wonder who was driving. This crowd would be more at home in a coach-and-four.'

Sylvia shrugged. 'I was always so astonished just at their being there in the car that I never worried much about who was driving.'

There were a number of other photographs on the wall, mostly bad ones in dime-store frames. Most were faked-up pictures of ghosts with a couple of paragraphs alongside by way of explanation. Sylvia shined the light on each in turn. There was a photograph of the ghost dog of Tingwick and another of the ghost dog of Garden Grove. Farther along was the Brown Lady of Raynham, descending a set of stairs, just like Uncle Roy's ghost woman, except that his was more convincing.

There were several artist's renderings of ghost cars and carriages, along with a dim photograph of a sort of Gumby vehicle parked behind a barn. Howard was happy to see that ghosts were as up-to-date as anyone, that early in the century they'd given up carriages and horses and taken to the highways in what were usually very fashionable cars – Daimlers and Austins and Rolls-Royces – all except Uncle Roy's ghosts, who had stolen a shabby old Studebaker. Beside a drawing of the ghost bus of North Kensington there was a photograph of the ghostly image of Dean Liddell, which had mysteriously appeared on the whitewashed wall of Christ Church Cathedral sometime in the early 1920s.

'Dean Liddell ...' Howard said. 'Wasn't that Alice Liddell's father?'

'Might have been,' Sylvia answered, giggling just a little. 'They have the same last name.'

'Ssh!' Howard cocked his head and listened.

'I was just joking ...' Sylvia started to say, but he clutched her arm and held it, and she was instantly quiet. They stood listening to the faint sound of the wind. 'What was it?' she whispered after a moment.

'I heard someone walking – on the gravel outside.'

'Just a squirrel,' she said, but she didn't sound convinced. They could see nothing through the shuttered windows. Both of them listened, but there wasn't a sound that there shouldn't have been. Sylvia started to giggle again. 'Where's your rock?' she asked.

He relaxed a little. It was his imagination again. He forced himself to ignore it, and then he wondered suddenly what he was doing out there in the woods in the middle of the night. Clearly he wasn't there to discover anything about the place. Daylight would be necessary for that.

Sylvia stood about a foot away from him now, still shining her flashlight on the sketchy visage of Dean Liddell. Howard put his hand on her shoulder and immediately felt a little less jumpy. She let it lie there, saying nothing and holding the light steady.

'Alice Liddell was Lewis Carroll's Alice – Alice in Wonderland,' Howard said.

'Really. And her father's face appeared on a wall? The family hogged more than its share of fame.'

'This is the only one of the ghost photos that doesn't look fake, isn't it?'

'How about Father's?'

'I mean besides his. Neither one of them looks like trick photography, anyway.'

'I'm ready to believe it,' she said. 'You're the doubting Thomas, remember?'

'Listen!' He had heard it again – the scuffing of shoe soles, the crunch of gravel. They stood absolutely still, but there was only silence again, as if something were waiting. And then, whisper-quiet, the back door of the museum swung closed.

'The wind,' Sylvia said as Howard stepped toward it, following the beam of her flashlight.

But there was a quick metallic clicking and the sound of the padlock snapping shut. There were clear footsteps outside now – someone hurrying – and low voices talking, maybe arguing.

Howard had a quick insane notion that it was Mr Jimmers, come around to lock him in for the second night in a row. Crazy as it had to be, the thought made him furious. He banged on the locked door, and then, in a rage, kicked it with the bottom of his foot. 'Hey!' he shouted at the darkness, but no one except Sylvia was paying any attention to him.

'Shut up and listen,' she whispered, grabbing him by the arm now. 'Someone's going through my car.'

It was true. They could hear a car door close, followed by the sound of the trunk slamming shut. Howard went from one window to another along the wall, trying to see out past the edge of the shutter, but it was no good. Through one he could see a sliver of moonlit ground, but that was all. Another door slammed.

He slid one of the windows open. 'I can kick the shutters out,' he whispered. 'They're just held in by a screw or a nail or something.'

'Why?' she asked.

'You're being robbed. What if they're going to steal your car?'

'What are you going to do, chase them up the road? Let them have the car and everything in it. Who cares? It's insured. Don't be a hero. This isn't worth getting beat up over.'

She was right. He saw that right away. He was still smarting from when she'd scared him outside, when he had thrown the rock into the dirt, and it seemed to him that kicking out the shutter would redeem him somehow. He listened again, to the sound of someone walking, probably two people. The footsteps receded now, fading into nothing. They hadn't stolen the car.

'Where are your car keys?' he whispered.

'In the ignition.'

That was puzzling. Why *hadn't* they taken the car? Clearly because they weren't garden-variety thieves.

'Are they both gone, do you think?'

'I don't know,' she said. 'Why wouldn't they be? Probably someone on the road, looking to steal a jacket or a blanket or something.'

He wondered. Somehow it felt as if it were something more sinister than that. 'What if they light the place on fire? With us locked inside?'

'Will you shut up about that!' she said, talking out loud. Then she whispered, 'Why would they do that? Don't invent things. This is bad enough. And if they do, then you have my permission to kick out the shutters – all of them.'

'Wait!' He held his hand up. There was the sound of a car engine trying to catch – except that the starter was bad, and it whined for a moment before the engine rumbled and the motor noise evened out.

'Stoat!' Howard said, and leaning back, slammed the edge of his forearm into the bottom of the shutter. It popped loose, but it was hinged at the top, and so it flopped back down into place, a nail in either corner bumping against the window casing. Hurrying, he bent the nails over sideways and then pulled one of the tables across. 'Come on,' he said, climbing onto the table and holding the shutter open. Sylvia climbed up next to him and handed him the flashlight.

'Careful,' he whispered. 'Check first.'

She stuck her head out, looking up and down the building. The parking lot was deserted. 'They're gone,' she said, and climbed through, dropping easily to the ground below and then standing up to grab the shutter. He gave her the flashlight and then climbed out himself, heading for the car. The keys were lying on the seat. The thief had taken them out to open the trunk and then tossed them back into the car. He could as easily have tossed them into the bushes, and Howard and Sylvia would have spent the next hour walking up the highway into Little River. This was very slick – carried out like a business venture, without any malice or larking around.

'Wait,' Sylvia said, hurrying back toward the rear of the building again. Howard went with her, watching carefully, trying to be ready if someone was hiding in the shadows. There was no one – only the scattered rocks and the door locked shut. Sylvia put the key in among the rocks and built the pile back up on top of it. 'Let's get out of here,' she said, sounding frightened now.

'Gladly.'

'How did you know it was him?' she asked. 'It might not have been Stoat. What do you have against Stoat?' She gazed at him evenly, and he had the notion that she was baiting him, being playful.

'His car engine,' Howard said. 'His starter's bad. It sounded just like that down at Sammy's this afternoon. You'd think a guy like that would be on top of things, would worry about being identified. Either he's sloppy or he doesn't care. Why should he? Apparently he didn't steal anything.'

She shrugged. 'Nothing that I can see. What the hell was he after?'

'You don't know?'

'I don't know. And quit looking at me like that.' She climbed into the car and started up the engine.

'I'm not looking like anything.' He shut the door and sat back in the seat, feeling easy at last. 'Let's go.'

'So what was he after?' she asked again. 'Can't you tell me? Is it a government secret or something? What are you, CIA?'

'No, I can't reveal my true identity. You can call me Agent X.'

'I'll call you brand X if you don't tell me what in the hell he was looking for.'

'They,' Howard said. 'They wanted the Hoku-sai sketch. The one that I came up after.'

'Where is it, then?'

'You tell me,' he said, 'and we'll both know. Could be that Jimmers has it. He's about the most suspicious person I've ever met.'

'He's pretty shady, all right,' Sylvia said. 'But he's just an eccentric. He's not up to anything – what? – illegal or something. Is this trouble with the sketch illegal?'

'I don't know. It may have something to do with Graham's murder.'

She looked at him, driving carefully along the dark highway, past the Little River Inn. 'Maybe Graham wasn't murdered,' she said. 'Word has it that he committed suicide.'

'Who told you that?'

'Who told you he was murdered?'

'Mr Jimmers … I think.' But *had* Jimmers told him that? Or had he only been joking? Jimmers had laughed like a prankster after saying it – hardly the response of a mail who believed his friend to have been murdered. 'I don't know, really. Anyway, you mean he *wasn't* murdered?'

'They found a suicide note in the car.'

'He wrote a suicide note and left it in the car? Then drove the damned thing into the ocean? What did he want, for the fish to read it?'

'I don't know. I'm just telling you that they found a suicide note – Mr Jimmers did. He gave it to the police in Fort Bragg. It was Mr Jimmers that found the car and all.'

'How'd he get down to the ocean, by boat?'

Sylvia shrugged. 'He got down there, that's all I know. The tide was up and the car doors were open – the fall knocked them open, I guess. Graham's body was gone, washed out with the tide, but the note was still in the car, clothespinned to the rearview mirror.'

'Uh-huh.' Howard realized that he didn't half believe in Graham's suicide. He didn't believe in murderers, either; what he believed was that he still knew almost nothing about what had gone on. But he had an idea, though, that he could find a way in the morning to learn more, and he determined to get up early, before the rest of the house was awake. 'I might as well tell you that Stoat threatened your father at the bar this afternoon. He pretty clearly was after something – the sketch, I think. And he implied that the problem of your lease could be fixed if Uncle Roy could come up with it. He offered him money for it, too. A lot, I think.'

'Father doesn't have any sketch. At least I'm pretty sure he doesn't.'

'That's what he said. Stoat didn't believe it, though.'

They drove in silence into Fort Bragg. It was almost midnight, and he was tired out. Sylvia was, too. He could see it in her face, which, this late in the evening, revealed her age just a little bit. He could see the strain of the passing years in the lines beside her eyes. 'Thanks for holding it together like that out there,' he said. 'I was pretty shaken up.'

'I was, too.'

'You were thinking. I was lurching around.' He patted her knee, not really meaning anything by it except that the physical contact, the warmth of her leg through her jeans, made him feel a little more solid. The world had been too full of ghosts.

'It's late,' she said, answering an unspoken question.

'Yeah, and I'm beat.' He moved his hand away, as if he had to in order to rub his eyes. They turned up Barnett Street, angling toward the curb in front of the house, in behind Howard's truck. Abruptly he sat up straight in the seat, peering out through the window. 'Shit,' he said.

'What, what's wrong?'

'The camper door's open. I left it locked.'

10

Howard awoke in darkness, jarred awake when the iron clock in the living room tolled five. That had gone on all night, and he had finally gotten off to sleep by smashing the pillow over his head and then had awakened two or three more times when the bell tolled. He rolled over, deciding not to get up, after all. Sleep was more important to him. Then he lay there thinking, waking up a little more each minute, starting to worry about trifles, as he always did when he woke up in the early morning.

Only now what he worried about seemed to be more than mere trifles, and it seemed to be more and more certain to him as the minutes dragged past that he didn't have very much idle time. He was being locked up at every turn, and his truck had been burgled twice – once by the gluers and now by Stoat and whoever else had gone through Sylvia's car. They hadn't taken anything this time, but the act itself was ominous. Things were happening in pairs and in triplicate, and somehow at five in the morning that seemed to signify. He climbed out of bed after another few minutes of mulling things over and pulled on his clothes.

Fog had drifted in during the night. It was gray-dark outside, and still. He went out silently through the kitchen door, trudging through the wet grass around to the front of the house, where he got Sylvia's flashlight out of the backseat of her car, eased the car door shut, and headed for the backyard again.

When he passed Uncle Roy's workshop, he hesitated for a moment and then pulled the splinter of wood out of the hasp and opened the door. He turned on the light and looked around, wondering what he could carry with him out into the woods. He only half believed Uncle Roy's horror stories, but somehow the fog and the early-morning twilight had started to work on him. He found a two-foot length of closet rod in among a stacked-up pile of scrap lumber. He swung it into the palm of his hand a couple of times, deciding that it would do the trick as well as anything. It was a bit of security, anyway – something to balance the fear that was seeping into him even as he stood there.

He went out again, leaving the door unlatched, and headed straight for the misty line of fir trees. The yard sloped up into them, fenced off by berry vines, which had been hacked away along the north edge so that there was a path into the woods. On the other side of the path lay a vacant lot, overgrown with vines and scrub.

Up close, the woods weren't quite as thick as it had seemed from a distance. Even with the fog he could see a good ways through the trees – far enough so that he was unlikely to come upon anyone unawares. He switched on the flashlight, but the glow was feeble because of the dawn leaking through the tops of the trees. In among the deep shadows the light helped more, though, and he was happy enough to have it. He suspected that he didn't have far to go.

He walked along for a time, conscious of the smell of evergreen and fog. You didn't often get that sort of thing down south. Here he was, up at dawn, trudging through the primeval woodlands. It wouldn't be a bad thing to make a morning ritual of this – in any sort of weather. He could buy some sort of oilcloth raincoat and a pair of galoshes, too, and try it in the rain, carrying a thermos of coffee.

Just when that pleasant notion occurred to him, the path forked. He stopped and listened to the stillness, a little bit wary now. The fog had thickened and seemed to be settling in rather than lifting. How far *had* he walked? He had been enjoying himself and not paying attention. There was a rustle back among the trees just then, and his heart leaped. He stood still, thinking of Uncle Roy's bears and lions. It hadn't been much of a rustle, though – barely enough for a rabbit or bird – just enough so that his hearty, up-at-dawn mood utterly evaporated and he was filled with unease. He told himself that the forest wasn't any different in the fog and the darkness than it would be in the sunshine. Then he tried to convince himself that surely the fog would begin to burn off as the sun came up.

He looked behind him, though, and saw nothing but a wall of murk and trees. He had no idea how far away the city lay or in which direction he had come. He had wanted to go straight on up the path, roughly along the property line – but which of the two paths confronting him now was the main path and which one branched off? Neither one was well traveled. For no reason at all he stayed to the left, going along quickly and quietly for three or four minutes until the path forked again.

Again he angled left. That ought to be safe. If he failed to find anything at all, he could at least make his way back by – what? – taking all the left forks again. Or was it all the right forks? – he would be returning after all. Would there necessarily be any forks at all? He would be coming back, but then he wouldn't be coming *backward*, would he? Most of these sideline trails would be leading away behind on his return, anyway, deeper into the forest. It would just muddle him up to pay attention to them.

Somehow it had gotten darker; either that or the forest was more dense. He was sure now that he had come too far, but he went on slowly, anyway, determined to turn back soon. There was something up ahead; he could see it dimly through the mist, a sort of clearing. Just then there was another path, too – this one leading away behind. It couldn't do him any good now, but it was the one that would cause trouble on the way back. There was a lot of autumn-colored poison oak, he noticed, climbing all over the stump of a tree, right there at the fork. He would remember that easily enough.

He walked on, as if hurrying now would get him out of the woods sooner, and within moments he found himself standing at the edge of the clearing he had seen through the trees. It was overgrown with grass and wild iris and skunk cabbage. The path ended there, just like that. Clearly he was deep into the woods – far deeper than Aunt Edith could have ventured yesterday afternoon. She had been gone for maybe ten minutes and seemed to have made a round trip of it – although now that he studied it out, he couldn't really be sure that it was *her* red jacket he had seen through the trees. It might have been anybody, kids maybe. This might easily be a wild-goose chase.

Someone had been using the clearing as a junk pile, too – so much for the primeval woodland idea. There were a couple of old car fenders tilted against each other toward the far side of it, although it was too weedy and misty to make much else out. There was something about the way the fenders were tilted together, though, as if they were meant to form a little shrine ...

Suddenly he was both curious and terrified. He ducked back behind a tree and stood listening. There wasn't a sound. Clearly this was too far out into the forest to be a mere junk pile; no one hauls car fenders into the woods just to throw them away. A child might haul them out there to build a fort, of course, although scrap lumber would have made more sense. He quit trying to make sense out of what he saw. This had something to do with what he had found embedded in the attic plaster night before last. There was no getting around it.

He stepped out from behind the tree, satisfied that there was no one around, and walked to where the two fenders stood, sunk six inches or so into the soft loam. There was freshly dug soil scattered across the top of the weeds. Someone had been working at the thing recently. Beneath the arched, mismatched fenders, someone had built a clever little wall out of odds and ends – small stones, an old glass inkwell, doll-sized lipstick tubes, a broken pocket knife, a rubber puppet head, half a dozen ivory dice, a couple of broken tin toys, and, among more of the same, his stolen paperweight.

Sitting on this junk-pile wall, his short legs dangling, was a ceramic Humpty Dumpty, its paint nearly weathered off and the white of its shell the color of an old meerschaum pipe.

Howard reached down to pick up the paperweight, but then stopped himself. Something in him didn't want to disturb it, any of it. There was something child-like about the collection – like the careful arrangement of small toys and collected objects, say, on top of a child's bedroom dresser, arranged just so for reasons that only the child could fathom. He was struck with the certainty, though, that the oddball little wall wasn't the work of a child. There was a magic in the arrangement and choice of objects. He could feel it in the air of the clearing. He had stumbled into an open-air cathedral, and he felt suddenly that he didn't belong there and didn't want to run into anyone who did. To hell with the paperweight.

He was determined now to head straight to the house. He would find a way to slip out that afternoon, maybe, when the fog lifted and the sun shined. He slowed down in order to make less noise. There seemed to be paths everywhere around the clearing, and the fog had settled in so that even nearby trees were ghostly and dim. He stumbled on a root and nearly fell on his face in the grass, dropping the flashlight to catch himself. He sprang up at once, shaking his hand and looking around, half expecting a patchwork zombie to materialize out of the fog. He had wandered straight off the path somehow, out onto another little patch of meadow.

This was no good at all. He was utterly lost, and had been within five minutes of leaving the house. The whole concept of direction, of north, east, south, and west, was imaginary. It meant nothing, had no application. Realizing it made him mad. He would sit down and wait. Wasn't that what someone advised? Sooner or later they would discover that he was missing and – what? Follow him into the woods, track him with dogs? It wasn't likely.

He could wait out the fog, perhaps – unless it didn't lift for two or three days. It was almost funny. He was thirty years old and lost in the damned woods. He didn't feel like laughing, though, or sitting, either, so he found the path and started walking again, searching futilely for his own footprints coming the other way.

The trail narrowed and weeds grew up through it. Clearly it wasn't very often traveled. There wasn't any sign of his footprints on it, or anyone else's, either. A fallen tree loomed out of the fog, blocking the trail and making it certain that he'd gone wrong. He turned around, took ten steps back, and found another trail, this one broader and well traveled.

Don't get frantic, he told himself, half out loud. Then immediately he understood that to be evidence that he was getting frantic. He felt the urge to run up this new path, just in order to get somewhere different, and so he consciously slowed his pace and forced himself to pay attention to his sur-roundings – to remember oddly shaped bushes and trees. It was daylight now, and the fog was ghostly white where the sun shined through. It was wet, too. Water dripped down the back of his coat from overhead branches. *Were* there bears in the woods? He asked himself that, wishing immediately that he hadn't thought of it.

Again the path forked, this time to the right – a better path, it occurred to him, although he couldn't have told himself why. He had to duck beneath low branches, hunching along through the gloomy twilight. There was sud-denly an ocean breeze – just the hint of one, as if maybe he had found his way back toward the edge of the woods, after all, and he hurried along, wonder-ing how long he'd been out there – a half hour, anyway, maybe longer.

The path ended at the clearing with the shrine again. He had blundered in a sort of zigzag circle through the woods, coming upon the clearing from the other side. At once he plunged back into the trees, with no idea where he was bound, and stumbled within seconds into a patch of forest partly clear of fog. He found himself atop a ridge, its overgrown slope running down into a weedy little pond, and then another hill beyond it, very steep and grassy. He clambered down the slope toward the pond, standing after a moment in marshy grass at the edge, watching water striders flit across the top of the water while he caught his breath, utterly lost.

Across the pond, floating on the shallow water and tied to a half-submerged tree, lay an old rowboat with a couple of trout poles and fishing tackle in the bottom of it, partly covered in a piece of oilcloth. Leading away from the boat, along the edge of the pond and then through the grass and up the opposite slope, was another trail. Through the trees he could just make out what looked to be the shingled roof of a cabin, the rest of the cabin hidden by the hillside. He picked his way down and around the pond, slogging through mud and wet grass until he reached the path on the far side.

He crouched along, moving slowly, watching the back of the cabin appear above the crest of the hill and ready to duck into the bushes at the sight or sound of anyone at all. There was a light on inside the cabin and smoke from a chimney. It occurred to him that he ought to have been happy, stumbling back into civilization like this, but he wasn't. This was hardly civilization. Likely as not, this cabin had been Aunt Edith's destination yesterday afternoon. He had come too far not to find out now.

Now that he needed it, the fog had mostly disappeared. He crept forward, toward the rear of the cabin where a long pile of split logs reached nearly to the windows. The intelligent thing, of course, would be simply to knock on the front door and announce that he had gotten lost in the woods and needed directions. Except that there was clearly something secretive about Aunt Edith's furtive trip, and at the moment he felt like being equally furtive. And there was the shrine in the clearing, too, not a hundred yards away, that lent the whole business a strangely dangerous air.

He peered in at the rear window, into a small bedroom containing little more than an unmade bed. Through the open door he could see into what was maybe a living room, just making out the edge of a stove and the corner of a small wooden table. Shadows moved across the edge of the table, but no one stepped into view. He would have to find a more useful window.

He edged down toward the corner of the cabin, ducking low behind the woodpile in order to take a peek before stepping into the open. He could feel the ocean breeze again, blowing uphill toward the cabin, and it struck him that if the breeze held up he could take a stab at following it toward town. A well-traveled path angled away in that general direction, and although the trees were too thick for him to be certain, that path must surely lead toward Uncle Roy's house – toward the city instead of deeper into the woods.

His footsteps were noiseless on the soft, weedy ground as he slipped past two curtained windows, neither one of which gave him any view at all of the interior. At the corner of the house there began a broad, wooden front porch, and the ground ran away downhill steeply there, so that in the very front of the porch there were four or five wooden steps. He would have to clump across the porch in order to see in.

He crept back down to the woodpile and from there back down the hill toward the pond, so as to approach the house from some little distance. It wouldn't do to seem to have been snooping around. Should he whistle? He squashed the idea as too theatrical. He would yell 'Hello' instead, a couple of times, and then head up onto the porch and knock heartily so that no one on earth could think him a sneak.

Putting on his best look of pleasant surprise, just for the sake of anyone looking out the window, he cupped his hands over his mouth and stopped cold, cocking his head to listen. He had heard the sound of a door slamming.

346

There wasn't any doubt. It must be well after six now. He had been mucking around in the woods forever. He jogged away in a crouch again, back toward the woodpile. Inside of three minutes, here came Aunt Edith, carrying a foil-covered plate of food and a pot of coffee. She hurried along, although she didn't look ill at ease; she looked attentive, as if she wanted to arrive with hot food.

She passed out of sight, and then momentarily he heard a screen door slam shut and then another door shut more softly. This time he hurried around the opposite side of the house, the side that fronted the deep woods, so that if his aunt went back out directly, she wouldn't catch him in the open.

A red wheelbarrow stood tilted against the house, surrounded by garden tools and piles of mulch and stakes and pots. The nearby garden was made up of moldery little rows of withered cabbages and anemic onions, all of it blighted somehow. He pulled the wheelbarrow away, settling it down onto its bed, and silently climbed up onto it so as to see in through a window just beside the edge of the front porch. Luckily the curtains hung a couple of inches apart – plenty far enough for him to get a quick glimpse inside.

There stood Aunt Edith next to an old black potbellied stove. Her plate of food sat on the table. Sitting in a chair, just getting ready to tie into the food, was old Michael Graham, thoroughly alive, although incredibly old and frail-looking. A walking stick leaned against the back of an adjacent chair.

Howard clung to the windowsill, lost in thought. What did this mean? The old man was hiding out here, certainly. That was clear. So he wasn't murdered and he hadn't committed suicide. The car-over-the-cliff business had been a ruse, a red herring to confound Stoat and his associates. Who knew that, besides Uncle Roy and Aunt Edith? Jimmers? Sylvia, clearly. Why hadn't they told Howard? Because he was from out of town – a casual guest. For his own good, obviously, they would attempt to keep it secret. There was no use him getting involved. So where was the sketch? It was a good bet that the old man had it. His mind spun, trying to add things up, to work out the mathematics of the puzzle.

Aunt Edith turned to leave, and Howard dropped off the wheelbarrow and scuttled back toward the rear of the house, hunching along past the woodpile again. In a couple of minutes, after she had plenty of time to get home, he would follow her. There was nothing more to learn – not without breaking into the cabin and searching it, which was utterly out of the question. He was sliding into deep waters, to be sure, and his best bet would be to wade ashore while he still had his feet under him, and give up any notions of being an amateur detective. He didn't owe the museum anything, anyway, and no one, certainly, owed him the Hoku-sai sketch.

He crouched there for one more moment, just to be safe, and in that moment he felt a tap on the shoulder.

11

For a moment Howard crouched silently, knowing that trouble stood at his elbow, but asking the universe for another ten seconds of relative comfort before he had to look doom in the face. He tensed himself and turned around. Doom had taken the form of Uncle Roy, who stood there in a heavy jacket, holding a field guide to West Coast mushrooms and a little basket covered with a handkerchief. He shook his head as if advising Howard not to talk and then nodded back toward home. Howard followed him down the path, feeling sheepish and still shaking a little from the fright.

Uncle Roy ambled along, stopping every now and then like an Indian tracker to examine the ground. He picked up a limp little mushroom and dangled it there for Howard to see. 'Panaeolus campanulatus,' he said. 'Don't eat this one.'

'I won't,' Howard said.

Roy pitched it into the bushes, wiping his hands on his pants. 'I've got a bunch of crap at the house that I've got to haul down to Bennet's. I figured you'd want to come along. You seemed keen on it last night. We'll run it over to his house this morning.'

'Sure,' Howard said. 'I was out for a walk. You don't get this sort of opportunity down south. There's no place to walk to, really.'

'That's a fact. That's why we got out of there. These woods, though … You're lucky you didn't just disappear into the fog, wander up into the coast range somewhere. It's a dangerous place. They've found the bones of hikers up there, picked clean.' He said nothing for a moment and then, matter-of-factly, said, 'You've found the cabin.'

This took him by surprise. 'Yes, I guess so.'

'I knew you would. I knew it yesterday afternoon in the truck there, when you brought up the subject of the sketch again. 'There's no hiding anything from a lad like Howard,' I said to myself. And then when I couldn't find you around the house this morning even though your truck was still out at the curb, I waited for Edith to go out with the old man's breakfast and I came along after her. Sure enough, there you were. "Howard's a shrewd one," I said to myself. "We've got to come clean with him." Look here. Look at this.'

He bent over and pointed at a brown, corky-looking fungus coming out of a rotted stump. 'That's a pretty specimen, isn't it?'

'Nice color at the end there,' Howard said, pointing to the pale blue edge of the thing and waiting for Uncle Roy to come clean with him.

'That's one of the pore fungi. What they call "artist's fungus." Believe it or not, it's tough enough to carve. You can make attractive household articles out of it – matchboxes, candlesticks. Not much market for it, though.'

'Lots of mushrooms out here in the woods, aren't there?'

'More than you'd suppose. You can just eat the hell out of most of them, too. You wouldn't want to, maybe. Half of them taste like rotten dirt. Take a look at these.' He lifted the cloth from the top of the basket. Lying in the bottom was a handful of small purplish fungi, misshapen and evil-smelling. 'I'll bet you a silver dollar that these are uncatalogued. Never seen or heard of them. I've been finding them over the last few days, growing out around the cabin. I call them witch flowers. Look at the shape.'

Howard peered closely at them. Sure enough, they looked like little disfigured lilies, as if someone had set out to make imitation flowers out of crayons and snail slime but hadn't seen enough real flowers to get the shape right. 'Smell like hell, don't they?'

Uncle Roy looked shrewdly at him. 'You don't know how close you are to being right,' he said, putting the cloth back over them.

The two of them set out down the trail again, still going slowly, Uncle Roy on the alert for mushrooms. 'About the cabin,' he said. 'We're putting up a guest there.'

'Right. Michael Graham. That's where Aunt Edith goes with the food.'

'Breakfast, lunch, and dinner.'

'I guess that means he's not dead, then.'

'No, he's not dead. That was a ruse that didn't work worth a damn. Might have gained us a week.'

Us? Howard wondered about that. Maybe Uncle Roy was coming clean at last.

'He's lame, though. He's old. Do you know how old he is?'

'No,' Howard said, and the phrase 'older than the woolly mammoth' sprang into his mind.

'Ninety-something. He has the right to be lame.'

'Lame, though,' Howard asked. 'From the accident? The car going over the cliff?' He felt abruptly foolish for having said such a thing. He hadn't been in the car at all. Maybe he was lame from some old war wound.

'He can hardly get around any longer without his cane. Does a little fishing when he's up to it, but most of the time it's all he can do to eat. He and I are old friends, you know.'

'Are you?'

'Oh, yes. Old friends. We go way back, to before Edith and I married. When it got bad for him … Well, he was too easily gotten at, if you see what I mean, out there on the bluffs and all, with no one around but Jimmers. We thought we'd better hide him. The woods are full of our people, too, coming and going.'

'I saw some evidence of that. But what do you mean "gotten at"? More creditors?' That was a safe word, one of his uncle's favorite euphemisms.

'Worse than that, actually. This sketch that you're keen on. You aren't the only one, you know.'

'Is that right?'

'Yes, and it's not just the money, either.'

'I can see that,' Howard said. 'The piece can't be as valuable as all that.'

Uncle Roy stopped for a moment. They were in sight of the house now. 'There's value and then there's value,' he said, nodding back uphill in the direction of the cabin. 'It's a rare piece, all right. I know why you've come out here, but let's not bother the old man as early as this. He's tired. Spends his time just holding his own. He usually comes down to fish around dusk. If we can swing it, we'll bring down a couple of poles and stop off for a chat, maybe this evening. I'm going to level with you, though. Your being here is a liability, of sorts. Don't mistake my meaning, either. I want you here. I think maybe you *have* to be here. It's entirely possible that you don't have any choice in the matter. You better brace yourself for that. But you're a suspicious character, aren't you, riding in like Perceval on a horse. What's his game? they're thinking.' He looked hard at Howard, clearly waiting for an answer.

'I don't know what my game is,' Howard said truthfully.

'I believe you. Maybe you don't have one. Maybe you do. No matter what we like to think, we don't always get to choose what games we play in this world. Sometimes they choose us.'

Uncle Roy set out again, and said nothing more until they were out of the woods. When he stopped again in the backyard in order to finish their talk in private, he had the look of a man who was choosing his words carefully.

'Anyway, you're something of a liability. What I mean is that word's out that you've come north, after the sketch, looking for Graham. Who are you, they're wondering, one of us or something new? It's pitched the balance all haywire, hasn't it? Now, we supposed that they thought Graham was dead, but from what Stoat was saying yesterday afternoon, they didn't fall for the wrecked-car trick. Stoat could as easily have been fishing, of course. But he's gone through your truck, hasn't he? And through Sylvia's car, too – undoubtedly because she was with you. He's onto you, then, and no denying it. What I'm saying is that I don't want you leading him or any of his people into the woods. That's paramount. You understand that, don't you?'

'Sure,' Howard said. 'I didn't know ...'

'You couldn't have. I should have told you, but I didn't want you dragged along, either. I'm beginning to think it's a whirlpool, though, with all of us in the same boat, going round and round together. We'll pull through if we look sharp, all engines full. Maybe you're the captain of this damned tugboat – the dread Captain Howard from down south. Time will tell. We're not alone in this, either. We've got confederates.'

'What did you mean "his people"? Is there a whole crowd of them, then, trying to put their hands on the sketch?'

'Too many of them for my taste. Stoat's not the most formidable of them, either. It's Heloise Lamey that we've got to watch. Say, I'm half starved. Let's hit the Cap'n England for breakfast – some of those million-dollar pancakes and bacon. You can buy. Edith cooked the old man a couple of eggs, and she'll want to fix us up, too. But I want to talk a bit – set you straight on some of this, if you know what I mean. Secrecy is paramount.'

'Surely Aunt Edith …' Howard made a stab at protesting, but Uncle Roy cut him short.

'True enough. She's a party to this, but not in the way you and I are. She's been looking after Graham, and so has Sylvia. I like to call them the "tent maidens."'

He grinned at Howard, finding this clever. Howard didn't get it, though.

'Like in the Grail romances.'

'Ah,' Howard said. 'Sorry. I'm ignorant of most of that.'

'Well, no matter,' Uncle Roy said. 'Live and learn, as the old saw goes. Anyway, they're both on the boat, too, but they don't come out on deck very often, and so maybe they haven't taken a good look at the sky lately. It all makes Edith pretty seasick, is what I'm trying to say, so we'll let her rest in her stateroom for the moment. But you and I can't sleep, boy. Not a wink. The barometer's dropping, and it's up to lads like us to haul on the bowline. That's paramount. We can't be slackers, or they'll catch us out.'

'I'm your man,' Howard said, trying to decide if he had learned anything particularly useful or new. Uncle Roy seemed to live in a world of euphemism and metaphor, and it left Howard with a hundred practical questions, all of them clattering around, colliding with each other. Maybe over breakfast …

'My advice right now,' Uncle Roy continued, 'is to lie low. You know nothing at all. That's the byword. Don't tip your hand. Forget the sketch for the moment. It'll be there right enough when the time comes. Or else it won't. I don't know quite where it is, and that's the solemn truth. Jimmers reported it stolen to the police, and for all I know that's gospel. He's a deep one, though, and in a business like this it's better if the left hand doesn't know what the right hand is doing. Do you follow me? They don't know which way to jump when you work it like that.

'This business of Jimmers' shed …' his uncle was saying as they trooped in through the back door. He cut off the sentence, though, at the sight of Aunt Edith washing dishes. 'Ready in five?' he asked Howard.

'Easy,' Howard replied, and went up the hallway to change his clothes, hearing his uncle in the kitchen saying something to Aunt Edith about them 'making a connection on the barn lumber.'

At midmorning, Howard found himself pulling into the parking lot of the ghost museum again, along with Uncle Roy, two propane lanterns, and a heavy flashlight. Uncle Roy had a 'hunch,' and he couldn't rest until he'd taken a look at the museum. But they must try to be back up in Mendocino before noon, he said, in order for Howard to meet Bennet, who spent his mornings working on his house. Howard intended to ask Sylvia out to lunch today, too. Time was short.

The place seemed doubly deserted in the wind that blew off the ocean, whipping the tree branches. A little flurry of pine needles and autumn leaves whirled across the gravel lot, pinning Howard's pants to his legs, and the hollow-eyed cow skulls on the pickets stared straight into the wind, watching the whitecaps through the trees. The whole place was inhospitable, geared to frightening people away – a perfect habitat for ghosts but a bad one, perhaps, for customers.

The rocks beside the rear steps were scattered over the ground. 'Sylvia piled those back up last night,' Howard said, suddenly tense.

'Of course. They came back is what they did. It's just as well you got out of there, although I suppose they gave you a chance to do that so as to avoid confronting you. They don't want outright trouble. Not yet. Key's gone, of course, the bastards.'

'No, it isn't,' Howard said, spotting the key in the dirt along the concrete foundation where someone had tossed it. 'Why did they lock it back up, do you think? Why bother?' He handed his uncle the key.

Uncle Roy shrugged, stepping heavily up the stairs. Now that they were around out of the wind and into a little bit of sunlight, he had started to sweat. 'Maybe they didn't find what they wanted but are afraid it's still here,' he said, unlocking the door and pocketing the key. He lay the propane lanterns on one of the tables and fired them up, adjusting the flame.

What there was left of the place had been dismantled. The framed photographs, one by one, had been pulled off the walls, taken apart, and lay now scattered over the tables and floors. Nothing was smashed or wrecked. The intruders hadn't been in any sort of fury. Again, the whole business was methodical, painstaking – something that Howard found troubling. It seemed to argue that their adversaries, 'the enemy' as Uncle Roy had referred to them during their cryptic talk at breakfast, were calm and organized and moderately sure of themselves.

In the little bathroom, the lid had been removed from the top of the drained toilet, and the medicine cabinet had been pulled entirely out from its niche in the wall and yanked apart. They'd taken the steel band off from around the mirror and pulled it away from its backing. They'd even looked into the hollow chrome-plated bar of the towel rack.

Out in the main room, the floor vents were pulled up. Howard looked down through the hole in the floor at the old gravity heater below, sitting in an open concrete box. With the flashlight it was easy to see where the dust had been disturbed on top of the dark metal. Someone had hung through the hole and had a look around down below.

'So they were looking for the sketch,' Howard said, helping his uncle gather stuff up. 'They thought it was framed up behind one of these photographs or rolled up and shoved into the towel bar or something. Thorough crowd. As I read it, though, their being here means they don't have it. Not yet.'

'Don't be so sure. If they have it, they need time, and this could be a ruse. Throw us off the track with a lot of tomfoolery.'

'Why would they have been so careful about it, though? I guess because paper is delicate, and they didn't want to tear it up, to damage it.'

'Or to *pretend* to care about not tearing it up, of course. The trick is to separate illusion from reality here, isn't it? This is a powerfully tricky lot of scum. Their purposes are never apparent. Nothing is.'

Uncle Roy squinted at Howard, making this last statement seem to apply to everything, to the north coast in general, to the wide world.

'Too bad about these pictures,' Howard said. 'They don't seem to be ruined, though. We can put them back together again.'

Uncle Roy smiled at him, as if he'd said something funny. 'That's the way to talk,' he said. 'These are all copies, actually. I took everything valuable along home two years back, when the place folded. You can only keep so much stuff.'

'How about the police?' Howard asked suddenly. 'The place has pretty clearly been ransacked. Let's call the police and put them onto Stoat.'

'Let's not,' Uncle Roy said. 'Let's not even think about the police. We don't want institutionalized help.' With that he shut the lanterns down, picked them up, and headed for the door. Five minutes later, after ditching the key in a new hidey-hole, they set out for Mendocino, Uncle Roy directing Howard through town and up onto Albion where they parked at the curb in front of the house with the Humpty Dumpty on the roof, the very house where Howard had nearly wrecked his truck yesterday morning.

The front lawn of the house was a wonderland of miniature windmills and whirligigs. A small, dark-haired man in a string-sleeve T-shirt worked out front, shoveling concrete out of a galvanized tub. Across the street, dressed in a sort of red kimono and a pair of Wellingtons, Mrs Lamey watered her roses.

Howard was surprised to see her there, in public, just like that, living across the street from the Humpty Dumpty house. It meant that she had a life of some sort, a favorite chair that she sat in, maybe a family. Up until then he had defined her entirely in terms of mortgages and percentage points. It surprised him even more sharply when she recognized him and waved, as if she were happy to see him. Well, he thought, business is business. Maybe this is watering the roses, and business doesn't apply.

He waved back. There was no use being troublesome. Then he gave his attention to Mr Bennet, who nearly broke Howard's fingers when they shook hands. He spoke with an accent, but just the trace of one, and Howard couldn't place it.

'I build things,' he said, hosing wet concrete off his shovel and seeming to sum up his life in that one statement. He gestured at the yard. It was a pincushion of gimcracks, all wind-operated: little men sawing boards in two, ducks flapping their wings, fish on wires swimming around posts, Dutch windmills and whirligig cows slowly cranking away in the wind off the ocean. 'They never stop,' he said. 'Something's always moving.' He lit a cigarette and puffed hard on it.

Bordering the house were beds full of wooden, painted flowers – tulips and daisies cut out with a scroll saw and complicated roses glued up out of individual wooden petals. There were wooden animals behind the wooden flowers, with heads that tilted and wobbled continually. The entire lawn was alive with movement, up and down and back and forth and sideways. The roof of the house was spiked with weather vanes, too, swiveled toward the east, and in the midst of them, with his legs crossed and wearing high-water pants and the familiar red-soled shoes, sat the plywood Humpty Dumpty, like a judge on a bench, leering across the street toward where Mrs Lamey sprinkled the roses. A strong gust blew straight off the ocean, and one of the Humpty Dumpty's arms lowered in a solemn sort of wave and then was jerked back upright by a spring.

Mr Bennet turned off the hose, ran his hands through his hair, and stepped onto the porch and then into the house. Uncle Roy followed, saying to Howard, 'I think he planted this whole passel of whirlibobs just to drive the old lady nuts. That's part of why she hates me, because I'm friends with Bennet. She thinks this place is a disgrace. Tried to burn him out two weeks ago, too. That's when we put the egg man on the roof. She can't stand to have the damned thing waving at her day and night. She tried to get an injunction against it.'

'Really?' asked Howard, honestly surprised. 'She tried to burn his house down?'

Uncle Roy nodded slowly and decisively, like Oliver Hardy, while grinning with the same sort of raised-eyebrow expression that had betrayed him when he was talking about the fleet of underground Buicks yesterday.

Mr Bennet pulled a steel coffeepot off the stove and poured coffee out into three heavy porcelain cups that were stained brown on the inside. The coffee was tepid and bitter and full of grounds, but Mr Bennet drank it with relish, as if it were the last cup he'd ever see, and smoked on his cigarette between sips. The place was only sparsely furnished, with plain wooden furniture, and the old area rug in the living room was pulled back across the red pine floor and rolled up onto itself. An oak dresser lay dismantled in the middle of an ocean of wood dust, and a belt sander sat inside one of the drawers along with three or four loaded-up sanding belts.

'Little project,' Mr Bennet said, nodding at the dresser. 'Woman up near the harbor owns it. I'm cleaning it up for her. Poor old lady.' He shook his head. 'Mrs Deventer,' he said to Roy.

'Oh, sure, Mrs Deventer.' Then to Howard he said, 'Mrs Lamey's trying to run her out of her house, too. Lamey owns the land on either side. They want to put up a bank, and Mrs Deventer's smack in the middle of the project. She'll hold out, though. She's Dutch, just like me.'

'What he means is a German with his brains kicked out,' Bennet said, nodding broadly. 'You ain't a Dutchman,' he said to Uncle Roy. 'Last week you were telling me you were – what was it?' He looked at Howard, as if he needed help sorting things out. 'A South Sea Islander of some nature. A Fiji, I think it was.'

'What I said,' Uncle Roy said, shaking his head tiredly, 'was that my grandfather *lived* in the South Seas. He wasn't any kind of native. He was in the hotel business.'

'That ain't how I remember it.' Mr Bennet pursed his lips and then changed the subject abruptly. 'I've been studying numbers,' he said.

Uncle Roy nodded in assent. 'He's going to crack the lottery.'

'It's something I call the Principle of Universal Attraction. Numbers are just like people, just like you and me. Do you know what I mean?'

'Like people?' Howard asked.

'Just like that. Like people going to a banquet, going down to the VFW for a fish fry. They walk in the door and they don't know nobody. Not a soul. Think about it. Hold it still in your mind. They mill around, don't they, and sit down somewhere, on one of them folding chairs. Pretty soon they strike up a talk with someone they don't know from Adam, and what does it turn out but that both of them like baseball. They can't get enough of the Giants. Or maybe they got the same kind of dog or their wives are up to the same damned foolishness. You with me so far?'

'Sure,' Howard said. Through the window he could see Mrs Lamey sitting on her porch, which was sheltered from the wind. She was reading a book now and drinking something hot out of a cup. Howard began to think that he'd sold Mrs Lamey short. Still, though, if she'd really tried to burn Mr Bennet's house down and if she was the sort of monster that Uncle Roy seemed to think she was …

''Nother cup of coffee?' Bennet gestured at their half-filled cups.

'Not unless you've got a pack of Rolaids to sweeten it with,' Uncle Roy said, nudging Howard in order to illustrate how funny the remark had been. 'Your coffee tastes like rat poison. What the hell do you do to it?'

'You don't know from coffee,' Mr Bennet said, waving at him in disgust and then ignoring him and talking straight at Howard. 'So anyway, numbers are like that, too, like people. You dump them in a box and away they go, searching out someone to have a chat with. Birds of a feather is what it is. Shake them up, spin them around, and here comes number forty-three, sitting down with number eighteen, and then number six and number eight, maybe, and number twelve making a third, feeling more and more comfortable with each other as the night goes on. Next Tuesday there's another fish fry, but this time, as soon as they're in the door, they're searching each other out straight off. The trick is to watch them, figure out who it is that's attracting who. That's all it is – attraction. Simple attraction. Not like love. I don't mean like that. This is a casual thing, day by day. You've got to study it hard if you want to peg it.'

'Mr Bennet went out to Vegas ten years ago and nearly beggared them,' Uncle Roy said. 'Went to town on keno, day and night. Wouldn't stop. They nearly had to shut down. Brought the whole damned town to its knees. Where was it?' he asked Mr Bennet.

'Place called Benny's.'

'Penny's, wasn't it? I thought you said it was Penny's.'

'That's because you don't listen worth a damn,' Mr Bennet said, draining his coffee mug. 'You and your Samoan grandfather.' Then to Howard he said, 'It ain't one of your Strip hotels, nor downtown neither. You don't want to draw attention to yourself, you see, in one of the big spots. They'll work you over in the alley if they catch on. Small joint, though, doesn't pay any attention. They think it's a run of luck. I took them to the cleaners, too. I'm going back again someday, when I've got the goods, the particulars.'

'How much did you soak them for?' asked Howard.

'Nearly five hundred bucks,' Uncle Roy said.

'I bought that truck with it.' Mr Bennet nodded out toward the curb. There was a flatbed truck with stake sides parked there, half on the grass. It looked like it had been through some rough times.

'We used it to haul a load of chicken manure up from Petaluma just last week.'

'That was two weeks ago,' Mr Bennet said. 'Nothing like chicken manure for the rosebushes. Put too much around them, though, and it burns the roses right up.'

Uncle Roy stood up to pour himself another cup of coffee, shaking his head sadly at the pot, as if it were a crime against the gentle art of cooking. 'People around here are big on organic gardening,' he said. 'You can sell a truckload of chicken manure to the Sunberries nearly any day of the year. Leaf mold, too. You can drive out toward Ukiah for a load of leaf mold out of the oak woods.' He shrugged. 'It's a way to earn a couple of bucks. We're saving a little up in a joint fund, isn't that right?'

His friend nodded. 'We need a stake for when we make the run out to Reno.'

'Tell him about numbers some more,' Uncle Roy said. 'I can see that he still doesn't get it.'

'The problem with numbers,' Mr Bennet said darkly, settling down to the task, 'is that there isn't any end to them. Do you get it?'

Howard said he did. He knew that much about them, anyway.

'I mean to say that they'll trip you up that way. You'll chase them like a dog after a mechanical rabbit until you drop dead. That's the Babel effect.'

'That's right,' said Uncle Roy. 'What he means is that you can't get there from here. There's no such thing as rich enough, nor anything else of the kind. Your man Stoat, now ...'

Mr Bennet looked up sharply at the mention of the name.

'Howard's all right,' Uncle Roy said, waving his hand. 'He's come in with us, lock, stock, and barrel.'

'Well, then,' Mr Bennet said, and shook Howard's hand solidly again. 'Good to have you.'

'So people like Stoat,' Uncle Roy continued, 'and your woman across the road there, they *want* things, don't they?' He looked very serious. ' "I want more and more and more," that's what they go around mumbling all day long. It's the song they sing. What do they *want*, though? They don't know. They can't put a name on it. It burns them up, though. It's a little taste of hell, isn't it, all this wanting. Is it another dollar? That's not it. They've got more than they can use. Another acre of land? What for? A mechanical eyeball in the middle of the forehead? What good would that do them? – they can't see worth a damn out of the eyes they've got. I know what it is, though, what they want. It's *apotheosis*. They want to be God almighty.' He slammed his open palm against the tabletop, and coffee sloshed out of his cup. 'Damn it,' he said, 'gimme a paper towel.'

Bennet handed him a sponge off the counter. 'The boy don't see the connection,' he said. 'He don't see the number business. You get too worked up to explain it worth, a damn.'

'I'm right, though, aren't I?'

'Right enough. It's a matter of patterns is what it is.'

'Everything is,' Uncle Roy said.

'Now take the gluers, for instance. What's their motto? "No rules." That's it, plain and simple. *Look* at them, wearing two different shoes, never driving into town by the same route twice in a row. And let me tell you something you won't believe. When one of the elders, one of the gluer saints, comes around, what happens?'

Howard shrugged.

'Everything goes haywire.'

'That's a fact,' Uncle Roy said. 'Picture frame corners open up. Aquariums leak. Streets don't even meet perpendicular anymore. Believe it.'

'Your table saw won't cut square,' Mr Bennet said. 'Don't matter how hard you try to tune it up.'

'It's anarchy, pure and simple – chaos, hanging around them like a magnetic field.' Uncle Roy sat back in his chair, squinting at Howard. 'It's elemental energy.'

'But what is it,' asked Mr Bennet carefully, 'when you've got anarchy written into the rulebook?'

'When you *compel* it?' asked Uncle Roy.

They waited for a moment, forcing Howard to answer. 'Well,' he said finally, 'I don't suppose it's anarchy anymore.'

'Give that man a cigar,' said Uncle Roy. 'There's more to it than that, though. Do you remember what Bennet was telling you about the numbers?'

Howard nodded again.

Mr Bennet hunkered forward in his chair, dropping his voice. 'What your Samoan uncle means to say is that there's *patterns in the chaos*.'

'What you might call "the Way,"' said Uncle Roy.

'The Dance.'

'And the Hoku-sai sketch …?' Howard started to ask, but his uncle stopped him by holding up a hand. He shook his head and jerked his thumb backward toward the window, toward where Mrs Lamey once again meddled with her rosebushes. She seemed to have her head cocked, as if she were listening to voices on the wind.

'We're not like the others,' Uncle Roy said, gesturing out the window. 'We're the king's men, aren't we? Isn't that what I told you? The circle's been broken. We mean to put it back together again before they have a crack at it. We mean to put the pattern in order.'

'And the lion will lie down with the lamb,' Mr Bennet said, with a note of finality in his voice.

'This is alchemy that we're talking about,' Uncle Roy said, clearly worked up almost to a missionary zeal. 'There's the one crowd, the Stoats and the Lameys who would turn lead into gold to line their pockets with, and worse. And there's another crowd …'

'Us,' said Mr Bennet.

'... who don't give a damn about metallurgy, except to drag this whole sorry world up out of the leaden age it's fallen to – back to a place that's a little bit sunnier, if you follow me.'

'Won't it just fall again?' Howard asked. Clearly his uncle and Mr Bennet were deadly serious, even though they'd lapsed into the mythological. They weren't talking platitudes and abstractions here. That was certain. They were driving toward some goal that they could see with their eyes, like the walls of El Dorado, perched on a meadow above the sea.

Uncle Roy shrugged. 'It will, certainly. Just like your Humpty Dumpty. But the path to the garden is a crooked one, hid by mist. You've got to be walking on it to see it clearly.'

'That's right,' said Mr Bennet. 'Your man *will* fall off the wall, won't he? That's his nature, and God bless him. Then some damned old fool will try to put him back together again, sure as you're born, and God bless him, too.'

Uncle Roy gave him a sharp look. 'Who are you calling a damned old fool, you damned old fool?' Then to Howard he said, 'But there's no choice in the matter, not really, not for men like you. That's paramount, isn't it? This matter of choice and no choice. You've got it and you don't. It sounds contradictory, and that's just fine. Sense is nonsense when you get around behind it, and the opposite, too. You can see that, can't you? I knew that when I saw you. Here's a lad who'll do his part. That's what I said. He's got the instinct. Like a salmon. That's why he's come north. Forget the damned museum. It's redemption you're here for. Break out that can of Glub's glue and start puzzling the pieces back together again. The other crowd's at it right now, hammer and tongs. Only it's the dark tower they're mortaring back up, piece by piece, and by God we mean to bring it down.'

'Earthquake and thunder,' Bennet said, putting down his coffee cup.

'Brimstone and fire,' said Uncle Roy. Then he hooked his fingers under his coat collar, looking very much like Humpty Dumpty himself, having had his say.

'Nearly noon.' Mr Bennet stood up abruptly and smashed out his cigarette into his empty coffee cup. 'You got the wigs for the corpses?'

'In the truck,' Uncle Roy said. And then he winked broadly at Howard. 'Don't make too much of this, my boy. Don't lose any sleep. Take Sylvia somewhere nice. Here.' He hauled an old, wrinkled ten-dollar bill out of his pants pocket and gave it to Howard. 'Have a drink on me. Life goes on in the midst of the battle. Otherwise what's the battle for?'

'Really ...' Howard said, trying to think of a way to refuse the ten. It was clearly leftover money from hustling food stamps.

Uncle Roy frowned. 'Take it,' he said. 'Wasn't I just telling you about making a run out to Reno? This isn't all nonsense, you know. This is no time for doubts. The sand's running out. The king is wounded, but we mean to put him right, or bring the whole shebang down in the effort. Have a drink on your poor old uncle.'

Howard nodded and stood up. 'Right, thanks.' He shoved the bill into his pocket. 'I'll just catch up with you later, then.'

The three of them went out, Mr Bennet locking the door. And after hauling the wigs out of Howard's camper, Uncle Roy and Mr Bennet shuddered away up the street in the flatbed truck. Howard watched them turn the comer, heading for the highway, and then stepped across toward where Mrs Lamey sat on her porch.

12

Mrs Lamey sat in an armchair, bent over and mixing up a potion of some sort in a ceramic bowl that lay on the floor of the porch. It was apparently fertilizer – fish emulsion from the smell of it. She glanced up at Howard as he came up the flagstone walk, between the tree roses. 'Well,' she said, standing up and wiping her right hand on her apron. Then she held it out so that he could shake it. Her face still had the pickle look, but it wasn't distorted by rage now, probably because there was no chance of being assaulted by rubber bats.

'I'm afraid I made a rather negative impression on you yesterday,' she said, not in an apologetic tone, perhaps, but with some hint of regret and shared responsibility.

'It was a difficult business.'

'Well, I oughtn't to lose my temper like that. But Mr Barton can be an irritating man.' With a momentarily bemused smile, she shook her head and said, 'I'm afraid he's not what they'd call fiscally responsible.'

Howard couldn't argue with that, although he hated the phrase 'fiscal responsibility,' because usually it meant nothing, and left everything out. He was intrigued, though, that Mrs Lamey was apparently apologizing in her way, making amends. She was puttering in the garden now, carrying on like a human being. Obviously she had discovered that Howard's check was good. 'Putting out a little fertilizer?' Howard asked. 'What's this can of rusty nails for?'

'For the hydrangeas,' she said. 'Do you garden?'

'Not much, no. A few tomatoes in pots, some houseplants, that's about all.'

'Well, if you bury rusted nails around the roots of hydrangeas, the pink blossoms come out blue. It's the iron in them. Sounds almost magical, doesn't it? You can change the color of roses, too, although not so easily. It's rather messy, but you get interesting results. I'm something of an amateur horticulturist, and put this together myself.' She gestured at the ceramic pot, and Howard could see, now that he was standing next to it, that it didn't contain fish emulsion at all. It was full of a heavy red liquid.

'Don't shudder when I tell you that it's blood,' Mrs Lamey said, putting on a pained expression. 'Any sort of blood works well enough, but fish blood is best. Wonderful fertilizer at the same time. And easy to come by, too, at the cannery. I put it around the white roses. You've got to soak the roots, though, and keep after them with it, if you want the full effect. I use safflower stamens to color white daisies yellow. I even raised a black orchid last year.'

'A black orchid?' Howard asked. 'How?'

'Squid ink and charred wood.' She nodded at him, with a look that suggested she was telling the solemn truth. 'The colors aren't natural, of course. But that's the beauty of it. Look here.' She led him across the patchy grass to where a little forest of pink ladies was blooming against the wall of the house. They stood there alien and huge, thrusting up through the dark soil, their blooms an alien, fleshy color of brown-pink. There was a rotten smell in the air around them, as if there were a dead animal under the house. 'These were a product of blood and rust,' she said, 'and a couple of other ingredients that I'll keep secret.'

'Fascinating,' Howard said. He couldn't think of any other word for it, except maybe 'morbid' or 'abominable' or some other word out of an old pulp horror story. The heavy blooms suggested something both human and unearthly, the effect heightened by a web of faint bluish veins beneath the flesh, reminding Howard uncomfortably of bloodstreams or, worse, tattoos. He thought of the 'witch flower' mushrooms that Uncle Roy had been collecting in the woods around Graham's shack, and in his mind he saw Mrs Lamey sowing fungal spores in the sea wind, watching them blow north across the road and into the forest.

'You're the curator of an art museum, I'm told.'

'Well,' said Howard, suddenly on his guard, 'that's close. I'm not actually curator. It's a small natural-history museum that dabbles in art. I'm not even certain I'm going back to it. I like it up here.'

'Do you? I'm *so* happy to hear that. I was afraid I'd rather put a damper on that. Here you were, newly arrived, and I lost my temper completely. I've been wanting to apologize ever since.'

'Don't mention it,' Howard said, walking back toward the porch. He didn't believe her suddenly. There was something in him that distrusted wide swings in temperament, and he suspected that she had come to some conclusion about him since their struggle at Uncle Roy's house yesterday. She had determined that he was important, and he wondered why.

Howard noticed the printed figures on her kimono for the first time: little squared-off mechanical gadgets and loose coils, blocked-out patches of computer circuitry and radio schematics and what looked like tiny robotic bugs. It was all highly stylized and hard to sort out, but the little figures seemed anatomical somehow – bits and pieces of internal organs reduced to webs or skeletons or very sketchy computer graphics. He was certain he knew who had designed the fabric.

Howard realized suddenly that if he were going to catch Sylvia in time for lunch, he would have to hurry. He checked his watch and looked surprised at what he saw. 'I guess I'll be off,' he said.

'So soon? I was rather hoping to show you my collection of miniatures. It's seldom that there's an expert in town.'

'I'll have to take a rain check,' Howard said.

'Good. I'll tell you what. I have a little … circle, I suppose you would say. A salon. We meet on Tuesday nights. You'd be surprised at the number of artists and writers living around here. It's not rare that people drive up from San Francisco and even farther south just to be part of my little circle. I'm a queen mother to them, you could say – their fiercest champion and critic both. They're my *real* collection of miniatures. All of them full of potential, like seeds that want a little water and soil. Why don't you drop past? The conversation is stimulating.'

'I'm not any kind of artist,' Howard said. 'I only meddle with what other people do – try to talk learnedly about it.'

'Learned talk is the order of the evening. Say around six.'

'I'll try, certainly. I'll bet Mr Stoat is a member of this circle.'

She burst into laughter at the suggestion – cackling and waving her hand almost coyly as if he'd suggested something bordering on indecent. 'Nobody calls him *Mister* Stoat except me. It's merely "Stoat." He's very defensive about that. You've met him, then?'

'Just briefly. Seems fascinating.'

'He's a little bit nervy, too. Don't let him bother you. He's very glossy and hard on the outside, but a terrible pussycat inside who thinks he's a panther. I can keep him on leash, but I don't suppose anyone else can. He's a genius, really, and a man of many talents. A fearful decadent, I'm afraid.' She winked at Howard and said, 'I'm glad we had this little talk, then. You'd make a welcome addition to my little circle. You'd fit right in. And I hope you harbor no ill will toward me for my shameless behavior yesterday afternoon.'

'Not at all.'

She stood for another moment regarding him, and suddenly he felt self-conscious and a little embarrassed, as if something more were expected of him.

'Do you know,' she said, 'you look a little bit like someone I knew once, many years ago.'

'Really?' Howard said. 'I have a common face, I guess.'

'On the contrary, it's … remarkable.' For a moment Mrs Lamey's features betrayed a look of profound longing and remorse, and it struck Howard, sadly, that this was the only honest expression that had crossed her face during their conversation. The rest was veneer. Even the gardening enthusiasm had sounded false, nearly demented. This wasn't false, though, even Uncle Roy would agree to that.

She smiled abruptly, dissolving the sorrow by an act of will, and said, 'Tuesday night, then.'

'Tuesday night.'

She held her hand out, limp-wristed and palm down, as if she expected him to be gallant and to kiss it. He gave it a small shake instead and hurriedly crossed the street, climbed into his truck, and turned the key, letting the engine idle for a moment. This last exchange had unsettled him, and although he didn't want to hobnob with anyone's 'little circle', he felt as if he had made a solemn and necessary promise to her, and he told himself that on Tuesday he would pay her a visit. He wouldn't have to stay long, and it would give him an opportunity to be a sort of spy for Uncle Roy.

Except that she was something more of a mystery to him now, and it seemed less likely that she and her salon were the 'enemy' that Uncle Roy had talked about at breakfast. His uncle was full of exaggeration and wild metaphor, a habit which made jumping to conclusions a dangerous thing.

Sitting alone in the car, free of persuasions, it seemed entirely possible to him that all this north coast plotting might have a very simple and mundane explanation – greed, likely as not, or a consequence of a lot of backwater types nursing grudges over the long years.

Then he remembered the shrine in the woods and old Graham hiding out in the cabin, and his own truck having been ransacked, and the talk about the attempt to burn down Bennet's house. After a moment he admitted to himself that what he really knew was nothing at all yet. Just to keep things smooth, as he drove away he waved out the window to Mrs Lamey, who was crouched in front of the hydrangea bush now, burying rusty nails. The Humpty Dumpty on Bennet's roof waved, too, as if in sarcastic imitation.

It was still early afternoon when they bumped down the drive toward Graham's house on the bluffs. Sylvia had taken two hours off and had sent Howard out to buy sandwich makings so as to supply poor Jimmers with a decent meal. They had a picnic basket full of food and drink in the back of the truck. Howard meant to beard Mr Jimmers on the subject of the Hoku-sai sketch. Either Jimmers had it or he didn't, and if he had it, then he ought to be willing to discuss Howard's claim on it. He was free to refuse to hand it over, after all; there was nothing that could be done to force him. Graham's properties were tied up by law for who knows how long from the date of his death – except that he wasn't dead, anyway, and so Jimmers had no business meddling with the old man's property. He no doubt thought he was protecting it somehow, which you had to admire.

Howard went round and round in his head, arguing all this out with an imaginary Mr Jimmers. The wind off the ocean drove right through his sweater when he stepped out of the truck, and there wasn't much heat in the noonday sun floating orange and cool in the sky. They could see Mr Jimmers out on the bluffs, hoeing in a little garden that was sheltered from the sea wind by a long lean-to of wavy squares of yellow fiberglass. They had clumped nearly up to him before he caught sight of them and stood up straight, resting against the hoe, still dressed in the shabby tweed coat but wearing a pair of heavy rubber boots now.

Off by itself stood the tin shed, locked and mysterious. Howard purposefully avoided looking at it so as not to arouse suspicion. Above them in the wall of the house, facing the meadow, was the mysterious door-that-led-nowhere, and the broken-off stairway built of stones that went two thirds of the way up the wall toward it.

'Swiss chard,' Mr Jimmers said, nodding down at the meager-looking greens poking up through the soil.

'Good, are they?' asked Howard.

'Wretched, actually, but easy to grow if you don't let the wind blow them to bits. Not enough sun, though, so you've got to grow a lot of them if you want to harvest enough to eat. You should have seen the garden in the old days, before Mr Graham declined.' He shook his head sadly, hacking at a weed with the corner of the hoe blade. 'Now it's reduced to these few rows of Swiss chard. It's a disgrace is what it is. But a man can stay healthy on a diet of greens. Taken in sufficient quantity, with eggs, they'll provide a human being with a full range of nutrients, a complete diet. Postum is made entirely of vegetable matter. Did you know that?'

'No,' said Howard. 'Really? Vegetable matter?'

'Wheat, mostly.'

'Speaking of eating,' Sylvia said, 'we've brought along this basket.'

Mr Jimmers dropped his hoe and set off toward the house, rubbing his hands together as if he hadn't eaten anything except Postum and Swiss chard in days. 'I'll just put on a tablecloth,' he said, prying off his rubber boots on the front porch. Sylvia slipped her shoes off, and Howard did, too, realizing too late that his socks had holes in the toes. Maybe it would make him look vulnerable, he thought, and would be a good ploy. He'd have to suffer cold feet again, though.

It was at lunch that he brought up the topic of the sketch. Awkwardly, and pretending not to care very much, he said, 'About the Hoku-sai, Mr Jimmers.'

'That would be the sketch on rice paper?' Mr Jimmers said.

'That's correct.'

'It's damned rare, you know.'

'I do know that. That's what explains my interest in it in the first place.'

'I mean to say that Hoku-sai woodcuts abound, but original sketches, especially from the Mangkwa, are rare as hen's teeth. And items with this history, I should think, are rarer still.'

'What Howard wants to know,' Sylvia said bluntly, 'is whether you've got the thing, Mr Jimmers, and whether you're willing to fork it over.'

Jimmers smiled hugely and raised his eyebrows at Sylvia. 'Have another slice of this wonderful cheese, my dear,' he said. 'I'm in a precarious position, of course. Mr Graham was never found, was he? Who's to say he's dead? He's *assumed* dead, of course, but the lack of a body rather complicates the dispersal of his property.' He winked at Sylvia before going on. 'And if I'm not really certain he's dead, beyond a shadow of a doubt, I can hardly go about giving his things away, regardless of quite possibly spurious letters.' He held his hand up in order to put a stop to Howard's protests. 'There are no end of awful people in the world, who would be entirely happy to think they've fooled Mr Jimmers and gotten their hands on this curious – ah, sketch, as you put it. What makes you think it's a Hoku-sai?'

'Isn't it?' Howard asked.

'Of course it's not. You see the problem, then. You're blundering around, aren't you? You haven't any idea what you want. All you know is that you want it. Should you have it, though? That's the question.'

'So my letter of acquisition, signed by Graham, means nothing to you?'

'On the contrary, my boy. It means ever so much. It means you might easily *be* the man who now or very shortly will own this valuable object that we've been discussing. For the moment, I mean to say, you are *not* the man. What we would like is not always what is, but it might be what will be, if I make myself clear.'

Mr Jimmers nibbled a piece of bread contentedly, as if it didn't take more than a good crumb or two to satisfy him. 'I wish I could find something here to offer you two by way of dessert,' he said regretfully. 'I had a paper bag full of horehound drops somewhere. I can't remember quite where. I haven't seen them for the better part of a year. Wild horehound, put together by the Sunberry people.'

'That's all right,' Howard said quickly.

'It's not all right, not entirely. I've become a regular Mother Hubbard. Nothing to offer guests. You're the first I've had, though, in years. I promise that next time I see you I'll have something nice. I've developed a taste for canned-spaghetti sandwiches on a superior-quality white bread. Nothing fancy, just bread, margarine, and spaghetti – canned spaghetti. Doesn't really matter what brand.'

So the subject of the sketch had been brought up and abandoned in the space of a single minute, buried beneath Mr Jimmers' spaghetti sandwich. He had half promised something, but Howard couldn't be sure what. What was it he had said? That Howard might well be 'the man' – as if Mr Jimmers were waiting not simply for someone with a letter of requisition, but for someone who knew the answer to a riddle, or would know the riddle itself, or would have the secret password.

'About the sketch, then,' Howard said. 'I understand your hesitation, and I hate to keep bothering you with it. That's the problem. I don't want to make a pest of myself, but I've got the letter from Mr Graham, which I believe to be perfectly authentic, and—'

'I'm certain of it,' Mr Jimmers said, interrupting. 'Perfectly authentic. May I see the letter again?'

'Absolutely,' Howard said, pulling it out of his coat and handing it across.

Mr Jimmers studied it, nodding and squinting, and then abruptly tore it into fragments and threw the pieces over his shoulder.

'Wait!' Howard shouted, getting up out of his chair. It was too late, though: the pieces lay on the floor. He sat back down, his mouth open. Sylvia was smiling faintly, as if she thought the whole production was funny, but didn't dare laugh out loud.

'Now you've got one fewer scrap of paper to worry about,' Mr Jimmers said to him. 'Avoid focusing your energies on trash. That wasn't worth anything to you. It was meant to draw you up here, that's all. This isn't a matter of museums. This is something more. You don't need letters of "requisition," as you put it. The whole world is tired of your letter of requisition. It makes them sick. Remember the promise in the adage – everything will be revealed in the fullness of time.' Then he held his hand up again, as if he would prevent Howard from commenting. '*The fullness* of time.'

He touched his mouth with his napkin and said, 'Come along. I'll show you something noteworthy – something that will relieve your mind immensely.' He tipped Howard a wink now, as if he were going to let the both of them in on a secret, and they followed him into the parlor with the fireplace, which was lit but had died down into a pool of embers. He threw in a handful of brown pine needles and blew on them and then laid a half dozen cedar sticks on top, which flared up immediately and began to pop and crackle, lighting up the little area around the hearth.

Mr Jimmers stood very still, listening, and then tiptoed to one, then the other doorway, and stood listening at each for a moment. Then, putting a finger to his lips, he eased a stone out of the face of the fireplace, reached back into the recess, and pulled out a carefully folded bit of paper.

Howard caught his breath. Here it was, still in its hidey-hole but no longer in its case. Mr Jimmers nodded at him and unfolded it with steady hands. 'Not another of this quality in the world,' he whispered. 'Never again will be.' Howard could see inked images through the paper.

'What do you think?' Mr Jimmers asked, holding the sketch up so that the firelight glowed through it. The confusion of folds in the paper appeared almost to be Xerox reproductions – the shadows of folds – and not authentic folds at all. It was very fine work, the rice paper yellowed with age and frayed along the edges. 'This,' said Jimmers, gesturing at one of the images, 'is the flowering staff. And these are meant to represent secret keys. This one is a cup and this is a coin and this is a tree by a river. And if you fold the thing in half twice, what you get is …' He folded it in half twice and said, 'A broken egg. Now watch.'

He folded the sketch again, warping it first and then shoving his hands together so that the center third of the paper disappeared behind the outside thirds, and then he turned it around diamond-wise and folded the top corner down. As if by magic the broken sections of eggshell became whole, and random spots and lines and shadings on the sketch formed a face on the patched-together egg. It sat now on the limb of the tree by the river and held the staff in its hand, its thin arms stretched out along smaller limbs on either side, almost as if it were crucified to the tree.

An electric thrill ran through Howard, and he was surprised to find that Sylvia had taken his hand, as if she felt that something was pending, some revelation. The firelight behind the rice paper made the images waver and jump as if they were seen through ocean water. Mr Jimmers let go of one of the corners of the sketch, snapped his fingers, and the fire flared in the fireplace, throwing out a great wash of greenish-blue flame that seemed to consume the rice paper sketch even as he held it.

Looking dumbstruck with surprise, Jimmers shouted and waved the burning scrap dramatically, as if it were scorching his hand but he couldn't manage to let go of it, and then with a wild flourish he threw it onto the stones of the floor and trod on it until the flames were out and there was nothing but a few black fragments left, smudging the gray stones.

'Damn it,' Mr Jimmers said, looking morosely at the bottom of his stockinged feet. 'It's that damned cedar – throws God's own amount of sparks.'

Howard realized that his own mouth was open. He had meant to shout, but there hadn't been time, it had all happened so fast.

'*What* a tragedy,' Mr Jimmers said. '*What* an unbearable loss.'

'You're joking,' Howard managed to say. He was certain suddenly that Mr Jimmers had pulled a fast one, with all the finger snapping and the whoosh of flame. He had pitched something into the fire to cause the flare-up and had pocketed the sketch and burned up a dummy of some sort. He bent over and picked up a fragment – one that still had a bit of unburned paper clinging to the black ash. There was a slash of brown ink on it – easily identifiable as the top of the flowering staff. So Jimmers had burned a *copy*. It couldn't have been the real one. Still, it had *looked* to be the real one. Howard waited for Jimmers to snatch it back out of his coat and laugh.

Instead he sat down heavily in a stuffed chair and buried his forehead in his hands. 'Alas,' he said.

'You can't really have burned it up ...' Howard looked to Sylvia for support. She shrugged and shook her head, as if to tell him to drop it entirely.

'Not a word of this leaks out!' Mr Jimmers said, almost frantically, jerking his head up and staring at the two of them. He wore a hunted look, the look of a man whose life was suddenly threatened by an unseen foe. He reached into his coat, hesitated, cocking his head. Howard nodded inwardly. Here it came ...

But Mr Jimmers merely pulled out a ragged old handkerchief and mopped his brow. 'I believe a drink is called for under the circumstances. A strong one.'

Howard couldn't disagree. He and Sylvia followed Mr Jimmers back out toward the kitchen, where Jimmers pulled the cork out of the bottle of Sunberry wine that Howard had tasted two nights back. He poured out two tumblers full, nearly killing off the bottle and announcing that he never touched the stuff. Sylvia sipped at hers, but Howard couldn't bring himself to it and set his glass down untouched, pretending to be distracted for a moment by something out the window. Then Mr Jimmers wandered off, seeming lost and depressed, and left the two of them alone.

'What about a walk along the bluffs?' Howard asked loudly, catching Sylvia's eye and jerking his head.

'You children go along without me,' Mr Jimmers said from the next room. 'I've got to think this through. I've betrayed my trust. I ...' He fell silent, and they heard him slump heavily into a chair. Sylvia folded up the tablecloth and repacked the dishes, leaving the remainder of the food for Mr Jimmers. When they peeked into the parlor a moment later, he was nodding in his chair, asleep.

Howard still half expected him to spring up and laugh, but that didn't happen; instead he began to snore, his head lolling forward over his chest.

13

'Where are you going?' Sylvia asked when they'd gone outside.

'For a walk on the bluffs, like I said.'

'Now?'

'Of course now. What's the hurry? You don't have to be back for another forty-five minutes. We just got had, that's what I think.'

Sylvia was silent, walking next to him with her arms folded across her chest. 'It looked like a trick.'

'Sure it was. He's got the damned thing in his coat. He's no more asleep than I am. What he's doing now is hiding the thing again, and I'll bet you a shiny new dime that it's not going back behind the rock, either.' Howard looked over his shoulder, back toward the house. They had gotten around toward the rear now. A trail led away through the berry vines, down along the edge of the bluffs where someone had long ago erected a picket fence, to keep people well back away from the edge, maybe. Howard walked down the path until they were hidden from the house by wild shrubbery. He pulled a key out of his pocket.

'What's that?' Sylvia asked.

'A key.'

'I can see that. What's it for?'

'Jimmers' shed. I'm going to see what's inside it. There were a half dozen keys on strings inside the back door. I slipped it off of the hook when he fell asleep in the chair. You were cleaning up the lunch stuff.'

'How do you know it's the right one?'

'I looked at the lock. It's a regular antique. This key is old enough and cut right. It's the only one of the bunch that's anywhere near working. The way I see it, the padlocks on all these outbuildings are probably keyed the same. It wouldn't make sense to carry a dozen keys.'

'What did Father tell you was in there?'

'A fabulous machine, actually.'

She nodded. 'It figures. What else would Mr Jimmers have in a tin shed? You know what Jimmers told me was in there?'

'What?' asked Howard. The whole business was beginning to look pretty dubious to him.

'The Platonic archetypes.'

'All of them?'

'That's what he said. He told me that nearly a year ago. Said the shed was packed with them – the archetypal bottle cap and chair and mustache and who-knows-what-all.'

'The wing-tip shoe.'

'The archetypal corkboard. Everything. He said he couldn't explain the physics, but it had to do with the sort of infinity you see in double mirrors, like in a barbershop.'

'I bet it does. I bet he did that trick in the parlor with mirrors, too. Uncle Roy called it a ghost machine. He's pretty certain that it had something to do with the crowd that stole Graham's car. I promised him I'd have a look at it if I could. Apparently Jimmers won't let him anywhere near it. Tell me something – is there bad blood between Jimmers and your father?'

'Well, yes.' Sylvia stood looking out over the ocean, her hair blowing back out of her face. She looked as if she were thinking of how to continue, so Howard waited for her, even though he was itching to have a look into the shed before Mr Jimmers woke up.

'Mr Jimmers and my mother were lovers.'

'Jimmers?' Howard asked, trying not to sound too incredulous. He tried to consider Mr Jimmers in that light, but it wasn't easy.

'Long time ago – shortly before I was born. You know who she wound up marrying, though.'

'You might have been Sylvia Jimmers.'

'Very damned nearly.'

'You wouldn't have been as pretty.'

Sylvia blushed just a little, which was encouraging. 'Actually,' she said, 'he wasn't a bad-looking man when he was young. It wrecked him, though, breaking up with Mother. She's still guilty about it – more than makes sense, really. I think she likes carrying guilt around like baggage. She wouldn't know what to do without it. She told me once that I had Mr Jimmers' eyes.'

'Really? I think Uncle Roy has them, in a jar in the kitchen. There was a lot of bitterness, then?'

'I suppose so,' Sylvia said. 'Nobody hates anybody, though. Same circle of friends and all – everyone winding up in the same place, finally. Mr Jimmers had a difficult time of it, though. He was hospitalized in San Francisco at least twice for mental disorders. He was brilliant, too. An engineer until he gave it up and began living in a garage in Fort Bragg. Spent all his time working on a flying automobile.'

'He was a gluer,' Howard said flatly. 'I'll bet you.'

'After a fashion, I guess. The compulsion seems to move people differently. Anyway, he was put away, and when he got out he fell in love again. You wouldn't believe with whom.'

'I give up. Anybody I know?'

'Heloise Lamey.'

'Not old Landlady Lamey!'

'The very one. Lasted something under two months. Father says that she wanted to use Mr Jimmers to betray Graham, but that he wouldn't knuckle under and she dropped him after some sort of scandal that resulted in Jimmers' disgrace. Jimmers disappeared for a time, back down to San Francisco, and then came back and has lived here at Graham's since. He came and went in the night, I guess, because nobody ever saw him. It was always assumed he was here, just sort of puttering around, watching the stars. Mother kept track of him. I remember coming out here with her once when I was a little girl, and her telling me that he was on a diet of sprouts and milk and vitamins. He even published a newsletter and started an organization, the Flat Constellation Society, but he was closed down for mail fraud. He was innocent, though. He believed it all.'

Howard nodded. 'I like that. An authentic crank is innocent of mail fraud, but a fake crank isn't. There's a certain logic to the idea.'

Sylvia gave him a look. 'You know what I mean.'

'Actually I do. Was this some sort of religion or something?'

'I've seen some of his newsletters. They were full of articles about saucers and the hollow earth and especially about machinery. He had a sort of Jungian slant, though – not your usual nut literature, except that he claimed to be in contact with hundred-year-old spirits. He didn't capitalize common nouns or put everything inside of useless quotation marks or things like that.'

'That's reassuring,' Howard said. 'I don't mean to be slighting or anything, but it sounds as if he and your father ought to have gotten along fine.'

'Somehow that didn't happen. They were rivals when they were in love with my mother, and they just carried right on being rivals. They used to play pranks on each other once in a while after it was all settled and over, as if it weren't really over at all. Mr Jimmers would have a truckload of manure delivered out to the museum, say, as a joke, and then Father would strike back at him by printing up a fake newsletter from the Flat Constellation Society, full of crazy limericks and psychotic illustrations. Then we moved south, of course, and they pretty much gave it up until we came north again years later. It's died down again now, but I think that Father is capable of starting it back up anytime.'

'I would have thought that Jimmers was a fan of the ghost museum. What did he think, that Uncle Roy set it up to make fun of him or something?'

'No, not especially.' She hesitated for a moment, pulling her hair back out of her face and tying it into a big knot. 'I shouldn't tell you this, since you're such a terrible skeptic, but it's altogether possible that Mr Jimmers rigged up the entire ghost car phenomenon. That was his crowd of hundred-year-old spirits driving the car. Don't ask me how. Don't even ask me how he fooled us with the sketch just now. Right before the museum failed, Father saw a glowing creature walking through the forest after dark. He was just closing up, getting ready to head home. He followed it, but it ran off up one of the lumber roads and disappeared. Father couldn't keep up with it. He drove straight to the newspaper office, full of excitement, and of course they treated it as a farce. The next morning a cow was reported stolen from a farm near Albion, and that same day it was found, right up behind the museum, sprayed with luminous paint.'

Howard smiled. 'Did Uncle Roy paint the cow? I love the idea of that – a glowing ghost cow terrorizing the north coast. That's good. A canny business move. It would have hauled the tourists in by the busload.'

'Of *course* he didn't paint it. If he had, he wouldn't have been fool enough to let it get away up the lumber road. And he would have made sure a few other people saw it, too. He thinks Jimmers did it, as a prank, to make him look like a fool. It certainly worked that way. The museum was just then going under, and the luminous cow fraud is what broke the camel's back.'

'I dare say it would. So did Uncle Roy strike back?'

'A couple of times. Nothing very inspired, though – not for a while. Sometime I'll tell you about his campaigns. I think he was tired of it right then. The cow incident hadn't turned out to be very funny. Mother got a little bit shortsighted about his capers, too. You could tell that last night. I'm surprised that she hasn't put a stop to the haunted house. The only thing that I can figure is that she's more tired out than he is. She can't keep up with him anymore.'

'She's fairly long-suffering, isn't she? In the best way.'

Sylvia nodded. 'In some of the best ways. Not always.'

Then after a moment Howard said, 'Let's make a move on the tin shed before Jimmers wakes up.'

'If you stay up here,' Sylvia said, ignoring what he said and growing suddenly serious, 'I know just exactly what's going to happen to you.'

Howard gestured at her, as if to tell her to go on, to reveal his future. 'Read my palm,' he said, holding out his hand.

'You're going to end up like Father and Mr Jimmers – spending your life worrying about secret societies and outer space and ancient mysteries. You don't believe in anything, and what happens when you don't believe in anything is that you've got no defense against all this weird crap when it puts itself in your way.'

'You're a fine one to talk, passing out mystical pamphlets and selling recipes for sun tea made out of rose quartz and stump water.'

'At least I can take an objective look at it. I've got some basis for comparison. You're utterly ignorant of it, because you've never considered it, and when something that doesn't fit comes along, you don't begin to know where to put it.'

Howard had the vague feeling that she was right, not because of any particular logic or nonsense about her being objective, but because right at the moment he was faced with a basket full of strange activities that he hadn't been able to fathom. This business about rivalries and wrecked love affairs put a new coat of paint on the horse, too, or on the cow.

'Thanks,' he said.

'For what?'

'For worrying about me. I'm not much on secret societies, though. You don't have to let that trouble you. There's good reasons for me to stay up here. That's what I think.'

'Uh-huh.' She looked at him suspiciously and then out at the ocean, lost in thought.

He put his arm around her shoulder and pulled her close, feeling like a teenager in a darkened theater.

'What are you up to?' she asked, looking him in the face.

'Nothing.' He didn't let her go, though.

She nodded. 'For a moment there I thought you were making a pass at me.'

'Maybe I was.'

'Remember that girl who used to live in the house behind you? Jeanelle Shelly. You were out of your mind over her. And how old were you? About six? You started in early.'

'I didn't "start in."'

She leaned against him, neither of them saying anything. Howard was struck by the feeling that they were still playing at being in love – him making his fumbling advances and her fighting him off with language, making verbal jokes, diffusing things by poking fun at him. Suddenly she looked at her watch. 'I've got to get back to town,' she said.

'I'm going to look at that shed. I'll hurry.'

Sylvia nodded, as if it had to be done in order for Howard and her father to rest easy. 'I'll take your word for it,' she said. 'What I'm going to do is head back to the house and keep Mr Jimmers company. If he wakes up, I'll give you a holler so that you know he's up and about.'

'Good.' Howard whirled the string with the key on it around his finger. 'It won't take a minute.'

'Wait,' she said. 'Look at this first. It's been here for years.' She led the way through brown, waist-high weeds toward three lonesome cypress trees growing in a clump halfway up toward the highway. In between the triangle formed by the three trunks sat a little gluer shrine, very much like the one set up in the woods by Graham's cabin. It was built of old junk again – perfume bottles, bits of ceramic tile, wooden dominoes, an old rusty fishing reel, a brass doorknob, all enclosed within a pair of arched automobile fenders, rusted and pitted to the point that they were almost lacy.

'This has been here for as long as I can remember,' Sylvia said. 'They just add new stuff sometimes and rearrange it.'

'There's one like it back behind your house, out in the woods.'

She nodded. 'That one's new. It appeared the day Father moved him back there. Nobody was supposed to know where he was, but they knew.'

'You wouldn't believe what I found in that one,' Howard said, 'back in the woods. My paperweight, sitting right there in plain view.'

'And you took it back?'

Howard shook his head. 'It'll be safe enough out there. I had the feeling, actually, that it had been put to good use. Don't ask me why.'

'Not me. It's funny, though, the weird sorts of things Howard Barton is learning to take on faith. What's next? Membership in the Flat Constellation Society?'

'Next is the adventure of the tin shed.'

'You're sure?'

'Too good a chance to pass up,' Howard said, and the two of them tramped back up to the trail again and then along the bluffs toward the rear of the house. Sylvia went around toward the front, disappearing beyond the hillocks of berry vines.

Where the rear wall of the house became one with the cliff, there was no backyard at all, just a narrow shelf of rock far above the sea. High above was the attic window, beyond which Howard had spent the night, sleeping in a chair. He found that he could pick his way along the slender ledge, just as long as he didn't look down. The stones of the house wall were rough and the mortar was deep-set, so there were handholds. And someone, ages past, had cemented an iron railing into the rocks in order to prevent anyone from going over, but one end of the railing had long ago rusted through, and it dangled uselessly now like a broken tree root a hundred feet over the water. Even a seasoned rock climber would have found it impossible to scramble down the wet and mossy shale to the beach below.

Safely back on the meadow, he hurried past Mr Jimmers' Swiss chard toward the tin shed, hiding behind it finally and peering back toward the house. It looked quiet enough. There was the chance that Mr Jimmers was simply being subtle again, that he hadn't fallen asleep at all but was giving Howard a chance to betray himself, but Sylvia would have had time to get back in by now, and she hadn't hollered ...

He crouched at the corner of the shed and took one last look. Then, staying low, he scuttled crabwise to the locked sliding doors. The key slid straight in and the lock opened easily, as if it were slick with graphite. In a moment he had slipped the padlock out of its holes in the door handles. He yanked on one of the doors, and it let out a screech of rusty protest, jiggling along its bent track just a few inches and then jamming tight. He pushed on the opposite door, along the bottom edge, wishing he had a can of sewing-machine oil to spray into the track and expecting momentarily to hear Sylvia yell.

The door jerked along a bit farther, and suddenly the opening was wide enough to slide through. He took the padlock with him, remembering his adventure at the spirit museum, and wafered himself through, easing the door shut again at once, all but about an inch so as to have some light to see by.

There was light leaking in under the eaves, too, enough to reveal Mr Jimmers' device. It was built of wood and brass and copper and leather – a product, pretty clearly, of the Victorian age, of the early days of the Industrial Revolution. It had foot pedals and an organ pipe apparatus alongside a broad, spoked wheel, as if from an oversize sewing machine. A wavy-looking, fish-bowl lens was set in the top. The whole thing had a sort of Rumplestiltskin fairy tale magic to it, a backwoods cobbler's notion of what a 'machine' must look like. There was a bit of writing carved into the wooden superstructure, which read simply, 'St George's Guild, 1872.'

John Ruskin again, Howard said to himself, rolling back onto his heels and squinting in concentration. Knowing that it was Ruskin who had established the unsuccessful St George's Guild didn't tell him anything at all about the machine. But the name of the guild itself was powerfully suggestive to him, and abruptly he thought of Sylvia and his just-ended conversation with her. How was it that she saw him and his desires so much more clearly than he saw them himself?

Here he was, hiding out in Mr Jimmers' tin shed, turning quite possibly innocent artifacts into fourteen-carat mysteries in the spirit of Jimmers and Uncle Roy. He was infected, and no doubt about it. Knowing that didn't help at all either, though. And with an almost helpless curiosity he reached across and gave the brass wheel a spin. The wheel revolved effortlessly, frictionlessly, as though now that it was put into motion, it wouldn't be inclined to stop.

Suddenly there was a shift in the quality of light in the shed. A dim glow emanated from the lens atop the machine. Howard spun the wheel faster and the light brightened. The wheel whirred on its bearings, and Howard was momentarily torn between trying to stop it, to end whatever was happening before it had gone too far, and to see it through, into the heart of some deeper mystery. He let it spin. There was the sound of bees humming, which sorted itself out into the low babble of voices like a roomful of mechanical men talking excitedly.

A pale fog materialized in the air over the machine. Particles whirled in it like dust motes. Vibrations shook the shed, and the machine, rocking on its springs, began to bang against the tin wall with a slow, rhythmic pounding, like the spinning of an out-of-balance washing machine. The noise and the spinning made him dizzy, and he was aware suddenly that there were stars on the ceiling over his head, pale and diffuse like stars at twilight.

The mist from the machine congealed into a spinning blur like a tiny human head, and there was the loud sound of footsteps walking down a long wooden corridor. The misty face developed features now, and Howard's curiosity turned abruptly to fear. The thing blinked, as if vaguely surprised to find itself there. Then its mouth began to work, like the mouth of a ruminating cow. The machine banged away at the wall of the shed, easily loud enough to awaken Jimmers and throw him into a panic. The babble of voices combined to form a single voice, deep and commanding, but mostly lost in the banging and whirring of the machine.

Howard heard his name shouted, and he reached down to stop the turning of the wheel, which thumped against his hand, still spinning heavily and freely. There was a body forming beneath the head now. Howard could see a waistcoat, a dangling pocket-watch chain. The ghostly shape was growing, too, exactly as if it were approaching him from across a vast distance. There was the sound of wind rushing through a canyon and the flapping of bird wings and of pages rustling in an old book. Then, as the wheel slowed, the image began to fade and the light dimmed. The voice ran down until it was nothing but a tired whisper and then the sound of bees buzzing again, and Howard slumped back onto a gunnysack full of mulch, realizing that he was faint with the stuffiness of the shed, with the heavy, dusty air.

Someone tugged at the shed doors. There was a furious rattling and screeching as they skidded open. The machine still banged away, but not so heavily now. Afternoon sunlight poured through the open doors, and the night sky overhead dissolved into the daylight as Mr Jimmers pushed past Howard's feet and slammed his hand against the hub of the brass wheel, stopping it dead. The ghost noises evaporated altogether and the foggy head was gone.

Left over, like a negative afterimage on the back of his eyelids, the floating, two-dimensional face still hovered there. Howard blinked, looked closer, and realized that the visage, somehow, seemed now to be painted against the corrugated tin of the shed wall, like an imprint taken with ghost-sensitive film. Slowly it faded and vanished.

14

Mr Jimmers' hair and clothes were mussed from his napping in the chair, and he stared at Howard now like a school-master thinking about birch rods.

'What on earth were you doing?' asked Sylvia, staring past Mr Jimmers' shoulder at the now-still machine. Howard could see that she was smiling.

She was taking on the job of scolding him before Jimmers had a chance to get going. 'The whole shed was *vibrating*. We heard it inside the house. What is that, Mr Jimmers, some sort of gramophone?' She looked at the device innocently.

'That's nothing,' Mr Jimmers said, waving them backward out of the shed. 'I mean that's just what it is. A gramophone. It's an early sort of television, really, that skims energy out of the ether. It's a delicate instrument, though. I can't have people meddling with it. There's people who would misuse it ... How on earth did you get in here?' he asked suddenly, squinting hard at Howard.

Howard handed him the key. 'Sorry,' he said. 'It was breaking and entering. Curiosity, mainly. Better call the police.'

'Curiosity,' said Mr Jimmers flatly as he padlocked the shed again and then dropped the key theatrically down his shirt. He smiled momentarily, as if to show that he had nothing against curiosity. 'We don't need the police. Not this time.'

Howard had begun to feel genuinely guilty. Now that he stood in the sunlight, with the workaday world clear and solid around him, the mystical adventure in the shed seemed suddenly to have happened in some distant time. What did he think he had seen? A ghost? 'I really am sorry,' he said again, and abruptly Sylvia grinned at him and mouthed the word 'See?' He ignored her. 'I didn't know ...'

'You're right about that,' Jimmers said. 'You didn't know. What other keys have you stolen from me?'

'None. That's it.'

'I'll vouch for him,' Sylvia said cheerfully. 'He means well, he's just a nitwit. He's always been like this. It's a sort of Dennis the Menace complex.'

This seemed to make Mr Jimmers happy. As if to celebrate, he kissed Sylvia on the hand and patted her head. 'Ask next time,' he said to Howard patronizingly and laying a hand on his shoulder. 'I'll let you have a glimpse through my telescope sometime. Perhaps you'd like copies of some of my literature?'

'Sure,' Howard said, relieved that he was being let off the hook.

Mr Jimmers didn't produce any literature, though. Instead he said, 'I've got nothing to hide, nothing at all. You can go through my effects with a flea comb. Nothing up *my* sleeve.' He tugged his coat sleeve up, revealing the thin fabric of his mattress-stripe shirt and the pale flesh of his wrist. He nodded at his hand, turning it over slowly, and said, 'Why did the turtle cross the road?'

Taken utterly by surprise at this lunatic question, Howard could only shake his head.

'Chicken's day off,' Mr Jimmers said very seriously. After making sure the padlock was secure, he picked up his hoe and began chopping at weeds again, working in his oddball garden. They left him there, Howard apologizing one last time and driving away miserably toward town. He hadn't been caught in any such stunts for twenty years and had forgotten how humiliating it was.

He tried to explain the experience with the ghost head to Sylvia, who made him repeat the more lunatic aspects of the tale. 'Do you know what I think it was?' she asked. Howard didn't know. 'A hypnogogic experience. A waking dream. You only *thought* you saw – who was it? John Ruskin's ghost? Talking like a swarm of wooden bees?' She nodded but had a perplexed look on her face, and he caught her looking at him out of the comer of her eye. She was evidently satisfied to know that Howard had been face-to-face with the Unknown, and had come away shaken and confused. It was as they were pulling up in front of the boutique that Sylvia remembered about the picnic basket. They had left it with Mr Jimmers.

'Damn it,' she said. 'It isn't mine, either, it's Rosie's, the woman who works for me at the shop. It's expensive as hell, full of her plates and tablecloth and everything. What'll I tell her?'

'I'll go back after it,' Howard said promptly, although not really liking the idea at all. He would have to confront Mr Jimmers again. It was the only gallant thing to do, though. 'It isn't ten minutes down the road. I'll fetch it back here inside of a half hour. Tell her … tell her that I drove off with it in the truck by mistake, and that surely I'll realize it and bring it back around. Then I will. Simple as that.'

'You're sweet,' she said, leaning over and kissing him on the cheek, then moving away before he had a chance to respond. With a mock-wicked look she said, 'You should have seen your face when Jimmers was yelling at you.'

'Pretty woebegone, eh?'

'Pitiful. I remember that look perfectly from when you were a child. Remember that time you got caught in the garage with Jeanelle Shelly? Don't deny it. Your mother sent her home and then gave you that lecture about being struck dead by God. Remember?'

'I … What? How did you …?' Howard couldn't speak. He realized that he was blushing fiercely, confronted now with this old, mortifying sin.

'I was listening at the garage door, out in the driveway. You remember that I was there when you came out looking shameful. Anyway, that was the sort of look you had this time around, too. Mr Jimmers and I saw the shed just vibrating like a tuning fork, and I said, "What on earth!" and Jimmers said, "My Lord!" and to tell you the truth I didn't know *what* we'd find. "He's got Jeanelle Shelly in there," I remember thinking. Actually I think I said it out loud, which must be what confused Mr Jimmers. He's wondering right now who Jeanelle Shelly is and where you've got her hidden now that you've had your way with her in the shed.'

Howard discovered that it was utterly impossible to respond, so he smiled crookedly, like a man struggling to be a good sport.

'Look at you,' she said suddenly, pretending to feel bad about Howard's deflated condition. 'I'm awful, aren't I? But you're such an easy target.' She kissed him again, again unexpectedly, and then slid over and climbed out of the truck, keeping him consistently off balance. Poking her head in through the open window, she said, 'Save the basket, will you? Before Jimmers turns it into a sanatorium for mice or something.'

She stepped away from the truck and waved at him as he backed almost happily out onto the street. He waved back and then drove off slowly, still able to feel a sort of electric tingle on his cheek where she'd kissed him. He looked into the rearview mirror, and there were red lip marks, which he wiped off with the sleeve of his sweater. Whistling now, he pushed his foot down on the accelerator and angled south onto the coast highway, feeling suddenly as if he, were man enough, after all, to confront the curious Mr Jimmers one more time.

Mr Jimmers wasn't hoeing in the garden anymore. The meadow around the house was windy and deserted, and afternoon shadows stretched away across it. Howard was tempted toward the tin shed, having learned only about half enough to satisfy himself. If it had only been full of gardening tools, he could have been happy and gone about his business on an even keel. He didn't have the key any longer, though, and he surely couldn't afford to be caught meddling around there by Mr Jimmers, who *would* call the police this time, machine or no machine. Or maybe take a shot at him with a load of rock-salt.

So he strolled toward the house thinking hard about Mr Jimmers himself. Who and what was he? A sideshow magician and crackpot professor of fringe science, or an artful genius of great power, toiling at a deep and authentic mystery? Too bad you couldn't just ask him. Howard stepped up onto the porch and slipped off his shoes, then raised his hand to knock.

The front door stood open a couple of inches. Howard paused, vaguely surprised. There was dirt on the sill and trailing into the house, knocked off of someone's crepe-soled shoe – someone who clearly hadn't been invited in under Jimmers' watchful gaze. Howard shrank back against the wall, out of sight of anyone inside who might see him through the open door.

Suddenly tense, he looked around himself. He saw the car now – a red Camaro pulled in behind the long wooden shed that housed the chain-saw mill and workshop. His first impulse was to leave – head straight for his truck and gun it the hell out of there, up to Albion where he could call the police from the store. His starting the truck, of course, would alert whoever was inside, and by the time the police arrived they'd be gone, and Mr Jimmers would be what? Dead? Robbed?

And maybe it was nothing at all. Steeling himself, Howard listened at the almost closed door. He heard nothing. He pushed it open, waiting for it to creak or slam or rattle, but it was silent, helping him out.

Ducking down into a crouch, he peered around it into the shadowy interior hall. He wished it were earlier in the day instead of nearly twilight, because he could see almost nothing inside.

He slipped in, anyway, hurrying across and pressing himself against the wall, where he would be mostly hidden but could still see a section of the parlor. From the light playing across the parlor carpet, Howard could tell that a fire still burned in the grate. The fireplace itself and Mr Jimmers' easy chair were both hidden by the intervening wall, though. There seemed to be nobody up and moving in the room – no shadows or noises.

He was halfway across the floor toward the doorway when he heard something heavy crash to the floor in an upstairs room, followed by the sound of a muffled voice. The place was being ransacked. He peered through the doorway into the parlor, and there was Mr Jimmers, slumped in his chair – tied into it with a length of rope. He sat with his head on his chest. Blood oozed slowly out of a wound on his forehead. Howard stepped across, picked up Jimmers' hand, and found his pulse, which was steady and regular. Jimmers' eyes opened, blinked, and then opened wider, in contusion at first and then narrowing with anger. He grimaced, as if the effort had hurt.

Howard shook his head and put a finger to his lips. 'It wasn't me,' he whispered, looking into Jimmers' eyes to see if there was any sign of concussion. 'Move your right leg.' Mr Jimmers shifted his leg, then moved his other leg and both arms in turn, without having to be asked.

'Did you see them?' Howard asked.

He shook his head once, slowly, and shut his eyes. 'They're upstairs,' Howard said. 'I came back after Sylvia's picnic basket.'

He felt foolish suddenly, explaining about the picnic basket, but he wanted to make very sure that Mr Jimmers understood why he was there. Jimmers nodded weakly, keeping his eyes shut, and fumbled with Howard's hand, pressing it a little. 'I'm all right,' he whispered, opening his eyes then and seeming to summon his strength. 'Leave now. They won't find it. They'll get out when they're through. Don't tangle with them. Leave me here. No police.' He drifted off, then abruptly whispered ''Mall right' again before giving up.

There was another crash upstairs, and the sound of heavy furniture being pushed around. Howard was helpless. His brain spun. Clearly he was involved in whatever was happening here, and not only because he had stumbled into it. This was what Uncle Roy had been talking about that very morning. This wasn't any sort of metaphoric vagary, like the business about the Tower of Babel or the attractions of numbers. Sides had been drawn in some sort of peculiar north coast war, and Howard had been drafted into it, on the side of Jimmers and old Graham and his uncle and aunt. And, of course, Sylvia.

But what did that mean? He had to take action – get Jimmers out of there. Except that maybe Jimmers was right. If Howard left him there, tied to his chair, the thieves would assume nothing and would go on their way, satisfied.

Or else they'd work Jimmers over. That was equally possible. And who were they? Was one of them Stoat? Would he stoop to this? Impulsively Howard bent over and went to work on the knots. It was thin nylon cord, though, pulled tight and knotted to each of the four legs. Whoever had tied Jimmers up hadn't known what the hell he was doing, and the knots were a mess.

Suddenly there was the sound of a voice again: the words 'We'll *ask* him!' It was clear and loud this time, as if from halfway down the stairs.

Howard realized that Mr Jimmers was mumbling something. Leaning closer, he heard the words 'gun' and 'closet.' Looking around, Howard saw the coat closet back out in the hall, near the front door. He pushed the rope ends under the chair and leaped across to pull the closet door open. There, behind three or four umbrellas, stood an old, beat-up shotgun.

He jerked it out by the barrel and carried it across to the wall, where he waited silently, listening and catching his breath. No one appeared. The voices were arguing now, from upstairs again. Whoever had been coming down had gone back up.

He looked at the shotgun, realizing that the cold metal of the barrel repulsed him. There was something deadly and final about it, and instead of making him feel that much safer, it meant that he was that much closer to real trouble.

His hand shook, and he closed his eyes and breathed evenly, trying to control himself, to think things out. He had used a shotgun once, to blast skeet off the stern of a ferry on a two-day voyage from England to Spain. He had got his share of the little clay disks and from a hell of a lot farther off than he would be now. He told himself that this was nothing he couldn't deal with.

Only there was a moderate difference between shooting a lump of clay and shooting a man – a difference he couldn't allow himself to experience. Maybe he had fallen into the middle of Uncle Roy's complicated troubles, but those troubles couldn't involve him in killings. Still, there was Jimmers hit on the head and tied into a chair. The gun was protection for both of them – better than nothing. It was a good prop is what it was. He wouldn't have to use it.

Having made up his mind, he hefted the gun again. It was wrapped heavily with old duct tape where the wooden stock joined the metal behind the trigger. The whole thing felt mushy, as if the tape weren't just to help with the grip, but actually tied the halves of the gun together. The tape was dirty and old, too, and sticky with glue, and the barrel was flecked with rust from sitting in the damp closet. The whole thing rattled, as if all the joints were loose. All in all it wasn't a very formidable sight.

So what? It would have to do. The mere noise of the shell being chambered would paralyze them with fear, especially if they were unarmed.

Feeling slightly more steely-jawed, he checked Mr Jimmers again, who seemed to be resting as comfortably as a man might in his condition. His forehead wasn't bleeding anymore. Howard went on past him, listening hard, padding silently in his stocking feet. They were still at it up above, taking the place apart.

He edged up the stairs, pointing the barrel of the shotgun up the gloomy well and wedging the stock against his stomach so that he could jam the shell home in an instant – if the gun was loaded. He turned it over, and through a little open door in the bottom he could see the brass disk at the end of a shell.

No one met him on the stairs. He heard them talking now, oblivious to him. He hesitated on the second-floor landing, looking for cover, and jumped at the sound of a door closing. He gripped the gun more tightly, forcing the wobbly stock against him. His hand slipped across the duct tape, which had gone from sticky to slick with sweat. The tape moved under his palm, and he could feel that the wood of the stock was cracked. Never mind, he told himself. It's a prop, a gimmick. If he moved quickly and found a place to hide, they weren't going to see him, anyway.

It was easy to tell which room they were in. The door was open and the light on, and he could see through it when he'd taken three steps up the hallway. He would duck into an adjacent room, one already torn up, and follow them down when they left. That way he could see who they were, identify them. And if they tried anything further with Jimmers, Howard could stop them. Better to let them get away clean, though, than to provoke any stupid confrontation.

'Shit!' a voice said suddenly. 'It's not here.'

'Can't be.'

'What now?'

'Upstairs,' the other voice said. 'The attic.'

Howard leaped toward the nearest bedroom door, but it was six paces away, and one of the two thieves was halfway out of the room and stepping into the hallway before Howard had his hand on the knob and was pushing it open. 'Hey!' the man shouted, as if half in surprise and half to alert his friend, who was still hidden in the room behind.

The man in the hall wore a disguise, a cheap shoulder-length woman's wig and a black Lone Ranger mask. There was makeup on his cheeks – putty that was piled up and then cut with gouged-in scars. He wore a black T-shirt and blue jeans. Howard froze where he stood, trying to put on a steel-edged smile. It wasn't Stoat. 'He's got a shotgun,' the man said evenly. His companion was silent.

Stepping forward slowly, the man in the wig gestured at Howard, who shuffled back into the center of the hall, putting another yard between them. He set his feet, squinted, and aimed the shotgun straight at the man's chest. His hand shook on the gunstock, though.

The man stopped, not liking the look of Howard's shaking hands. He threw his arms into the air, grinning with false surprise. 'Down, boy!' he said, laughing. 'Chill out. You've got us.'

Howard tensed, ready for him as the man took another step forward, gesturing with both hands and shaking his head as if trying to make Howard see reason. Howard didn't look like a killer; that was the problem. The man could smell it, like a wolf. Howard didn't have the instinct, and there was no way in the world to hide it. He should have made his move long ago; now it was clear he had no move to make.

'Give me the sketch,' Howard said suddenly.

'What?'

'Give me the sketch. I want it. I'm taking it.'

The man glanced hesitantly over his shoulder, but there was still no sight of his companion. 'Sure,' he said then. 'Aim the damned gun at the floor, though. It's not worth killing anyone over. What are you? Friend of the old man downstairs?'

'To hell with the old man downstairs. He's out cold. He'll think you have it, won't he?'

The man grinned. 'Smart,' he said. He leaned forward, staring into Howard's face. Howard stepped back again, tightening his grip on the trigger and slide. Sweat ran down his forehead, and he told himself that it wasn't supposed to have gone this far. People were supposed to live in terror of shotguns. He pushed the stock tighter against his stomach, clicked the safety catch forward with his thumb, and jacked the shell into the chamber. There was a throaty *kshlack-shlack* as the gun levered away from his stomach with the force of the slide slamming forward.

And then, as if in a cartoon, without any warning at all, the stock simply fell loose from the rest of the gun, dangling for a moment on the end of the pulled-loose duct tape before clattering to the hallway floor.

At the sound of the gun being chambered, the man in the wig had jumped backward toward the bedroom door, which right then was slamming shut. The door clipped him in the back, and he sat down hard, knocking it open again. Howard got a brief glimpse of someone's backside, crawling in behind a pulled-apart bed. Howard gripped the end of the barrel in his right hand, threw his arm back, and flung the useless piece of steel wildly at the open door. The man in the wig ducked against the doorjamb, throwing his hand across his face.

The piece of metal whirled like a boomerang, slamming into the plaster wall three feet past the open door. By then Howard was running hard, back down the hallway. He heard the steel thud against the wall and then the explosion of the gun going off. He pitched forward, onto his chest on the floor, and slid out onto the landing. Chunks of plaster clattered against the walls behind him, peppering the back of his neck, and something sharp hit his hand and bounced away, leaving a bleeding cut – a fragment of green bottle glass. With a hasty glance behind him, he was up and running before he had time to think about it.

Howard leaped up the stairs two at a time, toward the attic, thinking that he should have gone downstairs instead, but at the same time wanting to lead them away from Mr Jimmers for reasons that he didn't bother to think about until it was too late to change his mind. He heard a shuffling behind him and the thud of a knee hitting the stairs when one of them fell. Then he pushed through the attic door, slamming it shut and bolting it from the inside. He fastened the little panel window shut, too, before he began hauling furniture across in front of the door, panting and gasping and yanking on the chairs and the library table. He threw his shoulder behind a stack of lawyer's book-cases and inched the heavy cases across the floor, too. Then he heard the outside bolt snap shut.

He was locked in. For fifteen seconds he had wanted desperately to be locked in, but now that he was, from the outside ... He stood up and leaned against the stack of bookcases, trying to breathe evenly. He forced himself to think, willed himself to calm down. He was struck with the blind ignorance of what he had done – capering around with the ludicrous gun, nearly killing someone, himself maybe, out of stupidity. He should have got Mr Jimmers out of there while the others were occupied upstairs. They wouldn't have guessed anything fishy was going on below. He could have helped Jimmers to the truck and been gone in minutes, and to hell with them – unless they had come down the stairs and surprised him at it ...

He made himself stop. He had tried, anyway. Dwelling on mistakes wouldn't help now. When this sort of thing happened in the future, he would remember. Live and learn. If nothing else, at least these people would get the impression that Howard wanted the sketch as badly as they did. He had brought a gun along, after all.

The quilt still lay on the floor. There was the casement window. Hadn't he just determined that very afternoon that a man might risk climbing down? If the cloth ripped, of course, or if he couldn't hold on ... well ... there was precious little chance that he would fall straight down onto the little rocky ledge, merely to break his ankle, say. What he would do is tumble a hundred-odd feet down onto wave-washed rocks.

They were talking outside the door now, low and indistinct, arguing. The wigged man was accusing the other man of something – chewing him out for having tried to shut the door, probably, back in the hallway. Soon they would unbolt Howard's door and force their way in. They would deal with him as they had dealt with Jimmers. Probably worse. He was in the way, a dangerous obstacle, and competition to boot. That's what they were doing outside – deciding his fate.

He thought again about the quilt and the window. He picked the quilt up and tugged on it, unable to rip it. It was strong enough, certainly, and there was a scissors in the library table drawer. He could cut the quilt into six strips, tie them together. That ought to give him what? – thirty-five feet or so. He'd have to make it eight strips. What would he fasten the whole mess to? Something that couldn't be jerked through the window, that wouldn't come apart. The library table would do in a pinch. It would jam up against the open window, and its heavy oak legs would hold up fine.

It would work. He had determined that. But there was no way on earth that he wanted to try it.

The two outside were silent now, or had left. He hoped to heaven that there were other rooms for them to rout through, or that better yet they'd made their getaway, content to save the attic for another day. It was possible, too, that they had gone downstairs to murder Jimmers, or to rough him up, to make him talk.

Thinking hard, Howard strode across to the closet and threw the door open. He was struck again with the strange construction of the thing, built, as it was, into an odd little bit of outward-curving wall. The strangeness of it seemed to signify now, far more than it had two nights ago, when he was comfortable in his chair and eating a sandwich and there were no potential murderers lurking outside the door.

Clearly the rounded bit of closet wall that faced him now stood adjacent to the stairwell. He thought abruptly of the Humpty Dumpty window. What had been the point of that fishy section of window and wall? It had needlessly narrowed the stairs. Perhaps that window let out onto a room or passage behind the closet, a hidden turret. Clearly it was all part of the same secret structure. The closet itself wasn't more than twenty-four inches deep. The curve of the wall argued that the turret it formed was something much larger – eight or ten feet across.

He couldn't recall having seen it from outside the house, from the vantage point of Jimmers' garden or from where the back of the house was knit into the cliff. It was a secret room of some sort, and no doubt about it.

At once he began pulling stuff out of the closet – a boxed telescope, portable file boxes, dusty books, paper bags filled with receipts and scraps, cardboard boxes with the tops woven shut. He pushed it all behind him into the room, working frantically, warming up again with the exertion. He scooped out the last of the litter on the floor, so that the closet was utterly empty, and he stood staring at the walls of the thing, catching his breath.

There was nothing to see. It was just a closet, set in a round piece of wall. It was plaster on the inside, just like any other closet – dirty plaster streaked yellow with water stains.

If there was a secret passage of some sort beyond it, it must be accessible from some other part of the house. What was on the opposite side this far upstairs, though? Nothing. There was only the one attic room. He was certain of that.

Except there was the exterior door, the one you *could* see from Jimmers' garden, the one in his dreams that opened out onto nothing, with the broken stone stairs leading almost to it. That was it. There *was* a door, all right, and so arguably there was a secret passage, and it was an even bet that this was it.

But what good did it do him? Even if he was free and standing down on the meadow, without a twenty- or thirty-foot ladder he could get nowhere near the door, which was padlocked, anyway, just like Jimmers' shed – probably the same key.

He stepped out into the room again. The exertion had calmed him down. It was the quilt, apparently, or nothing.

Resolutely he found the scissors and hacked away, cutting as straight and clean as he could along the vertical seams and wondering whether the stitching would hold a man's weight or would ravel into threads when he was halfway to the ground. Cotton batting fluffed out from between the panels, deflating them, making the strips look flimsy and weak. He would roll it up and knot it in order to fake a little extra strength. He went on with it, growing more and more doubtful, each passing minute increasing his anxiety, the silence outside the room becoming more ominous.

When the quilt was cut apart, he stood up and stepped across to the casement, throwing it open, steeling himself before looking down. The tide was low, and the hulk of the Studebaker sat high and dry. The kelp-covered reefs were half dried out in the afternoon sunlight. There was a movement below, on the edge of Jimmers' garden. It was the man with the wig, working feverishly, digging up the Swiss chard with a spade.

Damn it, Howard thought. That might be it. What if they'd tortured Jimmers and he'd confessed to burying the sketch and covering the thing's grave with vegetables? If that was the case, maybe they would take it and leave. Maybe not. One way or another, Howard would be spotted in a second Rapunzeling down the wall. They would wait below and just give him a gentle push with the end of the shovel when he touched down.

The scissored-up quilt looked like hell to him, lying there on the floor. He stared at the closet again, thinking, for some strange reason, of Mrs Lamey and her dyed flowers. What was it? The closet still intrigued him, still drew him. He shoved into it again, rapping against the plaster this time, knocking methodically. It echoed thin and hollow beneath his knuckles.

15

It was a piece of wallboard is what it was, thin and flimsy, not plaster at all. Dollars to doughnuts it wasn't original. Graham wouldn't have had anything to do with wallboard back when he built the place, even if it had been available, which it probably hadn't been. Shoving his face nearly against it, Howard could smell the musty, dried mud odor of the recently applied joint compound and the chemical odor of new paint. There were brush marks where someone had painted-on the stains, probably with rusty water. It might have been done yesterday, last week. Whoever it was – Jimmers, probably – had made a thorough job of it.

Howard knocked again, listening close – rap, rap, rap along the entire length of the thin wall. There were studs at either end, with three feet of unsupported wallboard in the center, pretty clearly where a door used to be. It pressed inward half an inch when he pushed on it.

He leaned back, levered himself against the door frame, and kicked the wall with the bottom of his foot, which chunked through the wall, tearing open a ten-inch ragged hole. He kicked it again, widening the gap, and then grabbed the wallboard with his hands, slamming it back and forth, breaking out chunks and throwing them back through, into the dim antechamber beyond.

Along with the chalky smell of drywall dust, he could smell ocean air drifting up out of the passage. It led to the sea, then, probably to the base of the cliff, a cave through the bluffs themselves. Too bad about Mr Jimmers' quilt; there had been no point in scissoring it up. Howard had become a sort of thorn in the poor man's side. But if he wanted to make up for any of the trouble he had caused Jimmers, then Howard had to hurry, to get back to Jimmers before it was too late to help him.

For a moment he hesitated, though. To do it right, a sort of Huckleberry Finn job, he should knot up the quilt strips, anchor them to the table, and drop the end out the window. That would throw them off the scent. He should repack the closet, too, and then shut the door behind him when he made his escape. They would take one look into the room, see the tied-together quilt, rush to the window, figure things out wrong, and charge back down to see if he was outside somewhere, skulking around.

Either that or they would suppose it was all fakery and that he was hiding in the closet. They'd find the passage and be after him, if they cared about him, and he would have wasted twenty minutes screwing around being clever.

Without waiting another instant he bent through the hole, stepping on the pieces of drywall in his stocking feet, nearly slipping on them as they skidded across the floor. Jimmers' hankering after Japanese customs had begun to look something worse than silly, and Howard made a vow never again to give up his shoes. Still, socks were better than nothing, even if they had holes in the toes.

Now that his eyes had adjusted to the dim light, Howard could see that the tiny chamber beyond the closet was nothing more than the top landing of a spiral stairway. The Humpty Dumpty window hung in the wall adjacent to the first step. A diffused glow showed through it from the hallway beyond, and Howard could see the figure of a man just then moving across the window like a shadow – probably one of the two intruders, sneaking up the stairs. It might have been Jimmers, of course, free and coming to let him out, but Howard didn't think so. It was more likely that they had found nothing but Swiss chard in the garden and were looking to have a go at the attic. The bolted, barricaded door would hold them up, but not for more than a few moments.

Howard started down the stairs, taking them two at a time, hanging on to the handrail, which was an iron pipe that snaked down into the blackness. Within eight steps the night had closed around him and he couldn't see anything at all. He gripped the cold railing, stepping down slowly now, thinking of the ruined stairs that led to the high doorway above the meadow. What if someone, Jimmers, had done something to these stairs, too? – pried two or three of them apart with a crowbar so that a person coming along in the blind darkness would …

But that wouldn't make sense. Clearly the passage had been used, and recently, too. And someone had gone to some little trouble to hide the fact while sealing the passage off altogether. Why? Howard couldn't say, and didn't have time to consider the problem. There was a sudden, muffled banging from above, and then the sound of a voice shouting – the thieves yelling through the attic door, probably. He couldn't make out the words. The shouting stopped and the banging started back up, a loud, slow *thump, thump, thump* now, as if they were slamming at the door with something heavy, trying to batter it open.

Abruptly he found himself at the bottom of the stairs. Cool, wet air drifted up from below. The smell of the sea was stronger now, mixed with the musty odor of stone and decayed kelp, and he could hear the murmur of breaking waves echoing up through the tunnel. It was still utterly dark, and he felt around himself before going on, running his hands across rough timbers like in a shored-up mine. After a few feet of level ground, the passage ran off steeply again, with wooden steps set right into the dirt and rock. Howard followed them down, gripping the corroded pipe, listening for sound from above.

He just barely heard another distant thump and then heavy scraping – the table and chairs shoving away in front of the door. So now they knew. They could see the closet door standing open, the jagged hole torn in the wall-board. They would see the cut-up quilt, too, and know that he hadn't gone straight out, that he had wasted time first, that they were right behind him.

They wanted the sketch, though; they didn't want him. If they had already found it, they would profit by getting it out of there, simply taking off. He stopped and held his breath, cocking his head. Someone had come through the wall. He could hear them scrabbling around on the loose pieces of dry-wall. It was deadly silent for a moment except for the noise of his own heart beating, and then there sounded the thumping of shoe soles on the wooden stairs.

He hurried on, down into the ground, brushing the air above his head to try to find the tunnel ceiling. There was nothing, empty air. And then suddenly the steps ended, and his stocking feet slid on gravel, shooting out from under him so that he sat down hard on the ground, scraping the palms of his hands, his breath whumping out of his lungs. He pushed himself up, dusting the gravel off his hands, and took off again. He went carefully now, stepping gingerly on rocks, feeling his way, trying to hurry along in a sort of high-stepping caper. If he wore shoes, he might have run – the two behind him surely would – but the gravelly tunnel was too rough.

There they were. Howard heard a scuffling and a brief snatch of cutoff talk. In the echoing darkness of the tunnel it sounded like the disembodied voice of a ghost. There was no way to tell where it had come from. Thank God for the railing; he had something to hold on to, at least, and unless Jimmers was simply crazy, there ought to be nothing obstructing the passage at the bottom end, no boulders to stub his toes on. The sound of the ocean, clear and close now, argued against any sort of door across the tunnel mouth.

The passage leveled suddenly and he saw ahead of him a moonlit section of sand and rocks. He stepped outside, into the evening air, the sand beneath his feet crusty and damp from the receded tide. The cold sea wind blew straight onshore, into his face. The sun was low over the ocean now, almost swallowed up. A wall of tumbled rock on his right cut off the view of the smashed Studebaker and made it impossible for anyone to see the tunnel mouth from the meadow above. To his left the bluffs rose straight up toward the sky, loose and scrubby – impossible to climb. He might have been able to scrabble up a ways in order to drop a rock on someone's head, but he wasn't in a rock-dropping mood.

He waded straight out into a big tide pool instead, gasping at the cold water that swirled around his ankles and stepping up onto a dark shelf of rock that was a garden of limp, exposed sea palms. He slid on the slippery leaves, slamming his foot against a jagged bit of rock and then sliding sideways into a deeper pool, soaking his right leg up to the waist. His breath jerked up out of his throat, and he nearly shouted as he pulled himself out of the freezing water and scrambled in behind a table-sized angle of stone, gripping two handfuls of sea palm to hold himself steady.

Right then the two men appeared at the mouth of the passage, looking around themselves warily. One of them carried a stick – a table leg or something – and he held it out to the side, ready to bash someone. They turned to look above them up the bluffs just in case Howard was up there. Seeing nothing, they stood murmuring to each other, one of them shaking his head.

Howard kneeled in the shadow, hidden behind his rock. The ocean swirled in just then, rising to his waist, trying to push him forward. His breath shot up out of his lungs with the numbing cold of it, and he was nearly washed off into deeper water. The ocean rose higher, and his legs slewed around as he kicked to try to find a purchase against the rocks.

Then the ocean receded, leaving him sodden and hanging. He got his knees up under him, creeping toward higher ground, crouching to stay hidden while the two on shore still looked around themselves dumbly, surveying the cliff face once more and then looking hard out into the ocean – straight past him. They edged out onto the rocks, trying to get a glimpse across to where the Studebaker sat. But that meant taking a swim, or at least a wade out into the ocean, and their tiptoeing around made it seem as if neither one of them wanted to get wet.

They pointed Howard's footsteps out to each other and looked across the little bay. Howard stayed put, watching them between the rocks, thankful that the sun was low and the shadows were long. But if they came his way, they would see him, and he would have no choice but to turn and run – head for deep water and swim straight out to sea. The water was cold, but not cold enough to cause him any serious trouble, not for a little while, anyway.

They stood arguing now. One of them pointed oceanward, and Howard heard the other one say, 'Who cares?' very loud, and then turn and walk away, back into the tunnel. The other stood there for another minute, evidently considering things.

The water swirled up around Howard's waist again, pushing him up the rock, spinning him in a lazy circle. He held on, waiting it out, cursing the man who still stood there hunting him. The ocean was colder than he had realized, and with the wind blowing now he would be colder yet before he was out of it. Then the second man was gone suddenly, back into the darkness.

Howard held on. What if they were crouched in the shadows, waiting for him to make his move? They might be more desperate than he thought. It was possible of course, from their point of view, that Howard had the sketch with him, that he had found it in the attic and taken it. He suddenly regretted all the tough talk in the hallway when he had confronted the man in the wig. He shouldn't have mentioned the sketch at all.

Minutes passed. The ocean rose and fell. Howard's feet were like blocks of heavy, numb sponge, wrapped in soggy socks that bagged around his ankles. He could see the silhouettes of the two men now, far above him, moving around in the attic, back and forth across the windows. There was no going back up the tunnel, not unless he wanted to hand himself over.

Without wasting any more time, he stood up, balancing carefully. Starting to shiver, he picked his way seaward from rock to rock, his wet pants sticking to his legs. It struck him that the cove must be impossible to navigate, even in a small boat at high tide. Far outside he could see the white tumble of breakers.

He looked over his shoulder, back at the little bit of beach, where the tunnel mouth lay dark and silent. He could see only a black crescent of it now, and in a moment it was lost to sight completely beyond intervening rocks. He was safe. They would see him from the attic window if they cared enough to look, but by then he'd be too far off to chase. He had only to keep moving. In a half hour, he told himself, he would be in Jimmers' parlor; the fire would be roaring, and he would have his shoes back. By then, he hoped, the two men would be gone.

His socks were a ragged mess, pulled apart on the rough rocks. He couldn't feel much at all because of the cold water, which was just as well, because there were a couple of bleeding cuts on the bottom of his feet. He stepped along gingerly, forcing himself to slow down. He was tired and wobbly, and if he hurried he was sure to slip and fall. A twisted ankle would plunge him into deep trouble.

The tide seemed to be creeping higher, too. If he didn't want to find himself swimming against it, he would have to get out and around the long, rocky promontory that formed the south edge of the cove. It wasn't much farther to the tip of it – fifty yards, perhaps.

He could see where the water rushed out, leaving the low, kelp-covered shelf of the promontory high and dry, and then rushed back in again to cover it, slamming up against the vertical face of the upthrusting rock cliffs. He would have to avoid that, somehow – wait for a lull in the waves and run for it across the rocks; to hell with his feet. In ten minutes, probably, there would be nothing but ocean there, breaking waves, and getting past it would mean a long swim in rough water.

He set out across a bed of mussels and barnacles, hobbling gingerly on the things like a South Sea Islander across hot coals, his feet pressing them down. A broken shell knicked the soft arch of his foot, and he said 'Ouch!' out loud, not caring who might hear him anymore, which was no one. The house sat on the cliff far above and behind him now, lit up from top to bottom. A faint wisp of smoke rose from the stone chimney.

He skirted the tip of the promontory finally, crawling up and onto a dark, stone shelf. The ocean washed through, deeper with each succeeding swell. Waves that had been breaking farther out in shallow water rolled right through now to smash against the ledge that he picked his way across, and he was knocked off his feet and had to scramble to keep himself from being swept back out with them.

He wasn't certain where the rock shelf ended and the next cove started but he knew there was another cove there, visible to the south of where he and Sylvia had talked on the bluffs that afternoon. He pictured it in his mind, as if to make it exist for him by sympathetic magic. There was a trail that led down to it from above, switchbacking along the bluffs, through the wildflowers and tall grass, and he imagined himself staggering up that trail, out of the water at last.

Another wave washed through, humping up over the ledge and quartering toward him across the now-submerged kelp and smaller rocks. He braced himself, but it slammed him over backward, pushing him helplessly toward the cliff face where the water roiled and leaped and blasted into the air in heavy geysers. He flailed with his arms, trying to turn himself around, waiting to be knocked senseless. His head scraped sickeningly across a mussel-covered rock, and he could hear his scalp tear for a stinging-cold moment. Then the face of the wave smashed against the cliff, and the wave's energy turned on itself as the sea rushed back, dragging him along, surging away from the rock wall and hauling him off the edge of the reef and into deeper water before relaxing its grip on him.

He struck out hard, swimming parallel to the shore, his sodden clothes dragging at him. They had saved him a thousand cuts and scrapes, though. Pulling any of them off now would be madness. They would do something to cut the sea wind, too, when he got to shore.

He kept that in mind – getting to shore – as he kicked over the top of a wave and down the back side of it, still swimming. Again he pictured Mr Jimmers' stuffed chair in front of the parlor fire, and the fire itself, heaped with cedar logs, leaping and popping, orange sparks rushing up the stone chimney.

His arms and legs felt weighted, and he found that he couldn't easily open and close his hands, which he pulled through the water like frozen bricks. A wave broke, catching him by surprise and washing over his head. He fought to stay on the surface, coughing up ocean water and gasping for air, kicking his legs tiredly. He forced his arms to move, plodding along in a sodden crawl stroke and paying attention to the waves and to the rocks along the shore.

He could see that the cliffs moved slowly past him now. He was making headway – more than he ought to be making. He was being swept along in a current. Suddenly frightened, he began to swim straight in toward shore with fear-induced power, trying to pull a little energy out of the waves washing past him.

When he rose on one swell, he saw that he was straight off the next cove, which stretched lovely and flat and sandy for something like fifty yards. He kicked furiously into an onrushing wave, which sped him forward, picking him up and hurtling him past the black humps of exposed rock. He held his hands out in front of him and tucked his head against his chest, expecting to be slammed against the rocks as the wave jumped and foamed around him, carrying him shoreward now in a wild rush.

Then the wave abruptly dwindled, dumping him thirty feet from shore and washing out to leave him on his knees in the shallows. He tried to stand, but couldn't, and another wave tumbled through, sliding him in across the sand before rushing back out and leaving him there on the beach, sodden and gasping.

He rested for a moment before crawling farther up, the ocean licking at his feet. Then he lay there again, thinking that as the tide came up, the waves might easily submerge the whole beach, which was almost flat. He could see flotsam and seaweed scattered in the rocks above him, advertising the high-tide line. The sight of it compelled him to stand, and he staggered away toward where the dirt path joined the beach, trying to dust the sand off his hands against the side of his pants.

He plodded tiredly up the path some twenty or thirty feet before sitting down in the dirt to rest. His feet had started to thaw out, and it wasn't any sort of pins and needles tickling; it was a slow burning and itching, and the painful realization that they were cut up, and that he was walking now nearly barefoot through dirt. He still wore his socks, but there wasn't anything left of the bottoms of them except a few stretched bunches of thread. He stopped long enough to turn his socks over, so that the heel stretched across his ankle. At least his head, miraculously, was whole. There was a wash of watery blood across his hand when he touched his cut scalp, but the mussels, blessedly, had been just a little bit spongy, happy just to slice him up and tear out clumps of hair.

Twice again he stopped to rest, looking down on the cove and at the ocean that had both saved him and tried to drown him. Then he trudged upward, finally topping the rise and finding himself on the meadow, skirting the wooden fence where he had talked to Sylvia only a few hours earlier.

He was suddenly in dangerous territory, and he slipped along warily, boosted by the adrenaline rush of confronting the two robbers again. He couldn't afford to do that. But what would he do instead? Pitch their distributor cap into the weeds and drive like hell down the highway? Wait for them to leave peaceably and then go in after Jimmers?

He pushed through the vines at the side of the house, crouching behind the cement mixer and peering past it.

They were gone. The red Camaro simply wasn't there. Cautiously he hunched across the yard in the shadow of the house. The front door was shut, the house dark. Fearing that they'd moved the car and that he would blunder into them, Howard edged along the wall toward the garden. There was nothing – just the tin shed standing lonely in the moonlight.

He retraced his steps to the front door, opened it slowly, and listened for a moment before pulling off his socks and stepping in out of the sea wind. The house was silent, the fire nearly burned down. Mr Jimmers sat in his chair yet, just as Howard had left him. He was breathing evenly, obviously asleep.

Without a backward glance, Howard eased the stone out of the face of the fireplace, reaching into the dark recess. The hidey-hole was empty, the sketch gone.

'Move and you're a dead man,' a voice said, and Howard believed it, and stood very still, his nose six inches from the granite wall of the fireplace.

16

A minute passed in complete silence. Howard was aware of the cold stones of the floor and of the pitifully burned-down fire and of the stomach-wrenching truth that someone right now was deciding calmly what to do with him – shoot him, maybe, in the back, or merely beat him senseless with a club. He began to shiver again, violently now. Whatever energies had fired him when he was sneaking back into the house had waned, and it was with a growing sense of horror that he realized he was in no condition at all to put up a fight.

Still nothing happened – no blow, no further orders, not even a poke in the ribs. He risked standing up out of the semi-crouch he was in. No one protested. There was nothing but silence. He turned his head slightly. No one said a word. He had moved, and he wasn't a dead man. He had the eerie notion, though, that someone was standing directly behind him.

He couldn't bear it any longer, and he turned to look, ready to throw himself onto the floor, into the fireplace if need be. There stood Mr Jimmers, wide-eyed but otherwise deadpan and staring at his pocket watch as if counting off the seconds. He had cleaned the blood from his forehead and wore a big, rectangular bandage on the cut. Howard hadn't noticed it, sneaking around as he had been.

'A little experiment in human behavior,' Mr Jimmers said, putting the watch away. 'Taken a swim, then?'

'Yes,' said Howard. 'That's right. They chased me down to the cove, and I got away across the rocks.'

'And came back around to rob me?'

'Not at all. I wanted to know if they'd got it. What were we fighting about, after all, if it wasn't to keep them from getting it?'

'I burned it this afternoon. You saw me. Disbelieve your own eyes these days?'

'I thought it was, you know – a prank, a trick.'

'Ah! That's it. A prank, a trick, a cheat.' He smiled suddenly. 'They're gone. Empty-handed. I told them it was in the attic, after they locked you in. They came back down to rough me up. I'm not the sort, though, to be pushed around like that. I've got friends, and I warned them of it. Clever of me, wasn't it, telling them it was in the attic, hidden under the drawer in the library table? You should have heard me.'

Mr Jimmers waggled his eyebrows at Howard, and then said, 'Ouch,' under his breath, and touched his forehead gingerly, his face clouding over for a moment. Then he grinned again. 'It could be they think *you've* got it now – that you found it and fled. I said you were a skunk, a thief, a poseur from down south. I'm free of them. They're yours now. Here, sit down.' Mr Jimmers gestured toward the chair, but then seemed to see for the first time that Howard was soaked through, and he shook his head, as if withdrawing the offer. Instead, he threw two logs onto the fire and blew at them with a bellows.

'You'll warm up faster standing up,' he said. 'Cup of Postum?'

'No thanks. You're all right, then – no ringing in the ears or faintness?'

'Not at all. I'm tip-top. They didn't want trouble, assault charges. You know what they wanted. How about you, though? You've taken a nasty scratch on your head.'

'Assault charges?' Howard said. 'You called the police?'

'No,' said Mr Jimmers. 'Nor will you. You'll disappear south, back to the warrens of Los Angeles. I've thought this through, and I've come up with a plan that might save you. You'll leave your truck and all your belongings.

They aren't worth anything, anyway. We'll smuggle you up to the Little River airport and fly you out in a private plane – to Oakland, where you can catch a commercial jet into Los Angeles. You can't return to work, of course, or to your living quarters, but I can't imagine that you'll suffer any for that. It's possible that we can arrange some little stipend to see you over. I have a cousin in the cordage industry down there. He could probably find you a position.'

Mr Jimmers paced up and down, his hands behind his back. Howard stood cooking before the fire, listening in astonishment. 'Anyway, straight off you'll send someone in to steal your dental records. And when you don't reappear at Roy Barton's place, our thieves will be certain you've drowned with the sketch. Meantime, somehow we'll get a cadaver and soak it in a tide pool for a few days, let the crabs and fish have a go at it, then tow it a quarter mile out to sea and set it adrift. By the time it washes up on shore there'll be no one alive who can say it's not you if they don't have the dental records, which they won't, of course, because you'll have destroyed them. No, cancel that. Forget the dental records. We've got a corpse, don't we? We'll break its teeth out. Wait! Better than that, and easier, *we'll cut off its head*! To hell with dental records. Don't bother yourself with them. This is foolproof! We'll pull the wool straight over their eyes. You won't have anything to fear from these men. I had to pitch you into the soup there with the shotgun and all, which I notice you ruined somehow, but I'm hauling you out again with the ladle. Dry yourself off and get back to the business of living. That's my last word on the subject, and it's a good one.'

Howard said nothing during this appalling speech. The fire leaped behind him, throwing out a wash of heat, and he stepped forward and brushed at the back of his legs. He had no earthly idea whether Mr Jimmers was serious or playing Tom Fool. He didn't have the strength to ask and certainly not the strength to play along. Of course he wouldn't disappear south. If these thieves accosted him, he'd tell the truth – that he had seen Jimmers burn it. They could turn him upside down, empty his pockets, give him the third degree. What good would it do them? They hadn't killed Jimmers tonight. It stood to reason that they wouldn't kill him, either.

'Wait here,' Mr Jimmers said, hurrying away. He was back within minutes with a set of dry clothes, and Howard, suddenly, was itching to be out of there. Mr Jimmers was safe. Howard could catch Uncle Roy at the haunted house. He would know what Jo do next. In fact, Uncle Roy and Sylvia might easily be the next victims. There was no time to stand and chat with Mr Jimmers.

'Hold off on the cadaver,' he said to Jimmers. 'It's a good plan, but I see some bugs in it. I'll contact you.'

He took the dry clothes with him to the next room, and, feeling ridiculous but almost warm again after cinching up the too-short and too-broad pants, he thanked Mr Jimmers, latched on to the picnic basket, and went out into the evening, carrying his wet clothes in a plastic grocery bag.

'Honestly, Mr Stoat. Think about it,' Mrs Lamey said. Stoat sat on her living room couch, his feet propped up on the table. A second woman sat across from him, scowling toward the window as if she were tired with the conversation. Mrs Lamey went on, gesturing expansively. 'Those old properties on Haight Street are worth millions. Your friend the Reverend has made a fortune renovating dilapidated flats. I mean to tap it myself – tie into them with a bulldozer. You get tiresome when you pretend to have a social conscience, Mr Stoat. I know very well that you haven't any such thing. A conscience of any sort is like fetters, isn't it?'

'Dangerous talk,' Stoat said, shrugging. 'Never deny having a conscience. You might wake up one morning and discover you're right. And we're talking about the area around where the old Haight Street Theater used to stand, aren't we? Down around Haight and Cole? That's dangerous ground. The last developer got firebombed by urban terrorists, didn't he?'

Mrs Lamey made a long face. 'There's terrorists,' she said, 'and there's terrorists. It's all a matter of motivation. The good Reverend White, I believe, has some little experience with these terrorists. He has a great deal of motivation on call, pockets full of it.'

'Are you saying that—'

'I'm not *saying* anything, Mr Stoat, except that you need have no fear of urban terrorists, as you call them. All you have to fear is your bleeding social conscience.'

'There's no point in talking in labels and definitions, anyway. I've never thought of myself as having a "social conscience," as you put it. When you politicize morality you lose it. That's what I think. A standard-issue conscience is enough for me.'

'That's absolute shit,' the second woman said, breaking in. 'You're stone-scared, Stoat. Don't turn this into a study of philosophy. Face yourself.'

'It's tiring to face yourself, Gwen, if you don't like what you see in the mirror.'

The woman named Gwen wore a khaki dashiki, a necklace of wooden beads, a pair of old combat boots. She had long, straight, unevenly cut brown hair, as if she were working hard to affect the look of an urban guerrilla at a Halloween costume party.

'Let's ignore your conscience, then, shall we?' Mrs Lamey said to Stoat. 'What I'm talking about is some squalid empty lots and a run-down lot of flats occupied by human rubbish.' She held up a hand to silence Stoat, who had started to speak. 'What will happen, as it's happened time and time again in the past, is that one fine day a cigarette and a mattress will burn another half block to the ground and all those people will be on the street, anyway, if they're not dead. The entire area is an unsanitary warren of drug havens and bathhouses and human degradation. What I propose is to rebuild all of it, and human dignity into the bargain.'

'What you propose is turning two hundred people out of their homes in order to profit by it. Let's keep all this motivation talk straight, just like Gwen suggested.'

'It's a matter of perspective, isn't it?'

'It's a matter of something.'

'Don't pretend to be above it, Stoat,' Gwen said. 'You're a fine one to talk about profit. How long ago was it that you sold out? And didn't I just hear you propounding a lot of shit about there being no such thing as a social conscience? Now you're coming in on the side of the huddled masses.'

'On the side of the poor bastard who's trying to get by from day to day.'

'Shit happens, Stoat.'

Mrs Lamey frowned. 'My dear,' she said pettishly, 'could you try to be less fecal about this whole thing?'

'Shit, shit, shit!' Gwen said at Mrs Lamey's face. 'You and my goddamn mother. Let me give you a piece of advice. It's a couple of lines from my last poem. "You've got to be able to shit and look at it. That's all that matters."'

'All?' Stoat asked, blinking at her. 'I would have thought something else … a good bottle of wine …'

'*Fuck* what you would have thought.'

Mrs Lamey recoiled, like a snail touched with an electric prod. After a moment's silence she said, 'Forgive me if I try to get us back on subject. This little venture would return quadruple the investment within a couple of years. It's *quite* an opportunity. Now, here's a thought. If you want so badly to help the downtrodden, why don't you make them an offer – each and every one of them. Let them all be partners in this. For every hundred dollars each of them invests, we'll return two hundred dollars after two years, guaranteed. There's nothing more egalitarian than profit sharing. There's two hundred and fifty or so of them. Squeeze a hundred dollars out of them on the average and we'll have enough to rent a crane and wrecking ball.' She smiled at the dashiki-clad woman, who frowned back at her. 'You don't seem to want to agree with anyone today, do you, Gwen?'

'Agreeing doesn't agree with her,' Stoat said. 'I'd cut off her allowance if I were you, Heloise. Being a patron of artists and poets ought to give you a certain power over them. Here's one of them waxing obscene in your living room. Let's wash her mouth out with soap.'

'You took my money greedily enough when you were drawing your disreputable comic books and living in poverty, Mr Stoat. Leave Gwendolyn alone. She'll come into her own.' Mrs Lamey cast the woman a motherly look.

'Why don't you both suck on a gun barrel?' Gwendolyn said.

The door opened just then and in walked two men, one of them wearing a beard and dressed in a coat and tie, and the other in a fashionable knitted sweater and pleated pants and carrying a leather shoulder bag like a yuppie banker dressed for a country excursion. Mrs Lamey stood up, looking sharp at them. 'Did you locate it this time? Or did you simply tear the place up and hit the man over the head again?'

'Got a fix on it this time,' the second one said. He reached into the shoulder bag and hauled out Mrs Lamey's magical divining rod – the two lashed-together forearm bones. A rotten, musty smell issued from the bag and from the bones. The man held them gingerly, as a person might hold a loaded gun with a cocked hair trigger. It was clear that he found it a loathsome object and wanted to get rid of it as quick as he could.

Mrs Lamey took the thing from him, then strode across the room to lay it on a distant table, out of harm's way.

'Can't you shift it farther than that?' Stoat asked. 'Why does magic stink so badly?'

'Nearly everything stinks that badly,' Gwendolyn said. 'You've been holding your nose all these years. Let go of it once, you'll learn something.'

'Where, then?' Mrs Lamey asked.

'Near as we can tell, in the tin shed. Who would have thought he would leave it out there? We used triangulation to home in on it, just like you suggested. Took us straight to the edge of the bluffs. For my money it's either locked in the shed or thrown off the cliff.'

'And you extricated it, then, from this tin shed?'

'No, we didn't. The nut – what's his name?'

'Jimmers.'

'That's it. He spotted us out the window. Said he'd already called a cop. So we moved on. He might have been telling the truth. Shouldn't be any real trouble to get at it – pair of bolt cutters when the old boy's asleep.'

'No, we'll get it now, before anyone else has a go at it. There's more in that shed than … what it is we're after.' She stepped to the window. Across the street sat Mr Bennet's house with its garden of wooden gizmos. Bennet himself had gone off with Roy Barton two hours ago. His truck sat carelessly at the curb. The street was silent and empty.

'You know Sylvia Barton, I think,' Mrs Lamey said to Gwen.

'I did once,' she replied, speaking to Mrs Lamey's back. 'When she was sweet on Stoatie here.'

Mrs Lamey turned around, looking shrewdly at her. 'Your voices aren't so very different. Hers is pitched just a little higher. Could you mimic it, do you think?'

She shrugged. 'I suppose so. How's this? Hello,' she said, sounding something like Felix the Cat, 'I'm Sylvia Barton, raven-haired beauty.'

'Too high. I don't want a cartoon imitation. I want something that will fool our friend Jimmers.'

She tried again, modulating her voice until Mrs Lamey told her to stop, that she had it at last. 'Practice that,' she said. 'And you three, you're going back out to that house one more time. Please don't come back empty-handed this time. Bring me what I ask for or go home and make an honest living.'

'What about Jimmers?' the man in the suit asked. 'He'll be watching for us. What shall we do to him?'

'Nothing,' Stoat said immediately. 'There's no profit in violence here. If I'm going along, you can be damn well sure Jimmers is not going to get a glimpse of my face. I'm fairly well known around these parts. I'm not going in there waving a lead pipe. Sometimes it seems like I'm the only one around here that values subtlety.'

'Or fear, for that matter,' Gwendolyn Bundy said in the voice of Sylvia Barton. 'How's that? Do I still have it?'

'Just right,' Mrs Lamey said proudly. 'That's my girl. Mr Stoat is entirely right in this case. Leave your lead pipes in your car and leave your car where it is. Better yet, move it around the corner. I don't want you parking in front of my house anymore. You've bungled this twice, and that sort of bungling leads to troubles.'

'What, we're *walking* down to Elk?' the man in the sweater asked.

'I've arranged for transportation. You'll leave at once. When you get there, Mr Jimmers' car will be gone, with him in it. You'll have a good half hour to do the job and then disappear along with the goods. Don't dawdle, though. I don't want any possibility of a slipup. Gwendolyn, you're to phone Mr Jimmers. You're Sylvia Barton, and you've run out of gas – where?'

'Irish Beach,' said the man in the sweater.

'Too close. Point Arena. Just north of Point Arena, on the side of the highway. That's safe. Poor Sylvia will have to walk three or four miles back into town if he doesn't bring her up a gallon of gas in a can.'

'What if she can't convince him?' the man in the coat asked.

'She'll convince him. I promise you. I know Mr Jimmers and I know his past. He's a born champion, or wants to think so, and he has a special place in his heart for our Sylvia. By the way,' she asked Stoat, 'has she been notified that her lease won't be renewed come January?'

'Sent the notice off in the mail this morning. I'm not certain, though, why she has to be punished for the obstinacy of her crazy father.'

'The sins of the fathers,' Mrs Lamey said, 'will be visited upon the heads of their daughters. I mean to bring the whole family down in the manner of the Chinese communists. Get at the cousins and the aunts and the grandfathers, too, if I can find them.'

Stoat shrugged.

She turned back to the man in the coat. 'If worse comes to worst,' she said, 'then Gwen will have failed to convince him, and Jimmers' car will still be in the drive. In that case you'll have to terminate the immediate plan and figure out more forceful methods, even if they discommode Mr Stoat, who perhaps ought to wear an extra pair of socks to keep his feet from getting cold.' She looked hard at Stoat until he looked away.

Gwendolyn Bundy smiled widely. 'Poor Stoatie-Woatie,' she said.

The man in the sweater didn't look entirely convinced. 'What about this transportation business?'

'Simple as anything,' Mrs Lamey said, breaking into a grin and stepping across to the window again.

17

Howard slept in late the next morning, but woke up feeling better than he would have expected. His cuts and scrapes were superficial, and twelve hours of sleep had done a lot to restore him. Chasing around in the back of his mind was the idea that he knew something now that he hadn't known before, but he couldn't say just what. It was more likely a feeling of having fallen in among people with a common interest – as if he had been baptized at last and was finally part of a congregation.

Uncle Roy and he took the morning off and drove up along the coast to fish. They caught nothing but seaweed, though, and came home early in the afternoon to an empty house. Aunt Edith was off doing volunteer work at the hospital, and so when Uncle Roy drove off to the harbor to meet Bennet, Howard stayed home to glue decals onto the windows of his truck. It was a frivolous way to kill an hour, but it gave him time to think, and somehow gluing on the decals seemed right to him, appropriately strange. He was caught up in crazy activities, and this was no crazier than the rest.

Afterward, he went to work on the barn lumber, cleaning a good part of it up and stacking it against the wall. At six it was time to meet Sylvia at the worrisome haunted house. He half dreaded becoming involved in the project. Aunt Edith would probably have him arrested for contributing to the delinquency of an uncle. There was no way on earth, though, that once he was asked he could decline to help with it, or that he could even say anything serious against it.

He drove down to the harbor, finally, and found the old wooden icehouse. It had been painted white once, but the white paint had faded to a sort of uniform gray in the weather. There was a sign on top that read 'Snowman Ice' above a painting of a winking snowman in a hat. The place didn't look a lot like a haunted house, maybe because of all the activity going on around it – kids on bikes and tourists looking for fish restaurants and fishermen going back and forth in pickup trucks. It was run-down enough, though, with broken windows and a couple of old ground-draping pepper trees at the corner. Uncle Roy was hard at it when Howard arrived. Howard could hear the sound of a dull circular saw whining and burning its way through a piece of wood. Sylvia's car was there, too, parked in front.

The door creaked open when he pushed on it, and Howard walked into an entry hall gaudy with dark red, velvety wallpaper. The skeleton from the university hung from a noose tied to a brass chandelier fixture in the ceiling, its wired-together toes pointed at a threadbare piece of oriental carpet. The ceiling was high, easily twelve feet, but the skeleton's knees dangled at eye level, anyway, and Howard was tempted to give it a knock just to hear it clatter like a wind chime. It would be a mighty temptation on Halloween night.

Beyond the entry hall was a big, open room with a dirty wooden floor, littered and stained and water-warped. In the dark, maybe, the place wouldn't look too bad. Uncle Roy sat at a plywood table near a pair of tall windows, carving ornate pumpkins. A plugged-in circular saw lay on the floor next to a couple of little triangles of plywood that had just been cut off the corners of the table. The air smelled of sawdust and friction-burned wood. Uncle Roy scraped sticky orange strings and seeds onto a heap of newspaper. 'I figure we need quite a few,' he was saying when Howard walked in. Sylvia still had her coat on.

'Damn it!' Uncle Roy cried just then, and threw his knife down onto the plywood. 'Look at this! Hell. I've screwed it up.' He tilted his head back like an artist, regarding his pumpkin, and then sliced delicately at the comer of the thing's mouth.

'So you went fishing today?' Sylvia asked Howard.

Howard nodded, and she said, 'That's good. You've had too much excitement. You're on vacation.'

'Right. I'm feeling pretty good, really. Rested. My only regret is that I didn't get the picnic basket back on time.' He examined Uncle Roy's pumpkin, shrugging at it. 'Looks all right to me.'

'I've cut its damned teeth out,' Uncle Roy said, shaking his head. 'This knife isn't worth a damn. A knife has got to be sharp. That's paramount. Now I've gone and wrecked it.' He picked up the knife again and hacked the pumpkin into oblivion, sweeping it finally off onto the carpet and then slapping the knife blade back and forth across the plywood in an awkward attempt to sharpen it.

'Rosie forgave you,' Sylvia said, pushing up her jacket sleeves and looking over the pumpkins.

'Take one of those that sit flat,' Uncle Roy said to her. Then to Howard he said, 'Traded eighty pounds of pumpkins from the Sunberries for a couple of boxes of scrap leather I got off a pal of mine who's an orthotist. He gave me these, too.' He leaned over and picked up two rubber hands, which were surprisingly lifelike except for being dirty, as if they'd lain around waiting to be used for ten or fifteen years. Uncle Roy pitched the hands into a cardboard carton full of wigs and old clothes and said, 'Haven't heard from Jimmers, have you?'

'No,' Howard said. 'I was outside, though, most of the afternoon, with the saw running. Aunt Edith was down at the hospital.'

'She got her five thousand hours pin for volunteer work,' Sylvia said.

'That's right,' Uncle Roy said proudly. 'She's worth five women. Take my word for it. You sure Jimmers didn't call? I thought he might have. I thought maybe getting beat in the head yesterday had knocked some sense into him.'

'Nope.'

Uncle Roy fiddled his knife blade into the plywood, prying out a long sliver. 'They stole Bennet's truck today. Just this afternoon.'

'His *truck*?' Howard said. 'Why?'

Uncle Roy shook his head. 'Prank, I guess. What it is, is Mrs Lamey.'

'Mrs Lamey stole Bennet's truck?'

'She had the job done. Bet on it. It was revenge for us putting the Humpty Dumpty on the roof. He'll find it driven off a cliff down south somewhere.' Uncle Roy sighed. 'Poor bastard. And after he spent all his Vegas money on it. The whole kit and caboodle.'

'And you didn't call the police, of course,' Howard said.

Uncle Roy shook his head. 'It isn't worth that.' He fell silent. He studied a fresh pumpkin, scowling at it. 'What can we do about it?' he asked, as if he expected the pumpkin to answer. And then to Howard he said, 'Sure you don't know who they were yesterday? Not Stoat?'

'Not Stoat. Smaller man. Stoat might have been hiding in the other room, but I don't think so. That's not his style.'

'And today they steal Bennet's truck right off the street, colder'n a duck. The dirty bastards.' Uncle Roy squinted at his pumpkin and then thrust the knife blade into it, up near the stem, cutting out the lid. The knife caught and hung itself up. Cursing, as if he'd had enough trouble already with uncooperative knives and pumpkins, he yanked at it, jerking it entirely free of the pumpkin and lancing the blade across his thumb. 'Shit!' he yelled, tucking his thumb into his hand and holding on to it. He threw the knife down onto the table, then peeked at the cut thumb. There was a line of blood on it. He opened his hand all the way, relieved to see that the blood didn't well out, that it wasn't much of a cut. 'Lucky the damned knife wasn't any sharper,' he said. 'I'd have cut it right off.' Then, apropos of nothing, he said, 'Jimmers and his damned machine. I have half a mind ...' he started to say, but then he fizzled out and simply sat there looking tired. He stared at his thumb again and then wiped the blood off onto the pumpkin-spattered newspaper.

'Why don't we head home?' Sylvia said, putting her hand on her father's arm. 'Give it up for tonight. Let's eat some dinner.'

'Only days to go before we open,' Uncle Roy said, shaking his head. 'There's no time for dinner. I'm generating my second wind.' He forced a replica of a smile. 'Here, Howard – take a gander at this. This one is a knockout. Stick your hand into this bag.'

Howard obligingly shoved his hand into the paper sack, while Uncle Roy supported it on the bottom, which was soggy and ready to break through. 'Wet spaghetti?' Howard said.

'Guts,' said Uncle Roy. 'Doesn't it feel like guts? I got the idea at dinner last night. You can buy tripe down at Safeway, but it doesn't feel like anything at all. Wet spaghetti, though ... feels like guts, doesn't it? Had you going for a moment there. I saw it on your face.' Spaghetti leaked out onto the plywood through a tear in the bag, and Uncle Roy shoveled it back in and twisted the bag shut. 'That damned Jimmers,' he said. 'I'd hit the son of a bitch myself, if he was here. Sylvia, tell me this doesn't feel like spaghetti – I mean guts. It feels like guts, damn it. Gopher guts. How does that jingle go? Great big gobs of greemy grimy gopher guts ... It can't be "greemy," can it? We'll fill a plastic trash bag with the stuff – shove people in up to their elbows.' Then, cheering up abruptly, as if he'd just then remembered something, he said, 'Hey, Howard, I've got a couple of cow brains over in the ice chest. The real McCoy, too. Take a gander at them. Bring me a beer while you're at it, will you?' He wiped his cut thumb on the newspaper again, then picked up his pumpkin and sliced out a triangular eye.

Howard stepped past the pumpkin pile and pulled the lid off the Styrofoam ice chest. Uncle Roy seemed agitated, unable to concentrate, as if he were bothered not only by the truck being stolen but by whatever conversation he had had with Jimmers. He was avoiding all of it, though, perhaps because Sylvia was there.

Just then there was the sound of a car pulling up outside the door. It was Bennet, driving the station wagon. The two brains lay inside the ice chest, wrapped loosely in a plastic bag. Howard hauled a can of beer out and wiped it off carefully on his sleeve. 'Good-looking brains,' Howard said. 'Will they last?'

Uncle Roy flourished his knife. 'No, we've got to leave them in the freezer over at the Cap'n England. We'll cold-storage these pumpkins, too, once I've got them carved. Bring 'em in here!' he shouted suddenly toward the door, and he took the open beer from Howard, nodding happily at it. Bennet appeared just then, grappling two naked mannequins around the middle, both of them androgynous-looking males. He set them down on the floor near the pumpkins and then went back out and returned with two chrome-plated supports, propping the dummies up and securing them so that they stood looking at each other.

'Any word about the truck?' Bennet asked.

'Not a lick. I've got feelers out, though. We'll get it back. The scum-sucking pigs. They'll regret this one.' Uncle Roy looked at the dummies. 'Watch this,' he said. 'Where's that Japanese saw?'

Bennet disappeared into a back room, and Uncle Roy picked up a felt-tipped pen and drew a dotted line around the dummies' craniums. 'Saw the bastards up,' he said to Bennet, who had returned with the saw. Uncle Roy looked at the dummies with an artist's eye. 'Don't spare the horses.'

Bennet slid the little saw past the edge of his thumb, skiving into the head of the first dummy and parting its skull so that the top of its bald head came off like a cap. Uncle Roy fetched the brains out of the ice chest himself while Bennet worked on the second dummy.

'Watch this,' Uncle Roy said proudly, laying one of the brains into the trepanned head of the first dummy. The hiatus was too deep, though, and the brain nearly disappeared inside, down beneath the thing's nose and eyes. Undefeated, Uncle Roy crumpled up a page of newspaper, pushing pumpkin innards off onto the floor, and then, removing the brain, he pushed the paper into the dummy's neck and head, stuffing it full, then laying the brain back in. It rode too high now, perching there like a bird on a nest, so he plucked it out once again and slugged the newspaper a couple of times to smash it down, and then lay the brain back in. 'There,' he said, standing back and admiring his work. 'What do you think?'

'That's – something,' Sylvia said. 'Are you going to put clothes on him?'

'Of *course* we're going to put clothes on him – dress both of them up in these silver-glitter shirts we got down at the thrift shop. It'll be a sort of "men from the stars" display. "The Brainiacs."'

Bennet finished up with the second dummy, and then, as if in a hurry, said, 'Adiós,' and went back out toward the front, past the hanging skeleton. 'Got to pick up those plaster-of-Paris cats,' he said, before going out.

Uncle Roy waved at the back of his head, shouting, 'Hit Yum Yum for a dozen sinkers!' Bennet disappeared without answering and drove away in the wagon.

Howard looked at the mannequins, trying to summon whatever emotion it was that they were meant to evoke – fear? mystery? awe? Maybe when they were dressed and the lights were turned down ... Truthfully the place needed something more, and lots of it.

As if Uncle Roy were thinking the same thing, he seemed to deflate suddenly. Tiredly he sat back down in his chair and studied the face of a pumpkin. 'Alas,' he said. Then he smelled his hands, grimaced, and wiped them on the bib of his overalls. 'We need something big.' He looked out toward the street, sighing deeply.

'How about the corpses?' Howard asked, thinking to cheer him up.

'In there.' Uncle Roy gestured toward the back. 'Ready to shoot marbles.' He ran his hands through his hair. 'You tell me,' he said, looking at Howard. 'What do we need here? What would *you* do? What is it that kids want to see in a haunted house? What kind of crap puts the fear into them? Jack-o'-lanterns? Skeletons? Back in my day a good skeleton would have sent them screaming. Now they want blood. Sex. Both together, for Christ's sake. Nothing less. Blood and gore and flesh. I won't have it, though. I won't. This damned world's rotten. Morality's on the slag heap. Cut a woman up with a chain saw – that'll fetch 'em in. But a skeleton? That went out with the trash.' He looked up timidly at Sylvia suddenly, as if remembering there was company present, and said, 'Sorry to talk dirty.'

He buried his face in his hands, resting for a moment, composing himself. Howard stood silently, embarrassed for his uncle. In the morning, when Howard was fresh, he would put his mind to it. With a little imagination he and Sylvia could come up with something.

'I called down to Jimmers' place an hour ago,' Uncle Roy said to Howard, sounding beat and resigned. 'We're going to lose our shorts on this venture, me and Bennet both. It doesn't seem like that – a small show like this. But our shorts aren't worth much. They were worn pretty thin before we started out. What I did was I called Jimmers after Sylvia told me about the machine, and I flat out asked him for it. Told him it would bail me out. We could get away with any damned trash in here if we could crank that damned machine up as a sort of finale. They'd come in droves. We could give the press a sneak preview. The papers would be full of it, and we'd be rolling in cash. What the hell good is it doing him, rusting away out in that damned shed? Anyway, he wouldn't budge.'

Sylvia laid her hand on his arm, trying to stop him from working himself up. 'Maybe he'll come around,' she said. 'He's still remembering all those pranks you two used to play on each other. He's bound to be touchy when you call him out of the blue asking for a favor like that. Let him sleep on it. He'll see it different in the morning.'

'Well, he owes me, doesn't he? Drove me right out of business with that damned cow. No man likes being a laughingstock. This would have made bygones bygones. But no, he's a man who holds a long grudge. I'm half tempted to go out there and steal the damned thing, or wreck it, one or the other – just shove it off the cliff along with the goddamned Studebaker. I told him so, too.'

'You shouldn't have,' Sylvia said. 'Now he's mad at you.'

'Mad at *me*! I'll give him something to be mad about! Look at this damned mutant!' He reached out then and gave the dummy a shove, toppling it over, the brain spilling out onto the dirty carpet. Howard scooped it up, surprised at how rubbery and firm it was. There were hairs and bits of debris and dirt clinging to it now. Uncle Roy sat there with his face in his hands again, nearly in a state of collapse.

Sylvia set the dummy up, and Howard shoved the brain into its plastic bag and put it back into the ice chest. After that he popped the top on another can of beer and handed it to his uncle. Sylvia put her arm around her father's shoulder and said, 'You're anticipating things. You always anticipate the worst sort of defeats, and they wear you out. Just last week you were crazy with ideas for this place. Wait till tomorrow; they'll be there again.'

He looked up at her, gripping her hand. 'Just last week Halloween was about a year away, and there was hope. This is the end, though. I'm going to be living out of the back of the station wagon, down behind the Texaco station, just like Mrs Lamey says. Hell. I guess … I guess I'm just tired out.'

A sudden voice interrupted them. 'Knockety-knock,' it called playfully from the vicinity of the skeleton.

'Mrs Deventer,' Uncle Roy said, standing up and giving her a little half-bow. His remorseful face turned pleasant all of a sudden, as if he didn't want to burden the rest of the world with his troubles. Mrs Deventer stood in the doorway holding a pitcher of lemonade. She was short and gray-haired and dressed in thrift-store-quality clothes that didn't quite match up. A gaudy lot of costume jewelry hung around her neck, weighting down a long red scarf. She had the air of a five-year-old playing dress-up. All of that, along with her wild hair, gave her a naturally batty look. She was cheerful-looking, though, and the red scarf was almost dashing, as if she were geared up for a night on the town.

'Made in the shade,' she said, winking.

'By an old maid with a spade,' Uncle Roy said, winking back.

She feigned horror. '*Mister* Barton!' she said, stepping forward to set the pitcher and a stack of paper cups on the table. She looked askance at the dummy.

'Mrs Deventer,' Uncle Roy said, 'meet Brainiac, the man from Mars.'

'Charmed,' she said, reaching her hand out toward Howard. 'Welcome to planet earth.'

'Wait,' Uncle Roy said, pretending to be confounded, and then both of them, Uncle Roy and Mrs Deventer, laughed and laughed. 'You've heard me talk about Mrs Deventer, Howard.'

'Yes indeed,' Howard said, remembering. She was the one being squeezed by Mrs Lamey. Somehow she didn't look like a very formidable opponent.

'I've brought these cookies for all of you.' Mrs Deventer produced a sandwich bag full of cookies from the purse around her shoulder. 'Leave some for the children,' she said to Roy, and nodded toward Howard and Sylvia. Then to Sylvia she said, 'Is this one yours?'

Sylvia blushed just a little bit. 'Stray cat,' she said.

Mrs Deventer cast Howard a coy smile. 'Pleased.' She shook his hand again.

It struck Howard that Mrs Deventer wasn't anywhere near sober. She wasn't falling down, but she wasn't steady, either.

'My young man is taking me out,' she said happily.

The statement had a freezing effect on Sylvia and Uncle Roy both.

'Now, don't start in,' she said. 'He's pretty nearly saved me from ruin.' She directed this at Howard, as if to assure him that the opinions of Uncle Roy and Sylvia weren't worth very much. 'They'd have the place by now if it weren't for him, and you know it.' Her nearly giddy attitude had switched to something near anger. Howard was clearly the only disinterested party in the room. 'He's a godsend,' she said to him.

'Good for him,' Howard said, humoring her.

'Paid my taxes.'

'Good man,' said Howard.

'He's wealthy, you know. Pays my mortgage, too, when I can't afford it. He's looking out for me.'

Uncle Roy looked about to burst, but he kept quiet for another moment, for as long as he could, maybe, while he systematically chopped the latest pumpkin into cubes. 'That would be our friend Mr Stoat,' he said to Howard, not looking up.

Howard nodded, dumbfounded. Mrs Deventer was grinning again, though, at the mention of the name of her 'young man.' Here was trouble. Howard wondered if Uncle Roy knew just how much trouble. Paying her mortgage and taxes?

She turned to leave, slightly miffed, Howard thought, as if she had expected enthusiasm and gotten doubts instead. 'I'll just be on my way, then.'

Howard walked with her toward the door, wanting to be gallant, thinking it best to win her favor in some little way. 'Thanks for the lemonade,' he said. 'It was a pleasure meeting you. Live near here?'

'Right up on Dawson,' she said, bumping into the skeleton, which swayed back and forth like a tired pendulum. Outside stood an old two-tone Pontiac, pink and gray, looking as though it had just been waxed. It was gorgeous, not a scratch on it, except for the rear bumper, which was smashed in. 'Roy Barton is a good man, but he gets the most amazing ideas sometimes.'

'Well,' said Howard diplomatically, 'he wouldn't be Roy Barton otherwise, would he? He's pretty fond of you, you know. He's told me quite a bit about you.'

'Has he?' she asked, sounding pleased.

'Beautiful car.' Howard opened the door for her.

'My poor old Bob bought it back in fifty-six,' she said, her voice growing instantly husky. 'God rest his soul. I don't take it out much. Just once a month, up to Willits to visit my sister. There isn't even ten thousand miles on it.'

'Wow.' Howard ran his hand across the clean pink paint. 'Take care of it.' He was vaguely conscious of a telephone ringing nearby, over and over again. Mrs Deventer nodded, telling Howard through the open window that he was a good boy and looking about half wistful. She made several efforts to shove the key into the ignition, banging it on either side of the keyhole before sliding it in finally and starting the car. It died almost at once and then wouldn't start. There was the smell of gasoline as she pumped the accelerator. The telephone rang off the hook and then suddenly stopped.

'It's flooded,' Howard shouted. She had rolled her window up, though, and she smiled at him and said something that he couldn't hear. Mashing the accelerator to the floorboard, she twisted the key again, holding it on until the motor roared into life and a cloud of dark exhaust blew out of the tail pipe. She backed out quickly, swerving in the gravel, and then rocketed up the hill past a startled man in an apron just then coming out of the back of the Cap'n England.

Howard turned to walk back into the haunted house, working the Mrs Deventer problem over in his mind. 'Hey,' shouted someone from behind, and Howard looked back to see the aproned man hurrying toward him. 'Roy Barton inside?' he asked, out of breath.

'Sure is,' said Howard. 'What's wrong?'

'Phone call. Artemis Jimmers. There's been trouble; he's pretty well worked up.'

'Thanks,' Howard said over his shoulder. He was in through the door in a second, shouting for Uncle Roy, who was up and past him, hurrying out into the night. Howard and Sylvia followed along behind.

The pay phone hung on the rear of the restaurant, the empty black cover of a telephone directory dangling against the yellow stucco beneath it. A moth the size of a small bird fluttered wildly around the light overhead.

'Yeah,' Uncle Roy said into the mouthpiece. 'What the hell?' He listened for a moment, his eyes narrowing. 'You're completely over the edge,' he said, raising his voice. 'You're just exactly the nut I always said you were. That's right. You, too. I wouldn't touch your goddamn shed with a dung fork. Oh, yeah, well ...' He stopped talking suddenly and looked at the silent telephone. Then he listened again and hung up furiously.

'What on earth is it?' Sylvia asked. 'What's happened?'

'Somebody's stole his shed.'

'His tin shed?' Howard asked, finding it hard to believe. *Stole* it?'

'The whole megillah, lock, stock, and barrel. Jacked it up, slid it onto a truck, and drove off with it. Jimmers got a phone call luring him down to Point Arena. He thinks I put someone up to it. Anyway, he figured out it was a fake call, turned around to head back, and blew out a tire a quarter mile from home. When he pulled in they were just taking off down the highway. He followed them for a mile on the flat. Tore the tire to pieces, apparently. Turned the tube into a sausage, it got so hot. They left him in the dust, of course. Now he wants the shed back along with a new tire. He thinks it was me.'

'Why would he think it was you?' Howard asked.

'Because they were driving Bennet's truck.'

18

Graham didn't sleep much anymore. Sleep didn't come easy to him, and there didn't seem to be any great need of it, anyway. The hours of darkness dragged along. He couldn't fish at night. Getting down the hill to the pond was treacherous enough in daylight. A couple of times he had sat in his chair on the front porch in the middle of the night, watching the moon rise over the trees. But it was cold, and the cold tired him out these days. Sometimes at night he read – the Bible, mostly, a large-print edition he'd had to switch to a few years back.

How many years? He couldn't remember now. The years ran together like watercolor paints, and his memories surfaced in confused order, some days clear, some days dull. Most often at night he simply lay awake, letting his mind drift. In the morning either Edith or Sylvia would arrive with his breakfast and coffee. Midmorning he would work his garden, which, although it was new, seemed to be blighted somehow. He had his suspicions, but there was little he could do about it except work. There wasn't a lot of sun out in the forest there, especially not in the fall. But the cabin and garden were in a clearing, and he ought to have had some luck with leafy things, with lettuce and cabbage, even though there wasn't enough of the season left for the vegetables to mature. In a month it would be too cold.

But this trouble wasn't weather; it was some kind of rot that came up through the soil, which seemed always to be dry, no matter how often he watered it. Nothing at all had grown well for him for a couple of years now. He had expected most of this. He knew it would be so at the end – all the dust and the dying. It was the strange blight, the rot, the tainting and withering of the leaves that he wondered about. They had a bad smell to them, too, even while they were still mostly green.

This morning in particular he felt heavy and tired. He had awakened twice in the night with chest pains, but they'd subsided now. He had found himself awake a third time. He was out of doors, standing in the moonlit garden and wearing his long underwear and his hat. He couldn't remember having gotten out of bed. The dark woods stretched away on all sides, and in the clearing overhead the stars shined thick and bright like a thousand promises. He had his walking stick with him, and with it he was drawing wavy-edged circles in the dirt, like clouds in the sky.

He was filled with the vague notion that he had been dreaming the whole time he was sketching with the stick – a dream about salmon schooling in deep ocean water. And one of the fish, responding to some sort of deep and primitive calling, had turned landward, swimming lazily toward the river mouth where Graham had sat fishing with his pole and line. Someone had stood behind him in the dream, watching his back – a shadowy presence that had begun to fade, along with the dream itself, almost as soon as he hooked his fish.

It was just after 3 AM. The living room clock had tolled, and in another hour Uncle Roy would be in to wake him. It wasn't just the looming adventure of stealing back Mr Jimmers' shed that kept Howard awake. He sometimes worried about small things in the early morning – unpaid bills, long-avoided errands, elusive rice paper sketches which were pretty clearly not what they appeared to be. At home he got around the problem of insomnia by moving out to the living room couch – the change alone was usually enough to put him back to sleep. But he couldn't do that here. It would imply that his bed wasn't comfortable, and Aunt Edith would worry herself ragged over it.

The bed wasn't worth a damn, though. It sagged in the middle, and if Howard slept on his stomach for more than two minutes, he woke up in the morning with a backache that threatened to keep him in a chair. He lay on the very edge now, where the rail of the bed frame stiffened the mattress a little, and thought of all the things that he ought to be doing with his time but wasn't. Tomorrow he would clean up the rest of that pile of barn lumber, maybe steal a half dozen slats to throw under his mattress.

He had meant to be on vacation here, to sort things out, to discover whether his feelings for Sylvia had changed any. Well, they hadn't. That much was clear. It had taken him exactly two days to go nuts over her. Meanwhile she pretty clearly had found in him another man who needed looking after, like Uncle Roy – a slightly daft brother who had appeared out of the south, unable to keep out of trouble. And if he did stay in Fort Bragg, if he didn't return to his job at the museum, what would he do? He could move in with

Uncle Roy, of course, and be a burden. When his money was gone, he could hustle food stamps, maybe get a job at the mill and get laid off in the rainy season.

The thought of going home left him empty, though. There wasn't a single thing to entice him back down to southern California except a scattering of friends, who seemed to be more scattered with each succeeding year. His coming north had cut some sort of mooring line, and he was drifting. It was time to put on some sail, to break out the compass and the charts. He looked at the clock for the tenth time. It wasn't even three-fifteen. The big old house was cold, and he pulled the blankets up around his neck and listened to the wind.

He began counting backward from one hundred. Sheep were too complicated. After a while his troubles scurried off to the back of his mind, where they winked and waved at him, not quite out of sight. He could see them back there in the shadows, as dream images now, and his counting backward faltered at around forty-five. He started again, but soon slowed and then stopped, and he found himself dreaming about a ship that had gone aground on a rocky shore. He was on the beach, ankle-deep in the rising tide, thinking that there was something on board that he needed or that he wanted. He was a castaway, thinking to salvage rope and timber and live chickens from the staved-in ship. He turned and faced the shore, and above him on the cliff top was the stone house, dark but for a single light in the attic window.

He could see the silhouette of someone sitting in one of the Morris chairs, reading a book, and he knew all at once that it was him, at home there, whiling away a peaceful evening, impossibly content. A dream wind blew off the ocean, into the dark mouth of the passage beneath the cliffs, and when he turned around again to face the sea, there was no longer a ship on the rocks but the old Studebaker instead, a ruined hulk sitting just above the tide.

He clambered across the rocks toward it, his pant legs rolled to the knees, the ocean neither cold nor warm nor even particularly wet. The car's door hung open, its top hinge broken, the musty upholstery smelling of seaweed and barnacles. He climbed in behind the wheel, grasping the Lucite steering wheel knob and thinking that if only he had a chart he would pilot the car out through the scattered reefs and into the open sea.

Looking deep into the Lucite ball, he was convinced that something was drawn or written way down in there, floating in the depths like clouds in a fishbowl sky. He could make them out now – the constellation of images from the rice paper sketch. Then he perceived them to be words and not drawings at all – a message scrawled in the shaky handwriting of someone old and frail. 'Look in the glove box,' it read, and with a feeling of immense anticipation and reluctance both, he reached across and punched the button. The glove-box door banged open so heavily that the entire car tilted sideways, farther and farther until he began to slide toward the open passenger door, looking out and down toward the now-distant ocean, scrabbling to hold on to the rotten old upholstery and knowing that he couldn't, that he would fall.

Howard sat up in bed, having waked himself up with a cut-off scream. The gauzy remnant of an idea was fading at the back of his mind. He had the certainty that it was an important idea, and he trapped the tail end of it and fixed it there so that he could study it when he had a chance. There was something in his waking, as horrible as it was, that left him almost satisfied with things. Somehow the worries that had plagued him an hour ago had evaporated. He felt distinctly as if something were pending – that somehow, in some inconceivable way, his course was being partly charted for him. There was a knocking on the door just then, low and secretive. 'Howard!' a voice called. It was Uncle Roy.

A half hour later the three of them, Howard, Bennet, and Uncle Roy, sat in the station wagon, eating doughnuts and drinking coffee out of Styrofoam cups. The night was dark and silent except for the crash of waves and the sounds of chewing and sipping. They were parked on Elm, on the ocean side of the highway, down near the far end of the Georgia-Pacific yard. Hundreds of acres of stacked lumber lay drying in the night wind, fenced off with chain link and barbed wire from Glass Beach and from the weedy bluffs above it that stretched all the way out to the highway.

Directly across from them sat a white, flat-roofed wooden warehouse that must have been forty yards long and without a window in the entire length of it. There was nothing around it but weeds and berry vines growing right up against the sides. Around behind was a door with a small transom window above. No light showed through it. A single car was parked beside the door, hidden from the street – the red Camaro that had been at Jimmers' house yesterday afternoon.

According to Uncle Roy, Mrs Lamey owned the warehouse, which was empty, he was willing to bet, of everything except Bennet's truck with Mr Jimmers' shed on it, which they were going to steal back before the sun rose or know the reason why. Howard realized that he was in the company of committed men. What did that mean? he wondered. Probably that he'd be committed himself before the sun rose – to a cell in the county jail.

So now his vacation had taken a serious turn. His adventures at Mr Jimmers' place had been dangerous enough, but compared to this they hadn't been anything but play – guns or no guns. Here he was setting out to break into a warehouse, to steal back Mr Jimmers' shed, to steal a car, for God's sake. And what for? For Sylvia? Well, hardly. For Uncle Roy? Not entirely.

What he ought to have done was try to talk his uncle out of this venture. Aunt Edith would think he was a hero if he could squash it. This was called aiding and abetting. He was going to help Uncle Roy go to jail, too, and the whole haunted house caper would be in the trash can. Sylvia would kill him.

Uncle Roy patted him on the knee, as if he sensed that Howard was uneasy. 'Want to wait it out down at Winchell's?' He said it matter-of-factly, as if there were no shame in it.

Howard shook his head. 'It'll take both of you to get the truck out of there.'

'That ain't got nothing to do with it,' Bennet said, pitching half of a dough-nut back into the white paper sack. 'This ain't convenience we're talking about. Nobody owes anyone any favors. There won't be no turning back when you start up that car engine.'

Howard was silent, but not because he was thinking of turning back. He couldn't 'wait it out at Winchell's.' He was either in or out. There wasn't any in between – no choosing not to choose. He couldn't be a fair-weather con-spirator. And somehow, sitting out there in the old station wagon, getting set to strike a blow against the enemy, he felt for the first time in months, years maybe, that something mattered. It was as if one of his eyes had been shut for a long time, and now it was open, and things had dimension to them at last. He reached into his coat pocket, pulled out a pair of thin goatskin gloves, and put them on, flexing his fingers. Then he pulled his stocking cap down over his face, adjusting it and looking out through the eyeholes.

'God almighty,' Uncle Roy said. 'You look like an IRA assassin. If the cops come anywhere near you, ditch the mask and the gloves both. They'll shoot you on sight looking like that. You've got the name of the foreman up at the yard?'

'Jack MacDonald.'

'That's it. He's a good man. You'll be safe there. He's ready with an alibi, but I don't want to make him lie if we don't have to. He'll say that he sent you down to the Gas 'n' Grub for a couple of boxes of crumb doughnuts. He gave you three dollars.'

'In my front pocket,' Howard said.

'You need to look at his picture again?'

'Nope.'

'What is it you do at the mill?'

'Run a stroke sander.'

Uncle Roy was silent for a moment. 'In general, don't cross the highway if you don't have to. Leave the car at the other side of the train yard and look for us at the old library building. Make sure the bastard chases you, though. He won't think it's us making a move on the shed, not this quick, so it ought to be possible to draw him away for a couple of blocks or so. Farther if you can. Play hide-and-seek with him. We just need enough time to break in there and get the door open. My hunch is that he'll come back finally looking to call the old lady on the telephone. We'll have cut the wire, and he'll have to head down to Gas 'n' Grub to use the pay phone.'

He fell silent again. The time to talk was past. They had gone through it a half dozen times, and all of them knew that the plan was full of optimism.

'Let's go,' Howard said, opening the door and sliding out. He eased the door shut. Uncle Roy fired up the engine and backed away a half a block down Elm, where they would wait. Howard loped across into the weeds, patting the bulge in his coat pocket where two cherry bombs lay along with a throwaway lighter.

The streets were abandoned and the nearby houses dark. A car sailed past down the highway, bound for points north, but there was no one out and about except Howard, the night wind, and the two in the wagon. Aside from the cold, conditions were nearly perfect. He tucked his hands into his armpits to try to warm them through the gloves.

The Camaro was unlocked, which was a relief, since he wouldn't have to break a window. And thank heaven there wasn't any car alarm. That would have cooked his goose, although it would have made the whole theft more grand. It would have been wonderful if the keys were in the ignition, but they weren't. Trust to a thief to hold on to his keys. Howard would have to start it up without them, which was just fine.

He listened first at the closed back door of the warehouse and heard nothing. It was entirely possible that there was nobody at all inside, in which case the elaborate distraction was a noisy waste of time. But surely the car wouldn't be there if no one was guarding the place. He stepped out away from the building, checking the street for traffic one last time. There was nothing at all but nighttime silence – no pedestrians, no prowl cars. He waved once at the distant station wagon, and the headlights blinked the go-ahead signal.

Then he climbed into the car, leaving the door ajar. He found the ignition wires under the dash, and, with one last quick look around, yanked the wires out in a clump, mashing the bare ends together in order to jump out the ignition. The motor turned over and he pumped the gas lightly.

He let it idle for a moment, watching the door for signs of stirring inside the warehouse. Then he shifted down into reverse, checked the emergency brake, and backed away from the building, turning out again toward the street so as to have a straight run for it. He raced the engine a couple of times again, hoping that whoever was inside would simply hear it and come out. He considered honking the horn, but it was such an idiotically doubtful thing for a car thief to do that he gave the notion up at once.

The cherry bombs, though, would take his man by surprise. He would wake up and hear the car engine and think it was backfiring, and he would wonder who in the hell was fooling around out back. He would take a cau-

tious look out the door and discover in horror that … Howard wound down
the window, still watching the door, ready to roll out of there. He pulled out
both cherry bombs and held them side by side in his left hand, bending the
fuses away from each other. Then, holding them out the open window, he
flipped the lighter on with his free hand, lit both fuses, and pitched them
toward the door, rolling up the window furiously.

They exploded one right after the other, slamming out like gunshots. A
second passed. A light flipped on inside and then off again, and the door
opened. Howard raced the engine a couple of times before hurtling out
toward Elm Street, throwing up a rooster tail of dust and gravel. He waited
for an instant at the edge of the street, giving his man time to make sense of
things. Howard could see him through the dust, outside now, hopping on
one foot while he pulled a shoe on. Howard jammed his foot down on the
brake and accelerator both, then eased off on the brake, spinning the tires as
if stuck in a hole. The man ducked back in for as long as it took for him to
snatch out a coat, and then he was out through the open door again, pulling
it shut behind him and running fast across the weeds, trying to catch up with
Howard before the car took off again.

Howard bit his lip, waiting for the last moment, watching him come. In the
moonlight, the man's face was wild with loathing. It was the man who had
worn the fright wig out at Jimmers'. He had the same black T-shirt on, and
his build was right. He ran at a gallop, one leg working harder than the other,
and he wrestled with the coat in his hands as if he were groping after something. Howard spun the tires once more, slammed the transmission into
reverse, and backed up a wild ten feet, nearly running the man over before
shifting back into drive, the car lunging down onto Elm Street.

He headed straight toward the ocean, bouncing up onto the dirt road that
ran out to Glass Beach. The road went nowhere – dead-ended two hundred
yards down. Howard counted on the man's knowing that and following along
behind, thinking that Howard was a nitwit, that he knew nothing of the local
streets. He had to draw the man away, down the block, around the corner,
out onto the bluffs, anywhere.

In the side mirror Howard could see the station wagon moving without
lights. It angled across and disappeared from view behind the front of the
warehouse. His man was still following, running wildly after the fleeing
Camaro, which rocked from side to side down the dirt road, throwing Howard back and forth on the seat. The man had dropped his coat, but he held
something in his hand now – a gun.

Howard nearly choked, spinning the steering wheel hard to the right and
sliding in a wide doughnut across the dirt parking lot above Glass Beach,
clipping a fence post with the rear fender and fishtailing back out in the
direction of the highway, fifty yards down from his startled pursuer, who

stopped dead at the corner of Stewart Street, leaped up onto the curb, dropped down into a crouch, and pointed the gun at the windshield, straight at Howard's head, tracking the Camaro as it hurtled toward him.

Howard stomped on the accelerator, angling straight toward the curb and smashing himself down onto the seat, almost hidden by the dashboard. Fear of being shot pounded through him. To hell with the man's car. If he started shooting, there would be lights on all over the neighborhood and telephones ringing down at the station house. Howard's career as a felon would be assured.

The Camaro slammed into the curb, up and over it with two wheels, as Howard pulled it hard to the left now, back onto the street, when his man lunged backward against the fence and out of the way, and then at once was up and aiming the gun again, training it on the car as Howard slewed around the corner onto Stewart, heading south now toward the train station.

He sat up in the seat again and slowed down, watching in the mirror. There was too much stuff in the way – telephone poles and parked cars – for the man to get off anything but a wild shot, and Howard was confident that he wouldn't risk any such thing. 'Follow me,' Howard said out loud. 'C'mon. Chase me.'

He didn't, though. The man wasn't going anywhere, but stood looking back at the warehouse. He clearly couldn't see anything of the station wagon, but he seemed to be thinking hard. If he gave up on Howard now, then stealing the car would become suddenly pointless. Howard had to draw the man away. Right now.

He punched the accelerator and shot forward again, tires squealing. Then he slammed on the brakes, locking them up and yanking the steering wheel hard, the car drifting sideways and forward in a slow spin. Howard threw himself down onto the passenger seat, covering his head with his hands. Almost instantly the car smashed into a curb tree, tearing out a length of grape-stake fence that catapulted across the hood. The crash threw Howard forward, nearly onto the floorboard, his knee cracking hard against the steering column. The horn honked one desperate blast, and then all was silent except for the clank of something falling onto the street.

Howard groped for the door handle, throwing the door open and pulling himself out upside down. He rolled to his feet and loped away down Stewart, not looking back but pulling wildly at his ski mask, which had been yanked around so that he was nearly blind. His knee hurt like a bastard where he'd knocked it against the steering wheel, and he limped and hopped in a zigzag course, waiting for the sound of gunfire or for the hammering of feet on pavement.

He was in trouble if the man caught him – the whole enterprise was in trouble. But it was in worse trouble if the man had gotten suspicious and gone back to the warehouse. For another few minutes at least, this had to look like a car theft, not a break-in. Howard rounded the comer onto Bush, past someone's fenced-in back lawn. He stopped short, looking back now, past the comer of the fence, both relieved and horrified to see his man sprinting up the block, not twenty yards behind. There were people at the curb, too, wearing their nightclothes, gathering around the smashed car.

Howard ran toward the ocean, his knee shooting a fiery pain up and down his leg every time he hammered his foot against the sidewalk. It was run or fight, though, and the farther he could lure the man away … He cut across the street, up onto a lawn and down a gravel alley, running south again, toward the lumberyard. The gate was a solid three blocks away. He could hide, maybe. But where? The fences along the alley were old and rickety and high, and even if he had time to pull himself over one, he'd be trapped in someone's backyard.

He looked back and immediately threw himself sideways. The man was at the mouth of the alley now, down on one knee, taking aim. He was sixty feet back, maybe – too close. Howard zigzagged again, hobbling and nearly pitching forward when his knee buckled. There was the sound of a shot, and a metal trash can ahead and to the right was punched backward, its lid jumping and clanking.

Like a heavy wind the sound of gunfire propelled Howard forward. He was out in the street again, running up the center of a pair of railroad tracks toward the Georgia-Pacific yard. Everything was fenced with chain link and barbed wire, and there was a confusion of tracks running down toward the train depot and another up toward vast warehouses and stacked lumber.

Somewhere back in there was the gate. It was after five. Men would be going in and out. What would they make of him in his ski mask and gloves? He couldn't pull the mask off, though, not yet. Not while the man who chased him could get a good look at him. He vaulted over a waist-high cinder-block fence, sliding on gravel. His feet flew out from under him and he landed hard, his breath whumping out of him. A shot pinged off the top of the wall, showering him with rock, and he jumped up and ran again in a crouch, trying to keep low behind the wall. Nearly winded, he ran in a half-stagger, half-trot, fueled only by momentum and fear.

The cars of the Skunk Train sat in parallel lines on the several tracks between the depot and the machine clutter of the lumberyard, and he ran in among the cars, past the comical skunks painted on the sides. He couldn't outrun his assailant. He would have to lose him among the silent trains, maybe work his way back around toward the old library, where his uncle would be waiting.

He listened hard for the sound of feet scrunching on gravel, but there was only silence. Had the man given up? Howard tried to calculate how long they'd been chasing around. Not long enough if Uncle Roy and Bennet had run into any trouble breaking into the warehouse. Maybe the man hadn't given up. Maybe he was sneaking around into position. Maybe he didn't give any kind of damn about the car, but was simply hunting for Howard, just to take it out of his hide.

Dropping to his hands and knees, Howard looked beneath the cars. A pair of feet were walking cautiously along the outside track. The man hadn't given up. The feet stopped and suddenly there was a face peering back at him, and then, quick as a snake, the hand with the gun.

Howard was up and moving, and he heard the shot ricochet off heavy steel as he clambered between two cars, trying to get around beyond the trains. He ran straight back along the chain link, north now, toward Fir Street. He needed company, people around. They could grab him and lock him up if they wanted to, but unless there were bystanders, witnesses, the man would shoot him dead. He was certain of that, and the certainty gave him a second wind.

He rounded the corner, slamming away up Fir, across a set of tracks and past an old rusted crane and a water tower. There was the gate ahead of him and a half dozen men in flannel shirts and jackets, standing around. Howard ran straight toward them. 'Hey! Help!' he shouted through his ski mask. He couldn't think of anything else. The whole crowd of them turned toward him, looking serious, and a man stepped out of a little glassed-in guardhouse and stood there with his arms folded.

Howard felt as if he were running toward his doom and with more doom following along behind. He risked a glance over his shoulder. His pursuer was coming along confidently and easily, like a man who had just hit a home run and was circling the bases as a matter of form. He had pocketed the gun, and was now just an innocent citizen chasing down a vicious car thief.

For a wild instant Howard nearly stopped. He was trapped, fore and aft. Everything depended on the mythical Jack MacDonald, a man he had never seen. He wished he had paid more attention to Uncle Roy's description of the man, but somehow he hadn't meant things to go this bad. There was no place else to run now except up another alley, across another vacant lot, and that was so obviously futile that it wasn't worth a second thought. His job was done, and done thoroughly – thoroughly enough to account for the next couple of years, during which he would learn to make license plates, maybe stamp one out to replace the one on the wrecked Camaro that he had stolen.

He limped through the gate, exhausted, horrified to see a forklift bearing down on him fast, carrying a short, knee-level stack of plywood. The men around the gate closed in on him, between him and his pursuer, and the one who had come out of the guardhouse said, 'Did you get the goddamn doughnuts?' Then the forklift slid to a stop in front of him. Someone said, 'Hop on,' and at the same time pushed Howard forward so that he fell onto the ply-wood, sprawling on his stomach. He flailed for a grip on the edge of the wood, nearly sliding off as the forklift hummed away again.

Howard looked back in time to see the mill workers approaching his pur-suer, who slowed down, looking puzzled. 'He's got a gun!' someone warned, although there still wasn't any gun visible. The man stopped, holding up his hands as if in surrender as they surged in around him. A fist lashed out in a wild haymaker to the man's belly as someone pushed him hard from behind, and he went down with a look of profound amazement on his face, the men surging in around him. The one who must have been Jack MacDonald walked placidly back to his guardhouse and lifted the receiver on a telephone, and for the moment Howard was safe, borne away on the forklift deeper into the yard, back among loaded pallets and stacked lumber and idle equipment.

With a scream, Heloise Lamey awakened from a dream involving fish. She had stood on an almost deserted pier, where an old man was fishing with a pole made out of a stick and a bit of string. The end of his pole wavered in little circles as he sat there, leaving a misty afterimage behind, like chalk drawings on the sky.

In the dream she had looked over the railing into the clear salt water, see-ing nothing at first, but with the understanding that something was pending, that something under the surface of the ocean had shifted and was drawing near. There were shadows beneath the surface, too deep and dark to identify, but she knew abruptly that beneath the pier there was a great shoal of fish, and that the old man had hooked one and was pulling it in.

His line tightened and his pole bent, and the entire pier shifted with it, as if his fish were so vast that it would pull them, pier and all, into the sea. Mrs Lamey held on to the iron railing as the pier tilted. Her feet slid across the wooden floorboards. Her hands were torn loose from the railing, and she slid wildly past the old man, who still sat there placidly and steadily, holding the bent pole, playing the fish.

She screamed as she plummeted toward the shadowy green ocean, and the scream woke her up. She sat for a second, breathing hard, pulling herself together, reminding herself that it was simply a dream. She was shivering beneath her nightclothes. After a moment, when she could think, she reminded herself that it was the same dream she had had last night, too, and the night before, only this time the old man had caught his fish.

She climbed out of bed and switched on the light. It was four-thirty in the morning – early, but there'd be no more sleeping for her tonight, anyway.

She dressed and went downstairs to put on water for instant coffee. Then she stepped out into the predawn morning and found her pruning shears. She hurried around the dark garden, clipping off a bouquet of discolored flowers, wide enough awake now to make a joke in her mind about never going to visit someone without taking him a little gift.

19

There was a knock on the door. It was too early to be Edith bringing around the breakfast. It might be Roy Barton, smelling trouble and dishing up plots, but it didn't sound like his knock. Graham got slowly off his bed and pulled his pants on over his long underwear. Then he put on his hat and slippers, found his cane, and made his way to the door. It was just dawn, and the morning was gray and dim. He could see who it was, through the window glass, and he knew for certain what was wrong with the garden.

It had come to this at last, his showdown with Heloise Lamey. He knew what she wanted to take from him, but such a thing was impossible. It was out of his hands now. The die was cast, his successor chosen. The man had come north of his own free will, had asked to come. He was caught in the turning of things. Heloise Lamey, Michael Graham's half sister, was too late.

Together they walked down to the pond in the half-light of early morning. Graham leaned heavily on his cane, moving slowly on the hill, taking a step, setting his cane and his feet, and then taking another. She was impatient with him for being slow, so he stopped entirely to give her blood time to boil. He pulled a clasp knife out of his pocket and began to scrape his fingernails, working methodically.

'What are you doing?' she asked, exasperation in her voice.

'What?' He blinked at her, as if he only half recognized her.

'You wanted to fish. We were going down to the pond so that you could fish. Do you remember?'

He looked at her curiously. 'I moved up here in 1910,' he said slowly, gazing into the dark woods across the pond. 'Worked on the railroad. Built me a house down on the bluffs. One thing was that there was whales going up and down, twice a year. Like clockwork. Jimmers had a telescope. He could watch for hours.' He shook his head slowly, watching the look on her face. Her eye twitched and the side of her mouth rose toward her ear every time it did.

'You were going *to fish*, Michael. Try to grasp that. Forget about the past. It's the future we care about.'

He shook his head. 'Nothing but a mud hole,' he said. 'Used to be trout in it as long as your arm. Trout everywhere.'

She took him by the elbow, urging him down the hill. He let her lead him along, as if he didn't know quite where he was bound anymore, but would trust her to take him there, anyway. He stopped for a moment, though, when a knife edge of pain shot across under his ribs and down his left arm. Closing his eyes and breathing evenly, he wondered if this was it, if he would die without hearing what she had to say. He half hoped so.

The pain dwindled, though, and he forced himself to go on. Irritating her was easy, but tiring. What he wanted suddenly, more than anything else in the world, was to sit peacefully on the bank and watch the water striders play across the surface of the water. There was a duck on the pond, too. That was good, almost an omen. He stepped over the side of the beached rowboat, finally, and sat down heavily on the middle thwart, pulling his fishing pole out from underneath.

He hadn't ever caught anything at all in the pond, although there supposedly had been a time when it was full of fish. He remembered when that was generally true, when you could pluck abalone off the rocks of any cove along the north coast and the fishing boats hauled in tuna fish as big as milk cows. Salmon ran thick and huge in the river mouths and in the longshore currents in those days, and the lakes and rivers were full of native trout.

That was always the way, wasn't it? The seasons changed. Time passed. Things lived and died, and as you got older, there seemed to be more dying than living. Nothing was the same anymore, and you regretted the passing away of bits and pieces of the world.

He baited his hook slowly while she yammered at him, perched on the edge of the bow. He only partly understood her complaints and her desires. Her greed was lost on him. He couldn't believe in it like she did, because he didn't share it. He reached up and pretended to adjust the brim of his hat, while actually turning down his hearing aid. The morning was suddenly nearly silent, and her voice blathered along distantly, in a garble now, like the voice of a dissatisfied spirit. He could hear the blood rushing in his veins. He tossed the salmon eggs out into the pond, and they sank to the bottom, dragged down by a couple of small split shot.

She was suddenly yelling something. He nodded, jerking awake. The duck on the pond flew off in a rush of beating wings. He had dozed off and infuriated his half sister. There was no time in her day for his dozing off. 'What?' he asked, smiling. 'You what?' He turned his hearing aid back up, conspicuously this time, and she glared at him, her mouth set in a line. She seemed to be counting to ten, trying to keep an even temper. He could probably goad her until her heart burst, but he wouldn't. She might kill him then and there. She had it in her.

'I said that I'm prepared to take it. I've readied myself.'

'Take what?' he asked, trying to look puzzled.

She said something, but he didn't hear her because his throat suddenly was full of stuff, and he hacked up a clot of phlegm and spit it onto the grass, shaking his head tiredly and catching his breath. After a minute he could talk again. 'What?' he asked, pretending to be confused.

She stared at him, clearly horrified, either at all the coughing and spitting or at his seeming failure to understand her. 'I said that I've prepared myself,' she said slowly, enunciating each syllable roundly and loudly, like a person trying to force English into the head of a foreigner.

'How? For what?'

'I've had an operation. I'm infertile now. There was a secondary infection that affected my hip joint. It won't heal. I know what you know, Michael, and I've cultivated certain powers. I'm a vessel now, waiting to be filled.'

'The garden,' he said. 'I don't know why you bothered to blight it. It's part of the process, anyway, all the drought and the dying. Why do you try so hard to help it along? Why don't you simply let it alone to run its course?'

'There's no profit in letting things run their course. That's what I mean. That's what I'm talking about here. I'm prepared to take up the burden, to relieve you of it. You're dying. You know that, don't you? And when you die, there will have to be someone else. The Grail is rightfully mine. We're of the same flesh and blood. You have no more right to it than I have, and you know it. It was selfishness, your keeping it hidden all these years when it might have been put to use.'

Explaining things to her was futile. She heard what she wanted to hear, what her mind was long ago made up to. He would try, anyway, briefly. 'The Grail, is it? Don't be so confounded specific. It's not meant to be "put to use." The world is full of things that aren't *useful*, Heloise.'

'I'll be the judge of that.'

He looked at her. Talking to her was like shouting into a hole. Your words evaporated. 'I'm not sure what it is, and neither are you. There's danger in that. It's meant to be *kept*, not used. It's ... what? A scrap of paper that someone folded into a cup and caught some blood in. If I had it my way, he never would have brought it back from the East. It's a Pandora's box, and all you can think about is to tear the lid off it.'

He began to wheeze. Long speeches took it out of him. He closed his eyes and stayed as still as he could, trying to relax so that he could catch his breath. It came finally, along with another jab of pain which he tried to keep from showing on his face. After a time he opened his eyes and saw the growing impatience on her face. She had been listening hard, waiting for some scrap of information that she could bank on. There must be something in this old man that I can *use*, her face seemed to say, that I can profit from.

'Was it the reason for John Ruskin's impotence?' she asked.

He shrugged and gave his fishing pole a tug. His hook was stuck in something, as usual. People had thrown junk into the pond for years. Trees had fallen across it. There was no telling what was down there, except that it wasn't a fish. He pulled harder, managing only to set the hook tighter.

'And you. You've had no children. Why? You've lived like a monk.'

'I was never suited to be a family man.'

She looked at him skeptically, implying that he wasn't being honest with her, that she saw right through him. 'What I believe,' she said, 'is that it was Ruskin's impotence that made him a Fisher King. The Grail fell into his hands, and—'

'What *Grail*? You're literal-minded to the point of insanity, Heloise. You've driven yourself crazy, finally, with all your grasping and clutching. There's only a sheet of paper ...'

'I don't care what it is. Hear me out. Ruskin had all the necessary tools. He was a natural, and the task simply fell to him.' She looked out over the water, thinking hard, animated by her ideas.

'You're a born fool, Heloise. You can't see the forest.'

'It's you that can't see.'

'It doesn't matter what I see. I've spent my time building up my house. That's what the Scriptures advise.'

'The Scriptures! To you it doesn't matter. You've wasted everything. You have no future. I do, though. I have the whole world within my reach, and I'm warning you right now—'

'Wait,' he said, finally tired of her talk. He pulled on his fishing pole again. Whatever the hook had caught on was moving. Slowly he reeled it in, the trout pole bending almost double. It might just conceivably be an immense catfish – a lazy beast that had lain on the bottom of the pond for years. Heloise Lamey watched, her face expressionless, humoring him, waiting him out. A dark shadow rose toward the surface, and a cloud of mud and water-weeds churned up around it. It was a rubber boot, a knee-high sort of Wellington, rotted and covered with black mud and slime. He hauled it dripping onto the bank.

He turned toward her, blinking as if mystified. 'It's a boot,' he said. 'A rubber boot.' He chuckled at the idea.

'I can see that it's a *boot*,' she hissed, going pale with exasperation and urgency. 'Listen, old man. What I'm telling you is this. The world and the future are mine. You can stand in my way as long as you're alive, but your paltry little army of so-called friends cannot. When you're dead, there'll be a very brief and nasty conflict, I can promise you, and your friends will suffer needlessly. I don't give a tinker's damn what it is – a piece of paper or a golden cup. I'm destined to have it, I tell you. And it's your own obstinacy and foolishness that prevents it ... for the moment. If you would do your friends a favor, give it to me now.'

He wasn't indifferent to what she said. She might even be right. But it changed nothing. By way of answering, he unhooked his hearing aid entirely and threw it into the pond. Then, laboriously and without looking at her again, he wiggled the hook out of the toe of the boot, dropping the boot over the bow of the rowboat. He unscrewed the lid from the jar of salmon eggs and fiddled a couple out, baiting the hook again. He took his time about it. There was no rush. He was certain he wasn't going anywhere, ever again.

He sat for a moment watching the water striders scurry back and forth across the water like ballerinas. There was a quacking overhead. The duck that had flown off had returned along with three friends, and they landed on the pond, paddling toward him curiously.

Graham poured a quarter of the jar of salmon eggs out onto his hand and scattered them on the water, the ducks scooping them up enthusiastically. He noticed then that there were rabbits on the grass of the hillside, and a pair of gray squirrels chattering in a fir tree overhead. He could see a doe and her fawn coming along through the trees. A mole waddled down the hill past the rabbits.

Slowly, fighting the pain in his chest, he got up off the hard thwart and stepped over the side of the boat, onto the grass. He stumbled, falling forward and rolling over onto his back in order to look up through the trees at the sky. The forest was full of the sound of the world, ancient and wobbly and creaking toward the morning.

He remembered then that he had been talking to someone, but it seemed a long, long time ago, and the hillside was empty except for the mole and the rabbits. Whatever had been said meant nothing to him anymore. It was just wind now, sighing in the fir trees.

'She'll pay for the damned thing,' Uncle Roy said. 'Let your conscience take a rest.'

'Well, I still didn't want to smash his car up. I didn't see any other way, though. He just quit at the corner there. He knew he couldn't chase me on foot, and it wouldn't have made any sense for me to pretend to get stuck in another hole or something. What else could I do? I had to run it into the tree.'

'Hell, we were probably out of there by then. The whole job didn't take a minute. We clipped the padlock off with the bolt cutters, fired up the truck, and got the hell out, shed and all. Nothing to it. It would have been a dead bore if you hadn't wrecked the bastard's car. There's only one thing would have improved it – him being in it at the time, or in front of it, the dirty little creep.'

'Well …' Howard said.

'He starts shooting up the damned neighborhood! I didn't expect that. That was bad news. Secrecy is paramount in this business, paramount. He nearly tore the lid off the whole thing. The boys down at the mill worked him over pretty good, though. When the cops came, they said they thought *he* was the bad ass, waving his gun like that. Gave them a bogus description of you, and the cops tore around the yard for a half hour and then figured that you got out over the fence and headed down toward the airstrip. Fellow name of Dunbar who works out there saw you climb over. He swore to it. Somehow he gave out the same description of you that MacDonald and his boys did – short, overweight, baggy pants, and work boots. Two or three of them noticed you were missing two fingers on your right hand.'

Uncle Roy grinned, obviously happy with himself. If ever there was a campaign run successfully, this had been it, all except the shooting and Howard's getting hurt. Uncle Roy had a sort of underground army of loyalists around Fort Bragg. Howard had clearly seen only the tip of the iceberg that morning, and the respect he had for his uncle had increased. Jimmers' tin shed was safe down by the harbor, locked in the back of the old icehouse.

Apart from Mrs Lamey and her confederates, the only person who would suspect it was there was Jimmers himself, probably, and Howard had already found out that he wasn't the sort to call in the police. There could be no doubt that he would make his move to fetch it back, but it would come from some unguessable direction. And the harbor was a sort of enclave of Uncle Roy's people. The dilapidated house trailers and shacks down there were tenanted largely by poor fishermen and cannery workers and welfare unemployed, many of them living on land owned by Mrs Lamey and her associates. Coming in after the shed would be tricky even for Jimmers but would be doubly tricky for the enemy. Howard was half surprised that he had come to think of them as that – that he had fallen so completely under Uncle Roy's sway.

After a moment's silence Howard asked, 'What was she doing here this morning, anyway? That was weird, her driving away just now when we were pulling up.'

Uncle Roy shrugged. 'Watching the house. Harassment. Whatever. We've put a bee under her bonnet, or you have. This whole bottle of juice has started to ferment.'

'I figured she knew about us stealing back the shed, that she was waiting for us.'

'I don't see how she could have. She probably came around looking for money, saw that the car was gone, and took off again. We just happened to be getting home at the same time, and when she saw us, the two of us together, she got cold feet and just kept on going. These landlord types are like that. They come round in the early morning, hoping to catch you in your pajamas when you're naturally one down. They knock on loud enough for the neighbors to hear, thinking they'll shame you. All you can do is ignore them.'

Howard nodded. That seemed reasonable enough. Something in him had been startled by the sight of Mrs Lamey driving off at that hour of the morning, though, just when they were driving in. She hadn't even glanced at them or slowed down. Uncle Roy's explanation of it didn't quite wash. 'If I had it to do over again,' Howard started to say as Uncle Roy stood up and moved off toward the kitchen, 'I'd—'

'For now you could sit still,' Sylvia said, cutting him off. She pulled the Ace bandage tight around his knee and wrapped it half a dozen times. 'I think this whole escapade was a lot of stupid nonsense, all over that damned machine.'

Uncle Roy had disappeared, out clanking coffee mugs around in the kitchen. Outside, the sun was barely up, still hiding behind the trees. In a half hour it would be another beautiful, dry autumn day. Howard watched Sylvia happily as she clipped the bandage in place. She wore a woolly sort of bathrobe with big pink flowers on it, and her hair was a sleepy mess, falling half in front of her face. She had pretended to be exasperated with both of them, but she had clearly been more frightened than mad when Uncle Roy waked her up, asking about the bandage.

Howard felt like a knight, having gone out to slay the dragon, or something like that, and then come home to the fair Sylvia, who was tending his wounds. This whole north coast adventure was developing a Knights of the Round Table feel to it, and Howard realized that as stupidly romantic as such notions were, he was happily letting himself be swept up in it all. Sylvia pushed a low ottoman across and propped his leg up on it. 'It's a little swollen,' she said. 'Keep it elevated.'

She leaned against his thigh for a moment before pushing herself up off the floor and looked straight into his face. There wasn't anything flippant in her eyes, just worry, he thought – for him. He was filled suddenly with the urge to put his arms around her, to pull her closer and say something equally serious. In her loosely tied robe and wild hair she seemed to be still warm from her bed, and if ever there was a more perfect, custom-built moment to say what it was he meant to say ...

She spoke first, though. 'You don't really believe in this nonsense about Mr Jimmers' machine, do you? About it manufacturing ghosts?'

Howard shrugged. '*Something* pretty weird happened in that shed. I don't know what. I thought *you* were the spiritualist type, though. Now you all of a sudden don't believe in ghosts?'

'I believe that Mr Jimmers would go a long way to put one over on Father.'

'Really?' Howard said, surprised. 'Would he go *that* far? How about the wild phone call down at the harbor last night? And look who stole the damned thing. It wasn't us. Do you think he set up the theft with Mrs Lamey and her crowd just to confound your father? I don't follow this whole line of reasoning.'

Sylvia shrugged. 'I don't think he's got anything to do with Mrs Lamey anymore. My guess is that Jimmers outright hates her. He doesn't have any-thing to do with anyone but himself, and Graham, of course. But now that Graham's not living in the house, Jimmers is a loose cannon on the deck, and I have the feeling that this machine of his is going to roll all over the place smashing things up. I think he was mad, all right, when he called last night, because he thinks that Father stole the shed out from under his nose, and he can't stomach the idea. Secretly, though, he might be happy as a clam. Now Father's got Jimmers' loony machine and is proud of himself for having it. Father's guard is down. Do you see what I mean?'

'I see it,' Howard said, 'but I'm not buying it.'

'I've been thinking. Yesterday, when you unlocked the shed – I'm thinking that Jimmers knew you were in there all along. His surprise seems faked to me now, like he was hoping that you'd break in there, see something strange, and come away convinced.'

'Convinced of what? I came away convinced that I don't know what the hell to think.'

'That's just his style, isn't it? That's Mr Jimmers in a nutshell. Maybe he saw you as an easy mark, and you swallowed the whole ghost-out-of-a-machine notion and came home and got Father all fired up about it.'

'He didn't need any firing up. You know that.'

'Mr Jimmers couldn't have known that, though, could he? They hadn't spoken to each other in a year – probably haven't even seen each other.'

Howard thought for a moment. Mr Jimmers' emotions *always* seemed fake. You couldn't tell with Jimmers, which admittedly gave him an edge over you. But somehow the idea of Jimmers merely fooling them all didn't satisfy him. There had to be more to it than that. The idea of it all was comical, though. Here was Sylvia talking sense, and he himself talking mysticism. Go figure it, he told himself.

Uncle Roy came back in just then, carrying three cups of coffee, and Sylvia stood up to take one of the cups from him. She pulled her bathrobe tighter and tied it securely, the action reminding Howard of the opportunity that had come and gone. If the morning had accomplished nothing else, at least Sylvia was worrying about him now. He was an actor, finally, in this strange play, which, if Mr Jimmers had his way, would maybe turn into a farce.

'Tell me about Jimmers' machine,' Howard said to Uncle Roy. 'What are we going to do with it?'

His uncle sat there for a moment, sipping his coffee and gathering things in his mind, either because he was weighing how much he could safely say to Howard or, more likely, because what he had to say wasn't entirely credible. 'It's complicated,' was what he said finally.

Howard raised his eyebrows. 'I was thinking that it might be. What is it, though?'

'I believe it to be a machine that transports spirits through time and from one place to another.'

'I've been through this before,' Sylvia said, heading toward the stairs. 'You men thrash this out. I've got to get ready for work.'

'The ghosts of dead men?' Howard asked, waving haphazardly at Sylvia. They were getting down to it now.

Uncle Roy shook his head. 'Nope. The spiritual essences of live men – the men who built the machine for that very purpose. It's a device that could transport you and me across astral planes. Don't laugh when I ask you this, but have you read Burroughs' Martian novels?'

'John Carter? Thuvia?'

'That's the ones. They're a lot of colorful nonsense, of course, but the notion of out-of-body travel isn't. It's simple as that. You're a rationalist, and scoff at it, but since you asked me, I'm telling you the simple truth. Believe it or don't.'

'You know,' Howard said after pausing for a moment, 'I could have sworn that the ghost in the shed yesterday afternoon was John Ruskin – that portrait of him that you see with side-whiskers and with his hair white and ragged and his eyes all rheumy.'

'It was. I believe I can say that with some authority. What do you know about the Pre-Raphaelite Brotherhood, besides the fact that they were a lot of Victorian artists collected around Ruskin?'

'A bit,' Howard said. 'I know there were a couple of generations of them and that there were as many photographers among them as there were painters.'

'Lewis Carroll was one.'

Howard nodded.

'And Dean Liddell, Alice's father.'

'I saw the photograph on the wall down at the museum – the visage that appeared on the wall of Christ Church Cathedral. That was pretty intriguing. Did they figure out how it was done?'

'Done? Do you mean did they discover that it was a hoax? No, they didn't. It wasn't *done* at all. It was the real thing, and no mistaking it – the result of an experiment with the machine.' Uncle Roy paused heavily then, letting this sink in.

'I thought all the Pre-Raphaelites were artists of one sort or another. What did Liddell have to do with them?'

'He was a sort of soldier, actually. Carroll was living with George MacDonald at the time. Have you read MacDonald?'

'A couple of fantasies. I don't know much about him aside from figuring out that he was a Christian writer.'

'First of the great Christian fantasists. Back then there wasn't anyone writing in the fantastic vein who could touch MacDonald, unless it was Carroll. They got caught up in Ruskin's web, specifically in the dealings of the Guild of St George – Ruskin's efforts to destroy industrial society, which he saw as the Dragon, so to speak.'

'I've read a little about them. Didn't they build a few workers' cottages or something? It wasn't a crafts guild so much as a political action group – failed efforts, mostly. That's what I remember, anyway.'

'Well, that's right, mainly. They never destroyed industrial society, and they didn't produce much that was worth a damn when it came to art or furniture or any other typical crafts guild stuff. But then, as you say, the Guild of St George wasn't any typical crafts guild, and they did manage to skewer a dragon or two while they were at it. What do you know about James Graham?'

'Only what I found out after I looked into this sketch business. He was a photographer, mostly. Michael Graham's … what? Grandfather?'

'That's it. He's the *connection*. He was a member of Ruskin's crowd, very pious and dissipated both. He spent a long time in the Holy Land, taking photographs in the name of God. Lived in a tower overlooking Jerusalem. Holman Hunt lived there off and on, too, along with a couple of other Pre-Raphaelites who had gone native. Now, what were they looking for? What sort of pilgrimage were they on? It was Ruskin that sent them, and it was a long damned way into a desolate country. They were all engaged in a search, a quest. What were they looking for, though, really? The answer to that question is the key.'

Howard shrugged. He didn't have the answer. 'History has it that they were painting and taking photographs, that it was an artistic expedition.'

'History,' Uncle Roy snorted. 'You can have history. Don't pay more than a dime for it, though, or you've been cheated. This Holy Land quest was *passed off* as an artistic expedition, but what it really was, was a modern-day crusade, and nothing less. And I'm not talking metaphor here. I mean what I say.'

'What?' Howard said. 'A crusade? In what sense? They were looking for the Grail?'

Uncle Roy widened his eyes and blinked, laying his hands out in front of him, palms up, as if to say that he couldn't be blamed for their pursuits; he was only relating what he had heard.

'Did they find it?'

'They found something, and brought it back, too. And let me clarify a few things. It wasn't just industrialization that the Guild of St George wanted to annihilate. They weren't pitted against a generality or an abstraction. History has seen these lads as political and social failures – Ruskin and Morris and all the rest of them – and it'll see us as failures just as surely. The work we do will have to be its own reward.'

'I'd be surprised to find that history can see us at all,' Howard said.

'Who can say? Anyway, and more to the point, half of their story has never been told. It's too fantastic, too many high mucky-mucks brought low. Most of it was suppressed by people in power, who stayed in power, and later mapped out history in their own invented images.'

'What did they find, then, Graham and Hunt and all of these people who went East? The machine?' Howard was anxious to drag the conversation back down to earth. He thought he knew the answer to the question, but he wanted to hear it from Uncle Roy himself.

'The piece of paper. The sketch.'

'The Hoku-sai?'

Uncle Roy gestured. 'There's some that guessed it was a Hoku-sai. I don't think so.' He squinted at Howard, like a man who had secret knowledge, smiling just slightly, like a moon man with a Mona Lisa grin.

'You don't think it's a Hoku-sai? That's what I understood it to be. It's pretty clearly one of his sketches of the Takara-mono, the luck charms. And that's what Graham told me nearly fifteen years ago, too, when I was staying up at his place. That's what the hell I came up here for, to bring back a Hoku-sai sketch. Now you're telling me it's not a Hoku-sai at all? What is it, then? An imitation? A piece by someone nobody's ever heard of?'

'That's a good way to put it. Exactly that Someone nobody's heard of, just like you and me. Although the one who made the sketch wasn't the imitator, he was the originator. And if Hoku-sai was influenced by it, well ... what great artists aren't influenced in one way or another? As for why Graham lied about it, he'll have to tell you that much himself. That's not my duty.'

'Is it valuable, then?'

'To a museum? How do I know? You're the expert. It's old – predates Hoku-sai by a long damned time. So it has a certain value as an antiquity. Now, you wouldn't guess it to look at him, but Bennet is something of a scholar, in his way. He's looked into this, gone to ... *sources*. Bennet says this piece of paper was folded into the shape of a cup. Legend has it that it was inked with blood – not painted on, mind you, but splashed on. At Golgotha. It was smashed flat and smuggled out in someone's robe, probably. Later when it was unfolded, it was found to have been ... sketched, so to speak, with fundamental shapes. It could be folded again to derive other shapes, other pictures – a changeable pictograph, if you follow me. A sort of paper kaleidoscope inked with blood, entirely randomly. And yet the images that fall together are perfect representations of essential order.'

Howard sat in silence, trying to process this notion, but it was bothersomely schizophrenic to him. Suddenly he understood that there were patterns, whereas before there had seemed to be none – patterns, perhaps, in the random wash of gravel on a roadside, in the placement of leaves on a tree and stars in the night sky. Messages spelled out in hieroglyphics by a flock of birds passing overhead, by the ice fragments in the tail of a comet.

What was most puzzling and troubling was that Howard seemed to have been *sent* for. Finding the paper lily – had that been just a happy blunder, or had it been a mystically contrived step in a centuries-old process? And the dreams, the sketchy clouds full of suggestion, of travel, of compulsion. Even the signifying pelican …

Uncle Roy stood up and peered out through the curtains at the street, as if checking just for safety's sake before drawing them open. 'Let me say that you can no more avoid all this, now that you've thrown in your hand with us, than a meteor can avoid the gravity of a nearby planet. And I won't mince words. I won't lead you down the garden. Men have died in this struggle. Those were real bullets this morning. Lamey and her crowd aren't just a real estate cartel or something. What I'm telling you here is that you're the innocent pedestrian stumbling into the territory of a feud. You think you're selling encyclopedias door-to-door, and then there you are one day with a gun in your hand and a bunch of hillbillies spitting tobacco past your shoulder and calling you Brother Howard. Do you follow me?'

'I think so. Maybe you shouldn't tell me any more. If the sketch isn't what I thought it is, then there's nothing holding me here. I could drive back south.'

'Nothing holding you here but a car theft and a gimp knee … and Sylvia, I suppose.'

Howard's face got hot immediately, and he nearly denied it. There was no point in denying it, though. Silence was better. There was too much going on right now, and no room for complications. Uncle Roy looked monumentally grave all at once, and said, 'I'm going to ask you once more, nephew. Think everything through before you answer. Are you in or out? You could have sat it out down at Winchell's this morning, eating glazed doughnuts and thinking about that goddamn museum job of yours. Maybe you still can. Maybe we can rig it to get you out of here. There's sides drawn up, and when that happens a man's either in or he's out. There's nobody left on the fence except the stupid man when the hurricane blows. What do you say?'

Sylvia came in just then, along with Aunt Edith, both of them heading for the kitchen. Sylvia was dressed for work, wearing a sweater and jeans, her hair combed out and lipstick on. When she caught Howard's eye, she smiled, glancing down at his knee and shaking her head, as if his shenanigans confounded her. There was a rattling of cups out in the kitchen, and then a moment later the back door opened and closed.

'I'm in,' Howard said, after taking a look at Sylvia's face. 'Of course I'm in.' He felt at once relieved and at the same time like some sort of Secret Service agent heading out into the cold with only bits and pieces of information, because he couldn't be trusted with the whole business. 'So the sketch fell into Michael Graham's hands, and Jimmers, we guess, is keeping it safe. I understand that. But how about the machine?'

'Built by the Guild of St George hand in glove with Morris and Company. It was invented by a Morris acolyte named William Keeble, who later became a noted London toymaker. The man had very exotic notions. That was a few years after these sojourns in the Holy Land, when the battle was heating up. The sketch had been hidden at Red House, Morris' place at Upton, in Kent, which was built for no other reason than to hide it, although that's something that the historians won't tell you, probably because they don't know it. There was a well in the front yard, a slate-roofed brick well, very pretty. That's where they put it-down the well, in a bucket. Philip Webb, the architect, designed the whole shebang. Anyway, it's my belief that the machine finally was used to transport certain ... valuable objects out of the reach of the enemy at the time of Ruskin's death.

'That was in 1900, of course. The man had been stone crazy for ten years. There was a crowd that tried to stop them from burying him in Westminster Abbey. You can figure out why. He was laid out, finally, at Coniston, in the Lake District, but just between me and you, he didn't stay there.'

'He left?'

'There's some question about where his bones ended up. There was more than one attempt to get at them – a couple just recently. But they haven't been in Coniston for years. Never were, for my money.'

Uncle Roy studied his fingernails for a moment, then said, 'I got most of this from Jimmers, of course. And we both know what that's worth. Could be end-to-end nonsense.'

'Do we *want* the sketch, you and I?' Howard asked.

'Best not to think in terms of ourselves.'

'Fine. Practically speaking, though – do we want it? Do we need it?'

'Not me, certainly. I wouldn't touch it with a pole.'

'How about me? I seem to have been invited up here to find it or take it or help protect it or something. I don't know what.'

Uncle Roy shrugged. 'The old man might know. He's probably fishing in the pond right now, trying to hook a salmon.'

Just as he said this, Howard became aware that his chair was moving. The air seemed full of a vague rumbling, and for an instant Howard thought that a truck was passing outside. Then there was the sound of the house creaking and of objects rattling in cupboards. The curtains tossed and coffee sloshed in a wave out of Howard's still-full cup.

'Earthquake!' Uncle Roy shouted, and he was up and out of his chair, weaving toward the nearest doorway as plaster dust rained down onto his head.

20

Howard stood up, testing his knee, and at that instant there was a second jolt, as if something huge had struck the earth. Howard sat down hard, holding on to the arms of the chair and expecting the roof to cave in. He staggered to his feet and tottered into a doorway, bracing himself against the frame. The old house swayed and creaked, crack lines shooting ominously across the ceiling plaster. Glasses clinked together furiously in the kitchen cupboards, and there was the sound of a cupboard door banging open and of something shattering on the countertop.

Then it was over, and there was a dreadful, still sort of silence during which neither he nor Uncle Roy dared move. But the earth was solid. The morning had started up again. Outside, there was the sound of birds calling. A dog began to bark down the street. Howard stood up again and limped across to steady the chandelier, which was still swaying back and forth, dropping plaster dust from around the ceiling fixture.

The dog quit barking. Howard and Uncle Roy stood still for a few moments, waiting for it to start up again, but there was nothing. Together they went into the kitchen. Lying on the countertop, having fallen out of the thrown-open cupboard, was Aunt Edith's porcelain Humpty Dumpty, broken to pieces.

'Hell,' Uncle Roy said softly, picking up the top of the thing's head.

'Super Glue?' Howard asked.

'Could be useless in this case. Let's keep the pieces, though, just in case Sylvia wants to have a go at it.' Silently they put all the pieces in a paper sack. 'That was a good one,' Uncle Roy said, referring to the earthquake. 'I bet it was a five or six. Epicenter was close, too. You can tell when they're sharp like that. A real jolt.' They walked back out into the living room and sat down again, both of them edgy. For the space of a minute neither one of them spoke, then Uncle Roy said, 'What the hell were we talking about?'

'Fishing,' Howard said. 'You told me that Graham spends his time fishing for salmon. How can there be any salmon in that little mud hole?'

'There's not now. In wetter years the pond connects by a tributary to Pudding Creek. Used to run the year round, and the odd trout could find its way back there. That was before all this drought. Anyway, that's what he's doing, whether there's any salmon in there or not. He's got used to fishing off the rocks below his place. Plenty of salmon out there in the ocean, or used to be. Fishing industry's slow now, and going to get slower if all this offshore-oil nonsense starts up. That's Lamey, too, and your man Stoat. She's a hell of a squid, like I said – got a finger in every pie conceivable.' He shook his head, getting mad at the idea of Mrs Lamey. 'Anyway, used to be that the creeks were full of fish, back when they were full of water. Things change, though. Graham's the man to answer your questions. He asked me just yesterday whether you were a man who liked to fish. Ain't that something? Same question I asked you.'

'Quite a coincidence,' Howard said.

'Well, he seemed to guess that, about you being a fisherman. I'll warn you, though, that talking with him is rough. He's in and out, you know. Sometimes the light's on and sometimes there's nothing inside but a little flashlight bulb, sometimes outright darkness.'

'In the cabin?'

'Not in the cabin. In his head. He's been going downhill pretty quick. He's frail, like old cobweb. That's one of the reasons he moved back into the woods, out of the house on the bluffs. His days had begun to look numbered. He was tired, worn out. The struggle had got too much for him. Just getting up and pulling on his boots had got too much for him. There was nothing left for him but fishing. Could be he caught something when he wrote that letter back to you. It took a while, but he's finally reeled you in. He's set the hook.' Uncle Roy winked at him.

'Anyway, he's been living in the cabin off and on for more than a year, although we tried to make it look like he was still in his house, out on the bluffs. They caught on that there was something up, and so Jimmers pulled the suicide gag. It wasn't worth much. I would have done it different. Graham just wants some rest, and he deserves it, too.'

Uncle Roy yawned and stretched. 'I'm going to put in a couple of hours sleep,' he said, standing up and heading for the stairs. 'Later on I'm going down to the harbor. Probably be there all day. Now that you've, ah … come to all these decisions, maybe you ought to mosey out to the cabin and have a confab with old Graham. You might get some answers. Then again, you might not.' With that he shuffled away up the stairs, but had gotten just out of sight when the back door slammed open, banging into the clothes dryer.

'Father!' It was Sylvia, shouting. She ran into the living room, breathing hard.

Howard jumped up thinking of the stolen car, the police, gunfire. He flexed his game knee. He could walk on it fine – a little stiff-legged, maybe, but …

Uncle Roy appeared at the bottom of the stairs, ready for action. 'What is it?' he asked, breathing hard. 'What's wrong?'

Sylvia caught her breath. There was fear and grief in her eyes. 'Graham's dead.'

Howard stood paralyzed, struck with the notion that the world had stopped spinning, that time stood still. He knew that on the instant everything had changed. A door had shut. Another had opened.

'How?' Uncle Roy said, breaking the spell. 'Foul play?' He pulled on his coat while striding toward the back door. Howard followed along behind. 'Graham's dead' – the words played through Howard's mind like a closed-loop tape. He had heard the words more than once over the last few days, but now they signified – not only because this time it was true but because the truth had changed things.

'No. I don't think so,' Sylvia said. 'We found him on the grass, sort of trying to sit up. He'd been fishing. We called to him, and he just … went. There was an earthquake; did you feel it? It might have been that, I guess. Maybe he was frightened by it. Except that he looked like he was in trouble before the earthquake, faint or something. I think he was dying when we saw him. That's what it looked like. We tried to revive him – everything we could think of – but it wasn't any good.'

They hurried down the path, into the woods. The sun was up, but still below the tree line, and the woods were dark and dense. At least there was no fog. Within minutes they were there, at the clearing in front of the cabin. Howard must have gone far off course the other morning to have wandered for so long in the woods. The old man lay now at the base of the grassy hill, down by the pond. Aunt Edith knelt beside him as if guarding the body.

'The king is dead,' Uncle Roy said quietly, standing over him. Clearly there was nothing anyone could do for him. His face was relaxed, as if he'd died in his sleep and was finally truly at rest. It was deeply lined, the face of a man who had spent his life on a sea cliff. Howard hadn't realized that Graham was so old. He remembered him at something near eighty, still hale and hearty, sawing out rough planks with his chain-saw mill, running wheelbarrows full of cliff rock across the meadow. He looked frail now, and thin, although the lines cut into his face gave him a craggy sort of chiseled-out look, the face of a man sculpted by wind and ocean.

Uncle Roy nodded grimly at Howard. 'Let's get him up to the cabin.' He bent over and latched on to the old man's feet. Howard picked him up beneath his arms, surprised at how light he was. Gravity seemed to have given up on him already.

They moved off, Howard walking backward and Uncle Roy redfaced and breathing hard with the exertion of it. Beneath where the body had lain there was an unseasonable scattering of white daisies, growing up through the stiff grass of the hillside as if a little fragment of spring had risen to the surface of the land where the old man had died. It smelled briefly like spring, too – like wildflowers on a breezy, sunlit meadow in April.

Aunt Edith carried Graham's cane, a gnarled piece of manzanita, polished to a deep bloodred and wet with dew from where it had lain in the grass.

Slipping and sliding on the damp hillside, they finally reached the rear of the house and got onto level ground. The old man was heavier than Howard had thought. 'Hold it,' he said. His knee felt like rubber, throbbing with pain beneath the Ace bandage.

Sylvia stepped in and supported Graham's shoulders.

The three of them carried him around and onto the porch, setting him down carefully. Howard waited, wondering what was next. Old Graham looked so peaceful that there was nothing very different in it than if he had been merely asleep. Except that Howard felt a weird sort of affinity to him that he couldn't explain, as if this were his father lying dead at his feet. He could remember almost nothing about his own father aside from what he had gleaned from photographs – strange images of a man who was forever distant, lost to him.

He was struck suddenly with the uncanny feeling that he had been there before. He had stood just like that on a wooden front porch, looking down at a dead man. Then it was himself in his memory, lying on his own back, dead, looking up into faces of people who lived in a world that no longer contained him, a make-believe landscape on a movie screen. For one jolting moment he didn't know who he was, the living Howard Barton or the dead Michael Graham. He shook his head, nearly falling over. Uncle Roy clutched him under the arm in order to steady him, but Howard was already himself again, his confusion gone. He was dizzy, probably from the exertion.

'Couple of spades around back,' Uncle Roy said, collapsing into an armchair. Aunt Edith composed the old man's clothes, pulling his jacket straight and buttoning it up and then combing his hair with her fingers. With Sylvia alongside, Howard limped around after the shovels, and together they began to dig the grave in the center of the garden, careful not to disturb the few rows of lettuce and onions, even though they were discolored and blighted-looking.

After a few minutes, Uncle Roy offered to dig for a spell. Howard gave him the shovel gratefully. His knee was stiff as heavy cardboard, and he hobbled across to sit down by Aunt Edith on the porch again. His senses were strangely acute, as if every sound and smell were picture-framed, separate from every other. Something had happened to him. And it wasn't simply that a man had died.

Somehow the notion of burying Graham at once struck him as right and natural. Whether it was legal didn't matter. There wasn't any practical reason to wait. In fact, there was a sense of urgency in the air, as if the land were hungry for the body – not in any horrific sense, but in a dust-to-dust sense.

Dreamily, feeling vague and removed, he looked again at the resting corpse, and in that moment it looked to him to be made of dark loam, of forest debris and mulch, sprouting with oxalis and moss and weaved into shape with tiny roots. The porch floor around him was littered with acorns and oak leaves. Tendrils of berry vine grew up between the wood slats, winding across Graham's arms and chest like fibrous muscle.

Howard stood up, shaking the image out of his eyes. He was acutely aware of the sound of the forest around hint, of the wind in the treetops and the stirring of undergrowth, as if the woods suddenly were full of life – of crawling things, of creatures slipping up out of hidey-holes and thickets. The sun edged into view through a sort of avenue in the trees that led off toward the eastern horizon. The garden was stippled with sunlight, and the heat of it fell on his face, angling beneath the porch roof, bathing old Graham in golden rays. There wasn't any moss on the body, not really – no berry vines – just an old man who was dead, lying on the scuffed floorboards of the porch.

It was time to have another turn at the shovel. Exercise would help – physical exertion. Uncle Roy wasn't built for it, and was sweating freely despite the morning chill. He had taken off his coat and thrown it over the back of the wheelbarrow. Sylvia worked steadily, standing in the grave now, shoveling out loose dirt while Uncle Roy skived away at the side, widening it out. Howard found that he was suddenly too faint to dig, and he tried to pull himself together. Graham's death coming on top of the earthquake must have unnerved him.

'Come inside,' Aunt Edith said to Howard. 'You don't look well.' She opened the front door of the shack and stepped in, Howard following. On the table in the center of the room lay a bouquet of lilies, brownish green and bruised purple. A sickening odor rose from them. Edith swept them up angrily. She pushed past Howard through the front door again and flung them off the porch with so much force that the heavy, moist flowers flew to pieces in the air, scattering into the weeds. She came back in and pulled the windows open to air the place out.

'She was here, then,' Howard said. 'She killed him, didn't she?'

'She isn't strong enough to have killed him, although she wishes she were. Here,' she said to Howard, 'take his cane.' She looked old herself in that moment, and tired. She had an even-keeled air about her, though, as she handed Howard the stick, looking him full in the face. Her eyes were as green and deep as well water, as if she had endured great suffering in her time, and it had made her wise. 'He won't be needing it anymore.'

Howard looked down at the cane. He could use it, certainly, lame as he was. It looked old, polished from long years of use, and it occurred to him that if he were to take it out to the garden and thrust the tip of it down into the dirt, green tendrils would sprout from the old dry wood. He knocked it against the floorboards. It was stout enough to trust, and he leaned on it gratefully as they walked outside and clumped down the porch steps.

The sky was full of crows now, circling high above them, waiting and watching. There must have been thousands, tens of thousands. He could see them through the trees in every direction. Sylvia had laid her shovel down alongside the grave and was watching Howard intently, a little fearfully maybe, as if she saw something in his face that suggested his own mortality.

He shifted the cane in his hand, feeling a little dizzy. There was something sticky on it – sap? He looked at it more closely. Was it blood, leaking out of the cane as if out of a wound? The notion was crazy. He shook his head to clear it and leaned heavily against the cane with both hands, steadying himself and wondering suddenly if he was sick. He was certain that he didn't have any sort of fever, but his mind refused to focus. It was drifting at the whim of some vast tide, almost as if his normal concentration had come unstuck, and something else – the forest itself, or nature, or something even more boundless than that – was peering in at him from outside, assessing him.

He remembered the dream he had had for months now, the dream about the fireplace, the hot coal. And the dream suddenly was more real to him than the forest and the people round about. He stood staring into the fire again, the dark mill around him, the sound of the millwheel turning, and his knee throbbing with pain where he'd burned it. Only this time the mill didn't have walls or a roof except the dark tree line and a sky black with crows, and he was aware that even though people stood silently just a few yards away, just on the edge of the firelight, he felt alien and alone, with the sea wind blowing and the night sky turning overhead. He put his hand to his mouth and touched his tongue to the sticky residue on his fingers, the sap that had flowed from the stick. It was coppery-tasting, salty, like blood, and the taste of it made him feel faint. He sat down hard on the ground and closed his eyes, and the cawing of the crows fell down around him like raindrops.

Howard spent the day cleaning the rest of the barn lumber. What had happened to him in the woods was nothing but hyperventilation. He had told himself that a dozen times. He had been at a seance once, years ago, where a college friend of his had gotten excited and hyperventilated, making everyone think for a moment that a ghost had gotten into her. Someone had made her breathe into a paper sack, and she was all right again. This business up at the cabin was no doubt the same sort of thing – lack of sleep, a dead man, the strange conversation he'd had with Uncle Roy, the earthquake, the hurt knee. There were a thousand reasons for him to have gone temporarily off the deep end. Certainly there was no need to get mystical over it.

He was convinced that work was the antidote. After breakfast, Uncle Roy had gone off to meet Bennet, leaving the lumber to Howard. By two o'clock Howard had a big clean pile of it, all stacked and stickered alongside the house. There was nothing left of the pile on the grass but junk – firewood, boards too cracked and twisted to work with. He felt good for a half dozen reasons, although he was growing nervous as the afternoon wore on. It was Monday, and that meant that Mrs Lamey's 'little circle' was meeting tomorrow night.

Since he had last talked to Mrs Lamey, things had gotten vastly more complicated. They couldn't know anything certain about him, though. Not really. As far as Mrs Lamey knew, Howard was a free agent, or else represented the museum, and so was in a position to be lured away, into the enemy camp. He was a potential new recruit. Certainly the man who had chased him through the streets that morning hadn't identified him, although he would know by now that it had been no simple car theft.

The man was still in a holding cell at the police station, and might stay there for a while. He wouldn't be at Mrs Lamey's place tomorrow. The police weren't fond of his shooting up the neighborhood, and MacDonald down at the mill had testified that he had threatened the yard hands, waving his gun like a murderer, clearly out of his head. Of course it was his own car that had been stolen, so there were mitigating circumstances. Mrs Lamey, or more likely one of her paid acquaintances, would come to his rescue eventually. Palms would be greased, doors opened.

Certainly it would be dangerous for Howard to show up at her house, but not all that dangerous. They had nothing to gain from assaulting him. But maybe there was a potential gain from winning his favor. Of course there was. There was time enough to worry about it later, maybe lose a little sleep over it tonight. In an hour and a half, though, he was meeting Sylvia for dinner and then they were taking in a movie, whatever the hell was playing. Howard didn't care.

Whistling, he looped the extension cord and rolled the radial arm saw back into the shed. Then he pitched a coffee can full of bent nails into the trash and put away the hammer and pry bar. The stack of lumber sat there solid and clean, a thing of value now and not a pile of trash. It would be a tonic for Uncle Roy, money in the bank. The afternoon was fine – almost hot – and the ground around the house was hard and dry. He could hear the cawing of crows still, out over the woods. His knee felt pretty good. It had started to improve when he got the walking stick that morning. Howard picked the stick up from where it was leaning against the house and inspected it one last time. There was no sap on it, no blood. It was smooth and tight-grained. Shrugging, he knocked the dust off his shoes with it and then went in to change clothes.

21

Almost two hundred dollars in Roy Barton's pocket, and the sun was barely over the yardarm. The lumber that Howard had so kindly cleaned up yesterday had only fetched eighty bucks – not even twenty cents a foot. Still, it was all profit, and only Tuesday, to boot. No sense in even thinking about labor. What difference did it make to a retired man like himself? A dollar an hour, a nickel an hour – time wasn't money anymore and hadn't been for years.

He slapped his shirt pocket and started to whistle, but then he remembered his conversation with Jimmers that morning, and he quit whistling. News of the old man's death had nearly bowled Jimmers over. 'Shit,' Uncle Roy said out loud, wishing that it hadn't been him who had to tell Jimmers. Jimmers was fragile. Graham had been his only real friend, and now Jimmers was left alone … Uncle Roy shook his head. Things fell apart; there was no denying it.

He thought about the morning again in order to cheer himself up. He had driven around the city after selling the barn lumber, and had found a garage sale up at the end of Perkins Way that was hustling a lot of old construction debris, including a dozen French windows that the owner had torn out of his house. Roy had bought four wooden planes from the man, too, the irons all rusty and the wood gummy and dark.

The lot of it had cost him forty-eight dollars of his barn lumber money. It took him a half hour to pull the hardware off the doors – brass hinges and sliding bolts and glass doorknobs. He spent another hour on the planes, buffing out and sharpening the irons and cleaning the junk off the wood, then rubbing the wood and steel both with mineral oil. He sold the doors for sixty dollars to a man he knew of on Oak Street who was building a greenhouse, and the door hardware and planes to an antique store in town for another eighty.

It had been luck, though. The man was a fool to dump the doors for that kind of money. If Roy had taken some time with it – stripped the old paint off and refinished them, replaced a couple of panes of broken glass – he might easily have doubled his profit, tripled it. But, hell, who was he kidding? The truth was that if he had gotten fancy, the doors would have spent the

winter stacked in the weeds, just like the barn lumber had done. They would
have come to nothing. A quick turnover – that was paramount. Don't overreach yourself. Get in and get out.

He wondered idly whether there wasn't a book in it: *One Hundred Ways to
Make One Hundred Dollars, Overnight.* What did Xerox cost, a nickel a page?
You could have the copier bind the thing, too, inside colored boards, and
then distribute them yourself out of the back of the station wagon. Half the
north coast was out of a job, it seemed. People would snap them up. You
could leave half a dozen on a liquor store counter – forty percent for the
owner on consignment, sixty percent if he bought them outright.

That would be best, selling them outright would be. To hell with consignment; there was no profit in that. People would steal them or else the store
owner would say they did. He calculated profits in his head as he pulled into
a parking place in front of Sylvia's shop. What were there? Fifty thousand
people out of work along the coast? Twice that? He could buy an address list,
maybe, of all the poor bastards on food stamps, and send them a mailer. They
could afford a fiver easy enough when they knew they could parlay it into
something big. The sky was the limit, wasn't it? The whole damned country
was going broke. The future lay in a man's doing for himself, outside the
stinking system. Barter, co-ops, labor trading, neighborhood day care, backyard gardens, chickens in pens, goat cheese.

He pulled the wad of money out of his pocket, amazed at how a little bit of
dough set a man thinking. The horizon wasn't any kind of limit for an
onward-looking man. He hesitated out on the sidewalk, not going straight
into the shop.

Sylvia would only be happy to see him for a moment. She would know he
was up to something. She was too serious sometimes, though. What she
wanted was a longer view. Easy come, easy go; that was the nature of the
wicked world. It was better to be philosophical about it. If he himself was a
responsible man, he would give the money to Heloise Lamey; or rather, he
would give it to Edith and let her parse it out according to her budget.

He hated budgets. There was something small and mean about them that
killed a man's gumption and imagination. Spend it when you get it; that was
his motto. A man couldn't be running across town to save a nickel on a bottle
of ketchup or to put his few miserable pennies in the savings bank. By God if
you wanted a drink in the afternoon, because you were thirsty and because
that's what the Good Book advised – he couldn't recall the chapter and verse,
but he knew it was in there – then you either had a drink or you shut the hell
up forever after. Did you want to be happy, or work up a reputation for being
thrifty?

He walked into the boutique, and there was Sylvia, behind the counter,
folding up some sort of oriental swan out of paper. There was one other cus-

tomer in the store – a woman trying on a felt hat. Roy waved at Sylvia and then looked around at the merchandise, taking it all in. He nodded expansively. There was plenty to spend his money on.

In truth, he hardly ever came in. He didn't give a damn for women's clothes, and he didn't want to seem to be meddling in Sylvia's business affairs. This was her shop, after all. And, if they could keep out from under the thumb of the landlord class, the boutique would succeed where his enterprises had failed. If she made it through the winter, she'd be in the black. Come the spring, tourist money would start to flow, just like sap. Then all of them would rest easy. He was proud of her, and today he would do his best to help out.

He found a bulky, knitted sweater for a hundred dollars, Scottish wool dyed with berries – custom-built for the north coast climate. It was expensive, but nothing to a pocket-lined man like him, who had a daughter who was worth every penny. The sweater would do for Sylvia. Next he found a blouse for Edith, a dark green rayon blouse with a green and white scarf. It was youthful, and she would complain about that. But he wouldn't listen. The blouse and scarf would cost him another fifty dollars, which would leave fifty for dinner – sixty if you counted the secret tenner in his wallet. Altogether that would just about make the nut. Edith would murder him, if Sylvia didn't get him first. He nearly laughed out loud. This was rich. It had been too long since he'd lavished money on his family.

'What's that for?' Sylvia asked suspiciously when he laid the stuff on the counter.

'Wearing apparel,' he said. Then, noticing the felt-hat woman standing behind him, he said, 'Take the lady first, perhaps.' He backed away and nodded at the woman, who smiled and said he didn't have to do that, that she could wait.

He bowed gallantly. 'I anticipate trouble,' he said to her. 'This could get nasty.' She shrugged and stepped in front of him, chatting amiably with Sylvia and paying her thirty dollars for the hat before going out.

'What's the story?' Sylvia asked. 'What's this?'

'Sweater, blouse, and scarf. Nice, aren't they?'

'Very. What are they doing on the counter?' She narrowed her eyes at him. He thought she looked a little tired, not up to a contest of wills. He would walk all over her. She clearly knew very well what he was up to, though, and was going to try to humor him into submission.

'I did a spot of business this morning,' he said. 'Not much, mind you, given that it took me nearly three hours, but for once I'm a little flush. Where, I asked myself, does a man go to spend a little mad money? And the answer jumped into my head like a trout – why, down at the boutique!'

'Will you put the stuff back, or will I? What money? Did you do something illegal?'

'Illegal! Of course not. Ring these up, Sylvia. Don't argue with your old man. You can't refuse to do business with me just because I'm a senior citizen. That's pretty clearly ageist. There's laws disallowing that.'

'*Ageist*? Where on earth did you hear that?'

'Program on the television. I'm insisting on my rights here. Just because I'm an old man and your father doesn't mean …'

Sylvia smiled at him suddenly and shrugged. 'How much money?' she asked. 'I keep a strict accounting.'

'A heap of it. I'm spending it here to keep it in the family. Think about that. How do you think all these big-money families keep the coffers topped off? They buy and sell to themselves – keep the profits in the family and the goods, too. It's simple capitalism.'

'Sounds like inbreeding. Eventually they'd end up with mutations.'

'Mutations! Have you *seen* some of those people? There's not one of those Fortune 500 crowd that has a chin left. Fins, tails, spare toes – they keep the plastic surgeons hopping. The trick is that the surgeon is their second cousin. It's all in the family. What with kickbacks and tax write-offs, the whole thing's free. Money's just electricity for that crowd.'

'I can't argue with that kind of logic,' Sylvia said, having suddenly given up the fight. She put the clothes into a bag and took his money.

'I'm going to show your mother a night on the town,' he said.

'Not Cap'n England's,' she said. 'Not the fish restaurant.'

'What's wrong with the Cap'n's?'

'There's nothing wrong with it, if what you want is fried oysters and a slab of grilled swordfish. But if you want something more romantic … there's that new place out over the water, by the bridge – the Silver Salmon. All glass. There'll be a nice moon tonight. The woman who owns it comes in here a lot. I'll give her a call and reserve a table along the window.'

'Your mother will flip. It'll be hard enough to get her down to Cap'n England's.'

'We'll gang up on her.'

'That's just what we'll do,' Roy said happily. Together, he and Sylvia could accomplish about anything. He was tempted to tell her about his book idea, to lay the statistics out on the counter and watch her eyes shoot open. But he had learned long ago that you don't whisper that sort of thing around prematurely unless you wanted to bleed the magic off. He pulled out his pocket knife, took the sweater out of the bag, and cut through the plastic string that held the tag on. Then he shook the sweater out and held it up. 'This is for you,' he said. 'For your birthday.'

'My birthday's not till January.'

'I know. Today I'm rich. In January I'm a pauper. Or maybe not. The future's full of … something. Go ahead, try it on.'

Slowly Sylvia took it from him and slipped it over her head, standing in front of the mirror and pulling it straight. She took her hair out from the back and shook it down over her shoulders.

'Just your color, isn't it?'

She looked at him, saying nothing, her mouth set in an even line.

He waited for a moment and then realized that she wasn't going to say anything, not for the moment, anyway. 'What on earth are you crying for, daughter? What a little fool I've raised.'

She threw herself on him and hugged him, and then kissed him on the cheek and pushed him toward the door. 'You're impossible,' she said. 'I love this sweater. I've tried it on a dozen times. I've wanted it for weeks. How did you know?'

'I have impeccable taste.' He gestured at his own clothes – the worn-out tweed coat, the baggy trousers, the penny loafers. 'You'd do worse than to hire me as a fashion consultant.'

'Yes,' she said. 'I could do worse than that. Dinner at seven, then, for you and Mom. I'm making the reservations. Leave Mother to me.'

'She's yours until seven.' He went out into the afternoon sunlight whistling. There was Howard, coming along up the sidewalk, looking reasonably cheerful himself. Roy waited for him. 'I've just now left her, my boy. I've softened her up. It's not my fault if you can't accomplish anything now. My advice is to compliment her new sweater.' He slapped Howard on the shoulder, climbed into the station wagon, and sped off, carrying his package home to Edith and working out in his mind how he would force her to take it. He loved a challenge, especially when it came to women. When he set his mind to it, he was irresistible.

It was dark and the wind was blowing when Sylvia dropped him off that night in Mendocino, in front of the store. He would walk around the comer and up to Mrs Lamey's, while Sylvia went off to a New Age gathering up at the top of Pine Street. A Mrs Moynihan was scheduled to channel the spirit of her dead companion – a traveler along the astral planes whom she called Chet, but whose true name was secret. She consulted him on important issues because he had a more spacious view of things. He spoke a Celtic tongue, but the words were filtered through Mrs Moynihan's cranium and were uttered as modern English.

Last week Howard would have made fun of the whole business, but he held his tongue tonight. Last week was worlds away now. And in the lonesome darkness of the north coast night nothing seemed very funny to him. He agreed to meet Sylvia back at the store at eleven, and he walked west down Main, carrying his cane, although aside from the occasional twinge, he could get along well enough without it. Wasn't that typical? When he had it, he didn't need it; when he didn't have it, he limped around like Amos McCoy.

Mrs Lamey's house was lit up, and coarse, self-conscious laughter sounded inside, as if someone were laughing at his own vulgar joke. There was music in the air – some sort of electronically spawned, almost atonal melody that sounded as if it were being torn to pieces by the wind. Through the window, Howard could see three men sitting in the living room, and another man and woman holding champagne glasses in their hands and standing in what must have been the kitchen. Bennet's house sat cold and dark across the street, and would probably stay that way, since Bennet was up in Fort Bragg working late on the haunted house. Howard wished that Bennet were home, and Uncle Roy with him. It would have been nice to have an ally or two nearby. Things might very easily turn bad – maybe quickly.

There was a gust of sea wind, and the plywood Humpty Dumpty on Bennet's roof waved solemnly at him, as if in reassurance. Howard waved back, then turned around and walked up the street, back toward Main, paying attention this time to the dark neighborhood. Forty yards down he stopped in the shadow of a cypress tree. There was only one house beyond Bennet's, a wooden shack with a tiny front porch and patchwork roof. The place was dark.

On the other side of the shack lay the bluffs – hundreds of acres of grassy meadow that made up Mendocino Headlands. There were rocky islands offshore and dozens of little coves along the deserted shoreline. Howard wasn't in the mood to do any more swimming, though, and there was something in him that didn't like the idea of being pursued out onto the deserted bluffs, especially not with a game knee and with nothing to hide behind but dead, knee-high grass.

Somehow he was certain that it would come to something like that. He was full of the premonition that he wasn't here to spend a pleasant, chatty evening. There was something in the cold air that made him edgy – a brittle atmosphere that was tensed and ready to break like a sheet of thin glass. He could feel it in the jerky music on the wind and see it in the moonlit face of the grimacing egg man on the roof. In fact, he had felt it all afternoon, but had worked hard to convince himself that it was merely his imagination, that he was still reacting to whatever it was that had caused him to hallucinate yesterday morning out in the woods.

There weren't any houses right adjacent to Mrs Lamey's, only weedy lots that backed up onto an alley, which was half blocked by a partly torn-down Volkswagen bus settled onto a couple of four-by-fours. Its side door was missing and the old curtains around the windows were ragged and drooping. Fifty yards down lay a half dozen houses running down Kelly Street, which dead-ended into berry vines and grass. He heard laughter from Mrs Lamey's house again, followed by a woman's curse.

There was nothing more to be gained by studying the street, so he stepped out of the shadows and strolled across to Mrs Lamey's door, past the dis-colored roses and the pot of fish blood. He rang the bell twice so as to be heard over the noise. No use being timid.

Mrs Lamey answered the door, dressed in her red kimono and a necklace made, apparently, of dried flowers tied together with thinly braided hair. Her face was almost hideous in the light of the porch lamp, which betrayed a crust of ghostly powder and rouge and penciled-in eyebrows. Under her kimono she wore a turtleneck sweater that covered her wattle but didn't, somehow, mask her resemblance to some species of exotic turkey. 'Well!' she cried, clapping her hands. 'It's our Howard!'

Talk died in the living room, and the man and woman in the kitchen looked out toward the door. Even at that distance Howard could see the woman roll her eyes at the man beside her. She might have been a year or two over thirty and she had the face of a lean divorcée who smoked too much and whose life had become a running complaint. The man had a pale sort of dog's face with a sparse, adolescent mustache, although he must have been in his mid-thirties. He grinned back at her and raised his eyebrows, too, and they both walked out into the living room with the pretend expressions of people who wanted nothing more than to make Howard's acquaintance. Howard stepped in through the door and waited for Mrs Lamey to undertake introductions.

Stoat stood up from where he sat on the couch. He had the pale-looking skin of a person from an icy climate with more night than day, and he smiled at Howard with perfect teeth. 'You two have met,' Mrs Lamey stated, waving her hand back and forth between Howard and Stoat, who nodded very pleas-antly and sat back down, resuming his conversation in a low voice. Howard thought that there was something nervous in him, though. He looked like a man who expected a fire alarm to go off at any second but was pretending to act perfectly naturally.

Mr Jimmers' burglar, the man in the wig, wasn't there, thank God. That would have made for a bad moment. Probably he was still in jail. Either that or Mrs Lamey couldn't afford to have him around, given his new reputation. The other two men in the room were strangers to him. One had a shock of wild gray hair and a black businessman's suit and wore a red patent-leather belt and shoes. Everything about him was gaudy and vulgar.

The other – the one who was talking to Stoat – was a thin, ascetic-looking man in his twenties, maybe, who didn't look up when Howard was intro-duced. He wore a sweater tied casually over his shoulders and smoked a cigarette in a silver holder, his pinky finger waving in front of his face as if he were thumbing his nose at the wall.

So this is a 'salon,' Howard thought, shifting his cane from one hand to the other and shaking hands very heartily with the man in the suit.

'This is Reverend White,' Mrs Lamey said. 'The Reverend is on television in the Bay Area. Quite a ministry. Started out fifteen years ago preaching on a street corner in the Market District, and now he owns half the renovated mansions along Haight Street.'

'Glad to meet you,' Howard lied, wanting to wipe his hands on his pants and trying to work out the broken-backed logic of the introduction, to make the jump from street-corner preacher to landlord.

'His is the Ministry of the Profiting Christian,' Mrs Lamey said. 'And I'll warn you that he's a powerful debater. He'll win you over, Mr Barton, just like he's won me over.'

The man looked Howard up and down, clearly taking his measure. 'Gimp leg, Mr Barton?'

'Football injury. Nothing much. It acts up in a cold climate.'

'Carry a cane, though. Are you a Christian?'

'I'm more often a sinner,' Howard said evasively.

'Wrong answer. You'll have to work on that. Don't bother with the truth *all* the time. You'll develop a low opinion of yourself. Say "Yes, I am!" and you'll feel better about yourself. I can do something about that leg of yours if you want, but it'll mean a real commitment on your part. No more of this half-ass crap you're used to. I'm a man who says what he means and gets things done. That's quite a cane.' He bent over just a little bit, studying Graham's cane, then looked hard at Howard.

Mrs Lamey put her hand on the Reverend White's elbow and said, 'Be a dear, Lawrence, and pour Mr Barton a glass of champagne, will you? That's what needs to be done first. You can lay your hands on him later.' She favored the minister with a quick smile meant to dismiss him, and the man with the cigarette holder giggled. Mrs Lamey turned to the two who'd been dallying in the kitchen, introducing the man as a literary critic and reviewer named Glenwood Touchey, also from the Bay Area, who favored deconstruction and didn't hold with frivolous views about books. Howard knew only vaguely what that meant. The woman turned out to be a writer with an unmeasurably high IQ.

'Show him your Mensa card, Gwen,' the thin man with the cigarette holder said. And then to Howard he said, 'She's had it laminated.'

Howard smiled at the man, not knowing whether he was being funny or nasty. Probably nasty. 'Where can I buy your work?' he asked the woman, anticipating the answer. 'I'd like to read some of it.'

'Ms. Bundy is largely self-published,' Mrs Lamey said for her, as if saving her embarrassment. She put her hand on the woman's arm and gave her a squeeze as if in encouragement, and then let her hand trail away down her forearm until their fingers touched for a moment.

'City Lights carries three volumes of my poetry,' the woman said resolutely to Howard. She wore khaki clothes with a sort of political air, and had the long, straight hair of a practicing political activist. There was something in her eyes that said she despised Howard, along with all the other men in the room. 'You wouldn't find them very entertaining, I'm afraid – no sex, no fistfights.'

'Her poetry is very erudite,' Mrs Lamey said. 'Very avantgarde. An utter disregard for traditional poetic contrivances. She was among the vanguard of nonsense-syllable verse and what has been called flat meter. An investigation of the theme of the existential woman that common publishers can't begin to fathom.'

'Nor men, either,' the Reverend White said, sticking his head out of the kitchen and winking broadly. 'There's a number of us that can't fathom the existential woman, I'm afraid. I've probed the subject more than once in my time, and they're still a goddamn mystery.' He guffawed, hiccuped loudly, and disappeared back into the kitchen, still chasing Howard's champagne.

The man with the cigarette holder snorted just then, as if he had tried to laugh but the laughter had come entirely out of his nose.

'He's got money,' Stoat whispered loudly at Howard, jerking his head toward the kitchen. 'That's enough to recommend him.'

'And this is our artist.' Mrs Lamey extended her hand toward the man with the cigarette holder. 'Jason, be a good boy and say hello to Howard Barton. He's the curator of a very large museum in Los Angeles, aren't you, Mr Barton?'

'Not actually,' Howard said. 'I'm afraid it's a very small museum in Santa Ana, specializing in local history more than anything else. A lot of Indian bones and pot shards. It's got pretensions of becoming more grand someday.'

'I welcome a humble man,' the artist said, standing up and bowing at the waist. 'The world is full of poseurs. It's uncommon to run across someone who sees clearly what he amounts to and has the courage to admit it.'

Howard bowed back at him, swallowing the insult as the Reverend White handed him a champagne flute, which Howard passed in front of his nose as if to better appreciate it. He thanked the man, thinking that he wouldn't bother to drink it but would pour it into a potted plant when he had the opportunity. There was no profit in being either drunk or poisoned. He had pretty dearly fallen into a nest of snakes. The entire company seemed to be prepared for him. The introductions being made were for his benefit only; he had clearly been discussed, and the idea of it put him on guard.

Ms. Bundy, the poet, cast Reverend White a disparaging glance just then and wandered off toward the kitchen again with Mr Touchey ... Howard realized that he didn't like these people at all, except maybe Stoat, ironically, who was the only one among them who wasn't playing any sort of complicated game. Howard realized that he was in danger of becoming flippant, along with all the rest of them, and that wouldn't do. Not only was he outnumbered, but what he needed was to project the notion of being enthusiastic about the company and their no-doubt-formidable talents. Things had changed since his adventures at Jimmers'. He was there with a purpose now, although he had no idea what that was.

He sat on the couch and leaned his cane up against the arm of it, resting his hand along the back and feigning interest in the conversation that had sprung up again between Stoat and the artist, who Howard still knew only as Jason. He couldn't address the man as that, though, because it was too familiar, and he couldn't address Stoat as Stoat, either, any more than he could have addressed him as Elephant or Wildebeest. So he listened to the two of them carry on about performance art, and about a Bay Area artist whose name seemed to be Heliarc and who had, apparently, developed a way to plug himself into an electrical socket in order to shoot light beams out of his eyes and elbows.

'Really?' Howard asked. 'Light beams?' He meant it to sound sincere, but the artist gave him a sharp glance and then ignored him, lighting another cigarette off the end of the last one. Mrs Lamey had disappeared, but came out just then with a tray full of tiny sandwiches made of goat cheese, nasturtiums, and dill weed.

'Nouveau California,' she said. 'The cheese is from a farm up near Caspar and the nasturtiums are out of my own garden. You'll notice that they're green instead of orange. That wasn't easy, and I won't tell you how I accomplished it, but I will say that the flavor of these canapés is unique.'

'Just ate,' Howard said, as if he regretted it vastly but couldn't do anything about it beyond that. He patted his stomach and tried to imagine what gruesome liquids Mrs Lamey had stained the nasturtiums with – pulverized tomato worms, probably.

Just then there was a squeal, like a piglet with its foot caught in a gopher hole, followed by the sound of a champagne glass smashing down onto the kitchen floor, a burst of shrill laughter, and someone being slapped. Mrs Lamey looked up sharply, along with the two men, and in that instant, when their eyes were on the kitchen, Howard poured his champagne out into a potted plant and then set his glass down decisively on the coffee table as if he had drained the glass at a single gulp.

Ms. Bundy stepped out of the kitchen and into the living room, looking back over her shoulder, her face livid. 'You'd screw a chicken,' she said, 'if you could get close enough to it without making it blind or sick.'

Stoat bent over in Howard's direction and said, 'Gwen is very witty. That's the key to the success of her poetry.' He winked cheerfully. 'She doesn't like men touching her, though, even if it's Glenwood Touchey. They're a pair,

Glenwood and Gwen, but she's afraid he might heat up untapped passions. Her verses couldn't stand it. They'd have to be written on asbestos.'

Mr Touchey came out looking sour-faced, and the artist, taking his cigarette holder out of his mouth, said, 'Don't touch me, Touchey,' in an effeminate voice, which drew an intake of breath from Mrs Lamey, who asked very sincerely whether Ms. Bundy was all right.

'You old whore,' the poetess said to her, and stalked off down the hallway in the direction taken ten minutes earlier by Reverend White. Mrs Lamey looked sincerely hurt and then a little puzzled, like a mother insulted by her daughter. Moments later there sounded a titter of laughter from a distant corner of the house, which seemed to infuriate Mr Touchey and Mrs Lamey about equally. The artist winked at Stoat, and Howard stood up and moved off toward the kitchen, carrying his cane.

'Champagne out here?' he asked Mrs Lamey, nodding in that direction.

'In the ice bucket. Be liberal with it.'

There was the ice bucket on the kitchen counter. Howard poured himself a glass but didn't taste it, looking around at the furnishings and the layout of the kitchen. Through a glass door at the back lay a service porch, and beyond that a door, which, if he had things laid out clearly in his mind, must lead out to the backyard and the alley. Left down the alley would be Ukiah Street and Little Lake and the bluffs beyond; right would lead past the blocked-up Volkswagen bus, back toward Main Street. In a pinch, he could head up Little Lake toward the highway and reach Pine Street, where Sylvia was hustling crystals and herb teas.

No one had followed him into the kitchen, and he could hear conversation rattling away in the living room. So he poked his head around the door and into the ill-lit service porch, which was immense, with a couple of big pantry cupboards, a washer and dryer, and a service-porch sink. It was carefully organized, with a big metal-boxed first-aid kit hung on the wall alongside a fire extinguisher. The linoleum floor was waxed like glass. After glancing over his shoulder he stepped across and unlocked the back door, both a chain lock and a dead bolt, and then went back out into the kitchen, where he pretended to study a row of hanging pots and pans made of polished copper.

'Do you cook, Mr Barton?' asked Mrs Lamey from the doorway. She regarded him almost happily, as if something had happened to restore her.

'Can of Spam now and then,' Howard said. 'I'd love to have a set of copper pans, although they'd probably be wasted on me.'

'Well, truthfully,' she said, 'they're rather wasted on me, aren't they? I buy most of my food at the deli. I'm too busy for domestic chores. The kitchen was designed by one of the foremost decorators on the West Coast, though, a man from Palo Alto. Do you like it?'

'It's beautiful,' Howard said truthfully. 'I love the mossy color of the counter tile. It's perfect with this white linoleum. How do you keep it spotless like this? Is there some kind of trick to it?'

'Yes. Never cook in your kitchen, and avoid walking on the floor whenever you can. My decorator insisted on it, though. He drove up here personally to study the climate and landscape. He spent a week in town before he laid a hand on my kitchen. It was a matter of studying my personal space, vis-à-vis the concrete units of my existence. It was very complicated, I assure you, but I think he succeeded admirably. I learned a great deal from him – modes of perception.'

She paused for a moment as if summoning the right words, and then said, 'I've paid attention to *your* space, Howard, over the last few days, and the place you occupy in the local – what? – universe, you might say. I've become a shrewd judge of people, of human frailty. You're a puzzler, though, aren't you?' She took a good look at the cane right then, seeming to see it for the first time. There was something like surprise in her face, which, disappeared at once. She turned toward the sink with a distracted air, cranking on the water and rinsing the already clean porcelain.

Howard shrugged, trying to think of something to say about his 'space' but unable, really, to catch her drift. 'It's a strange world you all seem to inhabit up here,' he said. 'I felt a little like an outsider, a tourist, when I got up here a few days ago. I guess that's partly why I'm here, you know. To strike up a few new acquaintances, get to know a couple of people. Don't want to be the only living boy in New York and all that.' He smiled at her.

'New York?' she said, a little puzzled.

'Just a saying from a popular song.' What would Uncle Roy do in my shoes? he wondered, raising his still full champagne glass at Mrs Lamey. Then he asked, 'What on earth is that?' and squinted out toward the window of the living room.

Mrs Lamey spun around to look, expecting heaven knew what, and Howard dumped half his champagne down the sink. Outside, the moon was higher and the night had lightened. Bennet's Humpty Dumpty waved frantically at them from across the street, driven by the wind. Howard hadn't meant to call attention to it, specifically, but Mrs Lamey apparently thought he had. 'That's a nuisance,' she said. 'An eyesore and an insult.'

'This is first-rate champagne,' Howard said, grinning loopily at her and topping off his glass again. 'I'm drinking too much of it.'

'Nonsense,' she said, brightening up. 'That's an interesting sort of walking stick you have there. Is it decoration, mostly?'

'Not really. I'm sort of lame these days. Minor knee injury.'

'Do you mind if I have a look at it? It quite fascinates me.'

'Sure,' Howard said. 'I don't mind.' He handed Mrs Lamey the cane, knowing that he shouldn't but not really seeing how to avoid it. Still it was obvious that letting her examine the thing wouldn't cause him any real trouble.

Ms. Bundy came up just then and slipped a hand through the crook of Mrs Lamey's arm. Her face was flushed and her hair disheveled.

'Glenwood has come up with a first-class idea,' the poetess said, and she whispered it into Mrs Lamey's ear, giggling just a little.

'Oh, that's naughty!' Mrs Lamey said.

Ms. Bundy let go of the old woman and took Howard's arm now. '*He's* not any kind of wallflower,' she said. Her khaki blouse was unbuttoned halfway to her navel and she was clearly braless underneath. She rubbed against Howard's arm seductively, and she tossed her hair out of her face and cocked her head at him, giving him a sort of come-hither look. He knew that he ought to be repelled by it; the more pleasant the company became, the more dangerous it was.

The fingers of her left hand snaked around his waist, vaguely tickling him, and he grinned crookedly.

'He's not the daring sort,' Mrs Lamey said, smiling at the two of them and unconsciously licking her lips.

'Stoat has his video camera with him,' Ms. Bundy said. 'We can film it, all of it.' She adjusted her blouse, pushing it open indecently, as if by mistake.

'I don't know,' Howard said, horrified now. He thought about the back door. Thank God he'd unlocked it. He could turn and bolt. Right now …

'Oh, I see what *you* thought I meant,' Ms. Bundy said, tittering through her fingers. 'He *is* a naughty boy!'

'Let's go!' shouted someone from the living room, and Touchey strode into view, waving the video camera that must have belonged to Stoat. Ms. Bundy opened her blouse for the camera, kissed Howard on the cheek, and curtsied. The Reverend White appeared just then behind Howard, carrying a ball-peen hammer, his face flushed with drink.

Howard very nearly ran for it. It was the hammer that did it. But Ms. Bundy shouted 'We're off!' just then, and hauled Howard into the living room.

'Where?' Howard shouted back at her, determined not to show his fear. This was what he had come for, wasn't it? Of course it was.

'To kill the Humpty Dumpty!' Ms. Bundy yelled, and led Howard and the rest of them out into the night.

22

'Not going along, Stoat?' Touchey asked in a sneery voice. He stopped on the front porch, talking back into the house. Stoat stood up and headed toward them, shaking his head. Reverend White trained the video camera on Jason the artist, who looped his arm around Touchey's shoulder and struck a pose, turning to profile and drawing on his cigarette holder.

'Malicious mischief isn't in my line,' Stoat said. 'This sort of prank leaves me rather cold, I'm afraid. And it accomplishes nothing at all. It's frivolous. I don't *brawl*.' There was a pettish tone to his voice, as if he thought he was being picked on.

'Howard's going to pound it,' Gwendolyn Bundy said.

'*Pound* it!' Reverend White laughed out loud. 'I dare say he will if you don't keep your hand out of his pants.' He pinched Ms. Bundy on the flank, and she turned and slapped playfully at him.

'Come *on*, Stoatie,' she said. 'Don't you want to see Howard get tough? He's the spitting image of one of those quiet detectives with steel fists, isn't he? My kind of man. Drinks Scotch out of an office bottle and calls women dames. He's going to wax manly with Humpty Dumpty – show it no mercy at all. Isn't that right, Howard?' She grinned into his face and moistened her lips, flicking her tongue at him. Her breath smelled of champagne.

'That's right,' Howard said. 'No mercy at all.' He hesitated, though, on the porch, remembering Graham's cane – his cane – and he turned to look back through the window, into the well-lit living room where Stoat had sat back down in a sulk. Mrs Lamey had evidently put it down somewhere. She waved at him happily, like somebody's mother sending a pack of children out on a scavenger hunt.

The idea of losing the cane panicked him. He was a fool to have brought it here in the first place – although he couldn't quite say why – and he was a double fool for letting it out of his sight. 'My cane,' he said, slapping his forehead. 'I'd better get it.'

'Later,' Ms. Bundy said decisively. 'We're only going across the street. We're not going to make an evening of it. This is a sort of guerrilla raid. Slash and burn. We'll come back and play with your cane later.'

Howard was doubtful, but he let himself be led away through Mrs Lamey's front-yard garden. He had no idea what sort of high jinks they were up to, but it was true, apparently, that they were only going across the street. The sea wind was cold; there was no way they'd be out long.

'It's a battle in the art wars,' Glenwood Touchey said. 'All that cut-out crap in that front yard makes me sick.'

'Throw up for us, Glen,' Ms. Bundy said. 'Get sick. I love performance art.'

'I'll show you performance art,' Touchey said, skipping across the street toward Bennet's house and kicking a wooden pansy into the air.

'Hey!' Howard shouted, taken utterly by surprise, but his shout was lost when Reverend White howled out a drunken whoop and followed along behind Touchey, chasing him with the camera. Ms. Bundy pulled up a pair of long wooden tulips and tossed one to Jason. The two of them began to fence with the tulip stems, trampling back and forth across the lawn and through the flower beds.

All of them were kept quiet now, giggling and challenging each other in hushed tones. Howard stood watching. He had to do something to stop it, but, like Stoat, he didn't like the idea of brawling, and he didn't want to lose his cane, either. Their antics reminded Howard of when he and his friends had toilet-papered lawns when he was a teenager, except that this was malicious and somehow deadly serious. They were making a hash of Bennet's flower garden for some ulterior purpose that he only barely understood, unless it was just pure, idiot meanness.

'Come on,' Ms. Bundy said to him, lunging toward him with a tulip and jabbing him in the crotch with it. 'Don't be a jerk. Have some fun for a change.' Her blouse was half untucked and pushed all askew by now, another button having been lost in the tulip skirmish. It was clear that she was just warming up. Her eyes blazed, and there was a sadistic look in them that propelled Howard a step backward toward the curb.

It occurred to him abruptly that there were worse things waiting, that this smashing-up-the-Humpty-Dumpty prank was nothing more than a prelude for grander, more depraved things later in the evening – things involving him.

Mrs Lamey stood on her front porch now, watching. Her red kimono flapped in the sea wind, and her hair blew straight out away from her head so that skinny and painted and powdered in the light of the porch lamp, she looked like something that had crept up out of a subterranean bordello. She waved at Howard, as if to encourage him, and then stepped back into the house and shut the door, having nothing more to do with the nighttime frolic.

He shrugged submissively as Ms. Bundy grabbed his arm and wrestled him toward the Humpty Dumpty. She gouged him in the ribs and then thrust her hand into his pants pocket, pushing up against him and shoving her tongue into his ear, biting him hard on the lobe.

'Hey!' he shouted, pulling away and very nearly losing a piece of flesh. The

Reverend White stood panting next to a wooden, man-milking-a-cow whirligig, bathed in light from the video camera. One of his eyes jumped with a massive twitch, and there was a runnel of drool along his mouth. He handed the camera to Jason and then grabbed the cow with both hands, yanking it off its stake, throwing it over the house, end over end like a Frisbee. 'Raise a little hell,' he said to Howard, winking broadly.

Glenwood Touchey surged past just then with the hammer upraised, leaping up and swinging it at the Humpty Dumpty. The thing was too high for him, though, and the blow was a feeble one. He cursed, taking another ineffective shot at it. 'Damn it,' he said. 'Reverend!'

'At your service,' Reverend White said, bending over. Touchey climbed onto his shoulders, and his horse stood up shakily, staggering and nearly pitching over. Touchey yelped, holding on, and then when they were nearly steady he grasped the Reverend's collar like reins, and the two of them rushed at the Humpty Dumpty, which regarded them out of faintly Asiatic eyes, waving one last morbid goodbye at Howard, as if it knew it was about to undertake the fateful fall, had perhaps been waiting for it all evening.

Ms. Bundy grasped Howard's hand, pulling him forward. She had the look in her eye of a lecher at a pornographic film. He dug his heels in, though, looking around, and then shrugged out of her grasp and stepped across to the post that had held up the whirligig cow, just as Touchey slammed away futilely at the egg man with his hammer again.

Touchey cursed out loud, furious with the painted sheet of vibrating plywood. He had his left hand curled into Reverend White's hair now, and the preacher bucked and lunged, trying to shake him loose and yelling 'Ow! Ow!' so that half of Touchey's blows hit nothing at all, but swung wide, the force of them nearly throwing him from the Reverend White's shoulders.

Howard wiggled the stake out of the ground – a length of two-by-two fir painted white and some four feet long. Gripping it like a baseball bat a foot from the bottom end, he steeled himself, drew in a deep breath, and then shouted at Touchey, 'No! Like this!' Jason moved in, flooding all of them in electric light, camera whirring as Howard set his feet. Reverend White backed away gratefully, wheezing, anxious to give Howard a chance.

'Swing away!' he said. 'One for the Gipper!' He bent into a shaky crouch in order to tumble Touchey off onto the ground.

'Hey!' Touchey yelled, holding on like a rodeo rider, clearly nowhere near finished with the smirking Humpty Dumpty, and at that moment Howard said, 'Sorry, Reverend,' and whipped the stake around, slamming the preacher across the stomach.

The preacher crumpled at the waist, his breath shooting out of him like wind from a rusty machine. Touchey shrieked and flew forward, face-first into the dirt, scattering wooden flowers and helplessly trying to throw his hammer at Howard, who sidestepped, turned at the same time, and smashed the heavy stake across the top of Jason's video camera. There was a satisfying crack of something breaking, and a large black chunk flew off and skittered away down the sidewalk. Howard took a half-step back and swung again, smashing out the lamp in a spray of glass.

Ms. Bundy lunged in furiously, clawing at Howard, raking her fingernails across his neck. He spun around, swinging the stake deliberately high so that she was forced to fall to her knees as the club whizzed past overhead. Then, after aiming one last blow at Jason, who swung the ruined camera wildly at his head, Howard loped across the street, up Kelly toward town, flinging his club into the weeds of a vacant lot.

He was around the corner and into the darkness before they were after him, and without looking back he cut hard to the left, crawling into a row of bushes along Mrs Lamey's back fence.

Footsteps approached, passed him, and pounded away down the block. He thought he could hear more going off in some other direction. They'd gotten clever and split up, maybe, thinking to surround him. Taking the time to do it had cost them. He looked out carefully. There was no one around. He heard one of them shout from a good distance away. Apparently they were scouring the bluffs for him.

He hoisted himself up and over the wooden fence, dropping heavily to the ground beyond and wincing at the pain that shot up through his ankle and knee. He was surprised to find how much he had come to depend upon Graham's cane. Since he had given it up a bare half hour ago, the pain in his leg seemed to have tripled.

Without waiting another instant he limped in through the unlocked back door, shutting it noiselessly, and climbed straightaway into one of the big service-porch pantries. It turned out to be the hot water heater closet, and had a vent in the door that he could just barely see through. He steeled himself for a long wait, running through his mind the layout of the rest of the house. Somewhere in there lay his cane, and he wasn't leaving without it.

He might have taken the chance of going right in after the cane, except that Stoat still sat in the living room, talking to Mrs Lamey. Howard could hear their voices. He wasn't keen on the idea of fighting any more, not if he didn't have to. He discovered that his knees were shaking from the last battle. It was necessary to get the cane out of there without anyone getting hurt, especially himself.

Howard resigned himself to waiting it out. There was still an hour to go before eleven. If nothing at all could be done, he could easily slip out the back door and be gone, having made an utter hash of the evening. So much for convincing the enemy that he had the soul of a mercenary.

Gwendolyn Bundy was the first one home. Howard could hear her nagging at Mrs Lamey with news of Howard's treachery. Stoat laughed out loud, pretending to be confounded that this came as any surprise. He and Mrs Lamey had watched the whole escapade through the window. The lot of them had got nothing more than they deserved. He wasn't in the business of pulling wings off flies, he said. He favored crushing them outright – quickly. That's why God had invented fly swatters.

Then Ms. Bundy asked, 'Now who will we use?' Mrs Lamey was silent.

Use, Howard wondered. What the hell did that mean? Only that his instincts had probably been correct. They had been toying with him, tenderizing him in some foul way. Gwendolyn Bundy came into the kitchen. Through one of the vent slats he could see her haul the bottle out of the bucket and tilt it back, sucking the champagne out in long gasping drafts.

'You're hurt!' she said to someone. It turned out to be Touchey, whose face was covered with garden dirt.

'He's a dead man,' the critic said, slamming his fist down onto the counter and then turning on the faucet. He filled his palms with water and splashed his face.

'What a sad thing he's not a novelist,' Gwendolyn Bundy said, petting the back of his neck. 'You could work him over in the *Chronicle*.'

'Go to hell.' Touchey strode back out as the woman opened the refrigerator door, pulling out and uncorking another bottle. The voices of Stoat and Reverend White could be heard then, arguing, and for the space of five minutes everyone was talking at once.

Someone mentioned the 'staff,' which Howard understood to mean the cane, and suddenly the voices dropped and for another five minutes there was nothing but murmuring. Then there was silence, and Howard could hear footfalls echoing away up the stairs as the lot of them shuffled away.

The cane was upstairs, then, or so it seemed. There was no way on earth to get it, either, short of a massive sort of diversion – and quickly, too. Stealing a car wouldn't work this time. An explosion would be better. If only he had three or four of the cherry bombs left over. He could light them and then throw them into the downstairs toilet and shut the lid.

It was closing in on eleven o'clock. He couldn't wait all night to act. It was possible that Sylvia, finding him missing, might come around to investigate. The very thought of it got him down to business. Who would they *use*? That's what Gwendolyn Bundy had asked Mrs Lamey. Howard looked around wildly. What would *he* use? He could unscrew the gas line, climb out of the closet, and toss a match in. That was insane, though. The old wooden house would go up like tinder along with half the people in it. And the cane, for that matter. It would divert the hell out of them, though, and would add murder and arson to his rap sheet.

He'd have to get out of the closet. That was first. He peeked through the vent, and seeing no one in the kitchen, he stepped out into the service porch and straight off saw the first-aid chest hanging there on the wall. He opened it, hauling out a pile of gauze bandages and compresses and a bottle of iodine. Then he opened the next pantry, pushing around bottles of rug shampoo and detergent and boxes of Brillo pads. Shoved in among the clutter was a plastic half gallon of bleach, which he pulled out, listening for a moment. There was the sound of talking from upstairs, but it was nothing but a mutter. They would hear him if he started scraping around.

He decided that the moment had come to act. There was no time for a debate between the devil and the angel that sat on either shoulder. Providence had seen to it that Mrs Lamey had a well-stocked service porch, and it was clearly bad luck not to make use of providential gifts. That's what Uncle Roy would say, anyway.

He opened the bleach bottle and carefully drained the iodine into it, putting the top back on and swirling it around. Then he set the bottle into the service-porch sink and counted to sixty while he pulled out his pocket knife and opened it, shoving the blade into the plastic bottle a half inch from the bottom. Bleach dribbled out around the blade as he wiggled it back and forth, widening the hole until the bleach ran out in a rivulet down the drain. After a moment the flowing stopped, and Howard worked the knife lower, draining off most of the rest of the bleach. Then he twisted the knife sideways, cutting the whole top of the bottle off.

Left in the bottom was a chalky precipitate beneath a thin pool of bleach. He made a big wad of the gauze bandage and poured everything through it and down the sink, catching the precipitate and shaking as much of the moisture out of it as he could. What should he do with it? He wanted something sensational. Heat would do it.

Stepping hurriedly into the kitchen, he opened the drawers one after another until he found one that was full of ladles and spatulas and corncob skewers. The stuff inside clanked around when he searched through it, and he had to slow himself down and work carefully and quietly. There it was – a wire-mesh tea strainer. He stuffed the saturated gauze into the strainer and then closed and latched it, stepping across to turn on the gas stove.

In order to dry it out, he dangled the strainer over the heat, careful not to jostle it, and turning his face away so that if it blew up then and there, at least he wouldn't be blinded by it. He'd only done this once before, just a small one in a high school chemistry class, and the bomb had blown his desk open. He needed more than that now – something to send them running, to put the fear into them.

The stuff was nearly dry, and the whole business hadn't taken him six minutes. The rest was a matter of luck. Either it would work or it wouldn't. He shoved it into a sock from the clothes hamper, just to keep it from clanking too much, and laid the sock gently into the clothes dryer before turning it on.

They might hear it bouncing around in there, but that was a necessary risk. A couple of minutes on high heat ought to produce spectacular results. He slipped quickly to the kitchen door, and, seeing no one in the living room, went out through the front and crouched in the shadows of the porch to wait and think things through.

There wasn't any time for thinking. Almost at once there was a hellish explosion on the service porch. Howard had thought that the dryer would muffle it, but the sound was almost cataclysmic, like a dynamite blast, and there was the clamor of stuff crashing to the floor when something – the dryer door, probably – blew off and slammed against the opposite wall. The echo of it reverberated down the kitchen, and in the heavy silence that followed there sounded the clatter of footsteps on the stairs.

The entire crowd of them appeared in a rush. Crouching on the front porch, Howard watched them surge into the kitchen. Then he stood up and slipped in through the front-porch door, running for the second floor.

Someone shouted 'Shit! Look!' and someone else shrieked, probably Mrs Lamey, and then hollered something about the fire extinguisher. Howard heard it from halfway up the stairs. At the top, he pushed into the first room he came to.

It was big, wallpapered in a bloodred Victorian floral, and there was a circular bed very nearly in the center of the room. His cane lay on it. On the floor were a little propane torch, a saw, and Touchey's ball-peen hammer. They had been working at the cane – sawing pieces of it off. There was wood dust on the bedspread, and the tip of the cane was cut flat. The room was heavy with a resiny, sappy smell. The bits that had been cut off were gone.

Howard grabbed the cane and went out into the hall again, stopping at the top of the stairs to listen and catch his breath. He could just barely hear people talking down in the kitchen. Then there was the sound of the back door shutting. They would think he exploded the dryer and then went out the back. Maybe they would go out, too, thinking to follow … He tiptoed down the stairs, hugging the wall.

The front door still stood open, a long six yards from the base of the stairs. He stopped, hunkering down to take one quick look toward the kitchen door before running for the street, and in that moment Glenwood Touchey and Jason the artist stepped out of the kitchen, laughing between themselves, as if they thought that the blowing up of the dryer had been a wonderful trick. Then a look of doubt and suspicion crossed Touchey's face, and he stared at the open front door.

Howard jumped for it. There was nothing at all to be gained from waiting. He leaped off the bottom stair, waving the cane and landing on his bad leg, stumbling, and nearly going down. The two men regarded him momentarily with a look of wonder, as if they weren't sure what he meant by any of it. Then Touchey shouted, picked up a heavy glass ashtray, and threw it at Howard, missing him by three feet. The ashtray smashed through the front window in a shower of breaking glass, and Howard took a vicious swipe at Jason with the cane when the artist moved to cut him off.

Howard banged right into the screen door, knocking it open. He ran straight up the sidewalk and around into the alley. There was shouting in the house – Touchey and Jason hollering for help, not wanting to go out into the night alone. Howard climbed into the Volkswagen bus and crouched in the darkness between the two rear seats.

He could smell old vinyl and grease and upholstery stuffing as he waited there, thinking that this was either a good idea or a dead-bad one. They wouldn't expect him to stick around, now that he'd got his cane back. If they checked the bus, though …

He heard them running off, up and down the street. After a moment Stoat's car started up, its bad starter whirring for a moment before catching. Howard waited until there was silence and then peeked up over the top of the seat. The alley was dark and empty. The night was wearing on. Sylvia might already have finished hobnobbing with the spirit world and gone back to the shop. Climbing out of the bus, Howard headed that way, down the alley toward Main, sticking to the shadows and watching over his shoulder.

The store was dark. Sylvia was still up at Mrs Moynihan's. Howard set out in that direction, suddenly wanting to be there, too. Who could say what Mrs Lamey's little circle would attempt next? Listening for approaching cars and footfalls, he hurried up Main, all the way to Evergreen before turning up toward Pine. The village was dark and silent and the moon was high, lighting up the street. Abruptly he started to run, full of premonition, and just then a car turned up from Main, cruising slowly. Its headlights caught him, and the car sped up.

Vaulting a picket fence, Howard ran across the shabby front lawn of an old house. He rounded the corner into the backyard, bowling through a covey of metal trash cans and heading straight into the adjacent yard. He heard a door open and someone shout. A dog began to bark and then another joined it as Howard jogged on, past the backs of dark houses. Looking between two of them, he could see Stoat's car out on the street, keeping pace with him. There were three men in it – Stoat, Touchey, and Jason.

Howard leaned heavily on his cane as he jogged. There was a fence in front of him, blocking off the next backyard. He stopped, looking out again toward the street. A light came on in the top story of the house behind him, and he realized that there was nothing to be gained by trying to escape over fences. He headed for the sidewalk again and found himself fifty feet from the corner of Pine Street.

Stoat pulled up beside Howard as he panted along toward Pine, looking hard at street addresses. Howard had run himself out. That had to be clear to the three in the car, who shouted encouragement at him through the rolled-down windows, merely following along now, enjoying themselves, but none of them seeming willing to confront him on the sidewalk.

There was Sylvia's car parked in the drive of a rambling white house. Lights shined through the front window. Howard turned and jogged up the walk, knocking hard on the door. He could hear voices inside. Stoat's car stopped abruptly and backed crazily into the curb. The three piled out, heading up the walk after him as he whacked on the door again. It opened, and, as if in a cartoon, he nearly knocked on the face of a matronly-looking woman in a sack dress, who stared back at him half suspiciously.

Sylvia stood behind her, though, and at once said, 'Howard!' as if she were happy as anything to see him.

The woman smiled a little then, looking past him at the other three on the walk. Howard panted for breath, almost unable to speak. 'Won't you come in?' the woman said pleasantly.

'We'd love to,' Stoat told her, stepping up onto the porch. 'We're friends of Sylvia. We're visiting in the area, and Sylvia was nice enough to invite us around. We can't stay but a moment, though. I hope we're not too late.'

Howard stepped in through the door, past Mrs Moynihan, and drew his finger across his throat so that Sylvia could see it. Sylvia shrugged. What could she do?

A blond-haired woman sat on a sofa in a big room beyond, along with a man in a flannel shirt, with a beard and a large nose. He wore a half dozen big pieces of gaudy Navajo jewelry and had the flushed and broken-veined face of a heavy drinker. On a low coffee table lay a scattering of crystals, copper and silver jewelry, and a stack of paperback books and tracts.

'We've interrupted something!' Stoat said, as if he regretted being impolite. 'I was afraid of this, Howard.'

Sylvia had disappeared. Howard looked around wildly, hoping that she would appear to rescue him, but she was gone. 'Yes,' Howard said, trying to look apologetic. 'Are you a fancier of New Age philosophy, Mrs Moynihan?' He picked up one of the paperbacks. On the cover were three out-of-focus butterflies and the title 'Who You Are.'

She looked at him skeptically as he smoothed out his hair.

'Mrs Moynihan is not a "fancier" of philosophies,' the man with the beard said.

'Of course.' Howard smiled at him, wondering where the hell Sylvia was. She appeared just then from down the hall, and winked at Howard, who had no idea on earth what the wink meant. 'I met Rodia Davis at Esalen last year,' he continued, pulling the name out of a hat, talking wildly.

Mrs Moynihan widened her eyes. 'I'm sorry ...' she said.

'The woman who channels the spirit of the Carpathian slave. Wonderful book that she's written, out in paperback from Amethyst Imprints. Do you have a copy, hon?'

'No,' Sylvia said, looking doubtful. 'I might have one at the shop, though ...'

'Let's just go round and find it, shall we?' Stoat asked, putting his hand on Howard's shoulder. 'Seriously, we're interrupting things here. Coming along, Sylvia? Or should we pick you up in – what? A half hour, say?'

'A Carpathian slave?' Mrs Moynihan asked. 'That's fascinating.'

'I could have sworn that the Carpathians were a mountain system,' Touchey said cheerfully. 'Are you sure you mean Carpathian?'

Mrs Moynihan gestured at the couch. 'Do sit down,' she said. 'We were just finishing up, actually. Most of the guests have gone. This is Susan MacIntyre.'

The blond-haired woman on the couch smiled and nodded. There was a hammered-copper comb in her hair and she wore a quartzite ring as big as a goose egg. 'I've got to be going myself,' she said, standing up, and after a few parting pleasantries she hurried through the door and was gone.

'Glass of wine?' Mrs Moynihan asked.

The bearded man scowled and checked a wristwatch that was hidden beneath the sleeve of his flannel shirt. 'Coming onto eleven,' he said.

Sylvia gestured at him. 'This is *Mister* Moynihan.'

'Glad to meet you.' Howard leaned over and shook hands with the man, who looked more doubtful than ever. 'You know,' Howard said, 'you have an uncanny resemblance to Abraham Maslow,' which was a lie, or probably was. Howard couldn't recall ever having seen a picture of Maslow.

'Do you think so?' Mrs Moynihan said, looking sideways at her husband, maybe a little skeptically.

'Right on the money.' Howard sat down on the couch, settling in comfortably. 'A glass of wine would be spectacular, actually – as long as we're not keeping you folks up.'

'Of *course* we're keeping them up, Howard.' Stoat shook his head at him, as if he were a naughty boy.

'Jason here is an artist,' Howard said, nodding at the scowling Jason, who still hadn't sat down.

'A painter,' Mrs Moynihan said. 'How lovely. I paint myself. *Please* sit down.' Jason sat, dusting off the chair cushion first.

'Don't tell me that's your work on the wall there?' Howard asked, gesturing at two massive, unframed seascapes sitting side by side on the wall opposite. Together they composed a single scene of a rocky cove with waves the color and texture of cheesecake breaking on the rocks. A fishing boat stood out to sea, blocked in heavily with what must have been a rope end – the sort of picture that might easily have hung on the wall of a suburban bank.

Howard heard Touchey mutter something under his breath, and Jason seemed about to explode. 'That reminds me of Bigler,' Howard said, 'only the work here is much finer – far keener eye for detail.'

'Bigler?' Jason asked, accepting a glass of white wine. 'Who on earth ...?'

'Howard is the curator of a very upscale museum in Los Angeles,' Sylvia interrupted, talking to Mrs Moynihan. 'Getty money.'

'*Really!*' Mrs Moynihan said.

'Well,' said Howard. 'I can tell you this much: the oils on the wall there are very nice, no matter who painted them. Superb rendering of detail. Don't you agree, Jason?'

The artist said nothing.

'Mrs Moynihan painted those herself,' Mr Moynihan said. 'She's been hung in several galleries in town.'

'I'm certain of it,' Touchey said. 'Bigler, though. I haven't heard of him, either. Was he a Carpathian slave, too?'

Howard looked sharply at him, as if he had insulted Mrs Moynihan's paintings.

'I'm interested in hearing about that,' the woman said, too modest, perhaps, to carry on about her own paintings. Howard found that he liked her. There was something big and round and generous about her. 'What was the woman's name again?' she asked. 'I'd like to read her book.'

Howard searched his mind. He couldn't remember it, having pulled it out of the air in the first place.

'Rodia Davis,' Sylvia said helpfully. 'I think that's what you said, isn't it, Howard? Maybe you could search out a copy for Mrs Moynihan tomorrow.' She smiled broadly at him. Then to Mrs Moynihan she said, 'Howard is my father's nephew. He's a Barton.'

'*Is* he? Your uncle is a gravely misunderstood man,' she said to Howard. 'His spirit museum was a fascinating place. Men of real vision suffer in a culture that runs on greed and cynicism.'

'Isn't *that* the truth?' Stoat said, shaking his head sadly.

Mr Moynihan drained his glass. 'Mrs Moynihan is a channeler herself.'

'Are you?' Stoat asked, seeming genuinely enthused. Touchey and Jason sat silently, as if not trusting themselves to speak.

'She's in touch with an entity that is known only as "Chet," ' the bearded man said gravely, then looked around as if he expected one of them to challenge him. 'He was here tonight, in this room. It was not his corporeal self, of course. It was his astral projection.'

'Does he know Howard's Carpathian?' Touchey asked.

'He spoke to us for nearly twenty minutes tonight,' Sylvia said, ignoring him. Touchey snorted under his breath. 'Any tips on the market?'

'Glenwood!' Howard said, scowling faintly. Then, aside to the old man, he made the quick gesture of someone tippling, then winked and shook his head in a rapid little negative.

'Oh,' the man said flatly, shaking his own head.

Stoat checked his watch. 'Well, I'll be damned. Coming up on eleven-thirty. We've really got to be going. Thank you both so much for the wine.' He stood up, and so did Jason and Touchey.

'Well, that *is* a shame,' Mrs Moynihan said. 'Thank you for saying such nice things about my paintings.' Her husband stood up and collected the wine-glasses from the table, as if disposing of the glasses would also get rid of his unwanted guests. He wiped a water ring off the tabletop with the sleeve of his shirt, scowling tiredly.

Howard worked hard to think of something to stall things. He had to *act*, to do something to save them. It was too late for more conversation. He could hardly call the police; he had put in far too active a day for that. Sylvia looked at him suddenly as if puzzled. 'I think I've lost one of my stones,' she said.

'Oh, no!' Mrs Moynihan lamented. 'Sure it wasn't one of the ones that Susan bought?'

'No,' Sylvia said. 'It was a pyrite orb, about the size of a golf ball. I bet it's rolled under the couch or something.'

'Perhaps we can all have a look around,' Howard said to his three adversaries. 'It can't have gone far. Glenwood, crawl behind the chair, would you?'

'For the love of ...' Touchey started to say, but Stoat cut him off with a gesture.

'Have a look under the chair, Glen.'

Howard peered under the couch, pretending to search for the mythical ball of pyrite.

'We'll turn the place upside down in the morning,' Mr Moynihan said. 'No need to be crawling around the room now. Not at this time of night.'

Just then the doorbell rang, and Mrs Moynihan said, 'Isn't that a surprise? It's a regular party,' and she stepped across to open it.

'Christ on a bicycle,' Mr Moynihan said. He strode off toward the kitchen, muttering and carrying the wineglasses.

Howard hefted Graham's cane and moved in behind Jason and Touchey and Stoat, standing between them and the rest of the house. He was afraid it would be Ms. Bundy and Mrs Lamey and the Reverend White, having tracked down Stoat's car. This would be bad business. He shouldn't have come here at all. Now Sylvia was involved, along with the innocent Moynihans.

But when the door swung open, there stood Uncle Roy and old Bennet and the man from the restaurant in the harbor, who looked like a hod carrier and wore a stained butcher's apron smeared with what must have been blood. Behind them, half in shadow, were two men wearing the patchwork clothes of gluers. The one on the left could have passed for Moses in an illustration out of Exodus, except that in his right hand he held a tire iron that he slapped against his leg.

23

'Father!' Sylvia cried happily.

Touchey backed up a step, as if getting set to sprint for the back door. Even Stoat seemed to pale visibly, and Jason the artist was shifty-eyed and scared, like a nasty sort of petty criminal collared at last by the law. Howard jabbed Touchey in the back with the tip of his cane, and the man turned on him furiously. Howard widened his eyes and tipped his head toward the door as if inviting him out onto the front lawn.

'Hello, Mrs Moynihan!' Uncle Roy said happily.

'Good evening, Mr Barton,' Mrs Moynihan said.

'We've come to collect Sylvia and Howard.' Uncle Roy had a big, cheesy smile on his face, as if he'd just found out that the world was his oyster.

'What a wonderful young man her Howard is,' Mrs Moynihan said, looking dubiously now at Roy's friends. 'He's astonishingly knowledgeable. I believe he has some of his uncle's genetic material.'

'He's a peach,' Uncle Roy said.

'Where's my car?' Stoat asked suspiciously, looking past them toward the street.

Uncle Roy looked baffled. He shrugged and made a long face, as if he couldn't be blamed for whatever had happened to Stoat's car. Then he smiled broadly again and bowed like Mr Pickwick, gesturing toward the lawn. 'Come on out,' he said. 'We'll have a look around. I think maybe it was stolen by that damned Arab crowd that runs the deli up in Caspar. What was their name? Mohammed something or other. Same bunch that beat up Jimmers, I bet, and then came back and stole his shed.'

They filed out of the house then, waving goodbye to Mrs Moynihan, who closed the door behind them. 'Run these boys down the road apiece, will you?' Uncle Roy asked one of the gluers. 'Put them through the usual paces.'

'What?' Touchey said. 'Wait. I'm not going anywhere.'

Uncle Roy smiled at them. 'Little ride. Night air will do you good.'

At the curb sat a gluer vehicle, the Day of the Dead Chevy that had been parked up at Sammy's three days ago. The plaster-of-Paris skulls glowed ghostly white in the moonlight. Miniature skeletons wearing top hats and carrying canes sprawled across the hood in a heap as if they'd been shoveled out of a mass grave with a skip loader.

Glenwood Touchey began to back away, and then turned to run, pushing Uncle Roy aside and bowling past the two gluers. Old Bennet shoved out his foot and tripped him, though, and Touchey sprawled onto his hands and knees in the grass, grunting softly. The aproned man pulled Touchey to his feet again, obligingly dusting a few grass clippings off Touchey's clothes and then wiping his own hands on his bloody apron. Then he pointed toward the Chevy, explaining something to Touchey in a low voice, as if Touchey were a child being told about the terrible dangers of playing in the street. One of the gluers, his face set like concrete, latched on to Touchey's arm and hustled him toward the waiting car.

Stoat followed almost willingly, as if he would just as soon get it over with and not lose his dignity in the process, and Jason made a show of doing the same, although his face betrayed him and he looked dispirited, like a wet dog, and he glanced around nervously as if looking for a chance to run for it. It was too late, though, and he climbed into the car along with his two friends, the three of them sitting there wooden-faced, like mannequins. Touchey's hands fumbled on his knees, drumming out a nervous rhythm, and he bit at his upper lip, looking to the left and right and fidgeting around, staring hard at the door panels. Then, as if someone had poked him with a cattle prod, he crawled across Jason to hammer at the window, a look of terror on his face. Jason shoved him back into his seat, but immediately he was up again, trying to climb over into the front seat now.

'He's just discovered that there's no backseat door or window handles,' Uncle Roy said cheerfully to Howard, like a sportscaster delivering a play-by-play.

'Father!' Sylvia cried, putting her hand over her mouth. The gluers climbed silently into the front seat, rolling Touchey back over onto the laps of his companions.

Then Uncle Roy leaned down to speak through the passenger window, talking to the three in back. 'You boys are going on a little retreat,' he said, 'up to the hills. Diet of sprouts and berries. Fresh air. New outlook.'

'You'll wish you were dead!' Touchey shouted at him from the backseat, his face twisted by hatred and fear.

Uncle Roy looked at him for a moment, as if Touchey were a cockroach on a sidewalk. 'Put the *machine* on that one if he acts up,' Roy said to the two in front. 'But keep the electrodes away from his salivary glands. And for Christ's sake, don't turn it up above twelve volts this time. It isn't a goddamn hot-dog cooker.'

The Chevy rolled away up the street then, carrying the three stricken prisoners and their strange jailers. It turned south toward the highway.

Uncle Roy looked as if he'd just eaten a bad snail. He heaved a long sigh and rubbed his forehead tiredly. 'Poor bastards,' he said, watching them motor away. 'I hope they deserve all this.' He widened his eyes at Howard. 'Strike that. I *know* they do. One of them does, anyway. That one in the middle – his face was an advertisement.'

'That's him, all right,' Bennet said. 'I'll bet you a shiny new dime. Either him or the other one, name of – what was it? Marmot? What the hell kind of a name is that?' Bennet stood on the lawn with the man in the apron, who shrugged at the question. Both of them had their arms folded across their chests, like bodyguards waiting for a signal.

'What'll happen to them?' Howard asked. 'I'm not sure what they deserve, but—'

'Deserve?' Uncle Roy said. 'Lord knows what they deserve. The Sunberries are just going to give them a thrill. Silent bunch of guys, gluers. They won't say a word. That'll drive your men nearly nuts. They'll take them up into the hills above Albion, push them out of the car, and let them walk back down – not more than three or four miles. Call it six. They'll be snug in bed by three in the morning.'

He pulled a wad of bills out of his pocket and thumbed through them tiredly, sorting out the hundreds and straightening the wrinkles out of them.

'Could have got a sight more for it,' the man in the bloody apron said.

Uncle Roy grunted. 'Maybe. Say, Howard, you haven't met Lou Gibb, have you? Not officially?' He gestured at his friend, who shoved out his hand. Howard shook it.

'We ran past each other last night down at the harbor,' Howard said, 'but there wasn't any time for introductions.'

'Me and your uncle go way back,' Gibb said.

Uncle Roy nodded, managing to smile again. 'Gibb here owns the Cap'n England. Chief cook and bottle washer, too. Answers the phone out back for us. Nobody rings up a pay phone, mostly. So when it does ring it's probably for us, and Lou grabs it. When he got Sylvia's call tonight, he was doing a spot of business with those three gluers, trading for a few cases of hooch.'

'Two gluers,' Howard said.

'Well, there was the one that took Stoat's car. You didn't see him. We delivered the car out of bondage. Liberated it. Money for the cause. Next time Stoat sees the car he won't know it from Adam. The Sunberries were talking about turning it into a motorized flower bed. Here you go, Lou.' Uncle Roy counted out a few bills, pocketing the rest.

'Give it to Mrs Deventer,' Lou said, waving the money away. 'I don't need it.'

Uncle Roy nodded, not arguing with him. 'Eight hundred bucks, cash on the barrelhead. What do you figure is blue-book on a car like that?'

'Five thousand easy,' Bennet said.

'Yeah, but those Sunberries did us a hell of a favor, didn't they? They'll be ready to do us another one now, *quid pro quo*.'

Sylvia was pretty clearly seething. 'What the hell is going on?' she asked. 'Stoat didn't hit Mr Jimmers on the head. He wasn't even there. Howard said so.'

'That's right,' Howard said. 'None of them were.'

'You two shouldn't fret,' Uncle Roy said to Sylvia. 'Let me worry about it. Lou here wanted to beat them to a pulp right out here on the lawn. They got Mrs Deventer this evening, coming back down from Willits.'

'What?' Howard asked, shocked. Somehow he hadn't anticipated anything like that.

'What do you mean?' Sylvia said. 'Is she …?'

'No, she's not dead. Dead drunk, actually. That's what saved her. Crash tossed her around the floorboards like a rag doll. If she'd have been sober, and tensed up, there's no telling what would have happened. They took her up to the hospital and set her arm and then drove her back down to her house not a half hour before you called.'

'How do you know it was them?' Howard asked.

'Someone loosened the lug nuts on the right front wheel,' Bennet said. 'Must have done it while she was in at her sister's, up in Willits. Road up that way is nothing but curves.' He ran his hand through his hair and then shook his head darkly. 'I put new pads on the brakes a week ago, and I tightened them lugs down. I know I did. Now the blame falls to me. I'd be in it deep if she was hurt bad. They towed the car back down to her house.'

'There was trouble over at your place tonight, too,' Howard said to Bennet. 'They kicked your flower beds apart and tried to break down the Humpty Dumpty. I did what I could to stop it.'

'The creeps,' Uncle Roy said, heading for the station wagon. 'Let's get over there.'

Bennet shrugged. 'Not much lost if all they did was kick wooden flowers around. Nothing that can't be patched up.'

'If you boys don't need me,' Lou Gibb said, 'I'm out of here. I got three or four hours' work left.'

'Take some of this dough, damn it,' Uncle Roy said to him, turning around and pulling out the money again. 'Enough to pay for that Sunberry whiskey, anyway.'

Gibb hesitated, then took what Uncle Roy offered him, shoving it down into his pocket. 'Give the rest to Mrs Deventer, though.'

'Sure I will.' Uncle Roy nodded a goodbye to him as Gibb climbed into his own car and started it up. 'Hell of a good man, isn't he?' Roy asked. They watched Gibb pull away from the curb. 'There was a book I read once: one guy kept asking people what was the most surprising thing – that people could treat each other so good or so damned nasty. I think about that a lot. Then I run into people like Gibb, or Mrs Moynihan here, and I see that they treat people square and friendly and it doesn't take any kind of effort at all. It's like breathing to them. Nothing to it. What does that mean?'

'That some of us have a long way to go,' Howard said, yawning. 'It doesn't answer your man's question, though.'

'I guess not,' Uncle Roy said. 'Let's roll.' He and Bennet climbed into Roy's station wagon and drove off up Pine, swinging around toward Main.

Howard and Sylvia followed in Sylvia's car. It was midnight, and the streets and houses were dark. Trees swayed in the sea wind, and there was a winter chill in the air that made Howard think of the three men who would very shortly be walking home up the Coast Highway in their fashionable sweaters and shoes. For a moment he half hoped that they'd catch a ride with some late-night traveler, but then he thought of Mrs Deventer and her smashed-up Pontiac and the moment passed. Before they'd driven the four or five blocks to Bennet's house Howard was asleep.

The sound of a car door slamming woke him up, but he decided not to get out. There hadn't been all that much damage done, except to the whirligig cow. The others could deal with it. Howard felt as if he hadn't gotten any sleep in about six weeks. Tomorrow morning – this morning, that is – he would sleep till noon. He watched groggily as they moved around on the lawn. Uncle Roy was fired up, letting loose the energy now that he'd kept bottled up back at Mrs Moynihan's house. Howard heard him shout something, and then saw him stride toward the street, in the direction of Mrs Lamey's. Sylvia and Bennet chased him down, pushing him back toward the station wagon, but he broke away from them and hurried across to pound on her door.

Wearily Howard tried to climb out of the car. His knee joint felt packed with sand, and his leg was so stiff that he had to pick it up with his hands in order to shift it. It wouldn't do for Uncle Roy to start harassing Mrs Lamey at midnight. There were probably laws to protect landlords from wild tenants. He stood up in the weedy gutter, nearly falling down, and hung on to the car roof for support. He pulled the cane out and leaned on it. At once he felt lighter, and some of the pain and stiffness seemed to leak away into the vegetation beneath his feet.

Uncle Roy beat on Mrs Lamey's door again, kicking it finally with the toe of his boot. 'Wake the hell up, you old pig!' he shouted, cupping his hands and yelling toward the second story. The banging reverberated through the darkness. Sylvia and Bennet both pulled him away again, but it was like trying to shift a piano. Uncle Roy leaned past Sylvia and kicked furiously at the already broken front window. What was left of the pane shattered to pieces, tinkling to the floor inside.

'I know that's you, Roy Barton!' Mrs Lamey's voice called down from upstairs. Howard could see her face outlined in the dark, half-open window. 'The whole street knows it's you! I'll have you jailed for assault!'

'Try me!' Uncle Roy shouted back. 'Come down here and I'll shove your damned rent money down your throat!' Wrenching furiously loose again, he picked up the bowl still half full of fish blood and splashed it over the front door as if to mark the house in some grisly, Old Testament manner. He allowed himself to be pulled away toward the street then, still cursing, as Mrs Lamey slammed the upstairs window. Lights blinked on then.

'She's calling the cops,' Bennet said.

Uncle Roy breathed hard, nearly flattened by the exertion. 'Shit' he said, hauling the wad of bills out of his pocket again. 'Ditch this in your house.'

'Sit down somewhere,' Sylvia said to Howard when she saw him limping across toward them.

Bennet nodded at him. 'Come up on my porch and sit in the rocker.'

The four of them stepped onto Bennet's lawn, and it was then that Howard saw that the Humpty Dumpty had been wrecked. It lay crazily in the flower bed, smashing down wooden tulips. Someone had pried its arms and legs off and thrown them here and there around the yard, and its spring mechanism had been wrenched back and forth until it hung from half torn out screws, twisted and bent. The plywood head and body of the thing were cracked in half, and long splinters of fragmented plywood had torn away so that the painted face was mostly obliterated by what looked like jagged, grass-blade shadows.

'It's a wreck,' Bennet said. 'There's no fixing it, not busted in half like that.'

'Dirty, rotten sons of bitches ... Did you see them do this, Howard?' Uncle Roy looked at him, not angrily now, but as if suddenly worried.

'Not this, no. They kicked the flowers around a little when I was here. That's all. I broke it up and then sneaked back into Mrs Lamey's house and blew up her clothes dryer.'

'Did you!' Uncle Roy said, as if hearing good news at last. 'Why?'

'Well, they'd stolen Graham's cane, and I decided to get it back. So I blew up the dryer and when they all ran downstairs, I went up and got it. Then they chased me down to Mrs Moynihan's.'

'You were here, though, for some of this?' Uncle Roy gestured at the lawn. 'At first, yes.'

'How about the old lady? Was Mrs Lamey out here, too, raising hell?'

'No,' Howard said. 'She stayed home.'

'Of course she did. When you were gone she and whoever was left over came back out here and finished the job.' Uncle Roy stood thinking for a moment. 'Sylvia,' he said, 'get Howard out of here. Quick. We'll handle this. If Howard sticks around, she'll finger him, too – say she saw him with the other hooligans out breaking up Bennet's stuff. She'll get us all if we don't look sharp. We'll skin through, though, as long as that damned Stoat doesn't make it back down the hill while the cops are here.' He thought for a moment, squinting his eyes. 'Yes, that's it. You and Howard vamoose. Get home and put Howard to bed. He's earned his pay.'

Bennet stepped back out of the house just then. 'Coffee's on,' he said.

'Did you ditch the money?' Uncle Roy asked him.

'Under the floor.'

'Get four hundred back out, will you?'

'*Now* you tell me,' Bennet said. 'You aren't going to give me change, are you?'

Uncle Roy shook his head. 'There isn't going to be any change.' He waved decisively at Howard and Sylvia, gesturing toward the road. 'Get going,' he said.

Howard climbed gratefully back into Sylvia's Toyota, and together they drove down to Main Street and swung left toward the highway, cruising past Sylvia's darkened store. In his mind he didn't want to abandon his uncle. The rest of him, though – his muscles and joints and bones – was happy to. Anyway, Uncle Roy was good at this sort of thing. Howard couldn't teach him any tricks. And there was no doubt at all that Mrs Lamey *would* implicate Howard in something if she had half a chance to – the clothes dryer atrocity at the very least. She had invited him over with the most friendly and hospitable intentions, and he had blown her service porch up with a homemade bomb …

'Go to sleep,' Sylvia said. 'He'll be all right. Here.' She pulled a parka out of the back and handed it to him, and he stuffed it against the seat and door as a pillow, settling himself against it. 'What the heck happened to your neck?' She touched him on the spot where Ms. Bundy had raked him with her fingernails, and he winced at the raw streak of pain.

'I had a little fracas with another woman tonight,' he said sleepily.

'Another woman?'

'I'm afraid so. She was a feisty one, too.'

'*Another* woman? Who's the first one? You can't have another one without having one to start with.'

She was being playful, but Howard was too tired to carry on in that vein. 'Maybe you are,' he said, watching her face out of half-shut eyes.

She smirked at him, as if to say that she knew he was being silly, as usual. At least she hadn't denied it. But was she being agreeable or putting him off? This was no time to work through it. She looked worried and doubtful and tired, Howard realized. She was single-handedly keeping the whole family afloat, working overtime to sell her strange wares to the Mrs Moynihans of the world and trying to save Howard and Uncle Roy from themselves with what little time she had left over.

472

'You're a brick,' he said to her. 'Will you help me break into Jimmers' place tomorrow afternoon?'

'Enough!' she said. 'Give it a rest.'

'No time for that now. The merry-go-round's spinning too fast. We can't crawl off anymore.' She sighed, shrugging her shoulders as if she didn't trust herself to say anything. Howard squeezed her arm again. 'He *will* be all right, you know. It would be better for you to believe it.' She cast him a little smile and then winked, as if recalling just what sort of a man her father was.

Up on the highway they passed a patrol car turning down onto Lansing Street.

The whine of the power saw woke him next morning. It was eleven o'clock, and sunlight streamed through the window. Uncle Roy hadn't spent the night in jail, then. Howard had slept dreamlessly through the night and morning, and he could easily turn over now and drift off again.

There was too much to do, though. He bent his lame knee, and it was stiff and sore, although far better than it had been last night. He wrapped the bandage around it again, then grabbed the cane and hobbled to the window. Uncle Roy was bent over the saw, cutting up the rest of the lumber. He tossed a couple of pieces of scrap into the weeds and laid a clean piece on the pile, then stopped to drink from a coffee mug.

Fueled by the idea of coffee, Howard dressed and went out into the kitchen, taking the cane with him. He was determined not to let it out of his sight again, although he didn't know quite why. His knee loosened up when he moved, and he felt like the Tin Man, creaking back to life after rusting stiff in the rain.

Aunt Edith appeared, carrying a feather duster. She had the look on her face of someone longing for past, simpler times. 'Good morning,' she said. 'Coffee's probably cold by now.'

'Hot enough,' Howard said, pouring milk and sugar into the cup she handed him. She was looking steadily at him, as if taking his measure. He wondered what she knew about yesterday's shenanigans, and suddenly he felt as if he were twelve or thirteen and had been caught throwing eggs at houses. 'Uncle Roy all right?'

'He'll always be all right. He doesn't know how to doubt himself. He just rides along on his enthusiasms.'

'He got home late last night.'

'After two. He said that Bennet and him closed down the Tip Top Lounge, but he hadn't been drinking.'

'No,' Howard said. 'It wasn't that. There was a little bit of trouble down in Mendocino, and he bailed me out.'

'I know what kind of trouble, or can imagine it.' She brushed her hair out of her eyes, pinning it up so that half of it fell back down again. There was no hint of a smile on her face. 'He's one of the lilies of the field,' she said. 'He's blessed, I think. I'm worried about you, though. You haven't been here a week, and you're in trouble. I can feel it. It's deep, too. I know it's nothing of your doing. It was waiting for you up here, in the weather. You drove into it like a boat into a storm. You could probably leave – sail right back out of it.'

Howard was silenced by the abrupt finality of this last statement. He knew she wasn't being rude, that she wasn't ordering him out of the house.

'Talk Sylvia into going back down south with you. This is no place for her. She could make a go of it down there. I've thought about it, and if she opened a little store, in one of those big malls, there's nothing she couldn't accomplish. She could establish a chain of them. I was reading about someone who did that, a woman who sold cookies and made her fortune at it. It's too small for her up here. She hasn't got a chance. She's staying for us. We'd get by, though.'

'Maybe she thinks you're worth staying for.'

'Maybe she thinks you're worth leaving with.'

It was another statement that struck Howard silent. And it was a strange statement, too, coming from his aunt. But Aunt Edith, he was finding, often said just what she meant. He shrugged. 'I can't leave yet,' he said. 'There's something that's only half done.'

'What is it?'

'I'm not sure what it is, but I can feel it. You know – this thing with old Graham ...'

'What *thing*, Howard? Can you tell me? You don't know what you're talking about, do you?'

He shook his head. The saw started up outside again, and Howard could hear his uncle tossing boards around.

'Maybe that's good,' she said. 'Maybe that's some kind of charm. Take care of my daughter, though. She's not as tough as she thinks she is. We all lean on her.' Aunt Edith smiled proudly then, and in that moment her face softened and she looked like Sylvia. Then the saw blade shrieked outside and the saw abruptly stopped.

'*Chingatha!*' Uncle Roy shouted, and the lines of worry and care and work reappeared in Aunt Edith's face. They both looked out the back window, where Uncle Roy wrenched at a board that was cocked up into the jammed saw blade.

'I don't see any blood,' Aunt Edith said, pushing the window open. 'What happened?'

'Nothing,' Uncle Roy said, hammering at the piece of wood with his fist now.

'Turn the saw off, then. Watch out it doesn't come on while you're working with it.'

'Overload switch shut down. It *can't* come on. Damn it,' he shouted, looking around for something to hit it with and picking up a short length of two-by-four. His eyes were wide, as if he were going to show the jammed board a thing or two, and he smashed the two-by-four against the board, driving it down and out of the saw blade, denting and splitting the wood in the process. Once out of the blade, the board tumbled off the saw table onto the ground, and Uncle Roy slammed away at it another three or four times for good measure, splintering the board into rubbish. He stood over it, legs spread, his stomach heaving with exertion. Then he straightened up and yanked on his suspenders, kicking the pieces of board out of the way.

Aunt Edith still stared out of the open window, her hand over her mouth.

Uncle Roy gaped back in at her. 'Had to kill the patient,' he said. Then he felt around under the saw motor until he found the overload button. The saw whined and took off, and he reached up and shut it down with the on-off switch. 'Sometimes you have to beat the bastards up,' he said.

Aunt Edith stayed silent, but she gave Howard a look. He realized that he hadn't talked half enough to her. It was a shame that they couldn't have sat down over coffee and really chewed things over, gotten to know each other. There were a hundred questions he would have liked to ask her, about her and Mr Jimmers, about Sylvia's father, about the spirit museum and their lives on the north coast. Uncle Roy was just then coming in at the door, though, and it was too late. It would have to wait.

On the back corner of the kitchen cabinet sat a ceramic Humpty Dumpty – exactly like the one that had fallen and broken in the earthquake. 'Hey,' Howard said. 'Another one.' He pointed at it, and Aunt Edith picked it up.

'Same one,' she said. 'Sylvia went to work on it with a tube of glue. She's good with her hands – good at fine work. You can hardly see the cracks.'

Howard inspected it. 'Just looks like cracks in the glaze, doesn't it? I like that, actually – like old china in an antique shop. I like a bit of age in his face. He doesn't look so smug.'

Aunt Edith smiled at him. 'That's our Sylvia. She has that effect on people sometimes.'

'She got that from her mother,' Uncle Roy said, kissing his wife on the cheek. Then he shrugged, threw his arms around her, bent her back clumsily, and kissed her on the lips. 'Hah!' he said, straightening them both up. 'Wonderful dinner last night, wasn't it? Sylvia hit the nail on the head with that place.'

Aunt Edith smiled at Howard. 'It was,' she said. 'We don't go out very often. When was the last time, Roy?'

'Back in eighty-three, wasn't it? Remember, we went to that polka dive.

I could dance back then.' He winked at Edith. 'Dirty shame I had to go out last night, after we were through with dinner. Poor Bennet, he—'

'No need to lie,' Edith said. 'Howard's told me why you went out. There'll be other nights.'

'By golly, you're right.' Uncle Roy lit up, as if a momentous thought had just struck him. 'There's one later today, isn't there?' He kissed Edith again. 'Call me insatiable,' he said.

'Call you an old fool,' Edith told him, dusting the wood chips off the front of his shirt with her feather duster. She headed toward the door then. 'I'll just let you men talk shop. I've got cleaning to do while you two live the life of Riley.'

Uncle Roy watched her go. There was a look of longing in his face. He sighed deeply. 'Never underestimate the value of a wife,' he said. Recovering, he asked, 'How's the knee?' and poured the last of the cold coffee into his empty cup.

'Better, I think.'

'Sandwich?'

'Sure.' Howard realized that he was half starved.

Uncle Roy hauled out mustard and mayonnaise and lettuce and packages of bologna and American cheese. 'Well,' he said, 'we skinned out of it last night.' He went to the door and stuck his head out into the living room as if to see whether Aunt Edith was still around.

'What did you want the four hundred for?' Howard asked.

'Payola. I gave it to Mrs Lamey.' He stopped squirting mustard onto his bread slice and looked steadily at Howard, who widened his eyes in bewilderment.

'I told the cop that Bennet and I had just come up from Petaluma, where we'd got a load of chicken manure for old Cal down in Albion. You remember Cal. I said he'd paid us off, along with money he owed us for six more loads. And then when I dropped Bennet off, I figured that even though it was late, I'd knock on Mrs Lamey's door and wake her up, in order to pay her overdue rent money. That way she could get the money into the bank tomorrow, which is today, of course. Anyway, I said that I couldn't wake her up at first so I knocked harder, and she must have waked up out of a dream or something and thought there was a nut at the door.' Uncle Roy chuckled, layering meat and cheese onto the bread and smashing it all down with an inch of lettuce.

'So you gave *her* the four hundred?'

'Right there in front of the cop. Just handed it to her. Pissed her off, too.'

'Did they check the story, the chicken manure story?'

'Damned right they did. These hick cops aren't stupid. They called Cal up and grilled him, right then and there. Used Mrs Lamey's phone. We'd got to him first, of course, right after you left. Iron-clad story.'

'How about the window? Did she accuse you of breaking the window?'

'Of course she did. But what was lying in the bushes outside? An ashtray. Someone had pretty clearly thrown it through earlier. Why? That's the question I asked, right there on the spot. It was obvious that I hadn't broken the window at all. Someone else had done it, *from inside the house*. When I knocked on the door a piece had fallen out. She didn't deny it. Not for a moment. She didn't want cops snooping around there, getting suspicious. You should have seen her. Looked like something out of a nightmare. I'm pretty sure the cop wanted to lock her up on general principles. They don't like being called out at midnight to deal with a batshit old woman when nothing's wrong except she's been offered four hundred dollars.

'Then of course there was the fish blood all over everything. I pointed that out before she had a chance to. "What the hell's all this?" I said, stepping back. The cop looked hard at it. Stunk like a cannery. He thought it was some kind of creep joint. You could see it in his face. I reasoned with him, though – said she was an eccentric old woman but not dangerous. Luckily he didn't know who she really was. She probably owns the mortgage to his house. Anyway, it blew over and he left without any trouble. Between her place and Bennet's place, though, he was a confused man.'

Uncle Roy was smiling now, wolfing down big bites of sandwich and talking around them. He had won through again, pulled himself out of another scrape. His army of irregulars stretched down the coast, into Albion. The day had been full of victories, although it was unclear to Howard whether any of the battles had been decisive. 'How about the three that walked home?' Howard asked.

'To hell with them. Maybe they got run over by a lumber truck. And say, that reminds me, thanks again for getting a jump on that barn lumber. I made out all right on it. Bought a little something for Edith and Sylvia and took Edith out to dinner with what was left over. Squandered the hell out of it.'

'Good for you. Sylvia showed me the sweater. She's nuts about it.'

'She's a good girl. Sees things clearly. She gets her good looks from her mother, but I've had a little bit of influence on the way she thinks. I've worked hard to knock some of the practicality out of her. What I've been doing out back is trying to clean up the scrap that's left over. I figured to rip out another few feet of one-by-two, but it's so warped it keeps binding the blade up. It's firewood, I think.'

'That was my conclusion. We ought to chop it into lengths and stack it.'

Uncle Roy changed the subject, as if he'd gotten all the mileage out of the barn lumber he cared about. The practical business of turning it into firewood didn't interest him. 'I hated like hell to give Mrs Deventer's money to old Lamey last night, but what could I do?' He shrugged, to show that he'd had no other option. 'Anyway, I owe it to Mrs Deventer now, especially after what I told Lou Gibb.'

Howard didn't bother to question his logic, to ask what it was Uncle Roy owed himself and Aunt Edith.

Uncle Roy shoved down the rest of his sandwich and then washed his hands at the sink. 'Time to meet Bennet down to the harbor. What are you up to?'

'I thought I'd pay a visit to Jimmers', Howard said.

'He won't be there. It's his town day.'

Howard nodded. 'I know.'

Uncle Roy shrugged. 'Do what you have to.'

24

'We're certain he's not home, then?' Howard watched the ocean out the window as they drove south. The swell had come up considerably since last night, and the tide was higher than he would have liked. It looked as if he'd be getting wet again if they dawdled.

'Trust me. He comes up to town, up to the Safeway, once a week to buy supplies, and then he'll eat a late lunch down at the harbor. You can set your watch by it. He won't be home until dark. It's now or wait till next week, though, because if we show up while he's home, he won't let you anywhere near that passage. He'll thank you for bringing his clothes back and try to interest you in UFO sightings or disappearing rabbits or something. He'll be on his guard now, especially since the shed was stolen.'

The day was beautiful – sunny and dry, almost warm. Howard wished they were simply going down to the beach for a picnic. There wasn't time for that sort of pleasure, though – maybe. Mr Jimmers would be home before dark, carrying his bags of groceries. It wouldn't do to be confronted in the living room or to be trapped down on the beach and have to swim around the point again, especially if they were carrying the sketch.

They passed the driveway slowly, not turning off. Howard craned his neck to look back down toward the house, trying to catch a glimpse of Jimmers' car, just in case he hadn't made the usual Wednesday trip. He couldn't see anything at all, the car included. A quarter mile south, Sylvia pulled off at a turnout and cut the engine, and without waiting another moment they were out and walking back up the road just as fast as Howard could manage it. He felt almost spry, but he carried his cane in case he'd need it in the steep passage – and partly, he had to admit, out of superstition. He still didn't want to be without it. At the mouth of the driveway they held up, making sure there was no one out and about, and then slipped across and started down in the shadow of the woods.

For once, Howard thought, they could have used a little fog, if only to cover up all this breaking and entering. Abruptly he felt a twinge of doubt, but he shooed it out of his head like a pigeon out of the rafters. What he was going to steal didn't belong to Mr Jimmers, and neither did the house he and Sylvia were about to break into. Both of them belonged to a dead man who had summoned Howard north, it seemed, to accomplish just such feats as this.

Jimmers' car was indeed gone, and the place was deserted. Where the shed used to be, out on the meadow, there was a rectangle of moldery-looking dead grass and dirt with a few stalky tendrils of Bermuda grass growing up through it. The ground was broken where the comers of the wooden skids had been yanked around, and there were four rusty old bottle jacks left behind that were still lying there in the dirt. It looked as if someone had been surprised in the middle of the theft and had to run for it. They had probably jacked up the comers enough to back the lift gate under the skids, then winched it forward onto the truck bed while they were rolling back up the highway.

Sylvia wandered off, back to the house, where she was methodically checking the doors and windows. Before joining her, Howard took a quick look over the edge of the cliff, to where the Studebaker sat rusting on the rocks. A pelican stood placidly on the car's roof, watching the waves break. Howard wondered whether it was his pelican, and just then the bird looked up at him. Howard waved and then headed for the house.

'How convenient,' Sylvia said when Howard limped up, and she threw open one of the French doors that looked out onto the sea. The wind caught it and slammed it open against the edge of a table. She stepped back and gestured at the open door.

It turned out that simply walking in wasn't easy for Howard. Mr Jimmers' presence seemed to fill the place, even if he himself was in town, shopping at the Safeway. 'How can he be so sloppy?' Howard asked. 'We could be anybody. And after he got beat over the head, too.'

'We *are* anybody, aren't we?' Sylvia asked, pushing him through the doorway and into the interior. 'You're looking a gift horse in the mouth. What did you want to do, break something, kick the door in?'

'Well …' Howard said. 'You know what I mean.' The house was cold and musty and dim, lit only by sunlight through the dirty windows.

'Should we check beneath the rock in the fireplace?' Sylvia asked.

'It's not there.'

'You *know* that? What if it is there? We could be on the road in five minutes.'

'It's not there. I had a dream that revealed where it's hidden. I told you that.'

Sylvia grinned at him. 'I love that kind of dream,' she said. 'I had one once where this enormous brass baby's head advised me to call a particular telephone number in order to establish contacts. That's what it said, "contacts." It was a UFO dream, you know, like I used to get.' She took his elbow as she followed him up the dark stairs.

'Did you call the number? You must have. You couldn't bear not to.'

'Of course I called the number.'

Howard waited, but Sylvia said nothing more. 'Well? Who was it?'

'I don't know. It sounded like a Chinese man, at a laundry, I think, so I hung up.'

He waited again. 'That's it? That's the whole story?'

'Uh-huh. I got busy with something and forgot all about it. I think I had to wash the dishes.'

Mr Jimmers had made a small effort to straighten up the attic, or at least to get the closet door closed. Half the stuff Howard had hauled out still sat on the floor, though, and the cut-up quilt lay heaped by the Morris chair. The desk, which Howard had tried to bar the door with, was shoved sideways into the middle of the room, and more of the closet debris lay on top of it. He pulled the closet door open, revealing the arched hole torn into the wall and the dim antechamber beyond.

'This is it, then?' Sylvia asked in a hesitant voice.

'The secret passage.'

'What if Mr Jimmers didn't go into town? What if he's down in there somewhere, waiting for us?'

'Why on earth would he be waiting for us?' Howard asked, alarmed at the notion of Jimmers lurking below them in the darkness. 'Don't say that sort of thing.'

She shined her flashlight into the interior, and the light glowed dimly down the stairwell. 'Maybe he's got an axe down there.'

'Would you shut up?'

'Did you read about those severed heads they found perched on guardrail posts? That wasn't two miles south of here. They never found the bodies. It's my guess that Jimmers ate them.'

'Shine that light in here,' he said, 'and drop that sort of talk.'

'I bet it's sharp enough to split a hair with, like in the cartoons. *Your* head goes first.' She pushed him forward, handing him the flashlight.

'Shut that closet door, then,' he said. 'No use advertising that we're here.'

Carrying his cane, he bent hesitantly into the passage, playing the light around on the walls. In the yellow glow, Howard could see that the stairwell was paneled and roofed with wooden car siding, painted white, with a raised framework of sticks forming a pattern of circles and crosses on the walls. The wood was scuffed and dented and dirty as if furniture or equipment of some sort had been hauled up and down for fifty years. It had been a well-used passage, not just the scrimshaw of an eccentric architect.

The corners were hung with cobweb and there were rat droppings and stains along the edges of the stair treads, which were worn in the centers from use. The passage, apparently, had been a regular thoroughfare. Howard almost preferred the utter darkness he had found there two days ago, which had hidden the evidence of spiders and rats.

When the stairs ended, they followed the tunnel down through the cliff itself. Root tendrils grew through the ceiling, and for a distance of three or four yards after the last stair tread, the walls of the tunnel had evidently been cut away with picks and then had been shored up with timbers. The dirt gave way to stone, though, and the rest of the tunnel seemed to Howard to be a natural cave – wet and dark and cold. Here and there the walls were streaked with veins of whitish crystal, smooth and shiny, almost like heavy snail tracks. They could hear the muffled crash of waves now, and in minutes there was a sea wind in their faces and the smell of the ocean as they wound down around the last curving slope, skirting a pool of dark water left from the high tide, and stepping into the sunlight that poured into the tunnel mouth.

'I don't see any Studebaker,' Sylvia said.

'Not so damned loud,' Howard told her.

'Who's going to hear, the sea gulls?' She took his arm, leaning against him and gazing out into the empty sea. A foghorn sounded somewhere to the north, the faint sound of it carried on the wind. 'You're really tensed up, aren't you?'

He said nothing, but then nodded. In truth he felt just a little like he had in his dreams – just when they were beginning and the pieces of the dreams were still misty and disconnected and yet he knew, even in sleep, that something was waiting. In contrast, Sylvia seemed fresh and exuberant with her face rouged by the wind and her hair wild.

'Romantic, isn't it?' she said. 'I love deserted beaches.'

He nodded, feeling it, too. There seemed always to be such an infernal hurry – four days of it now, always with desperate destinations and the hands of the clock spinning and spinning. They had a good three hours yet before Mr Jimmers' return, though – time enough.

'We should have brought a blanket and a picnic lunch,' Sylvia said.

'That's just what I was thinking not a half hour ago. Why didn't we?'

The world was utterly empty of anybody but the two of them. There was nothing but the rocky cove and their little corner of beach, mostly sheltered from the wind and from the eyes of people above. The cliffs rose sheer and

stark behind them, faintly echoing the sound of lonesome gulls and of breaking waves. The sun shined down on the moving ocean, illuminating the pale
green waves that quartered across the reefs, throwing themselves into the air
in long sheets of spindrift foam.

Sylvia stood silently, holding on to his arm, watching the ocean, waiting,
maybe, for him to speak or move. There was nothing to prevent him from
kissing her, right then and there, except that suddenly he felt like a teenager,
his heart fluttering and his mind troubled by what might lie within the glove
box of the wrecked car. The dream anxiousness returned, and he looked nervously toward the rock shelf that separated them from the Studebaker.

'First things first,' she said, and he wondered what she meant, what came
first in her own mind just then.

He stepped up onto the rocks, though, and she followed, the two of them
picking their way easily over the top. There sat the Studebaker, as ever, the
front end crumpled, sun-dried kelp tangled around the tires. The doors hung
open on broken hinges, the window glass shattered, and the hood was torn
loose, hanging over the fender and crusted with sea salt. The windshield was
a spiderweb of cracks.

The back windows were unbroken, and the radiant heat of the sun through
the glass had warmed the interior. Sylvia clambered over the front seat, which
was thrown forward into the dashboard, and settled herself into the back.
Howard set his cane across the exposed engine, then pulled the front seat
roughly back into place and climbed in behind the steering wheel.

There was a steering knob on the wheel, just as his dream had predicted. It
was an oval of pale Lucite with an ivory ground. There was nothing in it – no
symbols, no messages. The sight of it, though, made him hesitate, his hand on
the button of the glove compartment. Again the unreality, the dream-likeness
of the whole business washed over him. There was something mythological
about it, as if at any moment some symbolic animal, a lamb or a kid or a cen-
taur, would descend the rocky cliff above. There was something timeless about
the moment, and he turned to look at Sylvia, who lounged on the seat, regarding him silently.

He opened the glove box. Inside lay a hammered-cooper rectangle about
a half inch thick. He lifted it out and examined it. There were two rectangles,
actually, pressed together, like a book without a spine. They were old-looking
and etched with verdigris, and were sandwiched very tightly over a rubber
flange. Four silver clips, cut into the shapes of tiny swords, were thrust
through each of the corners, somehow fastening the two halves of the case.
Cut deeply into the top plate was a rampant dragon with a knight on horse-
back before it, burying a lance into its heart. Below were the words 'The
Guild of St George.'

Howard hesitated half a moment, wondering how the sword clips were meant to work. They appeared to be corroded into place, almost fused to the metal plates. When he pulled at them, they slipped out impossibly easily, though – so easily that they might have fallen out if he had turned the case over.

The two halves parted just as easily, revealing the rubber flange laid into a channel inside as a seal. The sketch lay loosely on the bottom plate. It was almost translucent, the paper was so thin, and it showed a thousand creases, as if the paper were of such quality that it could be folded infinitely without any single crease being muddled by the rest. Sketched onto it were the figures that Howard remembered from Mr Jimmers' copy.

'It's an unfolded piece of origami,' Sylvia said suddenly into Howard's ear, startling him so that he nearly dropped it. 'I wonder what this discoloration is,' Sylvia said, leaning forward and looking over his shoulder. He could feel her breath on his neck. 'Looks like coffee stains.'

'Blood. That's what your father thinks.'

'Remember those *Mad* magazine covers?' Sylvia asked. 'Where you fold part of it over another part? Try to fold it the way Mr Jimmers folded it.'

On impulse Howard folded it lengthwise so that half the sketch disappeared. Lines joined, forming a picture.

'What is that?' Sylvia asked. 'A tower or something?'

Something blocked the sun just then, throwing the car into shadow. Howard leaned forward and looked through the cracked front windshield, surprised to see what looked like a raincloud, and perhaps more on the horizon. 'Or something,' he said. A rush of embarrassment colored his face. It was a domed turret, unmistakably phallic-looking.

Sylvia reached up and pinched his ear, running her hand down the front of his shirt, and he realized that the heat that he felt wasn't embarrassment at all. 'I think it's the Castle Perilous,' she said, slumping back into the seat and untying her shoes.

'I think we're *in* the Castle Perilous.'

'Or somewhere. Who cares?' She kicked her shoes off onto the floor and then shrugged out of her jacket. 'Warm in here,' she said, tossing the jacket down onto the shoes and pulling her sweater smooth.

He unfolded the sketch and centered it in its aperture. Then he laid the top plate back over the bottom, carefully sliding the tiny swords back into place with a faint click. He set the case on the dashboard. Sunlight shined onto it through the spiderwebbed window like lamplight through an aquarium full of diamonds, and the hammered copper glowed warmly.

Howard was filled with the inescapable knowledge that the sketch was his. It had belonged to Michael Graham, and to others before him, but now it was his, Howard's, for reasons he felt but didn't understand. The reasons didn't matter, though. His curiosity was beside the point.

Something vast – the energy of growing things, of the seasons, of the turning of the earth and of the stars themselves – flowed through him, filling him up like a goblet full of red wine.

He climbed hastily into the backseat with Sylvia, and she lay in his arms, the two of them sprawled together in the warmth of the autumn sun. She pulled his jacket off and pushed it onto the floor opposite her own and then began to unbutton his shirt. 'What do you need,' she whispered, 'a written invitation?'

He put his finger to her lips to quiet her. If he had needed an invitation before, he didn't now. He was surprised at how easily he slipped her sweater off, how roomy the backseat of the old Studebaker seemed to be. They might as easily have been in a palace. 'Remember that dead-end street?' he asked, recalling a shared moment of passion nearly twenty years past. 'Near the cornfield? Not as much room in the back of a Dodge.'

'You can't talk if I can't,' she whispered to him, and put one hand gently over his mouth while the other hand worked deftly at his belt. There was no sound after that except breathing and the swish of fabric on skin and of the rising and falling of the ocean. The world around them, outside of the wrecked car, ceased to exist, and the whole notion of time disappeared with it.

He lay beneath her finally, gazing through the rear window at the afternoon sky. They didn't need to hurry. There was still time. And even if there wasn't, even if Mr Jimmers was right then descending the coast road with his groceries, so what? The world had changed in the last hour, and couldn't be changed back.

He wondered if Sylvia was asleep now. She was breathing softly and regularly, like a contented cat. He had found her and the sketch both, in one languorous afternoon. The museum and his life down south were fast becoming little more than foggy memories, like the hazy recollection of a past life.

Puffy little clouds drifted slowly through the deep sky. Still half drugged with the smell of her hair and skin, he watched the clouds curiously through the rear window. There was something about them, about their shapes, that was deeply mysterious, like the five sketches on the paper in the copper case, like the suggestive pattern of a constellation in the night sky.

Two of the clouds floated above the three, all of them slipping slowly together until, for the space of a long moment, they formed the exact pattern of the clouds in his dream.

Startled, he half sat up, nearly tumbling Sylvia off onto the floor.

'Hey,' she said. 'You're pretty romantic.'

'Sorry. I must have fallen asleep.' He watched the clouds drift apart, his heart hammering.

'What's wrong?' she asked, brushing back her hair and looking at his face.

'Nothing. I thought for a moment that I was dreaming, that I dreamed this whole thing ...'

'What *thing*, exactly?' She grinned at him, hooking her hands over his shoulders and pulling herself up along him so that her breasts brushed his chest. 'This thing? You're not dreaming,' she said, 'I guarantee it.'

He moved toward the edge of the seat so that they could lie side by side, and she kissed him on the lips and cheeks, running her left hand up and down his chest, kissing his neck, shutting his lips before he could say something about Mr Jimmers' return, about the hour. And suddenly once again there was nothing to say, and time disappeared as they shifted positions, kneeling on their clothes, their body heat warming the car as the sun descended the sky.

'Time to be practical, maybe,' Sylvia said later, as they lay quietly together again at last. 'How come you wear two pairs of socks?'

'My feet get cold in the winter, especially when I'm in the same house as Artemis Jimmers.' He took his socks from her and pulled them on, one inside the other. Now that they had decided to go, to get on with their lives, he was impatient to dress and be out of there. He felt both conspicuous and late. 'What time is it?'

'Only four,' she said. 'No rush. I told you he probably wouldn't be home until after dark.'

'Famous last words.' He poked his head out of the car and surveyed the top of the surrounding cliffs. There was no one. He stepped out onto the rocks and pulled on his pants, holding the cuffs up out of the water in the shallow pools and watching the ocean. A wave surged up out of nowhere, rushing toward him, and he sat back down on the car seat, lifting his legs so that his feet rested on the floorboard. The tide had risen farther, and the ocean washed across the undercarriage of the car now, lapping at the open door. It swirled out again. 'Better hurry. Either that or leave your shoes off. You'll be wading.'

'Get out of the way, then,' she said. 'You're the slowpoke. I'd have been on the beach by now.'

He pulled his own shoes on, and then his jacket. Then he reached in and picked up the sketch, checked to see that it was tightly sealed, and waited once more for the ocean to recede. 'Bye,' he said, stepping down onto the rock, grabbing his cane off the engine, and loping toward the shelf that ran out along the tunnel mouth. He clambered atop it and waited for her, giving her a hand up, and then they climbed down the other side and stood for a moment on the little slice of beach that was left dry, shaded entirely now from the sun. He kissed her one last time, and they stepped into the darkness of the tunnel.

25

They walked along through the musty darkness, neither of them speaking, listening to the scraping of their shoes on the rocky floor of the tunnel. The flush of comfortable optimism that had filled the sun-warmed Studebaker had disappeared utterly, flown off like a wonderful bird in the few yards of their ascent back into the old house. As he wearily climbed the stairs, Howard's mind was full of a confusion of memories and rationalizations, excuses and half-built plans.

He leaned on his cane tiredly now and carried the copper plates with the sketch while Sylvia played the flashlight onto the stairs ahead of them. He imagined himself explaining to Uncle Roy and Aunt Edith that he and Sylvia … What did it mean? He would move out of the house; that was the first thing – maybe take a room at a bed-and-breakfast for the time being.

The closet door wouldn't open. Sylvia shined the light on it while Howard turned the doorknob, which twistcd uselessly in his hand, clearly a dummy. Unbelieving, he pushed in on it and pulled out on it, turning it left and right, thinking that it was simply worn out, that something would catch and the door would open.

'It's useless,' he said at last. 'The knob just spins. We're trapped down here. Why the hell did I close the closet door?'

'Because we found it closed and you thought you could open it again.'

'Do I break it down?'

'I don't see why you should.'

'Do you want to swim, or pound like hell on the door and hope that Jimmers will hear us and let us out?'

She looked at him steadily. 'There has to be another way out. You're the one who broke this hole in the wall. What did people do before that?'

'It was only recently walled up – maybe just a week or two ago – after the car went over the cliff, I'd bet. Before that there was probably a door in the back of the closet, but Mr Jimmers wanted to make it all less obvious, so he took out the door and walled it up.'

'Did you look for another way out?' Sylvia asked.

'No.'

'Think about it – Mr Jimmers has lived here for years, most of the time invisibly. You're the one who said that you didn't know he was here back when you came up in seventy-five. That's why I called him a mole man. He was living in secret rooms, probably beneath the house. It wasn't any big secret.'

'How did he get in and out?'

'That's what I'm saying, isn't it?'

'The stairs outside,' Howard said, suddenly remembering. 'That door's locked, too, and the stairs are broken off. No use trying to find our way to it.'

'That can't be it. If Mr Jimmers had come and gone through that door, you would have seen him, wouldn't you?'

Howard shrugged. 'Maybe, unless he hardly ever used it. Maybe he avoided coming and going when there was company in the house.'

'There was always company in the house – at least a few locals helping Graham build things. Father was out here himself half the time, along with Mr Bennet.'

They turned around and Howard followed Sylvia back down the dark stairs. What she said made perfect sense. Of course there must be another exit, what with all this tunneling, all the excavation. The place was riddled with secret passages, and apparently with secret rooms, too, if this had been Mr Jimmers' hideaway for so many years. He knocked on the paneling with his knuckles, hoping for some sort of telltale hollow sound. Sylvia shined the flashlight methodically, up and down the panels.

'Here it is,' she said suddenly. They were halfway down, on the top landing of the final flight, where the stairs doubled back at the level of the second floor. There were handprints on the dirty white paint, visible in the flashlight beam. Above the handprints, recessed into the wall so as to be invisible unless seen from straight on, was a light switch. Howard pushed it and light glowed down from overhead, shining through a muslin shade hidden in the design of the ceiling panel and lighting the stairs all the way down to the mouth of the underground tunnel.

He pushed at the paneling tentatively, and when nothing happened he rapped on it with his knuckles again. It thumped hollowly. 'This has got to be it,' he said, pressing again. 'Probably some sort of spring latch.'

Sylvia stood studying the design of the paneling for a moment while Howard tapped and pushed. Then she reached out and pulled on one of the circles of wood laid on over the top of the panel. It rotated beneath her hand. There was a click, and the panel swung open an inch or so, revealing a head-high opening into a small dark room. Howard pushed the panel open gently, standing back out of the way, half expecting something to leap out at them.

Half a dozen wooden stairs led down into the room. Sylvia shined her flashlight down them, playing it onto the floor. A rat scurried away, out of the light, disappearing behind a tumble of cardboard boxes. The room smelled of damp wood and moldering paper. Howard leaned in and felt around on the wall, opposite where the passageway light switch was recessed into the panel. There was another switch. He pushed it and a bare bulb blinked on, hanging from a cord in the center of the ceiling.

'Storage room of some sort,' Howard whispered, pointing out the obvious. There were dusty shelves of old books and piles of wooden crates and cardboard cartons. The room was windowless. They could hear the rat scratching in the comer near an old mimeograph machine that sat on a banged-up desk alongside an almost empty bottle of printing chemicals and a half dozen books. Pinned above it on the wall were dozens of star maps, overlapping each other and yellowed and drooping with age.

The pine floor was covered with a heavy layer of dust disturbed only by the footprints of rats, except for a clean, scuffed trail leading across toward a door surrounded by bookcases.

'This must be where he put together his publications,' Sylvia said, pushing past Howard to the desk and picking up one of the scattered books. 'Look, it's all flying saucer stuff. *Flying Saucers on the Attack, Aboard a Flying Saucer, Flying Saucers Uncensored, The Saucers of December. Saucer on a Hot Tin Roof.*'

'Let me see!'

'So what if I'm a liar? Hey, look. Here's Mr Jimmers' own book, *The Night of the Saucer People.*'

'You *are* a liar!'

'I swear. Here it is. Look at it.'

Howard stepped across and took the book from her. 'You didn't tell me he'd written a book. What a great title. What is it, fact or fiction?'

'Fiction, sort of. It's a novel about something that happened to him back in the forties. He worked on it forever, apparently, and finally had it self-published. It's dedicated to my mother even though it didn't come out until years after they parted – when he was out of the hospital for good, in 1958, 1 think.'

'Really? Let me see it.' He flipped through the first few pages, looking for a moment at the frontispiece illustration – a sleeping neighborhood beneath a night sky full of stars and with three lit-up saucers spinning in out of deep space. It was published, it said, in an edition of two hundred, in 1952 from the Phoenix Restaurant Press in San Francisco, priced at two dollars.

'You're way off on the date.'

'It might have been fifty-seven. I can remember it, though – I was in Mrs Webostad's class at that school in Lakewood we went to. That would have been second grade. It was my birthday and Mother had brought cupcakes to school. That's how I remember. Anyway, Mother found a copy of his book in the mail after school that day and started telling me all about this man named Mr Jimmers, whom she'd known before she married Father. It was the first time she'd said anything about him. We've still got the book at home. When I was a kid I used to look at it all the time because of the pictures in it.'

'Sorry,' Howard said. 'What about the pictures?'

'Nothing. I didn't say anything about the pictures. You weren't listening.' She turned toward the door in the bookcases. 'C'mon,' she said.

He stared at the dedication page, which said simply, 'For Edith,' and then below that, 'And for Sylvia.' His thoughts leaped ahead, too quickly to keep up with. 'Why,' he started to ask, but then stopped himself and flipped back to the title page to check the publication date again. Mystified, he slipped the book beneath his coat, into an inside pocket.

'Look at this,' Sylvia said, already gone on into an adjacent room.

Howard followed, down another flight of a half dozen stairs and into a room larger than the last. Along one wall was a heavy, scarred workbench with tools hung above it. On the floor sat an arc welder and drill press and grinder and heaps of brass and copper pipe and sheet metal. Rolled-up blueprints stood in a deep wooden box, crammed in together.

On the floor along the opposite wall, in an area otherwise clear of debris, crouched what was either an automobile or a vehicle from the stars. It appeared to be built around the chassis and body of an old Buick, with the top chopped and lowered to streamline it and the interior gutted and replaced with a single reclining, leather covered seat. The whole car rested on a circular plate, with vents cut through the running boards and bent pipes running into and out of the sides of the vehicle.

It was old and dusty, most of the steel rusted and the chrome corroded. It looked like a nearly finished project that had been abandoned and then had sat in place for twenty or thirty years. The exterior of the vehicle was the weirdest part of the thing. It was covered with a profusion of tin toys, gaudily painted in bright primary colors – hundreds of toys, cemented on randomly like a confused army.

There were great-headed babies riding wind-up tricycles past lunatic birds with whirligig hats. There were cross-eyed elephants driving automobiles alongside ape-driven zeppelins, train engines, biplanes, and hot-air balloons carrying entire tin families. Tiny tin soldiers and zoo animals, circus acrobats and strolling couples dressed in wedding clothes were glued among the windup toys as if wandering between giants. In the center of the crowd, towering above them, sat a big-eyed Humpty Dumpty with a crown on his head. His arms apparently rotated and he held a baton as if he were leading an orchestra. At the side of the car, as if it were an immense wind-up toy, was a square brass key.

'He's a gluer,' Howard said. 'That's what I said, remember?'

'Yeah. I never knew anything about *this*, though. I knew he went into the hospital that first time because he suffered from some kind of gluer compulsion that had got out of hand, but I didn't know he'd kept at it.'

'That's weirdly common around here, isn't it?'

'Ask Dad. He has a car of his own somewhere that he works on, or used to – I don't know where. He doesn't talk about it. It's like alcohol, I think. Some people get the habit worse than others. Some people glue in public; some of them are closet gluers.'

'Uncle Roy is a closet gluer?'

'I think it has something to do with knowing Graham.'

'With *this*, I think,' Howard said, waving the copper case.

'Father refers to it as the Humpty Dumpty complex, the desire to always be putting things back together.'

'Say,' Howard said, 'speaking of that – it was you who glued Aunt Edith's Humpty Dumpty back together again.'

'Uh-huh. Better to keep things whole.'

'You don't have a gluer vehicle stashed somewhere, do you? Covered up with origami fish or something?'

'A fleet of them, up in Willits. I sneak up there on weekends with Mrs Deventer. What happens if we turn this crank?'

'The thing flies?'

'Where to? Do you realize that he's built this intricate contraption in a cellar? If it did fly, or drive or something, he couldn't get it out of here.'

'He doesn't want to,' Howard said. 'What's important is the gluing. Go ahead and twist the crank.'

'You do it.'

'Remember that phone call you made, after the dream? Down to the Chinese laundry? The one where you hung up before you knew what the dream meant? This is a second chance for you. You can make up for that now, play out your destiny.'

Sylvia considered this for a moment, then shrugged, widened her eyes at him, and twisted the crank twice. The works were stiff, and it took both hands to do it. There was an instant clanging of dozens of tiny bells and the whirling of tin propellers. The creatures on bicycles pedaled furiously, the front wheels rotating while the back wheels stayed in place, cemented to the body of the car. Trains tooted and spun their wheels, circus animals beat on drums and banged cymbals, and the Humpty Dumpty waved his baton, orchestrating the whole seething mass of toys. There was a sound like a fan starting up, and the entire plate with the car on top lifted off the ground three or four inches. A gust of air blew out from underneath, ruffling their hair for the space of thirty seconds, until the toys finally wound down and fell still and the ship bumped to the floor.

'That's something,' said Howard. 'Isn't it? A wind-up flying saucer car. Jimmers is a genius.'

'It's indescribable. How long do you think it took him to build it?'

'Lord knows. There was a man who cut a chain out of a single toothpick.

I saw it at Knott's Berry Farm once, in a display of miniatures. Took him years, and he went blind carving it, too.'

'What does that have to do with this?'

'Nothing,' Howard said. 'I admire that sort of attention to worthless projects, though – doing things for the sheer sake of doing them.'

Sylvia nodded. 'I think it ought to be in a museum. Kids would go nuts over it.'

'Imagine riding in it,' Howard said. 'Cranking it up and driving it into Fort Bragg at eight in the morning, dressed in a foil hat. What's the rest of this stuff in here?' Howard gestured around the room, at the heaped pipe and sheet metal. He stood up and moved across to lay his cane and the copper case on the benchtop, and then pulled out one of the blueprints in the box, half expecting to find the plans for a flying saucer. What he found was a diagram of the ghost machine, drawn to scale, covered with symbols and illegibly written notes that he didn't understand. 'Oh-oh,' he said, holding it up for Sylvia to see.

She stared at it until she understood what it was. Then she shrugged. 'It doesn't change anything, really. Who cares where the damned thing came from? Somebody had to build it. Did you really expect it to generate ghosts?'

'I don't know,' Howard said. 'I guess I did, finally. If you had asked me three days ago, I would have laughed at the idea. Now I'm not laughing.'

'Good. Don't laugh. Think of the one human being on earth who might build a machine that generates ghosts. It's Mr Jimmers, isn't it? You're only skeptical because he built it in a basement on the coast. When you thought it was a hundred years old, you were half convinced. I don't think that anything's changed. Besides, how do you know who drew those plans? They look old to me.'

He shrugged. 'I don't. I wonder what else is in here.'

'I think we should leave Mr Jimmers' stuff alone. It's nearly six. If we were smart we'd find our way out of here. I don't feel right meddling with all of this. It's all private, hidden away down here like this. It's the last thirty years of Mr Jimmers' life that we're pawing through. I shouldn't have wound up the flying saucer.'

'No harm done, apparently. And if you hadn't wound it up, I would have.'

'Let's go,' she said, standing up. Howard rolled the drawing and shoved it back down into the box, then picked up his cane and the copper box. Together they went out through the next door and down more steps into yet another room, the flashlight illuminating a bed chamber with a single chair against one wall. There was a table with a lamp and hot plate and with open shelves above it lined with books and with cans of Spam and hash and hominy and Postum. A single faucet was piped straight out through the concrete wall. There was a small doorway leading into a toilet and yet another heavy, closed door like the one leading into the attic closet.

'That's it,' Howard said, stepping across to open it up. Darkness lay beyond. There was no knob at all on the outside of the door. It led out, not in. 'We need something to wedge it open,' he said. 'No telling where this goes. It can't go far, though. Shine the light through here.'

It was a tunnel like in a mine, shored up with old railroad ties. The floor of the tunnel seemed to run gradually uphill. 'Hold it for a moment,' Howard said, 'and throw some light on the shelves there.' He stepped back into the room, grabbed a can of Spam, and set it onto the threshold, letting the door close against it. Then they set out down the passage, through two hundred feet of darkness, until once again they came to a door, this one barred with a heavy piece of wood slotted into the timber of the door frame. An immense garage-door spring hooked the center of the door to the post it was hinged to.

Howard pulled the bar out of its niche and hooked it back into a tremulous sort of clip, like the hold-down of a rat trap. Carefully he leaned all his weight into the door, pushing it open a couple of inches before it jammed against something that sounded like dead leaves and brushwood. Fresh air whirled in around them, smelling of the ocean and evergreen trees and eucalyptus.

'Hold on,' Howard said, handing Sylvia the copper case and taking the flashlight from her. He loped back up the tunnel, put the Spam can back onto the shelf, and closed the door that the can had propped open. He hurried back toward the door into the woods again, anxious to get out.

In the woodsy darkness outside, tree branches swished together in the sea wind. There were no lights visible through the partly open door, no sign of the highway or the house, just the shadow of the woods in moonlight. Sylvia helped him shove the door farther open, skidding it through forest debris, the springs creaking and straining. They slid out, ducking beneath overhanging ferns and brush and letting the door pull shut behind them. The bar slammed down into place.

The door itself was set in the side of a hill, mostly hidden by vegetation and elaborately painted with depictions of twigs and leaves and ferns, most of the paint having been scoured off by weather and the wood beneath discolored to a granite shade of gray.

Up the hill above them a car roared past. They trudged along a tiny, disused trail, up onto the highway, and walked the quarter mile back up to their car. The sun was low in the sky, and the afternoon was dim with pending evening. They could see the house now, out on the bluffs. A light glowed downstairs and another upstairs. Smoke tumbled up out of the chimney. Mr Jimmers was clearly home and had been home long enough to get a good fire going. He had probably been strolling around above them when they wound up the device in the cellar; perhaps he had been there for hours, knowing exactly what Howard was doing downstairs and no longer interested in stopping him.

'Maybe we can just sit here for a moment,' Sylvia said, looking out over the ocean. The sky was clear and the distant edge of the ocean sparkled and danced in the dying sunlight. Howard put his arm around her shoulder, wishing that the Toyota didn't have bucket seats. 'Not just now,' she said, still looking out the window. She turned and smiled at him briefly, then went back to looking out the window.

The copper case sat on the dashboard. Howard picked it up. It was warm, maybe because he'd been carrying it. Its warmth felt like something else, though – as if it were alive in some strange way or charged with barely contained energy. He pulled the plates apart and lifted out the sketch, holding it up in the sunlight so that the paper was translucent. Clearly it had been pressed from a mixture containing leaves and flower petals. A stem of wheat lay outlined like a watermark within the paper, striated by the hundreds of creases.

'Let me see it,' Sylvia said.

For a moment Howard hesitated. He was filled with the notion that the sketch was his in some fundamental, mystical sense and that he shouldn't be passing it around to satisfy idle curiosity. 'Sure,' he said, feeling foolish. 'This paper seems so delicate, I can't imagine how it's held together through so many foldings. You'd think it would fall to pieces like an old road map.'

'I think it was meant to be folded,' Sylvia said. 'It's like a puzzle. I can see the start of a few different shapes here. I think I can follow these two folds and get the start of a simple balloon.'

'An egg, maybe?'

'I don't see an egg.'

'What else?'

'Maybe a fish. I don't know. I'd have to start on one of them in order to see steps farther along. Like following a map again or working your way through a maze. It's impossible to see connections unless you take them one at a time.'

'Go ahead and fold it.'

She looked at him and shook her head.

'Why not?'

'It's like Mr Jimmers' car in the basement,' she said. 'I felt like I was meddling when I wound it up.'

'This doesn't belong to Mr Jimmers, does it? It belongs to me.'

'It does?'

'Who else?'

She shrugged. 'I'd feel like I was ... *intruding* or something.'

'That's a strange word,' Howard said. 'Intruding on what? What do you mean intruding?'

'I don't know. What do you think this is, anyway?'

'Your father seems to think it's the Grail.'

'Then *you* fold the damned thing up. I won't have anything to do with folding it up.' She gave it back to him, but kept looking at it, as if she were studying it with something like longing. 'It has some sort of effect on you, doesn't it?'

'Like out on the beach there, in the Studebaker,' Howard said.

'We shouldn't have done that. We've known for years that we couldn't, or shouldn't.'

'Now we did. Simple as that. It was nice, wasn't it?'

'Nice, yes,' she said, 'but maybe not good.'

'Maybe it *was* good. What happens if I fold it lengthwise, like this?' Howard folded it down the center. There was no need to run his thumb and forefinger along the crease. It folded flat by itself, as if the fold were part of its natural state. The car shook in wind just then and Sylvia jumped.

'God,' she said. 'I thought someone had stood on the bumper. That thing makes me nervous as hell.'

'So what have I started? I could fold it into the shape of a diamond, I guess. I can't see past that.'

'Might be anything. You've got to picture it three-dimensionally. Haven't you ever taken those tests where you have to guess what an unfolded box will look like when it's folded up?'

'I always failed that sort of test.' Howard said. 'To me they always look like crossword puzzles for morons.'

Sylvia pointed out the passenger-side window. The sun was just then disappearing into the sea. 'Look at the sun now.' she said. 'The sky around it is hazy. The sun's almost red.'

'Sailor's delight.' Howard said. 'How did that rhyme go? "Midget at morning, sailor take warning. Midget at night, sailor's delight."'

She stared at the folded paper, concentrating on it.

'Pretty funny, eh?'

'Sure. What did you say? Fold it again, in half. Turn it into a small square. I think I see a cup in it.'

Howard folded it just as the wind shook the car again, sailing up and over the bluffs, bending the dead grasses almost flat and howling around the door frames. Sylvia pulled her coat out of the back and jammed it between the seats, sliding over beside Howard, snuggling up to him. 'Now open it up and tuck the two top corners in, diagonally.'

Darkness fell across the car now as if a vast shadow had blotted out any light left over from the now-departed sun. There was the sound of distant thunder, and Howard and Sylvia looked out through the windshield to find that great black clouds were roiling in double time over the water, soaring along madly in the wind, driving toward land. Lightning forked down toward the ocean, which leaped now with whitecaps. Long, black swells drove in to smash against the rocks with a concussion the two of them could hear even above the wind.

For the moment they ignored the partly folded sketch that Howard held in his hands, and they watched the storm sweep toward them, seeming almost to be pulling water upward out of the Pacific and into the clouds. Way out over the ocean a waterspout rose momentarily and then fell, and within seconds rain flailed against the car, obscuring the ocean entirely.

There were headlights on the highway suddenly, and a car swerved toward them, half on the wrong side of the road. It swung wildly back into its own lane, running up onto the right shoulder and glancing off the rock face of the cliff, the driver honking uselessly as he drove past, disappearing through the deluge.

Rain beat down now in vast waves, sluicing sideways into the car. It forced its way past the weather stripping around the doors and windows and ran in rivulets down the inside of the passenger door to pool up on the mat. Sylvia tried to crank the window shut, but it was already tight.

'It won't last long,' Howard half shouted, squinting to see through the murk and trying to be heard above the roar of rain drumming against the roof. He could see nothing in the sky now, only a black, low canopy. Water poured down the inside edge of the highway in a muddy torrent, wrapping around the cliffside and rushing beneath the car and over the cliff in a cataract. Howard switched on the headlights, but most of the light was thrown back at them, reflected off the heavy curtain of rain. A shower of fist-sized rocks tumbled down the cliff, scattering across the highway in front of them before being swept up in the torrent.

'We can't stay here,' Sylvia said. 'There'll be slides in weather like this. A few years ago fifty yards of road just fell into the ocean. It was a month before it was open to travel again. You had to drive inland nearly to Philo and then back out to Elk.'

'Fine,' Howard said. 'We *can't* go anywhere. We can't see ten feet.' He turned the radio on but there was nothing but static. Three rapid flashes of lightning lit the dark landscape like noonday, and Sylvia screamed, jamming herself back into Howard so that he was crushed against the door handle. An explosion of thunder masked her scream, and in the silence that followed there was a furious knocking at the window on the passenger side and a face peering in at them, its mouth working as if it were shouting something.

Howard lunged for the ignition, instantly remembering every apocryphal story about cult murders and escaped lunatics with hook arms. He twisted the key, wondering how the hell he was going to turn around on the flooded highway. Forget turning around. He threw the car into gear and edged forward, looking wildly at the face in the window. Sylvia was shouting at him, slugging him on the arm.

'It's Jimmers!' she shouted. 'Wait! It's just Jimmers!'

Howard stepped on the brake, his hand on the key again. She was right. It was Jimmers, his hair wild in the wind. Rain poured off his yellow rain slicker, beating against his back as he held on to both door handles for balance. Howard cut the engine and Sylvia unlocked the rear door, letting Jimmers pull it open as he fought against the gale. Rain hammered in around his shoulders as he crammed himself into the backseat, and the door smashed shut behind him, driven by the wind.

'Unfold the paper,' he gasped.

26

Howard looked at him, not understanding what he meant.

'The sketch. Unfold it.' He pointed at Howard's hand, which was still closed over the folded paper. Howard opened the paper up so that it lay flat again. Almost at once the storm began to abate. There was a flash or two of distant lightning but only the vague echo of thunder now. The wind fell off and the rain lessened to a sprinkle. Out over the ocean the starry sky shone through torn apart clouds that seemed to sail away in all directions at once, leaving the windswept sky clear again.

'Perhaps you'd better quit fiddling with it and put it away.' Mr Jimmers said slowly, as if he were talking to a man with a loaded gun.

Howard laid it back into its case, clipping the thing shut and setting it onto the dashboard again. 'What did I do?' he asked.

'Very simply, you called up a storm. Or started to at any rate.'

'*Started* to?'

'It was nothing alongside what it might have been. It was the lemon next to the pie.'

'The pie?' Howard said.

'It was my fault,' Sylvia said. 'I was the one who wanted to fold it.'

'Fault doesn't enter in.' Mr Jimmers wiped his hair back, wringing water down his raincoat.

'How did you know?' Howard asked. 'I'm just curious. Were you home all afternoon?'

'I went up to town to buy groceries and got back about a half hour ago. I spotted your car through the attic telescope and so knew it was you two banging around down below. And then when the storm rose out of nowhere like that, I went upstairs again, and there you were, sitting in your car on the roadside, meddling with the ... sketch, oblivious to the danger.'

'And you let us have the sketch, then, when you knew it was us in the cellars.'

'You knew where it was,' Jimmers said.

'What difference does that make?'

Mr Jimmers stared out of the window. Suddenly he began shivering, and Sylvia said, 'Start up the heater.'

'That's the stuff,' Mr Jimmers said. 'A cup of Postum would be nice, wouldn't it? I'm going to pop back up to the house and brew one, but you won't want to come along. There was trouble down at the harbor. I saw it from the road on the way back down here. You'll want to have a look. Fire department was there. It looked like a fire in among the trailers, maybe. A couple of eucalyptus trees were burning like torches.'

He paused for a moment to contemplate before going on, and then said tiredly, 'A week ago it wouldn't have mattered what you wanted. It wasn't mine to give, was it? But now poor old Graham is dead and someone's got to carry on. I believe that's you. It certainly isn't me.'

'Why isn't it you?' Howard asked softly.

'Because I'm a pawn,' Mr Jimmers said sadly. 'You're the king, aren't you? Promise me you'll remember something that I once forgot. Heloise Lamey is a dangerous adversary. The people who surround her are thugs and morons. She uses them as easily as she once used me. I thought I loved her once, years ago, and betrayed poor Graham by giving the sketch, as you call it, to her. I simply gave it away. I did it out of love, mind you. No one can say that I didn't. I had good intentions in some ways, but as they say, the road to hell is paved with that sort of brick. She threw me out when she thought she had what she wanted, and I knew I had betrayed my friend for nothing. Then it turned out that Graham had manipulated all of us by manufacturing a spurious sketch, and she had got nothing, after all.

'I was furious with him. He had seen the truth all along, seen straight through both of us, and yet had allowed me to betray him, and because of it I lost everything. I moved north and was living in the old Vance Hotel, on Second Street up in Eureka, when he found me at last and brought me back, saying that he was sorry to have used me to fight a battle in a war that I hadn't signed up for. He *hadn't* used me, though. I was sharp enough to see that. I had used him, and for purely selfish reasons. It's been my perpetual shame. I'm ... unworthy. I won't be the man to pretend to protect the thing I once betrayed.'

'That's the worst sort of rubbish,' Sylvia said. 'Tell it to the prodigal son.'

Mr Jimmers looked vaguely startled, as if he hadn't expected her to disagree.

It had sounded like he was reciting an apology that he had worked out over and over for twenty-odd years. 'Pardon me?' he said.

'That's all nonsense,' Sylvia said. 'It's true, maybe. The facts are. I'm not saying you're lying about what happened. But all these years of locking yourself away, living in your cellar – that's more a matter of feeling sorry for yourself, isn't it?'

'Well, yes, I suppose it is. How transparent I've become.' He smiled at her, putting on his old theatrical face but making a bad show of it. He looked hard at her for a few seconds before putting his hand on the door handle. For a moment Howard thought of pulling out the book that he had in his pocket, of asking Mr Jimmers about it outright. But he had already presumed too much, involved himself in other people's business.

'We ought to get down to the harbor,' he said to Sylvia.

'Yes, you should,' Mr Jimmers said.

'You'll be all right?' Sylvia asked him.

'Right as rain.' He stepped out onto the muddy roadside and half closed the door before pulling it back open. 'Remember what I said about Heloise Lamey. There's trouble on the boil. She'll see through this storm, too,' he said to Howard, looking grave now.

'They'll know you've got it, and they'll know you've used it.'

Muck-colored lilies, soft-throated and with curved, heavy-headed stamens, lay scattered across the bed, which had been partly covered with a sheet dyed red. A thick, milky-pink fluid leaked slowly out onto the sheet. The color of the flowers was nearly indescribable, as was their odor, which reminded Stoat of a pig farm. Their throats were almost black, fading to the brown-ocher of old blood at the outer rim of the petal.

A small earthen pot half full of muddy, grassy water sat on a little table beside the bed, as did a ceramic tray on which sat a slice of the cane that they had begun to cut up last night, before Howard Barton exploded the clothes dryer and stole the cane back.

'Those lilies have to be your most startling creation,' Stoat told her, not particularly happily. He sat in a chair near the window, peering out through the curtain at the street now and then. He yawned and rubbed his face blearily. 'You get used to the smell, I suppose.'

She said nothing, and after a moment he said, 'Maybe it's a necessary hazard to the occupation of power broker – living in the middle of bad smells.'

Still she said nothing, but went about her business humming. He seemed determined to make her speak, to make her acknowledge his existence. 'Curious thing about the water, too. I don't see why we can't bottle it. Make a fortune.'

She took a step back and surveyed the bed, looking satisfied with what she had accomplished so far. 'Because it's already stopped flowing,' she said to him. 'I found a half dozen indentations altogether – all of them in the back-yard of that little hovel halfway down the block. I assume that he ran through the backyard in an effort to elude the three of you, although I can't for the life of me determine why he bothered at all. Collectively you don't amount to much of a threat. The other boys sleeping the afternoon away, I suppose?'

Now it was Stoat who didn't respond, but looked out the window again instead. After a minute of silence he said, 'He'll be full of regrets before the night is through. You'll have some satisfaction out of it.'

'He who?'

'The fat man. The other one – Howard – what will he be full of? You tell me. Silver or lead?'

Mrs Lamey began to hum again as she worked away at one of the lilies, pressing the liquid out of it with her fingers so that it dribbled into the convex hollow of a tautened patch of silk cloth. 'Too late for silver,' she said. Then, after a pause, 'Pity the water dried up so quickly. The earth behind the house was soft, or the cane wouldn't have left any indentation at all. It was like six little fairyland springs – artesian water bubbling up through wells the size of a nickel and no deeper than your knuckle, flowing out into the grass. A cat was actually drinking at one of them when I came along and found them. It was a very satisfied-looking creature, quite clearly drunk, too. Dreams of springtime in its eyes. Within ten minutes of my coming all six were dry.'

'I don't believe that for a moment,' Stoat said facetiously, letting the curtain drop. 'Surely your coming had nothing to do with it ...' He fell silent. There was a look on her face that suggested she was in no mood to put up with him. 'What interest do you have in – what did you call it? Inglenook Fen? Why not some gesture more grand than that? Why not Lake Tahoe? Why can't you dry up Lake Tahoe?'

She shrugged. 'I rather like Lake Tahoe. I own considerable interest in a casino at Lake Tahoe. I don't require grand gestures, anyway. They're inartis-tic and they call attention to one, don't they? If we succeed this afternoon, though, I'd like to see what I can do with some rather large and useful reser-voir. Hetch Hetchy, I think.'

'Why *my* neighborhood?'

'The East Bay is so utterly dependent on that one source, isn't it? Imagine what two years of absolute drought would do to them? They would begin to *think* differently, and that's appealing to me. I would love to have been in Los Angeles in the thirties and forties and had a hand in draining the Owens Val-ley. For today, though, I'll concentrate on Inglenook Fen. It's always been one of my very favorite places – a remnant of the ice age. Did you know that?'

'Fascinating,' he said. 'Kill it as quick as you can.'

'I used to go out there to walk on the dunes. I've come to think of it as my own, I guess. I'm just a nostalgic old fool.' For a moment her face was over-come with a wistful, faraway look, as if she were remembering a distant, more pleasant time – days, maybe, when she could see some point in walking on the dunes, or perhaps when she had gone out walking with someone else, before that had all been spoiled for her. Just as suddenly as the wistful look had appeared, it was gone, and she applied herself to her work.

She finished with the lilies, having pressed all the juices out of them onto the silk, and she picked up a knife and swept it back and forth across the sur-face of the cloth, forcing the heavy juices through it, collecting the sieved liquid drop by drop on a circular mirror. 'Water is everything, you know. Money is nothing. Would you own north Africa, or would you own the Nile? And imagine the billions of gallons of water flowing south through this state right now, through the California Aqueduct alone, irrigating tens of millions of acres of orchards and vineyards and cotton and rice fields. What if one could shut off the flow, like water out of a sink? Imagine two or three snow-less years in the Sierra Nevada. No ice pack. No rain at all across the Northwest. Water is power. It's more than that. It's life and death.'

Stoat had fallen silent again. There was no arguing with her about that. She wasn't talking to him, anyway. She was talking to hear her head rattle. He wondered uneasily just how badly she needed him. An organization was necessary, perhaps, when you were in the real estate business, bleeding small animals like Mrs Deventer or Roy Barton, or when stalking bigger game – meddling with oil drilling rights offshore, lobbying the Coastal Commission. But this talk about water was something else. He had no intrinsic stake in that. In a moment she would simply dismiss him. There were secrets that she wouldn't reveal to him, and that was dangerous and tiresome. He hadn't bought in to that.

'Well,' she said. 'It's nearly time for me to be about my business. I'll see you at the motel later this evening?'

He nodded, putting on a smile. He was being invited to leave. There was no answering her, really – just obedience.

He closed the door after himself, and she waited, listening to his footsteps on the stairs. Through the gap in the curtains she watched him drive off. Then she dialed the phone. 'Glenwood,' she said into the receiver. 'It's time.' She listened for a moment and then said, 'Good. We want it all, this time – Jim-mers' device, all of it. We want to put an end to all their shenanigans. Do you understand me? Be thorough, but don't be foolish.'

Howard and Sylvia had to park up the hill and walk down to the harbor, past Mrs Deventer's house, where the half-wrecked Pontiac sat in the driveway. The road was cluttered with cars full of people who had come down to watch the fire and who were maneuvering now to get back out. Down below, fire trucks and equipment had blocked Harbor Drive, and firemen were spraying the burned-down remains of the old icehouse with hoses. A crowd of people milled around talking and speculating.

Sylvia started running, and Howard followed her, carrying his cane. There was no ambulance, no evidence that anyone was hurt. The haunted house had been burned pretty much out of existence, though. The walls were nothing but blackened studs and the roof had caved in right through the first-floor ceiling. The stairs were still there, leading nowhere, and with tendrils of white smoke curling up through them from where a fireman mopped up the last live embers with a fine spray. The wind off the ocean was full of the smell of wet, charred wood.

A squad car was parked behind Lou Gibb's fish restaurant, where old Bennet sat on an upturned plastic crate, pressing a bloodstained handkerchief across the back of his head. His hands and arms were smeared with ash, and his khaki pants were nearly black with it. He nodded in response to something a policeman asked him, and the man jotted notes in a spiral binder. Sylvia headed straight for them.

Howard saw Mrs Deventer herself just then, standing at the edge of a group of onlookers. Her right arm was in a sling and in her left hand she carried a closed umbrella. She wore an apron, too, as if she'd been baking cookies and the fire had interrupted her.

'Howard!' Bennet said when Howard and Sylvia strode up. Then to the policeman he said, 'This is Howard Barton. Roy Barton's nephew.'

'Where's Father?' Sylvia asked.

'He's fine. Went down to Caspar before this all started.'

The policeman stroked his mustache and sized Howard up suspiciously. Then he seemed to recognize Sylvia and brightened a little, growing chatty. 'You work at the boutique down in Mendo don't you?'

'That's right.' she said. 'I'm the owner, actually. I'm Roy Barton's daughter, Sylvia.'

'I bought my wife a shawl in there about a month ago. Bright green …'

'With big red paisleys. I remember it. Very Christmasy. Weren't you in with a little boy who wanted an ice cream?'

'That's it! That was me. I'll be damned.' he said, then turned to Howard, less suspicious now. 'And you're Barton's nephew?'

'Howard Barton. I'm visiting from down south. What's happened?'

Mrs Deventer's voice answered from behind him. 'There's been a fire,' she said.

Howard turned and nodded politely. 'Hello, Mrs Deventer,' he said. 'You must be freezing, out in this kind of weather without a coat.' He took his jacket off and held it out to her. Without protesting she slipped one arm into it, and pulled the opposite shoulder around, clutching it shut across the plaster cast on her left forearm.

'Young men are so attentive.' she said to Sylvia.

The policeman looked suddenly irritated, as if he had work to do and it wasn't being done. He ignored Mrs Deventer's remark about the fire and said to Howard. 'Looks to me like the old icehouse has burned down. It and a couple of trees. Mr Bennet here claims that he and Mr Barton were putting together some sort of fun house for Halloween.'

'We pulled a temporary license,' Bennet said. 'Didn't we, Syl?'

'That's right,' Sylvia said. 'I turned in the application myself.'

'Mr Barton was particularly proud of his store window mannequins,' Mrs Deventer said. 'He had some notion of filling their heads with noodles. I'm the one who cooked the noodles for him, aren't I?' She addressed the question to Sylvia, but clearly in order to set the policeman straight.

'Fine,' said the cop. 'The license isn't the issue. The license doesn't figure into the picture anymore, does it?' He waved at the smoking building. 'Mr Barton along with Mr Bennet here were involved in a little imbroglio late last night down in Mendocino. Don't know anything about that, do you?' He looked as Sylvia.

'Not a thing,' she said. 'Father sometimes has a little too much fun, I guess. He's harmless, though.' She cast the policeman a winning smile and he smiled back.

'We'd had a couple of drinks on the way back up from Albion,' Bennet said. 'Roy got a little loud with his landlady, that's all.'

'And today someone burns him out.' The cop's smile vanished.

'*Where* is he?' Sylvia asked, looking at Bennet.

The policeman spoke first. 'That's it, isn't it? We don't know where he is. Down in Caspar is what Mr Bennet says. We'd like to ask him a thing or two when he surfaces.'

'*Surfaces?*' Howard asked. 'What's he suspected of? What's he done?'

'Clear case of arson,' the cop said.

'You think he burned his own place down, his own haunted house? He's been working on this for weeks. Why in the hell would he do something like that?'

'Lou Gibb owns the place,' Bennet put in. 'They figure that he *hired* Roy to burn it down. Worth more burned to a cinder than turned into a haunted house. That's the logic. But who gave me this sock on the head? That's what I want to know. It wasn't Roy Barton. Thieves, that's what I think. I described the man that did it. Sneaked right up behind me. I stood up and saw him clear enough before he hit me, and it wasn't Roy Barton, not unless he was wearing a skinny-man costume. Unless of course Lou Gibb hired Roy to hire this man to hit me. If I'd have been thinking, I'd have hired him to hire me to hit myself, and we could have all kept our money and went home.'

The cop frowned. 'There's no call to get worked up, Mr Bennet.'

'I don't like all this hitting,' Mrs Deventer said. 'Why does everyone have to be hitting each other all the time? The television is full of it.'

'That's the truth,' Bennet said.

Mrs Deventer smiled suddenly. 'It was my young man who pulled Mr Bennet from the flames.'

'Stoat,' Bennet said.

'Was it?' Howard asked, not knowing exactly what this meant.

'Yes, it was,' Mrs Deventer said. 'He ran straight in and hauled Mr Bennet out of there. And very grateful for it Mr Bennet was, too.'

Bennet gave Howard a look. 'The boy ought to get an award,' he said.

The cop squinted at Bennet. 'You know,' he said, 'I can't figure your *tone* here. Your attitude. Man pulls you out of a burning building and you get hostile about it. That doesn't make any sense, does it?'

'No,' said Mr Bennet. 'I don't guess it does.' He looked sheepish for a moment. 'It's this knock on the head. It's been a rough night. Where'd that young man of yours go?' he asked Mrs Deventer. 'I'd like to thank him personally, give him a little gift.'

'He's not the sort to bask in glory,' she said proudly. 'It's not in his nature. He did what he could and went on his way. He's so thoughtful.'

'He's a prince,' Howard said.

The policeman waited Mrs Deventer out, smiling widely and nodding his head. 'Thank you for your insights,' he said to her. 'I'll see what I can do to get the boy a written commendation of some sort.' Then to Sylvia and Howard he said. 'You've got to admit that there isn't much motive for robbery here, regardless of what Mr Bennet says.' He gestured toward the wall of the restaurant, back into the shadows. 'No thief in his right mind wants this kind of trash.' There in a charred heap lay the remains of the two Brainiacs alongside the partly melted ice chest, which stood open now, the cow brains inside cooked white and standing in a half inch of milky water. Pieces of blackened skeleton lay in a pile, too, along with a half dozen jack-o'-lanterns that somehow had survived the blaze.

'My God,' said Mrs Deventer, covering her mouth with her hands. 'It's the dummies. And Mr Barton was so proud of them, too.'

'That's all that's left,' Bennet said sadly. 'Just the stuff that was sitting in the front room. I managed to get that much out. Rest of it's charcoal. The bastards pretty much wiped us out. Thank God Roy hadn't brought the eyeballs down yet or the equipment for the ghost woman on the stairs. If it hadn't been for that freak storm, the fire would have torn through the whole damned harbor in a wind like this. Rain put it right out, though. It was an act of God.'

Mrs Deventer nodded.

'That's true enough,' the cop said. 'First rain we've had, too, in months.' Just then there was a blast of static on the patrol car radio followed by someone chattering. He nodded at the three of them and hurried across to the car, climbing in and talking back to the radio. He slid entirely in and fired up the engine, then shouted through the open window on the passenger side, 'Tell Mr Barton to come downtown when you see him. Either that, or we'll be around to pick him up. Thanks a lot, folks.' With that, he drove off up the hill.

'They don't believe that nonsense about Uncle Roy and the insurance,' Sylvia said flatly.

Bennet touched his forehead gingerly. 'Of course they don't. Icehouse wasn't even insured. Gibb put up the money for liability insurance for a month, just until after Halloween. Then the place was coming down. A phone call or two would blow a hole in the whole theory. What they probably think is that we were up to something else here – hustling dope, maybe – and a deal went bad. That would make more sense, except that there's people swarming through here all the time – tourists, locals. Door stands open all day. We haven't kept any secrets here. What I think is that they'll end up writing the whole thing off to a nut. Come on inside.'

'I'll just be walking back up the hill,' Mrs Deventer said, starting out in that direction.

Bennet waved at her and then stood up and opened the back door of the fish restaurant, leading Howard and Sylvia into the kitchen, where Lou Gibb filleted fish at a long steel counter. A busboy sloshed a mop around the floor. Through the dining room door Howard could see that the restaurant was empty of customers. 'My doggone coat,' he said to Sylvia.

'Go get it,' she told him.

He shook his head. 'It'll give me an excuse to drop past her house. Let her wear it home. She needs it on a night like this.'

'Still waiting for the phone call,' Gibb said to Bennet, and then pulled three beers out of a refrigerator, handing one to each of them. 'I've locked up for the day. Sent everyone home. Sit down.' He pulled a stool away from the wall, nodding Sylvia toward it. 'You take off, Jack,' he said to the busboy, who put the mop back into the bucket, untied his apron, and stepped out the back door.

'So what's Father doing down in Caspar?' she asked.

'She don't know?' Gibb looked up suddenly at Bennet, who shook his head.

'He's not down in Caspar,' Bennet said. 'We're not sure where he is. We think he's all right. No reason that he shouldn't be all right.'

'What do you mean?' she asked, standing back up.

'They've got him. I couldn't say anything in front of the cop.'

'*Who's* got him?'

'We all know who's got him, don't we? It's her. The old woman. They knocked me on the head, grabbed him, and burned the icehouse. Out of spite, I guess. After last night.'

'Did they get the machine?' Howard asked.

Bennet shook his head. 'I drove it up to the Georgia-Pacific yard this morning. Turned out to be a good thing. MacDonald's looking out for it. He's moved it across town by now. No one knows where but him.'

'We don't *know* it's them,' Lou Gibb said to Sylvia. 'Might have been Jimmers. He was down here this afternoon, snooping around. He ate lunch and then went round back and had it out with Roy. They got pretty hot under the collar. Regular shouting match. Jimmers went off mad as hell. He might have come back and torched the place just as easy as anyone else. Maybe he finally went off the deep end.'

'We just left him.' Howard said. 'He didn't have anything to do with anything. Last thing he'd do is kidnap Uncle Roy or burn down the haunted house. Take my word for it. It doesn't matter how mad he might have been this afternoon.'

Gibb shrugged. 'I guess I know that. But it would have made things easier if it *was* Jimmers, wouldn't it?'

Sylvia moved toward the door. 'We've got to go.' she said to Howard as soon as Gibb had finished talking. 'At least I do. We can't leave Mother alone. They might have gone there, too.'

'She's safe,' Bennet said. 'I talked to her fifteen minutes ago.'

'I'm more help there,' Sylvia said resolutely.

'Call us first thing you hear anything,' Howard said, following Sylvia out into the evening.

Most of the crowd had dispersed by then. Harbor Drive was empty of parked cars and the only people milling around the burned icehouse were local children from the house trailers, throwing rocks at each other and dodging in and out behind buildings and fences and trees. Two firemen rolled up hoses while a couple more poked through the ashes along with a policeman and a city official of some sort wearing a suit and a pair of knee-high rubber boots.

Howard looked back at the old icehouse as they trudged silently up the hill. Burned buildings had always seemed lonesome and horrifying to him in some way all their own. There was something final and deadening and dark about them that suggested the worst kind of tragedy, even if, as was true of the icehouse, they were going to be torn down, anyway. It occurred to him that at least now Uncle Roy wouldn't have to face the failure of another doomed business venture. Except, of course, that the venture might have worked. Or at least if it hadn't, Uncle Roy ought to have been able to take a stab at it. Perhaps that's what made the burned icehouse such a sad thing – that one of his uncle's dreams had gone up with it, and it was dreams, largely, that kept Uncle Roy afloat.

They were almost to the car when they heard the phone ring, back down on the outside wall of the restaurant. They turned and ran without saying a word, watching Gibb come out of the back door to answer it, followed by Bennet, who cocked his head by the receiver, listening to the call. Gibb had already hung up by the time Howard and Sylvia got there. He stood scowling, deep in thought, and Bennet had sat down tiredly again on the plastic crate. 'It's them,' he said to Sylvia. 'They contacted your mother. She just hung up. They want the sketch in a swap for Roy.'

'We don't have the goddamn sketch,' Bennet said.

'Yes, we do,' Howard said, closing his eyes. 'And they know we do.'

Heloise Lamey drove north up the coast highway, through Fort Bragg. She smelled the tips of her fingers. Soap and water hadn't begun to eradicate the odor of the lilies. There was the smell of charred wood on them, too, separate and distinct from the lilies, like the smell of pruning fires on the wind. She wondered if the smells would ever entirely go away. She drove through Cleone, pulling off onto Ward Avenue and parking at the beach. From there she walked north on the old logging road until it disappeared beneath the sand. She set off across the empty dunes then, scuffing along through the gray sand.

The rotten lily smell hovered on the sea wind along with the smell of ashes, as if it had blown that afternoon through the second-story window of her house, drifted out across the bluffs and north along the coast, reaching long and smoky fingers toward Inglenook Fen. Could everyone smell it? Were people remarking on it right then, back in Fort Bragg, wondering what it was, what it meant? There was something satisfactory in the idea of people turning their heads, wondering, sniffing the air. Still, it was vanity that made her think so, and what she lived for was of vastly more importance than any momentary evidence of her power.

She topped a tall dune, looking for the distant, telltale stand of willows that ran down into the fen. The tiny lake itself was hidden by hills of sand, fed only by rainwater, as it had been since the ice age. Supposedly there were ice age microorganisms still in the fen, too, as well as water lilies and cattails. That was rather nice – the notion of reaching out a hand and brushing away not just any body of water, but this wild little isolated fen that was connected by rainwater to antiquity.

The dunes were empty of human footprints. Few people wandered out into the miles of rolling dunes, and the sea wind sculpted the sand continually, obliterating the evidence of life. Rodent prints and the splayed tracks of sea gulls stippled the sand in sheltered spots, and occasional clumps of horsetail ran down into the valleys. Here and there lay the scattered, bleached bones of small animals and the dried, white husks of dead plants. In the valleys the wide world round about disappeared utterly. There was only the sky and the sound of seabirds, and she was connected to her past and future only by the odor lingering in the air, more potent now, it seemed to her, as if it were hanging in an invisible cloud over the depression that contained the fen.

From one comparatively high ridge she could see the willows again, and she corrected her course, starting down into another valley and up the other side. She walked for twenty minutes, topping a little rise no different from all the others, except that below her now, walled in by dunes, lay the fen, protected from the wind and the sea.

Already the willows lined an empty stream bed in which the mud was drying and cracking. There was no longer any water emptying into the fen. Even as she watched, the cattails in the tiny lake seemed to rise up out of the water along the shoreline, as if they were growing. The smell of lilies and ashes was heavy in the air despite the sea wind. The water receded, emptying away into the surrounding sands, giving the illusion of a speeded-up motion picture. There was a tangle of roots and rotted vegetation around the cattails now, and the broad green leaves of the water lilies lay limp on the drying bed.

She sat in the sand and watched the fen evaporate, thinking of the central valleys, of the San Joaquin River, the Sacramento River, the Feather River. She pictured their dry beds, white stones hot in the afternoon sun. Farther north lay the Eel and the Trinity rivers and to the east flowed the Colorado, straight through the desolation of the great Southwest deserts. She sat picturing what it would be like merely to wiggle one's finger at this lake, say, or at that river or reservoir, and to see it begin to evaporate like water off a hot sidewalk, just like that into the air. And then she imagined rain in the desert, irrigating the Mojave. She would turn the Coachella Valley to dry dust, wither the grapefruit trees and the date orchards. She would grow rice in Death Valley. They could play golf in Boron and sift sand in an abandoned Palm Springs. Coyotes could have the resort hotels with their broken windows and cobwebby cinder block and empty swimming pools.

It was an ambitious afternoon, all in all – this small beginning out in the dunes. It made her hunger to possess the Grail, to have the power in full, to make these dreams as clear and solid as ice.

She realized she was cold suddenly, and the cold brought her up out of her dreaming about water. The fen was empty now. The wind scoured along the top of the dunes, blowing sand down into the forest of willows surrounding the bed of the dry fen. Slowly the sand began to cover the roots of the cattails and water lilies. She wondered how much time would have to pass before there was no evidence of water at all below the broken tops of scattered cattails.

It would be a long walk back to the car, success or no success, and there was a busy evening ahead. From her aerie atop the dune she could see black smoke rising over Fort Bragg – over the harbor, more exactly. That struck her as entirely satisfactory. Things were coming along. Her minions were going about their humble duties. She sniffed the wind, hoping to catch a hint of burning. That was asking for too much, perhaps. The odor of lilies and ash was faint, as if it had been a sort of magical catalyst that had finally been transmuted into something else, the remnants of it muffled by shifting sand.

She walked crab-legged down the edge of the steep dune, her shoes filling with sand. At the bottom she stopped and sniffed the air suspiciously. There was the smell of ozone on the wind now, of impending rain. She hurried up the next slope in order to get a view. Miles to the south, out over the ocean and driving in toward land, were heavy, black storm clouds – a clump of them, like someone's private hurricane. She could hear distant thunder.

The lily and ash magic had faded entirely from the sea wind now, and the sudden rainwater smell that had taken its place struck her unpleasantly as being its utter opposite, a sort of magical counterpoint. Overwhelmed with the sudden fear that the fen had somehow restored itself, she turned around and trudged back down into the valley, then up again to have one last look at it, to make sure of her work. It was empty – scummed over with a half inch of dry sand. With a growing smile, she watched the storm clouds suspiciously for a moment before starting out once again for the car.

Surrounded by sand and with the storm invisible beyond the dunes, she was suddenly greedy for dry things, for bringing another body of water into nonexistence – something that would matter next time, that would make people uncomfortable, change the way they perceived the world around them. The fen was gone, erased. It had no further value. The past was of no consequence to her.

She cursed Howard Barton out loud and cursed Stoat, too, for having been so damned slow about slicing up the cane. And then all of them running downstairs like fools at the sound of the explosion … If only she had more of it, more of the little disks of wood, she could return home now and start to work again, drying the standing and moving water out of the north coast like so many rain puddles.

27

'That's Jimmers' car,' Sylvia said when they turned the corner and drove toward the house. 'Jimmers is here with Mother.'

'Good,' Howard said happily, realizing that he was filled with immense relief but not, strangely, with surprise. Mr Jimmers had come through, out of nowhere. He would help them. Suddenly it seemed to Howard that they had a chance, after all. Although he couldn't have explained it easily, Mr Jimmers had become like a giant to him – an unpredictable force, one of the kings of the night, who watched the weather and stars through his tower window and navigated secret tunnels in the earth.

Sylvia pulled in at the curb, cut the engine, and jumped out of the car, heading for the house without waiting for Howard. Mr Jimmers met them at the door. He looked haggard and upset. His hair was wild, and he worked his hands together, forcing air through his fingers and making a sort of squeaking noise while he apologized for being there at all, for having come in uninvited. His clothes were rumpled and damp. Clearly he hadn't changed since going out into the storm.

'Where's Mother?' Sylvia asked, pushing past him into the house.

'Gone,' Jimmers said at once. 'She went after him.' He handed Sylvia a note, hastily written on the back of an envelope.

'Gone to get your father,' it read, and below that was the address and telephone number of the Sea Spray Motel.

'Damn it!' Sylvia said, sitting down on a chair and then standing up again. '*Why did she go?*'

'Because she loves him,' Jimmers said.

Sylvia shook her head. 'Of course she does. But she can't do anything at all. Can she?'

'She couldn't just sit here, either. Not your mother. She can at least try to be with him. I couldn't stay away, either. Not after our little discussion in the car tonight. I know what Edith's thinking, what she's feeling. She and I, well …' Mr Jimmers sat down shakily on the couch and stared for a moment before going on. 'She called thirty minutes ago and told me what they'd done, where they'd taken him and what they wanted. I rushed straight up here, and when no one answered the door, I let myself in and found this note. Should have waited for you, I guess.'

'No,' Sylvia said. 'Thanks for doing it. There was no telling what sort of trouble …'

'Exactly.'

Abruptly Sylvia began to cry, slumping in the chair again. Howard perched himself on the chair arm and put his hand on her shoulder, awkwardly trying to do some good. Edith's having gone after Uncle Roy made the whole thing about twice as hard, not just because now she was in trouble, too, but because she had set a Standard for them to follow. Aunt Edith had gone straight to the heart of danger and was right then confronting the enemy at the Sea Spray Motel, while Howard was lounging around the living room, unable to reason any of it out.

'Where's this motel?' Howard asked.

'Right up the street,' Sylvia said. 'It's on the ocean side of the highway, right above Pudding Creek. It's empty – being renovated, I think. There's new owners, or something.'

'I bet I know who.' Howard stood looking out the window, chewing his lip. His mind spun. What was called for here? A show of force? Trickery?

'How serious is Mrs Lamey?' he asked Jimmers.

'Deadly. I warned you.' He glanced at Sylvia, who wiped her eyes with the back of her hand. 'No use mincing words.'

'They'll kill him,' Sylvia said.

'Surely not both of them.' Howard appealed to Mr Jimmers. It was impossible to believe that things had gotten so desperate so quickly. 'They can't get away with murder. It's one thing to knock apart Mr Bennet's Humpty Dumpty, even to burn down the icehouse, but murder ...'

'Mr Bennet might easily be dead now if Stoat hadn't pulled him out of the fire,' Sylvia said.

'That's what I mean. *Stoat* pulled him out. They were anxious not to murder anyone, just to burn us down – and probably steal the truck back if Bennet hadn't been one step ahead of them.'

Sylvia shook her head. 'What if Stoat didn't burn the icehouse? What if Mrs Deventer is right?'

'You can't believe that,' Howard said.

'I *do* believe it. You can't, because you're jealous of him, and—'

'Wait a minute,' Howard said, interrupting her. Mr Jimmers studied his fingernails, keeping silent. 'I'm *not* jealous. That's not the problem. Let's not confuse the issue here.'

Sylvia looked at him steadily.

'All right. Maybe a little. Of course I am. Why shouldn't I be? That doesn't prove anything in any direction, does it? That doesn't make him innocent of any crimes. Who do you think loosened the lug nuts on Mrs Deventer's car? Stoat's the one who's always hanging around there. Maybe I *am* a little jealous, but that doesn't alter anything.'

'I just wanted to make you admit it,' Sylvia said, almost smiling for a moment. 'And I didn't say he was innocent of any crimes. I only said that I don't think he'd stoop to arson and murder. I don't think he had anything to do with screwing up Mrs Deventer's car. I saw him next morning downtown. He'd just heard about her accident. He was pretty shaken up.'

'Easy to fake,' Howard said sulkily.

'That's true, too. Anyway, what I'm saying is that they *would* be murderers, and that they almost murdered Bennet. Your being jealous of Stoat makes you underestimate them. That kind of thinking is dangerous here.'

No one spoke for a moment while Howard grappled with this notion. Finally Mr Jimmers said, 'She's right, you know.'

Howard shrugged. It was possible. Hell, she probably *was* right.

'I'm familiar with this jealousy business,' Jimmers said. 'It's a potent thing. It'll fill you up with false regrets. Take it from a man well seasoned in it.'

Howard nodded. 'I'll try to keep things straight,' he said. He smiled at Sylvia, though, rolling his eyes, and got a smile in return. Maybe there hadn't been any harm in clearing the decks. He could get on with it now. 'So what are we talking about here? What's the stakes?'

'Higher than you can imagine,' Jimmers said. Then, after a pause, he added, 'It was your coming here that brought it to a head. You were bound to come. There's no blame involved. But all of us knew something was coming, Roy included. Graham was fishing for someone, and out of the blue you called up and volunteered for the post. You were a natural. You can bet it didn't surprise Roy Barton any when they made their move. He was primed for it. I'm afraid that of all of us, you're the one who knows the least. So I'll be blunt. Right now the stakes are high and simple: they want you and the print.'

'That's the deal?' Howard asked.

'That's it in a nutshell.'

Howard shrugged. 'Then let's get on with it.' There seemed to be no option. He was moderately certain now what it was he had inherited, and he was equally sure that he didn't want it. What he wanted, he had come to understand, was Sylvia and a change in the way he lived his life. As unsettling and strange as the north coast air seemed to be, in the few days he'd been there he had come to like it. It suited him. Southern California had grown gray and hazy for him. 'Let's give the damned thing up, right now. We'll go up to the motel and deliver it like a pizza, trade it straight across for Uncle Roy. Then we'll all go out for dinner. Maybe we can squeak a couple of months' free rent out of the deal.'

Mr Jimmers sighed. 'She doesn't just want the *object*. She wants to *use* it. She wants its power. If she can't use it, it's worthless to her.'

'Let her go to town on it. She can use it like crazy. We need a little rain.'

'She couldn't even begin to get the pizza out of the box,' Jimmers said. 'She would need you for that. And you can bet she won't be satisfied with a little rain. She sees herself as the queen of the weather, and right now, she's too close to being right. If there's any going out to dinner tonight, you wouldn't be along for it, I'm afraid. She'll put you to some sort of ... use.'

'To hell with dinner,' Howard said, although doubtfully now. 'I'll grab a bite at the Gas 'n' Grub.'

'Father's been fighting this war for years,' Sylvia said. 'We can't just go up there and chuck it all in. He wouldn't want that.'

'No, he wouldn't,' Jimmers said. 'Nice of you to offer, though, Howard. It's exactly what I'd expect you to do. And more importantly, it's exactly what *they* expect you to do by now, or rather, what *she* expects you to do. "How serious is Howard Barton?" she's been asking herself. "What does he *want*?" As soon as she discovers that you don't *want* anything, not like she wants things, then she'll think you're easy to read. There's nothing particularly complicated about a hero. A hero will take another man's bullet without thinking it out first. And when he does have time to think it out, he'll take the bullet, anyway.'

Howard waved the notion away. 'That's somebody else you're talking about. I'm not big on bullets. But what do we do? How long do we have?'

'They've given us a deadline, actually. Very melodramatic. We come through by midnight tonight if we want to see Roy Barton alive.'

The Sea Spray Motel sat above the ocean, cheerfully painted in yellow and white and blue, with scalloped bargeboard trim along the length of the single-story row of rooms. Edith parked the station wagon in the deserted lot and surveyed the motel, not letting herself think, but simply keeping on. Roy was in one of the rooms, and she meant to find out which one. And then join him there. It was simple as that.

The night was lit by moonlight and neon, and she could see Pudding Creek just to the south of the motel, running out through a drain under the highway and then looping around toward the ocean. It was very nearly dry and it pooled up into a little slough between big sand dunes. A railroad trestle some thirty or forty feet high spanned the water and dunes at the mouth of the creek, and beyond the trestle the sandy beach was heaped with big clumps of brown kelp, looking like low, creeping shrubs in the moonlight. There was the smell of the ocean and of diesel exhaust from trucks on the highway.

Seeing a movement of drapes in a nearby lighted room, Edith stepped along up the concrete walk and knocked squarely on the door, holding her purse.

There was nothing for a moment except the sound of gulls and traffic. Then there was a swish of quiet movement inside and hushed talk, followed by a muffled shout – just the word 'Hey!' very loud and cut off by the sound of a hand slap and a grunt. Edith knocked again, hard this time. More silence followed.

'I have it!' she shouted, knocking once more. 'Heloise Lamey, I have what you want!' The light in the room blinked out, and there was the sound of a chain lock sliding and rattling. The door swung halfway open. The room inside was dark, and Edith squinted to see.

'Come in,' a woman's voice said.

And then immediately there was another shout, the word 'Don't!' followed by the sound of another hand slap and voice hissing out a warning.

Edith steeled herself and walked into the room. The door shut behind her and a man stepped out from behind it and switched on the light. Heloise Lamey sat in a chair by a wood-grain Formica table. There was a crossword puzzle and pencil in front of her, along with a couple of Styrofoam cups empty except for coffee dregs and lipstick stains.

'Timothy!' Edith said, surprised to see the man who had stepped out from behind the door.

He nodded at her, looking half ashamed of himself. Mrs Lamey glanced at him sharply, as if suddenly unhappy and doubtful. 'I didn't know that you and Edith Barton were on such familiar terms, Mr Stoat.'

'Years ago,' he mumbled. 'Knew each other briefly.'

'It *was* brief, wasn't it?' Edith said. 'I seem to remember, though, you having eaten at our table more than once. You must have forgotten that.'

He shrugged and moved away, sitting across from Mrs Lamey, his usual cool and haughty demeanor gone from his face and replaced now by something like the look of an embarrassed teenager. 'Lock the damned door,' Mrs Lamey said to him in a disgusted tone.

'It *is* locked,' Stoat replied. 'It locks automatically.'

'The chain lock, too.'

Edith turned around and slipped the chain lock into place.

'Thanks,' Stoat said politely, cutting it off sharp when Mrs Lamey gave him a vicious look. He shrugged, narrowing his eyes, and then started to pick at the rim of one of the coffee cups, tearing off little fragments of Styrofoam and avoiding the gaze of either woman.

'Well?' Mrs Lamey asked.

'I don't have it,' Edith said. 'That was a lie to get you to open the door.'

Mrs Lamey nodded slowly and wide-eyed, as if Edith were a first grader at share time. 'Then what do you want?' she said.

'I want my husband.'

'Well, you can't have him.' Mrs Lamey's voice drifted up an octave. 'Except in trade. That's what I told you over the phone. Things haven't changed any, have they? I expect I'll have to dispose of both of you now. You can't leave, you know, after walking in here like this. That was your second great mistake. Your first was to marry Roy Barton. What an unhappy and unfathomable thing. I can't say I understand it at all.'

'Of course you can't. You don't understand anything, not really. If you did, you'd know that I don't *want* to leave, not without Roy. Didn't I just tell you I wanted my husband? That meant nothing at all to you.'

Mrs Lamey stared at Edith for a moment, as if she were going to contradict her. Haughtily Mrs Lamey said, 'You know *nothing* about me. Nothing. How *dare* you judge me. I am ... I'm a ... *victim*, Mrs Barton.' She smoothed her hair, straining to keep her face composed.

'Aren't we all?' Edith said softly.

'Some of us more than others, I assure you,' Mrs Lamey said. 'There's no time for philosophy now, though. What you do or do not understand is of no concern to me. I told you that you can't *have* your husband, although why on earth you'd want a bloated old hulk like that I can't say.' Mrs Lamey was blinking hard now, staring at the tabletop, her lips pursed with tension. 'He was young and fit once, I suppose, which might explain something. But now … I'm afraid he's become a commodity now. Something to be bought and sold.'

'That's all there is to you, isn't it?' Edith said. 'Buying and selling. You're as simple as a wrinkled old dollar bill.'

Mrs Lamey gave Stoat a sudden furious look. 'What are you grinning at, Cheshire Cat?' she asked him, and abruptly he went back to picking at his Styrofoam cup, dropping the pieces onto a little heap inside. 'It's *you* that knows nothing and never has,' she said to Edith. 'You've lived an empty, wasted life. You've accumulated *nothing*. You've come to *nothing*, except perhaps the end, finally.' With an air of furious dismissal she picked up the crossword puzzle book, asking Stoat, 'What's a five-letter word for a confounding problem?'

'Bitch,' Stoat said flatly, standing up and heading for the door. 'I'm going down the road for another cup of coffee.' As he passed Edith he widened his eyes briefly, meeting her own and then looking hard at the door and throwing his head back a barely perceptible half inch.

'Try "poser,"' Edith said to Mrs Lamey, ignoring Stoat entirely. Stoat went out into the evening, shutting the door after himself. Then Edith asked, 'Where is he?'

Mrs Lamey nodded toward a connecting door to an adjacent room. Without asking anything more, Edith strode across to it, opened it, and stepped through. Beyond was a room identical to the first, except that Uncle Roy sat tied to one of the two chairs at the Formica table. In front of him was a Coke can and an ice bucket half full of melting ice. Lying on the bed was an oily-looking man in his twenties, smartly but casually dressed and with small, close-set eyes. He jotted notes in a spiral binder and didn't look up.

Edith ignored him just as thoroughly. A line of blood trickled from the corner of her husband's mouth and the side of his face near his right eye was puffy and bruised. She forced herself to smile at him, and he smiled back, wiggling his ears and then wincing. 'You shouldn't be here,' he said.

'I couldn't stay away. I missed you too much. This isn't one of your little business ventures, you know. You need me here.'

'That's a fact,' he said simply.

'And there's a lot we haven't said to each other,' she said. 'There's a lot we haven't done.' She sat in the chair across from him and put a hand on his knee, giving him a squeeze.

His chest heaved and he grinned lopsidedly, tried to speak, and couldn't. She reached up and wiped the corner of his eye, starting to cry herself, and then, suddenly angry, she began to untie the rope that held him in the chair.

The man on the bed looked up tiredly, as if the whole business were a bore. 'Would you *please* give that up?' he asked.

Roy nodded at her, and she sat up. 'We'll wait, then,' she said. 'Shouldn't be long.'

'Something happening?' Roy asked aloud.

'Jack MacDonald and thirty or forty mill workers are coming down here with something – what was it? Iron pipes, I think he said.'

She looked up at the man on the bed, who was very casually rubbing an automatic pistol with a rag now, buffing out fingerprints. He sighted down along the barrel, swinging it from the swag lamp to the ice bucket to Roy's head. Edith gasped and half stood up, as if she would push Roy's chair over backward. 'Bang,' the man said quietly, and then laid the pistol down on the nightstand next to the bed.

'This is Glendale Flounder,' Roy said to Edith. 'Something unfortunate like that. I misremember his exact name. He's a hoser of the first water, though. A literary critic out of San Francisco, who's got this thing about pistol barrels that would make Freud sick. Nearly shot his foot off a half hour ago. I had to show him how to release the damned safety. With her money you'd think she could afford pros, and instead she hires a bunch of goddamn artists and poets. It's enough to make you wonder. He's writing his novel right now. As we speak. I bet it's good. A laugh a minute. Excuse me. Glendale. What's the title again? I forgot.'

The man said nothing. His pencil scratched across the page.

'Don't antagonize him,' Edith whispered.

Roy shrugged. 'Say!' he said, brightening up. 'I've come up with a great notion, speaking of business.'

'Good,' she said cheerfully. 'What's your idea?'

'A sort of miniature golf course and amusement park, out between the airport and the azalea gardens.'

'Really?' Edith said in an encouraging tone of voice.

'A sure bet, too. Almost no risk. Limited capital outlay. There's a whole lot of Georgia-Pacific acreage lying fallow out there. Hasn't been used in thirty years. I figure that Bennet and me can build a stucco castle – big and gaudy but just a cheap facade, something you can see from the highway – and fill it full of video games. We'll lay out a pissant little golf course along the bluffs, indoor-outdoor carpeting and that sort of thing. A bunch of Bennet's whirligigs. That'll draw the families, you know. Families are paramount, even though financially speaking they aren't worth anything to you. It's the video games that pay, but we don't want this just to be some kind of teenage hangout.'

'Of course not,' Edith said.

'Anyway, picture a driving range out into the ocean. Maybe buoys out there as yardage markers. Turns out you can buy worthless old balls from courses all over the country for next to nothing, as well as seconds from the golf ball factory. The way I figure it, people will pay plenty for a bucket of balls if they can just knock them to hell and gone into the Pacific.'

Edith smiled happily. 'Yes,' she said. 'That would be nice, wouldn't it? A golf course on the ocean, like Pebble Beach. Remember when we took the Seventeen-mile Drive down around Carmel and stayed at that Spanish-style hotel? We had the worst food in the world at that Mexican restaurant.'

'Tasted like dog food,' Roy said. 'All that black, shredded meat. It wasn't beef; I know that much. Anyway, we'd' paint them, the golf balls – dip them by the basketful and then pick out the worst of them for the driving range. We'll buy secondhand putters and drivers. You see them all the time at garage sales. That's where you and Sylvia come into the picture.'

Roy stared off into space as if he were picturing the whole thing in his mind – a seaside kingdom above the ocean, built of stucco and electronics and wooden whirlibobs. 'Like I said,' he continued, 'the video games would draw the kids more than the golf would. You don't even have to buy the video machines – just pay a percentage. A man comes around once a week to service them and haul away gunnysacks full of quarters. They're doing this sort of thing all over the place down south. There was a big article in *Forbes* ...'

The phone rang just then in the next room, and Glenwood Touchey jumped up from the bed, slipped his pistol into his pocket, and pushed open the connecting door in order to listen in on the call.

'Who?' they heard Mrs Lamey ask. There was a moment's silence.

'Not *the* Artemis Jimmers,' she said, affecting astonishment. 'Well, yes, we *are* here at the motel. We're beating poor Mr Barton to within an inch, aren't we? You can have the inch, though, if you hurry. And please don't send any more emissaries unless you want to lose them, too. I believe I made it clear that I'm most anxious to consult with Howard Barton, not with his extended family. Listen very carefully now. When I hang up, I'm sending the Bartons away in a car, in very capable hands. If anyone shows up on my doorstep, anyone at all, except Howard Barton, I'm going to place a single phone call to the awful place that they've taken the poor Bartons. I'm going to let the phone ring exactly once, and then hang up. That ring will be the last thing that either one of them hears this side of hell. Tell that to the daughter, please. None of us can afford secrets.'

After this speech there was another silence. Through the door Edith could see Mrs Lamey's eyes narrow. Then she turned away to face the opposite wall as she listened. The door opened and Stoat came in, chain-locking it behind him and carrying a cup of coffee. He stood silently and expectantly, waiting for Mrs Lamey to speak.

'It's *what*?' she asked finally. 'A machine that conjures up ghosts? Built by John Ruskin? It only conjures up *his* ghost? Ah! It's because his bones are in it? That's rather cheap, isn't it?' She broke into a theatrical titter, turning around to look into the second room. There was no laughter in her face. 'Mr Barton has been telling me that your tin shed contains the Ark of the Covenant. He had me half convinced. I've never seen such a pack of liars as you two silly men. Really, you're both quite amusing. This whole situation is just as entertaining as it can be, isn't it?'

After another moment's listening, she held her hand over the receiver and said toward the second door, 'Mr Jimmers insists that you made up this nonsense about the Ark of the Covenant, Mr Barton. He claims you were lying to protect him, to keep the *real* identity of the machine a secret. He claims that we can use it to call John Ruskin up from the spirit world.'

'That's entirely correct,' Roy said, nodding broadly. 'I was lying about it all along.'

Into the receiver Mrs Lamey said, 'Mr Barton admits to having lied. We'll have to punish him for that.' She listened again and then said, 'But it's so very enjoyable, isn't it? No, I'm not interested in trading anyone for your machine. Yes, I've read your pamphlet about phone-calling the dead. When did you publish that, by the way? Back around 1961, wasn't it? And I'm just as familiar as I can be with the work that Mr Edison was doing on the spirit telephone when he died. He was a lunatic, too. They come in all shapes and sizes, Artemis, genius notwithstanding. I'll tell you what I'll do, though. I'll allow Howard Barton to bring the machine along, as a sort of gift. That's right. I'll take it into the bargain, since you've been gracious enough to offer.'

She hung up right then and sat looking at the phone. 'The fool's going to bring the machine back around, too,' she said to Stoat. 'Lord knows what it *really* is.' To Touchey she said, 'Get them out of here now. Gwendolyn is waiting for you. You two behave yourselves. Pay no attention to what I told that idiot over the phone. If I don't call by 2AM do what I've asked you to do.'

'The machine angle was a dead loss,' Mr Jimmers said unhappily as he hung up the phone. 'It was worth a try, though. One more quick phone call. What's the number of the pay phone down at the harbor? We've got to get someone down to watch the motel, to follow anyone who tries to move them out of there.'

Sylvia recited the number. 'I'll stay here for now,' she said after Jimmers made the call. 'Someone ought to be near the phone. Mother ... I don't know ... Maybe she'll come back. I'd want to be here. Why don't you two pick me up on your way back down?'

'Good enough,' Jimmers said. 'But watch out. Don't answer the door without knowing who it is.'

'They won't bother me,' she said. 'There's no reason for it.' Then she ushered them out the door as if she wanted to be alone, and Howard very nearly suggested that Jimmers drive back down to the stone house by himself. The night was windy, clear, and cold, and what Howard wanted to do was to spend the next forty minutes alone with Sylvia, just the two of them, before he had to confront Mrs Lamey at the Sea Spray Motel.

'We'll take your car,' Jimmers said, heading for the street. 'If they see my car parked out front here, they won't get up to any tricks. They know me.'

Howard was swept along by Jimmers' haste, and the two of them piled into Howard's truck, driving out to Main Street and turning south. There would be plenty of time to spend with Sylvia later, Howard told himself optimistically. Before the sun rose in the morning he and Sylvia would thrash things out. It was either that, or Howard would go home. There was no staying on the north coast unless his staying involved Sylvia.

'So Mr Bennet's truck is parked downtown now, behind the Tip Top Lounge,' Jimmers said. 'We'll pick it up on the way back. Key's under the mat.'

'Mrs Lamey won't fall for the fake sketch,' Howard said, pulling his mind back around to a more immediate problem. 'Not a second time.'

'Of course she won't. I'm betting on that. She'll make you *use* the thing, is what she'll do, and that can't be done indoors. She'll take you somewhere – not far, because she'll be in a sweat to get this business done. My guess is that the two of you will go down to the beach, and she'll insist that you demonstrate its authenticity right there. You can bet your eyeteeth that she's aware of your little storm this afternoon. If I'm right, it'll be a dangerous moment on the beach there, which is where you've got to take her. You'll insist on it. You've got to seem desperate to free Roy and Edith. She'll expect the thing to be a fake, of course, and if you don't come through with something – a rain squall or whatever ...'

After a moment's silence he went on. 'I'm tolerably certain she won't kill *you*, though. Not yet, anyway. It's Roy and Edith that we're worried about. She's *utterly* capable of any sort of atrocity. Remember that. She's terribly hungry, though, for what she's been chasing all these years. Graham's passing puts everything within her reach, and I'm thinking that she'll be nearly insane with all her nasty passions. That'll be to our advantage. You'll make use of it. She's got to be convinced that she's got the real article, though, which is where Sylvia and I play our part.'

'Do you think she'll move them out of there,' Howard asked, 'like she says?'

Jimmers thought for a moment before answering. 'No, she just wants to scare us away from calling in the authorities. We'll have to let our friend Bennet watch that angle. We can't worry about that now. We've got to pick up the fraudulent copy and get back up here.'

Howard accelerated to sixty, checking the rearview mirror.

'Damn it!' Mr Jimmers said. 'Why didn't I think to bring it in the first place? I don't like all this rushing up and down. It propagates confusion.'

'There wasn't time to think,' Howard said, watching Caspar hurtle past on their right. 'How do you manufacture these fakes? They look awfully good, don't they?'

'They look good enough to fool almost anyone. It won't fool Heloise Lamey, though, not once she gets a chance to study it out. We're depending on haste and disorder. It's an easy trick, forgery is. You use a photographic negative to expose a light-sensitive zinc plate, then etch it with nitric acid. Simple printing plate, really. The paper was authentically old. I bought it years ago in San Francisco from a dealer in oriental antiquities. You can fake up old-seeming ink out of common iron gall ink treated with chemicals – hydrogen peroxide, mainly. The process is absurdly simple and cheap for a man with time on his hands. Many a successful forger has used it. The trouble in this case, of course, is that an accurate forgery isn't enough. She'll want to see *results* from it, when what you have to offer her is a scrap of trash.'

His mind clouded by thoughts of Sylvia again, Howard only half listened to Jimmers' discussion of the art of forgery. He realized, though, that Jimmers was looking at him with a serious face, as if he expected a response of some sort.

'Sylvia's your daughter, isn't she?' Howard asked him, the question leaping out of him before he had time to temper it.

Mr Jimmers said nothing at all, but sat staring at Howard with a stricken face.

'I found a copy of your book this afternoon,' Howard said, rushing to explain. 'I'm sorry we were fooling around down there. We'd locked ourselves into the passage, though, and were trying to find a way back out. Anyway, I found what must be a first printing of the book, and the dedication is different from what Sylvia remembered it to be. You changed the dedication when Edith married Uncle Roy.'

Picket fences and moonlit hillsides flew past as they sat in awkward silence, and the silence made Howard realize that Jimmers was struggling to say something, but couldn't say it. Suddenly Howard hated himself. What an insensitive clod he had been just to blurt all this out. Why couldn't he have been a little bit subtle? He wasn't the only person on earth who had an interest in Sylvia. 'Sorry,' he said then. 'I shouldn't have thrown you like that, I ...'

'You need to know the truth,' Jimmers said shakily, 'and so does Sylvia.'

Howard slowed the truck, turning off the highway and into the shadow of the cypress trees, bumping along up the driveway toward the stone house.

'I ... Back then, I wasn't well,' Mr Jimmers said, staring out through the windshield. 'I told you about some of it. Sylvia is my daughter, but obviously

I couldn't bring her up. That was clear. Roy Barton could. He was happy to. Roy Barton has a heart like a whale. And I'm not being facetious, either. We've had our differences, but I won't say anything against the man now. He succeeded where I would have failed. There was no reason, back then, to saddle Sylvia with the stigma of having a father who ...'

Howard shut off the ignition, happy for himself but not very happy for Mr Jimmers, who had apparently finished talking. 'It must have been hard for you,' Howard said, the two of them sitting in the quiet truck.

'Yes,' Jimmers said, and then he opened the truck door and climbed heavily out onto the ground, walking away toward the front door. In the light of the porch lamp, he stooped to untie his shoes, his hands fumbling clumsily with the laces.

28

Jimmers and Sylvia, driving Sylvia's Toyota, dropped Howard off at the Tip Top Lounge, and from there he drove back up to the Sea Spray Motel in Bennet's flatbed truck. Leaving the keys in the ignition, he parked so that the truck faced the highway. He climbed out into the night and looked south toward the lights of town. The Toyota was parked near the Gas 'n' Grub, its front end just visible in the glow of the parking lot lamp. He scanned the dunes along Pudding Creek. There they were, Sylvia and Jimmers, waiting in the darkness beneath the railway trestle. Mr Jimmers waved slowly at him, and then the two of them vanished back into the shadows.

The tin shed sat on the truck bed behind Howard, full of garden tools, empty flowerpots, sacks of fertilizer, folded-up aluminum lawn chairs, and Mr Jimmers' oddball machine. Holding the fake sketch beneath his coat, Howard walked straight to room 18 and knocked on the door. The light went out inside. The curtain shifted momentarily, and the door opened partway.

Howard slid through, ducking toward the bed as a man stepped out from behind the door. The light blinked on suddenly. It was Stoat, looking tired and haggard. Mrs Lamey sat at a table, her hair pulled back in a tight bun that made her head seem unnaturally small and skeletal. 'Produce it,' she said.

He pulled out the print, still in its case, and laid the case on the table, one by one pulling out the clips and opening it up to reveal the sketch. He hadn't wanted to bring the case, but Jimmers had insisted. It would lend the fake sketch a certain credibility.

'There it is,' Howard said. 'It's yours, and you're welcome to it.'

Mrs Lamey picked up the copper case and examined it carefully, running her fingers over the cut-in picture and the words beneath it. Her hands shook, and she seemed to forget entirely that Howard was standing there.

'Where are they?' he said finally, losing patience with her. 'I want to see them now, this instant. I have friends on the beach. You can see them out the back window if you look. They're timing this whole thing. I'll call them off when I see Roy and Edith together, here and now.'

She blinked at him, almost in confusion, as if she were pulling her mind back from some distant place. 'They aren't here, are they?' she said. 'I told our friend Jimmers that over the phone. And if the friends you refer to are the two men in false beards pretending to surf-fish on the beach above the trestle, then we'll go out together to confront them. I *thought* one of them looked a bit like our Mr Bennet. *Very* artistic. I love the idea of your confederates masquerading as bearded fishermen. There's nothing like a touch of the dramatic to make death seem idiotic rather than tragic. Come along, then.' She stood up and removed the sketch from its case, squinting hard at it. 'If this is a false copy ...' she said.

'It's authentic,' Howard said. 'I've ... made use of it once already. If we're going out, anyway, I'll demonstrate it.'

'Wait here,' Mrs Lamey said to Stoat. 'And leave the television alone. Keep your ears open and watch out the window for foul play. You can't trust men in false beards.' Then to Howard she said, 'If there's treachery, remember that your aunt and uncle will die. Their lives depend on my making a phone call and uttering a certain phrase that you can't hope to guess. So you can't compel me. Violence is useless to you. I'm going to appeal to your common sense here, and say that if this works smoothly, when the sun rises in the morning Heloise Lamey will be gone from your pitiful lives.'

'I understand,' Howard said. 'Let's get to it.'

She nodded, picking up a leather satchel from the floor beneath her chair. A bad odor wafted up from it, as if it contained a dead animal. She hung the strap around her neck and shoulders, unlocked the door, and stepped out into the parking lot. Howard followed, hearing the sound of the door catching behind them and then of neon buzzing from the overhead lights. A truck roared past, fouling the air with diesel exhaust. 'Fetch the stick,' Mrs Lamey said. 'Mr Jimmers assured me that you wouldn't be so foolish as to arrive without it.'

Howard opened the truck door and pulled out Graham's walking stick. 'Let me get the feel of it,' Mrs Lamey said, taking it from Howard and hefting it. He was tempted to snatch it back, but there was no use pushing her, no use taking chances – not yet. She set out through a stucco breezeway, carrying the cane and with the leather satchel pushed around behind her back. Howard followed along like an obedient servant, the path being too narrow for them to walk side by side. Whacking the ground now and then with the cane, she angled across a weedy sort of back lot and down a sandy path toward the beach, walking hurriedly. The dark trestle loomed overhead to the left of them.

Howard could hear the breakers now, and could see Lou Gibb and Mr Bennet fifty yards north, their fishing poles thrusting up from holders jammed into the sand. The two men stood still, watching the ocean. Pretending to meddle with his fishing pole, Mr Bennet turned to look at Howard and Mrs Lamey. 'Wave the fool down this way,' she said.

Howard waved. Bennet stood still, waiting, pretending not to understand, then waved back, as if merely being cheerful. Howard waved again, gesturing him down the beach. The two men talked back and forth, and then Bennet trudged down toward them, wearing an Amish-looking beard not connected by a mustache. It made his face look like a hair-fringed egg, disguising him thoroughly. 'Stop!' Mrs Lamey commanded when he was ten feet away. 'Howard wants to tell you to go home. Reel in your lines and go. Be quick about it, because Howard and I have a bit of an experiment to perform, and you're inconvenient. Isn't that so, Howard?'

Howard nodded at Bennet. It was clear that Mrs Lamey was serious. She was talking in a brittle, forced-facetious tone that seemed about to crack. Howard was pretty sure she was on the edge, running cold and sharp, but with all her margin used up. She didn't have time to waste. Her whole twisted life had come to a focus on this moonlit beach, and everything about her seemed to suggest that this was no time for false talk or false beards. 'We've got to trust her,' Howard called, knowing that the word 'trust' wasn't what he wanted, really.

'Like hell we trust her,' Bennet shouted back. He scowled, standing solidly, his boots sinking in the wet sand. Mrs Lamey said nothing, but stared at him like a desert lizard until, with a dismissing wave of his hand, he turned and headed back up the beach, apparently having made up his mind. Mrs Lamey waited in silence until the two men had reeled their lines in, picked up their buckets and tackle boxes, and started up the rise that led to the highway. She stood watching them go, until a wave broke high up on shore, and the ocean swirled in around their feet, sending Mrs Lamey high-stepping toward dry sand.

The night was clear and starry and cold, and the wind off the ocean whipped beach sand across Howard's pant legs as he followed Mrs Lamey farther down toward where Pudding Creek trickled into the ocean, nothing but a few little rills a couple of inches deep. She seemed to be using the cane now, as if she were truly tired, and she headed straight toward a big driftwood log, where she could sit down and let Howard work.

The trestle stretched far overhead and threw an immense Crosshatch moon shadow across the beach. Somewhere back in that shadow Jimmers and Sylvia stood ready to play their part. Howard wanted to search the shadows with his eyes, to find a familiar and friendly face even if it was hidden in darkness, but he didn't dare.

Right now they would be trying simply to keep him in sight, to forecast his movements. All Howard had to do was make a show of folding the sketch up. Sylvia would work over the real sketch in secret, hidden back under the trestle.

Mrs Lamey tiptoed across Pudding Creek, where they would be partly sheltered from the wind. She stopped at the far side of the trestle, sitting down on a big driftwood log. She looked out over the ocean, listening to the night wind. Behind her, the cliffs rose forty feet or so, nearly vertically, the trestle connecting them with the smaller, sandy bluffs at the opposite side of the creek bed, behind the motel. Howard looked hard at the rocky cliff face, cut out of dark sandstone and hung with tough shrubs. A fringe of ice plant grew down from the top. It wouldn't be hard to climb the side of the cliffs if it came down to it ...

'Convince me,' Mrs Lamey said, startling him and settling herself on the log.

Howard nodded. 'You want a storm.'

'I want two inches of rainfall in the next three hours.'

'I can't ...' Howard began.

Mrs Lamey interrupted him. 'I know you can't. You can't do anything at all. You're an ignorant, passive instrument, is what you are. Just do *something*. You called up a storm this afternoon, probably by mistake. Do it again.'

'I'm warning you that I can't control it very well.' The truth of this statement occurred suddenly to Howard, and for the first time he began to doubt Mr Jimmers' plan. The storm that afternoon had nearly washed out the road, and in the space of only a few minutes. What would it have become if Howard hadn't stopped it?

'Of course you can't control it,' Mrs Lamey said, abruptly losing patience with him. 'It takes a stronger hand than yours. Use the sketch – whatever it is you did to it this afternoon. You didn't follow me out here to argue about it, did you? Think of your uncle, your aunt.'

Howard shrugged. 'All right.' He turned to face the trestle, his back to the ocean, trying to look as if he were summoning some sort of mystical power. 'Here we go,' he said to himself, and then kneeled in the sand, laying the sketch out on his thighs. Carefully, as if he were following some sort of method, he folded the paper from corner to corner, making a triangle. Then he folded it again, joining the opposite corner, cutting the size of the thing in half. He waited, squinting at it with an artist's eye.

Out over the sea the sky remained clear. There wasn't even the hint of a fog. Rain was impossible on a night like this. He folded it again, turning each of the corners into the middle, and then cocked one corner across and down to make a little tab of it, which he tucked into the opposite corner, creating a sort of circular pointy-fronted crown that might have fit a chicken. Still there was nothing. Mrs Lamey watched him dubiously. The look on her face suggested that they didn't have all night, that her temper was wearing thin.

'All part of the process,' Howard said. He looked up just then, having seen movement at the very top of his vision. There was Jimmers and Sylvia. They weren't under the trestle at all. They were edging along the cliffside, picking their way through the shrubbery, from rock to rock, and hidden from Mrs Lamey only because her back was turned. Howard lowered his eyes casually, wondering what in the hell they were up to. He studied the ridiculous hat. Then, laboriously, considering every crease, he unfolded it, opening it up to a full square before folding it in half again, lengthwise this time.

He risked a look toward the cliffs. Why on earth had the two of them come out of hiding like that? He couldn't see them now, but he knew they were crouched like cats behind the only bush big enough to hide them both. What did they intend to do, leap out and grab her? They couldn't be that stupid. Howard was struck with the notion that Sylvia had failed, that her folding of the print hadn't done anything at all, and he wondered how much power lay in the sketch and how much in himself.

'What are you up to?' Mrs Lamey asked ominously. And then, seeing something in his face, she turned suddenly around, scanning the hillside and then peering into the shadows beneath the trestle. The night was silent and empty, and the only thing that moved was the wind and the ocean. 'You have thirty seconds,' she said, looking at her watch. Her voice was pitched too high, as if she were about to come unhinged, to start shrieking.

'I've got it now.' Howard opened the rectangle into a square again and then folded it perpendicular to the first fold. He tucked the corners in, working as accurately as he could to make one of those finger-manipulated Chinese fortune-telling devices, remembering back to the fourth grade. He didn't dare look at the cliffside again, but he listened hard for telltale sounds. Mrs Lamey watched his face rather than his hands. He met her eyes once, and her face was filled with suspicion. The corner of her mouth twitched badly, as if it were being yanked by an invisible thread. She looked as if she knew she had been taken, that Jimmers had slipped her another fake, the old fool …

Howard barely breathed. The paper, delicate from age anyway, had been so overfolded that it was beginning to come apart. A crease line tore along the edge, and quickly he folded it at the tear in order to hide it, folding it over again on top of itself, and then again, abandoning the Chinese fortune-teller. The thing rapidly became a lump of paper, too thick to fold again without turning it into a mere wad. There was nothing to do but unfold it once more and start over, try to brass it out, maybe utter some mumbo jumbo. One way or another, though, the charade was about over.

The paper tore again as he was unfolding it, through three creases at once this time, leaving it webbed with two-inch-long slits. Quickly, before she saw that it was shredding, he folded it back in half, following no pattern at all, but merely covering up the sad fact that soon it would be worth nothing outside of a hamster cage.

She looked at her watch. 'Seven seconds,' she croaked. She was breathing heavily, as if hyperventilating, her eyes nearly shut with rage, and she pounded his cane into the sand between her feet, thumping out the seconds one after another. This will be it, Howard thought. Better to throw it in her face right now and run. Better to grab the cane and hit her with it, tie her to the trestle, then sneak back up to the motel and beat the truth out of Stoat, find out where Roy and Edith were being held. Bennet was right. They had been fools to play along with Mrs Lamey this far. She wasn't going to let them get away with anything.

'Well!' she said, as if she had just that moment been insulted. She stood up, making her pickle face at him, looking like a withered corpse in the ivory moonlight.

And just then the air was full of the smell of ozone, and a bolt of lightning and nearly simultaneous crash of thunder slammed out of the sky, illuminating the ocean in a yellow-blue flash. Mrs Lamey staggered against the driftwood log, going down onto one knee in the sand, and then pushing herself upright, her face stretched in an amazed mask of greed, satisfaction, and surprise.

'Give it to me!' she shrieked, pulling the still-folded paper out of his hands and shoving him pointlessly on the chest with the cane, as if to get the first blow in just in case he tried to fight her for it.

'Better unfold it!' Howard shouted, although it didn't matter a bit what she did with it. It was best to play the fraud out to the end, though. Raising the storm was only the beginning. Roy and Edith were still held prisoner somewhere, and it would have to be Mrs Lamey who released them.

She stood gaping at the stars now, ignoring him as if he were an insect that she had already destroyed. Stopping the storm wasn't conceivable to her. She *wanted* a storm – a storm to end all storms, a sky full of rainwater that would illustrate her newfound power. That afternoon she had dried out Inglenook Fen; now she would fill it again.

She still thumped the ground with the cane, as if counting out the seconds, her eyes narrowed, focused on the sky over the ocean. Mindlessly she licked her lips and then pushed out the side of her mouth as if to stop its twitching. Howard could hear her breathe, an almost frantic mewling sound, like a person in the grip of nearly terminal excitement.

Clouds dropped out of the empty night as if the darkness itself were congealing, and the air between the clouds and the ocean went black with falling rain. The storm clouds tumbled toward land, moving like a roiling black avalanche and seeming to suck ocean water straight up into the air in a hundred spinning twisters. Lightning tore through them, forking down into the electrified ocean as the night was shattered by the sound of peal after peal of thunder.

Then the ocean flattened and the wind fell off to nothing. The sound of the waves diminished so that between thunder cracks the night was weirdly silent except for the distant hiss of rain that washed across the surface of the sea. The rain was a black wall that surged toward them, obliterating the horizon.

Mrs Lamey remained motionless, gripping the worthless sketch in her fist as if it were a treasure map that the wind would tear out of her hands. Howard realized that she thought she was watching a manifestation of her power, seeing it materialize right there in the sky after she had plotted and schemed and dreamed about it for years. She was entranced, hypnotized, and it wasn't until the ocean began to recede and the first flurry of wind and rain hit them that she regained her senses and started to unfold the paper.

The tide ran outward in a visible rush of moving water and with a weird sucking sound punctuated by thunder. Submerged rocks seemed almost to leap up out of the ocean, sitting like dark little islands covered in kelp and eelgrass and barnacles with the sea swirling around them, its level falling like water in a draining bathtub.

Mrs Lamey tore at the sketch now, trying to flatten it out as the rain engulfed them, the wind tearing at her hair as she turned around and hunkered down against it, a vague look of fear visible on her face. The driving rain hammered at them, achingly cold in the grip of the furious wind. She turned and staggered back toward the log, huddling over like a beached seabird to deflect the wind and rain with her back and clutching her leather satchel in front of her now to protect it.

Howard shielded his face with his hand, watching the ominous ocean for one last moment before being driven back by the rain and wind. The clouds flew overhead now, lashing rain across the highway and forest, and the wind spun in a vortex, coming from all directions at once. The night was black, and the cliff beyond them was nothing but a sloping shadow. Two figures moved across it, clambering upward, slipping and crawling in an effort to gain the top.

At first Howard couldn't tell them apart in the darkness. He didn't care about that, though, as long as both of them were safe. One of the figures stopped right then, standing straight up and waving furiously down toward him with both arms. It was Jimmers, urging him to follow and gesturing wildly at the ocean.

Mrs Lamey was oblivious to everything but the sketch. She wasn't going anywhere, and clearly didn't want to. Howard grabbed her with his free hand, towing her by the elbow. She screeched straight into his ear, leaning forward and trying to bite it, twisting away at the same time and swinging the cane at him.

He grabbed the cane in the air and held on tight, hauling her forward with it. She kicked him hard on his bad knee, flailing away with her pointed-toed shoes like a machine, hitting at his face with her fist, which was closed around the sketch.

'I'll kill them!' she screamed. 'Leave me! Get out! It's mine!' She released her grip on the cane, tearing away from him, clearly convinced that it was the sketch he wanted, that he was trying to take it away from her. Clumsily she pawed at her leather satchel, casting him a look that seemed to suggest she could do him serious harm, that she had something inside the satchel she would destroy him with.

He backed off a step, gesturing at her that he was giving up. He had to calm her down, somehow, if he was going to get her out of there – which he was determined to do, since he still had no idea where his uncle and aunt were being held.

He looked up the hill just then, and in the glow of a lightning flash saw that Jimmers had Sylvia by the arm, endeavoring to pull her to safety. But in the moment that Howard looked, Sylvia yanked herself free, sliding downward across the ice plant on the seat of her pants until she jammed herself to a stop against a rock. She pushed herself to her feet, but then slipped on the wet ice plant and went down again as Jimmers crept back toward her, climbing carefully, holding on to roots and branches and rocks.

Howard saw Jimmers cup his hands to his mouth to holler at Sylvia, but the rain lashed down in a deafening tumult, and there was no hope of making her hear.

The wind blew just then in a gust that staggered Howard, as if it were compelling him to move, to act. The force of it spun him half around so that he faced the ocean again. The sandy seabed was visible as far as he could see through the rain-shrouded darkness. The rain drove into his eyes, though, half veiling the strange sight of the empty ocean bottom. He stepped backward, full of sudden fear, abandoning Mrs Lamey and making for the cliff. He couldn't have Sylvia coming to his rescue – not now, with the ocean going mad.

Mrs Lamey collapsed on her knees on the other side of the driftwood, where she bent down to shelter herself from the wind-driven rain. She was oblivious to Howard, and to Sylvia, too, who wasn't ten feet behind her now, nearly at the bottom of the cliff. Using the cane to support himself, Howard fought his way up to where Sylvia slipped and hopped down onto the sand, grabbing Howard's arm and hauling on it, helping to tug him to higher ground. Jimmers joined them, unwilling to abandon them even though it was everything he could do now just to save himself.

They set out up the cliff, climbing as fast as they could, slipping on the wet rock, hanging on to shrubs and giving each other a hand up. Rocks broke loose and skittered down the hillside behind them, raining down around where Mrs Lamey still crouched next to the log, the edge of which was partly submerged in the rising floodwaters of the creek.

Halfway up the hill, Howard turned to look. She was a shadow beyond the curtain of rain, and was straddling the driftwood log now, the leather satchel lying across her back. In the almost continual glow of the lightning, he saw that she was holding the fraudulent sketch in the air as if she were showing it to the storm. 'Look,' she seemed to be saying, 'I've unfolded it. Enough is enough. I'm satisfied.'

The wind took the fragile paper, though, and tore it to pieces in an instant, so that she was holding two rain-soaked banners that flailed themselves to soggy shreds.

Far out to sea loomed a shadow even blacker than the darkened sky – a tremendous wall of seawater rushing across the open ocean toward a half mile of empty seabed. Mrs Lamey saw the wave then, too, and stood up slowly, unbelieving, still clutching little handfuls of worthless rice paper. Turning again toward shore, she hunched forward against the wind, clearly intending to cross Pudding Creek in order to make her way to the path that led back to the motel.

Shouting at her pointlessly, Howard took a step back down the cliff. She wouldn't make it to the motel. He watched as she plunged into the deepening water of the creek, nearly up to her waist. As the floodwaters swept her off her feet, she struck out swimming, her hands still balled into fists, but the creek tumbled her forward and she disappeared beneath the surface.

Mr Jimmers caught Howard around the waist, hollering in his ear to let Mrs Lamey go. They had to get to higher ground. They couldn't save the old woman, not now. Howard knew that Jimmers was right. It was too late for Mrs Lamey. The fake-sketch idea would accomplish little beyond the old woman's death.

Then he saw Mrs Lamey lurch to the surface, and for a brief moment he thought she might make it. She staggered forward, slogging her way free of the creek at last, but bent over and coughing up water.

Howard turned around and started back up, pushing Jimmers ahead of him now toward where Sylvia waited, holding out her hand for Jimmers to grab. The slope lessened, and Howard found himself scuttling upward like a crab, clutching handfuls of ice plant to steady himself. Then the slope leveled altogether, and the ice plant ended at a verge of rough gravel. They lunged forward, up onto the train tracks, where they stopped. There was no higher ground.

The wind dropped then, the rain falling off with it, and in the sudden silence a distant roar filled the night air – not the deluge now, but the wave feeling the ocean bottom, pushing itself skyward, still hundreds of yards out. It rose vertically, a long, glassy, upended plane, the top of it lost in the night.

Then there was the far-off sound of water pounding into water, heavy and powerful in a long, ceaseless roar as the wave broke in a mountain of white foam, seeming to mirror the clouds overhead, which tore themselves to pieces now and vanished like steam into the sky. Clumps of shooting stars appeared and disappeared past the holes in the clouds, and for a moment it looked to Howard as if the entire universe were revolving overhead like a mill wheel.

Mrs Lamey turned at the sound of the wave breaking. She took two steps back toward the creek, then stopped, unsure of herself like a small animal on a highway. She seemed to see her mistake for the first time. The motel was too far away. And as the house-high wall of churning foam drove shoreward, it was clear that the motel was doomed, anyway. The wave would smash right through it.

Cramming the fragments of the sketch down the front of her dress, she made a wild dash for the log again, running up the edge of the creek toward where it was wide and comparatively shallow. She waded into it, looking back out to sea as the wave rushed shoreward, turning over and over on itself, flattening out in a wide, surging river.

Wildly she flung herself onto the log, up among the branches, hugging it to herself. The churning wave slammed across the beach, funneling into the creek and smashing thunderously across the face of the cliff. It picked up the big driftwood log as if it were a stick, and went booming beneath the trestle, swirling around the S-curve of the creek bed and blasting up and over the empty highway. In the dwindling lightning flashes they could see the log riding high on the top of the foam in a quickly revolving eddy, driving toward the dark forest. Mrs Lamey still clung to it as if crucified to its broken-off branches.

Suddenly the ocean was calm again, and moonlight shone through the scattered clouds. A little flurry of raindrops pelted down, and then there was one last timid lightning bolt that lit up the surface of the sea. In that instant Howard saw what he thought at first was cloud shadow on the ocean. But it was moving too quickly, swarming up toward the creek mouth – schools of fish moving just under the surface. They crowded up and across the inundated beach in the wake of the wave, leaping and splashing in the shallow water.

'Where are they!' Sylvia shouted.

'What?' Howard asked, half hypnotized by the sight of the wave and the fish.

'Are they in the motel?'

'No!' Howard understood her now. 'She moved them out.'

'How do you *know*?' Jimmers asked, looking suddenly panicked. 'That wave would have knocked the motel to pieces.'

'I don't,' Howard said, already moving down the railroad tracks, toward the distant motel. Carefully he stepped from tie to tie, out across the top of the trestle, which seemed to him suddenly to be as narrow as the top of a brick wall. With the road gone and the creek flooded, though, there was no other route. The ocean boiled and churned forty feet below them, and the trestle vibrated at its foundations, the water booming past the pilings.

A surge of vertigo washed through Howard when he looked down at the moving, moonlit water, and he had to look back up quick, fixing his eyes on what was left of the roofline of the Sea Spray Motel. He tried the trick of imagining that on the other side lay a warm room with a fire and a cup of hot coffee, but he couldn't manage it. The night was too wild, and it would be impossible for him to cross the trestle without focusing on each dizzying step, balancing himself with his stick.

He turned his head slowly to look at Sylvia, who followed two ties behind him. Mr Jimmers was behind her, farther back, though, and crawling on his hands and knees from tie to tie. His face was a mask of fear and concentration. Howard wanted to help, but it would mean having to shift past Sylvia, which was out of the question; they would both go over the side. And what could he do, anyway, to steady the man? Mr Jimmers would make it right enough – if a train didn't materialize.

They waited to let him catch up, and Mr Jimmers, seeing that he was slowing them down, stood up bravely, waving his arms in front of him in little spirals to keep his balance. He stepped along in a halting crouch, looking down fearfully. Then he stopped and wavered, trying to keep steady, and both Howard and Sylvia turned back to help him.

'Go back!' Howard shouted past Sylvia, who was busy making Jimmers get down on his hands and knees again. She turned Jimmers around slowly and ponderously, as if he were an elephant in a closet, and without saying anything he set out south again, desperate to get off the trestle and back on solid ground now that his mind was made up. 'Go with him,' Howard said to Sylvia. 'Take the car and get help.'

'No!' she shouted back in a tone that was utterly final.

The two of them waited, watching Jimmers struggle across the final twenty feet of trestle to where it merged with the hill. He stood up solidly and waved them on, then turned and set out along the tracks. Howard set out again, keeping his mind clear, taking it one step at a time.

Minutes later they stepped off onto firm ground themselves. Howard felt the cold now, exposed to the wind and with his clothes soaked with rain. He wore two shirts and a heavy sweater, but the wind blew straight through them. Sylvia, at least, wore her parka, which would do something to cut the wind. There was nothing to do but ignore the cold, though. With a little hurrying they could be back at Sylvia's Toyota in twenty minutes, cranking up the heater.

Below them the water was already flowing back into the ocean, and Pudding Creek was falling toward its banks. They could see a gaping hole in the highway nearly fifty feet across. Big chunks of asphalt lay on the mud. The ridge that the railroad tracks ran along had sheltered the coast to the south, and the lights of the Gas 'n' Grub shined as ever. There were sirens in the night, though, from fire trucks and police cars approaching along the highway.

'Where's the sketch?' Howard asked her suddenly.

'Mr Jimmers has it.'

He nodded doubtfully.

'It'll be all right,' she said, and then set out at a run for the motel, Howard limping along behind. The authorities would be stopped at the flood, and it was just possible that the two of them could search the place and get out again before help arrived that they didn't need.

In another moment they saw the motel from end to end. It was half swept away. Sheets of stucco hung from torn-away chicken wire, windows gaped empty. A single bed, still draped in its bedspread, angled out one broken window, driven through it like a boat. The broken wave had battered the motel to pieces, and only two or three rooms at the upper end appeared to be whole. Debris from the wrecked building littered the highway and parking lot, where the Sea Spray Motel sign lay heavily across the top of a piece of roof. Bennet's truck was gone, swept away, maybe, along with Mr Jimmers' tin shed.

At a glance they could see that the wrecked rooms were empty, mattresses and tables and chairs lying in puddles of seawater and smashed against walls. Half a dozen rooms had no furniture in them at all, evidently in the process of being restored. The doors of the final few, unwrecked rooms were locked.

Howard and Sylvia banged on the windows and shouted until banging and shouting began to seem pointless. If Roy and Edith were safe in one of the rooms, surely they would have thrown a chair through a window and gotten out long ago. Probably they *had* been moved, just like Mrs Lamey had said – a development that was either good news or bad; it was impossible to say. It was equally likely that Stoat had taken them off in Bennet's truck, deserting the sinking ship.

They could see red lights revolving down the highway, where police and firemen tried to negotiate the flood, which was still deep enough, due to the steep walls of the creek bed, to prevent their simply wading across. Several rescuers were halfway down the little road to the dunes, though, just above the trestle, looking for a crossing. In minutes they would be at the motel, wondering what Howard and Sylvia were up to, asking questions, taking up time.

'What do we do?' Howard asked. Roy and Edith were Sylvia's parents, after all. He couldn't insist that they abandon the search.

She shook her head.

'Break the windows out? We'd better be quick about it.'

'No,' she said. 'They aren't here. The place is empty. I can feel it. We're wasting time, and we can't afford to. We've got to figure out where they've been taken.'

They set out around the far side of the motel, heading down toward the beach so as to be hidden from the view of anyone on the highway. The sand was covered with debris, with kelp and rocks and seashells and dying fish, and they had to pick their way through it, watching the top of the trestle for a sign of anyone crossing that way. From the shadows of the trestle itself they watched the men wade through knee-deep water, not thirty feet off, making for the destroyed motel.

Howard recognized one of them as the cop that had grilled them down at the harbor. Would he find Bennet's wrecked truck and trace it back to them? Would he conclude that some heavy sort of mysterious crimes were being committed up and down the coast? And what if he did? The authorities could hardly blame Bennet or Uncle Roy for the storm and tidal wave.

There were more sirens suddenly on the highway, and a paramedic unit wheeled up, lurching to a stop, the doors sailing open. 'Someone's hurt, after all,' Howard said, feeling wretched all of a sudden. For the first time this whole fiasco had injured an innocent person, maybe killed someone. Howard felt as if he himself had been swept along on a tide this last week, except that somehow, just in the past couple of days, he had *become* that tide in some unfathomable and not very pleasant way. That, partly, was what Mrs Lamey had wanted for herself.

They crouched there another moment, in order to wait until the men had forded the creek and were entirely out of sight. Then they slogged out into the current themselves, angling downstream with the flow so that when they got to the opposite shore they were near the edge of the ocean. They hiked along past weed-covered rock for some fifty yards, nearly to Glass Beach, before they cut inland, toward the little rise behind the Gas 'n' Grub.

'Why did you and Jimmers creep down the damned cliff like that?' Howard asked when they were safe on the beach and the going was easy. 'You scared the hell out of me. I thought you were under the trestle, and then there you were, sneaking around behind Mrs Lamey.'

'The sketch wouldn't work,' Sylvia said. 'We were back under the trestle, something like thirty feet away. I was folding it up like crazy even before you started in on the fake. Mr Jimmers said that we ought to get a jump on you, that Mrs Lamey wasn't in a mood to wait, and that he wasn't entirely certain of the way to fold it. Anyway, nothing was happening, and suddenly Jimmers decided we were too far away from you, that you had to be right there, like in the car this afternoon. We couldn't just walk out into the moonlight, though, where she would see us, so we came around from behind her in order to get as close as we could.'

'She never knew she didn't have the sketch,' Howard said.

'That was the point, wasn't it?'

'I tried to save her. You saw that.'

'She was beyond saving, I think – wave or no wave.'

Howard shrugged. 'Maybe that's true. There was something about her, though, that wasn't as bad as all that. Something about the way she liked to putter around that house of hers, sit out on the front porch.'

'She should have stayed on the front porch,' Sylvia said.

Howard put his arm around her. 'You came back down the cliff to help me, didn't you?' he asked.

'Well, it did occur to me that you were doing a damned poor job of helping yourself, fencing with Mrs Lamey down on the beach like that when the ocean was going nuts.'

'Thanks,' Howard said. 'I needed the help. My knee wasn't worth a damn.'

'Seems better now. You're not limping as badly.'

'Walking in the sand is murder. It helps that it's wet, though. She kicked the hell out of me. And there's something in that sort of storm, I think. Wet weather's murder on it.'

They topped the hill and walked down the other side. Howard kept making small talk, secretly worried about Uncle Roy and Aunt Edith. There was no way to tell where they had been taken. Mrs Lamey seemed to own half the coast. She could have hidden them anywhere. Howard couldn't bring himself to believe that anyone would have killed them without word from Mrs Lamey, regardless of what she had threatened.

'Isn't that Mr Bennet's truck?' Sylvia asked suddenly.

For a moment Howard was filled with the happy notion that somehow if Bennet's truck were recovered, Roy and Edith would be, too.

But it wasn't Roy and Edith, or Bennet either, who stood talking to Mr Jimmers alongside Sylvia's car; it was Stoat.

29

Howard was suddenly tired. He shut his eyes and stood for a moment. Somehow he hadn't bargained for this, and he admitted to himself for the first time that Stoat scared the hell out of him. Stoat was too sure of himself, too fit, too unfathomable, and Howard wondered how much of this, along with the jealousy angle, had made him misread the man. As awful and dangerous as she was, Mrs Lamey was easier to confront.

But it was apparently time, finally, to find out what it was that Stoat wanted. Howard hoped it wasn't trouble, because Howard wasn't up to it. If it came to that, though, Howard would oblige him, up to it or not. Stoat didn't have a pistol or any other sort of weapon, not in his hands, anyway. If Howard could get around behind him without being seen, maybe he could give Jimmers a sign and the two of them could work this out together. They had made the mistake of playing along with Mrs Lamey, completely at her mercy and letting her order them up and down – something that had very nearly ended in disaster for all of them. They wouldn't make the same mistake with Stoat.

Stoat couldn't know what had happened to the sketch, or that Mrs Lamey was dead. Jimmers could tell him anything at all – that Mrs Lamey had taken it, say, and driven away north, up the highway. What on earth would Stoat demand from them? Money? It was blood out of a turnip. The man would have to be a living idiot. More likely he was confronting Jimmers out of pure nastiness, thinking to cut a last-minute deal in order to glean some little trifle out of his wrecked plans. Maybe it was the machine he wanted, although apparently he already *had* that. Whatever his game was, it was time that Howard found out.

He gestured at Sylvia to stay put. They were in the shadow of the building that housed the Mendo Machine Shop, and he would have to slip across fifteen yards of lighted parking lot unseen in order to sneak up behind Stoat. He moved as quickly as he could, ready to break into a full run if Stoat turned his head and saw him. Stoat was busy talking to Jimmers, though, pointing down the highway, one hand in his pocket now. Howard ducked in behind a battered old Cadillac that was nosed almost up to the rear wall of the Gas 'n' Grub.

If Jimmers had seen Howard and Sylvia coming up over the hill from the beach, he didn't let on. He revealed nothing, but stood listening to Stoat talk, nodding broadly, as if the man's speech fascinated him. Howard looked out from behind the Cadillac's fender, then looked back at Sylvia, who stood ten yards behind him with her arms folded in front of her. Her face was doubtful, but she seemed to be determined to let Howard have his way this time. She couldn't take the chance of interfering and then finding out that Stoat was the villain that Howard said he was all along. Her parents were at risk, and it was no time to exercise her natural generosity.

Howard waited another moment, steeling himself. He found that it wasn't easy, though, just stepping out into the clear and – what? – hammering Stoat senseless on the sidewalk? Throwing some sort of hammerlock on him? Putting up his dukes? It wasn't cowardice that held him up; it was that it was so visibly idiotic. And there wasn't any obvious *reason* to hit him in the head or clip him across the back of his knees. Stoat and Jimmers almost seemed to be pals. Howard stood up slowly, stepping out into the light and keeping a good grip on his cane just in case. He was ready if it came to it, but he would let Stoat make the first move – reach into his coat or something.

'My Lord, it's Howard!' Mr Jimmers shouted, throwing his hand to his mouth and grabbing Stoat by the shoulders, pulling the man toward the car and out of harm's way, clearly thinking that Howard was going to bean him with the cane.

What kind of behavior was that? Howard wondered. Had Jimmers and Stoat struck some sort of deal? Suddenly he remembered that Jimmers had the sketch again. He had taken it back with him from the train trestle. Was he selling them out to Stoat? Had he knuckled under?

'What's this?' Howard said to Stoat, watching him carefully. He heard the sound of Sylvia's footsteps, running up behind him. Stoat made no move to attack him or to run or anything else, but stood instead with a resigned look in his eyes. Puzzled, Howard waited him out, leaning against the stick now, a world of fatigue sweeping over him in a wave. Sylvia slumped against the fender of the Toyota. She looked wet, cold, and tired.

Without hesitation, Stoat took his coat off and handed it to her. Somehow the act of kindness irritated Howard, clearly because he hadn't been able to do it himself, and because coming from Stoat, it seemed to Howard not to be kindness at all, but a smarmy sort of pseudo-gallantry. He fumed for ten seconds before telling himself to quit being a fool – or to quit with the jealousy, just as Sylvia had told him. She had been right about that. He had to stop defining Stoat's actions from such a dangerously off-kilter perspective.

'I'm sorry,' Stoat said, speaking to all of them at once. He looked confused and strained, as if saying such a thing took an effort that he hadn't been trained for. His leading-man air was gone along with the starch in his trousers, and he looked rumpled and despairing and worn out, like a man just out of the jungle and wanting to rest up in some safe haven. Stoat turned around then and walked the several steps to Bennet's truck, opening the door and pulling out the jacket that Howard had given to Mrs Deventer down at the harbor – when was it? Months ago, it seemed. On the instant, Howard's fear and distrust of Stoat evaporated.

'Thanks,' Howard said, pulling on the jacket and realizing that his fingers were too cold to work the zipper.

'I was at Mrs Deventer's house when you two were down at the harbor talking to Mr Bennet and the police. She told me she'd forgot to give you this back, and so I took it, knowing I'd see you tonight.'

'She said it was you that saved Bennet at the icehouse,' Howard said.

Stoat shrugged. 'I guess I did. I should have done more. I didn't know it would come to that until it was too late to stop it. That was Glenwood Touchey's business. Heloise wanted the truck, and when she discovered that it had been seen in the back of the icehouse, and that the shed was still on it, she sent Touchey after it. I didn't know anything about it, or about setting the place on fire, either. She didn't trust me that far. She knew I'd balk finally. She was working to take Mrs Deventer's house away, too. That … that was something I *did* know about.'

'I figured that,' Howard said. 'By adverse possession. With you making payments for her and paying property taxes and seeming to live there off and on.'

'Yes,' Stoat said. 'The money came out of consortium funds belonging to White and her and myself and a couple of others. Touchey and Gwendolyn Bundy work for shares, although Heloise pretends that she's a patron and is supporting the arts, or some damned thing. She's lost touch. There's no telling what she believes anymore. Anyway, it's a long process. At best, adverse possession takes five years. And in this case it wasn't working worth a damn.

'Mrs Deventer was too decent to let me do anything consistent about making payments. Heloise thought she was just an addle-brained old woman who wouldn't recognize fraud when it was waved in her face, but that turned out to be wrong, and when it did, that changed Heloise's mind about the whole thing. We'd already determined that Mrs Deventer had no will and no living relatives except her sister, who's as old as Methusaleh.'

'And so Mrs Lamey decided to kill her,' Sylvia said, with a look of anger on her face, as if she were making her own hasty reevaluation of Stoat now, and didn't much like the result.

Stoat nodded, looking unhappy. 'I think Mrs Deventer knew all along that there was something going on. And yet that didn't seem to have any bearing at all on what she felt toward me. That's the worst of it. It was me that convinced Heloise we couldn't prevail, that we couldn't take the place legally. I was trying to help Mrs Deventer, but it turned out to be a mistake. I suggested we give it up. Mrs Deventer was seventy-odd years old. She wouldn't live forever. When the time came we could quietly buy the place from the state. Why all the rush? Heloise seemed resigned to it. I had no idea she'd hurt the old lady, let alone that she would have Touchey work the car over in order to try to kill her. He followed her up to her sister's house in Willits. The highway back is treacherous. It's all cliffs along the right shoulder. Heloise thought it was a good joke on old Bennet that he had worked on her brakes so recently. If there was any blame, it would be him who got it, and there'd be no way on earth for him to prove otherwise. The first I knew of it was the morning after the trouble in Mendocino.'

Howard believed him. There was no reason not to. Here he was, admitting all sorts of nasty guilt when he might just as easily have been halfway down Highway 128, running toward San Francisco. Stoat was sweeping away a lot of dust and cobweb, pitching out skeletons, and Howard wished that there were a table they could sit down at, with a pitcher of beer on it.

'So where are they?' Sylvia asked, interrupting his apology and sounding almost as if she were tired of hearing it. Her tone surprised Howard for a moment, but it didn't disappoint him. She seemed to have been right about Stoat. But, Howard was happy to find, that didn't make his activities in any way attractive to her. Nor did it guarantee that Stoat wasn't making up a grand lie here.

'I'm thinking they're not two hundred yards from us right now, right across there at the warehouse,' Howard said, pointing back toward Glass Beach.

Stoat shook his head. 'They're at Roy Barton's ghost museum. Touchey is there along with Gwendolyn Bundy.'

'How about White and the artist?'

'White's too smart for this kind of thing. He prefers safer investments. Heloise Lamey was caught up in spiritualism and magic. The Reverend White's a flesh-and-money man. Jason's just another artist she's carrying at the moment. She'll tire of him when she finds a new boy. He doesn't have any real interest in her plots.'

'She's dead.' Howard watched Stoat's face for a reaction. There was nothing on it except a vague relief.

'Then the world's a better place,' Stoat said. 'And things are easier for us.'

On the beach, an hour earlier, Bennet and Lou Gibb had watched Howard walk south toward the cliffs with Heloise Lamey. It was nearly impossible for Bennet to obey Lamey's order and leave, but he had to trust Howard. They were all taking orders from Howard now, although the boy didn't know it yet. The two men had trudged up toward the motel, carrying their poles and buckets. The parking lot was empty and the motel was dark. Bennet's truck should have been there, at least according to Jimmers, but it wasn't.

They had stood under the neon sign debating what to do, both of them filled with the certainty that there was no one left inside the motel, that Roy and Edith were long gone by then, along with the truck. Somewhere their friend was held prisoner. His life was threatened, and there was damn-all that they could do about it.

'Let's see who's home,' Bennet said, and the two of them beat on each and every motel door in turn until they had convinced themselves twice over that the place was empty. The action had moved south. Unless it had moved north.

Feeling empty and helpless, they climbed back into Lou's car, throwing in the fishing gear and pulling off the false beards they'd gotten out of Roy Barton's box of dummy makeup. They drove back into town, past the warehouse at Glass Beach, which was locked tight, apparently deserted. They circled around past Roy and Edith's house, but it was dark and empty, too. At the harbor everything was equally quiet except for the sound of thunder from the storm to the north of them and a few scattered lights still on in the trailers at the Sportsman's RV. There was no sign of life at Mrs Lamey's house or anywhere else in Mendocino, where almost everything had closed for the night. They drove back into Fort Bragg and stopped at the Tip Top Lounge for a late beer, then went tiredly back out to the street to keep looking.

Sirens wailed north up Main just then, and the two followed along behind, running out of highway within half a mile. The place was a mess of fallen trees and tom-up roadway. The mouth of Pudding Creek was inundated, and the Sea Spray Motel wrecked. Even at that late hour motorists were gathering to watch, and Bennet and Gibb pretended merely to be rubbernecking, and stayed in the car.

Bennet saw the cop from the harbor talking on his car radio, and reached into the backseat to retrieve his beard. There was no use being recognized now. Firemen seemed to have found someone – a body. Where had it come from? Had it just staggered out of the woods? It was lying in the wet grass. Bennet couldn't tell if it was dead or alive. He had to know, suddenly, who it was – or barring that, simply that it wasn't Howard Barton. Roy wouldn't be able to stand that. Heloise Lamey was treacherous, more than a match for the boy.

Moments later they heard the approaching siren of a paramedic unit. Cars began backing out of the way to let it in, and the crowd along the edge of the collapsed highway pushed back toward the shoulder. The paramedics went to work on whoever it was, the crowd closing in around them, people murmuring. More cars pulled up, spilling out people in pajamas and robes, who stood on the highway looking at the flooded creek and at the salmon flopping and dying on the edges of the washed-over dunes.

The cop from the harbor was long gone along with three other men, down the dirt road toward the trestle where they had waded through the shallows toward the motel. Bennet could see them poking around the wreckage now with flashlights. There was the sound of glass shattering as they bashed out a window with a broken-off wall stud and climbed into one of the remaining rooms, probably looking for victims.

Bennet watched the motel carefully, waiting for the panicked rush that would inevitably come if they found someone, if Roy and Edith *had* been there. There was no excitement at all, though, and after a couple of minutes the cop appeared from one of the open doors and set out toward the creek again, apparently in no hurry, leaving the firemen to work the place over more thoroughly.

Bennet turned his attention back to the highway. The paramedics weren't in any hurry, either. What did that mean, a corpse? The crowd parted momentarily, and Bennet got a quick glimpse of a leg and a foot. 'It's a woman,' Bennet said. 'Someone wearing a dress, anyway. I can't tell—'

'Hey!' Gibb shouted, nearly into his ear.

'What!'

'The truck!'

'Where?' Bennet shouted, looking back down the highway. There it went, pulling out from behind the Gas 'n' Grub, heading south. 'Let's go,' Bennet said. 'Step on it!'

Gibb backed the car around, honking his way past a dozen people. A child climbed up onto the highway right in front of them, happily carrying a three-foot-long salmon by the tail and mouth. Gibb braked hard, and the kid smiled into the windshield cheerfully, holding the fish up for them to see it. Three more children appeared, carrying fish of their own, and Gibb had to wait them out, too. Bennet drummed his fingers hard on the dashboard.

'Damn it!' Gibb said. 'The damn thing wasn't two blocks down.'

'What the hell was it doing at the Gas 'n' Grub?' Bennet asked.

'Search me,' Lou said. He eased past the last of the children, pushing the pedal down into overdrive. The car shot forward toward town. It was late, after one in the morning, and Fort Bragg was mostly asleep. A half dozen cars headed north toward the excitement, but almost no one was south-bound now. The highway was clear and straight. A pair of taillights shined about a mile down the road, and even at that distance they could see that it was Bennet's truck, with the tin shed shoving out a foot over either side of the bed.

'Give the bastards room,' Bennet said. 'Don't let them know it's us.'

30

It was pitch-dark as Howard and Sylvia bounced along down the highway, riding in their Trojan horse, the shed creaking and moaning as it sawed back and forth with the truck's movement. Jimmers rode up front with Stoat, who would have to make up some excuse for Jimmers being along with him. There wasn't enough room in the shed, though, for three people and the machine, too, unless they threw out all the garden supplies, and Jimmers couldn't see the point of that.

Howard sat on a pile of plastic nursery bags full of mulch, bracing himself with his shoulder against the cold, swaying wall. He would never have believed that a night could last as long as this one had. And it wasn't over yet. He was caught up in the rhythm of it, though, like a long-distance swimmer, and would be all right if he didn't think about the remaining miles. The truck swerved around an uphill curve, Stoat throttling down into second gear, and Howard tried to guess where they were on the highway, but it was useless.

Every now and then slivers of moonlight filtered through cracks, faintly illuminating the interior of the shed. In those moments he could see Sylvia sitting across from him on the aluminum lawn chair that she had managed to wedge open crookedly in the cramped space. Her eyes were closed, but Howard didn't think she was asleep.

Perhaps it was darkness, or fatigue, or the lateness of the hour, but Howard's emotional guard was down, and he knew it and welcomed it. Suddenly he wanted to talk. It was time to clarify things, to cast a light on elements of the mystery that were still in shadow. They had ten or fifteen minutes entirely to themselves, and he determined not to waste it, although he was equally determined not to be as clumsy and abrupt with Sylvia as he had been with Mr Jimmers earlier.

'What else do you know about Jimmers?' he asked her finally, breaking a long silence.

'I don't see all that much of him,' she said after a moment.

'He seems to be pretty fond of you, though.'

'He's always treated me like a daughter. Because of him and Mother, I suppose.'

'Is that it?' Howard asked.

Sylvia was quiet for a time. 'What else would it be?'

Then Howard told her about finding Mr Jimmers' book, with the altered – or unaltered – dedication and the screwy, too-early date. 'I knew that didn't *prove* anything at all,' Howard said to Sylvia. 'Not absolutely. But obviously I had to find out more. So last night, when we went back down to Jimmers' place after the fake sketch, I asked him outright about it. I told him that I had found the book, read the dedication, and figured out who you really are.'

'What did he say?' Sylvia asked, her voice hoarse.

'He wasn't surprised at all that I knew. I think he was relieved. On the way back up to Fort Bragg he seemed almost *happy* about it. Maybe you didn't notice it when we picked you up and headed down to the Tip Top Lounge, but he was about ready to pop with it. He didn't say anything to you while you were hiding out under the trestle.'

'No.'

'Well ...' Howard shrugged. 'There's the truth, though, if you want it. You're the only daughter of Artemis Jimmers.'

There was silence then. After a moment he heard her sniff. She was crying in the darkness. It was dark now, and he couldn't even see her face. He leaned over, reaching out to stroke her hair, but he couldn't judge the distance and poked her ear by mistake. She laughed then. 'Clod,' she said, sniffing again. 'At least now I don't have to claim you for a cousin.'

Howard didn't comment on this. 'And you didn't know?' he asked her. 'Honestly?'

'Of course I didn't know. If I had known ...'

'What?'

'If I had known ... I don't know. Maybe I would never have come back up north all those years ago. None of this would have happened. Where would we be now? Married? Living in an awful house in the suburbs somewhere, in Inglewood or Garden Grove or Pacoima. You'd be working at Delco Battery or Tubbs Cordage, supervising the night shift. I'd be barefoot and pregnant.'

'And now I'm not working at all,' Howard said. 'I'm a bum.'

'Not going back to the museum?'

'Nope.'

She was silent again.

'How does that strike you?' Howard asked. 'Are you excited at the prospect of me lurking around up here, getting in the way?'

'I'll have to ask my therapist,' she said. 'I could use some help around the boutique, I guess – sweeping up and all. Minimum wage until you learn the trade, though.'

'Could I talk to what's-his-name? Chet? I want to fly on his astral plane.'

'Mrs Moynihan would like that. She's another of your admirers, you know.' After a moment she said, 'It's not bad having two fathers, is it?'

'I don't know,' Howard said. 'I can barely remember what it's like to have one. Uncle Roy was pretty much my father, too. I feel a little shabby because of that. It isn't really my place to tell you all this. Uncle Roy and your mother kept it a secret all these years, and now I've torn the lid off it.'

Sylvia started crying again at the mention of Uncle Roy. Howard waited for a moment and then went on. 'They've been on the edge of revealing it, though. They keep hinting about me and you ... you know ...'

She sniffed again. 'I know,' she said finally. 'They think you'd make a fine husband. Mom told me that. I thought it was pretty weird at the time. Still sounds a little weird. Why didn't you tell me all this yesterday, when you found the dedication in the book?'

'Because of what happened on the beach. I didn't want to sound like I was rationalizing things, like I was making up reasons to justify our ... failing in love.'

'Our *what*?' Sylvia said. 'Is that the kind of thing you said to Jeanelle Shelly in the garage that time? Now you're saying it to me in a tin shed.'

'All right,' Howard said. 'When we were down in Jimmers' basement, you weren't paying any attention to me, anyway. All you wanted to do was play with Jimmers' tin toys. Why *should* I have told you? I wanted to keep it for *ammunition*, to be one up on you. I was going to hold it over your head if you ever started in on Jeanelle Shelly or the ice planetoids again. I should have guessed all of it from the first, anyway. You and Jimmers. You're peas in a pod. How could anyone think you *weren't* his daughter?'

'You just wait,' she said. He heard her yawn sleepily. 'My memory is long. We'll see who one-ups who.'

The truck bumped over a rut in the road just then, slamming from side to side and throwing Howard off his plastic sacks. He sat down hard on the plywood floor of the shed, hearing Sylvia's chair collapse at the same moment, and suddenly she sprawled across him in a tangle of arms and legs, clutching at him to avoid rolling into the closed shed door.

The truck slowed down then to turn off the highway. Sylvia lay against Howard, breathing softly against his ear, her hair in his face and her arms around his chest. She kissed him, and then said, 'Why didn't we think of this fifteen minutes ago? A tin shed is nearly as romantic as a wrecked Studebaker.'

With that, she kissed him again, long and hard, and he slid his hands up under her parka, along the small of her back. Her shirt was still damp with rainwater, but she was warm beneath the jacket. He held on to her as the truck crept across the gravel parking lot of Uncle Roy's Museum of Modern Mysteries and braked to a stop.

They quietly disentangled themselves then. Howard listened hard, full of sudden tension. One of the truck doors opened. There were footsteps, and then someone knocking against the door of the museum. Then came Stoat's voice speaking to someone. There was laughter, then the word 'What?'

followed by 'Why?' They were asking about Mr Jimmers. More talking followed, too low to understand, except that it obviously wasn't happy talk. Touchey's voice rang out clearly then, sounding irate.

Howard knew they would never get out of the shed without making God's own screeching racket, so he waited. But he would have to move fast when the time came – tear the doors open and vault right off the side of the truck. Stoat would let them know if it was safe – if Stoat could be trusted …

There was more talk and shuffling feet on the gravel now, but still no signal from Stoat. Howard heard Gwendolyn Bundy laugh and then ask, 'So where is he?'

'Back at the Sea Spray,' Stoat said. 'He's tied into a chair.'

'I'm going up there. He needs a playmate. You say he's *tied up?*' She giggled in what sounded like the voice of a tin can.

Glenwood Touchey said, 'Perhaps I'll go along, darling. We can—'

'Nyah, nyah,' Ms. Bundy yapped at him, interrupting. 'You can have him when I'm done. You're such a bloodthirsty little man! You can practice on the two you've got. Do you know, Stoatie, Glenwood wanted to take me in the woods just five minutes ago. And I mean *in*, not into. Do you want to know what he suggested?'

'Where is Heloise?' Touchey asked in a hollow voice, interrupting her.

'At home,' Stoat said, sounding relieved. 'The whole thing was a success. She's packing a bag and will meet us here.'

'Packing a bag?'

'A little vacation. She's worked hard, and there's a lot of planning to do. You know how big this thing is.'

'She owes me *money*,' Touchey said, his voice rising. 'She sure as hell *better* show up. She told me she'd be here a half hour ago. We've got people tied up in chairs and she's home packing a bag!'

'Settle down, Glen,' Gwendolyn Bundy said. 'Be a little soldier. It's late now to be full of suspicions, isn't it? I *told* you something was wrong when she didn't show up, but you were too damned stupid to …'

There was the sound of someone being slapped, and Gwendolyn Bundy let out a yelp.

'My ass I'm going to settle down,' Touchey yelled. 'She said you'd have the money, Stoat. *You're* her goddamn business partner. What's going on? She's got this precious sketch of hers and I'm getting stiffed, is that it? Or is it something else?'

There was a brief silence then, followed by a gasp and a shriek from Ms. Bundy and then the sound of Jimmers' door opening. In a rage, Touchey said, 'I've had my eye on you for the last week, you phony prick, and—'

'Put the damned gun away!' Stoat yelled.

Gwendolyn Bundy screamed, and there was the noise of a scuffle. 'You seedy little pervert!' she shouted. 'That's *just* what we need, your damned penis substitute.'

'Shut up!' Touchey shrieked, and there was the sound of another hand slap, and then of someone hitting the ground, followed by a single gunshot that echoed through the open night.

Howard tore the shed doors open, cursing himself for having waited. He threw himself over the edge of the truck bed, trying to take his weight on his good leg and expecting either to be shot by Touchey or attacked by Gwendolyn Bundy.

Mr Jimmers was just then coming around the front of the truck, waving his hands as if to settle everyone down. Stoat and Touchey wrestled on the ground, and Gwendolyn Bundy kicked furiously at them, not seeming to care who she kicked. A look of vast surprise and anger crossed her face when she looked up and saw Howard. For a moment he thought she would throw herself on him in a rage, and he put his arms out to ward her off.

She turned and ran around the corner of the building instead, out toward the highway. Howard let her go. Stoat and Touchey still rolled on the gravel, their feet kicking. Touchey's face was shriveled with insane anger, and he screamed nonsense into Stoat's ear.

Sylvia ran straight past Howard, heading for the door of the museum. Right at that moment Touchey fired the pistol again, wildly, into the eucalyptus branches overhead. Sylvia flinched, slamming herself against the wood siding of the museum and then dashing up onto the little porch and throwing herself through the open door, disappearing inside.

Touchey waved the pistol in his right hand, which Stoat held by the wrist, jacking the gun back and forth now and slamming Touchey's arm against the ground. Touchey gouged at Stoat's eyes and hit him futilely on the back with his free hand, gasping and mewling, his mouth biting air. Circling around them, Howard reached down and grabbed the gun barrel as if it were the head of a poisonous snake. With his other hand he pried Touchey's fingers off the grip.

Touchey went suddenly slack then, as if he had lost all his stuffing along with the gun. His mouth was pouty and sullen, like the mouth of a spoiled little boy set to cry. He sat up in the dirt and gravel, looking around. 'Gwendolyn!' he shrieked. 'Gwendolyn! Damn it! You damn bitch!' But she was gone, out into the night.

'She ditched you,' Howard said. 'Ran straight down the road.'

'Go to *hell*!' Touchey croaked at him, burying his face in his hands as he hooted out a long sob. 'You can't hold me here!' he shouted. 'You're *all* guilty of something.'

Stoat stood up, dusting at his pants.

'Hello,' a voice said. It was Uncle Roy, standing now in the doorway, Sylvia no doubt having untied him. He looked a mess, his hair riled and the side of his face black and blue. 'Where's the landlady?' he asked.

'Dead,' Howard said. 'Drowned.'

'I *knew* it!' Touchey shouted at Stoat, so full of fury that he could barely speak. 'Traitor! Stinking ... pig!' He picked up a handful of gravel then and threw it at Stoat, cocking his arm back as if he were swatting flies on a table-top. The gravel sprayed across Stoat's chest, and Stoat, suddenly furious, stepped in and clutched Touchey by the front of his shirt.

'That's enough!' Uncle Roy hollered. 'There's no point in holding on to him. He's old news now. Let the bastard go. We won't see him again.'

Stoat immediately pushed Touchey away, and the man sprawled back into the shadows of the eucalyptus trees. He stood there sputtering, looking hard at Stoat, as if he would gladly thrash Stoat then and there except for some very damned good reason. They waited for him to speak, but instead he stomped away, following in the wake of Gwendolyn Bundy, walking straight past his car toward the highway and looking back at them over his shoulder. At the corner of the building he turned briefly and, with almost lunatic inten-sity, made an obscene gesture so violent and wild it must nearly have broken his wrist.

'That's right,' Roy said to him, waving.

'He deserves more,' Howard said in a low voice, watching Touchey dis-appear beyond the edge of the building. He felt relief, though, at seeing him go, as if he were watching the departure of an irate door-to-door magazine salesman.

'All of us deserve more,' Uncle Roy said. He flexed his hands and worked his shoulders back and forth. 'I deserve a drink.' He took a step forward, out onto the little stoop, but nearly fell over and had to catch himself on the rail-ing. 'My damned rear end is asleep from sitting on that bench for three hours. What the hell took you?'

Right then, though, before anyone could answer, there came the sound of pounding feet from the direction Touchey had taken. A man shouted. Then, weirdly, the voice of Gwendolyn Bundy piped up in a high-pitched hen's cackle. 'That's him!' she yelled. 'He's the one who shot the fat man! He tried to kill the old Dutch lady, too!'

Howard sprinted across the back parking lot, followed by Jimmers, Stoat, and Uncle Roy. There, coming along past the picket fence and the vigilant cow skulls, Bennet and Lou Gibb swarmed toward Glenwood Touchey. Ms. Bundy stood behind them, her hands over her mouth, watching excit-edly. Touchey ran right into them, as if confident that his righteous fury would bowl them down.

It was Bennet who hit Touchey first, a roundhouse punch that caught him in the chest. Almost simultaneously Lou Gibb hit him in the stomach, and for a moment Touchey seemed to levitate there in a sort of airborne somer-sault crouch, before flopping to the ground, the two men closing in on either side.

'Hit him again!' Ms. Bundy yelled, dancing on the shoulder of the road next to Gibb's car. Howard sprinted toward them along with Stoat, shouting, 'No one's been shot! No one's been shot!' Howard pulled Bennet away, shak-ing his head wildly to make him understand. Uncle Roy limped up then, yelling things himself, but it wasn't until Mr Jimmers honked Lou Gibb's car horn three times that the two men stepped back, shrugging their shoulders and looking as if they would happily hit Touchey again and not ask overtime pay for it.

Touchey lay curled up on the ground, with his knees tucked up and his hands over his head, sobbing and shouting unrelated and purposeless obscenities.

'Roy!' Bennet said, grabbing his friend's shoulder. 'You ain't dead!'

'Not a bit,' Uncle Roy said.

'Then why are we beating this man up?' Bennet backed off another step, huffing and puffing, and Gwendolyn Bundy pushed past him, sinking to her knees next to Touchey. Tenderly she petted him on the back of his head.

'It's over,' she cooed softly. 'I'm so sorry. I thought … I thought … I was mad at you. I didn't think they'd … They won't hit my baby boy any more.' She helped him to sit up, pushing his face into her chest and hugging him, rocking him back and forth gently.

'Cripes,' Gibb said, a look of repulsion on his face. 'This kind of crap ain't natural.'

Gwendolyn Bundy turned on him furiously, her eyes pinched up. 'You're *brutal!*' she said, pulling Touchey to his feet. A thin stream of blood ran out of his nose. He gave everyone what was meant to be a hard look, his mouth a quivering slit, but then Ms. Bundy touched his cheek with her hand, and he howled and swatted at her. Together they walked off across the gravel, back toward their car. Ms. Bundy stroked Touchey's back as he leaned heavily against her, whimpering like a small animal, his hand stroking her thigh. They could hear her talking a sort of baby talk to him, and he yelped once more, as if she had touched his cheek again.

'I didn't mean to be beating on the man,' Bennet said apologetically. 'The woman said …'

Uncle Roy gestured at him. 'What that woman says would make you sick. It was him that burned the icehouse and worked over Mrs Deventer's car.'

'Maybe we ought to hit him some more, then,' Lou Gibb said.

But it was too late. Touchey and Gwendolyn Bundy roared past just then, Ms. Bundy driving, their car kicking up dust and gravel as she slewed around south onto Highway One. Then Mr Jimmers held out his hand to Uncle Roy, who pumped it heartily, clapping Jimmers on the back. Jimmers looked at Roy's face and shook his head. 'Did they beat you?'

'Beat me? Certainly they beat me.'

'The same lot as usual?' Jimmers asked, breaking into a grin.

'How does that go?' Uncle Roy asked. ' "Jesus, they beat me stupid." '

'That must be from a different book,' Jimmers said. 'You never could keep that sort of thing straight.'

'No, I couldn't. But it's tolerably good to see you. I've got that much straight.'

Aunt Edith and Sylvia appeared from around the side of the museum then. The moon shone over the treetops, lighting the road and the parking lot and illuminating Edith's face, which was full of relief. It was apparently over. No one was hurt. The crisis was past. She regarded Stoat, who stood a few feet off, leaning against the side of the museum.

'Timothy,' she said. 'Welcome back. Sylvia's been telling me about things.'

'I'm sorry,' Stoat said. He looked haggard and worn out, not particularly happy. Howard wondered what it was he regretted the most.

Uncle Roy stepped across and shook Stoat's hand. 'Who's not sorry for something?' he asked. Then, to Edith, he said, 'Stoat here wrestled the gun away from Glenwood Flounder, right out back in the gravel. Saved everyone's life probably.'

'Well,' Edith said. 'It's over, isn't it? Everyone is saved. The night is full of heroes.'

Bennet began to jabber at Uncle Roy just then, telling him about the road being washed away, and Mr Jimmers hugged Edith, talking very earnestly. Howard looked at Sylvia and smiled with pride. Her jeans were streaked with crushed ice plant and her hair was windblown and wild. He wanted to grab her right there on the spot and kiss her, sweep her right off her feet – the perfect end of a not-very-perfect day.

But the whine of an engine and the squeal of tires shut everyone up. Down the highway, from the direction of town, came a paramedics' van, weaving insanely from lane to lane but without any lights or siren. It drove straight toward them, the driver's face hidden in shadow, like the faces of the men in Uncle Roy's ghost car.

Howard stood there stupefied, unable to comprehend the meaning of the van's sudden appearance. Had someone innocently driven past and seen the commotion and called for help?

The van braked in a hard stutter, a half dozen jerks, as if someone were stamping the brake pedal into rubbish. It swerved into the lot, nearly clipping Bennet, who leaped out of the way when he saw who it was that was driving.

'God almighty,' Uncle Roy said softly.

The van door opened and Heloise Lamey very nearly fell out onto her face.

Uncle Roy and Mr Jimmers both stepped across to help her, Jimmers gaping in disbelief. She recovered before they got to her, though, sitting up very straight and fastening the two of them with a cold and wintry gaze. Slowly she opened her clenched fists, as if she had asked them to guess which hand held the colored bean, and with a triumphant laugh she displayed two water-soaked fragments of the fraudulent sketch.

31

The night was tremendously quiet, as if nature had been struck dumb. Even the wind had been stilled by Mrs Lamey's unlikely appearance. The only sound was the ocean muttering faintly in the distance, like a great, sighing ghost. The headlights of the paramedics' van lit up the woods behind the museum, and Howard half expected the luminous cow to wander out of the trees, chewing its phantom cud. It was Mrs Lamey who spoke first.

'Artemis Jimmers,' she said in a voice meant to be commanding, but which was shaking, and was too highly pitched. 'I've come for the machine and for John Ruskin's bones.'

She breathed hard, as if she had been running from something, or else was so agitated that she was hyperventilating. The leather satchel still hung around her neck, and she hunched forward as she stood there, as if weighed down by it. Her hair was startling – full of twigs and leaves – and her face and hands were smeared with muck from her pilgrimage up Pudding Creek. She turned and pulled a dry, clean, hospital-issue blanket out of the open door of the van and wrapped herself in it, clutching the blanket shut with the same hand in which she held the shredded fragments of the sketch. Her eyes glowed with light that was the result of a private, newly discovered wavelength.

'I have swum with the salmon,' she said, and then fumbled beneath the blanket, reaching her fingers into the satchel and pulling out her magical divining rod, which she waved in Jimmers' direction.

There was dead silence again as everyone stared mystified at the tied-together forearm bones – in stupefaction now rather than fear or wonder, since the bones didn't command the same respect that they might have earlier in the evening. Most of the debris that knotted them together had washed away, and aside from a few threads of bird feather hanging from a bit of adhesive tape, they might have been something scavenged from a garbage heap. Their terrible odor and their power to repulse people seemed to have been lost along with their nasty trimmings. She shook them in the air, though, back and forth in the manner of someone carefully salting a pot of stew.

'Of course,' Mr Jimmers said to her, watching the bones doubtfully. 'The machine. Yes. I'm not sure that you're any longer in a position to—'

'*Position?*' she gasped, her voice cracking. She took a step toward him, pointing the bones at him specifically. He flinched just a little, not liking the look of them suddenly, even in their declined state. But he held his ground, ready to parley with her like he would parley with a creature from the stars. She had come to menace them with her mere presence, which was very nearly enough.

'I was told by this man that the bones of John Ruskin were entombed within your device,' she said, cocking her head with great dignity and gesturing at Uncle Roy, who smiled, nodding at Jimmers.

'That's right,' Roy said. 'Ruskin's bones. All except for the fingers of his right hand. Those were ground up and used to seed clouds out in Iowa. That's what the machine is – a rain-making device built on the spiritual principle.'

She nodded slowly, as if this were reasonable.

'She's off her chump,' Uncle Roy whispered to Jimmers. 'Swum with the salmon?'

'I was promised the device in the tin shed,' she muttered, looking down at her hands, 'but I was given *this*.' She cast the watery bits of paper at their feet, snorting in disgust. 'Its power has been taken back. You're *nothing* now,' she said to Howard. 'You're a pitiful weak thing.'

'Christ!' breathed Uncle Roy, who obviously recognized what it was that she had thrown onto the ground. He stooped to pick up the pieces and looked at Howard with a horrified face.

Howard winked at him, and Uncle Roy relaxed.

'I'm damned if I'll give her the machine,' Jimmers whispered. 'Is there a phone inside? We'll call the hospital.'

Uncle Roy shook his head. 'No phone. Don't be so damned tight-fisted with the machine. Let's crank it up. Give her a taste of it. She's come a long damned way to see it, poor old thing. Look at her.'

Mrs Lamey began jigging the bones at them again, casting some sort of spell. Her mouth worked as if she were reciting something that would confound them all, except that right then one of the bones fell away from the other one and landed in the gravel. Howard was reminded of his adventure with the shotgun in the stone house. He felt suddenly sympathetic, and he bent over to retrieve the bone for her. She warded him off, though, and snatched it up herself, peering at it wonderingly and clutching the two bones in her hand, like chopsticks now, a look of uncertainty in her eye, as if she were watching her power literally fall apart. Like an insane orchestra conductor groping to remember a tune, she began to wave them at Jimmers again, taking up where she had left off.

It seemed to Howard that there was a horrible timelessness to her antics now, that she had forgotten what she was doing and so could see no reason ever to stop. The thought of her going on like that was unspeakable. The tension in the air broke, the tree branches stirred in the wind, and Mrs Lamey began to cry – a watery snivel at first, which gave way to shuddering and sobbing and wheezing as she pressed the bones to her chest, looking around her with pitiful, vacant eyes but apparently seeing nothing. There was no threat left to her, no magic or power.

Howard felt little satisfaction in that. He felt only the need to restrain her, and then to find her shelter from whatever empty thing it was that her world had become.

'For God's sake,' Uncle Roy said to Jimmers, speaking out loud, 'let her have a look at the machine. I think you owe it to all of us.'

Edith stepped across then along with Sylvia, and they took Mrs Lamey by either elbow, leading her toward the back door of the museum. No longer sobbing, the old woman glared at Edith, but without any real recognition. It didn't matter who Edith was. There wasn't a living human being on earth, Mrs Lamey's face seemed to say, that was of any interest to her.

The rest of them followed, Roy and Jimmers still arguing about the machine. But by the time they had gotten around back, and Edith had led Mrs Lamey into the museum, Jimmers apparently had made up his mind.

'I won't be responsible for it,' he said to Roy.

'I will,' Roy told him. 'Full responsibility.'

'It may have serious consequences on the spiritual existence of a very superior human being. There's no telling what will come of it ...' His warning was lost on Uncle Roy, though, and Jimmers could see that, and fell silent. Then, tiredly, he waved a hand at Howard, Bennet, and Lou Gibb. Uncle Roy stepped across to the paramedics' van, fired up the engine, and angled the van around so that the headlights illuminated the truck bed, where the tin shed sat with its doors gaping open.

Howard climbed up onto the lift gate and then turned to give Mr Bennet a hand up. Lou Gibb, Stoat, and Uncle Roy followed, although there wasn't room for more than two of them inside the shed. All of them, though, craned their necks to see through the doorway, where the machine sat as ever, half hidden by the fallen aluminum lawn chair. Together Howard and Stoat pulled bags of mulch out, laying them on the truck bed and clearing the doorway. Then they hauled Jimmers' machine out so that the others could get a grip on it, too, all of them easing it across to set it on the lift gate. Bennet lowered the gate to the ground, and they picked up the machine again and lifted it up onto the wooden porch, getting into each other's way.

'Too many Indians,' Uncle Roy said, stepping aside and letting the others wrestle with it. They had to tilt the device up sideways, holding on to it awkwardly and bumping their knuckles on the doorjamb. Mr Jimmers waved his arms and made valuable suggestions, grimacing at the pinging and ponging sounds echoing out from inside the machine.

In the museum, finally, they heaved it up onto one of the redwood tables, which creaked under the machine's weight. Uncle Roy held a propane lantern over it, and everyone except Mrs Lamey gathered around to inspect it. Free of shed debris now, it looked like a strange hybrid of sewing machine, harmonium, and vine-entangled shrub. It was studded along the back with what might have been crude vacuum tubes designed to look like bell jars. The frosted glass of the jars was cameo-carved with vines and oak leaves.

There were delicate cylinders, like metal reeds, sprouting from among the bell jars, and India-rubber squeezo bulbs dangling like kelp bladders along the back, making a sort of sighing noise, as if they were breathing.

The entire device was mounted on springs that were tied into what looked at first glance like claw-and-ball feet. Howard was only partly surprised to find that they were actually carved into the semblance of trees, with heavy, twisted root balls at the base, the springs twining out of their upper branches like foliage.

The case of the machine was decorated with more vines and leaves and with the logo of the Guild of St George. Even the springs and rivets were minutely decorated, so that as he stared at it in the silvery light of the lantern, Howard's vision was confused, and it seemed to him that he wasn't looking at a machine at all, but at something living and growing, like an ancient, tangled garden in miniature, or a carefully contrived archetype of all gardens and deep woods everywhere.

Howard realized that he had seen almost nothing in the darkness of the shed two days ago, when he had foolishly spun the thing's wheel.

Now he saw it clearly, though, and from a better angle, through eyes unclouded by doubt. It was obviously a Victorian-era, gluer-built machine. There was something in the heap of decoration and unlikely gadgetry that suggested, against all reason, a carefully ordered chaos – cosmically arranged doodads mixed up with a deep-woods thicket. Clearly this was the culmination of John Ruskin's work, the great masterpiece of the St George's Guild, the end product and object of the shadowy Pre-Raphaelite Brotherhood itself.

Edith and Sylvia went back to sit with Mrs Lamey on her bench against the wall. She still held on to the bones, clutching them in her hands and staring in the general direction of the machine. Her eyes were focused, though, on some distant place, as if the machine were a window on another world. Howard found himself hoping that whatever place it was, it was somewhere serene and safe.

He didn't feel any hatred for her at all, which vaguely surprised him. She was just a lonely, lost old woman wrapped in a blanket now, her life twisted and stunted by witchery and greed. Now that Howard had seen the power of the paper Grail and had gotten a good look at Jimmers' machine, he could understand the ambition that drove Mrs Lamey.

Jimmers stepped back away from the table and folded his arms. 'I can't say with any certainty ...' he started to say, as if uneasy again with the idea of 'cranking it up,' as Uncle Roy had put it.

'None of us *wants* any certainty,' Roy said, interrupting him. 'None of us minds a little uncertainty.'

'Just don't let any ghosts steal my damned truck,' Bennet said, nudging Lou Gibb in the arm.

Uncle Roy turned down both propane lamps, throwing the room into shadow. 'Let her rip,' he said to Jimmers.

Mr Jimmers hesitated for another moment, gathering himself, then he reached out and spun the wheel hard, slapping it faster and faster with the palm of his hand. He manipulated a lever and squeezed the bulbs in among the jars, and the machine made tiny splooping noises like thumb-sized frogs leaping into a pond.

This time Howard could predict what he would see and hear: the fishbowl glow of light, the distant footsteps, the humming, the sound of mechanical men deep in conversation. He thought of the ghosts in the Studebaker and Uncle Roy's spirit woman on the stairs. Was this the same sort of thing? A one-hundred-year-old hoax?

There was a sudden draft, and the temperature in the room fell ten degrees in a swoop, the back door slamming shut with a bang that made Howard jump. The lighted mist became a smoky wraith that swirled and congealed over the picnic table. Everyone still standing around the machine stepped back into the shadows, huddling together almost inadvertently, and Sylvia stood up from the bench and joined Howard, peering over his shoulder, her face full of wonder.

Mrs Lamey's divining rod clattered to the wooden floor, and Howard saw her stand up then, too, squinting, unable to believe her eyes. She stooped and picked up the bones, then took a half-step forward, talking under her breath. Jimmers held up his arm to stop her, and Edith stood up then behind her, putting a hand on Mrs Lamey's shoulder.

Through the swirling, machine-made cloud, a vague, nebulous shape appeared, seeming to grow in size and clarity, as if the white mist from the machine were a lighted avenue out of the heavens, and some vast, unruly force were rushing at them along that avenue, out of the void of time and space.

It was a human form that materialized in the light, apparently made out of glittering snowflakes. It seemed to be speaking in tongues, but haltingly, as if with a deficient command of that language.

The myriad voices from the machine fought to become one voice. They were broken apart at first, as if by some aural kaleidoscope, but then they fell together and became whole – the voice of a single, old, enraged man uttering what sounded like a prepared speech in a vast auditorium. 'Blanched sun!' he thundered. 'Blighted grass! Blinded man!' He paused to gather himself, looking around suddenly with a puzzled face, as if surprised to find himself there. He held out his glittering arms and examined the backs of his hands, opening and closing them stiffly. Then, gesturing with both arms in a broad arc, he went on, speaking in a tone of deep authority: 'If you ask me for any conceivable cause or meaning of these things, I can tell you none, according to your modern beliefs; but I can tell you what meaning it would have borne to the men of old time!'

He stopped again and looked around him, right at the little knot of men and women standing just outside the circle of lamplight. It wasn't clear that he saw them, and yet he seemed to be speaking to them directly, with a voice full of conviction and knowledge. Uncle Roy's face was hanging in disbelief, and Mr Jimmers looked as if the vision before them justified his entire existence. Mrs Lamey's eyes were narrowed, and she gasped for breath as if she had run a race.

The ghostly face was the visage of John Ruskin himself, white-haired and with the wide-open eyes of a prophet and seer. He fixed those eyes on Heloise Lamey, singling her out. Clearly entranced, she bent forward, hearkening to his words, and she reached out a hand, thinking, perhaps, that he would take it, that the two of them would stride out into the dark and windy night together.

The sound of bees rose on the air of the still room just then, and for a moment the ghost wavered and faded, his voice disintegrating again as the machine lost power. Mrs Lamey cast Jimmers a look of such wild alarm that Jimmers lunged forward and spun the wheel, and almost at once the image leaped into metal-etched clarity, every hair on Ruskin's head blazing white, as if he were ringed with fire.

The sound of a siren rose around them, and the beehive noise faded behind it. Howard thought for a moment that the up-and-down whining of the siren was the noise of the machine, somehow, that it was wound too tight and was spinning out of control.

Then there was the roar of a car engine and tires spinning in gravel. It wasn't the machine at all that was making the siren noise. It was cars outside in the parking lot, police probably, on the trail of Mrs Lamey and the stolen van.

The museum door flew open just as John Ruskin's ghost, nearly solid now, but still as white as moonlight and moving with the jerky rhythms of an old film image, reached both arms out, gesturing either at Mrs Lamey or else to underscore some telling phrase, to implore his audience to ignore the three men who stood in the open doorway now, and to pay attention to him and to his passions, 'By the plague wind every breath you draw is polluted, half round the world,' he told them. 'In a London fog the air itself is pure, though you choose to mix up dirt with it and choke yourself with your own nastiness.'

Mrs Lamey moaned loudly, cast off her blanket, and in her muddy, tattered dress she tore away from Edith and flew past Jimmers in a savage rush, knocking him sideways and leaping into the circle of light thrown off by the machine. She scrambled awkwardly up onto the end of the redwood picnic table, still clutching the bones and knocking one of the propane lanterns onto the floor. She stood up, reaching out her arms to grapple with the image of Ruskin, who continued to discourse about plague winds and apocalyptic storms. He seemed to be solid to her touch, and he turned his head and regarded her vaguely, as if *she* were the ghost, just barely visible to him now. His voice faltered and his eyes opened wide.

She teetered there on the table edge, nearly falling backward, but then hanging impossibly in the air, caught in the grip of some indecipherable force that defeated mere gravity. Jimmers shouted and threw out his hand, plunging it into the radium glow of the ghost light in order to steady her, to prevent her from falling. He howled, though, and jerked his arm abruptly backward as if something had tried to clutch his hand and haul him in.

Right then, her face a composed mask, Mrs Lamey stood straight up on tiptoe and very slowly rose above the table, her head thrown back and her face nearly grazing one of the open trestles that supported the roof rafters. She was washed in an electric-white aura that pulsated and spun, drawing the edges of the illuminated ghost of John Ruskin into herself like water drawn into a whirlpool, until his stretched face hovered beside her own, as if he were hidden behind her, peering over her shoulder. He seemed to be speaking only to her now, into her ear, as if she were the only person present who could hear him.

She shrieked and threw out her hands, casting the arm bones of Joseph of Arimathea into the far wall, where they clattered to the floor. Like a wind devil, the ghost light whirled around her, her hair standing on end as if she would be drawn straight up through the roof.

Uncle Roy's mouth hung open in astonishment, and the three men in the doorway – a policeman and two paramedics – stood gaping, too, as if they were on utterly unfamiliar ground, had found themselves suddenly on the moon and in the middle of some sort of alien ritual.

The ghost from the machine shuddered – a quick convulsion, the light rippling like heat waves – and then exploded, flying apart like a snowball with a firecracker buried in it. Fragments of light showered away in a spiral nebula, as the ghostly voice of John Ruskin shouted one last time and fell silent.

Mr Jimmers rushed forward now, in an effort to help Mrs Lamey, who had collapsed, and lay curled on the end of the table now like a sleeping cat, her head resting against one of the machine's feet.

'Stand clear!' commanded the policeman. He stepped into the lantern light. It was the cop from the harbor, looking both suspicious and baffled. The two paramedics pulled a gurney through the open door, then hurried across to lift Mrs Lamey onto it before checking vital signs. She lay there limp, like a doll with half its stuffing gone.

'Dead?' Jimmers asked in a hollow voice.

'No. Unconscious,' one of the paramedics said.

She stirred then, and her eyes blinked open. Her face was empty of animation, though, like a rubber mask. She began to gibber, barely moving her lips, and her hands twitched on the top of the sheet-covered gurney as if she were picking tiny weeds out of a flower bed.

'Mrs Lamey?' one of the paramedics said to her, looking at her eyes. He passed his hand in front of her face, then snapped his fingers.

She stared straight toward the ceiling, though, or at some point beyond it, oblivious to him, her face limp and her hands still plucking at the sheet. The paramedic shook his head at the cop.

'Finish up and get her out of here,' the cop said, 'and don't leave her alone in the damned van this time.'

'I think the van's safe from her now,' Uncle Roy said softly. He stepped across and turned up the lantern that still sat on the back of the table.

The cop looked hard at Roy, then at Bennet and Howard, realizing who they were, as if scattered puzzle pieces had fallen into place suddenly, only to form a picture so weird and complicated as to be beyond his comprehension.

'What's this now?' the cop asked. 'The whole damned gang, is it? You're Roy Barton, aren't you?'

Uncle Roy nodded, smiling cheerfully. 'Glad you arrived, Officer,' he said, shoving out his hand. The policeman looked at it dubiously before he shook it.

'Poor old Heloise Lamey,' Roy said. 'She burst in here ten minutes ago, right in the middle of all this.' He swept his hand around the room, as if to clarify the whole doubtful business. 'I don't know if you've met Mr Stoat. He's a financier. He's underwriting this whole venture.'

'Stoat?' the cop said flatly. 'What venture is that?' He looked hard at Stoat and then took a closer look at the machine.

'Ghost museum, haunted house,' Roy said. 'That doggone icehouse was a firetrap. We decided to shift out here when the place burned down.' Uncle

Roy gestured at the machine. 'Stage magic. You know how it is. The kids love this sort of thing. You've got kids yourself …'

The cop smiled and started to nod, as if then and there he would pull photos out of his wallet and pass them around. Then he looked abruptly suspicious again.

'Mr Stoat here is the man who pulled me out of the fire down at the icehouse,' Bennet said.

'Good man.' The cop caught sight of Sylvia then, who was sitting with Edith on the bench, back in the shadows. 'Hi there,' he said cheerfully. Sylvia waved tiredly at him.

'How many kids have you got?' Roy asked.

'What? Three. Why?'

'Put the officer down for three tickets,' he said to Howard. 'Gratis.'

'Right,' Howard said.

'What happened to your face?' The cop narrowed his eyes at Roy. 'Nasty bruise.'

'Stepped on a rake up in Caspar,' Uncle Roy said. 'I've been up there shoveling manure.'

'I bet you have. You can quit shoveling now, though. We're knee-deep in it.' He smiled for the first time. 'Jack Mac Donald's been telling me about you,' he said.

'Jack?' Roy said, surprised. 'You know Jack?'

'We play poker. Saturday nights. Friendly game.'

Roy looked at Bennet and winked. 'Don't need another couple of players, do you?'

'Well, we are a little short right now,' the cop said, smoothing down his mustache.

'Then we'll fit right in,' Bennet said. 'I'm only five eight and Roy here's nearly a midget when he takes the risers out of his shoes.'

Uncle Roy laughed, then looked at Mrs Lamey and stopped abruptly. She still gibbered and twitched, as if enlivened by a tiny electrical charge, with not nearly enough current to start her up. The two paramedics pushed her rolling stretcher toward the door, maneuvering her through it and down the couple of stairs outside, disappearing from sight.

'Poor old thing,' Roy said softly. 'She was always delicate. Like a thin piece of glass. Nothing but sharp edges, but it didn't take much to crack her.'

The cop nodded. 'She had a rough time up at the beach tonight. Freak storm up there did a lot of damage, nearly drowned the old woman, knocked her around pretty bad. She went haywire when they got her down to emergency. These boys left her alone for half a second, and she up and drove off in the van. Took some time to track her down.' They heard the door of the paramedics' van slide shut then. The engine roared, and there was the sound of wheels on gravel as it backed out onto the coast highway and motored away north.

'What I wonder,' the cop said, 'is why she came here. And what was she doing up on the table there?'

Roy clicked his tongue regretfully. 'She and Artemis Jimmers here were married. Years ago. She's been pining away for him.' He gestured at Mr Jimmers, who wore a long face, as if this were a personal tragedy.

'You're the one who lives down at the stone house, aren't you?' the cop said.

'Caretaker,' Jimmers said, 'since Michael Graham's tragic death.'

The cop nodded. 'My father used to lend Graham a hand, back when Graham was putting up the tower. I even hauled stone around out there when I was a kid. Old Graham was something. I learned to drink coffee there. He used to haul it out in a big ceramic jug with a spigot. I'll never forget that. Left the place to you, did he?'

Jimmers shook his head. 'Just caretaker,' he said. 'Holding on to the place until the rightful owner came along. Howard Barton here is the owner now. Lock, stock, and barrel. It's all down in Graham's will, giving me power of attorney. We're all supposing Howard will do the right thing and marry Sylvia, and the two of them can hoe chard out there together. Work the garden.'

Howard sat down hard next to Sylvia on the bench, looking at her in disbelief, his head swimming. Sylvia widened her eyes at him. 'Was *that* your proposal?' she whispered. 'Did you put him up to saying that?' Before Howard could utter a word, though, she stood up and rushed across to hug and kiss Mr Jimmers, then turned around and went after Uncle Roy, holding on to Jimmers' shoulders with one arm and throwing the other around Roy's neck, hugging them both together.

After a moment she let them both go. Grinning, but full of emotion, Roy picked up the knocked-over lantern and inspected it carefully. 'Mantle's whole,' he said to Jimmers. 'Can you beat that?'

'A mystery,' Jimmers said. 'Better document it.'

Roy pulled a book of paper matches out of his pocket and lit the thing with a shaky hand, turning up the knob until the room glowed with the light of both lanterns. Then he spotted the arm bones lying one beside the other on the floor, and he picked them up, looking them over.

'Relics,' Stoat said to him. 'The genuine article.'

'What?' the cop asked, cocking his head.

'Part of the props,' Roy said to him. 'A haunted house has got to be full of bones. It's standard stuff. Chains rattling in the closet and all.'

The cop looked doubtful, on the verge of speaking, when a voice from across the room interrupted him. It was Lou Gibb, his broad face full of astonishment.

'I'll be go-to-hell,' he said softly. He and Bennet were both staring at the wall, where the collection of framed photographs had hung.

Uncle Roy, followed now by everyone else, strode across to look closer at the dirty plaster. Two clean white images stood out against it, as if someone had splashed the wall with whitewash. They seemed almost to drink in the light from the propane lanterns. There couldn't be any doubt about what they were.

Roy touched one of the images hesitantly, as if afraid it would rub off, or would burn him, but it wasn't paint or charcoal or anything of the kind; it was shadow and light, captured and fixed onto the wall, a spirit photograph developed when the ghost from the machine had flown to pieces.

Roy turned around, smiling broadly at Edith like a little boy who has just recovered some wonderful lost object. It was John Ruskin's face on the wall, a satisfied grimace tugging at the corners of its mouth. Next to it, like the flip side of a coin from the spirit realm, was the astonished, wild-haired countenance of Heloise Lamey, her face showing jumbled traces of nearly every human emotion, as if her very spirit had departed from her body and was fixed now on the plaster wall.

Uncle Roy gestured grandly at the images, bowing like a maestro.

'Back in business!' he said happily, dusting his hands together before reaching out to clap Howard on the back.

ALL THE BELLS ON EARTH

For Viki, John, and Daniel

And this time,
for the Meyer Family,
Denny, Judy, Anderson, and Amanda

Mahalo
''Oh ke aloha ke kuleana o kahi malihini'

As ever, I'd like to thank a number of people for the help they gave me with this book: Tim Powers and Lew Shiner especially, for their friendship and for the right stuff at the right time, and John Accursi, who could make a fortune as a story editor. I'd also like to thank Chris Arena, who not only cheerfully put up with a thousand questions over the phone and over lunch, but who put up with them again when I called back for details. And thanks to Mark Ziesing, the king of Shingletown and the guru of catalogue sales …

For sheer inspiration, energy, joy, and faith in the future, I'm grateful to the kids of the Orange County Children's Theatre, who have added a whole lot of color to my life. 'Give a little love to a child, and you get a great deal back.' John Ruskin wrote that, and he was right.

PART ONE

The Dragon

Our full energies are to be given to the soul's work – to the great fight with the Dragon – the taking of the kingdom of heaven by force.

JOHN RUSKIN,
PRE-RAPHAELITISM

1

A wet winter night. Nearly two in the morning and the spirit of Christmas haunts the ocean wind, sighing through the foil candycanes that sway from lampposts along Chapman Avenue, through the ribs of the illuminated Santa Claus in the distant Plaza, along empty alleys dark with shifting, anxious shadows. Raindrops slant across the misty glass globes of streetlamps, and heavy, broken clouds drift across the face of the moon. For a few moments the terra-cotta roof tiles of St Anthony's Church glisten in the moonlight. The downtown houses appear out of the darkness: clapboard bungalows with shadowy porches and leafy flowerbeds, curb trees pushing up the side-walks, the houses dark except for the yellow glow of front porch lamps and here and there strings of Christmas lights left on all night.

The moon slips behind clouds again, and in the deepening gloom a human figure steps out of the shadows onto the peak of the church roof and walks carefully across the rainwashed tiles, bent low and carrying a stiff cloth bag. The bell tower rises before him, above the west wall of the church, its white stucco a pale ghost against the deeper darkness of the roof. Within the open arches of the tower stand the crossmembers and struts of the iron framework that supports a carillon of eleven heavy bells.

He climbs over the cast concrete railing in the east-facing arch and dissappears among the maze of shadows cast by the bells, and suddenly the silent night is broken by a tumult of flapping wings, and the sky above the tower is clouded with circling white doves.

Father Mahoney sat in the small sacristy of Holy Spirit Catholic Church and listened to the water dripping from the eaves outside the windows, which were tilted open to let in the melody of the rain. The room was pleasantly scented with the smell of the night air, mingling with the odor of floor wax and incense blocks. It was early in the morning – he wasn't sure just what time it was – but he rarely slept later than four these days, and over the years he had gotten used to seeing the sunrise as well as the sunset. And anyway, today he was seventy – he didn't have the leisure to be wasting a morning of this quality.

He heard a noise from somewhere off in the church, what sounded like the creaking of wooden joints.

Probably it was just the old church settling in the weather. He sat for a moment listening to hear it again, but there was nothing, just the sound of the rainy morning. Something about the rain improved the silence, something vast and deep that reminded him of the last notes of a hymn or the silence that followed the ringing of bells.

On the library table in front of him lay an open cigar box next to his cup of instant coffee. The box was filled with seashells. He picked out several kelp scallops and paired them according to size and color, but none of the pairs looked quite right. There had already been half a dozen Pacific storms this winter, and the shelling was better than any year he could remember. He had found two perfect chestnut cowries beneath the Huntington Beach pier last week – the first he had ever found. They sat on the table now, neatly arrayed beside the scallops and a handful of jewel-box shells.

He picked up an issue of *The Nautilus* and began to flip through the pages, but right then he heard the sound of wood scraping against wood, as if someone had pushed a pew out of its place in the church. He stood up and walked to the door, edging it open and looking out past the altar, seeing no one. He stepped across the choir and looked down into the nave, which was empty, the pews sitting square and neat and solid. After a moment he went back into the sacristy and sat down again, idly stirring the shells in the box with his index finger and gazing at the three stained-glass windows in the east wall.

It was in the early morning that he most liked to sit in the wood-paneled room and simply look at these windows, which depicted Christ and two angels ascending into heaven. Holly leaves with red berries bordered the windows, and the same color of red tinted the stigmata on Christ's out-turned palms. The windows looked out on a garden of tree ferns and maidenhair, and tonight the ivory light from the garden lamps muted the colors of the rain-washed glass, tinting the holly berries and the bleeding wounds an unearthly shade of deep red that reminded him of the sacrament. He couldn't help making these connections, seeing the spirit of one thing alive in something else; it was evidence of the great design.

There was the sound of car wheels swishing on the wet asphalt of the street, and he was momentarily thankful to be inside, where it was warm and dry and close. Picking up one of the cowries, he ran his finger over the smooth hump of its shell. And then, as he set it back down on the table among the others, the sacristy door creaked open.

A man stepped into the room. He wore an oversized coat and trousers, rubber gloves, and a pair of dirty white loafers with tassels. Covering his head was a rubber mask that resembled the face of a goat, complete with a protruding rubber tongue, curled-back horns, and a tuft of coarse hair.

The man in the church tower reeled against the railing, shocked at the rush of wings around him, at the wheeling birds that had been nesting in the belfry. Dropping the canvas sack full of tools, he held onto the smooth stucco of the tower wall with both hands. Although there was a floor beneath the bells, he felt himself to be standing at the edge of a yawning pit, as if the tower were a deep open well into the darkness.

Birds landed on the peak of the roof and stood in the rain before wheeling away again, disappearing into the deep shadows of a big cypress tree in the lot next door. In a moment the night was quiet, and he felt steady again. He let go of the wall, shoved his tools aside with his foot, and forced himself to attend to the bells. There was just enough light to make out the immense bolts that secured them – three bolts in each of the two biggest bells, which must have been three feet in diameter, their bronze walls some three or four inches thick. He groped in the bag of tools, his heart racing, and found a can of lubricant, then sprayed the heavily rusted nuts that secured the biggest bell.

It would be easier simply to cut the wires attached to the clappers and silence the bells that way, but then it would be equally easy for the bellringer to reattach the wires. He wanted something else to happen, something more permanent.

He took a big wrench from the bag and fit it to the nut, leaning into it hard, throwing his weight behind it. Nothing happened. It was frozen tight. The wind blew a flurry of raindrops through the arch, and he let up on the wrench, picking up the can of spray lube again and spraying the nuts heavily. A car drove past on the street below, its headlights glaring against the wet asphalt, and he cursed the driver under his breath.

Christmas lights winked off and on along the eaves of a house across the street, throwing a faint glow of blue and red and green across the dull metal of the bells. Somehow the colors horrified him, as if they were live things, tiny spirits dancing on the cold bells, mocking him, appearing and disappearing like goblin gold. The bells began to thrum in the wind, as if they had a voice, and for a moment he fancied he could hear a melody in the raindrops plinking against the bronze. The iron framework before him was dizzyingly complicated, and the bells swam in and out of his vision.

He dropped the wrench and reached for a crossbar in order to steady himself, but touched the surface of the bell instead. It was horribly solid, the bronze so cold that for a moment he thought he'd been burned. He jerked his hand away and grabbed for the railing, looking away from the bells and the reflected Christmas lights, out into the night where the palms along the avenue moved slowly in the wind. Like a tide beneath a pier, the shifting palm fronds made the tower seem to sway, and he held on desperately. A dove alighted on the concrete railing, stark white in the moonlight, and in a moment of wild rage and fear he swung his hand at it, lurching forward to grab it by the neck. The dove lifted off again, and the back of his hand struck the stucco corner of the arch.

The pain sobered him. He stood breathing hard, the rain in his face. He had nearly lost his mind there for a moment. It occurred to him abruptly that something was actively working against him, some power, filling his head with confusion – the rain, the colored lights, the doves …

The idea of it appealed to him, giving him a strange sensation of potency. He was filled with the certainty that he was laboring at the heart of an ages-old struggle, that with his bag of tools he might shift something so monumentally heavy that it made the ponderous bell in front of him nothing more than a dust mote.

Full of wild purpose, he picked up the spray lube, and held down the nozzle until all three nuts ran with oil. Then he fumbled in the sack again, pulling out a small propane torch. He lit the torch, adjusted the flame, and held it to the center nut. The oil burst into flame, and the flame ran out across the steel plate, flickering like witch fire, casting a glare on the walls around him. He held the torch to the nut, which had sat there immobile for sixty years, and watched the flaming oil burn itself out. Then, shutting off the torch, he fixed the wrench on the nut again and leaned hard against it. There was a spray of rust flakes and a loud squeak as the nut disengaged, but he didn't let up. He cranked the wrench around in a big circle, forcing it up the rusty threads until the nut fell loose, dropping to the floor. The second nut was easier than the first; there was no need to heat it with the torch. He eased the third nut up the bolt until, with a heart-stopping shriek, the bell twisted away from its steel plate, the bolt itself bending backward from the bell's weight. He stood for a moment, afraid to go on. If the bell came down now …

But the bell didn't fall. He counted four threads exposed above the remaining nut. Carefully he turned the wrench, easing the nut upward, the rusty iron groaning. Even when the nut was flush with the top of the bolt, he continued to turn the wrench, picturing the bell dropping, the terrible noise of it crashing through the floors below, slamming into the concrete floor at the bottom of the tower.

The top of the bolt slowly edged its way down into the nut. He counted the revolutions, stopping at the fourth, trusting utterly to instinct: another quarter turn and it would fall. The bell swayed there, defying gravity, thousands of pounds of cast bronze held by a thin curl of iron. One of the doves could dislodge it. The wind could blow it down.

He stepped backward and laughed out loud, picturing it, full of wild confidence now, of boundless exhilaration as he slid the wrench free, slipping it into the bag along with the torch and the spray can. Then he swung his leg over the railing, stepped out onto the roof again, and set out toward the back of the church. The moon shone now as if someone had turned on a lamp in the night sky. He hurried. It wouldn't do to be caught. Not now. Never mind what it would do to his life, to his career, if he were seen up here. It had quite simply been vital that the bells be silenced, but the awful compulsion that had led him out into the rainy night was already draining away …

A car approached from the west. He stepped down the back slope of the roof, trying to move out of sight, hunching forward to shrink himself. Suddenly he was off-balance, and he threw out his free hand, trying to grab the peak of the roof as his foot slipped on the wet terra-cotta and his leg splayed outward. He dropped the bag, throwing out his arms to catch himself as he fell forward. His fingernails scraped across the slick tiles and he skittered downward, scrabbling uselessly, moaning out loud.

In that instant there flew into his mind an image of himself lying dead on the ground, his soul sucked out of him, down through the dirt and rock of the cold earth, fleeing away toward some infinitely empty place. Terror and remorse surged through him, and for one appalling moment he thought he heard the bells themselves begin to toll.

Then his right foot struck the rain gutter that ran along the eave, and he hugged the terra-cotta tiles to him as he jolted to a stop right at the roof's edge. For a moment he lay there simply breathing, his eyes closed, feeling the cold rain against his back. Then, carefully, he looked behind him, down at the lawn and at the scattering of tools that had flown out of the canvas bag.

He hunched forward, crawling up the rusted metal valley like a bug, hanging onto the edges of the roof tiles and breathing hard now, desperately careful. The wild elation he had felt in the tower was utterly gone, all of it replaced by the terrible need to save himself, to get down off the roof, retrieve his tools, and make his way to safety without being seen.

When he was well clear of the edge, he stood up and quickened his pace, and within seconds was at the peak again, then past it, letting himself down the back side of the roof, which was hidden from the street by a row of trees.

The wet sidewalks reflected the glow from the old cast-concrete streetlamps on the parkway, and water dripped with a slow, hollow plink in the metal downspout at the edge of the porch. The wind was full of the promise of more rain. Walt Stebbins stood on the porch and listened to the night. He wore his pajama shirt tucked into a pair of pants that he'd pulled on hastily. He hadn't bothered with his bedroom slippers. The wisteria vine that climbed the downspout was bare of leaves, and the yellow buglight on the porch threw a tangle of moving shadows out onto the front lawn. There was a gust of wind, and the heavy vines scraped against the eaves of the house.

He noticed then that he'd left the Christmas lights on again – the third time that season. It was amazing how a few colored lights could run up the bill. He stepped down off the porch now and peered around the outside corner of the front bedroom, up the driveway toward the garage. The driveway gate was shut. It was a little section of picket fence hinged to the latticework wall of the carport, supported by a single steel wheel that made a gravelly, metallic sound when it rolled open.

That's what had awakened him, or so he thought – the sound of the gate rasping open across the concrete. A moment later a car had started up somewhere down the block, and, lying there in bed, it had seemed nearly certain to him that someone had been in the backyard, and had made a noise going out. Now he wasn't quite so certain. Ivy, his wife, would no doubt remind him of the time he'd woken up convinced he was in a submarine under the Indian Ocean …

And now that he thought about it, the noise could as easily have been the bare wisteria vines scraping the house. The garage door was locked. He could see the padlock from where he stood. The back doors of the house were dead-bolted. He walked softly down the driveway, listening hard, and slipped the latch on the gate, picking the wheel up off the concrete and swinging it open noiselessly. The backyard was quiet, the lawn pooled with rainwater. The stepping-stone path that led to the sheds behind the garage was wet, so there was no real chance of footprints. All in all, there was no indication of any prowler – nothing stolen, nothing out of order. If anyone had been back there, they were apparently only sightseeing.

Blame it on the wind. He went out through the gate again, lifting it to shut it and then easing the latch into place. It was too early in the morning to make noise. He stood for a moment on the sidewalk, looking down toward Chapman Avenue and simply taking in the rainy darkness. A car rolled past the end of the block, its tires humming on the wet pavement, speeding up to beat the light at the corner. The neighborhood was dark and silent, and the sky was like something out of a painting, full of clouds illuminated by moonglow. What a morning! He was thankful all of a sudden that the wind had woken him up and lured him outside, as if it had something to show him.

A flock of birds rose into the air from the roof of St Anthony's Church a block away, and for a moment they glowed impossibly white in the moonlight, flying in a circle around the bell tower before alighting again. Then he saw a movement on the roof – a shadow silhouetted against the darker hedge of trees beyond. In an instant it was gone.

A man on the roof? At this hour? Walt stood watching, waiting to see it again. Except for the birds, the church roof remained empty of movement now.

He seemed to have prowlers on the mind. The neighborhood was apparently alive with them. There was probably some kind of cat-burglar convention over at the Twin Palms Motel. The wind blew straight through the flimsy cotton of his pajama shirt, and he thought about his bed upstairs, about how Ivy would yell at him when he climbed in with frozen feet.

Rain began to fall, and he turned and hurried toward the porch. Then, on a whim, he stopped at the steps, bending over to pinch through a half dozen pansy stems before going in through the door, locking the dead bolt behind him and carrying the little bouquet upstairs.

Back in the bedroom, he watched Ivy sleep for a moment. She lay tucked up in the heap of blankets she'd stolen from him in the night. She was a restless sleeper, and had a sort of tidal effect on blankets, which invariably shifted to her side of the world by morning. His side of the bed was pitifully bare except for the corner of the top sheet. He glanced at the clock: quarter to five, nearly time to get up anyway. He looked around for somewhere to put the pansies so that Ivy would find them when she woke up. An idea came to him, and he turned around and headed into the bathroom, where he dropped a pansy into each of the toothbrush slots in the brass holder on the wall, entwining the handle of Ivy's toothbrush with the flimsy stem of the last flower.

Satisfied, he went quietly back out into the bedroom, took his shirt and sweater off the chair, and found his shoes and a pair of socks. He thought again about what he'd seen on the church roof. Something had startled the birds; he hadn't simply imagined the shadowy figure. Still, what could he do about it? Call the cops? It was raining like in the tropics outside now. There wasn't a chance in hell that they'd be interested in his observations. And it occurred to him that if someone *had* been on the roof, it was good odds that they were simply patching a leak during a lull in the storm – probably the minister himself. Surely it wasn't someone breaking in; you didn't break into a church by burrowing through the tile roof. He pushed the matter out of his mind and slipped downstairs again, anxious to put on a pot of coffee out in the garage.

When he saw the intruder in the doorway, Father Mahoney stood up, his throat constricting, a rush of fear slamming through him. For a single terrible moment he was certain that the man wasn't wearing a mask at all, that he actually had the face of a goat. He fought to control himself, but he simply couldn't speak, even when the moment passed and he knew he was wrong. There was something odious about the mask, something filthy that he simply couldn't abide, and without thinking he lunged forward, snatching at it, suddenly wanting to jerk it off the man's head. He felt himself struck hard in the chest and he fell heavily back down into the chair. There was a low laugh from within the confines of the mask, and he threw up his hands and ducked his head as the intruder drew a homemade blackjack from inside his coat – a length of pink rubber hose with a bulbous tip wrapped in cloth tape.

The intruder cracked it down on the corner of the table, leaving a dent. Father Mahoney winced backward, pressing himself into the chair as the man walked slowly around the desk, his head bobbing. The man leaned over until the mask nearly brushed the priest's ear. 'Fatty,' he whispered, his voice pitched weirdly high. He pushed the taped piece of hose into Father Mahoney's cheek and made little clucking sounds. Then he began to giggle, picking up a marking pen off the table and striding to the wall, where he jerked a painting of Job off its nail and let it drop to the floor. With the marker he wrote a filthy word on the white plaster.

He stopped giggling, turning around as if in alarm. He stood there swaying, his breath rasping within the mask. Abruptly he picked up the cup of coffee from the desktop and drank it through the mouth hole of the mask, half the coffee dribbling out from beneath the rubber chin and down his coat.

He pitched the coffee cup into the wall and slammed the blackjack across the cigar box full of shells, breaking apart the wooden panels of the box and knocking the whole thing to the floor, the shells scattering across the lino-leum. He picked up one of the cowries and looked closely at it, making little smacking noises with his lips, as if he wanted to taste it. Carefully, he set it at the corner of the table, and then smashed it flat with a single, quick blow, dusting the fragments onto the floor before smashing the second one the same way. Then, one by one, he hammered the scallops and jewel-box shells into fragments, working methodically, as if smashing the shells was the one great purpose of his visit. He trod through the scattered pieces of seashell on the floor, stomping around on them, crushing them to powder beneath his feet. There was something clearly insane about it, a drooling madness, and yet he moved with a singleness of purpose, as if the seashells were an enemy that had to be utterly destroyed.

'What do you want?' Father Mahoney asked finally. His voice shook. The man stood among the trampled shells, hunched over, his breath wheezing in his throat. 'We haven't got much money,' the priest said, 'not in the church. The offering ...'

The man pulled a short piece of nylon cord from his coat, made a loop in the end of it, grabbed Mahoney's wrist, and settled the loop over it, drawing it tight, yanking his other hand around and tying them both to the chair. Then he took a cloth bag from his pants pocket and pulled it over Mahoney's head. The bag stank, as if something dead had been stored in it, and Mahoney closed his eyes, the idea of praying only now coming to him through the haze of fear and bewilderment.

For uncounted seconds he listened to the man walking back and forth in the room, as if he were pacing, uttering an odd chanting noise that was almost idiotic, the meaningless demonic gibbering of a man who had given up all claim to humanity. There was the sound of the blackjack thudding against something wooden, then a loud grunt followed by the crash of heavy furni-ture toppling – the carved cabinet that held the Host and sacramental wine. Bottles broke against the floor, and Mahoney could smell the spilled wine.

Abruptly he found himself thinking that, thank God, the Host wasn't blessed, but then it struck him that the idea was almost foolish; he was thinking almost like the man in the goat mask – that God, somehow, could be damaged by this kind of pathetic vandalism.

Almost immediately there was another thump and the clank of something metallic falling to the floor. The chalice? It was gold; no doubt he'd steal it. There was a racket of sound: the hand-bells falling, the clanking roll of the censer, then the scrape of hangers on wooden rods – the vestments being yanked out of the wardrobe. A fold of cloth settled over his head – probably an altar boy's gown. He opened his mouth, sucking in air. The layers of cloth made it difficult to breathe, and he wondered suddenly if the man meant to kill him. The idea of suffocation terrified him, and he tore his mind away from the thought, forcing himself to visualize the picture in the stained glass of the windows.

Dimly he heard repeated blows of the blackjack and of glass breaking, and it came to him that the man was destroying the windows too, hammering the leaded joints apart, breaking out the glass. Surely he was making enough noise so that someone on the street would hear. But it was late, and the church and its buildings took up the entire square block …

Father Mahoney stood up, the chair legs coming up off the floor. He hunched away from the desk, bending his head to his chest to dislodge the cloth bag. 'Stop!' he yelled. 'In the name of God …!' He yanked at the ropes that bound his wrists, jerking up and down, full of fury now.

There was a silence, and then the sound of ragged breathing again, coming from somewhere behind him. Father Mahoney tensed, waiting for the blow, for the man to hit him with the blackjack. The hair on his neck crept, and he imagined the intruder standing behind him, the goat mask regarding him now, the blackjack upraised …

And then the sacristy door banged shut. He heard footsteps pounding across the tiles of the nave. The noise faded away, leaving the night silent again but for the sound of the rain.

2

George Nelson sat in his law office on the Plaza, waiting uneasily for the arrival of a business associate – Murray LeRoy. Through the window he could see the Plaza fountain and the small wooden nativity scene next to it. A lamp in the grass cast light on the nativity scene as a discouragement to vandals, but the light apparently hadn't done its job, because the packing-crate manger was kicked to pieces, its palm frond roof scattered into the street, and the plaster of Paris figures knocked over and broken. It was almost ironic: Nelson himself represented a citizens' group opposed to the display of nativity scenes on public property – the suit against the city was still pending – and here someone had come along in the night and done the job single-handedly.

He picked up the phone and dialed LeRoy's number. Nothing. LeRoy was already out, already on his way. There were only a couple of hours left before the arrival of Nelson's secretary, and before then he wanted to be finished with LeRoy. There were a number of reasons for cutting LeRoy loose forever. Mostly it was because LeRoy was a little unsteady these days.

In fact, if his behavior yesterday morning was any indication, the man was positively cracking up, and that was a dangerous thing. He had looked like he'd slept in his clothes, and he hadn't shaved for days. He was half drunk, too, at nine in the morning, and his head shook with some kind of palsy that had made Nelson want to slap him. Six months ago the man didn't drink except at weddings, and then he didn't enjoy it and was always willing to say so in a loud voice. Nelson knew that there had been good reasons for LeRoy to keep his personal life private, but he had the public persona of some kind of scowling Calvinist missionary, and that's what made his downhill slide so strange – he was making it so damned obvious. The thought wasn't comforting.

Nelson had no idea exactly what he'd do about it in the end, but this morning he intended to try to buy the man out. That was the simplest route – something he should have done two or three months ago when LeRoy first started to crack. He wondered suddenly if the business with the nativity scene had been LeRoy's doing. It would certainly fit the pattern. If the man were arrested again, he'd probably babble like the nut he'd become.

He heard a sound then, like the laughter of cartoon devils. 'Murray?' He stood up out of his chair, listening. He opened his desk drawer and slipped his hand in, sliding the loaded .38 to the front. Then he saw a glow beyond the window curtains, and he realized that what he heard now no longer sounded like laughter. There was a crackling, almost like fat sizzling on a griddle, and at that moment he smelled the burning. There was something sulphurous about it, something that nearly choked him even though the windows were shut and locked.

Abruptly it dawned on him that the building might be on fire, that LeRoy had torched it. Thank God the man had become an incompetent fool! He slammed shut the desk drawer and hurried out into the foyer, opening the coat closet and pulling out the fire extinguisher. In a second he had unlocked the door and was out on the sidewalk, yanking the little plastic cotter key out of the lever of the extinguisher. The streets were empty. He slowed down, fully expecting to find LeRoy himself squatting in the flowerbed and dressed up like a clown or a little girl. He angled out toward the street and peered into the alley, which was lit up now with flames.

At first it looked like someone must have dumped burning trashbags onto the pavement. The heat was intense and glowing with a corona of white haze that obscured the burning figure, whatever it was. The fire flickered, rising and falling as if something were literally breathing life into it. The effect was almost hallucinatory, and for a moment he seemed to be looking into the mouth of a burning, circular pit. He heard what sounded like voices, like human cries, and a sulphurous reek drifted skyward like a mass of whirling black shadows.

Clearly it wasn't trashbags. A big dog? The burning thing had a face like an ugly damned goat. He saw then that there were shoes at the other end of it. A man! He pointed the nozzle of the extinguisher in the general direction of the body and squeezed the lever. White dust sputtered out of it, but it was as if a whirlwind encompassed the burning body, and the chemicals blew away uselessly in the air. The flames didn't diminish; shouting at them would do as much good. He tried to get closer, but gave it up; there was no way that he intended to have his hair singed off over this. He pointed the extinguisher into the air and blew the rest of the contents in the direction of the flaming body, knowing it was pointless – no one could live through such a thing any-way – but wanting to make damn well sure that the extinguisher was empty when the investigators had a look at it.

There was something about the shoes ... He looked closely at them, recog-nizing them with a start of surprise – loafers, white, with tasseled laces.

God, it was Murray LeRoy! Someone must have dumped gasoline over him and lit a match. One of the shoes ignited just then, with an audible hiss, and Nelson backed away, turning around and heading up the sidewalk again, hurrying toward the door to the office, swept with relief and fear both.

This certainly solved the problem with LeRoy. He wouldn't be babbling to anyone now. But who had done this? In his mind Nelson ran through his list of enemies. Its being done outside his office, in the early morning like this, that was the bad thing. LeRoy must have talked to someone, said something. God, but to whom? Nelson and his associates were involved in a lot of shaky dealings, but nothing that would warrant something like this.

Inside he locked the door before punching 911 into the phone and report-ing the incident. He sat down then at his desk, taking out the .38. If someone wanted LeRoy dead this badly, there was no reason to think they wouldn't want him dead, too. But who, damn it? Argyle? He was capable of it. It dawned on him just then that perhaps there were other explanations. The city didn't have any real gang problems, but there'd been several incidents in the past couple of years of homeless people being mugged, and he seemed to remember something about a man set on fire somewhere – probably Santa Ana. Who could say how long LeRoy had been in the alley? No doubt he was drunk as a judge and was easy prey for a gang of sadistic skinheads who happened to be out joyriding.

And then there was the possibility that LeRoy had simply gone to Hell.

He pushed the idea out of his mind. There were flashing lights outside the window now – a paramedics truck. He returned the gun to the drawer and went out, carrying the fire extinguisher. The fire was already out except for a weird flickering on the surface of the asphalt itself. The paramedics stood looking at the body, or what was left of it – only a heap of gray ash and charred fragments of bone. One of the shoes sat on the ground, strangely intact, but the other was gone.

'You called this in?'

'What?' Nelson looked up at the paramedic. He realized that he'd been gaping at the shoe with its ridiculous tassel. There was an ankle bone thrust up out of it, charred in half, and he wondered suddenly if there was still flesh on the foot. The idea made him sick, and he turned away and looked across at the Plaza, at the big grinning Santa Claus waving at the traffic coming up Glassell Street.

'Was it you that called, sir?'

He turned back, pulling himself together. 'Yes. I tried to put the fire out, but this didn't seem to do any good.'

'Probably too much heat,' the paramedic said. 'If there's enough heat it can blow this stuff right back at you. It's like spraying a hose into the wind. You did what you could.'

Another truck pulled up, followed by a squad car, and in a moment the alley was full of investigators taking pictures and searching the ground, talking in undertones, their voices full of disbelief. There was a flurry of raindrops, and in moments the rain was coming down hard. Four firemen unfolded a tarp, trying in vain to keep LeRoy's ashes dry while a plainclothes investigator hastily swept it all into a black metal dustpan that he emptied into a plastic sack. Nelson saw that there was a dime in among the ashes, and something else that might have been a tooth.

Without warning, rainwater sluiced out of the drainpipes on either side of the alley and flooded out onto the asphalt. A fireman attempted to dam it up with a yellow slicker, but it was no use: the water washed the alley clean, and within two minutes there was no trace of Murray LeRoy left in the world except the heap of ashes and teeth and bone that lay with the godawful white shoe in the bottom of the plastic sack.

3

There was the sound of thunder somewhere far off, like a door closing on the season, and in the direction of the distant ocean the sky was the color of wet slate. The wind gusted now, carrying on it the first deep notes of the bells from the tower at St Anthony's on Chapman Avenue a block away, and for a moment Walt thought that the sound of the bells was a remnant of the thunder, echoing through remote canyons in the clouds.

Raindrops pattered down onto the concrete walk, and he ducked into the garden shed that stood beneath the canopy of an enormous avocado tree in the back corner of the yard. There was something lonesome in the rain this winter afternoon, in the smell of wet leaves and the low sound of thunder that mingled with the weather-muffled ringing of the bells.

They rang every afternoon during the month of December – something that Walt, happily, had never really gotten used to even though he and Ivy had lived in the neighborhood for upwards of twelve years. Hearing them was always a pleasant surprise, like coming around a corner and suddenly seeing a cherry tree or a hawthorne in blossom.

Abruptly he remembered that Ivy's aunt and uncle were due shortly – maybe even later this afternoon – and thinking about it took some of the magic out of the afternoon. They were on the last leg of their trip from the east. For a couple of weeks they'd been driving out from Michigan in a motor home, fully self-contained – toilet, refrigerator, awning, the whole works. They'd bought it last year with dividends from Uncle Henry's stocks and bonds. The idea was to spend the winter in California – specifically in Walt and Ivy's driveway, which, Walt had to admit, was better than them staying on the foldout couch in the den like last year.

'It's an Ex*e*cutive,' Uncle Henry had said to him over the phone, leaning heavily on the second syllable, and it had taken Walt most of the rest of the conversation to figure out what he meant, that it was the brand name of the motor home. He had tried to imagine the kind of vehicle it was, what it must look like, given its name – a desk in the back, maybe, with a Rolodex on it, and a swivel chair and file cabinet – an outfit suitable for a man of business. Last night Aunt Jinx had called from Kingman, from a pay phone in the parking lot of the Alpha Beta Market where they were spending the night.

Happily alone, at least for the moment, Walt looked out through the dripping branches of the avocado tree and knew that right now there was no place in the world he'd rather be. Even the threat of pending houseguests was somehow diminished by the misty weather. Solitude – that was the good thing about working out of the house, especially on a day like this with the rain coming down and with Christmas on the horizon. Ivy was earning pretty good money, thank God, and her income allowed Walt to run his catalogue sales business out of the garage. Once the business was really up and running, the money would roll in, and Ivy could flat-out quit if she wanted to. The Christmas season was already boosting sales, and he was counting on his most recent catalogue to turn things around for him.

'You hope,' he said out loud. Money – the subject had gotten increasingly unbearable to him. The truth was that he was past forty and still didn't have a real job. He worked like a pig, but somehow that didn't equate to bringing home the bacon. Ivy never complained, of course. She wasn't the complaining type. But a man had his pride.

Anyway, he wasn't in much of a position to complain about Jinx and Henry, no matter how long they intended to stay. He looked at his watch. It was just past noon.

He noticed now that there were a couple of dark red tomatoes on last summer's vines along the fence. The vines were still green, but it was a gray-green, not the emerald green of high summer, and of course there were no blooms left at all. The two tomatoes were probably fossilized by now. The basil in the adjacent herb garden had gone to seed, and the three basil plants had maybe six leaves between them, but the rosemary and sage would last out the winter no matter how lousy the weather got. And during the cool fall months the lemon tree at the opposite end of the garden had set on so many lemons that now the wet boughs were bent nearly to the ground beneath their weight. Avocadoes, lemons, lawns greening up in the rain – that was winter in southern California; no wonder Henry and Jinx got the hell out of Michigan every year and drove west. They must miss the hell out of California since they'd moved away.

Right then a spider, some kind of daddy longlegs, crawled out of the hole in the bottom of an overturned flowerpot on a shelf and stood there looking around, as if it had slept late and the thunder had awakened it. The pot had a sort of door in the front, a ragged arch where a piece had broken off. It occurred to Walt that the spider worked out of its house, too, and he wondered suddenly what kind of furnishings it had inside – a hammock, a pantry, shelves of books. If Walt had kids he'd be tempted to load the flowerpot up with doll furniture and tiny books and then pretend to find it like that, forever changing his children's notions about bugs.

Thinking about children, he wondered uneasily if Ivy would bring up that subject again tonight. She'd been on a kick lately about starting a family. Usually the subject came up around bedtime. He'd managed so far to fend her off with logic, just like he had in the past. But that couldn't go on forever. Ivy had a deep suspicion of logic. She said it was a leaky boat. Last night she had told him that there was nothing logical anyway about starting a family, and so trying to apply logic to it was illogical.

Even now the argument looked irrefutable to him, and he had the vague notion that he'd been defeated. Well, he was safe for the moment anyway, there among the sacks of planting mix and tools and clay pots, watching the heavy branches of the avocado tree shift in the wind, and listening to the swish of its big green leaves and the sound of the rain pelting down. A haze of mist rose from the shingles of the garage, and he could hear the drops pounding on the tin roof of one of the storage sheds, nearly drowning out the sound of the church bells. The bellringer was a hell of a dedicated man, out in weather like this in an open tower, yanking on soggy ropes whether any-one could hear the bells or not: art for art's sake, or more likely for the glory of God, like the old Renaissance painters.

Walt listened closely. It took him a moment to recognize the melody. It was 'In the Bleak Midwinter,' one of his favorites, and it really needed a big church choir to do it justice. He recalled the words to his favorite stanza, and was just on the verge of singing along when the bells broke into a clamor that sounded like a train wreck, the discordant echoes finally clanging away into silence.

4

The key to the third drawer was taped to the back side of the old metal desk. There was nothing in the drawer but the red telephone, and it hadn't rung for nearly ten years. Unless the phone rang, the drawer stayed locked. There was a phone jack behind the desk, and the phone cord exited through a hole drilled in the back of the drawer. Most of the time it was unplugged from the wall, the cord shoved back into the drawer. It was only when Flanagan was in the building alone that he plugged it in. And it was only when the phone rang that he called himself Flanagan. He had plugged the phone in religiously for the ten years that the phone hadn't rung at all. It was like walking along a sidewalk: once it occurred to him to avoid stepping on cracks, it became a small obsession. And until he arrived at his destination, he was a careful man.

As far as the phone was concerned, he hadn't arrived at his destination yet, but there was something in the rainy winter air this morning that made him fear that he was close. It was twenty years ago that he had helped send three men off in the general direction of Hell, and by now he understood that the pit he had dug for these other men was deep enough to contain him too.

So when the phone rang now, inside its drawer, it wasn't really a surprise, despite the ten years. He put down his pen, letting the phone ring four times before he reached behind the desk and pried the key out from under its tape. He unlocked the drawer, still counting the rings, and picked it up on the tenth.

'Flanagan.' The name sounded idiotic to him.

There was a silence. Then a voice said, 'Is it you?'

'It's me.'

'We have to talk.'

'We're talking.'

'I don't mean over the telephone. This kind of business can't be conducted over the telephone. I think … I believe something's happening.'

'I'm certain it is.'

'What do you mean by that?'

'What do *you* mean?'

There was a silence again, as if the man was forcing himself to be patient. His voice was urgent; something had happened to frighten him. 'I mean I want out,' he said at last.

Now it was Flanagan's turn to be silent. Was this what he had expected? He looked around at the old paint, the exposed extension cords, the water dripping in the sink that Mrs Hepplewhite optimistically called her 'kitchen.' He didn't have to do any calculations now; he had already done them a hundred times – how much hard cash he needed just to keep the church afloat. 'I can't help you,' he said, and he knew it was only partly right even as he said it. The flesh was weak.

'Name your price.'

'I'm not talking about price. I mean to say that I've never helped you. What you've done, you've done alone.' This was wrong too. He himself was as blameworthy as a felon.

'You know, Mr Flanagan, I don't think so. If I thought so, I wouldn't have called you. What have you taken from me over the years, twenty thousand?'

'I don't keep accounts.'

'Of course you do. We both know the truth.'

'The truth is, I'm not in that line of work any more, so never mind the past. You might say that I've changed; I've gone over to the other side.'

'The other side! And yet you answer to the same name and at the same old number. I wonder if some things haven't changed. How about the color of money? Has that changed, too?'

'I recommend that you ask God for help.'

'Let's not drift off the subject,' the man said. 'I'm willing to pay you a hundred thousand dollars, any way you like – through Obermeyer, cash in a briefcase, trust fund, you name it. I have a certain naive faith in you. Can you believe that? You've kept your word to me in the past, and I'm willing to take a gamble on you again. What do I have to lose? Stay near the phone while you think it over. I'll call back.'

5

When Argyle hung up the telephone his hand was shaking. He stood by the desk for a moment, getting a grip on himself, then stepped across and turned up the stereo. The children out on the playground had just come out for their midmorning recess. The sound of them shouting and screaming and laughing gave him a headache, or worse, and he'd found that tapes of special-effects type noises – train sounds, ocean waves, thunderstorms – served to drown out their voices better than music did. And these days the sound of music was nearly as intolerable as the sound of children. Nothing was free. Everything had its price.

He realized that his phone was ringing, his personal line, and he turned the stereo volume down slightly and picked up the receiver, sitting down at his desk. 'Robert Argyle,' he said. He listened a moment. It was George Nelson with news about Murray LeRoy – good news; LeRoy was dead.

'When?' Argyle asked. His momentary enthusiasm for LeRoy's death started to wane as Nelson went into detail, and he found himself staring at his desktop, recalling the conversation he'd had a few moments ago. Probably he should have offered Flanagan more money, pushed all his chips into the center of the table. 'What did the police say? Did they have any kind of explanation for it?'

'They found the metal parts of a Bic lighter in the alley and the presence of gas from the manhole that's right there. One theory is that the lighter leaked butane gas into LeRoy's pocket, and then when he lit his cigarette the gas followed his hand to his mouth and ignited. Apparently it happens more often than you'd guess. If he was wearing flammable clothes, he could have gone up like a torch. All of this is just conjecture, of course, since there aren't any clothes left to examine except one of those damned white patent leather loafers that he wears, with the tassels. Everything else burned to ash. Even his shirt buttons vaporized. The heat was incredible.'

'And the fire investigators buy this? The butane lighter and all?'

'There was the manhole, too. Apparently gasses might have built up out there in the alley. A spark can set them off. They think it's some kind of combination of this stuff, perhaps aggravated by chemicals like deodorant and cologne. I suggested kids – punks, skinheads, street gang, something like that – but they didn't like the idea. The city doesn't need that kind of talk. There's also a good possibility that it was a suicide, that he doused himself with flammable liquids and lit himself on fire. There was no gas can, though, no more evidence of suicide than anything else.'

'And you were the one that told them who it was, who you thought it was?'

There was a pause, then Nelson said, 'I didn't think I had any choice, and it turns out I was right. It seems that a couple hours before dawn, LeRoy broke into Holy Spirit Church, up on Almond. He roughed up the old priest and smashed some windows. Apparently our man had a *very* busy morning, dragging those white shoes all over town. I've got it on good authority that the priest described them to the police. I'd swear that LeRoy *wanted* to be caught, or at least didn't give a damn if he was recognized. There must be fifty people around town who'd know straight off the shoe was his. I couldn't see any choice but to identify it myself.

'Anyway, what I said is that I was expecting him at the office, that we were supposed to head across the street to Moody's for breakfast at six. I saw the flames through the curtains and ran out with a fire extinguisher, but couldn't do any good. Every part of that was true, including my trying to put out the flames. Of course I didn't know who it was then, but I didn't say so.'

'Who was the investigating officer?'

'Tyler, from Accident Investigations.'

'And he's satisfied?'

'There's no reason he shouldn't be. As I said, it's the truth, lock, stock, and barrel. Oh, and by the way, somebody kicked apart the nativity scene in the Plaza early this morning, too. We know that was LeRoy, don't we? That'll be his footprints in the flowerbeds?'

Argyle wondered suddenly if the question was simply rhetorical, or whether it was full of implication. 'Of *course* it was him, unless there's something you're holding back.'

'*I'm* not holding anything back,' Nelson said, and then paused again, letting his silences speak volumes. Argyle waited him out. 'One way or another,' he continued, 'I hinted around that LeRoy had been talking about destroying the creche, which is true again; half a dozen people heard him. You should have seen him last night, crying and swearing. His tears were pure gin. No wonder he burned like that; his cells were saturated with alcohol.'

'Do you believe that?'

'I'm a lawyer. I'm not in the business of believing in things. I simply wanted to make sure you understood the entire affair. As far as the police are concerned, the case is closed, and I can tell you that I'll breathe a little easier now.

But I think we ought to get together tonight anyway, just to make sure we've all got the same perspective on things.'

Argyle hung up the phone finally, moderately satisfied. It was certainly convenient to have a dead man to point the finger at, if a finger needed pointing. They could clean out LeRoy's house at the first opportunity. Probably there was nothing there to implicate either of them anyway. There was no reason to think they'd have any trouble with the police. Nelson was thorough and convincing – utterly treacherous.

He listened to the noise on the stereo, thinking about how close he had come last night to destroying himself, and at very nearly the same moment that LeRoy had fallen over the edge! What horrors had been visited upon Murray LeRoy? What urges and fears had driven him into the darkness at last? A surge of disconnected terror swept through him, the knowledge that he was somehow being swept into the same uncharted seas into which LeRoy had sunk, beneath black tides of compulsion and desire ...

He picked up the phone and called Flanagan again, but the line was busy now.

6

The wind kicked up, suddenly sweeping cold rain under the overhanging branches and into the open shed. The spider had disappeared, back inside its home. Walt hunched out into the rain and sprinted across the lawn toward the garage, rounding the corner into the carport, suddenly anxious to be in out of the weather and to crank up the space heater. His shirt was soaked. He reached for the door latch, but then stopped and jerked his hand away.

The garage doors were shut, like he'd left them, but the padlock was gone. He always left it hanging in the hasp, whether it was locked or not. And that's where he'd left it when he'd gone into the house for lunch; he was certain of it. He thought about last night, the noise that had woken him up. Suddenly it was clear to him: someone had come in, found the place locked up, and left again. Then today they'd come back, probably cased the house, waiting for him to go inside before making their move. They were bold sons-of-bitches, he had to give them that.

He listened for the scrape of shoe soles on the concrete floor inside, for the sound of paper rustling or boxes being shifted. All was silent; he could even hear the sound of the wind-up clock ticking on the workbench. He looked around for wet footprints, but there were none – which meant nothing, what with the rain and all. He reached for the latch, took a step backward, and pulled the door open slowly, keeping behind it, out of the way.

The door at the rear of the garage stood open to the rain. They'd gone out the back. Walt strode past piled-up cartons, a couple of which had been dumped out, their contents scattered on the concrete floor along with crumpled Chinese newspaper and clumps of excelsior. He looked around hurriedly. The stuff on the desk hadn't been touched – his cassette player, the Toshiba laptop. A twenty-dollar bill and a couple of singles lay on the blotter, in plain sight, money left over from a trip down to the stationers. The burglar hadn't touched any of it.

Warily, he held onto the doorknob and looked out into the backyard, half expecting to find someone crouched along the wall or sprinting across the wet lawn. But the yard was empty, the rain coming down steadily now. He picked up a claw hammer from the bench top and went out into the weather, angling across to where he could see past the corner of the new storage shed but keeping well away from it so he couldn't be jumped. Nobody. Nothing. Probably they'd gone out fast through the back door when they'd heard him coming around the side of the garage, and had climbed straight over the redwood fence.

He walked back across to the fence, and, sure enough, there were blades of grass on the rain-soaked middle rail. Someone had climbed over after walking across the wet grass. He pulled himself up onto the rail and looked over into the neighbor's backyard, but it was empty. There were two more houses beyond that, and from what he could see their yards were empty, too. Noontime traffic moved along Cambridge Street a half block down. He could see a couple of people hunched beneath the acrylic roof of a bus-stop shelter on the opposite side of the distant street.

On impulse he went back inside the garage and shut and locked the back door. He grabbed the padlock from where it lay on the counter and came out again through the front, sliding the padlock into the ring on the hasp and locking it. It occurred to him that the lock could be dusted for prints, but he saw at once that the idea was ludicrous. It didn't even look as if the thief had stolen anything, although he couldn't be sure without looking around a little at the stuff on the floor, maybe checking it against an invoice.

He rolled down the back window of his old Suburban and yanked out his umbrella, then hurried toward the corner. If the burglar had cut through the backyards, then the fences would have slowed him down. Probably it was a kid, looking for an easy score. But then why leave the radio and the cash? He looked hard along the sides of the houses, which were thick with shrubbery, wondering suddenly what he would do if he saw a pair of shoes beneath a bush.

But he didn't see any. Aside from a couple of cats on front porches, there wasn't a living soul out and about. He might have been the last man in the world. There was a rumble of thunder again, closer now, and rain poured down, dripping like a curtain from the rim of his umbrella. He tilted it into the wind, keeping the water out of his face and finally reaching the corner, where the gutter was flooded with water surging toward the storm drain. A bus pulled in across the street, blocking his view of the bus stop, which was empty of people when the bus pulled out again, maybe carrying his burglar.

Abruptly he decided to give it up. All he was getting for his trouble was wet shoes. He turned around, starting to head back up the sidewalk, when he saw a man round the distant corner, coming along down the sidewalk from the east. Walt changed directions, walking toward the man, who could easily be the burglar. Perhaps he had gone over the back fence of one of the houses behind Walt's own and made his way out to the street that way. The man didn't hesitate, but sloped along through the rain with his hands in the pockets of his coat.

7

The lunch counter at Watson's Drug Store was crowded, mostly with local businesspeople ordering hot turkey sandwiches and meatloaf and burgers. Ivy was supposed to meet a client for lunch, a woman named Linda Marvel, who honestly didn't seem to know what a great, sideshow-sounding name she had. She and her husband wanted to buy a bungalow on Center Street that was priced a little steep, and Linda had a moderate dose of buyer's remorse, although it was nothing she couldn't be talked out of. Right now she was nowhere to be seen.

Ivy stood near the magazine rack and looked at the people who occupied the tables. Lots of them wore coats and ties, and she was suddenly glad she'd worn her wool suit. She hated to look unprofessional when she was working. Better to overdo it a little bit than to underdo it. Half of the people gobbling lunch at the tables qualified as old-timers. That was one of Walt's great goals in life, to be recognized as an old-timer at the lunch counter.

Watson's had been there since the 1920s and had gone largely unchanged through the years – lots of chrome fixtures and red Naugahyde that was meant to be stylish back around 1945. They made big milkshakes on one of the old Waring machines, using real ice cream and whole milk and flavored syrups, and served it in those big stainless-steel buckets that easily held two full glasses. Walt always acted pettish when she wanted to share one, but she usually got her way by bringing up the subject of calories and waistlines. Today was strictly iced tea, though, unless Linda wanted to share one of the shakes, in which case she'd drink it for the sake of business. Any sacrifice for a sale.

Right now the Marvels lived out in Mission Viejo, and liked the 'personality' of downtown Orange, especially since the suburbs of Mission Viejo and Irvine had almost no personality at all. That's why Watson's Drug Store was perfect for their meeting. It had ambience to spare. It was a place where you saw your postman eating a sandwich and where the druggist knew your name. They still served vanilla Cokes at the fountain.

A couple in a corner booth got up and left, and Ivy pounced on the table before anyone else made a rush for it. She ordered an iced tea from the waitress and relaxed, sliding her purse and attaché case onto the adjacent chair. The house the Marvels wanted to buy was worth every penny of the asking price, even in today's market. It had already been extensively restored, and the tiled kitchen had a walk-in pantry, a Sub-Zero refrigerator, and a Wolf stove with a big copper hood. There was a fireplace in the master bedroom, and adjacent to that was a small room that had already been turned into a nursery, with a frieze around the walls depicting fairy-tale scenes, all of it framed in wood. The Marvels were the perfect owners for the house. Linda was three months pregnant.

Ivy realized she envied the woman – her baby, the house, the fact that her husband made a hundred and fifty thousand a year and they could afford this dream house without thinking about it more than twice. When she had shown it to them for the first time a week ago, Linda had become a sort of happy-faced zombie, drifting from room to room in a trance, until Bill, her husband, had said to her, in a voice that sounded like he'd been practicing in front of the mirror, 'Darling, say the word.'

That was it. Linda had said the word right there on the spot, like something out of a Doris Day movie circa 1955. She spun around and shouted 'Oh, yes! Darling!' and they'd kissed each other right there in the empty living room. Actually it *had* been fairly wonderful. Ivy had very nearly kissed him too. She'd been calculating the commission in her head all that afternoon, and what it added up to, from her perspective and Linda's both, was Bill being the hero of the week. He was handsome, too, in a weathered sort of way. Probably he was a creep in some other area: came home late and got drunk in front of the television.

The waitress brought her iced tea and a menu, and she told herself to cut it out. Still, she couldn't help thinking about her and Walt – how devoted he was to their house, their neighborhood. He was stodgy; that was the only word for it. The idea of change gave him heartburn. She had tried him out once – suggested that they move into a house that had just been listed with the agency. It was a steal. They could have moved up by a factor of fifty thousand dollars and not felt it once they refinanced, except for the increase in property taxes. But the very idea of it had left him speechless with dismay. He wasn't interested, he'd said, in the mathematics of investment, only in 'the damage' it would do to his soul.

What it boiled down to, she had finally decided, was that he couldn't give up his sheds in the backyard. Sheds were some kind of philosophy to him. Last night he had gone on and on about them, all worked up, about how the best sheds were built out of used materials, old boards and cinderblocks, and about how that made his new tin shed from Sears inferior, except that, he'd said very seriously, there was something 'nicely musical' about the sound of a new tin shed in the rain.

That's why he didn't need any children, Ivy figured; he had all these sheds in the backyard, each one with its own personality. Ivy had told him as much last night. She had advised him to go ahead and build one more shed, maybe out of brick this time, in order to organize them into a basketball team. They could play in the shed leagues. Ivy could be a team mom, and the two of them could drive the sheds back and forth to games in the back of the Suburban. Walt had laughed as if he thought it was funny and then had turned over and pretended to go to sleep. That was the end of the conversation.

She looked out the window at the street. It had started to rain. There was only one customer at the outside tables, and when the wind blew the rain under the canvas awning, he grabbed his half-full coffee cup and headed for the door.

Abruptly she recognized him, just at the moment that he saw her through the window. He waved at her and smiled, looking pleased, and although she hated herself for doing it, she smiled back. Probably she couldn't manage to look authentically pleased no matter how hard she tried. Thank heaven she had an excuse not to sit with him; it would simply be too difficult.

He came across to her table, and she stood up, taking his hand when he held it out and trying to hold onto the smile, too, reminding herself to let bygones be bygones, especially with a man like Robert Argyle, who, as much as she hated to say it, had acquired a certain amount of power in the city – multiple businesses, charities, residential and commercial properties … Because of Walt, she couldn't bring herself to refer to him as anything but Argyle. Walt had banished his Christian name and most often turned his last name into a joke, predictably having to do with socks. She and Walt had carefully avoided him over the past couple of years that they'd been neighbors. When it had been absolutely necessary, a nod or a monosyllable had been enough. Three years ago he had run for school board, and Ivy had to stop Walt from driving around the neighborhoods and vandalizing his campaign signs.

But, God, his face had gotten coarse over the years. He looked almost grainy, and his eyes were too active, as if he were afraid of something. Gravity hadn't been kind to him, and he was getting a little jowly. He was tall – taller than Walt, who was nearly six-two – and had always walked with just a slight stoop, as if he'd been timid and withdrawn as a child. His hair was still just as brown as it had been when they had dated in college. Walt's was gray at the temples, but Argyle looked older than Walt despite that.

He put his coffee cup on the next table, which was cluttered with dirty dishes, and then asked, 'Can I join you?'

She thought immediately of Walt's stock rejoinder: 'What's the matter, do I look like I'm coming apart?' and she nearly giggled out loud, realizing at the same time that she was nervous. There was too much history between them for it to be any other way. Sometimes things broke and you couldn't fix them. It was better to throw them away.

'Only for a moment,' she said. 'I'm afraid I'm meeting a client.'

'Good. That's nothing to be afraid of. In this economy, any business is good business.'

He looked searchingly at her, as if he were trying to see if there was anything in her face that he could read, some evidence that she still carried a torch for him, perhaps a candle, a lighted match … Whatever kind of man he had been twenty years ago, he was made of something different now. The years had turned him upside down and shaken all the good things out of his pockets, unless you counted money as a good thing, and in his case it wasn't. Aunt Jinx had called him a 'husk' once, when Walt was going on about him, which was the word Jinx used for worthless, empty men. Ivy wondered now if that was fair. The evidence was twenty years old. Maybe there was a statute of limitations on that kind of thing.

Argyle remained standing as he talked, and she realized that she'd tuned him out. '… a couple of industrial properties over on Batavia, if you're interested,' he said.

She nodded. What was this, a business proposition? 'I'm sorry,' she said. 'I thought I saw my client coming in. What were you saying?'

He looked at her for a moment before speaking. 'I was wondering whether you were interested in listing a couple of pieces of property.'

The idea struck her as odd. The last time she had spoken to him he'd – what? – propositioned her; there was nothing else to call it. She'd put him off pretty hard. Of course she hadn't told Walt, who would simply have gone out of his mind. So the suggestion that they have dealings of any sort, even business dealings, was a complete surprise. Her first impulse was to turn him down.

But if there was ever a time that she and Walt needed the income from commissions, it was now. Why not take the man's money? Walt was determined to make his business work, and he deserved to. Probably he *would* make it work, given enough time, because as screwball as some of his ideas could be, he had a certain strange genius for seeing the sense in nonsense, and making other people see it too. Not that catalogue sales was nonsense – Argyle apparently had done all right with his own mail-order businesses over the years …

'Perhaps I could drop by the office,' she said to him. Breakfast or lunch was out of the question.

'Tomorrow, then?'

'Make it day after tomorrow, can you? I'm going over to my sister's tomorrow.'

'That's fine,' he said. 'Morning? Say ten?'

'Ten's fine.' She wondered why she'd mentioned her sister. Her personal life wasn't any business of Argyle's, and hadn't been for a long time.

'How *is* Darla? I haven't seen her in …' He shook his head, as if he was unable to remember.

'She's fine,' Ivy said.

'What was her husband's name?'

'Jack.'

'They're still happy, then?'

'Tolerably. You know – ups and downs, like the rest of the world.'

'You're not giving anything away, are you?' He smiled wistfully. 'You aren't still hard on me, are you?'

There was no answer to the question; whatever she was, it had little to do with him. The waitress approached just then, carrying the iced tea pitcher. Argyle pulled his lunch check out of his shirt pocket along with a five-dollar bill and waved it at her, smiling broadly and starting to say something.

And at that moment the check and the five-dollar bill burst into flame, flaring up like burning phosphorus with a bright, white glow. He dropped it on the ground, jerking his hand back and shaking it as if he'd been burned. The waitress, without seeming to think twice about it, bent over and poured iced tea on the burning paper, which fizzled out.

She picked it up and looked at the five-dollar bill, which was charred black along one edge. She shrugged. 'Looks okay,' she said. 'No harm done.' A busboy appeared and wiped up the floor with a rag, and at that moment Linda Marvel came in through the front door carrying a dripping umbrella. Ivy waved at her and motioned her over, relieved to be saved from Argyle, who seemed to be embarrassed nearly to the point of apoplexy. He stood unblinking, gaping at the waitress, then opened and closed his mouth like a fish.

'I guess the candle …' He gestured, not finishing the sentence. He tried to piece his smile back together. Linda slid past him and sat down in the empty seat. 'Oh, yes,' he said. 'I'll just … I'll leave you two alone.' He rubbed his hands together, looking detached, as if he'd been tapped on the shoulder by a ghost.

'Did you burn yourself?' Ivy asked.

'No. Not at all. Thursday, then?'

'Fine. Ten.'

He nodded and fled, going out through the door and into the rain where he hurried away down the sidewalk on foot, pulling his coat shut and angling out into the street.

'Do you want the candle relit?' the waitress asked, pouring what was left of the iced tea into Ivy's glass. 'I don't know why it was lit anyway. Usually we don't light them until later. A customer must have lit it.'

'I don't think it *was* lit,' Ivy said. 'Do we need a candle?' She looked at Linda, who shook her head. 'I guess we don't care about the candle.' She touched the bumpy glass vase that the candle was in. The glass was cool.

The waitress shrugged, and Ivy looked out the window again, distracted now. She could still see Argyle, far down the block, hurrying through the rain in the direction of Maple Street, probably heading home. He cut a very small and sorry figure from this distance, and Ivy was suddenly struck with the notion that whatever power he'd ever had over her had been illusory. Had she changed? *He* certainly had. There was a loud crack of thunder just then, and the rain poured down in a torrent, concealing him altogether behind a gray veil of mist.

8

Walt recognized the man coming toward him. Hell. It wasn't the burglar at all; it was worse – a minister, the Reverend Bentley from the storefront church down on Grand Street who had the irritating habit of making door-to-door forays through the neighborhoods, looking for converts, passing out little tracts.

Walt turned around to avoid him, but it was too late. He'd been seen, recognized. Bentley hurried forward, as if he had something urgent to say. He looked rumpled and beat, and his wet jacket was streaked with dirt. The rain let up just then, and for a moment the sun showed through a gap in the clouds. The minister looked up at the clouds and smiled, as if he'd put in a request and God had seen fit to grant it.

'Henry and Jinx on the horizon, then?' Bentley asked, shaking Walt's hand.

Walt nodded. The Reverend Bentley was an old friend of Henry's; they went way back – lodge brothers of some sort. Walt hardly knew Bentley, though, and he was slightly surprised that the man recognized him so easily, looking half drowned and hiding behind the umbrella. 'They're due any moment, actually. They were in Needles last night, and were thinking about taking a detour through apple country, but I expect them any time.'

'Good,' the minister said, looking around. 'That's good. I'm going to drag that old sinner in front of the congregation and flush out his soul with a firehose.'

'It's high time,' Walt said. 'What brings you out on a day like this?'

'Trouble in paradise,' Bentley said. 'How's *your* soul, by the way? You look like a worried man, like maybe you swallowed some kind of sin.'

The question took Walt by surprise. The minister could be a hell of an irritating old interloper when he was on a mission in the neighborhood. He was something of a local joke, in fact, and his church had a congregation you could put into the back of a pickup truck and still have room for the dog. He did good works, though, taking food around to shut-ins and the like. Lord knows how he continued to fund his projects. He had a sort of meals-on-wheels van that Uncle Henry had driven for a few weeks last winter, dropping off hot lunches at the houses of neighborhood widows. Aunt Jinx had put an end to it, though, after talking to one of the widows among the vegetable bins at Satellite Market. Walt himself had donated a hundred bucks to the meals program in a generous moment. That was a few years ago, when money had been a little easier to come by.

'I guess it's still hobbling along,' Walt said.

'What is?' The minister was looking vaguely off down the street, not paying attention.

'My soul. You asked how my soul was doing.'

'Well … good. Keep at it, then. This is Babylon we're living in, make no mistake about that. There's a lot of temptations out there.' He looked meaningfully at Walt now, as if this tidbit of information had been hand-selected.

'That's the truth,' Walt said.

'I can tell you that a lot of people fall,' Bentley said.

'Like ripe fruit.' Walt shook his head at the seriousness of it.

'Don't be cocky.' The minister narrowed his eyes, convinced that Walt was making fun of him. 'Pride goeth, as they say. Here – here's a little something to read.'

He handed Walt a pamphlet, maybe three inches square, with a picture of a lion and a lamb on the front, lying down together with such wide, dopey grins on their faces that it looked as if they'd just been hit over the head with a mallet. The title of the booklet was 'Marriage as an Obstacle to Sin.'

Bentley took Walt's elbow suddenly and steered him toward the corner, pointing across the street, toward St Anthony's. 'What's going on there? My vision's not …'

Without waiting for an answer he let go of Walt's arm and hurried forward. Walt followed him, noticing now that there was a police car in the parking lot. Half a dozen people milled around near the base of the bell tower. It looked like the top of the tower had collapsed. At least one of the bells had fallen, and the bronze edge of it, shiny with rainwater, was shoved out of a gaping hole in the stucco tower. That was the noise he'd heard twenty minutes ago.

Bentley slogged through the water in the gutter, waiting for a gap in the traffic before sprinting across, two steps ahead of Walt. There was the sound of a siren from up the boulevard, and in moments an ambulance pulled up, slamming to a halt, its siren cutting off. The crowd parted, and for a moment Walt got a good look at the man who lay on the concrete floor at the base of the tower. Clearly the heavy bell had gone right through the upper floor, smashing the bellringer on the head and knocking him down the steep wooden stairs. The side of his head was crushed, and his mouth hung open unnaturally ...

A couple of kids came around the side of the church, and a woman in the crowd turned and corralled them with her arms. 'Stay back,' someone else hollered. 'One of the bells came down. It's still ...'

Walt didn't hear the rest of it. He turned away, walking back toward the street. The shadow on the roof early this morning – someone *had* been up there. Someone evidently had sabotaged the bell. Why the hell hadn't he called the police? Now the bellringer was dead.

Without thinking he stepped down into the gutter, heard a horn honk, and jumped back up onto the curb as a car whizzed by, the driver shouting something at him and flipping him off out the window, over the top of the car.

Walt waved. The picture of the dead man – surely he was dead – remained in his mind as he waited to recross the street: in his mind he saw the bell tower, the stairs leading away into the shadows above, a shoe lying on the second step, the bottom step smeared with blood, a woman's face mesmerized with the horror of it, her hand to her mouth as if to stop herself from screaming ...

Walt shuddered. He wanted desperately to go home, to change out of his wet clothes and warm up. It was raining again, but he didn't raise the umbrella. He walked a few steps farther, standing in the shelter of a big cypress tree and shielding his eyes from the water dripping through the branches. The two ambulance drivers stepped toward the back of the ambulance, carrying the body on a blanket-covered gurney. Presently the ambulance pulled out into traffic, switching on its siren and accelerating toward the west, probably heading for the emergency room at St Joseph's. Walt wondered if there was anything hopeful in the sound of the siren. Would they bother with it if the bellringer was dead? Would they cover the man's face if he wasn't?

He realized he was still carrying the tract that Bentley had given him, and suddenly the little folded bit of paper enraged him – a trivial little scrap of holier-than-thou advice in a world where someone had just been crushed to death in a blind instant. And at such a moment! Did the bellringer have a wife, a family? Did his wife consider marriage an obstacle to sin, or something considerably more than that?

Bentley was nowhere to be seen now; otherwise Walt would have thrown the tract in his face. He shoved it into his pocket instead, and then walked toward where two policemen stood talking, up under the roof of the portico at the front of the church.

And even as he stepped toward them he told himself that he could just as easily not say anything at all. It was too damned late now anyway. Speaking up now was nothing but useless humiliation, self-revenge …

But he forced himself forward, refusing to listen. One of the policemen turned and nodded at him, and Walt introduced himself, clearing his throat but still unable to get the gravel out of his voice, suddenly wishing to heaven that Ivy was there with him, holding his hand, that he wasn't standing there wet and alone and empty on this bleak December morning.

9

Walt unlocked the padlock on the garage door and pulled it open, taking Bentley's tract out of his pocket and tossing it into the galvanized bucket he used as a trash can. His hand shaking, he switched on the space heater and then filled the coffeemaker at the sink, spooned ground coffee into the filter, and plugged it in. He found his work sweater and put it on, only now realizing how cold he was, and for a long time he stood in front of the heater, letting the warm air blow across him while he listened to the sounds of the coffeepot and the rain on the roof.

The two policemen had listened closely to his story, which had taken all of forty seconds to recount. They nodded, writing down maybe two sentences along with his name and address. Neither of them seemed to see anything shameful in any of it. One of them, though, seeing that somehow this had wrecked Walt, had tried to make him easier about it. Even if they'd sent a squad car to the church, he said, they'd have found nothing. The prowler wouldn't have shown himself – even if he were still hanging around – and there was no way the officer would have climbed onto the roof in the pouring rain. And it certainly wouldn't have dawned on anyone that the bells might have been sabotaged. Sherlock Holmes couldn't have guessed it.

'Give yourself a break,' the cop had said, squeezing Walt's shoulder. And his being kind about it had turned out to be the hardest part.

Walt looked around the floor now, thinking suddenly that it was high time to get to work. Pouring a cup of coffee, he looked at the boxes on the floor. Random odds and ends had been hastily unwrapped and set around, as if the burglar had tried to be neat, and didn't want to break anything. Nothing about it made any sense. If the burglar wasn't after quick cash, then what was he after, one of the plaster-of-Paris tiki god mugs that sat now on the concrete floor? There were sixty or seventy cartons stacked up in the garage, maybe more; had the burglar meant to work his way through every blessed one of them?

He took a long sip of coffee, listening to the rain on the roof and wondering what Ivy would make of the break-in, if you could call it that; more like the walk-in. Then abruptly he saw that he couldn't tell Ivy about it at all. What was the use? They'd never been broken into before. The idea of it would only frighten her – intruders snooping around in the night, then breaking into the garage in midday. Every little noise would set her off. She'd wonder out loud if this was another one of the risks of doing business out of your garage. Walt wasn't making enough money at it yet to justify any kind of risk at all. From now on he'd keep the place locked up, just like you'd lock up any business when you went to lunch. And besides, this wasn't looking much like a real burglary anyway; it was certainly more curious than threatening.

It dawned on him then that the burglar had no idea what he was after; he had apparently opened a couple of boxes, discovered that the stuff wasn't valuable enough to steal, and then, hearing Walt come outside, had gone out through the back door in such a hurry that he didn't even see the stuff on the desk. This was some kind of random incident, the sort of thing that probably happened in dozens of garages every afternoon …

He turned a snow globe over in his hand. Silver glitter cascaded around a washed-out pink flamingo standing on one leg. There was no way the base of the thing was deep enough to be hollow. All of the stuff in the boxes was Chinese – from mainland China, but shipped out of Hong Kong – and somehow that suggested opium to him, heroin, whatever. But what sort of dope smuggler would be so dainty about retrieving his contraband? That theory just didn't figure.

Rewrapping the flamingo, he put it back in the box, then weaved the top of the box shut and scribbled the contents on the side with a felt marker. It was a crude system of organization, but there was no way he had enough space in the garage and in the sheds to unpack any boxes. Someday, when the business was humming, he'd open up in a small industrial building or in one of the old turn-of-the-century houses that were zoned for commercial use along Chapman Avenue. Meanwhile he'd make do with a garage and a couple of sheds.

In the second box there were bags of rhinestone-studded sunglasses, a dozen umbrella hats, and a gross of boxes of Magic Rocks, which were big stocking stuffers at Christmastime. All of the boxes were sealed, the bags were stapled shut. Nothing, apparently, had been tampered with.

One small box had been opened but not emptied; no doubt the burglar hadn't had time for it. It was stuffed tight with some kind of primitive, coarsely cut packing material that looked like the fiber from coconut husks. There was a bag visible at the corner of the box, folded up out of heavily waxed paper, as if someone had melted a candle over unbleached butcher paper. The ends were twisted tight and tied off with strips of the coconut-husk fiber. Puzzled, Walt untied the little parcel and folded it open. There was a bundle of sticks inside – sticks about six inches long, carefully stripped of bark. The glistening wood was a fleshy-looking pink, and the wood and paper both smelled of something – creosote, maybe. He parted the packing material and looked beneath it. There were three little bundles of wax-soaked cloth, tied off with string. He squeezed one, trying to determine what was inside, but it was impossible to say; it felt like a beanbag full of human teeth. The whole box, now that it was opened, smelled vaguely rancid, as if there was a dead mouse inside.

He sure as hell hadn't ordered any twigs, or sacks of teeth either. This was some kind of mistake. He looked at the invoice he'd razored off the cover flap of the first box, but there was nothing on it that sounded even remotely similar to this. He pulled out more of the packing material, exposing a box full of small vials with crimped-on metal lids. Inside each vial was a jumble of small seed pods and quartz crystals and colored beans packed in oil, as well as an inch-long segment of what might have been alabaster, crudely painted with the depiction of an elongated human figure the color of dried blood.

There was something awful about the vials – the discolored oil inside, maybe, or the yellowed alabaster that might as easily have been bone or fossil ivory. There were other boxes of vials in the carton, too – unsymmetrical, hand-blown bottles made of clouded glass and filled with amber-colored liquid, corked and then dipped in wax.

Nearly at the bottom lay a cloth bag with something inside – a small jar, maybe an ounce, sealed with a piece of canvas like a stiff fragment of an old ship's sail, tied off with twine and again dipped in wax. Despite the wax, the jar stank to high heaven, which explained the rancid smell, and Walt could see that ointment of some sort had oozed out from where the layer of wax was cracked. There was writing on the bag – two Chinese ideograms above a short phrase that might have been in English, except that it was so ill-written that Walt could barely make it out. He held it under the light, trying to puzzle through the words letter by letter.

After a moment it struck him, not one word at a time, but the whole phrase at once, and he dropped the bag onto the countertop. 'Dead mans grease' was what it said. There was no apostrophe, and the writing was mostly loops and slashes, but once he saw it, the meaning was clear.

Some kind of joke gift? A starter kit for suburban witches? He picked up the jar, slid it back into the bag, and tied the top shut. Then he pulled the rest of the packing fiber out of the carton. At the bottom lay a painted tin box. Stamped on the lid of the box were the words 'Gong Hee Fot Choy,' and beneath them was the painting of a bluebird on the wing, towing a banner that read 'happiness.'

Vaguely relieved, Walt pried the lid off the box. Inside lay a tiny folded pamphlet that reminded him immediately of the kind of thing the Reverend Bentley passed out. Under the pamphlet, protected by a ring of corrugated paper, lay a jar, this one smelling weirdly of gin and containing what appeared to be a dead bird. It looked awful, as if it had been dead a week before it was pickled in the gin. Abruptly, as if he had shaken the jar, the bird moved, or seemed to. He set it on the bench and stood back, shivering with a sudden chill. He must have imagined it. The bird floated there, turning slowly in the moving liquid until one of its open eyes seemed to be staring right at him, as if in contemplation.

He picked the jar up again and slid it back into the tin, then opened the pamphlet, which was written on some sort of parchment. It looked like instructions in about ten languages including Korean, French, Spanish, and German, two or three lines each, and a couple of other languages that were unidentifiable Arabic-looking swirls and dots. The English was illiterate – the kind of thing you'd find on badly translated directions for assembling a foreign-made toy.

'*Best thing come to you,*' it read. '*Speak any wish.*'

It was a good-luck charm, some kind of wish-fulfillment object that was apparently meant to bring happiness to its owner – although not, presumably, to the bluebird itself, which was as unhappy an object as he had ever seen.

He decided suddenly that the whole works disgusted him. How it had gotten mixed up in his order he couldn't say. There was something nasty and primitive about it, even without the jar of 'dead mans grease,' whatever the hell that was. He started to shove the stuff back into the box, cramming the packing fiber back in around it. His first impulse now was to throw it into the trash can, but then he decided he wanted it out of there altogether – better to pitch it into the bin behind the medical buildings on the corner. Probably it would be even better to incinerate it and bury the ashes.

It dawned on him then – surely this must be the stuff that the burglar had been after, this box of diabolical trash.

Walt turned the box over and looked for the first time at the mailing label on the bottom side. He saw at once that it had been misdelivered. It was addressed to a party named Dilworth at a residential address a block away. The number was the same as Walt's own, but the street was wrong. This had happened before. The address numbers on the downtown streets, both north and south, repeated so often that it was a mailman's nightmare. What was puzzling about this was that 225 North Cambridge wasn't owned by anyone named Dilworth; it was owned by a man named Robert Argyle – the one man in the world with whom Walt was not on speaking terms.

At one time he and Argyle had been close friends and business partners. And it wasn't just because Argyle had been in love with Ivy, either, back when they were both just out of college. Walt couldn't hold that against the man; it was almost the only thing about him that was sane. Argyle had turned out to be a corrupt, cheating son-of-a-bitch. Ultimately, he had ended up with the business, and Walt had ended up with almost nothing, except Ivy, of course, and the rotten realization that he'd been betrayed by a man whom he had once considered a friend. Hell, who had been his friend.

Argyle, gratifyingly, had gone broke after falling into some sort of trouble, and for years Walt had lost track of him. Then he had reappeared, buying the house at 224 North Sycamore – the most ostentatious house in Old Towne. It was built on a half acre – three stories, leaded glass windows, a wrought-iron elevator and detached servants' quarters. With his money Argyle could have moved up Chapman Avenue and bought one of the big homes on Orange Hill, but then he would have been just one more Orange County millionaire among the teeming masses of them. Here in his hometown he could be a tin god, a man who had made something of himself by working like a pig and behaving the same way.

And now fate had misdelivered to Walt a box meant for Argyle. Surely, he thought, there was some way to put this happy coincidence to use …

Clearly the name 'Dilworth' was a fraud, unless Argyle was renting out the servant's quarters these days. More likely it was some kind of blind – a way of protecting himself from being charged with improbable postal crimes if the contents were discovered.

Was it *Argyle* that had broken into the garage? The idea struck him like a stone. It was almost funny – a millionaire reduced to looting garages.

With his felt pen he crossed out the name 'Dilworth' and wrote 'Robert Argyle' above it. He picked up the tape roller and held it over the box. Then he put the tape down, opened the box again, and pulled out the bluebird of happiness, replacing it with wadded-up Chinese newspaper. He would keep the bluebird for a few days; he wasn't quite sure why.

Well, he *was* sure why. He'd keep it in order to make Argyle unhappy, mystified, and irritated. At the end of the week he would throw it down the storm drain at the end of the street.

There was the sound just then of a horn honking, and he looked out through the barely open door. There were Henry and Jinx, pulling into the driveway, right on time. Walt went out through the back door carrying the bluebird tin with him. Hurrying, he crossed the lawn to the garden shed, already having made up his mind. He found the trowel, then stepped across the muddy garden to the tomato vines, where he scooped a hole in the dirt, shoving the tin into the ground and covering it nearly to the top. Then he arranged the vines over it so that unless you looked right at it, from a couple of feet away, you couldn't see a thing.

'Bring me a decent tomato,' he said to the bluebird. Then he tossed the trowel into the shed and trotted back out toward the front of the garage. In the driveway, Aunt Jinx and Uncle Henry were pulling shopping bags full of wrapped Christmas presents out of the rear end of the motor home, which looked like a soda-cracker box on wheels.

10

Henry's hair was nearly pure white, and he kept it trimmed in a brush cut that gave him the look of a retired military man who would be going in for a haircut within the next day or two. He wore a polyester polo shirt, buttoned up, with a sports jacket and Sansabelt slacks and black loafers. He was short – shorter than Jinx – probably five-two or -three, but he made up for this by having the attitude that there was nothing a man couldn't do if he put his mind to it, and Walt always got the notion that Henry had put his mind to a thousand things in his life and had accomplished them all, even though it wasn't really clear what those things were. He was somewhere in his middle seventies, but it seemed as if he'd been retired forever.

He never gave any hint, though, that Walt, or anybody else, should be accomplishing anything in particular, and when Walt had told him, months ago, about the catalogue sales, he had said it sounded 'fabulous.' He would have said the same thing if Walt were starting up a shoe store or an amphibian import service. Henry seemed to assume that every other man on earth felt the same way that he himself did, and was up to the same things, and that with luck and perseverance they'd all succeed together. Because of that he had a built-in respect for nearly everyone he met, and struck up conversations with sales clerks and gas station attendants. Henry didn't have any enemies, and Walt liked him for that, although the blind trust that Henry had in the world seemed like a dangerous philosophy for a man of business.

Walt had always known that Henry and Jinx had money, largely because of family talk about Henry's investments and business dealings. And so the motor home was no surprise to him. There was a shower in it as well as a toilet, and a refrigerator that ran off propane or electricity, whichever was handy. The cabinetry was first-rate – lots of chrome, a twenty-inch television set with a built-in VCR.

'What do you think?' Henry said to him, waving his hand at things in general. 'Fabulous, isn't it?' Jinx had already disappeard into the house to see about dinner.

'Nice,' Walt said. 'Real deluxe.' He realized that Henry thought it *was* fabulous, too. He liked it. Things were right with the world, and this motor home was proof of it.

The screen door on the house slammed, and in a moment Aunt Jinx looked in, holding a bottle of salad dressing. 'I found everything I need for muffins and a salad,' she said, 'if that suits the two of you.'

'Suits me down to the ground,' Walt said. 'What else will we have?'

'Oh, that's enough, don't you think? I'll put chickpeas and tuna in the salad – a meal in itself. Is this what you two dress salads with?' She held out the bottle, which was nearly empty.

Walt nodded. 'Not much there.'

'I'll pep it up with a little canola oil. There's less saturated fat than in bottled dressings. No stabilizers, either, or MSG.' She climbed up the steps into the motor home and pushed past Walt and Henry in order to open a cupboard, where she found the oil and a small bottle of dark red vinegar. There wasn't a lot in the cupboard besides Styrofoam boxes of instant noodles. 'The muffins are made entirely without oil or salt and are high in bran. They're a first-rate source of roughage.'

'Good,' Walt said. 'That sounds perfect.' He hated it when people advised him to eat 'roughage,' like he was a cow or something. He imagined a big plate of chopped-up shrubbery.

'You'll be surprised how satisfying it is. And with the Christmas season starting up, we'll all be overeating. Fats, sugar ...' She shook her head. 'There's no better time to start a new regimen. I called Ivy at the office, and she's entirely in agreement. So you two quit nodding like fools and get it into your heads.'

'No,' Walt insisted. 'It sounds fine to me.'

There was the sound of drumming on the roof, and Walt realized that it had started to rain again. Aunt Jinx picked up a newspaper from the table and held it over her head before going back out.

'She intends to make men out of us,' Walt said, smiling at Henry.

'She's a juggernaut. I've lost five pounds.' Henry patted himself on the stomach and then pulled open a drawer full of clothes, shifted some socks out of the way, and found a small box of Cheez-Its. Together they ate the crackers, sitting at the table, while Henry fiddled with the television set, trying to improve the reception. 'It's got cable hookup,' he said. 'We'll have to get a roll of coax and a splitter down at Radio Shack.'

With the rain falling outside now, the motor home began to feel snug and comfortable, and Walt was disappointed when Jinx came back out and told him he had a phone call in the house. He followed her in, jogging through the rain, and picked up the receiver in the kitchen.

'Hello,' he said, listening to the staticky connection. It sounded like somebody rustling paper on the other end. 'Sorry, can you speak up?'

The man wanted something. It was a business call, and he was using a phone that was apparently wired into a beehive. 'I was wondering about a certain product line having to do with ... what shall we call it? Third-world religions – voodoo, Santeria. Do you carry anything along those lines?'

'I don't believe so,' Walt said. 'Anything in particular?'

'Herbals, perhaps?'

He thought about the stuff he'd found in the misdelivered box, and suddenly wondered who this was on the line. Argyle? It didn't sound like him, but of course it wouldn't make any sense that Argyle would call anyway; the call would come from one of his employees. 'I guess not,' he said. 'I've got nun finger puppets and plastic holy water bottles from Lourdes, night lights – that kind of thing.'

'Sounds basically like gag gifts. I wanted something more ... primitive. Authentic.'

'Was there some *specific* item you were looking for?' Walt asked.

'Not really, no. Charms, elixirs, primitive religious artifacts, that sort of thing. Do you have a catalogue?'

'A new one, in fact,' Walt said. 'I'll send it out tomorrow. Where are you located?'

There was a pause. 'Costa Mesa,' the man said. 'Two-twenty-five Fourteenth Street, 93341.'

Walt wrote it down and hung up after promising to send the catalogue. Then he went out into the rain and pulled the Thomas Bros. mapbook out of the Suburban, climbing onto the front seat and pulling the door shut. He was virtually certain that the zip was a fake, made up on the spot. He flipped to the index and scanned the addresses. Just as he thought, there was no 200 block of Fourteenth Street in Costa Mesa.

11

Walt flipped on the garage light at six in the evening, leaving Ivy to wash up the dishes with Aunt Jinx. Henry was watching the news in the living room, drinking a cup of coffee laced with Half and Half and about a pound of sugar as an antidote to the chickpeas and shrubbery. Actually, there hadn't been anything wrong with the food at dinner – nothing that a double cheeseburger from Wimpy's wouldn't cure. Of course, Jinx was probably right about what they needed, dietetically speaking. And probably she'd tire out soon.

It was pitch dark out and raining in flurries, but he decided he wouldn't bother with an umbrella. He picked up Argyle's cardboard carton and went down the carport toward the street, where the dim yellow circles of light from the streetlamps seemed, if anything, to make the night a little darker. The wind was blowing out of the east, and the sky overhead was heavy with clouds barely illuminated by a hidden moon. A car passed as he hurried toward the corner, but otherwise the streets were deserted. The bad weather kept everyone indoors.

He turned the corner and walked up toward Sycamore, and even from a distance he could see that Argyle's house was lit up. There were a couple of cars parked along the street and smoke coming out of the chimney, and for a moment Walt thought about turning around and heading back home. But there was no sign of anyone outside, and the porch light was off.

He decided to risk it. He crossed the street, angling toward Argyle's front porch, prepared to walk straight on past if anyone came out. Quickly he cut across the lawn, slid the box beneath the porch railings and gave it a good shove. It slid beneath a wicker chair where it lay hidden in the shadows. The box was nearly invisible; when Argyle found it he'd have to wonder whether it hadn't been lying there for a week.

Just then the porch light blinked on, and Walt ducked, sliding around the side of the porch toward a couple of big hydrangea bushes against the side of the house. Immediately he knew he'd made a mistake. He should simply have headed for the street – just another pedestrian hurrying home in the rain. Now it was too late. He felt like a kid, out marauding through the neighborhood at night. There was the rattling of a latch, and then the door swung open, casting light from the entryway out onto the lawn. Walt crammed himself in behind the bush, pressing himself into the shadows.

It started to rain harder, and he pulled his coat shut, waiting for them to leave, listening to shoe soles scraping on the wooden floorboards of the porch. Then there was silence for a moment, followed by low conversation.

Somebody laughed, and a voice said, '*I'll* say.' Then there was silence again, as if they were standing there watching the rain fall, hoping that it would let up so they could make a dash for their cars.

'I hate this damned rain,' someone finally said.

'It's the season,' someone else said.

'Well, I hate the season, too.'

'Too commercialized. I agree with you.'

'That isn't what I mean. God, I hate it when people say that. To my mind it isn't half commercial enough, not this year. Profit – that's the only thing about Christmas that does me any good, and here we are in the middle of it and nobody's spending any money.'

A third voice spoke, Argyle this time. 'Call me after someone's had a look at LeRoy's. Don't worry about waking me up. We want those jars.'

'Yes, *we* do.' It was the second man now, the one who didn't like Christmas. 'I'm still not clear on something. I understand that we've got a green light over there tonight, but if we can't – what shall I say – *clean it out*, are we absolutely certain …?'

'And it rained fire and brimstone out of heaven and destroyed them all,' Argyle said, interrupting him.

'That's just your style, Bob, to dismiss something like this with an irrelevant quote. It's easier than thinking, isn't it?'

Argyle laughed then. 'Relax, George. You're making a mountain out of a molehill. Just have your people take care of things over at LeRoy's and let me know. They won't be bothered over there tonight. When we've got what we want, we can *all* dismiss it. It'll *be* an irrelevancy. And have them look around good – crawl spaces, secret panels, throw rugs. Don't rush it. LeRoy had his own way with things, if you follow me. He went in for all the trappings. Leave the place clean.'

The rain let up abruptly, and Walt watched through the branches, hearing them descend the porch steps now, their shadows jutting out across the lawn. Something told him that he didn't want to know anything more than he already knew – which was virtually nothing – but he couldn't stop himself from wondering who the two men were. One of the cars was visible from where he was hidden, and when the door swung open the driver was illuminated for a moment by the dome light. Walt recognized him, from downtown. He was one of the Watson's morning regulars, which meant he probably worked in one of the buildings around the Plaza. He usually wore a suit, too; so he was likely a professional of some sort – lawyer, maybe, or chiropractor.

The engines started up and the cars moved off. He heard footsteps crossing the porch, and then a moment later the house door shut and the light went out. Walt peeked past the edge of the house, making sure the porch was empty. He saw immediately that there was no carton beneath the wicker chair; Argyle had retrieved it, probably wondering right now how long it had lain there, gathering dust. He hurried out to the sidewalk and headed home, his jacket soaked and his hair plastered to his forehead with rainwater.

12

Uncle Henry stood in the garage, eating a doughnut out of the box on the bench. He held out the box. 'I helped myself. Hope you don't mind.'

'They're probably a little dry by now.' There was only one left, so Henry must have eaten two of them. That didn't surprise Walt any; last winter Henry had developed a habit, and he was probably anxious to take it up again.

'They're just right,' Henry said. 'Dryness improves the roughage.' He winked.

Walt took the last doughnut, realizing that he was famished.

'Been out for a walk?'

'Yes,' Walt replied. 'I had to run something over to a neighbor's house, and the rain started up on me. Caught me on the way home.' He noticed that the sleeve of his jacket was streaked with dirt from leaning against the wet wall of Argyle's house. He'd leave it in the garage when he went in. There was no use trying to explain it to Ivy.

'Quite a setup you've got here,' Henry said, looking around.

'It's cramped,' Walt said, 'but it'll have to do till I can find a bigger place.'

Henry shrugged. 'There's a lot of overhead in a bigger place. You can deduct overhead from your profits. Pretty soon you're hiring help, buying trucks. Insurance goes through the roof. What's wrong with this?'

'Nothing,' Walt said. 'It's a little small-time, that's all. And I'm not zoned commercial either. I get away with it because there's no customers coming around – just UPS trucks, and they come through the neighborhood twice a day anyway.'

Henry nodded, looking around at the stacked cartons, ordered and numbered, their contents listed on the sides in felt pen – rubber chickens, false noses, glow-in-the-dark fish, garden elves … 'Quite an inventory.'

'Yeah, I'm cramped for storage. I just bought a jumbo tin shed from Sears and Roebuck for overflow. It's all set up, but I don't think I'll get around to shifting stock till after the Christmas rush.' There was nothing in Henry's attitude to suggest that he found any of this stuff laughable, as if to him it was merchandise to be bought and sold, and might as well have been shoes or automobile parts. Well, that was all right. Walt was content to let the custom-ers do the laughing. The world needed more laughing.

'To tell you the truth,' Henry said, 'I came out here tonight because I've got a small proposition for you. I've been thinking along a different line altogether – a way to make this business of yours fly without leaving home. No trucks. No warehouse. You hire all that out to someone else and take a profit right off the top.'

'Well, I hadn't thought …'

'That's the future, you know – electronics, the information highway. Everything out of your house with the push of a button. Are you willing to listen?' He squinted his eyes a little bit, as if Walt was going to have to make an effort here, but that it would be worth it.

This was exactly what Walt had feared – that Henry was going to try to rope him in on some kind of business deal. Last winter it had been asphalt and roof paint, sold door-to-door, but somehow it had never quite got going because the company had gone broke at the last moment, and Henry's sam-ple kits and sales-pitch brochures were suddenly worthless. To Henry it made no difference; you win some and you lose some. Walt couldn't afford to lose any. He hadn't ever leveled with Henry about it, though. Walt and Henry got along on a level of gentlemanly good humor and mutual support, and there wasn't much room for truth in it, not any kind of practical truth, anyway.

'Has it occurred to you that the real money might be in design?' Henry asked. 'Right now you're on the distribution end, the narrow end of the fun-nel. Have you read any of Dr Hefernin's books? Aaron Hefernin?'

Walt shook his head. He could hear the rain coming down. Out toward the street, the motor home was nearly invisible through the downpour. He switched on the space heater, listening doubtfully as Henry talked and won-dering what the sales pitch would finally amount to.

'The man's a genius,' Henry said. 'He developed what he calls the "Funnel Analogy" to explain business from the inside out. Look here.'

Henry picked up a manila envelope that lay on the bench and carefully shook out four or five stapled pamphlets. There was an illustration on the first one of a funnel, upside down, like the Tin Man's hat. Arrows went in one way and came out another, along with words and sentences and phrases. Below it was a paragraph that began, 'Welcome to the world of money, *real* money.'

'Eh?' Henry said, slapping the pamphlet. 'What do you think?'

Walt nodded.

'It's fascinating. Rock solid. I read this introductory pamphlet and sub-scribed to the entire series – nearly ten volumes so far. Each one clarifies another aspect of what Dr Hefernin calls "the business of business." Remember that phrase, because it's the key to this entire method. You see, most people fail for a simple reason: they don't understand the business of business. They understand food, let's say, so they open a restaurant. In six weeks it's kaput. Why?'

'Because they don't understand the business of business?' Walt said.

'Bingo! That's it! There's a dynamic that they don't see. They don't see the *big picture.*'

'Aah,' Walt said, nodding as if he were only now seeing the big picture himself. He picked up the pamphlet and looked at it closely, making out the words 'profit margin' alongside the arrow that moved up the funnel toward the top of the page. The word 'overhead' was contained within the loops of a spiral that looked almost like a snail crawling toward the margin. The caption at the bottom of the page read, 'When opportunity knocks, answer the door dressed to go out!'

'This is ... something,' Walt said. 'Where do you get these?'

'Subscription. The first pamphlet doesn't cost one red cent. It lays everything out on the page, take it or leave it. If you want to take it, the second pamphlet is fourteen dollars, but the information is priceless.'

'What does Dr Hefernin do, exactly? Is he a publisher?'

'Oh, my goodness, no. Publishing is only one of his ventures, but I'd warrant he's made a fortune on it.'

'I guess so,' Walt said. 'That's good money for a six-page pamphlet.'

'And worth every cent. How do you put a price on that kind of knowledge? Apply it, and it'll return a thousandfold. Here.' He held out another pamphlet entitled 'The Thousandfold Return,' this one illustrated with a picture of hundred-dollar bills, fanned out like a hand of cards. 'Think about this,' Henry said, nodding profoundly. 'Dr Hefernin is a wealthy man.'

'I don't doubt it,' Walt said.

'He's gotten a lot of *my* money, hasn't he?'

'Sure.' Walt gestured at the pamphlets. Nearly a hundred and fifty bucks for a few scraps of paper. You could shove all of them into your back pocket and not feel them when you sat down.

'Try this on for size: the more of my money he takes, *the more I ought to send him.* Do you know why?'

Walt shook his head. 'You've lost me.'

'Because *you can't argue with success.* Hefernin calls it "the miracle of the self-fulfilling prophecy."'

'Gosh,' Walt said. 'That ... *is* hard to argue with.'

'I mean to say that the proof is in the pudding. Put your faith in a man who warrants your faith.'

'Makes sense,' Walt said. He looked into the doughnut box, but of course it was empty. He'd already eaten the last one. He wondered suddenly if Henry was soliciting subscriptions for Dr Hefernin, if that was his 'small proposition.'

'I just want you to read these,' he said. 'That's all for now. They're brief, but I think they're convincing.'

'All right,' Walt said, taking the pamphlets and laying them on the bench. Things were working out pretty much like he had feared: first a salad full of garbanzo beans and carrot coins, now an envelope full of 'advice' that was actually part of an infinite come-on for more advice. And the come-on worked, which was proof that the amazing Dr Hefernin understood the business of business, and so you sent him more money to provide further evidence. It was like a school for pickpockets where they pick your pocket going in the door and then convince you that they'd done it to illustrate a point, and that you ought to pay them for it. Maybe the man *was* a genius.

'I'd like your opinion tomorrow,' Henry said.

'You'll have it.'

'Good, because there's more to it than I can tell you right now. I'm going to turn in. Driving wears me out. Jinx thinks I'm already in bed.' He started toward the door, then turned and said, 'There's no need to talk to the ladies about any of this, is there?'

'No,' Walt said. 'Not at all. Whatever you say.'

'They don't have much of a head for business sometimes.'

Walt thought about Ivy's last commission check, which had actually been very nice. In fact, along with everything else it was financing Christmas. He nodded shamelessly. 'I've never believed in operating by committee anyway,' he said, shifting things around to something he was comfortable with, but realizing when he said it that he was already entering into some kind of agreement with Henry. And it occurred to him at the same time that Aunt Jinx probably wasn't as crazy about all these Hefernin pamphlets as Henry was – if she even knew about them.

Uncle Henry went off down the carport, carrying his envelope. He heard the back door open, and then Ivy's voice: 'Are you staying out there all night?'

'No!' he shouted. 'Just locking up.' There was the sound of the back door shutting. He took off his jacket and hung it over the chair, then switched off the heater and the lights. He thought about the bird in the jar, buried out in the garden, and suddenly felt a little foolish about it – more than foolish. Apprehensive was the word. It was probably a bad idea to antagonize a man like Argyle, especially over something like a grudge that was nearly twenty years old.

The conversation he'd overheard an hour ago returned to him. There was something sinister in all that guarded talk, and for a moment he thought about retrieving the jar and running it over there. It wouldn't take half a minute, and he could be rid of Argyle for good and all.

'You out there in the dark?' Ivy shouted through the open door again.

To hell with the jar. He stepped out of the garage and started to close up. Ivy stood inside the back door, already dressed for bed despite it being early. She was wearing her kimono, loosely tied, the one he'd bought her in the Japanese antiques store in Seattle, and the red and black silk against her fair skin suggested something exotic to him tonight, something he didn't need to define. Her dark hair was pulled back loosely, into some kind of knot fixed with two glittery chopsticks.

He hunched through the rain, and Ivy kissed him as he came through the door. He could see that she was carrying two glasses and a bottle of champagne. The rest of the house was dark. Jinx must already have gone out to the motor home.

'Congratulate me,' Ivy said as they moved together toward the stairs. 'We've got a lot to celebrate.'

13

'An emergency marriage encounter?' Walt asked, pouring himself another glass of champagne. 'I like that – sounds like emergency car repair or something. They probably use duct tape and baling wire and cans of that tire inflator.'

Ivy gave him a dark look, so he cut the joke off short. 'A church counselor suggested it to Darla,' she said. 'And whether it sounds silly or not, it's the only thing anybody's come up with that's positive.'

'Except me,' Walt said. 'What I said was that Darla needs a lawyer and Jack needs a subpoena. I've been positive about that for years. Why does she hang around?'

'Because she's desperate. She loves him, I guess.'

'She's crazy about him is what you mean. Like in out of her mind.'

'It's easy to say that from a distance.'

'What makes it easy is knowing Jack, and she ought to know him better than I do. She's had to live with him all these years.'

'That's the purpose of the marriage encounter, isn't it? So you can get to know each other better. People are married for years and they don't have a clue about some of the things that matter most to their wives.'

'Or their husbands,' Walt said, but he knew it was the wrong thing to say as soon as it was out of his mouth. He put down his champagne glass.

Ivy was silent for a moment. He knew where the conversation was leading.

And he knew that he was going to have to be careful. Saying the first damned thing that came into his mind wasn't going to help unless he wanted a fight, which he didn't. He looked at Ivy, who had put on her kimono, but hadn't tied it. She pulled it shut now, as if closing a door, and he turned his eyes away, looking instead at the fire in the fireplace. It was mostly burned down now, but it was too near bedtime to throw another log on. He sipped the champagne and waited her out.

'Please don't go on at me about the size of the car tonight, okay? We've got to get past all that.'

Right like that she dropped into the middle of it. There was no way out except to get through it. 'All I meant by that was that children are expensive,' Walt said. 'That's all. I read somewhere that the average kid costs about five grand a year as a child. Then it goes up.'

'I don't plan on having average kids.'

'I don't either,' he said, ignoring her tone. 'When it comes to raising kids, it's a mistake to do things halfway. And that's my point, that's what I was saying about the car. A family needs room. Kids need *stuff*. This commission today is great, but it's only one commission. Things are tight, what with the economy and all. In a couple of years ...' He listened to himself, chattering like some kind of preprogrammed Walt robot, and suddenly he hated the sound of his own voice.

'Next year I'm forty,' Ivy said. 'And besides, we both know that this has nothing to do with money. Money's not the issue.'

'What is the issue, then?' Walt asked.

'You're afraid of raising children,' Ivy said. 'That's the issue – self-doubt. And you're self-centered. When a person's afraid of the world like you are, it's easier to be self-centered. It's safer, only worrying about yourself.'

He shrugged. It didn't seem worth denying. 'Bringing a child into a world like this ...'

'That's not what I meant. The world's better off than it has any right to be. I mean you're the one that's full of fear. Change scares the hell out of you.'

'No, it doesn't.'

'Yes, it does. You can't imagine having kids, and do you know why?'

'Why?'

'Because you don't have any. If you had a child, you could imagine it easily. It would all become clear to you. It would seem right. You're afraid of it now because you can't see it. It's the unknown. And I don't think you like the unknown.'

'That's not fair. Having kids doesn't *scare* me. I'm just practical about it, that's all. I don't get all hormonal about it.'

'Is that right?'

'Yeah. And you know what I mean. Don't pretend to be insulted on behalf of women.'

'You were pretty hormonal a half hour ago.'

'That's different. That was ...'

'Sex. I know. Someday maybe it'll be more than that.'

He gaped at her, not believing she'd say such a thing.

'And you know what *I* mean. Don't go looking for an excuse to explode. You've got all these dreams and desires, and I've supported all of them, haven't I?'

He nodded. Here it came.

'I'm happy about it, too, because you're the man I married. I did it on purpose. It wasn't a mistake.'

'I wonder ...' he muttered, but thank God she went right on.

'And what I want you to think about is who *you* married, because there's things that I want, too, and I've always wanted them, and ...'

She stopped. He could see that she was on the verge of tears, and he suddenly felt like a jerk. 'Maybe you're right,' he said after a moment. 'Maybe I'm afraid of not making it and of dragging my family down with me – finding myself a middle aged failure.'

'I don't think that's going to happen,' she said. 'Why can't we make it together? You know, the Marvels' signing the papers today wasn't the only thing good that happened.'

'What else?' He acted surprised and happy, trying to cheer her up. Maybe they'd gotten through the storm.

'You wouldn't guess who I ran into at Watson's.'

He shook his head. 'Jimmy Carter?'

'Bob Argyle.'

'What do you mean, "ran into"? Did you hit him with the car? I hope you killed him, because otherwise he'll sue us.'

'He wanted to talk business.'

'What kind of business?'

'He's got a couple of properties he wants to sell, commercial properties from what I could make out. There might be money in it. A lot.'

'We don't want his money.' Walt caught himself. 'Do we?'

'It's not *his* money, really, is it? All kinds of people profit from a sale of property. Why shouldn't I? Too many scruples? Scruples about what, exactly?'

'Well,' Walt said, 'all I can say is that I don't like it. I think he's still a damned criminal. It's a bad idea to get involved with him.'

'Who said anything about getting involved with him? We're not going into some kind of partnership. All I'm going to do is sell a couple of pieces of property. And that's why there's escrow companies and legal documents – to keep everything aboveboard. What can be criminal about it? And how do you know he's a criminal anyway?'

'I don't know what kind of depths he's sunk to, but it's probably deeper than we can guess.'

'How would you know? You've avoided him for years.'

'Let's just say I have my hunches. A leopard doesn't change his spots.'

'Let's just say that you're not a disinterested party. You've got a conflict of interest the size of an elephant. I've gotten the man out of my life, and I'd suggest you try to do the same.'

'If you mean that my interests are different from his, then you win the prize. What I want to do is *keep* him out of my life. So why don't you just tell him to go to Hell? No, wait a minute – he probably owns real estate there, too.'

Ivy stared at the ceiling, as if she were counting to ten. 'I don't know any-thing for sure yet,' she said, getting up out of bed. 'I'm going to talk to him Thursday morning. So there's no use fighting this one out right now. We might as well go to sleep and pick it up again tomorrow night. God knows we don't want to get into the habit of going to bed happy.'

She disappeared into the bathroom, and Walt reached over to the night-stand to shut off his light. It was a good thing no one was keeping score; he knew vaguely that she'd mopped up the floor with him tonight, forced him into corners. Christ, he wished she wouldn't cry in the middle of an argu-ment. That always got him. He knew that he was in great shape when it came to throwing words around. He could go on all night, beating her up with words till she couldn't take it any more. That was his strategy, wasn't it? He just didn't like to admit it. And so what if he was right? Was that enough to justify it?

Argyle! He'd been rid of the man for years, and now the dirty pig had pol-luted the whole day, popping up everywhere like some kind of damned jack-in-the-box.

Ivy came out of the bathroom wearing her nightshirt. She got into bed and turned out her light.

'Goodnight,' Walt said, bending over to kiss her on the cheek.

'Goodnight.'

'Sorry I'm so difficult sometimes.'

'So am I,' she said.

He didn't take the bait. Hell, it wasn't bait, it was a statement of fact. 'Give me time to think about all of it,' he said.

'Fine,' she said. 'Think.'

'I will.' He laid his head on the pillow and stared at the ceiling, knowing he wouldn't fall asleep easily, thinking about Argyle and what he was up to, his 'dead mans grease.' There was the sound of rain running in the gutters out-side, and somewhere in the distance the sound of sirens – fire engines pulling out of the station house down on Center.

It was a hell of a night for putting out a fire, he thought, raining like this … The idea amused him, and for a moment he considered waking Ivy up and telling her, but probably she wouldn't think it was all that funny anyway.

14

It wasn't yet dawn when Walt got out of bed. Moonlight shone through the blinds, and the morning was quiet outside, with no sound of rain. It was his routine to put on a pot of coffee in the garage and read the newspaper for a half hour before starting to work, but he didn't like to waste any real daylight on it. It was better to read while the rest of the world slept. For a moment, before going downstairs, he watched Ivy lying tucked up in the heap of blan-kets she'd stolen from him in the night.

After pulling his sweater on, he went downstairs and out through the back door. Except for a couple of big, swiftly moving clouds, the sky was full of stars, washed clean by the storm. In the east, toward the Santa Ana Mountains, the sky was gray with the dawn, and the twin peaks of old Saddleback stood out solid black against it. Everything smelled wet – the concrete, the soggy leaves in the flowerbeds, the morning wind that blew in off the ocean.

He stepped across the soaked lawn and in among the intertwined tomato vines in the garden. In the early dawn the vines looked black-green, dense with shadow, more lush than they had appeared to be yesterday afternoon. There was no sign of the tin box. It had sunk, probably, in the soft soil. Pull-ing up a tomato stake, he poked around in the dirt, wishing he had more light. Yesterday he really hadn't paid any attention to where he was planting the damned thing; he'd been in too much of a rush.

He bent down and parted the vines, soaking the sleeves of his sweater. His elbow bumped one of the two leftover tomatoes, which was heavy, nearly the size of his fist. He hadn't remembered them being as healthy as that, but then he hadn't really looked closely at them, either. Forgetting about the bluebird of happiness for a moment, he found the other tomato, which hung beside a cluster of about half a dozen green ones, unseasonably late. The green ones would never ripen, not this time of year. He picked the pair of ripe ones, real-izing suddenly why he couldn't find the tin – a tangle of vines covered the ground over it now: the rain or something must have weighted them down, and they'd fallen across the mud.

He pushed them out of the way and scrabbled around with his fingers. There it was – the lid of the box, nearly sunk beneath the mire. He wiggled it free and stood up, stepping past the herb garden toward the lawn again, carrying the tin and the two tomatoes. Then he paused for a moment, surprised at what he saw: the herbs looked bad this morning, wilted and pale. The sage and the rosemary had collapsed like old mushrooms, and in the dim moonlight they were white, as if blighted with some kind of fungus. The basil was just a couple of wet brown sticks now. Two weeks of nearly constant rain must finally have rotted the roots …

He carried the tin back to the garage, suddenly unsure what to do with it. It was still dark enough outside to run it over to Argyle's, where he could simply push it under the railing and come home again. Argyle could think anything he wanted to think.

He closed the garage doors before turning on the lights, then washed the tin in the sink and dried it off with paper towels. He set it on the bench and put the coffee on, then opened the tin and looked again at the bird, which floated in its slightly milky bath. The jar had leaked, and it smelled of gin, the whole thing reminding him suddenly of the worm in the bottom of a mescal bottle. The bird wasn't quite as badly decomposed as he remembered.

What on earth did Argyle want with such a thing? That was the twenty-five-cent question. Anything good? Walt couldn't imagine what. If it was for resale, then the man should be ashamed of himself, trafficking in rubbish. Walt had half a mind to show it to Ivy, just to illustrate what sort of a monster she was having business dealings with. But clearly he couldn't, unless he made up some kind of elaborate lie to explain what he was doing with the tin in the first place.

The two tomatoes sat on the bench, as nice as any he'd picked last summer. The rain was hell on the herb garden, but the tomatoes apparently loved it …

… which was nonsense, of course. It rained every winter, but it had never made any difference at all to his tomatoes. There was no explaining them away so easily. But making a wish on a dead bird – wasn't that about twice as loony? He wouldn't allow himself to believe it.

What if Argyle believed it? How badly would he want the thing back? The thought stunned him, and the tin looked suddenly different to him, perhaps more repulsive than it had, but mysterious at the same time, attractive in some dark and primitive way.

He looked out through the door. There was a light on in the motor home, and the day was brightening. Whatever he meant to do, he should simply do it, before Henry figured out he was awake and wanted to talk about Dr Hefernin and the pamphlets.

Abruptly deciding against returning the tin, he put it inside a drawer in the bench, then almost at once took it out and looked around for a better hiding place, just in case Argyle sent someone after it again. Climbing up onto the stepladder, he pushed aside the dusty junk piled in the rafters on a couple of sheets of plywood. He spotted his tackle box, opened the lid, and put the tin in the bottom, in among jars of salmon eggs and cheese bait and bobbers. Then he shut the box and wedged it in between his lashed-together fishing poles and a clothes-drying rack made out of wooden dowels.

He got down and looked. The tackle box was perfectly hidden from the ground, and it didn't seem likely that anyone would pull junk out of the rafters looking for the damned tin anyway. There were a thousand more likely places for it to be hidden – dozens of boxes lying right there on the floor. He'd leave the back door to the garage locked, and the same with the shed doors. The motor home in the driveway, with Henry and Jinx going in and out, would discourage anyone from coming in through the front.

Quietly, he went out through the door and down the drive, past the motor home to the sidewalk. The coffee was ready. All he needed was the newspaper – which, in fact, was nowhere to be seen. Usually it lay near the sidewalk, wrapped in plastic in weather like this. He stooped and looked under the motor home, but the paper wasn't there, either. Doubtful, he checked the front porch, then looked into the shrubbery. The last thing he wanted to do was call the paperboy on a morning like this, make him come all the way back out here with a single paper …

He saw Henry's silhouette on the window curtain of the motor home. He was sitting at the table – no doubt reading the paper himself. Walt considered knocking on the door, but he stopped himself. It would look like he was miffed, which he was, but there was no use carrying on like that with Henry, who deserved an early-morning newspaper as much as anybody else. Henry tended to read the hell out of a paper, though, taking it apart like a cadaver so that what was left was a scattering of wrecked parts.

Giving up on the paper, Walt returned to the garage and poured himself a cup of coffee, then idly turned the pages of one of Dr Hefernin's pamphlets, trying to memorize a few phrases for Henry's benefit. But his thoughts wandered to the jar, and it struck him suddenly that he ought to make another test of the thing. He thrust the idea out of his mind. There was something about toying with it that repelled him, that was almost obscene.

Immediately he saw that he was being silly. What harm could it do? And if he wasn't going to use it – whatever that meant – then there was no point in keeping it, in stirring up a man as potentially dangerous as Argyle. Probably he should haul it down and throw it into the trash bin at the end of the street like he'd threatened to do yesterday.

Very well, then, he would try it:

'Throw the newspaper into the bushes tomorrow morning so that Henry can't find it,' he said out loud, then immediately regretted it. His own voice sounded unnatural to him, hollow, like a voice out of a machine, and he wondered whom, exactly, he was talking to.

The question was vaguely disturbing, and he focused on the Hefernin pamphlets, chasing all thoughts of the bluebird out of his mind. 'Water Seeks Its Own Level,' one of the pamphlets was titled. It was full of advice on 'taking the plunge' but not 'getting in over your head. Don't thrash around,' Hefernin warned, and there was actually a sketch of a toothy-looking shark swimming along, the words 'insufficient capital' written across its back. Walt skimmed the article, searching for something concrete, something that wasn't all clichés and ready-made phrases – something that would warrant spending fourteen dollars and would make an intelligent man order another one. But there was nothing, only a few testimonials at the end regarding the huge sums of money that people had made by putting Hefernin's 'philosophy' into practice. The Reverend Bentley's tracts looked positively useful by comparison. Bentley nearly always promised you something final and discernible, an actual destination. It was generally always Hell, but at least he was decisive about it.

Walt turned the pamphlet over finally and looked at the business address. It took him a moment to make sense out of it, for it to sink in that the address was local – a post office box in Santa Ana. Why that was so startling he couldn't say; southern California was no doubt the capital of mail fraud, probably of every sort of fraud.

The door opened and Uncle Henry looked in, carrying the newspaper, which was so completely taken apart that it looked like it had thirty or forty sections to it.

'I stepped out for some air and noticed the light was on in here.'

'Good,' Walt said. 'I just put on some coffee. Sleep okay?'

'Well, not badly, anyway. It gets a little cramped in there after a few weeks. And the toilet …' He waved his hand, dismissing the toilet with a gesture. 'I see you've been reading Dr Hefernin.' He poured himself a cup of coffee out of the pot, widening his eyes at Walt, who nodded.

'Very interesting material in these pamphlets,' Walt said.

'That there is. We've established quite a correspondence, Aaron and I – first-name basis. And I can guarantee you that if you query the man you'll get a prompt response. That's another one of Hefernin's requirements – promptitude.'

'I read about that,' Walt lied, gesturing toward the bench. 'I'm in agreement with the man there.' He shoved the pamphlets back into their envelope. There was the bare chance that if they were out of sight, they'd be out of mind, at least for the moment. 'I see you've brought the newspaper. Anything earthshaking in the headlines?'

'Local interest story, actually.' Henry laid the paper on the bench. On the front page was a two-column article about the death of Murray LeRoy and the coincidental fire a few hours later that destroyed his house ...

'Say,' Henry said, 'I'm about starved.'

There was a photo of an alley downtown, nearly flooded with rainwater, people standing around, a man holding out a single white shoe hung with tassels. Walt read it through, hardly able to believe what he saw, remembering the way that Argyle had emphasized the second syllable of LeRoy's name when he'd stood talking to his cronies on the front porch last night.

Walt looked at Henry, finally making sense out of his words. 'Sure,' he said, skimming the rest of the article. LeRoy's house had burned when a gas leak was ignited by a pilot light. The man had apparently stored kerosene in his cellar, and the whole place had gone up so fast and hot that there'd been no saving it, although the fire department had prevented the nearby houses from burning.

'What about a couple of sinkers?' Henry asked. 'After that dinner last night ...' He shook his head. 'Oh, it was good, mind you. Nothing wrong with it. Jinx is dead right – penny saved, penny earned, as they say. There's no reason the same thing shouldn't go for calories, in a way.' He widened his eyes, as if he knew he was lying through his teeth. 'I've been eating like that for weeks now.'

'Boyd's All-Niter?' Walt asked, reaching for the lights.

'Just what I was thinking. We'll spend a few of those calories we saved last night.'

At the last moment Walt decided to leave the lights on, just for safety. If there was going to be another break-in, it would probably come soon. He snapped the padlock shut, and the two of them walked down the drive without speaking, past the now darkened motor home toward where the Suburban sat parked on the street. Just then a car rounded the corner, its headlights swinging around toward Walt as he opened the door and slid in onto the seat. He glanced at the car as it swept past, gunning toward Chapman Avenue.

'Slow down,' Walt said out loud. It was an old red Toyota with a dented fender and bent bumper. The Reverend Bentley sat hunched behind the wheel, looking straight ahead, his face hidden by shadow.

15

In his nightmare Argyle fled along a stone corridor deep in the earth. The shadows of insects twitched on the walls, and there was a metallic rasping and clicking like beetles in a can. Orange firelight glowed from vast rooms hidden behind half-closed doors, and from all around him there came the sound of moaning and shrieking and knocking, as if from something that had once been human but was human no longer, shrieks cut off sharp only to be taken up again in a monotony of pain.

There came into his mind the terrible certainty that he was running head-long *toward* something, not away from it now, running, perhaps, to embrace that pain. Soon the shrieks and howls would be his own. Inevitably there hovered before him, far away down the dim corridor, a disembodied head, its mouth working spasmodically, its face half turned away so that its eyes were hidden by an iron-dark shadow. There was the smell of sulphur and the corruption of rotten things, of death and hot metal. The face swiveled slowly toward him, and a voice whispered unintelligibly, like a sand-laden wind off the desert. He held his ears against it.

He woke up trying to scream. He heard his own voice rasp in his throat, and he launched himself forward, scrambling off the end of the bed, falling to the floor, his legs tangled in the sheets, his eyes adjusting to the moonlight in the dim bedroom. There was a slow and steady knocking, like someone beating on the pipes beneath the house, and a creaking sound like loose floorboards. Distantly, like ghost voices over a telephone, there sounded the echo of the shrieking and moaning that he'd heard in his nightmare, and he pressed his hands over his ears as he staggered to his feet, yanking open the top drawer of his dresser.

Inside lay two jars – common pint-size peanut butter jars, seemingly empty. He drew one out and shakily unscrewed the lid, and there was the faint, brief sound of a human cry in the closed air of the room. And at that moment the knocking ceased, the moaning and shrieking evaporated. The air was still heavy with sulphur and the smell of hot metal lingering like smoke, but that, too, was dwindling.

He was safe. For the moment he was safe.

He pulled himself free and pushed up onto his hands and knees. Although the window was open to the wind and rain, he was sweating hot. This wasn't the first time that he had fought to wake up from the dream. Each time it was more real, more solid, and even now the walls of his bedroom looked insubstantial to him, barely opaque, as if they were film projections on black basalt.

There was a noise like the rustling of insect wings in the depths of his mind, and staticky, disembodied voices muttering obscenities – infantile idiot gibberish.

He picked up the jar and twisted the lid back on tight. What had been in it was used up, and what remained was a useless leathery shaving of human flesh. He dropped the jar and its contents into the trash can next to the dresser, then walked across to the window, where he leaned out into the morning darkness. Soon, it seemed to him, there would come a night when the dream would take him with it, just as some similar tentacle of Hell had reached out to clutch at Murray LeRoy.

Stop it. He squeezed his eyes shut. This was nonsense. He would still beat it.

There weren't many jars left. He needed something else to offer – more spirit jars. Something. And soon it would demand something more solid than the dying exhalations in the spirit jars. But when? Each night was worse than the last: the shadows more dense, the sounds more anxious, closer. Yesterday morning the bedsheets had burst into flame – spontaneous combustion, just like the five-dollar bill at Watson's, just like Murray LeRoy.

He noticed suddenly that there were a couple of limbs broken off the hydrangea beneath the window, hanging by strips of bark. The dirt of the flowerbed was stomped down, the outlines of shoe soles in the wet soil clearly visible even in the moonlight. It took a moment to work it out: somebody had been there snooping around. And not the gardener, either; he hadn't been on the property since Thursday.

Argyle thought suddenly about the parcel he'd found last night on the porch. He hadn't looked closely at it, at the box itself; he'd been too anxious to get at the contents, and had simply slit the thing open and dumped it out, only to find that the item he wanted, that he had been waiting for, was missing.

It hadn't occurred to him that it might have been stolen. Now he was certain it had.

Someone had meddled with the address on the box. They'd crossed out the name *Dilworth* and written in *Argyle*. Why? Who would have done such a thing? The man in China who gathered these things for him knew him only as Dilworth. The post office? It didn't seem likely that they'd mark up the outside of the box like this. They never had before. He switched on the lamp on the dresser and peered closely at it. It was easy to see, now that he looked, that the box had been opened and then re-taped.

He looked closely at the handwriting in the rewritten name – the vertical, elongated letters, the way the *G* looked like a pulled-apart number eight, the way the *A* was crossed with a line about twice as long as necessary. It was Walt Stebbins's handwriting. Stebbins had got hold of the box, opened it, ditched the invoice, and stolen the only thing of real value in it.

How could he have known what it was?

Probably he didn't; he was just being a meddlesome hick, and this was some kind of pathetic joke.

Of course Stebbins could be compelled to return it. The thought came to him that perhaps he should spare Walt for Ivy's sake.

Ivy ... He stood for a moment, thinking about her, about them, him and Ivy – about the way things had been only a few short years ago – and suddenly he knew he was wrong: Walt Stebbins wasn't any kind of asset to her, and the world would be a happier place if he fell off the edge of it and disappeared.

He pulled on his bathrobe and walked out of the room, up the hall, and across a broad living room heavy with oak moldings and built-in cabinets. Another narrow hall led off the living room, and he followed it to a locked door at the end, switching on the hallway lamp and taking a key from his pocket. He opened the door and stepped into a room furnished with an easy chair and bookcases. On the floor lay a coffin-sized packing crate, the wooden lid covered with Chinese ideographs. He leaned over and opened the lid, tilting it back on recessed hinges. Within lay a body. It might have been his identical twin. Did it look dead, or merely asleep?

Without the item that Stebbins had taken from the carton, the thing in the box might as well be dead. What if he never recovered it? What if that fool Stebbins had destroyed it out of common stupidity?

Full of a sudden fear, he closed the box, locked the room, and went into his study, where he picked up the phone and punched in Flanagan's number. Of course the bastard wouldn't be in. He was never in. He kept you waiting and wondering ...

'Flanagan.'

The voice startled him. 'It's me,' he said breathlessly.

'I know who it is.'

'Can you help me? Have you considered my offer?'

'It would be better if you helped yourself.'

'So what? Do you want more? Is that it?'

'It's quite likely that you can't buy your way out of this, that you're wasting your money.'

Argyle laughed out loud. '*Wasting* it? That's rich. How much was Murray LeRoy worth when he went down that alley?'

There was a silence for a time. Argyle could hear Flanagan breathing. 'You haven't forgotten Obermeyer's address?'

'Of course not,' Argyle started to say, but Flanagan hung up on him.

16

Henry and Walt drove east on Chapman Avenue as the sun rose over the dark shadow of the mountains, which stood out now like an etching against the rain-scoured sky. Queen palms along the parkways stirred in the freshening wind, and big gray clouds sailed past overhead. Walt turned into the small parking lot of Boyd's All-Niter, a doughnut shop that sat at the edge of the several old neighborhoods that made up Old Towne – the downtown square mile of the city. The doughnut shop had been there for something like thirty years, and for a sign it had an enormous doughnut on a pole that stood at the curb, lit up all night long with neon. When he had climbed up onto his roof a few days ago to string up Christmas lights, Walt had seen the illuminated doughnut hovering in the sky above the housetops like a strange religious icon.

There were no other customers in the All-Niter, but the racks under the glass and chrome counter were half empty, which was strange at this time of the morning. Lyle Boyd was an old-school doughnut man who made no concessions to fashion or health. He served his doughnuts in pink, blue, and yellow plastic baskets, and although Walt couldn't quite define his feelings about these baskets, he had always found that they added something extra to the quality of the doughnuts – something that even a china plate, say, wouldn't confer. The baskets and the big doughnut in the sky added up to something large and almost mystical that compensated for Boyd's high prices – fifty cents apiece or four bucks a dozen. And also, Lyle Boyd didn't hold with Styrofoam cups for the coffee, but used heavy old white mugs that he'd bought at auction when Hosmer's coffee shop had folded up years ago in town.

They ordered doughnuts, a half dozen glazed, and Walt filled the mugs from a fresh pot – Boyd's coffee policy was strictly serve-yourself – and they sat down to eat, both of them disappointed to discover that the glazed doughnuts were a little off this morning, a little papery. Clearly they'd been sitting in the display case for a few hours. Generally there were hot glazed doughnuts by six, but the three cooking vats at the back of the shop were shut off and Lyle Boyd himself was nowhere to be seen. The woman behind the counter was new to the shop; Walt had never seen her before. She was at least sixty-something, and was probably retired, earning a few bucks on the side. She was pleasant-looking, jolly, with a full figure and what must be a red wig, and she wore a garish Hawaiian muumuu with a hibiscus flower print.

Henry had looked at her hard when she'd handed back their change, and he watched her now, over the top of his coffee cup. He had mentioned the 'business proposition' again, but then had eaten his doughnuts in silence, the woman apparently having distracted him. Another of his manila envelopes lay on the table, clamped shut with its clip and then sealed with a strip of tape, as if the contents were top secret. Walt was in no particular hurry to look inside.

'Excuse me for a moment,' Henry said, and he got up from the table and headed for the rest room door.

Walt nodded, turning back to the newspaper account of LeRoy's death: a one-time member of the city council and a highly respected local business-man, LeRoy had been 'troubled' in the last months and had been questioned by police in regard to several cases of church vandalism, the nature of which made it sound to Walt as if 'troubled' was too small a word; LeRoy had pretty clearly gone off his chump. He was suspected, the article said, of having loos-ened the bolts holding the bells at St Anthony's and causing the death of Mr Simms, the bellringer ...

Mr Simms ... The dead man he'd seen yesterday suddenly had a name, and Walt almost wished he hadn't learned it. He recalled the interrupted melody of the bells, how he'd felt standing under the roof of the garden shed while the rain fell, the words that had formed in his mind in anticipation of the next few notes: 'What can I give him, poor as I am?' The lyric almost sounded fateful now, and it occurred to Walt unhappily that there wouldn't be any church bells today at noon.

Why that should particularly bother him he couldn't say, but he had a wild, momentary urge to volunteer to carry on for poor Mr Simms, take a few minutes out of every afternoon just to do his part to provide a little solace in a world that didn't have nearly enough. But of course he didn't know the first thing about church bells except for what he'd seen in *The Hunchback of Notre Dame*.

The article went on to speculate that LeRoy might have committed suicide, immolating himself in the alley near the Continental Cafe after a night of rabid vandalism. A lawyer named Nelson had made a heroic effort to save him, but failed.

Walt heard laughter, and he turned around to look back at the woman behind the counter, who stood talking now to Henry. Henry nodded slowly, said something else that made her laugh again, and she put her hand on top of his hand for a moment and then took it away.

Walt coughed and got up, making a noisy issue out of pouring another cup of coffee. Henry looked at him and winked, and Walt smiled weakly. Prob-ably there was no harm in it – just another one of Henry's flirtations – but Walt had the uncomfortable feeling that Jinx would take a dim view of it, especially after the lunch wagon fiasco last year. He picked up the envelope and waved it, then looked at his watch. It was just six-thirty, and he was in no great rush, but Henry didn't know that. The old man bowed gallantly, and for a moment Walt thought he was going to kiss her hand, but just then the door swung open and two men came in, and the woman turned away to help them.

'She's in from Hawaii,' Henry explained, sitting down again and taking the envelope from Walt. He pried the tape up with his thumb and straightened out the clip. 'Lived in Honolulu since thirty-six and ran a restaurant called the Eastern Paradise out on King Street – best damned Taiwan noodles you've ever eaten – red chili sauce, kimchee on the side. Jinx and I spent some time out there ourselves in the fifties.'

'I remember,' Walt said. 'Couple of years, wasn't it?'

'Three and a half. I wish we'd held onto that little bungalow on Kahala Boulevard.' Henry shook his head, regretting the past for a moment. 'Right on the water – coconut palms, sand. You couldn't touch it today for two million. We took twelve thousand for it and felt lucky. Anyway, we used to eat at the Eastern Paradise every Tuesday night – bowl of Taiwan noodles and a cold beer. Pure heaven. I *thought* I recognized that woman when we came in. The years haven't touched her. Maggie Biggs, right here in Orange, It's like fate, isn't it?' He shook his head wonderingly, waving toward the counter with his fingers, tilting his head a little bit and smiling.

'Aunt Jinx will be amazed,' Walt said.

'Oh, I wouldn't mention it to Jinx,' Henry said hastily. He frowned, remembering again. 'I'm afraid there's skeletons from those years that we'd better just leave salted away, if you follow me. They'd just make a hell of a stink if we dug them up now.' He looked around slowly then, as if something had come into his mind.

The two other customers sat two tables back, eating doughnuts and talking in undertones. One of them was a big man, immense. There were a half dozen doughnuts in his basket, and he took one out and bit it nearly in half. He seemed to know Mrs Biggs, and he wore a flowered shirt, as if he'd just blown in from the Islands too. Suddenly Henry stood up, nodded at Walt, and gestured toward the table in the far back corner. Walt shrugged, getting up and grabbing the two coffee mugs and following him over.

'As soon as we apply for the patents I won't care,' Henry whispered, gesturing at the envelope. 'But for now …' He widened his eyes meaningfully.

'Of course,' Walt said. 'Keep it between us. What do you have?'

Henry slid a paper out of the envelope – some sort of drawing, apparently of a space alien. Then Walt saw that it was meant to be a dignitary of the Catholic Church, maybe the Pope himself, or some pope, but badly compressed, as if he'd lived on the sea bottom all his life or on a planet with heavy gravity. There was a dotted line across his throat and a thing coming out of the back of his hat, which was pretty clearly on fire.

'What do you think?'

'It's … It's good. What …?' He motioned helplessly with his hands. This was going to be worse than he'd feared.

Henry winked, took a pen out of his pocket, and wrote the words 'Corn Cob Pope' across a napkin, let it lie on the table long enough for Walt to take it in, then wadded up the napkin and threw it into a nearby trashcan. He sat there silently again, waiting for a response, casting an anxious glance toward the other two doughnut eaters, as if he feared that at any moment they'd leap up and rush the trashcan.

It struck Walt all at once. 'It's a smoking pipe?'

Henry nodded. In a low voice he said, 'Simple corncob pipe, really, carved to look like the pope. Novelty item.' He bent forward, pointing at the picture with the end of the pen. 'The stem fits into a hole in his neck, body's the bowl, smoke comes out here, through the fedora.' He indicated the pope's hat.

'Fedora? Are you sure about that? I thought his hat was something else – a miter or something?'

'Isn't the miter that stick thing he carries around? I couldn't see any way to work that in. It has something to do with holy water, maybe, but either way, it doesn't concern us here.'

'You must mean the smiter,' Walt said. 'That's what Catholics call the stick they used to beat the protestants with. What's this line across his throat?'

'It's a tip from Dr Hefernin, believe it or not.'

'Hefernin's in on this?' Walt's appreciation for Dr Hefernin soared suddenly. Apparently Hefernin was simply a world-class nut, which excused all kinds of sins.

Henry shook his head. 'I applied one of Hefernin's rules – "diversify your market."'

'Ah.' Walt nodded slowly.

Henry pointed with the pen again. 'Look here. Stem's detachable, and there's a hinge at the back of the neck. Cock the head back and load it with candy. It doubles as a Pez dispenser. We grab the youth market that way.'

'Shrewd,' Walt said, suppressing the desire to laugh out loud. 'I don't suppose you'd load it with candy once it's been smoked.'

'Absolutely not,' Henry said. 'That would limit your market again. My idea is that you'll indicate whether you want the Pez Pope or the Smoke Pope. A good share of the families will buy two – at *least* two. *We've* only got to have one model, though, with interchangeable parts. Overhead takes a nose dive.'

Walt was silenced. This made last winter's asphalt paint look reasonable.

'Speak your mind,' Henry said to him. Then without waiting he said, 'It's a dandy, isn't it?'

Suddenly, out of nowhere, Walt remembered last night's argument with Ivy, about the way he'd lain awake for who knows how long wrangling with it, with what had gone wrong. His wasn't the only point of view. That was the lesson he'd learned last night – the lesson he'd been learning over and over again, but couldn't quite remember whenever it was really *necessary* to remember. He forced himself to consider the fabulous popes from this new angle: what *would* people think about it? They'd gone crazy over gimmicks far more mundane. He looked at the drawing again, trying to picture someone smoking the thing in public.

'I'm virtually certain of one thing,' Henry said, sitting back in his chair and sliding the drawing back into the envelope.

Walt nodded for him to go on.

'The Japanese will buy it. The Pope's scheduled his first Japanese visit summer after next – part of a goodwill tour, a big powwow with the Buddhists. The Japanese are crazy for this kind of thing. They have a word for it – I can't remember what it is – Gomi-something. Have a look …'

He slipped several more sheets of paper out of the envelope, shuffling through drawings with carefully lettered subscripts and explanations. All of it was there: Pope Corn; Pope-sicles; Pope-on-a-Rope; something called Pope-in-a-Blanket, which was apparently a breaded hot dog; and Pope-pourri, a mixture of hyssop and myrrh and other biblical herbs that you put in a decorative Pope-shaped jar in the bathroom.

'All we need is seed money,' Henry said, speaking with utter confidence. He poured the rest of his coffee down his throat and clanked the mug down on the Formica tabletop. 'The sky's the limit.'

17

Ivy pulled onto Capricorn Avenue, the street where her sister lived in Irvine, a 'planned community.' The houses were all a uniform color – some variety of beige – and were landscaped with railroad ties and olive trees and junipers. Twenty years ago neighborhoods like this were going to be the future, but time hadn't been kind to them, and the aluminum windows and Spanish lace stucco and rough-cut wood had deteriorated at about the same rate that the houses had gone out of style. The neighborhood didn't have any air of financial poverty about it, just a poverty of imagination that was depressing, and for the hundredth time Ivy reminded herself that she couldn't live happily here, no matter how close she was to the supermarket and the mall. Darla hadn't exactly thrived here either.

A truck sat in Darla's driveway with a magnetic sign on the side that read 'Mow and Blow.' Ivy parked on the street and headed toward the house, past the three gardeners who worked furiously on the front lawn. There was the terrible racket of the mower, edger, and blower all going at once, the three men racing against the potential rain. The sky had gotten dark again, full of heavy clouds. All the blinds were drawn in the front of the house, as if no one were home, but that was just Darla's style – the house dark and the TV constantly on for background noise or distraction or companionship. Darla rarely paid any attention to it.

Ivy rang the bell, and her sister opened the door, saw who it was, and burst into tears. Ivy walked in, putting her arm around Darla's shoulder. The house smelled of dirty ashtrays and cooking odors, and on the television screen two soap opera people accused each other of treachery. Ivy shut it off and yanked on the drapes cord, trying to brighten the place up. The two-story house to the rear loomed above the fence, though, shading the sliding glass door. Rain began to patter down onto the concrete patio slab just then, and Ivy nearly slid the door open in order to pull the kids' big wheels and bikes under cover. It was hopeless, though; the backyard, a narrow strip of patchy brown Bermuda grass lined with weedy brick planters, was strewn with toys and knocked-over lawn chairs and an expensive-looking propane barbecue that had clearly been rained on all winter anyway.

'How are you holding up?' Ivy asked.

Darla sobbed out loud, wiping her eyes with the back of her hand. 'Jack's gone.'

'For good?'

Darla shrugged.

'Has he been drinking?'

She nodded. 'He agreed to go to the marriage encounter, like I told you, but then he started going out after dinner. And last night he didn't come home at all.'

'He's a dirty shit.'

'He's seeing somebody, some barfly. I know he is. I'm all packed.' She gestured in the general direction of the bedroom, then let her hand fall to her lap.

Darla looked pale, and she'd gained a couple of pounds since Ivy had seen her last, which was when? Last month some time, Ivy realized guiltily. Her hair needed some work, too, and she had yesterday's makeup on.

'You slept on the couch last night?'

Darla nodded. 'I waited up for Jack, but …'

Ivy tried to think of something to say to her, but realized she'd said it before. The junk-strewn backyard and darkened house was some kind of reflection of Darla's fate, something that had crept up on her over the years. Walt was right about Jack. Drunk or sober the man was a creep. It was no secret to anybody else; how could it be a secret to Darla? How could any of this be a secret to Darla? 'Where's Eddie and Nora?'

'At daycare.'

'You want me to pick them up still? It's your call. I said we'd take them, and I meant it.'

'Thanks.' Darla shook her head tiredly. 'What I decided ... I decided to go home for a while.'

Ivy looked at her. 'Home?'

'Ann Arbor.'

'With Mom and Dad?' Their parents had retired to a two-bedroom house on a rural lane. It was idyllic, all hardwood trees and gardens and pastures, but there was hardly any room for the children, for Eddie and Nora.

'I've got an interview back there,' Darla said. 'Receptionist at this doctor's office.' She started crying again. 'I just have to get out,' she said. 'Anywhere. Away from this. Goddamn Jack can have it if he wants it.' She waved her hand again, taking it all in.

'What about the kids?' Ivy asked. Suddenly it wasn't just a week-long marriage encounter; it was what? – indefinite? 'Are you thinking of taking Eddie and Nora back to live with Mom and Dad?'

'Jesus, Ivy, I don't know what to do. I booked a flight this morning with Jack's Mastercard. You said you'd take care of the kids for a while, so ... I guess I just need some space.'

Space. Ivy hated that word. Darla needed considerably more than space. What she was doing was running, but she had no idea from what, aside from Jack, who she should have run from years ago. Darla hadn't had a job in ten years. She didn't need to; Jack brought home the bacon along with the grief, and Darla had always been satisfied with that, or was supposed to be.

'It's okay with Walt, isn't it?' Darla asked. 'About Nora and Eddie? He's such a goddamn hero. How did you marry someone like him and I married something I scraped out of a garbage can?'

'Luck,' Ivy said.

'Men are such shits.'

'Some of them.'

'I didn't mean Walt. I just thank God Jack isn't their real father, the lying shit.' She shook her head. 'It killed me when Bill walked out on me and the kids, but at least he wasn't the kind of weak ... asshole that Jack is.'

'I talked it over with Walt last night,' Ivy lied. 'He's all for taking the kids.'

'You sure, sis? Because if you're not sure ...'

What? You'll what? Ivy thought it but didn't say it. She *should* have told Walt last night, but he was being such a – well, such a shit. Now he'd just have to be surprised. 'Sure I'm sure,' she said. 'What will Jack say about our taking the kids? He'll think that's his territory.'

'He can't have them,' Darla said heatedly. 'He ... I'm afraid he'll hurt Eddie.'

'Why?'

'He has before, when he's drunk.'

'Okay then, to hell with Jack.'

18

Argyle sat in traffic, the cars crawling slowly along the streets in the cloudy afternoon twilight, as if the air itself was thick and heavy. He had the wild desire to accelerate, to drive like a madman, to flee from the spinning darkness that seemed always to hover right outside his vision. The car in front of him stopped at an intersection, and Argyle braked again, closing his eyes, imagining himself mired forever in the winter gloom, his car immovable, the doors rusted shut, the engine frozen, his own withered visage staring out at the world from within the glass and iron cage. The thought came to him that he wouldn't make it to Obermeyer's at all, that he wouldn't be allowed to make the transaction.

He glanced into the car in the next lane, and for a split second saw the burned corpse of Murray LeRoy, wearing the goat mask, sitting in the passenger seat and staring back at him ...

He blinked hard, inclining his head toward the window. A woman returned his stare. She looked irritated and turned to say something to the man driving. He realized what she must have seen in his own face: the demented fear, the horror. He glanced quickly away, an afterimage of her bright yellow scarf burned onto his retinas. The colors of the world were too bright suddenly, too sharp and brittle, sharp enough to cut him, and the car seemed to close in around him like shrink-wrap, smelling of upholstery and paper and dust. The whir and rumble of the car engine filled the interior of the car with noise, vague and distant from beyond the firewall, almost like the sound of breathing, of whispering.

Something moved in the periphery of his vision, dark and vague and quick, like the shadow of a hand snatching a fly out of the air. He focused on the traffic light, at the cars swinging around out of the left-hand turn lane. There was a soft rustling, moth wings fluttering in a paper sack. He set his teeth, ignoring it, and glanced at the dashboard clock. The second hand was still. Nothing moved outside the windows. Again he heard the sound of some small dry thing, an insect sound, the tick-tick-tick of a fingernail on glass.

He turned his head slowly, his breath shallow, and looked into the back seat, ready to throw open the door, to abandon the car and run. Something *was* there? – a vague shape like a dark memory, the shadowy, larval form of something struggling to be born; or worse, of something bound and dying. The air was thick, hot, full of insistent whispering, smelling of scorched bone …

And then he was aware of a horn honking, and he realized that his mouth hung open and his breath was whimpering out of his throat, and he was staring at his briefcase on the back seat.

The driver of the car behind him gestured impatiently, honking again, and two cars farther back pulled out into the adjacent lane, gunning past him. Argyle pulled forward, both hands on the steering wheel now, and drove south on Grand Street into Santa Ana. He turned on the radio, finding an all-news station, cranked up the volume, and then lowered all the windows to let the wind blow through the car, as if the rush of moving air could carry away the thing that he'd seen.

Frank Obermeyer's house sat on a half-acre lot on North Park Boulevard, half-way between Broadway and Flower, a two-story colonial-style box built of red brick and white-painted wood. There were three pillars holding up the porch, a sort of solarium with broad windows with diamond-shaped panes. The house was shaded by big sycamores standing leafless in the winter afternoon.

Argyle didn't like Obermeyer. Argyle didn't like anything that he was afraid of, and he was afraid of Obermeyer. There was something wrong with him, not to mention the fact that he was a facetious son-of-a-bitch. He was too placid, too, as if he understood something that Argyle couldn't understand, and so Argyle could never be quite sure of him. It was like being afraid of a misfiring gun; sooner or later, without warning, it could blow your hand off. It was better to keep your distance, if you could.

He brushed his hair back and looked in the mirror, deep breathing a few times before getting out of the car and walking toward the porch, past a painted jockey in a flowerbed thick with pansies. It was entirely possible, he thought as he rang the bell, that he was the world's premier sucker. Obermeyer answered at once, as if he'd been waiting. He looked surprised and slightly amused.

'Bob!' he said, holding out his hand. He was short, his hair nearly white. There was something too cheerful about his eyes, as if he were always about to laugh.

'Hello, Frank,' Argyle said, stepping into the foyer. A staircase wound away toward a second level. There was a silk carpet on the floor and a landscape painting on the wall. From somewhere nearby came the sound of water running.

Obermeyer shut the door. 'Drink?'

'No,' Argyle said.

'That's right. You don't touch the stuff, do you?'

'Only on special occasions.'

'Good policy,' Obermeyer said. He led Argyle into an adjacent room and gestured at a chair. 'Have a seat. What brings you all the way out from the hinterlands of Orange? It must be ten years since you were here last.'

'I guess it has been,' Argyle said. 'Here I am again.'

'You look a little peaked, if you don't mind my saying so. Flanagan hounding you for money again?'

'I put a stop to that back in '86. Probably I was a fool to do business with him. What did I gain from it?'

'You gained the world, I guess. What were you looking to gain?'

'Nothing that I couldn't have gotten on my own, probably.'

Obermeyer shrugged. 'Who can say? But that's hindsight, isn't it? That's the joke. In the end we sell our souls for a pocketful of trash. Here's the question: did you sell your regrets along with it? I ran into George Nelson just yesterday afternoon. George told me that he had no regrets. He told me all about how you and he were – how did he put it? – accumulating personas, I think he said. All that business about the vice presidents.' Obermeyer laughed and shook his head. 'I love that kind of thing. What were all those vice presidents worth in trade to the Devil, do you think?'

'I'm afraid I don't know what the hell you're talking about, Frank. All I know is that Flanagan and I are doing a little business again, despite my better judgment.'

Obermeyer sat back in his chair and shook his head, as if the whole thing mystified him. 'Funny, isn't it? Flanagan was never anything more than a voice over the phone.'

'He's still a voice over the phone,' Argyle agreed tiredly. 'Same voice, same telephone number. Direct line to Hell. It's not even long distance.'

'That's *good*,' Obermeyer said, breaking into a grin. He sat forward, as if he were suddenly excited. 'Yes, sir, I like that. Imagine being a switchboard operator in Hell. What a fiasco! Machinery's hot as a pistol barrel, supervisor won't give you any peace, air conditioning's worthless, plenty of vacation time but none of the resorts are any damned good.' He sat back, folded his hands across his stomach, and widened his eyes, as if he were just getting started. 'They make you wear some kind of humiliating uniform with ...'

'I'm not in the mood, Frank.'

'No, I guess not. Neither was poor George when I talked to him. And Murray LeRoy ... Did you ever make a study of spontaneous human combustion?'

Argyle stared at him.

'Here's a scientific fact. Do you know what all those people had in common? No sense of humor. That's God's truth. Real laughter's not combustible.'

'The sooner I write out a check, the sooner you get your ten percent, Frank.'

Obermeyer shrugged. 'I've got the receipt already made out,' he said, and he picked up a slip of paper that was lying on the table next to his chair. There was a crack of thunder just then, like a sign from the heavens, and the rain let loose with a sudden fury, beating in under the overhang of the porch so that rainwater ran in rivulets down the windows.

Argyle pulled the check out of his pocket and handed it across, taking the receipt from Obermeyer. It was torn from a three-by-five-inch dime-store receipt booklet. 'For Services Rendered,' it said, and it struck him suddenly as the single most worthless-looking thing he had ever seen.

Obermeyer looked hard at the check, squinting at the sum. Then he looked at Argyle as if seeing him for the first time. And then, shaking like a pudding, he started to laugh.

19

Walt looked up at the sound of shoe soles scraping on the driveway, thinking it was Henry, back from his 'walk,' which had kept him away for almost two hours now. But it wasn't Henry coming up the driveway; it was apparently a postman, a large one – six-five or -six and with a face like a pudding, his immense bulk stuffed into a uniform that must have been bought down at Eagleman's Big and Tall, but was still too small. Walt put down the cellophane tape gun and walked to the gate to meet him. There was no use letting him into the backyard.

'Mr … Stebbins?' The man looked at a clipboard to get the name right. He had a voice like a gravel pit, and a big, pie-eating smile on his face. Despite the cool afternoon, he was sweating to beat the band, probably out of sheer bulk. He wasn't carrying any packages, and Walt could see his vehicle parked out at the curb, the tail end visible past the motor home – not a FedEx truck, but some kind of general-issue government Chevy or Ford.

'What can I do for you?' Walt asked.

'Postal Service. Investigations.' He pulled a leather wallet out from under his blue cardigan and flipped it open so that Walt could see his picture I. D., which was clearly him, his face so broad that his ears weren't included in the photo.

'How can I help?' Walt asked, knowing straight off how he could help. This was bad – if the man *was* a postal investigator and not some kind of fraud. The uniform, though, what the hell was that? He was dressed like a mail carrier, not an investigator. He looked familiar, too. Walt had seen him around town.

'Mr Stebbins, we're looking for a carton. Overseas mail, small, contents unspecified but apparently highly valuable.'

Walt nodded. 'Unspecified?'

'That's correct. It was insured in Hong Kong, and the handwriting on the documentation is illegible. Got rained on, ink ran. It's a mess. Utterly unreadable. We've got a signature from a postal clerk at the POE in Los Angeles.' He gestured with the clipboard.

'POE?'

'Port of Entry. Signature means it arrived, you see, and that's enough to establish our insurance liability.'

Walt snapped his fingers. 'Weren't you eating doughnuts this morning down at Boyd's All-Niter?'

The man squinted at him sharply, as if the question were a trick of some sort. Then he nodded.

'Me, too,' Walt said. This seemed vaguely suspicious, although why it should Walt couldn't say. Mail carriers and cops were both legendary for their doughnut consumption.

'It's a large claim, Mr Stebbins. That's why we're investigating.'

'So somebody *did* file an insurance claim?' That was interesting, if it was true – Argyle couldn't have made any legitimate claim against the loss of the box, unless that half-rotted bird corpse was worth something after all.

'Claim's been filed. That's why I'm here, Mr Stebbins.'

'What I mean is that he could probably tell you what's in the box.'

'He who?'

'*I* don't know, for Pete's sake. Whoever filed the claim. I'm still waiting to hear what this has to do with me.'

'*Does* it have anything to do with you? You seem to be under the impression that the claimee is male. Anything to explain that?'

'No,' Walt said. 'As far as I know the claimee is an ape. And don't you mean *claimant*?'

He shook his head. 'What you're suggesting is not that simple. We didn't actually talk to the party that instituted the claim. It was filed by number, apparently, before the party left town on business. Entirely routine, except for the size of the claim itself.'

'Well if I was the Postal Service,' Walt said, 'I wouldn't pay him a penny. The box was probably loaded up with rocks. My guess is that your man conspired with this postal clerk, who put his signature on … what was it? Some kind of bill of lading?'

The man nodded heavily. 'Like that.'

'Okay, and then he threw the box into the ocean. That's where you'll find your box – at the bottom of the harbor. For my money this is some kind of insurance fraud.'

'Mr Stebbins,' he said, 'we don't see it quite that way. We don't think fraud's an issue here. We're pretty sure that the box was delivered – *to the wrong house*. Just a simple mistake. And either the mistake hasn't been discovered yet, or else the homeowner *simply kept it.*' He inclined his head and squinted in order to underscore this utterance.

Walt nearly laughed out loud. No postal investigator on earth would come up to a man's gate in the middle of the afternoon and outright accuse him of theft. That kind of thing was probably actionable. Thunder sounded just then, way off over the mountains, and Walt heard the first big raindrops hit the roof of the carport.

'More rain,' the investigator said, easing off now. 'I guess the drought's over.'

'Laid to rest,' Walt said. He wondered suddenly about Uncle Henry, out in the neighborhood on foot. Probably he should drive around in the Suburban and try to find him to give him a lift home. Except that the old man was almost certainly down at the All-Niter … Walt was suddenly impatient. Life was too short to fritter it away hobnobbing over the gate with a man in a costume. 'So what *does* all this have to do with me?'

'Nothing,' the man said, holding up his hands. 'Don't get me wrong. For God's sake, we don't want that.' He gestured, dismissing whatever it was that Walt might have been thinking. 'What happened is that the delivery address is right here in the downtown, and it's close to the same as yours, you see. That's all. I've got … six more possibles.' He looked at his clipboard again, as if he wanted to be sure of himself. 'I'm just running down leads. I don't guess you've found any box, then?'

'No.' Walt shook his head, lying outright.

'Well that's good,' the investigator said. 'That's what I like to find. The last thing in the world I want is to find out that something's been … what the hell can I call it? *Stolen*, I guess. You know what I mean? A man's life thrown away over a thing like this. Family embarrassed. Jail time. It's a minimum sentence now, too, mail theft is.'

The rain was pounding down now, gurgling through the downspout that drained the carport roof. 'You've got a job to do,' Walt said. 'Somebody's got to bring these people to justice.'

'Then we see it the same way. But it pains me to have to do it. It truly does. Half the time it's what they call a crime of passion. A man makes the mistake in a bad moment, you know. He finds something in a box addressed to someone else, and it's too much for him. He wants it. And he's a good man, too – a good man who's made a mistake. But the judge doesn't care. The judge throws the book at him. Why? *Because the man ought to know better.* Postal theft is worth ten years of a man's life, but I'll be doggoned if he thinks of that. No, sir, he keeps the article, whatever it is.'

'I guess they call that temptation,' Walt said, shaking his head as if it were a pity.

'Let me tell you a sad story – one of my cases a couple of years ago. There was a man up in Bell Gardens who kept a little bitty crystal dog, meant for his neighbor. It came in from Czechoslovakia, cut by hand, you see. Worth a good deal. Well, he took one look at it and he coveted that dog. He thought, what the hell. Who'll know? And like I say, he kept it. I talked to that man just like I'm talking to you.' The inspector nodded soberly, letting this sink in. 'I suppose you can guess what happened.'

'They didn't let him keep the dog?'

'That man's doing time now, out in Norco.'

'That's a tragedy,' Walt said.

'Yes it is. And what I'm telling you is that it's my job to find the guilty party, if there is one, but it doesn't make me happy.'

Just then Walt heard whistling, a carefree rendition of 'Sophisticated Hula.' It was Uncle Henry, coming down the sidewalk, sheltered under his umbrella, which he was spinning in his hand, with the air of a man who had zeal enough to spare. He spotted Walt and headed up the drive-way, shaking out the umbrella when he came in under the roof.

'Thanks for your help, Mr Stebbins,' the investigator said. 'Keep an eye peeled.' He turned and headed down the driveway, nodding at Henry.

'Rain, sleet, or snow, eh?' Henry said to him.

'That's right,' he grunted. 'One or the other.' He hestitated, looking out at the curtain of rain for a moment, then moved ponderously toward the street in what was meant to be a hurry.

When he heard the car engine start up, Walt went out through the gate and peered through the front porch hibiscus, keeping out of sight. It was a government car all right, E plates and all.

He wandered back up the driveway, thinking things over. Putting the rifled box on Argyle's front porch looked like a monstrously stupid prank to him now – especially scribbling on it with a marker like that. Maybe Argyle *could* press charges for mail tampering or theft or whatever they'd call it. If Walt wanted to, he could throw the bluebird of happiness into the Dumpster behind the medical center right now, ditch the evidence, just walk down there and get the damned thing out of his life. They'd never prove anything …

But at the same time he thought this, he knew that he wouldn't. Right now he was going to keep the bird, and to hell with Argyle and the inspector both.

'Post office man, eh?' Henry said to him.

'Yeah,' Walt said. 'Routine investigation. Missing package, apparently.'

'They should have insured it,' Henry said, shaking his head. 'A stitch in time ...' He shrugged.

'Sounds like Dr Hefernin,' Walt said.

'You can bank on it.' Henry winked broadly. He was worked up, full of vinegar. 'Look,' he said, 'I met a man this afternoon whom I think you'll find fairly interesting.' He nodded slowly, unblinking, meaning what he said.

Walt braced himself.

'Man name of Vest. Have you heard of him?'

'*Vest?*'

'Sidney Vest. He's a financial advisor. What they call a lone wolf in the business. Used to work out of Merrill Lynch, but it was too crowded for him. He needed room to move, if you follow me – a bigger canvas. He's got *vision.*' Henry inclined his head, coming down hard on the word.

'Name is unfamiliar.'

'Well, it won't be for long.'

Walt waited to find out why.

'I let him in on the popes,' Henry said

'Was that wise?' Walt asked. 'Can we trust him?'

Henry waved his hand. 'I know I should have asked you first, since we've pretty much gone in partners on this. But I think he might be willing to underwrite the whole megillah, lock, stock, and barrel. He's got a couple of other ideas, too. He's a go-getter.'

'Maybe we should do some checking around,' Walt said. 'Something as important as this ...'

Henry shrugged, as if to say that checking around wasn't out of the question. 'Well, to tell you the truth, it smells like capital to me. What I did was set up a meeting – tomorrow for lunch, over at Coco's. I think you'll be surprised. The man drives a Lincoln Town Car, late model. He bought it for cash on the proceeds of a little sales venture he's got going. We can get in on that, too, if we want to. This man's the gift horse, Walter, and I mean to climb aboard.'

'Yeah,' Walt said. 'Sure. What the heck. Doesn't hurt to hear the man out, does it?' He listened to the words issue from his mouth and nearly hated himself. His first impulse was to tell Ivy about it, to try to work something out. But of course the news would get straight back to Jinx, who would put the kibosh on it, and forever after he'd have to live with having betrayed Henry, with being the man who scuttled the popes. He'd never be able to look the old man in the face again.

A horn honked, and Ivy's Toyota pulled up. The doors opened and two children got out – Eddie and Nora, Darla's kids. What the hell was this ...?

Walt waved at Ivy, who stepped out of the car and walked around to the trunk, yanking out two suitcases. Nora, who was four, looked like some kind of orphan child with her stick-skinny arms and gypsy eyes. She turned her face to the sky and opened her mouth, trying to catch a raindrop.

'Hi, Eddie!' Walt called to the boy, who waved back at him, then took one of the suitcases from Ivy, holding it with both hands. He was clearly wearing last year's pants, which were flood-quality now, and he needed a haircut. He had a long face, and even at five there was something in him that reminded Walt of an undertaker. Maybe it was his interminable seriousness. He let go of the suitcase with one hand and grabbed his sister's wrist, hauling her along toward the house, following Ivy.

'Looks like company,' Walt said to Henry. 'You remember Miss Nora, don't you?'

'Indeed I do,' Henry said, shaking Nora's hand. She looked at the ground, swiveling on the balls of her feet, and shoved her thumb into her mouth.

'And here's Eddie,' Walt said. 'What's up, Eddie?'

Eddie shrugged. 'The sky,' he said.

'That's pretty funny. What's in the suitcase?'

'Clothes and stuff.'

Together they stepped up onto the front porch. Jinx opened the door of the house just then and threw her hands to her mouth theatrically. '*My,*' she said. 'This *can't* be Nora and Eddie.'

'It sure is,' Walt said.

'Well, come in out of the rain.' She held the screen door open. The children went in timidly, as if stepping into the great unknown. Through the open door came the smell of something cooking on the stove – something awful, like a smoldering dust bin hosed down with vinegar. Walt couldn't place the smell for a moment, but then with a shock he realized it was beets.

Ivy came up onto the porch and handed Jinx the suitcase. 'Spare room, I guess.'

'All right,' Jinx said. 'And maybe we can find a snack. Bread and butter and sugar – how does that sound?'

Walt heard Eddie mutter something. 'There's more in the trunk,' Ivy said to him. 'Some toys mainly.'

'Okay,' Walt said.

'And can you take them down to the preschool on Prospect tomorrow and sign them up? It would save one of us driving out to Irvine every day. Unless you want to look after them at home.' She widened her eyes, as if this just might appeal to him.

'Look after them? What gives?'

'Jack's gone. Drunk. Darla thinks he's shacking up with someone. She's going back east.'

'Back *east*?'

'To Ann Arbor. She needs some space.'

'*She* needs some space? For how long?' This was unbelievable. Space? The house was turning into some kind of castaway's retreat. Had Ivy done this on purpose, to teach him some kind of obscure lesson?

She shrugged. 'I don't have any earthly idea how long. What could I say to her? To hand the kids over to social services? They're our niece and nephew, and I think they deserve better than that, better than what they've got.'

'Of course they do,' Walt said. 'I was just … It's just that it's Christmas and all …'

'And there's no room at the inn?'

That clobbered him. 'Of *course* there's room at the inn. That's not what I meant. What the heck, eh? The more the merrier. But really, Darla's just up and gone?'

'She's probably somewhere over Kansas right now.'

'And Jack just …'

'Jack's a shitbird.' She opened the door and went in, letting the screen slam. The discussion was over.

Uncle Henry stood with his hands in his pockets, watching the rain come down, lost in thought. 'We work the western angle,' he said at long last, nodding at Walt.

Walt waited, wondering what this meant: 'the western angle.'

'Pope-along Cassidy,' Henry said. 'On a horse.'

20

The ruins of the house that had belonged to Murray LeRoy sat a hundred feet off the cul-de-sac at the end of Water Street. It was a two-acre lot that occupied most of the street front and stretched north nearly to Chapman Avenue, where it was separated from the offices of lawyers and chiropractors and real estate agents by a brush-tangled wire fence and a row of immense eucalyptus trees.

The Reverend Bentley parked a block away, left his car beneath a streetlamp, and set out carrying an umbrella and a flashlight. A car rolled past, its tires throwing a sheet of water over the curb, and Bentley skipped back out of the way. He shook his umbrella at the driver. 'Damned pretzel-head,' he said under his breath. There was a light on in the office of St Anthony's Church up the street, but otherwise the night was lonesome and empty; rush hour was long over.

LeRoy's acreage had once been a walnut grove but was overgrown now with old grape arbors and unpruned fruit trees and fenced by an ancient windbreak built of weathered timbers and age-darkened redwood lath, all of it tangled with rusted chicken wire and vines. The blackened remains of the burned-down farmhouse lay deep within the grove, and during its ninety years it had been more visible at night than in the day, its curtained windows glowing through the wild shrubbery and the heavy trunks of the walnut trees. Now there was nothing but darkness through the trees, and Bentley couldn't see that there was a house there at all.

LeRoy had bought the two acres years ago, after a successful career in real estate and insurance sales. It was an R-4 zone, a prime spot for apartments or condominiums, but LeRoy hadn't ever sold it or built on it. He had lived there alone in the old house like a vampire, rarely seen, only rarely going out into the neighborhood – at least during the day.

Bentley angled across the cul-de-sac, took a quick look around, and slipped in through a garden gate in the fence, picking his way along a litter-covered path that led to the house. There was just enough moonlight to see by, and he had no intention of switching on his flashlight if he could help it, not until he was out of sight of the street. He didn't know quite what he was after, but he was certain that he would know it when he saw it, whatever it was. Somebody had sabotaged the bells at St Anthony's. Probably it was Murray LeRoy, who had obviously gone stark raving crazy there at the end. But maybe it wasn't; maybe it was someone else.

The remains of the house sat crooked on its foundation, pushed apart by the partially collapsed roof. The windows were broken out, the doors smashed open. There was the smell of burnt, water-soaked wood in the air, and something that stank – a broken sewer line, perhaps. He wondered if someone had set the place on fire – to cover something up? – or whether the house had simply caught on fire spontaneously, with no earthly help, just as LeRoy himself had.

Bentley looked around guardedly, trying to see into the dense shadows cast by the vines and brush and broken down outbuildings that sat behind the house, an old chicken coop and garden shed. Everything was deathly still. He could hear water dripping somewhere close by and the sound of small animals rustling through the dark carpet of leaves beneath the walnut trees. The wind moved through the palms out on the avenue, and from somewhere in the west there was the lonesome sound of a train whistle. The house and the overgrown grove seemed to generate its own atmosphere, something oppressive and dusky that curtained the acreage off from the cheerful old neighborhoods that surrounded it. Bentley was filled with the uncanny certainty that evil things had come to pass here, and the darkness of the nearly leafless, deserted grove was vaguely repellent to him.

He stopped himself from simply turning around and going back. This was nonsense, he told himself. It was the shadows that did it, the nighttime, the heavy vegetation, the terrible smell of the burnt, water-soaked wood. He closed his eyes for a moment to summon strength, then opened them again. He would see this through. He had no choice in the matter.

The front door was a blackened slab that lay on the boards of the porch, its twisted hinges still screwed to the jamb. Charred curtains hung in the empty windows, and inside sat the dark hulks of furniture. The beam over the door had fallen, and hung at an angle across the opening, as if to bar the door. Bentley walked around to the rear of the house, where a wide section of roof had caved in around the chimney. The rear door stood open, its white paint streaked with black. He shone his light inside, illuminating an outmoded old refrigerator and a green-enameled stove and oven that stood on legs.

He forced himself to go inside, stepping carefully up the wooden stoop, covering his nose and mouth with his jacket. The kitchen reeked of burned things, and the floor was heaped with blackened plaster, the ceiling crossed with charred lath, old wire hanging through it with the insulation burned off. There was something hellish about it – about the smell, about the waiting silence … Five minutes, he thought, then he would leave.

He moved into what had been the living room, shining the flashlight across the sofa and chairs. A wooden bookcase had fallen over, and the floor was strewn with burned books, swollen with water. He kicked through them, trying to make out titles, but there was nothing that signified. Among the books lay fallen pictures, their frames half consumed by the fire, glass broken. He pointed the flashlight at one of them – a painting of a man and a woman in a bedroom nearly empty of furniture. There was something off-key about the scene, peculiar …

The woman sat in a wooden chair, and the man's hand was entangled in her dark hair, as if he were removing the white ribbon that tied it back. Her eyes were haunted with shame and defeat; his burned with an almost lunatic brilliance that Bentley realized was meant to be lust. The bed in the painting was disheveled, and on the wall behind the bed hung a painting identical in miniature to the larger one, and even in this tiny painting within a painting, the look in the man's eyes was unmistakable. Meticulous care had gone into painting that face.

Bentley very calmly leaned his umbrella against the wall, then bent down and picked up a shard of window glass. Using the edge of the glass like a cabinet scraper, he eradicated both renderings of the man's face, rasping through the paint and then through the canvas itself, bearing down with more and more force until he realized that he was scraping a hole in the wooden floor. He stood up and shivered from a sudden chill, dropping the piece of glass. It dawned on him then that if the house hadn't been already burned, he would set it on fire himself.

There were two bedrooms at the rear of the house, one of them so choked with fallen roof timbers that he couldn't get through the door. The other was clear of debris, utterly bare, not even a carpet on the floor. He started toward the door, but at the threshold he was seized with a terror so profound that he stepped backward, bumping into the wall behind him.

Cautiously, he played his light around the empty room, trying to make out what it was that had affected him. The plaster walls were streaked with soot that rose flamelike toward the ceiling, and the wooden floor was broken open, as if firemen had pried it to pieces in order to get at the subfloor. He saw then that there were two eye hooks screwed into the back wall about a foot from the top – heavy hooks, the iron shafts nearly the circumference of his little finger. There were two more in the ceiling; one had a couple of inches of burned rope shoved through it. He stared at them, his mind flitting around them, wondering what they might be, what uses they might have been put to …

He turned away, glancing quickly into the bathroom, which was a wreck of broken tiles, the toilet torn away from the wall and hammered to pieces, the old claw-foot tub choked with plaster and glass and roof shingles, the wooden medicine cabinet yanked down. It seemed utterly unlikely to him that the fire would have made such a wreck of the place. The firemen, perhaps, had – what? – torn out the medicine cabinet and broken the toilet to pieces in order to put out the fire?

Still, there was nothing apparent, no single piece of evidence that told him anything certain. Convinced of that, he went out through the kitchen and down the stoop, into the clean night air. It had started to rain again, and he hoisted his umbrella, walking down toward the shed and the chicken coop. He spit into the weeds to clear the burned taste from his mouth. There were a couple of rusted old tools in the garden shed, but nothing else. It was just a lean-to shell sitting on the dirt. A wire fence ran out from the corner of it, caging the chicken coop, its roosts long ago fallen apart. The place had clearly been used as a dump for years, and was a litter of broken bottles and rusted cans, old eggshells and rotted garbage. Bentley stood beneath his umbrella and shoved at the debris with his foot, shining his flashlight on it.

He had the uncanny feeling that he had suddenly drawn closer to something, or as if something unnameable had suddenly drawn closer to him. Beneath the sound of the rain and the night wind there was a slow whispering, almost a breathing, that slipped into his consciousness as if through an open window. He looked up sharply, abruptly certain that he wasn't alone, that someone, something, stood close by, observing him. He saw that something was painted on the wooden slats directly in front of him. The paint was faded, obscured by darkness and weather. He shined his light on it, illuminating what appeared to be two crosses, except that the horizontal member was too low. He realized abruptly that they were upside-down crosses, and that beneath them was painted a five-pointed star, the points connected in a pentagram, all of it enclosed in a circle.

A broad wooden platform sat at the base of the wall, the legs wrapped in rusty chicken wire as if the thing was a cage, and sitting on the ground within the cage was a small iron kettle containing animal bones, as if it had been left behind from a cannibal feast. Beside it stood a rough chalice made out of pewter or some other lead-colored metal. A few feet away, hidden in the deep shadows, sat an open sack of quicklime, the white powder congealed by rain. Bentley stared at the bones in the kettle, suddenly and utterly convinced that whatever the empty room in the house meant, this meant the same thing. And he knew almost instinctively that the wooden platform hung on the wall was meant to be an altar.

He turned and fled, down the path between the white trunks of walnut trees and a long tangle of clumped vines. Rain flew in under the umbrella, and the cold water braced him. He stopped, panting in the middle of the path, realizing that he had panicked badly. The chicken coop and its diabolic scrawls couldn't harm him. 'I shall fear no evil,' he said out loud, but he was full of fear anyway.

Ahead of him, beneath the bare, overhanging boughs of a walnut tree, sat a wooden outhouse, apparently long disused. Ignore it, he thought. Surely there was nothing hidden in the outhouse. He had seen enough – more than enough. How this damned satanic foulness had remained hidden in this couple of acres of downtown land could be explained in only one way: LeRoy was protected. Whatever forces hovered in the air of the abandoned chicken coop somehow conspired to veil what had gone on here.

He stepped toward the outhouse cautiously. He would take a quick look at it and go, making a clean sweep of the place. He grasped the wooden door handle and yanked on it, but the door was jammed shut, and the entire outhouse wobbled on its foundation. He pushed on it to loosen it, then yanked again. Apparently the wooden door had swelled in the wet weather. Rain began to beat down hard now, soaking his shoes and pants, running down the collar of his shirt.

Suddenly filled with anger, with the shame of having been chased by fear from the burned house and then down this muddy path, he stepped back and kicked the door hard with the bottom of his foot, damning it to Hell. The entire outhouse tipped backward, hung there for a moment like the Tower of Pisa, then toppled over, slamming to the ground, the vent pipe breaking off when it hit the trunk of the walnut tree behind it. Bentley stood there breathing hard, half surprised at what he'd done, gaping at the fallen outhouse, at the sawn-out circle in the upended plank seat.

Then he saw that there in the dirt lay a heavy slab of wood, worm-eaten and rotted, lying where there should simply have been a hole dug in the ground. Collapsing his umbrella now, he poked the tip under the edge of the wood, reached under with both hands, and levered the slab over onto its back, revealing a dark rectangular pit in the earth. He hoisted the umbrella again, got the flashlight out of his pocket, and shined it into the hole.

The light reflected off a sheet of painted metal, a dirty ivory white with faded red hearts and curlicues painted on it. The paint was chipped away at the corners, and the metal was rusted and dented. It was the top of an old bread box. Bentley knelt in the mud, trying to keep the rain off with the umbrella while he reached down into the hole. He grabbed the rolled metal handle on top of the box and lifted it out of its shallow grave, clinging lumps of mud falling away into the hole. Whatever was inside clanked together like glass jars.

21

There was something unfair in the dinner arrangements that night, although clearly Walt couldn't say so, couldn't let on that he was jealous of the children's food. Nora and Eddie both had grilled cheese sandwiches that had been fried in margarine, for God's sake, and the rest of them – the adults, who ought to have more sense, and ought to eat what they damned well pleased – were sharing Jinx's 'sailor's meatloaf,' a casserole made out of albacore and broccoli and egg whites, stiffened with bran so that it cut like a pâté. Walt salted his plate for the third time and then passed the salt to Henry, who took it without a word. Everyone had boiled beets, too, which was probably unfair to the children, but Jinx hadn't really known about Nora and Eddie's arrival either, and the beets had already been boiling on the stove.

Nora, whose bobbed hair made her look like a character out of an old silent movie about street children, nibbled on the corner of her sandwich like a hamster. The freckles on her cheeks might have been dabbed on in ink. Walt winked at her, and she hid her face behind her sandwich and didn't move.

Eddie called the sandwiches 'cheesers.' Apparently they were the only thing he would eat aside from pizza, and he would only eat the sandwiches if they were made on white bread with a single slice of American cheese that was melted but not 'burnt.' Nora apparently ate nothing at all. Despite all her hamster nibbling, her sandwich was still nearly whole. Probably neither of them had ever tasted real food, since Darla couldn't cook. The one time that Walt and Ivy had eaten at Darla and Jack's, Darla had microwaved raw chicken slathered in ketchup, which had turned out to be both gray and inedible. In the embarrassed silence, Jack had called her a 'goddamn idiot' in a voice that was absolutely flat, no humor at all, and she had burst into tears and run into the other room.

Walt looked at Nora and Eddie and wondered how many of those scenes, or worse, they'd witnessed over the few short years of their lives. That creep Jack! Christ, the son-of-a-bitch needed a fist in the face. They were all living in Babylon or some damned place, and it was no small miracle that any of them survived, especially the children. The world was toxic to them. Walt was suddenly full of fear and affection for everybody at the dinner table, for Henry and Jinx tooling around the country in their portable home, sleeping under the mercury vapor lamps in grocery-store parking lots and eating noodles out of Styrofoam cups, for Nora and Eddie already cast adrift in a world that betrayed its children …

Nora's face was set in a glad-eyed smile, her cheeks pushing her eyes nearly shut, looking curiously at Walt as if he were the most comical thing she'd seen all day. He wiped his mouth and chin, thinking that maybe something was stuck there, a fragment of tuna fish or something. Nora set the sandwich on her plate with elaborate care and took a long drink of milk, still looking at him, and then held her empty glass out. Walt filled it out of the carton, and Nora squished up her eyes farther shut and made a rabbit nose. She'd been in the house now for nearly three hours and still hadn't spoken. Walt winked at her, turned his head sideways, and pretended to swallow his butter knife. She put her hand to her mouth, as if to stop herself from laughing out loud, and right then Eddie leaned across toward her plate, and with the palm of his hand he calmly flattened her sandwich so that it looked like something that had been pressed in a dictionary.

'Whoa!' Walt said to him. 'Cut that out. That's *Nora's* sandwich. Squash your own doggone sandwich.' But immediately he felt like a creep.

Eddie shrugged and shook his head, as if to say that it couldn't be helped. 'It's *'sposed* to be flat,' he said, finishing off his own milk. Then, as if to illustrate, he mashed his sandwich into his plate with the bottom of the empty glass. Rubbery-looking cheese pushed out from between the slices of cold toast. 'See,' he said. He held it up to show everyone. 'My mom puts it under a pan. On the stove thing.'

'I'm familiar with that,' Uncle Henry said helpfully. 'Same idea as a bacon press.' He blew his nose heavily into his napkin, which was shredded by the blast. Nora giggled through her fingers. Eddie looked very serious. The bacon press comment had vindicated him, although he couldn't have had any more idea about a bacon press than about a nuclear reactor.

'Edward,' Jinx said, nodding in the boy's direction, 'I'm happy to see that you've eaten your beets.' There were no beets left on his plate, only a pool of red juice.

Eddie nodded. 'I ate a turnip once,' he announced. 'They taste like sour dirt.'

At the mention of dirt, Nora giggled again and made her rabbit face at Walt.

'I nearly took a bus to work this morning,' Walt said, 'but I took my lunch instead.' He winked big at Nora, who hid her eyes with her hands and slid straight down out of her chair, very slowly, entirely disappearing under the table. Walt could hear her giggling under there, mostly through her nose. Ivy gave Walt a look that implied she couldn't understand why he had to talk like that, giving Nora fits. Eddie sat there stone-faced, acting incredibly grown-up and dependable.

Walt shook his head in wonderment, then lifted the edge of the tablecloth and peered at the floor under the table. Nora was crouched there, still with the cheeky smile, but with her thumb in her mouth now. He nodded toward her empty chair, suddenly afraid that this was going to turn into some kind of crisis.

'*I'll* get her,' Eddie said, starting to push his chair back.

Walt shook his head. 'It's all right,' he said. 'Here she comes now.' He widened his eyes at her, and she shook her head. Then he held his hand out, and to his surprise she pulled her thumb out of her mouth and latched onto his fingers, climbing out from under the table, back up into her chair. Walt picked up his napkin and, holding it out of sight, wiped the spit off his hand.

'Well, *I'm* through,' Uncle Henry said suddenly, standing up. Jinx looked hard at him and then nodded at his seat. 'What?' he asked.

'It's better to ask to be excused,' she said. 'Let's set an example.'

'Oh, yes. Of course.' He sat back down. Then, as if forgetting that he'd already quit eating, he forked up a cube of beet and started in on his plate again, making no move to excuse himself.

Aunt Jinx waited, looking vaguely astonished. 'Why, this is remarkable,' she said, speaking mainly to Ivy. 'What are they good for? Why did God bother?'

Henry was oblivious to the comment. With elaborate care he pushed together a piece of beet and a wad of casserole, salted it, and shoved it into his mouth. 'You can use an old flatiron as a bacon press,' he said, looking at his empty fork. 'Works as well as anything.'

There was a certain tension in the air now, a hovering cloud of uncertainty that made conversation impossible, and it struck Walt that like some baffling oriental tea ritual, the business of six people eating together was a deep and very nearly senseless mystery.

'May I be excused, please?' Eddie asked, looking at Walt.

'Certainly,' Jinx said, nodding deeply. 'And please clear your place. Put your plate in the sink. There's a good boy.'

Eddie stood up out of his chair, holding his plate in one hand and clutching his crumpled napkin in the other. Walt looked at him in astonishment: the entire crotch of his khaki pants was stained blood red in a blotch the size of a plate.

For a long moment the room was dead silent, and then Nora, wide-eyed and no longer smiling, pointed at her brother and said, 'Eddie blowed up.'

Walt got up from the floor of the dining room, and put down his rag and spray bottle. The beet stain wouldn't come out of the rug any easier than it would come out of Eddie's pants. He had to laugh, though. He had barely stopped Ivy from calling an ambulance. When the wad of beet cubes had fallen to the carpet, Jinx and Ivy still hadn't gotten it – that out of politeness Eddie had shoveled all the beets onto the napkin in his lap, intending to sneak the whole mess into the trash.

Walt remembered that one, a typical childhood ruse, way more effective than the usual business of shifting vegetables around your plate as if you'd eaten big healthful holes in them. When he was a kid he'd been a master of making food disappear in just that same way, but he had usually thrown the uneaten food onto the roof of his house, napkin and all. His father had found evidence of it once, when they were all out working in the yard on a Sunday afternoon – dried food in wadded up napkins lying among the dead leaves in the rain gutters. His mother, planting bulbs in the flowerbed below, had been utterly baffled. Walt's father had looked down at him from the top of his ladder, shook his head just slightly, and said, 'I bet it's from that meteor shower.' And that had become a sort of code for them later on, especially when they were served alien foodstuffs. He smiled now, thinking about it, how hard they'd worked that line over the years …

Then he thought about poor Eddie, mortified over the beet incident. It was no good saying anything to cheer him up for a couple of hours yet; it was better to let the mortification ease up. Later on Walt could say something to make things right, before the boy went to bed. He picked up the remains of Nora's flattened sandwich and took a bite out of it. Even cold the sandwich had a pleasant, salty taste. In a few minutes Ivy and Jinx and the kids would be back from their walk; despite their coats and umbrellas, they wouldn't be out long in the threatening weather. Henry had retired to the motor home, where he was probably polishing off a box of vanilla wafers and sketching out potential popes.

Walt sat down to finish the sandwich. The sad remains of the sailor's meatloaf sat in the serving dish, and he wondered vaguely if there was some way he could use it to terrorize Argyle. Nothing came to him. He poked at it.

Somehow the loaf was setting up, like a hybrid of rubber and plaster of Paris – probably because of the gluten in the oat bran. He pressed it with his fingers, fashioning a head out of it, pinching out ears and a hook nose, surprised to find that it kept its shape like modeling clay. He gave it a long neck and a thrust-out chin and deep-set eyes under a heavy brow, then picked up scraps of cooked broccoli and shoved the little flowerets into the top of the sculpture, over its ears, but leaving it mostly bald on top. It looked like the bust of some kind of German nobleman, very dignified and proud, but with a terrible case of chlorophyll poisoning.

Hurriedly he cleared the rest of the table, tossed the tablecloth into the dirty clothes, and then put the head back onto the table as a sort of centerpiece.

The door burst open and Nora and Eddie tumbled in, dripping with rainwater. Walt could see that it was pouring, and a gust of rain-laden wind blew into the room. Nora stopped abruptly, as if she was caught on something, then gave her still-open umbrella a tug, yanking it through the door, which was about six inches too narrow to accommodate it. The umbrella turned itself inside out, and Nora happily dragged it dripping into the room.

Walt took it from her and tried to invert it again by pressing it upside down into the carpet and leaning into it. 'Wind got to it,' he said to Ivy as she came in out of the rain. There was a popping noise as the wobbly little ribs snapped, and when he picked it up, half the umbrella simply hung there limp, like a victim of gravity. Ivy pulled her coat off and hung it on the coat rack. Then she took the umbrella from him and stared at it, nodding her head ponderously, as if to say that he'd done a tidy bit of work.

'You see?' Jinx asked her.

Ivy pushed open the screen door and tossed the umbrella out onto the porch.

'See what?' Walt asked.

'Men,' Jinx said. 'Never you mind. We were having a conversation. I really don't mean you, Walter. I needed an example and you obliged, that's all.'

'I was trying to fix the umbrella.' He looked at Ivy for support, and she squished up her face, making one of Nora's rabbit-noses at him.

'And while we were out you cleaned up the dinner dishes,' Jinx said. 'I wasn't being fair. I'm sorry.' She patted him on the forearm.

'That's all right,' Walt said. 'I don't mean to be touchy.'

'Did you put the rest of the loaf in the fridge? Henry loves to make a nice sandwich out of the leftovers.'

'Sure,' Walt started to say, already turning toward the table. If he was quick he could hammer it flat before Jinx or Ivy saw what had happened to it, no harm done …

But there was a hoot of laughter then, from Eddie, followed by Nora giggling insanely. They'd already found it. 'Such a funny!' Nora said, picking up the bust from where it sat on the table. She held it out by the neck so that everyone could see it. At that moment it broke in half, just below the chin, and the head fell heavily to the carpet where it lay staring up at the ceiling like a dead man, its features considerably flattened out by the impact.

'What in God's name?' Jinx asked, looking down at it in apparent disbelief.

'I ... bet it's from that meteor shower,' Walt said. He bent over to pick it up along with the bits of cooked broccoli scattered on the carpet.

Nora took it out of his hands, and she and Eddie hauled it into the kitchen together, Eddie trying to snatch it away from her.

'In the *sink!*' Jinx shouted. She fixed Walt with a stare, then waved her hand tiredly and moved toward the door. 'I'll turn in with Henry,' she said.

Walt chanced a look at Ivy, who eyed him sternly. But then she clearly couldn't stand it any longer and burst into laughter that she turned into a coughing fit before rushing away up the stairs. The front door swung shut, cutting off the sound of the rain, and Walt headed toward the stairs himself, glancing into the kitchen where Eddie stood at the counter now, beating the living hell out of the remains of the head with a big wooden spoon while Nora stood next to him on a chair, holding the egg beater and waiting for her turn.

22

Bentley thought suddenly of money, of treasure: not gold coins – this wasn't heavy enough for coins – but maybe rolled-up wads of twenty-dollar bills stuffed into jars and hidden in a hole beneath a privy!

He set the bread box on the dirt next to the hole, covering it with the umbrella. His hands trembling, he twisted the latch. The front of the box fell open. It was full of glass jars, all right – pint-size Mason jars, all of them lidded, all apparently empty, and certainly empty of money.

He picked one up and looked closely at it. Something lay in the bottom. He illuminated it with the flashlight. It was a tooth, a human molar with a silver filling. He set the jar down and picked up another, this one containing a lock of hair, curled together and bound with a single strand. He shone the light into the tin box now. All the jars were the same: each apparently contained nothing but a single small remnant of a human being – a fingernail paring, eyelash hairs, a tooth, a leathery little patch of skin.

Shutting the front of the bread box, he carried two of the jars toward the shed and ducked in out of the rain. He dropped the umbrella, shoved a couple of rusted trowels off onto the ground, and set the jars on a wooden shelf. He laid down the flashlight and picked up the first of the jars again. The ring twisted off easily, but the lid was tight. He pushed at the rim of the lid with the edge of his thumb but couldn't move it. Someone had done a fair job of canning …

The idea of these things having been canned horrified him and he set the jar down, his mind returning to the empty room in the burned house, to the iron hooks in the ceiling, to the foul picture on the floor in the living room. He laid the edge of the jar lid over a protruding nail head and pried at it. There was a slight pop, followed by an exhalation of escaping air and what sounded unmistakably like a human cry, small and immeasurably distant.

And just then, out of the corner of his eye, Bentley saw a light moving through the trees. He switched off his flashlight, then hurriedly screwed the lid back onto the opened jar. It was raining hard enough now so that the house and the trees beyond were obscured by a gray veil of drops. The moving light swung in a misty arc, two barely visible shadows hunching along behind it.

Making up his mind, Bentley moved away from the shed, pocketing his flashlight and carrying the two jars and his closed umbrella. He looked behind him. Whoever it was had stopped near the house. Their light swung his way, illuminating the path. He hurried the few feet to the bread box, picking it up and darting away again, crouching behind the fallen outhouse. Opening the front of the bread box, he tilted it back and replaced the two jars inside. The light was moving again, darting out along the little path toward the garden shed.

Bentley crept backward through the mud on his hands and knees, dragging the box and the umbrella along with him. His foot kicked the trunk of the big walnut tree, and he scuttled around behind it, peering out past the trunk. The two men had stopped to look over the shed. They'd see the trowels knocked down, rainwater on the wooden shelf, footprints in the mud …

Sure enough, here they came, bent over and casting the flashlight beam in front of them, looking for him. They both wore hats pulled low over their eyes. One was big, heavy, but Bentley couldn't make out his features in the darkness.

'What the hell's this?' the smaller one asked. He played the light along the edge of the outhouse, then shone it on the hole in the dirt. Bentley looked behind him. The shadows of eucalyptus trees loomed overhead, and the wire fence, choked with oleander, blocked his retreat that way. Wait them out, he thought, bending over and grasping the handle at the top of the box. If he had to, he'd run for it. He was in plenty good enough shape to get away – from the big one, at least.

'Empty,' the small man said, looking into the hole. 'Full of shit, just like you.'

'That's right,' the other one said tiredly. 'This hasn't been used for years, and it wasn't knocked over last night, either. This is what we're looking for, but someone got here first.'

'Yeah, well, I think we're chumps, out here looking around for something nobody don't even know what it is. Let's just bring him a goddamn bag of walnuts.'

'That's a *good* idea,' the big man said. He swung the flashlight slowly, aiming it into the trees. 'I think he's still here, whoever it is. The snoop. Look at this.'

He shone the light on the ground now, the two of them bending down to have a look at something – footprints probably, or the depression made by the bread box in the mud. Bentley nearly got up and ran for it, but he held on. What lengths would they go to in order to stop him? He thought of poor Simms, dead, and he knew the answer.

The thought of Simms galvanized him, and something stirred within him – a wild gladness, a righteous fire kindled out of nowhere. This was *it*. This was what he was *paid* for. Push had come to shove. He'd spent countless Sundays warning people about the Dragon; now it was damn well time to skewer the bastard!

He stepped out from behind the tree, waving his umbrella in the air. 'That's right!' he shouted. 'Here I am!' His voice was pitched high, from the excitement. He was giddy. Out of his mind. He shook his umbrella in the air like a Zulu, rainwater blowing into his face.

The two men looked at him, apparently mystified by his behavior, the small one shining the flashlight beam into his eyes and then down to the painted bread box. The big one said something to the small one, who nodded, and immediately the big one set out around the opposite side of the outhouse, clearly thinking to cut off Bentley's escape. The other one stepped forward, holding out his hand, palm up.

'Hand it over, pops,' he said.

'Absolutely,' Bentley shouted. And then, without another thought, he raised the closed umbrella like a lance and charged at the man, holding it stiff-armed in front of him. The big man turned around and lumbered back toward his partner, who threw both hands into the air in surprise, taking a wild swipe at the umbrella but missing it entirely. The blunt tip struck him in the chest, and the umbrella itself crumpled, its hollow stem bending in half as the ribs flew open, the thin fabric pushing into the man's face like bat wings as he staggered backward, slipping in the mud.

The fat man lunged toward Bentley, grabbing him by the arm, and the preacher flailed at his face with the open, broken umbrella, yanking backward and shouting scripture into the man's face, wild verses out of Ezekiel.

The man let go of him, treading backward and stepping on the fallen vent pipe from the outhouse, tripping and sitting down heavily across the outhouse door, which crumpled inward so that he sat in it like a drunken man sprawled over the sides of a canoe.

Bentley turned and slapped the destroyed umbrella at the small man again, dancing toward him and stamping at him as if the man were a bug that he could crush underfoot, and the man rolled away into a clump of bare vines, holding his hands over his head and yelling, 'Whoa, whoa, whoa!'

Just then the door of the bread box dropped open. Bentley felt the contents shift, felt the weight of the door banging down on its flimsy hinge. He snatched at the box, trying to right it, but the whole passel of jars flew out, into the mud, into the bushes, raining down on the small man, who sat up now, grabbing at the jars. Jars broke against rocks, against each other, and the night was full of the soft sounds of escaping human cries, audible even in the rain and the banging around. The fat man struggled up out of the outhouse, his arms swimming, lurching to his feet and bending forward in a crouch, hands out in front of him now as if he meant to squeeze Bentley in half.

Bentley flung the empty bread box at him, lashed the umbrella at his partner, then bent over and snatched up two of the jars. He turned to run, heading in among the ghostly trees. He didn't look back, but high-stepped it down the path, squinting against the rain.

They were following! Footsteps pounded along behind him as he wove through the trees, kicking through leaves, heading for the street with a jar in either hand. In school he'd been a sprinter, and although he hadn't run in thirty years, he poured it on now, putting his heart into it, sucking air into his lungs, half expecting the snap of a groin muscle or the sudden tightening of his heart seizing up. But the sounds of pursuit trailed away behind him. They were giving up.

And then he was out of the gate, into the street and loping down toward his car, running easily now, into his stride. Knowing he was safe, he looked back over his shoulder. No one was following. Why should they? They apparently had what they were after. Thank God he hadn't recognized either of them; that way they wouldn't have recognized him either. There was no way Argyle could suspect him.

He flung the car door open and slumped onto the seat, hauling in his legs, turning the key, and throwing the Toyota into reverse, careening backward toward the intersection at Almond, where he shifted into forward again and gunned away toward the Plaza. Then, on impulse, he turned up Shaffer Street, slowing down and switching on the heater, trying to catch his breath. He felt pretty doggone good, considering … He hooted out loud and slapped the wheel. By heaven he'd given the Devil hell, hadn't he? Grabbed him by the shirtfront and slapped his silly face for him!

He felt *real* good, was how he felt – better than he had for years. He glanced down at the two jars on the seat beside him, their contents visible in the glow of the streetlamps. In one lay what looked like a severed eyelid, lashes and all. His smile faded, and on impulse he pulled into the parking lot of the Holy Spirit Catholic Church. The light was on in the sacristy.

23

'Not until the children are asleep,' Ivy said, dodging away from Walt. She headed into the bathroom, where she stood at the sink, putting her hair up with a couple of silver clips.

'They're in bed,' he said. 'Snug as bugs.' He put his arm around her waist and wiggled his eyebrows at her.

'They're not asleep. They're wound up like tops.' She pushed him out and shut the door in his face.

'They're beat,' he said, talking at the door. 'In a few minutes they'll be asleep. We have some important business to discuss.'

'You mean monkey business, I think.' She opened the door and stepped out of the bathroom, wrapped in her kimono now. 'Listen,' she said.

From downstairs came the sound of a giggle, then the creaking of floorboards – someone walking in the dining room, probably heading for the kitchen.

'*I'll* handle this,' Walt said, nodding seriously.

'Thanks,' Ivy told him. 'I'm about dead. I might wait up for you, though – if I don't fall asleep.' She winked at him and sat down on the bed, switching on the table lamp and picking up her glasses and her book.

Full of anticipation, Walt headed down the stairs. He'd take care of this lickety-split. Sometimes kids just needed to be *told* what to do – no messing around, no choices. Raising children wasn't any kind of democracy …

There was a light in the kitchen. He looked in through the doorway. Eddie stood at the sink, trying to twist the chrome plug into the drain. The water was running full blast. Nora had clambered up onto the counter, where she was squirting a heavy stream of dish soap into the slowly filling sink.

'Hi,' Walt said, stepping up to the sink. 'What's up?'

'We're soaping,' Nora said, smiling big. She showed him the squeeze bottle of Ivory Liquid.

Eddie pushed his pajama sleeves up and dipped his hands into the water, swishing it around to make bubbles.

'Soaping what?' Walt looked around. The dishes were done, the counter entirely cleared off.

'Soap,' Nora said. 'See?' She picked up a double handful of bubbles and put her face into them. Bubbles clung to her nose and cheeks.

'That's good enough,' Eddie said, shutting off the water.

'I think maybe it's time for bed,' Walt told him. 'Why don't you start on this in the morning?'

Nora's face fell, and she slumped into a sort of rag doll position, as if most of her muscles had quit on her.

'Let's go,' Walt said. 'Let's hop into bed.'

Apparently they heard nothing. Eddie swirled his hands in the soapy water, piling the bubbles up into towers. Nora reached into the sink and flattened the towers with her hands. Eddie built them back up again, edging his sister out of the way and blocking the sink.

'Let *me*,' Nora said, trying to elbow her way in again.

Eddie stood there immovable, saying nothing but clearly determined now to keep her out.

Nora pushed him on the shoulder, but he set his feet and pushed back. Nora slapped him hard on the arm.

'Hey!' Walt said. 'That's enough now …'

Eddie dipped his hands into the sink and very calmly flung soapy water at his sister, who froze there on the countertop, her face suddenly full of a cold fury. She slid to the floor, her fists balled up, her pajama shirt soaked. She drew her hand back to slug him, but Walt caught her by the wrist.

'I don't *care*,' Eddie said, pulling the plug out of the sink. The soapy water swirled away down the drain.

'You *fuck*head,' Nora shouted at him, trying to jerk her wrist out of Walt's grasp.

'Whoa! Whoa!' Walt said. 'Haile Selassie! You can't talk like that! Not in *this* house.' He turned her around and marched her out into the dining room. Ivy stood on the bottom landing, a look of surprise on her face. He shrugged at her. Nora burst into tears, pulled away from him, and ran into the bedroom, slamming the door. He could hear her sobbing in there.

'Need help?' Ivy asked, widening her eyes.

Walt shook his head. 'I'm all right,' he said. 'They're just tired. This isn't easy on them.'

Eddie stood in the kitchen, drying his hands on a towel. Walt walked in and leaned against the counter. He folded his arms. 'Do me a favor, will you, man?'

'What?' Eddie asked, folding his own arms and leaning against the counter beside Walt.

'Apologize to your sister.'

'She wrecked my tower.'

'She just wanted her turn at the sink.'

'She said ... You heard.'

'She didn't mean it.'

'Yeah-huh,' Eddie said. 'She talks like that.'

'Well, I think she's kind of scared, staying here and all. You've got to help me take care of her. She's little, you know? Don't tell her I said that.'

Eddie shrugged. 'I guess,' he said.

'Good man,' Walt said. 'Let's go cheer her up.'

Walt opened the door and they went into the spare bedroom. Nora lay on her bed, facedown, as if she intended to smother herself in the pillow.

'I'm sorry,' Eddie said. 'About the water and all ...'

She didn't move, but her body shuddered from a quiet sob. Walt patted her head, wondering what to do. 'It's all right,' he said. 'No big deal.'

She put her fingers in her ears, closing out the world. He realized that she was still crying. What next? Pick her up? Roll her over? Threaten her? Where were her goddamn father and mother? That was the ten-cent question. One of them was pounding down another Budweiser and the other one was out looking for space. Shit. What a world.

'I'll be right back,' he said to Eddie, who climbed into his own bed. Walt headed upstairs.

'How's it going?' Ivy asked when he had gotten back to the bedroom.

'You better give it a shot,' he said. 'I'm a dead loss.'

'I bet you're not.' She got out of bed and kissed him on the lips. He had the brief feeling that he was being taken somehow, that Ivy had set him up in some complicated and devious way, and was playing him like a fiddle. She disappeared down the stairs, and he sat down on the edge of the bed to wait. Five minutes later he heard her coming back up.

'What's happening?' he asked.

'They're settled down. I promised them you'd tell them a story.'

Walt gaped at her. 'About what?'

'I don't know. Read them something out of that fairytale book in the living-room bookcase.'

'All right. But you're still waiting up for me, right?'

'Why, are you going to read me a story too?'

'Shucks, yes,' he said, heading for the stairs. 'Just you wait.'

'"There was once a man who had three sons,"' Walt read, trying another story. The first two he started had apparently been incomprehensible to the modern child. '"The youngest of the sons was named Dummling, and on that account was despised and slighted and put back on every occasion."'

'What?' Nora asked. She wasn't crying any more, but was sitting up in bed, wearing a pair of dry pajamas.

'What what?' Walt asked, smiling at her.

'What did that mean?'

'What I read?'

She nodded at him.

'Well, there's these three kids,' Walt said.

'Name of Dumbhead,' Eddie said, snickering.

Nora covered her mouth with her hand, giggling through it, happy again.

'"It happened,"' Walt read, '"that the eldest …"'

'The what?' Nora asked.

'The … oldest,' Walt said.

'The dummy one?' She looked confused, like she'd lost the thread of the story.

'He wasn't *dumb*,' Walt said. 'That was his name.'

'Why did they name him that?'

'Dumm*ling*. They named him Dumm*ling*.'

'Oh,' she said. She settled down in bed, waiting. Eddie picked at the flowers on the chenille bedspread. He looked tired, his eyes half shut.

'"It happened that the eldest wished to go into the forest to hew wood, and …"'

'Didn't he know he was the oldest?' Nora asked.

Walt nodded, unable to puzzle her out. There was something amazing about the question, some element of it that reminded him of the kind of special lunacy you run across in a Zen koan. Nora was apparently a sort of cosmic mystery. 'Sure he did,' Walt told her, closing the book. 'He just wanted to cut some wood, you know?'

'For his house?'

'For a fire and all.'

'It was cold,' she said.

Walt nodded. 'It was terribly cold. There was snow everywhere. So he got his axe and …'

'How do you know?' Nora looked at him, frowning. 'It's not in the book,' she said. 'It's not in the picture. You're making stuff up.'

'That's right,' he said. 'Don't you want snow in it?'

'Okay,' she said.

Walt winked at her. 'So anyway, he got this axe and went into the forest. And his friend, this guy named … I forget. Gooberhead, I think …'

Nora snickered.

'… showed up with a bag full of rocks. And Dummling says, "What's in the bag?" And Gooberhead says, "Smart pills."'

'Was it?' Nora asked.

Walt shook his head. 'It was a *trick*.' Eddie was asleep now, still sitting up in bed, but with his head slumped to the side. 'So Dummling says, "Let me have some," but Gooberhead wouldn't give him any.'

'He was *mean*,' Nora said.

'Wait. They were *rocks*, remember? So Dummling says, "C'mon, Gooberhead, give me some smart pills." And so Gooberhead opens the bag, and Dummling takes out a handful of the rocks and puts them in his mouth and tries to chew them up.'

'Mmm,' Nora said. 'Were they candy?'

Walt blinked at her. 'No, they were rocks, like I said. They broke his teeth out.'

'Oh!' Nora said.

'And Dummling says, "Hey! These taste like *rocks*." And Boogerhead ...'

Nora burst into laughter, pointing her finger at Walt. 'You said *booger*.'

'I meant Gooberhead ...'

'*Booger!*'

'Okay, but just never mind that. When Dummling says, "Hey, these taste like rocks," Gooberhead says, "See, you're getting smarter already."' Walt laughed a little bit. 'Pretty funny, eh?'

Nora gaped at him. 'Where's Uncle Henry?' she asked suddenly.

'Why, he's outside, in the motor home.'

'Is he old?'

'Sort of. I mean ...'

'He's funny. He looks like that head.'

'What head?'

'That cabbage head.'

'*What* cabbage head?' Walt asked.

'That *one*. That fell on the floor.'

Walt nodded. 'But did you like the story?'

'Yes.' She pulled the covers up to her chin. Eddie was sound asleep. 'But I don't like that Gooberhead man.'

'I don't either,' Walt said. 'He's a dirty pig. Go to sleep now.'

'G'night,' she said, turning over and snuggling down into the blankets.

He kissed her on the cheek, then eased Eddie down into bed, covered him up, and tiptoed out through the door, leaving the dining-room light on as a night light.

Upstairs, Ivy lay in bed. She still wore her glasses, but her book had fallen out of her hand, and she was clearly asleep. Walt set the book on the nightstand and eased her glasses off. She murmured something and slid down under the covers. He kissed her on the cheek, wondering vaguely whether it was still a husband's right to wake his wife up under circumstances like this, or if the politics of marriage had changed along with everything else. He decided to cut his losses. There would be other nights.

Somehow he wasn't sleepy yet, and he turned around and went back downstairs, where he switched on the Christmas tree lights. The room smelled strongly of pine. He sat down on the couch, watching the bubblers and the whirligigs come to life. Ivy had started buying old-fashioned-looking painted glass ornaments – Santa Clauses, grinning moons, clowns, comical dogs. There was a silver baby's head as big as his fist, with three different faces on it, each of the faces vaguely astonished, as if all of them had just that moment seen something wonderful and unlikely. He searched the baby head out now, finding it finally among a cluster of glass icicles, and it occurred to him that it was his favorite ornament because it was ridiculous, because it made the least sense.

He loved all of it, though, the whole thing together – the blinking lights shining through the icicles, the bubbles rising in their glass tubes, the colored balls glowing like tiny planets, the gaudily painted figures – and it seemed to him now, late in the evening, as if the tree signified all the light and color and magic in creation.

He laid his head back against the cushion. I'll just shut my eyes for a moment, he thought, and then get up and go to bed. And for a brief time, he could see the colored lights winking on and off even though his eyes were closed, and he wished Ivy were downstairs, too, sitting with him on the couch.

PART TWO

Doubt and Decision

A man was meant to be doubtful about himself, but undoubting about the truth.

G. K. CHESTERTON,
ORTHODOXY

The wood was green, and at first showed no disposition to blaze. It smoked furiously. Smoke, thought I, always goes before blaze; and so does doubt go before decision.

ANDREW MARVELL,
REVERIES OF A BACHELOR

24

'What do you make of them?'

Father Mahoney held one of the jars in his hand. It was the jar with the eyelid. He shook his head. 'I don't know. You say you heard something when you took the lid off?'

'A human cry. Just as sure as I'm standing here now.'

'Could have been the wind?'

'Could have been. I don't happen to think so.'

'What's your take on it, then?'

'I surely don't know. I don't mean to be morbid, but I wonder if when they take to digging up LeRoy's acreage they might not find worse things.'

Mahoney was silent.

'I don't mean to dump these on your doorstep like a couple of orphan babies, but to my mind there's no denying that we're both involved in something here.' He gestured around – at the boarded-up, stained-glass windows, the washed-down walls with the ghosts of filthy words still visible, waiting for a second coat of paint. 'LeRoy came after your church. Another one of them got the bells at St Anthony's and killed Simms. They aren't going away. Push is coming to shove. Now, we've had our differences in the past, you being a Catholic and all, but I've always known you were the real McCoy, and I hope I never let on any different about myself.'

'No, sir,' Mahoney said. 'I've admired your work here, Protestant or no Protestant.' Mahoney winked at him.

Bentley stood silently for a moment, as if he were working something out in his head. 'I'm going to tell you a few things, then. And afterward you can decide whether you want to stand by what you just said, or amend it.'

The priest nodded. Then very seriously he said, 'Would you prefer the confessional?'

'Damn it!' Bentley shouted. 'This isn't funny. I'm not *confessing* something. I'm telling you what happened.'

'Sorry,' Mahoney said. 'Honestly, I *am* sorry. I couldn't help myself. Go on with your story.'

'All right,' Bentley said. 'I'll make it plain. For a long time I led what you'd call a double life, and what I did in that other life was shameful.'

'All of us have done shameful ...'

'I'm not talking about that. What I did was worse. Murray LeRoy knew me, or thought he did, as a diabolical priest named Flanagan.'

'Priest?'

'Minister, then. It doesn't matter which. Anyway, I introduced LeRoy and another man, George Nelson, to the notion of selling their immortal souls, literally speaking. You know who Nelson is – the lawyer down on the Plaza who found LeRoy burning to death in the alley. Together they conscripted another man, Robert Argyle, who had fallen on hard times after some kind of trouble with the authorities. Argyle had certain … business connections, let us say, in the East. There were certain things he could acquire for them. Anyway, with my help, the three of them sold their souls to the Devil.' He paused, waiting for Mahoney to respond.

'*Sold* them?'

'That's right. For a price. A good one, too. I didn't really believe it myself at the time, just as you don't quite believe it now. I can see that much in your face.'

'You're telling me they thought they'd *sold* their souls? Like Faust? Was there a piece of paper? Something signed?'

'Well, no, not signed exactly. As a signature they bit down hard on a bar napkin and rubbed the indentation with charcoal. Along with that they gave me … tokens. I didn't ask for them, mind you. This was arranged by a third party, so to speak, a man named Obermeyer, who lives out in Santa Ana. Nelson's token was a lock of hair. From Murray LeRoy it was a severed fingertip. He was a sadomasochist of the worst type. Utter degenerate. Argyle offered a little vial of blood. These objects arrived in common household canning jars. And now you know why I don't like the look of these things here.' He pointed at the jars on the table.

'I don't like them much myself,' Mahoney said.

'I can see that you don't. And quit looking at me over the top of your spectacles like that. You don't know the half of it yet. Nelson and Leroy were already involved in spiritualism, dabbling in the occult, some of it pretty nasty. I had known LeRoy for years, and I didn't like him. His conscience, if he ever had one, had rotted. George Nelson was a complete idiot. The only thing he had going for him twenty years ago was that he knew he was a small-timer. He had a pitiful little divorce practice. He had come to know his own prospects, and he didn't like them a bit. As for Argyle, heaven knows what he would have come to without stumbling into this pit these other two dug for him. And me too, I guess. That's what I'm trying to say here. I worked on it myself, like a steamshovel.

'Anyway, the whole thing was simple. This man Obermeyer hinted around that he could set up this contract business for a fee, a commission. None of these men were wealthy at the time, but then the initial fee wasn't all that high, either. It was later, if they were satisfied, that they would pay me the real money. Of course I never expected to see it. This whole thing was a joke. I was going to pick the Devil's pocket and make a few dollars for the Church.'

'Well, pardon me if I'm a little skeptical about that last part,' Mahoney said.

'What *should* I have done with the money, bought a Cadillac?'

'Perhaps you shouldn't have taken it at all.'

'Then someone else would have. That's capitalism, isn't it? Somebody pays money out, somebody else gathers it in. I did the gathering that day.'

'I think I see. What you're telling me is that you sold your own soul to gain ... what? Not the world. You were above that. What you wanted was to do good works – Christian charity. You saw yourself as a sort of Robin Hood of the Church.'

'Well,' Bentley said. 'That gets close to it. I suppose I did. It's vanity, I know. But if I *did* sell my soul, by God I didn't sell it for my *own* gain.'

'I believe you. But you don't sound happy with it anyway.'

'Of *course* I don't sound happy with it.'

'Then what's eating you?'

'Well, it didn't end there. The three of them prospered, and I didn't, so I squeezed them a little bit, now and then, and kept the con alive. I always meant to quit, but then the lunch van would break down or the plumbing would back up, and I'd have my man call up Argyle or LeRoy and ask for an "offering." Heaven help me, that's how I phrased it. Argyle got richest, of course, so I squeezed him the hardest. And it worked, mind you, because they believed in me. And worse than that, they were *afraid* of me. How do you like that? Shameful, isn't it?'

'I suppose it is,' the priest said.

'Here's the bad thing: all three of these men got what they wanted. I conned them, you see, and yet it never *looked* like a con. To the contrary, they were satisfied customers. A few years pass, and what happens? George Nelson carves out a legal empire. He goes out to D. C. to lobby senators and does who-knows-what kind of damage. His law firm opens branch offices all across the country. There's even a law school named after him. After eighteen years he comes back home to take it easy, and he buys a big house in Panorama Heights. And Argyle? He's got the Midas touch. Whatever he sets his hand to, it returns to him tenfold. Half of it's fraudulent, outright criminal, but no one pays any attention any more, despite his past. It's as if he's got *protection* of some kind. LeRoy? Utterly debased. Real estate millions spent on filthy pursuits, right here in the middle of town. Life going on roundabout him like he's invisible.'

'Take some comfort in the fact that you *didn't* know,' Mahoney said. 'What did you *think* you were doing? Ask yourself that. I haven't got any grievance against guilt, but I insist that it be applied accurately.'

'No, there's no comfort in it, I assure you. You know why? Because I saw the truth. Here's the clincher: *There hadn't been any con.* They *intended* to give themselves up to the Devil, and I walked in and paved the way. I pretended to be some kind of satanic ... minister, and by heaven I *was that thing.* There is no king's X when you're dealing in souls. That's what I found out. I did the *wrong* thing, and I did it laughing and smiling. I saw something pretty clearly then. I saw that all of us, LeRoy and Nelson and Argyle and me too, all of us had the same ally – the Father of Lies. I cut it off then. I prayed that was the end of it.'

'Then now's the time to face the Devil down.'

'That's what I'm telling you. That's why I came here. I've botched it. I can't do it alone. I'm not strong enough. A few days ago Argyle called me on the phone, looking to talk to Flanagan again. He wanted to buy his way free, just like he'd bought his way in all those years ago.'

'And what did you tell him? The truth?'

Bentley shook his head. 'It didn't do any good. He offered me a hundred thousand dollars.'

Mahoney slumped backward in his chair, looked down his spectacles, and whistled softly.

'Just like that. Easy money. I told myself that the bastard was a dead man anyway. The Devil doesn't care how many checks Argyle writes out, or who he writes them to. Take the money and run before the man goes down the well, I thought – the damage is already done.'

'You didn't cash the check?'

'No, I didn't. But I took the money in weakness, and I'm a little afraid that ...' He shrugged.

'Well,' Mahoney said, picking up one of the jars. 'You've got my help. I'm in. And with the help of God we'll prevail, too.' He picked up one of the jars and peered into it. 'You've already opened one of these things. Now I will. Excuse me if I'm a little doubtful, but I want to know what we're up against.'

Before Bentley could protest he twisted the lid off the jar. There was the sound of a human cry, and then a fluttering sound, as if a bird had gotten into the church and lost itself among the rafters. Bentley felt a lightness in his throat that made him want to swallow. And, as if a wind were blowing straight through him, he was suffused with remorse and fear and regret and a dozen unnameable sensations that filled him utterly, then evaporated on the instant. Abruptly the fluttering was gone, the church was quiet, and he could hear the sound of the rain out on the street.

'Sorry,' Mahoney whispered.

'Well, now you know.'

Although what either of them knew, Bentley still couldn't say.

25

It was nearly midnight when the phone rang. Walt woke up instantly, lurching across the bed and snatching up the receiver before Ivy could get to it. He was certain it was Argyle, upping the stakes, maybe the enormous postal inspector ...

But the voice on the other end didn't belong to Argyle, or to the inspector either. It was vaguely familiar. '*Who* is this?' Walt asked.

'This is *Jack*, Walt. Your brother-in-law.'

'Jack!' Walt sat up in bed, motioning at Ivy, who was awake now, looking at him curiously. 'How the hell are you?'

'What in God's name is going on with Darla and the kids? She say anything to Ivy about taking off or something? I've been trying to get hold of her since this afternoon. The preschool tells me Ivy picked up the kids.'

Walt could hear noises in the background – someone talking, laughter, what sounded like glasses or bottles clinking. Jack was in a bar. He didn't sound drunk, not toasted anyway. Walt covered the phone and whispered the question to Ivy.

'Tell him the truth about Darla,' she said. 'We can't hide it from him. No use starting out with lies. Tell him to relax about the kids. We'll think of something.'

'Here's the deal,' Walt said, into the phone now. 'Ivy tells me that Darla flew back east, to Ann Arbor. You know, to stay with the folks for a little while.'

'Why the hell didn't she tell me?'

'She didn't *tell* you?'

'Not a goddamned word. When the hell was this?'

'Today, I guess. She called up Ivy to take over the kids for a few days. She didn't leave you any kind of note, maybe?'

'Not word one. And what are you talking about here? Nora and Eddie didn't go with her? They're over at your place?'

'No. Yeah. They're downstairs, asleep. Hell, I thought you knew all about this. Ivy told Darla that the kids could stay here for a few days, until Darla got herself together – whatever she's up to. I think she misses her folks, to tell you the truth, what with Christmas coming up and all. They aren't getting any younger.'

There was a muffled silence, and Walt could hear Jack mumbling to someone. A woman giggled, and then Jack snickered and said something else to her. Walt nearly hung up the phone.

'So what about the kids?' Jack said. 'What the hell am I supposed to do with the kids while she's back east? I've got a damned job. She apparently didn't think about that.'

Walt took a deep breath. Starting something now was the worst thing he could do. He'd have Jack over here in a drunken rage, pounding on the door. 'That's just it,' Walt said to him cheerfully. 'That's what I'm saying. We invited the kids for a visit. It's fine by us, Jack. We've been talking about having the kids over for what? – a year? Now's just about perfect. I'm working out of the house. Jinx and Henry are here for the winter. And you know Jinx, she's crazy about both of them.'

'I don't know,' Jack said. 'What did …? Shit. Darla told me *nothing* about this.'

'Well … heck. I don't know what to tell you about that. But we were looking forward to having the kids around for a week or so. Two weeks if we can talk you out of them. Just between you and me, man, I think Ivy's got some kind of female thing about this, you know what I mean? She's been riding the kid bandwagon these days. It's some kind of maternal thing – like a nesting instinct.' He grinned at Ivy, who scowled at him and narrowed her eyes. 'Anyway, she had this all worked out with Darla.'

'Yeah, okay,' Jack said. 'Everybody had the whole thing worked out except their damned father.'

Stepfather, Walt thought. The man who's down at the Dewdrop Inn with his part-time squeeze. 'Well, just don't worry about the kids, Jack. Jinx has got them both doing the damned dishes. And she's got some idea of taking them out to Prentice Park tomorrow, to the zoo, if this rain lets up.'

'Well, hell,' Jack said. 'I guess there's no harm. You sure you *want* the two of them?'

'*Hell*, yes. Like I said, Ivy's made all kinds of plans.'

'Okay, then. I guess so. Sounds like everything's copacetic. Tell the kids I'll give them a call tomorrow – tomorrow night, I guess. Busy day tomorrow.'

'I'll tell them,' Walt said. 'You want me to wake 'em up right now and …'

'No,' Jack said hastily. 'No need for that. I'll get back with you after I talk to Darla.'

'Good. You take it easy.'

'I will,' Jack said. 'You too.'

He hung up then, and Walt did too, breathing a heavy sigh of relief.

'Drunk?' Ivy asked.

'Not stinking. He's ticked off about Darla going back east without his permission, but I don't think he gives a damn about the kids being over here. It gives him a clear week or two.'

'That won't last. Once he talks to Darla, he'll be calling back.'

26

At three in the morning, Center Street was nearly dark. The streetlamps were off for some reason, and only a couple of houses had front porch lights on. Argyle nearly turned up the alley toward Grand, but then he noticed that Christmas lights were shining on a house near the end of the block, and instead of turning he killed the headlights, eased the car into the curb, and put the shift lever in park, letting the motor idle. He was tired, worn out, and he sat there for a moment undecided. He shivered in the dark. There was a hint of sulphur on the air, and his head was full of insects. He saw his own face reflected in the glass circle over the speedometer along with the foggy colors of the Christmas lights. It was the face of a corpse, milky-white, the eyes dead and staring. He licked his lips and looked away, hearing something now, above the droning noise that rose in his ears – a sound like iron doors slamming shut and distant human voices.

Fear prodded him into movement, and he turned and reached behind the seat. From the floor he picked up a broomstick with a coat hanger hook on the end, then took a quick look up and down the street before he opened the door and stepped out onto the curb. He trotted silently across the lawn, stopping beneath the lowest point of the eaves. Swiftly he slipped the hook over the string of lights and yanked on it, pulling the entire length down onto the bushes without a sound. The falling lights filled him with a sudden glee, and he grasped the cord between the hot bulbs and yanked on it. There was a snapping sound and the pop of a bulb breaking, and then the lights went dark. He dropped the cord, stomped on three or four bulbs, turned around, and trotted back to the car, climbing in and pulling away.

Thirty seconds! For a moment he felt invigorated, drunk with success as he turned the corner and gunned away up Palm Avenue. Then, as if a switch had been thrown, his stomach abruptly churned with fear again, and he looked into the rearview mirror half expecting to see an outraged homeowner running after him down the street, shaking his fist.

Nine houses that night; surely that was enough! Nine houses full of potential witnesses; nine times that he might have been caught; nine paths to utter ruination …

Would he kill to avoid it?

'Murder.' He mouthed the word, feeling the shape of it with his lips.

It had a ring to it, a certain … thrill. On the instant he was gleeful again, full of desire. The noises in his head were gone. One more house. He would make it an even ten, tonight. He thought of the lighted Christmas star that he'd pulled down at the first house he'd visited, and he laughed out loud, turning up past the Holy Spirit Catholic Church for the third time that night. He fought the urge to pull over, to pay the bells a small visit, but instead he drove on up the quiet street, making aimless right and left turns, letting his mind run until he found himself on Oak Street, drifting to a quiet stop in front of the Stebbinses' house.

Coming to himself again he was filled with a sudden panic, and he sped away. This was too much. They'd left their Christmas lights on! The fools! It was like an invitation to a dance. He turned left at the corner and circled the block, driving slowly past again. One last time. An even ten houses. Whatever power had been leading him around tonight, sniffing out lights, had led him here at last!

He wavered, caught between desire and fear. What an incredible blunder to be caught pulling down Christmas decorations at the Stebbinses' house! It would end it all – everything. Ivy would despise him. If he were accused of murder, of treason, of nearly anything, he could look her in the eye and imply that he'd had his reasons. But this – lurking in the neighborhood after midnight, committing the sins of a monster like Murray LeRoy – it would fill her with horror and loathing.

His hands shook on the steering wheel. His mouth was dry. His mind spun in an idiot whirl, empty now of argument. He turned up an alley and pulled into the deserted parking lot of a medical center, parking where he'd be invisible from the street. He got out of the car, carrying the pole, feeling the wind through his black wool sweater. Abruptly he realized that his mouth was working, as if he were talking to someone, to himself, and the idea of it terrified him.

And then, an instant later, he stood among the shadows at the edge of the Stebbinses' front porch. He scarcely knew how he'd gotten there. Hadn't he turned back to the car? For a moment he looked around blankly, horrified. His car was gone, the street empty.

He had parked in the alley! Of course. His teeth chattered, and he clamped them shut, fighting to control himself. The bushes and trees and front-porch furniture were charged with secret meaning, with some kind of horrible, mocking vitality. Across the street a rooftop Santa Claus stood like a sentinel, watching him through eyes painted on plywood. The Christmas lights on the eaves overhead shone like little pools of warmth and color on the lawn and on the concrete porch.

His mind lurched, suddenly rioting with ideas – what a man could do with a pruning saw, a can of paint, a hedge clippers, a can opener, something nasty to smear across stucco walls! The neighborhood was a vast canvas, a block of marble. Defilement! He tasted the word. And inside the houses – families asleep, children in their beds. Why not give them a face at the window, a sudden shriek and then away like a highwayman? Who would suspect *him*? If only he had a mask! They said that Murray LeRoy wore a goat's mask when he terrorized the old priest …

He had a vision of himself wearing such a mask, the chin and ears tufted with stiff hair, the tongue lolling out. Perhaps a costume out of stiff goatskin, something he could be sewn into … Full of a murky passion, he reached into his pocket and found a piece of a fat brown crayon that he'd taken from one of his own classrooms. Holding it in his fist, he scrawled an obscenity on the wall of the house, careful not to click the crayon against the wooden siding. Then he stepped up onto the porch and peered in through the front window, at the old furniture, the bits and pieces of their hateful, pitiful lives.

At that moment, like the tip of a knife blade, it occurred to him that Ivy lay somewhere inside, sound asleep. His head spun, and he staggered from the porch, still clutching the crayon. The pole lay on the lawn in the moonlight. Had he dropped it? His mind was murky again, and he realized that he was drooling. He wiped his mouth with his sleeve, and then, in obedience to whatever dark urges filled him like black water in a well, he picked up the pole and raised the hook toward the strand of lights.

Yank them down and get out! He leaped, hooking the strand, his weight tearing it loose from the eaves. He ran farther along the side of the house and yanked again. The lights swung, clattering against the siding, and he pulled again, throwing his weight into it. The cord snapped, and he sprawled backward, the lights blacking out.

He crouched on his hands and knees in the wet grass, panting like a dog. A light blinked on in the motor home parked in the driveway. He scuttled forward, out of view, crouching behind an overgrown camellia. There was the creak of the motor home door opening and the shuffling of bedroom slippers on concrete. Carefully, he parted the limbs and looked through the camellia. An old man stood on the sidewalk, wearing a bathrobe, looking around warily. He came along a few steps, then started up the neighbor's driveway, adjacent to the row of shrubbery. Argyle stood very still. He was deep in the shadows, dressed in dark clothing, well hidden. The old man wouldn't see him. He licked his lips, reaching slowly into his coat and putting his hand on the can of pepper spray in the inside pocket.

The old man looked straight at him – at the camellia, at the string of lights lying along the ground, draped across the shrubbery. He stepped gingerly across the wet lawn, toward the fallen pole. Argyle held his breath, slowly removing the can of spray from his coat. He licked his lips, anticipating the old man's reaction, the doubling up, the wheezing, the grunt of surprise when it blinded him …

The old man stood looking down at the pole, then nudged it with his foot, as if it were a snake. He looked again at the torn-down lights, figuring things out. Argyle carefully slid his hand through the branches, leaning forward and holding onto the trunk as the old man bent over to pick up the pole. There was a clear shot with the spray, straight into his eyes.

But just then the old man noticed the crayon writing on the wall. He stood up and stepped back, then turned around and hurried out to the sidewalk, disappearing past the corner of the house. Argyle stepped out of the bushes and peered toward the driveway, watching as the old man headed toward the backyard – toward an unlocked back door! He was going to waken the house!

Argyle grabbed the pole and ran, as quietly as he could, glancing back at the windows of the motor home for the telltale movement of curtains. He felt exposed, as if the dark windows of the houses were eyes watching him lope away, and again he was swept with the knowledge that he had risked everything, chanced Hell itself. He was suddenly nauseated, and he turned his head, twisting over, unable to prevent himself from being sick on his own pants and shoe. He dodged past the hedge, into the mouth of the alley, out of sight now, sick again – wildly, uncontrollably sick.

He ripped the car door open, falling onto the seat and starting the engine, backing wildly out of the parking stall and looking hard back toward the Stebbinses' house. A light was on in an upstairs room. They were awake. Were they calling the police?

He shifted into drive and moved away up the alley, turning right onto the first street, finally calming down, taking possession of himself again. Abruptly he recalled that he had nearly hosed the old man down with pepper spray. Why? Purely for pleasure, he thought. For fun. An unaccountable urge.

He passed slowly across the end of the block where the Stebbins house lay. The old man stood looking at the crayon mark, gesturing at the fallen lights. Stebbins stood next to him, his hands on his hips. Argyle's mood shifted again, and he smiled. At that instant Stebbins swiveled around and looked toward the corner, straight at him. Stebbins pointed, cocking his head. Argyle half expected him to take off running, to pursue him on foot, in which case …

He'd knock him down and run over his head!

He burst into laughter, unable to contain himself. Stebbins just stood there, wearing an idiotic nightshirt, his mouth open in disbelief. Argyle swung around onto his own street. Still laughing, he pushed the switch on his garage door opener and pulled into the dark garage, the door swishing closed behind the car.

27

The Reverend Bentley drove slowly past St Anthony's Church, where the bell tower was still cordoned off. They would apparently have to get a crane to hoist the fallen bell back up into place, and that would require pulling the top of the tower apart. And none of it could be done until after probes by police and insurance investigators, who couldn't have the slightest idea who or what to look for. The bells might be out of commission for months, which left the single bell over at Holy Spirit to chase out all the demons in Old Towne. At least Mahoney knew what he was up against. Desecrating Mahoney's sacristy had been one thing – almost infantile, really, the work of a madman. But this business at St Anthony's, the murder of poor Simms – and now the damned jars – all that was something else entirely.

'You might as well have murdered Simms yourself,' he said out loud.

This time he didn't contradict himself. It didn't do any good anyway. He'd gone round and round with it for years. He'd rationalized it. He'd wrestled with guilt, trying to deny that what was coming to pass was his fault. And now he had Argyle's check in the church safe. What would he do if Argyle combusted tonight, was simply gone out of the world? Would his money be too dirty to use? He had already committed a sin by taking it; how, exactly, would it compound things to spend it once Argyle had gone to Hell? It occurred to him that he might have held out for twice what he'd asked, but he pushed the idea out of his mind.

He turned left at the light on Cambridge, driving slowly, watching the houses along the east side of the street, looking for signs of anybody out and about. It was just past four in the morning – nearly the same hour that the bastards had gotten to Father Mahoney.

He pulled up to the curb and cut the engine, then sat in the dark car and waited, watching clouds boil across the sky. In the light of the streetlamp, raindrops swooped down toward the windshield. Bentley had spent the last two hours loading sandwiches into Ziploc bags for the church's Backdoor Lunch – one hundred and thirty-four of them, made out of bread donated by the local day-old shop. Each bagged sandwich went into a paper sack along with an apple and a foil packet of pretzels – lunch for the homeless. It was nearly the end of the pretzels. He'd have to go around to the Elks on Friday night and ask them to ante up another couple of cases. The sliced deli ham had come out of pitiful cash, as he liked to call it, and so had the apples. Usually Mrs Hepplewhite made the sandwiches, but she'd spent the night with Mrs Simms ...

Argyle's front porch light was on. Bentley decided to sit there for a few moments and scope things out. He that hasteth with his feet sinneth, he told himself, but actually he simply felt monumentally tired, and it seemed to him that he could easily lie down in bed and simply never get up again.

Last night, after his chat with Mahoney, he had spent two hours going over the books at the church. Doing good works wasn't cheap. Mahoney had understood that part of it. He was locked into a mortgage that had looked pretty reasonable just a few years ago, but now it was a buyer's market again, and you could find comparable buildings all over town for two-thirds the money. And besides that, the place was falling apart. It needed paint, plumbing; the electrical wiring was like an illustration out of a fire-prevention manual.

The rain came down in a deluge, and he switched off the wipers, listening to it beat against the roof of the car. That did it. Between the rain and the porch light and very nearly no sleep at all last night, it just wasn't a good morning for the business of spying on Argyle. Bentley was too damned tired to get wet. He reached for the ignition key, but just then, as if it were a message, a light blinked on inside the house.

Argyle was up before dawn again, like a man who had desperately important work to do. Bentley slid across the seat, eased the passenger door open, and slid out, shutting the door as silently as he could before jogging toward the side of the house in a crouch. He ducked in among the hibiscus and tree ferns, pushing his way through them until he was well hidden from the street.

Rain dripped from the brim of his hat as he crept forward, edging past a gas meter, pushing in among the rain-heavy fronds of a fern. The window shade was up a good inch, and the window itself was open. He could see the entirety of the room inside: books, stuffed chairs, an old table scattered with junk. On the floor lay what looked for all the world like a cross between a packing crate and a coffin. It was empty. Argyle was sitting in a chair, dressed in a pair of red pajamas, his back toward the window. He was utterly still, as if he'd just gotten out of bed to fall asleep in the chair. But there was something rigid and grotesque about his posture, as if he was a lifelike wooden puppet.

The moments passed. Bentley turned up his collar against the rain. This was worthless. He would catch pneumonia watching Argyle asleep in a chair ...

Argyle moved. His arm jerked upward spastically, like the arm of a man snatching at a fly, then flopped down again, the palm slapping against the arm of the chair with a sort of limp-wristed determination. He repeated the movement, started to rise, then slumped back down, his head lolling forward now so that his chin pressed against his chest. His neck was a grotesque, almost larval white against the red of the pajamas, and his hair, mussed up with sleep, seemed to sprout from the white scalp in tufts. The head bobbed, as if he were listening to inaudible music.

He's *drunk*, Bentley thought – and at four in the morning! Argyle's head swiveled from side to side then, unnaturally again, as if he had a crick in his neck that he was trying to work out, but couldn't. No, he wasn't drunk. He was in the grip of some kind of fit. A grand mal seizure? He tried to stand, but sat back down hard, and Bentley could hear the sound of gibbering now. A rush of laughter followed the gibbering, and then a low moaning, almost like a foghorn.

In a frightful rush, Bentley understood the truth. What he had feared had finally come to pass: like Murray LeRoy had been, Argyle was possessed, inhabited, manipulated by demons. 'Lord have mercy,' Bentley whispered.

Argyle stood up now, swaying on his feet like a marionette. Shakily, slowly, he reached up and jerked out a fistful of his own hair. Clutching it in his hand, he shuffled across the carpet, making a noise like flies buzzing against a window, one hesitant step at a time, until he slammed his foot into the wooden box on the floor and pitched forward across it like a stuffed dummy, where he lay heaving, his face mashed into the carpet, ghastly noises wheezing out of him. Then abruptly he fell still, apparently dead or comatose.

Bentley crouched there speechless, nearly unable to move. Rain swept in under the house eaves, thudding against his shoulders. He shivered in the chill air, certain that he had just witnessed a man's damnation, that Argyle had quite simply gone to Hell.

What did this require of Bentley? He was a minister, a man of God. Had he been led to this window merely to witness Argyle's descent into damnation? He felt tiny, exposed to the wind and rain and cold, and the darkness settled around him pitilessly, like an accusation.

He saw something then, dimly through the nearly closed door at the opposite side of the room – a shadow approaching, as if along a hallway. Someone else was in the house! He ducked out of sight, then peered up over the sill at the very corner of the window, keeping well back out of the way. His hands shook against the wooden sill as the door to the room swung open slowly, as if the intruder were doubtful, wondering what he might find. Whoever it was paused there in the shadows, then stepped forward into the room. Light from the ceiling lamp fell across his face …

Bentley croaked out a hoarse cry and fell over backward, tearing fronds off the trunk of the tree fern and scrabbling in the muddy flowerbed on his hands and knees as the rain pummeled his back and shoulders. He crawled along the side of the house, blinking the water out of his eyes. A hibiscus limb snatched off his hat, and he groped for it blindly, clutching it in his hand now and reeling forward, suddenly free of the shrubbery and staggering through the rain toward his car. He tore the car door open, slid in behind the wheel, and started the engine, glancing backward as he accelerated up the rainswept street, half expecting Argyle's corpse-pale face to peer out through the lighted window.

For it had been Argyle himself who had come out of the shadowed hallway and into the room, carrying two glasses of orange juice and dressed in red pajamas identical to the pair worn by the dead man on the floor.

28

The newspaper lay in the bushes that morning, hidden from view, just like he'd asked. It was early. The paperboy must have set the alarm for 3AM! Not bad for a dead bird in a jar, he thought. He smiled uneasily. Of course it was just coincidence …

But what if it wasn't? He stood on the sidewalk and thought about it, looking down the empty street toward the church. First the tomatoes, now the newspaper. The bluebird of happiness was apparently granting his wishes. The idea was lunatic, and he chuckled now, thinking about it. A man runs across a magical charm, Aladdin's lamp, and he gives its genie full rein, casting spells and calling down wishes. Does the man conquer kingdoms, attain vast power, amass a fortune? No, he makes the genie work out on newspapers and tomato vines, uses it to control the ant problem in the kitchen.

So give it back to Argyle, he told himself suddenly, and his smile faded. This idea had slipped into his mind as if out of nowhere: essentially he had *stolen* it, hadn't he? And normally he didn't *steal* things. And he didn't lie, either. And now he was up to his ears in both these crimes.

But hell, there wasn't anything *normal* about this. Here he was confronted by liars and cheats, with Argyle's baloney and the giant grinning postal inspector with eyes like a sand hog. Whose rules was he supposed to play by? What if a man found a grocery sack full of money in the bushes, and he *knew*, say, that it was dirty money, drug money – a lot of wrinkled fifties and hundreds, utterly untraceable. What would he do with it? Advertise? 'Attn, scum, found yr money in a shrub …' How *could* that be the right thing to do, in any way you could explain in under an hour? And anyway, this wasn't a bag full of money, it was just a dead bird pickled by some Third-World trinket company with an arcane sense of humor.

Unless of course it wasn't.

The door to the motor home swung open and Henry looked out, fumbling with his eyeglasses and dressed in a pair of pajamas and floppy-looking slippers. He spotted Walt out on the sidewalk and gave him the high sign.

'Paper?' Walt asked him. He stepped toward him across the wet lawn, pulling off the plastic wrapper and handing it over. *There*, he thought, abruptly relieved of his burden. It's out of my hands now. Like giving the sack of dirty money to the church, it expiates the living daylights out of the sin.

Henry looked at the paper, then tried to hand it back. He was too much of a gentleman to take it. 'Go ahead,' he whispered, clearly not wanting to wake up Jinx. 'You first. I can work a crossword or something.'

'No, heck,' Walt said. 'I've got work to do anyway.'

'Well, here. Take the sports or something. What do you read first? Financial page?'

'Not a thing,' Walt lied. 'I'm just going to stuff boxes with it. You might as well take a look at it first.'

'If you're sure ...'

'Sure I'm sure.'

'Thanks,' Henry said. He nodded and then shut the door, and Walt found himself standing in a fresh drizzle, his newspaper gone. Well, this took care of it. He could quit agonizing over the damned bluebird. Apparently the creature didn't work after all; he hadn't gotten his wish, had he?

He headed for the garage and cranked up the space heater, then climbed up the ladder and had a look in the rafters. Spotting the tin box, he reached in among the fishing tackle and pulled it out, opening the lid and sniffing the ginlike aroma that wafted out of it. The bird itself wasn't nearly as deteriorated as he remembered it. Its feathers were almost glossy now, a bright, clear blue, and its eyes were open and alert. Well, not alert, for heaven's sake. There was no use getting nutty about it.

He thought suddenly of the demons hightailing it out of Pandora's box, and he replaced the jar and shut the lid again, shoving it back in among the salmon eggs and the fishing lures, then stuffed the tackle box back into the rafters. Maybe later he would find an even safer place for it.

He climbed down and poured a cup of coffee, then sorted through the half dozen mail-order catalogues that had arrived in yesterday's junk mail – the competition. Walt was on every address list in the country by now. It fascinated him to think of it: his name and address reproducing itself like a slow virus along with thousands and millions of other addresses – long lists of them sold back and forth as if they were eggs in a basket instead of words and numbers. Somewhere, right now, enterprising people were pulling down a staggering fortune buying and selling names. The concept was almost mystical, sublunar capitalism in the information age.

Two months ago he himself had paid good money for three lists of a thousand addresses each – seven cents per address – which was about all the catalogue production and mailing he could afford to do right now. There was forty pages of offset printing along with darkroom work, collating, stapling, addressing, and bulk-rate postage, which added up to more than two thousand dollars per catalogue, and the cold truth was that within three weeks of the catalogue's coming out, orders dwindled nearly to nothing, and it was time to put out another one that was in some clear way different from the last, and him wondering all the time whether he ought to hustle another thousand addresses in order to expand things generally. But he had no real idea how much was too much – how many catalogues, how much inventory. It wasn't like planting corn; in the business of catalogue sales, the relationship between sowing and reaping was in no way clear. Probably Dr Hefernin could sell him a pamphlet on the subject.

He found the current Archie McPhee catalogue, one of his favorites, and the American Science and Surplus catalogue, which was offering overstock Water Weenies right there on the first page along with dental burs, radiation gloves, and something called a 'Toilet Seat Alarm,' the purpose of which wasn't made clear. There were sixty-five pages crammed with this kind of stuff, half of it electronic. Walt envied the hell out of that kind of inventory. His little collection of rubber skeletons and palm-tree hats was pitiful in comparison. Now that the tin shed was up, though, he could expand a little bit, make fewer trips out to the wholesale warehouses in Bellflower.

One of the catalogues was new to him – something called *The Captain Grose Collection*. It was expensively done, full color, offering 'antiquities and religious relics and reproductions of all natures, direct from the East.'

Walt sipped his coffee, fingering through the catalogue with idle interest at first, then with growing disbelief. It offered hundreds of sacred and sanctified relics: fragments of the true cross, vials of tears from a dozen different sources including the Savior himself, links of the chain that bound St Peter, droplets of blood from an inventory of martyrs two pages long, wine from the marriage at Cana, toenail parings from the apostles, Tubalcain's fire fender, the brass-shod broomstick of the Witch of Endor, one of the seven golden lampstands, a tooth from Balaam's ass, the preserved ears and snout of one of the Gadarene swine, a chip of the stone that the builder refused ...

He burst into laughter and shut the catalogue. This *had* to be a joke, an impossibly elaborate, lowball prank. But who on earth ...? He looked at the cover again, trying to estimate how much it had cost to print – the slick, full-color cover, the high-quality paper. It was put out by something called 'Millennialist Products, Ltd' He checked the address – Santa Ana! It was a local company. Immediately he thought of Dr Hefernin, but this wasn't in his line. In fact, this had a family resemblance to the stuff in Argyle's misdelivered box. Maybe it wasn't a prank after all.

Suddenly suspicious, he opened the catalogue again. A number of the items had no price – apparently you had to call an 800 number to inquire.

The priced items were classified as 'reproductions' that were 'strict copies' of originals in the Captain Grose Collection, with which these replicas were 'kept in close association.'

About halfway through the catalogue the listings changed, and instead of sacred relics and reproductions there was a list, much shorter, of 'profane' relics, 'offered strictly in the spirit of scientific inquiry.'

This clearly *was* the stuff in Argyle's box: the 'dead mans grease,' the twigs from the 'tree of living flesh,' figures of saints carved out of their own finger bones and preserved in oil, vials of blood ...

Walt dialed the number on the back of the catalogue. It was impossibly early, not even seven. Obviously no one would be there, although possibly they'd have a voice-mail ordering system ...

A man answered. 'Dilworth Catalogue Sales. Twenty-four-hour service.'

Walt was bowled over. *Dilworth!* Argyle after all! Nothing in the catalogue had ... 'Hello,' he said, scrambling to find something more to say, to keep the man on the line.

'What can I do for you?'

'I'm calling about the catalogue,' Walt said. 'The relics catalogue.'

'Mastercard, Visa, or American Express? There's a fourteen-dollar minimum. Any order over thirty dollars receives the "Get Out of Hell Free" card at absolutely no cost whatsoever.' The man's voice was perfunctory, as if he had reeled this nonsense off a hundred times that morning already. 'Are you interested in the card? I'll mark the appropriate box on the order form.'

Walt laughed out loud. 'I'll take ten,' he said.

'No can do,' the man said to him. 'One per customer. Nobody needs more than one anyway, do they?'

'Of course not,' Walt said. The man was serious! 'Just a little joke. Not very funny.'

'Mastercard, Visa, or American Express?'

'Visa,' Walt said hurriedly. Apparently the man wasn't in a joking mood. He thought about hanging up but he held on instead, thumbing through the catalogue, looking through the reproductions for something cheap. Hell, he could write it off. It was business. And it was only thirty bucks, after all, give or take. No way he was going to miss out on the free card. He reeled off his Visa number and expiration date.

'Delivery address?'

He gave the man his address.

'I need the description, catalogue number, quantity, and price, in that order,' the man said.

'All right. Let's see. Send me the "Ever-burning Brimstone," number S-883, quantity one, $8.95, and the "Reproduction Golden Lampstand," Q-452, quantity one, $26.50. Now what is that exactly? – the lampstand?'

'Revelations 1, verse 12.'

'Ah,' Walt said. 'From Revelations. Somehow I remember that those were *candlesticks*, but what you've got is lampstands?'

'The catalogue number you gave me is lampstands. That's Revised Standard Version. King James is candlesticks. Now, if you want the candlesticks instead of the lampstand, we offer those too, but they're a little more pricey, although they do come with good candles – aromatic.'

'No,' Walt said. 'That sounds nice, but I think I prefer the lampstand. I just can't … *Surely* it must be one or the other?'

'It's our policy to please the customer.'

Walt nearly hung up again. This was blatantly fraudulent. Fraud with its mask torn off. A moment ago the whole thing was funny; now he felt like a credulous fool. 'Look,' Walt said, 'what's the deal here? Seriously.'

After a moment the man said, 'What do you *think* the deal is?'

'To tell you the truth,' Walt said, 'I think I'm getting hosed.'

'Well, then that's the truth. You're getting hosed.'

'That's it?'

'Let's put it this way – sometimes you get what you *think* you pay for. It's like that here. All I can tell you is that we've had a *lot* of satisfied customers. You might be one of them, or you might be one of the other. The choice is yours. The choice is always yours.'

There was something about this speech that took the wind out of Walt's sails. Whatever else was true about Dilworth Catalogue Sales, this man clearly believed in it on some fundamental level. He was a salesman, not a shyster.

'Shall I enter this?' the man asked.

'Yeah,' Walt said. 'I guess so. What's the total?'

'That's $35.45 plus tax plus two dollars shipping … that's $40.10.'

'Great,' Walt said. 'Don't forget the card.'

'It's already on the order form – no extra charge.'

Walt hung up. He had just paid forty dollars for junk. It was a damned good thing that Ivy was going to work for Argyle. Lord knows how they'd get the bills paid otherwise.

He razored open a box and pulled out the contents, plastic bags full of dollhouse furniture – not the usual plastic trash, but high-toned wooden furniture, mouse-size. There were even little rolled-up rag rugs. He sold the heck out of these to dollhouse fanatics, usually adults crazy for little bitty things.

The motor home door slammed shut, and he looked out in time to see Jinx cutting across toward the front porch. The world was waking up.

'Bluebird,' Walt said, glancing toward the rafters just in case it was necessary, 'fetch me my golden lampstand this very day, a quarter hour before the sun reacheth the zenith.' He chuckled a little bit, as if to imply that what he'd said was a sort of joke.

29

'And what about the testimonials for the Sensible Investor? I don't want the same crowd we ran through the Startup America meetings last year. They'll be all right up in San Jose in the spring, but we'd be in bad shape if one of them was recognized as a ringer. We need some new faces. And tone it down, too. This is the nineties. A couple of years ago the public believed any damned thing. Now they don't want risk.'

Argyle studied himself in the mirror. He hadn't gotten a good night's sleep in weeks now. And he had a splitting headache. His late-night forays into the neighborhood inevitably made his head ache as if he'd been hit with a club. And the voices – the satanic gibbering and muttering in his nightmares, like someone had opened a door onto Hell …

'The testimonial crowd is entirely new,' the man on the other end of the line said tiredly. 'New faces, new stories. Don Little over at the temp agency worked that out along with the gimmick. You'd have to look hard to spot any kind of pyramid element. I'm surprised nobody got back to you with the prospectus.'

'I am too,' Argyle said flatly. But then he remembered. In fact someone *had* gotten back to him – weeks ago. He'd forgotten it, put the paperwork away in a drawer. His mind just wasn't with it somehow. Business kept getting shunted aside by this damned …

Abruptly he had the uncanny feeling that someone was looking at him, a feeling so profound that he swiveled around in his chair and looked behind him, although it was impossible: the wall was windowless, only three or four feet away. There was a sound in his ears like the rushing of wind and a creaking like a heavy body swinging slowly on a wooden gallows. Sweat ran into his collar as he sat staring, tensed, his head pounding, waiting for something to happen. Slowly he opened the bottom desk drawer. There were four jars in it, from LeRoy's collection. He untwisted one of the lids, releasing the sigh of breath, the last exhalation of life trapped within.

The sounds faded and disappeared. The presence in the room evaporated. There was nothing behind him but framed diplomas and thank-you trophies from Little League and from kids' soccer teams.

'Are you there?'

'Yeah,' he said into the phone. He looked at his list, trying to concentrate. 'What about the orphans?'

'They're gangbusters. We got IRS approval last week. The photo layouts are perfect – Filipino girl about four years old, crying at the edge of this vast dump, scrounging for garbage. She's got enormous eyes, like a kid in one of those paintings. Big crocodile tears.'

'Where'd you find her?'

'The girl? Pasadena. The photo shoot was at some kind of landfill out in Whittier. We trucked in a lot of crap to set it up right – rags and bottles and rotten fruit, that kind of thing. Big mountain of it. Looks like a typical third-world dump. Anyway, the girl's got this little busted-up basket with – get this – an old brown banana and a stuffed doggy in it. We took a rock and beat the hell out of the doggy, yanked its eye out, really made it look loved. It's purely pitiful. Girl's mother's a maid for Benson up there. You remember Jim Benson?'

'Benson?' Argyle groped through his mind, trying to remember the name. The words 'yanked its eye out' echoed in his head, going around like a nursery-rhyme refrain. 'Didn't Benson threaten to go to the press over the coupon giveaway? I thought he met with a couple of broken legs.'

'That was *Benton*, with a *T*. He's up in Camarillo now, state hospital, completely mental. This is the guy who did that great PR package for "Get Rich Yesterday."'

'How about the maid and the girl? Are they all right?'

'We put them on a plane back to Manila. No chance the mother will ever see the ads.'

'I didn't mean all right that way. I mean *happy*. The kid. The little girl.'

'Happy?'

'Yeah. Did you take care of her? I don't *use* children, not unless they're imaginary children.'

'Sure, we took care of her. Absolutely. We gave the mother two one-way tickets and a thousand bucks – a choice between that and deportation.'

'Send her another thousand. Five thousand. And the same in trust for the girl. And call George Mifflin in Manila. Tell him to keep an eye on both of them.'

'Whatever you say.'

'That's what I say. What kind of ads have we got?'

'Twenty-four so far, all in slick magazines. Save the starving orphans – the usual deal. Pathetic enough to make you cry. It'll draw like rotten meat. Beats the hell out of the legitimate ads, I can tell you that.'

'Good. That's it?' He could hear the creaking again, as if there were ghost children on the swings outside, and he realized that it was far hotter in the room than it should be. There was rain pattering against the windows now. He loosened his tie and unbuttoned his shirt, looking around uneasily. He could swear something was *here*, in the room, now.

Three more jars in the drawer.

'One more thing quick,' the man said. 'Benson's got a dynamite idea for an estate liquidation ploy. He wants me to run it past you.'

'Shoot.' Argyle looked at the desktop, working hard to listen. There was static on the phone, and the voice seemed to come from a long way away, as if the man were speaking on a string-and-can phone from some other room.

'Basically you donate your dead parents' estate,' he was saying, 'especially properties. The money goes – get this – *to buy wilderness land.* We run up a color brochure showing "holdings in trust" – so many million acres of north-west wilderness. Pictures of moose, buffalo, long article about the threat to the national parks system, mining, grazing, sale of public lands …'

Argyle lost track of what the man was saying. He loosened his tie and unbuttoned his shirt at his neck. His mouth was dry and his scalp itched, and he felt a vast pressure rising up within him, as if in another forty seconds he would simply explode. He tried to ignore it.

'We punch all the rich liberal buttons,' the man said, 'tap all the eco-fears, if you follow me. Guarantee your children's natural birthright into perpetuity and get a hell of a big tax write-off too. We do the whole scam Ponzi-style. Keep enough liquid income to cover ourselves in case we actually need to buy a little property. How fast can these people die, anyway? And we can show the inheritors the same piece of land over and over. It's foolproof. You got anything to add?'

'Add? I'd work Indians into it. That's always good. Picture of some old dead chief.

'Of course. We might risk the life insurance angle, too. That works like crazy for nursing homes and mausoleums; there's no reason it won't work for us …'

'Right,' Argyle said hurriedly. The room seemed to shake now, as if from heavy footfalls. The phone receiver thrummed in his hand. 'That's fine. Save the details for some other time.'

'All right. Now, on the 900 numbers. The crystal readings never got off the blocks. Standard psychic stuff is still the bread and butter. Soft porn's holding its own. That kind of thing's established, you know, but this fad stuff … What I'm saying is if it's current, then we've got to get on top of it quicker, get the product out there …' The man's voice droned on, running down accounts. '… breakfast cereal,' he said. '… computerized fortune cookie messages, garden-ing tips, dating service, Zantar the Psychic …'

'What?' Argyle was lost, baffled. His mind spun. He was hot, feverish. Was the man talking gibberish? 'Wait.' He croaked the word out, laying the phone down without punching the hold button. He put his hands to his ears, trying to press out the rushing and creaking, which had sprung up again as if some-one had put a cassette tape in the stereo. The sensation of being on view increased by the moment, and he looked around wildly, at the windows, at the lamp-lit playground equipment beyond, at the murky, shadowed corners of the office. He felt shrunken, tiny, like a specimen insect in a glass jar. The very air vibrated, and he was seized with panic, with the wild desire to run. Did he hear a bell tolling?

The windows ran with rainwater, and what had sounded like the rush of wind had evened into the unmistakable exhalation of heavy breathing. He felt a stirring against the back of his neck, as if someone stood very close behind him now, whispering softly.

He didn't dare turn around, but reached into the drawer again, turning the lid from one of the jars. There was a fleeting cry, swallowed immediately in the noise and the shaking. He opened another, and the spirit fled, the presence in the room undiminished, ravenous.

He was hot, burning up inside, his very cells on fire. Slowly he stood up, desperate simply to leave, to get out into the rain and the wind. He took a careful step toward the door. His shoulders hunched forward, retracting from the presence at his back. He knew damned well who it was. *What* it was. There was a stench of something burning, something sulphurous, and tendrils of smoke curled up from the carpet beneath his feet. With a wild shriek he lurched forward and grabbed the doorknob, which throbbed like a live thing. He slammed against the door with his shoulder, whimpering and shaking with terror. The door held. He was trapped!

Something wet slithered against his neck like the tongue of a lizard, and he screamed out loud, taking the knob in both hands and twisting it, falling to his knees on the carpet, his eyes screwed shut …

And the door swung inward, bumping gently against his knee. He opened his eyes. Abruptly the noises ceased, the presence in the room evaporated like steam. He heard the sound of rain against the window again. God almighty! He'd been out of his mind with fear, *pushing* on the door instead of pulling!

He realized then that the hallway outside the office door was full of children and their mothers, and he quickly pushed the door shut again. He took a long, shuddering breath and stood up, and right then he felt the wet fabric of his pants against the skin of his legs. He looked down, horrified. He'd wet himself in his terror.

The phone receiver still lay on the table, where he'd dropped it. His hands shook so badly that he could barely pick it up. 'You still there?'

'Yeah,' the man said. 'Everything all right over there?'

'Fine,' Argyle said, his voice husky. 'There's nothing wrong here. The storm's apparently got the phones all screwed up. Listen, you keep up the good work. I've got a meeting.'

'Good enough. I'll have Don send over a copy of the Sensible Investor prospectus. Anything else?'

The window lit up just then, and almost at the same time there was a crack of thunder that shook the walls.

'No,' Argyle said. He hung up the telephone and picked up his coat from the back of the chair. Holding it in front of his crotch, he stepped out of the door and into the hallway, where, for some unholy reason, Walt Stebbins sat in a chair by the receptionist's desk, filling out papers.

30

Ivy and Jinx left at seven-thirty, heading down to Watson's for breakfast, and Henry sneaked away down the sidewalk not five minutes later without saying a word to Walt, who felt as if he were surrounded by plots. Everybody had some kind of iron in the fire this morning – capitalism, hula-hula women, crayon graffiti – and he was left with the mundane chores. At eight he had to haul the kids over to the preschool and get them signed up, whatever that entailed, then stop at the grocery store on the way to the Old Hill Mailbox, where he'd ship the morning's UPS packages.

It had been a mistake to tell Ivy about having seen Argyle out driving around the neighborhood at the time of the vandalism. She had accused him outright of jealousy. Jealousy! Argyle's vandalizing the house had been beyond her understanding, but it wasn't beyond Walt's – although, clearly, what he understood he couldn't tell her.

The television was going in the house, and he could hear the sound of a rinky-dink cartoon jingle. The melody was vaguely familiar – from ages ago. A wave of nostalgia struck him, and he stopped to listen, laying the tape dispenser on the bench. It was Spunky and Tadpole! Great God almighty, he thought, in *this* day and age? Full of a sudden curious joy, he went out through the garage door and looked in at the window. Nora and Eddie sprawled on the floor in that weird rubber-legged way kids have, half sitting and half kneeling. They stared fixedly at the screen, Nora's head bobbing time to the music. Walt heard her laugh out loud and point; it was Tadpole, all right, just then coming along the road, carrying a fishing pole with a bigheaded fish on it. The fish was apparently dead, because his eyes were X'd out.

Walt abruptly recalled last night's adventure in the kitchen – Nora and Eddie setting out to make bubble castles in the sink. Why the hell had he broken it up so quickly and sent them to bed? Only one damned reason: monkey business; that's what Ivy had called it. Well, fat lot of good it had done anybody. He wished now that he had let the kids have a few minutes with the bubbles. Ten minutes would have seemed an eternity to them, nothing to him.

He could remember the long cartoon mornings when he was that age: the cold cereal, television programs stacked end to end like books on a shelf, the clock on the wall nearly falling asleep … It was one of the wild, doomed luxuries of childhood. Say what you want, but Spunky and Tadpole were vital in a way that was as huge as the sky, and so were bubbles in the sink.

He realized now that Nora was watching him through the window, making her rabbit face, and he waved at her before turning around and hurrying back into the garage, where he grabbed one of the plastic bags full of miniature furniture, and headed out toward the avocado tree, the sun shining in the east. The air was sharp and clear, and he sucked in a big lungful as he peeked under the flowerpot. The daddy longlegs was crouched against the roof. There was a ragged web spun against the back wall with a couple of tiny flies already wound up in it, waiting to be sucked dry. One of the trapped flies wiggled a little bit, but struggling was useless.

'Hello, Mr Argyle,' Walt said to the spider. 'Top o' the morning to you.' The spider seemed to retract at the sound of his voice, flattening itself into the corner. Walt wondered if he had a duty to the fly that was still alive; but probably there was no practical purpose in trying to do anything for it. And whatever moral value there would be in such a kindness was vague. Holding the pot carefully so as not to disturb the spider any more than necessary, he set two tiny chairs and a table onto the shelf and spread the little woven rug on the floor. Then he swiveled the pot around so that the broken-out section faced outward before he lowered the thing down over the furniture.

He returned to the garage, where he slipped a flashlight into his pocket. Then he looked in through the window again. The cartoon was just ending. Walt opened the back door and gestured to Nora and Eddie. 'Put your shoes on,' he said. 'I want to show you something.'

'Oh!' Nora said breathlessly, leaping up. Desperately she searched the floor with her eyes, holding one hand to her mouth. What she was looking for wasn't at all clear. 'What kind is it?' She looked wide-eyed at Walt.

'No kind,' Walt said. 'Just something. Out under the tree.'

Eddie leaned out and picked up Nora's shoes, which were in plain sight, and calmly handed them to her. She seemed relieved, as if a mystery had been cleared up. Eddie put on his own shoes without a word, carefully double-knotting the laces.

They followed Walt out through the door, across the wet grass. In the bright sunlight, rainwater steamed off the lawn in a mist. 'It'll be summer by noon,' Walt said, patting Nora's shoulder. She smiled big at him and nodded. 'Look here.' Walt pointed at a snail, heading for the dead herb garden. 'This is Mr Binion.'

'He has a name?' Nora asked. Eddie didn't look at the snail, but studied the palm of his hand.

'Oh, yes,' Walt said. 'There are many animals that live in these old neigh-borhoods.' He suddenly remembered his success with last night's story, and he cast his voice low and serious, waving his hand, taking it all in. 'At night,' he said, 'possums and raccoons use these fences as roads, going from one house to another in search of food. In the spring, toads appear from out of ditches, and families of salamanders come to live under fallen logs.'

'*What* kind?' Nora asked, squishing up her face. Eddie picked up a bent stick that had fallen from the avocado tree and swung it like a baseball bat. He looked away, deadpan, staring at some spot in the sky now.

'What kind of what?' Walt asked.

'Those things.'

'Salamanders?'

Nora nodded.

'Do you know what a salamander is?' Walt asked. Nora shook her head.

'It's a sort of newt.'

'Oh.'

'Like a lizard,' Eddie said helpfully.

'And like toads?' Nora asked.

'Kind of,' Walt said. 'A toad is its cousin. And do you know what?'

'What?' Nora whispered now.

Walt squinted at her. 'There was a toad out here last week that was wearing a hat and coat.'

'Oh!' Nora cried.

'And a mouse with a vest on. And spectacles.'

She covered her mouth with her hand, as if to keep from shouting out loud. Eddie rolled his eyes.

'What?' Walt said to Eddie. 'You don't believe me?'

Eddie shook his head, grinning faintly.

'I'll bet you a plug nickel,' Walt said. 'Try me.'

'Bet him!' Nora shouted. 'Bet him, Eddie!'

Eddie shook his head, still grinning.

'Well, let's just see, then.' Walt led the way into the garden shed, pretending to search around among the shovels and rakes. Nora followed him, taking exaggerated steps and biting her bottom lip. Eddie swung his stick with one hand, as if it were a sword now.

'What's this?' Walt said. He stopped in his tracks, double-taking at the overturned flower pot. 'What have we here?'

'What is it?' Nora said. 'The snail?'

'It's a *pot*,' Eddie said.

Walt pulled the flashlight out of his pocket and switched it on, then shined it in through the jagged door in the side of the pot. He could see the doll fur-niture in there. 'What on earth? Nora, take a closer look.'

Nora stepped forward, glancing at him wide-eyed, then stood on tiptoe and peered into the hole in the pot. Her breath caught. She'd seen it. Very slowly she turned toward Walt. 'Something's house,' she whispered.

Walt nodded. 'It's the house of the amazing Mr Argyle.' He motioned to Eddie. 'Have a look-see.' He held the light on the hole.

Eddie looked in, and Nora clutched his arm, trying to get in close enough to take another look herself. 'Don't pig up,' she whispered. And then, with his free hand, Eddie reached up and grasped the top of the pot, upending it, exposing the doll furniture, the quivering web, the buzzing little fly wound in gauze. The spider, big around as a silver dollar with its legs fully extended, rushed down the side of the pot and out onto Eddie's wrist. Nora screamed, leaping backward into Walt, and Eddie hooted with wild surprise, flinging the flowerpot into the fence and raking the stick down his arm to dislodge the spider. It fell into the dirt, and Eddy drew the stick back and slammed it down, yelling, 'Shit! Shit! Shit!' and flailing at the spider until the stick broke off short in his hand.

Nora shook with spasms of fear and shock, and Walt hugged her, trying to calm her down. Eddie stomped on the spider, or where the spider had been, grinding it into the dirt until he worked all the wild terror out of himself. Then he stood there breathing heavily, looking at the ground as if for signs of movement.

'I think you got him,' Walt said after a moment.

'What *was* he?' Nora asked, calming down now that the threat was passed.

'Daddy longlegs,' Walt said.

'A daddy?'

'A *spider*,' Eddie said.

'Is he Mr Argyle?' Nora asked. 'Like you said?'

'No,' Walt lied. 'I don't know what he's done with Mr Argyle.'

'He killed him,' Nora said.

'Oh, I don't think so,' Walt said.

'He killed Mr Argyle.' Nora started to giggle, finally covering her mouth with her hands.

Walt was relieved. She was apparently coming out of it. 'What's funny?' he asked her.

'Eddie said "shit," ' Nora said. 'Shit, shit, shit.'

'Yes, indeed,' Walt said. 'He had a reason to. You don't have a reason to, so don't say it.'

'I'm telling you.'

'I already know.'

'Poor Mr Argyle,' Nora said, and together they walked back toward the house.

Walt heard the sound of a distant church bell tolling eight o'clock. For a moment he thought it was the bells of St Anthony's, miraculously restored –

but it couldn't be. These were tolling somewhere across Old Towne, beyond the Plaza, probably the bells in the tower at Holy Spirit Catholic Church. He couldn't remember that they tolled the hours, but then maybe he'd never been listening for them, having always had bells closer to home. They took up the first notes of a Christmas carol, and carols were still ringing fifteen minutes later as he and Nora and Eddie drove east on Chapman Avenue, toward the Oak Lawn Preschool, the rain coming down hard again.

Walt ushered the children in through the door, past a half dozen mothers dropping off kids. One child stood in the hallway and sobbed out loud, and two others, apparently sisters, slugged and pinched each other, kicking like fiends on the carpeted floor of a classroom, or whatever they called it. There was a scream from down the hall, muffled by a closed door.

'I guess it's just another day in paradise,' Walt said to the receptionist. He introduced Nora and Eddie to her, and the woman handed him a couple of forms to fill out and then started chatting with the kids.

A door swung open off the hall just then, and through it, looking like a hammered mannequin, strode Robert Argyle, heading toward the open front door, and carrying his coat over his arm. He spotted Walt and seemed to go brain-dead for a moment, his face losing all powers of expression. Slowly he recovered, forcing a smile as he stepped forward, holding out his hand. Walt shook it for an instant and dropped it.

'You're surprised to see me,' Argyle said.

'Slightly.'

'This is one of my schools. I'm the director.'

Walt nodded, noticing suddenly that there was the rank smell of sulphur and piss on the air of the hallway. He squinted at Argyle, who still held his coat carefully in front of him. Forget it, he thought; this wasn't something he wanted to know.

'Who are these, then?' Argyle asked, gesturing at Nora and Eddie. The pre-school was quiet now, the hallway emptied out, the door to the classroom closed. The bells from across town were still playing carols, although it was too distant to make out the melody.

'This is Nora,' Walt said, 'and this is Eddie, my niece and nephew. Kids, this is Mr Argyle.'

Instantly, Nora covered her mouth with both hands, her eyes shooting open. She began to giggle. 'The one the spider ate?' she asked.

'That's right,' Walt said to her. 'He's not dead after all. Just like I told you.'

Argyle blinked his eyes hard, several times in succession, staring at Nora. Then he cocked his head, suddenly hearing something, his face white. Clearly it was the bells. They fell silent for a moment, and Argyle turned toward the door without saying another word, and right then they started up again, clanging away as if they'd ring right through until Christmas.

31

Robert Argyle had a business office in a big old flat-roofed Spanish-style house on Chapman Avenue. Probably he owned the house itself, which had been renovated and converted to office space, and which he shared with two law firms and some kind of consultant. His own office was subdued and unassuming – a couple of leather easy chairs, mahogany desk and file, Tiffany-style lamps, and a Berber carpet. There was no receptionist. Clearly it was more a hideaway than an office. Ivy had no real idea how much wealth he had managed to accumulate over the years; Argyle had never shown it off. It would have been nice to think a little better of him because of this, that despite his money he was a simple man, down to earth. And maybe he was.

She stood alone in the office, looking out the back window, down onto the old walnut grove where the house had burned. There was something horrible about a burned house. She saw now that there were police cars parked on the property. Men with shovels dug among the walnut trees in the grove, and others milled around, waiting.

'This morning's paper said it might be arson,' Argyle said, coming into the office behind her.

She turned around. 'Frightening when it's right next door, isn't it?'

He nodded grimly. 'Especially with this latest news.' He gestured at the work going on down below. 'I understand they've found what might be human remains buried out there.'

'Like a grave?'

'Not an old one, from what I hear. Maybe someone murdered – fairly recently.'

She shuddered. 'Not here – not in town?'

'That's the kind of world we seem to be living in, isn't it? There's not a lot of decency left.'

'Oh, I think there is, really,' Ivy said. 'The decency hasn't gone anyplace; it's just that a lot of the other is always in the news.'

'Of course you're right. This kind of thing is an aberration, isn't it?' He sat down, gesturing at a chair. Ivy sat down, too, facing away from the window. Robert didn't look as bad this morning, as tired and bedraggled, as he had in Watson's a couple of days ago. Then it struck her that he was covering it up – wearing an undereye concealer and a foundation. She glanced away, vaguely embarrassed for him. He smiled at her wanly. 'I get a little pessimistic some-times,' he said. 'A little lonely. I don't mind telling you the truth. I've always wanted children, but …' He shrugged, opening the desk drawer and bringing out a bottle of aspirin. He shook out a couple of the pills and swallowed them dry.

'Well, what about this property?' Ivy asked, steering the subject to business. There was no way she was going to discuss children with Argyle. 'It's commercial?'

'Industrial, really – out on Batavia. There's two of them, adjacent lots. I've been sitting on them for years. The whole neighborhood is concrete tilt-ups now, and a big self-storage yard. *Very* profitable area. Not much square footage left to rent. The lots, conservatively, are worth a half million dollars apiece. You'd be the sole agent.' He opened a drawer in the desk and took out a manila envelope, which he set in front of her. Her name was written across the top.

She sat for a moment, stunned even though she'd expected something like this. The commission would be somewhere in the neighborhood of sixty thousand dollars. 'Why don't you build on them yourself?'

He waved the suggestion aside. 'I'm lightening the load a little. Throwing the ballast overboard. How about you? Ship running smoothly?' He leaned back in his desk chair and appraised her with a look that was probably meant to be heartfelt. He looked goofy, somehow, like a nervous teenager.

'Ship's running very smoothly,' she said. 'Walt's got big plans for his catalogue sales business. Real estate market's turning around.'

'That's *good*,' he said, sitting up and smacking his palm against the desktop. He laughed, shaking his head. 'Big plans!' He paused for a moment, looking wistfully out the window now, as if something had just drifted into his mind. 'You know,' he said, 'after all these years, I still don't know what happened to the three of us. We were quite a team once.'

'It's all water under the bridge, Robert.'

'I don't think I ever had a chance to explain myself, my ambitions for … us.'

'There's no need to explain ambition to me. I'm acquainted with it.'

'No,' he said. 'Wait a moment. Hear me out. What I mean has something to do with big plans, with what you said. Walt and I have different ideas about that, about … size. Walt wouldn't have wanted what I wanted.'

'That's probably true,' she said, letting him talk. After all these years, an apology was overdue. He had behaved like a creep, even though essentially he was right. Walt didn't have his kind of ambition. Walt saw the world from a different point of view, from somewhere in outer space, usually, and the idea of the two of them as partners seemed impossible now.

'I knew we'd reached the end of things, of the partnership. But I didn't know that it would mean reaching the end of things with you. Even now, if I could change that, I would. Especially now.'

She shrugged. 'Things happen. There's no use carrying them around with you, is there?'

'If a man could change the past …'

'But he can't. Best just to let it go.'

'I could have made you happy, Ivy. Instead, I'm afraid I made all of us miserable.'

'Well, it's good of you to clear the air.'

He nodded and shrugged. 'Look at this.' He took a photograph out of the desk and laid it atop the envelope. It was he and Ivy, taken back when he was in his early twenties, not long after he'd gotten out of school. She was nineteen. The photo had been taken during the time of Argyle's first big success independent of Walt. He had promoted a vitamin supplement sales organization, which licensed salespeople who would pay a fee for the right to license further salespeople. All of them took a graduated percentage of profits, mainly from fees, and almost nobody sold any vitamins, which were largely worthless in the first place: 'natural vitamins' that were mainly gelled infusions of alfalfa and carrots. What it had amounted to, according to Walt, was money changing hands, shifting upward, filling the pockets of someone who was selling greed and lies. Half of Argyle's working capital had been Walt's money, which Argyle had eventually returned – tainted, according to Walt, who knew the difference between clean money and dirty money.

Walt wasn't in the photo. Ivy wore a sequined evening dress that Argyle had bought for her, simply to go out to dinner. It must have been a five-hundred-dollar dress even back then … It occurred to her suddenly that she'd made the right choice. Walt was the one, not that she had any doubts.

Argyle picked up the photo and stared at it. 'I wonder sometimes what would have become of us if things had gone differently. We would have made a formidable pair, you and I.'

'I guess it just wasn't destined to be.'

'Destiny,' he said. 'Sometimes destiny fools you, especially if you have too much respect for it. We can make our own destinies. That's one of the things I've found out. Who would have thought you'd be destined to sit across from me now, the two of us doing business together? Sometimes you have to *make* things happen. It's possible I can make things happen for Walt, too. It's no secret that my own companies have been successful. There's no limit to that commodity, you know, to success.'

'That'll be encouraging to Walt,' she said, imagining the conversation. Walt would have to take a pill to calm down.

'Mention to him that I'll help in any way I can, won't you?'

'Gladly.'

'And, Ivy … Let's start out fresh. The two of us.' He held out his hand.

Well, he hadn't exactly made a pass at her. She glanced down at the envelope on the seat of the Toyota as she drove up Chapman Avenue toward Batavia, and she imagined that it was stuffed with hundred-dollar bills instead of papers. Then she whooped out loud and slapped the steering wheel. Would she take the man's money? Yes, she would.

There was no use inventing motives for him. Maybe he didn't have any. He was lonely; anybody could see that. But that didn't mean that his apologies, or whatever they were, weren't real. Probably he meant what he said. And until she knew otherwise, there was no use assuming that he meant *more* than he said. Of course if she was certain that he had, that he was pulling something, then she'd have no choice but to hand him the envelope back and explain that they'd both made a mistake – again.

And she could do that as easily tomorrow as today.

32

Even though the white delivery van that arrived just before noon had the words 'Dilworth Catalogue Sales – We Deliver' painted on the side in red block letters, Walt stood for a moment wondering what it was.

A man in a khaki uniform got out carrying two boxes – a big one apparently containing the lampstand and a small one containing the brimstone. 'Membership card's in with the … brimstone,' he said, looking at the packing slip, which he handed to Walt along with a pen. Walt signed it and handed it back, and the man gave Walt a copy along with the two cartons, climbed into his van, and sped away. The box with the lamp in it was heavy as hell.

'Membership card?' Walt wondered out loud, watching the van roll away from the stop sign at the corner.

He looked at his watch even though he knew what time it was. The curious thing, he told himself, wasn't just that the packages arrived today; it was that they arrived *exactly when he'd asked*: before the sun rose to its zenith. He had thought he was being funny. If they had arrived a half hour from now, at quarter past, he could have dismissed the bird as a fake, a toy, but as it was …

As it was, what? What did this prove? Only that Dilworth Catalogue Sales was on the ball. Maybe there was a lesson in it – the virtues of lightning-fast delivery. Hefernin would recommend it. It was worth a twenty-dollar, illustrated pamphlet.

Ask for something more.

The thought occurred to him like a voice in his head, more a command than a suggestion, as he turned up the driveway toward the garage. Money?

He imagined wishing for a million dollars in small bills – just for starters;

later he could raise the stakes. How would it come to him? Out of the sky, floating like flower petals? Maybe he should complicate the issue in order to *really* test the thing – ask to find the money in a suitcase guarded by toads in a drainage ditch in Oz.

He chuckled, letting the thought slide away as he swung open the gate. Just then a voice sounded behind him: 'Mr Stebbins!'

It was the postman – not the 'inspector' from yesterday, but Phil, their real postman. Walt retraced his steps down the driveway and took the mail from him after setting down the two cartons.

'I don't know what happened to it,' Phil said, gesturing at the envelopes.

There were a dozen envelopes, already torn open – torn apart, rather – most of them containing checks. About half of them were so shredded and dirty that Walt couldn't even read the names and addresses imprinted on them. Obviously they'd been dropped in a puddle and run over. The tread marks were clearly visible, as if a car had rolled onto them and spun its tires. 'Hell,' Walt said. 'Wouldn't you know it, the damn junk mail's fine.'

'That's the way I found them this morning,' Phil said. 'I can't explain it, and neither can anyone else. Some kind of accident that nobody will admit to, I guess. I'm sorry. Looks like maybe they were dropped in the parking lot coming in from the truck or something.'

'Just *my* mail?'

He nodded. 'Far as I know. I'll keep on it. Maybe we can find out what happened.'

'Forget it,' Walt said. What good would it do? What he'd have to do is figure out where each of the checks had come from and ask for another, which would hold up payment for heaven knew how long, if he ever got paid again at all.

It dawned on him suddenly that Argyle was somehow to blame for this – either him or his man, the postal inspector. 'Say, Phil,' Walt said. 'Is there a *big* guy that's a postal inspector, works locally?'

'How big?'

'Size of a bus. Six-five, maybe. Fat, but big – call it three hundred and fifty pounds. Giant head.'

Phil shook his head. 'Nobody like that, unless he's new. Why?'

'Nothing,' Walt said. 'A friend of mine wanted to know. They went to the same high school or something.'

'Well, anyway, I'm sorry about the mail.'

'Not your fault,' Walt said.

'I can give you an affidavit from the post office acknowledging the damage.'

'Sure,' Walt said. 'I guess so. Thanks.'

Phil walked away across the lawn, sorting the mail for the next house.

Obviously this was the long arm of Argyle again, playing petty pranks. The guy was a mental case – writing dirty words in crayon, yanking down lights, trashing a man's mail. How he had gotten to it was a mystery, but dollars to doughnuts it involved the inspector. Well, this was it – an open declaration of war. Argyle was throwing it into Walt's face.

Back in the garage he razored open the small box, the ever-burning brimstone, which, Walt noted, wasn't even hot. Inside the cardboard was what looked exactly like a tiny cigar box, built out of cut-rate Asian mahogany with finger-jointed sides. The word 'Brimstone' was stamped in gold on the top of the box along with two little stylized flames containing ghostly faces that bore a family resemblance to the masks of comedy and tragedy. The eyes of one seemed to be suffering the tortures of the damned; the eyes of the other were almost insanely glad. Walt opened the box, half expecting a spring-snake to fly out at him. Instead, an inch-high flame rose slowly from the interior. The box was lined inside with metal the dull gray color of lead, and lying in the center of it was what looked like a chunk of lava rock. The flame smelled of sulphur, and he was reminded of Argyle standing in the hallway of the preschool this morning, stinking the place up.

He closed the box, wondering if the flame had gone out. When he reopened it, the flame rose from the box again, as if drawn upward by the hinged lid. He put his hand into the fire: it was hot, all right. He closed it and opened it – same thing: the flame sprang to life without even a whisper. The damned thing was like a refrigerator light that came on the instant the door opened, but you could only speculate that it went out again when the door was shut.

Walt noticed a folded paper in the bottom of the cardboard carton, along with a flat plastic-wrapped package. He unfolded the paper, which turned out to be a paragraph of information on the brimstone, printed in a smeary sort of ink, as if in someone's basement. 'Brought back from the everlasting fires of Hell,' the paper read, 'by intrepid explorers. Lights fireplaces, barbecues, cigars. Perfect for heating fondue. Useful as a night light ...'

He put the paper down and picked up the plastic package. Inside was his 'Get Out of Hell Free' card, a stiff, wallet-sized bit of paper with a place to sign his name. Along the edge were printed the words 'Dilworth Catalogue Sales, Member in Good Standing,' and the card was signed by Denton Dilworth above a couple of lines guaranteeing the card's authenticity. Beneath that were the words 'not to be sold or reproduced.' On the back of the card was a drawing of the faces in the flame, the same as the ones on the top of the brimstone box, like souls going up in smoke. Walt slipped it into his wallet, then opened the big box.

The golden lampstand, he was surprised to find, was wired for electricity. Somehow he hadn't counted on that kind of modern innovation. He screwed the several parts together, nicking the gilt paint when his screwdriver slipped.

There was pot metal underneath, and the base, which was the heavy part, was a thin metal shell that hid a saucer-shaped lump of plaster of Paris. All in all the lamp resembled a tall, dietetic candelabra, and it required three candle-flame-shaped bulbs, not to exceed fifteen watts. The bulbs weren't included in the price.

'What a haul,' Walt said out loud, stepping back to look at what he'd paid nearly forty dollars for. He tried to see something biblical in the lampstand, something apocalyptic, but the thing defeated him. Maybe he could give the brimstone to Uncle Henry as a Christmas gift.

Thirty minutes to go until the meeting with the man Vest at Coco's, and Henry wasn't home yet. He'd been gone all morning. Walt walked down toward the front yard, noticing just then that a car was pulling up at the curb – another government car, for heaven's sake. It was apparently the post office again, hounding him. A woman got out, small and gray-haired, like someone's old granny. She smiled brightly at him as she came up the driveway.

33

Walt and Henry sat in a window booth at Coco's, waiting for Sidney Vest, who would probably turn out to be another postal inspector. Unlike the big man, the woman this afternoon had been pleasant and undemanding – no threats, no jail talk. Her name, she'd told him, was Hepplewhite. When Walt had referred to the other inspector, she hadn't stumbled. 'Probably another operative,' she'd said, and then she'd given him her name and a phone number and left.

He glanced at Henry over the top of his water glass. Henry had the popes in a manila envelope. He was sparked up, looking over the menu like a trencherman, squinting his eyes and nodding, as if everything he saw looked first-rate. Something had given him an appetite. It was probably time to ask him outright about the Biggs woman, before lie did anything regrettable.

'I might try the chicken fried steak,' Henry said, winking at Walt and inclining his head toward the waitress, who was helping the people at the next booth. Henry leaned over and whispered, 'Nice gams,' and darted his eyes a couple of times.

Walt nodded, although the word meant nothing to him. Gams?

Henry leaned back and picked his teeth with a wooden toothpick he'd pulled from the dispenser on the way in. He had the relaxed air of someone who was in for the long haul, who had the afternoon off and was going to do some real *eating*.

'Women,' Henry said, heaving a sigh.

'Yes, indeed,' Walt said. He watched the street, looking out for a Lincoln Town Car.

'Who was that Italian woman, that blonde who ran for the senate or parliament or whatever the hell they've got over there? Reminded you of a couple of mush melons in a sack.'

Walt shook his head helplessly. 'Italian woman?'

'She took off her clothes and climbed into a public fountain. It was all over the newspapers.'

'Oh, sure,' Walt said, remembering. 'That was a few years ago. I think they call that a photo opportunity. What was her name? – something like Chicolina. I *think* that was it. I guess that was pretty much why they elected her, that prank with the fountain.'

'I've always liked the Italians,' Uncle Henry said. 'They understand beauty, the female form.'

'Did you know it's against the law to lie about a cheese over there?' Walt asked. 'A Parmesan cheese *has* to be made in Parma. Over here you can make a Parmesan cheese in Iowa.'

'Now, the blonde women are from the north,' Henry said, 'up around Switzerland … It's the cooler climate that fleshes them out.' He gestured with both hands, winking heavily. '*Bella, bella,*' he said.

Walt grinned weakly. 'Good pasta in the north.' Henry was full of beans. What was this, his hula-hula woman? Success? Anticipation? Certainly it was trouble with a capital T.

'I met a woman from Varese once …' Henry shook his head, as if the words had suddenly failed him, and Walt would have to imagine her.

'I wonder where your man Vest is,' Walt asked, still trying to shift the subject. He checked his watch.

'He'll show,' Henry said. He put his arm across the top of the Naugahyde booth and stared out the window at the afternoon traffic. 'Varese.' He rolled the word out of his mouth, stretching the second syllable.

Walt nodded.

'It was on a train.' Henry paused again, remembering. 'We were riding down to Rome. Crowded as hell, and *hot*. It was the first of August, and every Frenchman in creation was on the train heading south, speaking out of their noses like they do.' He inclined his head at Walt. 'Now, there's nothing wrong with a Parisian woman, although they're a little too thin.' He paused, looking as if he expected an argument on this one.

Walt widened his eyes. 'I was only in Paris once – with Ivy, of course. We found a bed and breakfast on a little street called the Rue Serpente – fresh bread and jam in the morning. And the coffee!' He clucked in appreciation. 'Good coffee in Italy, too.'

'Well, Jinx was in the first-class compartment, and I was out in the aisle getting some air, and here was this … this vision, absolute vision. Blonde like you wouldn't believe. Biggest …' He gestured with both hands, nearly knocking over the water glasses, indicating something that flew in the face of gravity. 'She was wearing her grandmother's nightgown.'

Walt glanced over at the waitress, hoping that … She was staring at Henry with a fixed grin. Walt smiled and shook his head, wishing he could make the pinwheel sign around his ear. He'd have to leave her a hell of a tip.

'This woman Chicoletta reminded me of her,' Uncle Henry said. 'She's an Italian *type*. Now, in the south, there's a touch of the Mediterranean in the women, a swarthiness. But in the north …'

Walt waited for the conclusion of the story, for what happened on the train full of Frenchmen, the woman in the nightgown, but Henry had abruptly fallen silent, perhaps lost in thought. 'Did you meet this woman?' Walt asked.

'What woman?'

'On board the train. The woman from Varese.'

'Oh, no. No. Not really. She got out in Milan, and the train went on to Rome. We stayed on it.'

'And you never saw her again?'

'Never. I wouldn't expect to, though. Never got back to Milan.'

'Then how did you know anything about her nightgown?'

'Well, she was *wearing* it. Here he comes!' Henry sat up straight and pointed out the window. An old green Torino was just angling into the parking lot. The paint was sun-faded, and the rear fender was banged up, with a taillight made out of duct tape and red cellophane. When the car hit the dip in the gutter, the entire rear end slammed down, as if the springs were shot, and a plume of black smoke exhaled from the tailpipe.

'I thought he was driving a Lincoln Town Car,' Walt said doubtfully. 'Are you *sure* this is the guy?'

'One and the same,' Henry said. 'I imagine that a man of his talents owns more than one vehicle. This is what you might call the practical art of understatement.'

Walt nodded. 'Hefernin?'

Henry winked and nodded.

Vest rounded the corner of the building on foot and headed up the sidewalk, carrying a briefcase. Henry waved at him through the window. He was short and stocky and looked a little too much like a well-fed chipmunk. He moved ahead with a will, like a man with places to go and people to meet, a man who was running a half hour behind. He came in and sat down in the booth, next to Henry, who introduced him to Walt. Vest gestured immediately at the waitress, who came around now to take their order. Walt studied his menu, not quite wanting to meet her eye.

As soon as the waitress was gone, Henry hauled out the popes. He had an even dozen renditions – side views, front views, measurements and notes in the margins. Vest looked through them for about thirty seconds and handed them back.

'What do you think?' Henry asked.

'I think I know a man who can help you out,' Vest said. He drained his water glass with a noise that sounded like he was sucking the water through his teeth.

'Henry rather thought that you yourself were interested,' Walt said.

'Oh, I *am*, but I've got a few things hanging fire right now. Don't count me out, though. Do you have a financial advisor, Mr Stebbins?'

'I hardly have any finances,' Walt said. 'About a nickel's worth of advice would cover it.'

'All the more reason to take care of business,' Vest said. 'Let me give you my card.' Vest handed over a business card, and Walt took out his wallet in order to put it inside. The little flip-flop plastic slipcase fell out, exposing his new Get-Out-of-Hell card.

'I can get you a twenty-six-percent return,' Vest said. 'What are you making now, bank interest?'

Walt nodded, and just then Vest noticed the card. 'Are you a current member?' he asked, tapping it with his finger.

'Well, yeah,' Walt said. 'So it says here, anyway. It's got the Dilworth signature.' He took the card out of its slip so Vest could see it more clearly.

'V. P.?'

'What? I'm sorry ...?'

'Are you a vice president?'

'No, I guess not. I just got the card, actually. I ordered a couple of items through a catalogue ...'

Vest nodded broadly, then drew his own card from his wallet, tossing it onto the table. 'I can get you started on the lamination process. There's a twenty-dollar fee, but it's worth its weight in gold. The connections are fabulous.'

'Connections?' Walt asked.

'Business connections. It's the best twenty dollars you'll ever spend.'

'*I'm* in,' Henry said, inspecting the card himself. He turned it over and stared at the faces.

'Actually,' Walt said, 'I didn't pay anything for this. It came free.'

'That's what I'm telling you. Yours isn't laminated. Take a look at mine. Take a look at this lamination.' He clicked it against the table. 'It's a chemically impregnated space-age plastic. It's actually impervious to gamma rays.

Won't burn. Floats. What I'm talking about is having your card *activated*, cleared for takeoff.'

'Takeoff? What is it actually?'

Vest sat thinking for a moment. 'It's like … what? Like the Catholic thing – the scapular. They wear it around their necks, you know, for salvation. Now, this card, *I* call it insurance. You're welcome to wear it around your neck, like the Catholics. I don't know how a hole punch would affect the lamination, though … You better hold off on that.'

'Why does all this sound preposterous to me?' Walt asked.

'I don't know,' Vest said. 'Do you own life insurance?'

Walt nodded.

'Nothing preposterous about that, is there?'

'I'm not sure,' Walt said. 'There might be.'

'There's where you're wrong,' Vest told him. 'A man can't have too much insurance, not a family man like you. Take my word for it.'

Their lunches arrived. After Jinx's meatloaf last night, Walt's burger looked like heaven. Vest had ordered a top sirloin, fries, and a salad – the seven-ninety-five lunch. 'Put aside a piece of that Harvest Pie for me, will you?' he asked the waitress.

'Anyone else for pie?' she asked.

Henry shrugged. 'I'm about famished.'

'Looks like pie all around,' Vest said cheerfully. He picked up his water glass and peered into it for a moment. 'Look,' he said seriously, setting down the glass. 'Thursday night after Christmas there's a meeting up on Batavia, at the union hall. I'm going to recommend it to you. It's a business venture put together by three of the most successful men you or I will ever meet. It's called the Plan for the Sensible Investor.'

'Now you're talking,' Henry said, nodding hard at Walt. 'This is the kind of thing I was telling you about.'

'There's a short testimonial first,' Vest said. 'Then they'll tap out the men who'll be cleared for takeoff. I think you'll be impressed with the ceremony. There'll be a general discussion about selling distributorships and about the officer hierarchy. If you're interested, you'll get a supply of coupon booklets right then and there. You're on your way.'

'Is this a sales organization?' Walt asked. Something was odd here – all this business about the card, the connection between Vest's nonsense and Dilworth Catalogue Sales. Argyle again, like the many-armed octopus, tightening his grip.

'Indirectly. The real object is *service*. That's the point of the coupon booklets.' He opened his briefcase and drew out a booklet the size of his palm. He flipped through it, showing Walt and Henry examples of the hundred-odd coupons – brake-job discounts, offers for free sodas at fast-food joints, two-for-one dinners, motel travel packages, cut-rate Vegas shows. 'These will save you a buck every time you go to the movies,' Vest said, indicating a discount card for a local chain of theaters. 'And look at this.' The back of the booklet was a Get-Out-of-Hell card, just like Walt's, but without the Dilworth affidavit and signature. This one was imprinted with the Sensible Investor logo instead, and had little squares around the perimeter that apparently could be punched out by merchants when you redeemed coupons. 'You can accumulate as many of these as you want,' Vest said.

'Why would you want more than one?' Walt asked, echoing the sentiment of the Dilworth man.

'For your children.'

'I don't have any children,' Walt said, heating up a little. Henry was clearly roused by this baloney.

'Then put a few aside for your grandchildren. Think about the future. *Look*, what I'm saying is that you can hold activated cards for *anybody you please* – dead relatives, what have you. The cards are *entirely* retroactive. And five percent of coupon sales are put into a fund for locating the missing children. This is a *service*-oriented organization, but it's got nothing against making a profit.'

'The missing children?' Walt asked, letting the 'retroactive' part go.

'That would be the children depicted on the milk cartons?' Henry said helpfully.

Vest nodded in Henry's direction. 'Like that except different, if you follow me. But the *real* money is in distributorships. I don't mind telling you that. None of us will make a dime by playing games here. When you buy the first program packet you're a distributor, and *five percent of your sales come to me*. That's right. You heard me right. *Straight* into my wallet. If I can pull in twenty distributors I'm what they call a "Hundred Percenter." That's the end of the rainbow. The pot of gold. Just four distributors and you're a vice president. That's what I was asking about when I saw your card. That's the Lamination Level. I myself was *four* vice presidents, and I've only been in the organization for two months.' He hit the table with his fist, to underscore things. 'Do you have a pen?'

Walt took his pen out of his pocket and handed it over. Vest tore a coupon out of the booklet and wrote an address in the margin. He handed the slip of paper to Walt, who tucked it into his shirt pocket.

'You're *four* vice presidents?' Walt asked. 'All by yourself?'

'I was. George Nelson is thirty-eight vice presidents. You know George?' Walt shook his head.

'Law office up on the Plaza? Well, he's a charter member. Inner Circle. One of the First Captains. The sky's the limit here. No ceiling. There's only one question to ask: *how rich do you want to be*?'

Their pies arrived, and Vest started forking his down in a hurry.

'How many vice presidents are you now?' Walt asked.

'That's not the point,' Vest said. 'The point is, I *sold* my vice presidencies back to the Sensible Investor. That's how it works. It happens that mine were bought by one of the Captains, and for *ten times their face value*, I made a couple of bucks on that one, and, listen to this, I receive two percent of the off-the-top profits into *perpetuity*. This is capitalism, gentlemen; there's no part of this that you can't sell at a profit. Surefire gain. What I'm thinking of doing is cashing out entirely. I'm from North Carolina, out around Raleigh. I'm going to take my nest egg and go home, buy a little place of my own.'

'Good for you,' Walt said. 'But this whole thing sounds a little like a pyramid scheme, doesn't it? Excuse me for saying so.'

'Perfectly reasonable question,' Vest said. 'But I can assure you this is no pyramid. This is *circular*, with levels. Look, don't take my word for it. Come around on Thursday and you'll hear the real McCoy, the horse's mouth, from men and women who are already making money. And I mean *money*.'

He stood up to leave. 'Thanks for the lunch,' he said, shaking Walt's hand.

'About the drawings ...' Henry said, picking up the envelope.

'Why don't you bring those around on Thursday night when you come?' Vest said. 'We'll see if we can't put something together.'

'Now you're talking,' Henry said.

'And what about the sales club?' Vest asked. 'Have you thought that over?'

'I certainly have,' Henry said. 'I'm ready.'

'Can you take delivery tomorrow? Betty's got a party set up already, gratis. You don't pay any percentage on your first party – profit's all yours, so you can't lose. It's a house right over here on Harwood, ten women so far and a couple more possibles.'

'Ten ...' Henry said, nodding.

'We're talking a *three-figure party*. That's not chump change. I'd jump in with both feet on this one.'

'By heaven, I will. Tomorrow's fine. Jinx is going out to see Gladys,' he said, turning to Walt, 'in Costa Mesa.'

Vest nodded and turned to leave, heading toward the door without a backward glance.

'I told you he was a go-getter,' Henry said.

'He's a ball of fire,' Walt said. 'What's this "delivery" he was talking about?'

'I mentioned that yesterday, I believe.'

'You said something about a business venture that Vest was going to let you in on. That wasn't this "Sensible Investor" scheme?'

'No,' Henry said. 'This is something else – *immediate* money. He's already shown me the ropes.' Henry paused, looking shrewdly at Walt. 'What do you think? Partners? It's ready money. I'll put up the three hundred to cover Vest's stock.'

'Sure,' Walt said weakly. 'I guess so.'

'Don't worry about me. The three hundred's entirely refundable if we can't sell the product. But that's not the issue. We'll sell it. You heard what Sidney said about that. He represents a surefire line of clothing articles. He books what they call "parties."'

'I've heard of that,' Walt said uneasily. 'So this isn't crystal or Tupperware or potted plants or something?'

'Women's lingerie,' Henry said, scraping his pie plate clean with his fork.

Sidney Vest bumped out of the parking lot just then, the old Torino boiling away up Chapman Avenue toward the Plaza. The waitress arrived, and Walt found himself paying for the lunch, for Vest's steak, for 'pie all around.'

Rain swept against the window in a sudden gust of wind, and Walt heard the bells start up again, over at the church. It was the top of the hour – two o'clock. If they rang true to form, they wouldn't let up for twenty minutes, which was perhaps getting to be too much of a good thing. Probably it was in the memory of poor Simms. Walt picked up his card from the tabletop and slipped it back into his wallet, noting for the first time that he hadn't signed it yet.

Maybe he'd wait …

And anyway, he didn't have a pen – Vest had taken it.

34

On the walk in front of the Sprouse Reitz store on Chapman Avenue stood several dozen Christmas trees nailed onto the crossed sections of bisected two-by-fours. A scattering of over-the-hill trees had been piled off to one side, and a boy in a T-shirt was just then dragging two of them around the side of the building toward a big trash bin, leaving a wide trail of fallen needles on the wet asphalt behind him. Walt parked the Suburban near the trash bins and rolled down the window. 'Throwing them out?' he asked.

An idea had come to him, an inspiration; why shouldn't he take a few trees home, for the kids – maybe set up some kind of Black Forest under the avocado tree?

'They're not really any good,' the boy said. His T-shirt had a picture of a trout on it, along with the words, 'Fish worship, is it wrong?'

An eccentric, Walt thought, immediately liking him. He was right about the trees, too; they *were* pretty clearly shot – not dried out, but mangled, with lots of broken limbs and twigs.

'What will you sell them for?' Walt asked.

'They're not really for sale. They just came in, but most of them are broken up like this because they fell off the truck or something. The supplier is going to refund our money for the wrecked ones. So ... I don't know.'

'So you're throwing them away?'

He nodded toward the trash bin. 'They compost them.'

'Well, I'll take a few off your hands,' Walt said. 'Say, ten bucks? I'll compost the heck out of them later.'

'I don't think I'm supposed to sell them ...'

'You're not really selling them, are you? I need a few for a sort of ... theatrical production, for my niece and nephew. It's hard to explain. I want to make a ... a Christmas forest, I guess, in the backyard, around this garden shed, which would be the woodcutter's cottage.'

The boy nodded, as if finally Walt was making sense. 'How many do you want?' he asked.

'Let's see ... we can load a few on the rack here and then shove a couple more inside the truck. Whatever I can fit.' He dug his wallet out of his back pocket then and pulled out a ten-dollar bill. 'Just drag a few more around here. If there's any trouble I'll say I was digging them out of the bin, and that you tried to stop me but I wouldn't listen.'

He handed the money to the boy, who dropped the two trees he'd been holding onto, took the bill, and stuffed it into his pocket. Walt got out of the Suburban, picked up a tree, and lifted it onto the rack, swiveling the two parts of the wooden base together. He loaded the second tree back-to-front with the first, then took a roll of twine from the back of the truck and tied the trees down, yanking them flat so that he could fit more on top. Finally he opened the tailgate and crammed two more inside. Even tied down, the trees added about six feet to the top of the truck, which looked like some kind of specially camouflaged alpine vehicle.

'Thanks,' he said, handing the twine back and putting away his pocketknife. 'Can I give you a hand with the rest of them? I really appreciate this.'

'I guess not,' the boy said. 'Thanks for the ten dollars.'

Walt headed into the store, feeling lucky. He wasn't sure exactly what he was going to do with the trees, other than that it involved Nora and Eddie. There was too much rain to set up the trees outside, now that he thought about it. And there was no way Ivy would let him drag them all into the house. What was that play, he wondered, in which the old man ended up living in an attic full of Christmas trees? It involved ducks, Walt seemed to remember – ducks and garden elves. Walt admired that kind of who-cares-what-you-think lunacy, but it seemed to him to be the special province of either the very young or the very old. A man his age had to watch out.

He looked over the Christmas ornaments on the way into the store, pick-ing out a couple of strings of illuminated candycanes suitable for hanging outdoors. He could decorate the porch with them. Then Argyle could come around and smash them to pieces with a stick. It would be an Argyle trap, a sort of monkey-and-coconut effect. Walt could watch through the upstairs window, and when Argyle really got going, Walt could point him out to Ivy: 'Look, isn't that poor old Bob Argyle dancing on the candycanes …?'

'Aren't those fun?' a woman asked him.

He looked up and nodded. She stood near one of the registers, an open bag of popcorn sitting on the Formica counter in front of her. Her wispy hair was blue-gray, and she wore a frilly kind of calico apron. The smell of popcorn was heavy in the store, and Walt noticed a big popping machine near the candy counter. 'I'm taking two strings,' Walt said.

'Good for you,' she said, full of good cheer. Walt was apparently the only customer in the store.

'Tell me,' he said to her, wishing that she didn't look quite so much like somebody's nice old granny. 'I notice that you sell parakeets.'

'That's right,' she said. 'They're at the back of the store, in the corner, past yardage. Pick one out and we'll get Andrew in here to catch it.'

'Well, what I need,' Walt said, 'and this is going to sound weird, is a dead one.'

The idea had come to him after he and Henry had gotten home from Coco's: he would give Argyle the dead bird after all, or at least *a* dead bird. He'd give it to him in a jar, too, filled with gin. 'I'd be happy to pay full price,' Walt told the woman. This involves – what do you call it? – a science fair pro-ject. Dissection. One of these eighth-grade science projects …'

… and it occurred to him that he might simply have asked the bluebird itself, up in the rafters, to supply him with another bluebird, a facsimile.

The idea simply leaped into his mind, like a suddenly appearing ghost. Almost at once he wondered if he could make a request like that at a distance, if the bird would grant it anyway, even though it was locked in a fishing tackle box in the rafters of a garage two miles away.

Abruptly he cast the idea out. *I don't want your help*, he thought forcibly.

'Well,' the woman said, 'it happens that I *do* have a dead parakeet. We sell a good number of birds, and once in a while we lose one.'

He winced. Success, just like that. *Had* the bluebird granted his wish? Did the mere *thought* command the thing's obedience? 'Parakeets can be deli-cate,' he said to the woman, trying to smile, to show his appreciation.

'Well, this one had some kind of cold. We separated him from the others and then dosed all of them with vitamins and antibiotics, but the poor thing died just this afternoon. I didn't know quite what to do with him. It didn't seem right just to toss him into the trash.'

Walt nodded sympathetically, following her toward the back of the store, past yardage displays and racks of notions and gizmos. She brought the bird out of the storeroom in a shoebox, lying in a little bed of tissue paper. It was blue, all right – bluebird blue.

'So it's been dead for a while?' Walt asked.

'A couple of hours. I didn't want to just throw it in the bin.'

'Of course not.' Two hours ago! That settled it. The bluebird couldn't have *anticipated* his wish. Could it? The idea was absurd, no matter how much the parakeet looked like the bird in the jar. Which it did, Walt realized, looking closely at it. No, it was impossible. This was outright coincidence.

'How much can I pay you for him?' he asked, getting out his wallet.

She waved the suggestion aside and rang up the two strings of candycane lights.

'If you're sure,' he said. Somehow he had counted on being able to pay for it. There was something almost immoral about it otherwise, what with the lie and all.

'Tell your son that I hope he gets an A on his project,' she said.

'I will.' Walt felt like a criminal. He took his package and the shoebox and went out into the rain. Somehow the act of lying to the woman had taken all the wind out of his sails, and the prank he intended to play on Argyle wasn't nearly as funny to him any more. The boy in the parking lot was tossing out the last of the trees when Walt came out, and he waved as Walt fired up the Suburban and drove slowly out toward the street.

After stopping at the liquor store for a pint of gin, he drove home and unloaded the trees into the new tin shed, intending to turn it into Nora and Eddie's own private forest. He rolled out a piece of green indoor-outdoor carpet and then stood the trees up in two rows so that their branches interlaced. Somehow the whole process wasn't as much fun as he had anticipated. He felt a little weary, as if weighted down by the idea of dead birds and by the tangle of lies that was like a net dropped over his head.

With a pruning clippers he removed the bottom limbs and the worst of the broken twigs. By now the shed smelled like a pine woods. He stood for a moment simply breathing it in, listening to the freshening rain beat down on the roof, then slid shut the shed door and went into the house. Jinx and Ivy were out, and apparently hadn't been home all day, since the mail still lay on the coffee table where Walt had tossed it earlier.

He noticed then that a folded sheet of paper lay on the living-room floor beneath the mail slot. He picked it up and pried out the staple. It was a Xeroxed flyer, hand done, offering a reward for a 'lost carton' possibly dropped from a mail truck in the neighborhood …

A thousand dollars would be paid for the carton's return, no questions asked.

35

On the flyer there was a description of the thing in the jar, which – the flyer claimed – was the corpse of a now-extinct sort of Chinese sparrow bound ultimately for the Natural History Museum in Los Angeles.

Walt laughed out loud. A thousand dollars! At that rate he would hand the thing over after all and hoot in Argyle's face.

Except, of course, that handing it over would establish his guilt. And there was no way on earth Argyle would pay him the money anyway, not now.

The more he thought about it, the more it smelled like a plot – probably something set up by the inspector. The extinct sparrow talk was obviously a lie. The bird was something else altogether, something that was clearly worth a *lot* more than a thousand dollars. Suddenly a thought occurred to him and he went outside again, heading next door, carrying the flyer with him. He checked with three of his neighbors before he was satisfied that nobody else on the block had gotten one – only him.

So this was a sting operation. They expected him to come panting along with the jar after having lied to a postal inspector. Probably that constituted some kind of vicious fraud.

Except of course that the postal inspector was himself a vicious fraud. Walt went up the driveway to lock up the garage, wondering idly whether two frauds canceled each other out. He crumpled the flyer and tossed it into the tin bucket, then stepped back and looked into the rafters. The tackle box sat up there as ever, gathering dust. The bird was in it. Somehow Walt knew that without having to check, as if the thing had a *presence* – exactly as if something were *living* up there in the dusty shadows beneath the roof beam, something small but with immense mass, so terribly heavy that the rafters groaned beneath its weight, and at any moment it would come smashing down. The idea of it gave him the willies.

A few hours earlier he had been on the verge of asking the thing for money. But he knew it was better to throw it into the ocean. His sudden fear of it in Sprouse Reitz had been healthy – sanity itself. He walked down the driveway to the motor home and knocked. Henry opened the door, saw who it was, and waved him in. Walt slid behind the table, looking out through the window at the rain. Henry's little space heater whirred away on the sink, and the trailer was close and warm.

'Coffee?' Henry asked, shutting off the television.

'Thanks,' Walt said, taking the cup from him. 'Rain won't quit.'

'It gives people something to talk about,' Henry said.

'Weather. That's the king of small talk.'

Henry shrugged. 'Everyone's interested in it. It's common ground.'

'It's safe, I guess.'

'Nothing safe about the weather. On the television they were just showing some homes out near Portuguese Bend – slid right into the ocean.'

'I meant as a topic of conversation. You don't get into trouble talking about the weather. It's not like politics and religion.'

'That's so,' Henry said. 'It's one of the only subjects people still give a damn for after ten thousand years of civilization. And it doesn't matter where you find yourself, Egypt, Peru, hell – *China*, for God's sake. People all over the world talk the same talk when they talk about the weather. It's the great leveler, the only thing time won't change in people. It's the same with food and drink. There's nothing small about any of that kind of talk.'

Walt blinked at the old man, who dumped several spoonfuls of sugar into his coffee and stirred it up. Somehow this all sounded tremendously sane, a side of Henry that Walt wasn't familiar with. The old man was apparently in a philosophical mood. He had come down off the wild buzz he'd been on at Coco's.

'Let me ask you something,' Walt said, suddenly deciding to confide in Henry. 'This is going to sound a little nuts, but did you ever have any interest in … what do you want to call it? Magic, let's say. Ouija boards, Tarot cards, that sort of thing?'

He nodded. 'Gladys used to read cards.'

'Really, Aunt Gladys?'

'Terrible bore. She was always showing you the horoscope, too, warning you about things, giving you advice.'

'You believe in any of it?'

'Believe in it?' Henry shook his head. 'I don't know about *believe*. I know I don't like it much.'

'Neither do I,' Walt said. 'What would happen, though, if Aunt Gladys was reading your cards, and you started to think there was something to it after all, as if the cards weren't just *pictures* any more, but really were … *windows*, say. That Gladys was actually communicating with something?'

'I'd walk right out of there.' Henry nodded for emphasis, setting his jaw. 'I'd say, "Gladys, you've gone crazy."'

'Well, this is interesting,' Walt said, 'because the damnedest thing has happened. I wonder what you'll think about it. I got this shipment, from Asia …'

Walt explained the bluebird, leaving Argyle out of the picture entirely and saying nothing about newspaper delivery or tomatoes or anything else that would make him seem certifiable. The details of the story seemed almost trivial now that he was recounting them, and he realized that the fear he had felt in the garage a few minutes ago had evaporated. 'The thing is,' Walt said at last, 'what if it *can* grant your wishes?'

'Then you've got to get it out of here. And I mean *now*. Otherwise I've got to tell you the same thing I'd tell Gladys. I'd say, Walter, you've gone crazy.'

'But what if there's a million dollars in it?'

'What if there's *ten* million dollars? It'll buy you the same thing – ruination. A ticket straight to Hell in an upholstered sedan chair. Bank on it. You'll ride to the Devil in comfort. Anyway, I've never pegged you as the kind of man who had his price.'

'Well, thanks,' Walt said. 'You want to have a look at it?'

'I'd be glad to,' Henry said. 'I'm happy to help.' He set down his coffee cup and took his sweater from a hook on the trailer wall. Together they went into the garage, and Walt climbed up into the rafters and pulled down the tackle box, setting it down on the bench and unclipping the lid.

'This is it,' Walt said. He took the jar out of its painted tin box and held it up to the light. The milky gin-water inside swirled around the corpse of the bird, and the surface of the liquid was agitated, as if the jar held a miniature, white-capped sea.

'It's apparently a dead bird,' Henry said. 'Nasty-looking fellow.'

Walt nodded, suppressing the urge to argue with him. The bird was actually a fairly beautiful specimen, the blue as bright as an afternoon sky. Abruptly he wished that he'd never brought the subject up to Henry at all. This was something he could handle on his own. He didn't need help. He set the jar on the bench and said offhandedly, 'Like I said, it's supposed to grant wishes. It's some kind of charm, like a rabbit's foot. I don't know why I brought it up, really.'

Henry looked at him over the top of his glasses. 'Throw it straight into the trash,' he said. 'That's no rabbit's foot.'

'You're right, of course.'

'There's something not right about it, some kind of juju. Get it the hell out of here. You don't want something like this around.'

'No,' Walt said. 'That's right. That's why I wanted to show it to you, to get your opinion on it.'

'Does Ivy know about it?'

'*Know* about it? No, I guess not.'

'Take my word for it. Don't show it to her. Get rid of it, somewhere off the property. If I showed Jinx a thing like this ...' He shook his head and reached into the open tackle box, pulling out a bottle of salmon eggs. 'What is this supposed to be, fish bait?'

Walt took it from him. Something was wrong with the eggs in the bottle. They were moving, as if swimming sluggishly in the gelatinous pink liquid. Walt looked closely at them, horrified to see that they were looking back out at him through round black eyes the size of flyspecks, and that each had a tail and fins, almost transparent. The jar pulsed in his hands, and he had the odd feeling that the sides of the jar bulged, that at any moment it would burst, spewing larvae through the air of the garage like a pod spewing out seeds.

'Damn thing's full of maggots,' he said, rolling the jar into several sheets of newspaper and twisting the ends before putting it in the trash bucket. He saw that the old bottle of cheese bait had turned a purple-black, like the color of a bruise, and he threw that into the trash, too, without looking at it closely. 'I'll toss it all into the Dumpster down behind the medical center on the corner.' He nodded seriously at Henry and picked up the bluebird, started to put it into the bucket too, but then stopped and set it on the bench again. 'What's tomorrow – Thursday? The bin doesn't get emptied till late in the afternoon, so I can toss it out in the morning.'

'Do it now,' Henry said. 'You wanted my opinion? Well, that's it. Get it out of here. Posthaste.'

'Sure,' Walt said. He put the jar back into its tin and laid the tin carefully in the bucket, picking the whole works up by the handle. Henry walked down the street with him, to the alley adjacent to the medical center. The bin was about half full. Walt dropped the tin in among tied-off plastic bags and jumbled papers and office trash.

'Good riddance to bad rubbish,' Henry said.

Walt reached in and yanked a trash bag over it so that no one would find it and fall prey to it as he had. He upended the tin bucket, dumping the rest of it in. By noon tomorrow the whole works would be landfill.

36

'The kids are tired out tonight,' Walt said hopefully, watching Ivy move around the bedroom, hanging clothes and straightening up. She looked at him, seeing through him immediately.

It was past ten, and things were blessedly quiet downstairs. Apparently the kids had finally settled in. Walt was a little disappointed that they hadn't given much of a damn for the Christmas trees in the shed. They'd gone inside and looked, but stepped right out again, as if they thought this was another spider prank or something. 'Why are there trees?' Nora had asked.

'You can play in there, if you want,' Walt had answered, and right then Eddie had suddenly remembered that there was something on television, and he had run back into the house without saying a word, not coming back out again. Nora had gone into the front yard and drawn hopscotch squares on the sidewalk with pink chalk and spent fifteen minutes hopping up and down on one foot. Then, over dinner, Nora had told Aunt Jinx that Walt had tried to make them 'go into the shed,' and Walt had found himself explaining about the forest of trees while Jinx regarded him with a look of astonishment and doubt.

'You and the kids ...' Ivy said now, shaking her head and closing the wardrobe door. 'You've gone head over heels.'

'Well ...' Walt said, trying to get to the bottom of the statement, which sounded loaded to him, like an attractive piece of fish bait. 'It's fun having the two of them as house-guests. You can spoil them, whatever you want, and then give them back to their parents and go on your way.'

Ivy was silent. 'I hope so ... Wherever their parents are at the moment. I guess I ought to call Mom and Dad and see how Darla's doing.' She sat down on her side of the bed. 'What I meant, though, is that I think you've got a knack for it, for parenthood.'

'It's a lot of work,' Walt said. 'There's a lot you give up.'

'There's more that you gain. They both think you're a peach.'

He shrugged. She nudged him in the ribs and winked at him, and he knew that this was her round; she'd out-scored him. There was no need to accuse him of fear or of being self centered tonight. It was enough that the kids thought he was a peach. She'd caught him in a vanity trap.

'You didn't tell me that it was one of Argyle's pre-schools,' he said to her, changing the subject.

'It was the only one nearby that allowed for drop-ins and temporaries in the kindergarten class.' She shut off the lamp now, so that the room was dim, the only illumination coming from the light in the downstairs landing. 'Did you speak to Robert?'

'Robert?' he asked. 'Oh, you mean Argyle. Only for a second. To tell you the truth, he looked like hell, like he'd been worked over by midgets. I'm not just making this up to give him a hard time. I'd have to guess that he'd been drinking hard. He stank too, like he had some kind of bladder disease.'

'He didn't look like that when I saw him at ten.'

'Obviously he'd been at it all night,' Walt said. 'Probably put away a couple of fifths. He went home and cleaned himself up for his meeting with you.'

'He said to give you his best. He was full of nostalgia, I think, for old times.'

'His best,' Walt said flatly. 'How good is that, exactly?'

'Maybe it's better than you think it is.'

Walt kept silent, thinking of Argyle out navigating the late-night streets, vandalizing houses. There was no use arguing about him, though. He wasn't worth it, especially if it meant exposing any of this business with the bluebird, which, happily, was a thing of the past, now that the bird was in the Dumpster.

'He even talked about how he missed having children, never getting married.'

'You talked to him about personal matters?' Walt asked. 'About having children?' This was astonishing. 'I don't suppose you discussed me? Us?'

'No. And don't get riled up. This was a business meeting. How much do you think the commission is?'

'Never mind the commission. I can't believe you talked about something like that. What business is it of his?'

'We didn't *talk* about it. He mentioned it in passing.' She slid farther under the covers, turning toward him and leaning her head on her elbow. Her kimono fell open, and she casually straightened it, but when it fell partly open again, she left it alone. 'I couldn't be a creep to him, could I?'

'It wouldn't be all that hard.'

'Well, maybe you're right. Maybe I should have been. Never mind about the commission, like you said. Money, who needs it? Filthy lucre.' She ran her finger down the sleeve of his nightshirt and off the tip of his finger. 'I like a man in a nightshirt,' she said. 'Especially a big roomy one.'

'I don't know where you'll find a big roomy man this time of night,' Walt said, brushing a strand of hair away from her face. 'But maybe I can be of service.'

'Maybe.'

'How much *is* the commission?' he asked, kissing her on the nose.

'It's nothing, really. Let's pretend I didn't even bring it up. I'll throw it back in his face tomorrow. I'll call him names, too. What shall I call him? A skunk?' She raised her eyebrows, then pushed herself up on her elbow and kissed him on the lips. 'I'll call him a *damned* skunk, and then I'll tweak his nose for him and box his ears. I always wanted to box a man's ears.'

'Tell me.'

'Maybe I'll tweak your nose too.'

'You won't have me unless you tell,' Walt said. But he slid his hand into her kimono and let it drift across her belly.

She lay down again, batting her eyes at him. 'I bet I will,' she said, and pulled his head down, kissing him again. 'I bet I'll have you right now.'

He had suddenly run out of things to say. He kissed her, slipping his hand down and loosening the tie on the kimono. She ran her fingers down his spine, putting her other arm across his shoulders.

And right then she sat up, clutching shut the kimono and pulling up the covers. He started to speak, but she put her finger to her lips.

'Listen,' she said.

He heard it then, the sound of movement downstairs. There was the patter of feet coming across the dining-room floor, heading toward the landing. It sounded like both of them. Soft footsteps sounded on the stair runner, and Nora and Eddie burst into the bedroom. Nora was breathless and wide-eyed, sobbing with fear.

'What's wrong?' Walt asked. Was someone downstairs? A prowler – the inspector! This had gone too damned far! He'd kill anyone who scared Nora and Eddie. Argyle! The dirty son-of-a-bitch ... Walt was full of adrenaline, worked up, wild with it.

'A b-bug,' Nora said, her voice shaking.

'A b-bug?' Walt asked.

'It was *big*,' Eddie said. He held up his hand, illustrating with his thumb and forefinger. 'Like this.'

Apparently the bug was several inches long. 'Where was it?' Walt asked, calming down now.

'On the floor,' Eddie said. 'It ran under Nora's bed. It's under there now.'

'Cockroach.' Ivy whispered the word in Walt's ear. 'Was it black?' Walt asked. 'Like a beetle, sort of?' Eddie nodded.

'What *is* it?' Nora asked.

'This house has *bugs*.'

'Every house has bugs,' Walt said. 'Bugs have to have a place to live, too. Many of them are involved in fertilization. They're part of God's great plan.'

'I'd kill it,' Eddie said, 'if I had a stick or something.'

'Uncle Walt will kill it,' Ivy said. 'Won't you, Uncle Walt? I bet it won't take a minute. Bring a shoe along to smack it with. We don't want it in the house.'

'Well, I *would* kill it,' Walt said, 'except that I think I know this bug. It's an Egyptian waterbug named ... Smith. E. Hopkinson Smith. He's very friendly. He was probably on his way to a party – to the ugly bug ball. You know, to find his friends. Was he carrying a bag of ...'

Nora burst into tears again, gasping out a sob that emptied her lungs.

'Oh, *I* don't think so,' Ivy said, giving him a look. 'Not under Nora's bed. I don't think this could have been Smith.'

'Of course not,' Walt said. 'This must be some other bug.' He could see he was defeated. Going on about bugs in trousers and top hats wouldn't do him any good, not now. 'I'll go mash him,' he said, climbing out of bed.

Nora suddenly began giggling. Like that the sobbing was gone, evaporated.

'What?' Walt said.

'You have a dress,' she said, pointing.

'It's a nightshirt,' Walt told her. 'Aunt Jinx made it for me. It's the family's plaid, from Scotland.'

'It's like a *dress*,' she said, climbing into his spot in bed and pulling the covers up to her chin so that only her head and her fingers showed. She made her rabbit face at him, crinkling up her eyes. Her bug fear was forgotten, just like that. Eddie sat down at the foot of the bed and yawned.

'Bring back the corpse,' Ivy said to him. 'I'll keep the children entertained.'

'No falling asleep?'

'Me?'

He gave her a hard look and descended the stairs, carrying a tennis shoe.

Going into the service porch, he grabbed a flashlight and a broom, then headed for the kids' room, where the light was on. Of course there was nothing under the bed. The roach, if that's what it had been, had slipped away through a gap in the floor moldings or gone into the closet. There was no way it would show itself. He was damned if he was going to spend all night on this quest. Laying the broom down, he raised the tennis shoe over his head and slammed it against the floor a half dozen times, then went out into the living room and opened the front door, shutting it hard. He put back the broom and the light and went up the stairs again.

'Got it,' he said. The children lay side by side on the bed, looking at pictures in a magazine.

'Let's see,' Nora said anxiously, sitting up.

'I pitched it out the front door,' Walt lied. 'Didn't you hear the door shut? I smashed him flatter than a molecule.'

Nora looked at him in silence, her mouth half open. 'You said he'd show us,' she said to Ivy.

'He will,' Ivy said to her. She looked hard at Walt, seeing straight through him. 'I think that Nora and Eddie will sleep better if they know the bug's really, *really* dead,' she told him.

'I'm sleeping up here,' Nora said.

'No, you're not,' Walt told her. 'Everyone in their own beds.'

'What if *it's* in my bed?' Nora asked. 'What if it's the bug again?'

'It is,' Eddie said. 'I think it was a kind of bedbug.'

'I don't think so,' Walt said.

'Maybe you could get its corpse,' Ivy said, 'from wherever you threw it. That would settle things, wouldn't it?'

'Sure,' Walt said. 'Of course it would.' He turned around and headed for the stairs again, still carrying his shoe, an idea suddenly coming to him. There were ten million roaches out on the streets at night, especially in the water meter box. He should have thought of that in the first place – not wasted his time looking for the actual bug. Any dead roach would do.

37

It was close to eleven o'clock. Bentley and Mahoney had been out walking the empty streets of Old Towne for over an hour, ringing bells. It had rained off and on, but now the rain was off, and Bentley tapped the wet sidewalk with his umbrella as if it were a walking stick. The Benedictus bell that he held in his other hand kept up a constant ringing that should have set off half the dogs in the neighborhood, but for some curious reason it didn't, as if the dogs understood.

Probably they should have split up, he and Mahoney, in order to cover more ground, except that alone they would be more open to attack. He looked behind him down the street, but it was deserted.

He relaxed and took in a lungful of the wet evening air. He liked to walk in the evening, especially in stormy weather, when he could see into softly lighted living rooms through open curtains: families sitting around warm and dry, watching television or reading, surrounded by the comfortable clutter of their lives. There were lighted Christmas trees in windows and cats on front porches and dogs looking out through screen doors, and it was easy to imagine that people were happy with simple things.

It wasn't all that long ago that bell-ringing was a common enough evening ritual, and in past centuries no one would have questioned the power of church bells to drive off evil. In the old days the sound of consecrated bells would have been as comforting to good people as it was intolerable to monsters like Argyle and LeRoy. Things had changed.

But here was the pot calling the kettle black, Bentley thought: it was only in the last few weeks that he himself had come to suspect that the vandalizing of neighborhood church bells *meant* anything. In fact, until this past week he had never given a second thought to the ringing of church bells. The history of bells was Catholic history for the most part, which, at least to his way of thinking, meant that it was nearly as hard to separate it from superstition as it was to chew the wrinkles out of a piece of gum. And look at him now: here he was, hand in glove with a priest, out in the rainy night, ringing a Benedictus bell and with more bells tied to his belt like wind chimes.

'Look at that,' Mahoney said, pointing his umbrella at the shadows alongside a front porch. A big plastic snowman, meant to be illuminated, lay on the grass, its face smashed in as if someone had yanked it off the porch and jumped up and down on it. Its electrical cord was wrapped around its neck in a sort of noose.

'Another one,' Mahoney said. 'Do you think it's him again?'

'Either it's him or …'

And just then, a car rolled slowly past the end of the block, heading east on Palm Street. It was the third time that evening that they'd seen it. The driver was a shadow, but it seemed to Bentley that the shadow was observing the two of them, and the preacher raised his umbrella as a greeting. The car sped up and was gone. Bentley didn't recognize the car, but he was almost certain it wasn't Argyle. The driver appeared to be a short man, maybe heavyset. Probably it was George Nelson, halfway to Hell in a hand-basket.

Bentley wondered again if he should have cashed the check that Argyle had given Obermeyer. Making the deal final – actually taking the money – might have stopped whatever it was that was coming to pass …

But that was nuts. Whatever was going on with Argyle had nothing to do with money, and it never had. A man could as easily sell his soul for a nickel as for five billion dollars, and you couldn't put a price on salvation – or on damnation, either, he reminded himself.

'What makes you think this thing in a jar is a demon?' Father Mahoney asked.

'What else would it be?'

'Do you mean a demon out of Hell? Beelzebub or Belial or one of them? Something with a name?'

'Well, there's no point in getting too specific about it. We don't care about the thing's credentials.'

'Why not something else?'

'What, exactly?'

'A bottle imp. A monkey's paw. A genie.'

'I don't believe in imps and genies. A demon's a demon the world around, as far as I'm concerned. What I know is that something has come into the country from the China coast, something Argyle has been waiting for. It was part of a shipment that included the golem, which I saw with my own eyes through the window. My sources believe this thing to be a demon, and *I* believe it to be a demon, and I believe that Argyle intends for this demon to ride his golem into Hell in order to give the Devil his due, which is to say, a soul. In a nutshell that's what I think.'

'And it's packaged as a toy?'

'Insidious, isn't it? Looks fairly innocent, apparently – some kind of good-luck item. You make a wish on it like you'd wish on a rabbit's foot or a star. Then it's got you. Pulls you in by appealing to your desires. What it means is damnation, which is nothing to Argyle – he thinks he's already damned.'

They turned the corner and headed up toward Cambridge. 'It's Stebbins that I'm worried about. I'm certain he's got it, and that he's lying when he says he doesn't. Looting his garage won't do us any good any more. He'll have the thing hidden by now. There's nothing left to do but confront him about it. We've got to appeal to his decency, and we've got to appeal to his fear.'

'Do you think he'll listen?'

'No,' Bentley said. 'I don't suppose he will.'

38

The motor home was dark, thank goodness, and it wasn't raining, although it smelled like rain, and the sky was heavy with clouds. Walt walked out to the curb and looked out into the street, where, on any other night of the year, there would have been a dozen roaches going about their senseless business. Tonight there was nothing; the streets were empty except for a few earthworms in the gutter. Somewhere in the distance there was the ringing of bells, small bells.

The wind billowed out the hem of his nightshirt, and he clapped his hands down against it, looking around him for the first time and thankful that he was wearing his shorts under the nightshirt. If a police cruiser were to appear ...

Hurrying now, he tucked his finger into the hole in the concrete lid of the water meter box and pulled it off, laying it on the grass. The streetlamp barely illuminated the inside of the box, which was about a foot deep, the meter itself casting a shadow across the bottom of it. He knelt against the curb, wishing he had brought the flashlight. There was movement down there, all right, small dark things creeping through the tangled roots of the Bermuda grass that had grown up through the bottom of the box. Of course there could as easily be black widows down there as roaches.

He shuddered and straightened up, looking out at the street again. *Surely* there was a lonely roach out and about, happy to sacrifice itself for something like this. The ringing of bells grew louder suddenly, accompanied by a random jingling, as if a Christmas-decorated horse and carriage had just then rounded the corner. Two men, he saw now, *had* rounded the corner and were approaching from up the street, coming along hurriedly, jingling as they came. One of them strode along a little in front of the other, and passed just then beneath a streetlight. He was heavyset and balding and wore dark clothing and spectacles – the image of Mr Pickwick. Walt realized with a shock of recognition that the man was a priest. The other man, for God's sake, was the Reverend Bentley, the two of them out on some kind of joint mission, probably ferreting out sinners.

Walt was seized with the sudden desire to run. Here he was in the street, barefoot, wearing a nightshirt, hunting roaches with a tennis shoe. What would he tell them? That this had something to do with sex?

Bentley spotted him and waved, and just then, as they drew near to the driveway, the priest set into a sort of dance, a fantastic, one-legged caper, waving his umbrella in the air as if he were casting out demons and hopping toward Walt with a look of wild glee on his face, his spectacles leaping on the bridge of his nose. Walt stood dumbfounded. Of all the late-night lunacy, this took the cake.

Nora's hopscotch! The old priest was simply hopscotching. Relieved, Walt shook Bentley's hand. Bentley was as sober-looking as Mahoney was gleeful.

'This is Walt Stebbins,' Bentley said to the priest. 'The man I've been telling you about. Stebbins, this is Father Mahoney, from the Holy Spirit.'

'My pleasure,' the priest said. He had a firm grip. Walt saw now that there were little clutches of bells clipped to both men's belts.

'Mr Stebbins once donated heavily to the lunch program,' Bentley said to Mahoney. 'I think we can use him if we can get him off his high horse.'

Walt grinned at him. *Use* him? What the *hell* was the man talking about?

'I haven't hopscotched in sixty years,' the priest said, breathing heavily. He took off his spectacles and wiped them on his shirt, then put them back on.

'We must look like a couple of crazy men to you.' Bentley squinted at Walt and jingled the bells.

'No,' Walt said, 'not at all.' He held onto his nightshirt, fighting the wind. 'I'm hardly in a position to ...' He gestured with the shoe.

'We're ringing bells,' Bentley said. 'In the middle of the night. Do you know why?'

Walt shook his head. 'I guess I don't, really.'

'Because the bells at St Anthony's were sabotaged and Mr Simms was murdered. That's right, I said *murdered*. Does this come as any surprise to you?'

'Well, I had no idea ...' Walt said. 'I haven't read anything ...'

'Of course you haven't read anything. And you won't, either. Do you know why he was murdered?'

Walt shrugged.

'*To silence the bells.*' Bentley nodded hard at him. 'Church bells, Mr Stebbins, are abhorrent to the ears of fiends and demons. Drives them mad. The streets of European cities used to be patrolled by bellmen throughout the night. Back me up here, Mahoney.'

'The Reverend Bentley is correct,' the priest said. 'These bells we carry are Benedictus bells, and with them we mean to drive the demons out of Old Towne. It's an old tradition, really, very old. "Mercy secure you all, and keep the goblin from you while you sleep." That was the chant of the bellman.'

Just then a cockroach came up out of the water meter hole and sprinted out onto the curb. Walt lunged at it, slamming it flat with the sole of the tennis shoe. He felt the cold wind on his rear end, and so he pinned down the hem of the nightshirt with his free hand again. 'Got him,' Wait said weakly, noticing that Bentley was frowning at him.

A light came on in the motor home, and the curtains were pushed aside. Aunt Jinx looked out at them, and Walt waved the tennis shoe at her as naturally as he could, as if he were just going about the usual business. Father Mahoney nodded politely. She shut the curtain again and the light went off.

'I don't suppose we'd better wake up Henry?' Bentley said to Walt.

'Better not to,' Walt said. 'He turns in early.' He nudged the smashed roach with his foot in order to loosen it from the concrete. The light was still on upstairs, and he could see a shadow move in front of the window, so it was good odds that Ivy was still awake.

'We'll tackle him tomorrow,' Bentley said.

'Good,' Walt said. 'It's getting pretty late.'

'What about you?' Bentley asked. 'Are you willing to do your part?'

'Sure,' Walt told him. 'I guess so. What part?'

'We're going to run the Devil out of town. Can we count you in?'

'I could contribute something, I guess.'

'Oh, we're not asking for money,' Mahoney said. 'We're looking for recruits.'

Walt blinked at them. He had gone through this once before with Bentley. 'I don't know ...' he said.

'Of course you don't know,' Bentley told him. 'Why should you know? I'm going to tell you something now. Can you stand to hear it?'

Walt nodded, feeling a drop of rain hit the top of his head. He was damned if he'd drown to hear it.

'It was me that burglarized your garage.'

'You?' Walt asked. And of course it was true. Everything was clear to him. Obviously Bentley had gone over the fence, then circled back around the block to where Walt had run into him.

'That's right. And by golly I'd burglarize it again if I had to. And I might, too, unless you make up your mind to come in on our side.'

'Why?' Walt asked. He knew the answer to his question even as he asked it. Of course Bentley wanted the jar. Everyone wanted the jar. Well, it belonged to Walt now, and everyone could go whistle for it.

And then he remembered – Uncle Henry had made him pitch it into the Dumpster.

'I was looking for something,' Bentley said. 'I have certain ... certain *sources*. There's a thing that's come into the country, into the neighborhood, encased in a jar, boxed up in painted tin. Do you know what I'm talking about?'

'I don't deal in jars very much,' Walt said evasively. 'I got a case of snow globes – flamingo globes, actually, filled with water. You know the kind of thing – glitter, a palm tree.'

Bentley waved the idea away. 'Don't meddle with me, son. There's no time for it now.'

'Why didn't you just *ask* me about this jar?' Walt said. 'Why break in?'

'Do you believe in the Devil?'

'I'm not sure what you …'

'Of course you're not sure. That's why I didn't ask you about it.'

He was serious! Well, so was Walt. It was his garage, and by heaven it was his jar, too. *Like* to call it … 'Who killed Mr Simms?' Walt asked abruptly. 'Do you know?'

Bentley looked at him for a moment, as if calculating, then said, 'We think we do. We believe it to be Robert Argyle, the financeer.'

'Well, that's hasty,' Mahoney said. 'We don't know any such thing.'

'He was an old friend of yours, wasn't he?' Bentley asked.

'Years ago,' Walt said, turning this whole thing over in his mind.

'Well let me give you a tip, straight from the horse,' Bentley said. '*He'll kill you too*. Don't think he won't.'

Walt realized that the shoulders of his nightshirt were wet. The rain was coming down in a mist, but harder by the moment.

'Keep a weather eye out,' Bentley said. 'We've got work to do. We can't stand here talking. If you find this jar, be *very* careful with it. Treat it like an unexploded bomb.'

'Take these,' the priest said, disconnecting the bells from his belt and handing them to Walt. 'Hang them up on the porch, like wind chimes.'

Walt took them. What the hell – it couldn't hurt.

A car turned the corner just then, from the Chapman Avenue end of the street, two hundred feet away. Its high beams were on, and Walt automatically turned his eyes away. The car accelerated suddenly, angling in toward the curb, straight at them, and Walt could see nothing but the blinding glow of its headlamps. He backpedaled, up onto the curb, felt a hand clutch the back of his nightshirt and yank him sideways. He sprawled onto his hands and knees, throwing the tennis shoe, and at the same time heard a heavy thud and squeal as the car sideswiped the curbside palm tree, then bounced down onto the road again and sped away.

Walt scrambled to his feet and helped Mahoney up. 'Thanks,' he said breathlessly.

The priest nodded. 'Which of them was it?' he asked Bentley.

The preacher shook his head. 'I couldn't see. Car's probably stolen. Anyway, it didn't have any plates. It's the same one we saw earlier, though – I know that much. I don't think it's Argyle. I think it's Nelson.'

'What on earth was that?' Aunt Jinx asked, coming around the back of the motor home now, dressed in a robe and wearing a pair of fuzzy bedroom slippers. She held a newspaper over her head to block the rain.

'Drunk driver,' Bentley said. 'Looked like he fell asleep at the wheel.' He winked at Walt and then widened his eyes, as if this attempted murder were a nice illustration of what he'd just been talking about.

'Is everyone all right, then?' Jinx asked.

'We're fine,' Walt said. 'No harm done.'

'Then go to bed,' she said. 'It's too late for all this powwow, drunks or no drunks.' She turned around and hurried away then, and Walt heard the motor home door click shut.

'I'll stop by tomorrow,' Bentley said meaningfully to Walt.

'Hang those bells up on the porch,' Mahoney said. 'Let the wind work on them.'

The two men turned and hurried away, jingling toward the corner, and Walt grabbed the tennis shoe, then pinched up the flattened roach and dumped it into the shoe. On his way back into the house he hung the bells on a loop of bare wisteria vine. Right now he would take all this lunacy at face value. Whatever else Bentley might be, he wasn't a liar. He believed, at least, that Argyle had murdered Simms for some kind of diabolical purpose. And with this car business ... *Something* was going on – perhaps something deeper and darker than Walt had thought.

On a sudden impulse he laid the shoe on the porch, turned around, and stepped down onto the driveway, tiptoeing past the motor home as quickly and silently as he could and then cutting across the street fast. Bentley and the priest were nowhere to be seen in the opposite direction; they'd turned the corner, maybe heading up toward Argyle's in order to use the bells against him. Walt shaded his face from the rain, ducking into the alley and opening the chain-link gate that cordoned off the Dumpster. He yanked a couple of trashbags out of the way, leaning over the edge of the bin, balancing there, the sodden nightshirt clinging to his legs, the scent of gin rising up around him like spilled perfume.

39

Walt raked leaves on the front lawn. It was just past noon, and the weather had cleared up some, although there was more rain forecast. It was going to be a wet Christmas. And a strange one.

It seemed to Walt that last night's adventure out on the sidewalk might have been a fabulous dream: the streetlight under a black sky, Father Mahoney hopscotching toward him down the dark sidewalk, Bentley with all his wild talk about murder and demons, the mysterious car with the license plates removed. The little cluster of bells that he'd hung from the wisteria was gone, vanished in the night, as if all of it, bells included, were a figment – all of it except the return of the thing in the jar, which was in his possession once again.

Throwing it away had clearly been a bad idea after all. Argyle wanted it. Bentley and Mahoney wanted it. So who was Walt Stebbins to be hasty with the thing? And right now it looked to him as if throwing it out was every bit as hasty as … what? *Using* it, maybe. Whatever that really consisted of. He wasn't entirely sure yet, not authentically so.

The bluebird was buried in the ground now, beneath one of the stepping-stones that led back to the garden shed. Henry knew about the tackle box, and that compromised it as a hiding place. Not that Walt didn't trust Henry, who, after all, thought that the jar was still in the Dumpster, but there were too many strange forces at work in the neighborhood to be careless. As an extra precaution, he had dropped the Sprouse Reitz parakeet into a pint-size Mason jar, filled the bottle with gin, and put it into the bluebird's tin box, then put the fake into the tackle box. If anyone broke in and stole it now – Argyle or Bentley – they could have it with his compliments.

He raked a pile of sodden leaves into an oversized plastic dustpan and dumped them into the barrel, and just then a horn tooted. It was the Reverend Bentley himself, just like he'd promised, pulling in at the curb, his face full of the same determination and urgency that Walt remembered from last night.

Walt waved at Bentley, who climbed out of the car and gestured at the motor home. Walt nodded. Henry was in. He had been out for a couple of hours that morning, but had come home an hour ago looking a little under the weather and had gone into the motor home and pulled the curtains. Whatever fires had been burning in him yesterday afternoon had dimmed considerably. Jinx was home, too, inside the house now, washing dishes.

The telephone rang, and Walt dropped the rake and went in through the screen door just as Uncle Henry appeared on the driveway, apparently having come out of the backyard. Jinx had already answered the phone. She handed Walt the receiver and went back to scrubbing dishes at the sink.

'Hello,' he said into the receiver.

For a moment there was no answer, and then a voice said, 'Walt? Is that you?'

'Yeah,' Walt said, 'who's …' But then he recognized the voice. It was Jack, liquored up. 'Jack! How the hell you doing? I figured you might call yesterday, like you said. The kids aren't here now.'

'*I'll* be the goddamn judge of that,' Jack said.

'What's wrong?' Walt said. 'Something up?'

'Don't give me any goddamn *talk*,' Jack said to him. 'I got through to Darla this morning. No more happy crap, man. That was all bullshit the other night. Shinola. *No one* does me like this.'

'Like what?' Walt asked.

'Like you know goddamn well what. What I call this is kidnapping, plain and simple. You took a man's children.'

'What I call this is drunk on your ass, Jack. Nora and Eddie are Darla's children, and she asked us to look after them.'

'I *raised* those kids, damn it. I paid their bills, and I know my rights.'

'You don't have any rights, Jack, except the right to sober up. It's just past noon, for God's sake. Put the bottle down. Give it a rest. You'll talk more sense when you're sober.'

'There's a few people I'm going to talk a *hell* of a lot of sense to,' Jack said. 'Or else my lawyer will. What I want you to do is have Eddie and Nora ready to go. Whatever crap they brought along, have that ready, too. I'll be around to pick 'em up.'

'Don't waste your time, Jack. You can't have them.'

'Look, fuck you and fuck whatever game you're playing. They're *my* kids. *I'm* the only father they ever had.'

'Then that's a hell of a dirty shame.'

'What the hell do you know about it? You don't have any kids. It takes a *man* to raise kids. I don't know what the hell *you* are, living off your wife, out in the garage all day yanking the goddamn crank, but you don't have *any* right to keep a man away from his kids. I want 'em now. If I have to bring a cop along I'll do it.'

'Bring a cop, Jack. You're drunk as a pig. I wouldn't trust you with a box full of tin bugs.'

'You listen ...' Jack started to say.

'Shut the hell up,' Walt said, his voice perfectly even. 'I want to ask you something about being a *man*. Where the hell were you all day yesterday? You call up night before last worried about Nora and Eddie, but you don't want to talk to them – you'll call them tomorrow. But where the hell are you tomorrow? Sloshed. Isn't that right? You've been living on pretzels and salted peanuts? Vitamin C out of the lime slice? I didn't even bother to tell the kids you called, because I *knew* you wouldn't call back. You're a king-hell asshole, Jack. Maybe you get it naturally. Maybe it comes out of a bottle. I don't give a damn either way. But you better get a handle on it. Because until you do, I swear to God I won't let you near these children. What you'll get if you come around here is a fist in the face.'

'You can't ...'

'And fuck you too.'

He hung up the phone without listening to another word. His hand was shaking and he could barely breathe. He'd lost it, gone right over the top. And now what had he done? Kidnapped the kids? Maybe Jack *did* have some kind of rights. You pay property taxes long enough on a house, and you *own* the house; did Jack *own* the kids in that same way? He realized that Jinx was looking at him wide-eyed.

'I'm sorry about the language,' he said, shaking his head. 'That was Jack. He's been drinking for a week now. Darla's gone back east to get away from him. That's why Ivy and I have the kids. I've got a real attitude about all of it.'

'Lord have mercy,' Jinx said, putting her hand to her mouth. 'Ivy told me something about that. And now Jack wants to take them back? He's just figured all this out?'

'That's about it.'

'Does he know which school they're at? Because if he does we ought to call and warn them.'

'No,' Walt said. 'And I don't think he can find out, either, unless he calls every preschool in the area. Even then they might not tell him anything. Security's pretty tight these days. I just don't want him coming around the house when the kids are here, not when he's drunk. I'd have to call the cops myself. Nora and Eddie don't need that kind of scene.'

'You watch out for him, Walter. Don't push him. Nora and Eddie don't need that, either.'

Walt nodded. She was right. Whatever else he was, Jack was telling the truth about raising Nora and Eddie, and that was probably worth something. 'It'll work out,' he said. 'Once he sobers up he'll calm down.' Unconvinced, he went back outside, where Bentley and Uncle Henry were sitting on the clamshell chairs on the front porch.

'Here he is,' Henry said, motioning toward the front porch swing.

Walt sat down, his mind racing.

'Lorimer was asking about the jar,' Henry said, keeping his voice low.

'Lorimer?' Walt looked at him.

Henry nodded at Bentley, and Walt caught on. 'Oh, of course,' he said. 'I guess we haven't really been on a first-name basis, have we?'

'I told him we threw it in the bin,' Henry said.

Walt looked from one to the other of them. 'I'm afraid that's true,' he said to Bentley. 'In the alley. I didn't want to tell you last night. Frankly, I was a little miffed about the break-in. Anyway, Orange Disposal hauled it away this morning. It's landfill now.' Actually, this was a lie, but Bentley couldn't know anything about trash schedules.

Bentley continued to stare at him, as if he were doubtful about all this. Henry watched Bentley uneasily.

'I'm afraid *I* made him toss it out,' Henry said. 'It looked … evil. Something about it … Anyway, we got rid of it.'

Bentley nodded finally, then sat back in his chair. 'You were absolutely right,' he said. 'You did the right thing. It's what I would have done with it.'

'Good,' Henry said. The old man looked nervous, somehow, like he was in trouble.

'Something wrong?' Walt asked him.

'No, no, no,' Henry said, wiping his forehead. His hand was trembling.

'You're not a stupid man,' Bentley said, looking Walt in the eye.

Walt waited.

'What did you do with the bells?'

'Hung them up,' Walt said, surprised at this turn.

'Where? They're still hung up?'

'No. I hung them right here on the porch. They disappeared. Someone stole them, I guess. The wind was still blowing them around at midnight, so it must have been early this morning.'

'Why would they do that – steal a few brass bells in the middle of a rainy night?'

'I ...' Walt shrugged. 'What were you saying last night?' Somehow Bentley reminded him of his fourth-grade teacher, Mrs Bender, drilling him for information, being as subtle as an ice pick.

'What I said last night was true. You can bet your immortal soul on it.' He leaned forward. 'What do you know about the connection between Robert Argyle and Murray LeRoy?'

'I wouldn't have connected them at all,' Walt said. 'I read about LeRoy in the paper, about his going nuts.'

'He didn't go *nuts*,' Bentley said. 'It's closer to the truth to say that he went diabolical, although maybe that's the same thing sometimes.'

Walt nodded, widening his eyes. *Diabolical*, here it came again ...

'Don't play the fool,' Bentley said. 'If you mean to say something, say it.'

'It's just that all this diabolical talk ...'

'Is what? You don't like it, do you? You don't want to think about damnation, do you? Not like that. It's too unpleasant. It's too *sharp*. It makes certain things too *clear*, and it's an easier world when you can keep those kinds of things a little bit out of focus. "Don't tell me too much," people say. "Let me believe the easy thing." Well, gentlemen, what I'm about to tell you isn't easy.'

40

'Go on,' Walt said to Bentley. 'We're listening.'

'I'll put it to you straight,' Bentley said. 'Robert Argyle *sold his soul to the Devil.*'

'Then the Devil got stiffed,' Walt said, 'because Argyle's soul wasn't worth a glass of milk, even back then when it was fresh.'

Bentley looked hard at him.

'Sorry,' Walt said. 'I didn't mean to make a joke out of it.'

'I'm not philosophizing here,' Bentley said. 'I'm talking about *what happened* – as if I said that Argyle signed papers to buy a house. I mean to say he made a bargain with Satan. Money, power, what have you.'

'I get it,' Walt said, picturing the transaction – the Devil in natty clothes, snazzy hat, probably driving a Lincoln Town Car and offering Argyle a twenty-six-percent return …

'Murray LeRoy sold his soul, too, at the same time.'

'Then you're right,' Walt said. 'It's not very funny.'

'And if you're with me this far, then I'll tell you something worse. Simms is dead on account of it. You can take that to the bank. All of this is my fault.'

'I don't see how,' Henry said, leaning forward in his chair. 'So far you're in the clear. Let these other men *go* to the Devil. That's their choice. That avenue's always open to a man, buyer beware.'

Bentley waved him silent. 'What I'm telling you is that I'm the man who brokered the deal, paper contract and all. Signature in gold ink.'

'What do you mean, "brokered"?' Walt asked.

'Middle man. I set it up – the mumbo jumbo. I made a few dollars, too; I can tell you that, although I won't tell you how much. I was even fool enough to think that some good could come of it – taking their dirty money. Maybe it did, too. I used it hard enough. It bought more lunches than you'd believe, and it paid a few bills, too. Both of those scoundrels worked for the Church. It's a good joke, eh? Don't you think? Their money was a means to an end, never mind where it came from. To this day they don't know who I really am. They don't know who they did business with.'

'Actually,' Walt said, 'if I understand what you're telling me, it was a *hell* of a good joke. Let me get this straight. You set up this phony soul-selling scam and made them *pay* for it?'

'Oh, they paid for it,' Bentley said. 'But paying *me* was the least of it. Now they're paying the piper. It's come full circle. Murray LeRoy was consumed by the fires of Hell – spontaneous human combustion!'

Walt nodded. Bentley was apparently off his chump after all, and just when it was looking like he had a first-rate sense of humor. 'I wouldn't worry about it. You conned a couple of monsters out of a few bucks over the years. They can afford it.'

'And so I thought. I had the best intentions. That much I'll claim. But the road to Hell is paved with that commodity, friend.'

'I guess,' Walt said skeptically.

'You don't grasp this,' Bentley said. 'I *used* them, didn't I? I played a hoax, a joke. And now I discover that the joke is on me. I was just larking around, slipping the wallets out of the pockets of a couple of prize idiots. But what I found out is something I already should have known: *the Devil doesn't kid around*. He's *got* no sense of humor. He's in *deadly* earnest.' He looked at Walt, letting this sink in.

'Still ...' Walt started to say.

'Still nothing. You're with me about halfway. You want to think that all this talk is some kind of tomfoolery. You're a good man, so you don't laugh at it, but you don't *believe* it either. You're thinking, what's this got to do with me?'

'Okay,' Walt said. 'What's this got to do with me? If you want to know the truth, I don't care if Robert Argyle goes straight to Hell. He can take the express. I'll pay to upgrade his ticket.'

'You make sure you don't go with him,' Bentley said. 'That's what I'm trying to tell you. This thing in the jar that I asked you about, that you and Henry threw in the bin?'

Walt nodded.

'Robert Argyle must not have it.'

'I tossed it out,' Walt said, feeling himself flush with shame at the lie. And to a minister, too ...

'Because if ...'

A car was pulling up at the curb just then, moving way too fast. Hell, it was Jack's T-bird! Jack banked the tires off the curb and shut the engine down, leaving the car angled into the street. The door flew open and he heaved himself out, coming around the back of the car, taking big steps, loaded for bear. He cut it too close, though, and his hip bumped the fender hard. He staggered, caught himself, and stepped up onto the curb with exaggerated care. He was drunk, all right, but he was trying hard not to look drunk.

'Hey, brother,' Jack said, nodding at Walt as he came up the walk.

'Hello, Jack.'

'You got the kids ready to go?'

Walt shook his head. 'They aren't here. I told you that over the phone.'

'Hi, folks,' Jack said, nodding to Henry and Bentley. 'This man's stolen my children, and I'm here to get them back.'

'Jack, the kids aren't here,' Walt said. 'You might as well run along.'

'*You* run the hell along,' Jack said, getting mad suddenly. 'I told you I wanted my kids. So you get my kids.'

'And I told you the kids aren't here. As long as you're drunk, they *won't he* here, either.'

'I'll by God *see* who's here,' Jack shouted, lunging suddenly at the door.

Walt stepped into his way, and Jack swung hard at him with the back of his hand. Walt ducked away from it sideways, and Jack's forearm slammed into his shoulder, knocking him into the Reverend Bentley, who was just then trying to stand up. Jack grabbed the handle of the screen door and swung it open, and just then the end of a broom thrust through the open door, the corn bristles shoving hard into Jack's chest and neck.

'Ow!' he shouted, stumbling backward, and Jinx stepped out onto the porch, carrying the broom with both hands like a rifle with a bayonet, her face set like a stone mask. She swung the broom sideways, hitting him in the chest with the flat of it, and he turned around and stepped off the porch, missing the second step entirely and sprawling down onto the lawn, knocking down Walt's trash can full of leaves. Jinx followed him, getting clear of the porch roof so that she could use the broom more effectively. She said nothing, just raised the broom straight into the air and pounded it down onto Jack's head as he scuttled toward the sidewalk yelling, 'Hey! Hey! Hey! Watch it!' He stood up, covering his head and angling around behind the T-bird, keeping it between them.

Jinx waited at the edge of the lawn now that she'd driven him off, ready for him if he made a move toward the house. Walt turned away so that Jack wouldn't see him smile. There was no vise humiliating him any more than he'd already been humiliated. The man would come back with a gun and kill them all.

The phone rang inside, and Henry stood up and made for the door. 'I'll grab it,' he said. 'Watch out for Jinx.'

Jack shook his fist, breathing in big gasps. 'I'll be back!' he shouted. He looked as if he wanted to say more, but couldn't find anything good enough.

'That's right,' Walt said, coming down to where Jinx stood with the broom. 'We'll see you when you're sober, Jack.' He put his arm around Jinx's shoulder. 'You okay?' he asked her.

She nodded.

'Who *was* that man?' The Reverend Bentley came down off the porch just as Jack tore away in his car, running straight through the stop sign at the corner of the street.

'That man is a *husk*,' Jinx said, breathing heavily. 'He isn't fit to be those children's father. Thank God he's *not* their father.'

'He's the weak brother,' Walt said.

Bentley nodded. 'He's been drinking.'

'Indeed he has,' Walt said.

Finished with her task, Jinx headed for the house again, just as the screen swung open and Henry stepped out. Somehow Henry looked hammered, worse off than Jack, as if he'd just been given some kind of terminal news. He smiled weakly at Jinx and patted her on the shoulder, but she pushed on into the house, not really looking at him, still fired up from the confrontation.

Henry glanced at Walt and shook his head.

'Bad news on the phone?' Walt asked.

'Lord, lord, lord,' the old man said, sitting down heavily. He craned his neck, looking back in through the window as if to make sure Jinx wasn't lurking by the open door.

'What is it?' Bentley asked. 'What's wrong?'

'It's the Biggs woman.' He gestured feebly, putting his hand to his face. 'It's very bad. The only good thing is that I answered the phone and not Jinx.'

'Biggs?' Walt asked. 'Who …?'

'From the All-Niter,' Henry said, gesturing up the street. 'Maggie Biggs.'

Walt sat down. This was it, just as he'd feared – the hula-hula woman. Trouble, and quicker than he would have thought possible. She was sixty-five years old if she was a day, so at least there wouldn't be any paternity suit.

'Talk to us, Henry,' Bentley said, forgetting for the moment about himself. Walt found that he liked Bentley suddenly, just like that. There was something okay about him, something that Walt hadn't seen before, probably because he'd never been able to get past the tracts and the preachery.

'I'm in trouble,' Henry said. 'Jinx deserves better than me.'

'Nonsense,' Bentley said. 'Let's have it. Whatever you've done, it can be fixed.'

'Not this time.' He shook his head, denying it. 'It's broken this time. I … I've been seeing too much of this … this Biggs woman. I guess you knew that, Walt. You tried to warn me. Well, she got her *mitts* on me. I guess you could say that and you wouldn't be far wrong.'

Bentley scowled, as if he didn't quite buy the mitts business.

'She claims I … had my way with her,' Henry said, 'and she's threatened to go to Jinx with it.'

'Had your way?' Walt asked. 'You've only known her for what? – two or three days?'

Henry shrugged. 'It's a dirty lie. It was *harmless*, I swear it. But Jinx won't see it that way, not anymore. She'll go to Goldfarb, and that'll be the end of it.'

'There's no need to swear,' Bentley said. 'We both believe you. My advice is to go to Jinx yourself. We'll stand behind you, by golly. Let's do it now!' He stood up.

'Good heavens, no!' Henry said. 'Sit down. And keep your voice down, for heaven's sake. After last winter …' He shook his head. 'I've been a damned fool. Why *should* she believe me?'

'Just tell her it's over with this Biggs woman,' Walt said in a low voice. 'It won't be easy, but you've got to come clean with her. Stop the trolley right here and get off.'

'That's the ticket,' Bentley said. 'If you've made a mistake, own up to it. As for this Biggs, do the manly thing – tell her it's over, it's all been a mistake.'

'That's what I did,' Henry told them. 'That's the whole trouble. Maggie Biggs lives out past Satellite Market, out on Olive. I went over there this morning and called it off, told her this whole thing was a mistake. But she wouldn't take no. She wouldn't listen. Now she's tracked me down. She'll tell Jinx some kind of lie just as sure as …' His voice trailed off.

'Did you … did you have your way with her?' Bentley asked.

Henry shook his head. 'I don't claim to be innocent in this,' he said, 'but by God I didn't touch her.'

'Then I think we can talk to her,' Walt said. 'She'll see reason.' This struck him as the empty-headedest thing he'd ever said. Clearly she wouldn't see any such thing. Maggie Biggs was doom in a muumuu.

'I'd be happy to go along,' Bentley said. 'I can be a persuasive prick when I want to be.'

'Thank you, boys,' Henry said. 'I'm on thin ice.'

Walt looked at his watch. It was still early. 'She called from home?'

Henry nodded.

'Will you take a look at that?' Bentley said suddenly. He pointed at the sky. Off to the west a plume of black smoke rose into the sky. There was the sound of sirens just then.

'Looks like the Plaza,' Walt said.

Bentley stood up. 'Let's go,' he said. Suddenly his voice was full of urgency, as if this smoke in the sky had something to do with what he'd been talking about, with what he feared.

Jinx came to the door just then, carrying her purse. 'Gladys is coming by to pick me up,' she said to Henry and Walt. 'We won't be late, but remember that I won't be cooking dinner.'

Henry nodded vaguely, and Jinx disappeared back into the house.

Bentley headed down the steps and made for the car without another word, as if he were going right now, with or without them.

41

The fire in the Plaza was out by the time Bentley pulled into a parking space near the Continental Cafe. There was smoke in the air, but only a thin blue-black haze blowing eastward in the wind. A fire truck and a paramedics unit sat at the mouth of the alley adjacent to Nelson and Whidley, and behind a barrier of yellow police tape a crowd of onlookers stood around silently, their arms crossed, a couple of them breathing through handkerchiefs.

Bentley climbed out of the car and hurried away, leaving the door open, his face stricken with fear and doubt.

'I'll wait in the car,' Henry said, dismissing the entire scene with a wave of his hand. 'I'm a little tired right now.'

Walt climbed out and shut Bentley's door, then edged along behind the crowd, standing on tiptoe on the curb in order to see up the dead-end alley. Bentley elbowed his way to the front, apologizing left and right, until he stood among the press of firemen and paramedics that hid the scene from the street. There was the awful and unmistakable smell of burnt bone on the air, along with something more – a smell like an electrical short, like charred wire and insulation mixed up with burnt sulphur.

'What happened?' Walt asked, glancing at the man next to him.

'They tell me somebody burned up,' he said, shrugging. 'I got here at the end of it. Lawyer, apparently. From the offices right here on the corner. Chemical fire, I guess. Burned him to a cinder just like the fire the other day. Same damned thing, except this didn't touch his clothes. Don't ask me how.'

Bentley turned around just then and surveyed the onlookers hastily, spotting Walt and waving him forward. 'Excuse me,' Walt said to two women in front of him. 'Investigation Division.' They smiled and stepped aside for him, and he said the same thing to the man in front of them, who scooted out of the way in order to let him pass.

Bentley stepped forward and took his elbow, shaking his head darkly. 'Take a look,' he said. 'This is what I've been talking about.'

Walt bent forward, looking past the shoulder of a fireman, down past the edge of the brick building. Immediately he wished he hadn't, and he looked away again, thinking suddenly of Simms's body at the base of the bell tower. A human skeleton lay huddled against the wall of the alley, its skull tilted downward so that its eye sockets stared at the asphalt, its fingers splayed out as if the dying man had tried to push himself to his feet.

The skeleton was fully clothed. It was wearing a three-piece suit, light blue.

Walt looked again, despite the horror of it. From what he could see – the hand and wrist bones, the skull and first vertebra – the man's flesh had been almost entirely consumed by the fire, and yet, except for the charred collar, the suit itself was unburned.

And draped across the back of the coat, just below the collar, as if it had been flung around by the force of the body falling, was a laminated card on a chain, the plastic lamination clean and smooth, as if to illustrate Sidney Vest's promise that the card was fireproof, 'ready for takeoff.'

A man in a tie and shirtsleeves snapped a picture of the corpse, and firemen moved in around it again, hiding it from Walt's view.

He realized that Bentley was staring at him. 'Now that you've seen, you believe, eh? No more doubting Thomas?'

'Believe what?' Walt asked.

'This was no chemical fire.'

Walt shrugged. 'That's what they're saying.'

'Who the hell are *they*? The police? What *they're* saying doesn't matter. *They* might as well say he was burned up by his own cigar. As for me, I know this man.' Bentley moved off now, angling through the crowd toward where Henry still sat in the car, staring straight ahead, lost in thought.

'Let me guess,' Walt said, following along. 'This was another of your men, your diabolists?'

'George Nelson.'

'*Nelson*?' Walt said. 'Well, I'll be damned. It's a small world.'

'You knew him?'

Walt nearly laughed out loud, suddenly recalling Sidney Vest's nonsense yesterday at Coco's. He could picture the newspaper headline: 'Thirty-eight Vice Presidents Broiled In Alley.'

'He was one of the First Captains, wasn't he?' Walt asked, repeating Vest's ridiculous phrase.

Bentley stopped dead, his face pale. 'What do you know about the Captains?' he asked.

'Nothing. A man named Sidney Vest used the phrase yesterday. I bought him lunch over at Coco's, and he tried to rope Henry and me into going to some kind of investment meeting.'

'*Vest*,' Bentley said, nearly spitting out the name. 'Don't have anything to do with the man.'

'No, I won't. I don't believe in getting rich quick.'

Bentley looked at him. 'This is no damned joke,' he said. 'Get that into your head.' He set out toward the car again, his face suddenly angry. But he hadn't taken two steps when, casting a glance at the Plaza, he suddenly darted forward, straight through the open door of the Continental Cafe, where he disappeared among the tables.

What the hell ...? Walt wondered, stepping to the door and glancing inside. Bentley sat at a table at the rear of the cafe, pretending to read a menu. His back was to the door, and he watched the street in one of the big mirrors on the wall. He caught Walt's eye and gestured emphatically, shaking his head.

Walt turned away, heading for the car again, just as Robert Argyle's Mercedes Benz pulled into an adjacent stall. Bentley must have seen the car coming round the other side of the Plaza. Argyle looked hard at Walt, squinting his eyes, clearly full of doubt, seeing him downtown at a time like this. He climbed out and nodded. Walt nodded back, leaning against one of the pine trees at the curb.

'Looks like another fire,' Argyle said to him, locking up the Mercedes with some kind of remote device.

'Another case of spontaneous human combustion, apparently,' Walt said, just for effect. The words hit Argyle like a blow. He licked his lips, as if he wanted to say something but the effort was too much. Seeing the reaction, Walt said, 'Whoever it was went up like a torch, just like Murray LeRoy.' He shook his head sadly. 'I've got a hunch I know what's going on, too.'

'What are you talking about?' Argyle said now, looking at him incredulously. His voice was creaky with strain.

'Devil worship,' Walt whispered, winking at him. 'I hear that George Nelson, this dead lawyer, *made a pact with the Devil* The news is all over town.
Now he's been burned up by the eternal fires. The Devil came for him and
took him straight to Hell – nothing left but calcinated bones and a three-piece
suit, the poor sap. Must have hurt like nobody's business, burning up like
that ...'

He quit talking, suddenly afraid that Argyle was having a stroke. Or worse,
that he was set to burst into flame right there on the spot. Argyle's face was
red as a crab leg, and the tendons in his neck stuck out like ropes. His eyes
stared at Walt, jumping in their sockets. His mouth twitched, and he made a
noise, but no words came out, so he clamped his teeth shut with what was
apparently a tremendous effort. Slowly he turned around and walked away
toward the alley, saying nothing. There was a clearing through the crowd
now, and Walt could see that they had the corpse on a stretcher. Argyle
stopped and stared at it, standing ramrod straight, like a wooden dummy.

Walt was aware suddenly that Bentley was gesturing at him from the doorway of the cafe, jerking his thumb toward the corner. Walt nodded, hurrying
away, rounding the corner without looking back. He waited in front of an
antiques shop, and in a moment Bentley's car pulled around and whipped
into the red zone. Walt climbed in, and Bentley motored away up Glassell
Street, turning the corner and heading west toward Olive.

'I thought Argyle didn't know you,' Walt said. 'Why all this secrecy?'

'He *doesn't* know me. Not in that capacity. But I had a little run-in with a
couple of friends of his night before last, out at Murray LeRoy's. I don't want
to be turning up too often – not yet, anyway. Did he speak to you?'

'Not really,' Walt said. 'Just small talk.'

42

Mrs Biggs lived in a Spanish-style rental, a small, flat-roofed house with a big
garage and an unkempt lawn that clearly hadn't been mowed or raked since
summer. There was an old Buick sitting in the driveway. The curtains were
pulled across the windows, and Walt found himself hoping that she wouldn't
be home, that she had walked down to Satellite Market or to the Spic 'n'
Span Cleaners and they'd have to come back tomorrow.

They sat at the curb for a moment, none of them making a move to get out.

'We're petrified, aren't we?' Walt asked finally. 'Mrs Biggs is going to work us over.'

'I'm afraid you're right,' Henry said. 'I didn't offer her money, exactly ...'

'Money!' Bentley said. 'Not a penny of it! We'll go straight to the police!'

'Good Lord, no!' Henry said. 'I don't mean *real* money. Just a little something ... to make amends.'

'Like a gift,' Walt said, taking out his wallet.

'I'm afraid I'm a little short right at the moment,' Henry said. 'Jinx is the banker these days, and she's a little tight with it. I'll cover any losses, though.'

Walt had four twenties in his wallet along with a couple of ones. That ought to about cover it. He opened the door and got out.

'Maybe I'd better stay here for the moment,' Henry said. 'What do you think?'

'I think that's a good idea,' Walt said through the window. 'Let us run interference for you. You don't have a twenty, do you?' he asked Bentley. 'That would give us an even hundred, just in case we need it.'

Bentley scowled at him and shook his head. 'It's *wrong*,' he said, hitching up his pants.

Walt saw the window curtains move. Mrs Biggs had been watching them. She opened the door when he and Bentley were halfway up the walk. She was wearing a muumuu and an orange wig with a flip like an ocean wave on the side of it. Somehow the wig made her head look small. She was pretty clearly assessing them, wondering whether she should parlay with them or send them packing. Suddenly she stepped aside and swung the door wide open.

'Step right in, boys,' she said, dusting off her hands. She shut the door. And then, making a show of it, she yanked the curtains open, revealing the interior of the house to the street, as if to warn them against trying anything fancy. 'Which one of you is the lawyer?' she asked.

'Neither of us is a lawyer,' Bentley said. 'I'm a minister, Lorimer Bentley.' He put his hand out.

'A reverend?' She gaped at him, taking his hand for a moment and then letting it fall. 'Well, he needs one, the old fraud. You know that he took unfair advantage of me?'

'He fell for you pretty hard,' Walt said, deciding to play the vanity angle. 'That morning when he saw you at the All-Niter – that brought back a lot of memories. He told me that you hadn't changed in ... How long had it been? Forty years? That threw him for a loop, seeing you there, an attractive woman from his past. He was like a teenager.'

'Well ...' She smiled at Walt. 'Still, he's a married man, isn't he? He ought to know better than to give a poor old woman the business. And a lie is a lie, isn't it?'

Walt shrugged. There was no use arguing with her. It was better to jolly her along, to give her what she wanted – up to a point, anyway.

She gazed at the rug for a moment, as if gathering her thoughts. 'Something happened to a friend of mine once,' she said, sitting down on the couch. She gestured at a couple of doily-draped armchairs, and Walt and Bentley sat down too. 'Her name was Velma Krane – with a K. She lived in Waikiki. This was in the days when there was nothing on the beach but the Royal Hawaiian and a few palm trees, not the tourist mess it is today. Today it's too much noise and buses and cheap T-shirts.'

'I hear it was beautiful back then,' Walt said.

'Nothing on the wind but plumeria blossoms and the smell of the ocean.' She gazed at the street, remembering. 'It was truly paradise.' She seemed to have lost the thread.

'Look here,' Bentley said, looking at his wristwatch. 'Let's get down to brass tacks. What you've threatened Henry with is simply not ...'

'Hold on, Reverend,' Walt said, waving him silent. 'Mrs Biggs has a story to tell, and I think we ought to listen. What about your friend Velma Krane? You were illustrating your point, I think.'

'Thank you,' she said to Walt. 'It's rare to find simple politeness these days. I appreciate a man who can listen – really *listen*.' She looked at Bentley pretty hard for a moment before going on. 'I guess you could say that Velma was just too ... *kind* for her own good. She befriended a man, took him in, fed him. And purely out of the kindness of her heart, too. He wasn't a rich man.'

Bentley sighed heavily and drummed his fingers on the arm of the couch. He looked at his watch again.

'I'm afraid your friend is impatient,' Mrs Biggs said to Walt.

'Oh, no,' Bentley said. 'I just fail to see how ...'

'I think that if we listen we'll discover how,' Walt said to him. 'Go on, ma'am.'

'Well, to make a long story short, a romance developed, and I'm afraid that she, that Velma ...' Mrs Biggs shook her head and looked at the carpet again. 'She was taken advantage of. Against my advice. Make no mistake about that – I warned her against him. I saw him for what he was. I said, "Velma, that man is a no-good Lothario." But she didn't listen. How could she? *She was listening to her heart.*' Mrs Biggs wiped her eye.

'And he left her cold?' Walt asked. 'This Lothario?'

She nodded. 'He was gone in the morning. He didn't take her money, but he took something more valuable by far ...' She paused, looking from Bentley to Walt.

'What was that?' Bentley asked.

'Her *dignity*,' she said to him, squinting hard to make it hit home.

Bentley had a fixed expression on his face now. His head swiveled slightly, and he glanced at Walt. Walt winked at him.

'And do you know what I told Velma?'

Walt shook his head.

'I said, "Velma, you've got to be compensated." That's just what I said. Those were my very words. Compensated.'

'I fully agree,' Walt said.

'Somehow I knew you would. I could see it in your face.' She stood up and patted him on the hand. 'I'll just put on the teakettle,' she said, and stepped across the living room, through the arched doorway that led to the kitchen.

'This is an outrage!' Bentley hissed at him. 'She means to take us straight to the cleaners.'

'I'll mollify her,' Walt said. 'It won't be much of a cleaners.' He went into the kitchen, drawing two of the twenties out of his wallet. Mrs Biggs fussed at the stove, an old O'Keefe and Merritt. There was the formaldehyde smell of gas on the air, and she waved a lit match at the burner, dropping it suddenly on the stovetop and shaking her hand.

'Pilot won't work?'

'It hasn't worked in ages.'

'Let me take a look.' He lifted the griddle in the center of the stovetop. The pilot was burning fine. It was probably the pipes clogged with grease or dust. 'I think I can finagle this if you have a rat-tail brush – like for cleaning out a turkey baster.'

'I have just the thing,' she said, opening a drawer.

'Henry said something about owing you a few dollars,' Walt said to her. 'I don't know what for – something he borrowed, I guess. He likes to pay his debts. Will this cover it?' He held out the two twenties. She took them out of his hand without answering and folded them into the pocket of her muumuu.

'When you're living on a fixed income …' She shook her head sadly. 'Velma had a little one-bedroom walkup. I guess I should feel lucky.'

She found the brush and handed it to Walt, who pulled apart the pipes in the stove. There was nothing very complicated about the plumbing in an old gas stove. A couple of minutes of sweeping out the dust was all it usually took, just to get the crumbs out …

43

Bentley came in and stood in the doorway. 'Henry's still in the car,' he said to Walt, nodding back over his shoulder.

'This won't take a second.' Walt laid the tube that ran to the pilot back into its slot and cranked the knob. Nothing happened. He fiddled with it, but after a moment there was the smell of gas again, and he twisted the knob back off. Something else was wrong. 'Let me check one more thing,' he said.

'You might as well make yourself useful too, Reverend,' Mrs Biggs said to Bentley. 'Have you ever emptied a trash bucket before, or do you just do the soul's work?'

'Of *course* I've emptied a trash bucket. Emptying trash buckets *is* the soul's work.'

'Then you're in luck,' she said, and she swung open the cupboard beneath the sink and gestured at the red plastic trash bucket. 'The cans are out behind the garage. Separate the recycle!'

Bentley hesitated for a moment, then moved into the room and pulled the bucket out from its cupboard. She opened the back door for him, and he went out. Walt took the stove top apart, piece by piece, setting it around on the floor, only then noticing that the undersides of the chrome top pieces were slick with dirty grease. 'Any newspaper?' he asked.

'Might as well wash it all up, now that you've gone and pulled it apart.' She put a stopper in the drain, cranked on the hot water, and found a box of Brillo Pads under the sink. Walt picked up the cast-iron burner grills and put them into the hot water.

Bentley came back in just then, carrying the empty bucket. He didn't look happy.

'Look there,' Mrs Biggs said, pointing at the linoleum floor. There was a litter of muddy dirt on the tiles. Bentley looked at the sole of one of his shoes, which was caked with mud from the backyard. '*Now your* work's cut out for you,' she said. 'Broom and dustpan's in the pantry. And take your shoes off first! Put them out on the stoop.'

Bentley stood staring at her. 'Henry's in ...' he started to say.

'In the car,' she said. 'We all know he's in the car. Let him sit there. It's the best place for him. As long as he's in the car he's not out wrecking the lives of half the women in the neighborhood. He won't get heatstroke, not on a day like this.'

Bentley set the trash bucket down, turned around slowly, and went back out through the door, where he slipped his shoes off.

'These preachers,' Mrs Biggs whispered to Walt. 'Too heavy for light work and too light for heavy work.' She shook her head.

'He's just out of practice,' Walt said. 'Do you have any kind of degreaser? Something in a spray bottle?'

'Just the thing,' she said, reaching under the sink again. 'You might as well do the job right.'

Bentley came back in.

'In the pantry,' she said to him, pointing toward a big cupboard near the door.

He opened it and got out a broom, then poked at the dirt on the floor. The dirt was too wet, though, and simply smeared across the linoleum.

'Mop's in there too,' she said. 'Hot water's in the sink. Use the right tool for the right job. I'm surprised I have to tell you that, a man your age. Maybe you'd better fetch Henry out of the car after all at this rate, the kind of job you do.'

She took a flyswatter from a peg on the wall and slammed the hell out of a fly that was just then buzzing against the window, then settled herself on a stool by the sink.

'He wouldn't have lasted a week at the Paradise, my place in Honolulu. Any of those little Filipino girls could clean circles around him.' She squinted at Bentley, who clearly kept his silence for Henry's sake. He edged past her, dipping the mop into the sink and then twisting some of the water out of it.

'That's still too wet,' she said to him, pointing at the mop with the swatter. 'It'll take a week for the floor to dry. You're not bathing a poodle here, you're just picking up a little dirt.'

He wrung it out again, leaning into it, nearly tearing the head off the mop, then he moved off across the kitchen again and slapped it around on the muddy floor.

'Watch out with that mop! For heaven's sake!' she said. 'Mind the cream pitchers!'

On a shelf above the back door stood a half dozen ceramic pitchers – cow and moose heads, a pig with a corkscrew tail, a Cheshire cat. All of them had holes in their mouths or noses where the cream could pour out. Bentley looked at them for a moment as if he didn't quite understand them, then went back to mopping.

'That's right,' she said, 'back away from it, don't walk through it or you'll get your socks wet and track it all over the rest of the floor. There, you missed some – along the baseboard.' She gestured with the swatter again. Walt sprayed the degreaser on the last of the stove pieces and wiped them down with a rag. The least he could do was leave it clean, since, he knew by now, there was no way he was going to fix it. He didn't have the foggiest idea what was wrong with it.

Bentley rinsed the mop again, then took one last swipe at the remnants of the mud. Turning toward the sink, he clipped the cream pitcher shelf with the mop handle, and the cow head pitched off the shelf onto the floor, breaking into three or four pieces.

44

Bentley stared at the broken cow head in disbelief. Mrs Biggs slumped, putting her face in her hands as if this had finally defeated her utterly.

'I'm *terribly* sorry,' Bentley said, dropping to his hands and knees. He picked up the fragments and tried to fit them together. 'Here we go, here's its eye ...' He groped under the edge of the clothes dryer.

'That was a *priceless* antique.'

'Let me pay you for it,' Bentley said. 'Honestly ... How *stupid* of me ...' He held his hands out, shaking his head helplessly at Walt.

'Maybe some Super Glue?' Walt said helpfully.

'That's kind of you,' Mrs Biggs said to Walt, 'but I'm afraid your friend has ruined it. I won't say that he did it on purpose, but ...'

'I most certainly did *not* do any such thing!' Bentley said, his face suddenly red. 'I'll be *happy* to take your word for it being valuable.' He hauled his wallet out, fingering the bills inside and drawing out a ten. She stared at it, as if it were some kind of Chinese phoney-dough.

'Don't in*sult* me,' she said coldly.

'All right. Fair enough.' Bentley took out a twenty and started to put the ten back, but Mrs Biggs pulled them both out of his hand.

'Fifty dollars should just about do it,' she said. '*If* I can replace the creamer at all. That object was made in *Germany* – prewar.'

Bentley looked at Walt again. 'That's it,' he said. 'I'm tapped out.'

'What do you need?' Walt asked, settling the chrome top back onto the stove. 'Another twenty?' He got his wallet out and handed over a twenty. Mrs Biggs took it politely.

Uncle Henry appeared right then, out on the driveway, standing next to the Buick and looking like a lost child. He waved at them.

'You might as well get the old goat in here,' Mrs Biggs said to Walt. 'He can at least lend a hand. He's got to be good for something.'

'Now look here,' Bentley said, starting up again. 'This has gone just about far enough. We've mopped your floor and repaired your stove ...'

'And broke my priceless heirloom, you might as well say.'

Walt opened the back door and gestured at Uncle Henry. 'Watch the mud,' he said as the old man came around the back side of the house.

'Is she still on the warpath?' Henry whispered.

'She's had it with Bentley. He's not much of a diplomat.'

'Roll up your sleeves, Henry, and scrub up this mess in the sink.' She shouted past Bentley and waved Henry in through the door. 'And you,

Reverend, why don't you see what you can do with a tube of glue, unless you've got the shakes. You don't look too steady. Not a secret toper, are you? Or is that what your big rush is all about? Too long away from the sauce?' She grinned at him for a moment before opening a drawer and pulling out a little green tube of Super Glue. Bentley sat down at the table without a word and went to work on the cow.

'That stove looks *fine*,' she said to Walt. 'Good as new. Now, how about that tea?'

'I'd like a cup of tea,' Henry said.

'Maybe not,' Walt put in, glancing at his wristwatch. 'It's nearly time to get the kids from school.' The stove *looked* first-rate, but there was no telling ...

'Oh, just one cup,' she said. 'Just to celebrate a job well done.'

Henry hauled one of the cast-iron grills out of the sink, dried it off, and set it over its burner. Mrs Biggs put the teakettle on top of it and twisted the knob. There was a faint hiss, but nothing happened beyond that.

'Takes a moment to run the gas back in through the pipes,' Walt said, knowing what he said was nonsense. The stove was completely buggered up. There was the smell of gas in the air, heavy now, so something was working, anyway. Walt picked up the matchbook on the counter and struck a match, slipping it under the edge of the grill. The burner ignited in a whoosh of blue flame, a fireball the size of the stovetop that singed all the hair off both of his arms. Walt danced backward, fanning at the stove with his hand, but there was no point; the flames were already out. He moved forward and twisted the knob, shutting down the burner.

'I guess this is a job for the gas company,' he said, shaking his head. 'Sorry. I gave it a try.'

'No harm done,' she said. She looked wistfully out the window. 'I don't suppose the gas company can come out today, though. Not this late. And I can't use the stove in this condition – it's like to blow up the house, isn't it?' She sighed. 'Lord knows I can't afford to eat out, though, not these days. I'll eat cold food, I guess, out of the fridge. I've got the rest of a box of frozen day-olds from the All-Niter. That'll do for the likes of me.'

'You've got fifty dollars,' Bentley said, trying to glue the cow's eye back into its head.

'That's pitcher money,' she said. 'You ought to know that much, unless that bourbon's ate up all your brain cells, too.'

'Maybe we could treat Maggie to a meal,' Henry said. 'I didn't bring any money, but ...'

'I've got another twenty in here someplace,' Walt said, dipping into his wallet again. Hell, he thought, looking at the two singles that were left. There was no use putting it off. Obviously she'd have those too, before they left; might as well burn it all down right now. 'Here you go, dinner on us.' He handed her the whole works, tipping his wallet toward her to make it clear it was empty of anything but moths.

'There we go,' Bentley said heartily, setting the repaired cow pitcher down on the table. 'Darned well good as new.'

Even from halfway across the room Walt could see that there was something wrong with it. A chip was apparently missing, and Bentley had tried to compromise by gluing the eye in a quarter inch too far down the nose. The effect was startling, almost demented, as if the cow were trying to look up its own nostril. Mrs Biggs picked up the creamer, flinching when she got a good look at it. 'Now it's ruined good and proper,' she said. 'It's trash now, isn't it? You've finished me off, Reverend.'

She began to cry, and set the pitcher on the counter. 'Never mind me,' she said, waving her hand. 'An hour ago I had a stove, a cream pitcher. I had my d … d … dignity.' She bleated out a sob, and Henry moved to her side, putting his arm around her shoulders.

Bentley closed his eyes, and Walt got the idea that he was counting, that maybe he would have to count several times.

'I was wondering,' Henry said softly to Walt. 'Maggie's Buick has been acting up, and she hates to take it over to Pinky's Garage again, not after what they soaked her for last time. Maybe you've got some idea …?'

'Acting up how?' Walt asked. Bentley turned away, cutting the air with little slashes of his hand, as if he were reading his congregation a hellfire sermon.

'Overheating,' Henry said. 'Isn't that it?'

She nodded, sniffling a little and fingering the cream pitcher again.

'She can't drive it ten blocks,' Henry said. 'She's lucky to make it to the All-Niter.'

'Probably just the thermostat,' Walt said. 'Nothing to it. We'll pull the hose and pop it out. We can run the thermostat down to Chief and swap it for a new one. Won't take a second, won't cost a cent.' He winked at Mrs Biggs, who had gotten her composure back.

'I'd be obliged,' she said. 'And I wonder if you'd pop into the Satellite for a few groceries, too? I know it's only a block down, but my sciatica …' She grimaced, and straightened her back with what was apparently a monumental pain and effort. 'Here.' She offered Walt one of his twenties back, but Henry stopped her.

'*We'll* take care of it,' he said. 'You buy yourself another one of these vessels.' He pointed at the cow.

Bentley stepped to the door, opened it, and went straight out without saying a word.

'Pissant,' Mrs Biggs said. 'That's the only name for a creature like that. And he calls himself a man of God.' She shook her head sadly, as if it were a shame.

'I'll make out the grocery list while you look to the car. There's some tools in the garage, but not many.' She inclined her head at Walt. 'Leave 'em as clean as you find 'em. That's what I always told the help at the Paradise.'

'Good policy,' Walt said. 'Leave it to us.'

He followed Henry out the door again. It only took a few minutes to get the top hose off the radiator and pull out the thermostat. But the hose had gone mushy, so Walt took it, too, and then pulled the bottom hose just to be safe, letting the green radiator water run down the driveway and into the gutter while Henry diluted it with hose water. They'd have to buy clamps before it was over, and a gallon of antifreeze. Still, unless the radiator itself was shot, the whole thing wouldn't cost more than twenty-five bucks, and maybe another twenty for groceries, give or take, and if that was the end of Maggie Biggs, they'd have gotten off cheap. Bentley had sat in his car the whole time, staring out through the windshield while Walt worked on the Buick. He popped the trunk from inside when Walt rapped on the window, and Walt dropped the hoses and thermostat inside.

'How much?' Bentley asked when Walt and Henry climbed in.

'How much what?' Walt asked.

'How much more of this damnation extortion till we're out of the woods? I tell you I've seen a few hard cases in my day, but she takes the cake, every blessed crumb of it.' He pulled away from the curb, shaking his head darkly. 'And I'll tell you what – you give these people an inch of rope, and they'll hang you. Velma Krane and her dignity! I'll bet you a shiny new dime there never was a Velma Krane. And that cow pitcher! Prewar Germany! That was a piece of plaster of Paris she bought down at Pic 'n' Save, and she soaked us for fifty bucks! What did she take you for, altogether?'

'Pull in here at the bank,' Walt said, digging out his automatic teller card. 'It's your call, Henry. Shall we see this through?'

'Absolutely,' Henry said. 'Damn the expense. If she calls Jinx …'

Walt hopped out of the can and drew five twenties from the machine, then handed three of them to Bentley when he got back in. 'There's grocery money and enough left over to cover the thirty you put out for the cow pitcher. Drop me off at home, will you? I'm late already to get the kids, and I don't want to get in dutch with Ivy.'

'Well … heck,' Bentley said. 'Never mind the thirty for the cow pitcher. *I* broke it.' He tried to hand two of the twenties back, reaching his hand over the top of the seat.

'It's not your fight,' Walt said, waving them away. 'Thanks for going along. If you can see this grocery list through to the end, you've done a day's work. Keep your money.'

'Maybe it *is* my fight,' Bentley said. 'I came around this afternoon looking to enlist the two of you in this little affair of mine, didn't I? I thought I was up against a pretty formidable dragon, but now I'm inclined to believe that Maggie Biggs gets the brass ring.' He stopped at a red light at Shaffer Street, in front of Coco's, and tucked the two twenties into Walt's shirt pocket. 'In for a penny, in for thirty bucks, as they say. Keep your money. It'll all come out even in the end.'

'That's the truth,' Henry put in. 'And by heaven I'll reimburse both of you after the sales party. That lingerie will *sell*. You've got nothing to worry about there. Vest will have delivered it by now.'

'*That's* good news,' Walt said, imagining the lingerie party for the first time, actually picturing it in his mind – he and Henry hauling foundation garments and knickers and brassieres out of a cardboard box, a dozen neighborhood women grinning at them, going into the other room to try these things on …

The picture was absolutely insupportable; he saw that clearly now. There would be no recovering from such an ordeal. If he was lucky he would merely be a laughingstock. More likely he'd be considered a world-class pervert. Bentley braked to a stop in front of the house. There was no box on the porch yet; Vest apparently hadn't arrived. Bentley was talking to Henry like a Dutch uncle, giving him advice, waving his finger. Walt tuned them out, his mind consumed by his sudden horror of the lingerie, of the party over on Harwood. God bless Henry, but sometimes he was like a doomful prophecy in an old Greek myth. Oedipus is humiliated at a lingerie party. What else *can* he do but gouge his eyes out?

The popes, Maggie Biggs, Sidney Vest – it was all too much. And it was his own fault, wasn't it? – letting things go on too long, full of futile hope. Well, this was it. Push had come to shove. Something had to be done right now. There was no more putting it off.

Then the answer came to him, like a radio signal from a distant planet. Out of nowhere he recollected Vest's chatter at Coco's, the talk about selling the vice presidencies, cashing out, moving back to North Carolina. It was all suddenly easy: Walt could put one over on fate and do Vest a favor at the same time. He made the wish right there and then: send Vest home now, he thought, talking to the bluebird. Kill the lingerie deal right this instant and send Vest back to Raleigh.

45

Ivy turned left from Palm onto Batavia and headed north, on her way to check out Argyle's lots. Within a couple of blocks the neighborhood changed from residential to industrial. There was almost no open land at all through-out the downtown area, and the few lots still available had gotten expensive during the boom years in the eighties when the price of real estate had quad-rupled. For a couple of years it just hadn't been prudent to buy, and prices drifted downward. Now, with diminished interest rates, things were starting to come back around, but very slowly. Argyle might have moved his two properties quick five years ago and done pretty well, but now prospective buyers would be looking hard for a bargain, and the money he wanted for the parcels didn't look like a bargain to Ivy. Selling them would be a long haul.

She turned into the driveway of an auto parts warehouse and pulled into a stall at the lonesome end of the parking lot, adjacent to one of the parcels, and then sat for a minute looking over the paperwork in the manila enve-lope, glancing up now and then to get some idea of the place. The dirt lots had turned into mud holes with all the rain, and there was a lake covering half the acreage.

She got out of the car and stood in the cool breeze, leaning back against the hood. This whole thing was baffling: suddenly she was at the edge of making real money, as if a door had opened for her. It was hard not to think of all the what-ifs, to start spending the money in her mind – and not just this com-mission, but those that might follow. It occurred to her suddenly that she had been treating Argyle a little hard, probably because she didn't want to fight with Walt about him. It was easier to let Walt have his way sometimes, although if she was going to do the kind of serious business with Argyle that it looked like she might do …

At the back of one of the lots were a couple of heavy old eucalyptus trees, the loose bark peeling off and littering the ground along with broken-off limbs. Kids had nailed boards to the trunks of the trees, and there were planks up in the lower limbs, half hidden by leafy branches. Somebody, anyway, would be disappointed if the lots sold and the trees had to come down. Such was progress. Out near the street, someone had dumped an old washing machine and some other trash – that would all have to be cleaned up. And she'd have to get a sign, too, which would be covered with graffiti in under a week.

A black pickup truck nearly as long as a limousine pulled off the road right then, onto the muddy shoulder in front of the farther lot. A man got out and stood looking, maybe fifty yards from Ivy. He was a big man – tall and heavy, like an enormous football player way over the hill. He was dressed nicely, in a coat and tie, and had curly hair cut like Nero.

He reached into the rear of the pickup and pulled out one of those bicycle-wheel measuring devices and walked out onto the lot, pushing the wheel along, avoiding the worst of the mud and heading past the edge of the lake toward the eucalyptus trees. When he hit the fence, he scribbled something into a little notebook and then traversed both lots in the other direction, ending up at the northwest corner. He scribbled again and then headed back out toward the street, along the back side of the auto parts warehouse in a route that would take him right past Ivy.

For a moment she was tempted to get back into the car, start it up, and drive away. There was something forbidding about him, out here in the lonesome afternoon. She felt conspicuous, as if she were standing on a street corner.

She stopped herself. It was simply his size, probably, that intimidated her. And whatever he was doing here, surveying the property like this, she really ought to know about it. It was possible he worked for Argyle.

He saw her and nodded. He was sweating despite the wind, and up close he looked even larger, easily six-five. His shirt, either good rayon or some very nice combed cotton, couldn't be off the rack; it must have been three or four yards of material. There was a monogram on the pocket, too.

'Beautiful day,' he said. His voice was husky, like a smoker's voice.

'Isn't it?' she said. 'The rain's kind of made a mess of these lots, though.'

'They'll dry out. Nice couple of lots.' He looked back at the ground he'd just covered and nodded his head.

'What's up with all the measuring?' Ivy said. 'I don't mean to be nosy, but it happens that I represent the owner of the lots. I'm just out here looking things over now that he's decided to sell them. I've got to get a sign up, get things moving.'

'Well, I'll be,' he said, holding out his hand. 'My name's George Peet. Short for Peetenpaul.'

'I'm Ivy Stebbins – Old Orange Realty.' He had almost no handshake for a big man – all fingers.

'This is a heck of a coincidence. Saves me tracking down the owner myself.'

'Are you interested in the properties?'

'That's right,' he said. 'So don't bother with the sign. I'll take 'em to go, if the price is right.'

'I'm sure we can make it right,' she said. She realized then that she must have been smiling like a drunk, but there was no way she could get rid of the smile; that would take some time.

46

Nora and Eddie came out of the preschool carrying notebooks covered in red and green foil. The other kids had them, too – catalogues of some kind, very ornate and costly looking.

'What's this?' Walt asked, taking one from Nora as they sat in the parking lot.

'Christmas paper and stuff.'

He opened it up. Inside were two dozen four-inch-square samples of Christmas wrapping paper – embossed foil, printed paper, paper stamped with religious messages. There were photos of Christmas craft pieces, too – wreaths and candles and tree ornaments and garlands. At the back of the catalogue was a price list and a three-page order form with blanks for names and addresses and telephone numbers. 'One Day Delivery Guaranteed,' the order form read.

'What's it for?' Walt asked, spotting the Dilworth logo on the samples page.

'Selling,' Nora said.

'You and Eddie both have one?'

'It's a fund-raiser,' Eddie said. 'To earn money for the school. Last Christmas they bought the dinosaur slide.'

Out on the playground stood a desolate-looking fiberglass Tyrannosaurus, six or seven feet tall, in a sand pit. The thing had little bitty worthless arms like a begging poodle, and sun-faded Orphan Annie eyes. Its back and tail were apparently a slide.

'That costed a million dollars,' Nora said.

'And they bought it with money from a fund drive?' Walt handed the catalogue back to her and started the car.

'At the Easter one they bought a computer,' Eddie said.

'Good for them.' Walt headed up Chapman Avenue, wondering what Ivy would say about this, whether she'd find it as contemptible as he did. 'What are you supposed to do, go around the neighborhood selling this stuff?'

'And on the telephone,' Eddie said. 'They have a list of what people we can call, like our dentist and our grandma. If we can sell ten things we get a prize. Ten things is a hundred dollars.'

'One of the prizes is a giant bubble thing,' Nora said. 'You can make these big big bubbles with it.' She held her hands out, indicating a bubble four feet across. 'It's a string on a stick.'

'Really?' Walt said. 'You earn a hundred dollars and they give you a string on a stick?'

'And soap,' Eddie said. 'And this kind of plate thing you put the soap in.'

'A kind of plate thing …' Walt said. He nearly turned the Suburban around and headed back to the preschool. This was unbelievable, like something out of Charles Dickens – a hundred small children peddling Argyle's pine-cone wreaths door to door in the rain, patriotically hustling funds so that the dirty bastard didn't have to spend his own money on a million-dollar fiberglass dinosaur. This was capitalism gone rancid – inbred money-mongering. Maybe the commies had been right after all. What had Ivy told him? – that Argyle owned something like seven preschools? So that was seven hundred kids at a hundred dollars a head! And how many times a year?

'Can you take us around, Unca Walter?' Nora asked him.

'Yeah,' Walt said. 'I guess I can. Except I've got a better idea. Why don't I buy all of it myself? Then you don't have to sell anything.'

'Really?' Eddie asked. *All of it?*'

'Sure,' Walt said. 'I'll take the whole pile.' Tomorrow he could take the cata-logues back down to the school and make Argyle eat them.

'But I wanted to do a fund raisin,' Nora said.

'You *can* do a fund raisin,' Walt said. 'A better one. This one will help some-one who really needs help bad right now. What do you think? Are you in?'

'Who needs help?' Eddie asked.

'This woman named Mrs Simms. Her husband, old Mr Simms, just died. He used to ring the bells at the church, but he died, and Mrs Simms was left all alone.'

'Then she's a widow,' Eddie said. 'A widow woman.'

'That's right. We've got to help her out. What we'll sell is … cookies. People give you as much funds as they want, and they get two dozen cowboy cookies wrapped up in Christmas foil.'

'But I want a bubble wand,' Nora said. 'I don't want cowboys.'

'Cowboy *cookies*,' Walt said. 'With raisins. That's what *they* get, the people who fork over money.'

'Fund raisin cookies!' Eddie said.

'Right!' Walt shouted happily. 'Eddie, you're a genius. We'll make Mrs Simms happy after all.'

'But what's our prize?' Nora asked sadly. 'We were going to have a prize.'

'You get a bubble wand for sure.'

'No matter what?' Eddie asked.

'No matter what,' Walt said, pulling into the driveway and cutting the engine. 'And for every ten dollars you earn you get another prize. Let's see. If you make a thousand dollars that's … a hundred prizes!'

'I'm going to start right now!' Eddie said, climbing out.

'You'll need a brochure,' Walt said. 'We'll run that up on the computer. And you'll need a pencil, too, and an affidavit of authenticity. I'll sign that. And order forms. Here, we'll use the order forms you got from school. They won't mind.'

He tore the forms out of the back of Argyle's Christmas catalogues, then tossed the notebooks into the rear of the Suburban. Later he could come out and soak them in the gutter for a half hour, then throw them onto the roof of the house to dry.

47

'That's the ticket,' Maggie Biggs said. 'A bluebird in a jar full of some kind of liquid – I don't know what kind. And what difference does that make anyway? Apparently there's only this one bird. You don't have to pick and choose.'

They stood in the alley behind the library. The high brick wall sheltered them from the rain, which angled in from the west, and out on the street the cars had their wipers on. Rainwater trickled out of a metal downspout. Henry stared at the bumper of a car parked in the library lot. 'Practice safe government,' the sticker read, 'use kingdoms.'

'I'm telling you this bird's been thrown away.' Henry forced himself to concentrate on what she was telling him. His mind was tired, and he wished to hell he was back in the motor home, taking a nap.

'What do you mean, "thrown away"?'

'He threw it into the bin yesterday afternoon.'

'Don't lie to me, you old fool. Why would he throw it away when there's people willing to pay for it?'

'Because it's an evil damned thing in a jar,' Henry said, suddenly angered that he'd been called down here in the rain, and after she'd promised not to call the house at all. Thank God Jinx had been out! 'I took one look at this bird and I *told* him to throw it away, and by golly he did the right thing.'

'That's where you're wrong. You'd better dig it out of the bin lickety-split.'

'Don't bully me,' he said, taking a stand.

'I'll do worse than that, and you know it.'

'You might as well save your breath. I suppose the bird's gone by now anyway.'

'*Gone!* How would you know? Did you look?'

'Well, no. It's just that ...'

'It's just that you'll have to look now, that's what it is. And quit being such a bag of pudding. For God's sake, Henry, give your infernal conscience a rest.

If he threw it in the bin, then it's trash now, isn't it? There's no crime in taking it back out. And your precious nephew *stole* it from my party in the first place.'

'Walter wouldn't do that.'

'Did he tell you how he got it?'

'Why, in a shipment, from China. He imports ...'

'I *know* what he imports. What I'm asking is did he *order* this bird in a jar?'

'He apparently found it in this shipment. There was just the one, and ...'

'And hold your tongue for a second. It was delivered to his house *by mistake*, and you know it's true, don't you?'

This was the same thing Bentley had told him! It *had* all been a mistake. Maggie Biggs was right about that much: it hadn't been Walt's to throw away, and that's why he'd been so damned guilty about it. Well, that part was too bad, and he himself had aided and abetted the whole thing. He had nearly *forced* Walt to do it. 'I guess it was my fault,' he said.

'Well, I don't doubt it. But if that's true, then it's up to you to make it right,' she told him. 'You hand it over to me and I'll return it to its rightful owner. If you want a signed affidavit, I'll give you one.'

'I don't guess ...'

'And let me tell you something else. This party I represent *wants this object*, and he wants it now. I can't be blamed for what he might do if he finds out it's been destroyed. I *like* your nephew. He's treated me pretty well. He buggered up my stove, but I don't hold that against him.'

'What do you mean?' Henry asked. 'What will this man do?'

'For goodness sake, *I* don't know. *I* can't be expected to think like a murderer, can I? That's not my province.'

'Murder!' Henry gasped.

Mrs Biggs shrugged. 'You didn't hear it from me. I'm not saying anything. Look, let's just say your nephew climbed in over his head. This is the big leagues he's playing in, and the poor fool thinks he's out on the sandlot with the kids. Now if someone were to put through a call to your wife, say, and tell her about us ...'

'*Us!* This is rubbish. Extortion, that's what Bentley called it.'

She snorted out a laugh. 'Bentley!' she said. 'I guess the Reverend's familiar with the likes of *that*. I won't dispute with the Reverend when it comes to the subject of pernicious activity. But I won't be threatened by the man, either. He comes into my home and breaks things up, vandalizes the place ...' She shook her head. 'So you watch your words. You wave the Reverend at me and by God I'll run the whole lot of you into the sheriff.'

'What I meant to say is that you were going to leave Jinx out of this. That was our agreement.'

'Oh, *I'm* willing to leave her out. She's got enough grief, I suppose. What I was saying is that to this party who's been cheated out of his bluebird, a phone call to your wife would be a warm-up. He'd *start* with that.'

'You've simply *got* to call him off.'

'Only one thing that'll call him off, Henry, and that's this bird.'

There was the sound of a trash truck then, Orange Disposal Company making its twice-weekly rounds of commercial bins. Mrs Biggs cocked her head, listening. 'Sounds like they're out behind the bank, don't it?' She clucked her tongue, as if it were a dirty shame. 'A couple of minutes and they'll be scooping that bird, won't they?'

They *were* behind the bank. Henry watched the bin rising in the air, upending into the open mouth of the truck. Without saying another word he turned around and started across the library parking lot toward Coco's. If he cut through a couple of lots and up the alley, he could make it to the bins at the medical center ahead of the truck. There was too much at risk to hesitate now.

'Bring it over to the All-Niter,' Mrs Biggs shouted at him.

He waved in agreement and then put up his umbrella. Shaffer Street was running ankle-deep in water, and he was forced to slog through it. The rain fell harder, pounding down now, beating through the pine trees that shaded the restaurant. He heard the trash truck again, and looked back just as the thing rounded the corner, pulling in behind Coco's kitchen. Henry stepped up his pace, racing with the truck now, angling his umbrella back into the wind, letting it shove him along. He had gotten Walt into terribly deep water, carrying on about damnation like that, nearly *forcing* him to throw the damned jar away. 'You'll ride to the Devil in comfort,' he had told Walt, and now by God he had apparently delivered his poor nephew straight into the Devil's hands! Good intentions! Bentley was right; sometimes they weren't worth a handful of chicken scratch.

The brick enclosure around the trash bins loomed up ahead of him in the rain. The truck was nearly two blocks behind now. He had plenty of time. He would save Walt yet.

He rooted through the trash, yanking aside empty cartons and stuffed plastic sacks. Immediately he saw the salmon eggs that had gone bad, wrapped up in wet newspaper like a party popper. The bin was about half full, nearly the same as it had been yesterday. It was too deep, though, for him to reach to the bottom of it. He looked around the alley, spotting a couple of cinderblocks against the wall of the medical building, and he hurried across and dragged them over to the bin, one for each foot.

He was *sure* that Walt had stuffed the bird under a sack of trash at the left-hand corner, but by golly it wasn't there now. He yanked a sack out, dropping it onto the wet concrete, then heaved out three cardboard boxes and another sack. The damned thing was simply gone! There was the noise of the truck gearing up again, and he looked up the alley. The truck was bearing down on him. He pitched his umbrella into the hedge behind him and rooted around with both hands, through wet computer paper and old magazines and coffee grounds. Nothing. It simply wasn't there.

Puzzled, he stepped down off the blocks, realizing the truth. The bird was gone. Someone had taken it. The trash truck heaved to a stop, and a man stepped down off the running board and said something to him in Spanish, gesturing at the boxes and bags on the ground. Henry shook his head, having no idea what the man had said.

The man shrugged and started picking up the boxes on the ground, chucking them back into the bin. Henry bent over to help, but the man waved him away. 'Is okay,' he said. 'No problema.'

'No problema,' Henry said to him, stepping back a couple of feet and watching for a moment, as if that were his duty. The man waved the truck forward, and Henry fetched his umbrella out of the hedge and headed up the street toward home, mulling the entire situation over in his mind.

So who had taken the jar out of the bin? A stranger? That didn't wash. The bird wasn't the kind of thing anybody would want.

It had to have been Walt.

Walt coveted the thing. He was under its spell. That had been evident yesterday, when he was going on about it, talking about bags full of money, trying to rationalize keeping the damned thing. This was what Bentley had tried to warn them about, and now the truth was crystal clear: Henry hadn't done *enough* to talk Walt out of it.

Maybe the best thing he could do now was to steal it back and give it to Maggie Biggs just like she said – let her murdering friends go to the Devil instead of poor Walter. Dollars to doughnuts it was back in the tackle box in the rafters – easy enough to take it back out again.

At home he climbed into the motor home. He was soaked, and before he caught his death he …

There was an envelope on the table. It was torn open, the contents gone. The return address paralyzed him with fear: it was from Myron Goldfarb, Jinx's lawyer friend. So Jinx had gone to Goldfarb! She intended to serve him with papers. She'd had enough of him at last.

Henry turned straight around and went back out into the rain. The least he could do was to save Walt before these monsters got to him too …

He heard the front door of the house bang shut. Nora, Eddie, and Walt came out and headed up the street. Henry watched them from behind the shrubbery at the edge of the porch, and when they were gone, he headed up the driveway toward the garage.

48

Walt let the kids go from door-to-door alone. It was nearly dusk, only fifteen or twenty minutes left till dark, but he couldn't stop them from setting out on the fund drive for Mrs Simms. There was something endearing about them going at it alone, like two guardian angels. He'd only be a fly in the ointment if he went along. With any luck, he and Jinx could kill the day tomorrow baking cookies for the neighbors.

He wondered suddenly if he were trying to salve his conscience with this thing. Well, so what if he was? It was good for the kids, and good for Mrs Simms, too. In fact, it was probably good for Argyle – some kind of object lesson. Nora and Eddie stepped down off the porch of the last house now, turning to wave at old Mrs Bord, who stood with her arms folded, beaming at them. Eddie waved the order form at Walt. By golly, they were doing it!

They headed up Maple Street, and Walt strolled down to the corner to keep an eye on them. There were only a couple of houses on Maple, and after that, if the day held up, they could hit a couple more on Cambridge …

An idea struck him just then, and he walked on down toward the next corner, watching the kids knock on the door of the Fillpots' house. No one would be home. Fillpot's Stationers, down on Glassell, didn't close till six. 'How's it going?' Walt hollered at them.

Nora and Eddie stood on the sidewalk, looking uncertain where to go next. 'Three,' Eddie said. He held up the order form for Walt to take a look at – thirty bucks; that was ten dollars a house! There were two checks and a ten-dollar bill. Eddie gave Walt the money to hold. 'I told the lady that everybody was giving ten,' he said.

'Good,' Walt told him. 'Keep it up. That's called salesmanship.'

'I get three prizes,' Nora said, making the rabbit face.

'Well, not quite,' Walt said. 'Not three prizes for each *kid*. What I meant was three prizes for each ten dollars. And if there's one extra prize, you'll have to share it.'

'Oh,' Nora said.

Walt pointed up the street, toward Argyle's house. 'See that big house down there?'

'The *really* big one?' Eddie asked.

'That's right – with the big porch. That's where the millionaire lives, the rich man. It's getting late, but you've got time for one more house. Why don't you try that one?'

'*I'll* talk this time,' Nora said, setting out up the sidewalk and trying to pull the order form out of Eddie's hand. He took off running, holding the form close to his chest where she couldn't get at it. She caught up to him at Argyle's porch and slugged him hard on the shoulder, then turned around and looked back at Walt, who shook his head at her. She and Eddie climbed the stairs and rang the bell.

Argyle's car was in the driveway, so he was probably home. If Bentley was right about him, then his reaction to the kids' homegrown 'fund-raiser' would be interesting in about ten different ways …

His door swung open and Walt stepped back away from the corner, moving out of sight behind the corner house. There was no use letting Argyle see him there; this shouldn't seem like a put-up job. After a moment he walked forward again and peeked down the street. They were just coming out through the door, and Nora was saying something to Argyle. She stopped suddenly, ran back to the open door, and he bent over so she could kiss him on the cheek. Then she ran off again, down the stairs and out to the sidewalk where both of them ran wildly toward the corner, Eddie carrying a check in his hand. Spotting Walt, Argyle waved cheerfully from the doorway, then disappeared back inside.

What the hell did *that* mean? That Argyle was being *gracious* about it? Walt nearly laughed out loud. The man had to be seething inside, confounded, wondering what this was all about. The best he could do was to put on a good face. His smile was some kind of terrible rictus. Maybe Walt could slip some arsenic into his raisin cookies tomorrow and just do away with him completely.

'It was Mr Argyle!' Eddie shouted, out of breath from running.

'Really?' Walt said. '*The* Mr Argyle?'

'From school!' Nora said. 'He gave us *money*! Show him, Eddie! Oh, he's …!' She jigged with excitement, bouncing from one foot to the other. 'He's such a good one!'

Eddie handed over Argyle's check, and Walt stared at it for a moment, unable to make immediate sense of it. He looked back down toward the house, but Argyle had gone back inside.

The check was for twenty thousand dollars, made out to Walt Stebbins.

'How many prizes is it?' Nora asked.

Walt sent the kids inside and headed straight into the garage where he tore the check to pieces, then threw the pieces into the tin pail, resisting the urge to spit on them. Argyle wasn't going to get away with it, whatever it was he was trying to get away with, him and his dirty money.

Walt packed boxes, crumpling newspaper and slamming the tape dispenser onto the box tops, zipping them shut, and slapping on mail labels. The afternoon had been a dead loss – first Maggie Biggs and then this damned encounter with Argyle. And that reminded him – tomorrow morning he had to fix the Biggsmobile! He ripped open a carton hard enough to tear half the flap loose. Inside lay a gross of bug catapults along with bags of rubber beetles. He shoved the box toward the garage door, separating it from the rest. Tomorrow he'd by God take it down to the preschool and hand a bug flinger out to every kid there. Every doggone one of them would get a prize. And not because they were day laborers, either, scraping together hatfuls of money for stinking creeps like Argyle, but because they were kids, damn it, and they *deserved* a prize.

Shit! The dirty son-of-a-bitch! Walt threw down the tape dispenser and kicked the leg of the bench. Argyle had done this on *purpose*, to throw it into their faces! First he murders Simms; then he turns the murder into a sort of monstrous joke, hosing everyone down with money. Well, it wouldn't wash. Twenty thousand bucks was *nothing* to Argyle. Argyle blew his nose on twenty thousand bucks. That's what this meant, wasn't it? The finger. Up yours.

He kicked the bench again, and his coffee mug fell over, spilling out a pool of cold coffee. And of *course* the check won't be any damn good anyway. The damned thing would have bounced over the moon, and Walt would have looked like some kind of criminal idiot.

The door swung open and Walt jumped. It was Ivy, smiling and happy, full of pep.

'What's this about a fund-raiser?' she asked. 'Nora and Eddie are out of their minds with it.' She came in and kissed him on the cheek.

Walt decided not to mention the Christmas wrap fundraiser at all. 'Just an idea I had. I wanted to put together a little something for Mrs Simms.'

'Well, I think that's wonderful. The kids are all full of talk about Robert Argyle. Nora tells me he gave them a million dollars.'

'Not quite,' Walt said. 'Everything's a million dollars to Nora. You know how she is.'

'How much, then?'

'Well, he wrote out a check, which I guess was a kind of joke. It pisses me off, too, because he obviously did it to needle me, and now the kids are all excited. I guess he didn't consider their feelings at all.'

'What are you talking about?' The smile disappeared from her face.

'See for yourself.' He gestured at the bucket, which was empty except for the torn-up check.

Ivy bent over and picked out the pieces, getting them about half arranged on the bench top before she made out the amount. She looked at him in disbelief.

'Obviously it's a joke,' Walt said.

'A joke? Why would it be a joke?'

'Of *course* it's a joke. You don't know the whole story. Argyle's running this bogus fund-raiser at school. Get this, he drags in *thousands* of dollars with these scams, putting children to work selling worthless crap door to door. Then he spends the money on computer equipment and Lord knows what-all. I'm sorry, but I just wouldn't stand for it. I won't play the man's games.'

'So you tore up a twenty-thousand-dollar check?'

'You're damned right I tore it up!'

'Don't cuss at me. Maybe you don't know this, but *every* school does fund-raisers.'

'Non-profit schools, maybe. That makes sense. And that's what pisses me off. That's how he takes people, sending kids around. People trust the kids, and so they don't think anything through. Money for a good cause, they think, and they fork it over. They don't know that Argyle's a filthy rich hoser who's charging six prices already at his so-called school. He's making a *mint*. But he can't buy his own computer? The kids can't have a slide, for God's sake, unless they earn it themselves?' Walt shook his head. 'What a stinking pig.' He picked up the tape dispenser again, looking for another box to go after, but there was nothing more packed.

'I think we've drifted from the point,' Ivy said evenly. 'I don't know anything about Robert's so-called fund-raiser. What I *do* know is that you tore up Mrs Simms's twenty thousand dollars and threw it in the trash.'

'It isn't that easy.'

'It isn't easy being Mrs Simms right now, either.'

'I've had a bad day, all right?'

'How bad was it?'

He gestured, unable to answer. He knew he'd been talking like a lunatic.

'Let me tell you about my day.'

'Go ahead.'

'I sold the property.'

'Which one? I thought she already bought it.'

'Who?'

'Mrs Fabulous. I don't remember her name.'

'You mean Linda Marvel. I don't mean that one. I mean the two commercial properties that Robert let me represent. Remember? I *must* have told you about it.'

'All right, all right. Don't get ironic. Of course you told me about it.'

'Because of Robert Argyle I – *we* – made something like *sixty thousand dollars* today.'

'Bring it in here,' Walt said, 'I'll tear it up for you.'

She stood there staring at him, as if for two cents she'd knock his teeth loose. After a moment she turned around and walked out.

49

'I'm sorry,' Walt said, sitting down at the foot of the bed. 'I was worked up. I lost my mind.'

She didn't look up from her book. 'Sorry is as sorry does.'

'Yeah,' he said. 'I guess so.' Clearly she was still pissed, saying insane things to avoid saying anything at all. 'Anyway, I don't know why I tore up the check. I honestly thought it was some kind of … ploy, I guess.'

'Ploy to accomplish *what*?' she asked after a long silence. 'Do you really think he'd go to that length to humiliate you in some weird way that nobody but you can figure out? The truth is, he's not half as bad as you say he is.'

'You don't know what you're saying.'

'Do you?'

'I'm pretty sure.'

'You're pretty sure. You're so pretty sure that you tore up Mrs Simms's check?'

'What can I do about it now, tape it back together?'

'Take it back to Robert and ask for another check. It's easy.'

'*Easy?*'

'Okay, *I'll* take it over there. *I'll* ask Robert to replace it.'

'No,' Walt said hastily. 'I'll do it. I'll see him tomorrow morning anyway, at the preschool.'

'I'd do it now.'

'You're right. I'll do it now.'

Walt walked out, down the stairs and into the family room, where Nora and Eddie sat on the floor playing 'Uncle Wiggly.'

'The Pipsawa nearly got me,' Nora said.

'Pipsisewa,' Eddie told her.

'Nuh-*uh*, Pipsawa.'

'He nearly got me too,' Walt said. 'I think he *did* get me.'

Out in the garage he gathered up the pieces of the check, and, forcing himself not to think too much about where he was going, he set out down the driveway.

Then an idea came to him, and he turned around, heading back into the garage and climbing up into the rafters in order to yank out the tackle box. Argyle could have the phony parakeet after all, as payola for his generosity. He grinned at the thought of it. Climbing down, he set the box on the bench and opened the latch. The parakeet was gone.

He looked around. Nothing else in the garage was touched. There was no ransacking, no opened boxes. Whoever had taken it had known right where to look.

Bentley? Of course there was no way Bentley believed that Walt had thrown it away. He was too canny for that. Had he gotten the information out of Henry, the old man having revealed the bird's hiding place thinking it didn't matter anyway? Of course he had. Walt's anger drained away. Bentley was on a mission. And it was a *good* mission, too, even if it did involve stealing another man's bluebird.

He went outside, angling around into the backyard where he pried up the corner of the stepping-stone. The real bird was still under there, snug and happy. It occurred to him then that the dead parakeet scam had turned out to be genius after all: even if he wouldn't have a chance of working it on Argyle, he'd at least got to work it on Bentley.

He walked down the driveway now, and headed up the sidewalk toward the corner. When he got down to Cambridge Street he could see that the lights were on in Argyle's house, and his car was still in the driveway. He walked boldly up to the house and stepped up onto the porch, where he rang the bell. There was no use being timid about this whole thing. Argyle opened the door, blinked as if in puzzlement, and then smiled at him.

'I think this fund-raiser of yours is something else,' he said immediately. 'I wish I'd have thought of it myself.'

'I bet you do,' Walt said. 'Actually, there's been a slight accident with the check that you wrote for the kids.'

'I beg your pardon?'

'The check,' Walt said. 'It got torn up.' He handed Argyle the pieces.

'This is astonishing,' Argyle said. He shook his head, dumbfounded. 'Enlighten me.'

'Well, the truth is, it got put in with the junk mail by mistake. We've gotten a lot of crap, flyers and like that, shoved through the slot recently. And so it got torn up by mistake.'

'I see.' There was the hint of a leer on his face, and he nodded broadly.

'I wonder if you could write out another one,' Walt said. 'That is, if you're still in such a generous mood.'

'Of course, of course.' Argyle gestured toward the interior of the house. 'Step inside?'

'I'll wait out here,' Walt said.

'Good enough. Checkbook's still sitting here by the door.' He turned away to pick up the checkbook, opened it up, and started scribbling in it with a pen.

'Why don't you make it out directly to Mrs Simms?' Walt said.

'Oh, I don't want that.' Argyle waved the idea away. 'I don't want any mention of *me* at all. Put this in the general fund along with the rest. How much have you collected so far?'

'Quite a bit,' Walt said. 'The world's a generous place when you give it half a chance.'

'We agree on that,' Argyle said. He handed the check over to Walt. 'There you go. Take better care of this one, eh?' He started to shut the door.

'Oh, oh,' Walt said, looking it over. 'Wait. Date's wrong. That's *last* year.' He pointed at the miswritten date. 'I don't know if the bank will go for that. It looks like the check's a year old.'

'I'll be damned,' Argyle said. 'Let me have it back.' He scratched at the check with his pen, then handed it over again, winking at Walt. 'Good as new.' He shut the door this time.

The date was corrected and initialed, but now Walt saw that the quantity was wrong. The comma was in the right place, but there were only three zeroes instead of four, so that it almost looked like twenty dollars, except with a couple of superfluous zeroes hovering off to the side. Walt was struck with the sudden notion that Argyle was doing this on purpose. He knocked on the door, and Argyle answered immediately, as if he'd been waiting there.

'Yes?' Argyle asked, wrinkling his forehead with doubt and surprise.

'What's the amount here?' Walt asked. 'The comma seems ...'

'Why, let's see.' He took the check again. '*Very* perceptive,' he said. 'But you always were good with numbers, eh? *Here* we go ...' He touched up the check again and handed it back.

'And I think you forgot your last name,' Walt said, blocking the door with his foot now. The signature read simply 'Robert P.'

'Forgotten my *name*?'

'Here on the signature.'

'Well I'll be ... *Aren't* I something!' He took the check again. '*Un*believable.'

Hit him now, Walt thought – a haymaker to the belly while he messes with the check again, then work him over good while he's on his hands and knees ...

Argyle gave him back the check. 'Everything's shipshape now, Cap'n,' he said, winking again. He clicked his feet together and saluted.

Wait stared at him, leaving his foot in the door. 'Looks like they'll catch the dirty little creep who sabotaged the church bells after all,' he said.

'That *is* good news.' Argyle furrowed up his face with concern, glancing unhappily at Walt's foot.

'Positive I. D.,' Walt said. 'Someone saw the bastard on the church roof, apparently. Police thought it was Murray LeRoy at first, but this new evidence changes all that. This was some other pathetic little shithead. They figure it's the same one that's been vandalizing the neighborhood, writing poo-poo words on walls with a brown crayon. Apparently he's *seriously* Freudian, if you follow me.'

Argyle didn't flinch. 'I'm sure it'll go hard on him if they catch him. And I believe your foot's in my door.'

'I imagine they'll throw away the key,' Walt said, shaking his head. 'What a stinking geek, don't you think?'

'I couldn't agree with you more.'

'Lowest kind of rat-eating scum, wouldn't you say?'

'Amen.' Argyle's face was a mask of barely disguised loathing now.

'A man like that blows like big rats,' Walt said, 'if you can call him a man at all, which I can't. Personally I call him a treacherous, pig-faced, insect-brained, murdering piece of dog waste. Isn't that what you call him?'

'First chance I get,' Argyle said. 'And now really, Walt, I don't want to hold you up. It's been *very* nice talking to you.'

'Maybe I haven't made myself clear,' Walt said. 'This dipshit who murdered Simms ...'

And just then Father Mahoney's bells started to ring again. It was time for the nightly round of carols. Argyle suddenly looked as if he'd been poleaxed. Walt smiled big at him and put his hand to his ear theatrically. 'Hark!' he said. 'The tintinnabulation of the bells!'

Argyle thrust out his hand, pushing Walt solidly in the chest, and Walt backpedaled a step before getting his balance. In that moment the door slammed shut and there was the sound of a dead bolt striking. For a second Walt considered lifting the brass flap on the mail slot and shouting more insults into the interior of the house, but he turned around instead, walking away toward the corner. He glanced back to see if Argyle was watching him, but apparently the creature had slunk back into its den. Tolerably well satisfied, Walt headed for home.

50

Ivy was talking to Darla on the telephone. Walt had already talked to her once that evening. She had called earlier to speak to Nora and Eddie. That had been a productive call. Afterward Nora had cried for ten minutes. Now Darla had called back to talk to Ivy again, trying hard to make sense of suddenly finding herself a couple of thousand miles from home. Flying back to Michigan ought to have clarified something, given her life direction, but so far it hadn't.

Walt couldn't puzzle Darla out. She apparently missed the kids so much she could hardly stand it, but she couldn't come home right now because she needed to 'find herself.' Walt imagined her fumbling through coats in a dark closet with a tiny flashlight, certain she was in there someplace. She had a duty as a *mother*, she had told Walt tearfully, but her first duty was to herself, because if she didn't love herself, then she couldn't really love anything, could she? Except of course she had loved Jack, she said, but he turned into a worthless son-of-a-bitch.

She had carried on this way for ten minutes, weeping like a faucet until Walt had wanted to tell her to shut the hell up. But then it had occurred to him, like a knock on the head, that in some terribly real sense, Darla *couldn't* shut the hell up. She couldn't help herself, not right now. That's what she was talking about, even if she didn't quite know it. He had been thinking that she was *pretending* somehow, that this was all weakness and theater, that if she wanted to she could just cut it out, straighten up and fly right. But what if she wasn't pretending at all? What if all of it was simply *true*, and that was the ghastly horror of it? The gulf between what Darla needed and what she possessed was so broad that she couldn't navigate it, not in the leaky little rowboat she'd put to sea in.

Maybe the truth was that *all* of them – himself, the kids, Uncle Henry, Mrs Biggs, even Argyle – were bailing like sixty, trying to stay afloat in their sorry little tubs.

'Where?' he heard Ivy ask now. 'A chiropractic office? Is it good money?' She nodded, looking at Walt and making a face. 'He's a what? A nutritionist? Not right now, I guess. I don't think Walt would want any vitamin supplements. How much? I'll tell him. Okay, sure,' she said. 'Take care.' She hung up. 'It looks like she's got a job, but no place to live,' she said to Walt. 'If you want, you can subscribe to a line of vitamin supplements. This chiropractor is looking for a west coast rep. You can buy a sales kit for five hundred dollars.'

'Don't let her talk to Henry.'

Ivy rolled her eyes. 'She sounds like she's down in the dumps.'

'So we've got Nora and Eddie for Christmas?'

'I get the feeling we've got Nora and Eddie till further notice, unless we want to hand them over to Jack, which I don't think we do. Darla tells me that Jack was a little rough with Eddie a few times. That's what she said, "a little rough."'

'What does she mean, "rough"? Did Jack beat him up?' Walt sat up in bed. He felt his face get hot.

'Your guess is as good as mine.'

'Well, then he better not come around here anymore, because if he does I'm going to ask him about it.'

'What do you mean, *ask* him?'

'Simple question before I hit him.'

'Don't start fighting with Jack, for God's sake.'

Walt didn't say anything. His mind had descended into a dark place, and he pictured Jack lurching up the front walk toward the house again, making demands. He half wanted the phone to ring right now. Sure, Jack, come the hell on over … Then step out of the dark with a fist full of dimes and make everything clear to him.

He realized suddenly that he'd never been this pissed off about anything in his life. Calm down, he thought, don't have a coronary. His heart was going like sixty.

'It's poison to sit there and dwell on this,' Ivy said. 'Lie down. We don't know anything for sure about what Jack did or didn't do. And it's not going to help Eddie for you to fly off the handle. If you want to help Eddie, there's better ways to do it.'

'I know.'

'Because Eddie might just depend on you in some way you can't foresee right now, and if you …'

'Okay, okay. I'm all right. I'm not going to hunt Jack down and kill him. But I think that if we're going to do something to fix his hash, we ought to do it. Because if it comes down to it, I'm not sure I care what's legal and what's not legal when it comes to Nora and Eddie. I think I could break the law, especially if it meant breaking that bastard's nose.'

'Don't keep thinking about breaking someone's nose. You're worked up.'

'Well, of course I am. It's the kids. Jack can insult me up one side and down the other and I'll laugh in his face, but he's going to damn well leave Nora and Eddie alone.'

'*Listen* to you. You've gone crazy,' Ivy said. 'Head over heels. You're all of a sudden a sucker for kids. You've been handing me this line all this time, being rational, and it turns out you're custom-built, out-of-your-mind father material.'

'Yeah, yeah, yeah. Take advantage of my better nature. Go ahead. I'm used to it.'

Ivy switched the light out, and together they pulled the blankets up under their chins. Walt lay there staring at the ceiling, which was faintly illuminated by the light at the bottom of the stairs. They left the light on routinely now, just in case Nora and Eddie had to come up in the middle of the night because of bugs or something.

Routinely … After three days it was routine? He was already *used* to that light. How had it happened so quickly?

'Anyway, I was telling you about the lots over on Batavia?'

'That's right,' Walt said. 'That went okay?'

'It was amazing,' Ivy said. 'Actually it was pretty weird. Good weird. I was out there looking things over, and this giant man appeared and started measuring the size of the lots.'

'A giant man?' Walt asked. 'How many eyes did he have?'

'How many eyes? What are you talking about?'

'I thought maybe he was a cyclops.'

'He had two eyes. It turned out he'd already made his mind up. He wanted *both* of the lots. I walked straight into it.'

'You deserve a little luck,' Walt said. 'You work hard.'

'So do you. We both work hard. And this is *our* luck, isn't it?'

'Sure,' Walt said. 'But I'd like to contribute a little bit of it once in a while too. Especially around Christmas.'

'Don't be so hard on yourself,' she said. 'And anyway, Mr Peetenpaul's in charge of making Christmas green this year. We can lean on the MasterCard and take care of it later when Mr Peentenpaul antes up the cash.'

'Pete 'n' Paul?'

'The giant man who's buying the lots.'

'That *can't* be his name. He sounds like a Mounds bar.'

'He's eaten a few, I think. I guess it's a Dutch name – all one word, Peeten-paul. He says to call him Mr Peet. He's got this voice like you wouldn't believe, like he eats sandpaper.'

'How big?' Walt asked, suddenly suspicious – the size, the voice, the impossible name …

'I don't know. A couple inches taller than you, I guess.'

'Grizzly-looking guy, with a beard? He wasn't dressed like a postman, was he?'

'A postman? No. Why do you ask? Why would he be dressed like a post-man, for God's sake?'

'Nothing. No reason. It sounded like someone I know, that's all.'

'You know a giant postman?'

'Met one recently.'

'Well, this was no postman. He was driving a pickup truck, but it was new and expensive. He was dressed for the office, too – very stylish for such a big man. I guess you could say he was overdressed.'

'Like he was playing a role?'

'What are you talking about?'

'Nothing.'

They lay there in the darkness. Walt listened to the rain ping against the sheet-metal chimney cap. The sound of the droplets radiated down through the flue so that it sounded like it was raining in the bedroom itself.

'What are you thinking about?' she asked him suddenly.

'I'm thinking that the Lotto's sixty million dollars tonight. I'd like to win. I'd spend the money like an idiot.'

'If our special numbers came up, and you didn't have a ticket, what would you do?'

'I dunno. Curse my fate, I guess. Then later I'd tell the story every chance I got. What it would do is turn me into a bore.'

'You wouldn't jump out of a window?'

'Not over money.'

'Good.' She was silent for a moment. Then she asked, 'What *would* make you jump out of a window?'

'Shame,' he said, not having to think twice about it. 'If I was Jack I'd jump out a window.'

'If you were Jack, you wouldn't have any shame.' For a moment she didn't say anything, then she said, 'So did you buy a ticket?'

'A ticket?'

'For the Lotto.'

'Sure,' Walt said. 'No quick-pick, just our lucky numbers. You don't want to dilute your luck when there's big money on the line.'

'Good thinking,' she said.

After another few minutes of silence he realized that Ivy was asleep, her breathing regular and soft. The house was quiet except for the sound of the rain. His thoughts slowly turned in his head, thoughts about winning the Lotto, about found money in a sack. Lots of money. Sixty million iron men. What was that worth, fractioned out over whatever it was – twenty years? He pictured Henry and Jinx back in Honolulu again, decked out in aloha clothes and leis and wearing go-aheads from Long's Drugs, listening to Don Ho music on a Friday night in Waikiki. Palm trees, trade winds, the scent of flowers on the air ...

Money: what was it but a means to an end? It was a door, wasn't it? Why treat it like a poisonous snake? You open the door and step through, into Oz or Candyland or somewhere.

He thought about the bluebird, buried out under the stepping-stone, down in the dirt with the ants and the earthworms. 'Sixty bucks,' he whispered. In his mind he made it a wish. It was easier than he thought, just like with the lingerie this afternoon. A thrill ran through him, a shudder.

That's all, just the sixty-dollar win. What was that? – four measly numbers in the Lotto? Sixty lousy dollars would just about pay him back for what Mrs Biggs had taken him for. He wouldn't be greedy. And it was safe enough for a simple test. The odds against winning it without help were tremendous. The odds of *calling* your win must be nearly infinitely bad.

So if he won, he would know, absolutely, and he would resign himself ...

... he would resign himself to making a decision. And you didn't make that kind of decision unless you were sure of yourself.

'You'll ride to the Devil in comfort.'

He heard Henry's voice in his mind.

And then, for no reason at all, he suddenly recalled watching Nora and

Eddie say their prayers before going to bed, God-blessing Mr Argyle along with everyone else.

How long had it been since Walt had said his prayers?

He was struck with the uncanny idea that he just had – but to whom?

He pushed the idea out of his mind, then turned over to go to sleep.

PART THREE

All the Bells on Earth

And all the bells on earth did ring, on Christmas Day in the morning...

'I SAW THREE SHIPS A-SAILING'
TRADITIONAL CHRISTMAS CAROL

51

Mahoney and Bentley headed up Shaffer Street toward the Holy Spirit Catholic Church. Bentley was dog-tired. They'd been out since eight o'clock, bell-ringing through the neighborhoods. The wind was blowing hard, and the sky was wild, the clouds torn to pieces by the wind, scattered stars winking and blinking in the clear parts.

'There's Orion.' Mahoney pointed his finger at the heavens.

Bentley looked, but he couldn't make anything out. 'I'll take your word for it,' he said. 'I never could see constellations. I suspect they're a hoax. I can spot the dipper and the Seven Sisters, which might as well be seven anything – the Seven Santini Brothers.'

'That attitude's a pity,' Mahoney said. 'Sometimes I imagine they're celestial seashells arranged on a beach.'

'That's real artistic,' Bentley said. 'I admire that kind of talk.'

Mahoney squinted one eye at him and took something out of his pocket. 'Nip?'

'Pardon me?'

The priest held out a silver pint flask. 'Scotch? Little belt after a long night's work?'

'No,' Bentley said, waving it away. 'Thanks, but I guess not.'

'Well, fine.' Mahoney tilted a swallow down his throat and put the flask back into his coat. 'Teetotaler, eh?'

'You make it sound like a crime.'

'You make it sound like a virtue.'

'Well, it comes tolerably close to being a virtue. But, no, I'm not teetotaler. I used to take a drink now and then, in company.'

'This liquor,' Mahoney said, tapping the flask with his finger, 'is what they call a single malt Scotch.'

'Don't patronize me,' Bentley said, listening to their footfalls on the sidewalk. 'I know what malt Scotch is.'

The rain began to fall now, and without saying another word both of them set off jogging toward the church, cutting across the street toward a rear door. Mahoney hauled a key ring out of his pocket and unlocked the dead bolt, letting them both into the sacristy.

'Man, that's rain!' Bentley said. Father Mahoney hauled off his dripping trenchcoat and hung it on a peg in the vestibule, then unhitched the bells from around his waist and set them on the desk along with his Benedictus bell. Bentley did the same. The rain poured down outside, drumming against the plywood cutouts that filled the two window arches where the stained glass had been removed for repair. The room smelled of fresh paint.

'So you're a Scotch man?' the priest said, sitting down at the desk. He waved at a nearby chair, and Bentley dragged it across and sat down too.

'Used to be a Scotch man. I'm descended from John Knox.'

'Is that a fact?' Mahoney said. 'The Presbyter himself? *Good* for you. I'll take a small drink in honor of your illustrious ancestor despite what we all know about him.'

'Scourge of the Papists,' Bentley said. 'Maybe I'll take one little blast, in recollection of how your crowd turned a good man into a galley slave.' He took the flask and poured a swallow down his throat, wishing he had something in his stomach.

Mahoney nodded and took the flask back. 'The thing is,' he said, 'when you're using Protestants as galley slaves, you need a *lot* of them – half a dozen to an oar. Knox wasn't worth much when it came to real labor. He was mainly a talker.' Mahoney put his feet on the desk and yanked at his collar, loosening it up.

'Well, he was a *good* talker,' Bentley said. 'He changed it all, the whole course of human destiny. The whole megillah.'

'Magilla Gorilla,' Mahoney said, nodding somberly and tasting the Scotch again.

Bentley took the flask from him, and for a time they sat there in silence, passing it back and forth. Bentley abruptly felt tremendously tired, worn out, and the Scotch had the effect of a hot bath on his muscles. 'Here's to all the people out there,' he said finally, 'who are doing the best they damn well can.'

'Amen,' Mahoney said.

Bentley felt the whiskey in his guts now, like a living heat, and he moved his shoulders to loosen up.

'John Knox wore bobby sox,' Mahoney said, giggling.

Bentley snickered, then glared at him theatrically. Then, in his best Bing Crosby impersonation, he sang, 'Too-ra-loo-ra-loo-ral ...' and then cut it off and snickered again. His teeth felt rubbery, and his head was heavy. He turned the flask over and pretended to read something on the bottom. 'The Pep Boys,' he said. 'Well, I'll be dipped in a sack of dung, that's a high-class flask.' He winked, handing it back to Mahoney.

The phone rang then – two rings, then nothing. Bentley stood blinking at it for a moment, suddenly regretting the Scotch.

'He's moving,' Bentley said. He stepped across and switched off the light. The sudden darkness seemed to amplify the sound of the rain, and for a moment neither man spoke. Light from the garden lanterns filtered in through the two remaining windows, casting a dim, rainy shadow onto the linoleum floor.

'He won't come here,' Father Mahoney said. 'Not as early as this.'

'Maybe,' Bentley said. 'But we ought to be ready for him anyway. He knows we're moving against him in earnest now. Edna Hepplewhite is staying with Mrs Simms, up near Pitcher Park. If he turns up Almond, past the park, she'll ...'

The phone rang again – one ring and then silence.

'That's Edna!' Bentley said. 'That's the signal. Argyle just passed the Simms place. He's making his rounds. You're probably right about him not coming here, but we'd better get up there into the tower anyway and wait for the go-ahead.' Bentley swung the sacristy door open. Through the hallway window the rainy street shone in the glow of the streetlamps. It wasn't even midnight. Argyle would have to be a desperate man to break into the bell tower now. How desperate was he? Bentley half wished that he had a baseball bat instead of a Polaroid camera.

'Front door locked?' Bentley kept his voice low even though there was no one except Mahoney to hear him.

'Locked but not bolted. He can get in with a credit card if he wants to. We'll leave this one the same.' Father Mahoney picked up the two cameras waiting on the desk along with a couple of penlights. He handed one of each to Bentley. Then the two of them set out through the darkened church, heading toward the door that led into the bell tower.

Bentley shivered. He felt a little sick to his stomach.

'Top or bottom?' Bentley asked.

'Top, I guess,' Mahoney said. 'Unless you want it.'

'Well, I'm a younger man.'

'Yeah, but you're tired,' Mahoney said. 'You don't eat enough fish and you drink too much.'

'Yeah, but if he kills me I don't mind. I'm right with the Lord. You, on the other hand, have a lot to atone for, being Catholic.'

'Probably you're right,' Father Mahoney said, smiling and winking. 'But if he kills you, at least there'll be a priest standing by to steer your soul toward heaven. If he kills me there won't be anybody around but a Protestant.'

'That's right,' Bentley said. 'A *live* one. Go ahead on up. You know the drill.'

'I know the drill,' Mahoney said. 'You hold up your end. I'll be fine.'

'How long will we give him?'

'An hour?'

'An hour it is. For heaven's sake, don't fall asleep either. And if the phone rings three times, it'll be Edna calling to say Argyle's gone home. That's the all-clear.'

'Good enough,' Mahoney said. He turned around and opened the tower door, shining his penlight on the ladder. He stepped inside and climbed slowly up into the darkness. Bentley swung the door shut, the hinges creaking, then turned around and slipped into the little broom closet next to the tower door. He switched on the penlight and sat down in the kitchen chair that he'd put there earlier, then shined the penlight around to get his bearings before switching the light out. Even the faintest light under the door would scare Argyle off. Or worse. He put the penlight into his shirt pocket and lay the camera in his lap, wishing that the chair had a cushion on it.

Minutes passed. He strained to listen in the darkness. He could hear water gurgling through a gutter somewhere beyond the wall and a steady, slow drip every twenty seconds or so, like rain leaking through the roof onto the ceiling above his head. After what seemed a long time, he took out the penlight and shined it on his watch, counting off the moments as the second hand revolved around the watch face. It would be a long old haul sitting here in the darkness for an hour. At least up in the tower Mahoney had something to look at …

He heard a footstep out in the church, and he held his breath, listening. The camera! He'd been fooling away his time when he should have been planning things out. He strained to hear something more, but now there was only silence and rain. Then there were footfalls again, closer now, and quiet – soft-soled shoes, someone creeping along. Up in the tower Mahoney wouldn't hear him, but he might easily have seen him pull in off the street.

There was silence again. Had Argyle seen something, some sign that they were there? Throw the door open and shoot, Bentley thought, before he gets spooked and runs.

He felt the front of the camera with his fingers, found the trigger, and started to stand up. The chair slid backward a half inch with a soft scraping sound, and Bentley froze, listening.

There was still movement out in the church, and then the sound of hinges creaking. The tower door! Argyle was going up the ladder!

Keeping his finger on the camera trigger, Bentley counted off ten seconds, then, fearfully slowly, he opened the door and peered around it. Sure enough, the tower door stood wide open. There was no sign of anyone inside. Bentley creeped forward, looking through the viewfinder, centering the doorway and ready to shoot. The bastard was on the ladder, all right. He could hear his shoe soles scraping on the rungs.

He waited for the flash from Mahoney's camera. Now! he thought. Take it now! Had the priest fallen asleep up there? Bentley edged closer to the open door, ready for Argyle to burst through and rush at him. A moment passed. He couldn't stand it. He stepped into the tower and looked up into the darkness.

Argyle was on the ladder, nearly to the top! Bentley aimed the Polaroid up the ladder, and just then the tower lit up in a blinding flash of light. He pressed his finger on the camera trigger, setting off his own flash. Through the viewfinder he saw something rushing down at him, and instinctively he threw his hands up, letting go of the camera just as Argyle slammed into him, crushing him to the floor. He flung his hands out, grabbing a leg, and grunted when Argyle stood up, stepping on his stomach. He held on, twisting the leg, trying to throw him, and right then he caught a glimpse of moonlight in the tower above and Mahoney's silhouette as the priest swung down onto the ladder, coming to help. Argyle's foot pressed into his cheek, grinding his head into the floor. He let go of the leg, and Argyle stepped away, kicking him once in the ribs before stepping out through the door, which slammed shut. Bentley pushed himself up onto his hands and knees just as Father Mahoney stepped down heavily onto his back in the darkness.

'What?' the priest shouted. 'Is it you?'

'Of *course* it's me,' Bentley said. 'Don't *pul*verize me!' He stood up, breathing heavily and groping for the door handle. He found the latch and pushed. The door skidded open a quarter of an inch and then jammed. Bentley yanked it shut and threw it open again, pitching his shoulder into it. Then he yanked it shut hard again. There was the sound of something sliding, and a heavy object slammed into the door – a pew, probably. Bentley flung himself into the door, but it wouldn't budge at all now. They were trapped.

'Give me a hand here,' he said to Mahoney. 'Maybe together ...'

There was the sound of guttural laughter, and Bentley put his ear to the panel. At that moment there was a flickering light from the crack beneath the door, and a burning slip of paper slid through – a couple of pages torn out of a hymnal.

Bentley stomped it out, and yelled, 'Listen!' at the closed door. But there was laughter again, and now a curling tendril of smoke wisped up into the tower.

'Holy Mother of God,' Bentley whispered, turning toward the priest. 'He means to burn us down!'

52

'Grab these photos,' Bentley said, bending over and pressing his ear to the door. Smoke drifted upward in a sheet now, and he could hear the crackling sound of the fire.

Father Mahoney retrieved the two snapshots that the cameras had spit out, along with the camera itself, which lay on the floor where Bentley had dropped it. He started awkwardly up the ladder, holding onto the camera and the rungs both, and Bentley started up behind him, hand over hand. Halfway up the camera slipped, falling ten feet to the floor where it smashed into several pieces. Mahoney stopped and looked down, and Bentley shouted, 'It's junk! Leave it!' and pushed on the priest's calf, hurrying him up.

Mahoney stepped clear of the ladder, and Bentley followed him onto the little landing that encircled the single bell. The windows on the four sides of the tower were covered with angled wooden slats, and Bentley had to look down through them to see the street. At the Church of the Holy Spirit, the bell was used only to toll the hours of the day. Above, hidden in the top of the tower, were four loudspeakers, which broadcast tape-recorded hymns and Christmas carols. Apparently it didn't matter that the bells were recorded and not played live. Devils and their minions couldn't appreciate the difference. They didn't have any kind of ear for it.

'We're safe up here,' Bentley said, 'at least for now. Let's see those photos.'

Mahoney took them out and shined the penlight onto one of them. For a moment Bentley thought that it was blank, but then he saw that it had some vague out-of-focus color to it – probably tan trousers. He had managed to snap a picture of Argyle's rear end, just about to fall on him. 'Give me some light on the other one,' Bentley said, taking the second photo from Mahoney and holding it up.

'Got him,' the priest said, illuminating the face in the photo.

Bentley's breath caught in his throat. The upturned face was hideous. It was Argyle all right, although it might have easily been Argyle's animated corpse. His eyes were rolled back, like the eyes of a dead man, and there was something drawn on his forehead – something unintelligible, scrawled on as if with a soft crayon and then smeared. His mouth was wide open, and his teeth were streaked with black, as if he'd been eating burned things.

Bentley nearly dropped the photo down the well, just to get it out of his hands, and at that moment he saw that he was wrong about being safe in the brick tower: dense smoke rose around them now, and it was noticeably warmer. Mahoney coughed, breathing through his coat. He took the photo and shoved both of them into his coat. Bentley grabbed one of the slats in the window arch and jerked at it. At the bottom of the arch the ends were slid into grooves, like the panes in a louvered window. He wiggled one out of its groove and dropped it onto the floor of the tower. Now there was enough open space to get his hands in, and he yanked out four more, so that they had a ventilation and a view. The wind gusted through the opening, but somehow, just when they needed it in buckets, the rain had let up.

'Let's wake someone up,' Father Mahoney said. He cupped his hands around his mouth and shouted 'Help!' at the empty street, but the wind, shuddering through the tower, blew the words away as if they were leaves.

'He-elp!' Bentley yelled. 'Fire!' But it was pointless, like yelling under water. He felt thick-headed and stodgy from the Scotch, as if his blood were half congealed, and he remembered now why he didn't drink. Of all the nights to throw caution to the damned wind!

The smoke was suddenly thicker, and Bentley's eyes smarted. He thrust his head out through the hole he'd made in the side of the tower, sucking in the rainy air. There was a noticeable crackling now, and smoke gusted up the well. We'll asphyxiate, Bentley thought. We're dead. Argyle has murdered us too.

'Tear these out of here,' Bentley shouted, and immediately yanked out more slats, dropping them down onto the ground. Mahoney pulled a couple out, and in a moment they were looking straight down at the lawn below. Bentley was suddenly dizzy, and he held on tight to the window frame. There was a ledge outside, a foot-wide brick frieze a couple of feet below the line of the roof. There was the yellow glow of the fire behind them now – the ladder burning, the tower door, wood paneling – and the wind through the hole they'd made seemed to feed the fire.

'Out,' Bentley said. 'Hold onto my hand and step out onto the ledge where you can hold onto the roof.'

Mahoney squeezed his shoulder in a gesture of thanks and bent out through the arch without a word. He stood teetering there, gripping Bentley's wrist like a vise, looking down at the lawn and the street.

'Grab the roof!' Bentley yelled, but Mahoney waved his free arm wildly, trying to balance himself, knocking his spectacles off and bending forward at the waist. Bentley, holding on tight to the edge of the window, and with the toe of one shoe wedged under the sill, swung himself out into the air like a man swinging around a post. With the hand that held Mahoney's wrist, he thrust forward hard, shoving the priest backward and onto the roof.

Mahoney shouted, releasing his grip on Bentley's wrist, his arms flailing, and sat down across the curb that ran around the perimeter of the roof. His feet flew upward and his rear end landed in the dark water pooled in the rain gutter. Bentley followed him, scrambling out onto the ledge and over the curb without looking down.

'Are you all right?' he asked the priest, who pulled himself out of the water and sat down.

'I ... Yes,' Mahoney said. He put a hand on his chest and heaved a deep breath.

Smoke poured out of the open arch now and threaded out between the wooden slats. 'I thought you were going down for a moment,' Bentley said. 'I couldn't think of anything else but to push you over backward.'

'I'm fine. That was ... that was close. Thank you.'

'Is there a roof access door?'

Mahoney shook his head. 'We keep it padlocked underneath.'

There was a ringing sound somewhere below, and by the time Bentley realized what it was, it had stopped – three rings, the all-clear from Mrs Hepplewhite. Argyle had gotten home safe.

At that moment there was the sound of a siren, and Bentley could see a paramedics truck and a hook and ladder pulling around a distant corner, heading toward them up Almond Street. They were saved.

Mahoney took the two Polaroid snaps out of his coat. 'We've got him dead to rights,' he said. 'What do we do?'

'Save it,' Bentley said, taking the photos. 'At least until tomorrow or the day after. I want to talk to him first. It's my duty. That's the face of an insane man, and it was me who set him down that path. I'm going to pay him a visit. I'm going to shake him up.'

53

Walt looked around for the newspaper, which would have last night's Lotto numbers in it, but it was too late, past seven, and Henry had long since grabbed it.

He climbed into the Suburban and headed for Satellite Market, wondering what he would find. Would the bluebird pay off? Part of him wanted to throw the ticket into the trash without looking at it, and not even check the winning numbers. But it was too late to think about that now. Ivy would check the numbers herself, and then she would ask him where the ticket was.

There was something about actually knowing the results, though, that was a little like the knowledge of good and evil, biblically speaking. It was a thing better left unknown, he told himself. But there was the market, looming up on the right, and he pulled into the nearly empty parking lot, got out of the truck, and went inside. Toni, the woman who worked the liquor counter, was just opening up, and the Lotto machine wasn't switched on yet, so he browsed through the racks of liquor, idly looking at the bottles of flavored gin and oddball creme de menthes.

Then abruptly he turned around and walked outside again, where he stood on the asphalt and looked up at the cloudy sky and at the foil Christmas garland strung across Chapman Avenue between the streetlamps.

Of course Henry had been right. Walt saw it all clearly – a real insight. This was no good, this wishing on a bluebird. Once you started to develop an interest in damnable things, the interest was liable to grow like a milkweed vine until it strangled you. One day you're satisfied with sixty bucks, and the next day you're Nebuchadnezzar or somebody, King of Babylon, and all you've bought for yourself is regret.

He went back into the store, his mind made up and made up solidly. He would look this demon in the face, size it up, and knock it down like a pot-metal milk bottle.

'Big winner?' Toni asked, taking the ticket from him.

'Just might be.'

She slipped it into the slot in the machine, which sucked it in, whirred a little bit, and spit it back out.

'Sixty dollars!' she said, handing him the winning ticket so he could see for himself.

He found that he couldn't speak. He took the ticket but didn't look at it. It was all true. What he feared had been proven true. The bluebird was *exactly* what it was advertised to be. Maybe that made it a demon, like Bentley thought it was. And here he'd been playing around with it, turning it into a prank to goad Argyle.

Use it against him. The sentence drifted unbidden into his thoughts, but he pushed it away, thinking about Sidney Vest despite himself, about being cavalier with the damned bluebird, making ignorant wishes on it …

And immediately that thought was replaced by another sort of knowledge – that he was rich, incalculably, infinitely rich. Once again he pictured the paper sack with a million dollars in it, but the million dollars was nothing now; it was like finding an old tuna sandwich. A billion was more like it, if they made sacks that large. His spirits soared and he nearly laughed out loud.

Toni handed him three twenties, and he nodded at her, then wandered away toward the liquor racks again, clutching his money. He stared at nothing, not daring to look at the bills in his hand just in case they wouldn't be bills at all, but would be slips of newspaper or something, and this whole thing was nothing but a dream.

He shut his eyes hard, opened them again, and looked. It was three twenties, all right. He wasn't asleep.

It dawned on him then that he was already wasting time. He could as easily already have won the sixty million as the sixty. What would he have to do to accumulate sixty million in Lotto jackpots now? The usual return was a measly three million a week, so that meant twenty weeks of winning. But of course they'd arrest him after he won the third time. He'd get away with winning twice – twice was a fluke. But the third time they'd smell a rat, and they'd round him up. What then? Would he be doomed? Why, no. He'd call in the bluebird. The thought was exhilarating and terrifying both. The world was suddenly his oyster. What would it be? Television appearances? Public speeches? Limousines? A house the size of the state of Maine? He laughed, giddy with the idea of limitless wealth.

He had no idea how to spend money! That was the truth of it. He was a piker, a lightweight, a hayseed. Could he learn fast enough? Of course the first thing was to buy Argyle out, lock, stock, and barrel, and then have him publicly humiliated in the Plaza, dressed up like an organ grinder's monkey. The bluebird would make it seem right and natural to people. They'd throw rotten fruit, eggs … Hell, it *was* right and natural.

Suddenly there came into his mind a picture of Nora bringing the shackled Argyle a cup of water, a look of profound sadness on her face. Instantly he was ashamed of himself. He unclutched his hand and dropped the twenties onto the floor.

For a moment there he'd gone nearly crazy! That's what Henry had been talking about! He took a deep breath. Well, to hell with that. He would leave the bills right there on the floor, like lucky pennies, for somebody else to find. He would walk away from them, from the whole shebang. From now on he'd despise wealth like a Hindu.

And this time he wouldn't just throw the damned jar in the bin either; he'd break it to pieces, dump the gin out onto the ground, put the bluebird in a paint can and pound the lid down and haul it out to the dump where he'd pitch it under the wheels of an earth-moving vehicle.

Yes, his mind was made up for good and all, and he felt suddenly better. A minute ago he'd been drunk with anticipation, with the love of money, but now he saw the futility in it. He looked at the twenties scattered at his feet …

What the hell, there was no reason not to take them after all, a pitiful little sum like that. But thank God he hadn't asked for the sixty million! Sixty dollars was different. It was simply the money he was owed from yesterday. How could there be any sin in breaking even? He didn't look for an answer.

'Well, for the love of Mike,' someone said just then, 'it's starting to look like the whole damn gang!'

The voice belonged unmistakably to Mrs Biggs. Walt bent over now and picked up the twenties, then turned slowly around. It was her, all right. She stood grinning at him, holding onto the Reverend Bentley through the crook of his arm. Bentley looked like hell, unshaven, his hair a wreck, eyes bloodshot, and wearing the same clothes he'd worn yesterday. He scowled and shook his head hard at Walt, as if to deny whatever Walt was thinking.

'Look who I found in the lot,' Mrs Biggs said. 'I said to myself, "Maggie, there's the Reverend, stopping in for a fifth, and it's just coming on to eight o'clock, too." But now I see *you've* beat him to it. Early bird gets the snort, eh? You starting a fresh bender, or finishing one up?'

'Neither,' Walt said. 'I stopped in to run a Lotto ticket.'

She looked at the money in his hand. 'Well then, hand it over,' she said, 'since it turns out you've pretty much wrecked my stove.'

Walt gaped at her.

'That's right. I had my friend Mr Peet in last night and he says it'll cost sixty dollars to fix it. He tells me the gas company won't touch it because it's buggered up. You apparently done something to it, which Mr Peet explained. I misremember what, except that it was sixty dollars' worth.'

'I didn't do *any*thing to it,' Walt said, 'except clean out the pipes. Sixty dollars!' Of course this was probably a lie. Mr Pete was a pipe dream, a figment, pure downtown hosery. She'd seen that he was holding three twenties, so that's how much the whole thing was going to cost, to the penny. Good thing Walt *hadn't* won the sixty million; he'd be handing that over.

She nodded slowly, fixing him with a sad look, but he held out against her. And when she spoke again her voice was small, as if she had finally given up, thrown in the towel. 'It's that way, is it?' she said.

'What way?' Walt asked. 'What are you talking about?'

'I kind of figured you were made of stronger stuff. I thought you had some backbone. I guess I'm a bad judge of character, although I never would have thought so ...' She dropped Bentley's arm. 'Go on Reverend, buy your hootch and skedaddle. Both of you. I'm through with the whole bunch of you.'

'I suggest we take her at her word,' Bentley said, gesturing toward the door. 'I just stopped in after some coffee filters, actually, and then I'm on my way.'

'Yessir,' Mrs Biggs said, wiping at her eyes now and turning to Toni, who was working over the bottles with a feather duster. 'Do you have a tissue, dearie?'

'Oh, for ...!' Bentley said. 'A public display! This is a dis*grace*!'

Toni hauled out a tissue box from under the counter, and Mrs Biggs took one and dabbed her eyes. 'Yesterday these two went to work on my old O'Keefe and Merritt,' she said to Toni, 'and I said to myself, "Now there's a couple of samaritans!" That's just what I said. And what came of it? You'd never guess.' Toni shook her head. *'Rubbage.'* Mrs Biggs said, and she nodded hard, making her point. '*I* didn't mind lighting that old stove with a match, did I? I'd been lighting it that way for years. And now they've *fixed* it, as they say, and I can't light it at all, or it'll blow up. This tribe comes in for a cup of tea, and now my stove's broke, my cow pitcher's broke, my car's broke. Another hour and I suppose they'd have finished me off. Maybe it'd be better if they had.' She put her face in her hands and started to cry 'Sixty dollars worth of grief!' she said.

Toni handed her another tissue.

'And the old man!' Mrs Biggs said, looking up sharply and shaking the tissue at Walt. 'That sweet-talking old devil. I guess everyone might as well know about *him*. Lord knows I *trusted* that man!' She glanced unmistakably at the money in Walt's hand again. Then she turned her head sideways so that Toni couldn't see her and winked at him – a shameless, greedy wink.

'Here,' Walt said, instantly handing over the money. Clearly this was simply a matter of payola. She wasn't going to shut up otherwise. She meant to drag Henry's name through the mud right then and there.

'And what about my automobile?' she asked Walt, suddenly forgetting about Henry.

'I've got the hoses in the car. Let's get to work. We're burning daylight standing around here.' He headed toward the door. 'Thanks,' he said to Toni.

Outside, he saw right off that something was wrong with the Suburban, which sat at an angle in its parking space, as if the back end had been slammed sideways a couple of feet. Walt strode across to the far side. The rear fender was caved in, and the end of the bumper, the last four inches or so, was bent all to hell. Someone had clobbered the truck and taken off. 'Hell,' Walt said.

'You'll just have to be a little soldier about it,' Mrs Biggs said to him. 'There's worse things that can happen to a person.'

'*That's* the truth,' Bentley said.

'Well,' Mrs Biggs said, 'another country heard from. I've got a couple of items on my list for you, too, Reverend.'

'Not this morning,' Bentley said.

'Why?' she asked. 'What have you got to do that's so all-fired important?'

'Sleep,' Bentley said. 'You'll have to count me out.'

'You mean Henry'll have to count you out, don't you? *There's* friendship for you. If it involves work, the Reverend's got to sleep. I saw that yesterday, the way you handled that mop.'

'What I mean is that I was up all night long and nearly burned alive in a fire.'

'Well, get used to it,' she said. 'That's pretty much the whole program down in perdition.'

54

It was past noon when Walt loaded his tools into the Suburban and fired up the engine, sitting there for a moment to let it warm up. At least he had gotten the radiator fixed before the rain started up – although he hadn't gotten a chance to help Bentley scrub out the trash cans with bleach and a broom; Bentley had cleaned the cans by himself after coming back from the beauty supply store up on Main Street. The rain had nearly drowned him before he was done.

Walt's sixty dollars was more than gone. He had gone down to the automated teller around eleven and pulled out sixty more. Right now Mrs Biggs had groceries enough for a month, a couple of rented movies for the VCR, and a new cow pitcher that Bentley had found down at Stiffworthy's Antiques. Tomorrow Wait was supposed to come around and look over the garbage disposal, which had shut down and wouldn't reset. The plumber had apparently said it was just a loose wire ...

Along with that, one of the garage door hinges was sprung, the crawl space screens under the house had to be replaced because possums were getting in, and in the bedroom there was a leaky window that 'wanted putty.' And as soon as the rain let up, according to Mrs Biggs, someone could get on with the work of scraping the eaves so the house could be repainted. She had hired a Mexican to do the work nearly a month ago, but the man had quit after half a day because he wasn't satisfied with three dollars an hour and all the doughnuts he could eat. And, she'd told Walt, that was 'under the table,' by which, Walt supposed, she meant the money.

He drummed his fingers on the steering wheel, then turned on the defrost and pulled away from the curb, heading up Olive and then left on Palmyra, passing a house with a life-size Santa Claus and reindeer in the yard, the whole display vandalized – knocked down and defaced with graffiti. No doubt it was more of Argyle's high jinks. He swung a left onto Glassell, back toward home. By his calculations he was down something like two hundred dollars total. Bentley was down another thirty for the cow pitcher, and it didn't make him happy. Henry was going to pay them back with the lingerie money, except that the lingerie had never materialized, and, as of this morning anyway, Sidney Vest hadn't returned any of Henry's calls.

'Henry's going to have to work out his own problems,' Bentley had told Walt after scouring out the last of the trash cans. 'I *can't*. I've done what I could, but trying to pay this woman off is like pouring water through sand. It was a mistake that we ever took her on.'

And of course Bentley was right. He'd been right yesterday. Walt had been the fool. What they'd done so far was the tip of the iceberg. There were worse things waiting. All morning long she'd been full of the Islands again – going back to Waikiki, maybe look up her old friend Velma Krane. Plane tickets were reasonable right now, during the fare war. You could fly round trip for about three hundred dollars. And who could say? – maybe once she was in Honolulu, by golly, she'd stay put. *Maybe all she needed was a one-way ticket and first month's rent on a little bungalow downtown.* Fifteen hundred would about do it, give or take. As for the house in Orange, hell, she could lease that out and make an income.

Walt hashed it over. What with Ivy's commission, it was almost easier to give Mrs Biggs what she wanted. Except that of course she wouldn't go to Honolulu even so. She'd hang around Orange and weasel more money out of them until Walt cut her off. Then she'd rat all of them out to Jinx.

Something had to be done right now. There was no more putting it off.

Already he knew the answer. It had been circulating through his mind all morning long. Sending Vest back to North Carolina had been the work of an instant. He was probably counting his many blessings right now, along with his money, which he was spending on cheap Carolina real estate. Vest, after all, had *wanted* to go. Walt's calling on the bluebird hadn't been a matter of greed; it had been a matter of doing a man a favor, if you wanted to look at it that way.

And if that was the way you were looking at it, then why not do the same favor for Maggie Biggs, who was pining away for the Islands? And there was Uncle Henry to think of too. Calling in the bluebird would be a blessing all the way around – everyone a winner. By golly, he'd kill two stones with one bird, he thought, laughing out loud, and he wished that he had someone to tell the joke to. Probably he'd never be able to tell it to anyone.

He made the wish quickly, just a blink of his mind, and turned up Oak Street toward home.

55

Mrs Simms lived on Washington Street in a white clapboard house with a wraparound porch, and when Walt and the kids pulled up at the curb, she was sitting on the porch in a wooden chair, very still, watching the rain fall, her lawn all covered with leaves. She had a shawl around her shoulders and her hands in her lap, and from the way she stared at the street, it seemed clear to Walt that all the money in the world wouldn't help her, not in the way she needed to be helped. She and Simms had been married for fifty years.

'It's *her*,' Eddie said, looking out the window.

'She's *old*,' Nora said. 'She's a million.'

'Not *that* old,' Eddie said. 'That's stupid.'

'Yes-huh,' Nora said. 'Isn't she a million, Unca Walter?'

Somehow Nora had taken to calling him Walter, just like Jinx. Walt had always been a little irritated when Jinx called him that, but Nora somehow made it all right. Nora was the great leveler.

'She's *close* to a million,' Walt said. 'Closer than we are, anyway.'

'See?' Nora said to Eddie.

'You don't get it,' Eddie said.

'Do too.'

'Do not.'

Walt held up the cashier's check that he'd swapped the rest of the checks for. Argyle's money had of course killed the fund-raiser. There didn't seem to be any reason to go back out after another forty or fifty bucks or whatever they might have managed to scrounge up, and then they'd have to go to all the trouble to bake more cookies.

'I'm going to let Nora carry the money,' he said, and he winked at Eddie.

'That's okay,' Eddie said. 'I'll stay here.'

'Nope. We'll all go,' Walt said. 'You ready?'

Without waiting for an answer, he ducked out into the rain, coming around the side of the car and opening the doors for the kids. Nora climbed out and took the check, then started out toward the porch, holding the check in front of her face with both hands as if she were hiding behind it.

'Mrs Simms, I believe,' Walt said, once they were out of the rain.

She smiled and nodded, holding out her hand. Nora shook it like a pump handle. Eddie touched it, then pulled his hand away. Walt introduced the three of them, and Mrs Simms said she was happy to meet them. Then Nora tried explaining the check, calling it a 'fund raisin,' but Mrs Simms was baffled. She took it and stared at it. 'Whatever do you mean?' she asked.

'It's a collection from people in the neighborhood,' Walt explained. 'It's on behalf of Mr Simms, because of the bell-ringing. People around here appreciated that. Nora and Eddie did the footwork. Every single person they talked to donated.' And that was true. There was no percentage in revealing that they'd only hit four houses before they'd quit.

Suddenly Mrs Simms was crying. She laid the check down on a little table next to the chair, then took her spectacles off and wiped her eyes with a handkerchief that she pulled out of her sleeve.

'Why is she crying?' Nora whispered out loud.

'Shhh,' Walt said.

'It's 'cause of her husband,' Eddie said.

Nora put her hand on Mrs Simms's arm, and Mrs Simms patted Nora's hand. She picked up the check again and looked at it. 'Who would have thought?' she said to Walt.

He shrugged. 'Give people a chance,' he said, 'and they'll show their true colors.' Somehow he felt like a heel, and it dawned on him just then that he himself hadn't contributed a dime to the check. He hadn't thought to.

'I'd like to know who donated,' she said. 'I intend to write all of them a thank-you note.'

'Well, there's so *many*,' Walt said. 'We didn't keep any kind of record ...'

'There was that one lady on the corner,' Eddie said. 'And the other one, too, that lived next door to her.'

'That's right,' Walt said. 'We can get you their names and addresses anyway. That's a start.'

'Well, I'd be obliged,' she said.

'And Mr R-guy,' Nora said. 'He gave the most.'

'Yes, indeed,' Walt said. 'That's true.'

'Will you step inside?' Mrs Simms asked. 'I could put on a pot of coffee.'

Walt nearly refused. He had things to do – boxes to pack for a last-ditch Christmas mailing, Christmas shopping, errands to run. He just didn't have time …

Then he realized what he was thinking. This was another case of there not being any room at the inn, wasn't it? He couldn't be a good Samaritan; *he was too busy*. Someone else could do it. Charity was something you measured in dollars and cents, but you didn't go to any trouble.

'Would you like a cookie?' she asked Eddie.

Eddie nodded, and Nora held onto her hand as they went into the house. Mr Simms had apparently owned a doily factory, because there were doilies everywhere, as if the furniture were wearing special clothes. And there were easily a hundred dolls in the living room and dining room, big ones and little ones both, with porcelain heads and glass eyes. There was a big dollhouse on a table against a wall – a three-story Victorian with tiny shingles and intricate wooden fretwork and corbels and gables. The rooms had little hand-woven rugs on the floor and Chippendale furniture, and there were tiny milk cartons and canned goods in the kitchen. Nora stood staring at the house, rocking back and forth on her heels.

'Here's a cookie from the freezer,' Mrs Simms said, coming out of the kitchen and pulling the top off a Tupperware container.

Eddie took one.

'You'd better have four, to start with,' she said, and Eddie took three more, then sat down on a chair and held the four cookies in his hand.

'Oh!' Nora uttered, pointing at a doll with blonde curls.

'Do you like that one?' Mrs Simms asked.

'Oh!' Nora said again. 'She's … Oh!'

'Would you like to have her?'

Nora swiveled around and looked at Walt, her eyes wide open in astonishment. 'Could I?' she asked. Eddie sat in the chair staring straight ahead.

'It would make me very happy,' Mrs Simms said to Walt.

He shrugged. 'What do you say, Nora?'

'Oh, yes!' Nora said.

Mrs Simms picked up the doll and handed it to Nora, who held it in her arms like a baby. 'I have something for you, too,' Mrs Simms said to Eddie.

She led them into a den, where there was a line of books supported by two heavy brass bookends on a table. The bookends were square-rigged clipper ships tossing on ocean waves. 'Do you like these?' Mrs Simms asked.

Eddie shrugged. He was still holding onto his cookies.

'Well, I want you to have them,' she said, 'along with this book.' She handed him an old copy of *Treasure Island* with a glued-on cover illustration of a pirate with a knife in his teeth. 'Will you take them? They belonged to Mr Simms.'

Eddie shrugged again and looked at the floor.

'What do you think, Eddie?' Walt asked, smiling at Mrs Simms. He looked at Eddie and mouthed the word 'Thanks.'

'Sure,' Eddie mumbled. 'I guess.'

'Can I have a cookie?' Nora asked. 'What kind are they?'

'Ginger cookies.'

Nora took one out of the Tupperware, nibbled at it, and made her rabbit face at Mrs Simms. Walt headed for the front door, and Mrs Simms followed them out onto the porch, thanking Walt again for the check.

'Perhaps you'd like to come over some time and help me with my dollhouse?' she asked Nora, who nodded hard. 'And Eddie, if you wouldn't mind looking through Mr Simms's coins, perhaps you could help me catalogue them. I need to make a list of them.'

'I could,' Eddie said.

'Well, that's just fine. God bless you,' she said to Walt, who nodded and stepped out into the rain.

The kids ran to the truck and clambered in, carrying their stuff, and Nora belted the doll into the center seat belt. 'She's nice,' Nora said.

'Yes, indeed,' Walt said. He felt like a complete fraud. Somehow he had set out to do the right thing with the fundraiser, and Argyle had turned him into a sort of messenger boy. By remaining anonymous, Argyle had made sure that the glory would fall to Walt, who didn't deserve it, and Walt had enough conscience to feel guilty about it. And who was he kidding? He had thought up the fund-raiser to spite Argyle and the preschool's Christmas wrap fund-raiser, hadn't he? And the wild success of it had pissed him off because it wasn't *his* success. And now Mrs Simms turns out to be some kind of saint, and he ends up driving away down Washington Street feeling like a hollow man. What a mess. Maybe Bentley had an illustrated tract to clear all this up: 'Guilt as an Obstacle to Sin.'

'You said we get a doughnut,' Nora said.

'A doughnut? Not after all those cookies?' Walt turned up Chapman toward the All-Niter. Nora and Eddie deserved a doughnut.

'I didn't eat my cookies,' Eddie said. 'I'm saving them.'

'I'm saving, too,' Nora said, making the rabbit face. But her cookies were already gone.

The parking lot at the All-Niter was deserted. It was too late in the day for serious doughnut eating. Walt swung the Suburban into a slot and glanced into the building, through the big window in front, on the lookout for Maggie Biggs. Had she vanished? Taken the slow boat to Waikiki?

Someone was coming out to the front of the shop from behind the counter, pushing through the little Dutch door. But it wasn't Maggie Biggs; it was Uncle Henry. Henry looked up just then, apparently spotted the Suburban through the window, and stood stock-still, as if trying to decide whether to come ahead or to turn and flee. Abruptly he hurried forward, out among the tables, where he slid into one of the booths. There was an empty doughnut basket and a half-drunk cup of coffee on the table in front of him. He picked up a section of newspaper and affected an engrossed look.

Walt got out and walked to the door, pushing it open and letting Nora and Eddie squeeze in under his outstretched arm. Eddie stood looking at the doughnuts and Nora ran to Uncle Henry, who feigned surprise at seeing them there. Walt decided to let it slide.

There was a lipstick stain on the coffee cup, so the stuff on the table wasn't Henry's; either that or he'd had company. Probably he was here for some purpose besides doughnuts. 'No sign of the lingerie yet?' Walt asked hopefully.

'No,' Henry said, putting the paper down. 'And there won't be, either. The party's off.'

'That's a dirty shame,' Walt said. 'Vest didn't drop the ball on us, did he?'

Henry nodded his head slowly. 'Something like that. I got through to his secretary this morning. She tells me that Sidney Vest fell over dead last night at a restaurant out in Villa Park. Choked on a piece of fish. They're shipping his body back home to Raleigh for burial.'

56

'Dead?' Walt asked, sitting down hard in the booth. The word croaked out of him. His head swam, and he shut his eyes tight. 'I don't believe it,' he muttered.

'Apparently it's true,' Henry said. 'Piece of halibut got him. He sucked it down his windpipe. They worked the Heimlich on him but it didn't do any good. I guess that when it's your turn to go ...' He shrugged philosophically.

'My God!' Walt shouted suddenly, just then remembering his other wish. 'Maggie Biggs! Where is she?'

Henry looked around uneasily, his face furrowed up. 'I'm not sure,' he said.

'What's wrong, Walter? What's the matter?' Nora and Eddie stared at him. He stood up again, looking from the counter to the door, ready to bolt for the car and drive the half mile to Olive Street.

There was a voice from among the doughnuts then, and Walt stood up and turned around. Mrs Biggs herself looked out from the door to the back room, eyeing him suspiciously. 'It's you, is it?' she said. 'What's all this fuss?'

'Are you all right?' Walt shouted at her. He strode across to the counter. She took a step backward, looking uncertainly at him now, and he gestured at her and shook his head. 'It's okay, it's okay,' he said, grinning weakly. 'Everything's all right with you, then?'

'Well, I suppose it is.'

'You're feeling all right?'

'What's your game?' she asked, squinting at him. 'Where's the Reverend?' She looked around suspiciously.

'He's ...' Walt realized that he sounded like a lunatic. 'The car, I mean to say.' Clearly Mrs Biggs was safe. The bluebird hadn't killed her, at least for the moment. 'The car's all right? Not overheating?'

'Not so's you'd notice it, no. You look like hell, sonny, pardon my French. Why don't you go sit down? Chew on a sinker.'

'That's right,' Walt said. 'Sure I will.' He slumped into the booth again.

'Who are these, then, your children?' Mrs Biggs waved at Eddie and Nora. Nora smiled big at her and held up her new doll. 'What'll you have?' Mrs Biggs asked, and then started piling doughnuts into one of the baskets as Nora and Eddie pointed at the racks. 'On the house,' she said to Walt. 'Couple of glazeys for you? Cup of mud?'

Walt shook his head. 'Put them in a bag,' he said. 'We'll take them to go.'

In his mind he revised his wish to the bluebird, calling it off, half expecting Maggie Biggs to pitch over dead right then and there. Don't kill her, he commanded the bird, talking loud in his mind. Send her home happy.

But was it enough? Could he be sure that the bird was listening? 'We'd better run,' he said to the kids, getting up and taking the bag from Mrs Biggs. 'Look,' he said to her. 'For the next fifteen minutes, don't go anywhere.'

'What is this?' she asked. 'What's going on here?' She looked at Henry now, sizing him up. 'Is this your doing?' she asked.

'I swear,' he said, shaking his head. 'It's a mystery.'

'Because if it is ...'

'Just stay here,' Walt said to her. 'Just for a few minutes. And don't eat *anything*. Don't take any medications. For God's sake, don't do anything dangerous, like climb a ladder or something. Stay away from the windows. Just stay *put* for a few minutes.' He pushed the door open and ushered the kids out, then jumped into the Suburban, fired it up, and headed for home.

*

'And that's all I want you to do,' he said out loud to the bluebird. 'Get her out of here alive.' It sat on the garage bench, freed from its grave under the stepping-stone. Nora and Eddie were indoors, making themselves sick with the doughnuts. He wondered if he should call the All-Niter and give Mrs Biggs the all-clear, but that would just compound the craziness of this whole thing. She had thought something was 'going on' as it was.

Was it?

The whole setup at the All-Niter was strange: Henry sneaking around behind the counter, acting furtive, pretending to have been eating dough-nuts, Maggie Biggs hiding out in the back room. If Walt hadn't shouted, she'd have stayed hidden; he was pretty sure of that. Maybe Henry was just down there giving her what's what, straightening her out for good and all. But that's not the way he had acted.

57

Bentley looked out through the walnut trees toward the street. From where he stood he could see up and down Chapman Avenue, get a view of cars heading both east and west. It was 2AM, and there was no traffic, and except for crickets the night was still. Away across the lot he could see the shadow of a backhoe left by the men who'd been digging up LeRoy's orchard. The shell of the burned-out house shone in the moonlight, and for the first time in over a week the sky was clear and full of stars, but the ground and shrubbery and trees were soaked, and it would take them days to dry out, which was a good thing, under the circumstances.

Father Mahoney sprinkled gasoline over the low, altarlike shelf in the chicken coop and then doused the painted scrawls on the plank walls before saturating the dirt beneath, pouring the gasoline over the chicken wire and the diabolical trash behind it. He flicked the last of the gasoline out in the rough shape of a cross, mumbling in Latin. Bentley listened to him, watched him making these liturgical gestures with a gasoline can. He had thought that the church had given up Latin, but it was possible that the priest had shifted out of English simply because English couldn't quite carry the neces-sary weight, so to speak.

Finally Mahoney set the now-empty can on the shelf and gestured at it. 'Leave it,' Bentley said in a low voice. There was no use trying to hide it. Fire inspectors would know this was an arson.

They had left Bentley's car at the Holy Spirit church and walked the six blocks to Water Street carrying the gas can in a plastic sack. If they were stopped on the way back, well, so be it: the police wouldn't arrest a priest and a minister. They'd say they'd been off visiting Mrs Hepplewhite, who was at home right now, waiting for the all-clear phone call when they got back to the church. If they made it to the church without incident, then Obermeyer would swear they'd spent the evening at his place if they needed an alibi later, which they wouldn't; who would suspect the two of them? The whole thing was Bentley's plan: as soon as the shed went up they would phone in an alarm from the pay phone on the Cambridge Street corner and then hightail it through the neighborhood on foot.

There was the reek of gasoline on the night air now, and Bentley looked around uneasily again, checking traffic, on the alert for cruising patrol cars. Mahoney stepped back and bowed his head for a moment, and Bentley did too.

The priest nodded at him finally, and Bentley lit the wick of a Stay-Lit birthday candle and checked the street one last time. Chapman was clear of cars, from the Plaza to Tustin Avenue half a mile east. Mahoney backed away, into the shadows of the grove. Bentley let the candle burn for a couple of seconds before he tossed it into the open shed, and then he turned and ran, but even so the heat from the explosion was so intense that he panicked and threw himself forward into an arbor overgrown with unpruned grapevines, and had to scramble to free himself. Mahoney was already high-stepping it through the trees, toward the oleander-choked wire fence at the rear of the lot.

Bentley ran after him, holding onto his hat and pushing in through the oleander, yanking the stiff branches out of his way. 'Go!' he shouted hoarsely, and then shoved the priest through the hole they'd cut in the fence ten minutes ago, out into the parking lot at the rear of a set of two-story office buildings. Bentley bent through behind him, careful not to snag his coat, and the two hurried across the moonlit asphalt as the glow of the fire rose up behind them.

58

'Oh, yes, it's safe as a baby,' Mrs Biggs said over the phone. 'I've got it hid where nobody'll think to look.'

'There's really no need for that,' Argyle told her. 'I'll take delivery today – as soon as possible, if that's acceptable to you. I believe I authorized Mr Peetenpaul to offer you two thousand dollars, but I'm happy to say that I'm *so* thrilled you've been prompt and professional, that I'd like to double that figure. I don't suppose you'd argue with that?' He looked out the window. They'd started digging up LeRoy's remains again, but the rain had them stymied. Most of the grove was a mud hole now. Somehow Argyle didn't think they'd find anything much anyway. It was only at the end that LeRoy had gotten stupid.

'Four thousand dollars,' she said. 'Well, that's mighty generous of you, I'm sure. And like you say, I won't argue. I don't believe in it. An argument's just words, isn't it? It won't pay rent.'

'There's a good philosophy,' Argyle said.

'But I might just as well tell you now that there's another party has an interest in this thing. Considerably more interested than four thousand dollars, I might say.'

'What are you talking about?'

'Only that there's a party who'll offer me more. And like I say, I won't argue. I let the money talk.'

Argyle sat up in his chair and evened his voice. This was a new turn. Peetenpaul had grossly misjudged this woman, which wasn't at all like him. 'You've misunderstood me entirely, Mrs Biggs,' he said. 'I'm not offering to *buy* this item from you and never was. I offered to pay you to retrieve it. The bird itself is very rare – the only existing example of its species. The Museum of Natural History in Los Angeles commissioned me to obtain it from sources in China, and I was successful in doing so. The bird, very unfortunately, was sent to the wrong address and this entire confusion resulted. For the sake of science, Mrs Biggs, and on the part of the taxpayer, I entreat you to allow me to send it on to its rightful owners.'

'That's not how it worked out, you see.'

'What's not? What do you mean?'

'Mr Stebbins threw the bird away.'

'I don't follow you.'

'He threw the thing into the Dumpster. Anybody could have took it out, couldn't they?'

'Am I mistaken, or did you say you were in possession of the item in question?' Argyle asked evenly.

'Oh, I'm in possession of it. That I am.'

'Then nobody else took it out of the trash?'

'No, I've got it.'

'And it wasn't carted away to the dump?'

'No, it was not. I'm telling you I've got it.'

'Good! For a moment there I was lost. So, to put this in perspective, you've got the item and you're not satisfied with the remuneration despite my doubling it?'

'Well, I don't know anything about remuneration, as you call it. I was thinking more along the lines of *purchase price*. What I mean is that I don't know who *owns* this thing, do I? All I know is it was me that found it in the trash. You talk about this museum and China and all, but that smells like rubbish to me. It looks to me like *I* own it, so don't quote the by-God tax-payer to me.'

'I must advise you to rethink your position, Mrs Biggs.'

'That's what I've done in regard to this other party, like I said ...'

'*What* other party?'

'This other gentleman. I misremember the man's name, but he's *very* keen on the item.'

'I don't for a moment believe in the existence of this other gentleman, Mrs Biggs.'

'That's as may be. You might just as well say you don't believe in the moon, for all the good it'll do you. What if I told you this other gentleman was the neighbor's cat and that. I'd feed this damned bird to it on a shingle as soon as give it to a cheapskate like you? What would you say then? That you don't believe in the cat? Because that's just what I'll do, and I'll do it in a cold second, too.'

'I'm getting a little tired of this entire charade, Mrs Biggs. How much do you want?'

'Two hundred and fifty thousand dollars,' she said. 'Cash on the barrelhead.'

He heard a bang then, as if she'd pounded her fist onto a desktop. A quarter of a million dollars! The amount struck him dumb. He sat looking at the telephone receiver, as if what he held in his hand had ceased to have any meaning. After a moment he managed to laugh, but it sounded unconvincing even to him.

'You might as well laugh,' she said. 'I'm onto you and your little game. I want small bills, spending cash – nothing bigger than a fifty and not all fifties, either. Put 'em in a suitcase. Some kind of quality leather, not vinyl or cloth. Have that big Dutchman of yours bring it around. I'll give him the bird right enough. *Comprende?*'

'I'm with you so far,' Argyle said.

'Then stay with me, because I've got one more thing to say. I've found out a thing or two about you, Mr Swindle-meister, about some of the things you've *done*, if you take my meaning, and I think it's a crying shame. I know who your friends are, too. Your whole crowd makes me sick. I've wrote it all down, all the dirt that's fit to print, and it's a sorry thing to look at, I can tell you. What I did is I sent a copy off to my dear friend Velma, and if I don't show up at Velma's with her share of the payment PDQ, then it all goes public. Every blessed thing.'

'I think I understand.'

'I knew you would. You're a man of business. And what I hope you under-stand is that tomorrow, if I don't have the money in hand, I mean to dry this bird out in the oven, salt its tail, and throw it to the lions.'

She hung up the phone then, and Argyle sat there with his head in his hands. He'd managed to get the bird out of the frying pan and into the fire. And it wasn't the money that frosted him, either. He could pay her the damned money easily enough; he would have paid Flanagan as much if the man hadn't gone soft on him. What pissed him off was the idea of being hosed like this.

But what could he do, short of having the old woman tortured? Not a damn thing. She'd do what she said.

He laughed out loud. He'd been flayed! Well, to hell with it. Once he pos-sessed the bird he'd be free, clean of the last twenty years, rid of the nightmares, rid of the black desire that drove him out into the neighborhood after dark …

Last night he had come to himself outside the church, standing on the sidewalk in the midnight wind and holding a burned-down candle. Appar-ently he'd bitten the burning end off it, because his tongue was blistered and there was wax in his teeth. He had fled home in a blind rush, where he had found his back door open wide, water running in the kitchen sink, all the stove burners flaming. His memory of what he'd done inside the church was a heap of fragments, like an image in a broken mirror: climbing in the dim well of the bell tower, stomping on a man in a dark room, smoke curling up from torn-apart hymnals …

He stood up from his desk now, picked up his umbrella, and left the office, locking the door and heading down the stairs and out onto the porch. Peeten-paul himself was just then pulling up along the curb, driving the new truck and dressed for business.

59

'You promised,' Nora said.

Walt glanced at her in the rearview mirror. She was frowning hard, look-ing straight ahead, her hands folded across her chest, her bangs a razor-straight line above her eyebrows.

'But I didn't know we would make that much, did I?' Walt asked. 'You've got the bubble string already. Today after school we can go to the dime store and you can pick out … let's see … three things. We'll do that every day for … two weeks. Three prizes a day.'

'How many is that?' Nora asked.

Eddie counted on his fingers. 'Kind of a lot,' he said.

'Nuh-uh,' Nora said unhappily.

'How many prizes did you promise the children?' Ivy asked.

Walt grinned weakly at her. 'About two thousand,' he muttered, 'give or take.' He turned left, onto Chapman, heading for the preschool.

'How many is that?' Nora asked, instantly happy again. 'That two-thing?'

'It's a *lot*,' Eddie said. 'A *really* lot.'

'But how many?'

'Count to twenty,' Ivy said helpfully. 'And then count to twenty again. And do it over and over *a hundred times.*'

Nora immediately started to count out loud, her head bobbing back and forth.

Ivy grinned at Walt. 'Old moneybags,' she said. 'Two thousand prizes!'

'I'll think of something,' Walt said, although actually he had already tried and he couldn't think of anything at all. Through his wholesalers he could buy carnival prizes in bulk for two or three cents apiece – plastic spiders and skulls, rhinestone rings, silver-painted plastic charms, window stickers – but there was no way the children would be happy with being handed three gross of each of these things. And even if that *would* work, it would still easily cost him hundreds of dollars.

'Fourteen, fifteen, fifteen,' Nora intoned, moving from there into a realm of numbers that Walt was unfamiliar with. She stopped suddenly. 'Mr R-Guy!' she said.

Walt looked. Argyle stood under the porch roof in front of his downtown office, talking, for God's sake, to the inspector, who was dressed in a coat and tie. He had gotten a haircut, apparently, and trimmed his beard.

'Why, it's Mr Peetenpaul,' Ivy said. 'That's the man who bought the properties.'

'Is it?' Walt asked broadly. 'Well, I'll be damned. It's a small world, I guess.'

She looked at him. 'What's wrong with you all of a sudden?'

'Well, it might be Mr Peetenpaul,' he said. 'But whoever he is, he didn't buy any properties. He happens to *work* for Argyle.' Walt widened his eyes at her, and she frowned back at him, as if she didn't quite understand. Nora kept on counting, bouncing in her seat now.

'How do you know he works for Robert?' Ivy asked.

'Trust me. I know. I'm not sure what Argyle's up to with this sales-commission scam, but like I told you, it's not as simple as you think it is. Watch out he isn't playing you for a patsy.'

Ivy was silent, looking at the street now, taking it all in. Walt felt vindicated by this, and then almost immediately ashamed of feeling that way at Ivy's expense. But hell, it was time that she had a glimpse of the real Argyle – Argyle the sneak and the manipulator. Now she didn't have to take Walt's word for it, which of course she hadn't taken anyway, to her own peril.

'I don't mean you shouldn't take his sixty grand,' he said, suddenly thinking of the money.

'I don't want to talk about it right now.'

'Okay.' He glanced at Nora again, a bright idea coming to him out of the blue. 'How's this?' he asked her brightly. 'We'll consolidate.'

Nora stopped counting. 'Wha-a-a-t?' she asked, screwing up her face at him.

'Consolidate. It means a putting-together, a gathering into a bundle, so to speak. The many become one, the one greater than the sum of its parts.'

'What's parts?' She frowned, as if she were concentrating. Eddie remained silent.

'I'll give you an example,' Walt said. 'Instead of twenty-five pennies, you get a quarter.'

'I get a quarter?'

'No, I'm just making up an example. Look …'

'A zample?'

'What I mean is instead of two thousand little bitty prizes, you get a couple of *big* prizes.'

'What kind?' Eddie asked now.

'I was thinking along the lines of a bicycle,' Walt said, glancing at Ivy, who didn't respond. She was still in a funk. 'How would you like that?'

'What did he say?' Nora asked Eddie in a loud whisper.

'He said we could have bikes.'

'And maybe a swing set for the backyard …' Immediately Walt thought of Argyle and his fund-raiser expenditures. 'Or maybe something else nice,' he said.

Nora began to hop up and down in the seat now, spring-headed, counting happily again. The preschool appeared, and over the tops of the cars parked in the lot Walt could see the head of the tyrannosaur, steadfastly guarding the sandbox. Somehow it looked like an old friend this morning. 'So much depends on a sad dinosaur,' he said, pulling into a space, 'glazed with rainwater beside the spring chickens.'

He laughed out loud. 'That's a poem,' he said to Nora.

'Don't … be … silly,' she said, rolling her eyes and opening the door. Eddie slid across the seat in order to get out on her side.

Walt climbed out into the rain and glanced at the front of the school, where someone was just then coming out the door. For a moment he didn't recognize the man, who was hunched over as if to keep the rain off his face. The man looked up, stopped, and then came on again, angling toward them now, his face full of anger and determination. It was Jack.

60

'Back into the car,' Walt said.

Ivy turned around in her seat and grasped Nora's arm, hauling her inside again as Walt reached for the ignition key, looking back to see that the kids were safely in. Eddie slid back into his spot and slumped down in the seat, not looking at Jack, but staring at the upholstery like he'd been drugged.

Walt was suddenly full of rage. This had gone on too damned long! He wrenched on the door handle, starting to get back out of the car.

'Don't,' Ivy said, grabbing his arm. 'Not here. Not now.'

He hesitated. The look on her face convinced him. 'Right,' he said, and slammed his door, shifting into reverse and backing out in a rush just as Jack started to run toward them. He changed direction then, heading toward the street, leaping over the parkway junipers in order to cut the car off when Walt pulled out of the lot. 'Bad move, asshole,' Walt muttered, swerving around straight at him, getting him in his sights. He punched the accelerator and Jack threw his arms up and jumped backward, stepping up onto the curb again and stumbling through the shrubs.

'Take it easy!' Ivy warned him.

'I'll knock him into the schoolyard,' Walt said, but the preschool was a half a block back now, and he eased up on the accelerator, watching for Jack's T-bird to pull out onto the road, chasing them. When it didn't happen, he relaxed.

Then he saw that Ivy was giving him a look, and it came to him out of nowhere that the kids were in the car, that he'd probably scared the hell out of them …

In his anger he hadn't given Nora and Eddie a second thought, but had lost his mind instead, involving them in his own war against Jack, as if they weren't deeply enough involved in the man's creepy behavior already. Whose side are you on? he asked himself.

'Sorry,' he said to Ivy. He glanced in the mirror and saw that Eddie was crying. Nora sat silently, her thumb in her mouth.

He scrambled in his mind for something to say, something to make it all right. Nothing came to him, except that there was something terrible and hard about taking care of children, and that no matter how good you might be with them one moment, you were sure to screw it up another. He slapped the wheel with the back of his fingers, making it hurt.

'Let's hit the All-Niter for doughnuts,' he said, shamelessly deciding to buy them off. 'Then we'll go down to Toy City and pick out a couple of bicycles.' He and Ivy could Christmas shop some other time.

Nora didn't take her thumb out of her mouth, but she nodded.

Eddie sniffed, and then in a shaky voice he said, 'I can't ride a bike.'

'Before the sun goes down this evening,' Walt said, 'you'll know how to ride one, or by golly your Aunt Ivy will stay up all night teaching you. She once taught an ape to ride a bicycle, and it was a two-wheeler, too.'

'An a-a-ape,' Nora said, smiling again. 'Nuh-uh.'

'Yeah-huh,' Walt said, turning into the lot in front of the All-Niter. 'After that she taught the ape to sing.' There were already several cars in the tiny lot, so he drove to the far end, shutting off the engine.

'Look there,' Ivy said, pointing. It was Peetenpaul's truck, parked at the rear of the shop and sheltered from the rain by a big pine tree. The man himself stood beside the open passenger door. They watched as he pulled off his black suit coat and tossed it inside. Underneath he was wearing a garish Hawaiian shirt – big red hibiscus blossoms on a blue background. He reached into the truck and pulled out a white linen jacket, folding it over his arm, then reached in again and drew out a leather suitcase. Then he took his keys out of his pocket, tossed them into the air, caught them, and threw them onto the floorboard of the pickup, slamming the door after them. He turned and hurried across the lot toward a waiting vehicle, yanking open the trunk and dropping the suitcase in on top of several others.

'I'll be damned,' Walt whispered. It was the Biggs-mobile, the old Buick! Maggie Biggs herself sat in the passenger seat. Peetenpaul climbed in the driver's side, backed out and swung around, straightening out and moving slowly past them, heading for Chapman Avenue.

Mrs Biggs wore a yellow muumuu and there was a flower in her wig the size of a plate, as if she were on her way to God's own luau. She spotted Walt as the Buick rolled past, and tipped him a big wink, evidently mighty happy to see him. She picked up something off the dash – what appeared to be airplane tickets – which she waved in his direction. Peetenpaul waved too, waggling his thick fingers and hunching over to have a look at Walt through the partly open window.

'Thanks, sweetie!' Mrs Biggs shouted, and then the Buick was gone, bumping out onto the avenue and tearing away east toward the freeway.

'What on *earth* was that all about?' Ivy asked.

'That was my old friend Maggie Biggs,' Walt said, astonished at this turn of events. 'I think her ship just came in.'

'She's a friend of Mr Peetenpaul?'

'I believe she is,' Walt said, 'although I just now found that out myself.' So Peetenpaul was the legendary Mr Peet, the man who had taken the stove apart after Walt had screwed it up! Postal inspector, real estate entrepreneur, plumber, eater of doughnuts … Walt shook his head, putting it all together at last. Somehow he was unaccountably happy at this turn of affairs. 'You know what I think?' he said to Ivy. 'I think that sometimes what we don't see would fill a tub.'

'Amen to that,' Ivy said, getting out of the car. 'For heaven's sake, let's eat.'

Nora and Eddie and Walt got out too, and the three of them jogged through the rain toward the All-Niter, where Lyle Boyd was just then sliding a fresh tray of glazed doughnuts onto the rack.

61

Bentley walked up onto Argyle's porch, this time in broad daylight, and knocked hard on the door. He carried his Bible, and he had a half dozen appropriate verses tagged with slips of paper. That was dangerous – most people would sooner let a door-to-door salesman into the house than a man with a Bible – but it was time to come clean, all the way clean, no punches pulled.

The door opened finally, and Argyle stood there looking disheveled, as if he had woken up from an afternoon nap. He squinted, perhaps half recognizing Bentley but not quite placing him. Then he smiled. His eyes narrowed when he saw the Bible. 'What can I do for you?' he asked.

'What can you do for yourself?' Bentley said, and it was instantly clear from Argyle's face that he knew him entirely now, that he recognized Bentley's voice.

'I'll be damned,' he said. 'It's Father Flanagan, after all these years. So you turn out to be the neighborhood bellringer, too, eh? The thorn in my side, and the man who just took a pile of my money. We meet at last. Pardon me if I don't shake hands until I know why you're here.'

' "What the wicked dreads will come upon him, but the desire of the righteous will be granted," ' Bentley quoted. There was no use opening the Bible. He knew that one by heart.

'So what?' Argyle asked.

'Well, for openers, my name's not Flanagan. That's so what. My name is Lorimer Bentley. What I pretended to be in the past isn't of interest to us any more. I've repented of that, and I suggest you do the same. That's why I've come here.'

'Repented? Was this before or after you cashed the check I gave Obermeyer?'

There was a clattering noise behind him in the house, and then the sound of a heavy object knocking against the wall. Argyle turned around and looked, and Bentley caught a glimpse of something – someone – moving across the room.

He stared meaningfully at Argyle and shook his head tiredly. 'As for your money,' he said, 'what you gave me in the past was well spent. If I had it, I'd give it back to you, but I'm afraid it's blood out of a turnip now. And I'm ashamed to admit it, too. I'm ashamed of the whole thing. I thought I was running a con for the Lord. It was pure sinful foolishness and stupidity.' Bentley took Argyle's hundred-thousand-dollar check out of his coat pocket and held it up between his thumb and forefinger. 'As for this ...'

Argyle snatched it out of his hand and tucked it away in his own pocket. 'Thank you,' he said. 'In fact, I no longer need your services. The situation has changed dramatically since I last spoke to you.'

'That's true,' Bentley said. 'It's gotten a hell of a lot worse, hasn't it?'

'For you, maybe. You should have been quicker on the draw with that check.'

'Take a look at this, if you can stand it.' Bentley removed a photograph from his coat now – Father Mahoney's Polaroid photo – and showed it to Argyle, who immediately shuddered at the sight of his own idiot face.

'So what is this?' he croaked. 'Some sort of extortion? The whole world's playing that game, eh? Even the Church wants in. Repentance you call it!' He took the check back out of his pocket and handed it to Bentley, who looked at it for a moment in astonishment, and then tore it to fragments, dropping them on the porch.

'You're a hard man to satisfy,' Argyle said.

'Not really,' Bentley said. 'I want your soul.'

'It's not for sale.'

'It was once.'

'You've got delusions of grandeur, haven't you?'

'I don't have any delusions anymore. And you didn't either when you called me the other day. You're in trouble. Take a hard look at this snapshot. That's the face of a man with one foot in Hell.' He held the photo up again, then abruptly tore it to shreds, too, and threw the pieces onto the porch with the torn-up check. '*There's* your extortion for you,' he shouted, losing his temper now. 'Keep your money. I'm here to right a wrong. It's not too late for either one of us.'

'You're right about that. It's a brand-new day for me.' Argyle smiled at him now. 'Anything else up your sleeve?'

'A new day! How? Because of that damned ... *thing* you've got in the coffin in the back room? If *that's* your plan – trying to fool the Devil with a golem – then you're a sorry damned fool. And I mean damned, too.'

'*What* a perceptive man you are,' Argyle said, a look of mock astonishment on his face now. 'So you're the one who's been peering through my windows! Well, you certainly are tenacious. I *like* that in a man.'

There was an immense crash now, like a drawer full of silverware hitting a linoleum floor. This was followed by the grunting of a human, or nearly human, voice.

'Destroy it,' Bentley said.

'Would you like to meet him?' Argyle's voice was full of enthusiasm. 'He's rather crude by some standards, but with a little help he'll do the trick. And I suppose it's true that if it weren't for you he wouldn't have any … life at all. I guess you'd call it life.'

'*I* wouldn't call it that, and I utterly deny having *any*thing to …'

'Well, come on in then and say hello.' Argyle opened the door, stepped back, and gestured Bentley into the house.

Even though he was prepared, Bentley was struck dumb by what he saw. The thing that sat in an overstuffed chair next to the fireplace was very nearly Argyle's twin, dressed again in identical clothing. But there was something coarse about it, something blocky and unfinished. It had a vague, lobotomized look on its face, and its flesh, if it *was* flesh, was waxy and discolored. The fact that its eyes moved and its mouth twitched made it all the more horrible.

'What do you think?' Argyle asked. He looked as if he relished the sight of Bentley's face.

'Destroy it now,' Bentley said. 'I'll help you do it. Lord knows how, but we'll do it. Destroy it or go to Hell.'

'Don't pass Go, eh? Don't collect two hundred dollars. Don't you think it's an astonishing likeness?'

Bentley breathed slowly and steadily, trying to compose himself. 'It looks like I imagine you'd look after lying dead in a ditch. Can I ask where you got it?' He glanced around the room, looking for something heavy. What would it take to kill a creature that wasn't alive?

'China. The Chinese are masters of replication. Do you know that they have carpet factories that will replicate any kind of picture onto a wool carpet? – your mother, a Picasso painting, a jet airplane, anything you want. This is the same sort of thing, after a fashion. A little more mysticism, perhaps. There's a grand, Kabbalistic tradition to it – several thousand years of mystical mumbo jumbo …'

'Spare me the details. I'm not an idiot.'

'All right. Let's just say that this is another case of the Chinese doing it more cheaply, that's all. Moderately cheap, anyway – at least the production end of things. Attendant expenses can creep up on you. All they need is a photo, some odds and ends of memorabilia. In my case, a ring, baby shoes, a couple of articles of clothing. It comes to you fully clothed, by the way. When it arrives it's not so … finely wrought, I guess you'd say, as our friend is now, but its general appearance improves as long as it's in close association with its master, shares its master's habits. It even brushes its own teeth.'

'It's a filthy abomination,' Bentley said, suddenly wanting to shut him up.

'Probably it is. I'll be glad to get it out of here, actually.' The golem shifted in its chair, the expression on its face undergoing sudden changes as if to mimic Argyle's own phony high spirits. 'Of course it's deficient intellectually,' Argyle said. 'I tried to teach it to play Scrabble, but it was no use. I wish I could say it cheated, but it was simply stupid. All in all it's been a tiresome houseguest: drops food out of its mouth, pisses on the toilet seat – thank heavens it doesn't smoke, eh?' He chuckled and shook his head almost fondly. 'Ah well, I suppose there's no use complaining, since it's just about to leave us. It's bound for a warmer climate, and I suppose it'll serve in Hell as well as the next man.'

'*Serve?*' Argyle spat the word out. 'This soulless thing? The Devil wouldn't want it.'

'Now, don't insult my houseguest!' Argyle said. He waggled a finger at Bentley. 'And you know absolutely *nothing* about its soul, such as it is. It has one, actually. It's lying around here somewhere, locked in a jar.'

'If you're talking about Walt Stebbins's demon,' Bentley told him, 'then I think I can assure you that you'll never get hold of it. It's beyond your grasp now.'

'*What* a dirty shame,' Argyle said, putting his hand to his mouth and widening his eyes. 'So you've come all the way over here, full of passion, to tell me that I've failed?'

'Worse than failed,' Bentley said.

'And what would you have me do? Follow George Nelson and Murray LeRoy into that damned alley myself?'

'Repent!' Bentley shouted at him, suddenly losing his temper.

The golem abruptly stood up and took a couple of halting steps forward, and Argyle reached over and pushed it solidly on the chest, propelling it backward into its chair again. 'You crawling little hypocrite!' he said to Bentley. 'You Johnny-come-lately. Your kind is all the same, pointing the self-righteous finger at everyone else while you go around doing what you damned well choose. By God, *listen* for once! I don't *need* your help. *I* am all the help I need!' He jabbed himself in the chest now. '*You* can damned well go to Hell, because I've got better things to do. Now get out of here.' He pointed toward the door.

'All right,' Bentley said evenly. 'Self-righteous, is it? What about poor Simms? Was he self-righteous too? Is that why you murdered him?'

'Get out,' Argyle said evenly. 'You understand *nothing*. Simms was an accident. I compensated his widow. If she needs something more ...'

'*Compensated!*' Bentley shouted. 'I'll show you compensation!' He dropped his Bible onto a tabletop, then bent over and picked up the fireplace poker, slapping it once against his palm. He took a step forward, threw his arm back, and swung the poker hard at Argyle's head.

62

Henry looked into the motor home, through the closed screen door. Jinx worked at the little counter inside, putting together a couple of sandwiches. There was a jar of mayonnaise out, lettuce, sliced ham … She caught sight of him, stared for a moment, then leaned toward the door and said, 'Don't stand out in the drizzle, for heaven's sake. Come on in. I'm making lunch.'

Henry nodded, pulling open the screen and climbing the steps. Jinx had a space heater going inside, and so keeping the door open was a waste of energy, except that both of them liked the rain, especially the sound and the smell of it. A long time ago they had come to the mutual decision to waste the damned energy when they felt like it. How many rainy days did they have left, after all?

He sat down at the table and watched the street. He was speechless, think-ing about this, about how he and Jinx had come to share this attitude about the rain. They'd driven just about every highway in the western United States in their day – slept in parking lots, eaten in diners; Jinx had a thimble collec-tion from everywhere, hundreds of thimbles, porcelain and copper and pewter. Every one of them contained a memory, too, like a little cup – that's what Jinx said; those were her own words. And now she'd been to see Goldfarb.

'You're quiet this afternoon,' she said. She wasn't giving anything away. He couldn't read her face.

'Yes,' he said, 'I guess I am.'

'What's wrong? Are you eating that bran cereal that I bought?'

'Oh, yes,' he said, waving away any thought to the contrary.

'Well, here's a sandwich. Did you want sprouts on it, or lettuce?'

'I don't guess I want any sprouts.'

She put the sandwich on a plate along with a couple of lettuce leaves and slid it in front of him, then sat down opposite him with her own sandwich. He took a bite and chewed on it without any interest, and then shoved the plate away.

'All right,' she said, 'what's eating you? You look like a lost soul.'

'I saw the mail,' he said. 'You've been to see Goldfarb.'

'Yes, I certainly have.' She looked at him curiously.

He shook his head at her, trying to find the right words. 'Whatever she … whatever they told you, it was a lie.'

'Was it?' she asked, putting her own sandwich down. 'How much of it was a lie?'

'All of it. I didn't *touch* that woman. You can ask Walt or Bentley; either one of them will tell you. She's a damned extortionist. She'll say anything at all, anything. I wish to God I'd never ...'

'Who *is* she, exactly? Not one of the lunchwagon women again?'

'No, she's not one of the lunchwagon women. You know her, actually. Maggie Biggs. She used to run the Eastern Paradise restaurant out on King Street in Honolulu back when we were in the Kahala bungalow.'

Jinx squinted at him. 'Who?'

'Short woman? Hair ...' Henry gestured with his hands to illustrate Maggie Biggs's hair.

'Hair?' Jinx said, nodding her head and pursing her lips. 'That too ...' Then suddenly she broke into a smile. 'What *are* you talking about?' she asked.

'Don't *mock* me,' Henry said, shaking his head at her. 'For God's sake, don't play dumb. You've seen Goldfarb. We both know that. I'm trying to clear the air. What I'm telling you is that there was no reason for you to talk to Goldfarb. Not *any* reason. I ... I love you like ... like ...' He realized that she was gaping at him. 'Like I don't know,' he said. 'I guess I'm a damned fool.' He got up and turned toward the door, taking his hat off the peg and reaching for his coat.

'Now where are you going?' she asked. Her voice didn't have any amusement in it any more.

'Walk,' he said.

'Now? In the rain?'

He shrugged. 'I guess I just don't know.'

'Henry, I called Mr Goldfarb about the children.'

'Which children?' he asked, not grasping this.

'Why, Nora and Eddie. What other children are there?'

'You called Goldfarb about Nora and Eddie? Why? What did they do?'

'They didn't *do* anything. Sit back down, for goodness sake, and I'll tell you about it. Walt and Ivy are in a dead panic about that damned Jack, and so I took it upon myself to find out what's what. That's why I called Mr Goldfarb. So I don't know anything about any woman with hair like you've described. You've quit seeing her, then?'

'I never *was* seeing her. That's what I've been telling you.'

'Good. I never much liked her anyway. She was too brash. I remember she used to sit on a stool at the end of the counter and order the little Filipino waitresses around. So I'm glad you haven't been seeing her. Who else haven't you been seeing?' She narrowed her eyes.

'Why, I haven't been seeing anybody else,' he said, puzzled.

'That's good,' she said. 'Neither have I. I don't want to; do you know why?'

He looked at her for a moment, trying to puzzle her out. She was apparently serious.

'Because I love you too,' she said. 'Just like you love me.'

He nodded at her. 'Good,' he said. 'That's good. And I do love you, too.'

'I know you do,' she said. 'Now sit down and eat your sandwich.'

63

Argyle threw his hands up and stumbled backward, grunting as the poker whistled past his face. Bentley whirled around and lunged at the golem, slashing at the thing's neck. The heavy iron head of the poker sank into its flesh as if into wet clay. Bentley wrenched it free and threw the weapon back for another blow, but just then Argyle slammed into his back, wrapping his arms around Bentley's shoulders and grabbing the shaft of the poker, wrenching it hard.

Bentley stumbled forward, clamping his free hand onto the heavy end of the poker, cranking it around like he was steering a bus and pulling Argyle off-balance. 'No!' he shouted, but Argyle held on, falling to one knee. Bentley stomped hard on his ankle and twisted the poker again, yanking it free, then stepped back and kicked Argyle in the small of the back. 'That's for Simms!' he shouted, whipping the poker behind his back with both hands now, as if he'd take Argyle's head off with it. He skipped forward and swung it hard, pulling it short again, scaring the bastard away. Argyle yelped, going over backward and knocking over a small table, scuttling away on his hands and knees, heading around behind a stuffed chair, where he stood up, waving both hands to ward off Bentley.

'Put it down!' Argyle shouted. 'For God's sake …!'

'Burn the church down, eh?' Bentley yelled, full of a wild rage, and he smashed a potted palm, hacking it to smithereens with the poker. Dirt and leaves flew in the air, raining down on the golem, and Bentley skipped across and hammered a vase on the fireplace mantel, then pounded the hell out of a table lamp, flattening the lampshade and smashing its porcelain base. He took aim at a piece of bird statuary, knocked a flamingo's porcelain head flying, and then lunged without warning toward Argyle again, stabbing the end of the poker into the chair that stood between them, tearing a long gash in the material and yanking out a big wad of stuffing.

Argyle made a sideways move, as if to run, and Bentley drove the poker downward like a saber and lunged in at him again, swinging his weapon in a wild tumult of blows as if he were knocking down an army. Argyle retreated into a far corner, his arms in front of his face, and without an instant's hesitation Bentley spun around and rushed the golem again, intending this time to finish it off. He swung the poker savagely, catching the monster full in the face as it attempted now to stand up out of its chair, its expression an eerie mixture of idiot confusion and of Argyle's own fear and hatred.

Bentley saw the poker drive into the thing's mouth and nose, saw a piece of its waxy flesh tear loose, heard the noise that came out of the thing's throat. It jerked backward, perhaps from the force of the blow, perhaps to escape, and sat down hard on the arm of the chair, then slumped onto the seat, resting its disfigured head against the cushion. There was no expression in its face now, only vacancy, but somehow that made things even worse, and Bentley was suddenly full of horror at what he'd done.

He stood there panting, drained of energy, holding the poker loosely in his hand. It was over. He felt degraded, monstrous, and for a moment he was nearly sick. He hadn't killed it. Probably he couldn't kill it. Its eyes wandered around the room as if it didn't quite know where it was, and it made a noise, a breathy, rapid whimper. Bentley had simply worked out his anger on it. In his mind it had been Argyle himself that had taken the beating. He wondered abruptly if the golem could feel pain. Surely not.

'Get out,' Argyle said to him, his voice croaking out of him like the voice of a strangled man. Bentley turned around, dropping the poker in surprise at what he saw. Blood ran out of Argyle's nose and from a cut on his lip, and there was a heavy red welt across his neck. Stigmata, Bentley realized. Mirror images of the golem's own wounds.

Full of self-loathing, Bentley groped for something to say, something to justify himself. Before whom? Argyle? God? He gestured at the golem, which lay in the chair like a dead man, its throat caved in, its face mutilated. 'I didn't mean ...'

'I don't care what you meant,' Argyle told him, smearing his bloody face with his hand. He looked at the stain on his palm. His hand trembled violently. His voice was wheezy and labored, and he coughed and tilted his head back as if to open his throat. 'Understand me when I say that I'm indifferent to you. Just go now. Go on. Get out. Get out. Get out.' He waved both his hands, wrists turned downward, as if to sweep Bentley out of the room, out of his life. Something had come into his eyes, almost a glow, as if in the taste of his own blood he savored his victory, his imminent success.

Bentley stepped across to the door. He was deflated, utterly fatigued. Argyle hadn't defeated him – he saw that clearly – he had defeated himself. He felt sickened and ashamed. The act of hurting the golem had humanized it in some odd, backhanded way. He felt as if he'd beaten a dumb beast, a cow or a sheep.

Pushing the door open, he stepped out onto the porch. Without looking back he descended the steps, out from under the porch roof and into a heavy drizzle. Right then something struck him hard in the small of the back, and he grunted and stumbled forward. It was his Bible. Argyle had thrown it at him.

Slowly he bent over to pick it up off the wet concrete. He steeled himself and turned around, reminding himself that the book was none the worse for wear, that Argyle couldn't hurt it. He opened his mouth to speak, to redeem …

But the door slammed shut, hard enough so that the entire front of the house shook on its foundation. Bentley stood looking at it for a moment, then turned around and walked toward the street, standing by his car for a minute before getting in, looking up at the rainy evening sky.

Mahoney wanted Bentley to go shelling with him tomorrow morning at dawn, rain or shine, and Bentley had told him that he didn't have time for it – too many duties, too much work. Well, suddenly he was ready for it. He couldn't remember how long it had been since he had gone anywhere merely for pleasure. What he needed right now was air – ocean air, brisk enough to blow the moths out of his coat. And according to Mahoney, there was no telling what you'd find on the beach after a storm.

64

Ivy found Argyle at his desk in his business office. He wore a turtleneck sweater, and he sat and stared with his hands folded in front of him, apparently in a contemplative mood. She carried the manila envelope full of the Batavia property paperwork. 'You've hurt yourself,' she said, seeing that his lip and cheek had been cut open. The wound was held shut with three butterfly Band-Aids.

'Golfing accident.' He gestured at the office chair and beamed at her, as if suddenly full of zip. 'I can't tell you how happy I am that you've come to me today.'

She stopped herself from pointing out how idiotic this sounded, how full of vanity, and instead she sat down and waited for him to go on.

'Everything is absolutely sailing along with the properties. They're rushing the loan papers; escrow's already moving. We could close in no time. Mr Peetenpaul is *extremely* happy.'

'I dare say he is.'

'Now,' Argyle went on, winking at her, 'I've got a little surprise for you.'

'What's that?' She kept her voice even.

'I'd like to advance you half the commission right now, if you don't mind, just to start sewing things up. How's that with you? Do you mind half the money now? No added tax burden, is there, if you get it before the first of the year?'

'No,' she said, standing up and wandering over to the window. 'I don't think it'll have any effect on taxes at all.' She saw that Murray LeRoy's property was dug to pieces now, areas cordoned off with yellow plastic tape flipping and dancing in the wind. A generator chugged away under a plastic awning, pumping muddy rainwater out of a hole, but she couldn't see any workmen or watchmen around the premises, and there was no longer any sign of earth-moving equipment. By this time next year the place would be up in condominiums, which was a shame.

She glanced down into the rear parking lot of the office building. The black pickup truck sat in a stall. 'Where is Mr Peetenpaul?' she asked. 'He seems to have become unavailable.'

'Oh, he's around. I can assure you of that. He's a busy man, what with his plans. I think we can depend upon him for more business in the future.'

'Is he here now? In the building?'

'No,' Argyle said, his smile fixed on his face. 'Here? Why do you ask?'

'Well, that seems to be his truck down there in the lot, doesn't it?'

'*Is* it? Oh, of course it is. I'm having it … detailed for him. My man's coming around this afternoon if the weather stays clear. Mobile detailing unit.'

'That's big of you,' Ivy said, sitting down again. She saw that Argyle had his checkbook out. Apparently he was going to write out a great big check right then and there. She was reminded suddenly of Walt's tearing up Mrs Simms's check in the garage the other night, and she could easily envision herself doing the same thing here, throwing the pieces in Argyle's face. She realized that she was thinking of him as Argyle again. Robert had disappeared. 'I saw Mr Peetenpaul at the doughnut shop yesterday, at the All-Niter.'

He nodded, as if this fascinated him.

'He seemed to be on his way somewhere.'

'To eat a doughnut, probably.'

'Actually, he didn't buy any doughnuts. He apparently abandoned his truck in the parking lot and drove away with a local woman, a Mrs Biggs. It looked for all the world like they were carrying airline tickets.'

Argyle stared at her now, as if he didn't quite take this in. 'A Mrs Biggs,' he said flatly.

'That's what I was told. I wonder what exactly happened to his truck after that – the way he tossed his keys onto the floor and just walked away. I wonder, did he come back after it? Maybe I was wrong about the airline tickets?'

'Well, I don't quite know,' Argyle said. 'I've been a little busy myself. I see that I'm not up on the details of Mr Peetenpaul's life. Are you certain about this … this Mrs Biggs? About the name, I mean? You saw the two of them leave together?' All the humor, even the false humor, had gone out of his face.

'I'm afraid I did. They seemed to be an item, actually. It almost looked as if they were taking off on their honeymoon, off to Tahiti or somewhere.'

Argyle looked away, thinking hard about something, his checkbook apparently forgotten for the moment. 'I'll be damned,' he said finally, then abruptly barked out a laugh. 'Mr Peet! That old son of a gun …'

'Look,' Ivy said, leaning forward. 'Don't bother with the check, all right? Let's quit pretending. A little bit of honesty once in a while wouldn't hurt much. I had hoped that after all these years things would have changed with you, but apparently they haven't.'

'I'm afraid I don't …' He shook his head helplessly.

'Walt was right, wasn't he? He said that Mr Peetenpaul was an employee of yours, and that this entire property transaction was set up to deceive me. I wanted to think differently, but it's true, isn't it? You've had something up your sleeve all along. You've been playing some sort of game, saying one thing, doing another. This has all been a deception.'

He looked steadily at her for a moment, as if he were scrambling to find something to say in his own defense. 'We had a contract,' he said, just a little desperately, 'and I intend to honor it. Humor me, Ivy, for old times' sake. Give me another chance.' He picked up a pen and reached for the checkbook. '*This* is no deception, I assure you.'

'I'll tear it up, Robert. I mean it. I don't want your money. As for another chance, I don't quite know what you mean by that, and I don't think I want to.'

'This commission could *make* you, Ivy. It could open doors for you. I've got powerful friends, wealthy friends. They buy and sell property for sums of money that would astonish you. And certainly this commission, as small as it is, would very nearly save Walt, wouldn't it? You were telling me about his business. Hanging on through the first year is *crucial*. This money could make Walt's dreams come true – get him out of the garage and into a commercial building, who knows where he'd end up?'

'Nobody knows,' Ivy said. 'What I know is that you don't understand the first thing about Walt, and you never have. He wouldn't touch your money twenty years ago, and he won't touch it now. Neither would I. Don't make me say any more about it. Please. And don't pretend to have Walt's best interests in mind, because you don't, and you know it. This whole thing was a mistake. Let's end it here.'

He shrugged and slumped back into his seat. After a moment he closed the checkbook slowly, but left it on the desktop. 'I did it for you,' he said. 'What does it matter who bought the property?'

'What matters is that *nobody* bought the property. You were trying to buy *me*. That's closer to the truth, isn't it?'

'Don't say that. I wouldn't do that. I can't explain what I mean, exactly, but believe me when I tell you that I'm undergoing *changes* in my life. Profound changes. I don't know what you'd call them – spiritual changes, I guess. I've finally managed to square things away. There's a … a spiritual bankruptcy, I guess you could say, that a man can apply for when he's in the sort of debt I'm in. I mean to say that I've filed Chapter 13, Ivy. I'm getting out from under a great … a great debt, a great weight. I'll be free of it. By tomorrow I'll … I'll finally be able to feel *good* about myself.'

'I don't have any idea what you're talking about, Robert. And to tell you the truth, I don't think you do either. I think you're the most incredibly self-deceived human being I've ever known. I'd bet a shiny new dime that by tomorrow you won't have changed in any way at all, although you probably *will* feel good about yourself, heaven help you. So *please* don't mention your commission again, or whatever you want to call it. Save your breath.'

He gestured at her, holding up both hands, then slid them under the edge of the heavy checkbook and tilted it at her, letting her see his name embossed in gold on the leather cover. 'You've *got* to understand what this would mean …'

'I'm *really* tired of this,' she said, interrupting him again. She stood up and leaned on the desk, looking down on him now. 'I'm going to say one last thing, and while I say it I don't want you to speak. I know that something's gone on over the past few weeks between you and Walt. I don't know what it is. I thought it was him making it up, out of jealousy or something, but I don't think so any more. So listen to this: if you so much as touch that man, if you come near our house, if you do *anything* to damage him or his business or anything else, I swear to God I'll find a way to hurt you.'

She laid the manila envelope on the desktop, then walked out the door.

65

Walt fitted candle bulbs into the Dilworth catalogue golden lampstand, then carried it out to the tin shed and set it in among the pine trees. He stepped back to take a look at the thing, breathing the scent of the pine and listening to the rain on the roof. The lampstand reminded him suddenly of the lamp-post in Narnia; there was something magically incongruous about it, even if it was made out of pot metal and plaster of Paris.

It occurred to him that he was rationalizing having spent good money on what was evidently a piece of junk, and he turned around and went back out into the rain, heading for the garage.

That was tough about Ivy's losing Argyle's big commission. At first Walt had tried to talk her into taking it anyway, the whole sixty grand, just like she'd made him take the check for Mrs Simms. Why not? – cash the check and then tell Argyle to his face what kind of a stinking geek he really was. Take his money and insult him both, so as to double the satisfaction. Of course, that wasn't the sort of thing Ivy would do, and he was proud of her for that. The only trouble was that he had pretty much convinced himself that spending forty bucks on this crap from the catalogue was no big deal, since they were suddenly rolling in money anyway. Now it looked like a big deal again, because suddenly they weren't rolling in money at all; they weren't rolling in anything but visiting relatives. It was going to be a drier Christmas than he'd thought. And by spring, if things didn't pick up considerably, he was going to be reading the want ads in the morning instead of the comics.

In the garage he shifted boxes out of the way and uncovered an old chair that Ivy was making him store out there. She'd bought it at a garage sale – too good a deal to pass by – but then they hadn't had any room for it, so it had gone into storage. He pounded on the worn tapestry seat a couple of times to knock the dust out of it, then picked it up by its wooden arms and carried it around to the shed, setting it down inside the door so that the pine boughs nearly brushed against it. Now all he needed was some kind of little table to set a drink and a book on, and the shed would be about perfect.

He wondered idly how he could hide the lamp cord, which right now snaked across the floor, ruining the effect. Maybe straight up through the roof. Or maybe a hole in the indoor-outdoor carpeting and then through the floor itself, run it into the garage through plastic conduit instead of using an extension cord.

He glanced out through the open door, at the concrete stepping-stones in the lawn. There was a patch of blackened grass around the stone that hid the bluebird, and some kind of greenish-looking puffball toadstools coming up through it, as if the ground had been poisoned. He thought about the mutated salmon eggs in the tackle box and Bentley's talk about demons.

Probably it was time to get the jar out of there, he thought idly, off the property altogether. How easy would that be? Was he tough enough? It was easy to refuse the demon when you had other options, but when the ice was getting thin, and your dreams were one by one falling through …

It was true that he had made a hideous error when he set the bird on Sidney Vest. Lord knows there was plenty of evidence that the thing meant trouble. It had given him tomatoes but killed his herbs. It had delivered his newspaper early and then sabotaged his mail. It had given him sixty bucks in the Lotto and then smashed up his car. He had asked it to send Sidney Vest home to Raleigh, and by golly the bird had done it. Thank God he had gotten to it before it killed Maggie Biggs, too.

And what exactly *had* happened there? The bird had apparently come through in fine style, and the result of that whole deal was that Ivy's money went down the rat hole. There seemed to be some kind of awful *cost* that went along with making a wish on the bluebird – an equal and opposite reaction that was utterly unpredictable and vicious.

He sat down in the chair and stared into the trees. Of course, he had no way of knowing that any of this was true. The herb garden, the mail, the bent fender, even Vest's death – all of that might easily be coincidence, and not even unlikely coincidence, either. The Maggie Biggs wish had certainly been successful, unless of course it *had* cost them the sixty grand.

Maybe there was a way to *phrase* things, he thought. He had gone about the first wishes haphazardly, like an amateur. It wasn't until he'd saved Maggie Biggs that he'd considered *how* to talk to the bird. Perhaps it was simply necessary to phrase the request carefully …

Just then there was a loud metallic knocking, and he nearly leaped out of the chair at the sound of it. Robert Argyle stood in the doorway under a black umbrella, the rain dripping down around him. Walt blinked at him for a moment, as if Argyle were a hallucination. Someone had apparently given him a fat lip. Well, good for them, whoever it was.

'Top of the morning to you,' Walt said, recovering. 'What brings you out into the rain?'

'Can I step inside?'

Walt gestured, inviting him in, and Argyle closed up his umbrella and shook the rain off. 'I want you to know there are no hard feelings,' he said.

'About what, exactly?'

'Forgive me for saying so, but you seem to have taken all this too personally, Walt. You shouldn't let morons like Lorimer Bentley feed you full of ideas. You've always been your own man. Keep it up. The Bentleys of the world can't see past their noses, but men like us have vision.'

' "Men like us," ' Walt said flatly. 'Why am I troubled by that phrase?'

'There's no need to apologize,' Argyle told him.

'Apologize? That's a relief. You don't know how good that makes me feel.'

'I'm happy to hear that.'

'That's why you dropped by, to tell me I don't have to apologize? Or do you have something else in mind?'

'Well, in fact I do – two things. First I want you to know that the Robert Argyle you've known for the last twenty years will shortly cease to exist, in a manner of speaking.'

'Well, I'll be damned,' Walt said.

'I guess you could say that I'll be the phoenix that rises from the ashes. It's a long story, Walt. By now Bentley's told you most of it, so there's no need to pretend that you don't know what I'm talking about. I guess … I guess I want to make amends, you might say. I want you to know that I forgive you for coveting the bluebird, which you have to admit was rightfully mine. I'm sorry that I had to resort to … to the methods I had to resort to in order to retrieve it, but honestly, I gave you every opportunity.'

'Yes, you did. No hard feelings.'

'Good. One more thing. As you know, Ivy and I have had what you might call a special relationship, and …'

'Don't push your luck,' Walt said.

'Pardon me?'

'You haven't had any sort of relationship at all with Ivy except in your piti-ful imagination. If you say another word about her … Look, just do yourself a favor and shut the hell up.'

Argyle stared at him. 'I certainly didn't mean …'

'Then what did you mean? Say what you mean and get the hell out of here.'

'I owe her a considerable sum of money, which she refuses to take for rea-sons that I don't at all understand. I happen to be very interested in absolving myself of debt right now; I guess that's the best way to put it. And I came here hoping that you and I might come to an understanding between ourselves.'

'Let me get this straight. You figure that Ivy has too many scruples to take your dirty money, but that I don't have those scruples. You "understand" me, is that it? Is that how you'd put it?'

'I didn't say that. I just think that as a businessman *you* understand …'

'Do you have the check?'

Argyle nodded. 'In my pocket.'

'Then you're right, I'll take it,' Walt said.

Argyle took a check out of his coat pocket and handed it to Walt, who looked at the sum. It was written out for an even sixty thousand. Walt crum-pled it into a ball and threw them out into the rain. 'Now take a hike,' he said. 'I've got nothing else to say to you, except that you ought to do yourself a favor and open your damned eyes. You don't look like any kind of phoenix to me; you look like a man who's lost his mind. I seem to recall that you used to have one.'

He bent over and picked up the plug end of the lamp cord, connecting it to the extension cord running out of the garage. The candle bulbs in the golden lampstand flickered on, seeming to waver like candle flames. For one eerie moment the darkness in the shed actually deepened, as if night had fallen. The bulbs shone like fireflies and the black shadows of the trees stood out against the shed walls like etchings. Then the glow from the bulbs spread – not as if the bulbs were gaining in wattage, but as if the light emanating from them was actually moving very slowly, billowing into a cloud like the smoke rising out of a genie's lamp.

Walt glanced up at Argyle, who stood staring, his eyes wide. His face seemed fleshless in the light of the lamp-stand, a grinning skull. His teeth were brown, like old ivory, and he raised his hands slowly, turning them over and looking at his palms in apparent disbelief, as if he could see his bones through his flesh. A noise came out of his mouth, a groan like the creaking of a door, and he turned on his heel and staggered out onto the lawn, where he bent over and picked up the balled-up check, putting it into his pocket without looking at it. He stood staring up into the avocado tree, his hands crossed on his chest like a man laid out for burial.

'What's wrong?' Walt asked him, getting up out of his chair. It looked as if the bastard was having a heart attack. 'You all right?'

But Argyle waved him away and lurched off in the direction of the gate, past the family room window, where Nora and Eddie sat watching the television. Argyle looked in at the children, and Walt heard him utter another groan. Then he staggered forward again, almost falling, and Walt followed, swinging open the gate to let him out. Hunched over, Argyle went away down the driveway, hurrying now, as if he were pursued by something. His car was parked at the curb. Walt watched him climb into it and drive away. Strangely, there was a passenger in the car. Someone had been waiting for him.

66

'Was that Mr R-guy?'

'Yeah,' Walt said, turning around. Nora had come outside. Eddie stood in the doorway.

'He was all bent,' Nora said.

'Yes, he was,' Walt told her. 'That's just what he was. He's one of the bent people. Come on over here, out of the rain.'

'Eddie drew Mr Binion,' Nora said.

'What?' Walt looked at her, baffled. 'Mr Binion?' Eddie stepped down onto the walk and hurried across to the carport to join them, holding out a piece of paper with a crayon drawing of a snail on it. The snail was apparently wearing a hat.

'Mr Binion,' Nora said. 'The snail.' She waved at the lawn. 'You know. Don't be funny.'

'Oh, that Mr Binion. Of course.' He looked at the picture. 'Yes, indeed,' he said. 'That's a good likeness.' Eddie was very nearly smiling. 'I'd like to have this,' Walt said. Eddie nodded.

'Can we play in the trees?' Nora asked.

'Sure,' Walt said. 'Of course. I just put up a light in there.' This staggered him. Mr Binion, the trees … It had worked. His nonsensical plans to entertain the children had worked.

He and Eddie followed Nora over to the shed door and looked in. The shed was filled now with the glow from the lampstand. The light hung in the air like a mist, like translucent gold. The shadows beneath the trees were as deep as caves, and the green floor stretched away like a meadow. It was almost impossible to say just where the shed walls were, as if the light created the illusion of vast depth and width. The interior of the shed might have held an entire forest, and heaven knew what beyond that – a place with running streams, grass, deep skies, and moving clouds …

He realized that Nora was holding onto his leg, still staring with wide wonder into the light. He put his arm around Eddie's shoulders and gave him a squeeze, and Eddie didn't draw away as he usually did, but stood still, holding the picture of Mr Binion.

How long they had stood there Walt couldn't say, but after a while he heard the gate scrape open, and there came into his mind the idea that Argyle had returned for some desperate reason. And then abruptly he was aware of the smell of something burning – an electrical smell, like a hot wire. He shook his head to clear it. There was a low, electronic buzz, then a snap and spark from the lampstand plug. The light in the shed wavered and dimmed, and the magic evaporated on the instant.

Walt pushed Nora and Eddie out the door, away from the pine trees, which would go up like Hell if they caught fire. He stepped forward, grabbing the lampstand cord. It was hot and soft in his hand. He stepped down hard on the extension cord and jerked, yanking the two plugs apart in a shower of sparks like a waterfall.

'Whoa!' Eddie shouted, looking in through the door from the middle of the lawn.

Walt dropped the hot cord and closed his fist over the burn on his palm, touching the metal lampstand pole with his other hand. It was hot too. The bulbs were melted in their sockets, and the molten glass had run down the sides of the sockets like a sugar glaze.

'What happened?' a voice asked behind him.

'Nothing,' he said instinctively, and turned around. Ivy stood between Nora and Eddie, sheltering the three of them under her umbrella and looking into the shed skeptically.

'It's these doggone cheap extension cords,' Walt said, smiling big at her. 'No harm done.'

'Not yet anyway.' Then to the kids she said, 'Go on into the house and find Aunt Jinx. I want to talk to Uncle Walt alone.' She didn't look happy, but it wasn't the lamp; it was something else.

The kids ran off, and when they were out of earshot Walt asked, 'What gives?'

'Jack. He's on his way over. He's apparently got a lawyer. And he's sober, too.'

'A lawyer?'

'Some crook, probably, but he means business.'

'That's good. I'll give him business.'

'Don't start it up,' she said. 'Stay cool this time, will you? Jinx's lawyer friend is on the way – Mr Goldfarb.'

'Good for him,' Walt said. 'I'll need a lawyer when I'm done with Jack. We might as well put him on retainer as soon as he pulls in. Call in a plastic surgeon, too, and alert the trauma center down at St Joseph's.'

'Cut it out, okay? Just stop. Can you watch the kids? Get them out here with you, maybe? Keep them tied up?'

He looked at her, considering this. Moments passed. 'Sure,' he said finally. He was big enough to give it a try, to hold onto his temper. 'Have them bring out some paper and crayons or something. I'll be the last line of defense. If I turn out to be unnecessary, then you can tell me I told you so. But look, Jack can't come into the backyard. If he does, I'll make him sorry for it. It'll be a bad thing, but I'm through talking with the man. He's poison, like a snake, and if he comes back here or into the house, if he gets pushy in any way, says or does anything out of line, then I'll feed him his head. So have Mr Goldfarb do his job, whatever that is.'

'He'll do it. Jack's history.' She kissed him, turned around, and hurried away.

He stood there for a moment controlling himself, realizing that what he wanted to do was hit something hard, break something, smash something. Jack could drink himself crazy every night; who cared about that? With any luck he would drink himself to death. But his hurting Eddie, that made him an end-to-end creep, a stain on the human landscape, a blotch, a poison. A little bit of remorse would have lightened him up – any little effort to do the right thing. But there wasn't any effort. His conscience had flatlined. How he had gotten that way just didn't matter any more.

Walt caught sight just then of the stepping-stone, the blackened grass, the toadstools. The bluebird sat buried beneath the ground like an accusation, like a cancer, like the evil filth that it was. It occurred to him right then that it was astonishingly easy to condemn another man's temptations – liquor, greed, lust, whatever they were – *because they weren't your own temptations.* And when you yourself fell, you'd find that it was your own temptations that had nailed you, and never mind anyone else's.

Suddenly seeing what he had to do, he shoved his hand under the edge of the stepping-stone and flipped it on end, then picked up the concrete slab with both hands and smashed the toadstools to mush, using the corner of the stone to reduce even the smallest of them to a pale green slime, which he beat deep into the earth. Then he threw the stone down and picked up the jar with the bird in it. Without looking at it, without listening to it, he drew his hand back and pitched it sidearm into the redwood fence, a fastball, dead center against a post. The glass shattered, spraying gin and shards in a wide arc. The bird fell straight down into the dirt of the flowerbed. He jogged into the garden shed and grabbed the shovel, then went back out and dug a hole in the wet dirt. He prodded the corpse of the bird into the hole with the tip of the shovel and buried it, packing the dirt back on top. Feeling considerably better, he threw down the shovel and went to meet Nora, who was just then coming out the door, carrying a book – the fairy-table book he'd read from the other night.

'Read us that one story,' she said. Eddie followed her, carrying the crayon box and paper.

'What story?' Walt asked, bending over to set the stone back into the hole. He stood up again, dusting his hands. 'What was it about? You don't really remember, do you?'

'Yes-huh,' she said. 'It was that dummy, who they made him eat rocks, and it made him smart.'

'I guess you *do* remember,' Walt said, putting an arm around each of the kids. 'I guess it's me who keeps forgetting.'

67

Jack and his lawyer arrived before Goldfarb, pulling in at the curb in a new BMW, clearly the lawyer's car. Jack wore a tie, and from what Ivy could see of him, he was clean and sober, just as he'd threatened. The front door opened behind her, and Henry stepped out onto the porch.

'I think I can handle this,' Ivy said to him. There was no use in Henry's getting involved at all. Jinx had agreed to stay inside the house, listening through the window. She could run information out to Walt if she had to, although Ivy wondered if it wouldn't be better to avoid that kind of thing. There was no use working Walt up if it wasn't necessary. And she was determined that it wouldn't be necessary.

'I'd just as soon stay,' Henry said quietly. 'For moral support. Walter thinks this man is a skunk, and I trust Walter's judgment in these matters.'

'So do I,' Ivy said. 'Thanks.'

Jack and the lawyer sat talking for a moment, then opened the door and got out, hunching through the rain toward the house, and then up onto the porch. The sun was going down, and Ivy opened the door back up, reached in, and flipped on the porch light and the Christmas lights.

'All right,' Jack said straight off. 'I suppose you've got them ready to go this time?' There was no smiling this time, no joking around.

'Who?' Ivy asked.

'You know who, Ivy. Legally you don't have a leg to stand on. Thank me for not charging you and Walt with kidnapping. And after that stunt in the street outside the school yesterday morning, with attempted murder, too.'

'I don't have any idea what you're talking about,' Ivy said. 'Who tried to murder you?'

'Get off it.'

'Were there witnesses?' She looked up toward the corner. Goldfarb was only driving out from Santa Ana; surely he ought to be here by now.

'You know damned well there weren't any ...'

'Watch your language, young man,' Henry said, interrupting him. 'We don't allow profanity on the premises. And I certainly won't let you swear at my niece. If I'd have known what kind of creature you were, I wouldn't have let you marry Darla, either, if I could have stopped it.'

'That's rather more to the point, isn't it?' the lawyer said, leaning in and waving the several sheets of paper in his hand. 'Since my client is in fact married to Darla Douglas, my client, Mr Douglas, is the legal guardian to' – he looked at the papers – 'Nora and Eddie Douglas. *Are* the children on the premises? I believe I called to alert you to our coming. You haven't in fact hidden them somewhere?'

'They're not hidden anywhere,' Ivy said.

'Then if you'll produce them, we'll be on our way. I assure you that neither I nor my client wishes to file any sort of charges against you. This is a court order,' he said, showing Ivy the papers.

'What kind of charges don't you and your client want to file against us?' She didn't bother to look at the papers. For all she knew, Jack *had* gotten a court order, in which case the kids were gone, and there was going to be trouble with Walt, who wasn't in a mood for court orders.

'Numerous possible charges,' the lawyer said. 'Take my word for it.'

'Let me ask you one thing, Jack,' Ivy said.

'Shoot. Make it quick, though. I've got places to go.'

'Why *did* you abuse Eddie? Darla tells me you like to beat kids up. Is that only when you're drunk, or do you like to do that when you're sober, too?' As soon as she said it she wished she hadn't. It was the kind of thing Walt would say.

Jack's eyes seemed to glaze over, and his face turned red. He stood there silently, maybe counting to ten. The lawyer put a hand on his arm, and Jack shook it off.

'I'll warn you against making false accusations against my client,' the lawyer said. 'Please don't attempt to provoke him. For the record, are you suggesting that Mr Douglas intends to harm these children?'

'Intends? I guess I'm not suggesting that. I certainly hope he doesn't.'

'Have you filed a notice of Manifest Bad Intent in regard to my client with Child Protective Services?'

She shook her head.

'Because this is a serious charge. I suggest you go through proper channels and eschew public accusations.'

'Let's not get involved in that kind of horsecrap,' Jack said. 'We're here to pick up Nora and Eddie. That's it. Case closed. And let me tell you something,' he said to Ivy, 'anyone charges me with anything, there's going to be more trouble than anyone wants.'

'Don't threaten us, young man,' Henry said.

'Please,' the lawyer said. 'Let's avoid escalation here. The fact remains that Mr Douglas is the children's legal guardian by virtue of his marriage to Darla Douglas. If you refuse to give up the children, this will become a police matter. I'm trying to avoid that for the good of everyone involved, including the two children. I'm sure you understand that.'

'I do,' Ivy said. 'Thank you. Maybe you think you're doing the right thing, but I'm afraid that in this case you're wrong. You might as well call the police on your car phone right now, because we're going to be entirely uncooperative.'

'You're damned right we'll call the police,' Jack said. 'We're talking serious jail time here. This is a court *order*. I've had enough. Get 'em down here,' he said to the lawyer.

'Surely you …' the lawyer started to say to Ivy.

'Call 'em now.'

'Go ahead,' Ivy said. She took Henry's arm and waited.

The lawyer shrugged, turned around, and headed down the steps toward the car. They watched as he placed the call, got back out, and returned to the porch. 'I'm sorry it has to go this way,' he said to Ivy.

'I'm not,' Jack said. 'And I'm not paying you to be sorry, either.'

They waited. The idea came into Ivy's head to offer them coffee and cookies, and she almost laughed out loud. Then she saw that there was something near hysteria in her thinking, and the thought scared the laughter out of her.

'Where are they coming from?' Henry asked her.

'The police department's down on Batavia. Call it five or ten …'

A Cadillac turned the corner off Chapman Avenue.

'Here's the cavalry,' Henry said. 'Thank God.'

68

It was Goldfarb in the Cadillac. He pulled up at the curb and got out, unfurling an umbrella and hurrying across to the porch. He wore a dark suit and tie and was short and heavily built, evidently Henry's age, but fit-looking. He glanced at Ivy and winked, then shook Henry's hand. Right then a patrol car rounded the corner and parked behind the Cadillac, and two uniformed officers got out. Before anyone spoke, the policemen joined them on the porch.

'It'll be all right,' Henry said to Ivy, who nodded at him. It looked like doom to her, despite Goldfarb's wink.

'I represent the Stebbins family,' Goldfarb said to the policemen. 'I'm afraid there's something wrong here that I don't quite understand. I'm here to help clear it up. Just to put things in order, let me say that my clients have been caring for the two children in question. Mr Douglas has attempted without success to take them several times. The Stebbinses refused to relinquish the children because Mr Douglas was both intoxicated and irrational.'

'The hell if I was ...' Jack started to say, but his lawyer shook his head to silence him.

'With all due respect,' Jack's lawyer said, 'that's all beside the point. We have a court order mandating the release of the children.' He handed the papers to one of the policemen, who looked them over, showing them to his partner.

'Do you have anything other than a fax copy, sir?'

The lawyer shook his head. 'I'm afraid not. I was out of the office, and my secretary was compelled to fax them to me.'

'Court's closed by now,' the second cop said, looking at his watch. 'Where's your office?'

'Los Angeles, I'm afraid.'

Jack looked at his attorney, who watched the officer's face as he looked over the fax again. The officer looked up at Ivy. 'You've been caring for the children?'

'Yes. What Mr Goldfarb told you is entirely true. Mr Douglas has been drinking heavily for days. My sister left the kids in my care.'

'Well,' the officer said, 'thank you for helping out, but Mr Douglas doesn't appear to be intoxicated now. According to this document, he's the children's legal guardian. At least until court opens tomorrow we'll have to assume the document's legal. I'm afraid you'll have to get the children. Are they here?'

'They're here,' Ivy said.

'Why do we assume the document's legal?' Goldfarb asked. 'I have reason to believe it isn't.'

Ivy looked at Jack's lawyer, who was stone-faced.

'That's a lie,' Jack said.

'May I?' Goldfarb held his hand out, and the officer gave him the fax. 'Well, this *is* odd,' he said after a moment.

'What the hell's odd?' Jack tried to grab the fax, but Goldfarb snatched it away.

'The judge's name. Benjamin Meng. He retired six months ago, didn't he? I seem to recall that he moved up north, up to Oroville. The date's just right, though, isn't it? How do you explain that? Has he come out of retirement?' He looked Jack's lawyer straight in the face, but the man said nothing. The second of the two officers turned around and walked down the steps and out to the patrol car.

'What I think is this,' Goldfarb said. 'I think you took an old copy of a court order, whited out the inaccurate information, typed in fresh information, then had it faxed to yourself in order to obtain a clean copy. You set this appointment up late in the afternoon because you knew that court would be closed and the document's authenticity couldn't be established. Am I right so far?'

'No,' Jack said. 'We're out here this late because *these* people' – he gestured at Ivy and Henry – 'have had the kids hidden away. I call that kidnapping. I call that taking a man's kids away, and if that's not a crime, then it's a sorry damned world we're living in.'

'But then of course they're not your kids, are they, Jack?' Ivy kept her voice even.

'I as good as raised them,' Jack said. 'What they had, I bought them, didn't I? They'd be on the *street* if it weren't for me. Deny *that*.'

'Okay,' Ivy said, 'I'll deny it. They never would have been on the street. They'd have been here. They *are* here, aren't they?'

Jack's lawyer still said nothing.

The second officer came back up onto the porch. 'Judge Meng retired last March. The order's bogus.'

Jack's lawyer shrugged. Jack shoved his jaw out, as if he were trying to bite his upper lip. 'This is all crap,' he said.

'Actually,' Goldfarb said, 'I've got a fax of my own from the San Diego County courthouse. Weren't you married to Darla Schwenk in San Diego County, Mr Douglas?'

'Yeah. So what?'

'There's no record of any such marriage. I believe you were actually married in Tijuana.'

'So what? That's legal. Isn't that legal?' He appealed to his lawyer who rolled his eyes tiredly.

'I'm afraid I've been seriously misled,' Jack's lawyer said to the two officers. 'I've got someplace to be by six.' He looked at his watch. 'So if I can't be of any more service here ...'

'Stay where you are,' the first officer said. 'You're going to be late, wherever you've got to be.'

'This,' Goldfarb said, showing them a second paper, 'is from the court of the County of Orange. There's no record of Darla Schwenk having been divorced at all from her first husband. I put through a call to a Mr Bill Schwenk, the children's biological father, and he sent back this notarized letter stating that there had been no divorce. The papers were never filed. He's still the children's legal guardian. In the letter he gives his permission to Walt and Ivy Stebbins to care for the children until their mother returns to claim them. The letter's a fax, too, I'm afraid, but as you can see, the original was notarized.' He handed all the documentation to the police, who looked it over hastily.

The front door opened then, and Walt looked out through the screen.

'Hi,' he said, coming out onto the porch. 'Jack! How are you? Is all this cleared up? I sure hope so.' He smiled brightly at Jack. 'I'm Walt Stebbins, Nora and Eddie's uncle,' he said to the two officers. 'If I can help ...?' He gestured with both hands.

'You can help by fucking off,' Jack said to him.

'Now, Jack,' Walt said, 'that kind of language won't do. You haven't been drinking again, have you?'

'You going to let them talk to me that way?' Jack said to his lawyer. 'After what I paid you? I want these people arrested. Kidnapping and assault.'

'You didn't pay me half enough as it is, Jack,' the lawyer said.

'Well, then, why don't you go to Hell, you shyster bastard?'

'Try to calm down, sir,' the first officer said.

'I know my rights, asshole. I can say anything I want, and you can't touch me, and you know it. To hell with you, man, and your friend too.'

'*Have* you been drinking, sir?'

'Shove it up your ass.'

'Oh, *no!*' Walt muttered, and Ivy elbowed him in the ribs.

'I'd like your cooperation here, sir. I believe there's reason for you to take a field sobriety test. If you're unwilling to submit to a test here, we can take you to the station and draw blood. The choice is yours.'

'The hell if you'll do anything like that. You know I'm not drunk. I haven't had a drink since last night. There's no damn way you'd take me in and risk my being sober. I'd ream you both out, and you know it damn well.' His voice rose, and the veins stood out in his neck. He looked furiously at Walt, who smiled like a Cheshire cat, and Jack threw his arm back to take a punch at him.

'Don't do it,' the second cop said. 'Don't even think about it. So far no ...'

'*Shut* the hell up,' Jack said, swiveling around toward the cop and poking him in the chest with his index finger. He tried to step past him then, to storm away, but quicker than Ivy could see exactly what happened, the second cop's arm shot out, spun Jack around, and Jack was on his knees on the porch with his arm bent around behind him. The other officer already had his handcuffs out. There was a double click of the cuff latches, and then Jack was hauled to his feet.

'Where are the kids?' Ivy asked Walt.

'With Jinx. In the shed.'

The police read Jack his rights as they led him through the drizzle toward the patrol car, taking his lawyer along with them.

'Assaulting a police officer,' Goldfarb said clicking his tongue. 'I'm afraid Mr Douglas made a rather grievous mistake. He must have wanted those kids very badly.'

'This doesn't have anything to do with the kids,' Walt said. 'Believe me, I know. This had to do with getting mad, which is pretty much the same as getting drunk, as I see it. You lose your mind either way.'

'Write that down,' Ivy said to Henry. 'Let's post it on the refrigerator.'

'Let's order a pizza,' Walt said. 'Drink, Mr Goldfarb?'

'Thanks,' the lawyer said. 'Don't mind if I do.'

They opened the door and went in. 'Darla called this afternoon,' Ivy said, looking at Walt.

'What'd she say?'

'She got a job working for that chiropractor. She's putting her life back together, she said, one piece at a time. I told her we were happy to keep the kids for a while, for however long she needs.'

'Good,' Walt said. 'And good for her.' He could see Nora and Eddie coming in through the back door, and he heard Nora's laughter. He was happy to see them. 'I hope Darla finds herself,' he said. 'I honestly do.'

69

It was dark when Argyle parked in front of the alley next to Nelson and Whidley and shut the car off. The unlit alley where LeRoy and Nelson had burned to death stretched away into the darkness, wet with rainwater. On the front wall of the architects' offices that formed the south wall of the alley, a long strand of pinlights spelled out the words 'Merry Christmas,' blinking on and off and casting a feeble light down onto the hood of his car. He was swept with the sudden urge to tear the lights down, to climb up onto the hood of his car and leap for them, to beat them to pieces against the bricks ...

He found that the door was open and he was standing in gutter water. A wet wind gusted out of the alley and into his face. Hurriedly he climbed back into the car. It was a weeknight, so there were only a few diners at the Continental Cafe, and all of them sat inside, out of the weather. The sidewalks were deserted, the streets virtually empty. No one had seen him. He hadn't called attention to himself.

The golem sat in the seat beside him. It looked as if Bentley had knocked the living sense out of the thing with the poker – whatever sense it ever had – and it stared out the window now as if it was drugged.

Since being blinded by the weird lamplight in the Stebbinses' shed, Argyle's vision had flickered in and out, and he wondered if he were working up to have a stroke, if that's what would get him. Was the alley as black as it seemed? The dead end couldn't be more than forty feet distant, but it was hidden in a shadow as black as ink. His ears rang with a leaden clanging sound, and very faintly he could hear what sounded like voices, weak and far away.

He opened a leather satchel on the seat and took out the tin box with the bird in it. It was a hell of an unlikely basket to have put all his eggs into, so to speak, and there was a solid chance that when he sent the golem down the alley, bird or no bird, it would do nothing but bump into the wall and fall over, which is pretty much what it had been doing for the past few hours.

There was the sound of footsteps on the sidewalk, and he looked up to see a man and woman walking arm and arm, heading toward the cafe. For a quick moment the woman looked just like Ivy, and he was full of a sudden shame, of the urge to hide the golem somehow, yank a sack over its head, ditch the bird in the jar, deny who and what he was and what had brought him to the mouth of this dark alley on a rainy winter night.

But it wasn't Ivy, and the two passed on by without even seeing him there. He closed his eyes for a moment, settling himself down again, clearing his mind. Then, seeing that the sidewalks were empty again, he unscrewed the jar lid, dipped two fingers into the liquid, and pulled the bird out by the tail, letting it drip onto the floor. The car was instantly full of the juniper smell of gin. The golem twitched, swiveling its head, looking out the side window at a passing car as if the creature had suddenly woken up. Good, Argyle thought. Something was stirring in it, some sense of purpose.

'It's time,' he said. It was anybody's guess whether the creature understood anything at all, but he had fallen into the habit of speaking to it, like a person might speak to a goldfish in a bowl. He reached across, grasped its chin between his thumb and forefinger, yanked its mouth open so that its ivory teeth separated, and shoved the bird's head down its mouth.

'Eat it, god*damn* it!' he said. Then he pushed the golem's head back with the palm of his hand in order to open its throat. He knelt on the seat and pried its jaws open even wider, corkscrewing the bird, pinning the golem to the upholstery where it jerked and twitched, mumbling blue feathers out of its mouth, its eyes shifting back and forth like clockwork.

The golem stood in front of the car now, its face turned half toward him, illuminated in the light of the Merry Christmas sign. Its clothes were disheveled from the tussle over the bird, its hair wild, its eyes demented. He could barely stand to look at it, standing there stupidly, like some kind of horrible alter ego, the wreck he might have become if his life had gone differently, if he hadn't managed to pull himself up by his own bootstraps, if he had allowed himself to become like Murray LeRoy ...

A shudder ran through him, and he forced the thought away. 'Go,' he said out loud. 'Go now.'

Its jaw hung open, unhinged in the struggle, so that it looked as if it were gagging. There was a lump in its throat where the bird had lodged. Argyle had tried to massage it down, but the flesh of the thing's neck had started to tear like soft rubber, and he'd left it, unable to go on with the process. The golem took a step down the sidewalk, heading toward the cafe Argyle started the car, shifting into drive, and looked around wildly. He couldn't let it wander off alone. It would have to meet its fate in the alley, whatever that fate might be. If he had to, he'd run the golem down, pin it against the wall, cripple it and drag it into the alley himself ...

It stopped suddenly, staggered, and turned around, looking up the alley now as if it had suddenly heard something there, a whispered command. Argyle fancied that he heard it too. The voices in his mind grew louder, and he clamped his hands over his ears. But the sound was simply magnified, rising like a chorus. He squinted, rubbing his eyes to clear them. Shapes like the shadows of bats seemed to flutter in front of the window, and he thought he could hear the sound of their rushing wings. A wind sprang up, sweeping dead sycamore leaves from the alley floor, and a sheet of newspaper tumbled out of the darkness and burst into flames, falling on the hood of the car. There was a scattering of raindrops then, and Argyle switched on the wipers, hunching forward to watch as the golem slouched away into the darkness and was swallowed up by shadow. He waited for it to turn around, to come wandering back out again, and he put both hands on the steering wheel, ready to slam forward and knock it to Hell himself if he had to.

Then, with a startling suddenness, there was a flash of dazzling yellow light and what sounded like a human cry. The golem turned in slow circles, flapping its arms slowly, caroming off either wall of the alley, engulfed in flame. The fire was white, like a chemical fire, and Argyle could feel its heat, incredibly intense. The golem fell to its knees, then straight over onto its face, curling up on the ground like burning paper. It was over. The thing was dead. The voices in Argyle's head were silenced. He looked up at the Merry Christmas sign, but he felt nothing, no dark desires, no compulsions. He climbed out of the car and hurried back to the trunk, throwing it open and hauling out a fire extinguisher.

Out of the corner of his eye he saw people coming out of the cafe, hurrying forward. 'Here!' he shouted stupidly, and ran to the mouth of the alley, squeezing the lever of the extinguisher. The rain beat down now, harder by the second, and he had the incredible urge to laugh out loud, to turn around and hose everyone down with the extinguisher. The golem was a heap on the ground, like a burning pile of trash, and the flames flickered lower, running up and down like witch fire across what had been the thing's back. There was a sighing noise, like wind through a grate, and the rain whirled around the burning corpse in a wild little vortex.

Argyle forced back his laughter, his joy. By God, he had done it! – deceived the Father of Lies, swindled the master swindler and got off scot-free. The Devil had taken it, lock, stock, and barrel.

70

'Some kind of windfall,' Lyle Boyd said, dipping cake doughnuts into pans of frosting. 'About a quarter of a million from what I heard. Her and her boyfriend headed straight for Honolulu, booked a room at the Royal Hawaiian. I don't guess she'll *ever* be back.'

'What was it,' Walt asked, 'inheritance?'

'Something like that.'

'How about her house over on Olive? She just lock the doors and go?'

'Realtor's selling it for her.' Boyd scraped frosting off the big wooden breadboard with a spatula. 'She'll make a couple of bucks there too. She owned that, you know.'

'She *owned* it?' Walt said incredulously. 'I had the idea she was just about broke, living on macaroni and cheese.'

'Hell,' Boyd said. 'That's what she let on. She sold that place of hers in the Islands and outright *bought* the house here in town. Then she started to regret it right off. She was always pining away for the tropics. Anyway, I imagine she'll clear another hundred thousand on it, all told. She's a rich woman, at least by my standards.'

'I'll be damned,' Walt said, looking out the window at the cloudy afternoon sky. 'I guess you never know.'

'That's the truth.'

A man and four kids came in the door just then, and Walt nodded at the man, then winked at one of the boys, who had to be about Nora's age. The boy's eyes shot open and he ducked behind his father, looking out at Walt from behind the man's leg.

Walt turned around and grinned at Henry, who tried to grin back, but couldn't. His face was full of trouble.

'What's wrong?' Walt asked. 'You're not thinking about Maggie Biggs, are you? It's almost funny, the way she took us to the cleaners. And now she's dancing the hula with Don Ho. Bentley's going to drop dead when he hears about it.'

Henry waved his hand. 'I guess so,' he said.

'What I wonder is where she got the money. I'll bet you a shiny new dime that she shook somebody down, and I'll bet you it was Argyle, too. She had something on him, her and Peetenpaul.'

Henry nodded weakly. 'I don't …' He stopped, gesturing helplessly.

'What's up?' Walt asked.

'I think I know how she got the money out of Argyle.'

'How? She blackmailed him?'

'I guess you could say that.'

'What gives, then? She didn't involve *you* in it, did she? She didn't leave you holding the bag and skip town?'

'No, not like that. Worse, I guess. She threatened to go to Jinx again. And more. I … I couldn't let her. I was afraid.'

'So …?'

'So I stole that damned bird of yours. You look in the tackle box and it won't be there.'

Walt blinked at him. So that was it. 'I guess you figured out that I'd gotten it back out of the Dumpster?'

'Next day. Maggie told me all about these men who wanted the bird – what they'd do to get it. To tell you the truth, I thought it was in the can anyway, so I played along. Then when it was gone, when I knew you'd gotten it out of the bin, I figured it had this … this *hold* over you, and somehow that gave me the right to steal it. That was wrong. None of us has any right to another man's possessions. We can make up whys and wherefores till the cows come home, but all of it's lies we tell ourselves to justify our sins. That's what I think. Anyway, I gave the bird to Maggie, and Maggie cut a deal with these men.'

Walt nodded at him, thinking about this. As usual, Henry was right. 'It was the wrong bird,' Walt said to him.

'I beg your pardon?'

'You gave her a fake. The bird in the tackle box was a dead parakeet in a Mason jar. It was a dummy. The real bird's … I took care of the real one.'

Henry sat there silently for a moment, thinking this out. 'It hardly matters, morally speaking,' he said finally. 'I thought I was stealing the real McCoy. This doesn't make it right.'

'Maybe not,' Walt said, 'but the way I see it, you tried to do the right thing, and more than once, too. I wish you *had* stolen the real one.'

There was laughter behind them, and the man with the kids was pushing out through the door again. 'I'd stay out of that alley, anyway,' he said over his shoulder to Boyd, 'unless you've got an asbestos suit.' He laughed again, and the door swung shut behind them.

Boyd shook his head and squirted Windex on the top of the glass dough-nut case. 'How do you like that?' he said.

'What?' Walt waited.

'That guy that burned up in the alley last night? It was an effigy.'

'A Fiji?' Henry asked, picking up his coffee cup. 'Well, I'll be go to Hell. That's tough on an immigrant. They come over here looking for the Ameri-can dream ...' He shook his head sadly. 'Wasn't there a Samoan family over on Harwood Street? Big people, I seem to remember. I wonder if they knew this man, poor devil.'

'I said an *effigy*,' Boyd told him. 'A dummy. Fire department got there and apparently this thing was made up out of dirt and sticks and melted wax and crap like that. Patrick just told me it had a goddamn *bird* in its mouth. Some kind of prank, I guess.'

'Sure sounds like it,' Walt said. 'Heading home?' he asked Henry.

'I think I'll sit for a while. I told Jinx I'd go Christmas shopping downtown. I'll have another cup of coffee first.'

'I'll drop you.'

'I can use the walk.'

Walt stood up and drained his coffee cup. 'I guess I better roll, then. I've got some unfinished business.' He couldn't help thinking about what Argyle had said about rising out of the ashes like a phoenix. There was something unlikely in the picture. They didn't let just anybody be a phoenix. You had to qualify.

71

Walt forced the spade down into the wet dirt with his heel, digging out a wide hole. He didn't want to cut the bluebird in half. It wasn't his to cut. He shook the heavy clods off the shovel and knocked them apart, but there was no sign of the bird, so he dug out another shovelful. Still there was nothing. Maybe the bird was so dirty it didn't look like a bird any more ... He moved the loose dirt around in the hole. The bird *couldn't* be deeper. He was already down into soil that hadn't been turned over in years.

He rejected the first notion that came into his mind – that Argyle had come back and stolen it after all. He had found the shovel exactly where he'd left it, and the filled-in hole had looked as he remembered, tamped down with the shovel and then stomped on. He prodded around some more, working the shovel carefully, slicing away at the edges of the hole. A patch of dirt suddenly loosened and fell outward, exposing the mouth of a neat, round tunnel. A gopher hole! Apparently a gopher had dragged the bird away.

Getting down onto his hands and knees, he peered into the little tunnel, but it was perfectly dark and he could see nothing. He dug out another shovel of dirt, and then another, following the hole until it disappeared under his neighbor's garage. He hacked away at it sideways, under the old slab floor, more determined than ever to drag it out of there. He had never intended to leave it buried, and he was damned if he was going to let it hang around and demonize the neighbor's garage.

He threw the shovel down finally and went after the flashlight, fetching it outside where he knelt in the dirt again and shined the light into the hole. It ended a foot farther on. The bird lay jammed against the back end of the tunnel, as limp and dead-looking as ever, but shiny blue, as if the dirt wouldn't stick to it. There was no gopher to be seen, no outlet to the hole. The faint smell of gin hung in the air.

He was abruptly certain that nothing had dragged the bird into the tunnel. It had somehow burrowed its way under there itself, going somewhere under its own power ...

Its wing twitched suddenly, and there was a papery sound, like dry corn husks in a sack. Walt jerked backward, averting his face, fearful that the bird would fly out at him, that it would escape into the evening gloom like a demon out of Pandora's box. He crammed the flashlight into the hole, stopping it up, and went into the house after the fireplace tongs. He carried the tongs into the garage, where he found a nearly empty pint-size paint can. He pried the lid off and poured the paint out, then he hurried back outside, carrying the can and a hammer, and took the flashlight out of the hole. He felt around gingerly with the tongs until he found the bird. Carefully he dragged it out into the open and peered at it in the waning light.

It seemed to vibrate in the tongs, as if it were charged with an infernal energy, and its eyes were clear and bright and focused on Walt's face, as if it were as interested in him as he was in it.

A picture slowly formed in Walt's mind, like a flower opening up. He saw Maggie Biggs sitting in her suite at the Royal Hawaiian, looking out over

Waikiki and sipping a Mai Tai, watching the afternoon waves reel in over the reef. A leather valise lay open on the hotel bed, neatly filled with bills. Mr Peetenpaul stood on the balcony in his aloha shirt. Far beyond him, the steep green sides of Diamond Head rose against a sky as blue as the feathers of the bluebird itself. The lazy strains of Polynesian music, steel guitars and soft voices, drifted on the trade wind. There was the smell of blossoms on the air, as clear and heavy as if Walt wore a lei around his own neck.

He looked across at the tin shed, empty of anything but dry Christmas trees, at the garage with its pitiful inventory of gag gifts, and suddenly he saw himself crumpling up Argyle's check, throwing it out onto the lawn, paying heavily for his principles. The bluebird peered into his face. Its eyes were full of possibility, full of suggestion. There was the sound of thunder, a rumbling echo that went on and on.

Speak any wish, he thought, remembering the promise on the little bit of folded paper that had accompanied the thing …

He was startled out of his reverie by the sound of bells, ringing out an evening hymn. Six o'clock. It was the bells at the Holy Spirit. It was raining again, and obviously had been. Somehow he hadn't noticed. And he was surprised to see that darkness had fallen, that his arms were weary from holding the tongs, which were clamped like a vise around the bluebird's neck.

'Go to Hell,' he said to it.

Then he dropped the bird like a plumb bob into the paint can, set the lid over it, and pounded it down tight. He took it back into the garage, where he crisscrossed the lid with duct tape, then headed out toward the street to where the Suburban was parked. There was a thumping noise from within the can, as if the thing were angry, and he hammered it against the steering wheel a couple of times to shut it up. He started the engine, switched on the wipers and angled away from the curb, heading toward Argyle's house in the downpour.

72

Argyle looked out the window at the dark street. Rain was falling again, heavily now. It was going to be a hell of a stormy night. Well, let it storm! He stepped across and put Edward Elgar on the stereo. Carrying the record jacket with him, he sat down in the chair that Bentley had torn up with the poker. When it came to music he still preferred vinyl to tape or compact disc, and over the years that his records had sat in their sleeves unplayed, he had kept them organized and perfectly shelved. Now he could play them again, by God, and he aimed to work through them steadily, savoring them, starting with 'Pomp and Circumstance,' which seemed somehow appropriate, given his success with the golem.

He felt like a new man. He *was* a new man. It was damned good to have the golem out of the house at last, to have this whole sorry episode finished. It was a brand-new day. He picked up a glass on the table, a piece of cut crystal with an inch of bourbon in the bottom. Bourbon was his one great vice, although he never allowed himself more than a single glass. Swirling the whiskey, he held it under his nose and breathed in the vapors, then set the glass back down onto the tiled tabletop without tasting it. There was plenty of time to drink it.

The strains of the music seemed to expand and fill the room. He smiled, recalling from down the years the first phrases of the piece, and he moved his hand like a conductor and bobbed his head, listening closely, thinking how the sound of the rain lent the music a certain something.

Then, abruptly, a pain shot across his forehead, and he closed his eyes and took his face in his hands. Thunder rattled the windows, then died away. The music sounded suddenly louder to him, as if the electricity in the storm had doubled the wattage. The pain passed, and he breathed deeply and gratefully. Clearly it was nothing. He set in to listen again, but the melody was slightly discordant now, slightly off-key. Of course, he hadn't heard it in years …

The music seemed to swell, compressing the atmosphere in the room like air pumped into a tire. He could almost see the walls balloon outward, vibrating with the bass. The windows rattled in their frames, the glass panes humming like an insect swarm. He felt the pain in his head again, coming on more slowly this time, a mounting pressure at the back of his eyeballs, pushing at his forehead and temples as if his brain were swelling.

He fumbled for the bourbon glass, choked on the liquor, and spat it out, standing up out of the chair and slamming the glass back down onto the table. And then, to his horror, the liquor burst into flame in the glass, and the flames slipped down the outside and ignited the whiskey puddled on the tabletop. He slapped at it, splashing the burning liquor onto the rug, knocking the glass itself over. His hand was on fire! He beat it against the back of the chair now, stamping at the rug. The music was unbearable, chaotic, raucous, like a cage full of parrots. Smoke rose from the wool rug, and Argyle fell to his hands and knees and pounded at it, the scorched wool stinking in his nostrils. He clutched his head again and stumbled to his feet, reeling across toward the stereo cabinet, a deep moan pushing up out of his open mouth. He heard secret voices in the music now, clanking machinery, howls of inarticulate pain, and a deep thumping in the very foundation of the house, as if some mechanical beast were coming for him, as if at any moment the earth would open and swallow the house, dragging him down to Hell.

He knocked the tone arm off the record, and the abrupt silence nearly took his breath away. He saw clearly that something had gone wrong. The golem hadn't worked. He had been betrayed. Everyone had betrayed him – Stebbins, Peetenpaul, the Biggs woman, that goddamn Bentley. Even Ivy had betrayed him! The whole crowd of them had conspired to ruin him!

He realized suddenly that the silence wasn't complete. In the distance, from the tower at the Holy Spirit Church, came the sound of the evening bells. For God's sake, they were still hounding him! He pressed his hands against his ears, and the whole world seemed to him to vibrate like a tuning fork, like a church bell, vibrations that would shake him to atoms. He strode away through the house, howling to drown out the noise of the bells, moving from room to room, turning on lights, every light he could find. He talked out loud, reciting old poems he'd been forced to memorize in high school. He realized with a shock of long-overdue recognition that he was utterly alone. There was nobody to call, nobody to help. That had been true of Murray LeRoy when LeRoy had been consumed. And of Nelson, too. Nobody had given a damn for George Nelson's death – not even his so-called friends. Especially not his friends! Argyle walked back into the living room now, looking behind him at the empty rooms of his house, at the lonesome shadows in the corners.

He fell silent, listening. The bells had stopped, but that wouldn't last long. There was a scuffing sound outside, on the porch, and he saw something move beyond the curtained window in the door.

'Yes!' he shouted, unable to contain himself. He didn't care who it was, as long as it was company. Even Lorimer Bentley would do. He stepped eagerly across the carpet toward the door, putting his hand on the knob and throwing the door open wide to let in the night air.

But the porch was empty when Argyle opened the door and looked out, ready to welcome the world into his house. 'Who is it?' he asked, peering out into the darkness beyond the glow of the porch lamp. 'Who's there?' He stepped outside onto the porch.

Something moved in the shadows, out near the sycamore tree that shaded the lawn. A human figure stood there, hunched over like a beggar out of an old illustration. It was dressed in rags, its face turned away. 'Get the hell out of here!' Argyle said to it. His voice shook. 'I'll call the police!'

The man's head swiveled toward him, and for a moment, when they reflected the lamplight, his eyes glowed red. Argyle's breath caught. The man's jaw was broken, unhinged. His – its – flesh was charred, its clothing ragged and blackened.

It was the golem, reanimated, returned from whatever place it had gone.

The front door slammed shut behind Argyle, hard enough to shake the house. He flung himself around and grabbed the knob. It was locked. And his pockets were empty! His house keys were inside, the back door locked, the windows bolted.

He was swept with the utter certainty that the creature had come back to fetch him. Had been *sent* back.

From beyond the Plaza, the bells at the Church of the Holy Spirit tolled the hour.

Argyle sat down in the rattan porch chair and gripped the armrests. He would stay right there. Whatever the thing wanted of him, wherever it wanted him to go, it would have to force him. By God, it would have to carry him. And it would have a fight on its hands first! He'd go kicking and screaming.

The chair burst into flames beneath him, and he threw himself out of it, smelling the stink of burned hair. He swiveled around, hooking his leg through the armrest and dragging the burning chair away from the side of the house. His shoe caught fire, and he hopped away, kicking the chair down and pulling off his sweater, whipping his shoe with it to put the fire out. The sweater itself burst into flames, and he flung it away from him, screaming out loud. The golem remained slouched in the shadows beneath the tree, as if waiting patiently for Argyle to finish up his earthly antics so that the two of them could get down to the business at hand.

73

Rain fell out of the sky like the end of the world, running in a sheet down the windshield, so that even with the wipers on high speed Walt got only small, momentary glimpses of the road ahead of him as he turned off Maple Street onto Cambridge. A river of water six feet across rose over the curb on the low side of the street, flooding out onto lawns, and above the drumming of the rain he could hear the sound of thunder and, impossibly, the weather-muted sound of the bells of the Holy Spirit rising somehow above the tumult – melody in the chaos of weather.

The paint can on the seat beside him bounced and jiggled, as if it were full of jumping beans. For a moment it levitated above the seat, hovering two inches over the upholstery and vibrating like a can in a paint shaker. He could hear a beating sound from inside it again, a thumping against the walls, and suddenly the can leaped completely off the seat and banged into the dashboard, falling to the floor and rolling against the door panel where it lay still.

He spotted Argyle's house through the blur of rain, and he angled across toward the curb. Through the gray haze of the downpour he saw that something was burning on the front lawn. Argyle danced in front of it, trying to beat out the fire, slapping at his own shoes with his sweater.

Walt cut the engine and scooped up the paint can, climbing out of the Suburban and bending back into the car to haul out his umbrella, which he hoisted against the rain. The flames that engulfed the chair dwindled in the deluge as Walt hurried across the lawn to where Argyle stood clutching his forehead, his eyes wide like the eyes of a lunatic. He fell to his knees on the wet lawn and clasped his hands in front of him as if he had suddenly decided to say his prayers.

Walt tilted the umbrella so that it sheltered Argyle's face from the rain, and he wished suddenly that he had Ivy along. He was in over his head here. Argyle was a wreck, hardly sensible. Walt grabbed him by the arm and lifted, and he reluctantly got to his feet, slouching under the umbrella. Walt turned him and navigated through the rain toward the porch, and right then lightning flashed. There was a simultaneous crack of thunder, and the night lit up like noontime.

In the flash of light, Walt saw that someone stood beneath the dripping sycamore tree, a hunched ruin of a man dressed in rags. His eyes were rolled back into his head, and his jaw hung slack so that his mouth lolled open grotesquely. Walt shouted out loud in surprise as the night plunged into darkness again. Walt squinted, his eyes adjusting. There was enough porchlight shining through the rain and tree foliage that Walt could see that the man still stood there, unmoving.

Walt dragged Argyle forward now, propelling him up the porch steps, under the eaves. 'Who the hell is *he*?' Walt asked. Rain hammered the porch roof and sluiced out of the downspouts. The street was very nearly a river now, and water lapped at the porch steps of the houses across the street.

'That's my *soul*,' Argyle said. He shivered, wrapping his arms around himself. Walt could hear his teeth chatter.

'Let's go inside.' Walt tried the door, not waiting for Argyle to voice his opinion. 'Door's locked.'

'Of *course* it is.'

'Where's the key?'

'Locked inside. It's no good. He won't let me in. It's over.'

'Who won't let you in? *That* character?'

The paint can thumped hard, jerking in Walt's hand. He set it down on the porch and stepped on it.

'No, not *that* thing. I've sold my soul to the Devil, and now I've got to pay up. Don't tell me Bentley's kept this a secret from you.'

'What about the phoenix?' Walt asked, trying not to get mad.

'What?'

'Rising out of the ashes,' Walt said. 'Like you were talking about yesterday.'

'I got a reprieve,' Argyle said. 'But it didn't last.'

'Well, listen,' Walt said. 'I've got something to confess.'

'You want Bentley for that – him or the priest from the Holy Spirit. I'd suggest the priest.'

'The bird that you bought from Maggie Biggs ...' Walt said.

'What's he *doing*?' Argyle's voice was suddenly shrill. He jerked forward as if tugged by an invisible rope.

The creature under the tree had stepped out onto the sidewalk. Walt saw what it was now; it was the thing that Bentley had described to him, the golem, the effigy that Lyle Boyd said had burned in the alley last night. The creature had apparently come back from the dead, or from wherever it had been. It moved away down the sidewalk, and Argyle went down the steps as if to follow it.

'Wait!' Walt said, picking up the paint can and following him out into the rain, putting up the umbrella again. 'Let it go. To hell with it.'

Argyle ignored him, moving off at a pace identical to that of the golem, the two of them drawn inexorably toward the distant boulevard.

Walt hurried up behind Argyle and kept up with him, sharing the umbrella. 'The bird that Biggs sold you was the wrong one,' he said. 'It was a dead parakeet I got from the Sprouse Reitz. Same color blue.'

Argyle groaned. 'I'm finished,' he said. 'Tell Ivy ...'

'I've got the real one right here.' Walt held up the paint can, which flew out of his grasp at that moment and clanked down onto the sidewalk, the rain beating on it as it hopped and jittered there. Walt scooped it up and tucked it under his arm, holding onto it tightly.

Argyle looked at him hard now, his mouth half open in disbelief. 'That's a lie,' he said, not breaking his stride. He licked his lips, and his eyes darted toward the paint can. Ten paces ahead of them the golem stepped down off the curb, into the floodwaters that flowed down Maple Street, and headed for the opposite shore.

'No it's not,' Walt said. 'It's the bluebird. If I told you any lies about it before, I'm sorry. I shouldn't have. It was wrong. But you were too, of course.'

'What do you want for it?' Argyle asked flatly. He looked ahead again, matching the golem's shambling stride. 'Anything. There's no time to haggle. Name it.'

'Nothing.'

'Damn it!' Argyle said. 'This is life and death! This is salvation.'

'This is *not* salvation,' Walt shouted. 'This is the opposite of that.' There was another lightning flash, and the figure of the golem was thrown into sharp clarity against the rainy night. The lightning seemed to glow straight through the thing's flesh and torn clothing, as if it were made of cheesecloth or cobweb.

'A million dollars.'

'No! For God's sake, Bob, open your eyes.'

'Name it. Whatever you want. Say the word and it's yours.'

'Damn it! No! Get it through your ...'

'Do you think I'm joking, Walt? Are you a goddamn self-righteous moron?'

'Joking!' Walt realized that Argyle was weeping openly now, his face contorted with it. Here he was talking like the Devil himself, and out of fear of the Devil! There was a noise from ahead of them, as if the golem had moaned out loud, and Walt wondered what would happen if he sprinted ahead and just tackled the bastard, stuffed it down the storm drain, shoes and all. He watched it step up onto the curb at the opposite side of the intersection, and, just as it did, Argyle stepped down into ankle deep water, following in the thing's wake, stepping where it had stepped. Walt kept pace with him, and they waded to the curb and up onto the sidewalk again. Clearly the golem was moving toward the Plaza, bound for the alley behind Nelson and Whidley.

Across Chapman Avenue the bell tower at St Anthony's rose into the sky. Dark sheets of rain slanted across the pale stucco walls. The curved base of the fallen bell was visible through the hole it had broken in the tower. Walt saw Argyle look at it, shut his eyes, and turn his head away.

'I heard that Mrs Simms is giving the fund-raiser money to the church,' Walt said to him. 'All of it. In order to restore the tower. Can you beat that?'

'I didn't mean to kill Simms.'

'I didn't say you did. I was just saying that ...'

'Give it to the children,' Argyle said.

'What? Give what? What the hell are you talking about?'

'The money. Take the money I'm offering to you and give it to the children, to Nora and Eddie. Put it in a trust fund, for God's sake, and they'll never have to worry about money for the rest of their lives. Do it for them if you won't do it for yourself. You *owe* me, Walt. We go back a long way I screwed up bad back then, and I'm paying for it now, any way I can. So just let me make amends a little bit, will you? Go ahead and do it for the kids. Or are your principles so high and mighty that you'd take the money out of their hands too?'

Walt looked away, muddled by the thought of it. Argyle's money could make all the difference in the world to Nora and Eddie – no hardships, no sweat. Did he have any *right* to turn something like that down, just on principle?

'A million dollars?' Walt asked, calculating what that would be worth, put out at interest – enough for a private college, a big house on Easy Street.

'That's right. What's wrong, not enough? You want more? Ten million?'

They were passing the back of Walt's own house now, one street away, and over the garage roof of the nearby house he could see the enormous shadow of the avocado tree where Mr Argyle the daddy longlegs lived. Used to live.

'No,' Walt said to him. 'There's not a thing that I want, not that you could give me. And there's nothing very high and mighty about my principles. They're small principles, but they're mine, and right now I'm in a mood to hang onto them.'

Argyle laughed out loud, but it wasn't a convincing laugh. They were approaching the corner of the street. The golem would turn right and head downtown, where it had an appointment with destiny. Walt determined to stick it out, to see this thing through, even though by now Ivy would be wondering where he'd gone. Jinx would be cooking dinner. The kids would be goofing around, coloring or playing Uncle Wiggly. Henry was probably out in the motor home with the space heater running, eating Cheez-Its, warm and dry and listening to the rain on the roof like another man would listen to music.

'Take it,' Walt said, and he handed Argyle the paint can. 'It belongs to you anyway. That's why I brought it over to your house instead of throwing it into the ocean. If you want my opinion about it, though, about all your little tricks here, I'll give it to you along with the can.'

For a moment Argyle was silent. Trudging along, soaked to the skin, he looked at Walt in apparent disbelief, as if being given the can had taken him utterly by surprise. Then Walt heard him mumble the word 'Thanks.' After a few more steps he said, 'I guess I already know your opinion.'

'Well, I'm going to give it to you anyway. That thing in the can there, that's not salvation. If it were *my* bluebird, I'd throw it out, just like Henry told me to do.'

The street was a river of rushing water, curb to curb, and the windy rain swept across it in flurries, reminding Walt of a monsoon. They passed the last house on the block, and moved out into the wind that blew along Chapman Avenue. Away to the west, the lights of the Plaza shimmered and winked through the rainy dark, and Walt could see the enormous white bulk of the cellophane snowman next to the Plaza fountain, waving up the avenue toward them, as if it were happy to see them out and about on a night like this.

St Anthony's Church was lit up inside, and the stained-glass windows shone in a hundred different hues, illuminating a window-shaped curtain of falling rain. From somewhere within came the sound of the choir, hushed by the weather and by the wood and plaster walls of the old church building.

Argyle's step faltered at the corner. He jerked to a stop, went on a couple paces, and stopped again. He looked around then, puzzled, like a sleepwalking man just shocked into wakefulness. The golem stood still, waiting, staring toward the Plaza. A car drove past on the street, its tires singing on the wet asphalt, and the driver looked at Walt and waved, although Walt didn't recognize him – probably it was just the season, and he was waving for no reason at all except some sudden impulse toward friendliness.

Argyle held the paint can in both hands and stood staring at it, as if he were reading the label. And just then the wind died, making an odd creaking sound like a door opening, and Argyle threw his hands into the air like Moses smashing the tablets. He stood just so for a scattering of seconds and then hurled the paint can straight down into the flooded gutter, where it sank beneath the current.

The earth shook, and Walt staggered sideways toward the curb, grabbing onto the streetlamp to keep from falling, and in the same instant a bell began to ring, so loudly that he let go of the lamppost and pressed his hands over his ears. A flock of pigeons rose from the ruined bell tower at St Anthony's, flying straight into the sky, where the clouds parted to reveal a wash of stars and an enormous moon. Walt realized that it was the fallen bell that was ringing, perhaps reverberating from the shock of the earthquake, its impossibly clear tones soaring out over the neighborhood.

The paint can surfaced and bobbed away on the tide, swept toward the open mouth of a storm drain through which the floodwaters rushed in a cascading torrent. In a moment the demon and the can it lived in were swallowed up, delivered into the subterranean river that would carry it to the ocean, gone out of Old Towne, out of their lives.

The tolling of the bell faded, and the night fell silent. Walt watched Argyle, who had his face in his hands now and was standing still. The golem lay in a heap on the wet sidewalk, its face staring up at the moon.

'I'll be damned,' Walt said finally. 'I think it's dead. It'll miss its appointment now.'

'I guess I will too,' Argyle said. He put out his hand, and Walt shook it.

Together they walked over to the golem. Its wreck of a face bore little resemblance to Argyle's any longer, and it lay limp and decrepit, an old mummy left out in the weather. Argyle nudged it with his foot, pushing it toward the gutter. Walt joined him, and together they slid the thing off the curb and into the torrent. It rolled away toward the storm drain, turning over in the flood before it slid headfirst beneath the sidewalk and vanished, its head compressing like a wet bag, moonlight glinting for one last moment on the soles of its worn-out shoes.

They stood in the silence, listening to the night, to the palm fronds rustling in the curbside trees. The choir started up again inside the church, and the rain fell off and then stopped entirely. Walt furled the umbrella, looped the fastener around it, and buttoned it.

'I guess I'll head home,' Argyle said to him at last.

'Your door's locked, isn't it?'

'I'm not sure. Maybe it's not locked at all. Not any more.'

'Come on over to our place,' Walt said, although he realized that he still didn't like the idea of an evening with Robert Argyle very much at all, which he knew was uncharitable. He'd have to work on that. Probably there would always be something to work on.

'I guess I won't.'

'Nonsense. Come on over and have a bite to eat. Nora and Eddie would love it. You know what Nora calls you?'

He shook his head.

'Mr R-Guy.'

Argyle smiled, and Walt smiled back at him.

'She's a case, isn't she?' Walt asked. 'She'd like to see you. What do you say?'

'It's …' He shrugged.

'Plenty of room at the inn,' Walt said. 'It's Christmas. It's the best time of the year to let bygones be bygones. We might as well start tonight.'

'Some bygones can't be forgotten,' Argyle said. 'This business with Mr Simms …'

'There's tomorrow for that. Tonight we both need dry clothes and something to eat.'

Argyle stood looking at him for a moment, then said, 'Okay, then.'

They walked up toward Oak Street and turned the corner, heading home. Walt could see his house halfway down the block. Ivy had strung the candy-cane lights around the porch. The light was on in the motor home, and Henry's profile was silhouetted against the curtain. What was he doing, Walt wondered, working on the popes? Reading Hefernin?

'I guess I better warn you that Henry's got a business proposition for you,' Walt said.

'For me?'

'I think you can count on hearing about it before the evening is through.'

'I'm not in business like I used to be. I guess you know that. I did some things …'

'Bygones, Bob. This plan of Henry's is different from the kind of thing you're talking about, whatever that is. This is some novelty items that Henry's cooked up, and he wants me to go in partners. He's convinced we'll make our fortune in Japan. What he's looking for is investors, start-up cash. You'd better be ready for him.'

'This wouldn't be the popes, would it?'

'You know about the popes?'

'Sidney Vest told me about it. Surefire moneymaker, he said.'

'Good old Sidney Vest,' Walt said uneasily.

'I'm surprised he didn't jump on it himself. I always say that when opportunity knocks, you answer the door dressed to go out.'

'If I didn't know better,' Walt said, giving him a narrow look, 'I'd guess you've read Aaron Hefernin.'

'*Read* him?' Argyle said back to him. 'I *am* Aaron Hefernin.'

Walt heard a child's laughter then, unmistakably Nora's, and she and Eddie both appeared from behind the motor home, carrying open umbrellas and followed by Ivy and Jinx, just come down off the porch for the evening walk. Nora shouted and ran on ahead, and Walt tossed his own umbrella onto the lawn. Dropping to one knee on the wet sidewalk, he opened his arms to catch her.

If you've enjoyed these books and would
like to read more, you'll find literally thousands
of classic Science Fiction & Fantasy titles
through the **SF Gateway**

✳

For the new home of
Science Fiction & Fantasy . . .

✳

For the most comprehensive collection
of classic SF on the internet . . .

✳

Visit the SF Gateway

www.sfgateway.com

James P. Blaylock (1950–)

James Paul Blaylock was born in Long Beach, California, in 1950, and attended California State University, where he received an MA in 1974. He was befriended and mentored by Philip K. Dick, along with his contemporaries K.W. Jeter and Tim Powers, and is regarded – along with Powers and Jeter – as one of the founding fathers of the steampunk movement. Winner of two World Fantasy Awards and a Philip K. Dick Award, he is currently director of the Creative Writing Conservatory at the Orange County High School of the Arts, where Tim Powers is Writer in Residence.